Praise for *To Forge a Nation*

Seeing historical events through the eyes of Amos Nordquist's heart firmly places the reader in the historical moment, often with a spiritual perspective...To Forge a Nation at times reads like a combined effort of Ken Follett and Louis L'Amour.

Dr. Daniel K. Perrin
Author and composer
Taken Generation

Mr. Munson has done extraordinary research. Well-written, often intense, the novel is a tour de force that leaves the reader with a vicarious sense of accomplishment – five talents well-invested – serving as reader encouragement and inspiration.

Dr. Joseph L. Castleberry, President
Northwest University
Author of *The New Pilgrims: How Immigrants Are Renewing America's Faith*

To Forge a Nation is an epic novel drawing on historical events of the late 19th and early 20th century in Sweden and the United States as built around the life, religious convictions, and social persuasions of Lutheran Pastor Amos Nordquist...[who] arrives during latter phases of the Civil War and then lives successively in Minnesota, the Idaho mining country, and finally Seattle and its rural hinterland.

Charles P. LeWarne
Ph.D. in History, University of Washington
Historian and author of books on Pacific Northwest history

To Forge a Nation

An Immigrant Journey
in an Immigrant Land
1859 ~ 1918

A Historical Novel

Carl Jon Munson

EVM

Earthen Vessel Media
San Rafael, CA

To Wendy

Contents

"Posterity – you will never know how much it has cost my generation to preserve your freedom. I hope you will make good use of it." – John Quincy Adams

Part One:

America Beckons

1859–1883

Prologue

A batholith is a large intrusion of solidified magma that did not reach the earth's surface as it cooled. Within solidified magma, subterranean fissures or dikes can form, eventually filled by younger magma and, as millions of years elapse, the entire batholithic structure is pressured by multiple geological forces including continental uplift, exposing the batholith. During the Mesozoic Era that's how the Montana/Idaho Bitterroot Mountains formed.

Subsequent eons of geological, glacial and atmospheric events ground, gouged, scored and eroded the old solidified magma, sometimes uncovering mineral wealth, often in exposed dikes. The earth's surface contains copper at 50 parts per million (ppm) and gold at 0.005 ppm, and finding gold lying along creek beds is unlikely, but in 1882 that's what happened in the Bitterroot Mountains, attracting men from everywhere.

January, 1884

Dawn sunlight pushed through the leaden overcast above the steep, snow-covered hillsides as one of those men, Amos Nordquist, lay sleeping in his soogan, or bedroll, spread on the unfinished boarding room's cold, rough-sawn floor boards, the room's woody dankness preferable to a snow covered tent outside. Nocturnal breathing formed frost on Nordquist's mustache, making him look older than his 43 years. In the pleasant predawn state sandwiched between deep sleep and wide awake, the vision of his wife, Anna, was talking to him, saying things he wanted to hear, and he felt her presence as if back with her in Minnesota. Were it up to her, he would be. She knew that bringing the word of God to uncivilized Murray, a town begun overnight, blooming in the light of the American West's last major gold strike, could be more readily accomplished by her husband than lesser men. She had uncharacteristically questioned, however, the wisdom, even sanity, of the church calling him across the Great Plains to some Bitterroot Mountain boomtown in the middle of winter, leaving behind a wife and three daughters.

Her concerns might have been justified when two weeks earlier Nordquist and his small party became lost in prairie snows while searching for the Little Big Horn battlefield south of Billings – a visit Nordquist wanted to make because he served under Custer at Appomattox. A scouting party of Christian Sioux, no longer trusting the machinations of their medicine man, gave redirection in exchange for medical attention to sick Sioux children. At the tribal encampment, with big, bearded, bearskin-clothed companion "Fur man" interpreting, Amos told Bible stories.

Story-telling was the primary form of Sioux entertainment and, to the displeasure of some older chiefs and younger braves, much of the tribe gradually gathered to hear about the miracles, death and resurrection of Jesus the promised Messiah, and stories like Noah and the ark (for which the Sioux had a similar story of a great flood), Moses on Mt. Sinai, Joseph's reconciliation with his brothers, and what would become the tribal favorite: David and Goliath.

Leaving the tribe, Amos and the other men in the party returned safely to Billings where Amos re-boarded the Great Northern train, travelling west to Thompson Falls, the end of the line. There Amos bought a horse, and two nights ago overcame a blinding blizzard on the Bitterroot Mountain pass from Thompson Falls to Murray.

Now, still half asleep, enjoying the vision of Anna for whom he would send after building a parsonage, he subconsciously brushed his hand over his mustache, removing some of the frost but upsetting his reverie, waking him.

Unwilling to leave the relative warmth of his soogan, he remained motionless. As a sense of urgency set in, however, he slid out from the bedroll and, still sitting on the cold wood floor, began forcing his boots over his stocking feet. His several pairs of socks had not been changed since re-boarding the train at Billings and would not be changed now.

Apart from his boots, Amos did not undress the night before, not even removing his heavy coat. Shivering nevertheless as he stood up, to stimulate his system he flexed as he considered his new flock: the expanding town's citizenry. Time to begin the Lord's work in Murray, he thought, opening and closing his big hands.

He suddenly sensed he was not alone. His eyes narrowed as the hair on his arms rose and he felt a clinging sensation like attic cobwebs, the sinister numen having dogged him from Sweden to America. The Old Evil. The feeling reminded him of when, years earlier as a cabin boy, his father's ship was berthed on the east coast of Africa with supplies for British-occupied Ft. Jesus, a Christian sanctuary on the Moslem island of Mombasa. Excited to finally be ashore, in the hot Kenyan air he raced in the sand along the water's edge, leaving the others walking behind.

As he ran, distancing himself from the armed seamen, his intuition and peripheral vision yanked his line-of-sight to his right. Panic instantly suffused him as he saw the island's alpha female-led clan of hyenas, eyes malevolent and dark above slavering grins, intelligently watching him from the brush and tall grass just above the beach. With so much death around Mombasa, hyenas had become accustomed to feeding on human flesh, even attacking isolated children or small adults when the opportunity availed, dragging them away before ravenously ripping and ravaging them, leaving little for ubiquitous Mombasa vultures.

As Amos stopped, locking into the alpha female's laughing eyes, the alpha female began to move forward. Terrified, adrenaline shooting through his system, Amos spun, cried out and raced like the Kenyan wind toward the distant adults who, seeing what was happening, in panic sprinted wide-eyed toward him, drawing pistols, the hyena clan leaping from the tall grass.

Tears blurring his vision as his feet raced in the sand, Amos stumbled, falling while still running, covering his head, anticipating the worst. But the fall was fortuitous, giving the men clear shots at the attacking hyenas. The alpha female in front yelped and rolled as she was hit with pistol fire before reaching Amos, and the beta female, fangs bared, was hit just as it reached him. But instead of sinking her teeth, she tumbled over him and lay on her side, her legs still moving for a moment. All motion stopped as she lay still in the sand four feet from his head while another hyena caught additional fire. The remaining clan turned and raced back up into the tall grass as vultures circling high in the sky began to slowly spiral downward, landing cautiously nearby on the beach.

The sensation caused by the alpha female's laughing eyes and the sensation of Old Evil were similar except Old Evil was an invisible, hulking thing whose presence injected creeping trepidation through Nordquist's skin like Bitterroot Mountain cold.

While the Old Evil no longer truly frightened Amos, the Spirit within him being stronger and opposite, the ghostly feeling in the cold room was more than annoying. Jaws clenched, Amos put his wide-brimmed, black leather hat over his black hair and, while pulling on his sheepskin gloves, walked to the room's door, and grabbed the latch. As he pulled, there was no movement; the heavy door of wet, rough-sawn boards was frozen shut. Seemingly trapped with Old Evil at his back, but over six feet tall and preternaturally strong, Amos ignored the crawling sensation, focusing on the door handle in his hand. He made no attempt to yank the door open, realizing that with his strength he might rip out the latch.

Grimacing, with his right hand he squeezed and pulled with measured, constant force while loudly pounding the upper door with his gloved, left hand, and kicking the base with his right boot until the door jamb surrendered its icy grip and the door jerked open, reciprocally banging against Amos's boot.

Amos half-grinned, took a deep breath and expelled it as he stepped through the doorway and out into the icy air, closing the door behind him. For a moment he stood focusing his senses to see if…the Old Evil had not followed. Would it be there when he returned? But when wasn't it around like a guardian daemon, constantly attempting to undermine his efforts, reverse his successes?

His breath vaporizing thickly before him, he brushed his hands together and slipped them in his pockets as his incisive eyes studied the snow-laden hillsides that surrounded the town of Murray like cold men crowding around a campfire, the aged mountains in turn watching self-absorbed newcomers whose conceit allowed them to call this rugged area "the new country" when there was nothing new about it.

The ragged ridges above snow-coated, treed hillsides reminded Amos of his native Sweden where snow and ice covered hillsides four-to-six months of the year; a severe land that created hard, uncomplaining people like Gustavus Adolphus, "the Lion of the North;" and Charles XII, "the Last of the Vikings," who led his formidable armies by both rank and example, meeting or exceeding their hardships during long marches, dropping to his knees twice daily for prayer, his great army following in kind.

Amos lowered his gaze, studying the nascent town: snow-covered tents, shanties of shakes and canvas, cabins of logs and shakes, and, with a new sawmill in nearby Eagle City – named "City" in hope of becoming one – frame buildings under construction in spite of the snow.

Warring with winter, men bustled about. The new harvest, Amos thought. Careful of his balance, he pushed through the snow toward the biggest saloon, Dutch Jake's, still in a large tent, perhaps once part of a circus, partially blending in with the mist-shrouded hillsides. As he lurched steadily forward, ahead of him hunched-over, shaggy, bearded men in heavy coats, leather gloves and wide-brimmed hats were quickly entering or leaving the saloon. Men teemed and swirled like blizzard flakes along a re-whitened street covered by packed snowfall over frozen mud, the surrounding snow-covered hillsides absorbing the sound. Pastor Nordquist intended to engage others in conversation, letting them know he was both a friend and a minister, here to serve them.

Later that day, Pastor Nordquist found three men willing to pray with him, asking for an outpouring of the Holy Spirit in Murray…until, while praying, it became evident they weren't sure what this meant. When Amos explained and asked them to pray with him for conversion, they again prayed without entirely understanding what they were praying for. After warmly shaking their hands, Pastor Nordquist studied them as they walked away uneasily glancing at each other, and as he had done for many others, silently prayed God would draw them to Jesus so they could experience the peace and joy of conversion, about which they knew nothing.

For the next two days, Pastor Nordquist spent most of his time in saloons, all still in tents, befriending others. As he did so, he met the men who came for the gold: men with hope who would work hard and sacrifice. But there were also the drifters – some leaving a previous town just ahead of the posse – who followed boomtowns mushrooming across the West, restless for excitement.

Some changed their names, some multiple times, fitting a new handle to an old axe, and Amos was never completely sure of to whom he was talking. Most men wore side arms, and some acted furtively, saying very little, obviously fearful of being identified. In conversation with such men, Amos wondered what they left behind.

While some had wives and loved-ones back east, and would eventually bring them west, most were alone – they rode alone, lived alone, acted alone, and anyone friendly toward them was viewed with suspicion. Saying you're a pastor would be great cover for a U.S. Marshal.

All conversation verified the Lord had one representative in Murray.

And no other Scandinavians were in town. In conversation, Amos's accent would unintentionally undermine the good intent of the English words he spoke.

He found few of the expanding Murray population were churchgoers, and in one way this simplified matters: he need not deal with denominational dogma. For Amos, as Charles Spurgeon once said, the audience wasn't in the pews, the audience was in heaven, and to Amos it mattered little if someone was a deacon or a drunkard if dead in their sins.

Many Murray newcomers of Irish descent, however, held religious convictions summarized, as one man responded, "If it aihn't Cath'lic, I aihn't t' be bothered." While Churchianity could be more difficult to overcome than unbeliever apathy, in the past Amos found most with religious leaning had an arable spirituality in which seeds of faith could be planted, cultivated and, with the Lord of the Harvest drawing them to Jesus, true Christian faith attained. And while Amos wasn't Catholic, he wasn't non-Catholic, as a later conversation would verify.

Undaunted, Amos pushed on. In a boomtown having reached several thousand people, there were an identical number of souls to be saved. Amos had no misgivings about going into Murray bars filled with coarse men of limited intellect. He did not proselytize, judge or preach, but, rather, tried to leave the honest impression he and they were kindred souls. Amos was a stark contrast to the men he met, however, and in varying degrees made others uncomfortable. Most treated him with respect but, to the vexation of Amos who wanted only their eternal salvation, kept their distance.

Amos observed that when it came to right and wrong, these didn't count for much in Murray. A group called The Committee avenged any prospectors and miners harmed, exacting an eye for an eye – and then some – as need arose. Otherwise, men lived according to frontier law, meaning no law. From stories heard while at sea years ago, Amos knew that in the absence of law and staying conscience, the base nature of men can take free rein and, when that happens, sins multiply like maggots beneath an outhouse seat. While discouraging sinful behavior was an indirect reason for Amos being in Murray, his overriding purpose was to present the message of the gospel – Christ's solution to the eternal consequence of that sinful behavior.

When witnessing, Amos found that ignorance of God's laws was not an obstacle. These men knew they were sinners and had fallen short of the glory of God; they just didn't care to be reminded. Many were painfully aware of their shortcomings and mistakes. The majority of men in Murray weren't there because of success elsewhere; many had failed time and again. But salvation? Hoping to salvage a life of failure, men focused on finding gold not God.

As Christ spent time with the downtrodden, Pastor Nordquist waded into the dregs of Murray: men with sordid pasts and limited, even hopeless futures. Prospecting was fraught with hardship, and a decision to work the new mines often fated an early death. Unsurprisingly, Amos continually sensed urgency… the end for many Murray men would come sooner than later. Meanwhile, the men worked, ate, drank and made merry; and, unsated, drank some more.

Three days later, Pastor Nordquist again visited Dutch Jake's Saloon. As he stepped inside, looking about at men standing at the bar or seated at tables, most looked back poker-faced. By now they knew the identity of "the big preacher." A string of ceiling lantern lights weakly illuminated the corner occupied by Angus MacGregor, a burly, red-bearded prospector dressed in dirty, bib overalls, worn leather hat and coat, and large, worn, work boots. Angus had been genteelly sipping Scotch for about an hour. Next to his glass was his bottle, about 3/4 full. Angus enjoyed pleasures of the moment and took his time. Angus was starting to loosen up and was getting tired of sitting alone. Angus MacGregor knew Pastor Nordquist's identity and, in Angus's relaxed, uninhibited state, Angus was ready to talk to someone who might provide stimulating camaraderie.

"Hey, yer Reverend, sir!" Angus hollered at a surprised Amos Nordquist.

"Hello. I don't believe we've met," said Amos, his Scandinavian accent prominent as he moved in the direction of Angus MacGregor, a recent immigrant from Scotland. "I'm Pastor Amos Nordquist."

"Angus MacGregor. M' pleasure," said Angus in his thick Scottish brogue, his smile contrasting the surrounding gloom as he stuck out his callused hand and shook Amos's with companionable affection. "Say, what religion did y' say you were?"

"I am a Christian, sir."

"Please. Sit down." Angus motioned with his head toward the opposite chair as he carefully measured one finger of Scotch into a shot glass while Amos pulled up the chair and sat down.

"This be m' bottle," said Angus reverently as he placed the bottle on the table. "Brought from Scotland, it was. Walker's Old Highland. A gift from m' friend, Alexander Walker. Rightly blended."

Angus looked intently at Amos and formally nodded.

"Dutch Jake keeps it behind the bar for me – and only me. Although I own the bottle, I keep track of and pay for each drink. T'is a fair arrangement. Were I t' keep it t' myself, drink for free, the bottle'd've gone dry long ago. This way the bottle's safe and the contents incrementally consumed. I sip Old Highland gradually, as is mete and proper." Looking up a Pastor Nordquist, Angus took a sip.

Angus formally nodded again, and Amos nodded back, not knowing what to say.

"What kind of Christian might you be, sir?" asked Angus.

"I am a Lutheran," responded Amos pleasantly, folding his hands on the table.

His hand wrapped around the glass, Angus looked at Pastor Nordquist, thinking. "D' ya mean like Martin Luther?"

Pastor Nordquist beamed, believing that perhaps he might have someone being led by the Holy Spirit.

"Yah, we follow the teachings of Martin Luther – that is why we are called Lutherans. But the term 'Lutheran' only refers to our church organization; the more correct term is 'Christian.' We believe that sin separated man from God, that the crucifixion of Jesus was the atonement enabling forgiveness of sin, and the resurrection that first Easter provides the basis for a newness of life here and also, following our physical death, eternal life with God."

Angus MacGregor listened intently, nodding in agreement with each point, and added another log to the small fire.

"We are Christians, you and I. You are a Lutheran. I am a Presbyterian. My whole family consists of Presbyterians. But I must tell you that I am not entirely sure what a Presbyterian is."

"Well, Reformed Presbyterians and Lutherans have a great deal in common. In fact, Reformed Presbyterians now are more like Lutherans were following the Reformation."

"Aye, then, why do you not become a Reformed Presbyterian rather than remaining a Lutheran? Because, if it is as you say," said Angus MacGregor, taking a sip of Scotch, "you would be more of a Lutheran if you were a Presbyterian than you are as a Lutheran."

Reverend Nordquist blinked at Angus MacGregor.

"Well, you know, maybe that is so, maybe not," said Amos quickly. "Perhaps, if we place more emphasis on God's saving grace, like the Reformed Presbyterians, then we become better Lutherans."

Pastor Nordquist was satisfied with his answer because, although it shed little additional light on the subject, he was a Lutheran minister, not a Presbyterian minister, and even though the purpose at hand, saving souls, was of paramount importance, at the moment he was not prepared to switch denominations. If Pastor Nordquist's response clarified the issue for Angus MacGregor, the next question posed by Angus would muddy the theological waters into which they were wading to an even greater degree.

"Was Martin Luther a Lutheran?"

"Well, you know," began Pastor Nordquist, "we follow the teachings of Martin Luther, but he did not call himself a Lutheran."

"Martin Luther was not a Lutheran. Is that what you said?" asked Angus MacGregor, sounding somewhat confused.

"Yah, we follow Martin Luther," answered Pastor Nordquist, "but he was not a follower of himself because he was himself, of course. I mean he was not a Lutheran – although certainly he believed what Lutherans believe because...he was Martin Luther." In his mind, Amos questioned where this conversation was going. "Martin Luther," added Pastor Nordquist, "believed that the sacrifice of Jesus Christ, the son of God, paid for our sins…"

"…just as the Presbyterians believe," interjected Angus MacGregor, holding up his right index measuring finger.

"Yah."

Angus MacGregor thought a moment. Pastor Nordquist waited, his forehead slightly furrowed.

"Of what denomination was Martin Luther if he wasn't a Lutheran?" asked Angus MacGregor, raising the glass of Scotch to his mouth.

"He was Catholic."

"Aye, a Catholic y' say," said Angus, relishing a sip. "If he was Catholic and you follow him, then you should also be Catholic or, because, as you say, since Reformed Presbyterians are more like Lutherans should be than Lutherans are, then it seems you should be either Catholic or Reformed Presbyterian if you are followers of Luther, as you say you are, rather than being Lutherans."

Reverend Nordquist was now convinced that this conversation into which he had entered with great expectations was quickly becoming a circus of semantics and might be doing more harm than good as far as the soul of Angus Mac-Gregor was concerned.

"Again, it is sufficient that we are Christians," responded Pastor Nordquist. "We do not worship Martin Luther, we worship God, and we believe that Jesus was the Christ, the Savior, the third person of the trinity. Immanuel: 'God with us.'"

Angus nodded in agreement, looking extremely serious.

"Was Jesus a Lutheran?" asked Angus MacGregor.

What? thought Pastor Nordquist, looking quizzically at Angus MacGregor. Of course he wasn't.

"No," sighed Pastor Nordquist with resignation. "He was born into a Jewish family. But, perhaps, as a Reformed Presbyterian, you are familiar with some of Jesus' miracles like 'Lazarus, come forth!'" Angus nodded. "And 'Peace, be still!' whereupon a disciple said, 'What manner of man is this that even the wind and sea obey him?' As I said, He was and is the promised Messiah…for both Jews and Gentiles, Lutherans and Presbyterians. Salvation is not attained by religious affiliation but through belief in Christ, renewal through the Holy Spirit – being 'born again' – experiencing the door of your heart open, welcoming the Lord while receiving the simple faith that His death – erasing your sins from the ledger, so to speak – enables you to live eternally with God."

"He came to save the elect?" asked Angus the Calvinist, eyebrows raised.

"Yah," answered Pastor Nordquist. "Salvation is not by good works – no one is that good. He speaks of those who did miraculous things in His name, yet He will say to some of them, 'Depart from me; I never knew you.' He also said to the disciples, 'You did not choose me, but I chose you.' Having been chosen by God is the greatest thing that can happen." Amos repeated sincerely with emphasis, "The greatest thing."

What Pastor Nordquist said came from the heart, void of any erudite religious rhetoric. While not evident, the sincerity and conviction of Pastor Nordquist impressed Angus MacGregor who, because of his Reformed Presbyterian upbringing, knew as much about Martin Luther and the Reformation as did Pastor Nordquist. Angus MacGregor had quickly grown to like Pastor Nordquist. At the same time, Angus MacGregor had been enjoying himself, sipping Scotch and playing word games with an infinitely patient Lutheran pastor.

"So if Jesus was not a Lutheran," concluded Angus MacGregor with a serious countenance, "then what Jesus Christ and Martin Luther had in common was that neither was a Lutheran."

Amos looked neutrally at Angus.

"Well, yah." Pastor Nordquist's rope was at its end. "But they weren't Presbyterians either."

Trying to keep from choking, Angus MacGregor put down his glass of Scotch, sat back in his chair and erupted with laughter easily heard above the raucousness at Dutch Jake's.

Pastor Nordquist looked at Angus with the traditional Lutheran look that indicates its bearer is having a difficult time discerning what is so funny.

The genuine uncontrolled laughter of Angus MacGregor was contagious and soon, although no one other than Angus MacGregor understood why he was laughing, a few men at the next table began to chuckle and, as Angus continued laughing, they also began to laugh. Within a few moments, those seated at nearby tables found the laughter irresistible and spontaneously joined in. Others seated further away were also at a loss about the cause of laughter, but gradually they too began to laugh, one-by-one forming a chorus of mindless hilarity – magnified by the absurdity that no one knew what was funny – until the entire saloon was laughing. Then laughing hard.

There was little in Murray to laugh about up to that moment and presently no more reason than before. Perhaps because the aggregate laughter was so totally pointless to most, or because human nature has a need for laughter and pent-up demand was being met, the laughter crescendoed to uproarious, uncontrolled howling, the infection for which there is no cure. The intensity of the hilarity did not die at that point but grew to gale winds force with men laughing so hard that their stomachs began to hurt. Tears streaming down their faces, some fell off their chairs and lay on the barroom floor still laughing uncontrollably. On it went for several minutes until men became physically exhausted and began to become laughed-out.

Gradually the gale winds began to die down.

Pastor Nordquist, sitting at his table, wiped away tears, and noticed how good he felt. This was the first opportunity he had to laugh hard since…he couldn't remember. He knew he never laughed this hard before. Angus also regained his composure, and looked at Amos for a moment, chortling intermittently, like a spout continues to drip after the cask is emptied.

"Y' hold a church service and I will come," volunteered Angus MacGregor, smiling while wiping his eyes. Men at nearby tables were doing the same, still wondering what the big preacher said that made the red-bearded prospector and, subsequently, everyone else, go into hysterics.

Pastor Nordquist beamed back at likeable Angus, hoping that in addition to Angus becoming a parishioner, the two might become fast friends.

Angus poured one last finger of Scotch in his shot glass and, in a voice loud enough for others to hear, asked a question that began laying the foundation for future camaraderie.

"Aye, now tell me: what brings a Scandinavian Lutheran pastor with a sense of humor all the way to Murray, Idaho?!"

With no conversation nearby, hearing the question, two beaming men at the next table began listening.

Angus pleasantly looked at the men and beckoned, "Gentlemen, join us!" motioning with his head. The two men looked at one another, and Amos smiled as the two picked up their drinks, walked over and sat down with Amos and Angus. Still smiling, Amos nodded at the bartender, held up one finger and mouthed the words, "Glass of wine."

He returned his attention to the table, introducing himself and Angus to the other men.

"What brought me all this way?" beamed Pastor Nordquist. "It's an interesting story. Do you want to hear it?"

"Aye, if you promise you'll leave nothing out," said Angus. The others nodded.

Pastor Nordquist leaned back in his chair as the bartender brought over a glass of wine. "That will be easy," he smiled, taking the glass.

Northern Europe, Mid-19th Century

1

It all began normally enough," said Amos, "one crisis after another interspersed with tedium like that about to end."

Late fall, 1859

As the large, North Sea swells rose and fell outside, holding the edge of the chart desk with his left hand for stability, 18-year-old Amos Nordquist walked the plotting dividers across the chart, estimating how far the Einar II was from home.

Amos put the dividers in a drawer and made a mental calculation as he roughly pushed the drawer shut. At their present course and speed, the Einar II was less than a day from the Skagerrak, the deep, black sea along southern Norway, and perhaps four or five days from Göteborg depending on rising wind and wave. Amos was concerned, however; over the last hour the seas had grown ominously rougher.

As the Einar II pitched and rolled, the hatch door opened behind Amos, the uninvited wind snatching the chart and pinning it against the bulkhead. Amos grabbed the chart as the hatch door slammed shut. Amos smoothed out the chart on the chart desk and felt a hand on his shoulder.

"Amos," said Captain Stig Nordquist, a bear of a man, "that storm to the north will be on top of us in less than a half hour and I need you on deck. I thought we might make it back without going through one of these, but no. Mizzenmast preventer braces needed to be reeved and hauled taut; tackles got upon the backstays. Go, get your gear on."

Following his father out the door, Amos hurried to the forecastle and raced down the ladder to his rack, underneath which he stowed his oilskins and southwester. The ship pitched and rolled heavily, occasionally yawing to left or right, the swells high, menacing mounds of icy, undulating ocean whipped and lacerated by the rising north wind beneath a blackening sky.

Fighting to keep his balance, Amos pulled on his gear, pushed to the boatswain's locker, grabbed coiled halyards, and climbed the ladder topside. As he steadied himself on the wet, heaving deck, the swells were huge and black, continually lifting and lowering the Einar II as if inspecting it for flaws. His back to the windward, Amos staggered along the weatherdeck and back to the aftcastle.

Reaching the mizzenmast, Amos lurched as a larger swell slammed and passed beneath the Einar II, lifting her upward amidships before thrusting her down into the next huge swell where icy spray exploded and shot aft from the forecastle, stinging Amos like wet buckshot.

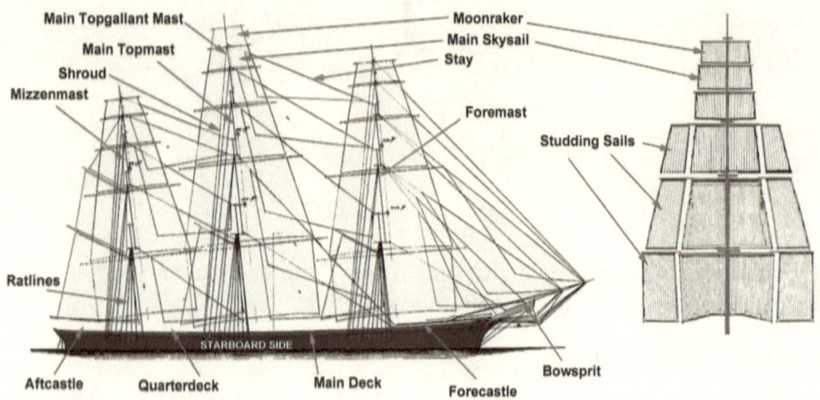

"Hurrah, men!" Amos shouted to other seamen. "Lay aloft and I'll send the rigging up to you!"

As men climbed the rigging, the square-rigged ship's bow rose high and dove into the next swell, sending an audible, resonating shudder along the deck as another blast of icy saltwater shot over the forecastle, weatherdeck and stern while the topgallant masts crackled and bent like horse whips. As Amos maintained his balance while feeding heavy lines to the men above, thoughts of men such as his grandfather, Lars, whom he had never met, and others lost at sea, came to him. Amos's stomach tightened. Too often these thoughts were presentiments – he had no idea how this spiritual intuition worked, but so often in the past, thoughts of events that had not yet happened were then followed by those events. Amos became wary, exercising extreme caution.

The Einar II raced toward the Skagerrak. By the first mate's reckoning they were less than a day from the Jutland peninsula of northern Denmark. Until moments ago, the sea and wind were tolerable. Two hours ago, all was well until the men felt it: a drop in temperature followed by that initially innocent sound the wind makes when she first decides to rise, like the sound of a group of schoolboys learning to whistle. Shortly the wind's anger had grown – who knows why? – and the men scrambled. It was as if the North Sea wanted to give them a reminder of its more natural disposition before they reached the western Skagerrak. But the seasoned crewmen were already familiar with the maddening North Sea and her temperamental mood swings and needed no reminder.

As the north wind howled about him on the dangerous aftcastle, equally maddened by an angry sea and lacerating sleet, Amos fought back, rapidly handling lines requiring the strength of two men, having done it since he was a boy. Seasoned in battles like this on the North Sea and the North Atlantic, a fighter with a familiar opponent, Amos punched and counter-punched. Like men possessed, all on board fought against rising wind, sleet and North Sea swells. All knew souls lost in seas like these.

"Lay aloft there and set the mizzen topsail!" shouted the mate. "Be lively, lads. It's the Skagerrak by noon on the morrow!"

As the men neared completion of readiness, Captain Stig Nordquist came on deck. Although the wind was fierce, his captain's hat brim clung tightly to his forehead above his thick gray eyebrows that, like his trimmed beard, resembled clipped strands of oxidized iron wire. Even if the men did not immediately see him, they sensed his presence. To the men, no other man, not one, was more intimately familiar with the North Sea than Captain Stig Nordquist, and for a split-second it seemed the angry waves reared like spooked horses, as if recognizing the man who had just stepped on deck, his gray eyes surveying the great swells like they were the familiar hillsides of Göteborg.

"Mr. Olson, is all made ready?" Captain Nordquist shouted over the wind to Oldemar Olson who had been mate on the Einar II since her maiden voyage five years earlier.

"Nearly ready, Captain," shouted the mate. "All is secure on deck; we're lowering the moonraker and the main skysail…"

"'Moonraker'?" shouted Captain Nordquist as he squinted toward the main topmast, his face lacerated by sleet. "Mr. Olson, get those men down from up there before they're blown down! This storm will become angry enough without being provoked! Set the lower main studdingsails; we need even more speed. If we can get to the Skagerrak, we might survive!"

"Aye, captain," shouted the mate over the wind as he staggered to the mainmast to signal down the seamen precariously beginning work on the moonraker and main skysail as Captain Nordquist, after a glowering glance about at the threatening swells, returned below.

The helmsman adjusted the course slightly as the wind rose, and as sails caught the wind full, the Einar II leapt through the water, the spars and masts crackling under the strain.

"Aye! There she goes! The smell of land!" shouted the mate. "Ahahhh! Now she's got the scent! As long as she cracks, she holds!"

Buffeted by wind, sleet and wave, the Einar II sprang through the North Sea like an African lion hound, and the men worked frantically and prayed – prayed for safe landing in Göteborg, and for helmsman Olaf Andersson who would be God's man on board, steering a dead-reckoning course toward the wide mouth of the Skagerrak well beyond the cloud-shrouded horizon.

The swells now exceeded 15 feet, causing the Einar II to rise and dive, creak and moan as if in pain, occasionally loud enough to be heard above the sound of high-pitched wind and sleet rifling against sails and through the rigging.

Late in the day, the sky grew darker, and when blackness covered the North Sea, nowhere were the ship's crew more dependent on an all-seeing God. The swells grew larger, and Amos Nordquist could hear and feel the shrouds and stays whine, but not yet fray or snap as the agitated, wind-whipped North Sea reduced the Einar II's relative size to harbor dory insignificance.

That night Amos's presentiment occurred. At 2:00 a.m. the main topgallant mast ruptured at the crosstree, with flailing, iced-over stays and shrouds holding it aloft. In the forecastle berthing quarters, awakened by the second mate, an experienced seaman attempting to get an hour's sleep groggily unstrapped himself from his rack, grabbed a coil of halyards, a block, marline spike, strap and a hurricane lantern from the bo'sun's locker, all of which he hung from his neck, and warily went topside in the darkness. Reaching the main deck, he staggered toward the mainmast and began climbing the ratlines aloft to the step where the main topmast and topgallant mast were connected. With a loose end, he tied himself to the topmast and, no more than a blind man in the blackness, his hands began feeling nearly-frozen lines that he would juryrig until a better job could be done during daylight.

The ice caused his fingers to gradually numb. He struggled as if partially paralyzed in the cold, wind and blackness, all the while fighting the convulsive ship's motion exacerbated by mast height. Nearly 20 minutes later, shivering exaggeratedly, and gasping for breath, he untied the loose-end holding him to the topmast, and began to descend. His juryrigging wasn't nearly enough, but he had done what he could.

His rigid fingers frigid, like a circumspect spider he slowly crept down the icy rope ladder. As the ship dove, the seaman compensated by pushing his weight backwards while attempting to grab the line with his left hand, but at that moment a large swell pitched the ship to larboard, whipping the topmast and shrouds through the air, causing his left foot to slip. As his left foot slipped, the mast swing reversed, ripping the seaman's right foot and frigid fingers from the icy ratlines, hurling him out into the blackness above the quarterdeck. Eyes enormous, flying through the air, panic seizing through him like shroud ice, he plunged violently into the black, raging ocean below.

In shock, he still desperately fought his way to the surface and, in the high swells and hurricane winds, gasped for air, screaming in terror at the invisible larboard quarter as it passed by. Flailing like ruptured stays in the wind, he screamed over and over, choking on seawater as he gasped.

But the ship sailed on.

Before the last icy wave rolled over him, his eyes adopted a ghastly, ghostly stare as he realized that life's brief hour, in an unplanned and unexpected moment, was done.

━━━━●━━━━

Early dawn drew a faint, gray line above the black, eastern horizon, and by the grace of God the winds and swells were not as great as during the hours after midnight. As daylight grew, Second Mate Gustaf Johansen made a headcount of deck hands and came up one short. After checking about the ship, the count was still one short.

The seaman? When had he last been seen?

Awakened in his rack, midwatch helmsman Jurgen Ericsson said he saw someone come up from below deck and perhaps head to the mainmast, but it was too dark, too foul, to tell. Was it the seaman? If so, what was he doing? Who sent him aloft?

"I did, Captain," said Second Mate Gustaf Johansen somberly, standing before Captain Nordquist and Chief Mate Olson in the captain's stateroom. The three men held on to the table, fastened to the stateroom deck, to maintain their balance as they stood formally.

"I'm assuming you believed it absolutely necessary," said Captain Nordquist. Johansen served with Captain Nordquist for many years; Captain Nordquist knew Johansen well.

"It was, Captain," Johansen said, his voice tight. "Do you remember the storm southwest of the Azores eight years ago? We had a similar mishap and, rather than take chances that night, we let it go without doing anything immediately. We lost the main topgallant mast and rigging, and the rigging to the other masts was compromised to the point where we had to send several men aloft anyway. We lost Eric Johansen who was…," Johansen looked at Captain Nordquist grimly, and could not finish the sentence, his lips forming a tight line.

"…your nephew," said Captain Nordquist quietly, remembering how Gustaf requested his brother's son be hired on as a crewmember.

"Had the storm not subsided," continued Johansen after a moment, "we might have lost many more…perhaps the entire ship and crew. Me. You."

Captain Nordquist nodded solemnly.

"I don't know what happened, Captain," said Johansen, looking down gloomily. He quickly looked up at Captain Nordquist, maintaining decorum. "I could tell from what I found aloft earlier this morning that he climbed to the rupture and did a commendable job, considering weather conditions and absence of light."

At that moment a large swell slammed, lifted and threw the Einar II downward, causing the men to grab the secured table with both hands. Regaining his balance, Johansen looked at Captain Nordquist for a moment as Johansen also regained his train of thought.

"There was no light to work by last night," Johansen continued. "Raging seas, heavy sleet, ice, and the wind was foul. But there was no other choice." Johansen's eyes looked down. "No one saw or heard anything." He looked regretfully at Captain Nordquist. "I'm sorry."

"I know you are, Johansen," said the captain, his steely, gray eyes looking levelly at the second mate. "You will go with me when I inform his mother and give her his belongings. Now securely seize the shrouds. Dismissed."

"Aye, captain." Johansen turned, left the captain's stateroom, and went to find another seaman to finish juryrigging the damage.

"How far are we from land?" shouted the second seaman over the wind before he started aloft.

"The mate thought we'd see land sometime this morning," Johansen shouted back. "It depends on headway made during the night…and leeway."

With the dexterity of a rhesus monkey, the slender, young seaman climbed up to where the topgallant mast was ruptured. He worked precariously for 10 minutes, the mast whipping in multiple directions as the storm continued. While tying a line to the crosstree, he glanced eastward and, miraculously, as the mate anticipated, there was a black sliver on the clouded horizon – land – the Jutland peninsula. His popularity among the crew would momentarily soar as he looked down at the weather deck and hoarsely hollered the venerated cry of seafaring.

"Laaaaaaaand-ohhh! Dead ahead!"

2

I n the frigid North Sea storm, the exhausted crew members turned and stared as they looked beyond the bowsprit.

An hour later they were close enough to recognize Jutland landfall and the gaping mouth of the Skagerrak to the northeast. The helmsman corrected to larboard, the masts catching the trailing storm winds full. The first mate's dead reckoning was accurate, and each man was grateful as two hours later, racing in from the North Sea, prevailing winds continued to whip the large, rolling swells covered with cobwebbed foam, while pushing Einar II's full sails on a straight line into the unruly Skagerrak.

His cold hands occasionally gripping the gunwale for stability, Amos Nordquist stood on the forecastle and watched the distant Jutland shoreline in the gloom as insuperable swells continued to pummel the Einar II. Amos thought of his earlier presentiment about someone being lost at sea. With the loss of the seaman, again it came true.

Amos stared at the black waves, feeling guilty because he sensed something was going to happen, but did nothing…but, then, what could I have done? And now what will we tell the seaman's mother when we arrive in port? As Amos wondered, Second Mate Gustaf Johansen came to Amos's side.

"We still have problems," Johansen said loudly over the wind as he also grabbed hold of the gunwale. "The rigging is torn and frayed between the main topmast and both the fore topmast and mizzen topmast. Several other lines are either loosened or stretched taut to the point of snapping. But I don't want to chance another man overboard. We'll do the reparations when we get to port. Should something become amiss, however, making it to Göteborg could become a challenge. We just have to pray the rigging holds until we arrive."

"If it doesn't?"

"We weather that storm when we sail into it."

Amos nodded and looked at the sea. The waves about them boiled, rose, surfed and blew as if multiple sea monsters were rising to the surface of the storied Skagerrak.

"Amos," said Gustaf loudly over the wind after a moment, looking up at

Amos, "may I ask a question?"

"Certainly," said Amos, wondering what the question was if Gustaf felt he needed permission to ask it. Amos had known Gustaf all his life.

"Your father. As long as I've known your father, I've never known where he's from. Göteborg?"

"While my parents came from small towns, they met in Göteborg. My father grew up in the köping Döderhultsvik," Amos said, looking at the boiling waves, gripping the gunwale with both hands. "As you know, it was a beehive of enterprise that, unlike much of Sweden, had never been enserfed although nobles had tried…unsuccessfully. Families owned their farms, everyone worked hard – they knew no other way – and were a tough, stubborn bunch, covetous of their freedom. When missionaries first came a thousand years ago, the people were loath to give up the old gods – Odin, Freya, Thor – and many missionary priests met with death or enslavement. Eventually, however, Catholicism overcame the old paganism, and my father's people gradually became tepid Roman Catholics."

"Is there another kind?"

Amos looked disparagingly at Gustaf who smirked. "Of course," said Amos with mild exasperation. "Anyway, in the early 16th century when Sweden separated from Denmark, the…"

"Praise God!"

"…when Sweden separated from Denmark, the new king, Gustav Vasa, wanted to sever allegiance to Rome and have everyone become austere Lutherans. That didn't go over well at all. It had taken 400 years for the people to collect and revere Roman Catholic trappings, some quite valuable. The king wasn't going to get any of that stuff if they could help it. In addition, the king wanted to restrict free trade with Denmark, replace the local form of government with an appointed governor, and increase taxation."

"And the people revolted."

"To say the least," said Amos. "The Småland peasants responded by violently wiping out the king's army which included a thousand German mercenaries. But in the end, the Lutheran missionaries returned, backed by a much larger German mercenary army, and everyone said, "What the hell," and reluctantly became Lutherans…although, now, if leaned on to change, the conflagration would no doubt flash again. Free, hardworking men and women descended from Viking berserkers are an independent bunch; don't like to be ordered around."

"An understatement."

"My father's success has a lot to do with the history of where he was born and raised."

"So it is with most of us – including his oldest son. But what brought your father to Göteborg?"

"Dad and Uncle Torvald thought Göteborg to be the future of Sweden – on the west coast in proximity to Amsterdam, London, Edinburgh, LeHavre." Amos nodded southwestward.

"How much time did he spend in Göteborg before he moved there?"

"He and my Uncle Torvald came to Göteborg frequently. Göteborg was becoming cosmopolitan. He told me that conversations in English were as common as Swedish." Amos looked at Gustaf. "The British lifestyle was, in fact, becoming the norm – hence the nickname 'Little London.' So, eventually Dad and Uncle Torvald left home and moved to Göteborg." Amos looked back at the surf-covered swells. "And here we are. Dad has done well for himself."

"And now, being Stig Nordquist's son has its advantages."

"Yes," said Amos, glancing at Gustaf, wondering why Gustaf said that. "Obviously, my father's coattails provide opportunities most men my age can only dream of…like he once did. At the same time," Amos looked severely at Gustaf, "I'm never entirely my own man enjoying a separate identity. I'm always Captain Stig Nordquist's son."

"Is that so bad?"

"No," said Amos, becoming annoyed. "I've often wondered, however, what I might be doing if dad had not realized such success." Amos gripped the gunwale and bent his knees as the ship was slammed by a large, cresting starboard swell that lifted and dropped the Einar II as if the sea were looking for something else. "Certainly, things could be worse, but at times I wonder: if it were only me, fending for myself, what would I be doing?"

"Things are as they are. Be grateful, lad. You are in a…"

"I'm not ungrateful, Gustaf," countered Amos, more annoyed, "just curious. One wonders."

"Amos, all I'm saying is there is nothing wrong with having the benefits that come from being Stig Nordquist's son."

Amos's countenance darkened as he looked at Gustaf. "What are you implying? When have I ever acted as if I was entitled to anything?" Amos asked loudly in a monotone. "I do my share."

"Yes, and you always have…usually more than your share." Gustaf looked up at Amos again, sensing Amos's anger. "But what I am trying to say is: when I watch you, I get the sense you believe you have to prove your station is deserved," explained Gustaf, looking at Amos's darkened countenance. "And, so, you've more than proven it many times. The others all know Amos Nordquist does the work of two men. And has the brains of three." Gustaf studied Amos as Amos looked back. "But the temper of ten."

Amos's expression remained unchanged.

"There are reasons no one gives you trouble, lad. First, you're a Nordquist. Secondly, the men respect you because you can do the work of any two of them, regardless of what needs to be done, so no one has reason to give you trouble. And lastly, if someone gave you trouble, there'd be hell to pay. Isn't that right?"

Amos turned his head and looked out at the sea. The swells and foam rose, erupted, blew, fell and rose again.

"Someday, Amos, in spite of your size and strength, that temper could get you in a real stew."

"I don't get unreasonably angry," countered Angus defensively with forced coolness. Yet while his response was calm, anger was irrationally racing around Amos's heart with a fury like that of a little dog, eyes bugging out in panic, frantically barking at backyard squirrels. Amos did not like his anger, knew it was irrational and, in contrast to what Gustaf just implied, was trying to manage it.

"But when you get angry," added Gustaf, "reasonably angry, if you wish, you get very angry and very unreasonable." Looking at Amos, Gustaf shook his head. "Dousing that fire takes some doing, lad. Don't let things get to you so easily."

Amos took a deep breath and let it out slowly. "I try. Trust me, I try. But sometimes… Dad and I have talked about it. Like that time two years ago when I broke that guy's jaw in Messina. Dad was beside himself. I misunderstood what the guy was saying."

"I remember that." Gustaf looked at Amos. "And even if he said what you thought he said, it still wasn't enough to warrant taking his head off.

"Amos, you're 18, big and strong. Those full crates you lift and carry around like they were empty, I can barely lift those by myself. And, hell, you're handsome and intelligent besides. The rest of us would be grateful to have half of what you were given. For you, anger isn't necessary. And you're a Nordquist. People automatically expect more of you. Automatically. Amos, 98% of the time you're a fine young man. Sometimes you're so empathetic, generous and unselfish I'd think you were Jesus Christ. But other times, noooo. That's not who you are. You're more like the other guy. Think. Count to ten. I don't know. I just worry that one of these days, your temper is going to get you into a situation…is going to get you killed," Gustaf said adamantly. "Unplanned. Wrong place, wrong time." The men gripped the gunwale as the ship wrenched hard to larboard. "It happens."

"Yes," sighed Amos. "I know. Dad's said the same thing. More than once." Amos gave another large sigh that seemed to quiet his inner cauldron.

"Why did you ask where dad was from?"

"Your father has been more distant during the last few days," said Gustaf loudly as the ship rose and rolled, and both men gripped the gunwale tighter. "I've seen him get that look in the past. Some big decision is on his mind. And I can't think of anything that it might be except…" Gustaf looked seriously at Amos. "Do you know?"

"I don't. But I've noticed it too. You can see him thinking…that nearly blank expression that reminds me of an encyclopedia cover. He hasn't said anything to me. When we're ashore I'll ask him."

"When you do, let me know what he says," Gustaf said as he studied the horizon beyond the bow. "I'll not speculate now, but I have my suspicions."

Amos looked at Gustaf who said nothing more. Amos looked back at the sea and thought about his father's changed behavior.

The foul weather gradually declined as they sailed further into the Skagerrak, and the following day the crew was able to better stabilize the rigging until they reached Göteborg.

All were elated when the islands north of the Göteborg outer harbor came into view on the distant horizon, then the Vinga lighthouse. The men considered Göteborg an oasis where the difficult-to-deadly struggles at sea, liberally interspersed with boring tedium, could be escaped for predictability, stimulation and relative safety found within civilized community on solid ground. While social order and polite society were at hand, however, the Old Evil was never absent, but hid like a Kraken in the shadowy depths below legitimate commerce where it watched and waited.

All hands were on deck as the Einar II sailed up the Göteborg harbor channel and, with the help of harbor boats, approached its moorage. From the quarter-deck, Amos watched the beehive of activity along the waterfront as men, horses and carts moved cargo between shore, dock and ships. Dock workers loaded and unloaded carts while anxious waterfront merchants hawked a variety of wares, and passengers waited to depart. As always, upon hearing a foreigner unfamiliar with the city call it "Goat'-borg," busy merchants would patiently correct the newcomer: "Yeh'-tuh-bawr-ee. Yeh'-tuh-bawr-ee." The first line was thrown over, and another until the Einar II was made fast to the pier.

After all was secure, the crew began going ashore. Repairs and cargo removal would begin the following morning. Apart from the in-port watch who would stay on board, the last two men to leave the ship were Second Mate Gustaf Johansen with Captain Stig Nordquist who carried the missing seaman's sea bag. Other ships would auction off a drowned shipmate's belongings, but Captain Nordquist would not allow this, ordering a drowned man's belongings be given to his family if he had one. At a short distance, Amos waited. As Gustaf and Captain Nordquist approached, Captain Nordquist looked at Amos and nodded.

"Amos, please join us."

As the three men walked along the waterfront, upon seeing Captain Stig Nordquist carrying a sea bag on his shoulder, town folk quickly stepped to one side. Men removed their hats and stood solemnly as the three passed.

The three men arrived at the modest home of the seaman, and stood somberly before the door as Amos knocked. The seaman's widowed mother, a short, fleshy woman wearing a housedress, apron and wooden shoes, opened the door as she was drying her hands on a towel. She looked up and was startled upon seeing Captain Stig Nordquist, standing between Amos and Gustaf.

The three men removed their hats and looked down at her without expression.

Her eyes grew large as she looked at them questioningly, then down at the sea bag beside Captain Nordquist, and her face blanched. Her jaw went slack and her mouth fell open. She looked up at the men, glancing from face to face in disbelief. Her husband. Now her son? Her face grimaced and her head dropped as the towel in her hands rose to cover her eyes. Teeth clenched, she dissolved into uncontrolled sobs, shaking like a sail in the wind as a ship comes about.

Amos did the only thing he could do at that moment: he stepped forward, reached down and gently placed his arms around her, holding her to him in her moment of great pain, rocking softly back and forth, attempting to somehow comfort her. He held her like this for some time until she finally began to regain composure. As Captain Nordquist and Gustaf Johansen looked on, Amos spontaneously placed his right hand around the back of her head and tenderly held her head close to his chest, his left hand on her upper back as, exhausted, devastated, she slumped in his embrace, her escaping sobs quieting.

After a few moments, Amos gradually let go and stepped to her side, gently taking her right arm as he looked down at her. She still held the towel over her mouth as her wet, reddened eyes looked up at him in heartbroken disbelief.

"Mrs. Eng, may we come in?" he asked.

3

Mrs. Eng's small living room was modest but spotless, with hand-braided, oval rugs and white shelves displaying various porcelain knickknacks. Arm covers embroidered in needlepoint hid threadbare sofa arms.

"Please sit down," said Captain Nordquist, and the others took seats.

"The sea is a hard taskmaster," Captain Nordquist understated. "Second Mate Johansen and I have both been in your position, Mrs. Eng. I wish I could tell you what happened to your son, but we have no idea." Mrs. Eng stifled an occasional sob as she continued to hold the towel over her mouth while she stared toward the floor.

"I sent him aloft in the early morning darkness to repair some damaged rigging," said Johansen. "We took a head count after daylight and he wasn't there." Gustaf, holding his hat in his hands, looked at Mrs. Eng with sympathy. "Something happened. I don't know what."

"I…have some…kroppkakor." Mrs. Eng spoke with effort, looking at Captain Nordquist. "I have no… And some tea. Would you like some?" She awkwardly wiped her eyes and below her eyes, temporarily eliminating the accumulation of tears.

"Yes," said Amos after glancing at his father who did not care for kroppkakor. Amos looked at Mrs. Eng's anguished countenance. "That would be very kind of you."

When Mrs. Eng returned, she gave each man a plate with one kroppkaka. Each man thanked her, took a bite and favorably remarked about the taste. Moments later she returned with tea. Each man was served.

"Would you like something else?" she asked. She had little else to give, but Captain Stig Nordquist was in her home and she should ask.

"No, Mrs. Eng," said Captain Nordquist. "This is excellent. Please, sit down."

Mrs. Eng sat and looked downward, buoyed by the presence of the men although part of her wished that she, too, were dead.

"Mrs. Eng, your son was a good sailor and a good man," said Captain Nordquist. "I chose him to serve aboard the Einar II. Gustaf and I know how you feel. My son, Amos, has never experienced the loss of a close family member – and, hopefully, will not, at least for some time to come." Captain Nordquist looked neutrally at Mrs. Eng. "There is nothing we can do now. Your son is gone. You, however, are alive, and we know you were financially dependent on your son."

"What am I to do?" quietly asked Mrs. Eng, looking at the floor, speaking more to herself than the men.

"Don't worry about that," said Captain Nordquist. "Nordquist Shipping Company will look after you."

Still looking away, wiping a tear from under her eye, Mrs. Eng nodded gratefully.

"Please stop by the Einar II tomorrow – I should be there," said Captain Nordquist. "I'll give you your son's pay immediately, and we can make further arrangements. Meanwhile, please feel free to schedule a memorial service at the church. We will take care of the expense. I guarantee the attendance of my family and the ship's crew."

Mrs. Eng momentarily began again losing her composure, and Amos quietly stood up, walked to where she was sitting, pulled a chair over and sat next to her, putting his arm around her until she got herself under control.

"Are you going to be Okay?" asked Amos.

"I think so," said Mrs. Eng weakly after a moment, still looking at the floor while wiping her eyes.

Captain Nordquist stood up and respectfully nodded at Mrs. Eng. Gustaf and Amos both stood, and so did Mrs. Eng. Amos looked at his father questioningly, implying they stay longer, but Captain Nordquist gave his son a solemn look, turned and walked toward the door. There was nothing more they could do; Captain Nordquist wanted to keep this unhappy moment brief. The others followed.

Captain Nordquist turned to Mrs. Eng. "I'll see you tomorrow morning at the Einar II," he said as he opened the door.

"Yes," said Mrs. Eng. "Thank you."

Captain Nordquist led the others out the door.

While the despondency of the moment waned, a few days later another tragic event would occur.

———————◄●►———————

In an 1859 seafaring town, a man who was a captain – a man who had braved much – enjoyed prominence and commanded deference becoming of such a man. From the expansive front porch of the hillside home that overlooked the harbor like a stolid patriarch, Amos Nordquist, dressed in a white seaman's shirt laced at the chest, and white duck trousers tucked into his black, knee-high, work boots, stood erect, hands on his narrow hips, and looked down toward the docks where his father, master mariner and ship owner Captain Stig Nordquist, one of the most respected men in Göteborg, sat ruminating on the Einar II quarterdeck. Feet apart, his black hair leonine in the wind, Amos studied his father from a distance, wondering what his father was thinking.

Amos revered his father. Among his father's many virtues was the propensity to never waste time. When seemingly doing nothing, Captain Stig Nordquist would be busy mentally engineering some project, plan or investment deserving his attention. Even in port, Captain Nordquist spent time on board, the place where he was most productive. Owner of the Einar II and two other ships, the Polstjärnan and the Nordenvinden, as well as a brigantine and a barque, Captain Nordquist was town nobility. He dressed accordingly, not because of pretentiousness but, as with so much else, Captain Nordquist had high standards of dress. This morning while overseeing repairs aboard the Einar II, Captain Nordquist wore pressed black trousers, a black vest with lapels, black frock coat and a black cravat. Tonight, when entertaining guests at his hillside mansion, he would wear a longer coat and change the cravat from black to white. He wore his captain's hat when supervising ship repair at the moment, but tonight, if leaving the premises, he would don a top hat. For many, such ostentation might seem affected but, as Amos watched his father from a distance, he admired his father's regal air. The fit was more than coat size or inseam length. For Captain Nordquist to dress informally would be inappropriate.

Seafaring had always been a hard life. Sitting, reminiscing about the past, weighing the rewards received and the measures taken, pipe in his mouth, Captain Nordquist appeared the consummate sailing master, the ancient mariner. Against Captain Nordquist's will, the lingering effects of numerous back injuries and nutritional deficiencies while at sea made him sit hunched over, and as he slowly rose from where he sat, it was no longer possible for him to reach his full height. Looking up at the east hillside, weathered crow's feet fanned out from the sides of his sun-narrowed, gray eyes, his wizened, craggy face the texture of the tanned, shrunken lambskin he occasionally brought back from France. His face reflected decades of worry, stress, depression, malnutrition, hot sun, saltwater spray and the vertiginous disorientation caused by the inescapable rolling ship's motion that makes landlubbers ill. Although he was getting on in years, as with all men having spent a lifetime at sea, Captain Nordquist was younger than he looked. His ambition exacted a measure of his health, while his wealth and social status, so overriding in the beginning, ceased being of overwhelming importance. He painstakingly accumulated wealth beyond his dreams, enjoyed its satisfaction, and after an adult lifetime of conscientiously practicing his chosen profession, was shifting his attention to what he deemed now more important.

As Amos Nordquist watched his father smoking his pipe on the quarterdeck of the Einar II, the most striking of Captain Nordquist's three ships, Captain Nordquist again looked up at the Göteborg hillside toward the stately mansion rising above the harbor. A beautiful home. Perhaps the nicest in Göteborg, and more than he ever needed. Where the great, hip roof would have peaked, there was a white crown, a widow's-walk ornamented with pilasters, adding character to the house but serving little practical use. The massive white front porch with an extended porte-cochere for approaching carriages insured the widow's-walk received little attention. In contrast, hidden behind the tree line below the front porch was the daylight cellar where use varied from modest to extensive, depending on whether Captain Nordquist was home or at sea. When home, his cellar served as a workshop, taxidermy lab, and a crafts parlor where Captain Nordquist undertook projects previously given considerable thought during months at sea.

In addition to a place for an assortment of projects when home, the cellar was a repository where Captain Nordquist stored unusual artifacts his wife preferred not be displayed upstairs. Some were invaluable – unique, sometimes bizarre weapons, and implements of pagan worship from places like New Guinea, Pago Pago and Madagascar, and queer, stuffed animals and sea creatures from Borneo, Sumatra, Ceylon and other faraway places, accumulated during a lifetime of seafaring.

It was the home in which, beginning at the age of four, Amos was tutored in Greek, Latin, and English, and later English literature – especially Shakespeare – using his father's top-floor study while his father was at sea, or the bright entry parlor when his father was home. Amos was quiet as a child and enjoyed being alone to study and write. At an early age Amos began writing letters to his father when his father was away. Amos kept these letters and gave them to his father as a present when his father returned. The letters proved to be a warm monologue, effectively a diary his father cherished and kept, rereading from time to time.

Amos was a good student, particularly in language. He valued words like gems – some were more valuable than others, some were of extraordinary value, and some were fake. Over the years, Amos gradually improved his wordsmithing to where he could distill volumes of verbiage to single grain epitome. He expected to follow his father in the shipping business and, when sitting at his father's writing table in the study, occasionally wondered how he could use his literary penchant in that capacity. Or was he to do something different?

From the quarterdeck, puffing thoughtfully on his pipe, in the world of his memory Captain Nordquist again revisited faraway places with strange-sounding names, some visited long ago, that contributed to his cellar treasure trove. His oldest son, Amos, never tired of the cellar, while Captain Nordquist's younger son, Anders, seldom went down there except, perhaps, to get some tool that, when finished with it, Anders would invariably leave somewhere else. While Captain Nordquist enjoyed thinking about distant lands, he did so because they were in the past. It was as if, at this moment, in his mind he would take one last memorable voyage.

And would not return to sea.

The fire of wanderlust that burned brightly in his youth was little more than a waft of smoke that, after the last ember has died, rises and dies itself. He was entirely done.

Captain Nordquist reached over and knocked his hand-carved, briar root pipe from Cameroon – the blackened stem a gentleman's arm with an upturned hand holding a hollowed, dark brown skull, the pipe bowl – twice on a gunwale to remove remaining ashes. He slowly placed the pipe in his coat pocket. The in-port watch, Gustaf Johansen, who had no home other than the Einar II, and Captain Nordquist were again the only men on board. Earlier, Captain Nordquist gave the others the rest of the day off to spend with their families. As Captain Nordquist walked along the deck to the gangway landing, stepped up and then shuffled slowly down the rough gangplank, he was introspective, unmindful of Gustaf and what was happening on the docks around him, no longer thinking of the past, but of the future.

He thought of how his patient wife, Kjersten, endured his prolonged absences at sea for so many years that at times, he knew, she felt almost widowed. Loneliness, a marital anomaly shared by all Göteborg wives of seamen and military men, encouraged strong mutual friendships and support among the wives. When unable to give or receive attention and devotion from their sea-faring husbands, they attended to the needs of one another. Kjersten Nordquist, wife of Captain Stig Nordquist, was the natural leader among the women. Loneliness was kept at bay – at least during the day – and her sense of self-worth heightened from helping the others. Now her life would become much fuller, Captain Nordquist thought, his attention and devotion would at long last be hers without interruption.

He uncharacteristically smiled and looked again in the direction of the hillside mansion, his weakened eyes unable to clearly see Amos studying him from the porch, wondering why his father appeared so happy. Captain Nordquist was going to retire, stay home and enjoy his time with Kjersten as well as with Amos and Amos's gifted younger brother, Anders.

Captain Nordquist reflexively reached in his pocket for his pipe, remembered he just placed it there, removed his hand without it, and returned to his thoughts. Early on, there was so much time without Amos, and then Anders. It pained Captain Nordquist to think of it. Little Amos with his toy boats and that grand, cherubic smile. Always wanting to please. And Anders, on the other hand, calculating how much more of his behavior his mother would tolerate. Captain Nordquist chuckled. As he walked slowly, remembering Amos as a shepherd boy in a Christmas play, Captain Nordquist's heart became full, and he blinked, quickly wiping away the evidence with his rough, right hand.

Captain Nordquist thought of becoming more active in church. Reverend Lute Olafson, the Lutheran pastor, had been a source of stability and comfort for Captain Nordquist's small family in his absences and, since arriving in port, Captain Nordquist himself. As he walked, Captain Nordquist shrugged unhappily. The sea had given some spiritual and many material rewards, but deprived him, his family, of as much if not more. Soon Amos's brother, Anders, would be the same age as Captain Nordquist when his father, Olof, disappeared.

Olof Nordquist's disappearance was a strange, unsolved mystery. During the Napoleonic Wars, loyalties and alliances ran together like watercolors, and France was attempting to force Sweden into betraying England. Olof, a strong, fierce man with English friends and loyalty to England, and who preferred battles at sea to humdrum merchant sailing, enlisted in the United Kingdom Royal Marines. On February 13, 1811, Olof was aboard one of several ship's boats from the HMS Pandora, sent to board and capture a French brig at Scaw Reef at the northern tip of the Jutland Peninsula. The approaching boats, however, upon discovering the French brig had run aground and was abandoned, turned back to the Pandora as freezing weather set in. The men reboarded the Pandora, but after being brought aboard and restowed, the Pandora boats subsequently froze to their cradles. Shortly thereafter, in the growing darkness the Pandora pilot, William Famie, lost his bearings, and the Pandora also ran aground on Scaw Reef, gradually listing heavily to one side – but with the ship's boats frozen to their cradles, crewmen could not escape, and, as the temperature plummeted, began slowly freezing as well.

Out of the darkened mist in the rough seas, a boat from an unseen vessel – assumed to be the frigate HMS Venus which had been with the Pandora much earlier – appeared and came alongside. The coxswain, a shadowy figure speaking the King's English, specifically ordered the small contingent of Royal Marines to come aboard. With the Royal Marines aboard, the boat shoved off, heading seaward, disappearing in the blackness.

The others aboard the Pandora waited, expecting more boats, but none appeared.

Two days later, boats from the Danish mainland siding with France came and took prisoner those Pandora crewmen still alive.

What puzzled Amos was that Royal Navy records indicated the Venus, then at a distance of several miles and, unable to see the Pandora, never sent a boat.

Records also indicated there was no other Royal Navy ship in the area. The Danes later said they sent no boat.

Who or what, then, Amos wondered, was the boat and the coxswain who took his grandfather and the other Royal Marines, never to be heard from again? What happened? Many years later, requesting an investigation, Captain Stig Nordquist received an answer: no one knew. Amos would often wonder about the superstitions of mariners, their tales such as that of the Flying Dutchman witnessed occasionally in the high southern latitudes off the coast of Africa. While many such tales were fantasy, how many weren't?

It was during that terrible time following Olof's disappearance that Captain Nordquist's mother became a full-time seamstress, taking in sewing to support herself, her daughter, Ona, and her young sons, Stig and his younger brother Torvald, and when the necessities of life seemed continually beyond reach, that Captain Stig Nordquist began dreaming of wealth and little else.

Captain Nordquist stopped walking and turned around to study the veterans of so many North Sea rages: the Polstjärnan, the Nordenvinden, as well as the stately Einar II moored at the end of the pier. He thought of his brigantine, the Handelsresande, and his handsome barque, the Kringflackande, both presently at sea. The Göteborg sailing vessels at berth along the docks made Captain Nordquist consider so many others that were not, and all the families waiting for husbands, brothers and fathers to return. It occurred to him that some would not. Captain Nordquist sighed, turned and studied the road directly ahead of him as he began walking while thinking of his sons.

Amos watched his father, obviously deep in thought. Amos considered how his father constantly weighed minute details, and how his father made everything work smoothly. During the past few days it seemed his father was happier than Amos could ever remember, and Captain Nordquist would often speak to Amos of God's love, God's power, God's glory, outward behavior quite new to Captain Nordquist.

Resting, Captain Nordquist looked at the ground and continued to think of Amos and Anders. He hoped each would do what was best for them, not what they believed he would want. Captain Nordquist looked skyward as if watching seabirds above Mexico's western coastline. To Captain Nordquist it now only mattered that his sons do what was important in the eyes of God, for what was important in the eyes of God was what was ultimately important. The rest? Captain Nordquist lowered his gaze and shook his head.

Hands in his pockets, head down, Captain Nordquist quietly pushed himself up the coarse, dirt road that led from the pier to the hillside path winding through trees, planted many decades ago, that formed an arboreal semi-circle below his large hillside home. He raised his head and breathed deeply as the stimulating aromas of sea and trees mixed in the breeze. Captain Nordquist thought about his small family and what he had done with his life, and about a related matter: his important will, his last will and testament.

It was not.

He had not formally changed it in five years, and while the will had not changed, much else had.

As he walked up the path, he concluded he would change the will within the next few days, leaving everything of importance to Kjersten, Amos and Anders. Captain Nordquist's brother-in-law, Sven Ostermänn, after all, made no effort to attend to either the fleet or, in Captain Nordquist's absences, Kjersten, as well as Amos and Anders, Sven's only nephews.

Captain Nordquist wondered why Sven did not act like family; why Sven did not view his brother-in-law's success with favor. It was a source of envy, which was understandable, but the envy bled into an irrational jealousy that poisoned Sven's attitude and behavior. Sven's compulsive behavior included several ill-planned and ill-fated business ventures. Captain Nordquist shook his head. *Sven is not a good businessman; how is that my fault?*

As Captain Nordquist reached the landing next to his grand front porch, he looked up expectantly in the event Kjersten, Amos or, perhaps, Anders, were at the top of the stairs. Kjersten and Anders were inside, but there was Amos, looking down at his father with an expression that reflected what Captain Nordquist perceived were Amos's inherent intelligence and kindness. *Amos reminds me of myself*, thought Captain Nordquist. He smiled as he thought it would be quite a compliment, were it true.

Breathing heavily from the walk up the path, Captain Nordquist smiled at his grown son, anxious to talk with Amos about future plans.

Captain Nordquist looked down to find the first stair step, feeling suddenly odd, physically unstable as if the ground had shifted; feeling a sensation as if the previous moment was somehow deleted from time. What? He reflexively began to step up to the first stair, but his foot slipped, and for a moment it appeared as if he was doing a slow dance step as Captain Stig Nordquist sank to the ground, dead of a heart attack.

4

The community, young and old, walked slowly down the street, forming groups as they approached the church for the funeral service. The church filled quickly until the pews were packed. Ushers placed available chairs in the center and side aisles until those were also filled. Later arrivals stood in the narthex or the church steps, and the church doors were left open so those standing outside could hear what was said.

White-haired Pastor Lute Olafson, of above-average height, wiry, and with a ready smile, summarized Captain Nordquist's extraordinary life, concluding with Captain Nordquist's recent parsonage visit when the Einar II arrived in port. Captain Nordquist was quite anxious about the future, said Pastor Olafson. Unsure of how much time he had left, Captain Nordquist was planning retirement, wanting to spend his remaining years with his family. During Captain Nordquist's visit, Pastor Olafson said, he asked Captain Nordquist if he had been converted.

"'Converted'?"

"The sacraments and the church do not bring salvation and eternal life with God," explained Pastor Olafson, hands folded as they sat in Pastor Olafson's study with coffee and pastries, compliments of Mrs. Olafson. "Being good, going to church, does not get you into heaven because, as the *Bible* says, 'All have sinned and come short of the glory of God.' Jesus says that you have to be 'born again,' and by this He means a new spiritual birth, a transformation that only the Holy Spirit can bring about." Pastor Olafson leaned forward and rubbed his hands together as he looked warmly at Captain Nordquist. "Are you open to such a transformation?"

"Is this conversion experience common in the Lutheran church?" asked Captain Nordquist. "I had not heard of it."

"No, unfortunately many Lutherans and others in all denominations have not experienced conversion. How important is it? How important is knowing you're going to heaven?" Pastor Olafson folded his hands. "It's that important. Previously, I believed my salvation was up to me – exemplary behavior, liturgical propriety, simply being a conscientious pastor – but I must say that in private moments there was continual doubt about my salvation because, try as I might, I never felt 'good' enough. But now, Captain Nordquist," Pastor Olafson held out his hands, "I *know* I'm not good enough, but also that I'm saved." Pastor Olafson smiled brightly.

"How do I experience this conversion?"

"There is no single way and no specific time, and it's not up to you," said Pastor Olafson.

"Well…then, what do I do?

"Jesus said, 'The wind blows where it wills. You hear its sound, but you cannot tell where it comes from or where it is going. So is it with everyone born of the Spirit.' And He said, 'No one can come to me unless the Father who sent me draws him.'"

"Interesting," said Captain Nordquist, his eyebrows knitted and hands folded, looking down at the coffee table. "That, I guess, is why I'm here."

Pastor Olafson told the assembly of how he and Captain Nordquist kneeled and prayed for Captain Nordquist's conversion and salvation, how the question of salvation, which for some time had hung on Captain Nordquist's mind like the line from Coleridge's poem, "instead of a cross, an albatross," began to dissipate, and later Captain Nordquist had no doubt of his place in heaven.

Pastor Olafson concluded by saying that before Captain Nordquist left the parsonage to attend to matters on the Einar II, he said he would be more involved with spiritual matters now that he was planning retirement, stating it was time.

"And indeed," said Pastor Olafson, looking about the gathered assembly, his piercing blue eyes narrowing before he dropped both hands on the pulpit, "it was time! But not the time Captain Nordquist expected." Pastor Olafson leaned forward, gripping both sides of the pulpit. "And so shall it be for many. The good news is: Captain Nordquist is saved. He's in the glory of our Lord."

Pastor Olafson looked down at many still-vacant faces, spread his arms toward them, and asked, "But what of you? Like Captain Nordquist, many here will not see the moment of death approaching, but, regardless, before that time comes, must also know the same saving grace Captain Nordquist experienced."

Pastor Olafson's convicting words convinced many to do more than listen. After the funeral service, many waited in line to speak with Pastor Olafson, holding up the formal burial proceedings. To expedite matters, Pastor Olafson spontaneously scheduled an awakening service for that evening.

Meanwhile, when the casket was taken outside to the church cemetery behind the sanctuary, the crowd was so large it seemed to Amos that most of Göteborg was there. The void was palpable: a great man, Captain Stig Nordquist, was gone.

The awakening service that night was full and included Kjersten, Amos and Anders. In closing, Pastor Olafson summarized his simple oration: "Many of you are here because the Father drew you here; otherwise you would have little, if any, interest in this matter – quite the opposite. The next step, salvation, then, may be yours. What is this next step? Perhaps it has already been taken." Pastor Olafson smiled as he leaned forward, again holding the pulpit sides with both hands. "Jesus' sacrificial death – nothing else – paid for your sins, and your salvation is obtained by…" Pastor Olafson stood upright and again gently held out his hands, "…simply accepting He did."

After giving a benediction, Pastor Olafson stood and watched people leave. But many remained seated. After a moment, he dropped his head, eyes closed, as he brought up his hands, his left fingers cupped over his right fist. Pressing them against his chin, he began silently praying for them all. Finished, he beckoned forward those seated.

⸻ ⬧ ⸻

The following day, Captain Stig Nordquist's heirs, individually or in groups of two or three, walked up the town courthouse steps and entered the large courtroom. The heirs sat somberly in the sepulchral setting as if waiting for the beginning of another funeral service. In contrast to the funeral service, however, the gathering for the reading-of-the-will was modest. In the cavernous courtroom with ceilings high enough to accommodate two more floors, any small sound – a sniff, a muffled cough – was amplified.

Rising, the burly, bass-baritone barrister boomed like the voice of God as, in the room's still air, his voice reverberated off the walls and a courtroom ceiling. Standing at the podium rising in front of gathered heirs, all eyes upon him, the barrister solemnly intoned the terms of the will, created when Amos Nordquist was 13, shortly after the Einar II was launched.

Apprehensive heirs sat silently, concealing their unease with stoic countenances, quiet as courthouse mice in contrast to the barrister. As expected, the mansion and all its belongings, most cash and gold, and most non-nautical investments were left to Kjersten.

Captain Nordquist's widowed sister, beloved Aunt Ona, a stout woman with a lovely smile and a reputation for Scandinavian pastry, attempted to mitigate her concern by doing needlepoint while seated with nephews Amos and Anders. Ona lived rent-free in a cottage owned by her brother and, as her fingers worked anxiously, she worried about what would become of her when someone else received ownership. If Kjersten, she would probably be fine, but if someone else, where was she to live?

"To my sister Ona, I leave the small residence at…"

Upon hearing that Captain Nordquist had left the cottage to her, Ona searched for her handkerchief to dry her eyes, grateful to her older brother. Amos looked pleasantly at his aunt, then momentarily placed his right arm around her and hugged her. Drying her eyes, she looked gratefully over at Kjersten and nodded appreciatively.

As the barrister read on, Amos's thoughts turned to his father's sailing vessels, three of which were in port and two, the Handelsresande and the Kringflackande, at sea. From what his mother told him, his father's last will and testament gave Uncle Sven an interest in four of the five. How would that affect the operational efficacy painstakingly fostered by his father, and from which his father had received much satisfaction? And wealth?

To Amos, Uncle Sven was distant, strange and pointlessly enveloped in a mist of furtiveness, a tall, shadowy figure whose appearance and demeanor were more that of a phantom than an uncle. Amos recalled Uncle Sven seated in a living room chair years ago, his eyes bitter and godless, watching Amos play on the living room floor. When Amos's parents were not in the room, Sven, staring at Amos, crawled down on the floor and pretended to slowly slither – sinister sibilants simulating a hissing snake. Terrified, Amos ran from the room crying, and, as he ran, he could hear Sven laughing, reveling in Amos's terror. After that, Amos never wanted to be alone with Sven.

Although Amos's mother and father seldom talked of Uncle Sven, Amos remembered overhearing a conversation about Uncle Sven when Amos was 11. They were discussing Uncle Sven's odd fascination with the messianic French Revolution. Later Amos heard Sven animatedly explain to Kjersten that the Reign of Terror – torture, beheadings, crucifixions – was fate purging the undeserving mighty from stations that rightly belonged to the truly worthy and gifted… among whom Sven considered himself, seemingly unaware that the revolutionary purges included people no different than himself. In life, Sven's efforts were ineffective and unsuccessful, yet he was petulant and supercilious. As Amos sat thinking, he considered how completely different Sven was from Captain Nordquist. Amos sighed quietly. Would Sven cause trouble for the rest of the family?

On a chair in the back of the courtroom, alone, legs stretched out before him, dark-bearded Sven Ostermänn, long and slender, sat motionlessly to one side, his coat soiled with tar and oakum, paint of various hues, varnish, oil, and burn marks, all bleached to lighter shades by sun and sea. For anyone else, the coat would have long since been discarded. Sven strangely viewed the coat as a quasi-military jacket, the blemishes citations, the tatters campaign ribbons, and patches badges of honor. Illogically, he wore the frayed coat with pride.

Amos remembered Sven's tattoos, and they intrigued Amos. Sven's arms, when uncovered, displayed ragged tattoos of a devil's head on his right arm, and a tiny map of Java and Borneo on his left, as if Sven needed others to know his wonted lifestyle and where he'd been – although the tattoos were now little more than discolored blemishes that could be mistaken for skin disease. The human body is a work of art while tattoos are artwork, Amos thought, usually bad artwork. No one gets tattoos for themselves. What would be the point? But why would anyone else care? And Sven's tattoos are ugly – if they weren't ugly at first, they are now, as all tattoos become, thought Amos, contributing to Sven's seemingly intentional effort at unsightliness. But why would anyone make an effort to be unattractive? Amos folded his arms. Why do people do any of the illogical things they do?

Amos shrugged, folded his hands, and with some effort returned his attention to the barrister itemizing multiple valuables.

Meanwhile, Sven sat motionlessly, his rat-like face sodden from drink, his mouth slightly turned-up in an expression of fixed pleasantness contrasting with his black, acrimonious eyes, hardened around the edges. Earlier when

Amos turned around to see who else was in the room, Uncle Sven, tarpaulin cap covering his hair, looked back for a moment with no change in pleasant expression. At a glance, Sven's eyes seemed anxious, however, and somehow his relaxed posture seemed rigid.

In the formality of the moment, Amos's attention returned to the front of the room. As Sven looked at Amos and his family, Sven's eyes narrowed and glistened as if being buffeted by sea winds, and, although Amos's back was turned to Sven, Amos sensed malevolence. He wondered why Uncle Sven made no attempt to greet his sister or sit with her when he entered. For that matter, unlike many others, Uncle Sven did not come by the house following Captain Nordquist's death. Where had Uncle Sven been? What was he thinking?

"'To efficiently continue the commercial enterprise begun years ago,'" intoned the barrister, reading the words of Captain Stig Nordquist, "'I herewith bequeath 1) 75% ownership in the good ships Einar II, the Nordanvinden, and the Polstjärnan, and the barque Kringflackande, all homeported in Göteborg, to my wife, Kjersten Nordquist, and, to facilitate the day-to-day responsibilities required by ownership, 2) 25% ownership in said vessels to my brother-in-law, Sven Augustus Ostermänn, trusting that he work diligently and conscientiously with my wife/his sister, Kjersten Nordquist, maximizing operational efficiency, seaworthiness and general productivity, and to provide any and all services as deemed reasonable and necessary by my wife/his sister for the vessels' well-being and the well-being of crewmembers. The brigantine Handelsresande I leave to my wife to hold in trust for my sons Amos Nordquist and Anders Nordquist until each reaches lawful age, whereupon each shall inherit one-half interest.'"

Amos did not hear what the barrister read next, thinking only about what he just heard. At the time the will was written, it made sense because his mother would have been unable to run the fleet herself. Her brother, Sven, was the logical co-owner to insure continued effective maritime operation. The course steered by Sven, however, subsequently took a different heading. Meanwhile, Amos grew to be resourceful and discerning, a natural leader capable of accepting the responsibility bequeathed to his Uncle Sven. But Captain Stig Nordquist's will said otherwise.

The barrister's reading also stated that Captain Nordquist left a substantial amount of money to his gregarious brother, Torvald. Amos remembered that with above-average vision, fortitude and perseverance, while in their early 20's his father and Uncle Torvald pooled their savings, bought well-located timberland, logged it, subdivided the land, and sold the smaller tracts. They used the proceeds to buy more timberland, do the same thing again, and it was this beginning that enabled Captain Nordquist to buy his first commercial vessel, the brigantine Handelsresande, used to transport goods and people between Sweden, Denmark and Norway.

Uncle Torvald took a portion of his timber proceeds share and went to America – briefly New York, then Chicago, and later Minnesota where he acquired two sections of well-located, river bottom timberland. He hired a Scandinavian logging crew, partially cleared some of the timberland, sold the logs, subdivided what he had partially cleared, and resold the subdivided parcels at affordable terms to Scandinavian immigrants coming to America in search of a better life. While engaged in logging and subdividing, he built a sawmill. He bought more timberland while gradually logging and clearing what remained of the first purchase, but now milling the logs, and continued this effort with the second purchase.

At first, Uncle Torvald enjoyed his success, and sent money back to his brother to reinvest in Sweden, but shortly stopped sending money because he found better investments in an expanding land of opportunity attracting tens of thousands of Scandinavian immigrants annually. As time passed, however, his letters evidenced that satisfaction from profitable enterprise was beginning to wane. With a spirit that suited his new surroundings, Uncle Torvald sought and found other interests. Uncle Torvald said there was an inspirational mindset in America, a stratum of idealism, both unique and prevalent, that energized much of the country, creating a communal verve not felt in Sweden. Life became big for Torvald Nordquist, and hearing of extraordinary events happening throughout the country, he decided he wanted to be part of the great American adventure.

As time passed, logging and subdividing were discontinued. He sold his land holdings and the sawmill. Having made a significant amount of money, he left Minnesota in search of whatever grand undertaking America would offer.

While his family in Sweden received few letters from Uncle Torvald, the letters that arrived were fascinating. At the moment no one actually knew where Uncle Torvald was, and his family was unable to contact him about his brother's death. Uncle Torvald was a significant benefactor in Captain Nordquist's will because of Torvald's and Stig's agreement that Stig reinvest Torvald's portion of the original timber money, as well as money initially sent back from America. For quite some time, Captain Nordquist conscientiously invested, reinvested, and re-reinvested Torvald's share along with his own, and the amount of Torvald's share grew exponentially. As a consequence, these many years later Torvald was entitled to a large monetary sum, over 50,000 riksdaler specie.

"Where is Uncle Torvald?" asked Anders a little too loudly as he sat next to his mother, leaning forward.

"We don't know," whispered Kjersten through a cupped hand. "The last we heard, he was somewhere in America fighting Indians." Anders's face beamed, and as he relaxed against the wooden bench back, the muffled thud reverberated in the huge room. Oblivious to the courtroom, Anders began to daydream. "Regardless of what he's doing," added Kjersten quietly, "somehow we must find him."

Although Anders actually had never met Uncle Torvald, Anders knew all about him. The occasional letter from Uncle Torvald told of experiences that made Swedish seafaring seem tame by comparison. During Sunday afternoon socials with family friends, when conversation about day-to-day subjects became dull, Uncle Torvald's experiences in America would be reintroduced, followed by cautious-but-imaginative speculation about his present whereabouts and exploits, fueled in part by recent news from the New Country. In his absence, he became a family legend, and the longer he stayed away and left fact-finding to the imaginations of others, the more the legend grew.

50,000 riksdaler specie. Probably chicken feed for Uncle Torvald, mused Anders. Fighting Indians. Anders contemplated the implications. George Washington. Patrick Henry. Daniel Boone. Torvald Nordquist.

As the final statements were read, Amos resigned himself to working with and for his Uncle Sven, a man who had grown distant, his presence and activities a mystery since Amos was younger. As the Nordquists slowly walked with the others out of the large courtroom into the formal waiting area next to the foyer, Sven Ostermänn, his hands in his pockets, stood watching, his pleasant expression unchanged.

"Sven," Kjersten happily smiled as she, Amos and Anders approached Sven, "we haven't seen one another for a while! But we'll be seeing one another quite often now, no doubt."

"Actually, I'd like to see you this afternoon," replied Sven formally, as if correcting her in his smooth baritone voice.

"Excellent suggestion," said Kjersten, pleasantly looking up at her younger brother. "Under the circumstances, I agree we should get together immediately. We have much responsibility to consider. This could be an opportunity for many things. Amos," Kjersten looked up at her oldest son, "will join us and we'll see what each of us needs to do to accommodate the wishes of my late husband, all of us working together." Kjersten smiled again, attempting to coax a genuinely warm response from her younger brother.

Sven's pleasant expression remained unchanged and his hyena's eyes affectless, as if not having heard. While Amos sincerely wanted to have a friendly, even loving relationship with an uncle who always seemed distant, Uncle Sven was still disinterested in closer family ties. Even though Sven instantly received partial ownership in Göteborg's most valuable fleet, there was no evidence of gratitude, no feeling of empathy toward the others with whom he now would be expected to spend significant time. If Amos's intuition of Sven's disinterest was accurate, what was Sven thinking? Meet this afternoon. More to the point, Amos thought, what does Uncle Sven want?

In public, Kjersten was stoic. Away from the public eye, however, she mourned deeply over the death of her husband to whom she was married since she was 17; mourned because of her loss and their loss, mourned for what was and what was to have been – for her, for both of them. Certainly, it was a time for mourning, but because it was a time for mourning, it was also a time to be comforted. The circumstances provided an opportunity to repair weakened bonds between brother and sister, and Kjersten wanted it so. Visiting his widowed sister in her sorrow, closing the emotional gap between them at an opportune moment, would have united them, but Sven did not appear, and another opportunity to strengthen their relationship sailed off, familial love swirling and disappearing like eddies in its wake.

"I will be by around 3:00 then," said Sven pleasantly but formally before turning and walking away without having said "Goodbye"…or "Hello."

Without expression, Amos watched Sven walk out the courthouse front door and down the steps, apparently in a hurry to get somewhere else and, perhaps, Amos intuited, momentarily distance himself from what he would need to face.

"Sven is an odd person," said Amos, turning to his mother. "I still think of him as 'Uncle Sven.' But," Amos again looked toward the door, "there are things about him that elude me…and, I must say, I can't find it in myself to completely trust him." Amos again looked at his mother. "You know, I never have…even when I was little."

"Yes," said Kjersten without expression, her head slightly tilted back as she continued to look toward the courthouse door after her brother was gone. "Your father would approve. Maintain that perspective when your uncle comes by at 3:00."

5

At around 3:00 p.m., the knock came at the large, front door. As Kjersten opened the door, the cold wind raced in ahead of Sven.

"Sven, please come in! Goodness, winter can't be here yet; it was just summer."

Kjersten closed the door immediately after Sven entered. Tarpaulin hat in hand, he walked casually through the living room, looking about at paintings and shelves displaying books, artifacts and souvenirs, many from places Sven had also been. Absently stroking his dark beard, Sven sat down on the center chesterfield in a corner circle of Venetian velvet-upholstered sofas surrounding a large coffee table: a wide circle of glass lying atop a lateral ship's wheel supported by a mahogany base with brass trim. The table centerpiece was an intriguing miniature six-masted schooner inside a large, glass jug.

Sven re-familiarized himself with the room for a moment and then pointed toward a stuffed, kleptoparasitic magnificent frigatebird, a bird whose appearance and behavior earned it the nickname "Man O'War," its red breast appropriately inflated, standing nearby on a short branch affixed to a wall plaque aside and above the gaping main fireplace.

"Frigatebird." Sven sat down, put his hands behind his head, and crossed his legs. "Odd name for that feathered thief. 'Birds of feather…?' Not that one. It's everyone for himself. Not part of any crew. Makes its living assaulting other birds, taking food they've worked for. '*Mort aux voleurs* [Death to thieves!],'" said Sven, repeating a cry from the bloody French Revolution. "Now, me," continued Sven, "I like being part of a crew. I like being part of team. 'Put the welfare of the crew ahead of personal gain and you'll still be better off,' I always say."

"Uncle Sven," said Amos as he entered the room, "hello. Until this morning, we hadn't seen you in a while." Amos sat down in one of the large, stuffed chairs across from Sven, as Kjersten sat in another, both facing Sven.

Anders came in and flopped into a sofa, attracting attention and earning a disapproving look from his mother. In response, he sat upright, as he was prepared to do, and smiled a greeting at Sven.

"Well, my goodness," responded Sven, sitting forward. "Anders, is that you?

By golly, you have grown!" Sven looked at Kjersten. "What a good-looking son you have there."

Anders just orchestrated another "what a good-looking son" comment, following up with a disingenuous expression of sincere rectitude.

It was true, of course; while Amos was handsome, Anders was striking. As with most European family trees, the Nordquist family was heavily influenced by European trade, and the Nordquist boys were consequently part Scandinavian, Scotch, English, German, and with an Andalusian grandfather, Spanish. It appeared that Anders received the best of each nationality, with predominantly Spanish overtones. Anders had no problem with self-esteem. Given the opportunity to be anyone in the history of the world, Anders would have picked Anders.

"Yes, Sven. I am very proud of both my sons," responded Kjersten, resisting the temptation to discuss Amos and Anders in more detail and, since Sven had not seen her sons for years, the urge to question why Sven was absent, unreachable, for so long. "We obviously have a lot of catching-up to do. How have you been doing, Sven?"

"Well, that's why I'm here," said Sven, softly clapping his hands together while looking at the ship's wheel beneath the coffee table glass. "Haven't been by in a while and I've been giving this whole thing a lot of thought. While I like being part of crew, I really have done nothing to deserve ownership in any of Captain Nordquist's boats, and I think the only fair thing to do is sell my interest to both of you."

He looked up pleasantly at Kjersten.

"Doesn't necessarily have to be for full value," Sven added. "Probably smoother sailing for all of us." Sven's affectionate expression seemingly plumbed the depths of kindheartedness. "You'd have complete control of the boats, and I'd have money to pay a few bills."

"That would take care of some pretty healthy bills," laughed Amos. Sven did not laugh, but still continued to look back pleasantly. Amos looked intently at Sven. "Uncle Sven, what did you have in mind?"

Looking down for a moment, Sven folded his hands. He looked up at Amos.

"I have a few bills and, under the present, eh, unfortunate circumstances – the passing of a good man, my brother-in-law, Stig – I figured I could help my family, and my family might see to help me through my own problem."

"Buying your interest. But I'm curious – perhaps it's none of my business – what kind of bills, Sven?" asked Kjersten. "How big?"

"Bigger'n I'd like to have," Sven nodded sincerely. Preserving a moment of politeness, the others nodded in return, although aware that Sven had just deflected the question. Amos's curiosity grew.

"With 25% ownership in the *Einar II*, the *Nordanvinden*, the *Polstjärnan* and the *Kringflackande*, were we to buy your interest, you'd have a lot more than you need to pay a few bills," said Amos.

"Sven, this is rather sudden. I have to think," said Kjersten. "We have ample savings, but you understand… At the moment, I'm uncertain I want to touch that money. We owe nothing on any of the boats, and I think it is safe to say that

Stig would not want them to become collateral for any indebtedness. And it was never his intention to…"

"I agree; all of that is correct," interrupted Sven, having anticipated her response, "but we both know the will was drawn-up a number of years ago and, now," Sven looked intently at Kjersten, "if Stig were alive, and were to re-do the will, do you think *I'd* be in it…like I am?"

Neither Amos nor Kjersten spoke.

"I'd expect you two to jump at the chance to be in total ownership! And here I am, trying to help all of us – giving you the chance to take total control," Sven's eyes narrowed, "and somehow you don't think this is wise? Think about it, now," Sven said as he looked at the others with an uncomfortable intensity, his dark eyes shifting back and forth between Amos and Kjersten. "As a practical matter, were I in your shoes, I'd think real hard about how I could get total control… while getting Sven, your own flesh and blood, his money."

"We could do it," shrugged Amos, looking at his mother. "I suppose we could have the boats individually appraised and…"

"No, son," interrupted Sven in a monotone, nodding as he spoke. "'Keep things simple,' I say. Don't need formal appraisals. I'm not going to get greedy. I'm your old Uncle Sven. Just check around tomorrow. Ask a few other owners or one of the ship brokers what they think the boats are worth, and…"

"Sven, please, I'd rather not do that," Kjersten interjected politely. "After all, we're not selling the boats on the open market. I'd rather not waste a broker's time and, however reasonable, we can't go by the opinions of local owners. In the first place, I'd prefer not to involve them in our affairs and, secondly, I would want a firm basis for value – not just speculation. No, we'd need to bring in a competent appraiser, someone recommended by Lloyds, and…"

"That might take a whole month, Kjersten." Sven was annoyed. The fingers on his right hand began drumming on his knee.

"Then it would take a month," replied Amos. "What's a month?"

Sven sat fidgeting in his chair, legs still crossed, his dark eyes staring at Amos. He looked away, his forehead beginning to glisten. He looked back at Kjersten. If she did not want to touch any of the family's savings accounts…

"We need not make this complicated. Go down to a bank," said Sven to Kjersten, "and talk to a banker. Those boats are worth a lot. Those boats received excellent maintenance." Sven looked at Amos. "Your father was a conscientious man. The banker knows that. You will continue to hire good crews. You two are very capable of taking over." Sven turned to Kjersten. "Simply borrow the money."

"Sven, we neither need nor want to borrow the money," said Kjersten. "We may not…"

"But it would be stupid not to." Sven held his hands out toward Kjersten and in a tight voice said, "You don't need money, and have money, so they'll lend you money. Ask the banker how long it'll take. Put a little pressure on him to loan the money quickly and he'll…"

"Uncle Sven, you're not listening to mom," said Amos, annoyed at his uncle's condescending attitude.

"Don't interrupt me," said Sven formally, obliquely looking at Amos. "Remember, I've been around awhile."

Amos was momentarily taken back. Sven's rejoinder opened the emotional valve that normally kept Amos's temper from seeping into his heart.

"Then you should have learned something about respect," countered Amos in a flat, hard voice, staring at Sven. Intimidation by Sven was out of the question. Intimidation, in fact, was something Amos had not experienced since he was 14, and since reaching adulthood, the opportunities for Amos's anger to flash like lightening were few. While Sven never saw his nephew antagonized, inadvertently Sven was giving himself that unique opportunity. "And I encourage you to act like a gentleman," added Amos, sliding to the edge of the chesterfield.

"I'll behave as I wish, of course" said Sven brusquely. "And I'll do the talking here since I'm the one who knows what he's talking about."

Uncle Sven wouldn't dare speak like that to my father, Amos thought. Were my father here, in fact, Uncle Sven would say very little. Dad would dictate how things would be done. That thought was followed by a related thought: Dad may not be here but I am, and I will do what Dad would do. Amos's eyes flashed as he stood up.

"Then you'll know that banks don't throw money around any more than we do," said Amos. Sven stared back. "They want documentation. *We* want documentation." Kjersten lightly patted the back of Amos's leg, attempting to calm him. Amos took the hint and slowly sat down.

"You too should want to know actual value," continued Amos. "Regardless of how we take care of the matter, the first thing that should be established is value – which would be a lot of money, hopefully much more than you need, and then we..."

"I can use as much as I can get," interjected Sven, annoyed that Amos would not be cowed, and startled at Amos's intimidating reaction. "And especially as soon as I can get it," Sven added more courteously. Then, ignoring Amos, Sven looked at Kjersten. "Kjersten," Sven said mawkishly, "I'd like you to go talk to a bank tomorrow morning and push to..."

"Sven, wha..."

"Uncle Sven, why do you need all that money so quickly?" asked Amos, attempting to get to the heart of the matter.

Sven looked at Amos. "I told you," answered Sven, his forehead glistening, "I have bills to pay."

The others waited for Sven to elaborate, but he just looked uncomfortably at the bookshelf as if reading the book titles.

Then he looked back toward the others and annoyingly repeated, "Bills to pay."

"Very well, Uncle Sven. You have bills to pay. What bills?" asked Amos obstinately. Obviously angry and in discomfort, Sven's eyes shifted about and he made no reply.

"Sven, what bills?" asked Kjersten.

Sven stared at the coffee table, thinking hard.

"Uncle Sven," added Amos, "the amount of money we're discussing justifies our knowing why you need it, and if you don't tell us honestly, your reticence reduces our incentive to quickly and cooperatively purchase your interest." Amos glanced at his mother as Sven's demeanor darkened. "And," added Amos, "I'm sensing that if we don't purchase your interest, and do it soon, something will happen...something bad. What might that be?"

Sven stared at Amos.

Sven mumbled unintelligibly under his breath as his body rolled slightly in discomfort, and he glanced to his left. His eyes again grew larger, his expression betraying the fear in his heart.

"Sven?" asked Kjersten, sensing his fear. "What have you done?"

Anders was sitting rigidly upright, listening.

Sven looked back, his eyes emanating both fear and anger like the eyes of a cornered bilge rat. *By not telling Kjersten and Amos... I have to tell them.* Amos and Kjersten were the only people in the world who could help and, as his eyes shifted back and forth between Amos and Kjersten, he knew they were his only hope. Sven looked wide-eyed down at the coffee table, shrugged, and failed to completely suppress a sigh. *I will have to tell the truth.* He looked at the others, and his expression slowly changed until he regained his former look of pleasantness, causing them to look back perplexed. Sven gabbled an answer.

"I had a chance to make a lot of money," began Sven. "A lot of money," he repeated almost breathlessly for emphasis, "if I could run a shipment of guns from Prussia up to Norway. I could make... I just needed a ship to..."

"Guns?" asked Amos, leaning forward. "To Norway? What are you talking about?"

"There are those in Norway who don't *want* to be united with Sweden," answered Sven, looking at Amos. "They *never* wanted to be united with Sweden. It's *their* country, *their* language, *their* destiny, and I had the opportunity to..."

"Uncle Sven," interrupted Amos, "we know that. We know about the Norse language – we speak it – and the Norse gods and the Norse things that are no longer Swedish. But you are Swedish," emphasized Amos. "Why on earth would you..."

"I'm Swedish?"

Sven put his right hand behind him on the chesterfield arm, pushed, and got to his feet.

"Really, son? Is that right?" Sven asked with a hint of contemptuousness. "And for the less discerning that might be as far as it goes." He shoved his hands in his pockets, his eyebrows rose, and he focused on Amos who looked back inquisitively. "For one, give Norway to the Norwegians. But most importantly, I had an opportunity. I was in the perfect place at the perfect time. I had a chance to get ahead, way ahead," he added angrily. "No, nothing like you. Not like Stig. But to a decent level of financial respectability. And you know that if I didn't deliver those arms, any one of a dozen arms merchants would have, and they would have made money. 'Swedish?' How was *that* relevant? How was that important?"

Lips in a taut frown, at first his eyes again narrowed as Sven defiantly looked back and forth at Amos and Kjersten, but, as he thought, his eyes again enlarged like full sails.

"Norwegians, Swedes, Danes…regardless of nationality, idiots are idiots!" Sven glared at the Amos. "Okay, yes, Norway, although not as much as Denmark, has its fair share of idiots. So let them go run their own damned country; what does it matter to anyone here? What do we get from Norway, Denmark?" Sven jabbed the air with his finger. "And what do they get from us? Swedes give so much! How many men did Sweden lose in Schleswig?" he asked, referring to the 1848-1851 First Schleswig War where Sweden sided with Denmark against Prussia. He stopped gesticulating for a moment and stared at the others. "How *many*? Four times more than all the other armies combined! Both sides! For what? For who?" Amos and Kjersten looked back silently. Still wide-eyed, Sven continued angrily, "Not for Sweden!" He held out his hands, palms up. "Why does Sweden help those *idiots*, the Danes, the Norwegians? Cut them adrift, I say. Otherwise we're even bigger idiots than they are!"

Sven stood defiantly, his eyebrows knitted as he looked at Amos. He took a half step forward, and his eyes burrowed into Amos who remained sitting back, looking up.

"Wars are waged for stupid reasons by stupid people," Sven added angrily, "the bourgeoisie with all its absurd convictions and pretentious, foolish religious beliefs somehow compensating for all that self-inflicted, degrading intellectual poverty. All those murky principles that *somehow*," he shook his right index finger, "invariably convolute into justification for going to war!" Then he jabbed the air with his finger as he said more solemnly, "Such stupid people *deserve* be taken advantage of. Opportunity knocked and," he held his hands out, "I was obligated to open the door! Once again there was *money* to be made from the folly of stupid people, and was I to just stand by? Do nothing? As usual? Someone would make it. I knew that! And that should have been me!"

"Was it?" asked Amos.

Sven looked sullenly at Amos.

"Sven," asked Kjersten again quietly, "what have you done?"

Sven's eyes remained large as he fought to find the right words. Without saying anything else, he turned and sat down. His eyes narrowed as he looked mulishly at Amos, and begrudgingly began to tell the story.

"I made a down payment on schooner brig, hired a crew, and…"

"Excuse me, Sven, you made…?" interrupted Kjersten. "But where did you get that much money?"

Sven looked at Kjersten and at first said nothing.

"I borrowed the money."

"From who, Sven?" asked Kjersten.

"A lender."

"From who, Sven?"

"A Russian!" said Sven angrily. For a moment Sven said nothing but, before either Kjersten or Amos could ask him anything else, he added, "Actually a group of Russians; a Russian consortium." Sven sat motionlessly, looking at the floor.

"They lend money and you pay it back. Simple as that."

"Interest rate? Loan fee? Collateral?" asked Amos.

Sven stared at the embottled schooner centerpiece on the coffee table.

"What did you use for collateral?" asked Kjersten. "I can't see where the schooner brig's seller would subordinate to these Russians. What else did you use?"

"My modest farm," said Sven almost blandly, looking obliquely at Kjersten without emotion. Kjersten's mouth opened slightly.

"Sven? 'My modest farm'? But you… you don't own that farm," said Kjersten. "Unless you purchased it lately. But no, you haven't. We've known the owner for years. I would know if he sold it to you. You still don't own that farm, do you?"

Sven looked at the others with the supercilious expression of one with superior knowledge, as if he and he alone knew the secret to successful alchemy or the location of Blackbeard's treasure. He pleasantly beamed defiantly at them and they became more uncomfortable.

"I showed them a deed."

"A forged deed?"

Sven's expression went blank as he looked at the books along the lower bookshelf while the others looked back, mouths partially open.

"They asked, 'What do you have for collateral?'" said Sven. "I gave them collateral. I said I had a farm. But they wanted more, something else. So," Sven sighed, still looking at the bookshelf, "I offered something else. I didn't think it would be that easy. I thought they were unused to being…" Sven's head tilted back and forth for a moment as he searched for the proper word, "…misled."

Amos sensed that Sven's conscience was not functioning, as if he was in a queer psychological state and to him this was all a game.

"So I thought to myself, 'They are stupid,'" said Sven. "Stupid Russians."

Amos and Kjersten looked at one another.

"'Something else,'" said Amos. "You said, '…something else' as collateral. What else?" asked Amos.

Sven's expression hardened as he looked at Amos. Looking to the side at the floor, he first wiped one eyelid and then the other with his right hand fingertips.

"What else, Uncle Sven?" repeated Amos, annoyed at Sven's disingenuousness. Uncle Sven is as slippery as *lutefisk*, Amos thought.

Sven did not look at Amos or Kjersten. His skin color became etiolated as his forehead glistened even more. The moment passed with no response; the silence grew more uncomfortable.

"Uncle Sven, what else?" Amos intensely repeated for the third time.

Looking at the coffee table centerpiece, Sven finally gave an answer.

"The *Einar II*."

"Sven…!" exclaimed Kjersten in stunned disbelief. "The *Einar II*? Sven… How could…?"

"I told them I had a half-interest," Sven shot back loudly, defensively waving his hands. "I knew I would eventually have an interest. I didn't know what it would be. Half seemed possible. It seemed to satisfy them. They wanted proof.

Fine. I would show them proof!"

"Another forged document?" asked Amos.

Anders sat quietly fascinated.

"I had it planned perfectly," countered Sven almost smugly. "I could cover everything. There was hardly any chance for a mistake. We signed papers," said Sven, who again stared at the bottled schooner centerpiece, thinking about the signing. "The Russians and I signed papers. They didn't appear to check records. They gave me the money, and told me they would be watching me. With part of the money, I made a substantial down payment on a schooner brig, the *Orvar-Odd*, home-ported in Oslo." Sven finally looked up at the others. "The *Orvar-Odd* was familiar to those in Oslo. A diversion. No one would think twice about its presence in Norwegian waters or any destination in Norway.

"I made all the arrangements to sail to Königsberg, load the shipment of weapons, and transport the shipment to a Norwegian militia who would pay me for both the weapons and transportation of the weapons. It was a risky undertaking, but when it was finished, I would have money, a schooner brig and a profession," said Sven animatedly. "I would be able to make up a great deal of leeway."

"But what happened?" asked Amos. Sven's damp face became expressionless.

"All went well until we neared the coast of Norway." Sven took a deep breath and let it out slowly. His forehead furrowed as his gaze dropped to the coffee table. "A sloop came up to the *Orvar-Odd*; the Russians were on board. As usual, they were dressed in black fur coats with black fur hats, and they looked at me with that perpetual scowl. I wasn't sure what they knew or what they would do. I tried to be friendly, but they just looked at me sullenly and they told me – *told* me – to turn the ship and its cargo over to them – they told me they knew I was committing fraud." He looked up. "'Fraud.' That's what they called it. They told me that the weapons, together with my interest in the *Orvar-Odd*, would constitute 80% repayment for the loan – the weapons alone were worth more than that – and I should return to Göteborg and find a way to repay the remaining 20%. I could not argue. I had no defendable, legal position, and no other way to stop them. They took me ashore, put some documents in front of me, looked at me as if I were spoiled cod, and said, 'Sign here, and here, and here,' and put me on a boat home."

"Put you on a boat home," echoed Amos. "It could have been worse."

"They wanted another 20%," said Sven.

"They did not harm you?" asked Kjersten.

"No, they just looked at me like… When I left, one man – his name was Leonid – muttered in English that I was 'maybe only good for fish food.'" Sven stared angrily at the coffee table, revisiting that moment. "They said they would be in touch soon."

Sven looked anxiously at the fireplace while attempting to say something, his mouth opening and closing like a rock cod's, but no words were formed. His forehead began to freely perspire.

"Uncle Sven," asked Amos, "who told you there were serious revolutionaries in Norway? I had not heard that."

"The Russians themselves told me," answered Sven, holding his palms out. "They would know. And they were willing to loan me the money to buy and deliver the arms."

Amos and Kjersten looked at Sven without expression.

"What did they do with the *Orvar-Odd*? With the weapons?" asked Amos.

"Perhaps they sold them to the revolutionaries. I don't know," sighed Sven. He bent forward, folded his hands, and looked at the floor. "The Skagerrak leads to many places."

"What you did, as far as it went, if not morally, legally and ethically repugnant," said Kjersten, folding her hands, "would be commendable; your initiative was extraordinary. I don't understand what has prevented you from expending this much initiative in legitimate enterprises. But instead you weaved a very tangled web, Sven."

"So, if I understand this," said Amos, "they enabled you to go through all the trouble of negotiating the weapons purchase and then shipping the weapons to Norwegian waters, where they, not you, delivered the weapons to…someone with cash who wanted them…and kept the schooner brig."

Sven stared at the coffee table centerpiece with resignation, his far away expression blank except for his eyes that were still fearful.

"They are dangerous men. And clever." Sven said, unfolding his hands. "Yes, I suppose…I was doing their work for them…for free." Sven slowly slumped back in his seat, not looking at the others.

"How do you plan on paying the other 20%?" asked Amos after a moment.

"Why am I here?" asked Sven, looking at Amos without expression. "When I first sat down, what were we talking about?"

6

I think we should pay the Swede a visit soon, Sergei, Leonid," said a relaxed Yuri, speaking Russian in his gravelly voice as he leaned back in his chair next to the greasy kitchen wall. The large, austere room smelled rank after years of frying fish and potatoes with the windows shut. The men were eating dinner.

The marred wooden table held a meal of pirozhki, a crepe-like dumpling filled with Yuri's favorite stuffing of boiled, chopped meat mixed with mashed potatoes; and okroshka, a cold soup of raw vegetables, boiled eggs, and ham, in kvass, a slightly alcoholic liquid made from dark rye bread. Having eaten the solid contents of the okroshka, Yuri lifted the bowl, tilted his head back, and loudly drained the remaining kvass, some running into his thick, black beard. Finished, he leaned forward and absently banged down his wooden bowl. He picked up the remaining pirozhki and bit into it like a wolf eel into a fleeing crab.

Chewing with satisfaction, Yuri added, "There has been enough time for Sven to approach his wealthy relatives. We have a signed document stating we have for collateral a small farm and 50% of a large ship, the Einar II." Yuri chewed a moment longer, swallowed, then smiled.

A smile from Yuri was uncommon; his teeth were bad and his pleasures seldom lighthearted. He allowed himself the pleasure of the moment as the others, continuing to eat while looking at the table before them, responded with nods of uncharacteristic amusement. While Sven's web was tangled, theirs was spun perfectly.

"For most people," Sergei mused, his eyes half open as usual, "a worthless document is a worthless document. Eh? But for us," he threw his hands up, letting them fall with a loud slap on his lap, "nothing is worthless. What is worthless? Is there anything worthless?" he almost laughed. "I have not seen it. Value is in the eye of the beholder, Leonid."

"Yes. Our investments are low risk…for us." Leonid glanced at the others who nodded. "Yet, properly invested, 20% can become 100%," Leonid shrugged. The three of them again nodded, their bodies briefly shaking from laughter within. "Yes, we shall visit the Swede and hear what is said."

"And when the answer is, 'No,' Yuri?" asked Sergei, leaning back in his chair, and folding his arms.

"Fish food?" scowled Leonid, looking up at Yuri.

"Leonid, of what benefit would that be at this moment?" asked Yuri tersely.

"As you know, the benefit is long-term, Yuri," answered Leonid, continuing the investment analogy. "Obviously, others will again know we must be taken seriously. How seriously would they take us if we did not 'service' our loans?"

"When was the last time repayment became an issue?" asked Yuri. "Not for a year. We will get our money, Leonid." Yuri looked directly at Leonid. "I must ask you: is it wise to kill the source of repayment before other options are exhausted? No. How would we get the remainder of what is 'owed' us? I am not worried about future borrowers – when the time is right, they will learn – I am only intent on getting what is available now."

"So what do you propose we do this time, Yuri?" asked Leonid.

"Before I can tell you that, Leonid, we must pay the Swede a visit." He began picking his teeth with a fingernail for a moment. Then Yuri folded his hands over his stomach, and looked at the others. "It is time to do that." Looking at the table, scowling, the others nodded.

***

Each in their separate thoughts, but of a single mind, led by Yuri, the three men somberly marched in unison, hands in the pockets of their long fur coats, each muskrat мужские шапки tightly fitted atop their heads as they headed up the path to visit "the Swede."

Arriving at the base of the large front porch, they made no attempt to muffle the thick clomping of their boots as, side-by-side, they walked-up the expansive wooden steps, sounding like the marching army in which they had once served, and then maintained an identical pace to the front door.

Yuri banged the big doorknocker several times too loudly, and none of the men noticed. They stood staring at the door as if by doing so they could see inside. When the door opened, they could.

"Hallå," Kjersten said formally in Swedish, looking back and forth, unsure of to whom she was speaking.

"Ehr, we need to speak to Captain Stig Nordquist," came the gruff statement in English.

"Captain Nordquist passed away several weeks ago," Kjersten responded guardedly in English. A sensation of fear welled up in her, and her eyes grew larger. "Who are you?"

The three, bearded bear-men, frowning, looked back menacingly. "It may be more important that we first ask: who are you?" asked the one in the middle. "Are you Captain Nordquist's wife – Sven Ostermänn's sister?"

"Yes," answered Kjersten.

"Sven Ostermänn is part owner of the Einar II? Yes?"

"Yes. What's this…"

"Sven Ostermänn owes us much money," said Yuri adamantly. Kjersten studied the men. "We need to collect the money," continued Yuri, "or we become your partners. We do not want to become your partners. We do not like partners…except us. You may not like to have us as partners, yes? So…we want the money Sven Ostermänn owes us." Yuri leaned forward slightly. "You must pay."

"When did Sven make this arrangement?" asked Kjersten, feigning ignorance.

"It does not matter," replied Yuri gruffly. "We want to get paid now."

"It does matter," countered Kjersten, hugging in the fear she felt. "Sven's interest only became recent…with the death of my husband. Before then he had no legal interest in the boats and…"

"Do you mean he committed fraud?" interrupted Sergei, his eyes narrow.

"Then he should go to jail," growled Leonid loudly, looking at Yuri and Sergei.

"Is that what you want?" asked Yuri. "For your brother to go to jail?"

"No, of course that is not what I want," said Kjersten quickly, her stomach tightening. She made a quick decision and asked, "Won't you come in?"

Won't you come in? Is that what she just said? The others looked at one another. No one ever invited them in. Most people just wanted them to leave. And would pay them to do so. Or they could come back to get paid. That was usually how it was.

"We will come in," said Yuri, walking by Kjersten as she held the door open, letting in the cold. Yuri glanced at the high ceilings rimmed with thick, crown molding, and the attractively decorated room. Artifacts and paintings were everywhere. It was a small museum. He was silently impressed. Kjersten led them into the brightly decorated parlor with a light scent of cloves. Amos, hearing the footsteps, came downstairs.

"Won't you sit down?" asked Kjersten formally.

The three Russians hesitated, glancing at one another, and slowly took seats in ornate captain's chairs.

Toward one side of the parlor were small portraits, white chair rails, white lace curtains, and white built-in shelves displaying china saucers, teacups and fine porcelain statues. Against the light blue and white wallpapered wall was a massive, elaborately carved, oak hutch. Yuri had never seen anything like it and stared at it. Throughout the parlor there was no sign of dust; everything looked as if spring-cleaning had been completed that morning.

Amos stood at the parlor entrance and looked at Kjersten questioningly.

Without expression, Yuri glanced obliquely at the others. Leonid said nothing, shifting back and forth uncomfortably in his seat. Sergei stared straight ahead, his expression surly, annoyed. Kjersten had not asked for their coats.

"Would you like tea?" asked Kjersten formally as if addressing three familiar women.

Tea? How was this happening? Tea? While Sergei glanced at the others, Leonid remained stoic, not knowing what to think or say.

"Yes, tea would be good," said Yuri. "Erh, Leonid, Sergei? Tea would be good, eh?"

"Da," shrugged Leonid, his eyes darting toward Yuri and then straight ahead.

"Kjersten returned with a tray of tea cups, a tea pot and Scandinavian pastries. Amos entered the room and stood next to the hutch. After placing the tray on the table, Kjersten poured tea for the others, walked to one of the remaining table chairs and sat down. Before speaking, with formality Kjersten poured herself a cup of tea. The three men in their fur coats worked to partake in a proper manner, but were awkward, overdressed and underrefined.

"How much does my brother owe you?" asked Kjersten, sitting formally across from the three men, holding her teacup.

The others subconsciously attempted to duplicate her posture. Amos watched the Russians warily. We're expected to protect Sven? he wondered. Is that their only leverage?

"He borrowed a lot of money," grumbled Yuri. "He gave us collateral he did not own." Yuri looked at Kjersten as if surprised someone would do this. "Your brother is not honest," said Yuri menacingly while attempting chew quietly. The effort undermined his menace. "We do not want to have business dealings with such a man," concluded Yuri. "We want our money. Where is Captain Nordquist?"

"Again, Captain Nordquist passed away," said Kjersten. "How much does my brother owe you?" she repeated.

Yuri glanced at Leonid and Sergei who glanced back. Yuri returned his attention to Kjersten. They had agreed to a large amount, an amount that had little to do with what Sven had borrowed or the value of the confiscated shipment and schooner brig equity. It was what, under the circumstances, they figured they could get. Yuri looked back at Kjersten, recalculated, and uttered an amount that was less.

Leonid and Sergei stopped chewing.

Yuri repeated the amount.

"It will take time to get that much money," said Kjersten, stalling. "You must understand…"

"You can use a ship as collateral," said Sergei. "Get a loan. Pay us back. It is simple."

He took another bite and appeared to study the remaining morsel in his thick fingers while chewing.

"How much is the Einar II insured for?" asked Yuri in a monotone.

"The Einar II is insured for much more than that, of course," answered Kjersten.

Amos said nothing. The cold light in Yuri's eyes twinkled, and he slowly nodded, looking at the tray while again chewing. Amos sensed Yuri relax, as if a dilemma had been resolved. Amos believed the insured value indicated more-than-adequate collateral value, much more than the Russians wanted.

"There, you see, you can…," began Sergei.

"My father," interrupted Amos, "would not have wanted the ship encumbered."

"The ship was, as you say, 'encumbered,'" growled Leonid, "when Sven Ostermänn borrowed money from us. We have documents proving it."

"That document is fraudulent."

"There, you see?" said Sergei, leaning forward. "Sven must go to prison."

"Unless we get paid now," said Yuri. "That is why we are here. To get our money back. Then the ship and the farm will no longer be, eh, encumbered."

"May I see the loan documents?" asked Kjersten.

"See the loan documents?" echoed Yuri. "I suspect so. Your eyesight seems good. Is it necessary for you to see the documents? What do you think? We have told you what amount we want. It is a fair amount. We could have asked for more." The others frowned at the table centerpiece. "If you want us as partners, we can become partners. If you do not want us as partners, we can become partners. It is not up to you. It is only up to you that you pay us money so we are thinking we do not want to be partners. Then we go away. Life goes on. Everything, everyone is safe," Yuri said in a reassuring voice.

"What do you mean, 'safe'?" asked Amos.

"'Safe' is what you and Sven are not if you do not pay us," said Sergei, still chewing. "We want the money. It is simple. You give us the money, we go away. Money. Bye bye."

"This is extortion," said Amos. "The law…"

"Are you saying," interrupted Yuri, "that we have no legal right to our own money? We loaned money. We have a document that shows the Einar II as collateral. You threaten us with legal action for expecting to be repaid." Yuri scowled. "I think it is you who are extorting us."

"I'll need time to think about this," said Kjersten, wanting the Russians to leave without being paid. She did not have to wait long.

"Then we will be back soon," concluded Yuri as he stood up. The others, who were finally becoming acclimated to the moment, paused, reversing acclimation, and slowly stood. "Very soon. You will have the money then," he added in the same reassuring tone-of-voice. "The tea?" he looked at his cup as he put it down, stood upright and looked at Kjersten. "Thank you."

The three glowering men walked to the front door; Yuri opened it and stepped outside. After the others passed, Yuri, leaning inside the door, nodded and said, "The Einar II will be good leverage."

He leaned outside and closed the door.

Kjersten interpreted this to mean she and Amos should borrow against the Einar II. Borrowing against the Einar II would be unnecessary. Captain Nordquist was prosperous, and Kjersten needed only to obtain cash from deposits in local banks or the safe upstairs. She did not want to pay the Russians, however, because she intuited their investment already had been repaid several times over and anything else was additional surfeit.

That evening with a full moon to the southwest, the lone Einar II in-port watchman, Second Mate Gustaf Johansen, began conversing in English with a foreigner on the pier who had bottles of cider and vodka.

The conversation was amiable, and Gustaf lit a couple of fire pots to provide a little light and atmosphere. In English, the man on the pier said he was a seaman who knew no one in Göteborg, and was simply going to the head of the pier to sit, drink and watch the harbor in the moonlight. He asked if Gustaf might join him. Lonely himself, Gustaf accepted and joined the stranger on the pier.

The two walked to the head of the pier aside the Einar II bow. Isolated from the shore and other boats by stacked cargo boxes and pallets, it was relatively private. The two became comfortable on a smaller, wooden freight box, placed the bottles between them, and continued mixing cider and vodka with conversation. Although Gustaf drank no more than his companion, he was a smaller, older man with a lower alcohol tolerance. Stimulated by alcohol and camaraderie, time sped until Gustaf became too drunk to think lucidly. For a short time he sat unsteadily on the box, blankly staring at the water with the expression of a dead flounder. His companion sipped an apple cider/vodka mix and talked animatedly about French prostitutes, but Gustaf heard little of it.

Gustaf's inebriation grew greater, and shortly after midnight he passed-out and rolled off the wooden freight box, cracking his head on the edge of the pier as he fell, then landing in the frigid water.

In the early morning hours, away from the shore and most other ships, anyone who may have heard the splash as Gustaf's unconscious body hit the water would probably have been unconcerned. As it was, if anyone heard, no one took notice. Minutes later, bubbles rushing from his mouth, Gustaf Johansen's lifeless body nestled face-up among the seaweed fronds gently waving toward the rippled vision of three men peering downward, the quieted, dark surface a looking glass in the moonlight.

The three spectral figures scrabbled about the Einar II like mice in a ship's larder. Having completed their task, they quickly but quietly walked down the gangplank, bears imitating cats. On the pier they quietly cast off mooring lines. They watched for a moment as the Einar II began its drift with the tide toward center channel. Satisfied all was going as planned, they continued their silent cat walk along the dark pier to the shoreline.

Slowly the majestic Einar II, Captain Stig Nordquist's most noble ship, and one of the most beautiful ships in all of Europe, distanced itself from other ships as the open ship's hold and stateroom began burning, misplaced firepots doing the devil's work.

The fires were slow to spread, but soon flickering shadows began a frenzied dance on spars and masts above the open hold, preceding the fire's appearance like fiendish court jesters in a demonic royal procession. There were no great treasures aboard, no sacrificial animals or elaborate weaponry as would be expected in a Viking funeral for a hallowed warrior about to be led to Odin's great hall, Valhalla. There was no one aboard.

Under cover of darkness the three men motionlessly watched from the embankment above a dilapidated, shoreline storage building, mesmerized by the growing flames on the great ship drifting slowly away from the pier. Now all masts were ablaze, multiple burning crosses of stark gold diffusion, hearts of white, on a black background of night. In the dark, the bright fire illuminated surrounding ships, schooners, barques and brigantines in a manner giving the illusion other vessels were shrinking back from the ghostly burning ship.

As the eeriness grew, the three men glanced at one another. They had been all over the ship. No one else had been aboard. Yet each man saw a human silhouette, hands in the pockets of a sea coat, and captain's hat squarely in place, standing in the white, roaring quarterdeck flames as if the three men watching were, in turn, being watched. As the Einar II burned like a terrible, floating pyre, the three men thought the same improbable thought: Captain Stig Nordquist is going down with his ship.

7

Amos repeatedly opened and clenched his big fists angrily as he stared at the water off the pier. How could this have happened? Arson was being considered by the Lloyds of London syndicate Names, but arson seemed so unlikely. There was no direct evidence of arson and no evident motive for arson.

Using blocks and winches, the submerged *Einar II* hulk was pulled as close to shore as possible. Firepots were found in the charred remains. Particularly on a cold night, sailors topside would sometimes light small firepots. If left unattended, there was always potential for accidental mishap. Sudden ship motion from a wave, the result of nature or another ship coming into port, any number of things could upend unattended firepots – with a predictable consequence, particularly if the watch had been drinking heavily.

The Nordquists had no motive for arson. Someone else? The Nordquists had no enemies of which they were aware. Göteborg police carefully considered the evidence. A nearly-empty vodka bottle was on the pier next to where the *Einar II* was berthed. There appeared to have been no foul play. Investigators told Amos their conclusion was Gustaf had been drinking, passed out, fell overboard – the bottle flying out of his hand as he fell – and drowned. The Göteborg police concluded the drowning was accidental. To them, it appeared the fire was also.

The Lloyds of London syndicate Names were prepared to pay for the loss of *Einar II*, burned beyond restoration. Considering the circumstances and the settlement amount, however, Lloyds first sent their own investigator to Göteborg.

Private inspector Adam Jones-Curran, a tall, slender gentleman with a closely cropped gray mustache, and a full head of immaculately trimmed gray hair beneath his bowler, arrived warmly clothed, puffing on his symmetrically-stemmed churchwarden pipe ("It makes reading much easier") when he first stood on the Nordquist front door landing. He exuded an air of benign indifference as he conducted and re-conducted interviews with the Nordquists, Göteborg police, dockhands and other crewmen. Amos got the impression Jones-Curran was quite thorough, experienced and competent and, from Göteborg police learned Jones-Curran had been lured away from Scotland Yard by Lloyds syndicates who found his services exceptional.

Amos in tow, Jones-Curran walked around the pier assiduously looking at everything and anything. He studied the location where Gustaf's body was discovered, weighing tidal direction, and the distance from where the *Einar II* had been berthed. A day later they did it again, Jones-Curran puffing thoughtfully on his sculpted pipe, asking seemingly unrelated questions ("How often do you replace mooring lines?") of Amos, and occasionally taking notes.

The next day, seated in the Nordquist living room, Jones-Curran asked a few additional questions.

"That bottle of vodka, did you notice anything unusual about it?" asked Jones-Curran, pipe in hand.

The expressions of Amos and Kjersten went blank as the two glanced at one another and back at Jones-Curran.

"Rare," said Jones-Curran. "Unusual to find it outside of St. Petersburg. Who imports vodka here in Göteborg?"

"There are several shops that sell vodka," said Amos, shrugging his shoulders. "Importing vodka? We don't. My understanding is that most of what is sold here is made in Poland. Why?"

"That was my finding as well. I'm told this is very good vodka," answered Jones-Curran in a clipped British accent, "appealing to a vodka connoisseur – oh, yes, evidently there are such people. I prefer sherry, myself."

"Would you like a glass?" asked Kjersten.

"Why yes, that would be most splendid of you. Thank you so much." Jones-Curran beamed pleasantly as Kjersten went to get a tray, a bottle of sherry, and three sherry glasses.

"The vodka in question has an alcohol content of slightly over 75%," continued Jones-Curran, eyebrows raised, "significant assuming you could not care less about the cost of vodka or vodka taxes. You see, in Russia, vodka is priced, and sales are taxed, according to alcohol content. Whoever bought this bottle of vodka was someone who, as the expression goes, 'knew their alcohol' and did not care how much it cost. I might go so far as to say the purchaser was not only well-off, but also drank vodka like it was water – which is what the word 'vodka' means, incidentally: water.

"What I *don't* believe is that the purchaser was our deceased friend," said Jones-Curran with cultivated donnish doubt. "From what I can gather, he wasn't a connoisseur of anything. The vodka was purchased by someone else, somewhere else, and brought here."

Kjersten presented the tray with three full sherry glasses, and Jones-Curran took the furthest glass.

"Interesting that although a few others were about, no one saw the deceased or anyone who might have been with him before he drowned." Jones-Curran took a sip of his sherry and for a moment weighed the taste. "I suspect someone was."

Amos sat up.

"I also believe," Jones-Curran continued, "they were drinking on the pier, not the ship. I believe this for several reasons. First, the bottle was found behind a large wooden box in a location that would have been unlikely if, as some believe, the bottle flew from his hand as he fell. Secondly, if he fell from the ship, it also would be unlikely – although certainly not impossible – they would have found his body where it was, considering the tidal current.

"And thirdly, believing as I do that the deceased was not alone, and the second man was probably a stranger (and, based on this vodka, not someone you would normally find wandering about lonely piers in the evening hours), from what I have been told I don't believe the deceased would have invited a stranger aboard.

"It appears to me that the second man enticed the deceased to the pier," concluded Jones-Curran, "the two drank excessively, the stranger expecting the deceased to pass out, but – and this is merely intuition – did not expect him to fall in the water and drown. I could be wrong. On the other hand, it would be naïve to completely dismiss the possibility."

"Very interesting," said Kjersten. "Who do you think the person was?"

Anxious for Jones-Curran's answer, Amos leaned forward and looked intently at the Lloyds of London investigator.

"I think it was the same person – or perhaps there was more than one, I can't say – who set fire to your ship – and who wanted to set fire to *only* your ship."

"What makes you think it was deliberate arson?" asked Kjersten, softly wringing her folded hands.

"The ship sank at a distance from the pier," said Jones-Curran, "and there were no charred remains of the mooring lines on the pier – nothing. This suggests that the mooring lines were cast off before the fire and ship were underway, probably moments after the fire was set. If the fire were accidental, as the authorities believe, ends of the mooring lines would still have been attached to bollards or cleats on the pier and, although burned, at the very least there would have been charred mooring lines remains, and, at worst, charred remains of the pier…and possibly other ships moored nearby.

"The motive? My guess is that the perpetrator did not want to damage any of the other boats, perhaps incurring greater legal exposure, while at the same time, were the ship floating free in the harbor, the distance would preclude anyone being able to fight the fire. No, he – or they – wanted complete and total damage, and to keep it isolated."

Jones-Curran puffed on his pipe several times, thinking, while absently studying the embottled schooner centerpiece on the ship's wheel coffee table.

"No," he concluded, looking at the others gravely, "it was not an accident. One or several people were involved. My question to you is the same as your question to me: who do you think the perpetrator was? Do you have any enemies?"

Amos sat forward and looked at Kjersten who looked at Amos and nodded.

"Are they from St. Petersburg?" she asked Amos.

"I don't know," said Amos as anger suffused his system like 151 proof vodka.

"To whom are you referring," asked Jones-Curran, his head tilted back and his eyebrows raised, "when you say, 'they'?"

Amos and Kjersten glanced at one another. Amos began to tell Jones-Curran the entire story about Sven and the Russians, providing as much detail as possible. Jones-Curran listened carefully, and occasionally took more notes as Amos spoke.

"Pity," said Jones-Curran when Amos finished. "No doubt it's them. The evidence and motive are there. Clever." Jones-Curran refilled his pipe. "Short-sighted but clever," Jones-Curran concluded as he relit his pipe.

"It's quite a tale. Arson. Extortion. Possibly sedition." Jones-Curran frowned, looking at the others. "I suspect these individuals may already be wanted by the law in many places. Based on their *modus operandi*, I also suspect Scotland Yard may have a file or two on them," he added as he gestured with his pipe.

"So, do be careful," he said sincerely, nodding at the others. "If they show up on your doorstep demanding money, to prevent harm to yourselves, your possessions, or your brother, give it to them. I might not so freely offer such advice if those wronged included only you two. A Lloyds of London syndicate, however, will also be involved. As I say, it was shortsighted of them to do that. A more cunning criminal would have found a better way. So just give them the money. Trust me. If you can afford to wait for the return of the money, in the long run it should prove to be the best course of action.

"I'll report my findings and opinions to Lloyds and Scotland Yard," said Jones-Curran. "I recommend you file a second report with the local police as well. Lloyds will work immediately to find the perpetrators, arrest them, and swiftly execute justice – which will include both Lloyds of London and you getting your money back."

Jones-Curran's left eyebrow lifted knowingly.

"We're actually quite good at that. In comparison to the common criminal, however, it is much more difficult to catch Russian criminals who do their dirty work and then hide underground like clever little moles. If they escape and travel to St. Petersburg, knowing the city was built on a swamp along the Gulf of Finland, and there are many places to hide, finding the perpetrators would take some time." Jones-Curran gestured again with his pipe. "Russian authorities, you see, are of no help, to say the least. In Russia, an unholy alliance exists between criminals and government, aided and abetted by bribery on one hand, and extortion on the other," he added, holding out each hand. "I say, sometimes it's a bit difficult to tell where one ends and the other begins, the odd difference being the internal system of tribal rules to which criminals adhere – quite rigid actually – while government rules are, by-and-large, ignored." Jones-Curran drew on his pipe.

"It's quite a system. Hopeless. Godless. Little wonder so many Russians drink heavily. With respect to greed, however, that street runs both ways, and someone will know who is where. Paid properly, invariably one rat leads us to another."

"Do you believe they are still in Sweden?" asked Amos.

"I suspect they are not heading to Russia quite yet because they probably need to complete this unfinished business here. They are hard money lenders, not seamen. Meanwhile, we have our sources in the local Russian community. But we will need to move quickly."

"This is all very new to us," said Kjersten, looking at the table with a distant expression.

"I should add there is no doubt in my mind," concluded Jones-Curran, "that you two are in no way involved. I will report this to the syndicate and, as you know, Lloyds of London always pays legitimate claims without fail. Yours is legitimate because you did not set the fire."

"Thank you. It's just so hard to believe this has happened," said Kjersten.

"While this has been an unfortunate affair, I must tell you I have seen worse. Much worse. In many such cases the claim was not legitimate. Arson? Sabotage?" Jones-Curran took a puff on his pipe. "Amazing the ends to which some people will go to illegitimately make money…or often, more to the point, keep from losing it. Either way, as you know, in the final analysis, crime does not pay."

Jones-Curran finished his sherry, complimented its taste, and stood up.

"What did you say was the name of the schooner brig your brother bought?"

"The *Orvar-Odd*."

"The *Orvar-Odd*." Jones-Curran smiled. "Ah, yes. You Scandinavians have a full coffer of myths. Quite commendable actually. You can tell a civilization by its myths. In any event, thank you for your time and cooperation," he said, picking up his bowler. "Your funds should be delivered in approximately two weeks."

Jones-Curran began to walk toward the door as Kjersten and Amos got up to see him out.

"Oh, and by the way, should these Russians return demanding more money, and you pay them as I recommend, immediately notify the police of the incident, as I said a moment ago. You'll need an official record of it when the opportunity to retrieve the amount arrives. Meanwhile, again," Jones-Curran's left eyebrow rose as he looked back at Kjersten and Amos, "I want no harm to come to anyone."

———————◄●►———————

As promised, Amos and Kjersten received the insurance settlement. That evening in the bright twilight shortly after sunset, Amos stood on the pier sadly looking at the submerged hulk, wondering why men become so attached to inanimate objects such as ships. "She." The name was *Einar II*, but the ship was still "she." Sailors never referred to a ship as "he" or "it." And indeed, he would miss her.

Amos thought of Yuri's physical reaction when Kjersten said the *Einar II* was insured for far more than Sven owed. Neither Kjersten nor Amos gave the reaction, even the question, any thought at that moment. We should have suspected, thought Amos angrily, but we were naïve, unused to dealing with shadowy men whose business acumen is amoral. Staring at the burned-out hulk, Amos felt violated, inhumanely manipulated by the men responsible for the fire. If Lloyds of London, who would involve Scotland Yard, was unable to find the three men soon, Amos expected there would be another loud banging on the door.

Meanwhile, remembering the threats made by the one named Sergei, Kjersten could not help but worry about the safety of her sons, herself and especially her brother, Sven. She decided to follow Inspector Jones-Curran's advice and pay the three men, hoping no harm would follow and that the amount would shortly be retrieved.

———◆●◆———

A few days later they heard it: the hollow, cacophonous "thump-clump-thump-clump" of a small advancing army coming up the front porch steps.

The sound made its way to the top of the steps, then across the landing to the door where for a moment there was silence followed by an unnecessarily loud banging of the doorknocker.

Amos was on his feet. This time Kjersten did not open the door. Amos swung open the door, and stood looking at the three bear-men who looked back without blinking. Amos was bigger than any of the Russians. For a moment no one said anything, but in response to the evident anger in Amos's countenance, Sergei's expression became defiant as if to say, "What do you think you're going to do?"

"We have come for our money now," said Yuri unemotionally to Amos as if nothing happened since their last visit. Smoldering with anger, Amos said nothing, continuing to glare as his mother came to his side and looked at the three Russians.

"Well," she said politely, her head lowered slightly as she looked at them, "it seems recent events have provided us with a large sum of money from which we might pay what Sven owes you." She cocked her head slightly to one side. "Were you aware of that?"

"You pay. We go."

"Will you?" asked Kjersten forcefully. "Will you never come here again?"

"I'm certain we are all of one mind in that matter," said Yuri formally.

She studied Yuri for a moment and, without a word, went upstairs as the others stood motionlessly and silently in an emotional standoff. The Russians looked at Amos, but none spoke to him. This young man is not intimidated, they thought. Is he that brave or is he that stupid, or are we losing our edge?

"Never come back?" scowling Sergei asked in Russian, snorting a derisive response.

Yuri looked at Sergei and then Leonid. "I like this woman," growled Yuri firmly in Russian, his eyelids taut beneath his thick eyebrows, his lower lip protruding slightly. "She reminds me of someone. Someone I respected. If we never loan her brother any more money, we do not come back."

"What do we care if this шведский идиот standing before us wants that we not come back?" asked Sergei, puzzled. "What do we care? Business is business. Why not?"

"It is not Sven's money, here; it is his sister's money," said Yuri, frowning. "And I like this sister of his."

"Never come back? Yuri, just say, 'Yes,'" said Leonid. "Who cares if we mean it?" Leonid looked up at Amos contemptuously. Amos did not move.

"She is not deserving of such a brother," said Yuri. "Do you really think that змей, Sven, will be back asking for another loan? He is dishonest, gullible, but not completely stupid. Again? No. Let's leave these people alone. We used this woman's brother to do our dirty work for free, collected a schooner brig and a large sum of money, and will, in a moment, collect another large sum." He shrugged his shoulders, studying Sergei and Leonid through weathered, black eyes, his coarse, black eyebrows, mustache and beard making him appear sinister even to them. "With that large sum of money, let's leave these people in peace. These are honest but shrewd people…and have connections. No doubt they have Lloyds looking for us. We should not press our luck. It would be unwise to further aggravate people who can potentially undermine our future plans. For business reasons, we should put them in our past."

The others, hands in their pockets, frowned at Yuri, and shrugged their shoulders.

"This is what we do," explained Yuri in English, turning to Amos. "We loan money to people who cannot get it from banks. And sometimes we give loans also as a means to different ends – as with this Sven. It is amazing how many bottom fish you catch with a lure made of money. Making the loan is easy; getting paid back is not. But we are good at getting paid back. It is simple: we do not make loans unless we know how we are to be repaid. We make that determination, not the borrower."

Yuri looked at Amos for a moment.

"We will make no more loans to your uncle. We will not return to your doorstep. Pay us, promise we will have no problems with you, and you will have no problems with us. It is what you want. It is what we want."

Sergei and Leonid looked at Yuri knowingly. Sometimes Yuri changed his mind. Anders, standing a few feet behind his brother, was wide-eyed.

Kjersten returned with an envelope, walked through the doorway, by the bear-men and out on to the porch in the cold air. She turned and, after the Russians had also turned to face her, handed the envelope to Yuri. Amos came out and stood next to her.

"Please count it," said Kjersten.

"Why?" asked Yuri. "Do you not agree we should never come back?"

"Oh, I *do* agree."

"Then it is all here." Yuri uncharacteristically nodded respectfully toward Kjersten as Sergei shot a steely scowl at Amos who continued to look at the Russians as if they were pedophiles by a schoolyard.

Saying nothing else, the three bear-men turned and walked side-by-side to the edge of the landing and down the stairs, the hollow "thump-clump-thump-clump" of three sets of boots resonating as Kjersten and Amos watched them reach the bottom of the stairs and walk away.

Extortion. Blackmail. Larceny. Amos began to ask himself, why should they even be alive? Some people deserve to die, he thought. As he watched them walk into the distance, and as the import of what they just accomplished began to grow, his anger increased. His mind raced. He continued to feel used, violated, and the anger smoldering in him became hotter. Anger fed on anger, and combustion flashed, transforming his smoldering anger into a fire of hatred burning dangerously. He thought of Gustaf Johansen. Amos's face contorted. I would be within my rights to go after them, he thought, and deal with them like rats on mooring lines. His clenched teeth began to show.

"Amos, let's go inside now." Kjersten looked at Amos apprehensively and motioned for them to go back inside. "It's cold out here."

Amos followed, suffused with hatred, the fire burning hotter. Kjersten waited to close the door behind them as Amos mechanically walked through the doorway, but then stopped.

At first he stood there, teeth clenched, but after a moment he turned and walked back out the door.

His mother walked quickly after him, reached out and grabbed his arm with both hands. As she held his arm, looking up at him, he walked toward the steps, pulling her with him – he was so strong. Grimacing, leaning backward, she pulled on his arm like she was pulling on a hauling winch line, attempting to redirect him back to the front door.

"Amos, you're in civilized Göteborg," she grimaced, "where the behavior you must be considering is unacceptable…and you are the son of Stig Nordquist, revered in life and death."

Amos did not stop, but pulled her with him, approaching the steps, and she looked up at him, suddenly afraid.

"Amos, please!" she pleaded. "What if you were to do what you want to do?"

He didn't seem to hear.

"Amos!" She continued to pull. "Amos!"

Almost to the steps, he resisted, but as his mother continued to loudly beg of him while desperately hanging on his arm, his resistance weakened.

"Attacking, probably killing three men," Kjersten cried, "regardless of who they are, would ruin your life, Amos! Truly, it would ruin your life! Please, turn around!"

He stopped at the edge of the steps.

Not here, now, but someday…, he thought revengefully, his teeth still tightly clamped.

After a moment he turned and, as he walked to the front door, still open, his mother released his iron arm. Once in the living room, he stopped. With both hands he reached up and slowly pushed back his hair as if just having awakened.

Looking inwardly, he greatly disliked how he felt at that moment – hatred fueling hatred, a bonfire of lethally destructive proportion – while knowing that revenge would ameliorate nothing, bringing only additional problems, probably serious problems he could not foresee.

Beginning to perspire, he forced himself to relax, and walked forward into the kitchen where he absently wiped his face with a towel.

He went to the pantry and looked in although he was neither hungry nor attentive to what was inside. How does this hatred harm the Russians? he asked himself. Of course, it doesn't; it consumes only me. As the reality of the moment forced itself fully into his consciousness, his face became expressionless, although his jaws were still clamped. The pantry before him became apparent for the first time.

Logic stepped forward and attempted to take anger's place but, like a drunken sailor asked to weigh anchor, restive anger hung around before slowly heading to the door.

As his anger gradually dissipated, Amos began to feel enervated, drained. It occurred to him he could do nothing about the Russians, and that his emotional state was not only pointless but self-destructive. His jaws relaxed. This is injurious, he thought. This is a poison in me. He shook his head, took a deep breath and let it out slowly.

Hatred, resentment and an attendant inclination for revenge could change him from a loving human being into an enraged animal, endangering him and others. How can I prevent this feeling? he asked himself, wondering whether an anger-obstructing pill could be invented. Although the anger continued dissipating, his head throbbed incriminatingly and he wondered how many violent deaths, massacres and even wars had resulted from an irrational spark of hatred in someone like himself. How different would be the world were this emotion corralled, bridled, broken?

As he stood there, he vowed to exercise supreme caution and self-discipline, and to never knowingly do anything that would undermine that self-discipline. Amos determined this memory would not be allowed to leave. This is a seminal moment, he thought.

⚊⚊⚊⚊⚊ ● ⚊⚊⚊⚊⚊

The next morning the sun shone through a rising mist as Amos went down to the pier to assist with preparations to float the burned out hulk. Air was pumped by hand into any available pockets left by the fire, as well as barrels fastened to the hull.

By early evening the hulk slowly rose. Using strong men in small boats propelled by large oars, the *Einar II* was towed away from the port shipping lanes to a harmless inlet at a distance. There it would be allowed to sink again to the seafloor, its tombstone a navigational buoy, where it would become home to all manner of small sea life.

Amos stood still, watching the charred hulk gradually distancing itself from the shoreline but not memory, part of him still unwilling to believe the whole implausible affair occurred. The *Einar II*. Anger began to curdle in his stomach, and he again fought against the feeling.

As the hulk was slowly pulled away, Amos closed his eyes, remembering the regal *Einar II* as she looked the first time he stood on the dock watching small boats pulling her out into the channel, the excited crew setting sails for her maiden voyage, and his father next to the helmsman.

He opened his eyes, and the vision oddly seemed more real than the reality before him. The unjustness of the arson – the betrayal of decency, the immoral self-centered lack of feeling, lack of conscience – would not leave him alone. The *Einar II*, subject of paintings, destroyed merely to cover an illegitimate business deal.

Standing directly above where Gustaf Johansen drowned, Amos looked at the water below him, thinking of Gustaf. Amos attempted to see beneath the surface where Gustaf's body had come to rest, but the sunlight was fading, the surface was black.

"Raise your spirits," rumbled a voice behind Amos.

Amos froze, listening for identification confirmation.

"You still have the others, the *Polstjärnan*, the *Nordanvinden* – and the *Handelsresande* and *Kringflackande*."

As if Amos were being forcibly submerged in a bath of revulsion, hatred began again seeping into his heart like seawater into a sinking ship, and then it began to pour in.

8

Y ou're an intelligent and fearless young man," continued the voice. "A grand future could be yours…you know much already about ships, sailing and maritime commerce. But there is much you should learn about people."

Incredulous, Amos took a deep breath and held it as his fists clenched and his jaw tightened.

"I will warn you. There are many like me," continued Yuri, stepping to Amos's side while watching the *Einar II* hulk being pulled at a distance. "Most people, in fact, if you consider degrees of sin." Amos glanced around. Leonid and Sergei stood about ten feet from Yuri. Yuri raised his right hand and stroked his black beard, thinking. "I might guess everyone."

Yuri looked sideways at Amos who did not look back.

"It is merely a matter of how far you want to go, how clever you can become." Yuri dropped his hand and shrugged. "It depends on what talents God has given you. I have been told the Bible says that. Develop your talents."

Amos's mouth opened slightly as his breathing became heavier. Unable to continue looking forward, Amos turned his head and glared down at Yuri who added, "So, I have made a fortune capitalizing on the weaknesses of sinners. It gives me much money and some pleasure."

"Why are you here?"

"Do you see that schooner brig over there? We just sold it. You heard it called the *Orvar-Odd*. We liked the name 'Seastar' better." Yuri nodded twice, his mouth turned into an accentuated frown, and he said matter-of-factly, "The 'Seastar' sold for 40% more than it effectively cost us a short time ago. Business is good."

"No, why are you here talking to me?" Amos completely turned, faced Yuri directly, and said, "You come down…" The words caught in his throat, and for a moment Amos's condemnation was too great for him to continue the sentence. Yuri looked back without fear, knowing this public place, but especially Amos's self-discipline, would prevent violence. Amos regained his self-control and continued, "You come down here and give me advice…" his mouth worked but for a moment no sound exited, "…on what's right and wrong?" Amos was almost apoplectic. "You?"

His tone of voice gave no chance for mistaking what he thought of Yuri. Decades of garbage, dumped over the sides of moored ships and from the edge of the pier, had accumulated in a seafloor covering of scum, the acrid, stinging stench of which made seamen nauseous when a line was inadvertently dragged on the bottom and hauled up. To Amos, Yuri was worse.

"Erh, it is as you say."

Yuri looked at the pathetic *Einar II* hulk and frowned.

"But, unlike most, we usually do not prey on the innocent," said Yuri. "We deal only with snakes like your uncle, mostly garden snakes wanting to become anacondas. And I warn you," Yuri's facial expression gained intensity as he again looked at Amos, "while the snakes in Göteborg appear as innocent as little earthworms, some are more dangerous than Congo rock pythons." Yuri stared at Amos for a moment, but his expression softened as if some humorous thought occurred to him.

"When opportunity knocks, we should go to the door. And in our work," Yuri glanced at Sergei and Leonid, "opportunity never ceases to knock. So many dishonest, scofflaw, get-rich-quick schemes. Varying forms of entrust, entrap and betray. You would think there was nothing else to do."

Yuri lightly nodded several times as if agreeing with himself.

"Ahh," continued Yuri, "those people are plentiful, imaginative, willing to work amazingly hard for a short while…willing to take risks… It is a shame not to capitalize on such a profound combination of admirable initiative and indefensible immorality." Yuri chuckled cynically. "If we remain tough and smart, the scheming Sven Ostermänns of this world invariably come along and, to our benefit, hoist themselves on their own petard."

He looked at Amos who stood unmovingly, stone-faced, simultaneously listening while working to control his anger.

"Do I too lack a conscience?" Yuri looked back toward the *Einar II* hulk. "Not so much as you may think. I don't need to be standing here."

"Then why are you?"

Yuri shrugged his shoulders as Amos continued to glare at him.

"Look at the present situation," said Yuri. "To you, terrible. But with the remainder of the insurance money, you and your mother can still buy another ship, a good ship." Yuri glanced at Amos. "You see, I know how much Lloyd's of London paid you."

"How…?" asked Amos. "How would you know?"

"How would I *know*? How would I *know*? What do you think? I know. It is only for you to know that I, too, do not take chances. I verified your father had the *Einar II* more-than-adequately insured. Had he not, we would not be watching the dead boat being towed away. You can replace the *Einar II*, and maybe you won't have your dishonest uncle as a partner. You are in a better business position than you were…you have no idea what headaches a partner like that dogfish, Sven, can bring. Especially if he is a relative. Betrayal? You think about that. We did you a favor."

Yuri took out his pipe and a tobacco pouch, dug the pipe into the tobacco pouch, filling the pipe, and pressed the tobacco in the bowl. Placing the pouch back in his pocket, he lit the pipe as he continued watching the *Einar II* hulk, waves lapping off its charred hull in the distance. Leonid and Sergei stood nearby, staring at Yuri, uneasily waiting for him to finish. It was unwise to remain there. They were eager to leave.

Tough and smart. Is there satisfaction from being tough and smart? Amos wondered. Is there any alternative? ...there is much you should learn about people. If so, Yuri is certainly an excellent instructor. But if this is a school, thought Amos, it has a curriculum of emptiness. Someone of depth and integrity would not continue this life and perception of humanity without pause. But that must be why, Amos intuited, Yuri is here, talking to me.

Leonid and Sergei, however, saw no point in what was happening, and grew more anxious.

"Yuri, we must go," said Leonid in Russian. "You know we should not remain."

"You should not take my admonitions lightly," said Yuri, ignoring Leonid. "Your father sailed to many places with danger all around. High seas. Inaccurate charts. Piracy. Dishonest clients, dishonest vendors, dishonest partners." Yuri nodded in the direction of men finishing work nearby in the fading daylight. "Thieves disguised as dock workers or security guards, infesting the docks like diseased rats. Emulating the devil, doing what he does best: they tempt, deceive and betray. Where there is much money, there are deceitful men who, in order to get it, will do whatever they can get away with...including extortion. Even murder. I see these things."

"You do these things."

"Ehr," Yuri nodded. He sighed and folded his arms, watching the *Einar II* extend its distance. Yuri shrugged his shoulders, glanced at Amos, and then looked away. The docks basked in the twilight. The moon rising over the eastern horizon behind them was bright, and the air was warm. Yuri felt good.

"Yuri, we must go," said Leonid anxiously in Russian.

"Wait!" Yuri answered brusquely in Russian, looking at Leonid. He turned his head toward Amos.

"In your position," said Yuri in his oktavist bass voice, studying his pipe, "it is proper to treat all men civilly and respectfully, but do not forget what I told you about varying degrees of sin. Stronger people prey on weaker people just as stronger animals do weaker animals. But animals never pretend to be anything other than what they are. People? What do people do?" Yuri turned and spat to one side. "Women accused of being witches are still slowly tortured, either hung or burned at the stake by men who deserve worse. Officials accused of treason – whether or not they are guilty seems never in question – are methodically drawn and quartered alive, their entrails then held aloft for huge, cheering mobs to see. Once, not too long ago, others were roasted alive over spits." Lips tight, eyes solemn, Yuri looked at Amos reflectively. "Attending the wrong church can be punished by being torn asunder by work horses in the public square as an on-looking audience – men, women and children – howl like banshees.

For political opposition, men are slowly tortured with red hot irons or coals, or punctured with spikes, or impaled in multiple directions with stakes, their tongues, noses, ears and other extremities sliced off. Others are slowly crushed with stones, or turned and broken on the wheel, or simply bashed with hammers by volunteers. 'Step right up.'"

Listening to Yuri's depressing litany, Amos's complexion etoliated slightly.

"Where are these things done?" Yuri asked rhetorically. "All over. Right now." He glanced at Amos and repeated, "All over.

"People?" continued Yuri. "People are what they are." Yuri stroked his black and gray beard, dropped his hand, and spat again. "Worse than animals." Yuri again glanced at Amos.

"You are a Christian, yes?'

Amos nodded.

"Always remember: the world rewards its own."

Eyes steely, Yuri added, "And carefully watch those who assure you there is no longer need for a lock on the gate."

Although he detested Yuri, Amos was listening.

"Many among us become someone's best friend by raising others' hopes – but when the others begin to trust, they are devoured like caviar." Yuri seemed to be studying the harbor. "Betrayal? All people need hope; so betrayal works well."

Yuri's pipe went out, but he was disinclined to smoke any longer. He banged his pipe on his heel, eliminating the ashes, and put the pipe back in his coat pocket.

"You must realize that although you hate me for what I did," said Yuri, "if you knew the others, I would be one of the more conscionable ones. Think about that. Think about how much worse it could have been. Here I stand beside you. Others? Once they get into you, as long as they can feed, they do not stop. They have no feeling, no conscience. Sharks among the cuttlefish. They take what they do not own, reap what they did not sow, and could not care less about the scarred, the lame and the dead left behind. You do not believe me?" questioned Yuri. "You believe me. If you do not, I pity you." Yuri looked at Amos who looked back without expression.

"You pity me." Amos folded his arms and looked at Yuri. "Why? Why do you care?"

Yuri's lower lip protruded more than normal. "In a moment I will tell you.

"Look at that ship," Yuri turned and pointed at the *Polstjärnan* silhouetted in the fading sunset, its masts also lightly reflected the growing moonlight. In the water the *Polstjärnan* rocked lightly, a great horse waiting patiently for its owner. "Beautiful." Yuri put his hands on his hips and studied the *Polstjärnan*, admiring its lines and weighing its capabilities. "Your father loved his vessels. He protected them. How do I know? They are beautiful boats. There are men who want them and, if given a very small opportunity, will get them. They have not. That is how I know. Your father has died. There are men who know about those boats, who are looking at those boats. Those men are thinking." Yuri looked intently at Amos. "Men much worse than I am. Have you made any new friends? Eh? You have an obligation to be tougher and smarter than they are. If you are to be as good as your father, you have no choice. It is your moral obligation."

Amos looked at Yuri for a moment. "Why are you here?" asked Amos. "Is all this supposed to convince me of something?"

"Convince you? Do you think I stand here because I need someone to talk to? You listen and you listen well."

"What you're describing is pointless rapacity," countered Amos cynically. Yuri looked back at Amos with disapprobation, putting his hands in his pockets. "Is there not something more important than merely taking things from others," asked Amos, "and keeping them until you die?"

"Erh, perhaps," answered Yuri, slightly rolling his head as he answered. "But I, myself, have not seen this heaven-on-earth. Quite the opposite; for many years I have seen what I have seen. What have I seen? People steal things they can afford to buy. Cheat when honesty would take them further. Lie when the truth would work better. Murder because, erh, it is simple; mercilessly expedient." Yuri shrugged his shoulders. "'Rapacity'? I know this word. Such is life. All of these things are some form of betrayal. People are people, not angels, and betrayal is what people do. People and betrayal. Oshroshka and kvass." Yuri shrugged his shoulders again. "If you do not..."

"Yuri, come!" said Leonid loudly in Russian. "We must go! We can't stay here. You know what can happen if we don't leave at once."

"What did I say?! One minute!" responded Yuri in Russian, giving Leonid an angry look.

"We have our money," countered Leonid anxiously. "Let's go!"

"One minute!" repeated Yuri, as if giving an order.

"Why are you here," asked Amos, "apparently trying to do a right thing? After doing a very wrong thing?"

"'Wrong?' How wrong was it?" Yuri stroked his beard. "Ehr, maybe it was a little wrong. But, as I said, you will be better off in the long run."

"Gustaf Johansen?" questioned Amos. "A lonely man who would give you the shirt off his back? A 'little wrong'?"

"It was not our plan that at midnight he fall in the water and drown," said Yuri, annoyed. "That he did himself."

"Of course, out of concern for the innocent, you tried to save him?"

"Ehr, that was not part of our plan either. We had other business to attend to." Yuri glanced at Amos. "And we did not think he would drown but, rather, if he had passed out, eh, the cold water would cause him to regain consciousness immediately. But we had no time to wait and see." Yuri shrugged his shoulders. "No," continued Yuri, "the 'little wrong' occurred because we came to collect after your father died." Yuri paused, thinking.

"His death? You did not plan on that; he did not plan on that. And neither did Leonid, Sergei nor I. But we made a loan, and had to follow through with our plan. Sven did..."

"Yuri! Let's go!" said Sergei adamantly, stepping toward Yuri.

"One minute!"

"Dammit, Yuri! We can't wait here any…"

"One minute, I said!" Yuri looked at Sergei menacingly.

"Sven did his part; we, of course, then did ours," said Yuri. "It is how we do business."

Yuri studied Amos for a moment, about to expose the small particle of good residing in Yuri's heart. In turn, Amos studied Yuri's eyes, puzzled.

"But I felt badly for you, a strong, young man with a great future," continued Yuri, his voice becoming solemn. "And especially your mother. A fine woman. A good woman. In all my years of collecting money, no one ever invited us in for tea." Yuri's expression brightened and, looking to one side, he shook his head. He returned his attention to Amos. "She is refined, smart; and obviously has high standards which she will not compromise. My own mother – I made her a promise before she passed away – was like that," added Yuri, looking at Amos without expression.

"My mother went without food and heat to insure I would have the best education possible. When it was done, she rationalized, she would rest and dote on…the grandchildren…she never had." Yuri studied the *Polstjärnan* while thinking of his mother.

"I have deep respect for such a woman. A woman like your mother." Yuri looked at Amos who looked back without expression.

"The best thing I can do for her now," said Yuri, holding his hands out, "is to counsel her son." Yuri put his hands back in his pockets.

"You must think about what I have said."

Yuri turned and faced Amos directly. In the distance there was the faint sound of men walking down the pier from the shoreline boardwalk.

"Yuri, enough!" Leonid implored in Russian. "We cannot stay! We are leaving!"

"We are just about through," replied Yuri adamantly in Russian. "Be patient!"

Leonid put his hands on his head in exasperation as Sergei, wide-eyed, mouth half open, bent slightly and imploringly held out his hands. The two men turned and began to side-step in the opposite direction while watching Yuri.

"I must go now," said Yuri as he turned to leave. Leonid and Sergei stopped to wait but Yuri stopped also. "So, you will take what I have said seriously? I know what you feel. There are times when it is very important to pay attention to what you feel inside, but sometimes it is more important to listen to your brain, not your stomach. Me? I try to listen to both, but then," Yuri raised his eyebrows and spoke more deliberately, "let my brain decide."

"Did your brain tell you to stay here and tell me all this?" asked Amos.

"Ehr, no," said Yuri after a moment, "that was another part of me…the part my mother liked." Yuri's lower lip again protruded unnaturally. "Before she died, she said she hoped I would have a son like me."

Amos stared at Yuri.

"So. What are you going to do now?" Yuri asked sternly, almost as a directive as he again turned to leave.

The sound of men walking down the pier was becoming more audible.

His back to Amos, Yuri walked toward Leonid and Sergei who turned quickly to leave the pier. As they did, the silhouettes of seven large men came toward them in the fading twilight and growing moonlight. As the two groups drew closer, it was evident that six of the men approaching the Russians were in uniform. Police. Each held pistols at the fore. As the police spread across the pier to block escape, one officer began barking orders in English at the three Russians as the seventh man, a tall, older man in heavy, civilian attire, stepped to one side and walked over to Amos.

"Good evening, Mr. Nordquist," said Adam Jones-Curran as the police officers began to manhandle the three Russians. "To insure your safety, could you be so kind as to step over here?"

Amos walked toward Jones-Curran, away from the Russians.

"We waited ashore for a while," said Jones-Curran, "but, seeing the two of you engaged in lengthy conversation, and what with it getting dark, decided to bring this entire, unfortunate affair to a close out here." Jones-Curran looked about at the silhouetted boxes, bollards and benches in the moon shadows of the now-familiar pier. "Somewhat appropriate, I would say."

Jones-Curran lit his pipe, absently waved and flicked the Congreve match in one motion, and turned toward the Russians and the police. As the three Russians were handcuffed, with a furtive expression on his face, Yuri searched Amos's darkened features in the moonlight.

"What were you two discussing?" asked Jones-Curran.

"Betrayal," answered Amos. "How strong people prey on weak people…like animals. How I should be 'tough and smart' and never again allow myself to be victimized by people like him."

"Interesting. Sounds like good advice, if you don't mind me saying so," said Jones-Curran. "Why was he giving you this advice?"

Amos looked thoughtfully at the Russians being forcibly directed toward the foot of the pier. Amos's head leaned slightly to his left, and returned upright. "A promise made long ago," Amos said after a moment.

The twilight was nearly gone. Yuri, Sergei and Leonid had been led away by the police to the front of the pier and disappeared behind dark silhouetted shoreline buildings gilded ghostly silver in the full moonlight.

Jones-Curran proved a point: it had been unwise to involve Lloyds of London. To the southeast, the moon formed a bright, wavy line on the black harbor surface giving Amos a sense that peace and normalcy had returned to civilized Göteborg. At the moment, however, Amos was unable to raise a feeling of elation. Jones-Curran turned, prepared to follow the others, but stopped.

"And by the way," said Jones-Curran, "in spite of appearances, the 'Seastar' is still the *Orvar-Odd*. We'll take care of that in the morning." Jones-Curran nodded and said, "Good evening" as he touched his right fingertips to his bowler and glanced again at the *Orvar-Odd*.

He walked away, pipe aside his mouth, looking about as if pasting the scene in a memory scrapbook. For a few moments, motionless and impressed, Amos watched the moonlit, silver-trimmed silhouette of Jones-Curran walk toward the foot of the pier. Amos put his hands in his pockets and, while thinking, turned in the direction of the *Einar II* hulk now barely visible in the distance, about to be sunk.

No, crime doesn't pay, Amos thought. Sin never satisfies. This thought was immediately followed by a third thought: and neither does hatred. I will reduce the incidences of betrayal, of men preying on one another, came the last thought immediately, and with it came an oddly warm resonance within Amos, a confident feeling of encouragement. His intuition told him it wasn't a question of who might take advantage of whom, or that no one would attempt to take advantage of Amos; it was that he should become a barrier to amoral and immoral behavior, preventing men from preying on one another like "sharks among the cuttlefish." Amos spontaneously nodded his head and, seemingly answering Yuri's last question, said out loud, "I will do that." The meaning of this statement was not clear to Amos. Within him it came as forceful direction, however, and Amos felt as he might if given a street map after wandering about in an unfamiliar city.

9

His left-hand fingers absently running through his thick hair continually, Amos sat hunched over the dining room table studying financial statements, making notes. Concentrating was challenging, exacerbated by Kjersten's wonderful baked bread, the arousing aroma wafting in from the adjacent kitchen.

While Amos inherited his father's office upstairs, when studying accounting records Amos would often take a seat at the grand dining room table, particularly when considerable paperwork was involved. The dining room ambiance heightened his senses. The high ceiling was edged with elaborate crown molding above mahogany paneled walls displaying large, gilded-framed, commissioned paintings of ships on which Captain Nordquist sailed, or faraway places visited. Prominently displayed was a painting of the *Einar II*, named after Captain Stig Nordquist's older brother, swept overboard in a North Sea storm when Captain Nordquist and Uncle Torvald were still young boys. Other than a brief mention of the terrible grief experienced by Amos's grandmother, Captain Nordquist never spoke of his older brother, Einar.

Along the north wall hung a large, intricately framed, beveled mirror brought back from London when Amos was ten. Facing waterfront and harbor, the south wall contained large, multiple-pane bay windows, peripherally ornamented with stuffed exotic birds, as if aviaries.

Along all walls were china-laden sideboards and shelves displaying crystal glasses and nautical artifacts. In the center of the room, Amos sat at a long, elaborately carved, mahogany dining table, part of a 16-piece set including two massive end chairs and ten smaller-but-elaborate side armchairs carefully transported from Italy years ago. Hanging above the table was an expansive crystal chandelier that once hung in one of the many rooms of Vienna's Upper Belvedere. Captain Nordquist's tastes were discerning, not specifically expensive, directed toward the best available. If an object were deemed too common, Captain Nordquist had preferred to wait, willing to spend more to obtain even greater value.

Although Amos appreciated his surroundings, he had no great hunger for wealth. Amos searched for meaning, purpose in life, and in the moments following the arrest of the Russians, he determined his life's work would be beyond affluence of the moment, toward value beyond wealth. He was unsure how that would be realized; he only knew he had received the presentiment his occupation would discourage men from preying on one another.

On the dining room table, the papers before him painted a favorable picture of assets and liabilities – indebtedness was almost non-existent – although with the destruction of the *Einar II*, total asset value declined. Liquid assets were still substantial, however. In addition to money already in banks, there was a relatively appreciable sum left over from what they had received from Lloyds of London. If Adam Jones-Curran was correct, restitution from the Russians could happen in short order. Meanwhile, they considered reinvestment options.

Amos sat grappling with numerous alternatives, aware of his father's overriding investment directive: maximize the efficiency with which money is spent.

To this end, Amos sat weighing a multitude of considerations among which was that Karl XV, recently crowned King of Sweden and Norway, would reduce taxation, levies, tolls, duties and tariffs – there was no war going on – understanding the extent to which these means of government funding stifled economic activity and, therefore, government funding. If the rumors were true, trade incentive would increase, demand for Nordquist Shipping Co. services would rise, and Amos would need to expand the Nordquist fleet beyond replacing the *Einar II*. Were the rumors true? There were always rumors.

As a child of five Amos heard a rumor of a giant snake-like creature in huge Lake Vänern east of Göteborg. Somehow in the distant past, the Lake Vänern monster, Amos was told, became separated from Skagerrak sea monsters. As a five-year-old, Amos felt sorry for the Lake Vänern monster which, having no monster playmates, was no doubt lonely – sad circumstances even for a monster. With no playmates, Amos wondered, what did the monster do? An older boy, age 10, told Amos on the best of authority that the Lake Vänern monster spent all of its time searching for five-year-old little boys to eat.

But even at five, Amos considered the suggestion highly unlikely since, Amos being Amos, "monsters" in his dreams behaved like extraordinarily large, family dogs with floppy, bifurcated tongues. In his imagination, Amos adopted the Lake Vänern monster as his pet. This relationship was favorable for both monster and master; the monster had a playmate while Amos had a pet monster, greatly reducing any sense of insecurity.

Finally returning to the moment, Amos smiled and nodded. As Yuri implied, in Göteborg there were snakes of a sort...but no monsters. Shuffling through the paper around him, Amos considered immediate options, resisting investment determinations based on unfounded speculation.

"Sven will be by soon to sign," said Kjersten, interrupting Amos's reverie as she took a loaf of bread from the oven, shook it from the bread pan and placed it on a wooden cutting board. She began slicing the hot loaf, emancipating fragrance, preparatory to placing the slices on a round, wooden, bread platter with "*Giv oss i dag vårt dagliga bröd*" (Give us this day our daily bread) carved in raised letters around the perimeter. As she continued to slice, the invigorating aroma filled the kitchen and overflowed into the dining room, chasing serious thoughts from Amos's mind.

"Oh, my," he said under his breath as Kjersten approached the dining room table with the steaming slices and a full butter dish.

Kjersten was justifiably proud of her bread, and anticipated Amos's happy reaction. She set the bread platter on the table as the first floor filled up with the hot-from-the-oven baked bread aroma. The aroma ascended the stairwell, and soon Anders came bounding down the stairs, hitting the landing with a resonating thud then racing to the table.

Sven would be by to transfer his interest in the *Polstjärnan*, the *Nordanvinden*, the *Handelsresande*, and the *Kringflackande* to Amos, Kjersten and Anders. After the recent events leading to Sven's salvation, Sven agreed with his sister's adamant admonition, fortified by Amos's malevolent glare, that transferring ownership was the right thing to do. But Kjersten's stomach was tight; with Sven there could always be problems.

"I still am unable to understand why," Amos said to his mother in between bites, "after the *Einar II* burned and we subsequently paid those Russians, we again could not find Uncle Sven. We saved his life, perhaps. Where was he this time?"

Kjersten folded and arranged some napkins. "Sven's well-being was my primary concern and why I made no attempt to negotiate with the Russians," said Kjersten. "Sven does not…think like the rest of us. The Russians held all the cards, and I could tell that while they might think twice about harming you or me, they were contemptuous of Sven. To them, human life has no intrinsic value; people are valued according whatever purpose they might serve. Were it to aid their purposes, Sven was disposable."

"Yes but, if for no other reason, he should have come by at some point," said Amos. "We were, after all, his only port in the storm."

The thought was fortuitous as the rhythm of sliding footsteps shuffled its way up the front porch steps, and shortly there was a knock at the door.

"Kjersten, how are you?" greeted Sven, stepping in as Kjersten opened the door. "How are you holding up? My, it smells good in here."

As Sven walked by her, Kjersten closed the door without replying. Sven, taking off his tarpaulin cap, turned and looked at her.

"I apologize for not coming by after you paid the Russians," he said. It was as if he had read her mind. "I just figured that, under the circumstances, it would be best if I stayed away for a while. I was certain my presence would not help things."

"That was, perhaps, thoughtful," responded Kjersten. "Although, Sven, you are family. You could have come by just to say, 'Thank you.'"

"I don't know for certain but we may have saved your life," added Amos who, with Anders, joined his mother at the entry.

"I know that," said Sven with an unctuous look of deep sincerity, "and it goes without saying that I can't…" Sven paused, thinking. "Words fail. I'm alive and well. What can I say?" shrugged Sven, looking at the others. Neither Amos nor Kjersten responded.

"The papers are on the table, Uncle Sven," said Amos, motioning towards the dining room. "The pen and ink are next to them."

Without another word, the four went into the dining room. Amos thought of what Yuri said about being tied to a dishonest relative. Kjersten was apprehensive, worried that Sven would equivocate, procrastinate, attempt to back-out. Leaning over, Amos pointed to where Sven was to sign.

"Well, it looks like all is in order," said Sven without moving. "You know, I was thinking that although you certainly came to my rescue, the amount the Russians received was a fraction of what my interest was worth." Rather than picking up the pen, Sven put his hands in his pockets. "Considering the disparity, I thought we could make a more equitable arrangement by providing me with an additional amount – not now necessarily but, you know, in the form of future payments. That's fair, don't you think?"

"Uncle Sven, weren't you the one who said if the will were drawn up now, you wouldn't be in it?"

"Well, yes, son, but fair is fair. If you were in my place, knowing what my interest is really worth, wouldn't you suggest that a more equitable arrangement be made?"

"Sven," said Kjersten, "please sign the papers."

"Kjersten, be honest, now. You're pressuring me to agree to something that is not only unfair but nearly larcenous."

"Uncle Sven, what did the Russian say to you when you signed over the *Ovar-Odd*?" asked Amos, arms folded. "As I recall, it was something about you only being good for fish food. We saved your life, Uncle Sven. What would they have done if we had not paid them? What would you have done?"

"I'm grateful for your loyalty," said Sven, "but, were the tables turned, I would have done the same for you."

"When? How? Uncle Sven, even under these recent circumstances you did not come by. You would help us? That's easy to say. Somehow, I doubt it. I strongly doubt it."

"Sven, the tables were not turned," said Kjersten with a steely look. "We were placed in a position where action on our part was required to keep you from harm. That's what one Russian subtly said: that we'd all be 'safe.' Sven, considering that we are standing here having this discussion, the arrangement is quite equitable." Kjersten pointed at the documents. "Now, please sign the papers."

"I find it hard to believe you are doing this," countered Sven. "You're pressuring me into signing documents that we all know are inequitable, unjust and unfair. I should get more. I should get much more. You made a big deal over getting an appraisal, and after the Einar II sank, you had all the remaining boats reappraised for insurance purposes. So, we know how much the *Einar II* was worth when it sank, and how much the others are worth presently. Add it all up. My 25% is substantially more than what you paid the Russians."

"Your 25% interest is 100% more than you deserve," said Amos angrily.

"Sven, your behavior is reprehensible," said Kjersten, putting her hands on her hips. "You earned none of that ownership interest...my husband's misfortune was your good fortune. No more, no less. You will get no substantial sum beyond what has already been paid." Kjersten pointed at the documents. "Please sign the papers."

"I don't believe I will," said Sven, folding his arms. "I believe I'll find a competent barrister and we'll see who gets what."

Kjersten glanced at Amos who was fighting to control his temper. Kjersten knew she had to diffuse the situation before Amos lost his inner battle.

"Sven, if you get a barrister, we will get our barrister, Ingemar Stenberg, who is, as you know, the best in Göteborg, because we've used him in the past to defend you. Through Mr. Stenberg we will press charges against you; and there will be other charges, charges you have been able to avoid until now because of us." Sven's jaw went slack and his eyes narrowed. "As you are well aware, the Russians were not the first we've paid – paid in lieu of you going to trial. That, however, will be history." Kjersten pointed at Amos and then herself. "A trial by jury will be convened, and witnesses called. What witnesses? Who do you think, Sven? You have more skeletons in your closet than clothes; and you have no doubt about what we know." Kjersten again folded her arms. "The consequences, of course, will be dire."

Kjersten glared at her younger brother.

"It's your call."

Sven did not move.

Kjersten again pointed to the documents. "Now, please sign the papers."

Sven continued to look at her, his forehead glistening.

After a moment he turned and woodenly walked to the table. "I guess I should sign," he mumbled.

"Precisely," said Kjersten.

As he did with the Russians, Sven bent over, picked up the pen, and silently signed and dated the documents in the appropriate places.

He stood upright and looked at Kjersten. Whatever his true feelings when he signed the last document, the weight on Kjersten's heart lifted like morning mist over Lake Vänern, and Kjersten inwardly sighed with relief.

"I apologize," said Sven. Amos looked mystified at Sven. "I guess I owe you a deep debt of gratitude," continued Sven, absently rotating his hat in his hands. "I suppose it's none of my business," added Sven, "but I hope that, after paying the Russians, you have a fair amount of the insurance settlement left over."

Amos's eyes were narrow and his mouth was open. To Amos it was evident that Sven just gambled and lost, but was prepared to lose. What move is he making now?

"The *Einar II* was the finest ship in Göteborg," said Kjersten, "and, of course, was adequately insured. My husband was very conscientious about our possessions. He once knew what poverty was…and made certain we would never come to the same knowledge."

"Yes," responded Sven, taking a deep breath while looking down at the papers he just signed, "he was a good man." Sven walked to the other side of the table, picked up a slice of warm bread and spread butter on it. "I'm certain he had everything covered and, for you, I'm grateful the settlement was adequate," Sven said before beginning to chew ravenously. He looked at the bread. "This is really good."

Looking at Sven, Amos thought Sven missed his calling: he should have been an actor.

"We are sound financially," said Kjersten diplomatically as she watched Sven hungrily rip bites like a leopard seal consuming a small penguin. "We have placed much of the insurance settlement in banks and have kept cash on hand for immediate needs such as..."

"Eh, do you feel safe – keeping loose cash around," interjected Sven, his mouth full. "Unlikely anything will happen but – "

"As you know, we don't keep it 'loose'; it's in the big safe upstairs, Sven," said Kjersten. "We're very careful."

Sven nodded, swallowed, and took another slice of hot bread and the butter knife. It was evident to Kjersten that, as she had anticipated, Sven was going to suggest something else.

Chewing again, he said, "Again, I apologize. I just thought that the difference between what you paid…well, you know."

Sven sighed, continued to chew and looked obliquely at the floor. He swallowed, looked up at Kjersten and his face contorted with seriousness.

"I know this is a bad time to ask – I'm not certain there is ever a good time – but could – "

"If you'd like to come upstairs for a moment," interrupted Kjersten, "I'll get some cash which should enable you to manage your affairs for a little while."

The tension on Sven's face disappeared and he adopted his courtroom countenance as he followed Kjersten upstairs to Captain Nordquist's office on the top floor.

Although Sven periodically came to the house over the past two decades, he had not been to this particular room for some time. The big, floor safe was the same one, recessed into the wall, and bracketed by bookshelves. Kjersten leaned forward and began to turn the combination lock dial. With Amos standing next to him, Sven watched. Kjersten opened the safe door, revealing a great deal of cash, valuable documents, gold bars and jewelry, and took out an envelope with 1,000 *riksdaler specie*. She stood up, closed the safe, turned the lock mechanism, and motioned to the others to follow her downstairs.

The four of them walked down the three flights of stairs without speaking. Rather than the living room or dining room, Kjersten walked to the foyer.

"Sven," said Kjersten as she turned and handed him the envelope, "it appears we are being benevolent, but appearances can be deceiving. You, for example."

Kjersten had given what she was about to say considerable forethought.

"I will not go into detail except to say this is the last money you will get from us," she said with quiet rectitude while looking at Sven neutrally as Amos stood at a short distance, arms folded, listening. "We would like to have you come around, be part of the family, and contribute to family matters, but I realize this is wishful thinking, and that you will not come here unless you need money."

Sven stared at his sister as if she had just exposed a dark secret of which no one was to know. He could think of nothing to say. The moment contained no warm pretense, only cold honesty.

"Very well then," she continued, "if that is your choice, you will simply not come here, because whatever-amount-you-need will not be available. Consider this before you involve yourself in any additional ploy."

Amos looked at Kjersten, clearly unprepared for what his mother was saying.

"Your ethical standards, not to mention the extent of your conscience," continued Kjersten, "are questionable. And if, in the future, you attempt any additional fraudulent schemes that somehow implicitly involve Amos, Anders and me, or otherwise leverage your family's good name for dishonest gain, we will not come to your aid or defense.

"Depending on what you do, your past could unravel, and we will do nothing to obviate the danger. You could go to prison." Sven continued to stare. "Is that clear?"

Sven's mouth was dry and partially open, his eyes slightly wider than normal. His forehead glistened. He said nothing. He reached out, took the 1,000 *riksdaler specie*, looked at Kjersten like he was going to say something, changed his mind, and changed his mind again.

"Prison?"

He put his cap back on and walked to the door. As he opened the door, he stopped and turned around.

"I'm sorry you feel that way," said Sven. "Very unbecoming, wouldn't you say? Take this money and don't come back. Blaming me for trying to get ahead. Blaming me for not coming around when all I was trying to do was to keep your own emotional burden at a minimum." Sven defiantly stood to his full height, looked at Kjersten and Amos, now side-by-side, and said, "And you criticize my behavior."

He pulled his eyes away from the Nordquists and looked in the envelope. 1,000 *riksdaler specie*. "Much more than I intended to ask." He looked again at the others. "Thank you, you who have more than you need. And, again, history repeats itself." Sven's expression became sullen. "Good day."

He glanced without recognition at Anders who stood wide-eyed behind Kjersten and Amos. Sven placed the money in a coat pocket, turned and left, gently closing the door behind him.

For a moment the others stood silently. Kjersten turned and walked to the living room, and her sons followed.

"Mom?" asked Anders. "Did you mean that?"

"Yes," answered Kjersten, her back to both Amos and Anders, and her hand on the end of the chesterfield. "Hopefully your Uncle Sven believed me. If he did, I may have erected an obstacle that will help keep him out of future trouble. But," she sighed softly, "we'll see."

Sven again disappeared. A month later, Amos and Anders rode to the farm Sven rented, simply to visit, to let Sven know he was still a welcome family member any time – just don't ask for money. As they approached, they saw a prominent note attached to the front door. Thinking it to be a note Sven had posted, Amos and Anders dismounted and walked to the door. The note read:

To all whom Sven Ostermänn owes money:

Sven Ostermänn no longer resides here and his where-abouts are unknown. If you have information of his whereabouts, please contact me at 25 Hjuviksvägen. A reward will be paid.

Nels Aardahl

Amos and Anders looked at one another, remounted, and rode to Nels's farm a mile away.

"Sven left before I could evict him!" said Nels Aardahl, waving his hands. "He's a scoundrel! He had dealings with some Russians that resulted in a temporary lien on the farm. Sold some of my farm equipment. But the last thing takes the cake. When you were by the farm, did you notice the cattle in the field?" Nels folded his arms as Amos and Anders shook their heads. "No? Well, there's a damned good reason you didn't. Sven sold them! All 35 head!"

"To who?"

"Wish I knew! Sold the cattle and left! I'm a little flabbergasted he's related to you Nordquists." Nels looked from Amos to Anders. "I'm sure that hasn't been any picnic. If you hear from him, tell him there's a warrant out for his arrest! Considering how long I've known you kids, Kjersten and Captain Nordquist, I'd rather not prosecute, but you tell Sven that unless he comes by to make restitution, he's going to wind up behind bars! The police are looking for him."

Amos surmised a number of people were looking for him. But where was he?

10

July, 1863

Four years passed like four months as Amos, Kjersten and Anders maintained a frenetic work pace. The *Einar II* was replaced by the *Nordland*, slower, less regal, but with greater draught and cargo capacity, a Fjord not an Arabian.

"We have another order for a shipment to the Union," said Amos. "Textiles." He shrugged. "The South sells cotton to Europe where it's made into cloth sold to the North."

"Too bad they can't cut a deal," said Anders. "The South sends the North cotton and the North sends the South machinery."

"There's a name for that," said Amos.

"What?"

"Peace."

"Well then I change my mind," said Anders. "Where's the delivery?"

"Wilmington."

"Wilmington?" asked Anders as if quizzing Amos.

"The Delaware Wilmington," said Amos, sipping his coffee, slightly annoyed.

"You're getting to know American pretty well, Amos. Considering all the time you spend there, I'm not surprised. I'm afraid if I went to New York, for example, I'd get lost in five minutes."

"It's well I know America, Anders. European trade as we once knew it is history. Emigration. So many Swedes, Norwegians…all Europeans…heading for America. The more who leave, the more market demand in Europe declines, and increases in America. Fortunately, we've established ourselves. We're doing quite well in the New Country."

"Who do you think will win the war? What then?"

"As you know, the South believes they have better soldiers – and to the man, perhaps they might – but the North has the better infrastructure, manufacturing, supplies, supply lines, and greater troop strength. On the other hand, as far as military leadership is concerned, while the South is set, the North is still sorting things out. Then, again, Lincoln might have the right generals now. A few days ago the North accounted themselves well in a big battle about 50 miles northwest of Baltimore."

"Where was that?"

"Someplace called Gettysburg."

"Never heard of it."

"That the South was that far north, however, tells you how the war was going. But perhaps now the momentum is swinging."

"The Southern blockades have become fewer. We used to worry about them."

"Yes, their ships get captured by the North, names are changed and the ships made to serve the Federals, but those Confederate ships aren't being readily replaced by the South. The South is fighting for sovereignty, but I wonder how long they're going to last. It takes more than an ideal to win a war."

"We'll see," said Anders. "The Minutemen did more with less during the American Revolution."

"Yes, but the British were not fighting on home ground – while presently the Army of the Potomac is," said Amos. "Big difference. And geography isn't the only problem the Confederacy has to worry about. Confederate currency is badly inflating. In fact, the purchasing power of gold is appreciating substantially both north and south of the Mason-Dixon Line. It seems that way everywhere."

"True," said Kjersten who had been listening. "The value of gold has been rising steadily against the ryksdaler and the paper dollar." She glanced at her sons while she folded another napkin. "Building a larger gold reserve would be wise. We'll put it in several banks."

"I'm not certain we should put it all in banks," said Amos. "There are failures, fraud…or more overt robbery. We should also keep more in the upstairs safe."

"We'll be our own bank," said Anders. "First, Nordquist Shipping Co., and now First Nordquist Bank." As others looked back without expression, Anders, arms folded, explained, "It's a pun."

"Starting a bank is the last thing I want to do," said Kjersten. "Let's focus on what we do best for the time being. With the money we make from what we do best, we'll accumulate more gold, deposit it in banks, keep some in the upstairs safe, and see what gains are made."

"Since we're discussing investment strategy – and what we do best – I have a second idea," said Amos, looking back and forth from Anders to Kjersten. "I feel like we should have already done this some time ago. I don't want to start a bank but, complementing Nordquist Shipping Co., I'd like to start an export business using our fleet for transport."

Kjersten also folded her arms as she looked at Amos.

"I already have the suppliers in Europe," Amos continued, "and the buyers in America. I know all the intermediate shippers in Europe. All European businesses are dying for opportunities. The timing is excellent and it would be a natural step to take now. I could handle the export business while Anders takes over Nordquist Shipping Co., and you, mom, could oversee what we do."

"I'm not certain I could 'oversee' exporting. I have enough of a challenge with shipping. I only came into this position because your father died."

"Mom, you know financial statements. You know a strong profit margin from a weak margin, and how it got that way. And you know a lot of people."

"I'm not sure," said Kjersten.

"We should do this. Undertaken gradually so that any mistakes result in only short-lived minor losses, this should ultimately be very successful."

"Anders," asked Kjersten, "what do you think? Do you believe you can run Nordquist Shipping?"

"Blindfolded."

"Let's try it without a blindfold for awhile," said Kjersten. "Your comfort level may not change, but mine might."

Nordquist Trading Co. was formed, trading selective goods, precluding damaging existing client relationships. As Amos expected, it became quickly successful, complementing and benefiting Nordquist Shipping Co. The Nordquist family of Göteborg was quietly making a great deal of money.

Amos, 22, took separate residence while Kjersten and Anders remained in the hillside mansion. Amos was becoming involved with Karin Olafsdotter, sailing master Olaf Hansen's beautiful daughter.

Anders, 20, was involved with everyone else.

Amos was looking forward to meeting Karin for lunch at a small Göteborg inn.

As Karin Olafsdotter walked down the main street of Göteborg's business district radiating urbane sophistication and earthy sensuality, pedestrian and horse traffic slowed in her vicinity. Her striking eyes and thick, golden blonde hair, distractions since she was a little girl, were like sunlight following a dark and dismal night. Walking erectly, a closed parasol in her hand, her long, conservative dress and coat failed to obscure a full figure. As she walked down the street, Karin attracted male attention like a queen bee attracts a swarm, exciting men, single and married, who gave her concupiscent looks. Although married men's wives knew there was no need for concern, the wives experienced a precipitate feeling of jealousy and threat. Meanwhile, single women inwardly both admired and fumed, and a few younger boys, some experiencing the first frisson of arousal, maladroitly gawked. Single men tipped their hats, nodded, smiled or effected whatever mannerism might contribute to a favorable first, second or last impression.

It would seem that Amos and Karin could be a perfect match, but the fit was imperfect because, while Amos was attractive, intelligent and a man of character, when with Karin he could be oddly awkward – farouche and uncommunicative if angry about something unrelated to the moment. Even when in an oft-pleasant state of mind, at the most crucial moments he would find himself at a loss for words when it was important he say something. That he say, really, anything – rather than remain silent – never occurred to him, although Amos thought long and hard about his romantic shortcomings, ultimately concluding only that, as Karin was who she was, he was who he was.

Anders had no romantic shortcomings; couldn't understand the problem.

Of the two brothers, the entire "lady's man" gene went to Anders, and while the love that Anders gave was directed toward himself, his older brother was falling in love with Karin Olafsdotter, she of many suitors.

As Karin walked toward the inn, fashionably late, Amos sat waiting, his impatience beginning to stir – he wanted to spend time with Karin, but his schedule dictated other responsibilities, and by being late, she reduced their time together. As she walked in the door, his impatience flew off like a Göteborg warbler, and he stood up, greeting Karin warmly. Karin sat down, prepared to be entertained, and Amos sat down, prepared to work at being entertaining.

Meanwhile, Anders attended to personal affairs at the Nordquist hillside residence. It was well Anders continued to live with his mother. The house was large, Kjersten's health was declining, and family and business affairs all directed they stay in close proximity. Anders was responsible for Nordquist Shipping, but was not as attentive to detail as his responsibility required. His mother would ask continual questions about details, forcing Anders to handle matters of potential oversight.

Over the years, the increase in Nordquist wealth created changed priorities and a changed lifestyle. For example, Kjersten, the consummate baker, no longer baked or cooked. As usual, that evening a three-course dinner was prepared by Arnauld, the French chef, and served by Higgins, the English butler.

In early 1864, Kjersten became bedridden for several days, the victim of… Dr. Johanssen was unsure. Dr. Johanssen visited each day and advised she stay in bed, keep warm, and eat and drink normally. He also provided a licorice-flavored tonic, the most active ingredients of which were alcohol and cocaine. Unsurprisingly, the concoction made Kjersten feel better.

During the second week that Kjersten was bedridden, Amos and Anders brought in a nurse to stay with Kjersten and attend to any needs of the moment. Concerned, Amos temporarily moved back into his old bedroom. In spite of the advice, the tonic, the nurse and Amos's presence, Kjersten's's health did not improve. Kjersten slept most of the time and, when awake, was incoherent, sometimes seemingly talking to her husband, Stig. She was unresponsive to questions she was asked. That evening, although awake, she could not eat dinner, again could not converse.

At one point when Anders came into her bedroom, Kjersten was staring obliquely at the ceiling, mouth slightly open as if her attention was focused on something up there. Anders looked up, but saw nothing.

"Mom?" asked Anders. "Are you all right?"

Kjersten continued to stare – her expression was oddly peaceful – unmindful of Anders' presence, possibly not hearing him at all. Anders tentatively stepped forward and for a moment studied his mother's expression, uncertain of what to do or say.

He bent over, still looking directly at her, and listened.

She did not move but was breathing normally. Anders wondered why she was staring at the ceiling without noticing he was there? What was she seeing? It was eerie, he thought.

He stood upright and looked at her for a while, attempting to discern what was happening.

He weakly attempted to get her attention again.

"Mom?"

No response.

"Mom?"

Kjersten peacefully closed her eyes, and for the first time Anders noticed how deathly silent the room was.

As she drifted into sleep, he had the odd-yet-somehow-edifying sensation they were not alone. He looked toward the doorway behind him, but no one was there.

He bent over his mother again and listened. Shallow breathing. It was 7:30 p.m.

For a moment he stood quietly, and then tensely turned. His legs and feet felt like concrete as he walked toward the door.

Before leaving the room he turned and looked again. He left the doorway, and quietly walked down the stairs into the living room where he approached Amos, seated and reading a newspaper.

"How's mom?" asked Amos, looking up.

"I don't know," answered Anders solemnly, hands in his pockets as he looked out the window. "Fine. I guess."

At roughly 9:30 p.m., Kjersten was awakened by someone standing at the foot of the bed. Instantly wide-awake, in contrast to the odd ceiling-stare earlier in the evening, she smiled, a pleasant, prolonged, youthful smile as if, well-dressed for the occasion, standing on a large passenger ship as it approached a pier, she spied someone whom she had looked forward to seeing for quite some time. Totally relaxed, she arose from the bed, happily greeted and left with the friend.

The funeral for Kjersten was almost as well-attended as was her husband's. Kjersten had many friends, especially from all those years when emotional support for wives was so often from one another.

She had touched many hearts, and Amos, while deeply sorrowful, was also deeply moved. It was, he hoped, as he might be remembered at his own funeral in the distant future.

Those in attendance included much of Göteborg's elderly – some of whom would soon follow – as well as younger friends, and Aunt Ona. Reminiscing was ubiquitous, and to Amos it seemed life was fuller when he was younger, when interaction with others in the community was extensive.

The presentiment he had sensed when talking to the Russian, Yuri, several years ago, was not forgotten, but neither was it further weighed and acted on. Amos reconsidered it at that moment. I have been "working," Amos thought to himself. I have been "making a living." I have been doing the benign clichés that describe the efforts men expend throughout an adult lifetime, seemingly necessary but, he thought, eternally pointless. In so doing, I've become reclusive. How does one become reclusive, but enrich the lives of others – beyond creating employment opportunities? A small voice inside Amos reminded him it was not enough, asking him, what are you going to do now? Now. Listening to the others, Amos felt angst and a desire for change.

After the funeral, Amos was emotionally drained, and that evening Amos and Anders went to their second floor bedrooms earlier than usual to relieve their weariness and momentarily escape their grief. Both immediately went to sleep.

In the dark early morning hours, Amos started, awakened by the sensation of someone being upstairs. He sat upright.

Who? Anders? Awake at this time?

The servants were in the servant's quarters. The nurse had returned to her home.

Wide awake, Amos sat perfectly still, barely breathing, and focused toward his open bedroom door, searching for some vague image in the darkness.

Nothing.

He listened.

No sound from without.

If he neither saw nor heard anything, he wondered, what was causing this sensation? One moment he was sound asleep; the next, he was completely awake with all senses on full alert. No initial grogginess; wide-awake. And no evident reason.

Then a sixth sense gave him an inexplicable infusion of fear. His muscles tensed and he stiffened, listening.

One minute passed.

Two.

Three.

He was just about to relax and lie back in the bed when he heard something. A creak. In the floor boards above him on the third floor. The wind?

Wide-eyed, Amos listened in the dark. A muffled shuffle – boots – barely audible, almost as if imagined.

No sound. Was it imagined?

No. There it was again.

Anders?

Even with reason to be quiet (it was 1:30 a.m.), being quiet would not cross Anders' mind. Anders, always self-absorbed, was never a quiet person.

Redirecting his attention, Amos listened very carefully, focusing on Anders' bedroom across the hall. Amos could hear Anders' heavy, nocturnal breathing.

Another creak. Almost identical but even softer. It was not imagined. Amos preferred the noise were louder, for the unnatural stillness of the noise implied the stillness was intentional, and if intentional then…

An intruder was in the house.

Amos sat up quietly for a moment, attempting to gauge the pace, the size, the emotion of the intruder. Something. Anything. The exact location?

Another creak, so quiet yet loud. Where? The office on the next floor?

Amos slid out of bed and, in his stocking feet, went quietly to his bureau, slowly opened the top drawer, and took out a loaded first model LeMat cap and ball revolver brought back from the United States, one pistol from a set of two received from an importer claiming the set formerly belonged to Confederate General P. G. T. Beauregard. The nine-shot upper cylinder fired bullets through the upper barrel; the central smoothbore barrel fired one burst of buckshot. Who first owned the pistols made no difference; what mattered was that the pistols were very effective at close range, formidable in case of a burglary – one was kept in the top bureau drawer in this bedroom, and the other in the top bureau drawer in Anders' bedroom. Pistol in hand, muscles tense, Amos's stocking feet slid slowly, silently, in the dark on his hardwood floor toward his bedroom door.

As he reached the dark hallway, Amos heard the almost inaudibly whispered epithet near the top of the stairwell, "*Jävlar* [damn it]."

In the quiet, Amos could hear it, the soft turning of the combination mechanism on the safe. Amos listened carefully, and intuited that the intruder was, at that moment, totally focused on the combination. And having no success.

Amos slid slowly, cautiously, to the second floor stair landing, stopped at the foot of the stairs to listen. Again, all Amos could hear was the nearly inaudible clicking noise of the combination lock slowly being turned. He could imagine the intruder with his ear pressed against the safe, listening to the tumblers as, one-by-one, each eventually fell into place.

Just as Amos began to test the first stair rung, he heard a weak "click" followed by the sound of the safe opening, normally a quiet creak, but now the same sound was as startling as a dropped ceramic plate breaking on a hardwood floor, and Amos reflexively stepped up several stairs fast as a fox. He stopped and listened.

As the intruder placed currency and gold in a carpetbag, Amos cautiously, forcefully, climbed the remaining stairs, each step deliberate, making no sound. Amos reached the top of the stairs, crouched and listened for a moment.

Amos stood upright and, on his toes, began to slide slowly, quietly toward the office as the intruder completed filling the bag, now quite heavy.

The intruder's kerosene lamp lit the study doorway, sending weak light into the hall. The lamp went out and the hallway went dark.

Amos reflexively crouched as the intruder stepped through the office doorway into the hall.

"Put your hands up!" Amos shouted.

The shouted order rudely awoke Anders on the floor below as the intruder spontaneously froze in the dark, and for a split-second the burglar did nothing before fishing awkwardly with his left hand for his pistol beneath his waistcoat.

"Put your hands up, I said!" shouted Amos. In the dark, Amos could not see the panicked intruder quickly drop to a crouch as he pulled out his own pistol.

Blam!

The blast sounded like the end of the world, the bullet hitting Amos below his right rib cage. As Amos sank to his knees, letting out a loud moan, he fired back – Blam! Blam! – hitting the intruder once as the intruder awkwardly ran toward the stairs with the carpetbag. Flipping a small lever on the end of the pistol hammer, Amos fired the lower barrel of "blue whistlers," hitting the intruder and causing him to lurch forward. Pumped full of fear, adrenalin, and lead, the wounded intruder continued down the dark stairwell to the second floor landing, unaware that the shouted commands awakened Anders, the exchange of shots directed Anders to jump from bed and immediately retrieve the second LeMat pistol in the set, and Amos's loud, recognizable moan and immediate drop to his knees told Anders that the man awkwardly descending the dark, third-floor stairwell to the second floor was not his brother.

Bleeding from the back, neck and leg, the panicked, wide-eyed intruder noisily reached the second floor landing and hobbled in the dark to the stairwell leading to the first floor as Anders jumped out of his nearby bedroom within a few feet of the burglar and fired.

Blam! sounded the first shot. "Uhrrahh!" the burglar rasped. Blam! came the second. He choked and, moaning, fell, loudly tumbling end-over-end down the stairwell to the first floor landing, lying motionlessly but still tightly gripping the heavy carpetbag in his left hand.

For a moment, Anders kept his LeMat pointed in the direction of the burglar at the bottom of the stairs, but the sharp smell of gunpowder brought Anders to his senses. Anders heard nothing other than muffled but continual moans from Amos who was in pain, attempting to walk down the stairs while leaning heavily on the railing.

Anders quickly turned and, in the dark, raced into his bedroom, tossed the pistol toward the bed, found and lit the bedside lamp, ran out to the edge of the second floor stairwell landing, and, shaking, cautiously held the lamp high as he looked down at the first floor stairway landing below in the lamplight.

The intruder's ragged waistcoat was stained dark crimson. No movement.

Still holding the lamp high, Anders raced to the stairwell where he ran up to his wounded brother, helping him down the stairs and into Amos's bedroom.

Although Amos was bleeding, the wound was not as serious as it might have been if the bullet penetrated more to the center and a little higher. Using his training as a young seaman, Anders first tore up a bed sheet, applied pressure to stop the bleeding as much as possible, and then dressed the wound using the strips of torn cloth.

Leaving Amos on the bed, Anders ran to his own bedroom for some street clothes. He needed to get Dr. Johanssen immediately.

Having quickly changed, lamp overhead, Anders raced down the stairs, stopping to see if there was any sign of life from the intruder lying prone on the first floor landing. Blood saturated the right side of the burglar's tattered coat, spreading on the oak floor beneath him. The burglar's face was obscured by his left arm, and the arm was anchored in place by the heavy carpetbag somehow still grasped by his left hand. Breathing heavily, Anders kept his LeMat pointed at the intruder's head, and cautiously pulled the carpetbag from the intruder's hand.

The intruder's left arm fell away from his face.

Looking down at the body lying at his feet, Anders began to quiver. The body moved slightly and Anders stepped back. The man slowly rolled on his side and as his rat-like face looked up at Anders with dark, godless eyes, emotion washed over Anders like waves in a North Atlantic storm. The eyes were joined by a weak smile as he mumbled something Anders did not understand.

"*Mort aux voleurs.*"

The faint smile faded and disappeared. Uncle Sven's head fell back, and his eyes rolled and stared at the Nordquist front door, the last thing they would see.

Uncle Sven was dead, leaving Amos and Anders with only one uncle, a man totally opposite of Sven: Captain Stig Nordquist's brother somewhere in America, the infamous Uncle Torvald.

11

1864

Blam! Blam!

Silence followed for a prolonged moment. No return fire.

"By Yiminy," exclaimed Uncle Torvald in his heavy Scandinavian accent, his skirmishing cap turned sideways, his dirt-encrusted mustache flowing aside of his open mouth, "I t'ink ve got dat vun last Norvegian, you know?" Torvald stood and shook his Spencer repeater overhead. "Yah, by Yiminy!"

"Swede, giddown!" hoarsely hollered one of the men.

Uncle Torvald began a little jig, however, singing, "10,000 Svedes, t'rough da veeds, chasing vun Norvegian," repeating something he'd heard as a child. The other Union soldiers guffawed in spite of their physical exhaustion and leather-hard emotions, the result of prolonged marches without sleep, sleeping in the rain and mud when sleep availed itself, periods with subsistence rations or scavenging, all in between bouts of deadly combat that saw Death select whoever it selected, including close comrades, but somehow not them.

Another forgettable skirmish ended. Two Union men wounded, one dead. The moment would be solemn were it not for Uncle Torvald's irreverent sense of humor. He referred to everyone on the other side as a "Norvegian." Consequently, some people thought he didn't like Norwegians. To the contrary, as with Germans, Scotsmen, and everyone else, to Torvald, Norwegians were fine. Many years earlier as a small boy, misconstruing a jig he'd heard, Torvald began using the word "Norvegian" to designate whatever he was shooting at, and subsequently the word had replaced "target." Over the years, there were rabbit Norvegians, squirrel Norvegians, buffalo Norvegians, possum Norvegians, Indian Norvegians, bandit Norvegians, and now Confederate Norvegians. Whatever unhappy, moving, breathing thing happened to find itself in his gunsights was a "Norvegian."

Torvald's irreverent personality and Scandinavian jargon were infectious and, consequently, a few others in his small corner of the Army of the Potomac had supplanted "Johnny Rebs," "rebs," or "Johnnies" with "Norvegians."

"Norvegians" were everywhere at Gettysburg months ago. When the accumulated smoke from hundreds of cannon and thousands of rifles and muskets, fired for days, finally drifted clear of the battlefield air, the South and North counted nearly 7,900 dead – large swatches of otherwise visible grass covered by dead men or what remained of them. Viscera, limbs, and torsos were splayed and mutilated, and warm blood puddled in some wagon ruts, runneling as if in an abattoir gutter. Among many still living, the ravages of battle would permanently scar both body and soul.

Nearly a half hour after the end of the 3rd day battle on East Cavalry Field, Torvald weakly looked about him. No one said, "Swede, giddown!" It seemed abnormally quiet until he realized how physically and emotionally spent he was, and that his ears were ringing so badly he could hear nothing else as he looked about. Bodies. Men. Horses. His horse was shot out from underneath him the previous day and he had grabbed the bridle of a riderless horse that galloped near him, swinging up into the empty saddle. About him now were the unblinking, vacant eyes of dead men staring; empty eyes that made Torvald's familiar compatriots eerily distant, further proliferating the degenerative malaise spreading in his soul like bloat in a carcass.

Stepping over bodies, some familiar, Torvald spotted a friend at a short distance and slowly walked to Sergeant Carl Tollefson, a medic, who lay on his back, motionless, emotionless. The night before the battle, while they were around the campfire, Carl told Torvald a little about Carl's life – as if Carl wanted someone to know. "I have a feeling," Carl said, staring at the fire without elaborating, but Torvald knew. Carl talked to Torvald about an idyllic childhood, growing up on a farm with a private lake. An only-son, his folks didn't want him to enlist but, like Torvald, he felt a responsibility to this new country.

As if Torvald were invisible, Carl's empty eyes stared beyond Torvald while Torvald stood over Carl's once-handsome face. Carl's open medical kit was beside him, along with a dead man Torvald did not recognize. Carl's jaw and much of his throat were gone, the vertebrae of his neck partially exposed in front through ripped flesh, strands of frayed, bloody pulp. Carl's hair and the ground under his head had been soaked with his blood.

Torvald stood and stared, beyond grief as emotional frissons shook his heart like the ground under incoming cannon fire, and his open mouth let out a loud shudder.

Carl's folks wanted him to be a doctor – it was why he was a medic – and Carl often talked about formal medical training when the war ended. But Carl grew up to become a mutilated corpse on the Gettysburg battlefield, and Torvald figured history might someday revere the men of Gettysburg, but in a few short years no one would remember Carl Tollefson from White Bear Lake, Minnesota.

To counter his sorrow, Torvald tried to remember Carl's smile. Torvald shuddered as he looked down.

Please, Lord, just his goddamned smile, Torvald thought desperately.

The memory of Carl's smile was overpowered by the stark reality of his ghostly eyes, his wickedly mutilated head and neck.

Beginning to feel queasy from despair and blood, for a moment longer Torvald continued to stare back, fighting against what he saw. Because it was so wrong.

Turning his head, Torvald grimaced hard for several moments, came to one knee, his hands wrapped around his vertical rifle barrel, the butt stock planted on the blood-soaked ground, and fought to keep his wits.

The following day, shaded and hidden from view at a distance, his back against the trunk of a large oak, Torvald sat and numbly watched the opposing Army of Northern Virginia's distant 14-mile-long train of suffering slowly and fearfully retreat like a badly injured animal, striking back at small Union forces pursuing like jackals. At that moment, the word "Norvegian" did not come to mind. For a while nothing came to mind as Torvald sat exhausted and incurious, staring blankly. He felt the brief, fatigued relief that came from still being alive, and absently wondered who Getty was, and whether Getty had the remotest idea that one day his burg could see anything like what happened here?

The following day, Union General George Meade was criticized in Washington for not vigorously pursuing General Lee and the living and wounded of the Army of Northern Virginia. Torvald understood the criticism, but considered how those well-intended critics had not gone through the hell Torvald went through, had not seen the horror Torvald saw. As Torvald sat leaning against the ancient oak, he sensed he was getting close to that moment when bloodshed could rise to a level where he might start to drown in it and, emotionally flailing to stay afloat, and having spent more spiritual energy than ammunition, his soul would go empty, raise its hands in surrender, and shout, "I'm out! I'm out!" He continued to stare blankly, knowing that when his soul cried out, he would somehow need to reload enough nerve to continue.

Now, months later, the Confederate army was being pushed south, and the Union soldiers began to suppress what many considered premature hope of eventual victory. The end would be welcome by Torvald. His enlistment, as with many Civil War enlistments, was naively undertaken. *Dulce bellum inexpertis*, he thought; war is attractive to those who know nothing of it.

That evening he sat next to a campfire with men still alive in his company, and motionlessly watched the flames dance and flick in the dark; shadows dancing fitfully on grim, grimy, bearded faces of seasoned soldiers lost in thought. In spite of the death, destruction and suffering, again Torvald concluded it was important he did this; important he enlisted. It should be done. America should be united. This America, these united states. It is important that all be preserved and perpetuated, he sensed, perhaps for challenging but favorable future vicissitude, like a musical score with which the composer is initially pleased but, coming back to it later, finds room for refinement and magnification if he eliminates one section and modifies others. Like an orchestra of accomplished musicians, with practice this great country will become even greater. But to do so, it must stay together.

Torvald proudly considered himself an American. America had grown on him. Torvald believed there was more ambition, more energy, more entrepreneurial spirit and creativity in America. America was a ship of independence and opportunity sailing in a current of Christian ideals and capitalist ideas. Europeans becoming Americans believed they could do great things, and America could do great things. It was a good place for people like him, he thought.

The situation was confusing because, from Torvald's perspective, the prisoners of war he met seemed like the men around him. Two countries? Different opinions, sure. Confederate prisoners considered themselves Southerners, but still acted and thought like Americans. South Americans? he joked weakly.

He glanced at the men about him.

This American melting pot accepts all kinds from everywhere, he thought while returning his stare at the mesmerizing campfire flames. Each person is different except for the need to overcome challenges…in a country that enables overcoming, forging newcomers like me into something homogenous and stellar.

Was, therefore, the 14-mile-long train of suffering necessary? Torvald's head rolled slightly from side-to-side as he tried to think. He was dog-tired.

Torvald slowly got to his feet, put his rifle over his shoulder, thought for a moment longer and concluded that when his enlistment was up, that was it. He carried a will with him, hoping it would not be needed. But he should be done soon. Head west. While the end of the war may only be a matter of time, the many Confederate bullets, perhaps one in particular, did not know that. "Yah, I should head vest," he said out loud. The West needed settling, and Torvald thought he might help make it so.

Standing motionlessly in the darkness, hands still in his pockets while firelight flickered across his grimy face, Torvald again thought about the Confederate train of wounded and dying men. One of these times, it might be my number that comes up. This was followed by a second related thought: before I do anything else, I should write a letter to my brother.

Torvald had not written home since he joined the army, and received no correspondence because no one knew where he was or what he was doing. Those in the old country wondered what happened to him. They worried; waiting to hear, wanting to know. His letter would be wonderfully welcome.

12

A month later the letter addressed to Captain Stig Nordquist arrived in Göteborg. Anders was wide-eyed, holding the letter. He took it up to the office where Amos sat studying a ship's manifest for a cargo to be delivered to New York.

"It's a letter from Uncle Torvald!" said Anders loudly, waving the letter. "Uncle Torvald, by golly!"

As Amos got up from his desk, Anders sat down in the leather couch next to the window and began excitedly reading to himself. Amos sat down next to Anders. Amos waited a moment but, impatient to hear what Uncle Torvald was doing, interrupted Anders. "Anders," said Amos, annoyed, "how about reading it aloud so we both know what it says. To begin with, where is he?"

"It says he's in the state of Pennsylvania. And he's been fighting for the North in the War of the Rebellion." Anders read some more. "He says his commanding officer is the bravest general in the army, someone named…."

"Read the letter, Anders," interrupted Amos. "From the beginning."

Anders anxiously read the letter, nearly 15 pages long, a brief history lesson, summarizing Uncle Torvald's exploits since he joined the Union army. The letter discussed the battles in which Uncle Torvald fought, his opinions of President Lincoln, General Sheridan, General Grant, the Confederates, the Union, and the lessons of life he learned from the death he saw. From reading brief newspaper accounts, much of the letter's content was familiar, but now more relevant to Amos and Anders because Uncle Torvald was a part of those accounts. From the letter, Amos and Anders did not know where Uncle Torvald was at the moment, but they knew what outfit he was with – Company A, 5th Regiment, The Michigan Cavalry Brigade…"The Wolverines" – and after discussing the letter, Amos read the letter himself, went to the desk, sat down and wrote an outline and then the first draft of a return letter.

Amos attempted to phrase the events of his father's death as delicately as possible for, although Torvald had been away for some time, Amos knew that Stig Nordquist's death would be as painful to his brother as it had been for Amos himself, particularly because Torvald had been away so long. Amos wrote he would be coming to America with an inheritance for Uncle Torvald. Hopefully the letter would reach Uncle Torvald before Amos did…but Amos knew that mail timeliness was not just cause for wager.

Both Amos and Anders re-read Uncle Torvald's letter several times over the next few days. Everything Uncle Torvald said implied he was in America to stay. In fact, the letter made America sound even more alluring to Amos – although not as alluring as Karin Olafsdotter, reason to stay in Göteborg.

Karin Olafsdotter was an enigma. Courted by the most eligible bachelor in Göteborg, she remained distant, keeping Amos at arm's length. Why? Amos wondered. What was it she did not like about him? Why wasn't she attracted to him? He realized he was a better listener than conversationalist, but was that so bad?

Karin found Amos attractive; he was tall, strong, handsome, kind and intelligent. Rich. All other young women in Göteborg would trade places with Karin in a heartbeat. The problem was Amos – in fact all of her suitors – did not make her feel as did another young man who was, uniquely, not a suitor. As easily the most beautiful woman in Göteborg – she made even the more-attractive ladies look plain by comparison – she was used to having her way with men, and sustained a confidence that this mysterious acquaintance, whom she knew well enough to greet informally when the occasion rose, could eventually be the man in her life if she was patient. Seated in front of her dressing mirror perfunctorily brushing her long glistening hair, this was her reverie.

What resulted was the eternal triangle – although two sides of the triangle were unaware the triangle existed. Only Karin knew that. Her behavior toward Amos, whom she liked and respected, was capricious. Amos thought Karin often enjoyed his company while at other times, although with him, she seemed somewhere else. Amos' love for Karin subsequently grew stronger from a combination of wishful thinking and intermittent reinforcement.

Export management required Amos make trips to America and back and, because of her capriciousness, and the availability of others ready to immediately take his place when he left, his absences did not help his relationship with Karin. Further complicating matters was the possibility Karin's fantasies might be the result of wanting something she could not have, although Karin always got what she wanted.

If there was a man Karin wanted, what obstacle stood in her way? If the acquaintance obviously already knew her well enough to effect a romantic triangle, why would he remain at a distance? Although he was Göteborg's male-equivalent of Göteborg's most beautiful woman, he remained at a distance because his brother was already involved with Karin. Otherwise, it wouldn't have bothered Anders to have another young lady, particularly the most attractive one in Göteborg, on the string. While Amos was essentially a one-woman man, Anders collected women like butterflies. Anders enjoyed variety and view. For Karin, if there was any man in the world whom a woman might want but could not have, it was Anders; but if there was any woman in the world that could monopolize the view, it was Karin.

"What are you doing tonight, Don Juan?'

"Sounds like the pot calling the kettle 'black'," responded Amos as he gently polished a silver serving tray. "Karin and I are going to have dinner with her mother and father."

"Ahhh. Sounds serious. Mother and father? Ehmmm. Too serious."

"Not as serious as I would like."

"That also sounds serious." Anders looked at Amos while languidly polishing silverware once in residence at the Vatican. "Are you feeling well?"

"Are you feeling anything?"

"I feel many things. I tell my paramours, 'Mi amor,'" Anders began affectedly, "let Anders take you to España. Majorca. Anders can show you many things." Anders tilted his head back subtly. "But Anders weel not beg." Anders smiled. "And what do you think they say to me? 'No'? Never. Amos, without feelings it would be impossible for one to make so many women eager to compromise Christian principle. Do I feel anything, you ask? Ah but I do. I feel. Every chance I get, Amos. It is," Anders gesticulated animatedly, "what I do best. You, my brother and friend, are spreading yourself entirely too thick."

"And you, my irrepressible, irresponsible younger brother, too thin… although in this room at this moment, it's getting a bit thick."

"Irresponsible?" responded Anders wide-eyed, feigning indignation. "At my age, I am acting extraordinarily responsibly. 'Variety is the spice of life!' Should I not add spice to my life? Should I not live life to the fullest? One woman?" Anders put down a spoon and held out his hands questioningly. "One? It is you who are irresponsible."

"Karin is a beautiful, intelligent woman," countered Amos. "Why should I spread my affections among many when there is only one I want?"

"Because it's fun, my entirely-too-serious brother."

"But does it bring real satisfaction, a deeper sense of fulfillment and contentment? Obviously it does not," said Amos, turning toward Anders with his arms outstretched, palms up. "You are never satisfied. What are the results of your womanizing? The broken hearts, the angry fathers, the disillusioned mothers? The lack of true love? How is there any pleasure-beyond-the-moment in what you do?"

"The moment suits me well, Amos. Spices, good man. The more you use, the better life tastes."

"When everything tastes good, eventually nothing tastes good," said Amos, returning to the silver platter.

"How so?"

"Look at your own example. You have many women, and that does not satisfy you because you cannot truly appreciate any of them. Were you to have one, and she meant the world to you, one would give you more satisfaction than many."

Putting down a polished platter, Amos folded his arms and looked at Anders.

"Think about it," Amos began. "There is great satisfaction, reward, when you treat one woman as a woman should be treated. You will never know how much of a man you are, Anders, until you have made a commitment to love one woman. While it is natural, it isn't easy. It requires effort. If done correctly, however, that woman will become as devoted and strong as the level to which you cherish her. Look at mom and dad. Dad was gone all that time, but when he came home, for mom it was worth the wait. Why? Dad made a commitment to love mom, and did so conscientiously their entire married life. Anders, one great thing you lack: commitment. Without commitment, the breeze needed to fill your sails comes and goes and, consequently, you are continually waiting for another breeze. But with commitment, the wind is constant and powerful, and the extent of your love life will amaze you. Especially you."

"Very well," said Anders seriously, polishing a fork, "if I meet the woman of my dreams – I should have been Solomon who had as many wives as he had dreams – I will get serious about commitment but, in the meantime, I will get serious about nothing."

"That's fair. No hurry. But when the right woman comes along," said Amos, looking levelly at Anders, "do the right thing. Remember: commitment."

Amos said no more, and washed his hands in the sink, drying them on a towel.

"When are you going to Karin's?"

"In about a half hour," answered Amos, tying his ascot. "What are you doing this evening? Possibly at this last moment you are trying to decide between three women you have asked out, and also trying to think of good excuse to tell the two you stand-up."

"Why should I leave anyone at home? With three women, there would be four of us; three's a crowd, not four." Anders laughed while Amos made no response to a remark that merited no response. "Actually, I'm taking the night off," said Anders. "I've nothing to do." He looked at Amos. "Do you believe that?"

"Certainly. If anyone needed a night off, it would be you," said Amos. "I have an idea. Since you and I have done nothing together for weeks except work, how about joining me at Karin's?"

"They wouldn't mind?"

"Why would they mind? They would probably enjoy you more than me. After all, you who are the master of invoking feeling could use your magic to invoke feelings of pleasure and delight. What a stroke of genius on my part: bringing you with me. We depart in a half hour. Get ready."

The evening at Karin's home was enjoyable, especially for Karin who spent most of the evening talking to Anders while Amos listened to Karin's father and mother. On the way home, Anders remarked that he enjoyed himself immensely, and looked forward to the next opportunity to have dinner with Karin and her family. The following day when Amos went to see Karin as scheduled, she was not there, and her parents were perplexed for they and Karin knew he was coming.

"She said she was going to see someone and would be back soon," said Karin's father. That was hours ago.

———————— •◦• ————————

"Guess who stopped by while you were gone?" asked Anders as he sat at the dining room table checking items on a list.

"Who?"

"Karin. She said she was looking for you, and I told her you were down at the dock overseeing cargo loading before the *Polstjärnan* and the *Nordanvinden* set sail for America."

Once again, the cargo they were to carry contained extensive amounts of cloth and linen to resupply Union clothiers. Timely delivery was important – Nordquist Shipping had built its business on dependability – and normally Amos would have assured no oversight occur if he were overseeing cargo loading.

He wasn't, however. While Karin was visiting Anders, Amos was at Karin's waiting for Karin to return.

"When I told her where you were," continued Anders, "she asked if she could come in. I was busy, but she's your petite amie, so I said, 'Certainly, come in.' She stayed for two hours. Normally fine with me – she is a vision – but I was busy. I finally almost asked her to leave – you know, I've things to do, it's getting late in the day, hint, hint. So she smiled, bid me adieu, and headed home."

"What time did she leave?"

"Around 5:30."

"She didn't head home. I was at her house. And I trust she knew I would be there. To see her." Amos and Anders looked at one another.

"I don't know what to say," said Anders, folding his hands.

"I don't either. I'll need to talk to her and discover what's going on in her mind." Amos said nothing for a moment, and then changed the subject.

"Are the *Polstjärnan* and the *Nordanvinden* checked out, seaworthy, full crew, good men? Any problems?"

"None I can think of," responded Anders as he leaned forward and placed his elbows on the table. "Sometimes I wish mom were here…you know, mom had such phenomenal attention to detail. She'd ask questions about things I'd given no thought. I worry about what I might not remember."

"You have an extensive check-list you use," said Amos, pointing at the list in front of Anders. "Is there anything on it that has not been considered?" asked Amos.

"I have this list memorized," said Anders, looking down at the sheets of paper, "but there are always things that aren't on the list; do you know what I mean?"

"Well, when you think of them, whatever they are, add them to the list."

The next day when Amos actually was down at the docks supervising the final loading of the *Polstjärnan* and the *Nordanvinden*, Karin again stopped by the house to see Amos. Anders answered the door.

"Hello, Anders. Is Amos in?" asked Karin. Her eyes are amazing, Anders thought.

"No," answered Anders. "Once again he is not here. Would you like to leave a message in the event he does drop by?"

"Yes, I would. I can't believe I did this – I must have been distracted – but yesterday I totally forgot he was coming over to see me and, well, I wasn't there…I was here." Karin looked up intently at Anders. "I must appear to be terribly absentminded and inconsiderate. I came by to apologize."

"That's quite all right, I'm sure. I'll tell him you came by. I would suggest that you, yourself, go down to the *Polstjärnan* and the *Nordanvinden* – that's where he is – and talk to him in person."

"Oh, I'm certain he's too busy if that's where he is," said Karin, looking at Ander's dark eyes as he leaned comfortably against the doorpost. "He's so con-scientious. It wouldn't be right to disrupt things."

"How would you disrupt things?" asked Anders slyly. "It's just you."

"Well, yes, it is just me," responded Karin without missing a beat, "and, under the circumstances, it would be better if I saw him later. I need to…I don't want to distract him. I'm certain with both the *Polstjärnan* and the *Nordanvinden* setting sail in three days, it is important that everything be in order, don't you think?"

"Yes, absolutely." There was a pause in the conversation. "Was there some-thing else you wanted to tell him?"

"Yes, but it would be better if I tell him myself."

"You're sure."

"Yes, very. May I come in? Perhaps he'll be by when he is done – in which case he and I can talk."

"Ah, very well; certainly," answered Anders, not certain what else to say. "Won't you come in? May I take your coat?" asked Anders as he closed the door behind her, admiring the view.

The two chatted for several hours, time that Anders would normally have spent wrapping up his end of the shipping responsibilities. The pleasure of the moment, however, dictated that more responsible behavior be postponed. There was always later. Amos, who again maintained a separate residence in Göteborg, did not come by. Anders and Karin talked well into the evening. Were she not already spoken for by Amos, Anders would have let his well-cultivated instincts take over.

The following morning, Amos came by to get a few accounting items from the office.

"Amos, I'm certain you're not going to like this," said Anders, sitting upright in his chair, "but Karin was by again."

"She was?" Amos looked at Anders without expression. "Did you invite her in?"

"Uh, no…well, yes, I did. After she asked. She thought you might be by after you were done at the dock, and she wanted to wait. She seemed anxious to talk to you."

"What did she want to talk about?"

"Well, initially she wanted to apologize for not being home yesterday. Apparently the whole thing slipped her mind. I sensed she wanted to discuss something that was serious – if for no other reason than she wouldn't tell me what it was. Anyway, dropping by to apologize may have been disingenuous, if you know what I mean." Anders paused.

"Go on." Amos sat down and folded his hands.

"Ah, I got the impression she…," Anders paused again, thinking of how he should phrase the statement, then sighed and continued, "…may have wanted to spend time with me." Anders shrugged his shoulders nervously. "I probably…she asked if she could come in and wait for you, so I agreed. I know this is awkward. I did nothing untoward but, nevertheless, my conscience seems to bother me because…"

"Like you say, 'She is a vision,'" interjected Amos.

"Yes," replied Anders with almost no expression. "She is that."

"Well, at least we know you have a conscience."

"My life is a balancing act."

"I suppose you could have taken advantage of the situation," said Amos, "but, of course, you wouldn't do that. Instead, you maintained a proper distance and, consequently, no harm was done…at least as far as your relationship with Karin is concerned. My relationship, however…" Amos turned his head to one side. "I have not wanted to recognize a problem exists, but have no alternative other than to discuss things with Karin," said Amos, looking at the table. "I hope my heart is not overruling my head in this matter." Amos looked at Anders. "It happens. Not to you, of course, but it happens."

Looking down, Amos laughed awkwardly.

"It is, ironically, well that this has happened." Amos looked absently at an opposite chair. "Sobering. I will need to see Karin, explain to her that her commitment and sense of propriety are wanting, and that, well, things need to improve. If, in fact, she is furtively making advances toward my brother, in spite of the old expression about love and war, her integrity may be less than what I have wanted to believe is the case."

Amos thought for a moment.

"Or maybe it's just me."

Amos looked at Anders.

"Or you."

"I'm sorry this has happened," said Anders glumly.

"Well, Anders, in spite of how alluring she is, I know I can depend on you to do the right thing. What would she mean to you anyway? Little more than an addition to your collection. Among the more attractive butterflies I would th…"

"Actually, Amos," interjected Anders, leaning back and speaking in an affected tone while folding his arms, "I think trout, not butterflies, might be a better metaphor."

"Trout?" responded Amos, looking at Anders dumbfounded. It was bad enough his heart was already aching; compounding his unhappiness was the implication that this amorous suffering was somehow caused by a fish.

Anders sat back, unfolded his arms, and comfortably folded his hands together. "I'd throw out my line – I have several, you know – and see if she takes the hook. I'd enjoy the sport, and throw her back." Anders concluded by beaming pleasantly.

"I see," responded Amos, looking at Anders with disapprobation. "A fishing analogy. Well, to begin with, I'd prefer you do no fishing in the first place. But, were you to do so, remember Karin is not a trout; she may be more like an incredibly attractive Kraken."

"Karin the Kraken."

"Yes, Anders," said Amos with some exasperation. "So, when casting your lines about, be careful you don't get eaten alive."

"A Kraken? Hmmm. Never dated a Kraken." Anders stopped and attempted to visualize the woman for whom the word "Kraken" was an apt description. Big? Multiple tentacles? No feminine image came to mind. "Foxes, yes." Anders ruminated. "Snakes. A few dogs," added Anders, eyebrows raised momentarily. "No Krakens."

Anders folded his arms as he looked seriously at the floor.

"I think that, under the circumstances," said Anders, "you should have the honor of being the only one in the family to have dated a Kraken. My hat is off to you." Anders pretended to respectfully remove a hat from his head. "I recognize this temporary difficulty with the Kraken-of-your-heart may be cause for anxiety," continued Anders insensitively, "and you may be tempted to drink heavily tonight – hemlock, perhaps – but as the family Don Juan, my advice is to consider other solutions, that is, other attractive, young women – many, if you have any sense – in the possible event you have been indulging in wishful thinking. Meanwhile I, on the other hand, will do my part as, eh hem, only I can." Anders folded his hands and looked at Amos sincerely. "You may call me 'Dr. Anders.' Oh, and on the subject of doing the right thing, I prescribe that 'when the right woman comes along, be prepared to do the right thing.'"

Anders clapped twice as if to say: And thus it shall be done. He smiled again and folded his arms.

"I'll send a bill."

As he looked back at Anders, Amos's head tilted slightly to the left, and he inwardly debated whether to say the right thing, which would be the wrong thing, or leave the wrong thing unsaid. Under the circumstances, he opted for the latter.

* * *

The *Polstjärnan* and the *Nordanvinden* set sail for America with Amos aboard the *Polstjärnan*. The new second mate, Henrik Haglund, and Amos leaned on the gunwale, watching the seas ahead and the landmass of the Grenen Peninsula, the northern tip of Jutland to the southwest. The wind was up, the seas were choppy, and as they passed by the Grenen Peninsula, the Skagerrak swells were average, causing the *Polstjärnan* and the *Nordanvinden* to rise and fall with predictable rolling motion.

"I'll be happy if it gets no worse than this," said Henrik with a sepulchral look. "But like a spoiled child, the North Sea never behaves well for long."

"On the other hand, there is a chance it will continue like this," said Amos. "In any event, we must always be prepared for the worst."

The worst, thought Amos, that which can get no worse. How bad is "the worst"? Unaware of what lay ahead, Amos, Henrik and the rest of the *Polstjär-nan* and the *Nordanvinden* crews unfortunately gave no thought to turning back immediately.

13

As Amos and Henrik spoke, an older seaman staggered along the rolling deck toward them. Former whaler, grizzled Bjorn Bjornson who never smiled, his face seamed with obsession, had an outlook on life as saturated with despair as the sea was with salt. Barnacled with pessimism, if the fog of gloom began to lift, he would find something, anything, over which to toss another net of impending doom. Entering the main strait of the Skagerrak enabled Bjornson to grab the next available anxiety.

"We're in *that* stretch of the Skagerrak," shouted Bjornson over the wind as he stood beside Amos and Henrik, looking intently at the swells. "Aye, t'is here it begins."

"Where what begins?" asked Amos loudly.

"Now we'll see whirlpools, vortexes…where none should be," shouted Bjornson, wide-eyed, "and sudden, swift currents arise that go a different direction from the main." With one eyebrow raised, Bjornson looked at Amos and Henrik, then back at the deep. "And of what do y' suppose these whirlpools and strange currents are evidence?"

Amos and Henrik looked at Bjornson, guessing what Bjornson was about to say.

"Centuries of missing ships, in good weather and bad," said Bjornson, "don't lie. They're evidence of what lurks below. There is only one explanation, and I've heard it many times – first-hand stories from sound men!"

"What are you alluding to, Bjornson? What did the sound men say?"

"No doubt you know the stories, sir. Sea creatures. Big. Big enough to attack a ship the size of the *Polstjärnan*." Bjornson looked wide-eyed back and forth from Amos to Henrik. "And have we seen any whales? No. None. When no whales are about, there's good reason: they know what swims below, and stay clear. And those giant sea creatures seldom attack a strong ship. No, they'll single out a weak one, one that has been damaged and can't readily defend itself."

"Bjornson, our ships are seaworthy, and we all share your concern about getting through the Skagerrak safely," shouted Amos loudly over the wind. "Tell the men we'll maintain top speed, and keep a sharp watch for any unusual surface behavior. Should we see any such behavior," Amos added, "we will defend our-selves with everything at our disposal."

"Thank you, sir," said Bjornson as he turned and, fighting the ship's rolling motion, staggered aft to tell anyone who would listen.

"Have you ever seen a sea monster?" Amos asked Henrik, figuring that since Henrik had seen it all, he would have seen a sea monster if such existed.

"Well, no, Amos, but, you know, sometimes I wonder. There are the stories. Huge sea creatures – yes, big as this ship. I've seen sketches made by men who've said that's what they saw. Men tend to exaggerate, of course, but there are the mysteriously missing ships. To be honest with you, I think high seas, ruptured topmasts, broken rudders, and frayed rigging are more responsible for missing ships than sea monsters. The stories can be quite compelling, however." Henrik mused for a moment. "I don't believe it's unreasonable to suspect there are things in the sea we don't want to encounter."

"I know what you mean," said Amos. "Most of the stories are exaggerated but, yes, there are a few that make you wonder. The Flying Dutchman, seen multiple times over two centuries."

"And ships found floating with missing crews," said Henrik. "No one."

Amos thought about that, and it made him think about the Horse Latitudes, the great, shoreless Sargasso Sea with its endless pastures of floating seaweed. A good place to hide, Amos had thought when he first encountered the drifting sargassum.

"Any idea why the compass quits working in the Sargasso?" asked Amos.

"No more than I know what that thing was that washed up on the beach in Bimini," Henrik half-laughed. "You were there too."

Amos nodded, staring at the sea. "It was a gruesome."

"And large."

"Not as big as when alive. Other sea creatures had obviously had an extended lunch."

"The stories make sense when they say sea monsters pick on damaged ships," said Henrik.

"Why is that?" asked Amos with a mystified look.

"Those are the ones that go down."

"Ah," smiled Amos.

Henrik also smiled as he looked into the troughs between swells and wondered, were he able to look far below the surface, what would he see? The ocean was vast, so much greater than the land, in places possibly deeper than the height of the highest mountains on land. It seemed unlikely that life beneath the surface ended with what sensible men believed. He'd heard too many stories for all of them to be false.

"Henrik," asked Amos after a moment, "do the stories say how a sea monster is able to discern a healthy ship from a damaged one?"

"Good question," answered Henrik loudly above the wind. Henrik thought for a second. "They must go bthrough some sort of formal training."

"Is there," asked Amos, "somewhere in the Skagerrak depths, a sea monster school on ship construction?"

Henrik looked at Amos, smiled and looked back at the sea.

"No doubt," said Henrik with a straight face.

"Are there examinations? Graduation exercises?"

"Probably."

"Do they have grade levels, perhaps depending on which sailing craft is being studied?"

"It's the only explanation."

The two men nodded, amused, as they looked into the sunlit waves, attempting to see below the surface.

The two ships sailed on unimpeded through the Skagerrak, the well-educated sea monsters able to discern the *Polstjärnan* and the *Nordanvinden* were in excellent condition.

The ships continued into the North Sea where wind and wave remained constant, and headed south toward the English Channel. After passing through the English Channel, they sailed out into the great North Atlantic where unforeseeable events were about to occur.

Both ships were approximately 175 feet at the waterline, a respectable length to most landlubbers, but insignificant should the North Atlantic decide to boil over. Amos looked toward a lucky shark's fin attached to the jib boom on the ship's bow according to superstition. Since sharks are at home in many seas, the crewmen believed the shark's fin would help the ship weather the wrath of a great storm at sea, for when the ship would turn toward rising swells, the first thing the ocean would see was a familiar shark's fin, ostensibly deflating the sea's wrath. If the superstition had merit, Amos thought, all ships would have a lucky shark's fin for, in extreme hurricane or typhoon seas, a ship can be under water as often as it is above. Amos turned his head and continued to blankly stare at the swells, hoping there would be no opportunity to test the superstition.

Amos thought about myths and superstition among seamen and nodded to himself while considering that men will grasp at anything that might protect them from an angry sea. As every young Göteborg seaman would learn, a landlubber has no idea of how terrifying the ocean can become. Amos thought about how, before he sailed, he could never imagine winds exceeding 60 knots or wave height equal to a main topgallant mast level; could not imagine the primal fear of dying that dictates immediate escape, followed by constricting panic from the realization there is no escape.

Amos and the two seasoned crews studied the waves and weather cautiously, hoping for normal tedium. The swells were average, as was the wind. If the rest of the journey were similar, the crews would be blessed with an unremarkable voyage. As implied by the replicas of carved ships' bows that adorned church pulpits in seafaring communities, thought Amos, so many voyages are not unremarkable.

At the age of eight, Amos began occasionally going to sea as a cabin boy, and now was well aware of the sea's mood swings. Once, eastbound in the Pacific while retracing their westerly route, Amos's ship found herself in the area where, when westbound, the ship and crew weathered a typhoon. Returning eastbound, they found the wind and sea both asleep. The ship drifted in complete calm – doldrums, the sea like glass. The only movement on the surface was a weak eddy along the waterline caused by the ship's hull drifting with a mild ocean current. No tradewind. For nearly two weeks there was no movement of water or air. The ship continued to drift, the vast Pacific like an autumn pond at sunset. They needed wind, and the superstitious among the crew began looking for ways to command the wind's presence.

Some older crewmen suggested an ancient remedy: tie the cabin boy to the main mast, facing the direction from which wind was desired, and flog him as penance for the sins of the crew. The cabin boy was Amos who was grateful such behavior was not tolerated on Nordquist boats. Defying the heat, the men on the ship busied themselves with whatever might need to be done. Many were tasks that normally would be done in port and, as the days without wind dragged on, the men worried about provisions running low. Toward the end of the first week in the doldrums, two humpback whales were seen sliding along the surface at a short distance, ignoring Amos's ship as if it didn't exist or, if it did, what of it? Young Amos watched the whales, looked about, and a thought occurred to him that was often reinforced later at sea: we are not truly meant to be here.

After passing west of the British Isles, the North Atlantic was not calm but neither was it agitated during the next two days as the *Polstjärnan* and the *Nordanvinden* sailed on. But the air. It didn't feel right, and the seasoned crewmen nervously studied the dark horizon clouds.

During the third day the mood swing came. It started suddenly and the crew immediately felt and saw the difference as the fitful sea awoke. All raced to make ready, assuring that everything was tied, battened or otherwise fastened down and, within a half hour, *Polstjärnan* and *Nordanvinden* helmsmen, pinching wind, put their helms to starboard, directing the boats into rising swells that had quickly grown to over 15 feet in height.

Rainsqualls fell from a blackened sky and the sea began behaving like a fuming titan enraged by the intrusion of these insignificant men and their petty boats. As the high-pitched wind began to scream in anger, rain rifled obliquely through the lines. And the wind became louder. And still louder as growing high seas swells began charging at the two ships. The *Polstjärnan* and the *Nordanvinden* shuddered and rolled, behaving less like streamlined sailing vessels, and more like discarded wine casks as the seas continued to grow.

20 feet.

25 feet.

30 feet.

The ships attempted to ride the huge, wind-whipped, foam-covered swells, climbing up one side and then diving down the other, the ocean swallowing the shark-fin-tipped, rapier jib boom which, in enfeebled self-defense, lunged and stabbed oncoming swells breaking high over the bow and washing aft over forecastle, quarterdeck and stern before the ship would again rise, ride up the salt water fulcrum, crest, nose over, and then slide down to be assaulted and brutalized again. And again. And again.

35 feet.

Crewmen topside had tied themselves with loose ends. While no crewmember in the two crews expected that the ships would ride out the storm unscathed, still it was possible, and each man did what he had to do to assure the ultimate survival of his ship and himself. If the helmsmen and crews could somehow keep the ships headed into these huge swells, and not be turned broadside, the ships and crews might somehow ride out the raging seas and hurricane winds.

40 feet.

Tied with loose ends, the helmsman worked furiously. As the sea became angrier, only the older seamen could remember anything like this. And it would get worse. As in battlefield foxholes, there are few atheists in a raging sea. All crewmen knew others who had met their Maker under similar circumstances… Amos's grandfather, Olof, for one. Perhaps Aunt Ona's husband…no one knew. All hoped God's will would somehow favor them, or perhaps they would have an unlikely douse of good luck. While luck could come from their own frantic efforts, God's will, on the other hand, was God's will.

50 feet.

The *Polstjärnan* and the *Nordanvinden* were effectively at the mercy of the wind and sea, and the seasoned crew knew they were in the hands of Almighty God.

Normally in a big storm, two ships would lose sight of one another, but not now. When the storm began, the *Polstjärnan* and the *Nordanvinden* were at a safe distance, but as the winds reached hurricane force, the *Nordanvinden*'s leeway pushed her closer and closer to the *Polstjärnan* whose leeward motion was less. The drenched and buffeted helmsmen fought to maintain headway into the on-coming swells. As the seas raged, and the masts creaked and moaned from the strain of sails by-and-large from winds now over 100 knots, the ships drew closer and closer as if subject to some magnetic attraction until they were in extremis, about to collide.

The seas rose and billowed, the black skies thundered and flashed, compounding fear. Fighting to avoid collision, the beleaguered *Polstjärnan* helmsmen over-corrected, inadvertently bearing directly into the wind, and instantly losing modest headway. Waves and wind quickly grabbed the defenseless *Polstjärnan* and whipped her broadside, slamming her violently into the *Nordanvinden*. Tied to hapless men struggling to stay aboard, loose ends were ripped away, and the men swept over the side into the deadly deep. The collision, severe in normal weather, was exacerbated by the combination of the ship's heaving and rolling in heavy, thrashing seas, and the extreme wind pressure in the *Polstjärnan* sails.

In the jarring collision, already under severe stress, the *Polstjärnan* forward lines, foremast and mainmast first moaned agonizingly, and then went by the board, slamming to larboard over the *Nordanvinden* bow as if thrown down by a giant hand – the result of gravity, hurricane winds which caught the sails full force, and ship's upward roll at that moment – while the falling foremast and mainmast caused the jib boom and every spar except the bowsprit to snap like pieces of kindling. The *Nordanvinden* had been struck forward by the *Polst-*

järnan, severing shrouds, sheets, booms, and sails that fluttered and flailed like flags, some gradually ripping loose in the hurricane wind, shooting over the deck like multiple apparitions.

The masts, booms, shrouds, and sails of both ships entangled, causing further chaos; the *Nordanvinden* and *Polstjärnan* were effectively lashed together without headway, absorbing additional body blows, and rapidly taking on water. Beaten nearly into submission, the *Nordanvinden* began to list heavily to larboard, pulling heavily on the *Polstjärnan* as if desperately grasping for help. But there would be no salvation from this moment, no possibility that what was done could be undone.

The sea was unrelenting and, shouting above the roar of wind and wave, the ships' captains ordered remaining men to lifeboats.

As the sea savaged the ships, launching lifeboats was treacherous, perilous. While one lifeboat successfully rode free when abandoning ship, several others swamped immediately, and still others shortly capsized as the ocean grabbed them. No help was available. The men cried out, holding fast to the capsized lifeboats until their fingers were ripped loose by the frigid North Atlantic, and towering swells plunged their bodies downward in the briny blackness to the bottom where they would become food for sightless worms.

The ships began breaking up, the raging North Atlantic angrily pulling on decks, hulls and masts until they were no more. Only a single lifeboat managed to remain afloat as, loudly exhorted by the tempest, the ocean thrashed like multiple enraged dragons.

14

As huge waves and hurricane winds slammed and battered the solitary lifeboat, eight panicked men gripped gunwales with flesh and bone pliers. As much as able, the men tried to keep their weight along the centerline like human ballast. Otherwise, they struggled to avoid being rifled overboard. As saltwater flew in, much would miraculously slosh out with the next jarring wave as the men held on.

As the night wore on, and against all odds the lifeboat remained upright and afloat, the men thought of nothing other than surviving another minute. Moans and inadvertent cries of terror were drowned out by the storm, and their fate seemed inevitable as, still, they held on while the great North Atlantic thrashed and battered them like threshing wheat. Not all could hold on. After an hour, losing his grip at the wrong moment, one man was rifled into the brine.

When a thin line of daylight appeared on the black horizon the next morning, hope encouraged the exhausted men. If they had made it through the night, perhaps, somehow, they might make it through the day. Exhaustion and sleeplessness were taking a toll. How long the storm would last, and how long they could last, were being weighed in the balance.

During the day the storm raged on, and the men were fatigued to the point of complete exhaustion.

Then came the night. The ocean ferocity was less, but still the large swells continued with relentless constancy, huge wave upon wave after wave. This continued until around 2:00 a.m. when, as if the sea had been merely sparring with the intent of lulling the men into an unguarded moment, suddenly an inordinately large swell loomed out of the blackness and slammed into the boat like an overhand right, shooting the boat to larboard and downward into a trough like a fighter lurching and falling to the canvas. The sudden, awkward blow at this fateful, fatigued moment wrenched two more men loose, pitching them overboard, their bodies instantly engulfed by the enormous black waves.

Seemingly sated, toward the end of the second night, the sea's anger slowly subsided, and by morning, gripping the gunwales was no longer necessary. Exhausted to the point of being unable to reason, the remaining five men lay sprawled in the rocking boat, their faces vacant, tired lungs breathing exaggeratedly, each drenched, shivering man barely conscious of how thirsty he was.

Amos Nordquist, one of the five survivors, looked heavenward at the morning sky an hour after sunrise, then at the others, and felt they were fortunate … but were they? He knew the men well, knew their families, and as he thought about the dim prospects of them ever seeing their families again, he inexplicably felt an urge to pray. Pray, an inner voice admonished. Pray with them. Too weak to explain, Amos sat up, looked at the men, and pushed out the words.

"Men."

His voice shivered in the cold. It was the first time in two days any of them had heard a vocal sound not resonating with terror.

"Men, I want you to pray with me."

Lying in the boat, they momentarily looked back at him, and again closed their eyes. Fatigued, Amos spoke slowly as he prayed, solemnly thanking God for enabling them to weather the storm, asking comfort for their families and the families of the men who had drowned, and asking God to send a ship to save them.

When he finished, the only sound was the dull roar of wind and sea. The boat continually rose and fell, no less than would a cork. Would they be saved? Although it seemed unlikely, as Amos sat staring at the fluid, never-ending waves, he comforted himself with the fact that God is well-versed in salvation.

Following the prayer, the sea's fury continued to subside, and although the lifeboat still rose, pitched and fell, instability declined. Huddled together to stay warm, the wet, exhausted men slept as if dead.

Sweeping the horizon in the event there was a ship in their vicinity, but seeing only the sea, Amos returned his gaze toward his surface sanctuary, this trifling lifeboat island. He studied the apparent serenity of the sleeping men for a moment, and before falling asleep himself, wondered what it would be like when they awoke.

As late afternoon approached and some of the others began to waken, Amos also awoke. He got up, carefully stepped over the men, and looked in the small lazarette, the storage locker in the lifeboat bow, where he found stored water and still-dry *knackebrod*, a Scandinavian, rye flatbread, in a tarred, waterproof box.

Based on the amount of water and *knackebrod*, and the number of men, now five, Amos determined the extent of rationing, quietly hoping these limited rations would last for several days. . .although he had no idea how long God would take to answer their prayer. "Where two or more of you are gathered in my name, there am I in the midst," Amos quietly quoted, reassuring himself that the Holy Spirit must be with them, even in the expansive North Atlantic. Arnie Arneson, a large man of considerable girth, looked at Amos questioningly, not quite hearing what Amos said. Amos just nodded at Arnie who said nothing, looking expressionlessly at Amos. Amos broke off a small piece of *knackebrod* and then another, while studying the men's faces.

"We have some food and some water," said Amos to the men, "but very little."

Amos passed the pieces around. As each man ate his small piece of *knacke-brod*, Amos wished there were also wine on board and then wondered, why did I wish that? There was none, of course, and Amos lifted the 3¾ liter jug of water and showed the men.

"This is what we have, men. If you drink too much now, there will be less available later when we may badly need it. I am going to pour a very small amount in this tin cup – Amos showed them the cup – the same amount for each of you. It will not be much. But since we have no idea of how long we will be adrift, it is wise to prepare for the worst and drink sparingly."

The men accepted this and, as Amos poured small amounts of water for each of the already thirsty men, no one complained. Finished, Amos took the water and *knackebrod* with him to the rear of the lifeboat where he sat down and rested against the transom.

Amos and the men looked about, studying the horizon. There was no sign of land or ship. The sky above was overcast, ominous; dark thunderclouds at a distance. Wave height continued to fall. The men remained silent. Gradually all again nodded off and slept.

Later, Second Mate Henrik Haglund awoke, opened his eyes, looked upward, and saw a great, wandering albatross floating effortlessly overhead, white against the dark gray, evening sky. Haglund awoke the others. The men marveled both because of the albatross and the fact it was unusual to see one this far north. To seamen, the sight of an albatross was a good omen, and the men's expressions reflected hope as they watched the bird. As Amos studied the men, his earlier apprehension diminished. The men made themselves as comfortable as possible, and returned to sporadic slumber as Amos, scanning the ocean for some sign of wreckage or anything else, wondered why this lifeboat was improbably spared.

At the beginning of the third night, the clouds moved on to the east, gradually uncovering a uniquely clear night sky awash with stars – so many visible stars that the extent was like breath on a mirror. The aggregation of stars provided enough light to see, although there was only a quartermoon. Amos tried to locate planets, and stars in different constellations. Polaris, the polstjärnan or North Star, the end star of the Little Dipper handle toward which the two outer bowl stars of the Big Dipper pointed, was observable, but the flood of starlight obscured other constellations.

My golly, look at it all, Amos thought with wonderment. Looking about, it seemed this sky was an astronomer's confectionary. And an astrologer's. He wondered if it was a night like this that so excited the magi well over 1,800 years earlier. There was so much there above him, more than he had seen before or ever imagined. He stared upward for a moment, and looked down at the men sleeping – perhaps they would want to see what he saw – but, seeing them at peace, he let them sleep.

His eyes wandered to the expansive, dark ocean that seemed endless in the starlight. What is overhead, however, makes the huge ocean seem of little significance, Amos thought. He glanced again at the men sleeping. If the rest of the universe made the vast sea appear to be of little significance, how important is this lifeboat and the men in it?

Amos shrugged slightly. Why does God even bother with us? Completely convinced, however, that God cares a great deal about men, and weighing his present circumstances within this great enigma, Amos laughed weakly, awaking Arnie Arneson who had been sleeping fitfully in his thick, wet pea coat, his red beard soaked with seawater collected along the bilge. Feeling ill, Arnie weakly opened his eyes and looked at Amos queerly. To Arnie there was absolutely nothing to laugh about. Arnie stared dumbly at Amos for a moment until the weight of his heavy eyelids closed them, and he returned to a restless sleep.

As Amos lay back against the transom staring at the stars, his thoughts rose, fell and wandered like the lifeboat. He remembered past conversations with older mariners who said that when adrift on the open sea, or during prolonged incarceration as a prisoner, maintaining physical stamina was significantly dependent on mental activity and strength of will, and that strength of will was in turn dependent on what could only be described as spiritual strength. Amos began to focus on epistemic challenges, knowing the mental exercise enhanced his survival odds, and began praying quietly for the others and himself.

After prayer under the starlight, Amos looked at the sleeping men who seemed helpless as lambs. These men are important, significant. But why? What makes it so? Amos thought of Dostoevsky saying that calling reprehensible human behavior "bestial" insulted beasts who probably have no capacity for creative cruelty. Amos then thought of Yuri who summarized his description of human nature with, "Most people…if you consider degrees of sin. I might guess everyone."

Amos remembered the time a rabbi told him the correct interpretation of Isaiah 64:6: man's acts of righteousness are as worthy as used menstrual rags.

Closing his eyes, he weighed his life thus far, and wondered. If we have any importance at all, Amos surmised as the boat rose and fell, it must be through God that our value is effected. Amos understood and believed in salvation through Christ, but also wondered: why go through all the bother? Why would God start all this in the first place?

He knew the answer would not be available in this lifetime, but, having time and need to think, as the boat dipped and rolled from one swell to the next, he attempted to find some reason ascribing importance to himself and the others. It seemed that in spite of human nature, foibles and history, he and the men had value and, perhaps, this somehow meant being saved from this ordeal.

Tired, his mind became inactive. He closed his eyes and, like the others, fell asleep in the lifeboat rising and falling on the broad North Atlantic.

The next day, the fourth day, came and went with no change in the tedium.

On the fifth day Amos began to worry about Arnie Arneson and Jens Hildegaard who were becoming churlish, their displeasure growing increasingly obstreperous. Amos looked at the men, wondering whether, as time wore on and the small amounts of water and *knackebrod* were gradually exhausted, the men would maintain lucid rectitude, or would someone brush aside the staying hand of Christian conscience in favor of survival in the moment, turning the lifeboat into a floating asylum where, having survived the ocean, men can sink to a level lower than the ocean floor. It has been done many times before, Amos thought. Yuri would not be surprised.

Amos had heard the stories, the tales of despicable behavior in lifeboats: wanton, wicked selfishness to the point of throwing others overboard. Amos had heard about the "custom" – the euphemism for cannibalism at sea – so-called because decades earlier it reached customary behavior in circumstances under which Amos presently found himself. There was the Dauphin lifeboat where the remaining two survivors, when found, were so unbalanced they would not willingly part with meated human bones that rescuers forcefully took from them. When the French frigate Medusa, carrying 400 sailors, soldiers and passengers, hit a reef off Africa, the sailors and soldiers fought over lifeboat space, killing one another and abandoning the passengers. The 150 soldiers, sailors and passengers still alive but not in the lifeboats, fought for space aboard a makeshift raft and, even as numbers dwindled, Darwinian behavior – mutiny, murder, ultimately cannibalism – continued. When rescuers found them after two weeks at sea, of the 150 only 15 were still alive. The stories made Amos disgusted and sickened.

During the sixth day, Amos noticed that hours seemed to go more slowly than entire days, as if time was a line with two fixed ends but the line, like a rubber band, could be stretched in the middle. It was an odd sensation, and Henrik Haglund spoke about it as well. Amos thought of Hell's clock: how Hell has a clock, the story went, that constantly ticks, …tick…tick…tick…, but the clock has no hands.

Parched and hungry, as the men in the boat talked for the first time that day, the conversation turned to food and drink. Knute Steinval, portly and bald, was the ship's cook. He invited them all to his home when they returned to Göteborg where he promised he would fix a meal fit for a king. The men listened hopefully except for Arnie Arneson who, his arm hanging on the gunwale, looked phlegmatically toward the sea. Amos was relieved the other men held out hope, but he worried about Arnie who was acting strangely.

On the seventh day, Arnie Arneson and Jens Hildegaard took their small rations of *knackebrod*, chewed and quickly swallowed with gloomy, martyred expressions. From their equally small portions, the other two men, Knute Steinval and Henrik Haglund, fingered their morsels, taking small bites over the course of the day – a nibble here, a nibble there – rationing the ration. All were suffering from dehydration, but it seemed to Amos that Knute and Henrik were determined to endure the ordeal, while Arnie and Jens lay loathing the suffering and anything else. There was no solution but to wait, hope, pray and think, and Amos began thinking about suffering.

As the morning passed, and the already difficult experience was becoming incrementally worse, Amos studied the men and again wondered where their suffering would lead. Amos considered he was quite capable of protecting himself, or enforcing civil behavior – the others knew it as well – but hoped it would not come to that.

Amos again thought of Yuri. He thought of the Medusa with 15 survivors. Amos stared at the sea and weakly shook his head. He was determined that such behavior would not happen here.

In contrast, he thought of great achievements accomplished because of suffering, and wondered what life would be like if men did not suffer. He again thought of Dostoevsky and how Dostoevsky valued his sufferings because they forced nobler, more compassionate behavior. It seemed to Amos that suffering was something to be avoided but, when unavoidable, suffering could be wind for the canvas. He thought of Christ's suffering, and Christ's request that God "let this cup pass from me." It did not; and Amos concluded it was necessary the Christ suffer, and suffer greatly.

Amos recalled the Latin root for both "crucifixion" and "excruciating" was the same: "cru," Latin for "cross." "*Eli, Eli, lama sabachthani?*" Christ's suffering was still bearable, thought Amos, as long as He felt the presence of the Father, but it would become beyond excruciating if God's presence were withheld. It was withheld, if only for a moment, maximizing the passion.

It seemed to Amos that since all men, regardless of stature or position, are made to suffer, it was imperative that change-for-good, an elevation of the personal or human condition, come from suffering, and perhaps the greater the suffering, the greater the opportunity to effect excellence and virtue. But a countering, second thought interjected itself: or the consequence could be implacable depravity. There is suffering in this lifeboat, thought Amos, and if a ship is not sighted soon, the suffering will grow worse. How will we harness this suffering? Or what might it otherwise bring?

The remaining water and *knackebrod*, modest in the beginning, would be gone shortly at the present rate of consumption, and Amos decided the already inadequate ration would need to be made even less.

Or did it matter?

From their fixed, funereal expressions, Arnie Arneson and Jens Hildegaard appeared to be considering the possibility it did not. The men were becoming more languorous and apathetic, and in their weakness, the continual rocking motion made them mildly vertiginous. Hungry, dying slowly of thirst, they were beginning not to care. Amos knew that lassitude could lead to either a decline in their will-to-live or *Medusa* behavior: jettisoning Christian principle, sacrificing the weakest to insure survival of the godless.

"What's God going to do now, Amos?" asked Jens Hildegaard after Amos led them in a morning prayer.

"God will do what He will do," answered Amos.

"Did that prayer help?" said Jens as if not hearing.

"If we do not pray, there will be no answer to prayer. It is important we pray."

"Then I wish He'd do something," muttered Arnie Arneson weakly, slurring his words. "I doubt He knows we're here...if He's there."

In the silence that followed, Amos studied Arnie's sullen, vitriolic eyes that reflected the bitterness in his heart and punctuated his lack of faith like an exclamation mark. From the few things Arnie said, it was evident his thinking was becoming unclear. Occasionally, Arnie would swear, and Amos concluded there was no point in attempting to comfort him.

During the daytime, temperatures were cool although the sun was out. The seas were rough, the high swells continuing as if the hurricane were just over the horizon considering whether or not to return and inflict more damage. Arnie's fevered imagination grew worse. Dehydration was extreme, but all knew better than to drink seawater.

Or so it seemed.

Unknown to the others, Knute Steinval was reaching into the ocean, furtively drinking small amounts of seawater. Inactivity, sunburn, additional salt, and poor nutrition started taking their toll, and Knute's legs were beginning to swell. In spite of it all, Amos was encouraged from what he perceived as the favorable extent of the men's self-discipline. Under the circumstances, he did not expect happiness. Each man took a turn watching the horizon with hope of seeing a ship, and all hoped that the sighting would not be at night.

On the eighth day, Amos thought hard about difficulties that might soon arise, and what could be done to stem them off. The men slept. Sleep provided escape from the reality of the moment. Dreams were of water, food, homes, wives and better times.

Later that night as everyone slept, Jens Hildegaard awoke. People were speaking to him, but the voices were from no one in the boat.

"Jens."

He listened.

"Jens. Your ordeal will be over in two days. Two days, Jens."

"If you weren't such a fool, it would be over now."

"This all could have been avoided, but you're so stupid, Jens."

Over the wind the voices concluded: "Two days, Jens."

Jens looked about in the dark and discerned nothing but the boat, sleeping men, and sea. I heard them plainly, he thought; I heard them clearly. He thought about what he just heard and, although he did not know the source, concluded the voices to be real. "Two days." His hands were shaking. At first Jens lay rigidly against the gunwale but, as the boat continued to rock, and nothing more was heard other than sea and wind, his eyes closed and he gradually settled into sleep.

The following morning upon awaking, Jens told the others what he had heard.

"Last night I awoke," said Jens, his throat dry, his voice whispered and rasping. "When I awoke, my father, it sounded like my father, maybe, and some others told me I have two days left. I heard them." Jens looked from face to face. "We have to hang on for two more days. Two days."

"You weren't just imagining?" asked Henrik, looking hard at Jens.

"They spoke to me plainly," rasped Jens. "I heard them just like I hear you. You're here, right?"

"Yes," said Henrik, "I'm here."

"Two days," said Jens, nodding, looking back at Henrik. "Two days."

Amos stared at Jens, not wanting to believe what he was sensing.

15

enrik looked at Amos. Amos said nothing about where such voices come from. It would be pointless. But he was concerned that Jens heard voices. The moment is difficult enough without visitors.

Knute's swelling legs became more painful. Other than the brief conversation between Jens and Henrik, no one spoke. Lips and mouths felt like chalk, and Arnie did not talk because, as if a hibernating bear, Arnie did not seem to completely wake up. Sometimes he mumbled words that were incoherent, and Amos worried about Arnie's physical and mental health.

On the morning of the ninth day they ate the last of the *knackebrod*. Knute's legs were in constant pain, and Arnie, sleeping fitfully, became delirious. Henrik Haglund kept moving his tongue and mouth without opening his lips, attempting to somehow stimulate saliva, but his abraded lips, mouth and throat remained like stale bread crusts. There was no longer elasticity in his skin, and the heat from the sun, although moderate, felt like an oven. His body begged for water as he stoically stared at the constant rolling swells. He thought of Coleridge's words: "Water, water, every where/ And all the boards did shrink/ Water, water, every where/ Nor any drop to drink." To divert his mind from his discomfort, Henrik attempted to remember the poem line by line, but dehydration made it impossible to think.

Jens, feeling no better than Henrik, continued to look out at the sea, looking for the ship he believed would come. The act of looking, searching, may have helped his survival chances, but caused discomfort, for his eyes no longer teared.

Amos felt worn, tired, his own physical suffering exacerbated by helplessness and worry for the others. To buoy his spirit, he thought of Karin.

Seated in the rear of the boat, propped against the transom as the small boat bobbed and rolled in the great Atlantic Ocean, Amos looked at the others and decided to tell them what they did not want to hear.

He rapped his knuckles on the side of boat to get their attention.

"We have no more water," Amos rasped quietly although as loudly as possible.

For a moment all except Arnie looked toward him.

"If a ship does not come soon, our lives will be ended; all that can be done until the end comes is to pray for one another and others, and to thank God for the lives we were given."

Amos looked levelly at each weakened man as they looked back.

"When a ship eventually finds this small boat, the crewmembers will look down at us, and I want them to see that we behaved well, that we acted as men should act.

"We suffer for a reason," Amos continued, "even though the reason is not evident. Now the greatest suffering lies immediately before us. And you must ask yourself: 'Who am I? What am I made of?' You want to live, as do I. Pray we will be found before the end comes.

"But if we are not found, in preparation for the moment when we each meet our Maker, in these final days on earth you will behave in a manner requiring no explanation or excuse when you stand before the Almighty."

Amos studied each man. Speaking required all the energy he could muster.

"While there is still the chance we may be rescued, it is very small, and most likely the end will come sooner than later. But whenever it comes, and you stand before God, prepare now to stand erectly."

The weakened men looked blankly at whatever was immediately in front of them, and considered what Amos said and the multiple implications. As the boat rose and fell in the North Atlantic swells, expecting a ship soon, with all his remaining energy Jens stared out at the sea.

On the morning of the 10th day, Jens spoke.

"Be on close lookout, for this is the day the ship will come and we shall be saved."

Arnie, delirious, stared wild-eyed at Jens as Jens' eyes painfully swept the horizon.

Soon it was noon; no ship was sighted that morning.

At around 1:00 p.m. on that sunlit afternoon, as Arnie lay sleeping closeby, Amos felt a frisson of dread.

What?

It was here.

The Old Evil. Amos's jaw tightened.

Amos remembered what Rev. Lute Olafson once said about evil and men at sea: "Dry land or North Sea hurricane, it matters not. Where there are souls, there will be a demonic presence going about Satan's work."

Arnie awoke up with a start, his eyes wild and large, and he awkwardly clambered to his feet, his girth shaking the boat as the others looked at him, bewildered.

"Arnie, what…?" rasped Amos, concerned.

Barely maintaining his balance, Arnie looked easterly for a moment and, wide-eyed, pointed at the eastern horizon.

"Land!" his voice cracked as he turned to the others. "There! Over there!"

Working to stand, Amos Nordquist looked where Arnie was pointing. Adrenaline slightly revitalized the men, and in their minds they began concocting ways of getting there – the oars were lost in the hurricane but they could row with their hands, or maybe make a makeshift sail. Shading their eyes, each man intensely studied the horizon in order to see the thin sliver or dot of land, and their thoughts raced, relieved that they would no longer be confined in a lifeboat with the endless, frenetic rolling motion, tedium and monotony.

It's probably an island, they thought. There must be water there. There usually is, isn't there?

Henrik Haglund, awkwardly stood, glanced at Arnie, and questioned simply, "Where?"

"Over there!" Arnie pointed, his right index finger poking repeatedly at the air.

All looked.

"Arnie, I can't see anything," said Jens cautiously, certain Arnie was right, not wanting to believe he wasn't. "Where?"

"There!"

The others looked at Arnie for a moment – he wasn't pointing the same direction. "You don't see it? I see it! It's there!"

The men looked at Arnie, and confused by Arnie pointing in yet a third direction, Jens asked, "Where, specifically, Arnie?"

"It must be Africa," Henrik rasped through dry lips. "He's pointed across most of the eastern horizon."

Younger than the others, and blessed with excellent eyesight, Amos saw nothing. From the last point of dead-reckoning while on board the *Polstjärnan*, he knew they were far from any land. They saw no land because there was no land.

"Arnie," Amos said, "you're mistaken. We're far from any known landfall." Amos looked at the horizon. "There's nothing there."

Yanking his eyes away from the horizon, Arnie glared wildly at Amos. "There is!" he rasped angrily. He looked at the others staring at him, and gave a deprecatory gesture, nearly losing his balance. "There is!" He clenched his fists. "We're going there!"

"Arnie, don't…,"

"We'll die if we stay in this boat!" cawed Arnie as he turned, shaking in his weakened state. "Don't you see that?"

Arnie then angrily muttered, "No, hell, you guys 'can't see anything.' What am I saying?"

He looked back and forth at the others for a moment.

"Well I'm going there!"

"Wha…?" Henrik began to ask, mystified, as, still shaking, Arnie sat down with a thud, dangerously rocking the boat, causing Amos to sit down quickly. Arnie pulled off his boots, took off his pea coat, and unstably stood up as the others looked at him, dumbfounded.

"Arnie…," said Amos, his apprehension rising.

Arnie's wide, wild eyes took on an ugly light as he stared in an easterly direction, and then he stepped forward, tumbling into the frigid water.

Arnie began swimming easterly as the others, uncertain of what to do, looked at Amos with expressions begging for direction.

It would be foolhardy to swim after him, Amos thought. If another man were actually able to catch up to Arnie in the windswept swells, Arnie would struggle and, as big as he is, the struggle would be fruitless. With the boat drifting southwesterly, the distance between the two men and the boat would increase, and with it the probability both would drown.

Then Amos saw Arnie struggling while attempting to turn around in the cold, choppy swells, looking for the boat. His normally tanned face was splotchy white like a leopard seal's, evidence Arnie's body temperature, above-normal moments ago, had dropped dramatically while in the water. To Amos's relief, Arnie, gasping, began to swim toward the boat.

Arnie rode up and down on the high, wind-swept swells, but after a moment stopped again. On Arnie's face Amos saw weakened, wide-eyed desperation as Arnie, breathing heavily, got his bearings. Amos knew that if Arnie did not get out of the water quickly, it would not be in the open boat that Arnie would die, but the open sea.

Jens lay back, exhausted from briefly standing while trying to see the "land." Henrik's head fell, his body further weakened, and his mind blank. It was up to Arnie to get back to the boat, but his bulk was working against him.

He started to swim again but began to founder, and for a moment sank as Amos, at the tiller, watched, his stomach in his throat. With the last of his will-to-survive, and with what little strength remained, Arnie struggled to the surface and weakly thrashed in the big swells like a harpooned sea lion, attempting to get his large body going forward.

Watching Arnie's struggle weakening in the water, Amos began to remove his boots, and his coat, preparing to dive in, swim seven or eight meters to Arnie and, God willing, pull Arnie back to the boat. Amos believed he could do it.

A wave rolled over Arnie as Amos stood at the ready, waiting for Arnie's body to reappear.

Seconds passed.

Amos continued to study the heaving surface, hope warring with visible evidence.

After nearly a half minute passed, the obvious convicted the men, and the other three looked at Amos.

Slumping, collapsing, Amos sat down still staring at the sea where Arnie was moments ago. Like his hallucination, Arnie was not there, and the excitement of the moment had further weakened the men, pushing them closer to the grave.

The others rested silently, weak to the point of insensitivity, but Jens – struggling as much emotionally as Arnie struggled physically – with his remaining hope again searched the horizon for the ship he believed would come.

Barely able to hold himself up with his arm over the gunwale, zombie-like, Jens alternately stared in one direction, transfixed, and then stared in another direction, gradually studying the entire horizon. His hope was keeping him lucid, and he continued to watch the horizon past sunset and into early evening twilight. Darkness began to fall and obscure the ocean, but still Jens fought to find an image, silhouette, beyond the monotonous swells. Shouldn't the ship be here by now? We had two days.

This was the second day.

As Jens anxiously searched the horizon, gradually his strength gave out and he rested his head on the gunwale, his mind blank.

And at that moment he heard a familiar voice.

Jens lifted his head slightly as he listened.

Father?

For a moment all Jens heard were mixed sibilants of wind and wave. Jens listened hard.

"Jens," said the voice.

"Father?"

"No ship is coming."

Jens's mouth slowly fell open and his eyes became wide as if he saw something on the horizon where there was nothing but dark gray froth and foam on vague ocean swells gradually disappearing in the evening darkness.

"No ship," the voice repeated. "No ship.

"You were told but did nothing to deserve rescue, and these men, who also knew, have all betrayed you."

Feeling as if he had been struck with a belaying pin, Jens's insides turned to water, his eyes fell. His arm slipped off the gunwale as he collapsed on his back as if sucker-punched.

"No ship."

His prolonged shudder was like that of a sinking ship as it totally submerges. He looked upward but saw nothing, his tortured soul quavering as if it was being brutally flogged, and he painfully closed his tearless eyes.

By the end of the next day, lassitude was extreme. Jens had not moved, and the others were too weak to check on him. As he rested against the transom, while looking at the remaining men, Amos thought of Arnie. Ocean or boat, maybe it didn't matter, thought Amos. We will die in these positions.

Water, Amos wished. Just a drop, Lord.

The Bible verse came to him where Jesus said: "Everyone who drinks of this water will thirst again; but whoever drinks of the water that I will give him shall never thirst; but the water that I will give him will become in him a well of water springing up to eternal life." Eternal life. As Amos thought of being in the presence of God, a comforting feeling imbued him.

The following day, only Amos was conscious. Amos was unsure if the others were dead or alive. In his mind, weak thoughts staggered forward, pushing away the mist before them. He thought of Karin. I will not see her again.

Later, in his mind, Amos carried on a short, imaginary conversation with his father, and from the imagined conversation Amos felt a slight increase in confidence and stamina.

Early that evening before sunset, knowing he was fading, Amos summoned all his remaining spiritual and cognitive energy. Resoluteness warring against semi-delirium, he prayed what he believed was to be his last prayer, thanking God for the life he had experienced, praying for the men with him, their families, Anders, and Karin, the woman he loved. He prayed she would find a good man who would cherish her, and for the rest of her life she would enjoy marital bliss.

Finished, ready to meet his Maker, propped against the transom, he stared vacantly for a moment, then turned his head slightly and again watched the sunset begin to form above the western horizon. It was eerily beautiful as if signifying a happy ending. Perhaps that starry sky will be out tonight.

Expecting he would not wake up in this life, he closed his eyes.

The boat, barely a dot on the great North Atlantic, rose and fell, dipped and rocked, as it drifted southwesterly, pushed by a following sea and the north wind. The light on the western horizon was gradually fading like stage lighting as the curtain descends.

The boat did this for nearly a half hour in the mid-twilight before the converted whaleboat from a British man o' war came alongside.

The whaleboat quartermaster leaned over the edge and, to protect his hand in the swells, gripped the inside of the lifeboat transom next to the oarlocks, pulling the lifeboat toward him so the two boats were rising and falling, touching familiarly. For a moment, he studied the dark shapes in the lifeboat, and it seemed there might be breathing – perhaps some were still alive.

He ordered a line tied to the lifeboat bow cleat and, following his orders, grim faced, hard muscled men began to pull on oars, towing the lifeboat through the big swells to the awaiting man o' war.

The sailors on the British ship studied the vague shapes below, staring silently as each man was taken out of the lifeboat and carried up the Jacob's ladder to the main deck and then below where Amos and Henrik were given water, and placed in berths, enabling them to sleep in some comfort for the first time in two weeks. For a period of time, Knute was force-fed water until he was consciously swallowing.

Jens, who spent the past two days anticipating this moment, was dead.

Of the many crewmen on the *Nordanvinden* and *Polstjärnan*, only three in one boat survived the storm and subsequent two-week ordeal, to be rescued by an aging British man 'o war returning to Portsmouth for decommissioning.

At Portsmouth, Amos sent a telegram to Anders, and began the return to Göteborg where another disaster awaited.

16

Leaning over the barque bow railing, Amos strained to find him.

Maybe it was the contrasting tragedy of the past few weeks or the euphoria of returning to Göteborg alive, but when Amos spied Anders on the pier in the distance, Amos thought to himself that Anders – who usually looked good – never looked better. Frock coat, ascot, top hat, preacher stovepipes. Amos smiled. If a man were to survive a shipwreck and two weeks in a lifeboat, and were to return home and be greeted by a brother dressed perfectly for the moment, this is how he would look. Exquisite. Anders, you are amazing, thought Amos, smiling.

Anders on the pier, in contrast, looked on grimly when the barque's bow finally nosed up to the pier, and lines were tossed to dock hands who pulled the lines and tied them to cleats.

As soon as he stepped on the pier, Amos walked rapidly to Anders, grabbed Anders in a bear hug, squeezing tightly and slapping his back before letting him go. Amos stepped back and gripped Anders' shoulders with both hands.

"There were moments when I was convinced this was not meant to happen!" said Amos unreservedly. "That I would never see you, never see Göteborg, again!"

As Amos removed his hands from Anders' shoulders and clapped his hands in delight, Anders expressionlessly reached out and took Amos's arm, pulling Amos away from knots of people forming on the pier. Walking Amos to the edge of the pier where their conversation would be private, Anders turned and looked at Amos, his eyes brimming with apprehensiveness.

"I have something I need to tell you," said Anders, attempting to hide his anxiety while looking directly into Amos's eyes with an expression that gave no clue as to what Anders was to say. So Amos guessed.

"You are going to tell me how happy you are that I'm alive," said Amos, laughing. "You're going to tell me this is one of the happiest days of our lives!"

"I'm delighted you're alive," responded Anders. "Of course. But there is a part of me that wishes I…" He paused and sighed. "That I, myself, were not."

Amos's expression slowly went blank.

"What…?"

"Do you remember when I told you that I worried about forgetting things?" asked Anders hurriedly. "Do you remember telling me to carefully check the list, and simply add anything to it that might be overlooked?"

"Yes," said Amos. "Why?"

"The list did not contain an important item because remembering it is not often required. I should have added it to the list anyway. I kept forgetting to do that. In the past, mom always took care of it. Nevertheless, I remembered the item; but then became distracted and forgot to take care of that specific responsibility." Anders paused, obviously agonizing over what he was about to say.

"Well? Say it," said Amos calmly. "What did you forget?"

Anders stared past Amos at the barque from which Amos had disembarked. Amos became impatient.

"What was it?"

Amos saw fear welling up in Anders's eyes.

"Do you remember the night that Karin stopped by to see you?" asked Anders. "The second time she did so, and you were actually somewhere else, and we both surmised she knew that and, therefore, had actually dropped by to…see me?"

"Vividly."

"I was working on some loose ends that night and – I'm afraid I was distracted."

"I thought nothing happened between you two."

"Nothing happened. You know. Nothing. Serious. Anyway," Anders continued without looking at Amos, "one thing, as the saying goes, led to another. Nothing…serious." Anders sighed. "So Karin left. But the distraction made me forget what I was intending to do. And the next day I went on to other things preparatory to your setting sail." Anders paused. "And completely forgot what I intended to do that night."

"Which was?"

Anders lowered his head slightly, still looking away.

"I…" Anders stopped and he looked at Amos. "I didn't remember until after I received a message your ship had not arrived as scheduled, that there was a huge hurricane. I was worried sick. Then it came to me…

"Merciful God," Anders muttered weakly as he turned away for a moment. He returned his attention to Amos. "I was in shock. I couldn't believe…I'd forgotten what I intended to do."

"Which was?"

"Renewing the fleet insurance."

Amos stared at Anders.

The fleet insurance. The *Polstjärnan*, the *Nordanvinden*, the *Handelsresande*, the *Kringflackande* and the *Nordland*. And now the *Polstjärnan*, the *Nordanvinden* and their cargoes, as well as most former crewmembers, were at the bottom of the Atlantic. The dead could not be returned to life, but the value of the ships and their cargoes would have been recovered.

Amos turned to one side, looking down at the worn, gray-black surface of the pier.

"We will need to return the cargo deposit," was all Amos could say. He looked at Anders. "And replace Uncle Torvald's inheritance."

Amos, forehead furrowed as he frowned, looked at the harbor, biting his lips.

"I worried about something like this," said Anders fearfully. "I worried about my inability to completely deal with details, and I…I knew something like this would eventually happen. 'Like this'? No," Anders looked imploringly at Amos, "nothing like this." Anders was almost shaking. "Nothing of this magnitude. When I realized what I had failed to do, I felt like walking to the end of the pier, drinking myself into oblivion, and joining Gustaf Johansen," said Anders.

Amos sensed that over the past two weeks, Anders' soul had been marinating in guilt and deprecation, but this didn't make Amos's stomach unwind.

"Karin came by every day to comfort me," said Anders. "When I explained what had happened, she also felt responsible…although the responsibility was all mine and I…"

"Everyday?"

"Yes, Amos. You see she…"

"Getting her to come by and see me once a week was like swimming in a suit of mail," said Amos, looking at Anders with an expression of dismay. "When I saw her, it was usually at her place, and then, as you know…"

"I very much appreciated her concern and support and…"

"…as you know," continued Amos, not allowing an interruption, "she wasn't necessarily there. In fact, during the last week I was home," Amos was stunned by the sudden thought, "you saw her more than I did."

"The reason, as it turns out, she was coming over to see you," said Anders, "was, in fact, to explain to you that…" Anders took a breath, "…to explain to you," Anders attempted again as Amos intuited what Anders was trying to say, "that she wanted to…to…"

Anders could not choke out the remainder of the sentence and, realizing what Anders was about to say, Amos finished Anders' sentence for him.

"…just be friends." Amos stared at Anders without expression as the pain in his heart summoned anger. "The most noble and profoundly demeaning insult in the entire female lexicon of demeaning insults."

Amos glared at Anders as the betrayal switch activated a venomous current through Amos's system, causing his anger to grow like an incoming tsunami, while his excellent mind tried to somehow make sense of what happened.

"How was the fishing?" asked Amos, his eyes expressionless. "Did you follow through with your plan to, eh, 'throw her back'?"

Anders stared at Amos, his mind working, wanting to speak but not having the right words. His mouth moved several times as if to speak but no words came out. Amos looked silently at Anders for a moment. He studied Anders closely, reading Anders' face, Anders' expression, and in a low monotone Amos asked, "And now are you going to continue seeing her?"

Anders swallowed. "Considering the present situation, I had not intended to bring this up until later," said Anders as he stood frozen. "None of this is proceeding as I would prefer."

Amos stared at Anders, listening.

"To answer your question, yes, I..." Anders turned his head to one side. "Yes." He looked at Amos and then quickly looked away.

"I will continue to see her," continued Anders earnestly, "because, unlike all the other women in my life, she and I are incredibly compatible. She is different. Very different. I've never met anyone like her. When I see her, it's like seeing an extension of myself."

"So, as I understand it," said Amos in a continued monotone, holding his anger at bay, his outward calmness misleading, "while I was adrift in the North Atlantic, suffering with severe dehydration, and anguishing over the possibility of never seeing you or Karin again, after losing two ships – uninsured ships – and their uninsured cargoes – you were here in Göteborg..."

"I did not know you were... I, I did not remember... I had forgotten to pay..."

Anders was perspiring. Amos was pulling on the reins.

"Then excuse me. I stand corrected," said Amos, his eyes boring into Anders, "you were here in Göteborg with Karin and were assuming – I believe this is correct – that I was on my way to America and would not be returning for months. Would it be fair to say: 'And, while the cat's away...'?"

"Amos, trust me," pleaded Anders. "My intentions were, at first, to do exactly what I said I would do. But then one thing led to another and..."

"Doesn't it always work that way?" interrupted Amos, teeth clenched. Emotional vitriol exploded in Amos's heart like an erupting volcano, compromising his rectitude, and for a split second Amos felt the urge to kill. For a brief, precipitate moment, he wanted to take his large hands, grab Anders' throat and squeeze until Anders could not breathe, until Anders was dead, and then pick up the dead body by the ankles and repeatedly bash the head on a pier bollard until...

In the moment this thought existed, Amos's heartache increased dramatically, and ached so badly his stomach grew bilious and his mind reeled until his better judgment managed to slap him emotionally. As his rectitude returned, his rage dissipated like gradually released steam.

Finally, Amos turned his head and looked at his younger brother.

"Can you understand my sense of betrayal, how I implicitly trusted you to...?

"Amos, I realized, as you had counseled me, that this was," Anders, whose stomach was also in knots, looked at Amos imploringly, "the right woman and..."

"I also counseled you to do the right thing...your counsel to me as well, as I recall." Amos's expression was a mixture of anger and puzzlement. "Somewhat naively, I guess, I left for America trusting that you would cover for me; that when I returned, my relationship with Karin would be on footing as solid as when I left. Instead..."

"It's not that simple, Amos. Your relationship was not on...was not going to improve."

"How do you *know* that?" asked Amos angrily. "Had you followed through, what would have happened? Again, 'attention to detail', Anders. If you had attended to the *small detail* of my relationship with Karin, how would things be now?"

"Amos, believe me, it was never, to me, a small detail." Anders spoke haltingly. "Amos, I realized that it was…how can I say it…it was…your relationship with Karin was never going to be more than it was. She told me she intended to tell you before you left, but then decided it was best to let you go to America, and tell you when you returned."

"Why?" asked Amos incredulously. "Did she say why? It's not like I'm the least eligible bachelor in Sweden," countered Amos. "In fact, I can think of only one other man with whom I might directly contend for Karin's affections." Amos looked for a moment at Anders.

"Assume you and I went to America together…"

"She likes you…and respects you…she… Amos, she simply does not love you."

Anders, speaking with even more difficulty because his mouth was dry, slightly turned his head while his eyes remained affixed on Amos. "In her mind, and heart, that was…is not going to change. To her, that was it…and to her it was…everything."

Amos looked at Anders and at first said nothing.

"I can believe," Amos began slowly and deliberately, exercising supreme self-discipline, "she does not love me." He had heard more unsettling news in the last two minutes, he thought, than in the last twenty years. "However, I have trouble believing …"

"Amos, as I say, this…"

"Dammit!" interrupted Amos loudly, startling several people nearby who looked at him apprehensively as, in effect, Amos told Anders to shut-up – no further explanation was needed or wanted. Amos then turned around and faced the other way, placing his hands behind his neck while trying to get his mind around all he just heard.

"We're both in love with the same woman," said Amos, as much to himself as Anders. Amos put his arms at his side.

"In a way, I can understand Karin's behavior." Amos turned and again faced Anders. "I must admit, however, it is more difficult for me to…understand yours. I understand your feelings of the moment; I have a very difficult time reconciling how they got from there to here. This is a bitter pill I am forced to swallow – losing Karin. And losing her to my own brother who…."

"Amos, this is not as you think! It is not as it appears! And as I said, this has not proceeded the way I would have preferred. It, what I did, did not happen intentionally. When I began to realize that Karin was the one – the right woman – and that she never was going to be serious about you…"

"Enough!" With his left hand, Amos deprecatorily waved Anders away, not wanting to hear any more.

Another emotion entered the fray. Amos always wanted what was best for Anders and, although what appeared to be best for Anders was also causing

Amos's heart to break, brotherly love was vying for his attention.

Needing a moment apart, Amos looked at Anders, took a deep breath, turned, and stepped a few feet away. He looked at the other travelers walking up the pier toward the graying, makeshift, shoreline buildings in which ship owners stored everything from jury masts to marlinspikes. Anders stood still and said nothing.

Eventually Amos turned and faced Anders at a short distance.

"So you're in love," said Amos to Anders. "I suspect this will be a new experience for you – I can't recall you having been in love before. With someone other than you, that is."

His mouth partially open, Amos looked for a moment like he would continue speaking, but slowly closed his mouth, and remained silent.

"Yes, Karin and I are very compatible," said Anders. "I wish there were two of her...one for each of us. But there isn't. She's...if I might be forthright, only interested in one of us and it is...not you, and, therefore, I'm..." Anders' mouth fell open. "Well...I could have opted to 'throw her back' but that would serve no purpose other than to...to..."

"...show solidarity with your older brother...which, you must admit, wouldn't be so bad. I would hope, were our situations reversed, it is what I would have done."

"I realize that under the circumstances," answered Anders adamantly, "it may seem improbable, but I'm not so certain, were you in my place, you would not have done the same thing."

"You're right," agreed Amos acidly, nodding his head. "You're absolutely right. It does seem improbable."

Anders looked at Amos with veiled exasperation, feeling that Amos would never understand.

"Amos, if she were not intent on discontinuing a romantic relationship with you – she said she had come to that decision before you left – and, and..."

Amos again turned and faced the other direction. Anders looked at his older brother imploringly, trying to will Amos into understanding.

"It's all very logical, Amos. It's..."

"And emotional." Amos put his hands in his pockets. This is Anders, Amos thought, Anders, my brother who would normally do anything for me. Anders.

"And I'm only beginning to fall in love with her, Amos. This is... I can only imagine what it will be like... Amos, I just hope someday you...someday this will all make more sense."

Anders paused and looked at Amos who was still facing away, listening to Anders...not just the words but also the emotion behind the words. Amos recalled his thoughts on suffering while in the lifeboat – change-for-good, elevation of the human spirit – how the opportunities of suffering must never be squandered.

"Amos, do you understand the lousy position I'm in?"

Amos sensed that while Anders was working hard to be stoic on the outside, inside he was almost apoplectic. Anders unconsciously folded his hands together as if begging.

"I, I truly want Karin," said Anders. "You told me that when the right woman came along, to do the right thing, and by that you meant I should exercise commitment, but while I am exercising commitment as you advised, under the circumstances, 'the right thing' is a bit muddled. I don't want to…to offend you. But I have offended you by developing a relationship with Karin…"

Amos turned around.

"Amos, she's committed to me…and not to you. I'm com…"

"Then go ahead, Anders," said Amos as he faced Anders.

Mouth dry and partially open, eyes wide, Anders stared at Amos.

"Develop the relationship. I won't be and, therefore, under the circumstances," Amos paused and sighed quietly, "you should."

Anders looked at Amos incredulously, as if Amos had just told him the fleet was still insured.

"You're serious?"

"Yes, I'm serious." Amos sensed Anders' emotional burden silently drop like a bolt of linen.

"I don't know anyone else who could see through this miasma except you, Amos. And it wasn't Karin's fault I neglected to renew the insurance. That was totally my stupidity. An incredible act of stupidity, yes, but stupidity only on my part."

"Very well, Anders." What's done is done, Amos thought.

Amos shoved his hands back in his pockets, took a deep breath, and looked knowingly at Anders.

"It seems," said Amos, hiding the pain he felt, "I am no longer the man in Karin's life – and perhaps…" Amos thought for a second, "…perhaps someday I will look back at this moment and conclude you did me a favor…although that is not how I feel now."

"Amos, I understand how you feel," said Anders quietly, looking down as he also shoved his hands in his coat pockets. "And I don't blame you. However, things are…as they are." Anders paused, looking up at Amos.

"I thought love was supposed to be wonderful. I find it wonderful, like nothing I have ever felt or experienced. I should think it doesn't get any better than this."

"Among the world's most potent elixirs, Anders," said Amos. "As we both know."

Amos folded his arms as he looked at his younger brother, the former Don Juan. None of this made Amos happy although, at the moment, Amos wanted to be happy, happy to be alive, and to celebrate being back in Göteborg. He motioned with his head, and the two began the walk up the hill to the Nordquist mansion.

I have experienced an extraordinary 10 minutes, Amos thought as they walked. The vicissitudes of life. I miraculously survive a two-week lifeboat ordeal in the North Atlantic, step ashore full of gladness, am told about the monumental insurance lapse, and the loss of my beloved to my brother…and God-only-knows what other gut-wrenching tragedy Anders might be keeping for later. The end of the world, perhaps.

"Anders," asked Amos, "is there anything else you need to tell me; any other tragic event that you believe I could not bear to hear until later?"

"You mean," considered Anders after a moment, "in spite of all I have just told you, you could still bear to hear about the end of the world?"

"No. No, you're right," said Amos, tight-lipped, "let's keep that one at bay for a while, shall we?"

"I'll pretend I didn't let it slip."

As they walked up the short dirt road toward the hillside, Amos decided to switch to the topic he was prepared to discuss when he stepped off the barque.

"Anders, I was at sea for many days before the hurricane hit; I was in a lifeboat for another two weeks. As I said, I was certain I would not live to see Göteborg again. In the middle of the Atlantic. Little food and water…as much as had been secured inside the lifeboat lazarette. No sail. No oars. Just the sea and time. After you've survived a hurricane, and are adrift with nothing to see except a few pitiful, deteriorating men and an unending repetition of large waves, you have time to consider and reconsider what you would do if you were to live through it. What is important and what is not. I had a lot of time to think. I came to some far-reaching conclusions."

"Sounds serious. What did you conclude?"

"I'll tell you when we get to the house…the home I believed I'd never see again."

Amos glanced at Anders. "Do you appreciate that house?"

"Ehhm," replied Anders, thinking, "…yeah."

"Anders, appreciate it."

<h1 style="text-align:center">17</h1>

"P lease, have a seat," said Amos, gesturing toward the two, stuffed leather chairs in the corner as he walked toward the massive oak hutch standing like a palace guard at the parlor entry. After removing his hat and gloves, comfortably seated, Anders watched Amos inquisitively.

Intricately carved hutch figures – menacing demonic faces with brass nose rings symbolizing condemnation and confinement – eyed Amos's approach. Like an elder before an altar, Amos stopped and stood reverently before the huge hutch. He reached up and pulled on a brass ring door handle. As the heavy, upper right door swung open, coruscating stained glass glittered in the afternoon sunlight that poured through diamond-shaped, parlor window panes. Amos reached in for one of two unopened bottles of Spanish sherry, gifts from their maternal Andalusian grandfather before his death many years ago. Each bottle was to be separately opened only for an occasion that was both very important and joyous.

Amos took a clean dishtowel from the hutch's green marble counter and wiped film from the bottle. Placing the sherry bottle on the counter, he stepped back, knelt down and opened the two lower doors. From the items inside, he took out an elaborately scrolled sterling silver serving tray with an ornate acanthus leaf embossed rim, brought back from America by his father. Roughly stamped on the bottom was the simple maker's mark "REVERE." Amos reached for a ¾ litre crystal ship's decanter, and two matching crystal sherry glasses, residual evidence of Captain Stig Nordquist's discriminating taste. Placing the decanter and glasses on the sterling silver tray, he cautiously grasped the tray's two end handles as if they, too, were crystal, and carefully stood up.

After placing the tray on the counter, Amos removed the decanter crystal stopper, turned and slid a dual-pronged Ah-So aside the cork and bottle neck, carefully twisting, pulling the cork, the lower half of which was beginning to disintegrate. He briefly sniffed the cork. The smell was favorable. He poured a splash in the first glass, swirled it briefly, nosed, took a sip, and paused, weighing the finish. Satisfied, Amos half-filled the two glasses, and poured the remainder into the decanter.

After stopping both bottle and decanter, Amos carried the tray with decanter and glasses to the parlor center table.

"Excellent," said Anders, having watched Amos's formal efficiency. "I'm uncertain as to why we didn't hire you sooner."

After handing one glass to Anders, Amos sat down in the other chair, leaned back and mentally revisited the North Atlantic.

Tension lining his face, his mind hundreds of miles away, Amos took a sip of sherry, and placed the glass on the end table next to his chair. He sat back, folded his hands, and looked levelly at Anders.

"What's the occasion?" asked Anders. "I'm feeling honored to be here."

"Anders," Amos began, "you've been in some rough seas, as have I, but the hurricane we faced a few weeks ago was not only the worst I have experienced but perhaps among the worst ever. The winds were incredible – in hindsight the wind and wave intensity and synchronization made them seem almost sentient." Amos shook his head both from thinking about the wind's ferocity and, at that moment, wishing he could escape the thought. "The wind. Were there no waves, and the ship motionless, it would still have been impossible to stand on deck. Still, swells as big as hills charged at us with unimaginable ferocity, almost as if intent on our destruction, livid these insignificant human beings and their little boats were so brazen as to trespass where no right had been given." Amos placed his hands on the chair arms and unconsciously squeezed.

"The sea and the wind methodically obliterated our ships, destroyed our cargoes, and attacked and killed nearly all of our crews. The sensation those of us who survived felt...I don't know that I can express it." Amos took a deep breath and quickly exhaled. "It was not that we were just in the wrong place at the wrong time, it seemed more like the storm patiently waited until a predetermined moment, and with a vengeance fell upon us."

Looking down, Amos shook his head in wonderment.

"A few of us were allowed to live...perhaps so we could go back and forewarn others of the sea's irritability and subsequent rage."

Anders noticed the subtle quaver in Amos's voice and realized Amos was far from over the ordeal. The combination of the storm and having lost Karin... Anders understood how distraught Amos must be; Anders was amazed that Amos was taking things as well as he was. A lesser man... Anders did not want to think of how a lesser man might behave.

"As the storm subsided, we were still alive and adrift with the limited food and water inside the lifeboat. We attempted to conserve as much as possible, and we took turns 'standing' watch in hope of seeing a ship in the distance. At night during the storm, it was darker than an Assassin's soul; nothing was visible – not the sea, not the boat, not the men, not the hand in front of your face. And the storm raged furiously. A thousand times I expected I would be gone in a moment.

"There were occasions when our boat would be hurled sideways into the air as if the huge waves were playing catch with one another, and we should have been instantly upended and lost. Somehow the boat always remained upright before more disaster occurred."

Amos leaned forward, looking at the floor.

"This went on and on and on." Amos paused to still himself. "…gradually the storm began to subside.

"Nights later, while the men were asleep, for the first time, stars were out. The contrast was dramatic: the nighttime sky became a canopy of infinitesimal lights, millions of them. To get my bearings, I attempted to study familiar constellations, and in so doing realized that proportionately this planet of ours – all that we really know – was relatively insignificant in contrast to the vast universe, and that the incredible storm – a greater force on earth I cannot imagine – was even less significant. And as a survivor of that insignificant storm, I saw myself, in turn, as of no consequence."

Amos looked at Anders who sat leaning forward, listening, hands gripped together as his forearms rested on his knees, his glass of sherry on the side table next to him.

"In the darkness, I considered our small boat adrift on great, rolling swells in a perceived huge sea that on a universal scale is so miniscule as to be almost laughable and, indeed, I did laugh. In spite of the destruction, death and suffering, I laughed. If any of the men were awake, they must have thought me queer. But, Anders, it was a lucid moment."

Taking his glass of sherry in his right hand, Amos looked at the glass for a moment, marveling it was there. With similar sensation he looked out the window toward the waterfront.

"I was actually beginning to see things clearly," he said after a moment, looking back at Anders. "We – you and I – own boats, we import and we export, making more money than most, but in the greater scheme of things, of what significance is any of it?"

Anders shrugged. "It's what we do. 'Significance'? I don't understand."

"You were Göteborg's Don Juan," Amos nodded. "To what great end has being the town's leading ladies' man led?"

"I have no idea," replied Anders, sitting back, almost smiling. "But if insignificant, it has been a very enjoyable foray into insignificance," he added, looking at Amos. "As insignificance goes, there are much worse insignificant things than being the leading ladies' man in Göteborg or any other Swedish town."

Anders beamed and picked up his glass of sherry.

"The opportunities presented themselves and, frankly, I would have been a fool not to capitalize on those opportunities. I simply invested," Anders explained, raising his eyebrows and his sherry glass as if giving a toast, "the talents God gave me. The Bible says to do that, you know." He took a sip.

"I do know. Not long ago I was given that advice by another paragon of virtue," Amos said dismissively. "Many are familiar with those verses, but I'm not certain the Good Lord had unwavering pursuit of the opposite sex in mind when he presented the parable."

"You don't know. Maybe He did." Completely focused on the topic, with an intense expression that precedes inspiration like hunger before foraging, Anders looked off, inadvertently spilling sherry on himself, thinking about the possibility that by doing what he did best, he had contributed to some grand, providential scheme. Were all to cultivate what God had enabled them to do best, thought Anders, isn't it possible they would be most closely conforming to God's will?

"In any event," said Amos, disturbing Anders reverie, "I'm glad you enjoyed yourself…and now, however, that you are off the market, I also hope your efforts at being a one-woman man are fruitful. Whether fruitful or not, none of this amounts to much. When you eventually pass on, as all men do, how will what you have done be of any significance?"

"Perhaps it won't," said Anders, playing the devil's advocate. "Perhaps none of this amounts to a tinker's 'damn.'"

"I think not," responded Amos. "There is a simple measure by which significance is weighed. It is not evident to most, but it became clear to me while I was adrift in the North Atlantic."

"What was made clear?"

"Most of what we've been doing, working so diligently to accomplish, is of itself insignificant, actually pointless. But what might make it significant?" Amos asked Anders.

Anders shrugged.

"You've never wondered?" asked Amos.

"I've never had the pleasure of surviving a major hurricane and floating about, near death, in the North Atlantic for two weeks. This has placed me at some disadvantage." Anders paused, thinking. "But, yes, actually I have wondered. In the greater scheme of things, what's the point?"

"Measurement of significance is very simple…obvious, actually," said Amos. "While people, events, may seem to have significance of the moment, it is only of the moment. We can become quite full of ourselves but, like a leaking balloon, our fullness dissipates, and the moment gradually fades from memory, forgotten like the rest, lost forever. In the greater scheme of things, eternally, people and events are of no significance apart from the Creator. That is, if the Lord is not part of the equation – or perhaps it would be better to say, 'if the equation is not of the Lord' – neither is significance."

"For example?"

"Perhaps the best means of explanation is to approach the subject from the perspective of one who does not believe in God – where God is never part of any equation," answered Amos. "Under those conditions, we should ask ourselves, is anything of significance? Where the non-believer is the beginning and the end, no, nothing really is. Ask yourself: 'How is relevancy established? What eternal end is accomplished?' The non-believer lives, he dies – as we all live and die – but, apart from God, life is, as Macbeth said, 'a tale told by an idiot, full of sound and fury, signifying nothing' – of no significance."

"Yes, Macbeth. Guardian of the high road," said Anders, studying the sherry glass in his right hand. "Continue."

"Incidentally, Anders, you've a spot of sherry on your tunic."

Looking down at his stained, white tunic, acting as if he were greatly agitated, Anders grabbed the fabric.

"'Out, damn'd spot! Out, I say!'"

"Clever, Anders."

Amos's eyes glittered like faceted jewels as he looked at his inimitable brother and chuckled while Anders solemnly studied the small stain.

"As I was about to say," interrupted Amos, "removing God from the equation, or vice versa, is not their choice, however."

"Wha'…Whose choice is…? Never mind, I think I know."

"And you'd be correct. In fact, the Bible is full of illustrations where non-believers, in spite their unbelief, were used by God to achieve His purposes. These actions then have significance." Amos raised his glass for emphasis. "But do the non-believers, used by God, profit from being used? Do their lives then become significant? Or is it merely the act that is significant and, unbelief sustained, their life's composition continues such that they do whatever they do because, well," Amos shrugged his shoulders, "what else is there to do?"

"Die," said Anders, raising his eyebrows momentarily as if to suggest his response was novel, knowing it was not.

"As we know, some take that route," replied Amos. "Most, of course, strive to overlook any sensation of insignificance, simply taking life as it comes, making the most of things, and ignoring the nagging 'So what?'s. Living because you are living, however, doesn't really count for much."

Anders listened.

"It seems God draws to Him whoever He chooses, for reasons not apparent," said Amos, "and while for a subsequent believer it is a great honor to be chosen by God for any purpose, for a non-believer, whatever happened just happened – no more, no less – and, therefore, apart from God, life is pointless; we're back to Macbeth. On the other hand," continued Amos, "with God, not only are all things possible, as Christ said, but all things are meaningful."

"When, if I might ask, is God *not* involved?" asked Anders, studying Amos seriously. "Isn't His nature such that nothing is possible apart from His will?"

"I'm again reminded," answered Amos, "of Jesus on the cross where he cries out, '*Eli! Eli! Sabachthani.*' 'My God! My God! Why have you forsaken me?' For a moment, at least, God the Father wasn't there."

"Ah, yes." Anders sipped. "Jesus said so." Anders held out his left palm. "And He would know. God the Father, therefore, somehow wasn't. But how? Why not?"

Amos gently wiped both eyes, and leaned forward.

"The reason at that moment had something to do with requisite suffering," answered Amos after a moment. "Evidently, Christ's suffering on the cross, as bad as it already was, would not be complete while He felt the presence of the Father. The Father's presence, therefore, would need to have been withheld, if only for a short moment. From this, I surmise that suffering, for whatever reason, is of much greater importance than most of us realize. For Christ, interestingly enough, the withheld moment was unexpected. I don't pretend to understand all of it…one of many questions I'll ask in the afterlife."

"Your point?"

"God's involvement can be withheld…and, therefore, so can significance."

"Did you feel God was absent in the North Atlantic?"

"Oh, no," Amos said softly, remembering while staring at the opposite wall chair rail as if it were the horizon. "No." Amos looked at Anders. "His presence became very evident to me." Amos thought of Arnie and Jens, and added, "Like Mombasa vultures among the dying, the other side was present as well. But while the hurricane was tragic, the tragedy did not preclude God's presence. It seemed just the opposite. While becoming physically weaker, my spiritual strength grew…which kept me alive."

Anders looked back, understanding, lightly nodding rhythmically.

"Sometimes," said Anders, "I think God works best through tragedy." Anders motioned toward Amos with his sherry glass. "Not necessarily Shakespearean, but many of the others."

"Clever again, Anders."

"Thank you." Anders' eyebrows rapidly rose and fell twice like bird wings. His self-satisfied expression intentionally accentuated, he took another sip.

"Uncle Sven's face came to me when I was drifting in the Atlantic," said Amos. "His life could have been so different. Since we – you and I – are considered, by worldly standards, successful, are we different from Sven? Let me ask you: does financial success bring with it significance or relevance?"

"Beats being broke."

"And then what?" asked Amos, unperturbed. "We have things. But what of it? We're born…we laugh, cry, work, play…we die. Forgotten with the rest?" Amos's eyes were wide as he put down his glass. "That's it?" asked Amos.

Anders shrugged.

"No, there's more than that," continued Amos. "How shall I put it? In the North Atlantic it became evident that it is only through the love of God that love is certified, only through faith in Him that hope truly meets reward, only through His orchestration that significance resonates, that the soul feels its worth." Amos looked intently at Anders. "Relationship to God is 'the measure of all things' because it is through God that all things have measure. And what is that measure? Meters, liters, minutes? No, it is the relative glorification of God Himself. Otherwise stated, the measure of anything is the extent to which it glorifies God."

"You should be in hurricanes more often."

Looking at Anders neutrally, Amos took a sip. "No, thank you."

"What are you going to do now?"

Amos looked back at Anders knowingly. "When floating in the North Atlantic, I sensed the storm was, in small part, God getting my attention, and that I improbably survived because it was intended I survive. The reason? You asked what I am going to do now. If the measure of anything is the extent to which it glorifies God, the Creator of the stars and the seas and the insignificant men who sail them, I should, therefore, place myself in the best position to glorify God, to become more like the servant with five talents than those with one or two."

"Isn't that rather dangerous?"

"Dangerous? Why would it be dangerous?"

"Because you have a multitude of talents, and God expects much from those to whom much is given," answered Anders. "The Bible says that. And remember the foolish servant buried his one talent in the ground, and was consequently cast into outer darkness," said Anders with mock gravity. "What if God determines you have effectively buried all five talents in the ground? What then? On judgment day, instead of saying, 'Well done, wise and faithful servant' – whatever it is He says – He says, 'You should have stuck with the one talent, buddy. But no, you had to have five. Well, outer darkness is too good for you.'"

Anders took a quick sip of sherry as Amos looked back mystified.

"You're screwed, Amos."

Amos put down his glass, looked at Anders and folded his hands.

"Anders, you have an uncommon knack for making the sublime ridiculous."

"It's a gift."

"Anders…" Amos paused, "never mind."

Amos leaned back in his chair while Anders, already comfortable, sherry glass in hand, did not move. Amos cleared his throat.

"So? What do you plan on doing?" asked Anders.

"How can I most effectively use of my talents? First of all," explained Amos, "the servant with one talent made no attempt to capitalize on what was given him. With whatever I have been given, I will make that effort. Secondly, I believe the servant who was given five talents was given a corresponding amount of opportunity. I will capitalize on opportunity provided."

Amos looked solemnly at Anders.

"Anders, I don't believe I have been led to this point of my own volition, and I believe that God will provide opportunities to effect His goals on earth through the talents he has given me, and will fortify my attempts to do so. Believing as I do, it will be my foremost objective to reach those goals without compromise. And, thirdly, I feel as if I have been literally prepared for this," added Amos.

"Prepared for what, Amos? What do you have in mind?"

"Anders, do you remember those Russians who visited us years ago?"

"Yes," said Anders as he took a sip. "Uncle Sven's business partners."

"One of them," continued Amos, "came down to the Polstjärnan shortly afterwards and talked to me."

"You never mentioned it."

"He gave me advice."

"What? What did he say?"

"He said I was naïve and I would be dealing with many men worse than he, men who would overwhelm me if I did not become more sensitive to the dark side of human nature. Ironically at that moment, you know, I wanted to grab him and throw him off the dock…but he was right.

"I took to heart what he said, and have been very cautious when dealing with others. I proceed on the assumption that if I give men the opportunity to betray my trust, they will. Anders, I naïvely disliked doing so at first – I always believed that a man's word should be his bond – but found that leaving nothing to chance, and putting agreements in writing regardless of with whom I was dealing, saved me considerable difficulty in the long run. Putting things in writing obviously makes it hard to forget what you said. And if a man balked at formally contracting what he had verbally agreed upon, he was not someone who could be trusted in the first place."

"What does this have to do with talents?"

"It almost seems like I was 'sent to school' to learn about dealing with people. I believe the acumen I have developed has subsequently become one of my talents. And when I was speaking with the Russian, I had the sensation my calling would become an obstacle to betrayal, preventing men from betraying and preying on one another."

"Preying on one another? For example?"

"For example, Uncle Sven was initially betraying the trust he thought he had from the Russians, preying on the Russians for material gain, committing fraud, unaware that they were betraying the trust he thought they were giving him while simultaneously preying on him. But men can prey on one another in a manner lower than animals: promising hope, then betraying trust – through anything from white lies to murder." Amos looked at the opposite wall and sighed. "A miserable existence."

"Amos, I agree. But now, forgive my asking, what you going to do?"

18

ead tilted slightly, eyes narrowed, Amos studied Anders, guessing what Anders was guessing, although Amos also intuited something else.

"Police work?" said Amos. "Practicing law? Private investigating?" Amos shook his head, looking to one side. "No. Not like Adam Curran-Jones." He looked at Anders. "Infinitely more lawlessness is thwarted by conscience than by law enforcement. The general answer is: I am going to do the Lord's work. The more specific answer is not yet evident."

"The Lord's work. The ministry?"

"Did you hear anything I just said?"

"But you know," Anders paused, "remember – before his last voyage – how Dad started going to church regularly…not just in-and-out on Sunday morning, but actively involved? Then shortly before he died – thank God he was converted – it was amazing he began to…"

"Wha'…wait a minute!" interjected Amos, sitting up. "'…thank God he was converted.'" Anders had previously been unconcerned with conversion. "When…?" Amos stared at Anders. "Anders, you're converted." Amos's eyes begged for explanation. "When did that happen?"

Anders slowly sat up in his seat, eyes wide.

"Interestingly, I've been worrying about it since you left. And letting the insurance lapse. And I must tell you I fought against falling in love with Karin… but it was like an undertow – struggle as I might, I couldn't help myself – and when I fell in love, while part of me was elated, a large part of me felt like hell, like the lowest form of life, because I had unintentionally…I wanted, somehow, to be forgiven…by you. And by God. I wanted…"

"So, you've been praying?" asked Amos, his dark eyebrows knitted. Previously, Anders only prayed when someone else led.

"Oh, considerably," stated Anders. "But isn't it odd? I just don't remember my conversion happening."

"Anders, remember, Jesus said, 'The wind blows wherever it wills. You hear its sound but you cannot tell where it comes from or where it is going. So is it with everyone born of the Spirit.' And remember He said, 'No one can come to me unless the Father who sent me draws him.' Anders, you were feeling like 'the lowest form of life' for a reason, and were finally convicted of your fallen nature – yes, even you – and were being drawn by the Father."

"You know…," Anders looked solemnly to one side. "You know, you're right." His lips tightened. He looked back at Amos. Anders calmly stood up, turned and faced the wall, his head tilted upward, thinking. Still holding his wine glass, he crossed his arms and looked down. "I can see now I was."

"Anders, this is fantastic." Amos put down his sherry glass, got up, went around the table, took Ander's sherry glass out of his hand, put it aside, and happily embraced his brother.

"I must admit," said Anders, taking a gulp of air as Amos released him, "it's also amazing."

Amos returned to his chair and slowly sat down as Anders also sat, folding his hands, looking expressionlessly at Amos who beamed at his normally narcissistic brother now uncharacteristically feeling uncomfortable in the spotlight, and oddly wanting to discuss something other than himself.

"Are you going into the ministry here in Göteborg?" asked Anders.

"I had assumed Göteborg. After the revelations an hour ago, however, I'm not so sure."

While continuing to look at Amos, Anders facial expression went blank except for his lips being bitten together.

"If not Göteborg, where?" asked Anders.

"At the moment I'm thinking about America," explained Amos. "Prior to the hurricane I thought many times about moving to America for business purposes, but I did not seriously consider doing so because of my relationship with Karin. Interestingly," Amos looked at Anders, "during the hurricane that obstacle was removed."

Head slightly lowered, Anders looked back uncomfortably.

"Again, while adrift in the North Atlantic," continued Amos, "I considered the things we just discussed, but was uncertain as to how my newfound conviction would manifest itself were I to survive. As I sit here in the wake of the revelation about Karin," Amos said, looking intently at Anders, "the path to America is unobstructed and, frankly, at this moment, considering how many Scandinavians are migrating to America, it seems to me that path is the one I should take. Once in America, I may still involve myself to some extent in imports," Amos conjectured. "It would seem…"

"You no longer seem extremely upset about Karin," Anders interjected.

Amos looked away as he took another sip of sherry.

"Consider the perspective. Getting over her will take some time but, well, how shall I say it? I know what I am to do." Amos looked obliquely at the floor. "And I know Karin. While it is important I be honest with others, it is paramount I am honest with myself." Amos again looked directly at Anders. "I'll be in the ministry, but she is not a minister's wife. I'm not being critical of Karin but, again, honestly…supporting the difficult work of God requires someone like, well…"

"…like Mom," interjected Anders.

"Yes," nodded Amos in agreement., "Mom would have been a great pastor's wife. She had the strength of character, the discernment, patience and faith. Even the Russian recognized that."

"So, with regard to Karin," said Anders, recovering the topic, "I guess I sh…"

"Don't misunderstand," interjected Amos. "Emotionally, this is a very difficult moment for me, Anders, but is what is and should be."

Anders sighed inwardly.

"If you're to go into the ministry in America," said Anders, "realistically, your business involvement will be modest at best." Anders looked at Amos for a moment. "As a practical matter, let's face it, you could become uninvolved. I'll then be solely responsible for the export business operation here, which worries me because of my lousy memory. But meanwhile, how are you to support yourself? Will you need me in that regard?"

"I've saved up quite a bit, and I don't anticipate large living expenses in America." Amos cupped his hands around his right knee and leaned back comfortably. "Locusts and honey are not in my plans, but neither shall I live like, well, I do. If priorities are kept in order, God's work doesn't make one affluent. The best – John the Baptist, the Apostle Paul, the Savior Himself – did nothing to enhance riches on earth," understated Amos. "They were slightly less sybaritic than that," Amos smiled as he sat back, taking his sherry glass. "I'll not need a paycheck. Although, as you know, Anders, people in God's work do solicit offerings."

"That will never be a problem, Amos. And you'll still own 50% of both Nordquist Shipping Co. and Nordquist Import Co. Dividends. Unless at some point you want to sell your shares to me." Hands folded in his lap, relaxed, Anders looked at Amos waggishly. "Financing would be no problem," Anders deadpanned. "I know some Russians."

"Then I'm set," smiled Amos. "But let's wait a while, shall we? A number of other things need to be considered first."

"Such as sorting out how I should run both the fleet and the export business," said Anders, worried.

Amos thought for a moment and quietly chuckled.

Anders looked at Amos perplexed. "What's so funny?"

"The question of operating the export business has an interesting answer."

Putting down his sherry glass, Amos leaned forward and folded his hands.

"Much of successful exporting is simply getting what you need at the price you want. I can't think of anyone who might be better at that than Karin Olafsdotter. Probably better than I. She's very bright. Charming. Obviously shrewd. Her family is already in the business. Down at the dock, I thought your involvement with her… I suspect much of what I thought and said reflected my feelings of the moment which were, well, rather raw."

"How do you feel now?" asked Anders seemingly without expression.

"The pain I feel at the moment will be with me for a while," answered Amos, looking down. "Like a deep wound. I must admit that at the dock I was nearly overcome with anger." Amos looked up at Anders. "My focus is clearer now.

Bluntly stated, Karin could be an excellent business partner, Anders." Anders studied Amos for any sign of deception, sarcasm. There was none.

"Again, I'm not certain I will completely leave the business," added Amos. "On the other hand, events may cause me to see things differently. So, perhaps you're right. I suspect I may have time for little else other than the Lord's work."

"The Lord's work?" questioned Anders. "I'm still uncertain of what you intend to do."

"Probably church ministry, but apart from doing it in America, we'll just have to see where I'm led."

"How God uses you will be interesting," said Anders after a moment, leaning with his left elbow on the chair arm. "You studied the Bible. When we were kids you did so and, I must admit, I wondered why. There was usually something much more entertaining available – for me anyway. Evidently not you."

Anders reached for his glass and held it up, inviting Amos to a toast.

"The Lord's work. Whatever it is, you'll do it well."

Having said this, Anders sipped, put down his sherry glass, got up out of his chair, went over to Amos, reached down and put his arm around Amos's shoulder, giving his older brother a one-armed hug.

"Things appear to have worked out," said Anders. Earlier in the day at the dock, Anders was in a great state of anxiety, feeling he had betrayed Amos, the one man he truly revered. Anders' agitated emotional state was a discomfited combination of fear, self-reproach, love, hope, and despair. He could not reconcile what he did with what he should have done and, then, what he wanted to do. The prospect of facing Amos made Anders' mind and stomach feel like he spent the morning gorging on lutefisk. But now it seemed all was far better than what might have been if he did what it seemed he should have done. Anders, grateful, shook his head.

"Yes, things work out…but never, it seems, without pain," said Amos as he stood up, walked to Anders and put his hands on Anders' shoulders. "At least that's my experience."

Amos dropped his hands to his sides. "Hopefully, however," continued Amos, "I will get to America without incident. Once there, I shall follow the leading of God as to where I should locate, and Uncle Torvald needs to be given his inheritance." Amos looked up at a painting, a portrait of his mother when she was a young woman. "No doubt the two are interrelated."

Anders agreed softly. "No doubt."

Amos returned to his chair and the two brothers again sat down. Anders picked up and studied his sherry glass.

"And no doubt there will be no more serious trouble," said Anders. "What else could happen?"

"What else?" As he looked seriously at Anders, Amos stuck his fingers together in front of his chest, pulling them in and out. "Anders, in the never-ending battles of spiritual warfare, the greatest obstacles are the ones we cannot see. What I am proposing to do will be met, at minimum, with duplicity, temptation, diversion, and retaliation. To foment my discouragement, I will be subjected to all manner of deceit and betrayal.

"Anders, in spite of the evidence all around us, many religiously believe no evil counterforce exists, no demonic influence, nothing like Satan and his minions. Disbelief is their faith." Amos nodded faintly. "Why is that? Why the Great Injunction?"

Anders looked back, not knowing what to say.

"Anders, what does the devil do best?"

"Well, he hates. He enables sinful behavior," said Anders, partially shrugging.

"Close. He does quite a bit of that, but it's not what he does best."

"What does he do best?"

"He lies, Anders," said Amos. "He lies beautifully. He lies wonderfully, convincingly, artfully. His lies flow inexorably and forcefully like a surging river current. While 'the truth is not in him,' still he knows the truth, manipulating truth perversely, tweaking the wants, sentiments and biases of us all, especially those who would abjure reality for the sake of an ideologically informed fantasy world where 'truth' is as wished, not as is; in the process never missing an opportunity to falsely accuse believers, and to convict the acedic of no reality beyond immediate perception, and no God…and, of course, no Satan."

Amos folded his hands as he looked at Anders.

"Prevarication, disingenuousness, duplicity and subterfuge, artfully using partial truths, are his forte, what he does best. Those who follow him become practiced at lying themselves, and to themselves, but often subsequently benefitting communally or materially. As someone once told me, 'The world rewards its own.'"

Amos looked at Anders without blinking. "That would not be me. The world will treat me quite differently.

"So, 'what else could happen?' you ask. With lack of foresight…or even with consummate planning," Amos placed his fingertips together, "anything and everything."

❯●❮

Amos walked up the porch steps of the parsonage, knocked three times, and waited for Pastor Lute Olafson to come to the door. Shortly the door opened.

"Amos! Come in!"

Amos removed his hat and entered, greeting Mrs. Olafson as she went to the kitchen to bring in some coffee.

"Please, Amos, sit down," said Pastor Olafson, motioning toward a couch while taking a seat opposite Amos as he sat down. "To what do I owe this honor?"

"I needed to talk with you. I've decided to go into the ministry."

"You have!" responded Pastor Olafson, wide-eyed, pleasantly surprised. "Wonderful!"

"Although I'm not certain in what capacity, I am certain I will be going to America."

"Amos, I'm delighted."

"Oh, my golly! Look at this!" exclaimed Amos as a smiling Mrs. Olafson placed a serving tray on the coffee table. Aside the silver coffee pot and china cups was a plate of golden brown, round- or heart-shaped hallon cookies with raspberry-filling centers that looked like large encrusted rubies. "Thank you, so much," said Amos as Mrs. Olafson stood upright, beaming. Amos hadn't tasted hallon cookies since his mother was alive. Mrs. Olafson nodded approvingly and returned to the kitchen.

"Pastor, I wanted to ask for some insight. It seems I've been going to church all my life without fully observing what you do."

Pastor Olafson laughed. "I remember when I made up my mind the same as you, Amos. And like you, I had been in another profession – I was a shipwright. I thought I knew as much as I needed to know, but it turned out there was so much I didn't know. So, let me share a few things with you, and save you some time.

"First, you're going to America. Much of Europe is going there, and it will be important that, as many begin a new life in America, they experience a new birth spiritually. There was a great spiritual awakening there in the mid-18th century, led by George Whitefield, Jonathan Edwards, Gilbert Tennent, and James Davenport, that greatly influenced that nation's founding fathers' conception of and emphasis on democratic thought, while encouraging non-compulsory religion, and – in the interest of truth – freedom of speech and the press. I pray there will be another awakening. And another."

"With respect to my American ministry," asked Amos, "what are some fundamental things to anticipate?"

"Heavy spiritual warfare. First, verisimilitude and paradox are in the ministry anywhere," Pastor Olafson replied. "Often what appears to be the case either is not or is much more than is apparent. Be on your toes."

Amos nodded.

"Second, never forget Who is really in control – you know the John 15:5 verse about the vine and the branches."

Amos again nodded.

"Good," said Pastor Olafson as he leaned over and poured some coffee.

"Amos, do you use cream and sugar?"

"Cream."

Pastor Olafson passed Amos some of the morning's fresh cream from Pastor Olafson's cow.

"As in Europe," continued Pastor Olafson, looking levelly at Amos, "many in America will believe that, for a variety of mistaken reasons, when they die they will go to heaven when, in fact, they have no idea of how one gets there."

"You mean they don't understand conversion."

"Satan, as he presently does, will provide ample diversions misleading many through perverted alternatives, aping God's work, obstructing conversion." Pastor Olafson waived his hand sagaciously.

"Ask people the most important question there is: 'Who is Jesus Christ?' Really. Who is He? Get people to seriously weigh an answer. Follow that with: 'Do you have peace with God?'

"Expect many will never have seriously weighed the first question, and do not understand the second. If He is drawing a person to Christ, however, God will tie the two questions together when providing the single answer to each."

Pastor Olafson reached for his Bible, opened it to a specific verse, and began to read. "Jesus said, 'Whosoever drinketh of this water shall thirst again.'" Amos sat up. "'But whosoever drinketh of the water that I give him shall never thirst; but the water that I shall give him shall be in him a well of water springing up into eternal life.'" Pastor Olafson again looked at Amos. "Amos, what did He mean by that?"

Amos sipped his coffee, thinking of the lifeboat.

"To begin with, while not recognizing their inner emptiness as such, everyone has a spiritual void to fill," answered Amos. "A thirst. To quench the thirst, many try diversions – literature, possessions, money, food, drink, science, philanthropy – but the spiritual void is never adequately filled unless we are drawn by God the Father and reborn through the Holy Spirit, the thirst quenched. These things were made clear to me while drifting on the Atlantic."

"Very good," nodded Pastor Olafson. "Amos, a moment ago I mentioned that Satan obstructs conversion by aping God's work, creating diversions. Here is a Bible passage from the Sermon on the Mount. It troubles many," said Pastor Olafson. "It troubled me until I understood what it meant." Pastor Olafson read.

"'Many will say to me in that day, "Lord, Lord, have we not prophesied in thy name? And in thy name have cast out devils? And in thy name done many wonderful works?" And then will I profess unto them, "I never knew you; depart from me, ye that work iniquity."'" Sipping his coffee, Pastor Olafson looked at Amos. "What was going on?" asked Pastor Olafson. "And how are this Bible verse and the previous verse related?"

"I…I'd rather not guess."

"The troubling second passage," said Pastor Olafson, "refers to those positioned in the Christian ministry by Satan."

Amos's eyes grew narrow as he looked backed puzzled.

"What more effective way to undermine your enemy," responded Pastor Olafson, "than filling his leadership positions with your own people? Churches and synagogues are rife with opportunities for Satan to insure potential converts receive no 'living water,' but hit only dry wells. Satan's myrmidons are misled men and women who surround themselves with the trappings of Christian-Judeo worship – vestments, pipes, chimes, bells and whistles – but whose actions glorify themselves, not the Trinity, and work to the benefit of Satan while directing parishioner focus on anything other than Christ. Many religious entrepreneurs play 'religion' quite profitably while misleading the flock. Hence: 'I never knew you: depart from me...'

"I must tell you, Amos, many times when sitting in someone else's congregation listening to a sermon, I have spontaneously wondered, 'What does any of this have to do with Jesus?' Or 'If he feels that way, why does he bother?' Why, indeed," said Pastor Olafson, forehead furrowed, as he looked at Amos with what, to Amos, were eyes of blue steel.

"Pastor, when people ask about it, how do you explain the Trinity?"

"Good question," Pastor Olafson nodded, looking at the coffee table. "In the great *Sh'ma Yisrael*, 'Hear, O Israel: the LORD our God is one LORD,' the Hebrew word for 'one', '*echadh*,' means 'one with unified parts.' A wagon wheel has hub, spokes and felloes, but in the case of 'the Lord,' the Creator, we have a single divine essence we as creatures cannot comprehend. Our vague perspective of the three spiritual parts, the Father, Son, and Holy Spirit, involves one divine essence that comes from the Father. John 1:14 says, 'And the Word' – *Logos* in the Greek – 'was made flesh, and dwelt among us…'" Pastor Olafson looked up at Amos. "'…was made flesh and dwelt among us.' This is what Jesus meant when He told the disciple Phillip, 'He that hath seen Me hath seen the Father.'

"But Jesus also says, 'I do nothing of myself; but as my Father hath taught me, I speak these things.' Out of His love for us, the Father sent the Son – the Christ – and His Holy Spirit – 'I shall pour out my Spirit on all flesh.' The Son and the Holy Spirit didn't just show up, and never act independently – ever – but are consonant with the will of the Father.

"Yet Jesus said to the rich man, 'Why callest thou me good? There is none good but one, that is, God.' In this verse Jesus did not say He was *not* good, because He was – far more than the rich man could understand – which was the point. And if He was good, and said only One is good, God, then who is the Christ?"

Amos nodded, thinking about how the difficult statements of Christ usually meant far more than apparent. For Amos, this was no longer surprising.

"Reasoning from what we understand based on all that is around us," said Pastor Olafson, "to whatever preceded creation – obviously not corporeal – and how pre-creation became, but how God has always been, very quickly pushes me to the edge of sanity, and I immediately need to stop the thought and back away from the edge. It's so big, so far beyond us."

"'Word.' Pastor," said Amos, "that tells me hardly anything. 'Logos.' I've tried to understand what, in context, that means. Either we don't have a word that properly translates, or the apostle John actually didn't either. I vote for both."

"Some say 'Verb,' not 'Word,' is a better translation. Personally, I've wondered if 'Mind,'" said Pastor Olafson, "not 'Word,' might have been closer to what John meant. Or did Word proceed separately from Mind, 'Word' then being completely accurate at the 'beginning'? And if so, what was meant by 'beginning'… that is, what was before then?" Pastor Olafson chuckled. "But, as you say, this 'Mind' is so great, so beyond our conceptual ability, we are unable to comprehend it. Jehovah: 'I am that I am.' An ostensibly meaningless tautology that somehow means something far beyond our comprehension."

Pastor Olafson looked at his coffee cup and shook his head, the edges of his mouth curled upward.

"Amos, it's a blessing the Creator draws the created to Him, because we are, in the greater scheme of things, spiritually deaf, dumb and blind, with no sense of smell or touch. Without being drawn, none of us would know where to go, even if we knew to come."

Pastor Olafson shifted his coffee cup to both hands. "We, the sheep, however, by His grace recognize the Good Shepherd's voice, but only by His grace, and are then able to believe what the Bible tells us. Otherwise, we wouldn't, couldn't."

"How would you sum up my responsibilities when I get to America?" asked Amos.

"Amos, when in America or anywhere, your responsibility will be to convince men of their sinfulness, of God's love for them in spite of those sins, and of their total dependence on Jesus for salvation – always much easier said than done. And if you pastor a church, as you most likely will, critics, naysayers, powermongers, complainers and skeptics will be your constant companions. You'll have to put up with questions like, 'How come the congregation isn't growing?' 'What are we supposed to do with all the new people?' 'Why is there so much emphasis on the Holy Spirit?' 'Why isn't there more emphasis on the Holy Spirit?' And the like. Listen to what is said. If the concerns have merit, deal with the problem, and enlist the concerned party to help you…which may quickly solve the problem. Otherwise, continually pray for God's leading.

"And when you are discouraged," added Pastor Olafson, "remind yourself that life following conversion becomes something you want everyone to experience.

"Ask for God's guidance as He works through you, knowing it is not you but God who convicts people as to Jesus' full identity, reminding them that, as with the thief on the cross next to Christ at Golgotha, it is never too late, and one's sins are never too great, for God to forgive."

"The thief on the cross," echoed Amos, thinking out loud, "an enigma for many because he went to heaven; his undeserved forgiveness and unmerited salvation contradict what so many believe necessary for entrance into the Kingdom of God."

"To our knowledge, although remorseful, the 'thief' – far beyond an ordinary thief – didn't ask for forgiveness, however, even though by his own admission he deserved to be crucified," said Pastor Olafson. "But he was drawn to Christ, as evidenced by his conviction the Man next to him was the Messiah, belief that could only come from the Holy Spirit. Considering who he was and the position he was in, his faith is counterintuitive to a nonbeliever. But the thief's demons were no match for the Holy Spirit, and the thief's means of salvation no different than ours," Pastor Olafson briefly raised his coffee cup in a toast, "praise God."

Amos pleasantly raised his own cup in response.

"At the same time, Amos, the act of asking for God's forgiveness, as we just mentioned, is evidence of the Holy Spirit's leading and, therefore, Amos – as I did with your father, your mother and you – when in America, at every opportunity ask others to pray for forgiveness, submitting to Jesus. Remind them that while the sacraments have their place, there is no religious object, person, rite or combination thereof that will save men and bring peace with God, only the faith that Jesus is who the Bible says He is, and did what the Bible says He came to do." Pastor Olafson looked levelly at Amos. "Could it be much simpler?"

"No," said Amos.

"So, Amos, in summary, when in America, focus on the 'living water,' the indwelling of the Holy Spirit evidenced by peace with God, while remaining alert to potential spiritual buffeting not only from the unchurched community reacting to diabolically-informed misperception, or from some in your congregation acting out of ignorance or selfishness, but also from those in the church hierarchy who may be blinded by self-importance or a lack of scriptural understanding, or both. I have experienced all of these," added Pastor Olafson. "If you do not experience spiritual attacks, Amos, you're not doing your job; if you raise the flag of Christ and no one shoots at it, you've not raised it high enough. Nevertheless, you'll need to include cynical community members, as well as restive congregational members, and self-important synod leaders, in your ministry. They need conversion too – and you will find that once they experience the Lord's conversion, they become wonderful witnesses for Christ.

"Amos, will you pray with me now?"

"Of course."

The two men stepped away from their seats and knelt on the braided living room rug before the coffee table. As led, they prayed for God's blessing on Amos's future ministry. As Amos prayed, he felt uniquely serene, evidence of being where he was supposed to be and at that moment doing what he was supposed to do in the presence of the Holy Spirit.

As Pastor Olafson stood up, at first he looked at Amos appreciatively; but his mind returned to a cautionary topic, and his expression grew somber.

"Again, Amos, remember, you will be opposed, perhaps even violently opposed. The opposition will be spiritual although it will seldom appear as such. The Old Evil will dog you, waiting for indirect opportunities to undermine your ministry, perhaps enabling others to accuse you of things you've never done. They may even want you dead; some believing they are acting according to God's will. When problems arise that seem illogical, improbable, and you ask yourself, 'How is this happening?' remember what I just said, and that the Spirit which is in you is far greater, and will bless and keep you.

"So, in a few words, as you go out to lead others, Amos, do not teach people to live before they are born, to be holy before they are saved. And play the music, not the notes."

Amos paused, and nodded.

As he turned and walked with Amos to the door, Pastor Olafson extended an open invitation to return for more instruction at any time before leaving for America.

Amos left the parsonage confident in what he was to do, but while Amos was usually able to accomplish anything to which he set his mind, this level of confidence was different.

———————— ● ————————

The *Nordland*, followed by the *Kringflackande*, sailed westward through the Skagerrak, the high-seas highway under which lived all manner of treachery, mostly imagined, but even then only weakly comparable to what, with no imagination, could be found on land.

Pastor Olafson's warnings were validated sooner than later. On the *Nordland* forecastle, Amos studied the seas and silently prayed this would be an uneventful voyage. He noticed that the visceral response to his prayer was silence, as if the answer was no answer. This bothered him. Was he not supposed to go to America? It seemed America was where he was being led. Another hurricane? His hands on the gunwale as he watched the surging swells passing by, he sighed. Improbable, not impossible.

The *Nordland* and the *Kringflackande* carried the same cargo as did the *Polstjärnan* and the *Nordanvinden*, to be delivered to the same customer. Before leaving Göteborg, their destination was revised to Wilmington, Delaware, reflecting the changing tide of the American Civil War, requiring the *Nordland* and the *Kringflackande* to travel further south through the Atlantic. Considering the size of Uncle Torvald's inheritance, Amos decided to keep it hidden on his person at all times.

The "Port of Wilmington" was playing a large role in the War of the Rebellion for both the North and the South because there were two Wilmingtons: the Delaware Wilmington served the North, and the North Carolina Wilmington served the South. Unaware he would visit both, Amos leaned against the gunwale and, once again with time to do so, wondered.

The hurricane directed him from the exporting business to the ministry, and the deterioration of his relationship with Karin facilitated the transition, as did the otherwise unfortunate loss of the *Polstjärnan* and the *Nordanvinden*. All of it was tragic; none of it was as planned – at least not by me, he thought. He stared at the frothing sea. And here I am. Whatever men's dreams and desires, he mused, God's will is done, and so often unpredictably.

As the *Nordland* and the *Kringflackande* sailed into the North Sea, swells raced toward the two ships like guard dogs sniffing for danger or weakness. For the crew, the increasingly frenetic motion of the *Nordland* was disconcerting so soon after the tragic hurricane. Superstitious *Nordland* crewmen watched the waves and glanced at one another. They thought about Amos, what happened to his previous ship and crew, and wondered, could it happen again? Two ships with full cargoes and 145 men went down. Now, beneath a blackening sky, large swells and whitecaps were everywhere, the *Nordland*, rising and falling, creaking loudly, the wind whistling through the shrouds. The crewmen watched warily, studying the large swells around them. Were they jinxed?

The crew knew it was a serious offense but, for the safety of everyone else, a jinx would be thrown overboard if crew members were of uniform mind on the matter. Certainly there was margin for error but, if the feeling was strong enough, crews chanced action over error.

Shortly, two crewmen would attempt to convince the entire crew the ship was indeed jinxed, and the jinx was Amos Nordquist.

19

Stendahl "Sunny" Sundquist and Solsten "Sol" Swenson, long-time companions but new to the crew, were critical of everything. With tongues like bo'sun's rasps, entering their presence was as pleasurable as diving into a migration of sea snakes. Their criticism took the form of repetitive rhetorical questions, the answers to which required extraordinary insight. Many questions simply had no answers.

The imbalance of Sunny and Sol's questioning gave them an edge enabling manipulation of more forthright crew members who, after enduring a barrage of questions, felt sifted like flour.

With hearts as treacherous as black ice on Göteborg tarmacadam, Sunny and Sol squeezed fault out of even the most favorable of events, and when events were unfavorable, their superciliousness was insufferable.

When not at sea, Sunny and Sol often ventured from "Little London" to the real London where they were members in a lesser men's club on Piccadilly near St. James Street. There they enjoyed immoderate surroundings and affected companionship that contrasted with rough, shipboard spaces and "beef-witted" crew members, enabling Sunny and Sol to act out accordingly although, in the eyes of the haut ton, still mushrooms in the rose garden.

Both men were intelligent, of average height, and slender with dark hair covering ears, neck, and partial forehead. Their facial features were attractive; their facial expressions prim. Unlike the other crewmen, they were usually clean-shaven and, when ashore, dressed as if leaving London's Burlington Arcade to attend an operetta.

Serving on a ship enabled opportunity for travel to far-away places occasioning unique and unusual sights and experiences, invariably embellished months later when discussed with other members at the club.

As the ship rose and fell, at a distance Sunny and Sol watched Amos Nordquist, lost in thought while leaning on the stern gunwale near the lifeboat davits.

"Solsten, why is that man repulsive?" asked Sunny, as if making a riddle. Sunny studied Amos carefully. "Would you look at him?"

"Why do you find him repulsive?" asked Sol as he studied Amos. Sonny and

Sol never made statements, and would carry on lengthy conversations consisting entirely of questions in response to questions.

"Why force fancy when one can delightfully despise?" asked Sunny, his eyes growing wide, glittering impishness, and his tongue running along his upper teeth.

Sol smirked and cocked his head as he looked back at Amos, sensing the same sensation as Sunny. "But, yes, specifically, what is it we find so naff [repulsive] about this man?"

"Isn't the saying, '*Le style, c'est l'homme même*'?" said Sunny, raising his eyebrows affectedly, "But if so, why would I still find this homme repulsive…yet not his clobber [attire] or his features?"

"Have we met him before?" Sol asked.

"If we did, wouldn't we remember?"

"What is it, then? Where does this, this…strange aversion come from? Can you explain why I simultaneously want very much to approach him while part of me demands keeping my distance?"

Sunny and Sol appraised Amos's handsome silhouette.

"Would you prefer he look more like Beau Brummell – his portrait at the club?"

"Beau Brummell?" Sol looked at Sunny. "God, Beau Brummell?" Sol smiled. "Oh, but could it be that, even at sea, he brushes his pots [teeth] and takes a daily bath like Beau Brummell?"

Sunny smiled back. "Is there a crew's bathtub aboard?"

"Wouldn't that be splendid?"

Both men knew that if a bathtub were aboard any ship, the tub would be in the captain's stateroom; there would be none for the crew. Most crewmen had never been exposed to continual sanitary living, in any event. In addition, fresh water was too valuable for bathing, while seawater turned soap into insoluble grease. In heavy rain squalls, sometimes men would wash on deck when temperature and sea allowed. The crew depended on nature for whatever improvised sanitation existed. The "head," another example, was a seat at the head of the ship aside the bowsprit base above an opening in the prow where, after use, waves and ship's motion naturally cleansed the unsanitary area, a problem in calm seas.

"If he brushes his pots," asked Sunny, smirking, "I wonder if his mouth is as clean as his clobber?" Sunny snickered wickedly as Sol's mouth opened widely until an unnaturally loud guffaw tumbled out.

"If he were shorter, wouldn't he look like Molly Mousie, that dilly boy on the corner by the club?"

The two men feigned laughter and again stared at Amos who, at a distance, immersed in mentally revisiting the hurricane, thinking of all the men who drowned, continued to absently watch the large swells, unaware he in turn was being watched.

"Isn't he single," asked Sol, "with no children?"

"Children?" Sunny said with a look of exaggerated nausea.

"Didn't I hear something about his girlfriend leaving him?" asked Sol.

"Unusual for someone that attractive and wealthy, wouldn't you say?"

Sunny rested his chin on his palm as he leaned on the gunwale, studying Amos. Sol nodded knowingly at Sunny, and Sunny looked back, his eyes narrowing. "Shouldn't we introduce ourselves?"

"Shouldn't we?"

The two men turned and walked along the deck in Amos's direction.

As they approached Amos, with frigid courtesy Sol asked, "Have we been formally introduced?" His tone suggested a breach of etiquette had occurred and someone was guilty of impropriety.

Pulled from his reverie, Amos looked at the men.

"No, the captain hired you," Amos smiled as he turned toward Sunny and Sol. "How do you do? I'm Amos Nordquist."

"How do we do?" asked Sunny. "Wouldn't that be an interesting topic?"

Amos looked at the two men as something inside him went cold.

"Have you ever been to Piccadilly?" asked Sol, his eyebrows inclined pretentiously.

"No, I haven't."

"But haven't you ever wanted to go there?" asked Sunny in a leading tone of voice.

"I've never thought about it. I've never been there. Why would I go there?"

"Wouldn't meeting a sophisticated, stimulating class of men…men with similar interests…appeal to you?" asked Sunny.

"Do you go there between voyages?" asked Amos as he studied the two men.

"Would we go elsewhere?" responded Sol, a light in his eyes.

"I don't know…but to answer your question directly, I have no desire to go there. I have no desire to spend time there."

Sunny and Sol's emotional momentum decelerated.

"Are you saying it beneath you to go there?" responded Sol,

"Or that we not go there?" added Sunny, folding his arms.

"Perhaps that's a good idea," interjected Amos before Sunny could ask the next question.

"A good idea?" countered Sunny.

"What would be good about it?" asked Sol.

"No doubt you could answer that better than I," responded Amos.

Sol and Sunny snapped a look at one another, and back at Amos.

"Shouldn't we all pursue cultivated living?" asked Sol, brimming with fastidiousness.

"Cultivated living?" Amos responded neutrally, also folding his arms. "I don't know what's going on in your minds, but if you wish to continue 'cultivated living,' it won't involve me."

Sunny drew his head back like a simian about to show his fangs, and looked toward Sol.

"Solsten? Shouldn't we leave this naff to analyze his ocean?"

"Might it be the deepest thing he'll ever consider?"

Sunny looked condescendingly at Amos; then the two men, chins aloft like spars, turned in unison and walked away.

Later that day, the subject of the worsening weather came up in conversation among the crew. Sunny introduced the question of a jinx, someone on board whose presence offended wind and wave, with the potential to send ship and crew to the bottom. When crewmen asked Sunny who he had in mind, folding his arms disdainfully, Sunny questioned why it was so difficult for the others to identify the offender. Sol asked why they did not consider Amos.

"Don't all of you remember what happened the last time he set sail?" questioned Sol.

"How many ships went down along with entire crews?" asked Sunny.

"And is that about to happen again?"

"Isn't the problem clear?"

"No, the problem is not clear!" interjected Second Mate Henrik Haglund, his face clouding over with anger.

"What isn't clear about it?" asked Sol condescendingly, arms folded, eyebrows raised, and head cocked to one side.

"Three things! Whether the sea is about to have a fit! Why we should throw someone overboard to appease the sea! And why it should be Mr. Nordquist – or anyone else – who gets scuppered! That's plenty that isn't clear!"

"And who else might it be?" asked Sol.

"Who else on board has a proven adversarial relationship with the sea?" asked Sunny.

Sunny and Sol peppered the listening crewmembers with questions about why the crew did nothing. When the others said they were watching Amos, along with the wind and the sea, Sunny and Sol milked the crew's irrational superstition with rapid responses alternating like steam engine pistons.

"Isn't it evident the sea dislikes that man?"

"When the sea becomes exasperated, and a tempest arises…?"

"…and waves come over the bow searching for someone…?"

"…wouldn't it be wise to give them what they…?"

"Enough!" barked Haglund angrily, temporarily disrupting the staccato questioning. "Return to your stations!"

Sunny and Sol looked about with imperious hauteur, turned and left to attend to their respective duties as steward's mate and ship's cook.

On the morning of the third day in the Atlantic, the sky turned ominously black, and the edgy men spoke apprehensively about the weather as they worked. Was it going to happen now? Caught up in their irrational gale of subterfuge, Sunny and Sol agitated for action, holding palms up toward a sky grown as dark as the sea, irritably warning that the weather gods of both sea and sky were nearing their wits' end, and the others had better take action. In Amos's absence, a below-decks confrontation developed.

"No, we will not!" shouted red-bearded Henrik Haglund, his teeth gritted.

"Oh? We have time to wait?" Sol countered.

"We'll take time, as much time as there is."

"And will you be like the others," asked Sunny, arms folded, "or will you take responsibility for sending this ship to the bottom?"

"We'll see who takes responsibility for what," Henrik answered angrily.

"Would it not be beneficial if someone on this ship took responsibility for *something*?" asked Sunny as he turned and looked at the men standing behind him.

"Wouldn't I be acting responsibly if I clamped you two in irons? And put an end to this nonsense?! Considering Mr. Nordquist is the ship's owner, what you are suggesting is tantamount to mutiny! Remind yourselves of the punishment for mutiny," said Haglund, grinding his teeth. "You worry about the seas; wanting to placate a storm and save your skins? I'd recommend you take your chances with the sea – for if you commit mutiny over something as groundless as this, and your death does not come from a storm at sea, it will come from the hands of able bodied men following an inquiry on shore. The gallows! You think about that, Mr. Sundquist, Mr. Swenson. Now return to your duties!"

Sunny and Sol looked sullenly at Haglund. The two men simultaneously turned in unison, as if in a drill, and marched away.

The confrontation ended, but Haglund knew the matter was far from over.

"You know," began Haglund, speaking to Yeoman Stein Soderberg after Sunny, Sol and the others had left, "those two are poison. Damn. Why were they brought on board?" Haglund packed tobacco in his pipe, raised the stem to his mouth, and lit the bowl. "This whole throw-Amos-Nordquist-overboard quest of theirs is borderline bizarre."

"Throwing anyone overboard is senseless," said Soderberg, also reaching for his pipe. "But especially Amos." Soderberg looked levelly at Haglund. "For whatever reason, it seems they want to get rid of Amos Nordquist. Really dislike him."

Soderberg reached for his tobacco pouch as Haglund drew on his pipe and added, "They barely know him."

"There's more to this than meets the eye," said Haglund. "It isn't just the weather, the sea or superstition. They're going at this a mite too hard."

Haglund took another draw from his pipe, and blew the smoke toward the topside ladder.

"And this might be a diversion on their part," said Soderberg.

"What do you mean?"

"The *Röda Hund* yeoman and I are old friends," said Soderberg. "My wife and I were down in Höganäs, and I visited him before we left. We were discussing the crew, and when I mentioned those two, he shuddered and shook his head. He told me they served on the *Röda Hund* and became so unpopular they were nearly keelhauled. They talked their way out of it."

"That doesn't surprise me," said Haglund.

"Happened a few years ago."

As Stein Soderberg packed tobacco into his pipe, he glanced up at Henrik Haglund.

"It wasn't just one of them," continued Stein, "but both. Like now, they got the crew all stirred up about something that was nonsense…making a mountain out of a molehill, if that. Some other people wanted to scupper the two of them, just throw them overboard, but cooler heads prevailed. The *Röda Hund* yeoman didn't dwell too long on it but, at the same time, Sundquist and Swenson don't seem to make themselves popular."

Stein shrugged as he lit his pipe.

"So, here they are."

"I'm afraid so."

"They always serve together?"

"Far as I know," said Stein.

Henrik absently unbuttoned his sea coat, turned around and stepped to a nearby table. Stein followed and the two sat down.

"I can see where people would want to throw them overboard," said Henrik, looking toward the bulkhead. "They're two of the most aggravating men I've met. I was close to grabbing both of them and throwing them over the side a moment ago…and placating the sea had nothing to do with it." Henrik looked at Stein. "Did the *Röda Hund* yeoman tell you why people wanted to throw them overboard?"

"Well, that's interesting," said Stein. "They were questioning why the *Röda Hund* could not spend more time in port near London, and why the crew was satisfied drinking in dingy pubs when there were more refined alternatives – implying the crew were riffraff. So, interestingly, the sea was becoming unseasonably rough. Many of the *Röda Hund* crew were convinced that smooth sailing would return if those two were to greet Davy Jones. But senior crew members convinced the others that throwing the two of them overboard would bring bad luck, not good luck, so keelhauling was offered as a compromise, but the captain belayed that too."

Stein looked away, drew on his pipe, and shook his head, wondering.

"If those two refined gentlemen don't learn to be half-way civil soon, luck will have nothing to do with it," muttered Henrik, "unless it's their bad luck. There's nothing wrong with Amos Nordquist; I've known Amos ever since he was little. If someone gets thrown overboard, it'll be those two."

With Sunny and Sol still fanning the flames, superstitious crew members remained apprehensive about the sea that day, and watched for any signal change in weather conditions.

No sooner had the crew settled down when a dramatic incident occurred.

The *Nordland* crow's nest lookout spotted a freak of nature: a huge, distant rogue wave headed toward the *Nordland* and the *Kringflackande*. While surrounding swells were three to five feet in height, this solitary wave was six to seven times as high. The lookout shouted to the men below, and the ship's captain immediately ordered items not already stowed, locked, tied or battened down to be secured. Seamen scrambled throughout the ship.

As Amos secured additional lines, he studied the distant wave as it moved toward the ship like an advancing hillside, recalling how he experienced something similar when serving as a cabin boy many years ago. His father's ship was approaching a Japanese port when the ocean around them, with average waves, seemed to somehow rise and in a moment fall. The sensation came from seeing a distant beach rapidly expand seaward as if someone pulled the plug on the ocean. A moment later, however, the beach disappeared along with the lower land as if it all sank beneath the sea. Minutes later the coastland gradually rose again, and the beach emerged.

What actually happened, Amos saw, was a wall of water obliterating the distant port to where they were heading. If they arrived earlier, the ship and crew would have been destroyed like ships and crews already in port.

The Japanese called this wall of water a *tsunami* or "harbor wave." What Amos presently watched was not a *tsunami*, but a rogue wave, a solitary giant wave at sea. It seemed to come from nowhere. What caused it? Amos wondered.

As the crewmembers raced to secure the ship, Sunny and Sol fired condemning questions at all within earshot, further aggravating an already tense situation.

When everything aboard seemed secure, at the last moment crewmembers lashed themselves to their racks or anything stationary.

The two ships came to starboard, sailing directly toward the wave as it approached. Each helmsman lashed himself to his helm, and kept each bow pointed directly at the approaching wall of water.

As the looming hillside grew near, all prepared for the impact. Amos felt the urge to pray, and prayed that when the wave hit the bow, the two ships would maintain headway and not be turned sideways, capsize and sink.

20

Bearing down on them, in a moment it was within firing distance, preceded by a deep trough as if the sea were genuflecting before the towering wall of water, the frothing ridge like a horse's mane as the wave raced toward the helpless ships.

As the ships' bows headed directly for the approaching giant, the men, lashed in, eyes wide, gripped anything stationary, fearfully holding on as the wave raced up to them. In an instant it was there, towering above them, and the men gasped in unison as the two ships' bows dove into the trough and then shot up the leading edge of the wave surging beneath them, the *Nordland* and the *Kringflackande* racing upward along the watery hillside to the wave's foaming crest, keels exposed from bow to amidships as the ships nosed over and dove down the other side, slamming into the trailing trough, the ocean exploding when enveloping the ships' hulls and portions of the superstructure.

As the ships' buoyancy pushed them back above the surface, seawater pouring through scuppers and gunwales, initially panicked crewmen began to rejoice then yell in excitement.

Many said a quick prayer of thanksgiving as all unlashed themselves, and began worrying about ruptured masts, spars and booms.

The damage to both ships was minor, however. By meeting the oncoming wave head-on, while the ride was terrifying, they avoided catastrophe.

In spite of only minor damage, Sunny and Sol unleashed a torrent of questions. The crew, generally relieved to be alive and grateful the damage was minor, became agitated at another barrage of condemning questions from the two men. No storm or wave on earth can dampen relief and joy like Sunny and Sol, thought Second Mate Henrik Haglund. Concerned about Sunny and Sol's agitating for a sacrifice to "the sea gods," Henrik went to find Amos.

"Amos, I haven't said anything because I didn't want to concern you. There's a problem."

"No doubt. That wave was incredible. I've never seen anything like that," said Amos, shaking his head and smiling with relief. "What happened?"

"It's not about the wave," said Henrik. "I expected much worse but, miraculously, very little happened to either ship or crew. This is a different problem."

As Henrik explained what Sunny and Sol were advocating, Amos's countenance darkened and, upset not-so-much that he was portrayed as a jinx but that anyone was, his anger began to simmer.

"Henrik, I'll get to the bottom of this," said Amos, turning around.

"Amos, that's okay. I'll be…"

Jaws clenched and eyes narrowed, Amos walked rapidly away before Henrik was finished, and searched for Sunny and Sol, finding them in the ship's galley.

"Men!" Amos said loudly, startling Sunny and Sol who froze and stared at him. "What are these rumors about throwing me over the side? That I am a jinx? That the sea will take this ship straight to the bottom if I am allowed to remain aboard? Have you heard this incredibly ignorant rumor?" Sonny and Sol stood frozen. "Surely you two urbane sophisticates must find it difficult to believe there are people on board who would advocate anything so primitively superstitious and lacking in reason!"

Neither man dared incur the disfavor of the other, and both worked to maintain a placid façade. Summoning courage, Sunny spoke first.

"And why," asked Sunny, swallowing, "would it be lacking in reason?"

"Isn't the loss of two ships and 145 men already evidence enough?" asked Sol, encouraged by Sunny's nerve. "Do we just ignore that? Do we…"

"I'll ask the questions!" Amos barked loudly, causing to two men to start. "What is going on in your heads? Your hearts? Why would you even believe there is such a thing as a jinx?"

"Have you never wondered why a tragedy occurs, but then occurs again?" asked Sunny.

"Isn't it possible that whatever-gods-may-be are reacting," added Sol, "and haven't you sensed this reaction: a loathing with no apparent basis but too strong to ignore?"

"Yes, I have," said Amos, eyebrows knitted, "But the basis may be more apparent than you realize. Gods? What 'gods' did you have in mind? Mithras? Poseidon? Njörðr? Ægir? Or is there another diversionary myth I am to believe?"

"Was Jonah a mythical character?" asked Sunny. "Didn't Jonah, on the way to Nineveh, cause the storm? And as the crew waited longer, didn't the storm grow worse? And didn't the storm immediately subside when the crew finally threw Jonah overboard?"

Sol's eyes narrowed as Sunny spoke.

"Jonah was running away from Nineveh," answered Amos, "not going to it as God had commanded him. I am going to America as I believe I am being led to do by God. There's an obvious difference."

"But have you never had a sensation, a voice in your head, warning that someone or something poses a threat?"

"I've never heard voices – fortunately, they'll have little to do with me – but I have sensed danger…and evil," said Amos. "In fact, I do at this moment… perhaps something you picked up in Piccadilly. Regardless of whether the accused is me or anyone else, if I hear any more of this lunacy, I will have you two placed in confinement. Do you understand that?"

Sunny and Sol looked at Amos mulishly, but said nothing as they watched Amos turn and walk away, each imprecating some ill fate that might befall Amos.

"Henrik," said Amos as he approached Henrik Haglund, "I just spoke with Sundquist and Swenson. I made it clear that if they agitate for throwing someone – me or anyone else – over the side, they will spend the rest of the voyage in confinement."

"Yes, sir. I'll tell the captain."

Sunny and Sol did not listen to Amos. Their questioning became ponderously vexing as they continued to remind crewmembers that they were given one last warning, a rogue wave, and that the sea's next action would spell the end of them all if they did not act immediately. Amos Nordquist needed to be scuppered or it would be the entire crew that would pay. Hearing again what was being said, Second Mate Henrik Haglund decided to put an end to it.

"Amos, they're still at it, but before I discipline them, I want to assemble the crew."

"Why?"

"I know you want them placed in confinement, but first I'd like to air this out – hear what the crew has to say."

"Although I think confinement would be fine with the crew," said Amos, "it's not up to the crew."

"At the same time, sir, it might be interesting to hear what the crew has to say." Henrik was determined to have the crew weigh in.

"Very well, then. Summon the crew."

Henrik called a meeting of crew members including Amos. They met on the weather deck, and Sunny and Sol were asked to repeat their accusations. Piqued, their rhetorical questions dripped with displeasure.

When Henrik could stand no more, he loudly interjected, "Sundquist, Swenson, you're absolutely right! Not appreciating you two has resulted in a wasted resource and wasted time. I apologize to both you and the rest of the crew for not realizing the certainty of your position until now."

Amos Nordquist stood among them wondering where Henrik was taking this.

"I have seen the ultimate warning – the day before yesterday it passed beneath our two ships – and I am now prepared to take action on your recommendation."

Sunny and Sol glanced at one another. The second mate finally admitted they were right, they were getting their due, and Amos would be getting his.

"Would you have me do what you have consistently questioned as not being done?" asked Henrik.

"Is there reason to wait?" asked Sol, eyebrows raised, head slightly tilted back.

"Absolute none," agreed Henrik with finality.

Henrik turned to four seamen standing at a short distance to his right.

"Someone, a jinx, is responsible for the huge wave that might have destroyed us," said Henrik, "someone with a history of disruption. As ominous as it was, the rogue wave may be a forewarning of something even worse to come. Knut, Magnus, Carl and Sten, do you see that man there?" Henrik pointed at Amos who looked back puzzled. "Do you believe the jinx is Mr. Nordquist?"

Henrik folded his arms as he awaited their response.

Amos stood slack-jawed as Knut, Magnus, Carl and Sten looked at one another.

Amos? They had worked for Nordquist Shipping Co. for years. Amos, his father, his brother. He was the ship owner. Are ship owners jinxes? And Amos, although an owner, was like one of them. Other than what they heard from Sunny and Sol, none of the four men saw or heard anything that would confirm Amos was a jinx…if a jinx existed. They understood Henrik's question. But… Amos?

They had escaped the rogue wave, and if someone was a jinx, wondered heavy-maned, giant Magnus from Jokkmokk, would that escape have happened? Or was the opposite true: their salvation was due to someone on board being blessed by the Lord? If so, who might that be? Mangus frowned at Knut, Carl and Sten, who frowned back. Amos Nordquist, if anyone, he concluded. Giant Magnus looked down at Henrik.

"No, Mr. Haglund, we do not," Magnus rumbled. Eyebrows knitted, the others nodded.

"Then neither do I," said Henrik.

Sunny and Sol were chagrined. What was this?

Henrik turned to the rest of the crew.

"However, as Sundquist and Swenson have so accurately determined, nevertheless we have a jinx in our midst. Perhaps, who knows, more than one. Yeoman Soderberg," Henrik turned to Stein Soderberg, "do we have a record of anyone with a history of disruption before coming aboard the Nordland?

"Yes, we do, Mr. Haglund," said Soderberg.

"Oh," responded Henrik. "And who might that be?"

"There be two such men, Mr. Haglund." Stein stood solemnly and pointed at Sunny and Sol.

"Both? And on what vessel?"

"The *Röda Hund.*"

"The *Röda Hund*?" protested Sunny. "Can you believe we were almost thrown overboard? How would that covey know any…?"

"Thrown overboard?!" shouted Henrik, silencing Sunny. "Why were you almost thrown overboard?"

Sunny and Sol began to press their innocence with a barrage of questioning, but Henrik cut them off.

"No, no! Let me rephrase the question. What reason do men usually have for throwing a crew member overboard?"

"Why would we be…?"

"Answer the question!"

"Is there a shred of evidence that we were…?"

"Answer the question! What reason do men usually have for throwing another member of the crew overboard?"

Sunny and Sol attempted to formulate a response, but although speaking, essentially said nothing. Impatient, Henrik drew his own conclusion.

"Then the 'jinx' is Swenson and Sundquist," said Henrik, moving toward Sunny and Sol. "Magnus, Knut, throw these two men over the side."

"Aye, aye, sir," said scowling Magnus and Knut as they also moved toward Sunny and Sol who backed away firing an enfilade of defensive questioning.

"Wait!"

The men turned toward the voice of Amos Nordquist who stepped forward. Scuppering Sunny and Sol was not what Amos wanted; he only wanted them placed in confinement.

"Mr. Haglund," said Amos, "I understand how you feel about these two men and am not surprised. The captain hired them because, although they have a history of, as you say, disruption, they are good at what they do." Amos spoke respectfully. "Yes, they are being seditious. As a Christian man, however, what you're proposing to do is wrong."

Amos stepped directly in front of the second mate and spoke in a quiet voice.

"Let me offer this compromise: Swenson and Sundquist will serve on board the *Nordland* in their present capacities until we reach America where I will replace them. Meanwhile, no one will make an attempt on their lives. At your discretion, you may place them in confinement apart from the crew." Amos looked at Henrik for a moment. "Is that clear, Mr. Haglund?"

"Yes sir." Henrik stroked his beard. "If I have leeway to confine them, may I do so at any time I deem appropriate?"

"You may."

"At my discretion?"

"As you wish."

Henrik said nothing as Amos stepped back among the crew.

Henrik Haglund frowned as he studied Sunny and Sol who insolently looked back obliquely, heads lowered and tilted to one side. Henrik turned toward Magnus, Knut, Carl and Sten, but decided this would require only one man.

"Then I will do so…now," said Henrik. "Magnus, escort these bilge rats to the ship's hold – place them in confinement."

Confinement. In the ship's hold. Sometimes extremely cold and sometimes sweltering, but always dank and rank – far from Piccadilly and St. James.

"For how long?" asked Sunny apprehensively.

"I'll let you out three times daily to take care of your duties; then it's back in the hold." Henrik folded his arms. "At least until I think you've learned to keep your mouths shut."

Placing Sunny and Sol in confinement would keep them off the crews' nerves; it also insured they would have considerable time to weigh retribution.

During early afternoon on the third day, two great humpback whales surfaced off the starboard beam. They swam ahead beyond the bow, maintaining the same course as the Nordland and the Kringflackande. Oddly enough, after several hours of leading the two ships, the whales did not leave. Superstitious crewmen considered the whales a good omen and, the weather remaining unchanged and Sunny and Sol out of sight and hearing, the voyage began to seem normal.

The whales stayed ahead of the boats, swimming leisurely to starboard as if wanting the ships to follow, often sounding – powerful, broad tails rising high and gracefully, the spray from their great flukes wind-whipped laterally above the surface, and then, as if pulled from below, the great tails would plunge vertically into the deep. Minutes later the huge creatures would rise again, blowing geysers upon breaking the surface. Amos and the men watched the whales, and marveled at their size, symmetry and seeming sentience.

Whales are unlike other sea creatures, thought Amos as he leaned on a forward gunwale watching. They seem to have identities, personalities, and know who they are. Amos knew whaling men who remarked that whales just seemed to know, like people know. Amos remembered that his father once said whales have memories – elephants of the sea – and could recognize ships from earlier encounters, even after many years passed. At this moment, it was as if the whales knew these ships, these waters, and these men, and like trail guides, were escorting the two crews through unfamiliar territory.

Watching the big whales, Amos considered that in spite of their size, blue whales, gray whales, right whales, humpbacks, and sperm whales are not the rulers of the sea. Killer whales can discriminately attack dolphins, calves, sharks, anything else that swims, but nothing attacks killer whales.

If any creature rules the ocean, thought Amos – apart from whatever causes Skagerrak vortexes, he smiled – it's the killer whale.

Amos remembered a fascinating scene in the Norwegian Sea along the northern Norwegian coast years earlier: adult killer whales acting as a team teaching a nearby juvenile killer whale who was watching motionlessly, snout vertical, eyes above the water, how to dislodge seals taking refuge on small, isolated chunks of ice.

Several adult killer whales came together forming a close group, side-by-side, at a short distance from the seal's tiny ice island, and swam toward the seal's small refuge, the motion of the large, side-by-side killer whales creating a trailing wave big enough to wash over the ice and dislodge the seal. But how, wondered Amos, did they learn this teamwork in the first place, much less communicate to the young killer whale what they were going to do, and that the youngster was to watch and learn?

They talk; they somehow talk, was all Amos could imagine. And he imagined the conversation.

"Now, you stay over there and watch carefully as we form a tight group, swim towards the seal's small ice refuge, causing a wave large enough to wash the seal off the ice," said the eldest killer whale. "Do pay close attention, please."

I wonder what their language sounds like? Amos silently asked himself. What he watched was obviously a teaching session, for the killer whale-induced wave did indeed wash the panicked seal off the ice, but the killer whales then seemed to hang around, allowing the seal to clamber back on the ice.

What then?

For the benefit of the small killer whale, the adults did it again.

When they were finished, Amos imagined the elder killer whale saying, "Make no mistake, this is how it is done. Do you understand now?"

"Yes I do," said the young killer whale.

"Are you certain?" asked the elder, unconvinced. "Observe once more."

And as the young killer whale again watched, the adult killer whales formed a tight group, swam toward the ice flow, creating a trailing wave large enough to wash the seal into the sea – only this time, to complete the lesson, the seal was summarily dispatched.

The lesson completed, all killer whales left, presumably to find another unfortunate. Had the young killer whale been inattentive, all was not lost, for Amos's knowledge of dislodging seals from chunks of Arctic ice was enhanced considerably.

The strong wind placed the *Nordland* and the *Kringflackande* ahead of westward schedule, but also created greater leeway, pushing them further south. The Nordland's sailing master, however, liked the headway they were making, and drew comfort from the accompanying leviathans. Course adjustments, he decided, could wait until the two ships were closer to North America.

At a considerable distance off the starboard bow, the great whale flukes rose again simultaneously, hesitated as if waving, and again plunged into the deep. Crewmen topside awaited the inevitable geysers, but minutes added to minutes with no change, and wave after monotonous wave barged southwesterly.

Nothing else.

The men continued to watch for longer than was reasonable, waiting.

But there was nothing. The whales were gone.

As the *Nordland* and the *Kringflackande* sailed on, the crews felt oddly alone.

For days the skies remained overcast until early one evening the clouds began to break up, and a twilight sky appeared, bright and multi-colored. Able to take a fix on the early evening stars, Henrik Haglund found leeward motion had been greater than reckoned, and if they continued their present course, they would arrive somewhere along the north coast of South Carolina. The course was immediately corrected, but when the *Nordland* and the *Kringflackande* sighted the east coast of North America a few days later at an early daylight hour, they were still far south of Wilmington, Delaware. Changing course once again, with a slight, westerly breeze, the ships crept slowly north.

At approximately 12:00 p.m. with the noonday sun illuminating the shimmering sea all about them, the two Swedish ships of sail, delivering goods to the Union, were spotted by a steam-driven Confederate commerce raider.

21

September 8, 1864

On the horizon, heading toward the *Nordland* and the *Kringflackande* in the bright sunlight was a black, steam propelled, Confederate side-wheeler, a fast-moving commerce raider which the captain reckoned would overtake them within an hour. There was no escape.

Amos knew the Confederacy had attempted to put together a Navy, preferably ironclad, but had little iron ore, limited means to ship the ore by rail to Southern refineries to be made into steel plates, and then ship the steel plates to the only Southern shipbuilding facility, in New Orleans, capable of mass-producing large ironclads. Alternative attempts to solidify working relationships with potentially sympathetic European nations, including Sweden, involved an inordinate amount of time and disappointment before being discarded. The brief exception was England which agreed to manufacture unarmed commerce raiders for a foreign government – without divulging who the government was. The unarmed commerce raiders were then sailed from England to a foreign port, such as the Azores, where they were armed, and placed under command of Confederate captains. This ploy lasted only a short time before being discovered, and was greatly protested by the Union and many in England, whereupon it was discontinued by the British government.

Amos also knew the Confederate strategy initially also included conventional privateers – private vessels issued a letter of marque and reprisal by the Confederate government, formally engaging them to capture and sell enemy merchant shipping, usually to the Confederate government, for profit. Used by all nations – the most famous privateer commander was Sir Francis Drake, whose patron was Elizabeth I – they were generally recognized by international convention and, if captured, although the ships and hard-earned cargo were lost, crewmembers would normally not be charged with piracy and hung. Some, however, including privateers themselves, believed privateers were little better than pirates, and hangings did occur. Privateers operating for the Confederacy found the limited profit not worth the effort and risk, and while formal Confederate commerce raiding using state-owned ships continued, privateering died out.

By 1864, as an evasive means against commerce raiders in dangerous waters, Federal merchant ships began flying flags of neutral countries, but Amos knew the ploy had become an open secret, and even then, if a merchant ship actually was from a neutral country but carrying goods for the North, the merchant ship might still be raided by the South, precluding supplies being delivered to the Union, those same supplies desperately needed by the Confederacy. Consequently, although the *Nordland* and the *Kringflackande* flew flags of a neutral country, Amos figured this made little difference to the approaching Confederate commerce raider.

The wind and the angle of the commerce raider approach discouraged the *Nordland* and the *Kringflackande* from turning out to sea, and the *Nordland* captain maintained the present course, considering his options.

Standing rod-straight, the captain sternly studied the distant enemy raider. To him this moment was incredulous. The incentive seemed moderate at best; the *Nordland* and the *Kringflackande* were carrying linen, not gold, not weaponry. Historically, however, raiders would take whatever they could lay hands on. Food, nautical items, textiles, and medical supplies were valuable, while jewels were of less value because they were hard to sell. Seldom-discovered gold was the optimum prize, but whatever could be immediately used or resold was of value.

Amos was equally surprised. He made previous trips without incident. This was not supposed to happen – perhaps two years ago, but not now. Obviously, they were further south than realized.

The crew raced about. Every firearm on board was brought to bear, and cannon made ready. Then the men watched as the long, black, sidewheel steamer, stacks billowing black smoke, became more ominous as the distance closed within a league, a little over three miles. The *Nordland* captain figured that the smaller, less defensible *Kringflackande* might be the raider's primary target, and gave orders for the *Nordland* to fall back, sailing close by the *Kringflackande* to starboard, making it difficult to isolate the *Kringflackande*.

The moment reminded Amos of when, as a cabin boy on one of his father's ships, they left the Nazareth River in Orungu along the west coast of Africa. They had traded for a shipment of ivory – tusks and large fragments. When asked about the fragments, the tribesmen drew pictures in the sand of giant creatures they called mokèlé-mbèmbé, one with a snake-like head, long neck, elephant-like body, and long, thick tail, and another with a small head, long neck, long tail, and a name that translated as "planks on its back." The tribesmen said mokèlé-mbèmbé lived in the jungle far up the river.

With the ivory, as they sailed northward along the coast, a pirate ship sailed out of a concealed cove in pursuit. Before leaving Sweden, however, Captain Nordquist had the prescience to have cannon set at oblique angles on the aftcastle and forecastle – whereas cannon were conventionally set in gunwales at 90 degrees, requiring an attacking or defending ship to be broadside if cannon fire were to hit anything. Captain Nordquist waited until the pirate ship came within 40 meters off the starboard quarter before ordering fire at the base of the pirate ship main mast when the cannon angle was optimum.

Amos held his ears as the cannon boomed at close quarters, hitting the main mast base before the pirate ship was in position to fire back, snapping the base, with the mast falling to starboard, ensnarling sail, shroud, and stays. Losing headway, the pirate ship began to fall back as the Nordquist cannons were quickly reloaded. In a moment they thundered at the pirate ship foremast, resulting in an indirect hit and damage to the forecastle. Although the pirate ship foremast was not completely ruptured, enough damage was sustained to where the pirate captain was made to furl foremast sails – allaying wind pressure – until the damage could be repaired. Partially shrouded in cannon smoke, the pirate ship fell far behind…where it would stay.

Through his long glass, the *Nordland* captain studied the Confederate raider, looking hard for any detail that might enable him to better prepare for battle. As he squinted, his trained eye took in everything about the approaching raider. It had two spar masts, one fore and one aft – schooner rigged – and two stacks along the centerline aft of amidships. The bow symmetry was oddly attractive; the hull long – over 200 feet – and sleek. It seemed well-designed for its job. But as the captain studied the commerce raider, something wasn't right.

At a distance, the raider looked threatening, but now, as the raider closed, its appearance became more and more innocuous. There were relatively few men topside, and those visible seemed unusually relaxed for men about to go into battle. And it was not heavily armed.

NCS Advance

As Amos and the captain watched, the long, side-wheel steamer soon overtook and passed the *Nordland* and the *Kringflackande* to starboard, obviously in a hurry to reach some North Carolina port.

"No," muttered the *Nordland* captain, "obviously not a commerce raider."

Standing next to the captain as the ship passed by them, through his long glass Amos could read the name on the stern. "*Advance.*"

"She's a blockade runner," said the captain.

The *Advance* was one of a dwindling number of Confederate blockade-runners attempting to deliver goods to a Confederate port – as the *Nordland* and the *Kringflackande* were attempting to deliver goods to a Union port.

For a few moments the captain kept his crew at their battle stations, and watched as the *Advance* distanced herself. Then he turned to the first mate and ordered all arms be re-stowed.

The crew did so with relief and a spattering of complaining because of the false alarm.

When passing by the merchant vessels, the *Advance* captain also studied the *Nordland* and the *Kringflackande* through his long glass. The *Advance* was owned by the state of North Carolina to enhance North Carolina commerce as well as the war effort, and was technically not part of what remained of the Confederate navy. In addition to the activities of Union blockades, the *Advance* captain was very familiar with shipping activities in North Carolina ports. He knew the two ships flying the blue and yellow Swedish flag were not expected by the state of North Carolina, and probably no other Southern state. Swedish merchant commerce with the Confederacy was non-existent, implying that while the flags were Swedish, the ships were not.

"What would a Swedish sailing ship and brig be doing off the coast of North Carolina?" wondered the *Advance* captain out loud. "If they're Swedish, I'm Gustavus Adolphus."

If the *Advance* slipped through the Federal blockade and arrived at its destination – expected to occur at around 1:30 a.m. the next morning – the *Advance* captain would report his sighting of two slow moving, weakly armed, merchant vessels under sail for the North.

Under cover of darkness, the black *Advance* steamed underneath a Union blockade, was detected, but outran a Union steamship, heading past the Smith's Island Confederate battery and up fortified Cape Fear River, arriving in Wilmington, North Carolina shortly after 1:30 a.m. on Sept. 9, 1864. Confederate authorities were duly notified of the two merchant ships heading north.

A short while later in the darkness, a smaller schooner-rigged steamship slipped out of the Wilmington harbor under sail, traveled downriver, around the south side of Smith's Island at the river mouth, and daringly into the Atlantic, hugging the coastline for a considerable distance, undetected, before firing up the boilers and heading out to sea. Using dead reckoning based on the *Advance* captain's estimate of merchant vessel position, the steamship went hunting the *Nordland* and the *Kringflackande*, ducks on a pond.

If the Union did not receive the cargo on board, whatever it might be, that was an accomplishment. If, however, the raider seized shipments and ships, the South would be thrice served.

In moonlight streaming between broken clouds, the *Nordland* and the *Kringflackande* were sighted to the southeast at about 3:30 a.m., several miles off the coast with most of the crew asleep. Seas were moderate. The raider steam engines were shut down, and the raider launched four boats, six men in each.

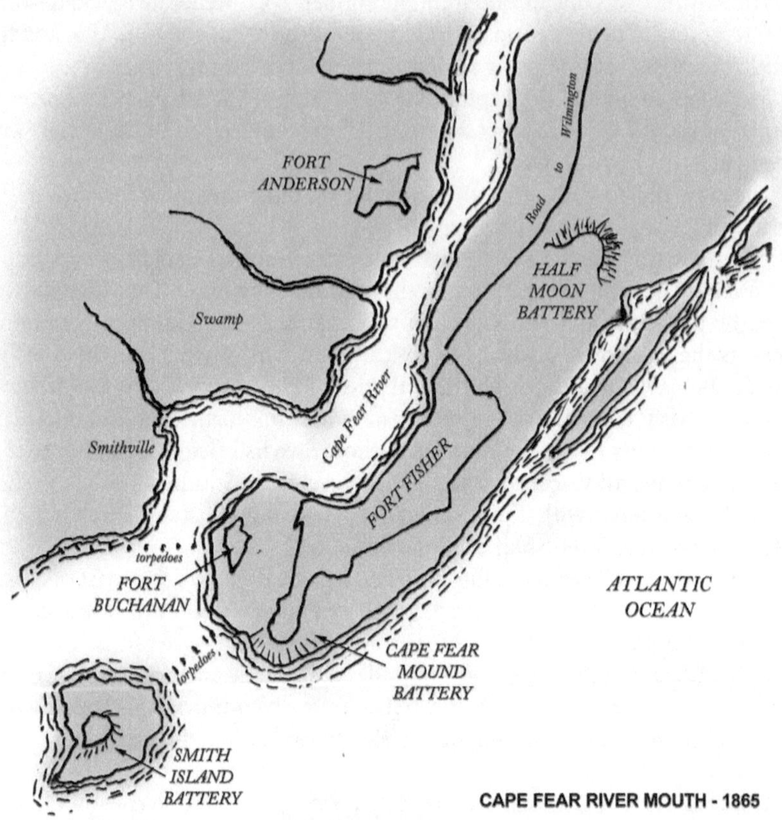

The *Nordland* and the *Kringflackande* were making slow, tedious headway, and the helmsmen were lost in thought, while the men on watch were half asleep. At approximately 4:00 a.m. in the moonlight, two boats silently approached the sterns of the *Nordland* and the *Kringflackande* while the remaining two boats lay-to at a short distance in the dark, awaiting a signal from the boarding parties.

Boarding quickly and silently, the Confederates commandeered each helm, subdued each watch, and signaled the remaining two boats.

All marauders aboard, they rudely awoke the ships' captains, signaled the commerce raider of successful boardings, and at gunpoint began forcing the awakened crew, including Amos, to the quarterdeck.

"Everyone up! Outta your racks!" shouted the marauder hoarsely. "C'mon! To the quarterdeck! Let's go!" He fired a round into the overhead, and the ear-splitting report in close quarters got everyone up and moving faster, no questions asked. "Up the ladder! To the quarterdeck! Now! Move!"

In the wake of the *Advance* scare, Amos looked heavenward and wondered, what is going on?

The commerce raider came alongside to starboard, and the marauders began putting full, oarless lifeboats over the larboard side every five minutes in order to scatter them adrift in the dark, keeping enough crewmen to form skeleton crews, inadvertently including Sunny and Sol in the *Nordland* hold. As Amos's lifeboat was lowered into the water, he quietly placed his right palm on his shirt directly over Uncle Torvald's inheritance, assuring himself it was there.

Returning the assault boats aboard the raider, under continued cover of darkness the raider steamed several miles to the shoreline and then north to the mouth of the Cape Fear River, immediately protected from Union blockade ships by the Smith's Island battery and large Ft. Fisher. Confederate contingents remained on board the *Nordland* and the *Kringflackande*, guarding the skeleton crews.

Meanwhile, the commandeered Swedish vessels headed west toward the coast, making better headway because of coastal breezes, and then north again. At about 9:00 a.m. ½ mile off the mouth of Cape Fear River, as the Confederates aboard anticipated, a Union blockade steamship bore down on them. The Confederate leader gave the *Nordland* captain a warning.

"If y'all wanna live t' tell your gran'kids about this, don't breathe a word about anything bein' wrong," said the raider leader. "Everything's fine. Y'all jes' got blown south. Understand?" The Swedish captain understood.

To prevent any bloodshed, the *Nordland* captain, as ordered, gave no indication anything was wrong and, his Swedish accent unintentionally prominent, told the Union captain they were blown substantially off-course, and were heading to Wilmington, Delaware.

"If that's true," said the Union captain, "I'd like to see your manifest."

The *Nordland* captain provided the ship's manifest, as ordered.

After allowing the *Nordland* and the *Kringflackande* to pass, the two Swedish ships slowly sailed off and, as the Union captain watched, furtively drifted toward the mouth of Cape Fear River. With the two ships at a considerable distance, the Union captain continued to watch, perplexed.

"Where the hell are they going? They're drifting dangerously close to Ft. Fisher gun range."

"It appears they're intentionally heading for the river mouth," said the executive officer.

The blockade crew half-expected barnacles below the waterline would be dislodged by the captain's profanity, heard throughout the ship.

Meanwhile the *Nordland* and the *Kringflackande*, under protection of Ft. Fisher guns, entered Cape Fear River, took a river pilot aboard, and slowly headed up to the port of Wilmington where the two cargoes were unloaded, and the raiders rewarded for a job well done.

Less than a week later on September 10th, the unusually lucky *Advance* would see its luck run out as it set out on its 21st run and was overtaken by a faster, heavily armed, Federal blockade steamship. As with so many of its sister blockade runners, the sleek *Advance* was subsequently made to serve the North, and ironically participated in Union assaults on Ft. Fisher that December and the following January.

Meanwhile, Amos was once again adrift at sea.

————————————◆●◆————————————

The wind caused a choppy sea to further scatter the lifeboats at distances precluding effective vocal communication in the darkness. All were drifting slowly toward the southern North Carolina coast.

That morning the overcast sky was pewter gray, and visibility was poor. On three occasions, ships at a distance were sighted, and the men undertook microcosmic mayhem, but to no avail.

By the end of the first day, the other lifeboats were so distant that it seemed all were going separate ways. Throats were dry, but this lifeboat had no water or food stored; an unfortunate oversight.

"Mr. Nordquist, we all could sure use a drink of water about now," said one of the men wishfully, speaking what others were thinking, while looking at the ocean surface.

"I know," responded Amos as he continued to look toward the west. "Let's pray about it. In fact, I want us to pray as a group at least twice each day until we're out of this difficulty."

They prayed for water, and good health.

One of the men asked Amos what it was like floating in the Atlantic after the hurricane. Amos told the story, discussing the problems, giving directions about what to do and not to do, using Jens and the others as examples. Although it was unnecessary, he warned the men not to drink any of the seawater all around them.

That evening they prayed again for water.

"How do you expect we're going to get drinking water, Mr. Nordquist?"

"Through faith," answered Amos. "Faith is God speaking to you. The Bible is full of examples where faith is rewarded."

"That was a long time ago."

"God is here now just as He was there then. Do you have faith?"

The other man shrugged.

"No? Do you expect to be rewarded for what you have not received?"

"How come God quit performing miracles?" the other man asked. "In the Bible there were all kinds of miracles."

"But not enough to get everyone's attention," answered Amos.

Amos again felt a summons to pray, and looked at the others. "We are to pray some more."

The men prayed again and when darkness fell, slept. During the early morning twilight hours they were awakened by rainfall, a light squall that seemed to calm the waves. The men used hats and hands to catch rainwater to drink.

The squall kept up for several hours, and when it had lifted, the men were no longer thirsty.

During midmorning, several flying fish, avoiding larger predators below the surface to the west, shot out of the water and flew over the boat. Their expansive dorsal fins a blur like hummingbird wings, they could fly above the waves at speeds approaching 60 knots for distances of up to 100 meters, using their tails as ailerons. Amos recalled many earlier voyages when he would arise in the morning, go topside, and discover dead flying fish on the deck. In the darkness, they would hit ship bulkheads with enough impact to instantly kill the fish. Their trajectory would take some of them a few feet above the heads of the men, and short-but-quick Gunnar Engvall stood up and caught one out of the air. The squirming fish in his hand, he looked triumphantly at the other men.

Food.

One of the men with a pocketknife cleaned the fish, cut it into small fillets, then cut the fillets into small strips.

"Flying fish sashimi," said the man, who had been to Japan. Amos nodded.

The boat was being pushed by wind and wave toward land, and hope grew commensurately with the gradual increase in land visibility. Amos knew they had drifted considerably north, and he could see, far to the southwest, stationary ships. Blockade ships. The men were north of the Cape Fear River mouth. As they were pushed by wind and tide, shoreline visibility was becoming clearer. Within a few hours the mild surf began to expedite their ride into shore until they were in water shallow enough for Magnus and Knut to slide over the side and pull the boat up to the beach.

Unsure of whether or not they would need the lifeboat again, once they reached the shoreline they pulled the boat well up on the beach and rested for about 10 minutes. Amos felt under his shirt. The inheritance and additional money were dry and securely in place.

West of the beach were salt marshlands, with hills beyond, and, after resting, he told the men they should walk through the marshlands to the mainland and look for a stream as a water source. The distance wasn't far, but after they reached a second beach on the other side of the marsh, they again rested.

"Do any of you men," asked Amos pointing westward, "feel strong enough to climb that embankment there, and climb a tree to look around? Perhaps there is some sign of community nearby."

"I'll do it," said Gunnar "Shorty" Engvall, all of 5' 2".

As the other men watched, Shorty got up, walked to the compacted sandy embankment and began scaling it slowly like a fly on a wall.

God bless Shorty, thought Amos, turning to the others.

"Henrik, Hans, Carl, Johan," said Amos, "I want you to walk south along the beach looking for anything of use or value, especially a stream flowing into the ocean. Sten, Magnus, Knut, you come with me. We'll head north. Men, we should all return to this spot just before the sun sets."

He turned in Shorty's direction and yelled, "Shorty, if you return here before we do, wait."

Amos heard Shorty acknowledge the command, and the men started out in their respective directions.

The men who walked to the south returned about an hour before sunset. They waited for Amos and his group, and Shorty Engvall. The north group returned a half hour later.

"We found a small stream about two miles south," said Henrik. "Water tasted brackish. Looks like there's also a fort further down. That's what's keeping blockade ships at a distance."

"But let's not go to the fort," suggested Henrik. "We may never get out of here. Did you find anything?"

"Yah, we did," said Amos. "There's a thickly forested inlet with a large stream about a mile or so up the beach. I walked up the stream a ways. It looks promising; from what I could see, it may be fed from a small lake further inland. When Shorty returns, we'll head on up there."

Amos and the two teams sat on a bleached log waiting for Shorty who appeared just before the sunset.

"What did you find? Water?" asked Shorty, bent over, his hands on his knees, breathing heavily.

'Yah," said Amos. "We'll take you to it."

"That's alright. I found some too." Shorty sat down, his mouth half open, and lay back on the sand still breathing hard. "There's something west. Quite a ways. I saw smoke. Probably 15-20 miles. Maybe more. Also, way out at sea to the south…some ships. Didn't seem to be…going anywhere."

"Union blockade," said Sten.

"Could be a Confederate port down there."

"Charleston?"

"No, no. Charleston is much further south," said Amos. "In South Carolina. And from what I've read, nothing gets in and out of Charleston anymore."

Amos led the men to the inlet and stream to the north. They would get water, and begin the trek west through the woods to whatever was west of them.

During late morning as they walked through the woods, they began to see signs of community – an occasional distant farmhouse, farm fences.

"I don't know," said Shorty. "A bunch of us walking through someone else's woods, and there's a war going on here. It makes me nervous."

"Are you afraid we'll get shot at?"

"Well, maybe. If not, someone's bound to wonder who we are and why we're here…walking through the woods. And what if some armed authorities come after us and ask? Or worse, don't ask. But if someone asks, what are we going to say?"

"We'll just tell them Yankees took our ship," said Sten, "set us adrift, we floated to shore and we're trying to find our way to whatever town is around here."

"What if they ask which ship, and discover we were really helping the North?" asked Shorty. "I don't need to get shot or go to some Confederate prison. And, if you don't mind me asking, where are we going?"

"We don't know," said Amos. "We won't know until we get there."

"Well, then, why are we going there?"

"Where else would you like to go, Shorty?" asked Henrik.

Shorty looked back and shrugged his shoulders.

"Right now, we'd better be careful. You know what I mean?" Shorty said nervously. "Even if we aren't spotted by authorities, well, I've read stories about hill people in this part of the world."

22

M r. Nordquist," said Shorty apprehensively after they walked a while, "before we left Sweden, I was reading a story in the *Göteborgs-Posten* about a Confederate prison, Camp Sumter." Shorty glanced obliquely at Amos, who continued to look at the beach before him as they walked. "We don't want to go to one of those."

"What did you read?"

"Well, I don't know how much can be believed – although actually written by a former guard, it all sounded incredible – but maybe there's some truth there."

"What was incredible?" asked Amos.

"It said prisoners were starving." Shorty glanced at Amos. "And it said Confederate guards were having enough trouble feeding themselves, much less Union prisoners. Prisoners are packed together like sardines, many sick because of no shelter or sanitation, and running through the middle of the camp is a creek used for bathing, drinking water, and sewage. But it isn't being used properly because the whole place smells like a cesspool. The story said the prison is by a swamp, rats are all around, and prisoners are dying from disease and dysentery. And on top of that, there is a gang of prisoners who bully and steal whatever they can from weaker prisoners."

While continuing to walk, Amos looked down at Shorty with a grim expression.

"We just had a run-in with Confederates," continued Shorty, "and wasn't that fun? If someone asks us who we are and why we're here, walking sort of lost, like we are, what are we going to tell them? Mr. Nordquist, I don't want to end up in a Confederate prison camp."

"Nor do I," was all Amos could say.

Hiking through the marsh areas, woods and thick underbrush took effort, but as sunset twilight began, they found a road that meandered westerly through woods. The men were prepared to dive to either side should someone approach at a distance. They saw no one and continued to walk, not talking, as night fell. After about three miles, they walked along a moonlit ridge overlooking a large river to the west. Along the river below in the moonlight they saw rooftops and street lamps over a wide swath fronting the river from north to south. They saw the roofs of silhouetted commercial buildings and homes including large southern mansions, and moonlit church steeples.

"Look at all that," said Shorty softly as he studied the scene. "What is this place? Look at the wharfs and ships along the river."

"Let's head down there," said Amos.

"We need to act like we belong here," said Henrik. "We can't be gawking around, looking like we don't know where we are. Somehow we need to look like we fit in."

As they came closer, in the dark they attempted to act like they were part of the community, walking two abreast, pretending to know where they were going.

Entering the town, they seemed unnoticed by the locals. In fact, however, the act was backfiring: by trying hard to be unnoticeable, they stuck out like blue and yellow lighthouses. Not certain of what to do, where to go, they chose the direction with the highest comfort level, walking toward the docks. Upon approaching the docks, it was evident this was certainly not Charleston. First, Charleston harbor was fed by three rivers, not one, and looked out toward the Atlantic, making Charleston easy to blockade. This city was inland on a large river leading to the Atlantic, and not easy to blockade. And, secondly, if nothing could get in or out of Charleston, the men would not be staring at the *Nordland* and *Kringflackande*.

For a moment no one said anything until Shorty, looking wide-eyed at the others, loudly whispered, "We can steal them back!"

Amos looked at Shorty, back at the *Nordland* and *Kringflackande*, and at the other men, their facial expressions reflecting a readiness to commandeer their ships at any moment.

"We can do it!" whispered Shorty excitedly. "We can set sails! No one knows we're here! And it's getting late!"

"Let's get closer," said Henrik.

The men continued walking toward the docks.

"Mr. Nordquist," said Shorty, "we can't get both boats underway. There are too few of us."

"Where are the others?" asked Sten.

The skeleton crews? Where were the skeleton crews that brought the boats into Wilmington harbor?

"They're still on board," said Henrik, looking at the two ships.

"How do you know?"

"Look down there. The ships are being guarded. See?"

Yes, that was it. Amos and the others could see that the *Nordland* and *Kringflackande* were being guarded by several young Confederate soldiers, probably no older than 13 or 14. The skeleton crews were still aboard.

At a distance, however, two crew members were returning, under guard, having spoken with a Confederate official. Seeing Amos and the men studying the ships at a distance, the two crew members stopped in their tracks.

"Are you certain there is no chance for a prisoner swap?" hurriedly asked one of the two crewmembers.

The head of the guard, an older sergeant who walked with a pronounced limp, looked at the crewmember.

"Wish we could," responded the sergeant. "But the boys up north don't wanna do that no more. Why you askin'? Ain't 'a gonna be swappin' you. That'd be no way repay how you helped us when we let you out of the hold."

The sergeant looked ahead toward the docks.

"But what if you had a prisoner who was very wealthy?" asked the first crewmember. "Wouldn't that create an unexpected opportunity?"

"What d'ya mean?"

"What would you expect to obtain in a swap for such a prisoner?" asked the first crewmember.

"Have you heard of the word 'ransom'?" clarified the second.

"You sayin' we got someone on board one a' those boats who's a mite well-off?" asked the sergeant. "How come you didn't say anything before?"

"Did I say he was on one of those boats?" asked Sol. "But then when is a prisoner not a prisoner? And when not a prisoner, how could that man quickly become a prisoner?"

"What the hell're you jabberin' about?"

"Would we have introduced this discussion were we unable to provide a wealthy prisoner?"

The sergeant looked at the men. I'm to beginning to dislike these two, he thought.

"How much wealth 'r we talkin' about?" asked the sergeant.

"How much wealth would you like?" responded the first crewmember. "To begin with, how about those two ships and several more?"

"And how about an international exporting business?" added Sunny.

"Which color do you like best? Red, white, blue, or gold?"

The guard thought for a moment. Damn, these two are annoying. Never say anything. Everything is a damned question.

"We'll go down t' the boats an' you two boys can point out the wealthy gent."

"What makes you think he's aboard?"

"Alright, then, wherever the hell he is," said the sergeant, exasperated. "Where is he?"

"First, shouldn't there be some form of reward? For us?"

"Like what?"

"Why not do something, eh, more accommodating?" suggested Sol. "Why not just all agree that if Stendahl and I identify the man with all that wealth, we go free?"

"Free t' do what?" laughed the sergeant. "What c'n you two birds do around here?"

"Can you think of any reason we shouldn't work for you? Wouldn't that benefit everyone?" asked Sol, nodding.

Sunny pointed at Sol. "Did you know this man is a competent chef cuisinier?"

The sergeant looked back at Sunny, puzzled, as Sol pinched the lapels of his coat, his head raised slightly, eyebrows arched.

"And did you know that this man," said Sol, nodding at Sunny, "is a formidable haberdasher in addition to being one of the most organized record-keepers, for both personnel and inventory, you will find?"

The sergeant looked at Sol. What the hell is a formidable haberdasher?

"Wouldn't you want someone highly skilled, highly organized and fastidiously conscientious?" asked Sunny imperiously. The sergeant looked at Sunny, at Sol, and back at Sunny.

"So, why wouldn't you want our services," quickly asked Sol, "providing more enjoyable meals and carefully monitoring your considerable inventory, saving you trouble and money?" The sergeant looked back and forth at Sunny and Sol.

"Sergeant, tell me, do you like record keeping?" asked Sunny.

"No one likes record keepin'," said the sergeant who was illiterate, able to write only his name, and had never learned to count past 25, the family farm never having more than 25 head of anything.

"Tell you what, you show me that wealthy gent an' I'll bring you up t' the lieutenant." The sergeant continually looked back and forth at Sunny and Sol. "Yeah, sounds like you two boys'd come in handy."

Sol turned and faced the harbor. Down the darkened street, about 50 feet away, Amos and the men stood quietly weighing the status of the *Nordland* and *Kringflackande*.

"Do you see those men in front of us?" asked Sol. "Do they look like familiar Confederate soldiers or townsfolk?"

"Nope. Never seen 'em before."

"Who do you suppose they are?" Sol looked at the sergeant who, in the darkness, continued to study the men 50 feet away. "Is it possible they're Swedish like us?"

Sol beamed as the sergeant looked at Sol, and then back at Amos and the others.

"They evidently made their way asho'wah an' foun' their way he'yah."

"Could the Cause benefit if I identified the wealthy one by walking up to him and simply patting him on the back?" smiled Sol.

"Yeah, that'd do it," said the sergeant, looking at Sol neutrally. "But wait here with these two so'jers before you go identifyin' anyone," said the old guard, "whiles I grabs a few more boys from the guardhouse over there."

The sergeant brought back four more young guards, and they followed Sunny and Sol down the street, approaching Amos, Shorty, Magnus and the others who were still in discussion about the *Nordland* and *Kringflackande*.

"Still," whispered Shorty, "no one knows we're here. We can slip down there without anyone…"

"Amos Nordquist? Well, isn't it wonderful you have arrived?" asked Sol

Swenson in Swedish as he walked up to Amos. Smiling, Sol reached out and patted Amos on the back as if the two were inseparable friends.

Amos turned and looked at Sol and Sunny.

"Whe'yah y'all from?" came a voice from behind Amos.

Amos tensed for a moment as he understood what was happening, and slowly turned around in front of six armed Confederate soldiers led by an older sergeant who, in contrast to the jittery young guards pointing their rifles at Amos and the others, saw no need to draw his revolver from its holster.

Amos spoke English well. As with all Scandinavians and Southerners, even with an excellent command of the English language, Amos's response would communicate more than just the words.

"Well," began Amos, "I suppose you can tell we are not from here."

Glancing at one another, the young Confederate soldiers guffawed at the English statement, edges frayed with a Scandinavian accent.

"Yeeup." The Confederate sergeant smiled pleasantly. "Yo'wah two friends he'yuh," the sergeant glanced at Sunny and Sol, "confirmed tha'yat a moment ago." He then nodded politely before he spat chewing tobacco to one side.

"Now, y'all wouldn't be interested 'n spendin' some mo'wah time on one 'a they'em they'ah boats, would y'?" he asked hospitably. The young Confederate soldiers raised their weapons slightly. "They'ah good boats. Made in Sweden, I he'yah."

The men looked at the *Nordland* and *Kringflackande*. Be it ever so humble..., Amos thought.

As the men were led down to the *Nordland* and *Kringflackande* to rejoin their shipmates, Amos glanced back at Sunny and Sol who were still standing in the road watching the men and guards walking toward the docks. Amos stopped, and the others stopped. Amos turned and spoke loudly in Swedish to Sunny and Sol.

"I assume you have chosen to unite with those taking us prisoner, is that correct?"

Sunny and Sol knew their perfidy was unconscionable, but had the temerity to display a façade of insouciant nonchalance. Sunny slowly put his hands in his pockets, and uncharacteristically neither Sunny nor Sol spoke.

Amos studied the two men as their countenance slowly changed to solemnity. Amos turned his back, the implication unmistakable, and the group under guard continued toward the docks. Betrayal was the basis of their scheming aboard, Amos thought, and is so now. As he walked, however, his inner voice commanded he pray. Amos slowly stopped, his spiritual sensitivity acute, and the verse from Matthew 5:44 came to him: "But I say unto you, Love your enemies, bless them that curse you, do good to them that hate you, and pray for them who despitefully use you, and persecute you."

"Y'all move along!" said the sergeant.

"One moment," said Amos who bowed his head, and, as led, silently prayed God would use this difficult moment to bless the still-watching Sonny and Sol, convicting them of the error of their ways. The Confederate soldiers stopped, uncertain of what to do, and the old sergeant, seeing Amos praying, waited impatiently. Sonny and Sol stood without expression, uncharacteristically staring numbly. Finished, Amos continued with the others.

The sergeant led the men to the *Nordland* gangplank, walked on board, turned and motioned for the others to follow. Amos was the last to step on deck.

"Welcome aboard," the old sergeant said. "I figyuh y'all already know yo' way aroun'. In case anyone wants t' know, yo'wah friends the cook and the record keepah'll be busy workin' fo' the Cause. One'll be cookin' okra, taters, goober peas, grits an' chitlins, an' the other'll keep a record a' how much garbage he takes out. S'pect he might even keep track a' how deep he buries it. Seems like the type." The sergeant nodded affirmatively as he looked at Amos. "And we he'ah yo'wah a vayaba fella. That's what those boys tol' us. A vayaba fella. When the lieutenant returns, he and you'll be gettin' t'gethah." The sergeant turned to leave, and walked down the gangplank.

"Now we really can steal them back," loudly whispered Shorty in Swedish. No one responded as they began to go below, but all were thinking the same thing.

"Mr. Nordquist," said Shorty after they were below deck, "all we have to do is wait a little while – maybe two or three days – until those soldiers get comfortable with us being here. Then well before sunrise, we attack the guards. They look pretty young, they'll probably be asleep, and besides," he added adamantly, "no one who's any good at soldiering is going to be guarding boats with a bunch of Swedish sailors on board. We can tie and gag the guards, then head out on the river before anyone else wakes up. We've enough men to do it all. And then who's going to stop us?"

Amos spoke with the captains of the *Nordland* and *Kringflackande* who agreed the attempt should be made. Who knew what awaited them in a Confederate prison should they be sent to one? Success would depend on the extent to which the Confederates became used to business-as-usual and would expect nothing.

The next morning more crewmen from other lifeboats were brought aboard, and the Confederates then began to keep an eye out for still others wandering into town. Later that afternoon there was another group, followed by yet another late that evening. By the following afternoon, both ships' crews had been reunited, and the Confederates, having no place to house them and little to feed them, kept them on board where they would have to take care of themselves until orders came for formal confinement.

Amos and the others were offered their freedom in return for serving the South.

"We'll need to think about it."

"No hurry. Take yo' tahm. The wah ain' gonna end t'morrah. Course, if y'all ain't a gonna help us none, we'll be needin' t' send ya somewhey'ah else. Gonna be needin' them boats."

The Confederates had already taken half of the ships' stores, primarily food and medical supplies. The rest would be taken when the sailors were transferred "somewhey'ah else."

Then something unexpected happened. Hearing there were two Swedish crews at the docks, harbor pilot Swen Bernquist who had migrated to Wilmington from Sweden two years before the war started, paid the crews a visit. Well-known around the Wilmington docks, the guards figured there was no reason Bernquist couldn't socialize with the crew.

"I miss my people," Swen said in Swedish to Amos. "I speak English, but the people here, even little boys, make fun of my accent which is so much different than theirs. I live here but am not accepted. You have no idea how good it is to just sit and talk with someone. I seldom am able to do this."

Swen and Amos sat on the forecastle, talking at length about how Swen came to America, what it was like living in the South, and how he became a river pilot on the Cape Fear River.

Swen went home, but returned to the *Nordland* with bags of apples and pears for the men. He first gave a bag to the guards, and they again let him walk on board. Smiling, Amos invited Swen to stay the night if he wished, and Swen was grateful because he didn't want to go back to his shanty on the other side of the river to be alone again, nor head down to the river mouth to wait alone for any blockade runners needing a river pilot.

The next day saw no blockade running activity off the Cape Fear River, and in the late afternoon Swen again went to the *Nordland* to fraternize.

"Swen," said Amos, "I like and trust you, but you need to know something. First, however, you must promise me you will tell no one anything of what I am about to tell you."

"I promise," said Swen solemnly. Amos studied Swen for a moment.

"Very well," said Amos. "We're going to hijack these ships. Take them back. We'll be doing that tomorrow in the early morning hours." Swen's forehead furrowed as Amos spoke. "Spending time with us could get you in trouble. It might be better for you if you left and did not return."

"Take them back? What then?" asked Swen, holding out his hands. "Do you think you can just float down the river and sail out into the ocean? It is not that easy!"

"We should have the element of surprise. We hope to be gone before they know we've left."

"You don't know what you're saying," replied Swen. "The river channel gets dangerously shallow in places – lots of places – and there are submerged obstacles, now including *cheveaux-de-frise* the Confederates dumped in the channel below Eagles Island. There are shore batteries all along the river, and if the alarm goes out, and you are fired on, you do not stand a chance. Even if you were to get beyond the shore batteries, torpedoes [mines] are along the river mouth… but you will never make it to the river mouth…" Swen paused, and his eyes narrowed as he looked away, thinking.

"Listen carefully," said Swen. "River pilots sail the outbound runners downriver and then wait at Smithville [Southport] under cover of darkness in anticipation of a blockade runner or two arriving at night. There will be no river pilots here in Wilmington at that hour. Except, perhaps, me." Swen's eyebrows knitted.

"You are intent on doing this tonight?" asked Swen.

"In the early morning hours. I thought we had everything planned, but apparent…."

"You didn't. Even if there were no Confederates, the river would stop you."

"Then we need to call it off."

"No," said Swen without expression. "I will stay with you tonight. We will leave together. This is good for me because it is time for me to get away from here. It is good for you because, without my help, you will not. Your plans to prevent detection, however, must somehow work perfectly; you're going to need some luck."

At 3:25 a.m., led by Magnus, Sten and Carl, the bigger Swedish sailors cupped their hands over the young, sleeping guards' mouths, easily overpowering the young guards in the dark, gagging and tying them.

In the full moonlight shining through broken clouds to the west, silhouetted sailors on deck readied to cast-off lines while others climbed the ship's rigging, preparatory to setting sails. No one spoke. Meanwhile, on the dock, the tied and gagged young guards struggled to escape their bonds.

Quietly at around 3:30 a.m., lines were taken aboard as several sailors in two harbor towboats, having tied towlines to each ship, pulled hard on the oars, gradually pulling the ships away from the dock as the young guards watched, frantically working to get free.

By 3:45 a.m., the *Nordland* and *Kringflackande* adequately distanced themselves from the dock, and the sailors in the harbor towboats quietly came alongside and climbed up rope ladders, leaving the towboats to drift. The men aloft began to set sails. As the sails caught a downriver breeze, joining the current, Swen Bernquist stood next to the *Nordland* helmsman giving instructions, the *Kringflackande* following closely in the *Nordland* wake.

"Amos, the wind and current are favorable, but, considering what we're attempting, this pace is still slow," the captain said an hour after setting sail. "If someone gets suspicious, we're in trouble. It's 4:45 and we're barely halfway down the river. Swen says there are multiple batteries between here and the river mouth. If any of those young guards gets loose, and they telegraph downriver, we're in trouble."

By then, most of the young guards had given up, and were waiting for someone to find them, one falling back to sleep. At around 5:45 a.m., however, one of the more determined young guards had managed to chew through his gag, and began shouting for help.

Several minutes passed before anyone awoke, and more time passed before anyone investigated. By then the ships were nearing the river mouth, quietly passing between Confederate Battery Lamb on the west bank, and Battery Buchanan on the east bank, while in the darkness approaching the New Inlet entrance to the Atlantic.

As the ships reached the mouth of the river, the river current ebbed as it merged with the Atlantic tide, and westward sea breezes countered the southeast river momentum, slowing the ship's speed. Amos and the others became even more anxious, seeing that escaping the river mouth would be extremely slow, possibly compromising the cover of darkness if any sentry at Ft. Fisher, directly north of them, had eagle eyes and questioned what was happening.

Back at the dock, an awakened man who finally investigated the shouting, found the bound-and-gagged young guards, roughly untied them, and after being told what happened, ran to find someone who could telegraph the batteries along the river and at the river mouth. Meanwhile the ships fought to escape the New Inlet entrance, crawling at a snail's pace beneath formidable Fort Fisher, the largest fort in the Confederacy. Amos looked up at the multiple batteries that kept Union blockade ships at a distance while protecting blockade runners leaving the river. If the Swedish ships' intentions were made known at that moment, the ships would be blown to smithereens.

Offshore were three lines of blockade ships and boats. The nearest line consisted of small steam driven vessels that Ft. Fisher gunners would target if the boats came too close to the shore batteries. These smaller vessels would signal the "bar tenders," the middle blockade line off the Cape Fear River shoal waters, when a larger blockade runner would leave the river mouth.

If neither blockade line was able to intercept a blockade runner leaving the river mouth, the third line of larger steamships, a member of which had stopped the *Nordland* and *Kringflackande* five days earlier, would take over. The three blockade lines continually signaled one another back and forth when pursuing blockade runners, their coordinated effort becoming more and more effective as the war progressed. The two, slow-moving Swedish ships of sail would be no match for the Union steamship dragnet if spotted in the dark.

As the telegraph clicked at Ft. Fisher, the watch heard it, and went to get someone who could read Morse code.

When the awakened telegrapher groggily sat down in front of the telegraph key, the ships were slowly heading out to sea, barely visible under a darkened cloud-cover. They had been spotted, however, by a front line blockade boat who signaled a bar tender who in turn signaled a third-line ship.

At Ft. Fisher, after getting the message, the telegraph operator and watch notified fort gunners who, manning cannon, prepared to open fire.

Slipping over the western horizon, the cloud-obscured moon was taking its modest light with it. The early light of sunrise would soon appear, but wasn't there yet. This was the darkest moment of the night. For Ft. Fisher gunners, locating the ships in the dark was difficult, and more time elapsed. The gunners at first prepared to fire, but lost the ships-of-sail in the total darkness, and rationalized that firing would be a waste of valuable round shot needed to protect inbound steam-driven blockade runners.

The gunners withheld fire.

Sensing what was happening, Shorty grinned at the other men who were unable to see him smile in the darkness.

"See. What'd I say? We made it," said Shorty.

The *Nordland* and *Kringflackande* were underway on the lightless Atlantic and, although their cargo was gone, the crew was elated, believing they would make it to the other Wilmington.

As dawn's early light broke over cresting Atlantic waves, the *Nordland* and *Kringflackande* were heading NNE, making slow headway, but expecting to get to Wilmington, Delaware in a few days. Freedom, Shorty thought. Now who will stop us? When the initial light of the sunrise first caused the waves to sparkle, however, it also enabled lookouts on the Union outer blockade ship to again find the *Nordland* and *Kringflackande*.

As the sun began to turn early dawn into pre-sunrise, the same Federal ship that stopped the *Nordland* and *Kringflackande* after they were commandeered by the Confederates was steaming in their direction. The commanding officer took over for the officer-of-the-deck as the steamship closed. Well aware these were the same two ships that slipped through five days earlier, the commanding officer muttered an epithet and turned to the boatswain's mate: "Forester, sound 'general quarters'!"

23

Another blockade steamship, a half league behind the first but further to starboard, joined the chase, both bearing down on the *Nordland* and *Kringflackande*. Amos thought, Oh, no, not again as he watched the lead Federal steamship approach.

Suddenly flame and smoke thundered from a steamship port bow cannon, a cannonball flashing over the *Nordland's* bowsprit, slamming into the ocean beyond, shooting spray skyward like a geyser. Holding the gunwale, wide-eyed, Amos had a premonition and looked upward at the flag flying from the *Nordland* signal spar. "Good grief," muttered Amos as he turned toward the captain.

"Captain!" yelled Amos as he pointed to the Stars and Bars still flying abaft the *Nordland* stern. "That's not our flag!"

In their haste to get out of Wilmington in the dark, no one thought of raising the Swedish flag. Flags nevertheless flew from each ship, compliments of the Confederacy. The captain swore, immediately ordered the Confederate flag retired, and signaled to the *Kringflackande* to do likewise.

As the blockade steamships approached close by, the crewmen on each sailing ship pulled down the Confederate flag, scrambled to find a Swedish flag to run up the halyard, and did so, not realizing it made little difference.

Recognizing the Federal blockade steamship from their previous encounter, Shorty jumped up and down waving his arms, attempting to alert the Federals that it was them! The Swedes! From the last time! As the Federal blockade steamships neared the *Nordland* and *Kringflackande*, incensed at being duped during the previous encounter, the Union captain already knew that.

The blockade ships pulled alongside, threw over grappling hooks, made lines fast, and boarded both the *Nordland* and *Kringflackande*.

"What's your cargo?" shouted the Union captain with asperity as he stepped aboard the *Nordland*.

"Textiles. But it's all ashore," said the *Nordland* captain. "The Confederates took it all."

"Was any attempt made to resist?"

"We were blown south, far off course, and when sailing north to Wilmington, Delaware, as you now know, we were taken captive…"

The *Nordland* captain explained everything – the whales, the hijacking, the betrayal, the commandeering – as the Union captain listened, reasoning that the story was so implausible as to be true, but he was in no mood to give the *Nordland* captain the benefit of the doubt. Considering these Swedes now wanted to sail on to Wilmington, Delaware, a Union port, the captain agreed – and stated that a Federal steamship would escort the Swedish vessels, precluding a second chance of "far off course."

"That would be wonderful," responded the *Nordland* captain with relief. "We just want to resupply, pick up some additional crewmen, and sail home."

That was not what the Union captain had in mind, however. Other foreign blockade runners had been made to serve the North. The captain could see no reason why it should be different for Swedes.

"Gentlemen, while you might eventually be heading home, these two vessels will not," said the Union captain. "While you may not be blockade runners – ships of sail do not do well in that regard – your formerly full holds are empty. And your story, while entertaining and plausible, gives me pause because it's as plausible as your story during our first encounter." The captain folded his arms. "I believed you then. You fooled me once; a second opportunity won't happen. You aided and abetted the enemy and, therefore, gentlemen, these ships now belong to the United States of America. If, in fact, you wish to remain on board," the captain added magnanimously, "you are welcome to enlist in the United States Navy, an act enabling American citizenship. If that is your wish, when you reach port the second mate will escort you to a yeoman. If not, you shall be granted clemency and allowed to find a ship willing to take you to Europe. Perhaps you'll be fortunate and find a Swedish ship. Perhaps not. If not, once in Europe, how you return to Sweden will be up to you." Finished, the captain concluded, "That will be all."

It wasn't all. As the Union captain began to leave, Amos stepped in front of him, and tried to enlighten the captain. The Federal captain, however, was already enlightened. His job was to capture vessels aiding the Confederacy and, to his way of thinking, he just did.

The *Nordland* and *Kringflackande* sailed to Wilmington, Delaware, tied up to the pier for a few days, and were about to be renamed the Northland and the Rover before Amos, with the help of a familiar U. S. Army supply corps colonel, convinced Wilmington Federal officials that his story was true, and he was able to reclaim his ships.

"What an ordeal," Amos said to himself, referring not only to the reclamation of the *Nordland* and *Kringflackande*, but also losing another cargo, nearly dying at sea in the wake of the hurricane, miraculously being rescued and returned to Göteborg only to find that the love of his life was now the love of his brother, and returning to America only to be captured by Confederates. He shook his head as he walked to the pier where the *Nordland* and *Kringflackande* were berthed, and wondered why the obstacles, and what would happen next?

He walked up the gangway to the *Nordland* and went below-deck to the crew's forecastle berthing space and, after descending the berthing space ladder, walked to his rack, took the Bible out from under the folded blanket, and swung up into his rack, at times one of the most comfortable places on earth in spite of being canvas. In the lantern light, he turned to the gospel of James written by James the Just, the brother of Jesus.

Before he started to read, Amos began to wonder what it was like to recline at table with the holy family. James was obviously intelligent and, as post-resurrection events indicated, a natural leader. What were the others like? What did they discuss? Some family conversations must have been riveting. It occurred to Amos that regardless of topic, one Person at the table knew all the answers. He would know about chairs, and Amos wondered why they didn't use them. Amos chuckled. Jesus' mother and father knew who He was. Did his other brothers? No, Amos remembered, while He was alive they did not believe He was the Chosen One and, therefore, during family conversations, Jesus may have been reticent, listening. Wise men usually do, Amos thought. As he began reading the first chapter of James, he felt an uplifting from verse 12: "Blessed is a man who perseveres under trial; for once he has been approved, he will receive the crown of life which the Lord has promised to those who love Him." A confident feeling suffused Amos. God was directing him, he intuited, and while his future way would not be easy, God would be with him. At that moment, regardless of what happened next, Amos recommitted to abide and persevere.

After repair, refitting, and replenishing stores, the *Nordland* and *Kringflackande* cast off lines and, with the help of harbor boats, pulled away from the pier.

His hands in his pockets, in the cold gloom Amos stoically stood on the pier facing the departing ships. He raised his right hand and held it in the air for nearly a minute, giving a formal send-off to the crew. He dropped his hand, slid it hand back in his pocket, and watched the *Nordland* and *Kringflackande* sail into the Christina River leading to Delaware Bay and the Atlantic Ocean. Amos was aware of the moment's significance as the ships' silhouettes grew gradually smaller. In future memory, this moment would bookmark the beginning of his life's next chapter.

When the ships were ragged dots near the horizon, he slowly turned and faced his new home, the United States of America. He stood looking at the young town with background hillside colors of gold, yellow and orange being brought out by fall temperatures and declining solar exposure, and wondered what his specific role might be in this new country. His next undertaking would be to find Uncle Torvald and, in the process, become better acquainted with what was beyond the multihued hillsides. And he determined his name would no longer be prefaced by "Mister."

October 1864

"Company A, 5th Regiment, The Michigan Cavalry Brigade," said the piece of paper. While in the process of converting kronae, formerly riksdalers, into United States notes, Amos showed the piece of paper to the Federal official in Wilmington.

"Emm. Sounds familiar, Pastor Nordquist," said the official. "Where are they?"

"Pennsylvania, last I knew. They were at Gettysburg."

The official looked back at Amos, and the official's eyebrows knitted. "Gettysburg. Been a while." The official thought for a moment. "Michigan Cav. Heard of 'em."

"That'd be the 'Wolverines,'" said another nearby official in a forced monotone.

"Yes," said Amos, standing upright, "that's their nickname."

"Got two nephews in that bunch."

"Do you know where they are?"

"A while back they was north a' Richmond. But, no, dunno where they are now. Could be anywhere. Wolverines're hell on hoofs. Best in the army…be glad they're on our side. The Wolverines' commanding officer is supposed to be the second coming of William the Conqueror. Young. 24 or so. Some of these officers now ain't been at it too long, but been at it long enough to show they're better 'n some of the old bunch. In fact, I think the general he serves under, Sheridan, ain't too much older. Why're you looking for 'em?"

"I'm trying to find my uncle who has been in that company for a while. He has an inheritance I must give him," answered Amos. "Gettysburg is the last place where I know he was. He wrote us a letter when the battle was over."

"Save the letter. Hope he's still alive. Here's a map," said the first official. "Got a horse yet?"

"No."

"There's a livery stable two blocks down the street. Here's where Gettysburg is," said the first official, pointing at the map. "Take this road and head over the Susquehanna River to Westminster…"

"Say, Fred, I don't know exactly where they are," interrupted the second official, "but they ain't at Gettysburg. They're prob'ly a ways south."

"Well, okay," said the first official, "then head south through Baltimore; but be careful – some of those people still ain't made up their minds which side they're on. Then ride down through the nation's capital. See here?" Amos again followed the man's finger. Unaware that the Michigan Cavalry Brigade had become part of the Army of the Shenandoah, the official added, "Ask people where the Army of the Potomac is." He looked at Amos solemnly. "They'll need your services, pastor," the official understated.

The following day, Amos bought a good horse – with the needs of the army, good horses were in short supply and expensive. Eyeing Amos carefully and hoping Amos wouldn't change his mind or want to dicker further, the old saddler held the reins to the large, chestnut Arabian Amos selected.

"Yup, he's a good 'un. Y' got lucky." The man looked at Amos and smiled impishly. "Yeah, I guess pastors don't get 'lucky.' What's the word y'all use? 'Blessed'? Well, whatever; ya got a good horse here. Most a' the cavalrymen would be happy t' have this 'un. Good horse c'n mean the difference 'tween life 'n death. And that saddle'll last forever." The old man tied the reins to livery stable post and asked, "Anything else y' need?"

"What else should I get?"

Stroking his beard with his right thumb and index finger, the man looked at Amos. "Tell you what. Your uncle's with the cavalry and you're headin' out t' find 'im. You'd better get outfitted like your uncle. Here, let's do this: let me write a list." The saddler wrote out a list of items and handed it to Amos. "Take this over to the general store, give it to Josh. He'll recognize the handwritin'. He'll take care a' ya."

At the general store, Amos found Josh and handed the list to him. Josh looked at it and nodded. "Bart sent you over?"

"I didn't catch his name."

"This is his writin'. He's m' brother." The man studied Amos. "Looks like you're gonna be spendin' some time on horseback. Wait here while I get these things." The man went around the store picking out things from shelves and returned to the front counter where Amos waited.

"Here y' go. One cotton cloth tent, a bit over one yard square. Tent stakes and pole. Poncho, soogan including blankets – one rubber. Coffee pot, fry pan, tin cup. Fork and spoon – saw ya already have a knife. Overcoat. Haversack and canteen. Here's your grub. Bacon, beans, flour, hardtack, salt, coffee. Sugar in the small white bag." The man turned around and studied the rifles on the wall behind him. "You'll need a carbine and cartridge box," he said with his back to Amos.

"I don't think I'll need a rifle," said Amos. "I'm already armed."

"One of these 7-shot Spencer carbines might come in real handy," advised the man, looking over his shoulder. "Better safe than sorry."

"No, thank you; I think I'm fine." It was a misjudgment Amos would later correct.

Collecting his supplies, Amos walked out the door to his horse tethered in front, placed his items in saddlebags and the haversack. He fastened the tent, pole and bedroll to the back of his saddle, mounted his new horse and headed southwest toward Baltimore.

After passing through Baltimore, still unaware the Wolverines were no longer part of the Army of the Potomac, he began asking people where the Army of the Potomac was.

"Excuse me," began Pastor Nordquist, "with regards to the Army of the Potomac, can you gentlemen tell me in which direction, and how far, I should ride to find them? I'm looking for my uncle who serves under a general named Custer. I have something I need to deliver to him in person."

"What's that?" The man cupped his ear with his hand. "You bringin' something t' Custer?"

"No, my uncle."

"Well," came the reply, "if you want to put yourself in proximity to the fightin', you should head south to Washington – just follow the main road – then continue through Washington and keep goin' until you get to Fredericksburg. I suspect once you get to Fredericksburg you'll have no trouble findin' someone who'll know where the boys are. Seems like wherever there's a battle, Fredericksburg ain't too far away."

Amos continued toward Washington, D.C. Although it was mid-day, the Washington, D.C. sky was overcast and dark, and the wind was gusting as rain fell. After he rode a little farther, Amos stopped another traveler heading in the opposite direction.

"I'm trying to find my uncle who is with the Michigan Cavalry, the Wolverines. Do you have any idea where they might be? I think they're with the Army of the Potomac."

"Nope, not with the Army of the Potomac. Used t' be. Now the Michigan cavalry is with Sheridan over in the [Shenandoah] Valley. When you get to the next intersection south, head west."

"My uncle's commanding officer isn't Sheridan; it's Custer."

"Well, t' tell the truth, they ain't much difference. Custer serves under Sheridan and I hear tell the two of 'em are hell on Johnnies. Yeah, head south a little ways and take the next road west."

Amos did as instructed and took the westward road pockmarked with rain-filled, horse-hoof holes and wagon-wheel ruts.

After a few hours of riding at a comfortable but steady pace, the improbable happened as Amos approached three grizzled Union Army veterans on horseback heading east. Their uniforms were frayed and dirty, beards matted, eyes intense, hard and untrusting. As Amos rode nearer, they studied him as if annoyed he was there.

"Excuse me. Do any of you gentlemen know where the Michigan Cavalry Brigade might be now?" Amos wasn't sure what a brigade was exactly, but had little doubt these men knew.

"You talkin' to us?" said one of the soldiers.

"Yah," said Amos respectfully in his Scandinavian accent.

"We thought we heard the word 'gentlemen,' and warn't sure," said one as the three men reined their horses to a halt. "Why you wanna know?"

"My Uncle, Torvald Nordquist, serves with them and I'm trying…"

"Torvald?" erupted one of the men as all three suddenly looked at Amos with interest. "'Torvald the Terrible'?" The man guffawed as the other two, leaning forward in their saddles, chuckled knowingly.

Amos's mouth opened slightly without speaking as he looked at the men who apparently knew Uncle Torvald.

"We just call him 'Swede," said another man. "Dunno why?" he added dryly. "Jest, well, somethin' about 'im."

The others cynically snorted.

The third man added unnecessarily loudly, "Like his accent, and everything he aims at becomes a goddam 'Norwegian'. Helluvanaim. Never misses. Almost feel sorry for the 'Norvegians.'"

The other two glanced at one another.

"Jest what the hell's a 'Norvegian'?" one asked Amos.

"Whatever Torvald aims at," answered the first soldier matter-of-factly before Amos could speak.

"What d'ya want with yer uncle?" asked the second soldier.

"I have something I need to give him. I'm told he is over in the Shenandoah Valley."

"Nope, not yet, anyway," responded the first soldier. "Maybe White House… but probably City Point by now."

"But he might be on his way back t' the north end 'a the Valley," explained the second. "Joinin' Sheridan. Little while an' we'll be beatin' the tar outta Jubal Early again. Don't know many that can take ol' Jubal."

"Hell, no," added a third soldier. "In fact, Sheridan's the only one, far as I c'n see."

"Ol' Jubal's luck turned bad," said the first soldier. "He kin lick jest about any outfit in anyone's army and what happens? He gets to fight a guy that's as hell-bent-for-leather as he is – an' Phil Sheridan never stops, never even slows down."

"Mebbe never sleeps."

"His stirrups is high, but he's dam' big on horseback."

"Forever ridin' along the lines or goin' t' the rear to roust the stragglers… stoppin' long enough to chew-out his officers."

"That man's fearless, and I'll tell ya somethin': they's gotta be two of 'im."

"Gotta have a twin brother."

"Identical."

"Cain't any normal man be everywhere at once like he is."

"Wherever he is," said Amos, "I hope to find him and his army. Can you give me directions?"

"Jest go where we come from," said the first soldier solemnly, pointing his thumb in the direction Amos was facing. "We're in Sheridan's cavalry with your uncle. Time for a furlough."

"High time."

"Maybe we shoulda stuck around but, hell, not much happenin' at the moment, and figured we could use a break."

"Been two years without one. Know what I mean? Goin' home for a short spell."

"Beat the rush, maybe. If not, hell, we'll be back."

"We were half figurin' they'd even be able to get it done without us, but I don't know…"

"There's a road what turns north a ways west of here," said the first soldier. "Now either Swede is back with Sheridan, or he's still down at the City Point hospital."

"He's still down at City Point?" asked the third soldier.

"I heard they took 'im t' White House, but White House is closed now, so he must 'a gone t' City Point."

"What happened to him?" asked Amos.

"Swede has this habit of standin' up when he figures the last 'Norvegian' is kilt. Better idea is to keep down until you know the shootin's stopped. Well, a few months ago down near Richmond he stood up and, bam, caught Minié balls in the shoulder and upper chest. Got hit pretty bad."

"Some boys got him off the field, put him on an ambulance. Heard all the closer field hospitals was filled. Dunno. I figure he wound up at City Point. I suspect they might wanna throw 'im in the infantry around Richmond. Don't think Swede 'd much care fer that. Anyway, last we knows."

Straightening up in the saddle, the first soldier said, "If I were you, I'd go to City Point. First, he might still be there. Second, if he's not, they'll know where he is. Dam' City Point knows more'n Washington."

The man looked ahead and looked at Amos again.

"Head back t' that north-south road you musta been on a bit ago. Go south. When you get to the next major road intersectin' that one, jest head east in that general direction," he pointed east southeast, "an' keep goin' until the next major road goin' south. Take it until you get to City Point."

"How far to this City Point?" asked Amos as it started to rain again.

"Four, five days' ride. It's the big Union supply depot northeast a' Petersburg. Ships bring tons of stuff down from up north, pull in to the docks, unload ammunition, weapons, field artillery, caissons, wagons, uniforms, hogs, chickens, bandages, flour – all kinds of war supplies – it gets put on trains and sent to supply outfits at the rear. Everything the Union army needs around here comes from City Point. Consequently, we ain't a'wantin' fer much."

"Confederates ain't got nothin' like it," said the third soldier, "unless you consider the [Shenandoah] Valley."

"How far's the Valley," asked Amos.

"Couple days ride in the direction yer headin'. It's not far…but it depends on where in the Valley Sheridan is now. When we left, he was up north in Winchester and probably still is. Winter, y' know."

"Dunno how long he'll stay there."

"Hell, no one knows from one day t' the next."

"He could be headin' south through the Valley right now for all we knows."

"The Rebs is down south."

"How bad was Torvald wounded?" asked Amos.

"He got hit pretty bad; but knowin' Swede, he'll make it. Shouldn't take too long for him to get healed and head back. Might even be doin' it now."

"On the other hand, City Point's got a real fine hospital. Big. Real big.

"Hospital site alone is 200 acres."

"Rebs aint' got nothin' like it."

"I wouldn't be surprised if Swede stays there a little longer'n needed."

"He'd do that?" asked the third soldier.

"Hailll, yes," the second soldier said with a feigned expression of bewilderment as if wondering why anyone would ask.

"And you'd like City Point," continued the first soldier. "Lotsa food. Bakeries. Butcher shops. Saloons. Women."

"Y' mean devils dressed like women."

"Well, lets jes' say, anything you want, they got…if the army ain't got it, the saloons and the sutlers do. City Point. The Union army's New York City."

"So, what'd'ya do fer a livin', civilian?"

"I'm in the ministry," said Amos.

The three men looked at Amos without expression.

"Wanna be a chaplain? Could always use another one."

"War goin' on," understated the first soldier.

"Then it is good I am here," said Amos.

"Now," added the first soldier, "if Swede ain't at City Point, and you head back t' find Sheridan's cavalry, and yer havin' trouble findin' 'em, save yerself some time and just ask fer Custer's bunch...Gen. George Armstrong Custer...ask the locals along the way. Custer got promoted to 3rd Division commander, but if the locals don't remember Sheridan, they'll remember Custer. Dresses like the King of France."

"Smells like the King of France," said the third soldier.

"Dunno that the King of France smells like that."

"Hell, he's French, ain't he?"

"Hard t' say," shrugged the first soldier. "But when you get told, don't ride too slow catchin' up with Custer or you never will. Like I say, Custer ain't headin' the Wolverines no more. But if you finds the 3rd Division, they'll sure-as-hell know where the Wolverines are. Hell, keep it simple: jes' ask fer Custer's bunch."

"People know," said the second soldier, leaning forward in his saddle. "Custer ain't someone y' c'n ignore. New recruits come in naturally scared 'a jumpin' in a war – the unknown, what might happen, maybe get killed – but one look at ol' Armstrong an' they're even more scared t' be cowards."

"That's what's called 'irony,' boys," said the third man with a smirk.

"What the hell does makin' irons have t' do with anything? We pressin' uniforms?"

"Pressin' rebs," replied the third man as he spat to one side, "flat as whore-house sheet. Their boys in the infantry are as good as our boys. But we get replacement mounts from time t' time," he said as he reached down and patted his horse's neck, "so their cavalry ain't no match for us."

"Not by a dam' sight," said the first soldier. "Spencers and Henrys have somethin' t' do with that, too."

"An' if you see ol' Armstrong or his brother, Tom," added the third soldier, "tell 'em the Holman brothers'll be back." The other two soldiers said nothing as the third soldier again spat to one side and said, "Don't s'pose they c'n end this war without us."

The rain began to fall heavily. Intent on moving on, the first soldier simply said, "Good luck, rev'rend."

The Holman brothers reined their horses to the right and continued east as Amos's horse stepped back out of their way.

As Amos watched them ride off, he wondered whether to follow them and head south to City Point. Or should he continue west, and then north as they suggested. It didn't seem anyone was entirely sure of where Uncle Torvald's outfit was, much less Torvald himself. Heading south to City Point would be pointless if Torvald had left – he was wounded months ago – or was never there in the first place. Amos ruminated for a moment longer, turned and looked at the Holman brothers down the road. He looked west again. If Torvald's wounds were healed, and he wasn't yet with the Wolverines, he could already be riding back to the Michigan Brigade. Based on what the Holman brothers said, and their own desire to return, it was, no doubt, where Torvald wanted to be. If I head south, thought Amos, and Uncle Torvald heads northwest, it will take over twice as long to find him if I have to double back. But if I head west, and he's not there yet, I can wait for him. Amos listened to his intuition, took a deep breath, and decided to continue west.

Amos rode west and after another few days reached the north end of the Valley. Further to the north was Winchester; while to the south was where the warfare had been between the armies of Phil Sheridan and Jubal Early. Perhaps Torvald is again with Sheridan in Winchester – if Sheridan is still there. But the Holman brothers just came from there and said Torvald wasn't there. If he was at City Point, perhaps by now he is returning to his cavalry regiment, riding north. But there is a chance the Wolverines are headed south again. Where the Rebels are. Following his intuition, instead of going north, Amos began riding south through the Shenandoah Valley, and the further he rode, the more evident it became that the war preceded him, the destruction growing from sporadic to intermittent to constant. It would get worse as he rode further.

24

The Shenandoah Valley and Blue Ridge Mountains began as multi-layered metamorphic rock beneath an ancient sea until the tectonic plates of North America and Africa, drifting like enormous flatboats on a lake of magma, collided around 500 million years ago. When the collision occurred, an older, lower layer tilted upward, sliding over the edge of a younger layer, continuing upward, forming North America's oldest mountain range, the Appalachians, believed to have been once as high as the 40 million-year-old Himalayas. Over the last 250 million years, however, glacial, atmospheric and geological forces wore down the huge mountains, forming a small vestigial remnant, the present Blue Ridge Mountains with some plants and animals found nowhere else, and the Shenandoah Valley with substantial accumulation of detritus, resulting in rich 19th century farmland.

The Valley subsequently became the "breadbasket of the Confederacy" because of fertile farmland combined with the disciplined productivity of Valley inhabitants, primarily Mennonites, Dunkers, Quakers, or other Christian sects whose religious beliefs precluded active warfare participation. While most refused to serve in uniform, however, they would supply food to the Confederacy and, consequently, the Confederate army had become dependent on the Valley. Union Commanding General Ulysses S. Grant wanted this supply source destroyed, and the Shenandoah Valley had been, as one witnessing minister wrote, "peeled."

When still in Europe, Amos became familiar with Currier and Ives lithographs of beautiful scenes in mid-19th century North America, but few more beautiful than the Shenandoah Valley in summer and fall. Climate, flora, geomorphic processes, and the industriousness and creativity of its farmers rendered it one of the most picturesque places in North America.

Now as Amos looked about while riding south, in Valley forests and fields fall's formerly luxuriant foliage was dead and buried beneath winter snows. The evidence of warfare, however, converged and grew large, running north and south, a mucky swath that looked like a huge, dark, festering scab on the earth's skin. During the early winter, 1864, after Sheridan's army had gone through the

Valley, Currier and Ives would not have considered the Shenandoah Valley for its beauty, but only as an example of the ravages of war. Amos rode southward, stunned at the extent of the devastation all around him. It seemed as if hellfire and brimstone rained down from heaven; the swath gradually widened until the face of the earth was burned and blistered from horizon to horizon.

In the downpour, Amos navigated around muddied ruts caused by hundreds of carriages and wagons and caissons – the ruts worn down by the tramping of horses, mules and soldiers – and in places the bases of large embankments were worn inward. In fields, everywhere, Amos began to see rain beating down on dead cavalry horses and occasionally dead livestock accidentally shot and not taken by the Federals. That morning, Amos saw the sprawled body of a dead soldier – empty eyes open in a grim, ghostly stare, still lying where he died, inadvertently overlooked by retreating and pursuing troops. Amos thought of burying the body, but he had no shovel, and thought eternal anonymity might be avoided if the formality were left to someone who could identify the body. As he looked about, everywhere were remnants of things formerly whole, now utterly destroyed.

Earlier, the first house pock-marked with bullet holes caused Amos to do a double take until he realized what he was seeing. Now as he traveled south, he saw charred remains of barns, storage buildings, corncribs, stables, mills, granaries, chicken houses, anything believed an active part of the former Confederate breadbasket that was the Shenandoah Valley. Amos absently thought of being burned. Was there anything more painful than being badly burned?

Some of the farm houses were vacant, former occupants having headed elsewhere, hoping to find some manner of subsistence with relatives rather than risking starvation during the winter. Already avoiding the front, stealthy Union stragglers and deserters, "bummers," moved in like cellar rats. Amos could see them peering from behind curtains.

As Amos traveled further south, there were more perforated houses, modest and grand, and even greater destruction as the advancing army became more proficient at devastation. Amos tried to imagine being in Sweden, riding down a country road in winter, and seeing what he now saw. Sweden fought in many wars. Except for their centuries-earlier pursuit of the Russian army under Peter the Great who ordered everything behind him burned to eliminate Swedish army forage, Sweden never experienced anything similar to this. Amos glanced around and more carefully studied what was left of the former farms he was passing. All about him, growing destruction and disrepair had gained an upper hand as men who would be working farms had either left or, in a few cases, joined the Cause and fought valiant battles in formerly unmemorable places from which many would never return.

Later Amos approached a large house turned into a Federal field hospital. Women were attending the wounded. The most seriously wounded were inside while those barely able to walk were covered with blankets, sitting on the cold open porch that wrapped around the sides of the house. Others were in tents beyond. Alongside the porch on cots and chairs in makeshift shelters were the ambulatory, some of who appeared to be in no better condition than what Amos might see inside. A heavy woman with an expressionless face gave the others direction, and apparently was responsible for whatever success they were having. The nurses moved with a sense of urgency at the direction of the heavy woman. It was a Union field hospital; this meant they probably had adequate food, supplies and medicine.

Amos rode up to the woman and said, "I can only stay for a short time, but I'd like to help."

"Anything wrong with your back, sir?" the woman asked.

"No," answered Amos. "What do you need?"

"Sir, I need you to come in here and help carry some of the men, inside, back out here on the porch, and then take some of these men inside. The faster we treat these men, the better."

For the next six hours, Amos effected triage, ministered to the men, and took care of multiple tasks requiring physical strength. The women were grateful. Although tired, he bade them farewell and continued on his journey to find Uncle Torvald.

Late the next morning, the rain had let up and Amos was further south when he saw two children – maybe 3 and 6, a little boy and his older sister – standing next to their front porch 40-50 feet off the road up ahead, not moving, as if frozen in the cold winter air. Just watching him come down the road. Their mouths were rigid and their bloodshot eyes reflected a combination of intense seriousness and deep apprehension. Amos rode slowly with a pleasant expression as he studied the children. What had they seen? They seemed beyond scared.

As he rode closer to the two children, the children still did not move, and continued to stand rigidly watching him like he was an apparition. Sensing he was not going to harm anyone, their expressions became less apprehensive, looking only as if they had been scolded. Amos studied them. Why did they not run inside? he asked himself.

The little boy's lips quivered. Without looking at her, the little boy took his sister's hand. Both children were dirty; bundled in clothes that had been patched, but not enough. They needed baths. Something to eat. Attempting to lighten the moment, Amos beamed at them. The grim expression of the little boy remained unchanged, but the little girl eyes became stern as if to say, "You've no right to smile."

Bullet holes in the porch post behind them made Amos again wonder how much they had seen. His heart became heavy and he reined his horse to his right, rode closer to them, and slowly dismounted. As the little boy gripped his sister's hand tightly, Amos walked toward the children while reaching into his vest pocket for the envelope next to Uncle Torvald's inheritance. The second envelope contained a large sum of money he had been carrying for his own needs. He was in Virginia, but the war and Confederate money were reaching a point where Federal dollars could be of more use to this small family.

At that moment, the children's mother came out on the porch. She was a slender woman in her late 20's, of average height, with her frizzled brown hair in a bun. Her once-attractive face looked haggard, worn, complementing her floor-length calico skirt, probably once a source of pride, now frayed and stained. In her hands was a muzzle loader.

"Ah'd appreciate it if you went no fuh'thuh, suh," she said without expression. The hardness in her eyes was expression enough.

Amos stopped, removed his hat, and bowed slightly.

"I mean no harm," said Amos. "I have a little money with me and thought I'd give a dollar or two to your children. I realize it's Yankee money but…"

"We need no Yankee money, suh," she said, her jaw becoming tighter. "This wah is not ovuh."

Amos nervously kneaded the brim of his hat as he looked at her and said, "I understand how you feel, but perhaps, for the sake of the children, you could accept my offer. No one knows what the future might bring."

She looked at him, ascertaining from his demeanor and accent that he was neither Yankee nor Rebel. Her eyes relaxed.

"Very well, then. Fowah the children."

Amos stepped forward and handed a $5 United States Note to the little girl, and then looked at the little boy whose head did not move, but whose eyes looked upward at Amos with the same expression as before. How much did they see? Amos again wondered. $5 was a large sum to give to strangers, but this woman and her children obviously needed more. Amos reached into his breast pocket and from the money he carried, pulled out another $5 U.S. Note and gave it to the little boy who looked at it for a moment, and resumed his baleful stare at Amos.

"Go give these to your mother," said Amos softly but commandingly.

"Children, Ah've told you befowah, you needn't gahd the house. Now come heah."

The little boy let go of his sister's hand, and the two of them turned and walked up the steps to their mother who held out her hand. The children gave the notes to her and she studied them skeptically, questioning whether they were real.

She concluded they were.

As their mother straightened up, the children turned and looked at Amos again.

"Suh, yo'wah identity is unknown, but at this moment it appeahs you maht be an angel of God." She said this quietly with no change in expression. How stoic they have become, thought Amos.

"It is my calling," Amos smiled weakly. "I am, however, as the Bible says, 'a little lower than the angels.'"

He studied the children for a moment and looked at the woman, tipped his hat, and pleasantly said, "I trust you will use the money wisely."

The woman at first said nothing, but her heritage demanded a response.

"We haven't much, suh, but you ah welcome to suppuh if you wish." She said this knowing that if he accepted, the one meal would consume much of what they had left.

Amos looked at her with admiration, sensing the depth of her character.

"That is very generous of you but, no, I have to find someone. Perhaps you could help me in that regard."

"Who ah you lookin' fo'wah?"

"My uncle. He serves in the Union Army. In," Amos got out the piece of paper and read, "Company A, 5th Regiment, The Michigan Cavalry Brigade. Have you heard of them?"

"Michigan? Ah wouldn't know."

"They call themselves The Wolverines," responded Amos. The woman's expression seemingly did not change, but Amos intuited from the return of hardness in her eyes, and the pause that followed his response, that she was familiar with the name, "Wolverines."

"Tha'yat bunch of cavalry have been through he'ah, suh. A while back. They fight like men possessed...and maybe they ah." She looked intently at Amos. "They'uh leadah has long hay'ah and dresses lahk a prima donna."

She paused, looking at Amos, her lips taut.

"They shot mah husband."

With that statement, the fortitude of the children broke and, as hard as he fought against it, the little boy's teeth bared in an agonizing grimace. He looked down as, unable to remain stoic any longer, he began to sob, followed by his sister, although both fought back, agonizingly trying to be strong, trying not to further burden their mother, and gradually through herculean self-discipline, fists clenched, their sobs turned to staggered whimpers as they looked at Amos with expressions suggesting their torment was as much this outsider's fault as the others.

Pastor Nordquist stared at the children, his heart breaking. After a moment the whimpering stopped, with no more sound except the winter wind.

"No need to," she continued, looking hard and tired. "Mah husband was just trah'in' t' pr'tect his family. Anyone of they'em would have done the same. But they shot him raht whay'ah you stand now. Called themselves 'Wolverines.'"

She took a short breath and let it out.

Her expression unchanged, her eyes looked away. "Proud of tha'yat."

She paused again as Amos, his hat still held in both hands in front of him, looked at her with sadness.

"Some a' they'm acted like killin' Confederates was no different than killin' mah'ce." The woman added, "Killin'. That's they'ah job. Mah husband had a gun, doin' what a real man's s'posed t' do. And he died fo' it. Dunno but what if he hadn't had a gun, he'd still be alahv. They'ah leadah strongly, angrily, reprimanded the man responsible for mah husband's da'eth and, as best he could, apologized to me. Removed his hat. Apologized to me. Sincerely." Without taking her eyes off Amos, she weakly sighed again while shrugging her shoulders. "Perhaps some mah't think tha'yat act of chivalry would pahtly balance the scale." Her hardened eyes looked at Amos intently, as for a moment her jaw again grew firm.

"No, suh. It did not. And he knew tha'yat. But, at tha'yat moment, b'tween us, they'ah wasn't anythaing eithuh one of us could do."

She looked down at her distraught children who were wiping their eyes, attempting to conceal their weakness, attempting to be brave. She looked back at Amos.

"Continue down the road, suh. Ah suspect you'll eventually fahnd them neah Richmond."

Her eyes narrowed with sadness as she paused again, then added sincerely, "Thank you, suh."

Amos looked intently at her for a moment, nodded, turned and put on his hat. He mounted his horse and turned back toward the road, glancing at the woman and her two children who stood on the porch looking back.

They seemed very alone.

His heart filled further, and he instantly pulled on the reins, turned his horse around, and rode up to the porch.

Without looking at the woman and her children, he slowly dismounted and walked up the porch steps toward her.

Although he gave it a great deal of thought, Amos was not certain as to how prayer worked. Evidently, when led to pray, Amos concluded years earlier, mere human faith then somehow plugs into the indescribable source that is the power of God, and evident miraculous things subsequently happen, not to mention miraculous things not evident, as well as things not evidently miraculous and, among those things not evidently miraculous, many giving the appearance of being not-answers. Amos believed multiple things happen in response to a prayer and it was for this reason that the Bible, encouraging us to harness the power of God according to His will, admonished we 'pray without ceasing.' To Amos, often it seemed the urge to pray, while coming from within, was somehow not mind-directed, and sometimes – distracted by non-spiritual matters of the moment – Amos did not notice the urge. But always, when he did, wherever he was, he stopped all else and prayed.

"Ma'am, I need to pray for you and your children. I cannot stay, but I cannot leave without praying for you."

Amos bowed his head and began.

"Heavenly father," he paused, "this woman and these children have seen and experienced difficult things that only You and they know about, but only You understand. I pray for their safety, and future security – that You will protect them – and I pray it is Your will these children grow up to lead normal, productive lives, feeling loved by You and their mother and those You bring into their lives, and will never again experience things like they have seen here.

"I pray You will provide a man to be with them, a man You have drawn to You, and who seeks Your guidance. Meanwhile, I pray You will comfort them and their mother, and I thank You for this opportunity to pray for them.

"Your will be done.

"Amen."

Amos lifted his head, studied the woman for a moment, stepped forward, slowly placed his arms around her, and for a prolonged moment gently hugged her. Stoically, as he expected, she only weakly responded. He knew at that moment, however, she needed to feel lovingkindness, needed to be reminded it was still in the world.

He released her, but with his large hands softly held her shoulders momentarily and looked at her intently.

Without a word, he gently let go, turned and walked down the porch steps back to his horse and remounted.

"I will continue to pray for you," he stated as he again turned his horse around.

He trotted toward the road, but this time did not look back. While you will leave, I am with them, was the sensation within him.

The following day he continued riding southward, far from Winchester, uncertain of exactly where he was, following the burned swath. In the late morning, the sky was again overcast, the air cold and damp. A few sycamore trees lined a distant river as Amos crested a ridge, riding down the other side where the burned swath gradually fell then rose over a hill, curving to the west like an enormous, dark ribbon. He again passed dead horses, another dead soldier, and all manner of things broken and destroyed.

At a short distance, he saw a train of hauling wagons heading toward him carrying wounded and dead. They also must pick up the fallen along the way, Amos thought.

The older man driving the first wagon was gaunt with a tattered, gray skirmishing hat pulled down tight over his forehead. The old driver's course beard was white, his thick eyebrows mostly black, and his eyes were severe, accentuating a hostile countenance. He saw Amos through peripheral vision, but looked beyond Amos as if Amos wasn't there.

The man sensed the contrast he and his freight presented, and did not like some civilian guessing at those circumstances. Were misery able to be packaged and shipped, thought Amos, this wagon train would be overloaded, and if there was a pace that defined the phrase, "deathly slow," it was their pace. Death was affecting everything Amos watched including the mules and their forward motion.

The train had several wagons in graying states of wooden weariness; the first one carrying dying men, the other wagons filled with blankets-with-boots, the covered bodies of men whose souls were possibly in discussion with their Maker, perhaps relieved and grateful, perhaps trying to explain. As the Amos drew closer, he felt more and more invisible as if being willed out of the scenery by the head wagon driver. The old man led wagons filled with the dead and dying. The condition of his mules forced traveling at a pace insuring Death would claim more.

Hopeless?

Amos would not pass by as some might at that moment. "Love your neighbor as yourself," Christ said. On the road from Jerusalem to Jericho it would remain for a despised Samaritan to help the beaten man, tending to the man's wounds and paying an innkeeper to care for the beaten man until the Samaritan returned. Who was the "neighbor"?' Amos felt a leading to reduce the unremitting burden bearing down on consciousness and conscience, and as the wagon train approached him, Amos reined his horse to a halt alongside the road and waited.

Seated inside the front wagon was a nurse who looked back at Amos with vacant, inward eyes as if the end of visual acuity began with the outside world. She was obviously deathly tired. It was worse than the death-oppressed look Pastor Nordquist saw from the two children, and he also wondered what she had seen. It was an undisciplined thought, for what she had seen was evident from where she sat at this moment, and from how she looked at him, at anything. Men were killed in front of her. Many not killed in front of her, died in front of her. At the pace they were traveling, some of those not dead soon would be, and there was nothing she could do to stop this although that was why she was there: to save the lives of men willing to die honorably, to alleviate the misery of men whose actions insured alleviation would never gain an upper hand.

The wagons were only a dozen feet from Amos. The first wagon emanated intermittent moans from bearded grimaces frozen-in-place. As the second wagon drew nearer, Amos could see dead men, most covered with blankets, but some partially visible, their heads caked with dirt. Amos leaned forward on his saddle horn as he realized what he was seeing: men who had been disinterred at some battlefield, and were being taken home for proper burial.

Amos didn't know what he should do, but was convicted he must do something for those still alive in order they remain alive.

25

Emaciated horses tied behind the slow moving wagons walked at the same deathly pace, heads down from weakness. Belonging to the men in the wagons, the horses were evidence the men once had possessions and purpose, although now it was only a matter of who would die first, horse or owner.

Amos rode up beside the head wagon driver whose eyes continued to see everything else, and forced his way to the front of the man's attention.

"Sir! I am Amos Nordquist. Pastor Amos Nordquist. Can I help you?"

The old man heard every word and remained slumped forward without responding, his dark eyebrows low like winter clouds over his defiant eyes.

"Pardon me," added Amos adamantly, "you need help and I want to give it."

For a split second the wagon master's eyes flicked toward Amos, but the driver remained mute. The nurse turned her head as her tired eyes focused and looked at Amos as if to say help was needed weeks, months ago. As the wagon train continued to roll without verbal response, Amos reined his horse alongside the nurse slumped wearily on the seat.

"There is a widow's house a few days north," said Amos to the nurse, "where you can set up a temporary field hospital, feed your animals and yourselves." Amos described the house of the woman whose husband had been shot by the Wolverines. "I will meet you there," he said forcefully. "You can temporarily care for these men, perhaps save a few that would otherwise die before you get to wherever you're going. Do you understand?"

The depressing rain continued to fall. The dim light in the nurse's eyes weakly flickered, perhaps the first time in weeks, and she nodded. The Confederacy was running out of men, supplies and time, Amos surmised, while the Union's collective juggernaut continued to build.

Amos reined his horse to the left and began cantering back up the road, intent on notifying the woman with the two children while he continued north, hoping to buy medicine at the Federal field hospital he passed nearly a week ago. He would return to the woman's house, perhaps arriving around the same time as the wagon train. It would be a hard ride, but the wagon train was moving slowly, too slowly to keep many of these men alive much longer. Daily, men were moved from the front of the wagon train to the rear with the dead, and gradually the dead were moving further forward, taking over the wagons. Amos would buy food and medical supplies from the Yankees in order to help the Rebels. It didn't matter. To Amos it didn't matter. Fortunately, to the head nurse at the Federal field hospital later, it no longer mattered.

Amos rode north along the muddy road, eventually riding up to the woman's house, her children again standing in front, watching him approach. Are they again standing guard, wondered Amos, some inherent part of human nature drawing them to duty? The children were relaxed now, however, and looked at him almost welcomingly. Hearing the hoof steps, the woman came out with her muzzleloader, but took a deep sigh of relief upon seeing Amos. As Amos removed his hat, the woman set the weapon against the porch post. Amos nodded politely, dismounted, and told her of his plan.

"Ma'am, these men have come a long way in their present condition, and I'm fearful more will die soon if they are unable to receive treatment and medical care. Could they use your house for a few days? Just to get them stabilized."

"Ah s'pose so but, even with yo'wah generosity, Ah have little he'yah fo' they'm," she responded quietly.

"I'll take care of that. I'll ride north and get medical supplies…morphine, opium, alcohol, bandages, splints, whatever I can buy," said Amos. "I know of a place where medicine might be made available. I'll ride back here and deliver the supplies to you before the wagon train gets this far. Meanwhile, you should make ready for them; there's a nurse on board who will tell you what to do once they arrive. Is there someplace around here where you might be able to buy food."

"Ah got kin up the road a piece and then fuhthuh no'wath from they'ah," she said hesitantly. "They buried food the Yankees didn't fahnd. They been helpin' me. They'll help a little."

Pastor Nordquist sensed uncertainty in her voice, reached into his vest, counted out some money, and handed it to the woman.

"This might increase their generosity. I realize where your loyalties lie but, from what I've seen, this war may be over soon – I certainly hope so – and this money will be very useful when everyone can attempt to live normally again. You tell them that…after you tell them why you need the food."

"Who should Ah tell them gave me the money?"

"'An angel of God' would still be nice," Amos smiled.

The woman weakly smiled back. It was the first time Amos had seen her smile, and he marveled at how different she looked at that moment, and how good that weak smile made him feel. Upon seeing their mother smile for the first time in months, in stark contrast to the facial darkness and heaviness they were used to seeing, her children grabbed and held her, emotionally absorbing her brief brightness.

Pastor Nordquist touched the brim of his hat, and rode at a brisk pace north in the rain until he reached the field hospital, bought provisions and medical supplies, and rode south again to the woman's house.

No evidence of the wagon train. "No suh, they haven't arrahved yet."

Amos headed further south to again find the wagon train.

Amos badly needed prolonged sleep, his horse an extended rest. The rain stopped earlier and the sky was clearing when, as darkness began to fall, Amos reined his horse into a grove of trees off the road where three men were already next to a campfire and, in the cold air, playing cards in the firelight. Two kerosene lanterns hung on tall stakes. The card game was apparently engrossing, for when Amos rode into the campsite, the men glanced toward him, beyond him for a moment, relaxed and ignored him. Amos thought of the old wagon driver. It seems people in this territory are oddly intent on ignoring strangers. Or perhaps I'm becoming invisible.

The evening sky was clear and cold, and a sugar moon was beginning to rise, illuminating the eastern horizon. In the moonlight, firelight and lamplight, Amos could see a lot of money on the ground, Federal money. Who were these men, and how did they get that much money – money that could be gambled away?

Amos dismounted, led his tired horse to a grassy field by a creek near the campsite, and took his bedroll off the back of his saddle. He unsaddled his horse, allowing his horse to graze, and walked back into the general area of the three card players.

At a distance he watched the men, apprehensive of who they were, for their language was vulgar and loutish. Finally one man called, and hands were shown.

"Gawdamsonofabitchallt'hell!"

Another man laughed maniacally, and pulled the money toward the considerable sum he already had in front of him.

"That's three hands in a row, fr'en'. You mus' be one dam' lucky sonofabitch," one of the losers said, picking up his hand and holding it as if he was still be in the throes of betting.

"You seen fer yersef, didn't y'?" responded the winner. "Yeah, guess I'm lucky." The winner spat chewing tobacco spittle to one side. "Stick around me an' mebbe some'll rub off on you."

"Don't know that I wan' any 'a you rubbin' off on me, fr'en'. I'll tell ya though, you win four hands in a row, an' I'm gonna wonder how you done it."

The third man nodded in agreement, unblinking, staring at the winner menacingly.

"I ain't got no control over the cards, boys. It's the luck a' the draw. That's all. You boys wanna play another hand?"

"Yeah. I do. I wanna see if you're dumb enough to make it four in a row," said the second man. The third man continued to stare.

"Only one way to find out how dumb I am. Hell, I might even be as dumb as you two boys." He picked up the cards, did a quick gambler's shuffle, and handed it to the second man. "Your turn."

As the second man reshuffled and dealt cards in the light of the fire, lanterns and moon, Amos continued to watch, sitting on a log about 20 feet away.

"You two boys think I'm lucky," said the winner. "Hell, it's all relative. I ain't lucky. Could be you're jest unlucky." He watched the second man deal. "Hell, you said it took you two tries at deserting the last regiment you joined." He spat to one side. "I c'n always do it the first night. Jes' kinda wander off. Trouble with you boys," added the winner, amused, "is you cain't act, you cain't be anybody but you, and if you is only you, like right now, they's gonna guard you real good until they throws you into the line. But me, hell, I can be ol' Abe Lincoln's twin brother! Hell, yes!" The winner became animated. "*Cain't* wait! Get me into that front line so I c'n kill Johnnies! Hell, you two birds probably always look like you do now...no commitment t' nuthin'." The winner looked pathetically at the other two. "That ain't good. No two ways about it."

Amos Nordquist was confused. "What regiment are you talking about?" Amos asked, self-conscious about his accent. "Why did you desert?" They had forgotten he was there. His accent helped; the men thought Amos innocuous.

"Cain't reenlist if y' don't desert, fr'en," explained the second gambler. Amos was more confused.

"Why…if you want to reenlist…," asked Amos, "if you intend to desert, why enlist in the first place?"

The others chuckled.

"Get a bonus for enlistin', fr'en," said the second man. "Big bonus. Hell, I've enlisted mebbe four times. Where d'ya think I get money like this?"

The man gestured at the cards, spat a mouthful of chewing tobacco to one side, and wiped his mouth.

"Cain't re-enlist if yer still in the ranks. Gotta desert. Then re-enlist some-place where they never heard a' y' before. How many times've you deserted?" the second man asked the third.

"Three times. Gettin' harder t' do. Army's getting' too dam' suspicious. Remember this last time I enlisted, they put us all in jail 'til they could get us on a train south. Then they stand guard o'er us the whole trip. I usually jes' jump the train, but they shoot you now if you do. Had t' go all the way t'…hell, I never knew. Under guard the whole time. Dunno if I'm gonna do much more a' this."

"You boys gotta be like *actors*," implored the winner. "See, actors know yer brains talk to other brains." He looked back and forth seriously at the other two. "Not out loud, but kinda silent like. You know? It happens alla time. I knows this. So you don't even be thinkin' about jumpin' the train. Don't *think* that. The whole time, be thinkin' you want to be on the front lines. Hell, ol' man Grant needs all the help he c'n get. An' you be thinkin' you wanna help 'im. Truly. That'll make everyone guardin' you think you're the most loyal man alive. Jest wanna shoot ol' Massa, free the darkies, and stop this secession. That's how to *think*. And while you is *thinkin'* right, be waitin' for a break…'n when it comes, take it."

The winner bit off another hunk of plug chewing tobacco.

"Works every time."

"How many times you re-enlist?" asked the second man.

"I started doin' this, oh, two years ago," answered the winner. "I suspect I've enlisted, on average, let's see…once every two or three months. In no hurry."

"Two years? Once every two or three months?" responded the third man.

"Hell, that's…that's more'n six times."

The winner looked at the third man curiously. "Yup," said the winner, "that's more'n six times."

"Then you don't need to be winnin' like ya been, fr'en', cuz you already have a pot full of cash. Right? And Uriah and me, we're jest about broke."

The second man put his hand face-down on the ground, stood up, pulled a pistol out of his coat, and pointed it at the winner.

"Put that away," said the winner, also standing up as he saw his trust betrayed. "Don't be gettin' any ideas. You c'n have the money. An' I only carries what I needs."

"What you needs. Well let's jes' check and see. Uriah, search 'im…then grab his stash there."

As the second man held the winner at gunpoint, the short-but-powerful-ly-built third man, Uriah, searched the winner, taking money and his gun, and picked up all the money in front of the winner.

He searched the winner's saddlebags for additional money – and hit the mother lode: over four thousand dollars.

Uriah and the second man looked at each other with the look of men who unexpectedly finally found what they were looking for. Uriah walked back to the second man, staring at the neatly wrapped cash in his hands the whole way. All three had been focused on their hands, the winnings, the robbery underway and, finally, all that cash in Uriah's hands. Amos wondered whether he really was invisible, because the three men seemed oblivious to the fact that, in the dark, Amos was sitting on a log 20 feet away watching the whole thing.

"Well, I'm glad you needs so much," replied the second man to the winner, "cuz this is one a' the best card games I've ever been in. Oh, I don' think I tol' you," said the the second man with treacly sincerity: "I always win. Uriah," he ordered, "you take your half and I'll take the rest."

Unable to count well, Uriah, without regard to bill denomination, dutifully sorted the gambling and additional money into two equal-sized stacks, and gave one of them to the second man.

"We might as well jes' ride north," said the second man, smiling. "Re-en-listin' is gettin' too dangerous…and, hell, now we don't need to re-enlist anyway. Not for a dam' sight. Whoohoo!"

The second man turned to the winner.

"You talk about us bein' unlucky? Hell, this is our lucky night! An' how's yer luck holdin' out, fr'en'?"

The second man tossed his head back and laughed acidly while Uriah held on to his hat as he guffawed, his failing teeth looking like a piano keyboard. The campfire illuminated a bitter light in his eyes, the consequence of a lifetime of feral acrimony and godlessness.

As the second man held the winner at gunpoint, Uriah saddled his horse, the second man's horse, and ran off the winner's horse. Amos' horse was in the nearby field, not visible in the dark. Neither, it seemed, was Amos who crouched behind the log, almost holding his breath. He had his pistols, loaded with bullets and "blue whistlers," in each hand, and hoped not to use them.

As the two men mounted their horses, taking their eyes off the winner, the winner, in and out of tight spots before, quick as a rattlesnake grabbed a hidden pistol from under his right pant leg aside his boot. As Uriah and the second man reined their horses around to ride off, the second man raised his pistol, aimed at the winner, and pulled the trigger just as the winner's pistol fired at the second man. The distance between the two was less than eight feet.

Amos watched wide-eyed as the second man fell forward on his horse and to the ground, blood oozing from of his forehead, and the winner dropped to his knees, his hands reaching toward a wound in the middle of his throat before he fell over on his face near the second man.

Uriah turned his horse in circles several times, uncertain of what to do, wanting only to leave. Seconds ticked. He had half the money; he also escaped from a prison work gang years earlier. His thoughts started with "leave," and the impulse was growing. Spurring his horse, Uriah wildly galloped off, quickly disappearing in the distant darkness as Amos, stunned, slowly stood`.

The sound of hoof beats dying in the distance, Amos cautiously walked by the campfire to the two bloodied men lying on the ground nearly side-by-side, the second man on his back looking blankly upward, a bloodied hole in his forehead, and the winner on his stomach, face to one side, the campfire dancing in his lifeless eyes. Amos dropped to his haunches, reached over and picked up the second man's cards left face-down on the ground. Queen of hearts, nine of spades, a six of clubs, a three, a deuce…he had nothing. If he dealt himself a better hand, intuited Amos, he and the winner would still be alive. As Amos looked at the second man, Amos remembered the second man's inside pocket was full of money.

Amos ran his fingers through his hair, thinking. Authorities? The two horses. The money. The war had made things relatively lawless. Anyone, including whoever might represent authority, finding the bodies would take the money, telling no one else. Amos thought that giving it to someone in authority would probably have a similar result – government men of character were carrying muskets and repeaters on battlefields. The money was originally payment from the Union army – enlistment bonuses. Amos reached inside the jacket of the second man and took out the purse containing a large sum. He considered returning it to the Union Army when he found Uncle Torvald.

Amos retrieved the two horses, lifted one dead body over the saddle on each horse and, cutting some strands from a coil of rope tied to one of the saddles, tethered the bridles to his saddle. He mounted, headed to the road, and slowly rode off to tell someone of what happened. He wasn't sure of whom he should tell, or if anyone would care, but it was what he should do.

After slowly riding in the moonlight for about a half hour, fighting to stay awake, Amos came across a country church not burned in Sheridan's decimation of the Valley. Black silhouettes of crosses and short rounded monuments gilded silver in the moonlight were evidence of a cemetery on the south side. Amos reined his horse toward the small parsonage, dismounted and knocked at the door. No sound. He knocked again.

"Who is it?" asked a voice with frigid courtesy from inside after the second knock.

"I am Pastor Amos Nordquist," said Amos, his Scandinavian accent unmistakable. "I am on my way to…Richmond. I witnessed a gunfight less than an hour ago. Two men were killed and I need to report this to the authorities. I do not know where to go. Can you help me?"

Amos hoped whoever was behind the door was a Samaritan, not a Levite. After a moment, the door opened slightly, vague fingers unlatched the door. Barely visible, a person inside peered out.

"If you will help me," said Amos, "I will be happy to pay you for your assistance."

The door slowly opened the rest of the way. A small, white-haired man with a lantern held over his head looked at Amos, and in a rasping voice said, "There is no more law in these parts. And no undertaker. The war has taken them all. And why would you be going to Richmond?"

"That might be where my Uncle is. I have something I need to give him."

"He's in the Confederacy?"

"Ah, no, he is in the Union Army."

"Then he's not in Richmond…not yet. Try Petersburg south of Richmond, southeast of here."

Amos made a mental note of this, turned and pointed toward the three horses. "Less than an hour ago, two men were killed." Amos looked back at the man grimly. "By each other. Over money. I need to bury them somewhere, and give the money to…its rightful owner."

In the moonlight, the old man looked solemnly past Amos toward the two corpses still on the horses.

"I am Reverend Joshua H. Harrison," was the quiet response. "After you unburden those animals, you are welcome to spend the night here."

The next morning, Reverend Harrison fixed Pastor Nordquist breakfast. Two scrambled eggs.

"I used to have more, but the foraging armies took almost all of it," said Reverend Harrison. "They burned my barn, my chicken coop…after they ate most of my chickens. Burned the hay bins. They apologized; said if it were up to them, they wouldn't be doing it – but it was not up to them. Took my three head of cattle. Took my only horse. I recovered four chickens from the woods over yonder. God's provision, no doubt. Still a few carrots in the ground. And by the grace of God, there are many ways to fix eggs." Reverend Harrison took another small bite. "Perhaps more than ways to fix men's souls."

Amos looked at Reverend Harrison and made no reply.

"My uncle served under a man named Custer," said Amos after a moment. "Have you heard of him? Apparently he dresses flamboyantly."

"I can't say I've seen him. There are many Union soldiers…lately far more than Confederate soldiers. Most look dirty and tired. I have seen no sartorial splendor."

Reverend Harrison took another bite.

"I suspect this war will end soon if anyone on either side has any sense," said Reverend Harrison after a moment. "Last night you may have noticed there is a cemetery here. After we finish eating, you may use it if you wish. Lately it has been used often. I take no side in this conflict. I offer only Christian charity. A place to sleep, perhaps. Minor medical attention. Whatever I am able. Most who accept it seem to be good men."

"I very much appreciate your hospitality," responded Pastor Nordquist. "I will reciprocate."

"It is not expected."

"You have a parsonage, sanctuary, four chickens and a graveyard. Occasional reciprocity would, no doubt, be appreciated."

Reverend Harrison said nothing.

After eating, Pastor Nordquist borrowed Reverend Harrison's shovel and buried the winner and the second man in the cemetery. Harrison was not exaggerating; there were many fresh graves. Since funerals are not for the deceased, Pastor Nordquist's first funeral oration and subsequent prayer were brief. Both pastors needed the edification of the Holy Spirit but, Amos thought, edification need not be long-winded.

As Amos prepared to leave, he said to Reverend Harrison, "You now have a sanctuary, four chickens, a graveyard, and two horses." Amos raised his eyebrows. "Do you have a buckboard?"

"I do," responded Reverend Harrison with more emotion than usual. "It needs repair but God, in His good timing, will provide that."

"His good timing is now," said Amos without pause. "Where's the wagon?"

Using muscle and ingenuity, Pastor Nordquist was able to repair the buckboard wagon to where it was usable again

"You now have a sanctuary, four chickens, a graveyard, two horses and a wagon," concluded Pastor Nordquist.

"Your generosity has been a God-send," replied Reverend Harrison beaming. Pastor Nordquist smiled back.

"God is very generous," said Pastor Nordquist. "As you know, often that generosity is unexpected." Pastor Nordquist looked about him, surveying the modest sanctuary, parsonage, and charred barn and chicken house remains, and weighed their potential in the light of Reverend Harrison being truly committed to God. "As the saying goes, 'God works in mysterious ways.'"

Pastor Nordquist saddled his horse and mounted while Reverend Harrison watched. Pastor Nordquist put his right hand inside his coat and pulled out the dead gamblers' purse with roughly $2,200. He held it, studied it, reached down and gave it to Reverend Harrison who perfunctorily took whatever it was that was being handed to him.

Reverend Harrison stared at it for a moment.

His eyes became solemn. He looked questioningly at Pastor Nordquist, and stared at the purse again, disinclined to believe what it appeared to be.

As he carefully opened it and looked inside, his facial expression changed from incredulity to astonishment. He looked up at Pastor Nordquist, speechless.

"Reverend Harrison, last night I worried about where I should deliver this money," said Amos as he sat on his horse. "This morning it became evident. No one would use it more wisely than you."

Pastor Nordquist touched his fingers to his hat, smiled again at the older man looking up at him, reined his horse to the left, and began to canter in the direction of the wagon train.

26

Later in the day, he found the wagon train and told the nurse and the old driver there was a church up the road where they should forage their mules and horses and attend to the wounded. Bury some of the dead if need be. "And there might be eggs to share among the weakest until you reach the widow's home where there are some beds, medicine and, hopefully by now, food."

Reverend Harrison said Petersburg. Just south of Richmond, the capital of the Confederacy, to the southeast. Further south, Pastor Nordquist found a road that headed east southeast and he followed it. Lost in his own thoughts, he rode blindly, hoping the route he was following would eventually lead to the Union army and Uncle Torvald.

What the Union army had not destroyed, the weather attacked. Rain fired down like sniper bullets, gradually turning to sleet and then heavy snow, making riding conditions nearly unbearable.

Amos continued to ride slowly, stopping in the evenings at abandoned houses, the owners unintentionally driven out by Phil Sheridan's disciplined forces whose orders were to burn everything except houses, and to leave each family enough food to last until spring – orders from people with apparently no idea of what purpose barns and storehouses served.

Amos discovered a road that paralleled railroad tracks heading east southeast, and that night again did what many army stragglers did: he borrowed someone's vacated house in order to get out of the cold. Behind the house, the dark sky and snow cover obscured the frozen, charred remains of the former barn and outbuildings, burned by Federal troops as ordered, probably as the family looked on in horror. He stepped inside the partially open front door holding his lantern over his head and found more destruction; the home had been ransacked by deserters, bummers. Exhausted, as Pastor Nordquist rested in someone else's bed that night, he began wondering who the family was and where they were, but sleep quickly overcame him.

The following day after making certain the residence was in better condition than found, he continued on his way.

Several days later he approached a larger home, a stately 2.5-story residence in which there already were others: Union soldiers with frostbite, chilblains or minor foot or leg wounds, injuries not bad enough to require being transported to a distant field hospital, but of sufficient severity to preclude marching for a while. Treated, dressed and left behind to heal until they could shortly catch up with their units, these men had nothing to do except dry-out, warm up, eat, sleep, plan and talk.

The four men watched a fire blazing in the family hearth and were comfortable to the point of almost imagining they were invited guests, as if the owner and family were still there, perhaps in the adjacent kitchen. The men discussed the mindless logic of war that included the swift, methodical destruction of farms painstakingly constructed and expanded over years, perhaps a lifetime.

"Boys, I gotta tell ya, I'm gettin' a mite sick of this. This destruction's gettin' senseless, y'know?"

"Yeah, I know," said the second man. "What'll these people do when the war ends?"

"If the dam' Rebs would jes' quit, none of this'd be necessary," rationalized the first man. "There ain't gonna be a split rail fence, beef cow or corn crib left in Virginia by the time this war's over." Holding his hands out questioningly, he asked, "Why not face the music? They ain't a' gonna win."

"They don't seem t' think that way," said a second man passively.

"On the other hand," responded a third man, drawing on his pipe, "y' gotta believe they'd be a lot more inclined t' quit if we weren't down here."

"Dunno," said the second man, quietly, also smoking his pipe. "Dunno that anyone thinks about quittin' now, no matter what. Seems like everybody's really dug in. We have a formidable enemy, as they say. An' so do they." He puffed on his pipe once. "Jes' look in the mirror."

After asking the men about accommodations, Pastor Nordquist left the discussion for a moment to put his coat up to dry and, going upstairs, inspect his bed for the night, a simple affair – once one of the children's – too small for Amos, but it was far better than the cold ground outside. The quilt was a work of art.

Leaving the room, he saw a Bible left behind on a chest of drawers. He picked it up and read the inscription in the front: "To beloved Wilfred from Mother and Father. Easter, March 31, 1861." Twelve days before Ft. Sumter was fired upon, Amos thought. Why hadn't Wilfred taken his Bible with him? Had the family left in a great hurry? Was it a simple oversight? Perhaps they had intentionally left it behind for whoever would find it, enabling its use while serving as a reminder that civilization once thrived here. As Pastor Nordquist perused the Bible looking at notations, verses underlined, he silently hoped Wilfred was still alive.

Amos took the Bible downstairs with him, identified himself and what he was, and asked the others if they would mind if he read from the Good Book. In the firelight, the others quietly nodded respectfully in reply, indicating it would not bother them at all. In the warmth of a hearth in someone else's home, surrounded by cold, wet darkness that momentarily hid burned buildings and dead animals, Pastor Nordquist read from the 4th chapter of Philippians about the peace of God that passes all understanding, and the men listened quietly. Then he turned to chapters 5, 6 and 7 in Matthew, the Sermon on the Mount, where Jesus explained His mission on earth.

After Amos had finished reading, for a while little was said, the men lost in their thoughts, thoughts that had not ventured forth in some time. Gradually conversation returned, and soon the subject was the upcoming presidential election between President Abraham Lincoln and General George B. McClellan, former Union army General-in-Chief whom Lincoln demoted. The men served under McClellan and still thought of him with fondness.

"Caleb, you were with McClellan in '62. You think you'll vote for 'im now?"

"Well," Caleb paused to think, "like t' say I would. But, y' know, that was a different time. Lotta change in two, three years. There was a war goin' on but, same time, compared to now, there wasn't a war goin' on. Not like now."

"What you mean t' say is McClellan ain't Grant."

"S'pose so, Brigham," responded Caleb, shrugging his shoulders. "S'pose that sums it up. Y' know – I'm not sure – we had everything we needed to go out and get it done pronto but, like some people say, I'm not sure ol' Mac wanted t' get shot at."

"Well, of course he don't want t' get shot at, Caleb. Who wants t' get shot at?" asked a third man.

"No one, Zeke, no one," said Brigham, smoothing his beard. Then he smiled. "But look at the four of us."

The others drew on their pipes as they stared at the fire.

"James, what d'ya think?"

"Trouble is," responded James, a stocky redhead with an unkempt beard, relighting his pipe with a lucifer, "you can't jest fiddle around and gradually figure out how t' do it when you first get in a war, Zeke. Wars have a bad habit of not wantin' t' wait. You gotta get things done right away as if you have *already* been doing it for two years, and now it's time to bring this thing to a quick ending. Only ya gotta think like that at the *beginnin'*. Ya *get* in, *clean* someone's clock, and get *out!*" said James, pounding his left palm with his right fist as he looked back and forth at the others.

"Now, James, that's easy to say," said Caleb, his eyebrows raised. "Ain't so easy t' go do."

"Well, let's jes' say that if we had Ulysses Grant in '62," responded James, "with what we had, but doin' it the way we are now, we might 'a won the war then. Instead, here we are jest beatin' on the Rebs. Jest beatin' on 'em. Runnin' 'em off from their homes. Burnin' barns and storehouses. Forever takin' their farm animals. An' they still ain't a'gonna quit. Everyone sufferin'. Zeke, frankly, I'da been a lot happier throwin' everything at 'em in '62. Coulda done that, y'know?"

"I sorta liked ol' Mac."

"Hell, back then we all liked McClellan, Brigham."

"So, y' gonna vote for 'im?" asked Brigham.

For a while the men thought, the only sound being the crackling fireplace.

"We been doin' this for what, about three years?" asked Zeke. "That right, Caleb?"

"Almost."

"We're what, about 20% of what we were – numbers-wise?"

"Our bunch? Guess so. Thems that didn't die from getting' hit by Johnnies, got laid out by disease…malaria, yellow fever, smallpox. Pneumonia. Typhoid." Caleb's face went expressionless. "Hell, we probably lost as many to sickness as got kilt. And some run away, but," Caleb shrugged, "lotta boys ain't comin' back. Remember those boys? O'Brien. Walker. Ames. Gilman. Calkins…" Caleb laid his head back against the sofa, his eyes distant, his mouth falling open slightly, and whispered, "…dyin' like flies at Wilderness."

"Miserable," muttered James quietly, surpressing his anger. "Dam' miserable." His mind flashed on friends lost at the Battle of the Wilderness and, as if having been under extreme compression, an agonized epithet exploded from his mouth, the violent sound raking the room's silence.

The four men, saying nothing, empathetically looked at James, then returned their attention to the fireplace, allowing the flames to remesmerize, individual thoughts returning to that battle, the second day and how vicious it became, and brave men lost.

"The Rebs ain't gonna quit, James?" said Zeke after a moment. "Well, *hell*, at this point, ain't any of *us* gonna quit *either*. Hell, no."

"Eventually someone's gotta quit," said Caleb, making the obvious point.

"Ain't gonna be us," said Zeke.

"That's what everyone's sayin', Zeke," said Brigham.

"So what yer sayin', Zeke," said James, "is come hell or high water, this war goes on…until the Rebs cain't go on no more."

"That's what I'm sayin'."

"Well, now wait a minute. Fact of the matter is," said Caleb, "you vote for McClellan, the war ends. That's what the Democrats want. Peace. Let the Johnnies start their own dam' country."

"Hell, that ain't what Mac wants. Ain't you read what he says? He still wants to win."

"Wonder if them boys asked him what he thought before they nominated him?" questioned James. "Don't think they did. Whole rest of the party? Peace at any price. Call it off. Let's go home. That Vallandigham with his copperheaded treason." James hit his right thigh with his fist. "Damnable disgrace!"

"Can't believe people like him exist. That miserable bastard's lower 'n a swamp snake," muttered Zeke. "Like he gives a dam' about peace. Or anything except bein' centerstage. Don't any a' those boys know anything? About doin' what's right even if ya gotta die tryin'? An' how about us? Do any a' those boys think about thems what's doin' the fightin' 'n why?" Zeke's face darkened as he stared at the fire. "Vallandigham. Someone up north should just shoot the son-of-a-bitch."

"Seems like shootin's still really the only answer, boys," said Brigham. "War's really not too complicated. We jes' keep shootin' Johnnies until they hang it up."

"Then that means we vote for Abe Lincoln," said Caleb.

"Nuthin' wrong with votin' for Abe," replied Zeke. "I don't know why so many people hate Abe Lincoln. Some of those boys seem to live another day just to hate Abe Lincoln."

"I noticed that," said Brigham. "Intense. Dunno why that is. Listenin' t' them, you'd think he was the devil incarnate."

"Well, I'll tell ya, boys: me, I like Lincoln," said Zeke. "He's solid, y' know?

"Someone's gotta make the tough decisions," said Brigham. "Easy to second-guess when you're not on the hot seat. So many people seem to think easy answers is really answers."

"Hell, some seem t' think their dam' questions is answers. Seem to have a tough time with anything that requires, y' know, character, sacrifice."

"Character and sacrifice?" responded James. "Hell, votin' for Lincoln'll give y' all the character n' sacrifice y' want. It means we jes' keep doin' what we're doin.'"

"Yeah, but now we're doin' it with ol' U. S. Grant," said Caleb.

"An' Sherman."

"An' Sheridan."

The men silently weighed the implication of what they just said.

"See, now we're there," said Brigham. "If those boys were runnin' the same army we had in '62…" He held his hands out palms up. "Wooo. Know what I mean?"

"It takes too *damned* long to find out who can really fight!" said James in frustration. "You seen Sheridan talkin' to the other generals. I swear they'd rather hit the Johnnies in a drivin' snowstorm than feel the wrath a' Phil."

"Yeah, I noticed that too. He ain't very big, but that's a general. That's a goddam' general there."

"An' Custer. Sheridan shoor likes Armstrong."

"Custer gets things done."

"So does his brother, Tom."

"Yeah," replied Zeke with a muffled laugh. "Cut outa the same cloth. Somethin' really drives those boys. But it ain't bein' nuts. They jest hold t' a certain standard, y' understand?"

"Dunno, Zeke. Gotta be a little nuts," chuckled Brigham.

"They's a war goin' on," Caleb added, nodding several times. "Gotta be a little nuts t' be any good at this."

"Yeah," said James, making himself more comfortable. "So, what – two, three years later – here we are."

Caleb got up, poked the fire, and put on another log.

"Well, boys? Time t' quit foolin' around. James?! Who y' gonna vote for?!"

"So we may be a little nuts, boys," said James, carefully weighing his words, "but I'm not crazy enough t' be votin' for Mac." He looked at the others. "It was a great time, warn't it? We were way bigger, stronger, healthier – potentially more lethal in '62 than we are now – and without becoming the cynical sons-of-bitches we've become."

"Yeah, but we didn't have City Point then – that's a real machine there – and, let's face it, y' gotta become a cynical son-of-a-bitch t' be any good at war," responded Caleb.

"I don't entirely disagree, but remember how many men we had?" James stroked his beard. "An' *good* men; not like that bunch that's a' comin' in now – here t'day, gone t'morra'. Back then, *hell*uvanarmy. If we knew then what we know now, with Grant we coulda rolled over the Rebs that year. But, in comparison to ol' U. S. Grant, like people say, Mac didn't use the army when he shoulda."

"Don't necessarily teach that at West Point."

"Grant was at West Point."

"From what I've read, not much."

"Hell, Armstrong weren't hardly there at all."

"Don't repeat what those idiots write."

"Can you imagine what Grant, Sherman, Sheridan and Gibbon woulda done in '62?"

"Yeah," replied James, "but unfortunately that's *all* I can do. Imagine. I see what we're doin' now. This is goddam' warfare. But this'll get 'er done."

Looking at the fire, the four men nodded simultaneously.

"So, James," said Caleb, drawing on his pipe, "if Lincoln's your choice, let me ask y': you votin' *against* Mac, or *for* Abe?"

"I'm not votin' against General McClellan. Wouldn't do that. But I'm not votin' for 'im either," answered James, staring at the fire. "I'm votin' for Lincoln. I don't care how much the Democrats hate 'im. No one likes war, but we've gone too far to turn back, an' I have no doubt we're doin' the right thing. An' now we have Grant, Sherman, Sheridan, Gibbon and them runnin' this here army. I like our chances. Given some more time, we're gonna end this thing an' we're gonna be damn' proud we stuck it out."

"Still, lotta people think Lincoln's gone," cautioned Caleb. "I suspect even ol' Abe might think so. Lotta people up north, newspapermen, tired a' the war."

"Why the hell're *they* tired?" asked James. "Hell, we give 'em somethin' t' write. And they ain't done no fightin'. Jubal Early gets close t' Washington an' all those boys ran and hid. Never seen no dam' newspaperman carryin' a gun. Dunno where they get their news. Must sit around in saloons interviewin' deserters…or one another, comparin' notes. Some of that stuff…where the hell was I? Tell y', I never had no newspaperman 'round t' ask me if I was tired."

"Well, if one did," asked Zeke, "what would y' say?"

"Hell yes, I'm tired!" James replied, angrily looking at the others. "An' I'll stay tired 'til this goddam' war is o'er."

James turned and defiantly stared at the fire.

"What are you boys gonna do?" asked James after a moment, holding his pipe in his teeth, and looking obliquely at the others. "Vote for Mac?"

The others responded with body language that unquestionably said, "No."

"Then, there y' have it," said James as he looked back at the fire. "If most people think that way, we'll get what we came for. The Union'll stand." He relit his pipe, puffing several times, put his pipe down and looked at the others. "We may not, but the Union will."

The next morning, Pastor Nordquist saddled his horse that was nibbling grass stubble painstakingly uncovered beneath the snow. At the recommendation of the men in the house, Amos began looking for a route that would lead to Petersburg. That's where Grant is, he thought, and where the men expected Sheridan would be eventually. After all, that's where Robert E. Lee and the Army of Northern Virginia are.

Late morning sunlight filtered through the thin, opaque clouds, brightening the snow cover all about Amos. The countryside was quiet. No gun fire, no campfires, no irreverent voices interjecting human presence, and the snow absorbed sound, save one. The soft plodding of his horse was all Amos heard as he rode, thinking of how Uncle Torvald's location, and now his own, were unknown.

Several days passed when in late afternoon, as the sky was becoming almost too dark to see, Pastor Nordquist heard the sounds of soldiers in the distance. Not the sound of gunfire and angry men in battle.

Amos heard singing.

They were singing. The sound was so dramatically civilized, gentrified, that at first Amos doubted the sound came from anyone's army, but as he gradually grew nearer, he knew this sound was the sound of soldiers. As he rode closer, he could see at a distance they were, again, Union soldiers.

But the singing wasn't just from Union soldiers.

On one side of a wide creek were the Union soldiers around several campfires. On the other side behind trees and brush, barely visible in the light of their own campfires, was a contingent from the Confederacy. These rivals, seemingly bitter enemies during the day, were singing together at night – singing the same song at the same time – one side to the west of the creek, and the other to the east, and it seemed the two sides were trying to make the two sounds blend without separation, as if to sound what they were unwilling to do.

> *We're tenting tonight on the old campground,*
> *Give us a song to cheer*
> *Our weary hearts, a song of home*
> *And friends we hold so dear.*

Pastor Nordquist marveled. What kind of war is this? Amos shrugged; he could make no sense of what he saw and heard.

He listened intently. The vocal talent was modest at best – many men could not carry a tune, and pitch was anyone's guess – but the conviction was unmistakable. The song ended. In a moment another began with one man starting and the others joining in. As Amos listened, this went on for quite a while, each song begun by the same Union soldier who seemed to be the unofficial song leader for both sides.

Grown weary from earlier events of the day, the song leader slowly stood up and looked over at the other side of the creek.

"'Night, Reb!" he said loudly.

"'Night, Yank," came a voice from the other side of the creek.

The two sides were retiring for the night.

"Howdy, stranger," said a Union soldier to Amos who was still seated on his horse. "What's your business?"

27

1865

"I am a chaplain," said Amos as he dismounted, "and I'm looking for my uncle who is with the…" Pastor Nordquist had ridden a considerable distance, could not remember the formal name of the group, and it was too dark for him to see the piece of paper he carried. "He's with the Wolverines," said Amos.

"Well, they ain't here," said the man. "But we could use a new chaplain. Other one got kilt two days ago. He was carryin' wounded to the rear; a lot a' our boys got wounded, some wounded pretty bad, so he was movin' fast, not thinkin' a' his own safety." The man paused thinking about it. "Before he got hit, he kept a list a' who died, where they was from and where they was buried. He made sure each grave was marked. I got the list. Gonna get longer. Another man a' the Lord'd help about now."

The man studied Amos for a moment.

"How well d'y' shoot?"

"My job is to minister and to heal – I have some medical skills as well as providing spiritual direction – but not to kill."

"Yeah, s'pose so," said the man, expecting the answer Amos gave. "Wouldn't be right for a man a' the cloth to be shootin' Johnnies. Hell, most a' 'em believes in God as much as any a' us. 'Fact, you might be able to do some good over there too. They's gettin' as many kilt as us…I hopes."

"Whatever spiritual edification I can give, I will," responded Pastor Nordquist without expression.

He tied his horse to a tree and, as the men seated around a nearby campfire watched, he set up his small, dirty pup-tent, took his soogan and laid it out on the ground under tent cover. The others said nothing, but seemed relaxed. Amos looked at the men, barely visible in the campfire light, attempting to somehow study their eyes, and a thought came to him.

"I've wondered," began Amos, "do some of you think having a man of God nearby brings good luck?"

For a moment the silence was as still as the air until one man spoke.

"Maybe a couple years ago. Not now. That superstition's a peacetime luxury…fer when yer not sure. After y' go through a couple years a' what we done, anybody still alive goes over to the Lord."

Amos nodded, set a spiritual bar by praying with the men without asking or being asked, slipped under his blankets and made himself comfortable for the night.

The next morning Pastor Nordquist awoke to another light dusting on snow-covered tents, caissons, cannon and wagons. It was bitterly cold, and men lay under blankets, unwilling to fully awake. Except at that moment the cook had coffee ready. The men were hungrier than they were cold, and the smell of hot coffee brought them out of their tents.

Breakfast was a simple affair although not as simple as on the Confederate side of the creek where provisions were low. Consequently, the business of the day got underway sooner than the Union soldiers would have preferred.

"Down, Yank!" came the perfunctory yell from the Rebel side.

A moment after the Union soldiers spontaneously gulped their coffee and began grabbing their rifles, a murderous Rebel fusillade began, heavier than usual, perhaps a response to the fact the Yanks had more to eat, and one Union soldier next to Amos was hit immediately.

The Federals fired back with greater intensity, but the Confederates were already dug in, and the return-fire brought no initial casualties. As subsequent firing continued, gunfire became more sporadic, less intense, as soldiers on both sides reloaded and became acclimated to another long day of skirmishing, simultaneously trying to kill but not killed.

Pastor Nordquist began to attend to the wounded man – Simon Harris from Shepherdstown, West Virginia, Amos was later told – but Simon was already dead. Awake – breakfast – dead, thought Amos. Then eternity.

Pastor Nordquist and another man cautiously moved the body to a sheltered area toward the rear of the camp where it would await burial along with others whose souls were removed during the day.

"Who is responsible for digging graves?" Amos asked.

"The burial detail. Units rotate. Some outfits have darkies for jobs like that. We take good care of our dead – assuming we win, which we been doin'."

"If we don't?"

"Well, sometimes the Johnnies bury our men – and sometimes in mass graves. Gotta be dug up later and identified by relatives or someone. When we win, its s'pose t' be our job to bury their men. How we do it depends on how much time anyone has. Try t' do it proper dependin' on if we have the time. Dig a long ditch sometimes, placin' men end-to-end, mark the graves as we cover 'em up. But sometimes ain't no time t' bury nobody.

"Wantin' to win has partly to do with not wantin' 'em to touch our dead. 'Stay the hell away from those boys.' For some reason, Johnnies don't extend the same courtesy to our boys they do their own," the man said cynically. "S'pose we ain't much different sometimes, but I dunno. Life's a big mystery, a miracle, you know? Life?" The man shook his head. "An' a lotta boys who get hit make the ultimate sacrifice. Gotta honor the ones who did. Y' cain't do that, y' might as well be dead yerself."

As the day progressed, there were casualties on both sides, the suffering of warfare exacerbated by the assault of more rain and sleet. Pastor Nordquist painstakingly helped the surgeon, assisting with the nauseating job of leg and arm surgery, and Amos's help was greatly appreciated.

"I never thought I'd be doing anything like this when I got out of medical school," the surgeon grimaced while cutting through a chloroformed man's bicep and tricep brachii muscles preparatory to sawing the humerus above a shattered elbow, the lower arm hanging loosely. "At first, I thought all this was beneath me, a temporary step down from where I saw myself being – a respected New York doctor – but let me tell you, this is real medical school! In regular practice, how would I ever learn what I've learned here? In regular practice, how many people would live because of me…like they do here? When you consider everything, and think what you're trying to accomplish in life, being a battlefield physician has to be among the most honorable professions there is." The surgeon reached for his surgeon's saw. "Sure, it's a miserable job – blood and bloodied body parts everywhere, and no sleep – but I've saved quite a few of these boys. And I suspect I'll save quite a few more," he added as, carefully positioning the saw at a spot and angle that only he completely understood, the surgeon began his cut. "But that's what doctorin' is all about, isn't it?"

Amos nodded, bent over the operating table, his powerful hands holding the chloroformed man's humerus perfectly still.

Men hit but not killed were brought to Amos and the surgeon, and men bled to death as Amos worked to keep them alive. Amos found names and home addresses pinned inside their shirts. As he carried dead bodies to the rear, he found the area was also used to treat sick soldiers, some of whom were near death and would die.

"Where's the previous chaplain's list of the dead?" Amos asked.

Toward the end of the afternoon as the sky again grew darker, the gunshots began to decrease as if it were the end of the workday. What now? Amos asked himself, the front of his shirt and pants completely blood-stained. More singing?

"Hey, Yank!" yelled a voice from the other side. "We're a mite low on grub over here. You got any taters you'd be willin' 't send o'er?"

The cook and the commanding officer conferred and concluded that they had a little to spare; more provisions were coming the following morning from rear, having just arrived from City Point. The commanding officer ordered two sacks of potatoes sent over to the Rebels. Volunteers were solicited; several men raised their hands. Two men were selected and, their boot laces tied together, and the boots hung around their necks, with the two sacks they forded the cold creek. After reaching the other side, Rebel counterparts took the sacks to the rear while the two Union soldiers sat down, dried their feet, put their boots back on, and went up the short embankment to the rebel camp where they disappeared for about a half hour.

The two men returned, took off their boots again, and again forded the creek. They rejoined their comrades-in-arms feeling no pain. They brought back what remained of a jug of homemade whiskey to share with the others. The others began sharing.

"Dam'!" exclaimed one of the Federal troops as he took a swig. "Dam' hospitable 'a those boys. We send 'em taters, they send back whiskey."

"Guess they must be gettin' pretty good if they can make it that fast," said a second soldier with a reputation for dry humor. His statement went over the heads of the others.

"What?"

"Listen, Jake," said another soldier, "don't always be doin' that dry humor here. Yer the only one who gets it. Hell, you say some dam' thing and then, if it's t' be funny, we gotta ask you t' explain, and then it ain't funny even if it was. That's frustratin'," added the soldier, comically gritting his teeth, "so jes' sheeeuht up."

"Nevertheless, dam' hospitable a' those boys," repeated the first soldier.

"You like that word, don't ya?"

"What? 'Hospitable'? Yeah. It's got a nice ring to it. You might try it out once in a while. Might even try doin' it."

"Hell, I can be *dam'* hospitable."

"Horace, what did they tell you? You wuz over there visitin' for quite a spell."

"Nuthin' new. They's gettin' tired of this war. Said they c'n keep goin' as long as we can, but their provisions're startin' to become a problem. Half their food – which apparently ain't much – ain't edible. Lotta boys have dysentery, pneumonia. Some got worse things. They tell me lately disease has kilt more 'a their boys 'n we have. Ammunition is startin' to get in short supply. And, a' course, weather's awful. They really appreciated the taters. They ain't got no City Point. Sheridan's wiped out the Valley. Hell, I don't know, in the long run maybe that'll be the difference. The sooner this thing's over, the better they'll like it. Guess they got a problem with deserters too."

"It sounds like they're demoralized," said Amos.

"Could be," responded the soldier named Jake, "but with no women around, don't make no difference."

There was a pause.

"What?"

"Jake, what'd I just say?"

"I was wondering," interjected Pastor Nordquist, smiling, "if they might have any need for a chaplain?"

"I think they'll take anything they can get," responded Horace. "Why not just wander over there and ask 'em?"

In the style of Horace and his companion, Amos forded the creek and spent the next hour and a half leading the rebels in worship. This included a sermon on God's omnipotence, and hymn singing.

> *He is coming with the glory of the morning on the wave.*
> *He is wisdom to the mighty; He is honor to the brave.*
> *Though the world make war against Him,*
> *Those with faith in Him are saved*
> *As God is marching on.*

The federal troops couldn't hear the sermon, but when the rebel troops began singing, everyone joined in.

Pastor Nordquist stayed with these troops for several days and found the experience extraordinary. Two sides, two Americas, mirror images of one another, with more intestinal fortitude than Amos knew existed anywhere, each side attempting to avoid dying for a cause, but each convinced their cause was worth the sacrifice. Otherwise, Amos surmised, each side seemed to respect the other, behaving somewhat civilly when not trying to kill one another.

No one quite knew where the Wolverines were. While all knew of George Armstrong Custer, whose relatively flamboyant appearance had become associated with his ability and reputation as a fighter, General Phil Sheridan's notoriety was greater. The men around Amos drew on their pipes, and made a point of telling Amos that, from their vantage point, Sheridan's and Custer's reputation was "part Phil's an' Armstrong's" but a big part belonged to his men. "Anytime an officer gets that reputation," understated one of the soldiers, "sure as hell ain't just him what earned it."

"Nobody reads about us."

"But I'll tell ya," said one man, "from what I knows, Custer don't expect anyone t' do what he wouldn't do hisself. Custer leads the dam' charges. He don't hang back at the rear like most officers. An' we wouldn't be where we are without Phil Sheridan."

The others spontaneously nodded aggressively. Truly determined, inspiring leaders seldom come along, and the Army of the Shenandoah had at least two: Custer and Sheridan. That's what the men thought.

"Find Sheridan," Jake told Amos, puffing on his pipe. "You want to find Custer? Find Sheridan; Custer won't be too far away. And Sheridan ain't in these parts at the moment…but you know he will be 'cuz here's where most of the Johnnies are."

The men crawled into their tents as mixed snow and rain began falling again. As usual, sleep came quickly and men dreamt of home.

The next morning before he had a chance to hear, "Down, Yank!" or "Down, Reb!" – exclamations that would dictate he stay another day to help with the dead and wounded, and the alive but sick – a shivering Pastor Nordquist saddled-up, mounted, pulled up his coat collar again, bid the others farewell, and continued to ride, unsure of where he was, but expecting that Sheridan's troops would be coming, like the soldier said. It seemed the solution to finding Uncle Torvald wasn't finding Sheridan or Custer, but finding the greatest concentration of Confederate troops, who would be attracting Sheridan and Custer as a weakened elk herd attracts wolves.

This day the sun was trying hard to break through the overhead cloud cover. The sky and surrounding landscape were a little brighter than normal, illuminating leafless tree limbs seemingly made of glass, uniformly coated with ice from the freezing rain that fell hours before.

Amos rode through miles of snow and crystal ice, the sun penetrating the thick cloud cover, illuminating the ground and hillsides. Looking around him, Amos squinted at the landscape instantly transformed into a gleaming crystal wonderland.

Amos could not help but smile. The crystal ice trees looked like life-sized Christmas ornaments, reminding him that Christmas was approaching, and he wondered how these two armies, civil when not in battle, would behave on Christmas Eve and Christmas day. It would not surprise him now if the two sides had Christmas dinner together. He had no doubt Rebel forces would be receptive to the idea.

Amos rode all that day along an eastern route, unaware he was getting close to the fighting around Richmond. The wind was constant, the sky mostly cloudy, and the sun shone fitfully like a spectator unwilling to watch. The thawing ground, kicked and beaten by traveling armies, was a quagmire, slowing Pastor Nordquist's journey.

He rode alone, and at times was concerned about his safety…not so much from errant Confederate or Federal gunfire but, rather, those wandering about with base turpitude, no moral compass: bummers, deserters, bounty jumpers – growing in numbers as more northerners, often criminals, derelicts, or even the mentally ill, were paid healthy sums to join the Union army, only to desert at the first opportunity. Amos thought about the conversation with the four soldiers in the deserted house. The veteran soldiers were discerning, disciplined. Amoral, undisciplined persons like the bounty-jumping gamblers who killed one another, were of greater danger.

He felt the revolvers under his coat and remembered telling the soldier that killing was not his job. Yes, he could shoot well, but, again, he hoped that would not become necessary. If it did, remembering the night on the stairs when he fired at an intruder who turned out to be his uncle, he knew he could do what he had to do.

On the day before Christmas, it again snowed and, because of the season, the fresh snow seemed appropriate, certainly preferable to rain and sleet.

Toward the end of the afternoon as night approached and Christmas Eve was upon America, Pastor Nordquist heard sounds of men in the distance. Amos rode toward the sounds from a large Union encampment in a wooded area by a river and, as he had done several times during his journey, introduced himself as a minister, a chaplain, and was welcomed, more so than before because it was Christmas Eve. The Union soldiers were singing Christmas carols, and again Confederate troops were singing with them at a distance. There was no shared dinner. As the sound of the last carol died away, men sitting around many campfires in the dark woods talked quietly or just sat and waited until the next song started.

From a different direction, however, Pastor Nordquist heard a new sound, ghostly in the night, and far enough away to where it seemed neither Federal nor Confederate. He sat silently on his horse listening, attempting to judge direction and distance.

A lone tenor voice. Mournful. Melancholy.

The voice was not like any he had ever heard, either here or in Göteborg. It rose from beyond the dark knoll to the south and filtered through trees silhouetted by campfires. The rest of the camp gradually grew silent, also listening.

Pastor Nordquist reined his horse to the left and rode through the pine woods in the direction of the voice coming over the top of a knoll. Cresting the dark, wooded knoll, Amos looked down at another group of partially visible Federal soldiers, lying on the ground or seated on logs or rocks, weakly illuminated by campfires. Pastor Nordquist saw wounded everywhere: heads, arms, legs wrapped in bandages heavily soiled. Some men slept and all were exhausted. They had fought well if for no other reason than they could not allow themselves to be taken prisoner.

...All is bright,

continued the lyric tenor voice flowing directly into

Round yon virgin, mother and child

as the surrounding, nearby troops – tenors, basses – in unison began to hum a soft contrapuntal melody that intuitively complemented and focused the tenor's age-old Austrian tune, making it sound novel and fresh.

Holy infant, so tender and mild.

The humming stopped for just an instant as if all were listening to the tenor sing

Sleep...

The background humming started again with a single unchanging note as the tenor continued the melody...

...in heavenly peace,
Sleep in heavenly peace.

The tenor was joined by other, but not all, tenors who in unison softly began the second verse.

Silent night, holy night

They paused for a split second, and then the entire company – tenors, baritones, rumbling basses – broke in with striking volume, harmonizing

Son of God!

as Pastor Nordquist's jaw dropped...

Love's pure light!

He sat on his horse mesmerized, with other nearby Union troops listening hungrily. The tenor voices were impressive, a wonderful blend, but the vocal essence belonged to the formidable basses whose soft, low resonance seemed to make the ground vibrate beneath his horse. One bass, a very big man seated at a distance away from the campfire but close to Amos, caught Amos's attention – not because of vocal volume or physical size, but because of a pleasant bass timbre that made Amos ache to hear more than he was hearing.

The music, voices singing as one, was beautiful, the result of years of Christmas carols in various black congregations throughout the South. How much musical training did they have? It took little time to create the arrangement to which Amos and the others now listened, bits and pieces of what already worked well, having been sung and re-sung, tuned and fine-tuned for at least two generations. The Army of the James, XXV Corps, U.S.C.T. liked the way it sounded, so they stuck with this arrangement; but had no idea how much the white troops, possessing the contrast of having become used to hearing themselves, appreciated this talent in the next encampment.

The concert continued until sleep beckoned all.

Pastor Nordquist spent Christmas with the armies and was again told that Sheridan and Custer were still in Winchester at the north end of the Shenandoah Valley close to where Amos had started, and that Amos had ridden to somewhere near Richmond. He was advised that before he automatically headed back, it would be wise to find out when and where Sheridan was going. Unfortunately, Sheridan's itinerary was unknown, so Pastor Nordquist stayed where he was at a Federal field hospital, attending to the sometimes ghastly responsibility of aiding the sick and wounded. He provided reverent burial services for the dead, in the process fortifying the morale of the living. All graves were marked, and Amos kept a list of the dead and their locations so relatives could find burial sites later.

That Amos stayed was fortuitous, for his worship services were desired and appreciated. Often, ironically afraid to say they were afraid, men came to him asking for prayer. Here he would stay for a while, waiting for news of Sheridan's cavalry.

The news eventually came as, in late February, Sheridan's cavalry again thundered south through the Shenandoah Valley.

On March 2, 1865, again in pursuit of Jubal Early, Sheridan directed Custer to attack Early at Waynesboro, far to the west of where Pastor Nordquist found himself, and Custer did so with efficacy, decimating Early's forces. After Waynesboro, as many expected, Sheridan rode ESE to join Gen. Ulysses S. Grant, the Army of the Potomac and the Army of the James in the siege of Petersburg a short distance from where Pastor Nordquist was presently encamped, with the intention of finally getting the best of Robert E. Lee's Army of Northern Virginia.

Toward the end of March, Amos was told Sheridan had joined up with Grant. Amos took leave of his outfit and, looking for Uncle Torvald, rode closer to the battles around Petersburg, but the raging combat ebbed and flowed quickly in the Richmond and Petersburg periphery, from woods to field to crossroads and, of necessity, Amos kept at a distance. Between March 31st and April 2nd, the fighting between the North and South around Petersburg was, even by War of Rebellion standards, vicious as the men in the Army of Northern Virginia put up a superhuman defense.

On April 1st at Five Forks, west of Petersburg, Sheridan and Custer rained blow after blow until they finally knifed through General George Pickett's left flank and, at the end of the day, one third of Pickett's men were casualties. There were, of course, also many Yankee casualties. One in particular.

The next morning, Robert E. Lee decided to evacuate Petersburg and Richmond, and head west to Appomattox Station where supply trains would await him, then south to hook up with General Joe Johnston's Army of Tennessee. Simultaneously, General Grant launched another major assault in the third battle of Petersburg, capturing "Fort Mahone" and, finally, the trenches around Jerusalem Plank Road. On April 3, 1865, Richmond, the burning capital of the Confederacy, belonged to the Army of the Potomac and the Army of the James.

Like a wounded animal fighting for its life, Lee's Army of Northern Virginia rapidly limped westward, with Sheridan, Custer and the Army of the Shenandoah again nipping like wolves. Pastor Nordquist kept following the gunfire, keeping his distance, unsure of what else to do.

On the evening of April 4th, a lull in the fighting allowed Pastor Nordquist to ride into the Union lines and begin asking about Custer. He rode on as directed, and on April 5th, after months of trying, found himself among Custer's men.

28

April 5, 1865

After asking several wiry, bearded, dirt-encrusted cavalrymen, mistrusting and distant, of the whereabouts of Custer's men, Amos finally found them.

"I apologize for bothering you," said Pastor Nordquist as he approached a soldier with an absent expression, inspecting his horse in the rain. "I am Chaplain Amos Nordquist, and I am looking for my uncle, Torvald Nordquist. If you know him, do you know where I might find him?"

"What outfit's he in?"

"The Wolverines."

"They're in the 1st Division. This is the 3rd. Try ridin' up the road a ways."

Amos rode a short distance along the muddy road and again asked about the Wolverines."

"Head down to the bottom of that ravine. Ask one a' them boys."

Amos rode the muddy road down the rise until he reached a group of men watering their horses at a rain-swollen creek.

"Excuse me but do you know where I can find Torvald Nordquist, my uncle?"

"Swede's bunch is over yonder by that big tree in the distance," the man responded solemnly, looking hard at Amos. The man pointed. "Y' see? Over there? On the other side a' those horses. Ask one a' those boys."

Pastor Nordquist looked and, as the rain fell, the moment seemed surreal. All this time and all this trouble to find Uncle Torvald, and now Uncle Torvald was literally a few hundred yards away.

Pastor Nordquist rode toward the men near the big tree in the distance and as he approached them, reined his horse to a halt and dismounted.

Leading his horse, Amos walked slowly on the spongy ground. As he approached the big tree, he stopped beside a drenched cavalryman with a mud-flecked mustache and beard who, although standing in the rain, was asleep.

"Pardon me. Do you know where I can find Torvald Nordquist?"

The man opened his eyes, adjusted his perception, and looked hard at Pastor Nordquist for a moment.

"Who're you?"

"I'm Chaplain Amos Nordquist," said Amos, speaking softly, almost in a whisper. "I'm Torvald Nordquist's nephew." Amos was hoping to surprise Uncle Torvald, but it had been so long since Amos had seen Torvald, Amos wasn't sure he could recognize Torvald immediately. "Do you know where he is? I have something for him."

"Talk to those boys over there," said the man, nodding in the direction of three other men talking to one another at a distance.

The first man quickly returned to somnambulance as Amos walked over to the three bearded men in grimy, blue uniforms with soiled, red neckerchiefs.

"Excuse me," said Amos as he approached them. "Do you know where can I find Torvald Nordquist?"

The men looked at Amos for a moment, at one another, and back at Amos. One responded.

"Buried him four nights ago. Five Forks. Who're you?"

Amos stood stunned as if hit with a rifle butt. Buried him. All this time and all this trouble, only to find that Uncle Torvald was killed four days before Amos arrived. I was so close. Amos looked to one side. If only I went in sooner, he thought. I should have... He looked back at the men, sad but angry.

"I'm his nephew," said Amos as he again looked away. The men stood farouchely studying Amos and waited for Amos to continue.

"I have something I came a considerable distance to give him. Something of value." Amos looked up at the tree branches above, struggling to make any sense of the moment.

"Swede got shot through the head when we hit Pickett's left flank a few days ago," one man explained. "More'n a few boys got hit."

"Tell ya somethin'," said another of the men, looking at Amos without blinking. "Ol' Swede was a good man, fine so'jer."

"Damn' shame," said the third man quietly. "Just when we might be gettin' close to the end of this infernal war, ol' Swede gets it."

It was more explaining than they normally would have done, but from his accent and what he said, it was evident Amos had come a long way to find his uncle. And Torvald Nordquist had been popular.

"He has some belongin's," said the first soldier. "We had no idea who t' send 'em to. You want 'em?"

"Yah," responded Amos after a moment; it was hard for him to think clearly. "That would be my honor."

Amos studied the three men who continued to look back respectfully, but with a uniquely steely countenance as if to say there were places for feelings. This wasn't one of them.

"Was he accorded a proper burial?" asked Amos.

"Proper?" echoed the second man. "Well, hell, maybe. We haven't been spendin' much time wi' funerals – what with the battles that keep springin' up the past few days, there's been little time for anything except fightin'. Dunno. Proper?" The man shook his head. "Nah."

"He's dead," concluded the first soldier in a low voice as he looked to one side and spat chewing tobacco. He looked back at Amos. "Funerals always struck me as bein' kinda late anyway. Probably should have funerals before folks die. Some kind of a ceremony. Say all the flowery stuff then. Let the Lord sort it out." He folded his arms and imperceptibly shrugged.

"Do you remember where he was buried," asked Amos. "I'm a chaplain."

"Five Forks," said the first soldier. "Kinda quick. Grave was marked. Should be able to find 'im if we goes back there."

"Ain't headin' in that direction," said the third soldier.

"You're welcome to join us where we're goin'," said the first soldier. "Could use another chaplain."

"At the moment," answered Amos with a sigh, "I can't think of what else I should do." He thought for a moment. "Yah, let me help you too while I sort things out."

One of the men got Swede's belongings and brought them to Amos.

"Use t' be more. We gave clothes to other boys who needed 'em. No reason not t'." The remaining belongings were in a haversack and consisted mostly of minor odds and ends including documents.

From the belongings, the man took out a skirmishing cap, a kepi, hit it a couple of times with the back of his hand, removed Amos's hat and placed the kepi on Amos's head. It fit.

"There y' go, chaplain."

"Wait a minute," said one of the other men who turned and walked over to his horse. He unfastened a rifle scabbard with the rifle in it. Walking back toward Amos he held out the scabbard and rifle. "These belonged t' Swede. Almost-new Spencer carbine. Barely used. I see you ain't got one. I got another." The man looked at the carbine and added, "I could keep it but, hell, I figure Swede'd want you t' have it. Might as well, considerin' y' came all this way. An' even if yer a chaplain, y' might need it."

"Like everyone else, chaplains are a helluva lot more useful alive than dead."

Amos looked down at the rifle in its scabbard as he took it from the man. He looked at the hard men who looked back evenly, emotionlessly studying him in the rain. He thanked them and slowly turned and walked to his horse with the haversack, rifle and scabbard.

Amos was once again in a position where he could lead worship, help with the wounded, and enhance morale among the living while providing burial services for the dead. General Phil Sheridan's passion was both relentless and contagious in his pursuit of Lee's army, and neither he nor his troops could rest. As Pastor Nordquist adjusted the cap on his head, there came a bugle call, "Boots and Saddles," to mount-up, and the cavalry was off into battle again as Pastor Nordquist, with no other evident option, rode behind.

Pastor Nordquist's prior services to Union and Confederate soldiers were gifts from someone passing though looking for an uncle. Up until this moment, Amos was not part of the conflict. Without having formally enlisted, now he was.

In the downpour, the cavalrymen rode hard through woods and along roads already turned to muck by retreating Rebel forces, the Union cavalry passing abandoned, empty, confederate caissons and wagons, dead horses and soldiers, artillery guns and ambulances with wheels broken or missing. They came upon exhausted, desultory stragglers no longer willing to fight, some just resting against a fence post or a tree trunk, unresisting, and staring as the rain beat down on them, prepared to surrender or, absent Federal clemency, die.

Further down the road, the soldiers passed several emaciated, abandoned horses lying in the muddy road, ridden until they dropped, unable to move. As others rode by, a cavalryman stopped next to two of the horses, perfunctorily took out his pistol, took aim and put each horse out of its misery. Unwilling to use ammunition on others, he rode on. Amos saw more horses in the muddy road, most already dead. And more stragglers. The weary Union cavalrymen sensed the Rebel lassitude and, having recently received fresh horses from the Harper's Ferry federal remount ranch, rode hard. Amos could not keep up with them and gradually fell back. Later in the day he identified himself as a chaplain and asked a nearby cavalryman the name of the man's outfit.

"First Connecticut, 1st Brigade, 3rd Division, Army of the Shenandoah. Where's your outfit, chaplain?"

"I don't have an outfit," said Amos respectfully.

The man looked at Amos and surmised that, in the chaos, Amos had become detached from his men.

"Well, until y' find where yer supposed to be, jes' follow us. Bible says t' pray without ceasin'. C'n always use another chaplain."

June 6, 1865

Amos would quickly learn that the Army of the Shenandoah was commanded by Maj. General Phil Sheridan, and the 3rd Division commander was Maj. General George Custer, promoted last September and no longer leading the Wolverines. It seems destined I am to be under Custer, thought Amos.

Forward cavalrymen spotted a Rebel wagon train further ahead and, in the division's vanguard, Custer gave the order to charge. Soon the cavalrymen were in another battle. As Amos watched from a distance, Custer hit the Rebels hard, but was forced to fall back as the Confederates took cover, returning a fusillade of fire. Men on both sides were cut down, falling dead or dying. Custer regrouped his men and hit the Confederates again, guns spouting fire, probing for weaknesses along the Rebel line. In the gloomy rain, the emotionally degenerative effect on the Confederates was equal to the physical decimation but, driven by honor and duty, the defending Rebels wouldn't quit.

The Rebels were running low on ammunition, Amos determined, because whenever Federal troops were close to trees and rocks where Rebels had taken cover, rather than fire their rifles at close range as usual, as Pastor Nordquist watched aghast, Rebels angrily jumped and sabered chests, shoulders, faces of Union troops. Others, unsuccessful at impaling, were still able to pull Federal troops off their horses, and vicious, frenzied hand-to-hand combat resulted in primeval roars, screams, and extensive, frenzied bloodshed as men who didn't know one another fought to the death.

Pastor Nordquist reined his horse around and galloped away at a distance, coming to a halt next to a small copse. As he again reined his horse around to watch, Amos saw a gray flash to his right and looked just in time to dodge the saber of a Confederate soldier, his visage hate-filled, who knew Amos only by his blue skirmishing cap with a stamped brass cavalry insignia. Dodging the saber, Amos fell from his horse, but jumped to his feet, the horse providing a temporary barrier between Amos and the Confederate soldier who raced around the horse, thrusting at Amos as Amos dodged and darted, barely able to avoid the Confederate saber.

"I am a chaplain!" Pastor Nordquist shouted, jumping to his right, holding out his hands. "I have conducted worship services for Confederate troops!"

Deaf to Amos's words and nearly as big as Amos, the bearded Confederate soldier's wide eyes emanated the insanity of a man again intending to kill. Amos realized the Confederate soldier didn't care who Amos was, and that Amos had the rudimentary options of warfare: kill or be killed. Amos dodged another thrust, grabbed the man's arm, and their momentum carried the two to the soggy grass where each struggled to overpower the other. Teeth clenched, the man gripped his saber tightly, attempting to wrest his right arm free from Amos's grasp so he could either stab or bludgeon this stranger with the blue skirmishing cap. Underneath, pushing and straining, Amos focused on the man's right arm gripping the saber.

The Rebel soldier wrenched his left arm free from Amos's grasp and, over the top of his right arm, hit Amos hard in the face, striking Amos's forehead and eyebrows, hurting Amos, but not enough to weaken Amos's resolve. Just the opposite. Amos's anger fully awoke.

Teeth clenched, Amos gained leverage, pushed and rolled over on top the man as Amos struggled to break the Confederate soldier's grip on his sword, but the soldier used Amos's momentum to force Amos on his back, and again hit Amos in the face, bloodying Amos's nose and mouth. The Rebel soldier wanted more blood than that and, as Amos's anger rose to the surface like magma, continued to maniacally swing at Amos with his fist while attempting to free his right arm from Amos's grip.

As the men struggled on the wet grass, there was no quit in the Confederate soldier. Amos had done nothing to deserve martyrdom and, with so much ahead of him, there was a great deal for which to live. King David was both a warrior and a man of God, Amos thought as he struggled. He didn't die. Someone, Amos knew, would die as a result of what was happening this moment. The fight was not Amos's idea but, flushed with anger and adrenalin, he determined that at the end, the dead one would not be him.

Gritting his teeth, blood flowing from his nose, Amos drew on his uncommon strength and retaliated, hitting the Rebel soldier in the face harder than the Rebel soldier hit Amos, and the Confederate soldier was fazed, but continued trying to get his saber free. Holding the man's right arm with his left hand, both men now on their knees, Amos again hit the man in the face as Amos dodged a similar but glancing blow from the weakening Rebel soldier's left hand.

Without letting go of the man's right arm, with his right hand Amos pushed the man backwards and quickly reached into his breast pocket where Amos had a wooden writing stylus with the steel nib in place. In one motion Amos pulled out the stylus and, as the man reflexively snapped forward after being pushed, Amos rammed it upward through the soft part of the man's lower jaw in front of his neck, driving the nib up through the top of the man's mouth and into his brain. The man's eyes became protuberant and, for a moment, his body shuddered and jerked backward trying to get free. Amos, teeth clenched, continued to push the stylus even though it would go no further. The man's free hand grabbed for Amos's hand now pushing the nub of the stylus barely protruding from the bottom of the man's jaw, most of it inside the man's cranium, but the man's eyes softened and went blank as if seeing something directly in front of his face. In a moment he saw nothing. On his knees, his body went limp, leaning forward, and then brushing against Amos as it fell to one side before landing on its front. Although he was dead, the man's body twitched for a moment, as if trying to get up. Then stillness.

Amos jumped to his feet, grabbed the man's saber and, as the rain poured down on both of them, stood over the man waiting for any additional move. The man lay motionlessly. His head was flat on the ground like the head on a bearskin rug, his eyes open but vacant and unseeing, the stylus not visible. Amos quickly looked around for any other Rebel soldiers. There were none. After a few moments, Amos cautiously knelt on one knee in front of the man and studied the man's eyes as rain ran down the man's forehead and through his eyes, giving an impression of weeping. Blood was spreading out under the chin and through one side of the man's lips, soaking through the wet grass beneath. Amos caught a small whiff of it and, between the sight and smell and feeling in his soul, he became nauseated as he knelt.

Amos stood up in the rain, feeling momentarily vertiginous. As his head began to clear, self-condemnation washed over Amos like a North Sea wave as two voices inside him argued with one another. How could you have…? No, there was no choice. But… No… Then all thought left, and his mind went blank, as if snuffed out like a candle.

For a moment he stood unsteadily in the rain. Looking at the dead man, sodden with guilt, Amos immediately felt an overwhelming need for forgiveness. He agonized that at this moment he had no right to come to the Lord for anything, however, considering what he just did and the ignominy he felt. He was completely unworthy. There was no reason, Amos thought, to expect God to listen to someone who had just killed another man. Especially when the murderer was a minister.

The thief on the cross at Golgotha came to mind, and Amos knew God would forgive even this.

As he stood in the rain, the enormity of what he just did, together with his evident lack of faith a mere moment ago, added to previous emotional heaviness that in concert began to overburden him. The residual weight from watching men die on the battlefield and in front of him as he sought to save their lives, and not reaching Uncle Torvald in time – all the tragedies and disappointments that had piled up like pallets on a pier over the past year, combined with just killing a man – created a burden too heavy for his heart to carry.

Feeling as if he were about to drown in guilt, grief and spiritual exhaustion, inside him the flood of emotion rose until Amos agonizingly grimaced, choked, his eyes closed tightly, and like a cresting river, emotion overflowed, eroding his waning stoicism like a weakening dike until his heart burst with anguish and Amos dropped to his knees on the wet ground, broke down and wept bitterly, his body shaking from racking sobs, perhaps as Peter wept after denying Christ.

After moments of tormented wretchedness, Amos gradually regained his composure, gritting his teeth to insure he had control of himself. As he sighed, his jaw relaxed, and his breathing shuddered. Unconsciously, he wiped his eyes, forehead, and his bloody nose with his left sleeve – not realizing he also had a deep cut below his right eye – and looked momentarily skyward. He dropped his head, and fearfully and fervently begged God's forgiveness.

Finished, he again used his left sleeve to wipe his eyes, inadvertently smearing more blood around them. Standing, he looked one last time at the man who had attacked him. Amos bent down and searched inside the man's shirt and pockets for identification – Amos thought he should notify someone – but there was nothing except a stale bread crust.

I can't stay, Amos thought.

He stood up in the downpour, slightly bent over, holding his right hand that ached terribly from hitting the Confederate soldier. The man is destined for oblivion, Amos concluded.

The man's attack and subsequent death seemed so pointless – but were they? As with most inestimable matters, Amos didn't know what he couldn't know, and he was so distraught that, although he wanted to continue to deal with the matter, at that moment he had no emotional reserve left. He stood for a moment longer, turned and walked woodenly toward his horse. As if the dead man's soul was pulling Amos back, each step seemed heavy and difficult. Amos turned, looked at the man – his color waning in the pallor of death – gritted his teeth, blinked hard, turned again and continued walking.

After Amos mounted, he pulled his carbine from its scabbard, and replaced the carbine with the saber he still held. He cocked the carbine, looked about, leaned forward and spurred his heels into his horse's flanks a couple of times, bringing the horse to a gallop. Carbine cradled in his arm, he raced to catch up with the rest of the cavalry, unaware that when he did, he would witness action determining the fate of the United States.

By late afternoon, back with the cavalry, Amos's right hand became swollen and throbbed painfully; Amos hoped he had not broken anything. His body was stiff and hurt all over. His lips were puffed, and his right eye was black and swollen. His head ached and, to stem the bleeding, he pinched the deep cut beneath his right eye. His nose felt like it was broken, but he couldn't be certain, and there was no time to see a medic even if one were available. He wanted to lie down, sleep, but again Union cavalry were forming up behind Custer to begin another attack of the thin gray line.

As Amos watched at a distance, Custer waved his hat, shouting, his horse turning in circles as if building up centrifugal momentum, bringing his men to a boil and a sense of invincibility as they in turn waved their hats while shouting, roaring, until Custer gave the order: "Charge!" The noise increased with the thunder of hooves as Custer and the men, shouting and shooting, raced toward Rebel lines, and the Rebels returned fire – volley after volley, cutting down many of the charging horde – with all the resources they had: rifle, grape and canister. But it wasn't enough, and Amos watched the Union cavalry break through the forward Rebel forces with a merciless bloodlust, their behavior possessed, apoplectic.

Men on both sides fell as if the battlefield were being swiped with an enormous scythe. The Federals, still yelling maniacally, galloped left and right as they encircled the wagon train, isolating and shooting or sabering Confederate soldiers and drivers, destroying equipment and wagons, setting fire to anything that would burn. The smoke-filled air did little to obscure the terrible sight of men in the grasp of fanatical madness: killing and being killed.

Within minutes the wagon train was destroyed. Sheridan and Custer immediately regrouped and set their sights on the Confederate infantry ahead.

Sheridan sent messengers to the trailing VI Corps, the nearest Federal infantry unit, which had been marching in the rain without sleep or food for the past day and was expecting a moment's respite. As Sheridan's messengers arrived, the infantrymen were sitting down in a wet, open field to eat and rest. When the messengers rode up to VI Corps officers with Sheridan's orders, however, the officers immediately shouted for the men to get up; the time had arrived to help Phil Sheridan beat Lee's army, and when they were done, they could eat all they wanted.

Grumbling but with little hesitation, the men were up and again marching, motivated by the word "Sheridan." From his exploits in the Shenandoah Valley, his unflagging self-confidence, and his growing reputation for indomitability, Sheridan's image had undergone apotheosis and, at this pivotal point in the war, the infantrymen were eager to be part of whatever Phil Sheridan would do next.

The VI Corps men marched double-time in the rain and muck to where Amos stood looking through a spyglass at distant, assembled Confederate forces across the opposite lower hillside behind the swollen creek below. While opposing numbers were still formidable, what Amos saw magnified in the spyglass was, on one hand, so weak as to be almost pitiable, but, on the other, a desperate enemy. The gaunt Rebels, some of whom for weeks had not eaten anything resembling a regular meal, and had nothing to eat now, looked motley, emaciated and grim, but ready to die and take Yankees with them. They were out of food, low on ammunition, low on stamina, worn to a frazzle, and the sense of duty that buttressed their courage was becoming as splintered as their wagons.

Amos watched General Phil Sheridan ride to the VI Corps infantry marching into view and, as Sheridan approached the infantrymen, a few veterans looked around to others, hollering, "There's Phil! There's Phil!" as if an opportunity had arisen to worship this mounted god of war.

The rest began to yell, sensing a crucial moment was at hand. Sheridan imperiously gave orders to infantry officers who momentarily turned their attention toward the Rebel forces on the other side of swollen Sailor's Creek. The officers then gave the Union infantry a command to form up for a frontal assault, while the cavalrymen rode into positions preparing to charge Confederate flanks.

The Confederate cannon fire was weak. Either they are almost out of grapeshot, cannon balls and canisters or they are saving themselves for another major battle, Amos thought as he studied the opposite embankment through a spyglass. It occurred to him this had the potential to be the last major battle, and the Rebels were awaiting the Union army charge before unleashing the fury of their 12 pounders. As he looked through the spyglass, Amos could see Rebel hatred, and was reminded of how, centuries earlier, when Russia finally recaptured the Kremlin after a two-year Polish occupation under siege, the Russians burned the body of the Polish commander, primed a cannon, and fired the man's ashes back toward Poland. Amos had no doubt the Confederates would do the same with Custer or Sheridan if they could, aiming toward Washington, D.C.

Arm raised, Custer gave the order, bugles sounded down the line and, as Amos watched, cavalry horses at first began to walk forward, breaking into a trot and then came the order, "Charge!" As if shot from cannons, the massive Union infantry and cavalry raced downhill at full gallop, the air filled with the thunder of hoofs, boots, and guns again spouting fire, Federal troops roaring like Saracen hordes at Guadalete, with the gathered Confederate force, driven by duty, desperately firing back.

29

Hundreds of flashing carbines, muskets and rifles made a cacophonous din as iron, lead, and gun smoke filled the air from both directions. As Amos watched, his hands unconsciously over his ears, infantry-men, cavalrymen, horses and small trees fell on both sides as the Union army raced downward toward the rain-swollen creek in the face of ball, bullet, wicked canister and grape shot. The leading Union troops and horses were hit left and right, as were the forward defending Confederate soldiers, but the Union charge was repulsed. From a distance, Amos watched Custer regroup his cavalry, turn the men around, and make another desperate charge into an immediate hail-storm of Confederate fire. Forward Union soldiers and horses were again cut down, and Sailor's Creek ran as red as the Nile in Exodus.

Regrouped, led by Custer, yet again the Federals charged and again many men and horses in front were cut down, but this time, rifles and pistols blazing fire, the rest bore into the Rebel line. The line became confused, convulsed and overwhelmed, and the hand-to-hand combat quickly became a rout as weakened Rebel troops either ran or finally dropped their weapons, many now out of ammunition, raising their hands in surrender.

April 7, 1865

For Sheridan and Custer's men there would be no rest, however. While the curtain began to descend on the Confederacy at the Battle of Sailor's Creek, no one could know that yet. In the drizzle, the pace was breakneck as the Union cavalry sensed what the retreating men in the Army of Northern Virginia were enduring, and the flanks of Union cavalry horses glistened with rain, sweat and foam.

As the cavalry rode west again, the muddy road they were galloping along was littered with discarded Confederate Enfield muskets and heavier arms including a 12-pounder howitzer. Why? Amos wondered as he raced behind. It occurred to Amos that ammunition had been exhausted, and these firearms were an open invitation to be killed if held while unrelenting Union cavalry charged in with fully loaded, 7-shot repeaters.

As the cavalry rode on, at a distance Amos could see isolated, unarmed Rebel stragglers – out of ammunition and hope – partially hidden behind trees, rocks and houses, somberly looking back, and it was evident to Amos that for some Rebel soldiers this war was over. But for others up ahead, a defiant remnant, it would continue as long as they could kill Yankees.

April 8, 1865

The next morning Sheridan's scouts reported Lee's desperately needed supply trains at Appomattox Station to the west. Pastor Nordquist listened as Sheridan summoned his best general, the 3rd Division commanding officer, and ordered Custer to get to General Robert E. Lee's supply trains before Lee did. Immediately Custer had everyone off at a gallop.

As they rode west, however, Amos saw an odd scene: two panicked, screaming women running from a large house toward the thundering cavalry, and Amos wondered if they had lost their minds. The women were imploringly waving their arms while running toward the approaching Custer who reined his horse to a halt.

"Your soldiers!" screamed the older woman. "They are robbing us! They are robbing and trying to murder us!" the woman cried, pointing at the house, begging Custer to stop whoever was doing this.

Custer's demeanor became dark, and he quickly rode up to the house, jumped from the saddle and ran up the front porch steps just as a Union infantryman ran out the front door. As Amos watched, Custer hit the surprised man in the face so hard the man spun and fell unconscious down the front porch steps. Custer turned and ran inside the house. Amos would learn that another Union soldier ran out the back door as Custer ran in and, unable to immediately catch the man, Custer grabbed an axe lying against the back-porch wood pile and angrily threw it at the soldier, hitting him in the back of the head. The soldier fell unconscious, bleeding in the back yard. Maybe dead.

Custer ran to the front of the house, down the steps, swung up into the saddle, ordered the provost marshal to place a guard on the premises, and said firmly to the older of the two women, "Madam, we do not allow this!"

Reining his horse to the left, he raced off, with Amos and the cavalry galloping behind him.

Approaching Appomattox Station from the south as the Rebels were about to unload provisions – food, medical supplies, ordnance and equipment – from four supply trains including one that just arrived, Custer's cavalrymen swarmed in like blue hornets, and the cavalrymen quickly overpowered the Confederate reserve artillery unit guarding the trains, scattering or taking prisoner the artillerymen.

Pastor Nordquist watched from a distance as the cavalry hit the three supply trains loaded with provisions for Lee's hungry, undersupplied men, and as Custer's men captured the first three supply trains, the engineer of the fourth supply train, having just arrived with steam to spare, put the train into full throttle in an attempt to escape, stressing car couplings so severely that one snapped, leaving the majority of supply-filled cars behind as the train raced from the station. Recalling the emaciated, gaunt look of the Confederate soldiers, Amos thought this might be a worse blow to Lee's army than Federal artillery, cavalry and infantry at Sailor's Creek.

Elated by the quick victory, and excited at being around familiar steam locomotives, former railroad men among the cavalry fired up the remaining three Confederate locomotives. As Pastor Nordquist watched, the Union railroad men proceeded to run the supply trains a short distance up and down the railroad tracks, blowing the whistles, ringing the bells, behaving like children on a playground ride. Shortly, Custer put an end to these antics, and ordered the trains run up the track, positioning the trains some distance away from potential Confederate counterattack.

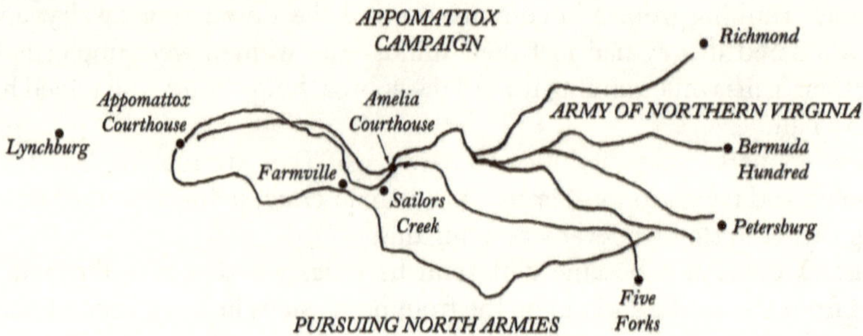

As Pastor Nordquist rode toward the congregating Union soldiers, he heard the familiar "switch-a switch-a switch-a" sound of an incoming shell, accompanied by musket fire from the dense pine and blackjack oak woods nearby as the forward units of Lee's army reached Appomattox Station knowing they could not lose these supply trains if the Army of Northern Virginia was to fight another day. Amos took cover as another desperate skirmish exploded, lasting a half hour until Custer's men drove back the Rebels.

As soon as the Confederates retreated, however, the ground began to shake from explosive bursts as cannon fire rained down from a confederate reserve artillery unit in the woods. Amos raced for the opposite thicket while several Federal soldiers fell wounded or dead, and others dove for cover. In the knell, when the Confederate cannons' position was finally determined, Custer mounted his horse, rode among his men giving the order for all to mount up and, as Amos watched, Custer's cavalrymen again swung into their saddles.

His horse again anxiously turning in circles, Custer waved his hat and shouted, "C'mon, boys! Let's have three cheers!" In response, the men also waved their hats while wildly shouting three cheers and, hell-bent-for-leather, led by Custer, they thundered toward a wooded area from which the explosive sounds of cannon and deadly canisters were coming. As Amos watched and listened, he thought of how the cacophony of galloping horses, cannon and rifle fire, becoming one with the shouts of raging men, further fomented the frenzied mindset instigating the behavior resulting in the cacophony.

As Custer's men rode within close range, confederate artillery began vomiting canisters, sometimes double canisters, filled with rifle balls, small chunks of lead, nails, pieces of wire and scrap iron. As cannons fired, the fired canisters would rupture, and expanding murderous enfilades – storms of iron – mutilated Yankee soldiers and horses, sending bloodied, shredded body parts flying about like an explosion in a butcher shop. Although other Union cavalrymen and horses, including another of Custer's, were killed, Custer jumped to his feet and, again unmarked, grabbed a horse whose rider had been killed, swinging into the saddle. After having regrouped his troops and being joined by a second brigade, he again rode along the men and horses while holding his saber aloft. He hoarsely shouted, reined his horse to the left, and dashed forward, leading a second charge of shouting men and thunderous hooves, but again the cavalry was met with a storm of canister iron and cannon. Amos was certain Custer would finally meet his Maker, but Custer was again miraculously unscathed and, undaunted, later led a third and, just before dusk, rallying all three brigades, a fourth murderous charge.

That is the most fearless man I've ever seen, thought Amos as he again watched from a distance. And so obviously visible. It's miraculous he hasn't been hit. Perhaps he thinks like Stonewall Jackson – feeling as safe in battle as in bed because God has fixed the time of his death, and when the time comes, as it did for Jackson, it comes, regardless of the circumstances.

As he watched, Amos marveled how battlefield madness melds men into a seemingly larger, singular organism, a body acting at the direction of its mind, the dominant field commander. From prior conversations with Custer's men, it was evident they almost worshipped Custer and, in the heat of battle, with no consideration for their personal safety, would do anything for him.

As darkness began to fall, the air thick with lead and sulfur, the Confederate artillerymen and supporting infantrymen were overwhelmed. Slack-jawed, exhausted, wide-eyed and badly beaten, some of the Rebels stood along wooded paths and narrow roads with hands in the air, but in the dark, most retreated north toward the courthouse while firing back at pursuing Yankees.

The Confederate canister fusillade did incredible damage, and soon Amos was again in a field hospital, a large tent, working with a Union surgeon, a doctor in civilian life – Amos knew not all surgeons were – amputating arms and legs. The army found that amputation had the highest survival rate, providing the procedure was done soon after the wound occurred. Moments earlier, Amos used chloroform to anesthetize the next man, being careful to place the cone-shaped, chloroform-saturated towel lightly over the man's mouth and nose, allowing the chloroform to mix with air as the man breathed, and being careful not to use too much which could lead to lung paralysis and death. As the man lay in deep sleep, the surgeon was removing a splintered leg, two lanterns hanging overhead. Ignoring body lice and dysentery, Amos held down the leg as the surgeon did his macabre job on a blood-stained table consisting of a door supported by two upright barrels. In a barrel behind the surgeon was a small-but-growing bloody accumulation of arms and legs from earlier amputees. Two more barrels were ready for use; earlier filled barrels were outside somewhere, the contents being buried.

"Y'know, chaplain," grimaced the surgeon, covered in blood and perspiration, "in prior battles I've seen more men wounded in a shorter time, but this is the worst, ever, I've seen men mutilated. God have mercy." He gritted his teeth due to effort, sight and smell, but he was nowhere close to being finished.

The stump was cauterized and dressed. That done, Amos removed the man from the table, exchanging patients with the help of orderlies. When Amos carried the next man to the table, while the man had on a Union skirmishing cap, Amos could tell from the man's ragged, gaunt appearance he was a Confederate. Amos again cautiously administered chloroform. To Amos and the surgeon, it made no difference. Theirs was the opposite end of the war.

While the surgeon began to cut off the man's pant leg with scissors, his surgical knife aside the man, Amos immediately attended to another man brought in and lying on the ground in a terribly ghastly state. His hands bloody from previous amputations, Amos worked with urgency to clean away dirt and re-place the man's intestines in the abdominal cavity as the man, still alive but in shock, lay moaning, bleeding badly, and on the verge of death. Slightly nauseous, Amos gritted his teeth as he worked. The odds were terrible, and Amos chided himself after weighing whether he should stay with this man or attend others with better chances for survival. Although Amos knew the soldier would live no longer than a few moments – the surgeon could do nothing for this – Amos stayed with the man because it was the right thing to do. When the man died moments later, Amos carefully picked him up and gave him to orderlies who took the body outside as the surgeon, having finished tying off a tourniquet, and then cutting through the flesh aside the Confederate's wound, reached for his saw.

Most of Custer's men finally encamped for the night. Meanwhile, to the east in a forced overnight march, several exhausted infantry corps of the Army of the Potomac and Army of the James pushed themselves up the muddy Richmond-Lynchburg Stage Road, the pace so difficult that many infantrymen collapsed as the corps raced to meet up with Sheridan and his cavalry by mid-morning.

It's amazing how the men endure, thought Amos who noticed how men seemed healthier in the field than in camp, and could recover with a day of sleep after a week of continual skirmishing.

Amos had reached that point of exhaustion. Too tired to think clearly, Amos crawled under his blankets at nearly midnight, but before he could fall asleep to the sound of gunfire in the distance, Amos saw Custer riding out of camp.

"Where's the general going?" asked Amos.

"Headed over to the other field hospital," Amos was told. "Gonna spend time with their wounded." The last thing Amos saw was Custer disappear in the darkness.

By early morning twilight, the two exhausted marching Union armies were within a short distance of the little village of Appomattox Court House. Unaware of what was happening not far from the courthouse, Rebel troops assembled at the base of the rise that ran along the Richmond-Lynchburg Stage Road, and at around 9:00 a.m. surged up the rise, attacking cavalry under Union Brevet Brigadier General Charles H. Smith who fought a delaying action while being reinforced by other units during the battle. From the Rebel perspective, the delaying action gave the impression of a much-needed Confederate momentum swing, even a victory. It also gave formidable Union infantry divisions, however, more time to reach their positions.

Pastor Nordquist sat on his horse near the rear ridge of the rise. As the Confederate soldiers advanced, faced bloody counterattacks, fell back, and advanced again, for his own safety Pastor Nordquist reined his horse around and rode further back. As he gained distance on the rise, through his peripheral vision he noticed distant movement, and rode a little higher to get a better view of what was happening. What he saw were great masses of tired but determined Federal troops marching into the courthouse vicinity. He could see officers shouting orders, and large groups of Union soldiers form up, gradually joined by others, until at a distance all Amos saw were blue lines of Federal infantry, cavalry, and artillery, even though he could not see others approaching further to the east: the Army of the Potomac II Corps together with the VI Corps double-timing up the Richmond-Lynchburg Stage Road. To the west, among Maj. Gen. Edward Ord's assembled Army of the James troops now blocking Lee's western escape route was the XXV Corps, the USCT, including one outstanding tenor.

Pastor Nordquist looked warily about, sensing a great massacre was about to unfold. Unaware of what was occurring at a distance around them, the Rebels kept coming up the rise, and Amos felt the urgency to warn them, to tell them to stop. Surrender at once!

As Amos watched, however, with what little energy remained, the beleaguered Confederate troops continued to fight their way up the rise, and when it seemed they had driven through part of the Federal cavalry near the crest of the rise, some cut loose with Rebel yells.

Then they saw what Amos saw. Many became slack-jawed, slumping as they looked about at the distant blue seas.

To the south was General Charles Giffin's V Corps, southeast was Sheridan's cavalry, to the west was the XXIV Corps led by Chancellorsville and Gettysburg veteran Maj. Gen. John Gibbon, and from the northeast, Maj. Gen. George Meade's troops were causing the wet ground to shake as they came running into position. The Confederates were inside a bowl – Federal troops around much of the rim – with a narrow, northwest escape route open…but there was no escape to the northwest because the Rebels could not continue unless re-supplied, and the supply trains were to the south. Unaware the supply trains were captured by Custer and his men, some Confederate officers believed the only option was to fight their way through Federal lines to the south. This would be suicide, however – a fact not lost on Federal troops. Pastor Nordquist overheard a Federal soldier grumble about the pointlessness of continued combat.

"Right here 'n now it's 'checkmate.' Ain't that evident what's gonna happen?

Ain't it obvious that thems what get kilt from now on, dies for nuthin'? An' those Johnnies're gonna git slaughtered like lambs in July. Lord in heaven. What's the point?!" The Federal soldier glowered at the Confederates in the distance below and, teeth clenched, quietly muttered, "C'mon. Jes' gawddam surrender."

As Amos watched, Brig. Gen. Joshua Chamberlain's infantry brigade marched toward General Sheridan's cavalry, and Chamberlain rode up to Phil Sheridan to get orders. Amos could hear the always-intense Sheridan punctuate his directions with a loud, guttural command: "Now smash 'em, I tell you, smash 'em!"

To the east, General Meade's grime-covered men, running on adrenalin, were nearly into position. General Gibbon's and General Charles Griffin's men, looking down on the Rebels from higher ground, were ready. Skirmishing fire between Confederate and some Yankee units continued, but most of the Union army waited. A bugle sounded from Sheridan's cavalry and, as Amos watched, cavalrymen swung their horses around and fell into lines, readying rifles. Amos expected that in a moment more bugles would sound, Sailor's Creek would be reenacted, and General Lee's fragile remnant, having placed itself in a suicidal position, would go the way of Masada.

Amos watched Union commanders raise their arms preparatory to giving the command to charge. All eyes grew intense and time seemed to stand still.

As Amos watched, however, a Confederate captain unexpectedly burst out of the Confederate lines below with a white flag of truce, a towel tied to his sword, flying high above the Confederate's outstretched arm. Amos watched the Confederate captain race toward the nearest Union officer, Lt. Col. George Briggs of the 7th Michigan Cavalry who, in turn, led the Confederate captain to Briggs's former commanding officer, General Custer.

Union commanders slowly let their arms fall without giving the command to charge. Out of Amos's sight, other Confederate flags of truce were delivered. The sporadic fire below Amos gradually ceased as men from both sides watched, eyes intense, mouths slightly open.

Pastor Nordquist strained to see what was happening as the Confederate rider met Custer, said something, and Custer dispatched two of his officers to go with the Confederate captain.

The officers soon returned, and Pastor Nordquist could tell what they said to Custer was not received favorably. Custer discussed the matter with the always-intense Sheridan who continued to look downhill toward the Confederate forces. Sheridan turned to Custer, speaking adamantly, and Amos watched Custer spur his heels into his horse, and gallop in the direction from which the two officers returned. It was evident to Amos that Sheridan gave Custer orders to take care of the matter personally.

A short while later, Custer returned at a cantor and took a position next to Sheridan. Custer's countenance was neutral but repressed, like a young man at a dance after being rejected. Pastor Nordquist watched Custer explaining the matter to Sheridan. Sheridan's expression remained imperious; whatever Custer attempted to do, failed. Pastor Nordquist would later find out Sheridan sent

Custer to demand a formal surrender from Confederate Generals Gordon and Longstreet, neither of whom had authority to surrender General Lee's troops, even if willing to do so.

Meanwhile, General Meade, under the weather, declared a temporary cease-fire from his ambulance.

The ceasefire atmosphere was at first apprehensive, for no one knew exactly what was going on. As if in a dream, sensing what seemed to be happening, a few Union soldiers began yell, to cheer, a cheer immediately picked up along the Union lines until it exploded into a din almost as loud as the muskets, rifles, galloping hooves and roaring men that would have been heard had the charge begun.

Gradually, Yankee troops began to relax and Pastor Nordquist watched a Federal cavalryman ride slowly, cautiously, over to the Rebel troops, dismount, and began talking with one of the enemy, apparently someone he knew.

As the moment wore on, a few other Union soldiers also joined Rebel soldiers.

At a greater distance, Pastor Nordquist saw several Union and Confederate officers, apparently familiar with their opposite numbers, but never having formally met, introduce one another, fraternize anxiously for about a half hour, and then return to their respective lines.

Pastor Nordquist shook his head. What kind of war is this?

A few Rebel troops started walking away.

Pastor Nordquist was perplexed. Where were they going? Then it occurred to him where they were going.

Home.

No Federal troops stopped them.

Pastor Nordquist began to ride closer to the opposing lines. As he rode further down the rise, Sheridan and Custer galloped by.

A rumor began circulating that General Lee was meeting with General Grant not far from where Amos sat astride his horse. Rumors were always rampant in the army, and Amos was initially skeptical. Under the evident circumstances, however, Amos continued thinking about the rumor, considering it might be true. He had not spoken at length with anyone since joining the 3rd Cavalry Division and found himself wishing he had someone to talk to about this moment. His wish was immediately granted.

"You a chaplain?" asked the big, dirty, heavily bearded Union cavalry sergeant riding up to Amos.

"I am."

"You sure? Somehow you don't look like a chaplain."

"I'm not sure what a chaplain is supposed to look like, but I assure you I am one."

"Dunno. Some of the boys think you're a Rebel spy." Amos leaned over his saddle and obliquely stared at the man. "They say they seen you go over to Rebel camps a time or two."

Amos turned his horse and looked levelly at the man, not knowing the man was from a misfit backwater family where bullying and fighting were common-place, and those fights seldom lost, a perverse source of family pride.

"I did. I gave sermons and led worship service. I've done it for both sides."

"Kinda strange don't y' think? We're at war and you fraternizin' with the enemy."

Amos looked about. "Fraternizing with the enemy," replied Amos, "has not been all that unusual in this war." As Amos turned toward the man, Amos asked in a monotone, "What can I do for you?"

"Surrender, maybe. I think you're a Rebel spy. Callin' yourself a chaplain'd be good cover."

"If I'm a Rebel spy, I haven't done a very good job. I haven't obtained a single secret and I have killed a Rebel soldier." His anger rising, Amos pulled the Rebel saber from the rifle sheath. "See this? The soldier who owned it is dead. Unfortunate. Unnecessary. What would you like me to do with this?"

"I don't much care what you do with it," said the man who then spat to one side, mistakenly thinking the chaplain a big drink of water.

"You wouldn't mind if I stuck the tip in your big mouth and shoved it down your throat?" Amos retorted, his eyes on fire. His jaw clamped, he leaned forward and his horse began to walk toward the man.

"You wouldn't mind that? I could do it." Amos's eyes grew narrower and his teeth began to show as he talked. "After all, I'm a Rebel spy."

Amos angrily approached the man who waited, about to get down from his horse and give this so-called chaplain the beating of his life. Shootin' Rebs was one thing, but the back-water soldier hadn't had a regular fight in months. And he half hoped the war was wasn't ending. He was in his element.

Without taking his eyes off the man's eyes, Amos shoved the saber back in the scabbard. As Amos came up next to the man, before the man could move, Amos's right hand shot out like a darting snake and grabbed the big man's neck, constricting powerfully and restricting blood flow as Amos brought the man's left ear close to Amos's mouth. Although the man's horse moved, Amos's right arm did not.

"If you want to live out this war," said Amos quietly through gritted teeth as the man tried with both hands to pull Amos's hand loose, "turn around and ride back to your line." Although the man at first pulled and yanked frenziedly, Amos's right hand remained tightly constricted. Increasing pain and dizziness began to make Amos's point. He was not going to put up with this nonsense. "Do it now," Amos added. Amos shoved the man upright and let go.

The man, on the verge of passing out, wove unsteadily in the saddle as he regained his bearings. Gradually mental clarity returned and, grimacing, the man blinked several times as, still woozy, he held his neck. He looked at Amos who glared back, and the man reined his horse about. Amos watched the man ride unsteadily back to his ranks, his fellow soldiers watching, but saying nothing.

Except one soldier. Family pride was now at stake.

"Hey! Hey, ya goddam Johnny-lover!" yelled another man, trotting toward Amos, muttering epithets, unmindful of either where they were or the circumstances. "Who th' hell y' think y'are? Ain' no dam' chaplain! Not by a long sight!"

The ugly light in his eyes flashed as the man dismounted, grabbed Amos and pulled him off his horse.

"You laid a hand on m' brother?" snarled the man as he threw a straight right and hit Amos on the left side of his face, "Now I'm layin' a hand or two on you!"

Hurt, Amos staggered, fell and rolled over, but as the man moved forward, Amos quickly got to his feet, nimbly fending off blows while clearing his head. Dancing away as the man kept coming, Amos decided talk was pointless and, the better part of valor being discretion, to discreetly end the confrontation.

As the man came at him, Amos again danced back, but quickly stepped in, shooting chain-lightning left jabs, the man's head snapping back multiple times. With surgical precision, Amos inflicted pain and bleeding. As the man attempted an off-balance haymaker, Amos slipped under it and came over the top with a blurred left followed by a straight right, dropping the man as if his legs had turned to soup. The man lay unmoving, and the men watching behaved no differently; the man was not popular. Amos's right hand, not entirely healed from his previous fight with the Confederate soldier, began to again throb painfully.

Maddened by the pain in his right hand, Amos walked to the unconscious brother – about the same size as Amos – and in spite of the pain, angrily grabbed and picked up the man like a big sack of grain, hoisting him up to one shoulder. Amos walked to the man's horse, and using legs and arms, lobbed the man over the saddle as if practiced at it. Amos turned the horse in the direction of the other men, whose expressions begged for explanation as to who Amos was. No one had ever beaten either of the Bales brothers, much less both in quick succession. Amos rudely slapped the horse's flank, and the horse trotted back to the others who continued to look back without moving.

"What was that all about?" Amos asked himself out loud as, holding his right hand, he studied the men for a moment. "Why would anyone think I was a Rebel spy? What was behind that?" Amos mounted and reined his horse to the left, again proceeding slowly toward the lines. Maybe not 'what' but 'who,' Amos intuited.

"Chaplain?"

Pastor Nordquist looked around as a dirty, bearded Union cavalryman, after watching at a distance, casually rode toward Amos. The cavalryman had such an intimidating appearance of hard intensity that Amos was immediately apprehensive. Even if his right hand did not hurt, Amos didn't want another altercation, but as he watched the cavalryman approach, Amos was prepared for the worst.

In his late 20's or early 30's, the soldier had a two-inch scar that traveled diagonally from above his left eyebrow to the bridge of his nose, and a patch over his left eye. The dark color of the scar indicated the wound was not an old one, and Pastor Nordquist wondered how horrible it must have been to lose an eye like that. The cavalryman was about the same size as Amos, sat upright in the saddle, a centaur, and when he came to a halt a short distance away, faced straight ahead, not looking directly at Amos. Protruding from a sheath attached to the man's belt, his Bowie knife handle was nicked and worn. The scraped, light brown leather sheath was darkly stained at the top. As the soldier held his reins, Amos could see the ends of three fingers were missing from the man's left hand, severed below the knuckles. The seasoned veteran's soiled tunic and breeches were hastily re-sewn in several places. His large, worn, muddy boots looked like someone buffed them for hours with a curry comb. The severity of the man's appearance made Amos think this man could fit into any army anywhere at any time in history. Without expression, Amos apprehensively waited for the man.

30

Yer Swede's kin, ain't y', " said the man in a low monotone as his horse took a few steps forward before stopping again.

"Yah," nodded Amos.

"Knowed Swede pretty good," said the man. "Don't know if you knowed it, but ol' Swede – just thought you should know – never liked killin' folks."

"I'm not surprised," said Amos. "No one likes to do that."

"I don't mind," said the man.

Amos said nothing. The man continued.

"See, he would always call the Rebs 'Norvegians,' but he called anything he shot at a 'Norvegian,' even rabbits and deer. I got the impression he might be tryin' t' cover up the fact that Rebs is people. Dunno how t' explain it, but when he said 'Norvegian,' he warn't talkin' about anyone from any country. I asked him once what was a 'Norvegian?' He said it was 'no one.'"

The man reined his horse alongside Pastor Nordquist and looked down the rise.

"I think it bothered 'im that he was…well, killin' somebody…somebody's brother, somebody's son, grandson. Tried makin' it a game, maybe; pretendin' what he was doin' wasn't real. Dunno. Never bothered me much. Not at the moment. I guess it shoulda, but I just aim and shoot. Not much to it. Jes' pull the trigger. Bible says not to kill, but I kilt a bunch a' those boys. They done the same. In the Bible there's a lotta Old Testament men-a'-God who were warriors. And there's a lot a' Bible-believin' men on both the North and the South…Lee, Stonewall Jackson…I hear General Chamberlain was a Bible teacher or somethin' somewhere up north before he became a so'jer. A lotta us."

Still looking straight ahead, the man weighed his choice of words.

"Seems like war and men 'a God go together like rifle muskets and Minié balls," the man said in a low, gravelly voice, "and that don't make sense t' me." He looked at Amos for the first time. "I wanted to ask y': what makes believers like Lee, Jackson, General Chamberlain and the rest of us so dam' natural at this? Don't seem right."

The two men sat in silence, both looking straight ahead, while Pastor Nordquist collected his thoughts.

"Are you familiar with the Bible?" Amos asked.

"Hell, everyone's familiar with the Bible," was the unnerving response.

"Do you remember what the Lord did when the Pharaoh refused the Lord's request through Moses to allow the Israelites to leave Egypt so that they might freely serve God?" asked Pastor Nordquist. Amos had no idea what the man's response might be.

"Yeah, I knows. First God turned all the water in Egypt, includin' the whole Nile River, into blood. Couldn't drink any of it. Fish all died. Stunk t' high heaven." The man snorted.

"And God said, 'By this you shall know that I am the Lord,'" said Pastor Nordquist. "Then what happened?"

"Where's this goin'?"

"I'll show you." Amos freely studied the man who did not look back. "You seem to know the Bible. After God turned the water into blood, what happened?"

"Well," the man answered after a moment, "Pharaoh's magicians were somehow able to turn some water into blood too…dunno quite how…since all the water in Egypt had already been turned into blood…but…"

"Magicians? I question what really happened," said Amos.

"Anyway," continued the man, "Pharaoh sees 'em do whatever they did, then God re-hardens 'ol Pharaoh's heart, and Pharaoh ag'in says the Israelites cain't go."

"Then what happened?" asked Amos.

"God brought plagues, one after the other – first millions a' frogs, then dust-turned-to-lice," the man's nose winced as he imagined that scene. "Then flies." The man cleared his throat. "And Egyptians started droppin' like flies – but nothin' happened in the land of Goshen where the Israelites were." The cavalry-man thought for a moment. "After each plague, ol' Pharaoh told Moses that if Moses would ask the Lord to stop doin' what He just done, the Israelites could go. Head on out. So, Moses would ask, and the Lord'd stop. Then each time after stoppin', the Lord'd harden Pharaoh's heart ag'in, and ol' Pharaoh 'd change his mind ag'in and tell Moses, 'Nope, y' gotta stay.' This went on after each plague. You know all this, right?" asked the soldier.

"What you are saying is true," said Pastor Nordquist. "At one point, the Lord, through Moses, tells the Pharaoh that the Egyptians would all be dead if God wanted them dead, but then God went on to say, '…for this cause I have allowed you to remain, in order to show you My power, and in order to proclaim My name throughout the earth.'"

"Yeah," the man drawled in his low, gravelly voice. "Guess y' do." The soldier looked at Amos. "Ma taught me t' read usin' the Bible. Only book in the house," he added as he looked away. "Read it more'n a few times."

"Can you tell me what happened next?"

The soldier flicked a caustic glance at Amos, as if to say, "What'd I just say?" but looked straight ahead.

"Yeah, I c'n tell ya what happened next. By then, God was playin' Pharaoh like a fiddle. Since God hardened ol' Pharaoh's heart each time, and Pharaoh changed his mind each time – as God determined – the last thing God commanded was the Passover," answered the man, looking back at Amos with the same steely, enigmatic look Amos saw when first meeting Custer's men. "The angel a' death passed o'er Egypt and kilt the firstborn of everythin' that was not part of the captive Israelites – the Israelites put lamb's blood on their doorposts and were spared. But the Egyptians lost husbands, wives, grown sons and daughters, children, animals…all firstborn. S'pose to have been the worse thing t' ever happen – or ever will happen, Bible says – in Egypt. Still, seemed God wasn't gonna let ol' Pharaoh give in. Kinda like some of those Johnnies over there."

"You're right," said Pastor Nordquist. He looked at the man and asked, "If God intended to harden Pharaoh's heart to the plagues and death each time, what was God doing?"

"Provin' a point."

"What point?" asked Amos.

"That He's God, His will is done. Nothin' else was higher or more powerful, not even one a' the most powerful rulers – a so-called emperor-god – in history. It was like He and Pharaoh had an agreement, but God would cause Pharaoh to break the agreement – sorta like he had no will of his own – and then God'd backhand him. Then they'd do it again." The man looked ahead sullenly. "A lot a' people got kilt in the process. God c'n do that," said the man. "But He tells us we cain't. So, here we are; jes' finished killin' a bunch a' Johnnies and vice versa. What's gonna happen t' me?"

"Those events in Egypt show life and death belong to the Creator who has power over life and death," said Amos. "All things are possible through God, and nothing is greater than God's will. He effects His will through us, whether softening hearts or hardening hearts, and can choose to do so, as you point out, even through death, including death in war."

"Okay but that's Him. Me? I kilt a lot a' Johnnies." The cavalryman looked around. "Now, maybe this war is over." The man looked at Amos. "I'm still here. I want to know: where do I stand with the Lord?"

"You recall the Bible said that 'Saul has killed his thousands, but David has killed his tens of thousands'?"

"Yeah but, now, I also recall David got into trouble fer killin' so many folks. The Lord told 'im, 'I'm a' gonna use your son, Solomon, – which meant 'man a' peace' – cuz you're just a little too good at this; you got too much blood on your hands,' somethin' like that."

"With the Lord, what seems apparent to us, so often isn't exactly as it seems," Amos said. "Certainly, God does not condone bloodshed. The Messiah said that 'those who live by the sword shall die by the sword.' It is important to make the distinction, however, that many who believe they must take up the 'sword,' do not 'live by the sword.'"

"Ol' Swede, maybe."

"Exactly," said Amos. "'The sword' was not part of his nature. Events are what God determines them to be and, again, God effects His will through those events, using participants in those events to accomplish his purposes."

"Wonder how God used the Wilderness?" wondered the man out loud, not looking at Pastor Nordquist. "Miserable goddam' battle – I been in this war since Shiloh, but I never seen anything like that. Ain't no use in even tryin' t' explain t' someone who weren't there." The man paused. "War'll be over, and 50, 60 years from now, no one'll know that second day; no one'll give a dam'. What'd we do it for? Bunch a' Yanks and Johnnies shootin' each other at point blank range in the woods an' the brush – brush catches on fire; smoke so thick ya cain't see – wounded lyin' on the ground gettin' burned t' death, an' no time t' reload so it becomes a matter a' who c'n stab each other the most. Dead so thick in some places y' c'n walk across 'em without steppin' on the ground." The soldier paused. "Merciful God." He slumped slightly for moment but sat upright again. "About as close t' hell as anyone c'n come in this life."

The man's eyes narrowed, and he whispered something inaudible, gritted his teeth, and his full-fingered right hand reflexively reached left for the handle of his Bowie knife. "How does… Makes no dam' sense at all," he muttered.

"If that misery, death and suffering had not occurred, where might we be at this moment?" asked Pastor Nordquist.

"Dunno. Dunno anyone knows."

"I heard a conversation a short while ago," said Pastor Nordquist, "where some men were discussing what would have happened in '62 if Grant had been in charge instead of McClellan who, the men said, was too focused on risks to make opportunities."

"That was Mac," the soldier muttered.

"They figured there was a good chance," continued Amos, "considering all the Union had available for warfare, the war could have been substantially concluded that year if Grant was giving orders, and Yanks were to fight like they have these past many months. Wasn't Grant the Union commander at Wilderness?"

"Yeah. He was. First time he was in charge. And first time we saw some real tenacity from a commanding officer. Lee's Army of Northern Virginia usually got their way until Wilderness. Grant made damn sure it didn't happen then. We had a miserable time, but we got 'er done."

"What if you didn't? What about the direction of the war? What about the November election?"

For a moment neither the man nor Pastor Nordquist said anything. In the silence, the soldier was weighing the Battle of the Wilderness at Spotsylvania in the context of Pastor Nordquist's questions, reasoning to himself.

"So…y' think…" The man stopped speaking, took a breath, and slowly expelled it, still thinking.

"S'pose if we hadn't gone through the Wilderness," he began again, "at this moment my guess is we'd still be fightin' the Rebs…an' maybe the war would go on for a spell…more people'd die – maybe me – an' people'd get more 'n more tired a' the fightin'. Some a' those boys up north, you know who I mean, would take advantage of that – and instead a' winnin' like now, maybe…well, you see where I'm 'a goin'. The present and, especially, the future'd be entirely dif'rent."

"Most likely."

"Nah," the man countered. "Def'nitely." The man looked away.

"Reasoning about God and war isn't easy," Amos said as he and the man started forward. "Warfare involves killing, but we are to protect the innocent and defenseless. Of necessity, courageous men must put their lives on the line to defend country, families, heritage. It has always been so; t'would be folly to think it will not always be so. The question is: how do we prolong peace in between wars? Jesus said, 'Blessed are the peacemakers,' but the word 'peacemakers' includes soldiers, very large numbers of them. As *Pax Romana* indicated, to maintain peace for a considerable period requires a large, disciplined army and the will to use it, while, ironically, those who would eschew having any army, who would 'avoid war at all costs,' will invariably dearly pay those costs, encouraging oppression and aggression and, consequently, betraying humanity by enhancing the prospects for strong men to successfully prey on weakened men."

The cavalryman nodded as Amos turned toward him.

"What's your name?" asked Pastor Nordquist, momentarily changing the subject.

"Real name's Joab." The man did not volunteer a last name.

"Joab? Really?"

"Really. Named after King David's right-hand man. But nobody calls me 'Joab.' Too familiar. I ain't the familiar type. Most don't know my name is Joab," said the man as he glanced at Amos.

He volunteered nothing else.

"What do they call you?" asked Amos after a moment.

The man continued to look straight ahead.

"'Blade.'"

Amos glanced at the man's Bowie knife. The name fit.

"Blade, I suspect you will agree that motive, what's in a person's heart, has considerable bearing in this matter," said Amos, returning to the subject.

"Yeah," said Blade as he rode, still looking straight ahead. "Tell ya a little story. When those Johnnies were shootin' at us, they're mostly just bein' so'jers like us. Sure, they wants t' kill us, but ain't nothin' personal. Takes a while t' figure that out. But, I tell ya," Blade glanced at Amos, "when they's shooting at our colored troops, it gets real down and personal. They aim real careful. If you wuz t' say motive is how it's measured, I think that's when the line between so'jers and murderers gets crossed…cuz a lot a' those boys 'd take that shot even if there weren't no war."

Pastor Nordquist looked at Blade and nodded in understanding.

"Motive has bearing," said Amos, "but when God forbade killing, on the other hand, He did not follow that commandment with a list of exceptions." Amos thought for a moment. "To the contrary, Jesus said to love one another – that the entire Law and the Prophets depended on loving God and one another – but, on the other hand, He said there is no greater act of love than to die for another, as Jesus, assuming our responsibility for our sin, did for all of us."

"Bunch 'a boys died in this war." The soldier weighed their sacrifice on behalf of posterity. "Didn't die jes' for themselves," said Blade, continuing to look straight ahead. "What the hell's the sense in that? Even when a man has no family, no home, no future, he fights for the other men in his platoon, his company. That's a lot of it." About to say something else, Blade first looked at Amos with that intense, steely expression, and came to a halt. Amos also came to a halt and, sensing Blade's inner turmoil, leaned slightly toward the soldier, waiting for whatever Blade was to say.

"Chaplain, I'll be straight with y'. Compared t' most, I'm 'good' at this. Dam' good. Sometimes I think I must have been born t' kill. But I'll tell ya…," Blade looked straight ahead again, "y' know how I said I didn't mind killin' no one? Well, yeah, individually, y' just do it – him or me; do what y' gotta. But doin' it over and over and over…blood always flowin' and dead men's eyes starin' back…I dunno…it starts t' saturate into y' like blood from someone's ripped guts draining in the goddam ground; builds inside like a goddam manure pile. You're around it all the time and it…" Blade ostensibly made himself more comfortable in the saddle and turned toward Amos. "Chaplain, how many more a' these do we gotta go through?"

The reins in his hands, Amos rested his hands on the saddle horn, looked at the ground and up at the soldier.

"As you know, Jesus said, 'There will always be wars and rumors of wars,'" quoted Amos, "and as long as there are wars, there will be ample occasions where men make the ultimate sacrifice doing what they believe they must do, defending those they love and the principles they want their posterity to live under."

"It gets real blurred though," said the soldier. "Shenandoah Valley? Coulda done without any a' that."

"Yah," said Amos. He sighed softly.

Thinking of his original question about believers and war, Blade looked at Amos for a moment, and again looked straight ahead.

"So, y' don't know, do y'," said Blade.

Amos looked at the cumulus clouds above the distant hills before them, looked at Blade, and said, "In this army not all Christians are good soldiers, but an inordinate number of good soldiers are Christians. Makes no sense? Well, there's a reason why Christians are good soldiers, having to do with what Christians believe and think. To begin with, men die physically in war, but we are already dead in our sins." Pastor Nordquist looked straight ahead again. "'For all have sinned and fallen short of the glory of God.' Abstaining from sinning, including killing, is our goal, but we will never reach it." Pastor Nordquist looked at Blade. "Ever lied? Ever stole anything? Ever taken the name of the Lord in vain?"

"Done 'em all," answered Blade.

"Well," said Amos, "add killing Johnnies to the list and it would seem you're deeper in the hole. Salvation, however, is not based on a point system. Sins. Men's on-going imperfections accumulate. Based on a providential checklist, heaven would be out of the question for all of us. Battle of the Wilderness? You and a lot of men shouldn't have a chance for salvation." Blade nodded. "But remember the 'thief' being crucified on one side of Jesus?"

"Yeah," said the man, still looking straight ahead. "Seems he made it. Right at the last moment."

"Yah," said Amos. "The thief said he deserved to be crucified. He had a conscience. This admission also indicates he was probably a lot more than an ordinary thief. He might have sinned beyond what you and I have done combined."

"That'd be a bunch."

"Jesus told the man he would be with Jesus in paradise," continued Pastor Nordquist, "simply because he knew the Lord, believed He was the Messiah."

"If he knew the Lord, had faith, why'd he do all that sinnin'?"

"That's my point. It's not up to us! We continually do what we should not do. Me. You. The thief on the cross. Why did you kill all those Johnnies?"

"I kin answer that, but I'm not sure the answer'd wash with th' Lord." The soldier's voice was tight.

"Do you believe that Jesus is the Messiah?" Amos asked Blade.

"Yup."

"Then salvation is yours. Like the thief on the cross, regardless of your sins, you have salvation."

"Mmhhhhh," moaned Blade in a low, tortured, guttural growl that seeped out from deep in his soul as he seemed to again be adjusting himself in his saddle. "Sometimes I wonder." He took a short breath and let it out. "You got no idea what I done. How do we know for sure? Yeah, I know what the Bible says." He paused and his eyes narrowed again. "Guess it's in the hands a' God."

"Yah," said Amos, looking at Blade. "It always has been. God is the source of all, everything; the 'alpha and omega.' And your faith is from Him."

Blade's burden of sin, however, had grown so large it crushed any sense of salvation. If God chooses, Blade thought, why would He choose me? No damned reason, he answered to himself.

"Let me ask you a related question," said Amos, sensing Blade's dilemma. "You're a believer. If you weren't, we wouldn't be having this conversation. But some believe the first Easter was merely an historical event, one more Roman crucifixion, and a waste of time to reconsider every year. What about you? How do you feel about Jesus' sacrifice on your behalf that first Easter?"

"Grateful."

Pastor Nordquist let that sink in, for a moment saying nothing else.

"So do I," said Pastor Nordquist, sensing the bridge was just crossed, the man understood. In spite of all his sinful behavior, Blade would stand before God sinless.

Blade glanced at Amos, a glint of hope reflecting off the soldier's steely countenance, and again looked straight ahead, weighing what was said.

"Christians and war?" continued Amos. "'Rifle muskets and Minié balls'?" Amos shook his head softly. "Blade, look around us. Look at these men. In war, no one ever fails to wish they were somewhere else. Before battle, all are enveloped with fear. In combat, none wants to die but, nevertheless, they've placed themselves in that position. After a battle, those still alive have further burdened or seared their consciences. Why do Christians do it? There is a consistent answer. Let me ask you something: what's the worst thing you can do in war?"

"Kill someone."

"No, that's the perspective of a civilian. From a soldier's perspective, what is the worst thing a soldier can do?"

"What're ya gettin' at?"

"In battle, you are supposed to kill the enemy. You said you killed a lot of Johnnies. You did what you were supposed to do. Isn't that correct?"

"Yeah," said Blade. "It was."

"Was it right?" asked Amos rhetorically. "We've already covered that. Your conscience wouldn't bother you if it was right. But as far as soldiering goes, what is the worst thing a soldier can do?"

Blade thought for moment.

"Turn traitor," he said.

"Anything worse than that?" asked Amos.

"Nope," said Blade without equivocation.

"I agree," said Amos, nodding. "Betraying your own men is the worst thing a soldier can do. It's the extreme act of selfishness. When faith is victimized, that is betrayal, not only in war but under any circumstances." Amos looked at Blade whose facial expression was in agreement although he did not look back, apparently thinking of an example.

"Betrayal is interesting," added Pastor Nordquist. "Every sin initially involves an element of betrayal. Trust and faith fill our lives – everything we do involves one or the other – and if you look at any sin closely, always at the heart of the matter is an element of betrayal. Lying, covetousness, adultery, stealing…you name it…at the core of each is betrayal. Someone sells you a new saddle, and after the sale you discover the stitching is bad. We don't think about it as faith, but you trusted the seller was selling you a good saddle."

"Or I wouldn't 'a bought the saddle."

"So, when you discover the saddle is poorly made, if anger is your second sensation, what is your first?"

Blade nodded as the two continued to ride slowly.

"Or you get up in the morning," said Amos, "and discover the rocking chair on your front porch was stolen during the night. You left the rocking chair out there because you had faith it would not be stolen. Who would be so low as to do that? But someone did. What is your first sensation?"

"Mmhm," nodded the soldier.

"Betrayal goes on continually; it's an enormous spiritual problem," said Pastor Nordquist. "How big is betrayal? Let me ask you something: how did the Romans find Jesus so they could arrest him?"

"Judas. He betrayed Jesus," said Blade as he glanced sideways at Amos.

"Betrayal. Right there in the crux of things," said Amos as the horses stood motionlessly. "Coincidental? Jesus? In the Bible? Hardly. There were an infinite number of alternatives whereby the Romans could find and identify Jesus. But, no, God elected betrayal; Jesus said to Judas, 'Friend, do what you have come for.' It wasn't a suggestion. Would there have been a more appropriate way for the Romans to find Jesus? No. Betrayal is the compromise of faith, of trust, and would have been most appropriate.

"So, Blade, you ask why Christians seem better suited for warfare than those with no conviction? The reason is because of what happened to Jesus, as well as many other biblical teachings. Christians, whether they realize it or not, are unusually sensitive to betrayal, and the degree to which it reflects selfishness and spiritual weakness. Don't misunderstand me; these men around us – Rebel or Yankee – who believe that Jesus is the Messiah, and who have followed their conflicted consciences, doing to their fullest extent what most believed was necessary, would otherwise rather have stayed home. They're here because of conviction, honor, a disinclination to betray – the extreme act of selfishness." Amos glanced about. "They've come this far – I have no doubt they'll stay here until the war's done."

Pastor Nordquist looked around at the motionless Confederate and Yankee troops waiting as an ethereal clock ticked away the end of the Civil War. Blade sat silently, erectly, his great burden lifted, having understood salvation through God's grace – but he was still trying to piece together all that went on, with little success.

"So, what's it all about?" asked Blade. "Why'd we do it? Gotta be more t' this 'n meets the eye."

"In the greater scheme of history," Amos concluded, "something, probably many things, much greater will come from all this suffering. 'What Satan meant for evil, God uses for good.'" Amos glanced at Blade who glanced back. "What will they be? I don't know." Amos looked forward again. "I wish I knew more. From what I have seen, however, I have little doubt the Lord has effected greater ends through the suffering you and these men who have endured." Pastor Nordquist nodded at both Rebel and Yankee troops.

Blade continued to look straight ahead, studying the Confederate troops below him. They appeared gaunt, spent and withdrawn but, his soldier's intuition sensitive, Blade knew most would go back into battle even though doing so meant death. Must be a few Christians, Blade thought.

On a rise aside a map-dot village called Appomattox Court House, Pastor Nordquist leaned forward in his saddle as he, Blade and the two armies quietly waited on the leading generals to conclude one of the most passionate but enigmatic conflicts in world history: the American Civil War.

31

April 9, 1865

As Pastor Nordquist and Blade looked at the cold, wet soldiers, Amos realized what day it was: Palm Sunday, when Jesus rode into Jerusalem as a coming king, fulfilling Zechariah 9:9: "Rejoice greatly, O daughter of Zion; shout, O daughter of Jerusalem: behold, thy King cometh unto thee: he is just, and having salvation; lowly, and riding upon a colt, the foal of a donkey," written 500 years before Christ was born. Amos knew a donkey colt in that place and era meant a king coming in peace; while a horse, typically used, signified a warrior king.

Amos, Blade and the warriors around them were beginning to sense the approach of peace. The pastor from Sweden inexplicably found himself at this place at this moment, and couldn't help but wonder why, for what reasons in the long run, this war was waged, although Amos had no doubt the reasons were multiple and extraordinary.

As Amos thought about this, a surreal moment occurred. At a distance an animated Union cavalryman excitedly galloped down the Richmond-Lynch-burg Stage Road waving his hat and yelling, "It's over boys! It's over! Lee's surrendered!" Yankees in the rider's wake exploded in jubilation, firing rifles, throwing caps, coats, even ammunition in the air, some dismounting and dancing, all the while yelling, yelling at a volume that rent the heavens – while at a short distance many vanquished Rebels sat sullenly watching, while others swore, teeth bared, angrily throwing down weapons carried for years.

Some, unable to come to grips with this moment, having endured more suffering and sacrifice in the last two years than most men endure in a lifetime, dropped to their knees in the rain and mud, and unashamedly wept as if their hearts would break. Others who dropped to their knees, simply gave thanks the ordeal was over and somehow they were alive.

Federal celebrating along the lines came to the attention of General Grant who ordered it stopped.

At a short distance, Amos watched a small group of Confederate troops tearing off pieces of the battle flag they'd fought under. The victors would not get it. Rather, each man would carry a piece with him for the rest of his life.

For most, the war had just ended, but for one group at Appomattox Court-house, nothing had changed. Amos's attention was redirected as he looked up at another horseman galloping toward him.

"Chaplain!" a medical officer shouted. "Been lookin' all over for you. The surgeon needs you!" Amos had learned the effective ranking officer anywhere around a battlefield was not the commanding officer; the man whose word is law was the surgeon. "Got more wounded men!" shouted the medical officer. "They got this far! Let's keep a few of 'em alive!" For the medical corps, the war continued.

When Amos and the others got to a hospital tent alongside the Rich-mond-Lynchburg Stage Road, the Union and Confederate dead were laid side-by-side, some with arms spread out as if mocking the living for failing to make the supreme sacrifice. The awful, mixed smells of blood and dysentery were rank, and Amos thought of the sergeant who earlier said, "Ain't it evident what's gonna happen? Ain't it obvious that thems what get kilt from now on, dies for nuthin'?" His jaw clenched, Amos looked about at the bodies, saddened by their death, but convinced their sacrifice would result in something far greater for those not yet born, and convinced posterity would somehow owe a deep debt of gratitude to these men because they had not died for nothing.

Amos joined assistant surgeons, medical officers, and volunteers from both Union and Confederacy as they went from man to man among the wounded laying on the muddy ground, expediting transportation of the living to field hospitals. As Amos walked by him in the hospital tent, a badly wounded young soldier, no more than 16, held out a muddied note – "I go to prepar a place for you" – to give to the soldier's mother. After handing the note to Amos, the young soldier stared at the tent ceiling as if listening to the rain beating down. In a moment Amos returned, studied the young soldier for a moment, then reached down with his fingers, closing the soldier's eyelids.

Grant gave another order in response to an earlier request by General Lee at the moment of surrender. The Union army would share their rations with the Rebels, most of whom had not eaten a decent meal in months. The Confederates ate gratefully, silently impressed with the extent of Union provisions, unaware that a significant proportion of the food being shared came from the Confeder-ate supply trains captured by Custer's men at Appomattox Station.

———————— ●————————

Nightfall. Taking a break from the gory floors and stench of the field hospital, Pastor Nordquist stood outside looking about at the distant, quiet men around campfires. The day was done. The war was nearly done. Much had changed, but no change was greater than the change in the seasoned veterans who with each battle had grown more hardened and older than their years, permanently distancing themselves from those who never carried a rifle. The spent veterans on both sides congregated as if, from Pastor Nordquist's perspective, having prepared to do so for some time, one or two talking quietly, but most standing motionlessly in exhausted silence, weakly visible in the campfire light. Somewhere in the darkness a Division band was playing a variety of tunes – "Yankee Doodle," "Hail Columbia," and "Dixie" – but, although the band played, Amos heard no singing.

April 12, 1865

The last formality, the laying-down-of-arms ceremony required by General Grant, was to be coordinated by former Bowdoin College humanities professor and medal-of-honor winner Brevet Major General Joshua Chamberlain, 36.

The following morning sky was again overcast, and the cold morning air made April 12th seem more like February 12th. As Pastor Nordquist watched, 6,000 Union soldiers formed two, long, parallel lines along either side of America's bloodiest arterial, the Richmond-Lynchburg Stage Road, a swath of muddy, blood-soaked ground winding up the hill from the west and through the middle of Appomattox Court House. Down the hill and across the valley on a hillside to the west, a procession of Rebel soldiers also formed on the Stage Road and, like a long, frayed, gray rope pulled by duty, began moving along the valley, wading through the shallow Appomattox River, and up the hill toward the small village. At that formerly insignificant place, they would stack their muskets and rifles, severed appendages after years of war. The weariness of war, not only of that day or even that week, but a weariness accumulating over years, was shunted aside, and in relative stillness the Rebel soldiers moved perfunctorily, on the march for the last time.

As Amos waited, with methodical cadence the grim Rebels marched in the appointed direction, their feet providing syncopated percussion complementing the beat of a snare drum, and at the top of the hill the Yankee soldiers stood silently in the rain, motionlessly awaiting the approach of the long Confederate line of exhausted solemn men, some of whom had yelled, "Down, Yank!" before opening fire.

Marching up the muddy road, although ragged and spent, the Rebels were still erect, eyes clear, and it was evident to Pastor Nordquist that these men who endured so much had a unified spirit of indomitability, and could have endured more, for their look was of defiance not defeat. At the very least, Amos thought, sitting in his saddle, most Rebels were men of resolve and character, having fought for a much smaller army with great leadership, but no answer for the juggernaut that was Sherman, Sheridan, Gibbon, Grant and City Point. More than one Yankee soldier inwardly marveled at the fortitude of their former adversaries, and hoped that somehow, they could become truly reunited, an honor for both sides, the same army under the same flag.

The long queue of Southern troops, someone later guessed maybe 24,000, a fraction of what was once the Army of Northern Virginia, maintained ranks as they marched up the muddy road to the ridge of the hill at the edge of the village, following mounted, former attorney, Maj. Gen. John B. Gordon, 33, wounded twice during the past week. A serious man under any circumstances, as he rode, he would not look directly at the Union lines up ahead of him on either side of the road but looked darkly at the muddy road before him.

As Pastor Nordquist watched frayed and ragged battle flags swaying overhead, the decimated Confederate division columns, led by the old Stonewall Jackson Brigade, were shouldering muskets and heavy emotional burden as, after years of conflict, Confederate General Gordon, expecting to endure the humiliation of the vanquished, approached the two long lines of motionless, former adversaries standing at attention on either side of the Richmond-Lynchburg Stage Road.

As the Army of Northern Virginia remnant neared the hillcrest, the snare drum became more audible, the tramping feet maintaining cadence. Pastor Nordquist could hear no other sound as mounted Union General Joshua Chamberlain watched General Gordon and the Rebel troops approach.

As General Gordon reached the ridge of the hill and approached the first Union men including General Chamberlain, Amos heard Chamberlain give an order, a trumpet sounded, and instantly along the entire Union line Union officers barked orders, soldiers snapped to attention, and Union carbines in successive regiments went to carry arms – rifles held perpendicular to the shoulder – the soldier's marching salutation…an honor expected for a Union official but…not…

General Gordon, startled by Chamberlain's order followed by the Union bugle and the sound of arms shifting in unison, looked at Chamberlain, and for a moment their eyes locked as Gordon realized what was happening: this was not to be a moment of humiliation.

Gordon, an excellent horseman, reined his horse to the left facing Chamberlain, ordered, "Up, Marye," and the horse reared as trained. As the horse reared, Gordon pulled his saber from its sheath, raised the saber aloft, and as the trained horse dropped and bowed, touched the saber to his toe, saluting General Chamberlain and the Union command.

Reining Marye about, facing his own marching army, Gordon shouted orders that successive Confederate brigades pass the Union lines accordingly. As ordered, Confederate muskets successively went to carry arms, returning the Union honor – honor for honor – as the Confederates uniformly marched, not as the vanquished but as equals, between the two lines of Federal troops along bloody Richmond-Lynchburg Stage Road through the modest village of Appomattox Court House, the muffled tramp, tramp, tramp marching sound joined only by the occasional sound of hardened men stifling emotion.

In the irrational miasma of the moment, among some Yankee soldiers arose a wishful inclination to yell, "Down, Reb!" one last time. "Down, Reb!" But quiet prevailed. Pastor Nordquist sensed this terrible and bloody but, at other times, oddly civil war was over and, at that moment, as was General Joshua Chamberlain's intention, Chaplain Nordquist could not tell who won and who lost.

--------•--------

As the Confederates stacked muskets, carbines, rifles, and other implements of war, the procedure went smoothly except for the stacking of battle flags. These

Rebels never surrendered those flags in battle and abhorred doing so now. One Southern soldier defiantly looked about at Yankee soldiers in ranks on either side of the road, held his battle flag aloft, shook it and shouted, "Boys, this is not the first time you've seen this flag! I've borne it at the front on many victorious fields of battle! And I'm not sure but that I'd rather die than surrender it to you now!" Amos heard General Chamberlain tell the man that it was with regret Chamberlain had no authority to allow the Confederate soldiers to keep battle flags. As Amos watched, for Confederates the moment was agonizing – Amos could feel it – and, as the men stacked their arms and battle flags, Amos saw on a nearby house veranda a young Southern woman, maybe 16 or 17, a handkerchief in her hands, watching and uninhibitedly weeping.

Eventually it was done. Confederate soldiers were given parole documents affording them safe return home, and the surrender of Lee's army precipitated the surrender of General Joe Johnston's forces in North Carolina, as well as other remaining scattered Confederate forces.

Amos was later told that the Gray Ghost of the Confederacy, John Singleton Mosby, and his men, however, did not formally surrender; but on April 21st regrouped one last time and disbanded near Salem, Virginia, disappearing among the city folk and farmers, much as they might have following one of their many raids during the war.

The former Confederate soldiers all began going their separate ways, intent on repairing the devastation wrought.

Pastor Nordquist began going through Uncle Torvald's belongings, initially interested in ownership documents supplementing Torvald's last will and testament, the primary document in the collection. Torvald's executor was someone named Nels Hanseth, a Lutheran Church executive up north. The will was not complicated; Torvald simply left everything to the Lutheran Church in Minnesota, and it was evident where the Lord needed Amos to go next. Extensive railroad and bridge destruction in Virginia and West Virginia meant Amos would ride north on horseback. It would be a long ride but, unknown to Amos, along the way he would have sage company, a former slave and Union soldier with the weight of the war still on his broad shoulders, "Fatha Abraham" Cole.

32

April 14, 1865

Pastor Nordquist remained in Appomattox Courthouse concluding his duties as a volunteer Union army chaplain. As he packed a haversack for the ride north to Minnesota, a soldier pulled back the tent flap and stepped in, his eyes tight as he choked out, "Lincoln's been shot."

The peace settling on Appomattox seemed to shatter like dropped crystal, and for the stunned soldiers it was as if they were suddenly being pushed back into the bloodshed. "Dammit!" shouted one of the men. "What the *hell's* the *matter* with people?!"

Following initial bursts of disgust and disbelief, the men looked at one another at a loss, and over the next hour depression and sadness gradually infused the encampment like tears on a handkerchief, all other emotions over-whelmed. Amos thought about the straggler named Brigham who had said: "So many people seem to think easy answers is really answers," and wondered what bizarre ideas the person who killed Lincoln was thinking. What will happen to the U.S. now without Lincoln?

April 15, 1865

On the 15th of April, Good Friday, the weather was cool with a gentle breeze wafting through regrowing foliage and field grass as Pastor Nordquist, after leading a service for the men, saddled up and began the trek north, follow-ing the same route through the Shenandoah Valley he took in the winter. With the snow gone, however, the burned-out barns and outbuildings were stark, a contrast magnified by the newly luxuriant forest foliage and greening fields as nature retaliated.

Families gradually returned to their homes and were cleaning up debris while reconstructing outbuildings and rebuilding lives. Initial despondency, resentment and anger were followed by stoic resignation and determination to put the war behind. The human spirit and the Valley united, and men and women worked long, hard hours attempting to eventually restore what once was.

Many others were heading north, however, led by hope of a better life, and most of those were former slaves – landless, illiterate and uneducated. Having little, Amos surmised, they had little to lose.

Pastor Nordquist passed several former slave families proceeding on foot or in wagons, while ahead of him riding a work horse was a very large Union soldier who somehow looked familiar. The soldier was softly humming in a low, mellow, bass voice, occasionally singing lyrics, and even at a distance the sound was comforting. Amos strained to recognize the melody and rode closer to the man who had the broadest shoulders Amos had ever seen, as wide as would be for two men. The song was a Negro spiritual with which the Swedish pastor was unfamiliar.

> *I go to the judgment in the evening of the day*
> *When I lay this body down,*
> *And my soul and your soul will meet in the day*
> *When I lay this body down.*

After about a half mile, Pastor Nordquist rode even with the Union soldier, listening to the singing and humming.

"That sounds good," said Pastor Nordquist. "You seem at peace."

The big man glanced at Amos, surprised.

"Well, boss, I s'pose t' a certain extent everyone is at peace now this wah's ovah," replied the big man respectfully in his low voice.

"Where are you going?" asked Amos, his Scandinavian accent prominent.

"Headin' north. Not sure just where yet. I'm not quite sure what I'm goin' back to, an' what I'm t' be doin' next. Lotta unknowns; lotta things that remain to be seen. I was just thinkin' about that. Think I know. Sometimes it helps t' hum or sing when I'm a' thinkin.'"

As Pastor Nordquist listened to the big man talk, Amos noticed his face appeared to have been burned, a war injury Amos surmised…but, looking closer, the burn marks on the big man's left cheek seemed oddly uniform.

"What happened to your cheek?" asked Amos.

The big man looked at Amos without expression, as if to ascertain whether Amos was serious, and what or whether to answer. Amos sensed the question may have been inappropriate.

"I apologize if the question is offensive," Amos said immediately.

"Ohhh, no. No suh. It's not offensive." The big man looked at Amos. "You really don't know, boss?" asked the big man.

"No," said Amos politely.

The two of them rode a short distance, the big man looking straight ahead, thinking but not singing. He turned and looked at Amos's kepi or skirmishing hat.

"What outfit were you with, boss?"

"I was a chaplain for different outfits. I actually provided services for both sides."

"Actually, I knew that," smiled the big man. "I thought I recognized you right off but wanted t' be sure. Around Christmas. Down near Petersburg. You surely did enjoy listenin' t' us sing. Mm mm." The big man beamed brightly for a moment. "An' you provided services for us too. We greatly appreciated that! That was, eh, unusual."

"Unusual?"

"Most white chaplains don't do that. Where're you from? Not here."

"I recently arrived from Sweden. To deliver something to my uncle who was killed in some battle four days before I found his outfit."

"That's a shame, chaplain." The man sat back in his saddle. "What outfit?"

Amos thought for a second. "Custer's."

"Oh, Lord," said the big man softly, his large eyes becoming even bigger. "Your uncle was with Custer's cavalry. Oh, my. They were the best. They'd ride right in shootin' and yellin' an' give no mind t' danger. Sometimes scare the daylights outta the other side. No braver bunch a' so'jers in the war. We weren't too far away from 'em near the end."

Amos looked at the big man and nodded. He wondered about the big man's background.

"I went north through the underground railroad northern Christians were runnin' before the war started," said the big man, intuiting Amos's thoughts. "Then the war began an' after a while I heard there was a colored unit bein' formed, so I joined. The South had their Cause, an' I had mine. At first, y' know, we considered ourselves a regular part of the Union army," said the big man, looking at the road ahead. "But as time wore on, it sometimes seemed like there were three armies: Union, Confederate, and us. I'll tell y' though, while sometimes we wondered if we were part of the Union army, there was never any doubt we were not part of the Confederates." The big man hummed pleasantly in his low bass voice. "Ehm ehm. No doubt whatsoever."

The two rode without talking for awhile, and Pastor Nordquist was uncertain what subject to bring up if he were to break the silence.

"I c'n tell you're not too familiar with the way some things have been done around here," said the big man. "You're gonna need t' get used t' a few things… not that you gotta do 'em, but just know they're goin' on. This burn? This scar?" The big man pointed at his left cheek and paused, giving Pastor Nordquist a closer look. "That's a brand. Like when you brand cattle."

Amos was stunned. A brand?

"My second massa did that." The man looked straight ahead again. "Paid a lot a' money t' buy me an' then, t' make sure everyone knew I belonged t' him, he used the same brandin' iron on me that he used on his lambs and pigs. He was an odd man. Had t' brand everything." The big man sighed and slumped forward slightly. "Hurt? Lord a' mighty, that hurt. Oh, my." The big man put his hand over his cheek as he looked straight ahead. "I've felt a lotta pain from a lotta things, but no single thing hurt mo' 'n that."

The man pointed at the brand.

"Those are the initials 'BR.' Stands for Browner Ranch. He raised cattle, horses, sheep, cotton and us."

Expression unchanged, the man looked over at Amos who was learning about a different world.

"Oh, yeah," said the man, "he bred us just like everything else. Early on, I had the strength a' three men an' massa look at me, an' from then on I was expected t' stud w' young girls." The big man looked at Amos with pensive lassitude. "Some may think that's a fine job," the man scoffed, shaking his head, "but it ain't. No way for a Christian man or anyone t' behave." The man looked straight ahead. "I had no choice. No suh. With me as the fatha, Massa could make a lot a' money. I either did what I was told, or he would have me shot, no questions asked. Like shootin' a horse, boss. Most owners were decent folk; Massa Browner wasn't.

"I'm fatha t' all kinds of babies an' never got t' see most 'a 'em…the mothers, pregnant, would be sold at auctions. Massa get mo' money fo' a pregnant girl, 'specially if I was the fatha – he'd have me there t' show people. Sometimes sell for as much as $1,500. Massa buy young girls, mebbe 13, 14, an' I was t' get 'em pregnant. Then he'd re-sell 'em.

"Dunno how many children I got. Other slaves called me 'Fatha Abraham,' sorta after President Lincoln…and, a' course, Fatha Abraham in the Bible."

Abraham took a deep breath and slowly exhaled, and although he faced the ground in front of him, his mind was far away.

"Fatha Abraham." Abraham's low voice rumbled as he spoke, "Abraham. Abraham Cole. That's my name."

"It's an excellent name," said Amos sincerely, wishing there was something else he could say.

"Never had no girlfrien'…Massa wouldn't allow that. No distraction." Watching the road before him, Abraham thought about those days. "No, I didn't like doin' that at all. Girls, real young, innocent – girls I didn't even know – bein' made t' get pregnant by me – like two horses – an' then havin' my babies. An' when the babies, my babies, get older, they get taken away from their mothers an' sold… Y' know, after a while a' that, I got t' feelin' bad. I got t' feelin' real bad deep inside, an' that feelin' has never gone away." Abraham looked at Amos. "Kinda like this brand here." Abraham briefly pointed at his cheek again. "That's when I ran away, went north.

"Didn't seem t' bother ol' Massa though," the big man added, continuing to look straight ahead. "Some a' those babies were his, not mine." Amos looked at the big man. "Oh, yes. You could tell right off. Specially quadroons. Fo' a young colored girl, beauty's a…"

"Excuse me," said Amos apologetically. "I'm unfamiliar with the word 'quadroon.'"

"Usually means the father is white, and the mother is mulatto…which should mean the baby is mo' white than black – 'least that's how I see it – but, no, that's not how other folks see it.

"Anyway, fo' a young colored girl, beauty's a curse cuz' she ain't allowed to say 'no' to Massa. It ain't done in the open, a' course, an' the other slaves who know don't dare say anything. With Massa Browner, you say anything and bad things happen…

"Miss Ivy, she just stayed away from the whole slave-tradin' business – she didn't like it at all – but she'd watch, an' if any a' those babies looked like Massa, oh my goodness. She'd get madder than d' devil, but then they'd be sold straight away." Amos's eyes grew wider as he looked at Abraham. "Oh yeah, that's right. Massa, he sells his own children."

"Sells them?" asked Amos, again not knowing quite what to say. "But…not without their mother."

"Oh, yes. Mothers cry and beg, but it doesn't matter. The pickininnies get sold…they's all cryin' too. But slave traders don't care; just part of doin' the sale. It's about the money, not us."

Abraham somberly looked upward above the road at nothing in particular.

"People up north, some of 'em, wonder why colored girls have so many children. Oh, yes. They ask that. Answer? Simple enough." Abraham shrugged. "Colored girls are expected to have lots of children so Massa c'n make mo' money. Sellin' colored children ain't no different 'n sellin' lambs, colts, calves. An' you never know when it's gonna happen. They say, 'no, never goin' t' sell you'… an' then somethin' comes up, and Massa needs money, where's he gonna get it? We're like money in the bank. You c'n sell a good Negro as fast as a good horse. Sometimes get more money too.

"Anyway," continued Abraham, "I'm ridin' back north. Been thinkin' I'll find a job teachin', teachin' former slaves how t' read and write."

Abraham looked at Pastor Nordquist.

"What's your name, boss?" asked Abraham. "If y' don' mind me askin.'"

"Amos Nordquist; Pastor Amos Nordquist. I'm pleased to meet you. I had no idea these things are happening. I suppose I should have known, but I didn't."

"Oh yes, and I could go on and on," responded Abraham. "This war was a step in the right direction, but it ain't gonna be the whole solution. Nevertheless, lotta bridges can be crossed now that couldn't be crossed before. You probably wouldn't know that educatin' slaves was illegal." He glanced at Amos and then looked straight ahead again. "Oh no, couldn't be teachin' us how to read and write or do arithmetic. But Miss Ivy, she liked me early on, an' she had a mind of her own. Lotta white folks in the South thought like Miss Ivie, jes' not enough of 'em. So, she'd come down when I'd be doin' my chores in the barns and stables, an' she'd take me t' one side an' spend time teachin' me how to read and write, add and subtract, multiply and divide. She enjoyed doin' it, I got pretty good at it after a while, an' Miss Ivy, she was real proud a' me." Abraham flashed a smile that seemed to brighten the surrounding landscape. "It may not be evident t' you, boss, but Miss Ivy teachin' me t' read helped me t' talk a lot better than most slaves."

"That's extremely important," said Amos, speaking from experience. "How you speak immediately defines you."

"Yes, but then Massa, he found out she was teachin' me and, oh my, the things that were said to me," said Abraham, again looking straight ahead as his countenance clouded over. "He claimed that I did things w' Miss Ivy that neither Miss Ivy nor I'd ever think a' doin'. He ordered his ranch hands to tie me up – they bound my arms and shackled my feet, bein' that I was so much bigger'n any a' them, and then threw a rope around my neck, tied the other end to a big ol' draft horse like this one," Abraham pointed to his horse, "and dragged me down by the oak tree with huge branches near the river, maybe hopin' my neck'd break along the way. I expected t' die. My neck was a mess. See these scars?" Abraham pointed at his dark neck to scars that were not immediately visible unless observed closely. "They don't seem as big as they once did. But they're from bein' dragged down there.

"They were gonna lynch me," continued Abraham after taking a deep breath. "Almost sorta did it on the way, but Miss Ivy, dressed in her riding habit, rode up with a repeater – an' they all knew she knew how t' use it and would – and first she said she would shoot anyone who moved. So, no one moved. Then she ordered one of the men to unshackle me, and take the ropes off my neck, arms and hands. Then she asked them why they were doin' this – I think she already knew – but none of 'em would answer because they knew it was all lies, and those lies involved Miss Ivy.

"Well, when they wouldn't say anything, she dismissed every one of 'em. Fired 'em all on the spot. An' that night, Lord a'mighty. Massa, he might as well have gone t' live in d' barn with the animals. Hellfire and brimstone would probably be better than the wrath a' Miss Ivy when she got real mad…an' she got real mad at Massa, oh, many times. But that night she was screamin' at him. Screamin'. Oh, she was mad! We could hear 'em. She kept sayin' 'despicable' over and over. I swear if he hadn't ducked out, she'd a killed him fo' sure. After that, I s'pect she would a' left him but was afraid of what would happen t' us if she did."

For a short time neither Amos nor Abraham said anything. Abraham started humming, and Amos wondered.

"So now I'm headin' back north," said Abraham after a while, breaking the silence. "They have schools up there for slaves. Slaves, like white folks, are never goin' to amount to much if they aren't educated. An' not just a little educated – y'know, bein' able to read a little – but educated enough t' where they c'n read 'most anything and understand it. That's the key: understandin'. Once you understand, ain't no tellin' what you c'n do. An' then you gotta do it. Work. Produce."

Abraham stopped talking, thinking some more, before again thinking out loud.

"So, I think that's what I'm gonna do. Find a teachin' job. If the Lord doesn't have one ready, mebbe I'll start a school. Dunno." Abraham looked at Pastor Nordquist then looked toward the road ahead.

He should do that, Amos thought.

"See, problem with slaves is they have no idea how to be anything 'cept slaves. Never known anything else. An' t' most a' them, what slavery means is you gotta work, and what freedom means is you don't. But everyone's gotta work; ain't no easy jobs. Witnessin' and testifyin' on behalf a' the Lord?" Abraham held his hand out toward Amos. "When's that ever been easy? Every job's hard if you do it right." Abraham looked back at the road. "Gotta get the slaves exposed to other things and pointed in the right direction, boss."

Amos nodded and thought it wouldn't be enough for Abraham to just find a teaching job; he needs to start a school, a system.

"Just cuz we won this war doesn't mean things are goin' t' change around here," said Abraham after a while, looking around. "That's also been on my mind. In fact, losin' the war is goin' t' make quite a few of these people more difficult than if the South won." Abraham looked at Amos. "You understand? The Cause? Many of these people don't wanna change things, and they definitely don't like losin' … 'specially to a bunch that includes ex-slaves. Salt in a wound. I reckon we're gonna have our hands full with some people." Abraham's eyes grew wide, and he sighed. "Oh, yes."

Abraham looked straight ahead again, and Pastor Nordquist also seemed to be looking straight ahead, although not actually looking at anything.

"I have no doubt that right now, as you and I are talkin'," said Abraham, "there are people workin' on plans to undo what's been done. Laws don't change people's hearts. Only conscience does that."

Pastor Nordquist beamed and nodded knowingly.

"So, now that we have this moment of opportunity, what do we do?" Abraham asked as he gestured with his left hand. "We have to make the most of it," said Abraham adamantly. "We have to change attitudes – both white and slave attitudes." Abraham shrugged his broad shoulders, looking at the road ahead. "Dunno. I worry about that," added Abraham. "But just like there are lots of people who don't wanna see things changed, there are also lots a' people, like Miss Ivy, who wanna give the slaves a hand. So, what's gonna make the difference?" Abraham looked at Amos. "Most a' the time if you wanna get somethin' done, you gotta do it yourself…can't be dependin' on someone else…an', as I see it, that's how it is now. Not the gov'ment, nobody. If real change is t' come, while white folks are pullin' one way an' pullin' the other, the slaves have t' do everything they can to change themselves. Do that by becomin' skilled…good as the next guy. Maybe better. Production talks; runnin'-your-mouth never got nuthin' done. Gotta let your walkin' do your talkin'."

Abraham paused for a moment, looking at the road, thinking to himself, while Amos thought how listening to Abraham was inspirational; and a door was open now; Abraham should walk through it.

"Gonna take a while. Considerin' the obstacles, I hope we c'n get it done." Abraham sighed. "Should be able to get it done." He looked at Amos and chuckled. "Gotta try, boss."

As they rode north through the Shenandoah Valley, Pastor Nordquist marveled at families who returned to their farms, intent on restarting their lives. Several near the road stopped working and watched the white man with the Yankee skirmishing cap, and the large, black man in a Yankee uniform ride by. The symbolism varied according to perspective. Some blamed both; some blamed neither; and while some thought it odd, one or two seemed to appreciate the apparent camaraderie between the two men. But quite a few more did not and said so. The acrimony made Pastor Nordquist uncomfortable, but Abraham's expression was one of determined affirmation and, as Abraham lightly nodded without looking at the men, Amos intuited the men inadvertently had further reinforced Abraham's resolve.

As Amos looked back at people while he and Abraham rode, his heart grew heavy, and Amos became more determined to do whatever necessary to discourage people from preying on one another. Meanwhile, humming as he looked straight ahead, Abraham struggled not so much with what he must do as with how he must do it. The social and political obstacles, black and white, created by 200 years of American slavery were formidable, and at that moment while many white folks would be a significant problem, Abraham was more focused on the vision and time horizons of the slaves themselves. Few of them, he thought, were blessed with owners like Miss Ivy, and Abraham knew that his own academic limitations were still significant. Abraham sighed. While there was so much to do, it had to be done right.

Although the reasons were not evident as they rode along, Pastor Nordquist would hear Abraham sigh often. At first Amos felt like there was nothing he could do, but then he heard his inner voice, by this time neither still nor small, shouting to pray! Out loud! With Abraham! Reining to a halt in front of a still-vacant, former Mennonite farm, Pastor Nordquist told Abraham that they needed to stop and pray.

"Thanks, chaplain. That's all I wanted t' hear."

The two of them prayed for folks, black and white, for the Shenandoah Valley farmers, for the country. They prayed for each other and their goals, Pastor Nordquist entreating God to give Abraham fortitude, direction, and opportunities, requests Amos knew the Holy Spirit would grant – they were, he sensed, the reason the Spirit had moved him to pray. When they were through, Pastor Nordquist had a sense of peace, not because he expected things would get better immediately, but because he prayed as instructed and, somehow, he intuited, in the long run this would somehow change things favorably from what might otherwise have been.

Pastor Nordquist was nevertheless annoyed with himself because he knew the Holy Spirit was trying to get his attention for much longer than should have been necessary. Pray without ceasing, he reminded himself of the Bible's admonition.

The two men rode on until it got dark, and then camped together that night.

April 16, 1865

The next morning, they resaddled and again headed north.

"Abraham, do you know what day it is?"

Abraham thought for a moment, and then his eyes grew large. "Lord, have mercy," he said as he looked at Pastor Nordquist. "What with all that's been goin' on, I plumb forgot. Easter Sunday." Abraham looked upward and said, "Forgive me, Lord."

"Abraham, God knows your heart. You're fine. And the first Easter had a lot to do with that," smiled Amos.

"What with you bein' a chaplain, a pastor, maybe we should have our own little service," suggested Abraham, "here alongside the road."

"I don't think we'll need to be quite that informal," said Amos, looking up ahead. "There appears to be a small church up there." Abraham looked far up the road at what appeared to be a small, country church. "Right about now," added Amos, "I suspect they're in full worship."

The two men rode to the small church, its front door open, and indeed, a worship service was in progress. As they dismounted and tied their horses to a hitching rail, the sound of a choir was wafting through the door like a summer wind, voices alive, blending in a unique soulful sound, the up-tempo rhythm helped along by clapping hands.

> *Well, we' goin' up t' see King Jesus!*
> *Gonna take him by the hand!*
> *Gonna tell 'im all about our troubles,*
> *Travelin' through this land.*

Abraham smiled in response to what he heard, a happy sound, as he and Amos stepped inside listening. From the back, the congregation appeared to be older men, women of all ages, and some young children, but there were a few young men. The choir was mostly women. The congregation was enjoying the choral music, occasionally waving hands and fans otherwise used to cool the warming morning air. As the song ended, one young man in the congregation sensed the presence of Amos and Abraham, turned around and immediately smiled.

"Abraham Cole! You get yo' big self in heah!"

"Well, hello, Eugene! Good to see you again, already. My golly, look at all these fine people," said Abraham, sweeping his hand over the congregation. "Hope y'all don't mind if we join in."

"Heavens, no!" said Eugene. "An' who's dis fine gennelman you brought wid you?" The rest of the congregation turned further around to look.

"This here," began Abraham deferentially, "is Pastor Amos, a Union chaplain, headin' back north. Eugene, does Pastor Amos look familiar to you?"

"Ohhh, yes!" smiled Eugene, eyes wide. "You was the one who preached t' us down by Richmond."

"How do you do, Eugene." Amos reached out in greeting to shake Eugene's hand, and Eugene reciprocated.

"I gotta say I was a mite low then," said Eugene, "but what you said to us got me feelin' alright again. Praise God.

"Pastor Amos, Abraham Cole," Eugene turned toward the head of the aisle, "this is Pastor Washburn."

"How do you do," smiled Amos, reaching out and shaking Pastor Washburn's hand as well. "Abraham and I apologize for interrupting."

"Oh, no. No one passin' by here is an interruption. This is the Good Samaritan Church, and we don' want no one passin' by." Pastor Washburn stepped slightly to one side. "An' since you is a minister, would you be inclined to say a few words? These people surely mus' get tired a hearin' only me."

"Oh, no, no, no." "No, now that's not true," the congregation responded. "We're blessed," and so on, and Pastor Washburn, looking like Moses speaking to the Israelites, held up his hand for quiet.

"You mean t' tell me you would mind," said the gray-bearded pastor dressed in black, "if this minister, who by the grace of Almighty God has come to us this Easter Sunday mornin', spoke to you from his heart?!" His eyes grew wide. "Is that what I'm hearin'?!"

The congregation erupted with exclamations that Amos speak! Deliver the word! And do it now! Pastor Washburn nodded approvingly, and sat down, as did Abraham, and except for hand fans moving air, the congregation sat motionlessly, respectfully waiting for Amos to begin. He had arrived just in time to give the sermon.

As Amos walked to the head of the aisle, the choir in front looking back expectantly, the Holy Spirit told him to begin where he left off near Richmond when speaking to Abraham, Eugene and other members of the XXV Corps, USCT, Army of the James, weeks earlier.

His Scandinavian accent prominent, he preached his first sermon in a church, a Negro church somewhere in northern Virginia, and whenever he made a point, which was often, the congregation would erupt with acclamations of understanding.

Would that all my sermons hereafter be so readily received, Amos thought prayerfully while waving as he rode away. And may my heart be equally blessed.

Pastor Nordquist and Abraham rode together the length of the Valley, and along the way Abraham taught Amos a song named after the river that ran through the Valley.

> *Oh Shenandoah, I long to hear you*
> *Away, you rollin' river.*
> *Oh Shenandoah, I long to hear you,*
> *Away, I'm bound away, 'cross the wide Missouri.*

It was a simple, beautiful melody, especially when Abraham sang it. Abraham said it was about a man who left the Shenandoah Valley, heading west across the wide Missouri River, leaving his two loves behind: the girl he loved and the Valley he left.

Amos encouraged Abraham to start a school, teaching the students not only the three Rs, but preparing the better students to eventually also teach, growing a school system for ex-slaves, and again they prayed. Finished, Abraham smiled, nodded at Pastor Nordquist, and affirmed: "I'll do that!"

Amos and Abraham bid one another a fond farewell at the north end of the Valley near Shepherdstown, a small town made smaller by the war, and Amos remembered that Simon Harris, the first man Amos had seen killed, was from Shepherdstown. As Abraham headed northeast, Amos asked some people about the family of Simon Harris. They'd been uprooted and left; no one knew where. Maybe northeast, maybe further west. Since no one knew, Amos found a local church, a graveyard next to it with both Civil War and Revolutionary War dead, went inside and left a note with the old pastor about Simon's death and the body's location, should the Harris family return. Then Amos rode north northwest.

Newspapers along the way printed photographs of President Lincoln's funeral train, his body in his presidential rail car – never used before – as it began its trip on April 21st from Washington D.C. to Springfield, Illinois, Lincoln's birthplace, for the president's burial. Along the route, large crowds lined the tracks in early daylight, late darkness, and all through the night, watch fires burning. All remained silent, women daubing their eyes with handkerchiefs, men uncovering their heads, as the train passed by.

Amos learned that an actor, John Wilkes Booth, after shooting President Lincoln, had dramatically jumped from the balcony at Washington D.C.'s Ford's Theater to the familiar stage below, oddly shouting something in Latin to confused theater patrons.

Booth escaped the theater, and during subsequent days evading the law, the actor, having lived in an ideologically informed world of fantasy, and having spent a professional lifetime pretending to be what he was not, couldn't understand why his name was becoming synonymous with treachery.

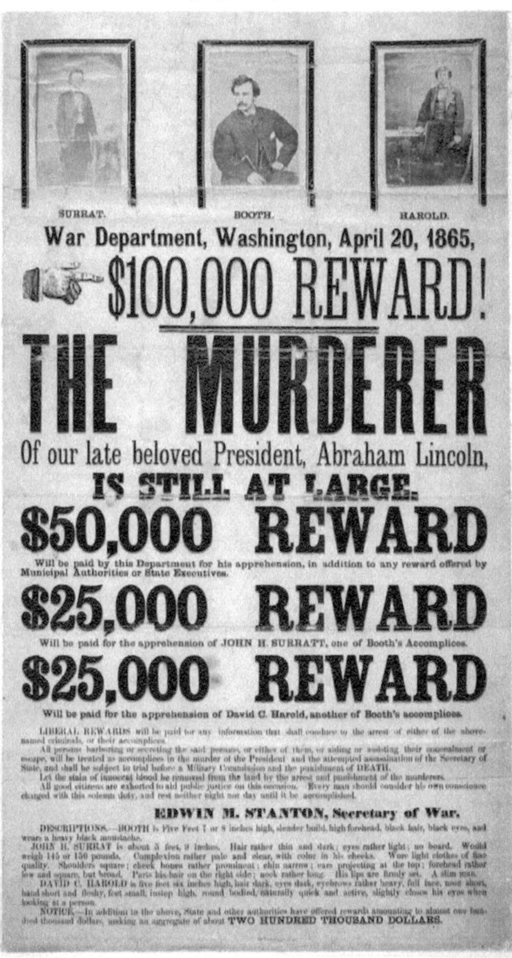

"And why?" Booth questioned in his last diary entry. "For doing what Brutus was honored for? What made [William] Tell a hero? And yet I, for striking down a greater tyrant than they ever knew, am looked upon as a common cutthroat. My action was purer than either of theirs."

Back in Appomattox the war-weary soldiers, responsible for so much bloodshed on the battlefield, were at a loss to make sense of it. "I understand what he thought he was doin," remarked Blade numbly, "but I don't quite understand why he thought it."

On April 27th, Amos read that Booth was killed the previous day while avoiding capture.

Amos eventually found Nels Hanseth, the affable Lutheran Church executive, who gratefully praised God when Pastor Nordquist presented Torvald's substantial inheritance and simple last will and testament that would provide an even greater offering. And Hanseth was ecstatic when Amos spoke of his desire to minister in an area flooding with Scandinavian immigrants.

Amos now fully expected he would begin formal duties as a pastor. There was a slight hitch, however.

33

Amos's initial impression of Nels was "country parson" personified. When conversing, Nels' eyes looked over the top of rectangular reading glasses perched at the end of a straight nose. Nearly as tall as Amos, Nels was clean-shaven with a strong jaw, and a ready smile accentuated by a light in his eyes that danced beneath gray eyebrows and a high forehead, above which nestled a full head of graying hair. Nels usually wore a black, 3-piece suit with a traditional watch fob attached to a vest pocket, and his white shirts had detachable collars, either Pembrook or stand-up depending on his preference that day, from which would hang a black, silk string tie, often double stranded. He wore a simple, black plug hat when outdoors.

Nels was spending considerable time attempting to lure East Coast and even Swedish pastors to Minnesota, but the trailblazing challenges were more than most wanted to face. Of those who came, some were able shepherds of their flock, but others, God's frozen people, were as uninspiring in Minnesota as they were in more populated areas – with similar results. Nels found Amos to be intelligent, resourceful, determined, hardworking, well organized and, with a heart for the Lord, someone willing and able do the more challenging church development work. With his entrepreneurial background, Amos was an able executive, respectful and motivating when dealing with others, and sensitive to what should be done and its timing. Amos and the inheritance from Uncle Torvald were answers to prayer.

Together they settled Torvald's affairs and, at Nels's behest, planned Pastor Nordquist's initial effort, planting new congregations in the central eastern part of a state. Amos's job was to organize a congregational nucleus, begin services in a home, start church facilities construction with volunteer help, finish the facilities, grow the congregation, turn the church over to a new pastor, leave and start the next one.

"Were you affiliated with the Gustavus Adolphus Foundation in Göteborg?" asked Nels in Swedish as they walked along the dirt street to a nearby general store.

"No, not really," said Amos. "My father contributed a little to the Foundation, but for the most part we were uninvolved. It was only a short time before my father died that he experienced the baptism of the Holy Spirit, and truly began going to church."

"Better that than go beyond," said Nels. "But for so much of our lives, there is also so much – *visibilium omnium et invisibilium* – so many give so little thought."

"I'm not certain what that means."

"'All things visible and invisible.'" Nels looked at Amos as they walked. "Where were you ordained?"

"Ordained?"

"Yes."

"I've not been ordained," said Amos. He looked at Nels seriously. "Is it truly necessary? Aren't there many in the ministry here in America not ordained? Like the Läsare, they followed the teaching of the apostle Paul in Ephesians: 'And He gave some as apostles, and some as prophets, and some as evangelists, and some as pastors and teachers, for the equipping of the saints for the work of service, to the building up of the body of Christ...' It doesn't say anything about formal ordination."

"While the Civil War has ended," said Nels, "America is still very much in a state of flux. Within this unsettled, national community are many who pass themselves off as men-of-God when, in reality, they wouldn't know the Savior if He staggered up with a cross over His shoulder. This is America: the land of opportunity…and from colporteurs to church leaders there are opportunities aplenty for religious flim-flam. Satan sees to it that those opportunities are not squandered."

Nels stopped walking, turned and looked levelly at Amos.

"I find no reason to believe you are anyone other than who you say you are, and are motivated for no other reason than the call of God. As a matter of propriety, however, you will become ordained."

"I see," said Amos who thought much less of ordination than did Nels. "Was Jesus ordained?" asked Amos.

"Not by the Lutheran church, Amos," said Nels, "but, yes, He was most certainly ordained."

Nels let that sink in. He began walking again.

"Although none of us will ever come close to being as ordained as was the Christ, we have been spiritually ordained in a lesser manner." Nels glanced at Amos, intuiting what Amos was thinking. "And, yes, Amos, there certainly are some in the ordained ministry who should be in horse trading. For the sake of legitimacy and credibility among the flock, however, both spiritual and earthly ordination are necessary. To denigrate formal ordination in our synod is to indirectly imply that ordained pastors are pharisaic – which is hardly the case. To effectively do the Lord's work here, you will become ordained." Nels paused for effect. "Do you understand?"

"Yes," said Amos. "I understand." Amos laughed.

"Did someone say something funny?" questioned Nels.

"I was just thinking about what you said with regard to religious flim-flam… and a former acquaintance named Yuri."

"Was Yuri a religious flim-flam artist?"

"No, but he probably loaned money to a few." Amos started to consider how Yuri would plan repayment, but the thought was quickly severed by Nels.

"Amos, there are an inordinate number of quacks in our profession, and historically there have been instances of irreparable harm, not just people being abused, but leaders carrying things to the point of murderous insanity, zealously cheered on by a bizarre religious ecstasy, sometimes resulting in unspeakably monstrous acts. Church and secular history are full of this."

When Nels looked at Amos his eyes were ablaze with anger, and he stopped walking.

"But what truly causes this phenonenom? Amos, men hear voices, voices claiming even to be the voice of God, although what the voices say is never godly. If, as others claim, 'it's all in their head,' does that mean there was no voice? 'No voice' is not what they heard, consistently heard, persuadingly heard. And where is that sentient spot where mind greets sound? Is external stimulus necessary or is there an easier, more direct way?" Nels drew the logical conclusion: "There obviously is." Nels started walking.

"Can you give an example," asked Amos respectfully, not entirely understanding.

"Unfortunately," Nels threw his hands up and again stopped walking, turning to Amos, "thousands, if we had time. Let's try the Münster Rebellion where protestant religious leader Jan Matthys, often literally hearing a 'voice' – 'of God,' the voice said – expelled the Catholic bishop, killed 'apostates and infidels' disagreeing with Matthys and, inspired by the voice, renamed the town the 'New Jerusalem' of Ezekiel's prophesy and John's vision in the Book of Revelation. Townspeople would then come to Matthys for direction in all matters. Matthys, in turn, would listen carefully to the voice and give direction accordingly, his word law, because Matthys was repeating what 'God' had said. Atrocities were freely commited.

"Was it all an act? No!" said Nels loudly. "He heard a rationally persuasive voice – not a bunch of babble – giving specific direction and followed that direction. When the expelled bishop gathered an army and besieged the town, Matthys, told by 'God' he was the second Gideon and victory was foreordained, naively took thirty equally-naïve followers out through the gates of Münster to face the besieging army, and, along with the thirty men, was killed and savagely mutilated." Nels again started walking.

"Opposing religious fanatics," muttered Nels. "It seldom gets worse. And if you look at everything closely, it was almost a set-up, as if 'God,'" Nels held up two fingers on each hand to indicate quotations, "had found someone else who could better betray and torture the people of Münster than Matthys. So Matthys was discarded."

"Who replaced him?" asked Amos.

"As food ran out during the siege – you might learn about this in seminary – Matthys' successor, charismatic Jan van Leiden, once an actor, also began to hear the 'voice of God,' but claimed to have visions from heaven as well. So he declared himself a prophet, renaming the community 'Zion,' legalizing polygamy – he had 16 wives – claimed he was born in the lineage of King David, and adopted all the trappings of a monarch, brooking no dissent whatsoever, while the townspeople continued to starve and die miserably during the siege. When the bishop's army eventually attacked, many more townspeople died, and Jan van Leiden and two cohorts were captured, publically tortured, and executed. Their remains were stuffed into barred cages for public exhibition and hung from the steeple of St. Lambert's Church where, to this day, although the bones are gone, the cages remain."

Nels let out a deep sigh.

"Hideous. Despicable. Münster was being played like a Silbermann pipe organ." Nels glanced at Amos. "By who? you might ask. The 'voice' or 'voices' have been so prevalent over the ages that suggesting mere imagination is naïve foolishness. The voice or voices are there, are heard although not biologically sourced but spiritually sourced. That source is not God, however, and if not God, then who?" Nels stopped walking again and looked at Amos who nodded.

"The Old Evil has many manifestations," understated Amos.

"Indeed," said Nels, looking solemnly at the ground as they began walking again.

Amos took a deep breath and sighed. "How long does it take to get ordained?"

"The ordination process has been modified to intensive study of crucial topics over a reduced time period, followed by a still-challenging examination," answered Nels. "If the need for pastors were not so great, the ordination process would be much longer, but, as I say, America is in a state of flux. Gaps need to be filled, and in Minnesota, like lakes, ministerial gaps are everywhere."

Amos used the Lutheran Church headquarters as his mailing address. He sent a lengthy letter to Anders and received a lengthy letter back weeks later. Anders wrote that steamships were becoming more prevalent, and that Nordquist Shipping Co. should sell the fleet of sailing ships in favor of faster and more dependable steam-powered vessels. Amos agreed and, in a return letter, suggested action be taken sooner than later because, as years passed, ships-of-sail could become obsolete, and their value and the number of buyers could decline substantially.

Over a short period of time, nostalgia pulling on his heart in protest, Anders sold the Nordquist Shipping Company ships-of-sail one-by-one, replacing each with a new steamship. Each steamship had a new propulsion devise appropriately named the "propeller." The new ships were christened with the old names – although one would be named "Einar III" – and a photograph of each applicable, older ship-of-sail was prominently hung in each captain's stateroom. The replacement steamships were expensive, and more expensive to operate, but made the company more competitive, able to earn more money in less time. The new ships complemented the export business that, Anders wrote in the letter, was thriving under the direction of its manager, Karin Olafsdotter, who had excellent attention to detail and, unsurprisingly, a knack for gaining customers.

No longer directly involved with the Nordquist Shipping Company, Amos focused on the spiritual welfare of Scandinavian Christians in Minnesota. He worked continually and conscientiously. Spiritual growth was his responsibility, but the Lord's work also helped keep his mind off of Karin. His love for Karin was slow to wane, he was lonely, and although he fought against it, he thought of her even though she was involved with Anders.

By the end of the first year, his first congregation was set and could continue with another pastor while Pastor Nordquist, now ordained, planted a second congregation in another area. Although the undertaking was successful, he was depressed.

Meanwhile, Karin Olafsdotter, as Amos paradoxically dreamed in Sweden, became Karin Nordquist. Anders asked Amos to be the best man, but the timing and time away from his duties were, in combination, bad enough for Amos to decline. Amos felt terrible because he wanted to be there, and he did not want to give the impression animosity lingered over being rejected by Karin. He wanted Anders and Karin to be happy.

He also wanted to be happy himself, but that was simply not how he felt. There was a large void in his heart. Amos knew there were two ways to stop the pain: be patient and gradually get over Karin or meet someone else. During a time of changes, the second biggest change in Amos Nordquist's life was about to occur.

⸻ ● ⸻

At the peak of the Ice Age, ice sheets one to two miles thick covered North America and northern Europe. In some locations their enormous weight severely depressed the earth's crust through a process known as isostasy, causing the crust to warp, pushing the affected mantle down and away from where glacial weight was greatest. In addition, as the ice floes advanced, retreated, and advanced again, gargantuan sheets of ice scored enormous swaths in the earth's surface including a prehistoric strait that covered much of present-day lower Scandinavia from the Kattegat Sea to the Gulf of Bothnia. With isostatic rebound (uplift due to all that weight melting), over geological ages the Swedish strait gradually disappeared, replaced with rising land mass holding many thousands of present Swedish lakes including 2,183 sq. mi. Lake Vänern containing some remnant Ice Age fish not found in other lakes.

In North America, the enormous, prehistoric, proglacial Lake Agassiz formed, covering portions of Manitoba, Ontario, Minnesota, North Dakota, and Saskatchewan. At its greatest extent, it covered 170,000 square miles, over five times the size of remnant Lake Superior. Isostatic rebound and glacial scoring created thousands of small Minnesota lakes – proportionate to what occurred in prehistoric Sweden. As a consequence, with similar climate, flora, and the presence of lakes everywhere, including Lake Superior's large western arm providing similarity to Lake Vänern, Swedish immigrants arriving in Minnesota felt they were still in Sweden.

Spring, 1870

When starting the next congregation, Pastor Nordquist found that among the problems he faced, language would again be at the fore.

There were many in the community who wanted to keep written and verbal communication in Swedish, no different than the homeland. In many communities, such as Chisago County, the spoken language was Swedish, and newspapers and books were in Swedish. Social convention was such that newcomers might wonder whether they were really in America. Pastor Nordquist heard some call it "*Svenskamerica*."

In order to adequately present the word-of-God, Pastor Nordquist would use Swedish during church services and Sunday school. During the school week, Swedish and Norwegian were secondary. The language of America was neither Swedish nor Norwegian; it was English, and English was also the international trade language. Pastor Nordquist knew that educating the children in an English-speaking environment would eventually provide an advantage, enhancing future potential for productivity and happiness. He not only wanted students to know and properly enunciate English, he wanted them to speak English as if they had grown up speaking it in an educated environment. Attaining this lofty goal was improbable, Amos knew, but improbability did not diminish merit.

During the week, Pastor Nordquist interviewed several applicants for the paid position of schoolteacher: teaching the church schoolchildren during the week and coordinating children's Sunday school and adult Bible studies with parental volunteers on Sunday. Among some in this congregation, Pastor Nordquist again expected restive behavior but, nevertheless, for the sake of the children, English would be the primary language in school. Accordingly, Amos wanted to hire a multilingual Scandinavian immigrant with high level of English fluency – and without much of an accent, if possible. After six interviews with first generation Scandinavians, recent arrivals from Sweden who spoke English reasonably well, but Swedish much better, it was evident he would need to hire someone who fell short of this ideal.

With one interview remaining, while he conveyed no message to either Nels Hanseth or any prospective candidates, he was certain he would hire the fifth person he interviewed, a young lady with a weak Scandinavian accent and a favorable English background. While her mother was Swedish and they came from Sweden, her father was a former British seaman, and English was spoken at home. While she wrote and spoke English adequately, and read books in English although not extensively, her weak Scandinavian accent had a cockney tinge that resulted in a peculiar inflection. During the interview, her expression was the exuberant façade of the unqualified, and she often looked away while answering questions, sometimes awkwardly. Pastor Nordquist felt sorry for her and surmised from the interview that she would be only a couple of steps ahead of the brighter students in class when teaching. She seemed determined, however, and was the best qualified of the candidates.

Amos sat behind a small, scratched and marred desk in a storage room on loan from the proprietor of the local store until the church and parsonage were completed. Like the store owner, the room was austere and gloomy. There was a window above Amos that provided enough daylight for clerical work or, in a moment, another teaching position interview. Waiting for the seventh and final candidate, a lady named Anna Hildegaard, Pastor Nordquist reread a list of textbook prices, and perused a copy of McGuffey's 4th Reader. Since he was already certain of whom he would hire, he expected the interview would be brief, after which he would notify the candidates and Nels Hanseth of his decision.

When Anna Hildegaard lightly knocked at the open storage room door, her startling green eyes caught the light from the window directly above Amos's head, and their color immediately reminded him of the emerald-green hutch doors in the Göteborg mansion parlor. Other than his jaw dropping slightly, his expression went blank.

Anna Hildegaard was 22, an advanced age where some parents might begin worrying about their daughter never marrying, possibly becoming an old maid. One look at Anna, however, provided ample evidence she would never make it to old maidenhood.

She was 5' 9" with a waterfall of thick, glistening blonde hair, and her soft skin had a dark, out-in-the-sun tone that remained all year. Her educated parents came to America from Sweden before she was born. She grew up speaking three languages: English and to a lesser extent Swedish and Norwegian, depending on who she was with. She also knew French. She had graduated from college where her closest friends spoke cultivated English.

To Amos she was a vision, as if she had stepped out of a dream. Her eyes were mesmerizing. How could anyone's eyes be that beautiful? thought Amos. Her figure was full and fit. Later, in his mind, Pastor Nordquist would sum up Anna's overall appearance in two words: gorgeous symmetry. Everything emanated strength and beauty. She stood to her full height, looked down at Amos, his smiling dark eyes catching her attention, and pleasantly asked in perfect English, "May I come in?"

"Yes, please do," he said, a rush flushing through him like a flashflood as he stood up while gesturing toward the beaten, wooden chair that sat in front of the old desk. Without taking her eyes off Amos, she smiled, walked confidently forward and said, "I'm Miss Anna Hildegaard. How do you do?"

"Very well, thank you," replied Amos with a slight quaver in his voice. "Won't you sit down?" He cleared his throat.

"Thank you."

As she pulled the chair out slightly, and gracefully swung into it, Amos sat down woodenly, his protuberance unavoidable, awkwardly distracted by the unexpected beauty of this woman.

"I'm Pastor Amos Nordquist. I'll be the pastor here until the congregation is settled and a permanent full-time pastor can take over."

"You'll not be with us very long then," said Anna, studying his dark features.

"No. Probably around a year," he answered. "Then I will leave and do it all over again."

"Why did they choose you to do this, that is, start new churches?" she asked.

"I have certain God-given talents with respect to construction, construction coordination, and organization in general…in addition to the usual pastoral duties. It is how I best serve God. I am like a harbor pilot: I get the ship underway and then someone else sails it."

"I would think that getting the ship underway might be more challenging than much of the subsequent voyage." Anna smiled pleasantly. "It's a good analogy. Have you sailed many places?"

Amos noticed she had no accent.

"I was formerly in the export and shipping businesses while I was in Sweden," answered Amos. "I have taken a long leave-of-absence, you might say. I have sailed the seven seas; been around the Horn of Africa; Cape Horn; crossed the Atlantic, oh, dozens of times."

"I've never been at sea, but I've read of the dangers," said Anna. "Were you ever in a hurricane?"

"Yes, several. The worst was also one of the worst ever," said Amos. "The two ships my brother and I owned went down. The few of us who did not drown when the ships went under were adrift in a lifeboat, but not all in the lifeboat survived. It was when we were adrift on the North Atlantic that I reconsidered my priorities and concluded that, in the greater scheme of things, should I survive, what I had been doing was not what I should be doing. To make a long story short," Amos smiled, holding his large hands out, "here I am."

Amos folded his hands on the table as he wondered who was interviewing who?

"Let me ask you something," he said quickly. "Do you have any teaching experience?"

"I have taught Sunday school, of course, and as a senior I taught small children in the grammar school affiliated with Oberlin College where I graduated. This past year I also was given the opportunity to lecture on Milton and Shakespeare at Oberlin."

Amos's mouth again fell open slightly. Overqualified? The thought had not occurred to him that he would interview someone who might be.

"I found that the best learning experiences often come from teaching," continued Anna. "Would you like to know anything about Hamlet?" she smiled. "King Lear?" She studied his dark eyes. "Romeo and Juliet?"

"I am a familiar with all three," said Amos. Then he also smiled. "And MacBeth. Growing up, when my father was at sea and I was not, my mother insured we – my brother and I – received a liberal education."

"Excellent," said Anna happily. "I expect that if Milton, Shakespeare, and the Bible are not already part of our curriculum, we'll use them to whatever extent complements the proposed curriculum.

"I should mention I also enjoy history," she continued, "and language to a certain extent, but certainly the most important language – forgive me if you disagree – is English. Used properly, as a means of expressing abstract thought with clarity, English is very cerebral, have you noticed? If you look about the United States, while most of us directly or indirectly came from somewhere else, English is the language of the intelligentsia and national leaders, and I believe all in America eventually will speak it. While Thomas Jefferson may have had an affinity for Bordeaux wine, the Declaration of Independence was not written in French. I'm not sure it could have said quite what it said if written in French, do you? And how might that have affected the early maturation of America?"

"That's an interesting question."

"Do you speak French?"

"I speak several languages and, in fact, French is one," smiled Amos. "When I was younger, I worked on the docks of Göteborg and interacted with many men from many countries including France."

"How interesting," responded Anna, her eyes growing slightly larger, momentarily re-distracting Amos. "My parents met in Göteborg and, although I have never been there, I know quite a bit about Göteborg. You said you were in exporting and shipping. What were the specific circumstances under which you decided to…?"

What was to be a short, formal interview lasted two thoroughly enjoyable hours for Amos. After Anna left, Amos looked at the drab wall opposite the desk and marveled at how plain, colorless and empty the room seemed, more than before. The next morning Amos notified all concerned that he had hired Miss Anna Hildegaard.

The sanctuary and parsonage were completed, and Pastor Nordquist took up temporary quarters in the parsonage. Classes were conducted in the sanctuary basement. Miss Hildegaard was a delight for the younger school children (the girls quickly grew to idolize her) but also a distraction for the boys ages 12 and older…and younger. Aware of this, she organized specific ancillary assignments and projects, respectfully delegating responsibility for their implementation, coordination and completion to the older boys in the class…who would do nothing to disappoint Miss Hildegaard.

The older boys became, in effect, teaching assistants, supplementing Anna's efforts, learning to tutor the younger children to meet specific goals Anna set. Since some of the best educational experiences result from teaching preparation reinforced by the teaching effort itself, the older boys learned a great deal more than if Miss Hildegaard did everything. Through delegation, hers was a very efficient classroom, and progress was extraordinary in comparison to what was the case within the first school organized by Pastor Nordquist.

Although many students spoke limited English, school sessions, texts and homework were primarily in English. As a practical matter, during the first two school months, significant time was spent on correctly writing and speaking English, and these lessons were reinforced throughout the year. There were frequent, brief-but-courteous Scandinavian explanations for students with weak English, but it was expected all would work diligently at English mastery. In his first congregation last year, most parents understood and appreciated Pastor Nordquist's motive, but the weakest students were often the children of parents who did not.

With parental discouragement instead of encouragement, Peter Busse, for example, simply quit coming to school. Pastor Nordquist subsequently rode out to the Busse farm to convince the Busses that absence from school was in no one's best interests.

34

1870

Pastor Nordquist was bigger than most of his parishioners and, after knocking on the Busse door in the late afternoon, Pastor Nordquist stepped back two steps, hat-in-hand, not wanting to appear intimidating. Mrs. Busse came to the door.

"Oh. Pastor Nordquist," she fretfully responded in Swedish upon opening the door. "Oh," she continued, looking up, holding the door open, "what can I do for you?"

"Peter has been absent from school for several days and I was concerned," said Pastor Nordquist sincerely. "Is anything wrong?"

"Right now, Peter and his father, Pete, are out in the barn," answered Mrs. Busse. "They're the ones you need to see."

Mrs. Busse glanced at the barn and looked up at Pastor Nordquist.

"I practically begged Peter to go back to school – it was my idea in the first place – but his father thinks this learning-everything-in-English is nonsense, by golly. Pete doesn't speak English and, I guess, thinks what's good enough for him is good enough for Peter." Mrs. Busse, a small woman with an affixed look of puzzlement, placed her fingertips against her cheek. "Most Swedes know some English…and many people we met coming here spoke English. It was difficult for Pete because someone would say something to him, and he couldn't respond. He thinks some of them made fun of him, but wasn't sure because he didn't understand, and couldn't tell from facial expressions because he wouldn't directly face them in the first place."

Mrs. Busse looked back at Amos while nervously pressing some strands of her unkempt hair back into place.

"I think Pete is a good man, but I also think Peter should learn English. At least as much as possible." Her fingers went back to her cheek. "I'm afraid Pete doesn't see it that way. And whatever Pete thinks is what Peter thinks, if you know what I mean."

"Perhaps I should go back to the barn and speak with them," said Amos.

"As long as you do it in Swedish," responding Mrs. Busse with a slight cough, placing her hand over her mouth and looking away.

After Pastor Nordquist thanked Mrs. Busse for being candid, he turned and walked back to the barn.

Pete Busse was a hard-working man of modest, uncultivated intellect whose insecurity placed him continually on the defensive, and much of his defensive mindset consisted of mentally standing guard, just in case. He came far enough in life with enough success to where he would make no attempt to learn English. The Busses had one child, Peter, who was the sunlight in Pete's otherwise overcast life. Pete and Peter were about as close as a father and son could be.

"Mr. Busse? How do you do?" warmly greeted Pastor Nordquist in Swedish as he stepped into the barn. Pete Busse was inspecting the udder of a cow, Peter beside him. Pete looked at Pastor Nordquist like he was a federal marshal with a warrant.

"What can we do for you, Pastor Nordquist?" asked Pete as he stood up. His expression quickly turned from surprise to insolence, and his stomach turned sour as he surmised why Pastor Nordquist was there.

"Peter has not been in school for several days," answered Amos, "and I was hoping nothing was wrong."

Pete glanced at Peter, his son, and then back at Pastor Nordquist.

"No, nothing is wrong," said Pete firmly. "Peter is staying home to help with work around the farm."

"I appreciate that work needs to be done," said Amos, "but it is obviously in Peter's best interest to be educated. Without an adequate education, he will be at a disadvantage. The country is changing, and when he is well into adulthood, the things we teach him now will insure he is not limited when opportunities present themselves. In fact, if Peter stays in school and works hard, he will have an advantage over others. We are preparing him for the future."

"Where everyone speaks English?"

"Yes," answered Pastor Nordquist. He folded his arms. "The day will come when fluent English is indispensable. Peter will be prepared for that day."

"I don't see that coming," said Pete. "Around here everyone speaks Swedish. It's no different than being in Sweden, by golly. Peter says English is hard to learn; he says he'd rather be here helping around the farm. Isn't that right, Peter?"

Peter obliquely looked at Amos, looked away and nodded.

"And I enjoy having him here," added Pete.

The onus is on Pete, thought Amos, who believes all is perfectly fine when, in fact, he simply does not know what he does not know. Consequently, the same is true for Peter, but Peter is a young student while Pete's an adult who should know more and better.

"Pete, what will happen when you need to barter, buy or sell livestock or crops in English?" asked Amos.

"I'll go somewhere else."

"What if the deal of the moment is too good to pass up?" asked Amos. "Will you know it's too good to pass up?"

Pete said nothing.

"What if a catalogue printed in English, as most are," asked Amos, "appears to have a photo of something you may need badly, something that might make farm operation much easier? Can you read English well enough to determine that the item is indeed what you need? Will you be able to order it?"

Pete looked defensively at Amos and again said nothing.

"If an important letter arrives and it is written in English," asked Amos, "what will you do? Find someone literate in English to translate? Certainly, that's what most people unfamiliar with English would do but, as with an English catalogue, you can do better. You can have your son, Peter, translate. Think of the future, yours and his. While Swedish is prevalent here, it is not so elsewhere in Minnesota because, Pete, this is not Sweden. The language of America is English, and gradually everyone will speak it because the great majority – led by the rich and powerful – already do."

Pete looked numbly at Amos and made no response.

"English is an excellent language," continued Amos as he walked up to Pete and Peter, and leaned against a stall rail, folding his arms again. "How can I say it? I speak several languages and, as languages go, English is not only an extraordinary medium for communication and innovation, it is an excellent means of discovering the riches of one's mind, like a lamp in a cave filled with treasure. In comparison to other languages, it more readily enables the formation and exchange of creative ideas. English is a vehicle by which literary, philosophical and scientific ideas can rapidly evolve and advance. Milton, Shakespeare, Poe, and Keats were not Swedish. While Swedish certainly functions adequately, and we have some prominent works of literature and science," Amos gestured with his hands, "if Swedish were intellectually and creatively comparable to English, we might possibly have many more. While not much is said or written about it, Pete, much of the success in America was, and will continue to be, enabled by the language with which most Americans communicate. Proper English and innovative thought are to one another like spring planting and autumn harvest."

Pete listened with begrudging respect while Peter listened with interest.

"So, you see, by not being literate in English," continued Pastor Nordquist sincerely, "you greatly limit your options and, especially, your son's options. This farm is a good one, and Peter is a smart student." Peter's expression darkened as he looked away. "Peter may not think so," countered Amos discerningly, "but, like farming, education is work – learning is never easy if the subject is worthy – and if Peter were as conscientious at school as he is here on the farm, he would perform remarkably. By Peter knowing English, you, Pete, will be in a position where your options are never limited by what you don't know. You will be able to depend on Peter to translate, and you will be proud to have him do it." Amos beamed at Pete. "Your farm will operate more efficiently. Your life will be fuller…not to mention Peter's life. That is why we're emphasizing English in school. School is for practical education. Peter will be learning something that is very practical, indeed, absolutely necessary if he is to make his life a success, maximizing the talents God has given him." Amos knew Pete was familiar with the parable of the talents. "In life, fulfillment of individual potential, and ability to communicate, are directly related. Peter learning proper English will help you and your wife, but especially will enhance Peter's ability to take advantage of future opportunities. I know you want the best for Peter. Encourage him to come to school and learn all we have to offer."

Amos sensed his words about the futures of Peter and the farm, together with Pete's love for his son, could carry the momentum.

"Peter, if the way were made clear, would you want to go back to school?" asked Pete, turning to his son.

Amos's heartfelt monologue had made an impression on Peter who looked at his father. For a moment he studied his father's face as Peter's hands absently bent and twisted some rope. Peter shrugged his shoulders as if to say, "I guess so."

"Would you or wouldn't you?" asked Pete. Amos held his breath.

"Yes, I would," said Peter. Pastor Nordquist beamed.

"Then get back in the classroom tomorrow morning," said Pete with a determined look. "I can take care of things here. You take care of things there. And don't let me hear you saying school is too hard."

Pastor Nordquist lightly nodded encouragingly at Peter, reached out and warmly shook Pete's hand, and Pete reciprocated with affable appreciation. Amos smiled, thanked Pete, touched his fingers to his hat, turned and walked out of the barn.

Pete just broadened his son's future horizon immeasurably, thought Amos, much further than either can know. People around them will be edified, the world a better place.

Peter was in school the next morning and, with encouragement from his father, thereafter worked diligently to learn English, slowly going from the bottom of the class to becoming one of the better students.

⸻ ●━ ⸻

While Anna and Amos worked together daily, and Amos's feeling of excitement when around Anna settled down, the excitement never left, and in the evenings he would look forward to being with Anna the following day. She enjoyed his company as well, impressed by his intelligence, work ethic, kindness, and depth of character which included his commitment to God.

Prior to coming to this area, Anna had many suitors. Her presence in this relatively remote part of Minnesota was due in part to her desire to disappear from the lives of not one but two eligible young men who would not take "no" for an answer. Amos's gentlemanly comportment, versatility, insightfulness and quiet self-confidence impressed Anna. What most impressed her was his sense of masculine responsibility: he told her during the course of conversation during lunch one day that he (correctly, in her opinion) believed the responsibility for the welfare of any relationship between a man and a woman was foremost the man's, and Amos's behavior with her was evidence this statement was made from conviction. As time progressed, her respect and fondness for this church-planting pastor deepened, and she constantly noticed how good-looking he was.

As their appreciation and fondness for one another grew, so did the small congregation in the new sanctuary, and student enrollment in the church school. Success begat success. After nine months, Pastor Nordquist notified Nels Hanseth that it was time to bring in a new pastor before the congregation became too emotionally attached to the one they had.

This wisdom would work for the congregation. It would not work for Anna.

"When do you think the permanent pastor will be installed?" she asked Amos.

"If the call provides suitable candidates, within a month or two," said Amos, stirring cream in a cup of coffee. He looked up at Anna pleasantly, reassuringly. She understood what he was communicating – all would be well – but this did not change her unspoken feelings about his leaving, while unknown to Anna, since duty dictated he leave, he kept it to himself that he did not want to go.

"Then where will you go?"

"My understanding is I will go further north to another growing settlement where there are no churches and no ministry at present. Nels has said nothing specific yet."

Wanting control of her destiny, Anna had given what she was about to say considerable thought.

"You've told me more than once," Anna said as she sat down, "that you like the job I do, and that you've never seen a school function more efficiently and effectively."

"I've told you that several times, Anna. You're doing a wonderful job." Anna absently wrote with a pencil on a sheet of paper as he spoke.

"Will you miss me?"

His mouth slightly open, he looked down at her, uncertain of what to say although part of him begged him to open his heart. She was so beautiful he sometimes wished he had a second pair of eyes in order see more of her at once.

"Very much," said Amos with a quiet intensity that told Anna "very much" was an understatement. He had misgivings about leaving, although he said nothing to anyone, continuing to trust in God for direction. That direction would be coming quickly.

"I would miss you too," she responded as Amos looked at her, confused by the word "would." Did she know something he did not? Was he not going to leave? "I believe there is a very good alternative."

"Alternative to what?" he asked.

"Us missing one another."

"And…what is that?" he asked, his heart racing.

"Jon Tolefson is 19. As you know, he began school late, but caught up quickly and is now my best student and assistant – the younger students like him very much. He will graduate soon, of course. He is bright, organized, writes and speaks English well, and knows the system I use perfectly." She paused, looking at Amos as he looked back. "Give Jon my job, let him continue it here – it would almost be a travesty for him to do something else. Then, when you go to plant a new church, I will go with you and set up the next school, implementing the same system: a wonderful system, don't you agree?"

Amos's thoughts about Anna had been romantic for months but, considering their respective positions and the awkwardness that could result if he overstepped his boundaries, believed it inappropriate to say anything. He decided to vault the boundaries.

"It's a wonderful system…," said Amos quietly as his heart pounded, "…and you're a wonderful teacher." Amos knew he needed to keep talking. "I would be delighted to have you join me…wherever it is I am to go." Amos looked at Anna, and Anna looked back. After having thought about it for so long, Amos finally asked, "Anna, how do you feel about us?"

"How do you feel?" she answered, returning the ball to his court, looking into his dark eyes, her beautiful green eyes not blinking.

"I want you to come with me…," said Amos, his stomach in knots, his heart a locomotive, "…and when we're finished establishing a church and a school, I would want you to come with me again."

"And then?"

"Again."

Amos didn't know what more to say, and there was a pause until Anna spoke.

"And then?"

Amos looked at Anna, studying her beautiful eyes, sensing what she wanted him to do. But was he mistaken? Was he about to make them both very happy or was he about to make a fool of himself? What he thought she wanted him to do, he would do. Covering his excitement with a thin veil of self-discipline, he got up from his seat and, as she watched him, walked around the small table, reached down and took her left hand, urging her to stand up. When she stood up and faced him, never pulling her eyes away from his, he slowly but lovingly embraced her, placing his right cheek aside her ear, pressing the side of his nose into her soft hair as his large, right hand tightly held the middle of her back, and with his left hand he reached down and pressed in on the small of her back. She was sensually imprisoned and unwilling to escape even if she thought it might be fun to try.

"'And then?'" he echoed, his eyes inches from hers. "And then I believe I will ask you to marry me." If he just made a fool out of himself, her response would tell him.

After a brief moment, she let her head slide forward and, looking to her left, rested her right temple on his shoulder.

"It's good to have plans," she murmured with a slightly masked smile.

As she lifted her head to look up at him, he slowly and uniformly squeezed her as if he were a python, as if she would come apart if he didn't. With enough electricity to make each heart race at breakneck speed, imbued with passion, he kissed her, slowly at first, and as she kissed back, his strong arms constricted further as their passion increased. The kiss lasted…he had no idea how long it lasted – it made up for all the moments when both thought about it but Amos, fearful of forcing inappropriate behavior on a church colleague, never made the attempt.

Later Amos would think the wait was worth it. It was a very memorable first kiss. In their waning years they still talked about it, and in the interim attempted to duplicate it. While passion, physical contact, constriction and affection could be duplicated, however, the first time only comes the first time.

Following the first kiss, Amos relaxed his arms slightly, studied Anna's green eyes and formally asked one the world's two most important questions.

"Anna. Will you marry me?"

"I will," she whispered, looking lovingly into his eyes before she buried her cheek into his chest.

She had known for quite some time that he was the one and, moments ago, weary of waiting, pushed their relationship forward like a teacher with a recalcitrant but promising pupil. Except Amos wasn't recalcitrant. He lifted her chin with his index finger and gave her a memorable second kiss. As kisses go, it might have been better than the first except the smoldering passion-exploding-into-fire would never be duplicated.

Less than a month later, the wedding ceremony was conducted by Amos's good friend, Nels Hanseth, and was attended by Anna's family, much of the community, and all the schoolchildren. Unlike most weddings, the best man really was – at least according to him – the best man. This afternoon, however, Anders happily surrendered the lead male role to Amos. Anders's wife Karin, feeling very pregnant, did not make the journey to Minnesota. In Anders's absence, she would look after the businesses.

When comparing Anna and Karin, the thought that he might have married Karin made Amos shake his head. He was marrying who he should marry, a wonderful woman and, considering where he was, what he was doing, and how important it was, he could think of being married to no one other than Anna… and besides, he thought, that aside, inside and out Anna is the most beautiful woman in the world. When on the day of his wedding he intuited that none of this was accidental, that God planned this union long before Anna and Amos ever met, it became obvious to Amos that God takes relationships between men and women more seriously than do men and women, and that marital relationships are, therefore, sacred. Amos wondered why this sacredness was not starkly evident earlier, why it took him so long to see this simple truth. Perhaps, he concluded, he needed to do it first.

"And will you, Anna Hildegaard," continued Nels Hanseth, "take this man, Amos Nordquist, as your lawfully wedded husband…"

It was among the two happiest moments in Amos's life, both of which concluded with Anna saying, "I will."

35

July 1873

Anna kept busy in spite of being in her 37th week of pregnancy. *I look like a world-record butternut squash,* she thought while looking at a smaller one on the drain board.

"Don't you think you should stop and rest?" asked Amos. "The baby will be here any moment…and then you will wish you had taken time to relax."

"That's why I continue to make myself useful," said Anna as she scrubbed an iron pot. "Once the baby is born, I won't have time for…so many things I can do right now."

"Just tell me what to do," said Amos. "I'll do it."

"Amos," answered Anna, "at the moment, for most of these things it's easier to do them myself." She did not feel like debating. "After the baby is born, believe me, you will have plenty of opportunity to do more."

Anna grimaced slightly.

"Oh, here they come again…I just wish these contractions would either go away or stay. They come, hang around for a few minutes, just long enough for me to get apprehensive, and then they leave. It's maddening."

"You remember what Mrs. Olson said: it's your body practicing for the real thing," said Amos as he stepped next to his wife and began placing dishes in the cupboard so Anna would not have to do it. "She would know, having had five children herself, and being the midwife at enough births to fill several school-houses. She said those false contractions are a sign that all will go well when the baby comes."

"Yes, but I'm getting tired of the training exercises," said Anna unhappily. "And looking like I've purloined a watermelon. I just want my baby to be born."

Anna impatiently reached for a towel to dry her hands.

"And you still believe it's a girl," said Amos, folding his arms as he looked at her.

"Oh, yes," said Anna, looking down at her midsection. "It's a girl."

"I still wonder how you can know."

"Of course, I don't know; it's what I believe," said Anna, "but my belief is based on…a feeling, like I already know my baby." She looked down. "My baby," she repeated as she gently held her large midsection with both hands.

Anna reached out for the additional laundry to fold and studied Amos's face.

"I know all men want a boy at first, Amos, but my intuition tells me we're having a beautiful little girl." She emphasized the word, "beautiful."

"With a very beautiful mother," smiled Amos, "unsurprising."

"Thank you, Amos," said Anna as she placed the laundry on the table.

Anna's hands again slid down to the lower part of her large, extended, abdominal area. She held that area for a moment as if it were a large sack of apples.

"The contractions have stopped. Errrhh." She looked up at Amos, aggravated. "This is driving me to distraction, Amos."

Amos and Anna had no sexual relations or bed sport recently because of her condition, and Amos felt sexually repressed. To Amos, in spite of her being pregnant, Anna was gorgeous, desirable, and he still wanted what he wanted.

"Well, Anna," said Amos, "Mrs. Olson said there is an enjoyable way to induce labor if we want to." A light danced in his eyes. "An intimate liaison."

"Sex? With me? Like this? Now?"

"Wouldn't you really like to go into labor soon?"

"I would really like to get this over with soon, but, Amos, as you can understand, I don't feel very desirable at the moment."

"You are always desirable, Anna," Amos smiled sincerely. "It's among the things you do best."

"I do want to start labor…I'm feeling so oversized and overweight and overdue… But Amos, at the moment I'm about as sexy as that butternut squash," Anna pointed toward the small squash on the kitchen drain board, "and fifty times as big. You won't enjoy sexual relations with me."

"I will."

"You won't."

Anna thought about how she and Amos had sexual intercourse as often as was safe, making up for those days and nights when they abstained. When it was safe, Amos made her feel like the world's most desirable woman. Fertile women were the norm in Anna's family and as she considered she had not become pregnant during their first two years of marriage, she thought it remarkable. A miracle. Thirty-seven weeks ago they threw caution to the winds. The moment would soon arrive when they would welcome their first child. If her intuition was correct, they would name the baby Inga, the name of Amos's grandmother and Anna's aunt.

Amos went over to Anna, gently took her right arm and slipped it behind his left upper arm and over his forearm, her hand resting on his wrist, as if they were about to walk out on a dance floor. Realizing what he wanted to do, she pulled away.

"Amos, look at me." Anna looked down in alarm.

"You're gorgeous."

"I'm not gorgeous, I'm enormous. A giant butternut squash with legs. And what about the baby? The baby might be injured if you get too aggressive."

"I promise I'll only be aggressive in one place," said Amos, folding his arms and smiling. "Otherwise, I will be a model of decorum."

"You'll be a model of a brigantine in a hurricane. Amos, 'decorum'? You don't make love like that. You're normally all over me, and normally I love it... but now...Amos, you can't do it like that...and I'm not feeling desirable."

"I can change that."

"Oh, can you? Mr. Casanova."

Under his concupiscent gaze, Anna folded her arms and looked away, and began considering an attempt. She looked back at him.

"But what about the baby?"

"I'll be careful."

"Talk is what it is, Amos."

"Anna, do you want to induce labor or not?" Amos asked. "I'll compromise. I'll be careful about the baby; I won't be careful about you."

"Amos, I don't know."

"I'll be very careful." He looked at her seriously. "I'll tell you what. If at any time you feel anxious, like something is wrong, tell me and I'll stop."

She studied his face.

"You promise?"

"I promise," he said, assuming that once they began, like him she would not want to stop.

She nodded. He is so sensational, she thought to herself as if wanting it to be a secret.

He led her into the bedroom. As they got into bed, she felt awkward because of her size, and considered, from Amos's perspective, what it must be like to have relations with an inverted hot air balloon. He kissed her passionately, however... my golly, she thought as she passionately kissed back, determining she would somehow match his ever-amorous physicality. From his facial expressions as they began to enjoy one another, she did not sense any drop-off in arousal, regardless of her physical condition. Positioned on top of her, his arms out straight on either side of her head, taking pressure off her abdominal area, he was obviously still Amos.

As she lay on the bed enjoying her husband's determined attack, thoughts flashed through her mind for a few seconds. Whether a pastor's wife enjoyed sexual relations more than, say, a miller's wife? A butcher's wife? It seemed to her that the spiritually disciplined life she and Amos led complemented and magnified the sensual pleasures they were gifted. Since God made women and men for each other, Anna thought, in appropriate circumstances the Holy Spirit could award enhancement, and it seemed He often did. Their honeymoon had been incredible. Oh, my golly. God had a hand in that, she thought as her own arousal increased.

Being continually close to God, was intercourse generally better with a pastor?

It was not a question she considered while a single virgin, thinking about the kind of man she wanted to marry. She thought heightened venery depended only on the persons, that is, herself and her husband. Now her intuition told her that the increased spiritual fecundity that came with being a pastor's wife might enable greater fecundity of another sort, more than experienced by other wives. It was an interesting thought. It seemed to be happening at that moment. She knew from church history that Martin Luther had something to do with Lutheran pastors not being celibate. As her bed groaned and creaked, in her mind Anna said, Thank you, Martin Luther, and then smiled at the unlikelihood of having such a thought at that moment. Anna and Amos continued with concupiscent alacrity, and gradually her excitement grew to where they could no longer be constrained. She fought to hold back, but still her arousal grew and then a frisson shot through her like a lightning bolt, rising in intensity and exploding like a bomb as she climaxed, her strong body shuddering like a church steeple in an earthquake while she moaned loudly in pleasure.

As sexual intercourse gradually came to an end, Amos, breathing heavily, beamed down at her, his arms still out straight but aching with fatigue. He bent his elbows, allowing him to kiss her softly and slowly with tender gratefulness for all that she was and did. He pushed his right arm straight again, and cautiously rolled over on his side next to her, continuing to breathe heavily.

"If that doesn't get labor started," he said in between breaths, "I don't know what will."

She looked back lovingly, somehow certain they had succeeded. And if they had not, she mused, oh well.

Moments later, Amos sat up, leaned over, lovingly kissed her once again, and slid his feet out of bed. His already-broad latissimi dorsi flared as he bent down and picked up his clothes from the floor.

"I'll be out in the barn for about an hour," he said as he put on his clothes. He turned to pull on his boots, stood up, and said with a smile, "I will expect you to be in labor when I return." His emotions soared with that thought as he turned around, walked out of the bedroom into the living room, the kitchen, and out the back door, closing it firmly behind him as she lay listening, not to him but to her heart.

It did not take an hour.

"The contractions are back," Anna said to Amos when he came inside. Amos looked at her without speaking, waiting for her to explain further. "They're regular, about seven minutes apart. I felt the baby's head drop."

Amos's eyes grew wide as his mouth went slack; then he relaxed and clapped his hands, rubbing them together. "I'll go get Mrs. Olson," said Amos as he turned and raced out the backdoor, slamming it shut behind him.

He ran toward the barn, whistling for his horse, Scirocco, grazing in the pasture. Maggie Olson, the community midwife, lived three miles away.

After Amos saddled Scirocco and rode off, Anna began to get things ready for the delivery. Warm water, towels, wash cloths, baby blankets. The contractions were becoming longer and coming faster now, and it was evident the baby would pay no attention to anyone else's time schedule.

Anna could feel continued softening in her vaginal area. She went into the bath chamber to check herself, and as she sat down on the chair in the corner, she could feel the baby's head pushing forward. Someone's in a hurry, she thought. Anna began to worry that Amos might not be back in time with Mrs. Olson. This is happening too fast.

She stood up and looked in the bath chamber wall mirror and was slightly surprised at her panicked expression. My water, she reminded herself, has not yet broken.

She turned away from the mirror, walked out of the bath chamber and went back into the bedroom. She considered lying on her back when she delivered, but Mrs. Olson recommended she be on all-fours or on her knees, perhaps hanging on to something in front of her to keep the womb at an angle. It was more natural and usually quicker, Mrs. Olson said.

On all-fours, delivering a baby. It doesn't get more immodest than this. But it will only be Amos and Mrs. Olson. Mrs. Olson has seen it all. This is no time for modesty. God has given me a beautiful baby and the means to deliver it. I am young and strong. She patted her large abdominal area and said out loud, "Pretty soon, little one."

After pushing Scirocco over the three-mile distance, Amos arrived at the Olson residence, a two-story house with high white walls, window boxes, black shutters, and a colorful blossoming flowerbed around the house like a moat around a castle. As Scirocco reached the front gate, Amos swung off the horse, dismounting on the run. The front porch was the drawbridge over which Amos raced and knocked rapidly on the door.

No answer.

He knocked again.

Still no answer.

Anxiously, Amos peered in a window. It seemed no one was home.

Avoiding the flower beds, he ran to the back of the house, and began looking around. Nothing; no one.

Amos placed his hands against the sides of his head, thinking about what he should do. Where would she have gone? He had no idea. Without knocking he ran into the house…maybe someone was there but asleep…or maybe she left a note, something to indicate where she went.

He walked quickly into the living room and stopped to listen for any sound. The room was silent, as if watching him.

"Mrs. Olson?!" he shouted.

No sound.

"Ira?!"

He turned, raced out the back door, and began to run toward the rear outbuildings when white-haired Ira Olson, hard of hearing, came out of the stable.

"Ira!" shouted Amos. "Ira!" Ira looked at Amos and knew what Amos needed. Ira Olson quickened his pace.

"Maggie's not here," said Ira. "She's over at the Siguurdsons visiting Maude and their grandson. Mighty fine little boy. Just…"

Ira didn't need to finish his sentence, for Amos was already racing around the side of the house. He jumped on Scirocco, leaned forward spurring Scirocco's flanks and shouted, "Go, Scirocco." The horse, still catching its breath, reared and bolted out the Olson driveway and down the dirt road like the bell had rung for the start of the second race. The Siguurdsons lived another two miles away.

As Amos and Scirocco neared the finish line that was the Siguurdsons, Mrs. Olson and Maude Siguurdson, a large, older woman who formerly taught school and now occasionally helped Anna, were having tea and pastries on the front porch while chatting and watching the Siguurdson's grandson attempting to crawl on a blanket. Anna Nordquist's pregnancy was well known in the little community, and most knew Anna was due to go into labor any time. Fortuitously, Mrs. Olson and Mrs. Siguurdson were just discussing it.

Upon spying wide-eyed Amos on Scirocco racing down the driveway, without saying a word, Mrs. Olson put down her teacup, stood up, bid Mrs. Siguurdson goodbye, and walked rapidly to her Stanhope carriage.

"I will follow you," Mrs. Olson said to Amos as she climbed into the carriage.

"Well, wait a minute," said Maude Siguurdson at a distance, "I'm coming too."

She picked up the teacups and brought them into the kitchen where her husband, Sig, was sharpening a knife.

"Would you watch 'Three' [Ira III] until Lillian returns? Should be any time now."

When Maude returned to the porch, she saw Mrs. Olson racing out the driveway in pursuit of Amos on Sirocco.

"I'm still coming," said Maude defiantly. "A new baby? I'll be there."

She walked in a rapid, waddling gait to one of the family horses, led it toward her buckboard, hitched up the horse, took the reins, climbed on and sat down hard, the buckboard giving a painful groan. She snapped the reins aggressively, and the buckboard rolled out the driveway and down the road, stirring up a cloud of dust that followed the cloud of dust from Mrs. Olson's carriage. Amos was now well ahead of Mrs. Olson.

Up the road, other families heard and saw Pastor Nordquist riding at a pace rivaling that of Dr. Samuel Prescott, William Dawes, and Paul Revere on their midnight ride.

In a few moments, Mrs. Olson's carriage followed – and everyone knew what Mrs. Olson did.

Moments later, Mrs. Siguurdson's buckboard bounced down the road stirring up more dust.

"Anna's in labor," the women all said as they watched Mrs. Olson and Mrs. Siguurdson race after Pastor Nordquist.

The other families hitched or saddled up and followed in hot pursuit.

The blessed event was going to bless and be blessed by many in the community. Within four miles of the Nordquist residence, those toward the front of the race kicked up a yellow-tinged dust cloud that blurred the vision of those in the rear. It rose well above the bushes along the fence lines and was visible at a considerable distance. Many in the rear put bandanas and handkerchiefs over their mouths as they raced down the dusty country road.

Anna was attempting to maintain her composure as she stood next to the bath chamber tub, an enameled pig scalder with legs and a draining hose that ran through a hole in the floor and outside to the cesspool. It was normally used only on Saturday night, but she looked at it, reconsidering that, as a practical matter, it might be used as a birthing place.

While standing next to the tub she felt a sudden "pop" and then, swhooooshh, water poured from her as if, inside, a miniature dam broke. It was immediately all over her legs, and the bath chamber floor.

Where is Amos?

She grabbed some towels, cleaned herself up, and awkwardly bent down to wipe up the floor. Amos, please hurry. She was not controlling the situation, the baby was. Fearful she was already coming close to giving birth, she grabbed an armload of clean towels, forsaking the tub, and walked awkwardly to the bedroom.

She placed several towels in two neat, overlapping rows on the bed where she thought the baby might land should she have to give birth alone.

She sat on the edge of the bed for a moment, laid back, slid her legs up on the bed, and turned over carefully on the towels, being careful not to push them out of place. Getting on her knees, she reached up for the small headboard. She held it with her hands while kneeling – her womb at an angle – and her baby working its way into the outside world.

She stayed in that position and waited, praying, Please, God, make this a wonderful moment.

God and the baby were there. But no one else.

Amos knew Sirocco was tired, but the pace could not be helped. It pained him that his baby might be born without him, and Sirocco, sweat glistening on his flanks, sensed his master's panic.

Where do souls come from? Anna wondered for a moment in between contractions as she intentionally hyperventilated. We know where souls go. Where do they come from? Are they created at conception? Or have they always existed somewhere? For a moment, she imagined an enormous white warehouse with an intricate, front entrance of festooned, fluted Greek columns. Above the great entrance was a huge sign that said in elaborate, Old English letters: "Eternal Souls."

The next contraction began; Anna gritted her teeth and painfully pushed. Realizing how far the baby came in such a short time, she became totally focused on what she was doing, giving no more thought to anything else. With each contraction, Anna again hyperventilated, the excess oxygen partially deadening her pain. Her abdominal area, loins, the insides of her thighs ached. Her skin was moist from becoming uncomfortably warm, and she was already feeling exhausted. They don't call this "labor" for nothing, she thought. Eve. Thanks a lot.

The baby's head was close to crowning. Another contraction. Anna's mouth was open and she was damp with perspiration. Then with all the energy she could muster, she pushed.

"Uhhhhhhhhhhhahhhhh."

As the contraction faded, she again panted aggressively, oxygenating her system.

Moments later as the next contraction began, she gritted her teeth. Mad with determination to give birth, she held her breath and, with a loud, formidable moan, began to push again.

As the contraction ended, she considered the position of the baby's head just above the bed. I'm alone; perhaps I should lie down on my side, she thought. Not yet.

Foam was forming on Scirocco's flanks when Amos saw the distant trees above the parsonage.

The top of the baby's head, its hair wet and dark, protruded from the vaginal area. Anna, exhausted, was near the end of another contraction. Only a moment more.

Foam flowed freely from Sirocco's mouth as he raced down the driveway, Amos already preparing to dismount.

Before Sirocco reached the front porch, Amos was off the saddle and on the ground, running up the steps and into the house as Anna began another contraction. As the front door banged behind him, she heard him cry, "Anna!"

"Amos," Anna gasped. "Oh, Amos. Get behind me. Catch the baby. Ahh-huhhhhhh. Don't let her fall."

Amos quickly sat down on the edge of the bed and, turning toward Anna, put his hands out. He'd helped birthing calves, colts and lambs, but this was different. Still, it was not a completely unfamiliar situation, and this helped him steady his nerves and racing heart.

Moments later, Mrs. Olson came through the bedroom door, followed shortly by Mrs. Siguurdson. Mrs. Olson looked at Anna, the top of the baby's protruding head, the towels, water and Pastor Nordquist.

"Well, Pastor Nordquist, it seems your wife has been doing quite nicely without us."

Mrs. Olson took a washcloth, dipped it in some lukewarm water Anna placed beside the bed earlier, and wiped Anna's forehead and face.

"Pastor Nordquist, quickly, wash your hands, and when you return be prepared to catch the baby."

Pastor Nordquist returned a moment later and held out his hands as if to catch a ball being thrown from the side.

"No, put your hands out as if you were already cradling the baby," directed Mrs. Olson excitedly. "Your baby may just quickly drop out. But when the mother is in that position, a baby can shoot out like a cannonball."

Mrs. Olson paused, studying the baby's head, and continued, "How do you feel, Anna? Anna, you are about to give birth to a wonderful little baby. Oh, I love this moment!"

"Baby," was all Anna could say, her body in the throes of heavy labor, her voice weak but high pitched as she concentrated on only one thing while continuing to cling to the headboard, exhausted but preparing to push again. Her arms were tired and her back ached.

Others arrived at the house, and a few women stood near the bedroom door, listening to assess the situation. Realizing the baby was mere moments away from leaving Anna, they stood wide-eyed, holding their breath as Anna breathed heavily.

"Anna," said Mrs. Olson, "from where the baby is, I think the next push could be the big one. Oh, we're almost there, dear! Breathe heavily now," said Mrs. Olson excitedly. "Panting. That's it."

"Another…contraction," gasped Anna, her forehead damp.

"This is it, dear," responded Mrs. Olson. "This one should do it."

Anna's fingernails dug into the headboard.

"On the count of three…" Mrs. Olson paused watching the baby's head. "Okay, dear, one…two…three!" Anna gritted her teeth and began.

The men on the porch turned around and looked toward the open front door, and the men and women in the living room looked toward the bedroom when they heard Anna's exceptionally loud moan followed by…

"WOOOHOOOOO!" exclaimed Amos as the baby shot into his hands. The women by the bedroom door spontaneously clapped their hands, laughing, chattering with excitement in concert with the wonderful sound of the newborn baby crying.

"What is it?" yelled one of the men in the living room.

"A little girl!" yelled Mrs. Siguurdson."

The men turned and looked at one another, thought of Anna Nordquist, and nodded. The odds were 50–50 but, by golly, another Anna would be good.

Anna, her mouth open, breathing heavily, took her hands off the headboard, and slowly got herself in position on her side.

Amos started to take another washcloth to clean off the baby, but Mrs. Olson gently put her hand on his and said, "Oh, no, Dr. Nordquist. God put that sticky, white stuff there for a reason. We'll just leave it there for a little while."

Amos looked at Mrs. Olson for further direction.

"The little girl will need to be fed," said Mrs. Olson patiently. "That was quite an ordeal for someone not even born yet."

Amos smiled and handed Inga, still crying softly, to Anna who placed the still-crying baby next to her breast and moved her nipple to the baby's mouth. The baby had no trouble with what to do next, and the room quieted.

Amos partially covered Anna with a blanket, wiped her head with a damp washcloth, and stood next to the bed, looking down at his new daughter. What an amazing thing, he thought as he studied his baby girl.

He bent down and kissed his wife on her temple.

"Maude," said Amos, turning around to Mrs. Siguurdson happily wiping the tears from her eyes, "would you do me a favor?"

"Oh." She smiled as she regained her composure. "Certainly. Whatever you wish."

"Ask the women to go into the kitchen, the root cellar, and the pantry, and fix supper – anything you wish to fix from what we have – for everyone here. This is a wonderful time for me," his smiling eyes glistened, "and I am proud to share it with such a fine community of friends as have gathered. Please tell the others that I will be out in a while. Tell the men to make themselves at home if they haven't already." The other women immediately left for the kitchen.

"My pleasure," said Mrs. Siguurdson who walked out of the bedroom and into the living room. There was no need to tell the men to make themselves at home, and in a moment Amos heard Mrs. Siguurdson's school teacher voice sing, "Okay, ladies…"

Amos pulled a chair closer, sat down next to Anna, reached out, took her damp hand, and silently prayed, thanking God.

Next to him, Mrs. Olson tied off the umbilical cord that no longer sustained the baby, and in a moment would cut it. Later the placenta would pass, and the young mother could clean up in earnest. Mrs. Olson pulled another chair next to the bed and also sat down.

"I'm willing to bet you thought we might not make it to the party," Mrs. Olson said politely to Anna.

"To tell you the truth, I was feeling a little abandoned," Anna responded, her eyes still closed. She opened her eyes and looked at the table clock. The intensity of the ordeal had made the time fly. Even though moments seemed like forever, she hardly believed she had been in serious labor that long.

"But you seemed to have everything under control," continued Mrs. Olson. "Ohh, t'wouldn't' be the first time a woman gave birth to a baby alone, but I must commend you." Mrs. Olson nodded seriously at Anna. "It was obvious to me when I walked into the bedroom that this baby was coming into the world without a hitch." Mrs. Olson folded her hands and looked pleasantly at mother and child.

"Of course, it doesn't always happen that way. I helped deliver a little boy several years ago for a young woman as strong and healthy as you. Problem was: the baby was afraid of being dropped, and so he decided to come out feet first. Something like that gets tricky, you know." Mrs. Olson looked at Anna neutrally. "The baby…and the mother…both lived, but it was touch and go for a while. That's when someone like me comes in handy.

"We had two doctors there: at first, a nice young man, but he couldn't figure out what to do, and an older gentleman, although not as old as me." Mrs. Olson chuckled. "The older doctor arrived about the same time I did. He and I got things straightened out, but what needs to be done under such circumstances is not always intuitive. I have helped a lot of mothers and babies through the ordeal."

For a moment Mrs. Olson silently reminisced.

"Don't get me wrong. You did a great job today, Anna. But, trust me; it's good to have experience nearby."

Anna kept her eyes closed, said nothing, but thought, yes, that would have been nice.

Anna passed the placenta, and Mrs. Olson took it in a towel outside. Anna knew that in some pagan cultures, burying the placenta involved ceremony and ritual. East central Minnesota was not a pagan culture. Amos would bury the placenta in one corner of the cornfield.

When Mrs. Olson and Amos returned, she directed Amos to help Anna become comfortable. When asked if she wanted anything to eat or drink, Anna had a drink of water; she said she was more exhausted than hungry and would eat later. She nursed for a while until the two of them, mother and child, fell asleep.

When they awoke sometime after supper, Mrs. Olson prepared a warm bath and Anna got up and walked into the bath chamber, bathed and cleaned herself up. She observed that her mid-section was deflated, but not as much as she wished.

She dried off, dressed, made herself presentable, and walked to the bed where she picked up little Inga who had remained asleep, and dressed her in a tiny dressing gown and cap.

With Inga who was still sleeping quietly in her arms, Anna walked toward the bedroom door. To get her facial expression working right, Anna stopped, practiced a smile, and walked into a living room filled with neighbors who, upon seeing her, spontaneously applauded. Inga remained quiet, not seeing, but sensing.

As Anna presented her baby to the young and old of the community gathered there, many clucked, ooh'd and ahh'd. The little girls present wanted to hold Inga. Some did and pretended. As the older girls held Inga, they wondered more serious thoughts. Younger mothers considered having another, while older women smiled, nodded and remarked how quickly it all goes by.

After the others left, mother and father lay on the bed with sleeping Inga between them. I wonder who she will be? Amos thought as he gently touched Inga's button nose with his right index finger. He pleasantly looked down at the sleeping baby and warmly whispered, "Who are you, Inga?"

36

Early 1882

The years blew by like Great Lakes gale winds and, in addition to planting churches and starting schools, Amos and Anna Nordquist were raising three daughters: Inga, Esther and Rachel.

Amos thought about the seventeen years since the end of Civil War, since Amos and Abraham Cole parted company. Amos wished he knew the whereabouts of Abraham Cole so Amos could write Abraham a letter telling him about Amos's family and the struggles and rewards of church planting in Minnesota. And, of course, discover what Abraham had started.

Letters continued back and forth across the Atlantic. With the perfection of multiple, expansion, steam engines, Anders again sold company ships and replaced them with new and larger vessels. The Golden Age of Immigration had arrived. Many in Europe were leaving for America, and the Nordquist Shipping Company was doing its part to help emigrants become immigrants. Anders was also merging Nordquist Shipping with other companies in an effort to become part of something more formidable and profitable.

On the other hand, Amos, sitting in his study, anticipated nothing more than life-as-usual. This is good, he thought. I enjoy this predictability and orderliness. Then the thought, unwelcome, came to him: like the predictability and orderliness I enjoyed before two uninsured ships and most of both crews went down in the North Atlantic. Amos's expression went blank as he folded his hands, then slumped in his chair.

The Old Prospector, as everyone called him, lived down the road from Amos, and was a local legend. Years earlier, he had been west panning for gold in the Rockies, found some, but considerably less than people said. He wisely took his wealth and returned to Minnesota where he bought a small lake, built a log cabin, and retired to fish. He didn't like to be bothered, so no one did, but he enjoyed talking to Amos who checked in on him periodically. Smoking a corncob pipe, he explained to Amos that, "'The gettin' it' part ain't never reward enough. Lookin' fer gold is a hard life. That 'great outdoors' stuff goes jest so far. No gold?" he shrugged. "What's the point?"

Amos had read stories of gold strikes, usually greatly embellished, that drew men west and held them like a spell. Most would never experience even the small success the Old Prospector had, but in a place Amos had never heard of, someone named Andy Pritchard was about to become a major exception, changing Amos's life significantly.

June 1882
North Idaho

Spellbound, Andy Prichard momentarily looked in disbelief at what he held in his hand. Resting on one knee beside the rippling Bitterroot Mountain creek, his dirty hat guarding his face from the overhead sun, Prichard couldn't believe what he saw. Maybe this was a dream. All this time and trouble. He blinked twice.

But it was still there.

He sighed and slumped forward. In a moment, he slowly stood. With his left hand he took off his hat and wiped his forehead with the back of his left forearm while still looking down at the contents in his right palm. He put his hat on, wiped his eyes and looked down again. Turning slowly to his right, he looked up and hollered to his pard.

"Hey!" He paused a moment. "Get over here 'n see what I jes' found!"

"What d'ya find?" yelled Phil Markson, disinclined to move from where he had just re-affixed his hope.

"Gold!"

The other partners panning at a distance stood up wide-eyed, looking at Prichard. Simultaneously Markson, Bill Gerrard, Mike Gillette and Bill Dempsey trotted in Prichard's direction. To see for themselves. To see the gold. To see what would be the beginning of the last major gold strike south of the Yukon.

In the Bitterroot Mountains, north Idaho's Eagle Creek babbled excitedly. Ages followed ages like waves on the sea before this moment finally arrived. Andrew Prichard discovered gold near the junction of Eagle Creek and another creek soon to be named Prichard Creek. Prichard staked several claims in the area, one of which he named the Murray Claim after a relative of his wife. Prichard and his pards rode west out of the Bitterroot and Coeur d'Alene Mountains into Spokane Falls to formalize their claim staking. They carried a buckskin pouch containing two pounds of gold.

On the way, Prichard and the men occasionally passed other prospectors aside forest creeks, kneeling over pans and sluice boxes. He looked down at them as he rode and said nothing. He wondered if any would experience luck like his. The odds weren't favorable; more fortunes were lost than made in the search for gold. Rather than tip his hand, Prichard kept his mouth shut, hoping to be among the few upon whom Fortune would smile but not laugh. Arriving in Spokane Falls during the early evening, Prichard and his pards quietly entered a Spokane Falls saloon, sidled up to the bar and ordered the standard elixir.

"What'll it be, gents?"

"Whiskey."

"Whiskey."

The others just nodded.

The bartender, new to Spokane Falls like most, pushed a bottle across the bar. Ain't many real mixologists out here, thought the bartender. No need.

The bartender poured each man a shot glass of whiskey. Collecting the fare, he turned his attention to other patrons in equal need of imagination. For a few moments neither Prichard nor his partners spoke. As Prichard stood, leaning against the bar, he glanced at the stranger standing next to him who looked back, wanting conversation.

"Jes' get into town?" the man asked. It's a logical opener, thought Prichard. Everyone has, in varying degrees, just gotten into town.

"Yeah. Been up in the Coeur d'Alenes prospectin'." Prichard didn't volunteer any additional information.

"Any luck?"

"Well...yeah," said Prichard. The words escaped his mouth before the sensible side of his brain could grab his ego.

"What kind 'a luck did ya have?" asked the stranger, poker faced.

"Discovered gold in one of the creeks up there." Lord, that did it, thought the sensible side.

The bartender moved closer to Prichard and the other man.

The word "gold," if accompanied by appropriate phrasing, could swiftly drive its way through a traffic jam of louder noises. When Prichard said he "discovered gold," several pairs of ears belonging to prospective prospectors and others seated nearby were already straining to hear the rest of the conversation.

"Ya don't say," responded the stranger who stared at Prichard like Prichard had three eyes. "So where, if ya don't mind my askin', did ya find the gold?"

When the stranger asked Prichard "where...did ya find the gold?" with no one talking within immediate earshot, the word made its way into other ears at a further distance. Wide-open eyes begged for reiteration and reply.

As surrounding social intercourse transformed from dull conversation to keen attentiveness, the word, repeated, would be able to drive farther faster as the din diminished, swiftly delivering the message to the dimly lit corners of the room. Attention spans were uniformly disrupted, with each span getting in line, following the others like lemmings. With contagion, the entire saloon grew quiet.

"As I said," Prichard repeated, knowing he was making a monumental mistake, but still unable to rein in his mouth, "we were prospecting up in the Coeur d'Alenes, maybe closer to the Bitterroot Mountains, and I was pannin' this creek bed. I was lookin' in the pan an' there it was. Gold dust. And a gold nugget flashin' at me like a miniature lantern. I looked in the pan some more an' saw another nugget. Then another an' another. I picked 'em out of the pan and looked at 'em. I didn't get excited though. Sorta like dreamin'. Real strange. Jes' sorta slumped. Guess I couldn't believe my good luck. Never had much luck before."

Prichard took a sip from his glass and said nothing more. The others waited, staring, clearing their throats, until finally Prichard felt obligated to say something for a moment.

"Strangest thing, seein' that. Like a dream. Not real. I jes' kept lookin'. Felt mighty strange. It was – as if by magic – gold."

The normally reticent Prichard again paused, unintentionally allowing the last word to echo in multiple mental caverns. The silence remained quiet, but muscles tightened and eyes strained. Someone spontaneously spoke, asking the question on every man's mind.

"Where…where was it?"

"Well," Prichard, not wanting to be either specific or impolite, took a breath, "it's east of here a piece – mebbe 60, 70 miles or so – up in the hills"

"Where? What was the name of the creek?"

Prichard looked at the sea of eyes around him as his common sense yelled at him to shut the hell up! No more!

"Well, what did it look like?"

"The gold?" responded Prichard. "Well, look…"

"No, not the gold! The creek! What did the creek look like? Where was it?"

The word was delivered out into the street and within moments men came barging through the door until the saloon was full of men. The barroom was rowdy, loud and confused.

"Dammit t' hell," said Prichard under his breath, mad at himself. He turned angrily to his pards and yelled, "What d'ya say we clear outta here?"

Each man quickly swigged down his whiskey and pulled away from groping hands, heading toward the front door.

"This is nuts," muttered Prichard loudly. "Can't believe how people act when there's a chance of gettin' rich real quick."

"Well, yeah…but that's why them an' us are all out here," said Bill Gerrard.

"I could almost feel sorry for 'em." As he pushed toward the door, Prichard looked about without expression.

"Andy, ya gotta remember: that was us a few days ago," said Phil Markson.

"But most a' these boys are wastin' their time," added Gerrard. "Won't find nothin'. Dam' shame."

"Dam' fool," muttered Prichard, annoyed at the crowd but mostly his ataxic tongue. I should have used more sense, he thought. I should have kept my big, damned mouth shut. I usually do. Why, when the most important event in my lifetime happens, do I go off at the mouth?

Head down, he pushed his way between some tables.

"Guess 'cause it was," he mumbled.

Prichard pulled someone's hand off his arm as he continued in the direction of the front door, trying to ignore someone else who wanted to know exactly where he found the gold.

"Ya think I'm dumb enough to tell you?" Prichard shouted in order to be heard. "I already said too much."

Leaning forward, one hand over his hat and the other hand over the pouch under his shirt, Prichard plowed through the mob like an icebreaker, his pards following in his wake. The icebreaker pushed hard into the heavy current at the front door through which men were flowing, all with the same purpose: to find out where the gold was.

As Prichard looked about him, he knew that as close as most of these men would come was the Dream, alluring as a boomtown harlot. But what were the odds? Most prospectors eventually gave up, but some would become addicts, investing their talent pursuing the Dream for an entire lifetime, eventually dying broke and broken.

And the Dream is what these men flowing through that front door are after, thought Prichard. Still, Prichard was surprised by the extent of unfettered behavior. He continued to push, breaking out onto the boardwalk and away from the current.

But while Prichard and his partners left, the news stayed and was amplified.

***

In contrast to Andy Prichard who was a quiet man, theatric Bill Keeler, a prospector who met Prichard in the hills prior to the day of the discovery, loved being the center of attention. With long hair and a long, untrimmed beard, Keeler looked as if he'd either lived in the mountains all his life or was an Old Testament prophet reincarnated. Keeler and his partner appeared in Spokane Falls several days later proclaiming to all who would listen, and there were many, that he struck gold on "Prichard Creek."

"I tell you boys, I never seen nothin' like it!" he shouted, standing on a chair in the barroom. His eyes were open wide as if he'd just seen the ghost of John Sutter walk in the door. He put his hands in the air out in front of him, palms down, waist high and, as he stared at the space between them, let them slowly drift away from one another. He looked down at the crowded barroom and intoned, "Just layin' there in the creek bed and along the edges of the creek and even in the brush."

The room grew quiet as Keeler's eyes grew even bigger, as if he had just discovered something.

"Here!"

He reached into his haversack, pulled something out, and in the silence stared at the other men. "Look at this," Keeler said just above a whisper as he raised his buckskin pouch and poured a little bit of gold dust into an outstretched hand as men who were watching strained to see.

Eyes wide, mouth half open, the prophet carefully poured the gold dust from his hand back into the poke, and slowly raised the pouch above his head until he resembled the Statue of Liberty.

"Gold!" he shouted. Congregating men in the shadows froze, staring like defensive housecats. "Gold!" shouted the prophet. His eyes wild, he pointed in the direction of Prichard Creek. "It's yers, boys!" saliva spraying from his mouth as he hoarsely shouted, "The hills up thar are lousy with it!"

In the growing tide of excitement, as Keeler pointed to the east, some men bolted for the door. Prichard Creek. It was not formally named and was not on a map, if there was a map, but within a day hundreds more were heading in its general direction, excited not only by the personal exclamations of Bill Keeler, but by the Associated Press which picked up the story and flashed those exclamations to a nation. Properly headlined editions could also strike gold.

Nels Hanseth sat at his desk reading the paper. Big gold strike. Interesting, he thought. Been awhile. North Idaho. Nels got out his map.

East of Washington Territory up north in Idaho Territory. No doubt a growing congregation of souls to save, he thought. A little farther west is Seattle. Nels studied the map. Amos and Anna have been planting Minnesota churches 13 years. Minnesota is growing, but not like it was, and probably nothing like north Idaho, Tacoma or Seattle right now. "I'll need to pray about this," he thought out loud.

News of the gold strike travelled east and south, and during the next 15 months a settlement grew in proximity to Prichard's gold strike. Growth was slow at first because Hayes City – as it was called for two months, then changed to Eagle City – a town of tents in the remote Bitterroot Mountains, was hard to find. With waning mineral wealth in other Western gold and silver districts, prospectors pulled up stakes and headed in that direction, nevertheless. When the Northern Pacific Railroad was completed on September 8, 1883, and the railroad began trumpeting the gold strike and the availability of train travel to Thompson Falls in western Montana, the trickle turned into a flood.

Coeur d'Alene

THE WONDERFUL

RICH MINERAL WEALTH

OF THE

COEUR D'ALENE

MOUNTAINS,

And the tributaries of the river of that name, has been

HERALDED TO THE WORLD,

And old prospectors and miners who are conversant
with the banner districts of

California, Montana

And

Colorado

STAND AMAZED

AT THESE NEW FIELDS, WHICH ARE

UNEQUALED

IN RICHNESS AND EXTENT,

**The yield being practically inexhaustible, rendering
impossible any overcrowding of the district by reason
of too great an influx of prospectors and miners.**

THERE IS

MORE THAN ENOUGH FOR ALL WHO COME

37

September 8, 1883
Independence Creek, Deer Lodge County, Montana Territory

Along with a thousand others, Chong Tsing Wei, 23, and, at a respectable distance, former Congressman William H. Clagett, sat in the newly con structed stands watching the Northern Pacific Railroad Golden Spike Ceremony near Independence Creek in Deer Lodge County, Montana Territory.

Twelve years earlier while representing Montana Territory in Congress, a bill of Clagett's resulted in the National Park Act, and Yellowstone National Park. It was the high point of Clagett's life – although at that distant moment he thought it was just the beginning of bigger things and dreamed of much higher public office. When Clagett was not reelected to Congress, however, his dream collapsed like a failing train trestle.

While watching 300 seasoned men in two railroad gangs lay the last 600 yards of Northern Pacific Railroad track, he pondered what he should do next. When this celebration was over, Deer Lodge County could grow because of the railroad, but it was unlikely that his political fortunes would improve. While he loved the mountains, the rivers and the big sky, he knew if he stayed in Montana Territory, his political ambitions had as much chance of going anywhere as installed railroad ties. He needed a new constituency in want of a veteran Congressman.

Meanwhile, Chong Tsing Wei and his friend, Ho Ching Chin, found the track-laying effort doubly entertaining. Without foresight, this track was already laid…but torn up a few days before the big ceremony.

"Perhaps a mistake was made," suggested Mr. Ho, speaking Cantonese.

"No," responded Mr. Chong quietly, also in his native language. "This is just for show. With all these dignitaries present, some form of entertainment was necessary."

"Nevertheless," replied Mr. Ho, raising his head slightly, "it seems silly. Everyone here knows that the tracks were already laid. Who are we fooling? The dignitaries? They must be foolish dignitaries."

"It's like a stage play," answered Mr. Chong. "We all have imaginations. It makes no difference whether we know the tracks were already laid. Everyone will watch the play…pretending tracks are being laid for the first time…and be entertained. The truth of the moment is not always important. People often elect to 'know' according to how they feel." Mr. Chong looked at Mr. Ho and respectfully nodded.

"I should think it would be the opposite," responded Mr. Ho, his eyebrows raised.

"The two are interrelated," said Mr. Chong. "Desire modifies perception. It is often like these people watching those men laying railroad tracks, pretending the second time is the first time. Fact is subordinated to desire; conventional wisdom is too often what we want to believe – whether or not it is true. We choose to 'know' that which we want to be knowledge."

"That is foolish," responded Mr. Ho.

"People are foolish," countered Mr. Chong.

"I am not foolish," Mr. Ho responded.

"You," Mr. Chong answered, turning and nodding politely, "are one of few exceptions."

Mr. Ho nodded politely in return.

"Confucius say," began Mr. Ho, "'The superior man cannot be known in little matters, but he may be entrusted with…'"

"Never mind what Confucius said," uncharacteristically interrupted Mr. Chong. "We were talking about knowledge."

"Confucius had many knowledgeable things to say!" countered Mr. Ho.

"Confucius had many thought-provoking things to say," said Mr. Chong. "I wouldn't categorize all of those sayings under 'knowledge,' however."

"Sometimes you need to twist your brain to find the truth," responded Mr. Ho.

"Usually it is quite the opposite," answered Mr. Chong. "Truth is usually simple, but it is difficult to find because of things that distort truth such as ignorance, inaccurate perception, faulty information, poor logic, and twisted brains. Mr. Ho, this conversation is twisting my brain. Could we just watch these people who are pretending to lay tracks for the first time?"

"Certainly," responded Mr. Ho who added, "I'll bet you $10 that the final rails fit perfectly."

"Oh, that is a risky wager on your part," said Mr. Chong.

Mr. Ho's eyebrows again rose. "Perhaps that is why everyone here is in such high spirits. They can pretend this is happening for the first time while knowing that – because this has already been done, scripted, if you will – a mistake is unlikely to be made, and the show will certainly have a happy ending."

"Mr. Ho," said Mr. Chong, giving a great sigh, "I salute you on your profound perception of human nature. Now, with your permission, let us watch this expensive and flamboyant exhibition of pretense."

Working toward the center from either end, 300 men laid the 600 yards of track in 20 minutes. At 5:18 p.m. on September 8, 1883, H. C. Davis, the Northern Pacific Passenger Agent who drove the first solid gold spike at the opening of the

Northern Pacific construction on February 8, 1870, drove the same spike into the track while the 5th United States Infantry artillery fired a salute. The three blows given by Mr. Davis were heard at all telegraph offices from Minnesota to New York through wires attached to the spike. Cheers rose from the celebrities in attendance including the governors of Wisconsin, Minnesota, Dakota Territory, Montana Territory, and Oregon. Henry Villard, Northern Pacific Railroad President, and Ulysses S. Grant, standing next to Davis, applauded.

Along with the cheers, there were cannon peals, and more martial music from the 5th United States Infantry band. The celebration noise reverberated from the surrounding hillsides. As the festivities began to subside, a few of the guests began making preparations for a return journey to the East Coast. The majority, including Chong Tsing Wei, would continue westward.

Trained in structural engineering, Mr. Chong came to the United States to build railroads. Chinese laborers were recruited extensively during the initial phases of railroad construction west of the Mississippi because Chinese labor was readily available, inexpensive, compliant, and believed to be more productive due to the Chinese work ethic. Mr. Chong was more valuable to men like Henry Villard and, later, Mr. Chong hoped, James J. Hill, because Mr. Chong could speak English, enabling him to act not only as a structural engineer, but also as a translator for the English-speaking foremen. While many Chinese understood some English, linguistic challenges made responding properly difficult. "Me sabe, me sabe," was the standard response when asked to do something. Mr. Chong could speak English well enough to where he did not feel self-conscious about his accent. His ability with the English language also generated some respect from foremen who regularly used his services and, through increasing familiarity, treated him differently than they did Chinese laborers.

Mr. Chong brought with him to the United States an engineering skill enjoyed by none of the foremen and, in fact, few personnel in railroad construction. From his structural engineering and construction training, he could design and direct construction of trestles and bridges, indispensable in difficult terrain. With his engineering skills and ability to speak both English and Chinese, Mr. Chong's presence became essential to railroad construction efforts. Unfortunately, because of his relative prominence, he was anathema to construction Sinophobes and distant from Chinese laborers. With the exception of his friend, Mr. Ho, Mr. Chong was close to no one.

He spoke with John Frank Steven, James J. Hill's chief surveyor, and learned that Hill intended to eventually run a railroad line over the Cascade Mountains to Seattle. Expecting his services would again be required, Mr. Chong, well-dressed, took the first of four Northern Pacific trains heading west following the ceremonies. Although Chinese, his former position enabled him to be a passenger, the only Chinese passenger on any of the four trains.

Representing the linking of America, the dignitary-filled trains passed through Missoula, Montana during the night and arrived at Lake Pend d'Oreille the following day. Wanting to impress celebrity passengers and hopefully place their town in a favored light, townsfolk at different stops prepared for weeks for the moment of the train's arrival.

The Spokane Falls townspeople were ready to present a grand reception but expected the trains would arrive in the morning rather than late in the day. Before the first train finally pulled into Spokane Falls, most of the crowd had gone home. The trains passed under three triumphal arches, and if Pastor Nordquist were aboard, he would have appreciated the inscription on the third arch: "Spokane Falls, the Minneapolis of the West."

Proceeding at the pace of an army convoy, the trains eventually passed through nearby Cheney, the town lavishly decorated with flags of every nation. Unlike the townsfolk in Spokane Falls, Cheney residents waited patiently for the arrival of the trains. After a brief stop, the trains continued on, later passing through Sprague, extensively decorated like Cheney, but also including a prominent portrait of Henry Villard and an immense transparency of a railroad locomotive.

The tracks turned south and Wallula was reached around 1:00 on Monday. The town spent an entire month in preparation for this moment, and the decorations in Wallula surpassed those of Spokane Falls, Cheney or Sprague.

Upon arriving at The Dalles on the Columbia River, the first train was greeted by an arch at the intersection of Court and Front streets, under which the train passed. Holding a large portrait of Henry Villard, the arch was surmounted by the Angel of Victory bearing a laurel wreath. The crowd was so dense, and the reception so well coordinated, that the first train, with Mr. Villard aboard, came to an unscheduled stop. A committee of young girls then boarded the train and presented each guest with a bouquet of flowers from the 400 bouquets prepared. The welcome included cheers and salutes from the local citizenry as well as music by the ladies' silver coronet band.

The Dalles welcoming committee formally greeted each train in the same way but, as in all cities, the last train created the greatest excitement because it was the train carrying Ulysses S. Grant, former Union Army General-in-Chief, a position considered much higher than just former president.

The ceremonies, decorations and entertainment provided thus far were dwarfed by what the passengers encountered when they awoke the following morning in Portland.

Mr. Chong looked out the window at a city buried beneath a mass of evergreens, bunting, banners, flags, models, portraits, and transparencies. Portland was awash with the flags of the United States, Germany, England and other nations.

The city, business firms and private individuals outdid themselves, rivaling each other in the extent and cost of their decorations. From early morning, the streets were lined with humanity watching a parade so extensive as to impress even those who had organized the pageant. The parade was led by 78 Oregon pioneers, some of whom had crossed the continent a decade before the start of the Civil War. Following the pioneers were more than 100 horse-drawn parade displays decorated and inscribed with all sorts of appropriate models. Those were followed by six companies of the 21st U.S. Infantry Division, mounted and dismounted policemen, a dozen marching bands, and Battery E of the 1st U.S. Artillery Brigade.

The entire city participated. Mr. Chong never imagined anything like it.

The following day, the first train of the entourage left for what, passengers were told, was "New Tacoma" – implying that somewhere was an old Tacoma. Actually, Mr. Chong would discover, there was. Some Tacoma people did not like the way things were done in Tacoma and started New Tacoma just north of Tacoma. A few years later, however, the competing factions set aside their differences and merged to form new old Tacoma.

Arriving in Tacoma, passengers found the entire city dressed up as if for a major holiday. The immense triple arch spanning Pacific Avenue had on its southern face the triumphant one-word inscription: "Terminus."

From Wednesday through Thursday, the passengers were entertained either in Tacoma or on board the steamer *Queen of the Pacific*. Mr. Chong walked around the city, inspected Commencement Bay, and participated in an excursion. Dressed similarly to other dignitaries but saying nothing to the others, he was content to see what there was to see.

Upon returning to the north end of downtown Tacoma, Mr. Chong felt comfortable with the surroundings and was impressed with the views of Commencement Bay and the huge, snow-covered mountain that many years earlier Capt. George Vancouver had named Mt. Rainier after his friend, Capt. Peter Rainier. The Tacoma people, however, continued to call it by its Indian name, Mt. Tacoma. While standing on a Pacific Avenue corner, Mr. Chong decided to converse with a tall, older man whose face he did not recognize and who, Mr. Chong believed, must be a local resident.

"This is a very nice place. I like New Tacoma very much," Mr. Chong volunteered to the man as a compliment to Tacoma.

The tall man with a huge, iron-grey mustache gazed back with a blank, languid look as he studied Mr. Chong and how he was dressed. The man was curious about how Mr. Chong learned to speak English but said nothing and looked away.

Although Mr. Chong was well aware of the animosity with which individuals of European descent treated Chinese, he had grown accustomed to a modicum of respect because of his position in railroad construction. The tall man with the iron-grey mustache had never seen Mr. Chong before and, within the aura of class consciousness that covered the country like a ubiquitous toxic plume, the man was annoyed that Mr. Chong spoke to him. Mr. Chong attempted to elicit a friendly response from the man.

"Where do you live in New Tacoma?" asked Mr. Chong pleasantly. Mr. Chong inadvertently introduced an additional source of antagonism to the already difficult chemistry between himself and the tall man with the iron-grey mustache.

"Tacoma. It's jest Tacoma," the man growled.

"Oh. Just Tacoma; not 'New Tacoma.'"

"An' I don't live here."

The man began to twirl the end of his mustache as his face clouded over like a winter sky above Commencement Bay. He decided to continue the conversation.

"Where y' from?"

"I work on railroad for three, four years designing bridges, and translate English," Mr. Chong responded with some pride.

"That's not where you're *from*. I asked, 'Where y' *from*?'"

"China."

"Well, y' ain't working on the railroad no more, are y'? Yer not buildin' no more bridges are y'?

"No, I came on the train to New Tacoma, uh, Tacoma," Mr. Chong responded respectfully.

"You're not trying to get smart with me now are y', Chinaman?"

Mr. Chong was not exactly sure what this question meant.

"I do not understand what you mean."

"I mean these parts ain't got no room for no smart-mouth Chinee. If you know what's good for ya, you'll get back on that train and, after you get off somewhere else, head back t' China."

Recently Mr. Chong had felt no fear because of his race, but now fear flushed through him, and his initially favorable impression of Tacoma dissipated like locomotive steam.

"I'll leave now."

"Y' do that," the man growled.

The large man with the iron-grey mustache glared at Mr. Chong without blinking, without moving. Chong turned and, head down, walked toward the train terminal. Tacoma is not a good place for me. Perhaps Seattle will be better, Mr. Chong thought.

But perhaps not.

The following Friday afternoon, the first and second trains arrived in Seattle. Mr. Villard made a speech and embarked on the *Queen of the Pacific*.

Mr. Chong decided to stay in Seattle to speak with a local representative of James J. Hill.

The remainder of the passengers departed in different directions, some returning directly to the East Coast, but most planning to visit the new national park at Yellowstone, compliments of William H. Clagett, and other interesting sights before heading home.

Thus ended the grand celebration.

———●———

Chong Tsing Wei aimlessly walked up 2nd Ave. in Seattle toward the intersection with Madison St. The future seemed bleak. Despondent, hands in his pockets, he made eye contact with no one, and wondered what further purpose he might serve in this new country. He thought of the man with the iron-gray mustache. Perhaps it was hopeless for him now; perhaps he should return to China. Mr. Chong knew he could serve many purposes here, however. He was good at what he did in railroad construction, and in his lifetime the opportunities to do what he did best would never be greater than at this moment in this country. He thought hard about which direction to take and, again, concluded, yes, he should offer his services to James J. Hill's organization. He would help build the Great Northern Railroad.

Late fall 1883, Eagle City

Among those who read about the Prichard Creek gold strike was former Arizona Territory Deputy Marshal Wyatt Earp.

Tombstone, Arizona was dying; full of drunks, con men, prospectors down on their luck, and men who were simply unwelcome in more civilized parts of the country. The OK Corral shoot-out was behind Earp, but not the animosity lingering among some of the town folk. Wyatt lost two brothers, Morgan and Virgil. Doc Holiday was gone; put in a sanitarium. Tombstone was never much of a place to do business. It was time to move on. Earp left Tombstone and rode to multiple destinations, not staying long in any.

In fall 1883, James Earp and Wyatt Earp rode into Eagle City on the east side of Prichard Creek. The community at that moment consisted of tents, large and small. Until permanent buildings were built, the Earp brothers put up a large tent and picked up where they left off in Tombstone. The name of their establishment was the White Elephant Saloon.

Meanwhile, following the Golden Spike Ceremony, William H. Clagett read about how people were flocking to the gold strike on Prichard Creek, and wondered if it might not be his next big opportunity. Clagett corresponded with acerbic Samuel Clemens who encouraged "Billy," as Clemens had called him since Clagett was a kid, to continue seeking public office in the new territories. Clemens was a friend of Clagett's father, Thomas Clagett, a judge and newspaper editor who published editorials so critical of McClellan during the early Civil War that Union soldiers stormed into his office, confiscated his printing press, and threw it into the Mississippi River.

Like his father, William Clagett was a practiced orator and comfortable at the fore. Deducing that this new gold strike would attract another growing population in need of leadership, Clagett rode into disorganized Eagle City a short while after the Earp brothers, quickly became familiar with the general area, and introduced himself to as many as would shake hands. Soon he did what came naturally: he gave an impassioned public speech letting all know, beyond the gold, the area's potential for greatness. In the absence of a mayor, town council or law enforcement, Clagett filled the leadership void and began giving direction. Before Eagle City began to permanently take root, William Clagett directed arriving prospectors and tradesmen to begin construction of a new settlement five miles up Prichard Creek to the east at a location closer to where, Clagett said, there was more gold.

Few prospectors questioned his judgment. He was, after all, a former United States Congressman, the only one in town, and if there wasn't any gold nearby, well, there was probably gold around somewhere. It was a gamble, but since most of the land around Eagle City was already claimed, newcomers and others followed Clagett. The site of the new settlement approximated the location of Prichard's Murray Claim, and the new town being constructed in the early snow of a north Idaho fall was initially called Murrayville, then just Murray, attracting a cast of characters more remarkable than Tombstone, Dodge City, Leadville or any other Old West town, although Murray's story would remain bottled up for well over a century.

38

Monday, November 10, 1883, Minnesota

Momma," said Inga who was interested in languages, "I've noticed that a certain Swedish word for wet snow has no directly equivalent word in English. Slush is something slightly different."

"Snow has a greater effect on life in Norway, Sweden and Finland," said Anna, "so there are some Scandinavian words and phrases relating to snow for which there are no direct English equivalents, but words like 'flurry,' 'blizzard,' 'powder,' 'slush' and 'drifts' provide as much verbal imagery as we need for snow's varying states."

From the girls' perspective, the snow provided a holiday mystique that covered Minnesota like an enchanted blanket. The girls went on sleigh rides where they admired powder-dusted, river rock chimneys on farmhouses aside small lakes or full creeks rushing down from nearby forests. When returning, the Nordquist windows glowed from the large fireplace and candles brightening the family hearth inside. The white Lutheran church with its multi-paned lancet windows and modest bell tower/steeple looked perfect and inviting when coated in winter snow. The settings were idyllic, and that night Inga wrote descriptive verses of moonlit snowiness outside.

> *'Neath full winter's moon of pale shining light,*
> *Snow blankets glisten with sparkles of white*
> *Growing brighter and gayer as moonbeams alight,*
> *Wee faeries aglow dancing bright in the night.*

Winter was a wonderland for Inga, Esther and little Rachel. On the other hand, such verses were at a distant station from idioms like "deathly cold," "cabin fever" and "solstice insanity," ominous phrases that actually fell short of depicting how dismal, even deadly, winter could become.

Minnesota winter temperatures turned the countryside into an icebox, and inside the fireplace-heated church sanctuary, Pastor Amos Nordquist reached down and picked up a piece of paper from the church floor while still wearing his heavy overcoat. Large Minneapolis congregations had maintenance men and janitors who would perform this task after services, but in Pastor Nordquist's rural congregation, most operational tasks fell to him. These responsibilities had their drawbacks, but also their rewards. The paper Amos Nordquist held had a child's drawing of…him.

Amos's smile radiated slowly like the winter solstice sunrise as he studied the drawing of himself standing in the pulpit, delivering yesterday's sermon. He didn't think his ears were that large…nor was his mouth, although he had little doubt there were those who did. Amos chuckled and began to put the paper in the garbage can, but changed his mind, and neatly placed it on a nearby pew. He would affix it on the wall above his office desk as a humorous reminder that others did not always see him as he did.

While carrying the garbage can up the aisle to the front pews, Pastor Nordquist thought about Alma Johanssen, mother of three, wife of Elbert Johanssen. Alma used to be a pretty woman and, although Elbert worked hard to support her, he had always been affectionless. Wordless. Elbert was unable give affection as other men did, and Amos sensed something happened years earlier that blunted Elbert's ability to be loving. Alma's life was that of a companion, caretaker, farmhand, cook, and a mother until early last winter when her children went to play on the ice for the first time that season.

It should have been safe. Others were out on the ice. Temperatures had been below freezing for some time.

As she did in the past, she allowed them to go on the ice, but not far from shore. The short distance had not mattered. In one unguarded moment she kissed her three children and sent them out to play.

Late that cold, dark afternoon, Elbert and two men from the congregation further broke open the ice near the shore and retrieved the little bodies.

Then one night several weeks after the children's funeral, while Elbert slept, Alma walked out of their sod and log cabin into the dark, snowy expanse, lay down, and went to sleep forever.

Pastor Nordquist stood motionlessly reliving the memory.

At the second funeral, an ashen Elbert stared condemningly inward. After her children died, his wife kept going until heartache, winter depression, silence and absence of affection pushed her out the door. Pastor Nordquist worried about Elbert; quiet Elbert who seldom spoke. What had he never spoken of; what event, what secret thing, was kept locked in his heart?

Several Sundays passed and Elbert was not in church. Normally this would not have bothered Pastor Nordquist, but his intuition told him something else was wrong.

A month after Alma was buried, following church, Amos, Anna and a cousin of Elbert, Emmy Soderquist, went by sleigh to Elbert's snow-covered cabin, but did not find Elbert home. They waited for a short while, but there was still no sign of Elbert. Pastor Nordquist decided to look around. Behind the snow-covered dwelling, Amos saw a deep depression through chest-high snow, obviously made by someone pushing through it. The depression was mostly covered with new snow, led to the west, and was not visible from the front or sides of the cabin. Amos pushed along through the depression. At a distance the depression stopped. Pastor Nordquist pushed forward to the depression's end and began to push and brush the snow away. He found Elbert buried under the fresh snowfall, curled up on his side, his expression slightly contorted with his teeth bare, as if grimacing. Elbert's closed eyes had ice around the edges, and his cheerless face was as white as the snow around him as he lay frozen in the same place Alma died.

Standing motionless in the sanctuary, Amos replayed the events in his mind. Pressured by the most extreme adversity, a tenacious human heart can rise to extraordinary levels, Amos thought, but if badly broken, can will itself to die. If only the heart were as simple to fix as loose shingles or a frozen pump.

He bent down and picked up some items left after church, and placed them in the garbage can at his side, thinking that most of the solution rested with the 11th Commandment: "A new commandment I give to you, that you love one another; even as I have loved you, also love one another." This meant loving oneself as well; and while most had no problem doing that, some did. Pastor Nordquist used the 11th Commandment as a sermon topic many times. The admonition to love is potentially such a great source of happiness, thought Pastor Nordquist as he finished cleaning the sanctuary, and, like prayer, a cure for more ills than we know about. Pastor Nordquist long ago concluded that, far from being the demands of an oppressive Creator, the commandments were given to make people happy. Their disobedience certainly has the opposite effect.

Even for Minnesota, the weather outside the sanctuary was particularly cold as the temperature began dropping with the declining distance between the late afternoon sun and the southwestern horizon. With low temperatures, no snow had fallen for nearly two weeks. Pastor Nordquist walked with broom and garbage can toward the foyer, opened the church rear-entry door, stepped out into the cold while quickly closing the door behind him, and crunched through the frozen snow behind the church, where he placed the covered garbage can, its contents to be used when starting fires in the church's big fireplace. He turned and walked along the icy path to the large, parsonage back porch, heavily stocked with firewood.

Steadying himself against the wall next to the kitchen door, he took off his snow-encrusted boots before loading up his arms with firewood. His arms full, he awkwardly opened the door, stepped inside and shut the door with his right foot, allowing only brief entrance of winter.

Pastor Nordquist found himself instantly vacationing in a wonderfully warm, aromatic country kitchen – a home within a home – that Anna occupied much of the day. Presently she was making applesauce while dinner cooked. The smell of the wood-heated oven was, of itself, pleasant, but when mixed with aromas of cooking applesauce, a baking chicken-and-vegetable pie, and cookies nearly done on the stovetop, the integrated aromas were, for Amos, payment for working several hours outside. A kitchen is a wonderful place, he thought, breathing in the mixed smells. Applesauce, the last edible stop along the path from blossom to compost.

When Amos dumped the firewood into the wood box aside the oven, it sounded like a building collapsing. Amos took off his gloves, hat and overcoat, hung them next to the back door, and walked to Anna who was peeling more apples on the wooden drain board next to their slightly chipped porcelain sink. He stopped and stood behind her, momentarily placing his palm on her shoulder, signaling his presence. She stopped peeling as he held her waist with both hands.

With his right hand he reached around, gently removed the apple peeler from her hand and placed it on the drain board. After he held her for a moment, he turned her around and lovingly embraced her.

She pressed her cheek against his chest, and the two of them gently swayed as she plugged into his outlet of affection. He lifted her chin with the crook of his right index finger and kissed her for a prolonged moment – it made her feel beautiful and desired – while she held him tightly. After a second or two, he let his hands slide down to her waist, and looked down at her lovingly. She looked back gratefully. Whatever might befall them, she knew she would always have this.

"I need to finish, dear," she whispered after a moment, implying that he release her so she could get back to work. No reaction. "As you know full well, Nels Hanseth could arrive at any time."

Amos allowed his hands to drop to his side, kissing Anna on the forehead before she turned toward the drain board.

"It's always nice to see Nels, of course," said Anna, again peeling the aging apples. "From his letter, it sounds like he has something important he wants to discuss."

"Yah," replied Amos, standing next to her and washing his hands, "this is more than a normal business and social call. If he wouldn't say specifically why he is coming, it's important. Those synod people are very busy. All the new churches in so many new places."

"I know," said Anna. "Hoping against hope, but I suspect he wants us to move again. I wouldn't mind staying in one place for a while."

"Well… I guess he'll tell us when he arrives. It's a long way for him to ride here, especially in the winter. I just want to make his stay worth the trip. The rest, the Lord will handle."

At a distance, the horse and rider slowly approached the surrounding snow-covered fields and trees beginning to turn silver and gray in the late after-noon. It had been a long ride, but the times and distances dictated such journeys. Although the area was becoming more populated, there was no stage or rail to where the Nordquists lived. Roads in winter were sometimes reduced to trails, and mail was delivered weekly to a distant general store that also served as a post office. In winter, the pace of life was as slow as tree growth. Whatever Nels had to say was important enough to require saying it in person and, considering Nels' position in the synod, Anna was 99% certain of what the message would be.

Nels Hanseth's responsibility was great: he directed church planting. He sent his friend Amos Nordquist to the Nordquists' present rural location, and at that time told Amos and Anna, again, the position would not be long-term.

Nels, who greatly respected Amos, said he needed a man with Amos's physical, intellectual, emotional and spiritual strengths for larger responsibilities. Amos's versatility enabled him to confront and overcome challenges that lesser men-of-the-cloth could not surmount when starting a new congregation in an isolated but growing area. Amos, Anna and their daughters dutifully left more comfortable surroundings many times and traveled considerable distances north and west where Amos coordinated new sanctuary and parsonage construction. Anna, tired of moving, did not want to move again.

As Nels Hanseth approached the Nordquist parsonage, weighing what he needed to say and the reaction it might bring, Anna had no misgivings about priority. It was Nels's responsibility to insure that the Great Commission be exercised. What Anna didn't want, she knew, came secondary. She sighed heavily, resigning herself to the inevitable, and prepared to welcome a truly gracious human being into her home.

Nels, still strong and agile although in his 60s, had decidedly Scandinavian features and, with his graying hair, strong jaw, kindly countenance and ready smile, looked like the godly man he was. Although they first met in Minneapolis, Nels' family was originally from Vänersborg, a small town on Lake Vänern northeast of Göteborg. Amos was familiar with Vänersborg. Quietly dedicated to serving God, their compatibility was great, their families grew close, and their bond was strong.

Nels knew very well what was going through Anna's mind. He would present his case accordingly, knowing that whatever was needed, with God's guidance Amos was willing to do. Shortly before sunset, Nels rode up the long Nordquist driveway.

"Nels! Nels! Welcome! Are you okay?" hollered Amos from the front porch as he gingerly navigated the icy porch steps to embrace Nels.

"Well, I just rode about twenty thousand miles, by golly," laughed Nels in his heavy Scandinavian accent as he dismounted. With his gloved hands, he pressed his arms and shoulders to insure they were still there. "I guess I am in one piece."

"Nels!" hollered Anna, the front door partially open, "Come inside out of the cold!"

"Yah," encouraged Amos, "you go in the house and I will take care of Flicka here."

Nels walked up the steps, stepped inside, closed the door, gave Anna a long hug, and entered the living room where he subsequently received hugs from the Nordquist daughters, Inga, Esther and little Rachel who greeted "Grandpa Nels" with delight.

"Ah, you are all growing up! Getting so big," laughed Nels.

"We haven't seen you since we lived down by Kindred," said middle daughter, Esther, age 6, excitedly. "Why did you come up here?"

"Well, I will be telling your mother and father shortly," answered Nels, anxious to do exactly that.

"Good," said Esther as Pastor Nordquist came through the back door, "then let's eat dinner now."

"It would help, of course," said her father as he walked into the living room, "if you would put dinner on the table now that Mr. Hanseth is here. Nels, join me in the living room while the girls get things ready."

While the girls began setting the living/dining room table, Anna, Amos and Nels sat at the table and talked about changes since they last visited, especially how much the country was growing.

"I must tell you that immigration of Scandinavians, everyone, is unbelievably extensive," said Nels. "Nearly a fifth of all Swedes in the world live here now."

"Is that so?" said Anna. "My goodness, I knew the proportion was significant but not that significant."

"Yah. As you know, it is possible to live in certain areas of Minnesota without ever needing to read, write or speak anything but Swedish. Books, newspapers, stores…it is no different than Sweden."

"Well, yah, but how long is that going to last?" asked Pastor Nordquist. "This isn't Sweden. The language of America is English."

"You know, that is sure true, by golly," responded Nels, "but you know what helps? Quite a few Scandinavians, like us, of course, already speak English – and many are learning fast because, in comparison to other immigrants, we have an advantage due to high literacy levels in Norway and Sweden. We come here already knowing how to read and write." Nels was proud of this. "Swedish, Norwegian, shoor," added Nels. "But, as you know, the languages and alphabets and linguistics are not all that different." Nels smiled. "So, English? We have a head start." Nels clapped his hands together. "Over time you will quickly be seeing a lot of English-speaking Swedes."

"I hope they speak English better than you," said Esther as she placed fresh, hot bread on the table.

"Esther!" said Anna brusquely, openly disgusted as the others stifled smiles. "That will be just enough!" Turning to Nels, about to stand up, Anna began apologizing, "Nels, I apologize. I'm so sorry. She's…"

"Don't be concerned," interrupted Nels, placing a restraining hand on Anna's arm, precluding the immediate remedial measures Anna was about to take. "I will improve," he laughed.

"As I was saying," Nels continued, "the American melting pot that is now so boiling, while concentrated in the cities, is spilling out all over the country." His face became expressionless. "Boomtowns in the West are experiencing a continual influx of prospectors, miners, merchants, cowmen, bartenders, blacksmiths, trappers, gamblers, you-name-it! But few representatives of the Lord." Nels looked at Amos and then Anna. "This concerns me."

Anna's eyes grew larger as she obliquely studied Nels while repositioning her silverware. Oh, no. What is this? The West, thought Anna. Boomtowns. Where does he want us to go? Thoughts flashed through her mind. Gamblers and murderers. Prostitution. Larceny. Alcohol and angry men in lawless places.

"There is lawlessness," said Nels, intuiting Anna's thoughts. "But in a boomtown where God's word as yet has no place," Nels added, "what should we expect?"

39

Anna looked at Nels, conflicted, understanding the need her husband could provide but genuinely concerned about his safety and the negative effect this environment – where men could be insensate, dissolute, and treacherous, and the few women in town were capitalizing on being the few women in town – could have on her daughters, all of whom, like their mother, would be very attractive. This move would be more than an inconvenience.

Her mouth partially open, Anna looked down to one side and sighed softly. Certainly, God's word is badly needed but…

"I know about what you have read, and I know this concerns you," said Nels, looking at Anna, "especially when considering your three beautiful daughters. Going to places without law and order is frightening. The population growth – present and future – in some of these places, however, is too great to overlook. And what we do is too important not to do," said Nels adamantly. "Amos is too innovative and productive to keep under a bushel here. It is a challenge. I could choose a lesser man, or choose no one and remain comfortable, but that is not what we are about, is it?"

Nels looked intently at the others. "Let me tell you what I think, and the options." Nels turned his chair in order to more directly face Amos and Anna.

"Right now, there are several places filling up with men," said Nels, "but two places, while they have many saloons, to my knowledge have no churches. A third may have a new, small congregation at best. The three places are Miles City in southeast Montana, Eagle City in northern Idaho Territory, and Seattle in Washington Territory.

"Miles City is a cow town. Lots of drinking and gambling. Seattle and the surrounding region – Puget Sound, they call it – are growing leaps and bounds. Eagle City doesn't even have buildings yet…just tents, from what I know. But there was just a major gold strike there, and prospectors and all kinds of other people are arriving daily."

Anna listened warily.

"Who's already there?" she asked as her daughters finished putting food on the table.

"As far as specific persons, I don't know," responded Nels, unaware that Eagle City had attracted very interesting people, some famous and some infamous. "I just know that both Miles City and Eagle City need the word of God and need it in a hurry."

"Of the three towns, which one's safest?" asked Anna.

"People can sin anywhere, but I'd say Seattle is safest. Miles City? Yes, things get out-of-hand occasionally, but usually settle down. Places where gold is discovered, like Eagle City, have a lot of contention, claim jumping, and big-stake gambling, to go with the drinking and raucous behavior. Men come because there's gold, and as more gold is discovered, there's more wealth in circulation, and sometimes that stirs up greater contention. Without any law enforcement, there is more larceny and murder than in a cattle town."

"When do you expect law enforcement in these places?" asked Amos.

"Seattle already has it. Miles City may be getting it; there appears to be an element of civility in Miles City."

The Nordquist sisters began seating themselves around the table.

"Eagle City? Like I said, people are still living in tents; the town's just getting started. There hasn't been enough time to expect organized law enforcement." Nels sighed. "Except there's an interesting group called 'The Committee.' It's made up of prospectors. They provide retribution should anyone harm a prospector – minimum, an eye for an eye. If you kill a prospector, they'll kill you; if you steal from a prospector, they take from you…or they'll take from you and throw in severe physical punishment. My understanding is they don't protect anyone other than prospectors."

"It sounds like an interesting place," said Amos, drawing a stark look from Anna.

"Except for The Committee, there are no laws and no formal law enforcement," said Nels, his eyes narrowing. "It's a dangerous place, by golly."

"Which one is in greatest need of God's word?" asked Pastor Nordquist.

"Eagle City," responded Nels. "I say 'Eagle City' because it is growing the most rapidly, but without formal direction, and therefore has the greatest need for Christ and Christian morality."

Nels looked at Amos seriously.

"I wouldn't want you to take your family there right now."

"Then you want me to go to either Miles City or Seattle."

"No, that's not what I meant," said Nels. "This is a decision that should be made with direction from the Lord, a decision that requires vigilant prayer and careful listening to that still, small voice. The distance is great. Until a parsonage is built, we have no place in Seattle, Miles City or Eagle City for either you or your family to stay. I do not think it wise to take your family with you."

"Leave them here?" asked Amos in disbelief.

"Only until you are settled – at least have a parsonage built and, perhaps, have begun sanctuary construction. You should have conducted several worship services in your living room, establishing a small but growing congregation, a settling influence in the community. Above all, you should become comfortable enough with your circumstances to where you believe it's time to send for them. You will be pioneering."

Nels glanced toward the dinner table and the impatient faces of the Nordquist daughters, seated and waiting.

"Miles City or Eagle City or Seattle – when should I make my decision?" asked Pastor Nordquist.

"I suggest you decide between Miles City and either Eagle City or Seattle when you reach Miles City and have spent a few days there," said Nels Hanseth. "You'll have to trust God for the direction when in Miles City, according to the circumstances you find there. Meanwhile, as I said, pray constantly."

"Sounds exciting," said Esther with a little bounce. Anna looked at Esther wanting to say, "Too exciting," but said nothing.

"Daddy," asked Esther, "why do they have the name 'City' if they're not cities – one doesn't even have any buildings?"

"It's an attempt to entice East Coast people to come to the town – start businesses," said Amos. "Perhaps the town founders think that placing the word 'City' in the name enhances the possibility that their little town will attract more notice. In some cases, East Coast millionaires might consider investing."

"Do the East Coast millionaires really believe a place with just tents is a city?" asked Esther skeptically. "If they're that dumb, how did they become millionaires?"

"There are," said Nels with a chuckle, "some millionaires who have just been very fortunate – there is no other way to explain it – but most millionaires did not become millionaires by being incautious. No, most everyone, and certainly most millionaires, are not fooled. I suspect people who start small settlements, naming them Something-City, are hoping they will become actual cities within a short period of time…although I'm not certain what difference the name would make. Certainly Boston, Philadelphia and Minneapolis are cities even though not formally named as such."

"Well, then," began Esther, "the smart thing is don't include the word 'City' in the name if you want a little place to become a big place."

"Esther," said Inga with quiet impatience. "You should let Mr. Hanseth talk."

"Esther," said Anna, "Inga is right. Let Mr. Hanseth continue. I'm very interested in what else he has to say."

"Amos, pray," said Nels. "Pray for discernment when you get to Miles City. I cannot tell you at what moment you should make your decision, Amos. Again, follow God's leading, and if you sense no discernible direction, my intuition is that Eagle City is probably the most fertile field for a new ministry. Frankly, there are others I can send to Miles City, but you, Amos, are the only man I would send to Eagle City."

"And Seattle?"

"First spend time in Miles City and, if you elect to continue west, then Eagle City. If not Eagle City, continue to Seattle."

"So ultimately it's my decision to make."

"With the leading of the Lord."

"Nels, no disrespect intended," said Anna, "but I wish the decision could be made sooner. I'd just like to know what's going to happen."

Amos looked at his wife, looked down at his plate and stretched his arms.

"I can tell you what is going to happen," said Amos knowingly. He paused.

"Well? What?"

"Dinner. Nels, after riding '20,000 miles', are you hungry?"

"Yah," smiled Nels. "I didn't come all this way just to do the work of the Lord."

Amos looked at Anna. "See the effect your cooking has on people?"

"I'm sure," said Anna. The pervasive country-kitchen aroma was affecting everyone.

"Dad," said Esther, "I'm hungry. Can you say the prayer?" It was not a question.

Amos deferred to Nels who then prayed an all-encompassing prayer as if it would be his last chance on earth to entreat and thank the Lord. When Nels finally finished, Esther, rolling her eyes, dove in.

"When should I expect to leave?" asked Amos just before taking his first mouthful.

"Unfortunately, Amos," responded Nels, chewing, "God's timing is often 'now.' When it comes to spreading the word of the Lord, we never have time to wait."

"I know nothing about the routes to Miles City or Eagle City or Seattle," said Pastor Nordquist. "I know nothing about what to expect along the way."

"The new railroad simplifies things although there are still hazards," said Nels. "I'll be honest. I've read about trains developing mechanical problems… boiler explosions. There have been landslides, avalanches. Floods. A short while ago the Missouri flooded; a great many livestock and several people were swept down the river. Trains first went over the Missouri River on barges during the summer and on tracks laid over the ice in winter – some people apparently didn't mind taking chances – but that stopped when Northern Pacific built a bridge. Still, what should be an uneventful trip could be otherwise. And if you choose to continue west from Miles City, you'll travel to Thompson Falls at the base of the Bitterroot Mountains where you'll need to buy a horse and follow a trail north through mountain passes to Eagle City. The trek is not too long, but in the middle of winter, the distance will seem great."

Nels put down his fork for a moment.

"That is why I'm asking *you* to do this, Amos. It is an important assignment, but there are not many in the ministry whom I could trust to overcome the obstacles and challenges along the way. I have no doubt you'll accomplish what you need to accomplish, and the Commission of the Lord will be greatly served."

The dinner was made more pleasurable by the contrasting weather through which Nels had ridden, but Anna had lost her appetite, and her stomach felt as taut as the frozen clotheslines outside the back door.

"Will Daddy see any Indians?" asked Rachel, three, her beautiful, long, auburn hair shimmering like polished bronze.

"Possibly," said Nels as he smiled at Rachel, "but no doubt they will see him first." Nels sat back.

"There have been no problems with the Plains Indians for a while – that incident with Custer will probably not be repeated – and I don't expect any danger of that sort along the way. If I did," Nels looked at Amos, "I would not be sitting here."

"Daddy used to know General Custer," said Esther with animation. Amos looked at Anna. "Daddy was a chaplain in General Custer's army during the war! And if Daddy were at Little Big Horn, ahhhlllll the soldiers would still be alive because, if Daddy were there, God would have saved them from the Indians."

"Fortunately, Esther," said Anna, "your father was not there to test that theory. Otherwise, neither he, nor you, I might add, would be here."

"Will Daddy be going near Little Big Horn?" asked Inga.

"Yes," answered Nels, "very near, in fact."

Anna sat expressionlessly looking at Nels, not eating.

She knew the untamed American West needed taming, and taming required God's word be delivered by brave, resourceful men like her husband. She heard the stories of western towns, and at that moment simply wished she knew what was true. Eagle City where men were arriving from all over…yet there weren't even permanent buildings at the moment. And no law enforcement. Except for a group known as The Committee. Which must have come into existence of necessity, and which remains in existence for the same reason. Was Eagle City what it sounded like?

The day after a somber Christmas, as his wife looked on apprehensively from a short distance, Amos studied his packing list one more time, attempting to discern any items not absolutely necessary for the 600 mile trek from northern Minnesota to Miles City and, more probably, another 600 miles to northern Idaho where extensive gold discoveries were occurring, attracting prospectors by the thousands – with an equal number of souls to save.

December 27, 1883

Seated in a living room chair, Pastor Nordquist once again concluded all list items were essential. He studied the list many times, but the departure hour was fast approaching; one more look to assure his burden was light, and it was time to leave. Amos read of pioneers who began the western journey with belongings, all initially considered essential, only to abandon items along the trail in an effort to arrive alive. He would be on a train much of the way, but still would take only what was absolutely necessary, no more.

While difficult winter weather conditions would not be escaped as he rode the train through the Dakotas, the Great Plains and beyond, he was confident there would be no mishap. Anna did not share this confidence, however, and worried about him. Eventually under better weather and, hopefully, social conditions, she and their three daughters would follow her husband.

"Amos," began Anna anxiously, looking at her husband. "It's the middle of winter; you'll have to ride long distances through wastelands…." Her facial expression mirrored her concern. "I don't know who you'll meet." For a moment she looked away.

Her eyes became moist. She knew from many Minnesota winters that her husband could handle inclement weather, should something unexpected happen. What upset her was everything else, those ubiquitous "what-if"s buzzing about Anna's brain like Minnesota mosquitoes, pestering her unmercifully.

"Amos, are you sure you have thought of everything you'll need? Is there anything else? I'm so sorry to be like this but…"

Again, her voice faded as she looked at Amos with trepid anxiety, shrugged her shoulders and sighed. Amos put down the list.

"As I have told you several times now, many others have gone before me and have arrived safely," assured Amos. "The path is worn. The trip will be long, but I will be very careful. This is the Lord's leading. Trust Him for my safety."

Amos looked at his wife lovingly as she looked back at him with love liberally mixed with apprehension.

"I will be fine, Anna."

Amos stood up and walked over to his wife, placing his arms around her as she tried to maintain her composure while wishing she were dreaming and that he was not really leaving to start a new congregation in a place neither knew much about, perhaps someplace called Eagle City in Idaho Territory which, as far as Anna Nordquist was concerned, was on the dark side of the moon. She wondered why anyone would have gone there for any reason, but then considered some might ask the same question about her relocating in northwestern Minnesota. There were families and permanency in northwestern Minnesota, however. Presently there was none of either around Eagle City, and the community developing in Eagle City, she considered, might be worse than no community at all. Her stomach was in knots. She badly wanted to know what lie ahead.

Part Two

Northwest Turmoil

1884–1889

40

December 29, 1883

After leaving Brainerd, Minnesota, as the train rolled west, Pastor Amos Nordquist was looking out the coach window at a dusting snowfall, but by the time the train approached Dakota Territory, he was being mesmerized by a high plains blizzard, the snow so thick, he couldn't see where it was coming from.

Amos glanced around at coach occupants, all studying the thick snowfall outside. Across the aisle was a woman with her young daughter, perhaps six, and in front of Amos sat a well-dressed, older gentleman with a white mustache, silently grateful to be traveling in an enclosed railcar, trying not to wonder what would happen if something broke down.

At a stop west of Fargo, while the engineer and brakeman checked train car couplings, Pastor Nordquist felt restless, stood up, put on his hat, and stepped off the train for a moment in the driving snowstorm to stretch his legs. Muted by the falling snow, the wind sounded like the heavy breathing of an approaching giant, a ghostly "Hhhoowwhhhhaaahhhoowhhhh…," repeated over and over as if admonishing Pastor Nordquist to turn back! Standing slightly slumped over in his heavy fur coat, his hands deep in his pockets, Pastor Nordquist sensed the eeriness, the presence of his ancient nemesis, and did not heed the warning; he was not going back, for while the snow and wind made visibility impossible, the spiritual path before him was clear.

During the second day of the journey, temperatures dropped, and the snowstorm, as if becoming too cold to continue, stayed to the east, allowing the train to enter a land blanketed by sunlit snow cover, bright enough to hurt Amos's eyes. Beneath the icy, blue prairie sky, wisping winds began the job of shooing snow into drifts, and the passengers were more relaxed as the train continued toward Miles City in eastern Montana Territory.

As the hours passed, Pastor Nordquist thought, planned, considered, reconsidered and reminisced, for there was little conversation among passengers. Amos worked on designs for his next parsonage and the church. Simplicity is the essence of good design, he reminded himself. He also organized liturgy and prepared sermons.

The food on board was interesting, and his entire effort thus far seemed rewarded when he was served a new dessert: ice cream with a chocolate sauce poured over the top, and "crème Chantilly" around the edge. My golly, thought Amos as he tasted it. Wouldn't Anna love this?

Heading west without incident, the train arrived in Miles City which was as Nels Hanseth described. There were already representatives of the Lord, however, providing spiritual leadership countering cow town temptations. The battle in Miles City was already underway.

Pastor Nordquist looked apprehensively westward from Miles City over the expansive snow-covered prairie, and considered traveling another 600 miles to the Bitterroot Mountains in winter. Am I being called there or am I not? he asked himself. He stood looking westward, deliberating, and turned toward Miles City. He prayed, asking direction. The sensation within him was not encouraging; his destination was not Miles City. Without further consideration, Amos decided to continue on to Eagle City. He reboarded the train, took a seat, and thought as he sat, arms folded, apprehensively looking out the train window, *alea iacta est*. The die is cast.

On the morning of the 4th day as the train ran along the Yellowstone River roughly 150 miles west of Miles City, the new town of Billings came into view. When the train slowed as it pulled into Billings, Pastor Nordquist looked out the window at a young community with construction expanding almost as fast as prospective residents arrived although, apart from the railroad, there was no evident reason why they were arriving.

"Folks, the train will have to stay here in Billings at least two nights, possibly more," said the conductor. "We have some maintenance issues, and have to wait for parts from back east." There were groans of resignation. Amos decided to walk around the town, interested in what was in Billings. Why Billings? he wondered as he stepped off the train. Since he didn't immediately see a barber shop, he went to the next profession most able to answer his questions.

"Well, it's an interesting story," said the bartender. "Folks didn't want to chance comin' out here because of the In'jins. But when the In'jins became peaceful, folks started comin', slow at first, and then more. Over yonder," the bartender pointed to the east, "a little less'n a couple of miles is the little town of Coulson along the river. Now, Coulson was here first by about five years. Weren't no Billings. Folks in Coulson expected the Northern Pacific would go through Coulson because that was how the line was laid out. Lotta people bet the farm on the railroad goin' through Coulson. Problem was, Coulson would be the location of the railhead for future railroad expansion, and for cattle and freight shippin' all over these parts. Could wind up bein' the biggest city in the state."

"That doesn't sound like a problem," said Amos.

"Well it was a problem for the people in Coulson because the profitability was so obvious that some of the bigwigs in Northern Pacific decided they could make another bundle of money startin' their own town. Greed makes the world go 'round, y' know.

"One of those men was Heman Clark who was the Northern Pacific Railroad railway contractor, the guy in charge of laying down the rails. This whole Billings thing was his idea. Then there's Thomas Oakes, vice president of the railroad, and Frederick Billings who was the past president. They were in a position to tweak the railroad line a tad, bypassin' Coulson. So they bought land from the railroad, the government, an' 'homesteaders' no one ever heard of." The bartender smirked and wiped his mouth. "And assembled enough land t' lay out a pretty fair-sized townsite where we stand. Named it Billings." The man chortled. "Dunno why. Just had a nice ring to it, I guess. Billings, Montana.

"Well, then they start promotin' the proposed town, an' other land speculators start comin' around. The railroad line is headin' this direction, and everyone knows who Frederick Billings is. Actually a real decent guy. He don't live here, but he's been here plenty. So, people are figurin' this town's here t' stay and could get big. Icing on the cake is that Frederick Billings funds a new library and the new Congregational Church over yonder. To people back East, if ya got a library and a Congregational Church, that's a real town, no two ways about it. All permanent-like. Well, that's all it took. People been comin' in droves. An' some are wanderin' over from Coulson. Not much future there, I'm afraid.

"See, people think that while other western boomtowns gotta fend for themselves, Frederick H. Billings'll take care of 'his' town. Maybe, maybe not. I wouldn't get too concerned anyway. We got the railroad. And this big Montana world here? We're smack dab in the middle of it. Gonna stay in the middle of it. For me, business has never been this good anywhere I been. I suspect Billings, Oakes, Clark and them all made a pretty bundle too. Probably done better 'n they even dreamed."

"I understand the Little Big Horn battlefield is somewhere southeast of here," said Amos. "I have a special interest in it. Who should I talk to about seeing it?"

"Dunno why you'd want to see it. Nuthin' much there. Tombstones. All covered with snow. But go see the In'jin agent down the street." The man pointed south. "He might be able t' help y."

Amos thanked the man, finished his glass of wine, and left to go down the street.

"There are still a few hostiles," said the agent, "but most have learned to keep their distance rather than causin' trouble. The hearts of some Sioux are bad; others good. Gotta get to know 'em. Like everything else here, I'm relatively new, so I don't know too many yet, but those I've met seem honorable. Still, gotta be careful."

"Major, is it safe to ride south, perhaps visit the Little Big Horn battlefield?" asked Amos.

"Yeah, I suppose, if you have that much time. But right now there's not much to see. Snow covers everything. That big gent there," the agent pointed at a large man standing near the door, his back to Amos while looking out the window, "seems t' know the territory pretty well. If you pay him, he'll take you down there and back."

Amos thanked the agent, and walked over to the large man. If Pastor Nordquist was a man-of-the-cloth, the guide was a man-of-the-fur for he was clothed in dark fur from head to foot, with a black beard and thunderstorm of black hair pushing out from under his black fur and leather hat. He looked half man and half bear,

"Hello," said Amos. Without unfolding his arms, the large man looked sideways at Amos. "I'm told you know your way around these parts pretty well."

"Know my way around a lotta parts pretty well."

"Could you take me down to the Little Big Horn battlefield?"

"Why you wanna go there? Nothin' t' see. Place is covered with snow."

"I want to be there, study the surroundings; perhaps get a sense of what happened. Sometimes it helps to stand on the ground – feel it – where something happened in order to get a better sense for what went on. Spiritual intuition, maybe. How much will it cost me?" The big fur man became more attentive when Amos mentioned remuneration. "How long do you think it will take?"

"Depends on how fast we ride," said the man as he turned toward Amos. He stroked his beard with big hands the texture of buckskin. His forehead – what could be seen of it – looked like a laterally eroded hillside. "Takin' it easy? Three, four days over and back."

"I might not have that much time. I'll need to check with the train I'm riding. Could you wait here a few minutes?"

"Sure. Weren't plannin' on goin' nowhere."

Amos left the Indian agent's office and walked to the railroad station a short distance away.

"I'm interested in seeing the Little Big Horn battlefield," said Amos when he found the conductor. "Do I have enough time to ride down there and back? It will take three or four days. How long will the train be here?"

"Thought it was gonna be two days, but now I don't know," answered the conductor. "Your timin' might be good. We have to wait for a new part and it looks like that part won't be here until the next train arrives or, more likely, the one after that. You might have time."

"How much time is that?"

"Usually longer than anyone expects. Could be three, four days, maybe more. Won't wait for ya. Get back as soon as possible.

"What happens if I'm not back on time?"

"Maybe catch the next train. Take your luggage with you if you get off."

"I don't have much luggage…travelin' light."

The conductor shrugged his shoulders. "Head on down there if y' know where your goin'. May not be much else t' do for a few days."

Amos walked back to the Indian agent's office thinking about a horse and provisions.

"We have time to go down to the Little Big Horn battlefield," Amos told the large man. "I'll need to rent a horse and buy provisions but, after that, there's no reason we can't leave at once."

"You sure you want to ride down there? Like I say, ain't nothin' there. Snowin' again outside. Cold. Ain' gonna be much t' see."

"I was with Custer toward the end of the war," said Amos, his expression brimming with resolve. "No doubt this will be the only chance in my lifetime to see the battlefield, and we're so close to it. I want to take advantage of the opportunity."

The big fur man studied Amos for a moment and nodded. Three other men in the room, listening to the conversation, asked to join Amos and the large guide. Two of the three men, Amos would learn, were range riders, "cow-boys," done with a cattle drive. The third man was about to check into a Billings hotel, but figured he'd wait until after he saw the battlefield.

The guide and the other three men had horses tied up in front of the Indian agency. Amos walked with the four men as they rode to the nearby livery stable; the fur man knew the owner.

"We got three here," the owner said to Amos, "all about the same size and temperament. Names are Tumbleweed, Dapper Dan, and Olaf. Same price. Which one ya want?"

"Olaf."

Based on cash up-front and the fur man's word that the horse would be returned, Amos rented a horse named Olaf. The men bought food – flour, bacon, beans, coffee, sugar, salt, potatoes – at the General Store. The fur man and the others already had cooking utensils, rifles, ammunition, tents and soogans. Amos bought a knife, fork, tent and soogan at the store; he would need them anyway when he arrived at Thompson Falls en route to Eagle City. Equipped, the five men rode south, forded the Yellowstone River, and headed east southeast.

As they rode, the range riders said little and talked only to one another; loquacious behavior in comparison to the big fur man who said nothing to anyone. Pastor Nordquist furtively studied the fur man from time-to-time and figured the man was probably more at home away from civilization than most people would be at "home," and was uncomfortable in polite society. The fur man's large, black horse with a thick winter coat seemed to have similar temperament. Amos's horse, Olaf, wasn't small, but the fur man's horse seemed as high at the withers as Olaf's ears

Several hours later, they were far from town. Amos looked around – snow covered everything. Fur Man also kept looking around. Others had ridden to the battlefield in the past, and the trail would be obvious to someone like Fur Man who could read "sign" – broken twigs, bent grass, scraped dirt – as well as the Sioux. Unknown to the others, however, Fur Man was having trouble because of the snow. Apart from topographical variations, everything appeared the same. Signs of animals – matted grass, scraped brush – were occasionally seen although only Fur Man recognized them. At one point, antelope appeared on a distant ridge, but disappeared in a blink. Snow fell lightly, silently re-covering recent sign. Fur Man doesn't seem like the type who would get lost, Amos thought hopefully. Amos attempted to engage the fur man in conversation.

"So," began Pastor Nordquist as an opener, "are you a resident of Billings?" The fur man looked at Pastor Nordquist as if Pastor Nordquist just woke him up, causing Pastor Nordquist to repeat the question pleasantly. "Are you a resident of Billings?"

"Billings?" said the fur man in a rumbling voice. "Hell, maybe. Dunno. As good a place as any. Maybe I'd stay awhile, but I might not. A man should have someplace t' go back t'. It's a thought."

While talking, the fur man looked about as if expecting to see someone or something.

"Pretty safe in town. Not that 'safe' is the greatest thing in the world. We're headin' toward a spot that gets both whites and In'jins fired up. We'll see what kind of reception the locals afford along the way."

"Locals?"

"A few years ago," said Fur Man, "people like us weren't any too popular in these parts."

Fur Man slowly looked about again.

"The Sioux cover a big area. Add the Cheyenne and the Crow, and the five'a us might as well be lil' prairie chickens. Red Cloud, Gall, Sitting Bull, Crow King, Kicking Bear, younger chiefs…" Fur Man nodded his head several times. "They're tryin' t' figure out what they want to do now. The gov'ment ain't been any too good at holdin' up our end of any bargain, y'know." Fur Man looked at Pastor Nordquist with concern. "Pressin' the Sioux. You cain't jes' change a people's whole way 'a life overnight. Dunno that the Sioux are gonna sit tight the way things are goin'. Lot of 'em never have. In'jin agents use the word, 'Unreconstructed.' They's the ones I worry about. Not a good situation."

Fur Man looked directly at Pastor Nordquist, and seemed to be warming up to a conversation.

"You know what the worst thing is that coulda happened to the Sioux?" asked Fur Man. Pastor Nordquist looked back, anxious to hear comments from someone who appeared familiar with the plains Indians. "I'll tell ya," said Fur Man. "We're headin' toward it: Little Big Horn."

"My understanding is," said Pastor Nordquist, "the Indians did pretty well at Little Big Horn."

"Yep," replied Fur Man. "And then what?"

"Well," responded Amos, "I don't know."

"One word," said Fur Man. "Heard it for quite a spell. 'Retribution.' Whole goddam' U.S. Army comes after 'em. Timin' couldn't a' been worse for the Sioux: killin' a Civil War hero on the eve of the nation's Centennial. People back East wanted to up the ante and then some," Fur Man looked at Amos knowingly, "and they wanted it done pronto. Woulda been better for the Sioux if ol' Custer had himself a little skirmish and hightailed outa there, but, no, he and his whole bunch gets massacred. Worse thing the In'jins coulda done. Now, t' them it didn't seem so at the time but, afterwards, ehm, no doubt about it. It was Custer's Last Stand but, dunno, might turn out t' be theirs too in the long run."

Amos nodded, thinking about what Fur Man had said.

"Sioux consider this land theirs," continued Fur Man, "but maybe it ain't. Maybe they took it from someone else. Sioux weren't always up in the Black Hills, fer instance. Kiowa were there for quite a spell until the Cheyenne pushed 'em out. Then the Sioux pushed the Cheyenne out. Long time ago."

"Who did the Kiowa push out?" asked Amos after a moment.

"Good question. Someone. Don't know. Wish I did. Them Hills got a history."

Fur Man looked about again. All Amos could see was rolling prairie, hills, gullies, and a line of trees at a distance, probably along a creek, everything white and snow-covered. Cold.

"Normally I can follow someone's trail, read sign as well as some can read a newspaper," said Fur Man, "but this snow ain't helpin'. The key ain't seein' what you *should* see; it's seein' the little things what shouldn't be there. That's what 'sign' is. In'jins can follow a trail none of you boys can see. So if they want to tail y', snow or no snow, they will. Nuthin' y' can do about that except be ready."

Amos glanced around.

"Funny thing about the Sioux, the Crow, the Cheyenne," said Fur Man, refocusing on the snow-covered ground that slowly flowed by, "when you think about them bein' around, and decide they ain't around, that's when they is. How many? Usually more'n y' think even if y' think they's around." He looked at Amos. "Custer found that out."

Pastor Nordquist looked about, attempting to hide his naïve anxiousness. He looked at Fur Man who looked back without expression, understanding Amos's reaction.

"Sometimes I c'n tell," said Fur Man, "but sometimes, well, let's just say, the Sioux c'n surprise y'.

"I'll tell you who knows most of the time: ol' Black Jack, here," added Fur Man, reaching out and patting the thick neck of his huge horse.

"What breed is he?" asked Amos.

"Only one of his kind, far as I know," said Fur Man. "Father was a Percheron, bred for war back in the day, and the mother a Kentucky Saddler. Damned helluva horse. Smart as hell. Ain'tcha?" Fur Man patted Black Jack again.

"Ol' Black Jack" – Fur man put emphasis on "Jack" – "his ears'll stand up and he'll start actin' a little spooky an' be lookin' in a direction where it ain't exactly obvious there's anything to look at. In the past when he does that, I'd pull out my rifle and we hightail it outa there. Right now, though, shouldn't be much to worry about. Sioux been peaceful for a spell. No immediate reason t' think that's about t' change. But, like I said before, there's still bad blood, an' y' never know."

Fur Man looked to the right while studying the ground.

"I knows some of 'em," said Fur Man, looking back at Pastor Nordquist, "probably a lot fewer 'n knows me, I suspect."

The men continued on for several hours until it was getting too dark to see clearly. Camp was pitched beneath a rock overhang, and a fire lit. While the others grouped together, Amos took out his soogan and made ready for the night. A coffee pot, hung from a big stick, was put over the fire for coffee. Bacon, pan bread, and potatoes were fried and gulped down.

"Keep the horses close by," Fur Man told the others. "Get 'em over here – I don't care how dam' tired y'are. In'jins don't like to travel in weather like this – who does? – but y' never know. Always gotta be ready. Sioux highly value horses, especially good horses like the ones we got."

The men complied although it was cold, real cold, and everyone wanted to get some sleep. As the men repositioned their horses, Black Jack's ears stood up and he began acting spooky, more like a small dog than a large horse.

"Make sure the picket pins are pushed in strong! Tether your horses tight!" said Fur Man to the others. "The Sioux are real good at retrievin' stray horses… or horses that could be stray with a little help!"

"Maybe we should stand watches," suggested one of the others apprehensively, imagining berserk braves pouring over surrounding ridges.

The sky had cleared, stars were everywhere, and the moon was full. The snow reflected the night light, further brightening the scenery. Anyone creeping up in the night would likely be spotted.

They decided to each take a turn. If nothing else, it would prevent the element of surprise; perhaps discourage an unfortunate larcenous act in the middle of the night.

Fur Man looked at the range riders securing their picket pins. "So, you boys come up from down around Texas, New Mexico?"

"Yep."

"Apaches? Commanches?"

"Yep," said one of the men neutrally as he took the saddle off his handsome piebald gelding.

"They like t' collect horses too," said Fur Man with a smirk. "Like shod ones best, I hear."

"Hell, shod or unshod, Apaches and Comanches get horses an' run 'em t' death," said the first range rider.

"Run 'em t' death, then eat 'em," said the second.

"Sioux are different," said Fur Man. "Take care of their horses. Value good horse flesh. So let's not give 'em any valuin' opportunities."

Amos's watch was from midnight until 2:00 a.m., but otherwise he slept restlessly, awaking from time-to-time. Nothing happened that night, however.

"False alarm?" asked Amos the next morning as they prepared to hit the trail again.

"What did I tell y' yesterday?" asked Fur Man. "No, friend, that weren't no dam' false alarm! Ol' Black Jack's got eyes in his ears. When he acts like that, they're out there. We're bein' followed. I'm not worried about bein' attacked," added Fur Man as if to reassure himself. "But while the Sioux are presently peaceful, a few of 'em will sure as hell take any opportunity we give 'em to add to their herd or food supply." Fur Man gestured a wide sweep of his arm. "Take a look around. Where are we?" Fur Man looked back at Amos. "Middle a' goddam nowhere. Good place for 'em to make a move. We don't need that happenin'."

The five men continued on. Weather conditions were unchanged, but snow drifts were becoming smaller. Before the railroad was built, pioneers carried belongings in wagon trains. Around noon Amos and the four men passed the bleached bones of some maple furniture – nice furniture once – someone's tie with the past, discarded to insure a future.

As he rode with nothing else to do, in his mind Pastor Nordquist again built the sanctuary, remodeled his conceptual parsonage kitchen, and generally entertained himself with thoughts of his family and what would be awaiting them when they followed him to Eagle City.

About three in the afternoon, Black Jack stopped cold in his tracks, his nostrils flaring and his ears straight up. He began to paw the ground and snort as if attempting to say something to Fur Man. Fur Man understood perfectly, and patted his horse while staring wide-eyed in the direction Black Jack turned and faced. The two of them had been in some tight spots, and Black Jack's memory was good.

Fur Man urged Black Jack forward, away from the others. He stared without blinking, attempting to see what Black Jack sensed, smelled or heard. The wind whipped about wisps of fine snow powder, and caused some exposed prairie grass to cringe and shudder, but, otherwise, there was no movement. Fur Man pushed Black Jack to a slow cantor while, at a distance, the others watched, wondering what was happening.

Fur Man, listening to his feelings, pulled on the reins. Horse and rider came to a halt a short distance from a rise on the prairie. For a moment nothing happened.

Then they were there.

<h1 style="text-align:center">41</h1>

Six Sioux braves sat motionlessly on horseback along the ridge line as if there the entire time, invisible until the leader flipped a switch. Expressionless and dressed much like Fur Man, they studied Fur Man and the others, knowing where the men were heading.

While the others watched, the Sioux leader rode down the ridge toward Fur Man who remained where he was. As the Sioux leader approached Fur Man, the leader slowed his horse to a walk as the braves, still motionless on the ridge, continued to watch without expression. From Pastor Nordquist's vantage point, it appeared as if the Sioux leader and Fur Man knew one another. While there was solemnity, there was also an air of familiarity when the two communicated using both words and sign language. After a couple of minutes, Fur Man pulled the reins to the right, turning Black Jack around, and rode down to the men while the Sioux leader remained where he was. The other Sioux on the ridge, as if petrifactions, watched without movement.

"They want to know if we have a *pejula wacasa*, a medicine man," shouted Fur Man as he rode up to the others. "Fur Man looked at Amos and the others. Any a' you gents a doctor? Know anything about doctorin'?" Black Jack was nervous and Fur Man had a difficult time keeping him facing the others. "Anyone here know much about doctorin'?" yelled Fur Man again to make certain they all heard him.

For a moment there was no response. Pastor Nordquist looked at the others, thinking maybe there was something he could do although he was not a physician.

"Why?" asked the man who was going to stay in a Billings hotel.

"They have some sick kids," responded Fur Man. "The Sioux love their children; children mean everything to 'em. Missionaries came here two years ago. There was a sick brave, real sick. The Sioux medicine man said the sick brave's spirit was preparin' to travel to the land of ghosts, so the tribe painted the brave with death paint and waited for the brave to die. One of the missionaries was also a doctor and knew what the problem was, treated the sick brave, and the brave got well.

"The In'jins believed the doctor had 'strong medicine' or 'great medicine,' which don't mean just somethin' in a bottle; it means the doctor has power over nature…supernatural power. 'Specially bein' a missionary. But you don't have to be a doctor or medicine man to have 'strong medicine'; the 'medicine' of a great warrior is said to be strong.

"The medicine man claimed the missionaries were in cahoots with the evil spirit living in the sick brave, and tried to talk the tribe into killing the missionaries, but the tribe didn't believe him. That don't mean the Sioux are gonna turn their backs on what they've been doin' for generations. But any people will switch when there's obviously a better way, especially when kids are involved.

"At the same time, hell, medicine men are all a bunch of con artists. I've watched 'em. Magic bear claws; snake skins. Grabbin' at straws. Maybe they believe what they're doin', but, in my way 'a thinkin', if anything good happens… hell, I don't know. Sometimes y' wonder.

"Medicine men are losing power. Gotta be slicker 'n ever now. Some Sioux'll kill medicine men whose 'medicine' fails.

"This bunch don't trust medicine men, but they trust white doctors. Trust is important with the Sioux. They want our medicine again."

"If we refuse?"

"You a doctor?" asked Fur Man. The man made no response, obviously awaiting the outcome of some momentary inner struggle.

"Yes," said the man. Then he repeated more deliberately, "Yes, I'm a doctor. I plan on setting up practice in Billings."

"Well, to answer your question," responded Fur Man, "if we refuse, they'll just let us go our merry way. But if we help 'em, they'll point us in the direction we should be goin'." Fur Man looked at the others for a moment. "The snow makes everything look pretty much alike and, well, White Eagle there," Fur Man nodded in the direction of the lone Sioux awaiting a response, "tells me we've drifted a piece further south than we should be, and that if we keep going like we are, first, we'll miss Little Big Horn altogether, and second, if we get too far south, our troubles'll just be startin'. White Eagle tells me we'll waste time, provisions and strength goin' the way we are, and we'll waste more time, provisions and strength when we have to double back and go a long ways t' Little Big Horn – if we're still wantin' an' able t' go there."

Fur Man leaned forward in the saddle – Black Jack, champing at the bit, took two steps, but stopped as Fur Man gently tugged the reins.

"In exchange for medicine, White Eagle will take us to where we wanna go. So why don't we spend a day or so helpin' these people…make some friends," Fur Man looked about at the barren landscape, "and save ourselves a lot of time and trouble, maybe a life or two, in the long run?"

The doctor nodded but said nothing.

"I'll take that as bein' a 'yes'," said Fur Man.

"You don't expect us to follow those savages," said one of the range riders. "You sayin' we should just ride on out with a bunch of coup counters?"

"Your hearin' okay?" asked Fur Man. "Maybe you need a doctor too? You follow those Sioux if you're smart. If you're stupid, hell, just keep goin.'"

Fur Man looked at the others for a moment.

"Oh, I forgot somethin,'" he added. "Don't suppose it hurts t' ask: they also wanted to know if anyone here is a *wichasha wakan*, a holy man, missionary?"

"Well," responded Pastor Nordquist, "I am a pastor. Why do they ask?"

"The Sioux are real spiritual. And this bunch here, they're Sioux who've become Christians. White Eagle, his brothers and cousins." Fur Man gestured toward the Sioux up on the ridge. "They're among the best braves, but they're sorta considered, well, different within the Sioux tribe. The rest of the Sioux, those who want nothin' to do with the white man, and who intend t' stick with the old ways, are, I guess, silently at odds with this bunch. They're peaceful with us cuz they're Christians – that's how they believe – but the old chiefs don't like it that this bunch don't, well, dislike whites. Peace is peace, but In'jins is In'jins and whites is whites." Fur Man's eyebrows knitted. "Well, now, in their tribe these Christian Sioux are doin' all right, but the pagans – they's a lot more a' them – don't like bein' around the Christians, an' consequently this bunch is kinda fendin fer themselves a little right about now."

Fur Man glanced over his shoulder at the watching Sioux.

"So these Sioux Christians y' see over there," he continued, "they'd like a holy man – or pastor – t' be a storyteller while the doctor treats the kids. Been done before. Guess they figure the tribal elders won't mind as long as you don't stay. You wanna tell some Bible stories tonight? Seems like a golden opportunity, considerin' you're a pastor and all."

"I would be delighted to do that," smiled Pastor Nordquist.

"Are you two crazy?!" asked one of the range riders. "How do you know what they'll do? This bunch we're supposed to help is already unpopular. They could be leadin' us into a trap. We could get scalped. Anyone here heard a' Custer?"

"First of all, Custer warn't scalped!" barked Fur Man. "A lot 'a men were, but not Custer. At least not George; Tom got scalped and then some. Boston too. Second, if the pagan tribal leaders wanted to do that here, ain't none of us would need a barber about now." Fur Man calmed Black Jack.

"No, sir, they ain't a gonna scalp us. I know White Eagle from before. He used t' be a hostile, but ain't no more. His word is good. They'll trade hospitality and directions for Bible stories and medicine. An' they wouldn't take us back t' the tribe if we'd be in danger."

The others watched apprehensively as Fur Man kept Black Jack from turning and facing in the direction of White Eagle.

"Your horse don't seem t' agree."

"That was then. Y' got medicine?" Fur Man asked the doctor.

"I have a little medicine with me presently, but most of it won't arrive until I start my practice. Of course, what medication might be needed won't be known until I can examine the children."

"Whatever you have'll have t' do," said Fur Man.

He pulled Black Jack around to face in the direction of White Eagle who waited about a hundred yards away. Fur Man glanced over his shoulder and in his gravelly voice shouted, "Follow me!"

In the western Great Plains, the small group of men began the trek somewhere to a Sioux tribal encampment so that a doctor with a small amount of medicine could treat some sick Sioux children, and a Swedish minister bound for Eagle City could administer spiritual healing and edification.

"Funny about that scalpin' at Little Big Horn," said Fur Man to Pastor Nordquist as they followed White Eagle. "They counted many coup, scalped a lot a' men, mutilated most – Sioux believe that the soul of a mutilated body can't go t' heaven, gotta walk the face a' the earth forever – but they didn't scalp Custer. Dunno why not. I'd a' thought if they scalped anyone, it a' been him. They didn't touch the body though."

Fur Man looked at Amos.

"Makes y' wonder what they thought," said Fur Man. "If they don't scalp someone like Custer, it usually means they're afraid of the man's spirit which they believe to be very powerful. 'Strong medicine.' And believe he was a great warrior, chief. Fearless. Don't touch."

"That's very true," said Amos, recalling Sailor's Creek.

"And some say even though Custer led cavalry into the Black Hills, he also didn't like the way we was breakin' treaties, and said so. Mighta been why the army bureaucrats sent him there."

"I've heard that," said Amos.

"Maybe the Sioux knew that too." Fur Man shrugged. "Wouldn't surprise me.

"But they got no problem cuttin' up an enemy," added Fur Man. "Another story – dunno if it's true or not – but it gives y' an idea a' how much they must 'a respected George Custer. One of the Sioux at Little Big Horn – Rain-in-the-Face, I'm told – cut out the heart of one of our more well-known boys and ate it."

Amos looked at Fur Man aghast. "He what?"

"After a battle, sometimes a Sioux warrior will cut out the heart of an enemy warrior known to be exceptionally brave – from the Sioux perspective it's an honor for the man killed – and eat it in order to obtain some of the enemy warrior's strength, strong medicine. I was told that's what happened to Tom Custer's body. No reason t' think it ain't true, but, since I weren't there, thank God, I don't know fer sure. But I guess George Armstrong Custer's medicine was so great they wouldn't even touch the body."

As Amos weighed this information, the men rode for a while without talking until Fur Man mentioned something else.

"Strange thing about medicine men. Most of 'em don't really do much, but I watched one go into a deep trance," said Fur Man, "an' somethin' mighty strange happened. You hear 'im speakin' different, sayin' stuff he couldn't 'a known…and it didn't even sound like 'im."

Fur Man looked at Pastor Nordquist.

"That's because it wasn't him," said Amos. "'Spirit guides' are who they've always been: demons. But they're very good at convincing people they're someone or something else."

"Like what else?"

"Anything that works. It depends on the person being possessed."

"The spirit of the bear or deer or wolf is what I hear," said Fur Man. "Sometimes they're supposed to be spirits of clouds or trees. Even rocks."

"Animism is alluring. Many things…"

"What the hell's animism?"

"The belief that all things have souls, spirits – and, obviously, the belief these spirits can act as supernatural guides. If a rock were believed to have a spirit, that would be animism, a supernatural phenomenon, and, subsequently, irrationally attractive to many having spiritual sensitivity but ignorance of the trinity. Spiritual voids beg to be filled." Amos looked at Fur Man neutrally. "Rocks? People have worshipped 'rocks' for thousands of years. Why? They are enticed into ascribing supernatural to the natural. Who entices them?" Amos's eyes narrowed. "One guess. It's well to remember that many things irrationally attractive are not what they seem. Satan has his diversions, many of them. Superficial 'beauty' is often the bait, a subsequent bestowal of power the hook, and 'spirit guides,'" said Amos grimly, "all have fishing poles."

"Yeah, I reckon so."

"Satan has a great many diversions to keep men from knowing God. My job is to get people understanding and pointed in the right direction." Amos pointed his finger upward. "Then God, not me, draws them to Jesus, Jesus the Messiah, and by His grace they are converted and saved."

"Sounds simple enough," said Fur Man, not looking at Amos.

"It is." Amos studied Fur Man. "Tonight, you and I are going to have a brief Bible study, and then pray together."

"Well. Dunno. I ain't the church-goin' type."

"Learning to love God, to love the Bible from cover-to-cover, doesn't require a church, just an open mind and an open heart. Of course, the indwelling of the Holy Spirit in your heart is more expedient if there isn't someone else already living there."

Fur Man thought about that.

"I should add," Amos smiled, "there is a 'rock' necessary: *petra*, the rock of revelation."

Fur Man looked puzzled. "What're you jabberin' about?"

"You'll find out," smiled Amos, sensing God's leading. "'Strong medicine.' Through God's grace, you'll find out."

For three days, the doctor treated the children and, with Fur Man interpreting, taught the Sioux women what to do after he left. Meanwhile, the vivid imaginations of the Sioux insured that Pastor Nordquist became a star entertainer telling stories about Moses and the 10 Commandments, David and Goliath, John the Baptist, Jesus calming the Sea of Galilee, Jesus feeding the 5,000, Jesus raising Lazarus from the dead, and Jesus' own death and then the resurrection. Since storytelling was the primary source of entertainment among the Sioux, Pastor Nordquist's audiences were full. I've told Bible stories in many places, he thought, but none like this.

While in the encampment, Pastor Nordquist with sadness learned that among the Sioux pagans, in response to the Christian story of Jesus, a counter-story about an Indian messiah was circulating, reflecting the deep bitterness and resentment of many tribal members. From his study of history, Amos knew that when an advanced people subjugates a more primitive people, the primitive people initially fight back. When that fails, they try accommodation. If that also fails, all that is left is either assimilation or retaliatory fantasy. The Sioux story foretold of an Indian messiah who would cause the prairie sod to roll up over the advancing soldiers, prospectors, pioneers and settlers. Those not crushed by the sod would be transformed by the messiah into buffalo, antelope and deer to serve as game for the Sioux. There would be no more white men, and life would be as it was before the white men came.

Pastor Nordquist sighed. Preyed upon, hated, their sacred places violated, and their customs and beliefs ridiculed, the bitterness of many Sioux was deep. In contrast, Pastor Nordquist taught that the love of the Savior was universal for all – white and Indian – and the Messiah wished all to behave according to the "new commandment" that we love one another.

Pastor Nordquist looked about him; he thought about staying. All needed to know about Jesus, but Pastor Nordquist was only one man, and God's word was required everywhere. Pastor Nordquist could not stay, even if he were welcome to stay. He had his directions from Nels Hanseth.

Late during the next afternoon in the Sioux encampment, Pastor Nordquist stood with Fur Man and looked about at the Sioux people, their horses, lodging, the fires burning, children playing. Old people sitting quietly and watching the two men. Nothing more. Simply sitting and watching.

Through his storytelling, Pastor Nordquist became popular with the children, and this popularity seemed to create a bond with some of the Sioux, particularly the young mothers and, at a distance, a few older chiefs who saw his heart. Many braves remained cold and aloof.

"While I don't see real peace with the Sioux anytime soon," said Fur Man, looking at the Sioux, "I s'pect it's gotta happen. Injins understood soldiers, warriors – war is part of the Sioux way of life – and were physically, mentally, emotionally and spiritually prepared t' hold off the cavalry. But the prospectors, pioneers, settlers? Too dam' many of 'em. They kept comin' like ocean waves. Buildin' fences, runnin' cattle, plowing the land. Individually they all came and they stayed in spite of the danger because, well, that's the white's way of life. Now the government people are still wantin' t' stick the Sioux on a reservation like they done with the Blackfeet, Crow, Hunkpapa and some of those tribes down south like the Creek and the Chocktaw. The government tells the Sioux they'll be safe and taken care of. Government officials think that will appeal to these people." Fur Man snorted derisively. "That's cowshit. Fine for the women, the chiefs say, but not the braves. 'Taken care of.' That's the last thing these Sioux braves want."

"Why is that?" asked Pastor Nordquist.

"Sioux manhood and tribal existence are intertwined. The Sioux braves ain't what we call 'braves' for nothin', " answered Fur Man. "To them, you ain't a man if you have to be taken care of. Braves provide the security for the women and children; do the huntin', the hard work, and the fightin'. Take that away and, t' them, you take away their manhood. Simple as that."

Fur Man unfolded his arms and put his hands in the pockets of his fur coat.

"Even White Eagle don't want no part of it. He asked me if I wanted t' have the government take care of me too?"

"I have no doubt of your response," said Amos.

"Dam' right!" answered Fur Man in a tone that brooked no denial. "Don't need no goddam, skinny-arm, pale face, bow-tie watchin' out for me!" He spat on the snow to his right. "White Eagle says the Sioux have more respect for so'jers, guys like Custer, 'braves,' than the government officials. Sioux say the government boys treat the Sioux braves like women because the officials don't know what it's like bein' men!" Fur Man's eyes narrowed. "He says they see… what's that called when you ain't a man no more?"

Amos thought for a moment. "Emasculated?"

"Yeah, like that. He says that if things continue the way they are, this whole country'll be like that. No bravery. No courage. Everything meekly done according to rules and regulations dictated by the goddam government. White Eagle says then eventually the whole country becomes a nation of women."

Fur Man looked at Amos who looked back.

"The young chiefs and the braves want no part of it. In fact, for a Sioux brave, that prospect is about the worst thing he can think of. These people were supposed to be on a reservation a long time ago. Ain't happened yet. So, peace?" Fur Man looked away. "Not the way we're goin'."

Fur Man folded his arms again. The two men continued to look about the encampment. The old people continued to watch.

The following day when it came time to go, Pastor Nordquist's heart was heavy. These people all need to accurately answer the most important question anyone can ask: who is Jesus Christ? Amos prayed for their leaders, their children and their relationship with the Lord, asking that God draw them to Himself, that they might be born again. Amos encouraged the Christian Sioux leaders to continue telling the tribal children about Jesus the Messiah, and of Jesus' love for them. Amos need not have worried.

"The Sioux are spiritual as hell," said Fur Man whose heart, but not his language, had been converted two nights earlier. While listening to Amos tell the story of Jesus walking on water, and who Jesus was, and the importance of faith, the Holy Spirit convicted Fur Man, and while he looked and spoke no differently, he was a different person. "Y' oughta ask White Eagle to say a prayer."

"I will," said Amos to Fur Man. "Would you do the honor?"

On behalf of Pastor Nordquist, Fur Man asked White Eagle to pray, and as White Eagle prayed, Fur Man translated for the whites.

Hands uplifted, from the depth of his soul White Eagle prayed in accordance with the admonition in Matthew 23:37-39 for all to love God, and for love among the Indians, and between the Indians and the white man. He entreated the Great Spirit to enable all men to love one another as Christ directed, and according to the story Amos had told two days earlier.

Until that moment, Pastor Nordquist believed the Great Spirit was a pagan concept, but as White Eagle continued his prayer to the Great Spirit, *Wakan Tanka* (Holy Great), Amos intuited White Eagle was being led by the Holy Spirit, and the prayer was being offered up to God the Father by another name.

When White Eagle finished, Amos looked at White Eagle and thought, God the Father and Christ the Son have many names in the Bible. "Wonderful, Counselor, the Mighty God, the Everlasting Father, the Prince of Peace," thought Amos, in his mind repeating the line from Isaiah 9:6-7 and reiterated in Handel's *Messiah*. Add "*Wakan Tanka*" when used by a Christian Sioux.

Amos smiled to himself. Untold generations of Sioux have not had the blessing of biblical history and direction, but, here, White Eagle and I are both Christians and, just now, both led by the person of the Holy Spirit. Amos folded his arms, smiled inwardly, and asked, why am I surprised? Faith knows no race or color. Jesus Christ and his purpose on earth are being embraced by some of the Sioux. Amos looked warmly at White Eagle whose serious expression remained unchanged. This is a great moment, Amos thought.

Seated on Olaf, Pastor Nordquist's last act with the Sioux was to give a benediction, blessing the Sioux tribe as they stood looking back, not literally understanding his English words, but spiritually intuiting their intent and Amos's feelings, and knowing *Wakan Tanka*, who reads men's hearts, understood.

Amos concluded with a short Sioux phrase: "*Wakan Tanka kici un* [Holy Great bless you]." God bless you.

Led by the Sioux remnant leader, White Eagle, the five men traveled east northeast to a location where White Eagle stopped and surveyed topography and geographical landmarks. He nodded and pointed toward an eastern rise. That was the place. Little Big Horn. That was where it happened. Pastor Nordquist could see distant granite gravestones rising above the snow.

White Eagle looked at Fur Man and said something the others did not understand. Before they turned to leave, Fur Man thanked White Eagle for his hospitality. White Eagle said something to Fur Man who turned to the others and said, "He says we have shown that whites and Indians can be of support and comfort to one another, and he thanks us for our kindness and generosity." Amos and the others nodded.

White Eagle sat upright and motionlessly on his horse as he watched Fur Man, Amos and the others turn and ride toward the east. Arriving at the site, Amos gave Olaf free rein and looked about as the horse walked circumspectly among gravestones on the snow-covered slope.

Amos sensed it – not the enraged fury of vicious bloodshed on a battlefield, but a reverence for the dead – white and Indian – who made an enigmatic sacrifice on this ground. What is there about sacrifice in battle that brings future reverence? Amos wondered. Why does it work that way? It is so for Gettysburg, Antietam, Shiloh.

During the next half hour, little was said as the men slowly rode around the site, following feeling. Finished, they turned and rode back to Billings, lost in individual thought, closer for the experience, but saying little to one another. Upon reaching Billings, Amos returned Olaf to the livery stable, picked up his bags, bid goodbye to the others, took Fur Man aside and the two prayed with and for each other.

"How well do you read?" asked Pastor Nordquist before he left Fur Man's company.

"Well enough, I s'pose. 'Nuf t' get by. Why?"

"Read this. You'll 'get by' better." Pastor Nordquist smiled as he handed Fur Man his Bible. Fur Man looked at the Bible, then up at Pastor Nordquist. Fur Man was literate but not by much. He thought of the spiritual and literacy edification, and nodded.

"Reckon I'll get by much better."

Pastor Nordquist also nodded, reached out and shook Fur Man's hand, turned and headed for the third train – the original train had left three days earlier – readying to leave for Thompson Falls, the last stop. Fur Man stood watching as Amos showed the conductor his ticket, the conductor nodded, and Amos boarded the train.

That evening as the train headed west, from a passenger inclined to converse Amos learned that all of the land around Eagle City was claimed. The pack train he would join from Thompson Falls up through the Bitterroot Mountains to Eagle City would first stop in the new town of Murrayville, five miles east of Eagle City, and that Murrayville was where most of these passengers were going.

⸺ ● ⸺

Looking out the train window, as Amos watched the snow-covered, western Montana woodlands flow by, he weighed whether to remain in Murrayville or continue to nearby Eagle City as originally planned, and decided that, as with Miles City, he would make that determination after reaching Murrayville. At the moment he knew nothing about Murrayville. Before arriving, however, he would have an unexpected encounter with the most beautiful and extraordinary woman to grace any Old West settlement or boomtown from Tombstone to Dodge City. Like the others, the woman was also headed for Murrayville. Her presence would affect his decision. Her presence would affect a lot of decisions.

42

January 1884

Head down, Amos Nordquist slumped over his saddle, his black hat brim protecting his face from the lacerating Bitterroot Mountain blizzard. His horse plodding slowly in the snow, he weighed years of events that led to this spot, events so unlikely they seemed fantasy, and how Bitterroot Mountain blizzard darkness was as black as in a North Sea hurricane.

He shivered. But the shiver had nothing to do with the cold and wind as in the darkness the burdened pack train horses followed one another at distances less than a rifle length. Ahead of Amos, a woman on foot, her two-year-old son strapped to her back, struggled forward into the howling, freezing wind, barely lifting her feet. She took one more step and stumbled, trying to keep her balance, but fell to her hands and knees aside the dark, wooded trail in the snow. As the pack train continued to move along the snow-covered trail, a rider ahead of Amos, Molly Burdan, carrying a hurricane lantern, dismounted next to the fallen woman, weakly visible in the lantern light.

"Ma'am, get up," Molly coaxed, placing her mouth near the left ear of the fallen woman in order that the woman might hear her above the wind. "I know that you can't go much further but you can't stay here either," implored Molly, "or you'll be dead by morning."

Shivering, the woman collapsed on her side, her back to Molly. The little boy was heavily bundled and seemed asleep. My God, life must have been hard for someone with a small child to brave this weather on foot, attempting to reach what she must think is something better, thought Molly. And now, after what she must have gone through, she's close to giving up.

Pulling her horse to one side, Molly hung her hurricane lamp from a tree bough. Feeling carefully with her gloved fingers in the weak light, Molly untied the two-year-old boy strapped to the woman's back and lifted the little boy, cradling him in her left arm as, with her right arm, she attempted to pull the woman to her feet while loudly but courteously encouraging the woman to get up. As the woman slowly rose to her feet, Amos Nordquist and another man in the pack train stopped and dismounted to help.

"Gentlemen," Molly yelled over the wind, "lift her up on the back of my horse!"

Molly switched the sleeping two-year-old boy to her right arm, forcefully mounted her horse, and took the hurricane lantern in her right hand.

The two men lifted the woman onto the back of the horse behind Molly.

Molly could sense from how weakly the woman clutched her that, as was evident a moment before, the woman's will to live was fading. In addition to the woman's exhaustion, she was not dressed to survive a blizzard. It would be a couple of hours before sunrise, and at least four more hours before they reached Murrayville. Molly wondered whether the woman could make it that far and, if the woman were to collapse and fall off the horse, what could be done? Even if uninjured, and with help, she might be too weak to remount.

The violence of the cold wind continued unabated, and the destination was no longer Murrayville, which now seemed halfway around the world, but the next bend in the trail. And the one after that.

Amos Nordquist rode behind Molly, the little boy and the weakened woman. To Amos, the wind and snow seemed almost sentient, as if sensing difficulty and conspiring to hinder the pack train's progress. Was the bitter weather intensity the same elsewhere in the mountains? Like this? His horse pushed forward, plodding wearily behind the two women, the little boy and the lantern.

Amos was impressed with the character of this Good Samaritan in front of him. Meanwhile, the Good Samaritan felt the woman's arms weakening, and worried the woman might fall. The little boy was growing heavier in Molly's right arm, and holding the reins in her left hand while steadying the hurricane latern was becoming awkward.

As the pack train pressed on, in the weak lantern light, Amos saw Molly rein her horse to the right as they passed a makeshift lean-to constructed by previous travelers in a small, sheltered alcove along the trail. As Amos came alongside Molly Burdan's horse, Molly turned and shouted above the wind, "Sir! Help me get her down, please!"

Quickly dismounting, Amos reached up and, when Molly gently prized the woman's hands apart with her left hand, caught the woman as she fell from the horse.

"Sir, place her in front of that lean-to!" shouted Molly.

Wrapping his arms around her from behind, hugging the woman's dead weight, Amos lifted her, turned and carried her to the front of the lean-to.

Carefully dismounting, Molly held the heavily bundled, two-year-old boy closely to her chest as her high boots sank into a snowdrift. With effort she pushed through the snow toward the lean-to and hung the lantern from a lean-to bough. Underneath the lean-to and still holding the little boy, she dropped to one knee and, with one gloved hand, pushed drifting snow away. She motioned Amos to put the woman underneath in the cleared spot. He did so, stepped back and stood upright.

Over the wind she yelled, "I will take care of this woman and her child! You go with the pack train in the event someone else needs help!"

Amos looked down at her facial features in the dim hurricane lantern light for a moment. Her beauty was striking.

"Are you sure I can't help you?!" he shouted over the blizzard, pronouncing the words as politely as he could.

Looking up at him, Molly Burdan shook her head. "No! Thank you! I want you to stay with the pack train until it reaches town! There may be others who need help!" she added commandingly.

In the contrasting bleakness of the Bitterroot Mountains blizzard, it seemed to Amos Nordquist that this must be a lady of some prominence; from the inflection in her voice, it was obvious to Amos that she was used to telling others what to do and having it done. Having been a pastor for many years, however, Amos Nordquist was used to people telling him they didn't need help when they did or, alternatively, asking for help when they didn't need it.

"You're sure I can't help you?!" yelled Amos again, allowing her a second opportunity to ask for help.

"I want you to help the others!" she shouted back.

While it was not evident any of the others needed help, her response made it clear to Amos that she was in command of the situation, as she probably was many times in the past. With most women, he would have stayed under any circumstances, but the forcefulness in Molly Burdan's voice convinced Amos she needed no help.

Amos mounted his horse and sat in the saddle for a moment as he watched for some additional assurance all would go well.

Molly carefully placed the young boy at the woman's side. The woman weakly reached out and held the little boy as if nothing else mattered. In the bitter cold, Amos watched Molly remove her expensive fur coat, placing it over the woman and the young child. She nodded at Amos, signaling him to continue on with the pack train. She tethered her horse to the lean-to, turned and took down the lantern, placing it on the ground next to the woman and little boy. Crouching down, she slid underneath the other side of the coat, with the young child warmly sandwiched between the mother and herself.

Pastor Nordquist watched for a moment longer as Molly reached out, lifted the hurricane lamp glass enclosure, and the wind blew out the flame. Ignoring the freezing blizzard, he sat in the saddle, looking in the direction of the two women and the child. It was too dark to detect movement if there was any. He turned his horse and pushed into the wind, continuing on with the rest of the pack train.

By early morning the pack train reached town and the storm subsided, occasional snowflakes drifting downward as residual excess. Concerned about the two women and the little boy, Amos told several men about what occurred on the trail the night before.

"They might be in trouble," concluded Amos, looking commandingly at the others. "If those two women and that little boy don't show up shortly, I'll need a couple of you to follow me back up the trail. We'll need to borrow an extra horse from someone who's not going with us." The men assented as they looked at Amos, wondering who he was.

As Amos waited and worried about the two women and the little boy, he looked about at the infant town – tents, shanties of shakes and canvas, cabins of logs and shakes, all blanketed with several feet of snow – and with a new saw mill over in Eagle City, some frame buildings under construction in spite of the snow. The growing town, sprouting through the snow in the Coeur d'Alene Mountains end of the Bitterroot range, was surrounded by whale tooth ridges hiding mountain streams and small, gleaming lakes that lay about like broken mirror pieces. Few in the pack train continued west to nearby Eagle City, a few months older than Murrayville.

From discussions with different people as he waited, Amos discovered there was already a pastor in Eagle City, but none in "Murray," as the locals called the new town, and that some Eagle City people, like Coulson with Billings, were leaving for Murray. Murray was gradually replacing Eagle City as the Coeur d'Alene Mountains commercial node. Amos heavily weighed staying in Murray rather than continuing to Eagle City.

After a half hour, impatient, Amos approached the other men and said, "There's no point in waiting any longer. We need to head up the trail and find the two women and the little boy." Amos again looked commandingly at the others. "Who's with me?"

Responding to Amos's chivalry, forcefulness and sense of urgency, several men headed to their horses, mounted up, and Amos described how far they should expect to ride. As he spoke, however, his concerns dissipated when he saw Molly Burdan riding out of the trailhead east of town.

"Hold it!" Amos reined his horse, and held up his left hand. "It's them!" said Amos with relief, and the men stopped and watched the approach of the women. The well-bundled, little boy was seated in front of Molly, holding the saddle horn, and his young mother was seated behind Molly. Eyes closed, head turned, the right side of the mother's face rested against Molly's back, her arms wrapped tightly around Molly's waist. In contrast, Molly's face had a pleasant, confident expression as if to say, "I'm here, gentlemen. You expected otherwise?"

As Molly's horse approached, aware of what had happened and attracted by Molly's uncommon beauty and regal demeanor, other men gathered and watched. One took out tobacco and paper, and rolled a smoke. Reaching the gathering, Molly reined her horse to a halt, and begin to lift the little boy as she nodded toward a nearby, gray-bearded older man who, after a moment's hesitation, quickly stepped forward. Molly spoke in motherly tones to the little boy as she carefully handed the two-year-old to the man while Amos dismounted and with another man helped the boy's mother down from the rear of Molly's horse.

Molly, however, did not move. She sat erectly, continuing to look pleasantly at the men, her auburn hair partially evident beneath her large, dark hat, scarlet scarf and fur coat. Her exotic, ice blue eyes studied the crowd without blinking. She was a very beautiful woman, mesmerizing, and even without the evidence provided by her act of mercy on the trail the previous night, the men sensed uncommon emotional and physical strength. The stares focused.

"Gentlemen," she said forcefully, "find them lodging and feed them." Her voice had a low, sensual, satin quality. Her attractive, commanding presence contrasted starkly with the sullied, bearded men who stood about like unkempt courtiers before a demanding queen. "Spare no expense, and bring the bill to me. I will be staying in Cabin 1 on Gold Street."

As two men stepped toward the mother holding her son, Pastor Nordquist walked to one side and watched the men lead the young mother and her son to Dutch Jake's Saloon, the best saloon or anything else in the infant town. Studying not only Molly Burdan, but also the expanding gathering of men, Pastor Nordquist was intrigued by her demeanor and, like everyone else, wondered who she was and why she had come to Murray.

Another intrigued gentleman was Phillip O'Rourke, a tall, powerfully built, well-dressed, young Irishman who, like all the men present, was immediately attracted to Molly. O'Rourke smiled broadly, looking like a screen persona a later generation would know as Rhett Butler. While help wasn't needed, when O'Rourke offered to help her from her horse, Molly seemed pleased, as if this was what she expected. With O'Rourke's assistance, she formally dismounted in front of the crowd.

"We heard about what you did last night," said O'Rourke as he gently let go of her hand. "That was a fine deed, it was. What's your name, ma'am?"

"I'm Molly Burdan," she said with an inflection suggesting the others might know of her. The name was not immediately familiar, and the people dug through their memory banks attempting to locate her identity. Congenial, self-confident O'Rourke, always comfortable around the opposite sex but rough around the edges, let his masculine instincts take over and said the first thing that came to mind.

"Well now, for the life a' me, I'd never a' thought it," O'Rourke joked. "Molly B'Dam'. I ask you, what a terrible name for a fine lady like yourself: Molly B'Dam.'"

Molly Burdan saw no humor in O'Rourke's statement, and was inwardly annoyed, but this was not the moment for base emotion. As one of the men led her horse, she looked about pleasantly at the crowd of men, many of whom stood prepared to accommodate any additional wish she might have, as others just looked, wondering. As if to finalize Act I, she thanked the men, and reiterated she already had arrangements to move into Cabin No. 1, the first of several self-contained cabins being quickly constructed along the southern edge of town as rental units.

The cabins were the first buildings on Gold Street, parallel to and south of Main Street. Both streets were just given names. How did she know about them? Why was she in Murray? Pastor Nordquist again wondered. Why did she feel it necessary that all know where she would be staying?

The woman who would become the Queen of Murray had arrived. As Pastor Nordquist turned to walk away, he stopped as he heard Phil O'Rourke chuckle, as if making a concluding statement: "Molly B'Dam."

Molly Burdan, Amos mentally corrected as he studied the grim, bearded men standing about, still staring at Molly and intermittently speaking to one another in hushed tones. As he studied the men – their expressionless, penetrating eyes –

Amos felt a familiar frisson of fear, and his expression went blank except for his taut lips as he again sensed the sinister, menacing presence of Old Evil.

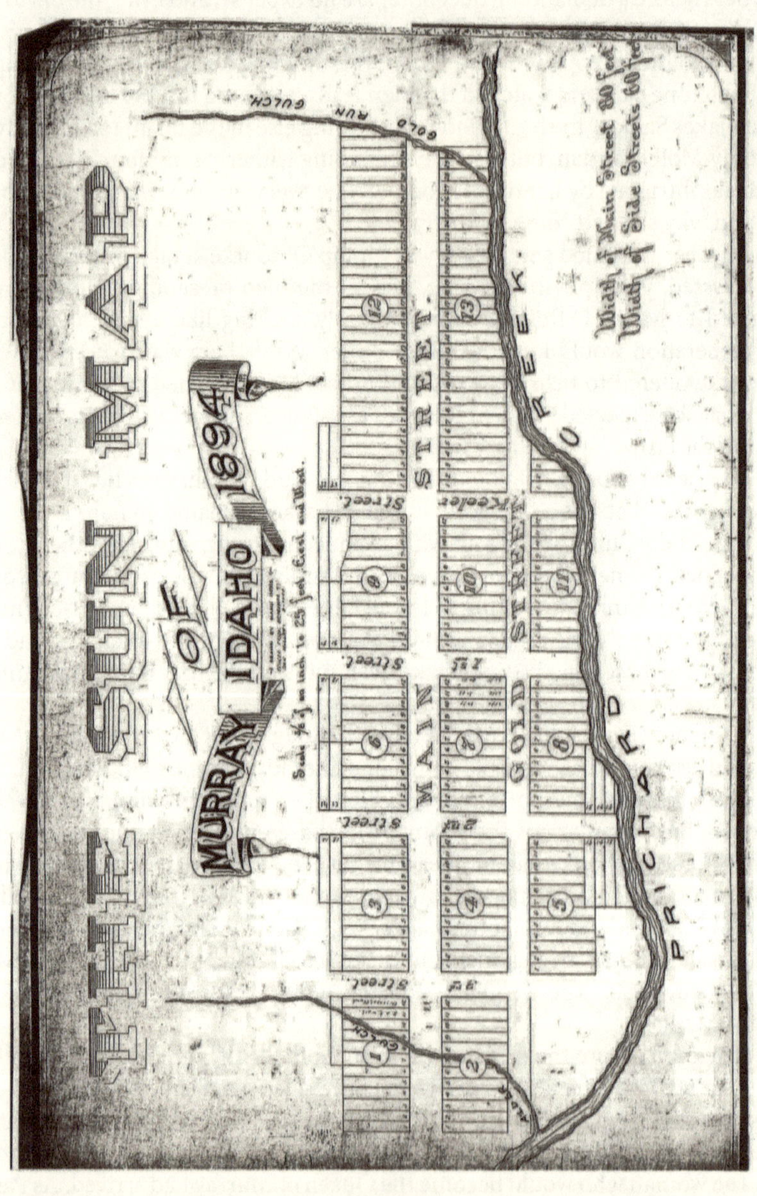

Murray was a hard, godless place, as Amos had expected. That was why he was there. In the wake of a big gold strike, the expanding settlement of Murray experienced outbreaks of raw emotion, remarkable in their extreme, as old rivals and new arrivals forced their way into one another's lives like unsupervised 3rd graders. No lawmen, no judge, no courthouse, no church, and no jail were evident. Five new saloons served armed patrons in an unfettered setting averaging, at the moment, one homicide per week. An occasional week might see no serious violence, but peaceful recesses were short-lived, followed by a flurry of lag-time violence. As the population grew, the time between homicides gradually contracted like the distance between a stalking mountain lion and a young doe. In lawless Murray, emotions and motives leading to these murders were numerous, ranging from long-standing feuds to momentary irritation.

An example of the latter occurred one week before Pastor Nordquist arrived. During the black, winter night, the icy wind moaned irritably. Inside a new Murray tent saloon, rancid cigar and pipe smoke was so thick that a non-smoker became one. Partially obscured patrons appeared like apparitions in the dimly-lit tent, and at the other end of the makeshift bar the small, overworked woodstove seemed to withhold its own heat to stay warm. Men were dressed no differently inside than in the icy air outside.

Grimy Oregon John, standing next to the bar, finished his drink, wiped the scrubble on his face and, avoiding the darkness outside a little longer, numbly looked around for anything of interest. Friendless, nearly penniless, he saw free entertainment at a table in the other corner of the tent where a high stakes poker game was in progress. All participants were professional gamblers, and each gambler had dealt cards to the others on more than one occasion. There was a small mound of cash in the center of the table. Oregon John became interested.

Professional gamblers in the Old West were generally uncongenial men of questionable character, and had no sympathy for others. They produced nothing; their gain was someone else's loss. Money was the primary objective but not the only one. Professional pride was at stake as well. It was simply a matter of who was best. Each man believed in luck, intuition or, beyond that, whatever it took. They reserved no empathy for a novice and, like stags in rut, could develop an intense dislike for one another. A high-stakes poker game sometimes bordered on warfare, and the familiarity among this group bred veiled malevolence.

His modest mind a mist from whiskey, Oregon John awkwardly staggered between tables and chairs toward the gamblers.

He stood there, an unwashed contrast to the modish gamblers, staring at all the money on the table. He loosened the front of his heavy coat to make himself more comfortable. Settled in, he placed his right boot on the lower rung of the closest chair, occupied by a black-mustached gambler wearing a porkpie hat and black fur coat.

The gambler had lost a substantial amount of money during three straight hands which he expected to win, considering the cards he held, and as with all gamblers, his tendency toward superstition made him wonder why this injustice was happening. Lady Luck never toyed with him before. Not like this. Why now? And he didn't like the expressionless look he was getting from the gambler on the other side of the table. He didn't need humiliation.

Stone faced, angrily searching for an answer for his bad luck, the gambler noticed Oregon John's boot resting on the lower chair rung. The gambler looked up at Oregon John for a moment, long enough to study his sodden face. Without a word, the gambler calmly put his hand face down on the table, reached inside his coat, pulled out his Remington Derringer, and cocked it as he turned.

"Blam!"

Gun smoke exploded from the Derringer as the shot bore into Oregon John's chest. Hands flying to his wound, Oregon John staggered backward, mouth open as the small hole over Oregon John's heart spewed blood on John's hands, but the bleeding quickly stopped as John's heart stopped, his lifeless body dropping to the floor like an armload of firewood. As startled onlookers quickly backed away, with extraordinary self-discipline the other gamblers at the table, as if deaf, held their hands motionlessly.

The saloon rowdiness momentarily died down until the owner and the bartender took Oregon John's lifeless body outside for burial in the morning, assuming the frozen ground wasn't too hard. No one at the table said anything; no one's cards moved. As the gun smoke thinned out, the other gamblers waited.

Muffled raucousness returned. The gambler slouched back in his chair and reloaded his Derringer. Sitting up, he raked the others with his eyes as he placed the pistol back inside his coat, picked up his hand and sat back. Onlookers relaxed. Some figured his luck might change now.

Oregon John was a drifter, a part of the Murray underworld, not a prospector. Had Oregon John been a prospector, the first gambler would have faced "the Committee" who would dispatch him as quickly as he killed Oregon John. No questions asked. The Committee was uncompromising. Self-appointed, unrestricted and unchallenged, the men on the Committee savored their power, and took an eye for an eye or more when the opportunity presented itself. In the early days of Murray, the opportunity stepped forward often, and the Committee dealt in naked retribution.

The next opportunity for the Committee to take action happened the following morning. A prospector squatted in the snowfall next to a Prichard Creek tributary north of town, focused on the pan of gravel he was shaking lightly under the water, encouraging the heavier elements to settle and the lighter materials to be swept away. As the icy water rushed around and over the pan, a trapper quietly came up behind the prospector.

"How y' doin', fr'en? Find anythin'?"

The startled prospector started to turn around as the trapper, as if chopping firewood, reared back with a small tree section about the thickness of a baseball bat, swung and clubbed the prospector hard. Teeth clenched, the big, bearded trapper brought down the club again and again, bashing in the prospector's skull, killing him for his burro and grubstake.

The trapper used a club instead of his rifle because, he reasoned, there would be no loud report, and no one would know what was happening. Had no one known, the trapper would have avoided the Committee, but the prospector, as with many prospectors, had a partner or "pard" who, working around a bend in the small creek, heard his pard's initial cry and went to investigate.

He gasped in disbelief when he found the prospector bleeding in the snow, the bloodied club along the edge of the creek not far away. Looking about fearfully, he saw the murderer with burro and grubstake disappear behind snow and trees that lined the trail heading down the mountain. Thinking quickly, rather than chance pursuing the murderer alone, he ran the other direction into town, a considerable distance, to find Committee members.

"Boys!" shouted the pard, out of breath as he staggered into Dutch Jake's Saloon and over to a table occupied by two Committeemen. "Boys!"

He gasped for air as he bent over, hands on his knees.

"Gotta git the others!"

The pard gulped more air.

"It's terrible!" he grimaced. "Ol' Asa's been beaten t' death…over yonder… down the trail! Somebody stole' our jackass…an' grubstake! Whoever they was…ain't gone far. Jes' down the trail."

The two Committee members swigged down their drinks, ran to the door and out into the frozen street, the exhausted pard staggering after them, holding his side. They found two more Committee members, borrowed a horse for the pard, mounted up and, with the pard leading for direction, rode out of town.

When they came to the spot where the prospector lay dead and bloody in the snow, the pard pointed to the bloody club tossed in the snow at the creek's edge. One of the Committeemen rode through the snow-covered brush, dismounted, grabbed the club, swung back up onto his saddle and, with the others, rode back up the embankment. Without a word, the five turned and in tandem galloped down the trail.

A little over a mile away, caught red handed, at gunpoint the trapper was tied, bound, tethered and, with a pistol aimed toward his head, led back to Murray where, as a crowd gathered, at the far end of Gold Street, Committee members took turns using the same club to beat the trapper unconscious in the snow.

"Hell, that's enough," said one Committeeman, breathing heavily. He looked around at the gathered crowd, then down at the unconscious trapper lying on his back, bleeding in the snow. "This is what happens t' goddam thieves and murderers!" the Committeeman shouted in a hoarse voice of finality.

The crowd looked back wide-eyed. Mouth partially open, the Committeeman turned to another Committeeman, took a breath, and snarled, "Woody, put this skunk out a' his misery!"

His expression hard and uncompromising, Woody drew and cocked his .44 revolver.

"Blam!"

Expressionless, for good measure he fired again.

"Blam!"

After two shots in the heart, his gun at his side, Woody looked down at the dead man and, as he slid his revolver back in its holster, turned and looked about at the crowd of dirty, bearded men looking back from under worn hats. Woody fixed his eyes on one man.

"Jedadiah!" shouted Woody to a startled onlooker as the gun smoke wafted away. "Well?" Jedadiah looked back wide-eyed. "Git yer dam' wagon and go bury this bushwacker!"

Old Jedadiah ran awkwardly down the street while the crowd stared at the bloody trapper's beaten, ghoulish face as if it might come back to life at any moment.

In a few minutes, Jedadiah the gravedigger pulled up with his wagon and, with help from three other men, tossed the big body up on the wagon. He jumped on to the seat, snapped the reigns, and the wagon rolled away, headed to the cemetery where Jedadiah would dig another long, deep hole.

The task took nearly four hours due in part to the frozen ground. Finished, Jedadiah pounded a thick, 3½-foot stake in the ground to show someone was already down there. Again, there would be no formal gravestone. No one knew; no one cared.

Jedadiah the gravedigger then went to Dutch Jake's Saloon, got the pard, an extra horse for the pard, and the pard's burro. They rode down the trail to get the dead prospector's body and repeat the process. It was becoming a busy day, but Jedadiah had seen busier.

The deceased prospector's burro and grubstake went to his pard; the trapper's belongings of any additional value went to the Committee as compensation for services rendered, and to defray Jedediah's burial fee.

Between the murders of passion and the murders of retribution, the quickly improvised, makeshift town cemetery was proportionately growing almost as fast as the town. Committee retribution kept cemetery sprawl in check, ironically because the underworld cast knew the Committee meant business – there was no staying court or judge in town, so most would-be murderers at least thought twice before giving in to impulse where prospectors were concerned.

When hearing the stories, Amos learned that, aside from the Committee, the only Murray quasi-public official was Jedadiah, the part-time gravedigger paid by the Committee. In winter, if Jedadiah couldn't get the job done immediately in the graveyard, a dead man's legs would be placed together, knees bent, his arms folded over his chest so that when his body froze, the frozen corpse could be easily dragged to and planted in an eventual grave.

The fate of the trapper, the prospector and Oregon John reflected the infant Murray social fabric, a maladroit patchwork of expediencies borrowed from more civilized communities. Murray wasn't planned. More like a full house in a poker game, it just happened. With the population of hard, self-serving fortune-seekers expanding daily, a mayor, judge, town marshal, and added law enforcement were rapidly becoming necessary. Meanwhile, the Committee did an exemplary job avenging prospectors robbed or murdered around Eagle City and Murray.

During the middle of January, 1884, when Amos arrived, the population of Murray, including prospectors, speculators, gamblers and others, exceeded 1,000 and was growing rapidly, while nearby Eagle City was stagnating. The Northern Pacific Railroad, although not running through Murray or Eagle City, was the fastest way to get to the region from the east, and was extensively promoting north Idaho through pamphlets, posters and ads. The railroad sold an anecdote for discontent and insecurity that was hard to turn down: hope, and even in the cold, defiant, north Idaho winter, each day brought more into the town of Murray including Wyatt Earp, his wife Josie, and his brother Jim. The Earps unwisely chose to continue to nearby Eagle City, however.

In spite of the winter, by February the Murray population exceeded 1,250, a result of people either coming over the Bitterroot Mountain trail from Thompson Falls or simply leaving nearby Eagle City. Most were there for the gold, but the others, a sizeable minority, came to lie, cheat, and steal as opportunities presented themselves.

February 2, 1884

Like many at first, the Earps didn't take the growth of Murray seriously, and began conducting business-as-usual: claim staking, card dealing, liquor sales, law enforcement, and prostitution. Inevitably, vested interests in Eagle City, including the Earps, became concerned about the growing competition with Murray, and to create some excitement, threw a community party in the largest of the 12 Eagle City saloons. The affair was hosted by Martha "Calamity Jane" Cannary and eight hostesses. Paid in cash and whiskey, Calamity Jane got dead drunk and passed out on the sawdust floor. While a rousing time was had by all, after the affair was over, Murray residents went back to Murray.

The Earps had come to Eagle City with the idea of finally staying in one place. From numerous claims, Wyatt started four gold mines – the Consolidated Grizzly Bear, the Dividend, the Dead Scratch, and the Golden Gate – and also became a Kootenai County Deputy Sheriff. When a large gun battle broke out over a claim that was jumped by some friends, Wyatt and Jim Earp, their hands upraised to stop the shooting, walked into the middle of the gunfire and gradually talked everyone into simmering down. One man, Bill Buzzard, had two bullet holes in his hat, and an innocent bystander, not quick enough diving for cover, was wounded in the leg during the 10-minute gun battle, but otherwise results were unlike O.K. Corral.

"I've been down this road before," shouted Wyatt to the men on either side, "and it don't lead nowhere! Stand up and put down your guns! None of you boys shoots worth a dam' anyway!"

Over 50 shots had been fired, filling the air with gun smoke, and no one hit except the innocent bystander.

March, 1884

A little over two months after he arrived in Murray and became familiar with the community, Amos bought a site between Gold Street and Main Street for a church and parsonage. The seller was former congressman William Clagett who spent most of his time steering the public weal and profitably countenancing the new town of Murray over nearby Eagle City.

Parsonage construction was slow because structural components were scarce. When raw iron rods were available, Amos made nails by hand, a skill he learned as a boy from a ship's carpenter in Göteborg.

Nevertheless, Amos' timing was good. The town was taking hold. A few weeks after Amos arrived, Murray welcomed two lawyers. While the town was in its infancy and there was yet no courthouse and no judge, when Amos learned of the barristers, he smiled. This is fortuitous, chuckled Amos. A town that can't support one attorney can always support two.

43

Late March 1884

As prospectors, merchants, and the underworld flowed into Eagle City and Murray, five miles apart, the two boomtowns blossomed and watched to see which would bloom and grow or gradually wither and die.

With spring came improved weather conditions and an escalating influx of prospectors. Most residences and commercial establishments were still in tents. The temperature was usually above freezing during the daytime and often at night as well, causing Main Street to completely thaw. Horses, wagons and huddled pedestrians slogged through mud with the consistency of a chocolate milkshake, and the mud distanced feet into yards while accumulating in bars, stores and residences.

Improved weather conditions enabled greater importation of building materials such as nails and stoves, allowing new building construction to accelerate, accommodating the expanding population. The new Hood & Co. sawmill in Eagle City was sawing up to 14,000 board feet daily, but the majority of the uncured lumber was going down the road to Murray. Having participated in the construction of many sanctuaries and parsonages in Minnesota, Pastor Nordquist spent much of his waking moments either building his own home, as building supplies availed themselves, or working on other new buildings. His activities enabled him to meet many men in construction, earning respect and friendship because of his competence, work ethic, patience and affable smile.

He had neither congregation nor church building, planning to use the parsonage as a temporary worship facility until the sanctuary was completed. The church would certainly not be the first Amos constructed. In the past, however, many hands were willing to help with the construction. In Murray thus far, other than Amos, there were none.

Amos periodically stopped into Dutch Jake's Saloon to visit with any acquaintances, and especially his new friend, Angus MacGregor. Inside, he would occasionally see the beautiful lady most of the town now referred to as "Molly B'Dam," the Good Samaritan on the trail from Thompson Falls. He would always respectfully say, "Hello," and she always courteously returned his greeting.

She was always dressed well and had a regal air that commanded respect. What Molly Burdan did for a living was now no secret. Although he disagreed, conventional wisdom believed hers to be the oldest profession, not his. From others in the bar, principally Angus MacGregor, Amos learned she was originally from Ireland, then New York where she was briefly married to a handsome ne'er-do-well who lived off of his wealthy parents. At the time of the marriage, Molly was a barmaid. Unwilling to accept the station of their new daughter-in-law, her husband's wealthy parents refused to attend the ceremony and would not give their son his substantial allowance as long as he remained married to her. Obviously, the parents' demands were met, thought Amos, because here she is in Murray, a single woman.

If she is Irish, thought Amos, she is probably Catholic. Amos saw Molly welcome indiscriminate young women from other areas of the country, and lease additional Gold Street cabins as quickly as they became available. Aware of her need, the owner wanted top dollar and had no problem getting it. Accommodations for additional girls were absolutely necessary, and the expense increase was a small percentage of the increased profit margin as, like similar establishments in Seattle's Lava Bed and San Francisco's Barbary Coast, work continued around the clock.

That evening, Pastor Nordquist went to Dutch Jake's Saloon for dinner, hopeful of obtaining the company of Angus MacGregor. Although MacGregor was absent, several acquaintances were present. Phil O'Rourke and three of the boys were playing poker at a center table.

Amos sat down at the next table and watched. O'Rourke absently held his cigar in his mouth as he studied the hand he held. From the other side of the table it was hard to tell when O'Rourke had a bad hand or a good hand – his visceral reaction to either was the same.

After ordering dinner, Pastor Nordquist sat back, facing the card game. He was intrigued by the simultaneously serious but uncommunicative expressions on the men's faces as they studied one another's eyes and cards, the latter considerably larger than in later years, did not have rounded edges, and face cards had only one face. Pastor Nordquist did not gamble but knew a seasoned gambler could sometimes identify someone else's cards by the way they were held.

The next hand was dealt, and as well-dressed O'Rourke picked up his cards, his eyes showed no emotion, his face no expression. He held the king of spades, the queen of spades, the six of hearts, the three of clubs and the seven of diamonds.

O'Rourke tossed three cards on the table and was dealt three more. He picked up the three cards and without expression slipped them into his hand.

The three other gamblers responded similarly and returned to their furtive stares, reevaluating what the others held. What each gambler held was significant. Besides whatever O'Rourke had, two of the others had two pairs – queen high and king high. The fourth gambler sat quietly with a full house – aces and eights.

Bad hands could be disconcerting, and the self-discipline needed to hide a gambler's disappointment would sometimes be all that his temperament could handle. But good hands, really good hands, good hands brought with them responsibility. Good hands demanded dispassion, sobriety, intellect, nerves of steel. Exceptionally good hands demanded all the discipline a gambler could muster. The full house stood in a shadow.

Meanwhile, during his life, O'Rourke had played a lot of hands, and sitting in what began as a penny ante poker game with nothing much at stake, he wondered, why am I dealt one of these? It isn't for practice, he thought, because I might never get another one. On top of the tension he felt, he worried about the effect this would have on his luck. Lordamighty, all my luck for the next year or so is right here in this hand. I either make the most of this now or quit playing.

O'Rourke was on edge, and the feeling quickly found its way around the table because the others were also on edge; all had favorable hands. With intuition honed radar-sharp by years of card playing, each maintained a stealthy stare, listening to gut-level feel. Pastor Nordquist watched the expressionless faces and, after dinner was delivered to his table and he gave thanks, continued to watch as the gamblers thoughts started, stopped, and zipped about like dragonflies over a pond.

Jernigan's got something, thought the first gambler. His eyes are plainly saying it's good. Other eyes flicked left and right. O'Rourke's tense, so O'Rourke's hand is big. But how big is big?

It's like knowing the other guy has hooked a big fish, thought the second gambler, long before you see the damned thing. You know it, you feel it. He studied the faces, the hands, and in a heartbeat glanced at his own, quickly looking up again.

The initial sensation evolved. As the men studied each other and scrutinized the backs of hands, caution, even skepticism, crept into the hearts of each. Do these boys have something really big? Or just better than average? The odds aren't there, thought the third gambler. But that's the funny thing about odds.

The fish began to make its run…and when O'Rourke opened with a little more than usual, the others were in, each raising the others. O'Rourke responded by cautiously raising them as much as he felt would not discourage the momentum. The amount of money on the table gradually began to take on serious proportions, fueled by two with two pair – queen high and king high – and a full house: aces and eights.

While looking at his hand, the third man cleared his throat. O'Rourke glanced at the third gambler like the man recited a speech. Between clearing his throat and the subtle change about his eyes that accompanied the thought, in gambler communication the others clearly received the message. His hand is good. But how good is good? Eyes smiling as usual, O'Rourke looked again at his hand. To the others, not just his smiling eyes but the way they smiled, and the forgotten, now-unlit cigar in his mouth, confirmed O'Rourke had a strong hand.

But so did they.

No one spoke. The game moved rapidly. O'Rourke kept the dead cigar in his mouth as the men continued to put money on the table, and each man's concentration and will to win grew stronger.

As the card game progressed, a dirty hulk of a man, big as a mountain, slogged through the mud toward Dutch Jake's. His nickname, Lightnin', reflected his comportment. As Lightnin' careened through the front door, he did not slow down, but blindly ignoring anything in his way, lurched towards the bar, stopping short of running into it, and straightened up as if suddenly seeing it. Eyeing the room through a self-induced fog, he put his left hand on the bar for stability and then, with uncalled-for flair, with his right hand waved a leather pouch of "diggings" – gold dust and nuggets – over his head before slamming it down on the bar. The pouch contents had a value in that year of roughly $1,000, considerable wealth.

"Whiskey!" shouted Lightnin', the dim light in his eyes flickering like a small candle.

The nearby card game stopped. They knew Lightnin's physical size dwarfed his intellect, and the combination of the two sometimes meant trouble. Phil O'Rourke, if he wasn't smiling or laughing outright, usually had laughter in his eyes. The laughter came naturally and was part of the reason people immediately liked him. From the card table, his hand carefully hidden, annoyed at the interruption, the laughter stopped, and O'Rourke momentarily glared at the huge man's disruptive antics.

The big bartender, his hair parted down the middle, a huge handlebar mustache covering taut lips, and eyes made bloodshot by hours of contact with thick cigar and pipe smoke, walked to where Lightnin' stood, and put both hands on the bar.

"Whiskey," repeated the bartender. "Scotch 'r Irish?"

The bartender dealt with more than his share of drunks during the past hour, and was in no mood to put up with Lightnin', regardless of how much wealth he brought in with him from the fir and pine covered hills around Murray. Lightnin' blinked blankly, confused for a moment. It had been weeks since anyone asked him a question…needing an answer. When the question registered and Lightnin' realized what little difference it made, through a dirt-encrusted, full, dark beard he flashed a gap-toothed grin at the glowering bartender, looked around the barroom, saw the looks of the men at the tables, glanced at his poke, looked back at the bartender and, realizing the effect that he had had during the last 10 seconds, began to laugh. In contrast to his appearance and behavior, the laugh had genteel, almost musical, bass-baritone charm delivered from a part of Lightnin' that would have little to do with the rest of him.

"Both!" ordered Lightnin' at a decibel level which could be heard out in the street. "Drinks're on me, boys! Scotch 'r Irish, name yer paisin!" For emphasis, he pounded the bar several times with his big grimy fist, shaking the bar and the $1,000 poke sitting on top of it.

The four men at O'Rourke's table returned to their cards, ignoring him. Let the others drink. To someone immersed in the throes of gambling, here was something almost as important as life itself. Each man believed he had a chance to win big.

O'Rourke raised again. As the others reevaluated the strengths of their hands, O'Rourke's mind momentarily wandered as he thought about how winning can bring multiple satisfactions. Obviously, the money. But there is also the pleasure of finishing first. First is big. Banks all over the East Coast never use the word "Last" in their name. Being first makes someone better than the next man, and all that implies.

And winning means you're lucky.

Few emotions motivate stronger than hope, and luck is hope improbably realized, O'Rourke ruminated, thinking of a conclusion he'd drawn years earlier: if it's probable, it isn't luck. And when this improbability happens a few times, others believe that person is lucky, and he's someone special. People begin to hang around him; watch what he does; hope to get there themselves. Without moving his head, O'Rourke glanced at Amos and other men at a short distance all watching the game. I'm about to attract some followers, O'Rourke thought, looking back at his cards, his eyes again laughing, his cigar still unlit.

Amos watched the four men, wondering how it would end. He already knew intermittent reinforcement of gambling behavior is seldom more effective than with a few insignificant wins followed by a single, great gambling success. Amos could not know, however, that two years earlier the third gambler won big in a Dodge City poker game, and the residual contagion infected him and all exposed. Two years later, he was still infected, and the hope of hitting another big one, however improbable, was irrepressible, monopolizing the man's judgment. Here he was. It could be done, he knew. Now, maybe it's time for a second big score, he thought.

Of course, most gamblers, like the remaining three men at the table including O'Rourke, never scored big; they won some and lost some and knew when to hold or fold. Some men didn't. Amos remembered being in Lahaina at the age of 14, watching a card game between six whalers where after already heavy losses, unwilling to quit, a gambler went even deeper in the hole, trying to "earn it all back," losing everything. Gambling, as Oregon John found out, could get deadly serious.

As the game progressed, around the table hope grew greater with each raise. But gradually the other three men sensed that O'Rourke's fish was as big as they initially intuited…for the simple reason that O'Rourke didn't seem too concerned about what hands the others held. A man must have a decent set of cards, they thought, when he don't seem to care much what the rest of us have.

After a while, the stakes started to become uncomfortably high for the two gamblers with two pair. Two pair was generally a pretty good hand, but it was becoming evident that O'Rourke and the third gambler held better cards. The two gamblers with two pair, first one then the other, folded. The full house stood erect. Aces and eights.

O'Rourke is either the best bluffer or holds the best hand in the territory, the third gambler thought. An ace-high full house isn't a bad hand though; good enough to win almost any time. The gambler glanced to his left and right. Pastor Nordquist was watching. The men at nearby tables were watching. The gambler looked back at his hand. *Maybe I've gone too far…or maybe I ain't gone far enough.* He looked at the other two gamblers, who looked back. No one spoke out loud, but their expressions spoke in unison as if to say: do or die, friend.

The third man raised O'Rourke who reciprocated as silent surrounding men watched motionlessly.

The third gambler decided to proceed more cautiously. Each time the third man raised O'Rourke slightly, O'Rourke, without much hesitancy, saw his raise and raised him back.

Might be a little slower on the draw, O'Rourke thought.

The gambler with the full house hesitated. *What does O'Rourke have?* the gambler wondered. *The gambler was almost out of money. It was time to call.*

Sensing the end approaching, O'Rourke, also getting low on cash, laid his hand face down on the table, re-lit his cigar, leaned back in his chair and blew more smoke into the gray haze above the card table.

Pastor Nordquist watched, hands folded in his lap.

O'Rourke looked pleasantly at the other gambler and politely waited. O'Rourke thought about something he read where someone named Seneca said luck was where preparation met opportunity. *Hell, preparation,* O'Rourke thought. *Real luck doesn't have anything to do with preparation.*

The third gambler's black slouch hat complemented his black sideburns, handlebar mustache and week's growth of black stubble. *I just bet the farm on a full house,* he thought. *Aces and eights.*

He leaned on his right elbow, forearm on the table with his cards face down. He stared hard at O'Rourke's hand, attempting to see something that might tell him what made O'Rourke so confident. He looked out of the corner of his eye at the neighboring table. They looked back. In fact, saloon rowdiness had subsided. It was quiet as everyone watched. Even Lightnin', his forearm resting on the bar with a forgotten drink in his hand, looked at the third gambler without expression. The money on the table told the story.

The gambler looked at the pot. *Good Lord, that's a lotta money,* he thought. *He recalled his big success two years ago. Been lucky before. This whole Murray business 'd be worth it if this was mine.* All eyes were on the third gambler. He stared at O'Rourke who responded by calmly blowing a large, smoke ring that hung over the table like a full moon.

The gambler matched O'Rourke's last raise. "I'll call," said the gambler. As the full moon seemingly hid behind a gray cloud, O'Rourke didn't move.

The gambler slowly laid his full house on the table. "Full house." He looked at O'Rourke. "Aces and eights."

It was a good hand. Everyone watching thought it was a good hand, and there was murmuring as onlookers nodded at one another. O'Rourke's expression did not change, and everyone in the bar leaned forward a little.

The fish began to surface.

Men seated at a distance got up from their chairs, walked toward O'Rourke's table and stood within a general radius of five feet, watching.

O'Rourke's smiling eyes looked at the third gambler as O'Rourke slowly laid down the 10 of spades.

Then the jack of spades. Followed by the queen of spades.

Cigar aside his mouth, O'Rourke looked at the tense expression on the third gambler's face as O'Rourke laid down the king of spades. When the last card slowly came to rest like a fallen maple leaf, the third gambler's head fell as his heart sank. The ace of spades.

A royal flush. The gambler's chin came to rest on his chest, knowing second-best meant last. Initial exclamations crescendoed to an uproar as surrounding men whooped and yelled, some spontaneously throwing their hats in the air upon seeing The Hand in front of popular Phil O'Rourke. It was a big fish, the biggest those present would expect to see, and bigger than most others would ever see.

O'Rourke began pulling the money toward him, cigar firmly fixed in the corner of his mouth.

The third gambler's chin remained on his chest as he weighed the chance he took, and the money he lost. Aces and eights. It was a good hand. Wasn't it? He wanted to turn back the clock. No. Hell, no it wasn't. His hope destroyed, he had no luck, and the moment felt like a nightmare. Coming out of his stupor, he reached for his drink. His head jerked up, the drink rose to his mouth and, his head rolling backwards, was downed in one gulp. His chin fell to his chest as the whiskey glass in his hand rudely slammed to the table, then fell on its side like a defeated chess piece.

The show was over, but the cast party was just starting. Everyone remembered their drinks, compliments of Lightnin', and after a few more rounds, men in Dutch Jake's were celebrating like it was St. Patrick's Day in Dublin.

Pastor Nordquist sat with his hands folded in his lap and watched. The third gambler sat in the same position, head down as if dead. Pastor Nordquist wanted to comfort him but wasn't sure of what to say; the man was numb, and oblivious to everything around him.

Beginning with Lightnin', the raucous behavior attracted the attention of the Queen of Murray who learned such situations, like being dealt a good hand, were profitable opportunities if she played her cards right. As Pastor Nordquist studied Molly from a distance, she stood alone at the end of the bar, patiently watching a discussion between another man and Lightnin' who, mindlessly laughing, was spilling his drink without noticing. In Molly's experience, since the time man began using mineral wealth as an exchange medium, the adage that "a fool and his money are soon parted" had remained as constant as the laws of gravity, and the velocity at which money departed increased exponentially with the presence of three catalysts: loneliness, whiskey (Scotch or Irish), and a beautiful woman. Molly Burdan did not go to Dutch Jake's to charm the fruit of his hard labor from Lightnin'. She came to watch. Measure the man. A steel trap does not pursue its prey.

Curious about her past and amenable to the pleasure of female companionship, Pastor Nordquist considered whether or not he should attempt conversation. As a pastor, he spoke to and counseled dozens of young women, and was certainly no stranger to public speaking. Yet he was hesitant to approach her. She stood there watching an inebriated Lightnin' as well as other men in the room, and it seemed that this was her sole purpose for being there. Pastor Nordquist was not sure he should disturb her.

As he stood up, prepared to either leave or formally introduce himself, she sensed his attention and pleasantly turned toward him. With a subtle nod, she beckoned him to step forward as if he were being granted an audience. He removed his hat and introduced himself as Amos Nordquist.

44

I understand you are a man of the cloth," Molly responded.

"Well, yah, but I have not been very active in the ministry since I arrived in Murray. I have been busy with construction of my parsonage where my first church services will also be held."

Pastor Nordquist had not been close enough to Molly to truly appreciate the extent of her beauty. Now they were face-to-face. Her light auburn hair was thick and full with a metallic glimmer that shimmered in the weak light as she turned her head. Her preternaturally ice-blue eyes emanated an intoxicating mixture of beauty, strength, and poise. Her intelligence was evident from complex, fluent sentences and perfect diction, indicative of a razor-sharp mental edge. Her soft bronze-tinged skin was flawless, as was her nose, and her high cheekbones complemented her supple mouth made sensuous by mirror image lips resting anxiously like leopards before a hunt. Her soft, determined jaw worked in partnership with her mouth, completing the magnification of her sensuality.

Her radiance was overpowering. Men speaking with her often lost their ability to concentrate on what they were saying or hearing, sometimes not responding to what she said until she politely repeated herself. She had an unusually small waist and relatively narrow hips. Everything else was well developed. Buxom with wide shoulders on a proportionately short torso, she had no need for the padded undergarments of the era.

The myth-making juggernaut that rode east out of the Old West made celebrities out of vinegary Belle Starr and grizzly Calamity Jane. In contrast, the beauty, intelligence and sophistication of the most unique woman to grace any Old West town from El Paso to Dawson City remained unknown outside of northern Idaho. The physical and charismatic contrast between Molly and her sorority sisters was stark. Intuiting the emotional quicksand into which he might step if not careful, and continually reminding himself of his position, Pastor Nordquist conscientiously exercised self-discipline.

"I am also working in preparation for the arrival of my wonderful wife and three daughters next year," he smiled.

Molly's pleasant expression became blank, her eyes enigmatic.

"This is a tough town. I hope your wife is prepared for the life she will experience here. How old are your daughters?"

Pastor Nordquist studied the change in countenance. "11, 7 and almost 4," he responded.

Her statement about Murray being a tough town, and her expression, were discomfiting. In the beginning he questioned the wisdom of bringing his wife and daughters to this north Idaho boomtown filled with prospectors, hard rock miners, gamblers and others enterprising in various forms of vice. But it was his responsibility to minister to the downtrodden, the outcast. The Messiah did no less. Pastor Nordquist believed the Holy Spirit, defending his calling and his ministerial position, would serve as protection against the powers of darkness.

Molly continued to look at Pastor Nordquist without expression, without blinking. Without knowing precisely why, Pastor Nordquist felt further discomfort, as if he were in the presence of something other than the Queen of Murray. As the silence that followed grew louder, Molly's beautiful blue eyes began to smile. She liked this pastor. She had studied him like everyone else. He seemed sincere, unaffected, intelligent and nonjudgmental. Good looking. Uncharacteristically of women during her era, she extended her hand.

"Pastor, may I formally introduce myself," she said with precise intonation. "I'm Molly Burdan. It is my pleasure to meet you."

Surprised, he gently took her hand and sensing some pleasure upon feeling the long Kelly green velvet glove she wore, Pastor Nordquist courteously acknowledged her introduction, slightly relieved she took the initiative, but still apprehensive about the sensation a moment ago.

"I am pleased to meet you too," responded Amos. "I was behind you in the pack train when we came from Thompson Falls. You may not remember that I offered to help you...you said it was unnecessary. Are you familiar with the story of the Good Samaritan in the Bible?"

Pastor Nordquist asked this question to introduce the subject of the Bible, to compliment Molly, and to find out more about Molly's spiritual convictions, if any.

"Yes, I have read the parable of the Good Samaritan," answered Molly Burdan with an expression of familiarity as if she and Pastor Nordquist had known one another for years. "You know, of course, that the Savior provided this parable not only to encourage helping the despised and unfortunate, but also to show the hypocrisy of the religious leaders who, before the Good Samaritan stopped to help, passed by the man who had been beaten and robbed."

"Yah, that is true," responded Pastor Nordquist.

"I appreciated your offer to help," Molly continued. "I responded in the way I thought appropriate at the moment but, frankly, in hindsight, I should have accepted your offer that night. I didn't think of it at the time, but getting that woman on the horse the next morning took some effort," she laughed.

Pastor Nordquist looked down. I should have been more adamant, he thought.

"I should have insisted," he responded sincerely. "Forgive me."

"You are forgiven," she smiled with a combination of pride and sincerity. It was not often that a woman in her position was asked to forgive a man of God.

"You appear to be familiar with the Bible, Miss Burdan," Pastor Nordquist stated while wondering whether the prefix "Miss" would be corrected by the lady. There was no evidence she noticed.

"With respect to Samaritans," responded Molly, "you know the Sanhedrin considered them less than human. In addition, the church leaders at that time would not normally speak to women. Were you aware of that?"

"Well, yah, that was so."

"Among some in the ministry, it is still so," stated Molly Burdan, her eyes narrowing. "But it was not so with the Savior. Among the many with whom He spoke was a Samaritan woman who gave him water to drink when he was thirsty. You are familiar with the story of the woman at the well, are you not, Pastor?"

"Jesus accurately tells the woman, whom he has previously never met, that she had five husbands and that she was living with a man who was not her husband," responded Pastor Nordquist, a little uncomfortable freely discussing dissolute infidelity with an extraordinarily beautiful woman. "The story appears in the fourth chapter of John."

"John 4:4-29," said Molly.

Pastor Nordquist looked at Molly with pleasant surprise, and accepted this response for, without referring to his Bible, he was uncertain of the exact verses.

"Do you know what else it said?" continued Molly. "When the disciples arrived, they were amazed that he had been speaking with a woman. This is an interesting contrast, don't you think? That the Son of God would have no reservation about speaking with not only a Samaritan or even a Samaritan woman, but a Samaritan woman who had been married several times and was, at the time the Savior spoke to her, living in sin."

"Well, yah," responded Pastor Nordquist, "but you remember the woman said the Messiah was coming. In spite of those sins, her heart had been opened to the truth of God, that is, the messianic covenant…ironically standing in front of her. You know that Martin Luther unintentionally began what was to be called the Reformation following the reading of Romans 3:28."

"'Therefore, we conclude that a man is justified by faith without the deeds of the law,'" said Molly. "And in his personal Bible Martin Luther wrote the Latin words…"

"'*Sola fide*,'" said Pastor Nordquist, repeating the Latin words for "only faith." Molly Burdan and Pastor Nordquist both laughed.

It was evident she had studied the Bible, especially those portions which dealt with women. And she knew church history.

"I understand the woman at the well," concluded Molly, looking aside without turning her head. It was a rare moment. Molly Burdan paid Pastor Nordquist a great compliment by allowing him a glimpse of something concealed. She sensed he was who he said he was. His perception of Molly B'Dam' was not as clear, however. He waited. She said nothing more.

"You must continue," he said.

A moment passed with no response from Molly Burdan. It was evident she would say nothing further. It seemed to Pastor Nordquist that like the woman at the well, Molly Burdan had faith. He studied her eyes intently for additional insight. The bright light in her eyes a moment ago was gone, and once again her beautiful eyes and face were emotionless. Pastor Nordquist asked Molly of what denomination she considered herself.

"I was raised a Catholic." Molly paused. "Following my divorce, however, the Catholic Church would have nothing to do with me. It's not just the Catholic Church…many churches are that way. I call myself a Christian." She looked away.

Pastor Nordquist thought to himself that from what he knew of her, she is a woman of faith who has been married, evidently treated inhumanely by her former in-laws and former husband, and is divorced. She has been with many men; more than the Samaritan woman. Pastor Nordquist saw in her eyes a related emotion: pain. It was not a hurt that came from being offended or even on-going abuse. It was a deeper, spiritual pain resulting from a clash of relentless conscience with conscious inclination to sin. The interim pain, Pastor Nordquist knew, could be temporarily anaesthetized with a combination of worldly popularity and material wealth. At the moment, Molly Burdan, in her finery and with her aristocratic air, however, stood in front of Pastor Nordquist feeling almost naked.

As her left hand rose to the side of her face, her eyes softened, and for a moment she stared in the direction of the floor on the opposite side of the barroom. Defensively, she looked up, shooting a probing glance at Pastor Nordquist, whose eyes caught the probe and held it.

"Indeed, Miss Burdan, none of us is spiritually what we want to be. As you probably know, the Bible says that 'all have sinned and fallen short of the glory of God.'"

Her face remained expressionless as she looked at him. I've said too much, she thought; it does not serve the present to resurrect the past. Simultaneously, Amos wanted to reach out in love, comforting her, while another part of him said to keep his distance. Then her eyes instantly regained their steeliness, as if something had flipped a switch in her heart.

She had heard it all before, but a part of her still wanted to hear it again.

"The Bible says," Pastor Nordquist continued, "in Ephesians 2:8: 'For by grace you have been saved through faith; and that not of yourselves, it is the gift of God; not as a result of works…' And in the 7th chapter of Luke, Jesus forgave a sinful woman, one who had displayed her love toward him, wiping his feet with her hair made wet by perfumed oil and tears. At that moment Jesus said to the Pharisees: 'For this reason I say to you, her sins, which are many, have been forgiven, for she loved much; but he who is forgiven little, loves little.'"

Molly continued listening carefully to what Pastor Nordquist said about love and forgiveness, and said nothing although, not completely understanding God's grace, what he just said seemed backwards: shouldn't love precede forgiveness?

"You have been forgiven much," Pastor Nordquist said to Molly, "and, therefore, love much. Love flows from your heart's well of faith, a gift of God, evidence of your forgiveness, signifying your salvation," he concluded, feeling, as he sometimes did, another voice speaking through him.

Molly Burdan's face was still expressionless, but seemed softer than a moment earlier.

Pastor Nordquist glanced about Dutch Jake's Saloon to see if Angus Mac-Gregor had walked in, but Angus was nowhere to be seen. Turning to Molly Burdan, Amos courteously thanked her for the conversation and, as he turned to leave, looked at her and said sincerely, "May God bless you."

Following the momentary lead of her heart, her beautiful eyes softened in response but, as he walked away, she maintained her silence. Watching him, the war inside her continued as it had for years, and a dark part of her grew indignant, offended, a grasping voice reminding her: remember the others? Remember what they did? Is this so-called man-of-God any different? Who are these men, and who are they to preach to you of love and salvation? What do many really want? In her heart, empty self-righteousness began to leaven, and she turned away.

As Pastor Nordquist started to leave, he inexplicably stopped, staring momentarily at the barroom door in front of him, inwardly debating whether to leave or stay in case. . . What was it? Angus? Was that it? Or something else. As Amos stood, he felt a sensation of someone standing behind him and he turned around.

All Amos saw was Molly talking to Lightnin', her back to Amos, not looking at him. The numinous feeling grew, and as Pastor Nordquist looked around him, the hair on the back of his neck and forearms began to stand up. An older man with a bushy mustache, seated to his right, looked up at Amos curiously, but otherwise Amos saw no one nearby.

He momentarily stood frozen in place, but then began to experience a gradual emotional transition to normalcy as Old Evil sloughed off. While Amos began to feel more like himself, he also felt spent, like he might after delivering a difficult sermon. He took a deep breath, turned around and stepped forward, continuing out the front door of the saloon.

While walking up the dark, muddy street toward the small boarding house where he was staying, his thoughts remained on Molly B'Dam. Molly would prove an enigma for Pastor Nordquist. She had strong spiritual leanings, but was entrapped by past memories and the convictions those memories created. Molly knew the gospel story and believed that Jesus was the Christ, her savior. And she knew what she should do, but did not. To Pastor Nordquist, it seemed this was how it was all over Murray. There was little hypocrisy; most people did not pretend to be one thing one moment and something else the next. They were who they were. They just freely sinned. In Murray, it was easy. The spiritual atmosphere was saturated with hope and "luck." Pastor Nordquist saw it every-where – the prospectors, the miners, the gamblers, the merchants, the women. The sensitivity to providential preference was thicker than cigar smoke above a card game.

Meanwhile, Lightnin' bought more rounds for the house. He liked his popu-larity. By early morning, an extremely inebriated Lightnin' found himself on The Line run by the Queen of Murray.

45

The following afternoon Lightnin' awoke hung over. As he pushed himself out of bed, he felt like miniature miners were digging shafts through the convolutions of his brain. When he looked where he had placed his poke last night, it was gone. At first he thought he was still asleep, and rubbed his eyes. No. He was awake. He looked again. Gone. Betrayal. Realizing he had been taken for $700 to $800 in gold, his anger exploded like rock blasting dynamite.

In a rage, convinced that the culprit was Molly B'Dam, Lightnin' hastily put on his pants, shirt, shoes and coat, and stormed out the door, through the mud, and into the next cabin where the big man accosted the girls, roaring like thunder, spewing obscenities. If his behavior when first entering Dutch Jake's Saloon the previous night was less than genteel, his behavior now made last night seem like finishing school. One of the girls slipped toward a closet to get the rifle the girls kept, just in case. Stomping back and forth, Lightnin' shouted repeatedly, "Where is she?! Where is she?!"

In mortal fear, they would have told him if they knew. Only Molly knew her itinerary, and at that moment, threatening the girls was pointless. As she returned from business, however, Molly heard the commotion and went to investigate. When she opened the cabin door and saw an enraged Lightnin', she expected to control the situation as usual, and with an affectation of fragile femininity, walked on stage, standing in front of him.

In his backwoods manner, Lightnin' raged back and forth in front of her as if at any moment he might grab her and snap her in half like a piece of kindling. He'd done it with men.

But he couldn't touch her. A lady like her needed to be protected, and the laugh in Lightnin' knew this. It took exceptional fortitude for Molly to maintain her composure, stand her ground, but she did, displaying the same regal bearing she brought into town following the blizzard.

Her defense was simple: deny and delay. She maintained steadfastly she did not take his poke.

Lightnin' shouted that was a lie. Molly would not change her story, and gradually Lightnin' exhausted himself. Frustrated, he began to back down and, when he wavered, several of the girls, offended by his behavior and as angry as Lightnin' was moments ago, began firing verbal salvos in Lightnin's direction.

Outnumbered and overmatched, Lightnin' began to withdraw. Being taken to the cleaners was bad enough, but being ridiculed for losing his shirt was more than his already-wounded ego could endure. He stood for a moment, his balance unsteady. He looked at Molly, and at the girls' hateful expressions, their language now searing. His poke was gone; and his hope was gone. His ignominy overwhelming, he turned and lumbered numbly to the door, opened it, and walked out into the chilly Murray air, owning little more than the clothes he had on.

As town folk heard about this later, rumors started, and someone speculated that Lightnin's missing poke materialized somewhere on The Line. Molly returned it, someone said, and she had no idea who took it. Returning gold, however, was not why Molly was in Murray.

As she watched him go, Molly felt pity for the man who just called her every name he knew, and claimed she stole his poke. Now he was broke, and his hope and exuberance of the previous evening were also gone. His manhood and existence were ridiculed by her girls. This whole thing had gone too far. She hadn't wanted to wound him; she just wanted his gold. The night before, she rationalized he'd find more. Now she wasn't sure he was going to make it out of the hole she dug. Most of the names he called her were true, and when she said she did not steal his poke, she lied. She shouldn't have stolen his poke. She shouldn't have lied. Her conscience was again becoming a nuisance.

It doesn't matter; this is what you must do to get on top, said Molly's dark side. If someone gives you an advantage, take it. Survival of the fittest. Never say you are sorry or wrong. If lying gives an advantage, lie. If cover is needed, cover with another lie...

Her conscience countered by continuing the logical sequence: ...to where everything you do is a lie, and you live a lie.

Her dark side reacted defensively, shooting back an answer – morality is for weaklings – she did not believe.

Molly's conscience replied in no uncertain terms that morality was not for weaklings – quite the opposite – and told her she did a cruel injustice, she was not among those with strength. Her conscience itself was evidence that the trials of humanity amounted to more than survival. She again went against her conscience and for an instant her regal ruse smirked at her. She felt humiliated. She was ashamed of what she had done. It was so common.

She walked, deprecating, back to her cabin. Words like honesty, integrity and decency, she thought, do not apply to me. To return the gold she had stolen, however, would nullify a very substantial single-evening financial gain, and undermine her ruse, the regal image she maintained in Murray that gained the respect she wanted, and which she would lose if it were proven she had stolen the hard-earned poke of a miner. To return the gold would show her hand.

Good Lord, she thought to herself...the Committee. Lightnin' was a prospector. She was one of the Murray underworld, no matter how upstanding she pretended to be.

How…? She did not continue the thought. She was doing exactly as she planned to do. Moralizing was pointless. Her hypocritical lifestyle had become spoiled and demanding, and in continued anger she rushed the short remaining distance to her cabin, anticipating losing her composure, exposing the resurfacing sense of worthlessness she could usually buy off.

Lightnin' went back to Dutch Jake's, but with no money for friendship, did not go inside. He slumped almost lifelessly in a chair outside the door staring at the cold, muddy roadbed that was Main Street. As he looked at the street, rain began to shoot down in bullets, a thousand bursts in the Murray mud. Lightnin' was still emotionally numb, but after a while his soul began to feel again, if only to feel bad. With effort he forced his way to his feet, adjusted the collar of his old, dirty coat and, looking downward, slogged out into the downpour where the laugh in him caused him to stop, his worn boots sinking in mud to his ankles. But he did not feel like laughing. He felt like unburdening his wretchedness.

He took off his weather-beaten, black plug hat and, blinking his eyes repeatedly before closing them, turned his face toward the downpour, his mouth moving involuntarily.

Moments later his face fell as his teeth clenched. His breaths were staccato as he stood long enough to regain his composure. "Hell," he whispered.

Reattaching his hat to his cold, soaked head, he tramped and stumbled through the dark mud to the edge of town, and then back up into the steep hills overlooking Murray, to a shanty where he lived with a dog-faced, old miner who seldom spoke. His pard.

— • —

Anna wrote to Amos every day, and letters reached Murray in batches. In addition to news of the community, the school, the church and the girls, every letter reiterated Anna's desire to be with Amos. And she did not like waiting. She fully expected he would have the parsonage done by the end of summer, and then she and the girls would head west to join him. Unhappy with general planning, each letter requested the same thing: she wanted a specific targeted date where she could expect to board a train for Thompson Falls, and that date should be before the beginning of the school year.

Amos could only reply what he replied before: while he shared her desire to reunite as soon as possible, he could not predict with certainty when the parsonage would be ready and, even if he could, he wasn't sure when Murray would reach a level of civility where he felt comfortable bringing his wife and daughters to the town. In his return letters, he did not provide specifics.

Early Summer, 1884

Three months passed since the poke-stealing incident. The parsonage was nearly finished. Anna was anxious to get started.

On a cloudy afternoon, Lightnin's pard, an older man slowed by arthritic pain, stepped out of their mean, one-room hillside shanty, and navigated the hillside trail into Murray to find a doctor if there was one.

As the small, old man came to the edge of town, the chaw in his mouth was forgotten. He saw a wooden box next to the road ahead and walked to it, needing to sit and let his legs recover. After ten minutes, he stood and walked down Main Street to Dutch Jake's Saloon. Stepping inside the door, he looked about and, eyes wide and unblinking, shuffled to the bar, stopping short of it. He looked up expectantly like a hungry cat at a back door. Both hands held his ragged hat, and he fidgeted with the brim as he stood motionlessly, hoping someone would notice him.

"What's eatin' ya, old timer?" asked the big bartender with the black handle-bar mustache as he washed a glass, expressionlessly studying the pard.

The pard mumbled self-consciously, unable to look directly at the bartender, "Lightnin'… Lightnin's been gittin' weaker an' weaker, an' he's been laid up sick in bed fer almost two weeks."

"Sorry t' hear that."

"Dunno…," Lightnin's pard began to say in a scratchy voice so unused to itself that it stammered and stopped for a moment. "Dunno but that he might have the fever."

His worn hands alternately squeezed the old hat brim, as if milking a cow like he did as a boy, while he momentarily looked uncomfortably at a nearby chair. Bushy eyebrows raised, his aged eyes flicked up and then down in the direction of the bar as he stood uncertain of what to say or do next. The bartender put the glass on a shelf under the bar.

"Mountain fever." The bartender put both hands on the bar and looked down at the small man, sympathizing. "Two weeks, y' say. Lotta boys that get mountain fever die from it. Stumpy Wicks just did. Dam' shame."

The pard said nothing as the bartender washed another glass and asked, "Lightnin' an' Molly gettin' along? We all heard he accused her of stealin' his poke." As he studied the glass he was washing, the bartender's eyebrows rose. "Shouldn't be talkin' like that unless he c'n prove it."

Lightnin's pard glared toward a chair and thought of a dozen responses without saying anything. Finally Lightnin's pard looked directly at the bartender. "We…gotta do somethin'."

His hands continued to alternately open and close on his hat brim as he looked from the bartender to the men at the bar, and back. While most of the men nearby ignored the old man, one of the nearest men at the bar, Sam Owen, offered sympathy.

"Yer Lightnin's pard," affirmed Sam. "Mountain fever. Tell ya' what, ol' timer. Not much any o' us c'n do right now. So's how about a drink? Calm yer nerves. Here," Sam turned and looked at the bartender, placing a coin on the bar, "Jack, give Ol' Timer a drink. He needs a drink, don' y' think?"

"Wouldn't hurt," said the bartender as he poured a glass of whiskey.

Not knowing what else to do, Lightnin's pard took the drink and for a moment stood there; then turned towards the door as if waiting for someone. It seemed he should be expecting somebody, although he wasn't sure why he should. All the distant acquaintances he knew were the two he just met in this room. The boys at the bar continued their reverie, occasionally glancing at the small man as he stood with his drink; waiting.

Sam Owen left the bar and headed down to Gold Street. He mentioned Lightnin's pard to one of Molly's girls who went to Cabin 1 and knocked on Molly's door. Molly answered.

"Molly," said the girl, "Sam says some old guy over at Dutch Jake's is worried about Lightnin'. Must be Lightnin's pard. Says Lightnin's got mountain fever. Had it for a short spell."

Molly's eyes showed no emotion as she thanked the girl and closed the door. Molly's movements became quick and fluid. After throwing her ankle-length coat over her shoulders and carefully fastening the buttons, she tied her hat ribbons neatly under her chin. Passing briefly in front of the mirror next to the door, she simultaneously studied and made minute adjustments. She looked herself in the eyes with the steely intensity that had unnerved many a man. Her jaw momentarily clenched. Relaxing, she turned, opened the door and stepped out into the Murray afternoon. She proceeded at a rapid but formal pace to Dutch Jake's Saloon.

As Molly walked erectly through the front door of the bar, Lightnin's pard stiffened, spilling the drink. She stopped for a moment to read faces and when she came to the pard, her features softened. She walked slowly forward as if she were a gamekeeper attempting not to frighten a small animal, and stopped in front of him.

The contrast in appearance between the two was stark. Lightnin's pard was short and homely, had a dirty, ragged hat, a worn shirt and frayed coat, pants that probably hadn't been changed in months, and a beard caked with dried chewing tobacco. At least one tooth was missing.

"Are you Lightnin's partner?" asked Molly. At first Lightnin's pard only looked at her. He blamed Molly for Lightnin's condition, and unlike everyone else, he didn't like her. "I need to speak to you privately," said Molly. "Could we step outside for a moment?"

The others in the bar watched curiously as royalty and commoner walked silently out the front door, and down the boardwalk toward the corner of the building. Near the corner, Molly stopped and came to the point.

"I want you to take me to Lightnin'," she said in a quiet monotone.

Lightnin's pard had no cultural background and little contact with members of the opposite sex. While men like Phil O'Rourke attracted attention, even admiration, the pard was invisible. He looked at her virulently, massaging the wad of tobacco in his mouth with his tongue. He turned his head to one side and spat contemptuously on the ground next to the boardwalk, reflecting years of accumulated bitterness. As the bitterness welled up in his heart and frightened away his self-consciousness, he looked up at her with controlled anger.

"I want you to take me to Lightnin'," she repeated again in the same monotone, but with greater emotional intensity. "The fact of the matter is," said Molly, "neither you nor Lightnin' have any money."

"Yup, that's right," Lightnin's pard looked at her sullenly, "an' you know why."

"Is that not reason why I should help now?"

Lightnin's pard wanted nothing to do with Molly but, on the other hand, Lightnin' needed help and she could get it. His small, tired eyes looked at her defiantly from under bushy eyebrows flecked with dirt.

"Yeah," he said, "y' should."

"Good," she said softly. "Here's what I would like you to do…"

Either as an act of modesty or fearful that the townsfolk would put two and two together and realize she stole Lightnin's poke and lied about it, she demanded Lightnin's pard tell no one about her intent to help Lightnin'.

The next day at her expense, Lightnin's pard loaded two burros with provisions and what little medicine Molly could buy, and rendezvoused with Molly near the trailhead. The two of them began the trek up the mountain trail leading to the small shanty above Murray.

As they drew near, Molly studied the shanty, a blemish on the face of the wooded mountainside. It was a crude, rough structure, patched together from small logs, clay, branches, mud, straw, slate, canvas and discarded lumber scraps from construction projects in town. About the size of a bedroom, Molly thought it might serve well as a primitive funeral hut.

Arriving at the shanty, she swung gracefully from the saddle, tied the reins to a tree, walked to the open door, and stood for a moment at the entrance before going in. She could understand how, after existing like this for weeks or even months, a miner might want to come into town and cut loose. Existing isn't living. This would be challenging, but, as she stood there, the ends of her mouth curled upward and she felt an increased sense of rectitude. It was the right decision to ride up and attempt to nurse Lightnin' back to health. As the burden on her conscience lightened, her sense of self-worth rose.

Molly and the pard went into the dark, dank shanty, into the musty, rank odor that emanates from hard-working men with neither bathtub nor change of clothes. Molly stifled the urge to hold her nose. The door was open, but beneath the forest canopy above, the cabin's interior was as dim as an unlit jail cell.

Without any explanation, Lightnin's pard walked out the door and into the forest. He returned with a dozen candles from a nearby dig that he and Lightnin' were working. In the meantime, Molly began to unload provisions, setting them in one corner of the cabin. Finished, she started cleaning up the shanty, dropping disposable items in a gunny sack.

After Lightnin's pard returned with the candles, she instructed him to dig a deep pit, about 20 yards away from the cabin, wherein were thrown old cans and miscellaneous garbage. The pard covered the pit with 2½ feet of dirt, a depth possibly precluding surface odor attracting bears roaming the tree-covered hillsides around Murray.

Lightnin's gaunt body lay semi-conscious, sprawled over several old blankets serving as a mattress on a makeshift bunk. Eyes closed, breathing lightly, occasionally Lightnin' would cough and it was evident from his grimace that coughing was painful. With some clean cloth brought to the cabin among the provisions, and water brought in from a nearby creek by Lightnin's pard, Molly washed Lightnin's face and neck, wistfully wishing the tenderness and affection might contribute to restoration of his health.

It might have had an immediate effect. Lightnin' coughed weakly and no grimace followed. She also made a mixture of water, quinine, whiskey and laudanum, the latter a bitter alcoholic preparation containing opium alkaloids, primarily codeine and morphine, the remedy of the day, which she tried patiently to get him to swallow bit by bit as the afternoon wore on.

From past experience, Molly knew sickness resulted from a variety of causes including cold, dampness, spoiled food, contaminated water, and contact with those already sick, but, she believed, also loneliness and depression. Molly knew people died from broken hearts, broken lives. Just died. "Mountain fever." Molly felt compelled to pray. Mere tenderness and affection would seem inadequate to bring about remedial results, but prayer and feminine mystique supplemented by the elixir began to weaken whatever it was that gripped Lightnin'.

As dusk approached, Lightnin's pard lit more candles in the cabin and asked if Lightnin' was going to make it. Molly looked at Lightnin's pard with the same lack of expression she had shown in her discussion with Pastor Nordquist. She had no idea. During the night, driven to heal, she continued her efforts to nurse Lightnin' back to health. She wanted him to live and, although extremely tired, did not stop.

Eventually Lightnin' regained consciousness and awoke. Looking up at the woman he thought his nemesis, Lightnin' mumbled weakly, "Molly B'Dam'?"

The corners of her mouth rose as she beamed at him without responding, continuing to softly wipe his face and neck with a damp cloth. Molly B'Dam's presence would have a favorable effect on any man; Lightnin' was no different.

Shortly after regaining consciousness, for the first time in many days he ate something. Another day passed and he was strong enough with the help of his pard and Molly to sit up in bed. The next day he was able to walk weakly out into the sunlight with his pard and Molly. At a short distance from the cabin, Lightnin' stopped and looked down at Molly.

"Molly, why'd ya come up here?" He stood unsteadily and waited as Molly composed her thoughts.

"I did something of which I am not proud," replied Molly with perfect intonation as she looked at Lightnin', "and needed to atone for that action."

"Why don't y' jes' give 'im back his poke?" rasped Lightnin's pard pointedly.

Molly glanced at the pard, but said nothing. The thought had occurred to her. It was the right thing to do, but inconsistent with her plans, her purpose for being in Murray. And she would not explicitly concede she had taken the poke. The struggle continued. Why should this single larcenous act be treated any differently than the others? she thought. Conscience be damned. This was a fair exchange, Molly silently rationalized, again steeling her heart. Lightnin' keeps his life; I keep his money.

Lightnin' said nothing more. He was alive. But he inwardly questioned why a lady like her would steal a miner's poke in the first place.

Saying nothing more, Lightnin's pard turned and walked to the cabin doorway.

Lightnin' looked at Molly wanting to say that this was a good deed she had done.

Lightnin's pard stopped at the cabin entrance and watched.

Molly turned her head to one side; this one act of compassion was overshadowed by many acts of selfishness and, even in this case, her compassion was stained with selfishness. It was just a deal, she thought to herself. That's all. The silent communication was effective. Expressionless, Lightnin' lumbered into the cabin. As Lightnin's pard watched him walk by, the pard figured from Lightnin's gait that he was pretty well healed.

While Molly told Lightnin's pard to keep the entire affair quiet, days later Lightnin' told the story to another prospector he met in the hills. Molly B'Dam' was célébrité and any newsworthy information about her would be repeated and usually embellished with each telling. How she saved Lightnin' from death was soon a topic of town discussion. Why did she do it? Lightnin's pard wondered. She stole his poke; if he was dead, no one could know. Except me. Why would the Queen of Murray ride up into the hills to save the life of a man who called her every foul name there was? You think someone might have asked. He shoved his hands in his pockets. When people already like how they feel about something, he thought, they don't ask.

━━━━━━━━━ ◆ ━━━━━━━━━

"It's been six months since you left, Amos," Anna wrote, "and your letters seem to imply the parsonage is well along, perhaps nearing completion. Could we finally make plans now for our trip to Murray? It seems like a dynamic place with the population growing so rapidly. And with you still being the only minister in town, you have your work cut out for you. I can see now why Nels Hanseth was so anxious to send you immediately. But I should be there to help you. It's important that the girls and I leave while the weather is good, and the school year is not imminent. I apologize for continually asking about this – I'm sure you'll let me know when all is ready – but I would like to start planning in earnest immediately."

Amos read the letter with mixed emotions – he wanted her and the girls there at once. And the parsonage was almost ready. But the town of Murray was not; far further from it than Anna was from Amos.

46

Molly Burdan grew tired of the prevarication. A week after returning from Lightnin's cabin, she lay on her bed, asking herself familiar questions like she were two people. The most familiar question was: how much longer will this theater continue?

She came to Murray to make as much money as fast as she could. That was the reason she was there. While the plan was for the show to go on a little longer, she was feeling a growing need to leave sooner. Yet she was becoming more and more attached to Murray, an emotional development not anticipated. Her wealth accumulation goals, which were to permanently place her in high stead somewhere else, were not yet met. Molly's thoughts were directed at expeditiously bringing the curtain down. This meant making more money sooner.

She lay on her bed in Cabin 1 and thought hard. I must find a way to end this. She stared at the ceiling. She felt nothing out of the ordinary. But it closed in on her, a sensation so strong she slowly sat upright. She felt condemned. Until now it was also not apparent how badly she wanted out of the life she led.

How can I generate over a year's income in moment? she asked herself. What else do I have to sell – that everyone would want, not just a few?

As she forced herself to acknowledge the only thing she sold, she inexplicably became vertiginous, and put the back of her right hand over her forehead as the ceiling seemed to move. For a moment she closed her eyes, lay back on the bed. I sell one thing.

As the sickly yellow tint returned, she rolled over and buried her head in her pillow.

For a while she lay motionlessly. Her head ached, and her stomach felt cramped. The room seemed eerily colder as if someone had piled ice in the middle of it. She thought of nothing. After a few minutes, she rolled on her back again. The yellow-white miasma was absorbed by the four watching walls and, without interference, she returned to thinking.

What I sell, sells consistently, she reasoned. There has been no down-cycle…there won't be any as long as the gold holds out. How long will that be?

The population appears to be stabilizing, she thought with concern, and growth in the amount of money, new gold, is waning, not what it was even six months ago.

Her thoughts, which up to this point introduced themselves apprehensively, began to freely wander into her consciousness. No time for diversification. She sighed. "None," she said out loud with finality. It isn't what I should sell but, rather, how I should sell it, she considered. Alternatives? What should be altered? She placed both hands on her forehead and thought. Only one idea, a very common one, stepped forward: same thing, better package.

She put her hands behind her head. How different? What repackaging would sell?

She gently bit her lip.

Something outrageous, she thought. Spectacular. The headache began to return.

She held a deep breath much longer than necessary and let it out like a deflating balloon. She felt light-headed. The edges of the ceiling were again tinged yellow, moving slowly. She paused, letting her mind go blank, waiting for the vapors to grow indifferent and leave.

Several minutes passed and she felt sick. Why do I feel so bad? Does sinning eventually come to this? she wondered. She softly moaned and attempted to make herself more comfortable.

Repackaging sex? How?

For a moment she smirked – the topic was bizarre – but again she forcefully redirected her thoughts, snapping the reins to her brain.

It would need to be a scheme where the men not only buy but feel obligated to buy, and would pressure others to buy as well. What would that be? Prostitution somehow seasoned with peer pressure. Venery venerated.

She thought hard.

For those with no conscience, but who usually don't buy, a feeling that they must buy to preserve face, even honor.

Also I need to entice those with higher standards…those who would never participate. I'd have to provide a scheme where they would feel compelled to buy, but not compelled to use. What? What could that be? she wondered. It occurred to her.

Philanthropy.

Prostitution as fundraising.

Her heart rebelled and she felt simultaneously pained and numbed as if she had been struck on the head. Briefly gritting her teeth, she relentlessly pushed forward.

All at varying rates – depending on ability to pay.

Those are my parameters. In summary, she thought, what I sell should bring not only base sexual gratification but also heightened self-esteem and philanthropic fulfillment. Impossible?

She put her hands behind her head as she looked at the ceiling. It is possible, she thought. Anything's possible. And men are that way. She folded her hands together over her tight stomach.

She pulled her hands apart, rolled over and buried her head in her pillow again. Then in a moment Molly was again on her back, wide-eyed, staring up at nothing in particular.

She sat up, her arms braced behind her. For a few seconds she remained motionless, thinking.

She swung her feet off the bed, stood up, and in her silk nightgown absently walked over to her mirror and perfunctorily combed her hair as her mind worked, ignoring her tight stomach and burdened heart.

When gorgeous Molly Burdan first decided to follow the profession, the parlor house accommodations and their rewards as well as her independence gave some satisfaction. As time progressed, and sex became simultaneously more expensive and cheaper, she would inexplicably feel iniquitous, even ugly. Her dependency on selling sex was slowly searing her conscience and, in a weaker woman, conscience interference would have ceased. Her conscience refused to quit, however, choosing to counterattack with uncomfortable bouts of angst and heartache. Things that once seemed enjoyable, even exciting, gradually became depressing and dark.

It was obvious the muck into which she had waded was becoming deeper faster, as if she was beginning to slide toward a drop-off in a lake, and she needed to quickly turn and head for solid ground.

At the moment, however, she had a financial goal, and a need to make a big sale to reach it. After deducing the correct marketing parameters, as she flexed her well-developed imagination, a novel idea slouched to the back door of her mind, avoiding her conscience on guard in front. In due time, Molly would envision a unique, incredible, repackaging solution.

August 18, 1884

Meanwhile, adulation of the Queen of Murray continued.

While Pastor Nordquist enjoyed his brief conversations with Molly B'Dam and kept her in his prayers, he believed the communal need to adulate and praise was greatly misdirected, and wondered what it was in human nature that needed celebrity adoration. Another of many diversions. He was having little success convincing townsfolk of Someone with far greater merit for adoration: their Savior. People listened politely and went on doing whatever they did. As more people came to Murray, Pastor Nordquist felt like a spawning salmon in a swollen river. His effort, usually difficult, was more difficult than usual.

His house was finally finished. While it was not a large residence, with the living room becoming the nave, and the dining room serving as a modest chancel, Pastor Nordquist's house was big enough to accommodate a very small congregation. Pastor Nordquist planned to hold his first worship service there at 11:00 a.m. the following Sunday, and hoped his home would be large enough for all who came.

September 22, 1884

In conspicuous places around Murray, Amos posted hand-made bulletins announcing the first church service, and also personally invited all acquaintances. That following Sunday morning, 30 folding chairs borrowed from the back of Dutch Jake's Saloon, all that Dutch Jake had, were placed in five rows of six in the living room. Pastor Nordquist worried that five rows were not enough; perhaps men would need to stand while women and children sat.

As 11:00 a.m. began to draw near, Murray residents started arriving at the Nordquist front door, a door left open while Pastor Nordquist stood on his front porch greeting anyone who came and, at a distance, many who did not. The total congregation, out of a population of over 1,500 people, amounted to 19 people that first Sunday morning, and those included his friend, Angus MacGregor, saloon owner Jacob "Dutch Jake" Goetz, several prospectors and miners whose ages varied from 17 to over 60, and a person with above-average biblical knowledge, the Queen of Murray.

Along with Molly B'Dam were two of her girls. Weighing the probable backgrounds of those in attendance, Pastor Nordquist chose for his sermon the enigmatic topic found in John 8:1-11: God's justice and mercy harmonized. Prior to the sermon he read the scripture to the congregation:

> *1 Jesus went unto the Mount of Olives.*
> *2 And early in the morning He came again into the temple, and all the people came unto Him; and He sat down and taught them.*
> *3 And the scribes and the Pharisees brought unto him a woman taken in adultery, and when they had set her in the midst,*
> *4 they said to Him, "Master, this woman was taken in adultery, in the very act.*
> *5 "Now Moses in the Law commanded us that such should be stoned; but what sayest Thou?"*
> *6 This they said, tempting Him, in order that they might have to accuse Him. But Jesus stooped down, and with His finger wrote on the ground, as though he heard them not.*
> *7 So when they continued asking Him, He lifted up himself and said unto them, "He who is without sin among you, let him cast the first stone at her."*
> *8 And again He stooped down, and wrote on the ground.*
> *9 And they which heard it, being convicted by their own conscience, went out one by one, beginning at the eldest even to the least, and Jesus was left alone, and the woman standing in the midst.*
> *10 When Jesus had lifted himself, and saw but the woman, Jesus said to her, "Woman, where are those, thine accusers? Hath no man condemned thee?"*
> *11 She said, "No man, Lord." And Jesus said unto her, "Neither do I condemn thee; go and sin no more."*

"What did Jesus write on the ground with His finger?" Pastor Nordquist asked his small congregation. "And why did he do that? Why didn't he immediately respond to the Pharisees' question? When he eventually did respond, the consciences of the scribes – lawyers at the time of Christ – and Pharisees, beginning with the oldest, convicted them that their position was hypocritical, and that none was justified in executing this law. Gradually all walked away. To say that none was justified in executing the law is to say all were condemned by the same law they were set to uphold. I suspect whatever Christ wrote on the ground coincided with that determination."

Pastor Nordquist walked along the front row looking at the seated parishioners.

"Where else in the Bible have we witnessed the Lord's finger writing on something?" asked Pastor Nordquist, eyebrows raised as he stopped and turned, pausing, allowing the others to think for a moment. "Before replying, Jesus stooped and wrote on the ground as if implying: this spiritual situation is not new; we have been here before, and the message is still the same. And although Scripture does not say one way or the other, the Pharisees and scribes must have seen and recognized what he wrote."

Pastor Nordquist looked about at the faces before him.

"No one is certain what Jesus wrote but, in context, my guess is Jesus wrote the Aramaic word for the Hebrew '*tekel*' found in '*Mene, mene, tekel, upharsin,*' – numbered, numbered, weighed, divided – the message for Belshazzar in Daniel 5 which Daniel translated to mean, 'God hath numbered thy kingdom, and finished it. Thou art weighed in the balances, and art found wanting. Thy kingdom is to be divided, and given to the Medes and Persians.'" Amos placed his right arm over his left. "'The writing on the wall' may have also been the writing on the ground," he said, and began walking to his right. "This statement applies to the scribes and Pharisees in our text…and," Amos looked about as he returned to the small podium, "everyone in this room, including me." He folded his hands on the open Bible resting atop the pine board lectern he'd made the previous week.

"How are we saved? '*No man, Lord,*'" Pastor Nordquist repeated the woman's words. "'*Lord.*' Perhaps, through the leading of the Holy Spirit of God, the woman already knew who this man was. 'Neither do I condemn thee,' He said. Did He," asked Pastor Nordquist, "have a right to condemn her? He did. '*He who is without sin among you, let him cast the first stone at her.*' Eternal salvation is determined by and through Jesus, and He could have condemned her, but did not. 'Neither do I condemn you.' He forgave her.

"Will it be so with each of us? With respect to our interpersonal relationships, I prayerfully hope so. With respect to our relationship with God, that is not our choice. But, if not, what should we do?" Pastor Nordquist asked, looking at Molly. "What did Jesus say? '*Go and sin no more.*' Did He expect her to stop sinning?" Molly looked back without expression. "No, in context He expected her to no longer commit adultery, but His admonition was intentionally more general. We are in a state of unregeneracy and cannot lead blameless lives, but we can honor God, showing Him our love, by trying." Molly listened, again convicted of what she should do, to the exclusion of what she should stop doing.

In concluding his sermon, Pastor Nordquist emphasized that "salvation is only through the grace of God. The law seemingly leads us along a path toward perfection ultimately resulting in salvation, but this is another mirage in a desert of sin. Rather, salvation is impossible to earn by being good or charitable or obedient because, due to our imperfection, our well-intended actions will never be sufficient. God's grace, manifested through the price of salvation paid by the death and resurrection of Jesus Christ that first Easter, accomplishes what the law fails to accomplish but, in this regard, upholds the intent of the law." Pastor Nordquist folded his arms. "We cannot expect a form of legal salvation, therefore, but, praise God, we have salvation through the grace He exercises according to John 6:44: 'No man can come to me, except the Father which hath sent me draw him: and I will raise him up at the last day.'" Molly nodded faintly; her mind knew this; and her heart knew beyond a doubt she was being drawn. Her aching conscience reminded her constantly. Just a little longer, she rationalized.

Pastor Nordquist looked at Dutch Jake, then Molly. "When we open the door to our heart, seeing the Lord before us, and knowing we are forgiven, we pray, Lord, enter. I want to 'Go and sin no more,'" Pastor Nordquist concluded as he lovingly looked at the faces in front of him, the flock he came to shepherd. Pastor Nordquist folded his hands and led his small congregation in closing prayer.

Throughout the sermon Dutch Jake tried hard to listen, but, as he had in similar circumstances throughout his life, frequently daydreamed. Angus MacGregor, on the other hand, elaborated in his own mind on each point of the sermon. Molly B'Dam' listened with an unchanging, neutral expression. In time-honored Lutheran tradition, hymns had been sung, but only Pastor Nordquist, Molly B'Dam' and Angus MacGregor appeared to know them. At the end of the service, Pastor Nordquist, with a warm smile, held out his arms and gave the benediction, blessing his congregation.

While Dutch Jake physically attended the service, Pastor Nordquist sensed that the Dutchman's spirit was often elsewhere. Alternatively, there was no doubt in the pastor's mind that Angus MacGregor would want to spend time during the afternoon discussing the sermon, an interesting topic for Angus.

Molly B'Dam's neutral expression remained unchanged throughout the service, and it occurred to Pastor Nordquist that Molly was holding her convictions close to the vest.

As his small congregation began to file out, Dutch Jake smiled, but looked off in the distance, not at Pastor Nordquist, as he shook the pastor's hand upon leaving the Church. Angus MacGregor sat in his chair with no intention of leaving. The last individual to leave was Molly B'Dam' who, in a regal manner, offered her velvet-gloved hand to Pastor Nordquist, smiled courteously, and engaged him in small-talk.

"That was an excellent sermon, Pastor Nordquist."

"Well, thank you," Pastor Nordquist beamed, believing that he might have helped construct a spiritual in-road. "I am sincerely pleased that you liked it. Perhaps we can discuss it further in the near future," he suggested.

"You realize, I'm sure," responded Molly B'Dam', "that the text you used for your sermon – the story of the Pharisees and the adulterous woman – is omitted in many ancient manuscripts. It may not have been originally part of the Gospel of John," Molly added, studying his eyes for the impact this statement would bring.

Pastor Nordquist's face darkened. "Well, yes and no. Leave it out and in context there is an obvious void. And it is completely consistent with the message of the New Testament. Do you still think it was added later?"

"Possibly," she answered honestly. "In any event, the sermon topic was important and you did an excellent job of delivering the message." To Amos, the last sentence sounded perfunctory.

Molly walked out the door as Pastor Nordquist watched her, slightly perplexed and slightly annoyed. She knew the Bible, he concluded. But how strong was her faith? It seemed to Pastor Nordquist that she believed, but then, at other times, it seemed as if the Holy Spirit was far from her. As she walked away, he chuckled at the irony of what he and Molly had in common: both were "fishers of men." This thought was quickly replaced by a second related thought. In his enthusiasm for winning souls during his first worship service, a more worldly necessity was overlooked: he forgot to take an offering. In the greater scheme of things, it was unimportant, and Pastor Nordquist continued to watch Molly walk toward Gold Street, knowing that forgetting to take an offering – in fact, overlooking any opportunity to make money – would not have occurred with Molly. It was obvious her priorities at the moment were much different than his. Gold, silver mean a great deal to Molly, he thought. Considering her evident knowledge of God's word, why is that? Why the extreme? There was a reason, Amos learned, a searing event in Molly's past.

47

Before they were married, Molly's narcissistic, hedonistic former husband lived off an allowance from his wealthy father, slept much of the morning, and spent his evenings gambling in expensive, exclusive clubs.

Following their quick marriage, her father-in-law and mother-in-law disapproved of their son marrying beneath his station to a common barmaid, and severed his substantial allowance, declaring it would be restored only when the marriage was annulled. Her husband's imperiousness, reinforced through years of complaining long enough to get his way, had become as fast as steel in concrete. He refused to get an annulment.

His usual tactics were not successful this time, however. The allowance continued to be withheld, and, intending to maintain his income level through the only other means he knew, Molly's husband gradually gambled away what they had. On the verge of being evicted from their residence, her husband took the next step: he approached a young acquaintance with old money.

"I have, by way of passing," began Burdan one evening, "an immediate need with which you could be of great assistance, old man." Burdan glanced about the expansive, Victorian living room, darkened corners shrinking from inquisitive gaslights.

"And what might that be?" asked his acquaintance, a small concupiscent man with slick, evenly-parted black hair, a sharp nose, and etiolated skin, evidence that, like a shrew, he only came out only at night.

"Well, it seems that I'm a little light this month," said Burdan, unconsciously wiping his hands on his sleeves, "and, ah, wondered if you could extend a small loan? Well, not exactly small. More medium sized, I would say."

"'Medium sized,'" the acquaintance echoed with nasal resonance. White piping outlined the quilted, black felt collar and cuffs of his silk smoking jacket as he sat almost enveloped in a regal overstuffed chair. He drew again on his pipe, exhaled, and murmured, "What's the collateral?"

"Collateral? Well, I suppose…," Burdan paused, searching for the right words. "Well, I'm not certain that I have anything that you would want. Certainly nothing you would need." Burdan looked at his acquaintance who continued to say nothing while looking up at his obdurate grandfather's portrait, and puffing on his pipe. Burdan's acquaintance recognized an opportunity, an advantage, and was mulling it over.

"Anyway, what do you say?" Burdan asked.

His acquaintance said nothing, although Burdan sensed his acquaintance had something he wanted say. After a moment's heavy silence, his acquaintance replied.

"Very well, Burdan, there is one thing you have, I must admit, I covet a great deal." He tapped his pipe twice thoughtfully in the partially-filled ash tray. "Collateral in the form of a service, actually." He began refilling the pipe bowl. "In fact," he looked up at Burdan very seriously, "incentive for future loans as well."

Burdan's expression became one of optimism tinged with puzzlement as his acquaintance turned and again looked at the grandfather's portrait, the pipe returning to its accustomed position. Burdan was at a loss.

"I can't imagine what that might be," said Burdan after a moment, attempting to beam pleasantly.

"Well, Burdan, stop and think," said the acquaintance. "What is the one thing which you have, that other men do not have, but which all men would want?"

Burdan looked at him perplexed. "I'm, I'm afraid I don't know what you're referring to."

"Oh, come, Burdan. Do I have to spell it for you?"

What do I have, which other men do not have, but that all men would want? Burdan repeated in his head.

"Well, old man," Burdan finally blurted out with a nervous smile, "I'm afraid you have me. What is this treasure I possess, of which I am completely unaware?"

The acquaintance removed his pipe, exhaled, and looked at Burdan with insouciant temerity.

"Your wife."

As the acquaintance looked away, replacing the pipe stem in his mouth, Burdan's face blanched as he stood astounded, not quite believing what he heard. My wife is the most beautiful woman I know and…but…well, she… is my wife.

"My wife?"

"You need money?" the acquaintance asked, not looking at Burdan. "Your wife."

Burdan's hands awkwardly fumbled in his pockets, staring wide-eyed at the acquaintance. "For, for what?" Burdan stammered.

The acquaintance's eyes narrowed.

"What do you think? 'Old man.'"

"But, that's, that's…ridiculous," joked Burdan. "She is, after all, my wife. I can't… you can't… be serious."

The acquaintance was used to obtaining the affections of women the same way he obtained everything else: he bought them. But this time, if he played his cards right, he would get what he wanted and his money back. Pipe in hand, the man gazed at Burdan neutrally, turned his head and placed his pipe back in his teeth, struck a Lucifer and relit the bowl. The acquaintance took another long draw on his pipe, and again slowly exhaled. The smoky sweet smell of pipe tobacco filled the room as Burdan sat speechless.

"How much do you need?" the man asked in a leading tone of voice.

Burdan sat frozen, microscopic beads of perspiration forming on his forehead. He was pressed; he needed money immediately, and if he did not get cash from this acquaintance, he was uncertain of where else to go.

"How much do you need?" repeated the friend with feigned consternation. "Please. You asked for a loan. Now have the courtesy to tell me how much you need."

Morgue-like silence fell. Burdan carried on a conversation within himself, as if speaking with others.

"For how long do you want her?" he finally asked in just above a whisper.

"What? I'm sorry," responded the acquaintance, "I didn't quite hear you."

"How long do you want her?" Burdan heard himself say in a normal tone of voice.

"It depends on the loan amount. If the amount is not too great, one night." In the weak light, a continual, thin wisp of exhaled smoke accompanied the subsequent succinct sentence – "Just one night" – rising eerily on both sides of the man's nose and in front of his small, malevolent eyes.

Molly's husband said nothing, staring at the acquaintance. Then he mumbled a dollar amount, more than initially intended.

"That, I'm afraid, will require collateral of several nights. Say, three."

"Then three."

His acquaintance placed his pipe on the ash tray, got up, disappeared for a moment, and returned with cash. Money was not a problem, particularly for three nights with Burdan's gorgeous wife.

"I'm not Rockefeller," the acquaintance said when he returned and, as Burdan stood up, held out an envelope filled with cash, "but for the particular service you are providing, as the expression goes, there's more where this came from. This is, by the way, 50%. I'll give you the other 50% after three days. Old man." Still standing while holding out the envelope in his right hand, the acquaintance weakly smiled without laughing, and Burdan forced himself to reach out as he stood up. He took the money, pulled the lapel of his coat, and placed the money in the left, inside breast pocket.

"We'll work out the time and date after you speak with your wife," said the acquaintance as he watched.

Without responding, Burdan backed away. As the acquaintance walked back to the overstuffed chair and sat down, Burdan put on his hat, turned and walked to the spacious entry, opened the grand front door and let himself out. The acquaintance clasped his hands together, biting on his pipe, looked at the portrait of his grandfather, and mused he'd played this hand well.

Arriving home, Burdan began the abuse of his position as head of the family.

"Molly, I have some business to discuss," said Burdan in a thin voice.

"Oh." Her beautiful eyes brightened as she dried her hands on a towel. "Have you found a job?"

"No, I mean business." He looked back at her, and his jaws tightened. "Serious business."

Burdan yanked a chair away from the table and, warily looking at Molly like a lion tamer, motioned for her to sit in it. He watched her put down the towel and walk to the chair.

As she sat down, he grabbed and pulled up another chair, lifted his boot and rested it on the chair while still standing, looking down at Molly who looked back perplexed.

"I made a deal last night that will get the rent and gas caught up, and put food on the table," he said. "It will also give me a little to wager; this deal tells me my luck's turning. I knew it would." Molly stared at him, mouth slightly open, worried about his gambling. "Like I said, I made a deal. I made a deal and I have to stick to that deal. Do you understand?"

Why is he emphasizing the need to stick to his word? she wondered. "Of course," said Molly. "What was the deal?"

In his mind, Burdan struggled to find the right words.

"It's a business deal." Burdan would not look directly at Molly. She saw he was obviously uncomfortable, conflicted.

"Well, then," she asked, her eyes smiling with encouragement, "what was the business deal?"

"You will need to help me in this." He looked at her again, and his eyes grew narrow. "Will you do that? Will you help me?" he asked heatedly.

"Of course. You're my husband. I'll do whatever I can."

As Burdan's mouth became dry, he heard himself say what he was to say. "I have only one thing that any other man would want. You. So I have arranged a loan. In exchange for the money, I agreed you will spend three nights with the man who gave me the money."

Molly looked up at Burdan dumbfounded, searching for an explanation. She was married. Her lips parted, and her eyes grew larger. Was he serious?

"You're not serious," she said, almost as a question.

To her what he was suggesting was unthinkable. To him, however, it was not only thinkable, but without alternative.

"There is no other choice and I do not want an argument!" he replied furiously. "Do you understand?! Let me repeat: I have made an agreement with an acquaintance and I intend to uphold that agreement!"

"No," she responded, "I can't do that." Eyes wide, her fingers pressed against her cheeks. "I can't; I can't do that."

His eyes grew small and his nostrils flared as he stood over her. "We need this money! You will not dishonor me with a refusal! Do you under*stand*?!"

She was young and still pliable. Burdan continued to berate her, and she again responded defensively. "No, I can't," she said weakly, her hand partially over her mouth. Looking up at him, stunned and now afraid, she asked, "How could I? I'm your wife." She began to say, "You know you're supposed to…" when he angrily raised his hand and slapped her hard enough to knock her off her chair.

"What did you say?! What was that?!" he yelled, teeth bared, as she lay on the floor, her face contorting in pain, looking up at him unbelievingly. "Do you want to repeat that?!" On the floor, her body went limp as she broke into sobs. Isn't this man my husband? But what is he now? Tears flowed down her throbbing cheek as her heart began to break.

He swore at her and, stepping forward, kicked the chair in front of her, breaking one of the rungs. His patience and manhood wasted, he yelled at her, "Get up!" He grabbed her wrist and pulled her hand away from her reddened eyes as he yanked her to her feet. Grinding his teeth, he put his nose less than an inch away from hers. "Are you going to do it!!?"

The verbal and physical abuse pushed down on her, and the poverty-stricken condition in which she found herself dictated she do what he said. Her Catholic convictions forbid adultery...but expected obedience to her husband. Sobbing, she was cornered and scared. Her right cheek throbbed, and abrasions were beginning to welt on her forehead, and her heart was breaking. Her disheveled hair wet with tears, her stomach feeling like it had gone through a meat grinder, she stood looking through blurring tears at a man turned demon.

"Well?! Are you?!"

The pain in her wrist overwhelming, and the pain in her heart excruciating, sobbing, she looked at him through teary vision, crushed. When she whimpered, "Yes," the light in her eyes flickered for a moment and then died.

48

olly didn't leave Burdan immediately. It wasn't done. Other women endured worse. But in the months that followed, the feelings of betrayal, humiliation, lovelessness, and entrapment were exacerbated, becoming unbearable, and Molly determined to escape the man to whom she felt chained. Reflecting her altered heart, she chose an escape route that would eventually lead to Murray, Idaho. She would no longer completely trust another man, and vowed to never again live in poverty or suffer humiliation, but the opposite.

While her esteem rose in the eyes of Murray residents, to attain the financial goal she was determined to reach, she continued to compromise standards held close to her heart since childhood, and endured remorse from lost innocence and absence of true respectability.

August 1, 1884

Amos was on the verge of giving Anna the go-ahead to begin the journey west to Murray. The town was still hard and uncivilized, but he missed her too much, and she was becoming increasingly more impatient. That evening he sat down and began writing a letter telling her it was time, but during the following day something happened that changed his mind.

Molly B'Dam' had the best girls in Murray but, with a population of two thousand, the vast majority of whom were single men, Molly's girls were not the only girls. Several of the bars employed women who waited on tables and showed guests to rooms upstairs where occupancy lasted less than an hour. While Molly had strict etiquette rules for her girls, among other professional women in Murray such rules were the exception. At most bars in town, bars that Pastor Nordquist would visit, the job of attracting men created competition between women. In some saloons, the undercurrent of suppressed acrimony was as strong as a Coeur d'Alene River undertow. The Gold Dust Saloon, for example. Early that evening, Pastor Nordquist walked into the Gold Dust, looked around, saw Angus McGregor in conversation with an unfamiliar man, smiled, and joined the two at a nearby table.

Among the girls working at the Gold Dust, Edith Carter was particularly temperamental, with a tongue that could double as a dagger. Edith had worked at the Gold Dust almost two years, longer than any of the other girls, and the other girls learned to give Edith a wide berth. Edith's past was unknown, and while no one knew her age, she looked like she was 30, more or less. She had a narrow waist and shoulders, a small chest, and was disproportionately wide in the hips. At 5' 7½", she was taller than some of the men she serviced. Her attraction to men was her face: appealing black eyes, high cheek bones, turned-up nose, dark complexion, and a mouth of straight, white teeth. She had a beautiful smile when it suited her purpose. Her make-up was always applied meticulously, and she would rather die than be seen without it. Her thick, jet-black hair highlighted her facial features like an attractive-but-inconspicuous frame highlights a portrait. When she spoke, her naturally low, sensual tone was arousing.

In the Gold Dust pecking order, through her petulant and implacable manner, Edith made certain all girls understood who was at the front. If one of the girls was entertaining a barroom patron, and Edith decided she wanted that particular man, she would move in on the encounter, and the other girl would move off to the next candidate rather than risk a confrontation. Confrontations with Edith were ugly, unwinnable and unprofitable.

In the Darwinian atmosphere at the Gold Dust, each girl developed some level of rivalry with every other. With no astute Molly Burdan to adjudicate disagreements, a few rivalries were as heated as molten bullet lead. Among the Gold Dust girls, Edith Carter was both the most successful and the most hated.

Sibyl Boudica was as tall as Edith with an olive complexion and black hair that fell well below her shoulders. Sibyl arrived in town two weeks earlier and, while no one knew her age, Sibyl looked to be in her early 20s. She mentioned she was the youngest of six children, and the only girl. She was slender, more symmetrically appealing than Edith, and had large, brown eyes that gave her a deceptive appearance of innocence. She was pleasant with the other girls and, in the competitive atmosphere of the Gold Dust, Sibyl had yet to cultivate any hostility. Sibyl might have found a better fit as one of Molly's girls, but Sibyl believed she didn't need someone like Molly, that she could make her own way and more money under the Gold Dust arrangement.

Sibyl could be headstrong, and as the youngest child and only daughter among six children, she was continually fighting until she got what she wanted. Sibyl was inflexible when expected to do something she did not want to do. It was why she left home in San Francisco, eventually traveling to Portland where she got a new job in the oldest profession. She came to Murray from Portland with the same intent as all the other girls: make as much money as quickly as possible until the gold was panned out, and then leave.

That evening as Amos entered the Gold Dust, Sibyl was sitting with Charlie O'Toole, a slender, good-looking young saddler and horse trainer who could be uniquely munificent when able. Sibyl entertained Charlie before and considered him her claim.

Meanwhile, Edith was having no luck with the stranger to whom she was talking. She decided to leave him and see what else was available. She saw Charlie O'Toole, and paid little attention to Sibyl. Sibyl and Edith did not yet know one another well; Edith decided to show Sibyl who was in charge, killing two birds with one stone. Edith affectedly sauntered over to Charlie O'Toole, stopped next to him, glanced at Sibyl – who looked back, but did not move – and looked down at Charlie.

"How are you doing?" asked Edith in a come-hither voice, running her right index finger slowly along Charlie's shoulder. "How would you like to be with a real woman?"

Before Charlie could respond, while staring bullets at Edith, Sibyl mimicked Edith's voice, "How would you like to go screw yourself?" Sibyl overly puckered her lips, as if blowing out a candle, when she said the word "screw." Used to being treated with deference, Edith's face darkened, and she glared at Sibyl. Sibyl glared back as she added, "It could be the best sex you've provided in, well, ages." Two men at the next table guffawed, but two other girls nearby turned and stared. No one resisted Edith's wishes, much less dared to openly insult her.

"No, thanks," added Charlie O'Toole warily, turning his head for a moment to see Edith, attempting to ward her off like a glancing blow, "this dance is taken."

The insult was permanently nailed in place by rejection. Like a bulbous vase, Edith's ego was large but fragile, and her eyes flashed as she walked with disciplined leisureliness around the table to where Sibyl sat.

Sibyl watched Edith come slowly toward her, and sensed Edith was going to up the ante. Sibyl's jaw set as she stood up and met Edith face-to-face. Sibyl had legitimate first claim to Charlie, but that became ancient history when Edith shoved Sibyl hard enough to make Sibyl lose her balance and fall to the barroom floor.

As Sibyl fell on the floor wide-eyed and open-mouthed, her first thought was that no one, especially not another woman, did that and got away with it. Her second thought was to remove either Edith's hair or eyes from Edith's head. Quick as a cat, Sibyl was on her feet as male patrons scurried like barroom mice to watch, some knocking over chairs in front of them. From where they sat, Angus and Amos could see commotion, but not exactly what was happening.

Sibyl went after Edith, grabbing Edith's thick, black hair with both hands, and pulling Edith's face toward her, bashing Edith's nose into Sibyl's forehead, a tactic Sibyl learned from her brothers. The wide-eyed men nearby began to cheer and shout like berserk banshees while the other girls, all of whom had little use for Edith Carter, began shouting encouragement to Sibyl. As Edith reflexively pulled back, her hand over her nose, Sibyl shoved forward hard, causing Edith to fall backward, rolling over the floor like a kicked barstool.

In the pandemonium, Edith quickly got up and dove at Sibyl who dodged to one side and jumped on top of Edith, pushing the side of Edith's face into the floor as they fell. As Edith rolled over in an attempt to get at Sibyl, teeth clenched, Sibyl hit Edith in Edith's already bleeding nose. The nose pain caused Edith to go mad with rage, grabbing, screaming and attempting to pull Sibyl close enough to get Edith's fingernails into Sibyl's large, dark eyes.

As the two women struggled and rolled on the floor, the men jostled for position and soon some took exception to the aggressiveness of others. The Gold Dust Saloon cauldron began to boil over. Encouraged by the emotion and madness of the moment, a fight and then a second, broke out among the men. Repressed anger and resentment rose to the surface and erupted as two other girls with a seasoned history of enmity became caught up in the moment's passion and went at each other. Those two girls were joined by other girls as women quickly picked sides or took on whoever they hated most.

Chaotic bedlam reigned, with security of drinks, chairs, tables, men and women jeopardized. Blood flowed from both Edith's nose and the painful gash in Sibyl's finger where Edith just bit it. With her fingernails Edith also cut Sibyl below Sibyl's right eye, but neither wound slowed Sibyl's determined maniacal assault.

As Amos and Angus stood up, the bartender and bouncer raced over to separate the girls, but so many other fights broke out so quickly that the two men stopped, looked around and, seeing there was no chance of restoring peace, began to move chairs and tables to safer locations. The bartender sent the bouncer to find the sheriff, new in town. Here was the new sheriff's introduction to Murray.

Shortly, the new sheriff raced through the front door, fired a couple of rounds into the ceiling to get everyone's attention, and shouted, "Everyone on their feet!"

Amos and Angus, not involved in the melee, began pulling the others – men and women – apart, but as other combatants regained their composure, two women continued to fight.

The sheriff ran over and dragged Sibyl off Edith while Amos grabbed Edith as she climbed to her feet. The women's resistance was subdued because both women were exhausted. Their clothes were ripped, their hair disheveled, and each was suffering from cuts and abrasions. Heaving heavily while being held by the sheriff and Amos, Edith and Sibyl glared at one another. When Amos loosened his grip, Edith broke free and rushed at Sibyl. As Sibyl turned quickly to avoid Edith's fingernails, Edith knocked Sibyl and the sheriff into a poker table, causing the sheriff to lose his grip as both he and Sibyl fell. Edith was quickly on top of Sibyl, and Sibyl tightly grasped Edith's wrists, but Amos grabbed Edith from behind and not-too-gently pulled her to her feet – pulling up Sibyl as well, since Sibyl had not let go of Edith's wrists. Wrenching Edith free from Sibyl, he placed Edith back where she had been standing as the sheriff again grabbed Sibyl, telling her to stay put. With fire in her eyes, Sibyl stood, chest heaving, and glared at Edith.

Souls on ice, both women gave the appearance of backing off. As Amos firmly held Edith, however, Sibyl broke free and bolted toward Edith before the sheriff angrily grabbed the end of Sibyls long hair and pulled her back. "Stand still, dammit!" he yelled, holding her tightly as he let loose a flurry of invectives toward both women and the encouraging male onlookers. Mouths partially open, still breathing heavily, hair obscuring their vision, the two women stared venomously at one another, but neither woman made any further assault attempt.

Edith and Sibyl were physically escorted to different rooms, and the rooms were guarded as a precaution. The Gold Dust bartender treated Edith's nose, wiping it with alcohol, and giving her a clean bar towel to press on it until the bleeding stopped.

Drawing some satisfaction from knowing she gave more than she got, Sibyl cleaned and bandaged the painful gash in her bitten finger and the cut below her eye.

After getting to the bottom of the fracas, the sheriff told the owner of the Gold Dust that both women could not stay in Murray; one or both would have to leave.

Edith received the worst of it and tacitly understood she no longer ruled the Gold Dust roost. The next day, with some town folks stopping to watch, Edith ignominiously left town. As Amos watched her ride off, he wondered what kind of upbringing she had, why she was the way she was, and where she was going. Seattle, someone said. Amos's emotions were multiple: disgusted the incident occurred, sorrowful that Edith had such an obviously hard life, but, for her sake and the sake of his family when they arrived, thankful Edith was leaving Murray.

Amos wrote to Anna and told her it would be a while longer, that events in Murray were not conducive to her and his daughters coming just yet. He did not go into detail.

Anna read his letter with great disappointment. She was sure she and the girls would be leaving within the month. Now she had to wait longer. Why? What was going on in Murray that would be so serious as to prevent their coming?

September 28, 1884

But Amos missed his family, and every night he would lay thinking of his wife and children before going to sleep. Even though his wife, Anna, was 1,200 miles away, Amos felt a closeness as if she were in the next room. Those thoughts also renewed his strength each morning while, at the same time, although his friendship with Angus MacGregor and other townsfolk was enjoyable, varying degrees of loneliness were Amos's companions.

For Amos, as with most literate adults, letter writing was both the means of communication, and a creative and cultural medium, and he approached each letter in a manner rivaling preparation of a timely sermon before a large congregation. He wrote letters he knew would be reread, collected, and reread again, not only by the addressee but, perhaps, friends and relatives, even future generations. Upon sitting down to write, he would often imagine his family in front of him as if he were speaking to them. He would prepare by creating a quick outline of topics. Sometimes, as ideas and subjects came faster than outline continuity could accommodate, he quickly made notes on another sheet, later inserting those thoughts logically in the outline, and editing the outline. Even if Amos was born in an English speaking country, it was unlikely his letters would improve remarkably. The first draft was never the final draft, and the final draft was always more succinct than the first. As Amos knew she would, Anna saved the letters, reread often, sustaining the heart of Anna Nordquist in her husband's absence.

Amos finished his outline, wrote the letter, edited it, and wrote the final draft.

Sept. 28, 1884

Dearest Anna,

I think of you constantly.

These thoughts flow like water in the desert, sustaining me in the drought of the moment. When it seems my love for you could become no greater, still it grows, and the distance between us continually reminds me of how much I miss you.

When alone in the evening, I often envision our last night together. You are an extraordinary woman in every way imaginable, and I am deeply honored God brought you to me; that it would be my responsibility among all men to protect, support, love and cherish you. Yet, surely no other man could possibly appreciate or enjoy this sacred responsibility more than I.

In my absence, I trust in God to protect and nurture you and the girls. I miss them, and the heartache I feel when alone, envisioning my family, is ample incentive for the hard work necessary to bring us together again. Remind the girls that I love them and that I am working diligently toward our reunion as soon as the moment is right. For that end, no labor is too great.

The parsonage serves as residence and sanctuary until we build a church. You will love the new kitchen. It is, indeed, much like the Osterlund kitchen, and will be your gift. I continue to conduct worship services in the living room every Sunday and, although attendance is still modest, most of those who come have been converted by the Holy Spirit.

Another day has gone. My wishes are few: to be with my beautiful wife and children, and to bring the gospel to all in Murray.

The harvest is plentiful; as is my love for you. It is unfortunate you and the girls cannot come to Murray yet, but the moral climate here is worse than Nels imagined, and must improve before, in good conscience and regardless of how much I miss you, I can bring you here. As much as I hate to say it, you may need to wait until spring. Travel in fall and winter is dangerous. Train travel is greatly romanticized by the railroads when, in fact, the engines can be undependable, and passenger cars, unheated and unventilated in winter, fraught with illness. Occasionally, robberies occur. While there is now a road through the Bitterroot and Coeur d'Alene Mountains, fall rains can make the road occasionally impassable, and in winter, that road will be snowbound and endangered by avalanches.

> *When I headed west, I was one man seasoned by Swedish*
> *and Minnesota winters; you will be a mother traveling with three*
> *young daughters. Acclimation after arrival will be more difficult*
> *than in warmer weather. A winter journey to Murray would be*
> *unwise so, no dear, not yet.*
>
> *But I promise that, regardless of what the circumstances are,*
> *you will come in the spring. I could not bear to wait any longer.*
> *Meanwhile, please be patient.*
>
> *Good night, dearest Anna. I love you. I will write again*
> *tomorrow*
>
> *with love that grows daily,*
>
> *Amos*

As Anna read the first part of the letter, the words and sentences danced before her – the Osterlund kitchen – and with renewed anxiousness to see her husband, Anna was ready to start packing at once. When she came to the part where he told her she would have to wait – in fact, wait until spring – her eyes flashed, her mouth dropped open, and she threw down the letter but then picked it up again. Turning, her teeth gritted in frustration, she walked to the couch, sat down with a grim expression, placed the letter on the center table, put her hands over her eyes, and angrily broke into tears.

When her crying quickly waned, Anna picked up the letter, wiped her eyes, and finished reading. Done, she sat on the sofa and stared. If he said spring, she would leave in the spring. Yet she also couldn't help wondering if she was going to see Amos again. Of course I am, she thought, her jaw set, because, with the girls, I am going to leave in the spring. She had the entire trip planned, it was just a matter of when, and she just made up her mind when.

Meanwhile, Pastor Nordquist began reconsidering the foundation of a sanctuary. Based on the weak interest from so many to whom he witnessed, he would build a small church; a larger building seemed unnecessary. His present congregation was no different than at the first service. Worship attendance in Pastor Nordquist's living room typically ranged between 25-to-30 people, no more.

Dutch Jake no longer attended. During the weekdays in Murray, Pastor Nordquist would occasionally see Dutch Jake approaching at a distance. Upon spying Amos, Dutch Jake would nod and head in a different direction or engage business associates in conversation too serious to interrupt. Whenever Dutch Jake would feint behavior to avoid Amos and the subject of the Almighty, Amos would think of the parable in Luke 12:16-34: "…You fool! This very night your soul is required of you… Where your treasure is, there will your heart be also." Dutch Jake was a wealthy man.

Unknown to the rest of Murray, Amos was also a wealthy man. No one in Murray knew about Nordquist Shipping Co. or Nordquist Trading Co. Both corporations had grown extensively with Anders at the helm. Gregarious, handsome Anders had charisma, vision and indomitability, and his attractive wife, Karin, had beauty, charm and excellent business acumen. They made a great team and a lot of money.

Meanwhile, Angus MacGregor buoyed Pastor Nordquist's spirits because Angus's interest in spiritual matters was endless, and his sense of humor always kept spiritual discussions in proper perspective. Angus's continual happiness made Amos's labor more enjoyable even on the worst of days. Nevertheless, Pastor Nordquist was disappointed with the fruits of that labor.

In a letter of frustration to Nels Hanseth, Amos briefly questioned the parsonage's adequacy for attracting worshippers, and speculated that perhaps "a real church building" might be necessary to draw an indifferent Murray populace into worship services. On the other hand, if he couldn't create more interest, construction of a new sanctuary might be pointless, regardless of size.

Amos was becoming frustrated.

He was always able to accomplish his goals, but not in Murray. One of Nels's many excellent letters arrived three weeks later. Nels discussed several matters, and placed Amos's church-planting efforts in perspective.

> *Do not be frustrated. First of all, it's not up to you. As you know, God makes that determination, and the Creator of the universe is quite capable of drawing people to Him.*
>
> *In the early Christian church, as evident from Romans 16:5, worshippers also met in modest structures, usually homes. As the church increased in size, so did church architecture, and over centuries the conviction arose that if a church building, not to mention liturgy, were to be pleasing to God, then magnitude and complexity would need to be on a scale worthy of the Almighty, were that possible. Consequently, places of worship gradually evolved like men in those little human evolution drawings, beginning very small and simple and, over a period of time, ending with extraordinary complexity.*
>
> *By the early Middle Ages, naves, transepts, quires, chancels, lofts, towers, and undercrofts combined to form huge cathedrals – bishop's headquarters containing the cathedra or bishop's chair. These enormous structures required decades to build, providing imposing places for high mass. The unintended result, like the great curtain isolating the Holy of Holies in the Jerusalem temple at the time of Christ, was to position church leaders, vestments, and religious accoutrements between God's people and God.*
>
> *When European Christians started coming to America, the trappings of established European Christian churches were left behind, and worshippers again congregated on Sunday mornings in more modest structures, usually homes, or, among pioneers, no structures at all. They simply used God's creation. Worshippers again had fewer obstacles between themselves and the Almighty, and worshipping again became personal.*

> *Your modest living room, Amos, will serve quite nicely for those who are called.*

Amos appreciated Nels' spiritual insight and began the week with a brightened outlook.

Molly B'Dam' continued to attend church regularly. "Your sermons are edifying, Pastor Nordquist," she would tell him. Molly's beauty and cultivated *persona* create a saintly public image, Amos thought, but her heart is coated with recalcitrance – and he thought of his Appomattox Courthouse conversation with Blade about God and Pharaoh.

As he watched the north Idaho snow accumulate to such heights as would entrap deer and elk, Pastor Nordquist often thought of his family who would come in the spring. With a sheriff, deputies, and an ongoing influx of East Coast civility, the tide of lawlessness was going out.

Meanwhile Amos read about unsettling events in Tacoma, location of the Northern Pacific Railroad terminus, unaware of the extent to which these distant events would soon affect his family and him.

49

Tacoma, February 1885

With the end of railroad construction, many Chinese laborers, like other Tacomans, were out of work. The town of Tacoma officially had 6,936 people of whom only 532 were Chinese, but their effect on unskilled labor demand and supply was making it difficult for unskilled laborers of European descent to make a living. Although some Chinese such as storekeeper Lum May, merchant Kwok Sue and labor contractor Sing Lee had been in Tacoma since the early 1870s, and had no problem until recently, now that the railroad was completed, many Tacomans simply wanted all the Chinese to leave. Tacoma was a nest of Sinophobe hornets about to swarm.

Lum, Kwok and Sing spoke English well. Kwok's and Sing's wardrobes were no different than Mayor Weisbach's. The vast majority of Tacoma Chinese, however, dressed in the same blue jackets and trousers daily, and while Lum, Kwok and Sing were exceptions, they were exceptions whose living depended on the remaining Chinese, the majority of whom were lower class from the Guangdong (Canton) province where poverty was pervasive, peasants desperate for work, and readily available for anywhere.

Most Chinese lived just north of the downtown waterfront along the railroad tracks near Half Moon Yard, the land leased from the Northern Pacific Railroad. A smaller settlement was along the beach at Old Town where salmon cannery and Tacoma Mill laborers lived. Around 100 worked in the 18 downtown wash houses doing laundry.

Chinese living and sanitary conditions were poor. Part of the problem oddly stemmed from their resourcefulness: the Chinese kept chickens, geese, pigs, and small animals, and fed the animals by obtaining slops from others in town, carried home in two buckets suspended from a pole, an act benefiting other Tacomans during a time when there was no garbage collection service. The Chinese lived in tightly grouped, scrap lumber shanties where lack of ventilation entrapped odors of slops, animal waste, unwashed humans, dried fish and meat hanging from ceilings, and contaminated water ponding beneath the wooden floor, if there was one. The smell of opium was occasionally in evidence.

While the Chinese earned very little, many still sent a portion of their earnings back to families in China – a significant reason for having come – precluding improvement in their Tacoma circumstances.

The unsanitary conditions offended Tacomans of European ancestry and, combined with Chinese customs and habits considered odd, even repulsive, like scalding live pigs after first cutting out their tongues for braised pork tongue, the social chasm between the Chinese and other Tacomans, together with latent animosity on both sides, grew and grew some more.

During the previous winter, due to lay-offs, 67 Tacoma families needed to be supported by charity. They blamed the Chinese. For all the complaining about the Chinese taking jobs, however, the ironic consequence was that many non-Chinese Tacomans would not take jobs done by Chinese. Some honest labor had become too menial. Employment as a maid fell out of favor, for example, because many Chinese women did that.

On February 7th, Eureka, California ran their Chinese out of town. The *Tacoma Ledger* and the *Tacoma News* each gave Eureka the front page.

Tacoma opinion makers disingenuously used half-truths and anecdotal gossip as justification for Chinese expulsion. One of those, *Tacoma Ledger* interim editor, "John Wilkes Booth look-alike" Jack Comerford, lit a huge racist bonfire and daily fanned the flames.

> *Why permit an army of leprous, prosperity-sucking, prog-*
> *ress-blasting, Asiatics to befoul our thoroughfares, degrade the*
> *city, repel immigration, drive out our people, break up our homes,*
> *take employment from our countrymen, corrupt the morals of our*
> *youth, establish opium joints, buy or steal the babe of poverty or*
> *slave, and taint with their brothels the lives of our young men?*

"Y'know, all this stuff in the paper makes sense," said a Tacoma man who just read Comerford's editorial to an illiterate friend. "But here's the real problem: I can barely live on the $1.75 a day they pays us, an' these Chinese'll work for $1.00 per day, sometimes as low as $0.60. Now, near as I can tell, either we work for $0.60 to $1.00 a day or tell the Chinese t' leave. Tell ya what: I ain't workin' for no $0.60 a day. Y' know? $0.60? That's nuts."

"Chinee, they can do that," said his friend, his expression perplexed. "Dunno how."

"Me either. An' I don't particularly care," responded the first man as he scratched his bearded cheek with his knuckles. "The Tacoma Ledger says they gotta go. Trust me," said the man as he jabbed the page with his finger. "Right here."

"I heard they's a' gonna be a big meetin' over at the Opera House."

"'S'pose," muttered the first man. "Always gotta be so dam' formal about everything. What's t' talk about?"

February 21, 1885

At the instigation of Tacoma Mayor Jacob Weisbach, Tacoma's first public meeting on the Chinese question took place at the Alpha Opera House on the evening of February 21, 1885. Although coordinated by Mayor Weisbach, the chairman was Pierce County Probate Judge Eli Bacon who doubled as a fireman, and the unwitting secretary was U. S. Marshal and Tacoma Guard Captain Albert Whyte. A Tacoma First Presbyterian Church soloist, Whyte neither opposed the Chinese presence nor foresaw the can of worms about to be opened.

While the primary basis for resentment was economic, to offset the nagging unfairness of what was being considered, the congressmen offered other tithes.

"These disease-breeding vermin," said the first man to speak, "this tattooed race of pig-tailed, slant-eyed lepers, lives in horrible degradation on the upper side of the Northern Pacific wharf. Something needs to be done about the spread of these squalid living conditions. Their diseases are a threat to our children!"

People quickly spoke to one another as the crowd acclimated itself to the severity of the man's statement. A stooped older man with round spectacles stood up to speak.

"Now, now, just a minute," interjected the older man, gently patting the air with one hand for emphasis. "Don't you think you're movin' a mite too fast? They still got a legal right t' be here." His eyebrows rose. "It ain't like they've been robbin' an' stealin' an' the like."

A disapproving murmur moved through the crowd. The counterpoint came quickly.

"Stealing our *jobs*!" spat a heavy-set, red-bearded man as he stood up. With an elephant seal's nose, and a prominent scar on the right side of his forehead, his appearance was intimidating. "If that ain't stealin', well, hell, what is?!" As Red Beard spoke, his breath suffused surrounding airspace with the sour acridity of a weakly ventilated chicken house, and, incongruously, those seated next to him, although agreeing, leaned away.

At a short distance, the small bespectacled man, taken back by Red Beard's anger, momentarily responded, "Now don't get all fired up jes' yet. Let's first talk this over sensible and see..."

"Ain't nothin' sensible about supportin' no Chinee!!" roared Red Beard adamantly. "An' that's all you are, frien': a white Chinee!" Red Beard spat on the floor. "Hell, the only thing worse 'n a Chinee is a goddam' *white* Chinee!"

Among those present were representatives of the clergy, Rev. J. B. Thompson and Rev. John Ward, who found the red-bearded man's continual use of the words "hell" and "goddam" disconcerting.

"Now just hold on a minute," responded the small man. "I didn't..."

"No, you hol' on a minute, white Chinee!" interrupted Red Beard. "They's about 7,000 folks what believes the bes' thing for this town is send dem infeedels back t'w'ar they come from." Looking angrily at his adversary, brooking no denial, with his right forefinger Red Beard punctuated each syllable in his next sentence: "And-that's-what-we-in-tend-t'-do!"

"Now hold your horses, hold your horses," interrupted City Councilman and brickmaker John Burns, getting up from his chair. "It wouldn't look good back East if we just run 'em outta town. Think about that. On the other hand,"

Burns looked about him, holding his hands out, "if the town council were to simply adopt a sanitation ordinance that said that they can't live like they do, in the interests of public health we could tear those shacks down. 'T'would be a legal thing and it'd help Tacoma's reputation for bein' a clean place t' live."

The rest of the crowd murmured without agreeing. No one knew for sure whether it would be legal, "legal" being a favorable East Coast reaction.

"Well, then," continued Councilman Burns, looking at Issac Anderson, Tacoma Land Company executive seated a few rows away, "maybe the Tacoma Land Company could provide land for a colony somewhere." Those in the crowd who wanted to take immediate action, like Eureka, began to grow impatient. "Or maybe we could just put 'em on a ship," concluded Burns, accommodating crowd bias, "and send them back to China." There was scattered applause and a few mild shouts of approval. Seeing the crowd reaction, Burns, who employed two Chinese laborers, sat down while making a mental note to take things further at the next meeting. Meanwhile, not all agreed.

"No, gentlemen, that sort of action should not even be considered this evening," was the solemn response. It was Reverend Thompson, standing in his clerical attire. The crowd was sitting, waiting, and the dull background susurration of mixed whispers and shifting feet sounded like rain on a maple copse. As Reverend Thompson began to speak, the dull noise became fainter as if the sound was in the next room and the door was slowly being closed. Reverend Thompson was against violence. He was aware, as were most in the crowd, that some Chinese were no longer heathens because Mark Ten Suie and Un Gow had written broken English letters to the Ledger complaining about being labeled "heathens." In their letters to the editor they told of being introduced to the Bible, being drawn by the Father to Jesus, being formally baptized, and having experienced the renewal that comes from understanding scriptures that make race irrelevant and faith primary in all matters. Few at the Alpha Opera House completely understood Mr. Mark's and Mr. Un's conversion experience. "Whereas some suggest that the solution involves the imposition of violence," continued Reverend Thompson, offering a compromise, "rather than resort to violence, the Chinese should be segregated. Let them live peacefully elsewhere in a location where they have no influence in our day-to-day living."

The crowd listened to Reverend Thompson's compromise, but considered it not much different temporally than the Burns recommendation. As attention spans contracted, background noise increased as if the door was being reopened. Reverend Thompson, disappointed, sat down.

Next to Reverend Thompson, Reverend Ward rose, hoping to put the matter to rest. Reverend Ward would introduce another compromise, a logical imperative: isolation of another sort.

"If merchants and property owners withhold services or employment," suggested Reverend Ward, "then the Chinese will leave of necessity, of their own volition, for they will have no reason to stay." To Reverend Ward it made sense: create circumstances which gave the Chinese no alternative, and they would leave of their own accord. It would be like nothing ever happened. The air hummed a little louder as the door opened more.

It was evident to the more discerning that any plan keeping the Chinese in Tacoma for any length of time was unacceptable to the crowd. Rev. Ward sat down.

After several others spoke, a resolution was passed that the Chinese must go, and Judge Bacon was chosen to organize an Anti-Chinese Committee of three men from each of the city's three wards. The snowball began to roll.

February 28, 1885

The Anti-Chinese Committee met, with Judge Bacon being elected chairman, and Knights of Labor member William Christie secretary. The committee designated subcommittees, the first to create formal agreements not to sell or lease real estate to Chinese, nor employ or patronize them. Tacoma residents would be expected to sign this agreement, a list made of any residents who would not, and abstainers were to be ostracized and fired or boycotted.

A second subcommittee, consisting of Mayor Weisbach, Rev. Ward, and regular *Ledger* editor Randolph Radebaugh, was to prepare press releases, primarily for the *Ledger*, on the "habits and characteristics" of the "Mongolian population."

The third subcommittee was to compile reports on Chinese sanitary conditions in each of the three wards.

March 6, 1885

The newly formed Carpenters and Joiners Union met at Mechanics Hall. President Dixon Mitchell introduced a resolution condemning City Councilman John Burns for using two Chinese to lay water pipe on Pacific Avenue to Burns' brick manufacturing plant:

> *Resolved: that the Carpenters and Joiners Union of Tacoma*
> *condemns the said action as unworthy of any man claiming to be*
> *a friend of white labor, and an insult to white workingmen on the*
> *part of a city councilman who asks for the votes of white labor-*
> *ers..."*

"This is terrible," Burns said to his business partner, Al Mills, when told of the condemning resolution. "This is awful. Bad for politics, and real bad for business."

"What'll we do?"

"Well, a' course, we gotta fire Lee and John!"

"Who's gonna dig the ditch?" asked Mills, holding out his hands.

"Hell, we'll just hire some Indians," Burns shrugged. Northwest Indians had worked aside whites long enough and attained enough reverse cultural assimilation to effect the perception – magnified by the fact Indians were not Chinese (at least not for many millennia) – that Indians were an equivalent to white labor.

Burns and his partner fired the two Chinese laborers, and hired two Indians. There was an immediate problem: the Indian production pace rivaled the flow of molasses uphill. The hourly wage was a little more than Burns had paid the Chinese, but the productivity was three times as expensive. And Burns needed the water immediately.

"This is gonna take forever," sighed Burns, hands on his hips, as he watched the ditch dig progressing slowly. He turned to Mills. "Hell, c'mon, Let's just finish the job ourselves."

"You kiddin'?"

"You know any cheaper way t' get it done?"

After firing the Indians, Burns and Mills took up pick and shovel and finished the job themselves. But meanwhile Councilman Burns' public image had received a black eye, a blemish he was determined to remove.

March 14, 1885

As the Sinophobia snowball rolled and grew, another Tacoma Anti-Chinese Committee meeting took the effort to the next level. At the suggestion of The Holy and Noble Order of the Knights of Labor organizer Dan Cronin in Seattle, Tacoma member William Christie proposed a combat information center, a bureau from which all Tacoma Sinophobes could coordinate pressure on both Chinese and employers, coercing employers to replace Chinese laborers with white.

50

In Seattle, Chong Tsing Wei heard of the Tacoma Chinese predicament and was concerned because of his experience two years earlier during the Northern Pacific Railroad excursion. Since then, with savings from years of work on the railroad, together with his knowledge of construction, using Chinese labor, he built several houses in the growing, adolescent city of Seattle. These he sold, and then built a smaller, attractive Victorian home for himself on Broadway Hill to the east of the Seattle waterfront. His neighbors seemingly treated him with indifference and, because of his status, other Chinese immigrants, most living in poverty near Elliott Bay, treated him with respect but not as an equal. He was close to no one.

Do my neighbors view me any differently than last month? he wondered as he peeked through the living room curtains. In March 1885 he believed he was still being ignored, but this was not the case.

"You know, Gene, he's got a nice lookin' place there," said Stanley, looking out the window as he stood, drawing on his pipe. "Most people wouldn't mind livin' in that place."

"Too bad the other Chinese don't try livin' like that," said Gene, seated nearby, pipe in hand.

"Livin' in somethin' like that takes money, Gene," said Stanley as he turned away from the window and looked at Gene. "You think the other Chinese have money? If they had money, they wouldn't be here."

"Then why's *he* here? He ain't a labor contractor."

"Must be doin' somethin' else that makes money. You ever notice how he dresses?"

"Don't dress any different 'n you or me."

"Actually, he dresses better, Gene." Stanley tilted his head back slightly as he completely turned and studied Mr. Chong's home. "I figure this guy didn't come from China."

"Where'd he come from?"

"From the way he dresses and that house," Stanley bit on his pipe, "I'd guess that while he's Chinese, he's from England. I hear he speaks English as well as you and me."

"Well, him bein' up here on Broadway Hill could lead t' all kinds of problems. What if a bunch of 'em livin' down south of Jackson Street decide to come to up here too? This whole thing has the potential to get out-of-hand, Stanley. Can't allow that."

"Well," asked Stanley, "what you propose we do?"

"Hell's bells, Stanley," said Gene, irritated, swiping the air with his pipe, "what's Tacoma doin'?"

April 1, 1885

Anna Nordquist and her daughters boarded a train in Minneapolis, and began a westward journey that would eventually bring them to Murray.

Near the end of April, a stagecoach brought Anna and Inga, now 12, Esther, 8, and Rachel, 5, over the Thompson Pass Road. Pastor Nordquist knew the stagecoach was coming, but was uncertain of on which day it would arrive.

"Stage a'comin' into town!" hollered someone out in the street. "People and mail!"

With fanfare of a 4th of July parade marching band, the stagecoach was rolling down Main Street.

Like so many others, Amos raced out and looked down the dirt street. Are they on it? He stopped and shaded his eyes with his hands – yes, they are! – he could see Inga through the stagecoach window! As he momentarily kept his hands above his eyes, Amos broke into a great smile that was not to leave for several minutes.

Amos dropped his hands and ran toward the slowing stage. Just before the coach stopped, upon spying her father, Esther opened a door, jumped off the coach, and ran toward him yelling, "Daddy! Daddy! Daddy!" until she jumped into his arms, and he whirled around and around like a circus ride.

Rachel and Inga were next, followed by Anna whom Amos hugged tightly, swaying back and forth like he was in a dream, unwilling to let go, afraid to wake up. All five of them – together again. This must be somewhat how heaven feels, Pastor Nordquist thought.

After hugging and holding one another, the five family members gradually disembraced and beamed at one another. It was as if, after being imprisoned, they were free.

Anna turned and looked around at Murray. In contrast to her visions of a unified Sodom and Gomorrah, the small town appeared innocuous. As she looked about, she saw two tall, slender, unshaven men with large, worn hats and bushy mustaches, leaning against the posts outside a nearby saloon. They were looking at the Nordquists. No, realized Anna, they were looking at Inga. Actually, staring. Twelve-year-old Inga, tall for her age, quiet and studious, was in the throes of becoming very attractive. Younger than she looked, she preferred listening to talking and, while she seldom spoke, she actively weighed and probed passing visual and verbal stimulants. Inga also noticed the men and, with a flush, turned away.

Firing off a defiant look at the men, Anna gathered her daughters together and asked Amos the direction of the parsonage. While Amos went to get a cart to carry his family's belongings to the parsonage, Esther and Rachel chattered with one another as Anna and Inga stood with their belongings, uncomfortably feeling the stares of other nearby men.

Like her husband, Anna practiced compassion and love on an on-going basis. At the same time, she was discerning and wise to worldly ways from which it was her duty to protect her daughters. Anna Nordquist was an excellent judge of character. Pastor Nordquist introduced Anna to Angus MacGregor, and after she spent less than five minutes with Angus, she knew who he was and was not. Angus subsequently visited and left the Nordquist residence as it pleased him. Like her husband, Anna found Angus to be a delightful person.

There was another person in town who Pastor Nordquist believed Anna should be prepared to meet.

"I must tell you," Amos began, drying dishes with one of the new towels Anna also brought from Minnesota, "the most prominent person in Murray is not the mayor."

"Does Murray have a mayor?" asked Anna.

"No, not yet."

"Ah!" responded Anna mischievously. "The most prominent person in town is…the pastor!"

"Oh, no," said Amos. "For the town's sake I wish that's how they thought, but I'm afraid not."

He placed another plate in the cupboard.

"Well, Amos," Anna said after a moment, "realistically it seems to me that this Jacob Goetz – 'Dutch Jake,' as everyone calls him – runs the show if anyone does."

"Well, no." Amos paused, seemingly studying the serving dish he had just dried.

"There is a woman in town, an attractive madam," Amos glanced at Anna, returning his attention to the serving dish, "who is very influential." Amos looked directly at Anna. In his letters, he had withheld details about the Murray cast of characters, not wanting to cause his wife worry. Knowing she was alone with the girls and looking forward to their reunion, Amos composed letters sustaining strength and giving encouragement.

"She is attractive, intelligent, charming and gracious," Amos continued. "She treats the prospectors and miners with respect, and they revere her."

Anna removed the dishtowel that covered the bowl just placed on the drain board.

"She has been attending services regularly," Amos added, "and has studied the Bible. We have had some interesting conversations about the Bible."

Anna took *fattigman* dough from the bowl, pressed the dough downward on the floured drain board with her palms, and with a rolling pin began flattening the dough while attempting to refocus her initial perception upon hearing of a church-going madam.

"As Christ said," continued Amos, "'it is not those who are healthy who are in need of a physician.'"

Anna said nothing in response, preferring to listen to what her husband was saying as she attended to her baking.

"As you know, some believe Mary Magdalene," added Pastor Nordquist, "may have had a similar background, but Jesus had no misgiving about having her in his presence."

"On the other hand," responded Anna, "what some believe about Mary Magdalene could be unfounded conjecture."

"Well, yah, but you will agree," said Pastor Nordquist, "that Rahab, the great, great grandmother of King David, was a harlot."

Anna nodded.

After Amos folded and placed the towel to one side of the drain board, he turned to face Anna. "This woman is named Molly Burdan but, outside of her presence, most people call her 'Molly B'Dam'. She is someone you will inevitably meet."

"She must be a very interesting person," said Anna, flattening the *fattigman*.

Anna put the *fattigman* aside and began kneading *krumkake* dough, ostensibly watching what she was doing, but, in fact, her attention was totally on what her husband was saying. She had heard the stories back East about the miners, the gamblers, the underworld cast, and ladies of the evening. It was indeed a field ripe for the harvest.

But no place to raise her daughters.

In Anna's mind, prostitutes were disqualified as role models; and coarse young men who gravitated to a gold strike but not church services were disqualified as eligible bachelors.

Her concern increased two-fold during the following Sunday morning worship service when she found herself in the presence of the Queen of Murray.

Anna Nordquist was not formally introduced to Molly Burdan, and need not be. This was the woman, Anna knew, of whom her husband spoke.

It was not the attraction of Molly's beauty or refined attire, but a different emanation Anna discerned when first seeing Molly Burdan in church. Sensing she was being studied, Molly's face became expressionless as the eyes of the two women looked at one another for a moment as only women can. Molly returned her gaze forward, as did Anna. Out of the corner of her eye, Molly studied Anna's daughters. Pretty Rachel, the youngest, sat energetically swinging her feet, her light auburn hair – nearly the same color as Molly's – glistening brightly as her body rocked in unison with her feet. How wonderful it would be to have three beautiful, young daughters, Molly thought to herself as she furtively glanced at the girls.

Rachel sensed Molly's momentary attention, and looked back. Molly beamed at Rachel. Rachel looked pleasantly at Molly who turned slightly in Rachel's direction. Anna, sensing Rachel's distraction, looked down at Rachel and whispered, "Rachel."

Rachel returned her attention toward her father speaking in front.

When the service was over, everyone filed out of the parsonage except

Angus and the Nordquists. The last to leave was Molly B'Dam, dressed exquisitely in an Edwardian peach-colored satin and lace jacket, matching touring hat, and French double layered skirt with white underskirt, who again beamed at Rachel, pleasantly raising her eyebrows as if to say, "Well, young lady, we should get to know one another." The expression was spontaneous, but when Molly saw Anna's protective look, the pleasant expression faded. Molly shook Pastor Nordquist's hand, and walked out the door.

"Who was that nice lady?" asked Rachel. "She looked wonderful."

"She's someone who works here in town," said Anna, offering no further explanation.

"What does she do?" asked Rachel, unable to imagine what someone that beautiful and well-dressed would do in Murray. Anna deflected the question, suggesting that Rachel help Esther clean their room, but it would not be the last time always-curious Rachel would ask.

51

June 9, 1885

At the recommendation of the Anti-Chinese Committee, in an era when across America fraternal and civic organizations were blossoming like dandelions in spring, the all- encompassing Anti-Chinese League was formed in Tacoma. Intended for eventual Chinese expulsion coordination all along the west coast, Mayor Weisbach was elected League president. The League's purpose once again was to organize those favoring Chinese expulsion, and identify those who did not.

———— • ————

Meanwhile, when people talked, unsubstantiated speculation morphed into "fact," and new rumors became the latest news around Murray.

Longhaired Jim Courtright, the Ft. Worth town marshal and gunfighter who kept both feet planted firmly on either side of the law, had gotten in over his head, and was heading to Murray.

The rumor was false.

Wyatt Earp and his brothers were becoming disillusioned in nearby Eagle City, and were considering looking for greener claim staking, card dealing, saloon keeping, law enforcement, and prostitution.

That rumor was true.

The Earps had staked numerous claims, but none were paying off. The White Elephant Saloon was moved from the tent into one of the few buildings constructed in Eagle City, but the new town was gradually left behind in the wake of Clagett's induced exodus. When the Earps determined they would close-up shop in Eagle City, they also determined nearby Murray had more-than-enough gambling establishments. While Warren Earp, who had joined his brothers a few months after they arrived, needed to stay for a while longer, completing unfinished business, Wyatt, Jim and Josie left – Jim for California where his sick wife waited. Wyatt and Josie drifted to Colorado, and then briefly to Raton, New Mexico where winter weather would suit them better than Colorado. Many others were leaving as well, and Eagle City, with an earlier population of nearly

3,500, slowly waned, eventually vanishing. Had the entrepreneurial Earps stayed another month, however, they might have capitalized on an improbable mineral discovery – bigger than anything that happened in Colorado, North Dakota, New Mexico, Arizona, California or Idaho to date – one that was unforeseeable and evidence that, as Phil O'Rourke mused during the poker game, real luck has nothing to do with preparation.

Early August, 1885

Pastor Nordquist was perspiring heavily as he worked on the parsonage roof in the 95 degree August sun. For a moment he stopped, resting on one elbow while sitting on the steeply pitched roof, and looked up at the blue sky, at first thinking about the hot weather, then changes in the weather. No rain had fallen for a while, but in three months the roof he was reinforcing would be covered with snow. By the end of winter, the snow accumulation could be as high as 10 to 12 feet. Amos thought about how changes in weather can be anticipated, providing time for preparation, but unexpected small changes can also lead to unexpected big changes, whether weather or anything else. When I traveled to Murray, he thought, the train to Thompson Falls was forced to stay in Billings for several days waiting for an engine part. I decided to visit the Little Big Horn battlefield south of Billings and, while following Fur Man over the snow-covered prairie to Little Big Horn, we drifted incrementally westward. If continued, we could have ridden far southwesterly of our destination, and might still be there if not for White Eagle.

Pastor Nordquist sat up as he began bending tin flashing while resealing the edge of the roof around the chimney. He thought about sudden, big changes. They were by nature unexpected. Like a royal flush, improbable. He thought about the North Atlantic hurricane many years earlier, and having drifted for two weeks in a lifeboat, one of three survivors. And because of that I am no longer in the shipping and export businesses in Göteborg, Sweden. I'm a Lutheran pastor. In Murray, Idaho. He beamed and shook his head.

He pushed some flashing into a chimney mortar groove, and wondered out loud, "What next?"

The thought was fortuitous, for an extraordinary event was about to occur.

As Pastor Nordquist continued to work, a short distance away Prichard Creek babbled affably, basking in a wealth of attention in return for a payout of nuggets and gold dust. Communal focus was on Prichard Creek and the surrounding creeks and hillsides, and not on tributaries of the Coeur d'Alene River South Fork in the big valley southwest of Murray. The gold in and around Prichard Creek was being gradually panned out, but, even if it were not, no one knew all the Prichard Creek gold would be insignificant in comparison to the enormous treasure buried in the folds of ancient hills that accompanied the South Fork and its tributaries along their trek 10 miles to the west.

So the South Fork waited for the world's most unlikely candidate to become the luckiest prospector anywhere ever – a broke, tired old man who, following church services, Amos would greet with, "Good morning, Mr. Kellogg."

52

For Murray's sixty-five-year-old Noah Kellogg, life wasn't as hard as it usually was; it was worse.

Gold discoveries were becoming fewer – the gold becoming panned out – and Murray population growth and new construction waned. A carpenter, Kellogg was having difficulty making ends meet. His most recent employer was unable to make payroll and issued scrip in order to meet its obligation to Kellogg and other employees. The scrip was worth, at most, $0.35 on the dollar in Murray stores and bars, placing Kellogg in an even worse position. Alone, with no resources and no other options, his only choice was to try prospecting along with so many hundreds of others…if he could find someone willing to provide a grubstake.

During his time in Murray, he developed acquaintances with Phil O'Rourke, Jacob "Dutch Jake" Goetz, and Cornelius "Con" Sullivan, three prominent men in town.

"Mr. Kellogg. How are you this afternoon, sir?"

Like Pastor Nordquist, they called the old man, "Mr. Kellogg." And "sir." These words, together with the familiarity that had developed, generated a loyalty of which O'Rourke, Goetz and Sullivan were unaware. There was nothing commanding about Kellogg's presence or pedigree. He was an average carpenter, but no more than that. Prospecting? He had no understanding of geology or mineralogy. He was neither a successful nor seasoned veteran of prospecting… in fact he never prospected in his life. Noah Kellogg was uneducated, unsuccessful, unwanted, in poor health, and broke. In the final accounting, his entire life, nearing its end, was going to amount to nothing.

Kellogg had no reason to be a proud man, but in spite of what he was not, he had pride, and when his misfortune sank to its lowest ebb and he needed someone to provide a prospector's grubstake, rather than compromise the respect received from O'Rourke, Goetz and Sullivan, Kellogg approached others including Origin O. Peck, a tall, gaunt contractor for whom Kellogg had done carpentry work. Kellogg sought out Peck and found him at the office of Dr.

John T. Cooper, a rotund, former British Royal Navy surgeon, originally from Scotland, attracted to Murray by the prospect of getting rich as the town's doctor. Cooper's competency, however, was evident from the fact he was in Murray.

"Mr. Peck, I'm out of work and out of money," said Kellogg, looking at Peck and at Cooper who stood nearby, arms folded. "I'm thinkin' of doin' some prospectin' over around the South Fork. Would you be willin' to go in with me?"

Peck was receptive. He'd known Kellogg for a while, appreciated Kellogg's character and work ethic, and wanted to help. Peck turned to Dr. Cooper.

"John," said Peck, "I think we might be able to grubstake Kellogg, here. He's a deservin' sort. Trustworthy. What d' y' think?"

"What do I think?" responded Cooper with a grim expression, arms remaining folded. "I think we not waste our time, that's what I think. No."

"I've known Kellogg for quite a while," countered Peck, "and I believe he'll work hard and remain true to his word."

Cooper tilted his head back, looking down his nose atKellogg.

"D' y' know whether or not he'll find gold?" asked Cooper impertinently.

"Well, no, of course not. That's the chance we take."

"Then I say we not take the chance. Send the blinkin' mongrel on his way."

"But Kellogg's different. I think his odds are better than most."

"Why?"

"Well, he's conscientious and hard-working. Dependable. What else can we expect him to be?"

"Lucky. Is he lucky?" Cooper sniffed loudly. "If he is, why is he standin' here lookin' like a mangy mongrel, and askin' us for a grubstake?" Cooper looked at Kellogg like Kellogg was a patch of smallpox.

"Away with him, Peck. Send the bloke on his way."

While Kellogg said nothing, he quickly developed a strong dislike for Cooper. After some wrangling, Cooper agreed to join Peck in providing Kellogg with a grubstake of $18.50 worth of food and utensils purchased on credit at Jim Wardner's new store, and a $3.00 jackass with an attitude. In return, Kellogg was to share 50% of his findings with Peck and Cooper.

By normal standards, it was a meager grubstake. Already offended by Cooper's severity, Kellogg felt further insulted. Kellogg believed that Cooper was a cheapskate and, due to perceived penury, might be tempted to short-change Kellogg in business dealings. But at that moment Kellogg had no choice. Of the men he had approached, Peck and Cooper were the only ones willing to back him.

Alone again, Kellogg prospected for a few weeks along the South Fork corridor. He pushed himself, but his health wasn't good, and he gradually became physically and emotionally spent. He kept going, but found nothing.

I've no success, but why would it be otherwise? he thought. I've never had success in anything.

When his grubstake was depleted near the end of the month, Kellogg scraped bottom. His dim, dismal, depressing life could not possibly sink any lower than this. He would have to return to Cooper and Peck because he had no money and, having again demonstrated an aptitude for failure, no other options.

As he slowly trekked back up to Murray, he was exhausted to the inner marrow, and simply putting one foot in front of the other seemed like climbing a Coeur d'Alene mountain peak. Don't give up, he told himself, breathing heavily as he trudged up another hillside, the jackass in tow. Talk to Cooper and Peck, he thought. This might be my last chance…last chance at anything.

August 28, 1885

Kellogg respectfully explained that he needed more supplies to continue. Peck listened sympathetically while Cooper leaned erectly against the wall, arms folded, looking severely solemn. The two men disappeared into the back room, there was muffled conversation, and they returned. It was obvious that Cooper was unhappy about it, but they agreed to give Kellogg another month's grubstake. While Cooper returned to the back room, Peck and Kellogg left for Wardner's store, again buying provisions on credit. When Peck and Kellogg returned, Peck laid the provisions on the table. As Peck did this, Cooper came out of the back room, again folded his arms, and stood near Kellogg.

"Kellogg," Cooper intoned after a moment, "how can it be? You've been up in the hills with no one else to care for. For God's sake, mon, take better care of what we give y'!"

Kellogg's jaw went slack and his lips parted slightly as he looked at Cooper.

"We're generous men," added Cooper. "You're damned lucky to ha' met us. Take these provisions, and go easy on 'em, Kellogg."

Peck looked intently at Kellogg who still said nothing. Peck expected he would.

"Everything okay?" asked Peck, encouraging a response.

To Cooper's annoyance, Kellogg still said nothing. He was penniless and little more than a walking corpse but, still, he needn't be treated like dirt. Peck began placing the provisions in a knapsack.

"Y' think these things grow on trees?" questioned Cooper insolently. "Is that it, Kellogg? No, Kellogg!" Cooper's eyes were round and his inflection sing-song. "No. That's right, they doon't!" Cooper clucked his tongue sagely. "Y' manage your provisions like a tyke." Kellogg's jaw tightened and he malevolently glared at Cooper as Cooper insensitively pointed towards the door and barked, "Now weigh anchor!"

Kellogg did not move.

"And bring us some gold," Cooper added.

Staring at Cooper, Kellogg still did not move.

"Good luck, Noah," said Peck, nodding politely as he held out the knapsack.

Kellogg looked at Peck, took the knapsack, and looked back at Cooper. Turning slowly, Kellogg's body preceded his gaze that left Cooper a moment later.

Regardless of how harmless the insult, the pride of Mr. Kellogg was again bruised, and at that moment Kellogg determined if he were to find any silver or gold, Cooper and, by association, Peck would have none of it.

Kellogg trudged back to the hills above the South Fork. Early in the evening, exhausted, Kellogg made a bed of fir branches, laid a blanket on the branch bed and went soundly to sleep.

September 6, 1885

It was already mid-morning when he awoke, still tired. His body ached. As he slowly got to his feet, stood unsteadily and gained his balance, he saw his jackass had slipped its tether during the night and was nowhere in sight. Kellogg sighed.

After searching for a while, it was evident his luck as a prospector, once bad, was worse because, in addition to having found no gold, he couldn't find his jackass. As Kellogg sat disconsolately, staring at the ground while thinking about what to do next, the jackass began braying in the distance, and Kellogg painfully got to his feet. He started climbing back up the tree-and-brush covered hillside in the direction of the noise.

Late in the afternoon, the jackass and Kellogg were reunited, but once again Kellogg was exhausted from climbing the hillside through the brush. Dog-tired, he sat down on a small ledge, lit his pipe, and absently gazed through the trees down into a gulch. He began thinking about the only man to whom Kellogg was ever close, his brother, Milo, who recently passed away.

Before he died, Milo Kellogg told Noah of a dream about a place where they would strike it rich. Impossible, Noah thought at that time. I'm a carpenter, not a prospector. Noah listened respectfully as Milo described in detail, as if it were real, his dream. Although Noah thought Milo's imagination was getting the better of him, it was an interesting story and the description was vivid and now, interestingly enough, Noah was prospecting. As he sat resting, puffing on his pipe, he recalled Milo's description. Eerily, the gulch below Noah looked exactly like what Milo had described, and at that moment Noah decided to call it Milo Gulch, wishing with all his heart and soul his brother was there with him.

For a moment Noah Kellogg sat introspectively and considered his present difficult circumstances. Life, he thought, played a cruel joke on him. He worked hard, incredibly hard at times, but it all came to nothing, nothing at all, and he was soon to become another member of the expansive legion of those entirely forgotten.

Here he sat, somewhere – God only knew where – without anything. Nothing. The total sum of his life's efforts was: nothing. He effected no significant changes, accomplished no notable goals, and at this lowly, forsaken place, even what little he had, the jackass and grubstake, were not his. In the sunset of his life, he despondently concluded his existence had been pointless.

Alone, despondent, he again wished his brother, Milo, were alive and sitting next to him. Noah's imagination was vivid and a moment later, in Noah's reverie, Milo came and sat down beside him, the two brothers studying Milo Gulch, and Noah imagined the two of them talking about their present circumstances and what they planned to do next. Although completely imagined, it was a happy moment for Kellogg, the first in some time.

Were it possible, ghosts of luckless prospectors from time immemorial, a spectral city populated by souls who found neither wealth nor happiness in this life, would have come from the ends of eternity to watch what happened next.

Still deep in his reverie with Milo, Noah reached back to steady himself and, when he did, the rock on which he placed his left hand gave way slightly. It felt odd. Kellogg turned and looked.

Surface galena.

Kellogg knew that finding galena was to silver what finding a treasure chest was to treasure. As adrenalin shot through his system, Kellogg awkwardly clambered to his feet. Wide-eyed, he grabbed his pick, and began digging where his hand was a moment before.

Galena.

And more galena. And more.

It seemed nearly pure. Kellogg stood erect, turned and, eyes still wide, studied the tree-covered hillside. His jaw dropped slightly as he looked into the sun, and for a moment he didn't move.

Why didn't I see it before? he wondered as he stared. Even I know what this is.

His jackass had led him to a great dike, geological evidence of potential mineral wealth, crossing the hillside from east to west at a right angle with Milo Gulch. Kellogg's teeth came together and clamped with emotion as he began to breathe heavily. He continued to stare, unable to immediately come to grips with something that was such a contradiction to everything else that had ever happened to him.

Kellogg imagined Milo was still there standing behind him, and Kellogg, staring around at the hillside, whispered, "Milo, my God, what have we found?" In Kellogg's imagination, Milo beamed.

Kellogg took another deep breath and bent over, digging some more. Beneath him appeared to be a vein of extraordinary size. But how much was there? Kellogg dug in different distant spots along the dike with similar results until the sun went down.

The next morning just as the sun came up, as wide awake as a child on Christmas morning, Kellogg continued spot digging, following the vein down the hillside, across the gulch and, around noon, up the face of the opposite hillside. He continued into the afternoon.

Nothing changed. It was all the same.

Kellogg stood, breathing hard, looking back and forth from one end of the dike to the other. Enormous. Just enormous.

Before evening, Kellogg carefully and properly staked the claim and, again exhausted, headed back toward Murray. As he pulled the jackass tediously through the brush while proceeding down the hillside, he momentarily questioned his sanity, stopped, turned around and stared.

But it was still there. It was all still there.

He pulled on the jackass's hackamore, turned and continued down the hill wondering how big the discovery might really be and, if it was as big as it seemed, could he handle it alone? I know I can't, he thought. How much will this change my life? He could not begin to imagine.

As planned, Kellogg said nothing to either Cooper or Peck because of the disrespectful treatment he received from Cooper whom he mistrusted, suspecting that greed with a little grubstake was evidence Cooper could become very difficult when real wealth was at stake. I might get cut out of the deal, thought Kellogg. But, no, not me. Cooper will be out.

Kellogg gradually made it back up to Murray and tied his jackass to the hitching rail outside Dutch Jake's. Taking a deep breath, Kellogg walked into the saloon and spotted Dutch Jake sitting alone rereading the National Police Gazette. As Noah Kellogg approached, Dutch Jake looked up, eyes smiling, and lowered the magazine.

"Mr. Kellogg. Mr. Kellogg," said Dutch Jake. "I haven't seen you in a while. How are you today, sir?"

"I'm…," Kellogg began, but no other words followed.

Physically and emotionally fatigued, hunched over, Kellogg just looked at Dutch Jake; Kellogg could not accurately answer the question. Nor did he immediately sit down.

"Dutch," Kellogg took a deep breath and expelled it, "you're my friend and, since you are, I've a proposition for you."

"A proposition?" Dutch Jake put the paper on his lap. "And what might that be, Mr. Kellogg?"

'I have…" Kellogg paused and looked around. It was obvious that what he was about to say needed to be said confidentially.

"Mr. Kellogg, please sit down," Dutch Jake nodded congenially, gesturing toward the nearest chair.

Kellogg pulled the chair out next to Dutch Jake, and placed it on the opposite side of the small, round table. As Kellogg quietly sat down, he put a small-but-heavy sack on the floor next to him. Kellogg initially did not lean forward, maintaining some formality, and he spoke quietly, almost in a whisper, commanding Dutch Jake's total attention.

"The jackass I had as part of my grubstake," began Kellogg, "wandered off while I was sleepin'. So, the next morning I woke up, saw the jackass was nowhere around, heard it in the distance, and I headed out after it. After I finally got to the jackass, I sat down to rest. Lit my pipe and sat back thinking about my brother, Milo. That's when I came across…" Kellogg paused and leaned forward, "…when I came across…" Kellogg's jaw moved involuntarily as he searched for the words.

"And what might that be?" encouraged Dutch Jake.

Dutch Jake knew that Kellogg was normally not excitable. Dutch Jake put the magazine on the table and also leaned forward. Glancing around furtively, Kellogg pulled an ore sample from the sack and returned his gaze toward Dutch Jake.

"Galena," whispered Kellogg as he held the ore sample out for Dutch Jake to see, looking intently at Dutch Jake's eyes as Dutch Jake looked at the ore sample.

"Huge," said Kellogg quietly but intensely. "Just…huge. Dutch, there's gotta be a load of silver there. More'n one man can handle. Hundreds of thousands of dollars. Maybe more."

Dutch Jake cautiously reached out and quietly took the sample, studying it, turning it over in his hand. His face was expressionless as he placed it on the table while looking levelly at Kellogg who took the sample, furtively placed it back in the sack, and then looked at Dutch Jake with equal intensity.

"I can't claim this one alone, Dutch. That much wealth attracts too many claim jumpers and other problems. Greed makes the world go 'round, but once the deal is on the table, keeping the deal alive usually requires a pard or two. You're my friend. I want you to go in on it with me."

Dutch Jake stared at Noah Kellogg. "I'd be honored."

It was an understatement, and with those words Dutch Jake sealed the deal.

"But Dutch, there's a problem."

Noah Kellogg told Dutch Jake about his experience with Cooper and Peck. Dutch Jake thought a moment.

"Mr. Kellogg, if we play our cards right, no, that shouldn't be a problem. We'll need to involve Phil O'Rourke because, should this ever go to trial, and we need favorable public opinion – you know how juries can be – O'Rourke is the guy who can get it."

Dutch Jake beamed and sat comfortably upright.

"Where did you find it?"

"Hillside down in the valley. About 15 miles southwest of here. Dutch," Kellogg still looked deadly serious, "this 'un ain't small."

Although successful, Dutch Jake had the uncommon gift of being aware of his limitations and never fancied himself as an overly shrewd businessman. And he wasn't greedy. In addition to Phil O'Rourke, Dutch Jake wanted to involve Con Sullivan.

"Mr. Kellogg, if this is as big as you think," said Dutch Jake, "and we might have trouble with Cooper and Peck, it would be wise to also involve Con Sullivan. He's a smart businessman…it wouldn't change your share of the ownership."

Kellogg also liked Con Sullivan. "That's fine by me," said Kellogg. "I was figuring 50% for me. You split your share with the rest as you see fit."

"That sounds more than fair," said Dutch Jake.

It is, thought Kellogg, with Cooper and Peck out of the deal.

Subsequently, Kellogg, Dutch Jake, Con Sullivan and Phil O'Rourke, together with Harry Baer, a partner of Dutch Jake's, and Alec Monk, a partner of Con Sullivan, trekked down to the head of Milo Gulch. During the time they were on the trail and around the Gulch, they consumed the food in Kellogg's grubstake. Taking ownership of the discovery through two claims they named "Bunker Hill" and "Sullivan," the men knew it was an extraordinarily rich deposit but had no idea of the magnitude of wealth that would be theirs and future generations.

September 7, 1885

Although already informally active in the Sinophobe movement, local chapters of The Noble and Holy Order of the Knights of Labor, begun in Philadelphia, were formally incorporated in Seattle and Tacoma by Seattle carpenter Dan Cronin, commissioned to do so by the Philadelphia general headquarters.

The formerly unknown Seattleite, now in a position of power, began overseeing chapter activities in both cities with the express purpose of further coordinating expulsion of the Chinese.

Coincidentally, that night in the hops fields northeast of Tacoma a gang of laid-off whites and Indians fired into the tents of replacement Chinese workers, killing three and wounding three. The remaining Chinese disappeared into the surrounding woods. Eight of the aggressors were charged with murder; none were convicted, and no Chinese returned.

September 9, 1885

On September 9th, Kellogg returned to Dr. Cooper's office. Peck was not around.

"I've no more food," Kellogg told Cooper. "I'm returning the remaining provisions you gave me, and the jackass."

Cooper, who was drinking, stared at Kellogg, waiting for an explanation. Cooper and Peck had given Kellogg 35 lbs. of bacon, 10 lbs of beans, and another 15 lbs. of sugar, flour, and coffee. How did he go through all that food? wondered Cooper. Kellogg stared back and said nothing else.

"That's it?" asked Cooper incredulously.

"Yes. That's it," Kellogg responded.

"Givin' up?" added Cooper, annoyed at Kellogg's reticence.

Kellogg stared at Cooper.

"Jackass tied up, is it?" asked Cooper.

Kellogg nodded slightly.

"I know nothin' of prospectin'," added Cooper, who paused for a moment and, one hand still around the whiskey bottle on the table, looked at Kellogg as if studying a dead possum, "but I guess you're a poor one at best."

"Then you'll have no objections," said Kellogg tersely, "if we end our agreement."

Cooper, drunk enough to be even more unreasonably irritating than usual, looked at Kellogg as if Kellogg just insulted Cooper's mother.

"'End our agreement,' 'e sez," responded Cooper, looking at an imaginary acquaintance. "'End our agreement.'" He looked directly at Kellogg. "After you waste the provisions you were given. Why don't you just tell me to throw money away?!"

Kellogg angrily retorted, "Dr. Cooper, I think you've said enough. As of this moment I'm through with you."

"Then put the remainder of your provisions on the table!" loudly ordered Cooper. "Someone wi' a li'l more determination'll be needin' 'em!"

Then Cooper scoffed, again wondering: how is it he ate all that food? What did he do the entire time? Eat?

Kellogg angrily placed the items belonging to Peck and Cooper on the table. Without saying another word, Kellogg turned and walked toward the door. As he opened it, without expression he turned and looked at Cooper for a moment, not to remember what Cooper looked like, but to give Cooper an opportunity to remember what he, Kellogg, looked like. Neither man spoke. As Kellogg stepped outside and closed the door, he squeezed the handle with finality before he let go.

A short while later Peck came by Cooper's office.

"Peck, you'll never guess who came by," said Cooper, arms folded.

"Who?"

"Your friend, Kellogg. Turned in what little remained of his grubstake and tethered his mule outside."

"What was the problem?" asked Peck, surprised.

"The problem was we gave him the grubstake in the first place," said Cooper condemningly. "I told you it would be a waste of money. Didn't I say that?"

"Yes, but," Peck looked at what Kellogg had left, "where's the rest of the grubstake?"

"That's it," said Cooper nodding at the knapsack, tools and pick on the table.

"The food?"

"Ate it all."

"Ate it all? He couldn't have ate it all."

"I don't know what else he did with it. T'ain't here," continued Cooper, arms still folded. "Maybe the wretched bloke sold it. We had no business giving it to him in the first place. Isn't that what I said?"

"It doesn't make sense," said Peck. "Kellogg didn't eat all that by himself. And Kellogg's not the kind to quit. This doesn't make sense."

"Good riddance. Last time I ever do that," said Cooper, dropping his arms and shoving his hands in his pockets as he tilted his head back and looked down his nose at the taller Peck. "Shouldn't have given him anything in the first place. Then he comes back for more. An' I says t' you, 'No,' a second time, but you says give 'im one more chance. Another bad decision, Peck. You can't trust that man."

"Kellogg has always been trustworthy."

"You can trust him to fail, maybe. He has 'failure' written all over him. And I said so at the time. Didn't I say so?"

⬥ ● ⬥

"Pastor Nordquist," said Angus McGregor, "Have y' yet heard about the big strike down in the valley."

"Oh?" Amos turned toward an approaching Angus. "No, I hadn't. New gold strike. Been awhile."

"No, sir. Silver. From what I was told, most of the silver in the world is down there."

"Who found it?" asked Amos.

"I dunno. Just a minute. Let me ask Mike," said Angus. "Hey! Mike! Who was it that found the big vein?"

"Some old guy," answered Mike. "Named Kellogg."

"Some old guy named Kellogg," repeated Angus as he turned to Amos.

53

S ome old guy named Kellogg?" repeated Cooper when told the news. "When did he find it?"

Cooper did the math. Cooper and Peck subsequently filed suit against Noah Kellogg, Dutch Jake, Phil O'Rourke, *et al*, in order to obtain 50% of the strike which Cooper and Peck knew was theirs since the discovery was made while the agreement between Noah Kellogg and themselves was in effect.

Their efforts were of no avail, however, for the jury, all friends of Phil O'Rourke, were directed by collective prejudices in the time-honored manner, and ruled for Kellogg in spite of the evidence.

During that evening, drinks were on the house at Dutch Jake's Saloon.

Amos sat down at a corner table with a glass of wine, listening to inebriated conversation around him. The merriment was contagious and, with plenty of men willing to talk to him, Pastor Nordquist was enjoying himself.

"C'n y' believe that'd happen to ol' Kellogg?" said the man seated at the next table, talking to anyone who would listen, but who didn't actually know Kellogg. "Kellogg! Sheeyit!" Amos turned and looked at the man whose mind was groping about as he spewed slurred sentences interspersed with obscenities. Amos didn't recognize him. "Why the goddamhell don' somethin' li' that happen t' *mee*, goddamit?!"

Amos's spirit became suppressed then depressed as he listened to the man.

"Jesus Christ! Why th' goddam hell…" was repeated frequently, and Amos fought against his anger. This person obviously has no clue about what he is saying, Amos thought as he listened the man. Perhaps this is neither time nor place to minister…but no, I'll speak to him.

Amos swung his chair around. When he reached over, tapped the man on the shoulder, the man, spooked, reflexively grabbed his gun, and was on his feet, awkwardly turning around, standing unsteadily. He had the draw on Amos who also stood, at first stunned, looking down at the man.

"You got a problem, frien'?" asked the man, wide-eyed. "Tap me on the shoulder and yer liable t' die."

"And why is that?" asked Amos coldly. "You've never been tapped on the shoulder?"

"Y' goddam' right I have. Ain' gonna happen again!"

The rest of the saloon turned and, in the sudden quiet, motionlessly watched the man aim his gun at an unarmed pastor.

"Hey, ya damned *fool*!" shouted the bartender, reaching for something behind the bar. "That man's a pastor, he ain't packin', and I don't know who you are or where you're from, mister," the bartender placed the object over the bar surface, "but this here shotgun says you'd better put that 6-shooter away!" The bartender knew how to handle this: have a bigger gun. As the man aimed at Amos, the bartender aimed at the man.

"You hear me, mister? I have absolutely no patience with your type. I'm a gonna count t' three. One!" Other patrons began to scatter as the bartender crouched slightly, resting his left elbow on the bar, taking careful aim.

"How th' hell was I suppose' t' know he was a goddam' pastor?! Las' time someone tapped me on th' shoulder, when I turn' around the goddam' basserd smashes m' head with a rifle butt." Staring sullenly at Amos, the man let his arm drop and re-holstered his Colt .45.

"I wouldn't need a rifle butt," said Amos.

Amos's temper had flared up, and he was trying to put out the flames as he stared at the man.

How did this man get to where he is? Amos wondered. He curses by rote, and just pulled a gun with mindless reflexivity. He's clueless about civil behavior and, especially, the heart and love of the Creator of the universe.

While the man was clueless, it was Amos's job to provide clues. As Amos looked at the man, Amos's heart grew heavy for the man, obviously scarred and empty, leading a feral life. This saloon was his church. His invocation and litany were: "Jesus Christ! Why the goddam hell…" Amos wondered how different the world would be if every time God's name was spoken, it was never in vain but in praise; how infinitely happier everyone would be. We wouldn't recognize the place, Amos thought. Perhaps because I'm describing heaven.

Amos put his hands in his pockets as he studied the man who, simmering down, had momentarily turned around and picked up his bottle. Already drunk, and further used-up by the emotional surge of the brief confrontation, the man turned around again and unsteadily faced the big preacher.

"Didn't mean any harm, reverend," slurred the man as he looked up at Amos.

Amos could tell from expressions on other faces at the man's table that the stranger had worn-out his welcome. As saloon raucousness returned, the bartender, seeing Amos in conversation with the man, put the shotgun back behind the bar. The man, spent, stood unsteadily, looking at Amos's nearly empty wineglass on the table where Amos was sitting.

"What're y' drinkin', reverend?" asked the inebriated stranger, holding the open bottle of whiskey, trying to be friendly. "I thought ministers weren't s'pose t' drink?"

"The apostles and the Messiah drank wine, but in moderation," said Pastor Nordquist as he sat down in his chair. "I might have something to drink, but I exercise the Aristotelian mean. If the occasion warrants it, I'll have a glass of sherry or wine, but never very much."

"I suspect ol' Arishtotle," said the man as he steadied himself, cradling the bottle in his left arm while holding his right index finger in the air, "got blotto a time or two. I read some a' Arishtotle." His eyes grew wider. "An' Sock'-ratees. An' y' know, 'tween you 'n me, Arishtotle wasn't so mean. Nope. He wuz like a goo' fr'en. An' if you was like a goo' fr'en', you'd have another drink an' invite me t' siddown."

"I won't have another drink," said Amos. "I enjoy myself much more when I am in control of my faculties."

"Me, I don't worry 'bout that. 'Cuz," unnecessarily explained the man, "I have no faculties t' control. Too time-consumin'…havin' t' run aroun' controllin' goddam' faculties like I'm runnin' some goddam East Coast collich like Princeton…," the man took a deep breath, "…Theeeeyological Seminary." He staggered but caught his balance. "I went there for almos' a whole goddam' year," the man nodded, "but they showed me the door."

Teetering, the stranger pointed towards the barroom door, took a swig, and wiped his mouth.

"Ast me why I wuz there. I tol' 'em it's cuz I kinda liked learnin' 'bout all that stuff. I figger," the man shrugged, "tha's a goo' reason; seemed like a goo' reason t' mee. They tol' me I should also try *actin'* like that stuff. So," said the stranger as he put his hand on the table, "here I…am. *Urp.* I don' think half that stuff happened anyway. Know any Latin?"

"I know a little," chuckled Amos, looking at the floor and up at the man. "My primary languages are Swedish, Norwegian, English and Danish. I can also speak German, Spanish, Dutch, Flemish, French and a little Russian."

"I should join you cuz I," offered the stranger, "can speak a lotta stuff too."

"No, thank you," said Amos. "I'm sure you are an impressive polyglot but I have to…"

"*Actchooally*…I'm Scotch and Irish," asserted the man, teetering slightly, as he looked at Amos levelly, feigning formality, "an' if that ain't impressive, I dunno what is."

This man is quite different than he originally appeared to be, thought Amos. Idiots don't get into Princeton. And he has a sense of humor.

"The Scotch is evident," said Amos who also had a sense of humor. "I must be going. But, tomorrow, if you do want a good friend, meet me here at noon and I'll buy you lunch. I have some things you need to completely understand."

"Why not have 'nother drink an' jes' discush 'em now?"

"Because the Princeton Theological Seminary faculty is the least of your faculty worries. Tomorrow. Noon. Here. Okay?"

"Shhhhhure." The man's head fell slightly, and he looked like he was about to pass out. "Why naw?"

Amos finished the small amount of wine remaining, bid the stranger, "Good evening," and left.

The barroom atmosphere remained circus-like and whatever enmity was held between various citizens of Murray dissolved in the continuous laughter pouring out the establishment windows.

After studying the case for several days, Judge Norman Buck changed some of the jury's findings and provided Cooper and Peck with a ¼ share in what was now popularly being called just "Bunker Hill."

The decision was appealed. Cooper and Peck wanted the whole 50%.

But Judge Buck's ruling was upheld. Cooper and Peck would get half of 50%, making them rich because throughout it all, favorable change was occurring. As litigation dragged on, the value of the Bunker Hill Claim continually rose. When the lawsuits were over, all litigants benefited when Simeon G. Reed, a Portland financier, purchased the Bunker Hill property from the court-determined owners for $650,000, a huge sum for the times, but a sum that would later prove to be one of the biggest bargains of the era. Kellogg found an extraordinary vein of silver-bearing ore at a single location from which, neither Kellogg nor his partners nor Simeon G. Reed could have foreseen, over the next 100 years more than one billion ounces of silver would be extracted.

For his efforts, which were limited, it was rumored that Phil O'Rourke received nearly $100,000, while formerly destitute Noah Kellogg was said to have received three times that much. To Pastor Nordquist this made sense since, under all ownership agreements, Kellogg was to have 50%.

News of the silver discovery in what would be called the Great Silver Valley southwest of Murray brought more prospectors and miners to the area. An influx of new people entered stores, saloons and the cabins on Gold Street – Wall Street for Molly as she and her girls continued to provide services around the clock.

September 11, 1885

A gang of at least 10 men with rifles broke into the dormitory at the Newcastle coal fields northeast of Tacoma, and chased 49 Chinese coalminers into the woods before the men burned the dormitory and cook house to the ground. No one was arrested, and no Chinese returned.

September 19, 1885

White miners drove off Chinese coal miners at Black Diamond, also northeast of Tacoma, injuring nine. No one was charged, no Chinese returned.

September 28, 1885

With the intent of Chinese expulsion from the entire western Washington Territory, the greater Puget Sound Anti-Chinese Congress convened in Seattle, gathering in Yesler Hall at the corner of 1st Avenue and Yesler Way. The three City of Tacoma delegates included Mayor Weisbach who was elected chairman.

The Holy and Noble Knights of Labor leader Dan Cronin, however, was the primary organizer. The order of business was simple: formal expulsion of Chinese laborers and their families.

Dressed in a black coat, vest and tie, watch fob hanging across his vest, Cronin appeared calm as he spoke confidently to others at the rear of the hall before the meeting began. The commissioned Knights of Labor organizer, expecting no opposition, told the others how simply things would go this evening.

"No need to draw this thing out." Cronin folded his arms, as he waited for the minute hand to hit the hour. "I already talked to Weisbach and the others. Tonight, we'll just keep the speeches to a minimum. Heard all that stuff already. Tonight's about organizin'. We'll select delegates who will go home and call mass meetings in their communities on October 3rd. At those meetings they'll organize local citizens committees who will then speak directly to the Chinese and their employers about leaving by the deadline we already talked about." Cronin looked at the others and concluded with asperity: "All Chinese are to be out of Washington Territory by November 1st." Arms still folded, Cronin looked toward the front of the Hall. "Simple enough."

When time came for the meeting to start, Cronin excused himself and walked to the front.

"We all know why we're here!" began Cronin as he stepped in front of the crowd, his voice amplified and his diction clear. Like an unrolling aisle carpet, room silence fell from front to back. "It isn't like nothing has ever been said or done before tonight so let's not waste a lot of time! Let's just get on with the business at hand!"

Having the undivided attention of all present, Cronin concluded, "It is hereby resolved that the infidels must go! The Chinaman has served his purpose; now let's get rid of him peacefully. Is there a motion to…"

"I must strenuously protest the intent and purpose of this gathering!"

It was Battery Street Methodist Episcopal Church Pastor Louis Banks, a slender, older man of uncompromising conviction. Reverend Banks' receding hair, high forehead, and dark eyebrows gave him an appearance of determination and discernment, while his stern, piercing eyes could look into another man's soul. Dressed in black except for his high clerical collar, standing before the crowd, Reverend Banks was immediately recognized by those present. Out of conviction that by helping "the least of these" Banks was fulfilling a directive from Christ, Banks had organized soup kitchens and clothing drives for Seattle's down-and-out. He visited widows and the sick when their situation was difficult. Banks practiced what he preached, behavior that could include driving the moneychangers from the temple. Reverend Banks had read about what was happening in Tacoma – with seemingly little resistance from the clergy.

"The motive here is abominable," continued Banks loudly. "Infidels! You men make such a display of behaving according to Christian principle. But your throats are open graves; your lips spew deceit! All this amounts to is a display of sinful iniquity!"

Banks looked at Cronin angrily.

"Where in the Bible is there anything said which might justify your intentions this day?!!" Reverend Banks face flushed as he condemningly shook his finger at Cronin. "What chapter, what verse, can you cite that might lend credence to your sinful actions, your hardened hearts? None! You are no more than hypocrites, men of grievous character, vicious vipers, all of you!"

"Now hold on, Reverend!" countered Cronin, holding his hands up.

"No!" retorted Reverend Banks. "I will be heard! The intentions of this body are anything but Christian!"

"Now wait one minute, Reverend!" countered Cronin angrily. "Don't you know who those people are? Do those heathens fill your pews every Sunday morning? No sir, they don't; not one of 'em."

"Quite to the contrary!" shot back Reverend Banks, his eyebrows raised. "We have two Chinese families attending our services. And in time, sir, there will be more…although there are some in our congregation who, like many in this room, seem to have a difficult time accepting the lowly, despised Chinese who had no more say about their heritage than you or I. Those two Chinese families speak only minimal English but, I dare say, they have come to a better understanding of who Jesus Christ is, and salvation through God's grace, than you do, sir! And now, would you stand in the way of…"

"Just a minute, just a minute!" interrupted Cronin, waving his arms. "Two families? Look around you, Reverend. Who are the Christians? Whose side are you on?" Others seated nearby, arms folded, looked sullenly at Banks. "We're not here to fool around; we're here to get this done!" This statement met with slight applause, and Banks looked reprovingly at some seated nearby.

"Is there no compassion among those present?!" asked Reverend Banks loudly as he turned and faced the room. "No one present who will help 'the least of these'?"[1]

For a moment the room was quiet until another Knights of Labor member countered that allowing infidels to reside in Seattle was to accommodate the devil. This resonated with many in the crowd. While it sounded righteous, more importantly it was what they wanted to hear, what they came to hear.

Before Banks could respond, another man in the second row stood and asked Reverend Banks if he didn't feel hypocritical for advocating harm to many he previously helped. As others openly agreed, Banks began to feel the weight of futility, objectivity being butchered by irrational bias, the room an epistemic abattoir.

Reverend Banks was about to answer the charge of hypocrisy when Seattle City attorney, utopian socialist George Venable Smith, ignoring Banks, stood up and, taking advantage of an opportunity to get in front of a crowd, walked to the head of the aisle while exhorting the crowd to rid the community of the Chinese whom Smith labeled unwitting pawns of the capitalist aristocracy. Cronin was annoyed that opportunistic Smith was giving a speech; the time for speeches was over. Cronin glared at Smith who he personally disliked. Smith did not notice.

While Smith had a small, almost frail build, his ego was as big as oxen pulling logs to Yesler's mill. Smith had only one decidedly masculine feature: his small mouth staggered under a huge, black, border hedge mustache, above which dark, expressionless round eyes, like miniature binoculars, spied on unwary strangers perhaps in need of a leader.

As Smith droned on, Reverend Banks, disheartened and seemingly alone in his opposition, turned and slowly sat down.

But Banks was not alone. Providence provided another to pick up Banks' fallen standard.

---

[1] Matthew 25:40

As Banks sat down, Judge Thomas Burke stood up, glaring at Smith, and seeing Judge Burke, attorney Smith immediately quit speaking.

Well-known to all present, Burke was a powerfully built man with an infectious smile, an Irish accent, and an enormous intellect. He was well-liked and respected. In the next decade he would become the state attorney general, and several decades later would cofound Seattle's Museum of Natural History. As Judge Burke stood, ambient crowd noise declined until the room was silent. Burke began speaking in a logical manner as if in a courtroom.

"We are all in agreement," Judge Burke began, "that the time has come when a new treaty should be made with China restricting Chinese immigration to this country."

Reverend Banks watched. Burke's eyebrows knitted as he walked toward the front of the room.

"But by the lawless action of irresponsible persons from outside, the people of this city are called upon to decide whether this shall be brought about in a lawful and orderly manner or by defiantly trampling on the laws, treaties and Constitution of our country."

It was obvious that Judge Burke, by advocating obedience to the law, opposed what the most in the crowd wanted to do and expected would be done. Moans and muffled protests were heard. Judge Burke reached the front of the room near George Venable Smith, and turned around.

"Would you, men of Seattle," asked Burke, "even if you had the power, overthrow the law of the land and set up brute force and violence in its stead?"

Silence.

"For the first time in the history of this territory," continued Burke, "an attempt is made to divide the community into two classes – laborers on one side," he said, holding out his right hand, "and all other workers on the other," he concluded, holding out his left. "This attempt is as wicked as it is un-American." Glancing at Cronin, then Weisbach, Burke added, "The man who would now seek to divide us on Old-World lines is an enemy to all."

There were many Irish immigrants like Burke present – some of whom were treated inhumanly while living on the East Coast – and he reasoned with them.

"I cannot conceive how it is possible," Burke said, looking at several men near the front, "that any man of Irish birth could be so base, could be guilty of such black ingratitude, as to raise his hand in violence against the laws, the Constitution or the treaties of this country. If the Irishman is true to his own nature, he would love justice and his sympathies will go out in overflowing measures to the weak, the lowly, the despised and oppressed. He will not deprive any of God's creatures, not even the defenseless Chinaman, of the protection of that law which found the Irishman a serf and made him a free man."

Some present had as little use for the Irish as they did the Chinese. With no desire to hear anything from anyone defending the law and, consequently, a Chinese presence in Seattle, from the rear of the hall a few scattered catcalls ("The Paddies c'n git out too!") broke the silence. The Irish present turned and glared. Judge Burke was undaunted and took a step forward as he eyed those to the rear.

"Those who come from other lands to live here must obey the laws, and respect and honor the institutions of our country or go back to where *they* came from," stated Burke matter-of-factly.

Many present openly disagreed, and the noise crescendoed. Sensing opportunity, George Venable Smith stepped in front of Burke.

"I hope the workingmen will be patient and listen to what Judge Burke has to say!" yelled Smith, waving his arms in an effort to quiet the crowd.

Judge Burke saw Smith's action as a self-serving attempt to enhance Smith's political stature. Seattle City Attorney Smith was a Seattle Sinophobe leader; much Sinophobe planning occurred in Smith's office. In addition, Smith's reputation and behavior in and out of the courtroom indicated that whatever he said was determined by the opportunity at hand. Judge Burke was familiar with attorney Smith.

"Excuse me, Mr. Smith! Excuse me!" Burke said angrily as he roughly shoved the smaller Smith to the side.

Regaining his balance, Smith stood frozen, aghast that his simple ruse just backfired in front of a crowd. As Judge Burke straightened his lapels, he glared at Smith. "I can assure you I need no one to intercede for me with a Seattle audience!"

As Smith, like a tar baby with a huge mustache, remained completely motionless, Burke turned to the others, all of whom were silent.

"I recognize the insidious and unworthy appeal to workingmen," said Burke. "But to them I say that if there is anything certain in human history, it is that of all men, the workingman has the most vital interest in upholding the authority of the law. 'Where law ends, tyranny begins,' and where tyranny reigns, the workingman is a slave! By conducting ourselves as true Americans pursuing lawful measures for the redress of any grievance, real or imaginary, this little trouble that in the mirage of passion now looms so large will soon vanish like a bad dream, and we shall all wonder what we were so wrought up about.

"I thank you for this patient hearing," Burke concluded, looking about the room. "I knew you would listen to me whether you agreed with me or not, even though I say things ever so distasteful to you."

As Burke returned to his seat, the room remained silent.

All present knew Judge Burke was right. Smith remained speechless and, like lions in the den with Daniel, the Knights of Labor seemed unable to open their mouths. While it was not what most wanted to hear, the force of Judge Burke's persuasiveness, punctuated by his uncompromising treatment of City Attorney George Venable Smith, diffused an explosive situation.

As the crowd slowly got to their feet and gradually began to disperse, some men glared at Burke and considered thoughts which, if put into action, would be cause for bringing those men before Judge Burke or someone like him.

"We'll see if these people take to heart what I said," sighed Burke to an acquaintance. "I fear many will not, and this peaceful moment will be only a lull before a storm."

While Burke discouraged the Seattle Sinophobes, nothing changed in

Tacoma. Most railroad people and employers of Chinese did not favor Chinese expulsion, primarily because it would be unprofitable, while other Tacomans simply considered the movement morally reprehensible. The Sinophobes, however, led by the mayor, two judges, a city council member, and numerous citizens of prominence, held sway.

September 30, 1885

Outside of western Washington Territory, not everyone was impressed with what was happening. The Portland *Oregonian* editorialized that the Seattle organizers were "men of no note or character" belonging to "the vicious, liquor-guzzling, unthrifty class who want to work as little as possible," and the Anti-Chinese Congress "could only take place in a frontier community, governed like a mining camp, under a very primitive civilization."

"Sounds like they nailed it," laughed a Tacoman after reading the statement to his Seattle friend.

"Hell, that's you guys as much as us, dimwit." The Seattleite drew on his pipe, and forcefully blew out the smoke. "Someone outa nail the *Oregonian*," he suggested. "'Vicious.' Hell, we're nice guys," he deadpanned.

The Tacoma *Ledger* and the Tacoma *News* subsequently editorialized that all workingmen everywhere boycott the *Oregonian*, but this seemed to carry little weight among workingmen in Portland.

54

King County Sheriff John H. McGraw was as concerned as Burke, a concern magnified by the Seattle City Police Department's support of the Sinophobes.

To aid the County Sheriff's Department, the local militia, the Seattle Rifles, began patrolling the streets, and the next morning's train brought in 350 soldiers from Brigadier General John Gibbon's 14th Infantry Division stationed in Vancouver.

Commander of the "Iron Brigade" at Antietam, whose soldiers bore the brunt of Pickett's Charge at Gettysburg, and infantry commander during the final battle at Appomattox Court House, Gibbon was held in awe by Sinophobes and law-abiding citizens alike. While Gibbon's presence was all that was needed to maintain civil order, in the absence of city police enforcement, Sheriff McGraw deputized a large number of non-Sinophobes, and organized them into a local Home Guard, passing out rifles to any needing them.

For good measure, that afternoon the Coast Guard revenue cutter *Oliver Wolcott* steamed into Seattle's Elliott Bay.

Shortly thereafter, a grand jury indicted seventeen Seattle Sinophobes including George Venable Smith for conspiring to deprive the Chinese of their rights. This only strengthened Sinophobe resolve, and they determined that sooner than later there would still be a Chinese exodus.

After the show of force, federal law enforcement left town, the fire far from out.

October 3, 1885

As the Anti-Chinese Congress determined, all representatives would organize their communities on October 3rd. An October 3rd Tacoma mass meeting, preceded by a torchlight parade of 500 men, was again held in the Alpha Opera House. The meeting perfunctorily endorsed the Seattle platform, and a Committee of Fifteen was elected to coordinate Tacoma Chinese expulsion by November 1st. The committee included Judge Bacon, Judge James Wickersham, Knights of Labor member William Christie, carpenter John Budlong, and Henry Bixler, president of the Independent Carpenter's Association.

City Councilman John Burns, criticized earlier in the year for employing Chinese, to solidify his position as a Sinophobe, presented an expansive resolution that boiled down to four words: the Chinese must go. This resolution was followed by a similar although far more succinct resolution by George Fuller also favoring expulsion, but adding an emphasis on lack of coercion.

"What's he talking about?" one attendee whispered to another. "The Chinese're gonna go if we ask 'em, all nice an' civil-like?" Chewing tobacco, the man folded his arms and leaned back. "And I'm General Custer's son-in-law." Custer's son-in-law, the two men knew, together with the two other Custer brothers, Tom and Boston, also died at Little Big Horn.

"Are ya?" asked the other man, suddenly wide-eyed, feigning surprise as he leaned to his left.

"Shaddup."

Pioneer Ezra Meeker, a hop farmer believed to be the wealthiest man in the Territory, stood up and spoke on behalf of the better element. With Meeker were Tacoma Land Company President Isaac Anderson, Tacoma National Bank Director George Atkinson, hotel owner William B. Blackwell, and former Tacoma Mayor Gen. John Wilson Sprague. As Meeker proposed a resolution opposing Chinese expulsion, the audience, hearing the opposite of what they wanted, responded with angry boos and catcalls, momentum building as Meeker continued speaking. The clamor became great enough that Meeker stopped speaking, flummoxed, looking about at many he thought were friends.

"One moment! Just a moment!" shouted Mayor Jacob Weisbach, rising slowly to his feet, straightening his lapels, then motioning for order before things got out of hand. Weisbach had organized the meeting. Meeker slowly sat down while in the crowd several men continued to deprecate him.

"You fine people of Tacoma, as one might expect," began Mayor Weisbach loudly in his thick German accent, "talk about solutions that respect the rights of the Chinese." The mayor put his hands on the back of the chair in front of him and leaned forward as he waited for everyone's undivided attention. "But what about the rights of the rest of us?" His voice grew even louder. "What about the people who have invested toil and hard-earned money in this city?" His eyebrows rose slightly as he again stood upright and held his hands out. "Don't they have rights?"

The crowd response was predictable. This was what they were waiting for. Years before coming to the United States from Germany, Mayor Weisbach was imprisoned for five months because of his political views. When released early in his sentence under the condition he leave Germany, he went to China where he refined his perception of oppression, believing the poor were victims of two extremes: their own lack of initiative and the big corporations who capitalized on that lack of initiative.

"The first inalienable right is the right of self-preservation!" Mayor Weisbach shouted.

This statement was met with enthusiastic applause. Before the applause died away, Mayor Weisbach, with practiced timing, began his next line.

"This community also has rights," he said forcefully as if defying some imaginary oppressor. "The right to protect themself!"

Applause.

"I don't know who deserves to bear the greater weight of justice here," shouted Weisbach, "the Chinese or the big corporations that brought them here!"

The crowd loudly agreed, and Weisbach waited for the noise to subside to a level where he could be heard.

"They came here," he shouted at the crowd, "to steal your cream, and on their return to China, to laugh at your folly!" To anyone listening carefully, this statement made little sense, but, in the heat of the moment, the crowd found it insulting. "I do not condone violence but," countered Weisbach, "it behooves us to rid ourselves of this curse. If the people are in earnest, if they are free Americans in fact, they will not yield up their homes and businesses to the filthy horde!"

Some in the crowd rose to their feet as they applauded. The obligatory discussion had ended. Reverend Thompson and Reverend Ward watched uncomfortably as the audience voted overwhelmingly in favor of the Burns resolution.

Meanwhile, in nearby Wilkerson, townfolk approached local Chinese, said nothing, and fired rifles in the air. The message was effective. The Chinese immediately packed up and left.

Puyallup hop pickers, told to leave by the following morning, also packed up and left.

The more patient South Prairie residents gave the Chinese three days.

The news about Wilkerson, Puyallup and South Prairie was reported in the *Ledger* and the *News*, and none of it was lost on either Tacoma Sinophobes or Chinese.

October 8, 1885

At a Chamber of Commerce meeting attended by several prominent employers, Councilman John Burns forwarded yet another resolution that said in part: "…we cordially and fully endorse the action of the so-called workingmen's movement for the expulsion of the Chinese."

"So if I understand what you're saying, John," said former mayor John Sprague, seated across from Burns, and now working for Tacoma Land Co., "you want us to fall into lockstep with Weisbach, Christie and that crackpot Budlong…just throw up our hands and say, 'We're with you boys,' even though we aren't."

Sprague leaned forward, taking his folded hands from his lap and putting them on the table as he looked at Burns.

"In principle, I don't like how they think," said Sprague, "and what they're doing. It's unquestionably immoral and unAmerican." Burns' mouth opened slightly as he stared at Sprague. "Men have given their lives," added Sprague, "to insure things like this don't happen here." This statement carried import, coming from a former Civil War general and medal-of-honor winner. "And from a business vantage-point, expelling the Chinese makes no sense whatsoever. We need to keep things affordable for people moving here, and business profit margins are tight enough as it is."

"General," said Burns, addressing Sprague by his army rank as many did, "some larger employers are just too far removed from their employees, and they don't really care about the workingman." Burns added, "You know that, sir."

"Well, yes, and that's not good, "said Sprague. "But smaller employers, if forced to hire all-whites at the wage they want…well, effectively nobody gets hired because the business won't stay afloat. What then, John?"

"If their bottom line is that small, maybe they shouldn't be in business," said Burns without expression.

"Or maybe they should," said Sprague in a formidable tone of voice as if again giving orders at Vicksburg. "Andrew Carnegie started out as a messenger boy at $2.50 a week. Rockefeller started out as an assistant bookkeeper! General Sherman's father died when the general was nine – eleven children and no inheritance." Sprague folded his arms. "I'm damned glad no one ever told them: 'Listen, you can't do that, so don't even try.' Or if someone did, they didn't listen." His eyebrows knitted, Sprague unfolded his arms and squeezed his hands together as he added, "With hard work and resourcefulness, little people – Carnegie, Rockefeller, Sherman – become big people.

"It would be one thing if the Chinese were trying to overthrow the government or end capitalism…that's what that crackpot Budlong wants, but we don't show *him* the door…," said Sprague, wide-eyed, lightly throwing his hands in the air, letting them land on his lap, "but the Chinese are here just trying to make a better living than they could in China. Doesn't that sound somehow familiar?"

Burns said nothing.

"And 'infidels'?" Sprague laughed cynically. "Chrisitanity isn't a private club, John. Anyone can join. As you know, some Chinese already have. And by the grace of God, many more will if welcomed and treated with Christian charity, rather than ostracized and denigrated. Contrary to what Weisbach says, the Chinese aren't a threat to our way of life; their values are not incompatible with ours. Our core values based on biblical precepts are not being challenged…at least not by the Chinese! With respect to the Constitution, the Bill of Rights, ask yourself this, John: who's a bigger threat here, a Chinaman working 16 hours a day in a Commerce Street washhouse…or Weisbach?"

Looking downward, Burns weakly raised his right palm. "General, pardon me, but …"

"No, I'll finish," said Sprague with deprecatory wave of his hand. "In this land of opportunity, these Chinese work incredibly hard," continued Sprague adamantly, "and make the most out of what little they have. But that's the formula." Sprague held out his hands. "That's always been the formula, John. And now where will it lead?" Sprague lightly slapped the table with his right palm for emphasis, his forehead furrowed as he said, "The small, Tacoma Asian population will gradually assimilate into Tacoma society, as some already have, and from their industriousness, resourcefulness and resolve, in the long run the economic and social benefits to Tacoma will be far greater than if there is a coerced mass exodus in the days ahead! Leave the Chinese alone, let them eventually prosper – which they inevitably will – and in 100 years what will Tacoma look like? Can we even imagine?"

Lips taut, Burns looked back impatiently as he waited.

"But do what you people would have us do," continued Sprague, "show that resourcefulness-and-work-ethic the door, and how much does Tacoma lose? What's the ultimate loss? Think, John. Imagine. What might be the contrast in, say, 100 years?!"

But Burns had neither imagination nor concern apart from concern imagining Tacoma overrun by Chinese in blue work pants and coats. Miffed as Sprague said "100 years," Burns began to roll his eyes, turning his head aside in an unsuccessful attempt to hide his displeasure, further aggravating Sprague and some others.

"Am I boring you, John? Well, let me pick up the pace a bit. For one thing, don't give us that damned – and I mean 'damned' – mantra," continued Sprague with forced outward calmness belying his anger, "about how we have a 'moral obligation' – completely convoluting biblical morality – to send the Chinese packing because they're somehow 'subhuman.'" Clenching his teeth at first, Sprague stared darts at Burns and, lowering his voice, said with equal intensity: "Good God, John; here we are about to invoke the great irony of extreme racism: the madness of labeling other ethnicities 'subhuman,' an act which invariably precedes behavior so reprehensible that it is, itself, 'subhuman.'" Sprague stared at Burns. "And is that the road you're proposing we take?"

Tight-lipped, Burns looked back at Sprague with displeasure, remaining silent, his head cocked to one side, waiting for the former mayor and Civil War general to finish.

Sensing Burns' recalcitrance and hardness of heart, disgusted, Sprague glanced at the other faces around the table. "I don't know what everyone else thinks," Sprague looked back at Burns, "but I won't vote for another of your resolutions. I can't help but think that doing the right thing will have the best results for Tacoma in the long run. And that's how we should think: in the long run. I fear that if we don't, our grandchildren, great grandchildren, and thereafter will never enjoy the probable consequences; just the opposite."

"Well General," responded Burns primly, "in the long run, expulsion may not be the right thing, but at the moment it's the *only* thing. I'm more concerned about what the consequences will be today. We either fall in step or we get boycotted out of business…or worse." Burns held his hands out. "These Tacoma laborers are about 90% of the workforce and are not above taking the law into their hands. You all know about that barrel factory over in Puyallup, the owner refusing to fire Chinese, hire whites. He was a man of principle. Until someone put a bomb under his building. So, yes, if he didn't fire the Chinese, hire whites, he'd have no business for which to hire either one. It's the same for most of us. As you know, life has hard choices, General. Do we adhere to ideality, 'doing the right thing,' or do we consider our families – the ones we have now – embrace reality, and do what we have to do?"

The meeting was long and acrimonious, but the Burns resolution was eventually adopted by the Chamber of Commerce, and Burns' status as a Sinophobe was further solidified.

October 9, 1885

Proud of their eminence and perceived moral high ground, the Committee of Fifteen, formed to formally coordinate expulsion, had a portrait taken.

Committee of Fifteen members visited all Tacoma Chinese residences on October 9th, explaining to the Chinese their lack of options. Some Chinese began leaving, and some employers began discharging some of the others.

Some Tacomans, however, aware of Eureka, Wilkerson, Puyallup and South Prairie, decided the Committee of Fifteen should be getting the job done faster. A secret Committee of Nine formed, led by anarchist John Budlong and Knights of Labor member William Christie. Following an organizational plan successful used by radical European socialists, each original member organized a second circle of nine, wherein each circle member organized a third circle of nine, and so on, but circle contacts were to be undisclosed, and consequently, in the event of arrests, no one knew more than 16. This did little to limit exposure and liability, but the surreptitiousness added piquancy to the organizational effort.

The Committee of Nine also set an expulsion deadline of November 1st, vowing that if the Committee of Fifteen did not get the job done by then, the Niners would step out in the open and wrap it up.

October 10, 1885

The Knights of Labor sponsored another torchlight procession to the Tacoma Alpha Opera House where an angry Jack Comerford, who had been fired by regular editor Randolph Radebaugh for going too far in Radebaugh's absence back east, stood up and railed against Sprague, Blackwell, Anderson, Radebaugh, Meeker and anyone else he wanted others to believe was not completely on board with expulsion. Comerford's list would have been a little longer, but Reverend Bill McFarland had just arrived in town.

October 17, 1885

McFarland had just moved from Salem, Oregon to pastor the new Presbyterian Church, and begin the first Washington Territorial Deaf School in its basement. He previously had started a similar deaf school in Salem.

Reverend McFarland knew nothing of Burns or his resolutions, and having previously read and cut-out Comerford's diatribe with a pair of scissors – "*Why permit an army of leprous, prosperity-sucking, progress-blasting, Asiatics...*" – had no use for Comerford. At the next public meeting, acting far more naïve than he was, McFarland stood up and questioned Sinophobe motives, aggravating those present who believed dissent was behind them.

"Leprosy?" McFarland questioned as he held out his hands incredulously while looking about the room. "Leprosy?" he repeated in a cultivated baritone voice.

As McFarland stepped into the aisle, someone whispered, "Who's he?"

"Dunno," whispered the man in the next seat. "Ne'er saw 'im before. Why's he keep sayin' 'leprosy'?"

"While I've certainly heard of cases occurring elsewhere," intoned McFarland, his Scottish accent prominant, "being new to Tacoma, I decided t' see for myself because leprosy is a serious matter, a subject not to be irresponsibly bruited about!"

Maybe he's a doctor, some people thought.

"If outbreaks of leprosy are in our community," McFarland pinched his lapels, "those afflicted must be isolated – which appears to have already been done – and helped."

The crowd stared at him, puzzled, many with mouths partially open. What's he talking about? Helping the afflicted if they're Chinese?

"But I also wanted t' see the brothels," said McFarland before anyone could react. "I've never actually been in one, and, unlike the former interim editor of our paper, wouldn't even know if I was." Some men reflexively smirked.

"I've never been in an 'opium joint' either. The former editor [Comerford, seated a few rows away with arms folded] would find me terribly inexperienced." The Tacoma *Ledger* former/fired interim editor, Jack Comerford, jaw clenched, looked at McFarland with withering disapprobation, wondering: who the hell is this guy?

"Not wanting to appear embarrassingly naive," continued McFarland, "especially if I were to address an august public gathering like this one, I thought: here's my opportunity." McFarland's eyes grew wide as he smilingly looked about the room. "So I went down to where the 'heathens' live, and looked for myself! I took a congregation member, Un Gow, with me to translate."

The crowd looked back in dismay. Another pastor? With an Asiatic? Jesus. More arms folded.

And he actually went down to those vermin-infested shacks and exposed himself to all that filth? Those near McFarland glared at him with contempt.

"I must admit to you, however," continued McFarland apologetically, still smiling. "I still don't know what a brothel looks like…or an opium joint, although I'm not really sure what opium smells like." From their unchanged, motionless expressions, obviously neither did most in the room. Nodding his head dejectedly, McFarland again held out his hands. "Apparently, either those clever heathens were adept at concealing the evidence our more discerning former editor was able to discover, or he did an excellent job concealing his identity, or both." Surrounding expressions were churlish. "And, alas," said McFarland, holding up an admonitory finger, "I found no leprosy either! The whole excursion was, well, wastefully unfruitful."

McFarland turned and roughly clasped his hands together, his eyes raking another part of the room now filled with expressions ranging from grim to menacing. There were cat-calls from the back. Hearing them, McFarland's formerly pleasant expression slowly changed, reflecting the expressions of those around him.

"I came here to tell you the facts and, in the light of a first-hand inspection," he preached, "expect we will have a change of heart, and allow the Chinese to stay, continuing to launder our finery, collect our garbage, raise our livestock, weed our crops, repair our landscape, dig…"

"Hey! Hey! Hold on!" shouted one man unable to hold back, standing up, but Pastor McFarland, eyes wide, again holding out his hands as if reasoning, sarcastically said: "But why not?! If, as you say, they will work for less than half of what others will, I say, hire them! Isn't a change-of-heart then to your benefit?!"

"Not to our benefit, preacher!" shouted someone in back. "It's what they'll take that's the problem! As if you didn't know!"

"Well, then," responded McFarland with continued subtle sarcasm, "has anyone offered to pay them more?! Trust me," he added, his voice dripping with seeming sincerity, "they would compromise in a heartbe…!"

"We don't wanna pay 'em nuthin'!" angrily shouted a young, bearded man in grimy bib overalls, rising to his feet. "Jes' git that buncha coolies outta Tacoma! Outta Tacoma!" he repeated angrily, pointing to McFarland. "An' you feel free t' join 'em!"

"You're implying they should work for nothing?" retorted McFarland in a serious monotone, his hands at his side. "Don't you realize that with what little they make, most barely survive?"

"We don't want 'em t' survive!" shouted Red Beard as he stood up. "Get 'em the hell outta Tacoma! Out! Simple enough! And let me tell you something," said Red Beard, jabbing the air with his finger, his eyes stabbing McFarland, "you keep *talkin'* like that an' you c'n plan on losin' yer whole dam' congregation, if y' still got one!"

"Then I'll preach until there are only two in the room: me and the Lord!" rejoined McFarland loudly, standing to his full height, eyes on fire.

"Hell, yeah, you do that!" shouted Red Beard. "Have fun preachin' t' the Lord about heathens. Like He don't know. An' after y' lose yer congregation, I'll tell y' what else yer gonna lose, ya goddam, self-ri…!"

"Hold on! Hold on!" shouted peacemaker Mayor Weisbach who again had organized the meeting. He stood and turned toward McFarland. "You're a little late to the party, preacher. This discussion ended months ago. The Committee of Fifteen will take care of this business; you take care of yours." McFarland did not know about the Committee of Fifteen. But Weisbach did not know about the Committee of Nine.

Stifling dissent, a few days later representatives of the former Committee paid a visit to Pastor McFarland. Clomping up the stairs like the Russians at the Nordquist Göteborg residence years earlier, three members of the Committee of Fifteen also knocked more loudly than necessary. When Mrs. McFarland opened the door, they walked in.

"Evenin', ma'am. Where's Pastor McFarland? Need a word with 'im."

"He's not here. And you can't just come barging in here like this."

"Sorry, ma'am, we just did," said their leader as he looked about before turning to Mrs. McFarland. "You're new in town. You need to understand how we do things here. Besides your husband keepin' his mouth shut from now on, there's somethin' else. We understand you got an Asiatic housekeeper. That right?"

"Yes. Lena [Li Na] is upstairs. She comes in once a week. Is that what you came here to talk about?"

"We came here t' talk about a lot of things. Pastor or not, your husband's walkin' a fine line. Just hopin' he doesn't trip. He might. Seems t' be the only one in town with no sense."

Fortuitously, McFarland was not home. The Committeemen left without violence. Mrs. McFarland, however, had made no compromises. Lena stayed upstairs.

When McFarland arrived home that evening after making rural house calls, and was told what had happened, he was livid. He determined that next Sunday's sermon would be on the Chinese Question, and over the next few days he let everyone know.

That Sunday, the church was packed. During his sermon on the unhappy history of the state as god, as an example of government gone amok, with righteous indignation he told the congregation about the visit, and that if he was home, "I would have tossed every one of them out in the street!" That he could have done so was unlikely, but less likely than that he might not have tried. He castigated the Committee of Fifteen and all involved in the expulsion effort, and as he spoke, led by attorney Thomas Nixon who was also YMCA Secretary, several men and women stood up and began to walk out, whereupon McFarland leaned forward in the pulpit, slammed his hand down and thundered, "If you can't take the truth about yourselves, then get out!"

Several looked back at him condemningly, even threateningly, and he shouted, "Yes, go! Go!"

As they turned their backs to leave, placing his hands on the front of the lectern, loud enough for half of Tacoma to hear he added: "I will preach on until the benches are empty!"

At the next public meeting, the man of God raised hell, his vitriol earning him no friends; quite the opposite. Consequent threats to himself and his family prompted McFarland to visit soloist Albert Whyte at the Captain's Tacoma Guard office.

"Albert, I've received threats, and one of them just might be serious. I own no guns, and unfortunately I need to arm myself. Do you have anything I can borrow?"

Captain Whyte had just received a shipment of .45 caliber U.S. Colt Single Action Army revolvers from the territorial adjutant general.

"Help yourself," said Whyte, looking levelly at McFarland while gesturing toward an open box.

"Show me how to use these," said McFarland after selecting two.

"Come with me." Whyte took him out back and taught McFarland how to load, aim and fire.

A determined McFarland subsequently made house calls with two loaded .45s holstered under his unbuttoned overcoat.

55

October 18, 1885

The church service had ended, and the congregation, including Molly Burdan, had left. Growing more and more curious, Rachel again asked, "What does Miss Burdan do? How come you won't tell me what Miss Burdan does here in Murray? She isn't married. And look at her: she dresses like a queen." Although she had an excellent imagination, Rachel couldn't imagine what Molly did, and with her mother having kept the topic at bay until now, was dying to know.

Anna thought for a moment before truthfully answering, "She entertains men."

Rachel thought about that. She imagined men coming to this beautiful woman's home and being entertained with hors d'oeuvres and polite conversation.

"Do men pay her for that?"

"Handsomely."

Rachel began to feel sorry for the men in Murray who must be very lonely if they would pay this beautiful woman to do what the Nordquists would do for free.

"We should do that then," said Rachel.

"Do what, Rachel?"

"What she does: entertain men."

Anna's eyes grew large although the rest of her face remained expressionless.

"We could make cookies and pies. You're a great cook, mom. Everyone says so. We could have the men over and entertain them ourselves – you, Inga, Esther and me – and then they wouldn't have to pay for it."

"Rachel…," Anna's mind was racing, "…she does more than bake cookies…"

"Well, whatever else she does, we can do that too…and probably do it better."

Rachel was painting her mother into a corner. Anna considered that she, Anna, probably *could* do "it" better. Anna was proud of her God-given sexual prowess. Her husband certainly never complained. But she was also convinced sex was infinitely better with marital commitment, love and intimate passion.

Anna could not, however, simply agree with Rachel that, yes, Anna could do it better – when doing it at all was out of the question.

"She does things that Christian women should not do," said Anna, "and, therefore, we would not do what she does, were we to entertain men."

"But she was in church, so she must be a Christian. If she's a Christian, why can't we do what she does? The men in Murray must be very lonely, and it would be good if they went somewhere nice that didn't cost anything. Christian charity. Maybe we could get her to volunteer sometimes."

"Rachel, even though she goes to church – and we want her to go to church – what she does is something my daughters should never consider…and you're too young to have it explained to you in detail."

"Explain what?"

"Rachel, do you realize how attractive Inga is?"

"Yes."

"Is that lady more attractive than Inga?"

Rachel thought for a moment. *Inga is pretty, but this lady, somehow, seems even prettier…but maybe because she's grown up and dresses nice. But Inga's sure pretty. And so's mom.*

"Mmmm no. You and Inga are just as pretty." Rachel looked brightly at her mother. She was proud of her mom and older sister.

"Thank you. Do you see how the men in this town look at that lady…or Inga, for that matter?"

Rachel's eyebrows knitted. Yes, she had noticed. They seemed to always be looking. And the way they looked was strange…like they had never seen a girl before.

"Why do they look at Inga like that?" asked Rachel.

"Because your sister is beautiful. But would you want any of those men to kiss Inga like your father kisses me."

Rachel's eyes grew large as she became momentarily shocked at the thought.

"Would they do that?"

"Oh, yes."

"They shouldn't be allowed to do that."

"Then, you wouldn't want to entertain them by allowing them to kiss you?"

"No. Yeeuck." Rachel wiped her mouth. "Does that lady do that? Kiss men if they pay her?"

"Yes," said Anna. "Sometimes, perhaps," she added, having heard kissing is often not allowed by prostitutes.

"Oh," said Rachel. "My."

As she thought about it, Rachel was becoming very curious about how much that lady could make selling kisses. *If she was paid "handsomely," thought Rachel, then why…? What does she do…that…? Oh, but she's so pretty. That must be it.*

Rachel shrugged her shoulders. *There are lots of things I don't know, she thought; the proprieties of kissing, for one.* Rachel's curiosity was again aroused. She saw her dad affectionately kiss and hug her mom. It seemed normal enough, and it made them happy. After the men were entertained, Rachel thought, they must be allowed to kiss that pretty lady goodbye. But surely only on the cheek. And they could also hug her. To show their appreciation, they probably left money in a collection plate by the door. Like church. And some must be generous.

Yes, that must be it.

To Rachel, the lady did not look like someone who would be anything other than genteel.

"She seems nice, to me," said Rachel as she looked seriously toward the door where Molly was moments ago. "She's sure pretty," said Rachel. "My."

"Looks are deceiving, Rachel. Now, come. Let's help Inga and Esther start lunch."

Rachel nodded, still thinking.

For Molly, her interaction with Anna and Rachel was a double-edged sword. While the Queen of Murray did not abdicate her throne, there was one person in her majesty's realm, Anna Nordquist, from who obeisance would not be forthcoming. Although Molly maintained a noble air and, in public, always conducted herself properly, the presence of another woman in Murray with superior claim to nobility, an equally beautiful woman who was the wife of a minister, with three lovely daughters, provided stark contrast. The contrast reinforced what Molly already knew: to be what she wanted, she must leave with enough wealth to start over in a position of respected prominence somewhere else.

Occasionally Molly would see Anna with Rachel and, as the obvious became more inescapable, to silence the mild moaning of emptiness, the Queen of Murray increased her ostentation. She selected from her wardrobe favorite dresses, hats, coats and costume jewelry. To further cultivate her popularity among her subjects, on one occasion Molly B'Dam walked into Dutch Jake's Saloon looking fantastic, and ordered drinks for everyone. The esteem with which the realm held its Queen continued to rise.

The emptiness in her, however, also grew, pricking her heart like frostbite. As she cultivated her popularity, in public the emptiness could be pushed into the corners of her heart and silenced, but when she was alone, the emptiness pushed its way back into the center, refusing to be ignored. With each bout, the contrast between where she was and what she wanted became more pronounced.

Gradually the façade became worn and she discontinued the act. The clothing and jewels were put back in their place within Cabin 1 on Gold Street, and Molly did not venture forth quite as often.

Early one evening, Molly saw Anna and Rachel walking down the Murray boardwalk near Dutch Jake's and believed this was an opportunity to speak with Anna – Anna and Molly had not yet spoken after church – and perhaps have the enjoyment of conversing with Anna's effervescent daughter. Molly loved children, and Rachel was particularly fetching.

"Hello, Mrs. Nordquist," said Molly pleasantly but guardedly as Molly approached Anna and Rachel, unsure of what Anna's reaction would be to Molly's greeting. "I haven't had the pleasure of meeting you or your daughter although I see you in church on Sunday mornings. I'm Molly Burdan."

"How do you do," responded Anna neutrally as she stopped and looked at Molly. Both women were equally attractive although Anna wore little make-up. Anna was taller; and Molly was dressed in fashionable finery while Anna's clothes were common. Both women knew it was inevitable they would speak at some point, and Anna did not want to be impolite. She also did not want to spend much time with Molly B'Dam when Rachel was along.

"You have beautiful daughters," said Molly, beaming down at Rachel. "You are very fortunate. Were circumstances different, I might be where you are." Molly's pleasant expression faded slightly as she looked at Anna. "I might still be. One can hope."

"For your sake, I hope so too," said Anna, keeping the conversation unspecific. "I love my daughters and my husband. It is as a marriage should be, and I wish all women were so blessed."

Molly nodded politely in agreement and looked down at Rachel.

"Hi," said Molly, turning toward Rachel. "I'm Miss Burdan. I already know *your* name."

"How do you know my name?" asked Rachel.

"Your father would often talk about his family before you arrived in Murray. But you're even prettier than I thought."

"You're pretty too."

"Why, thank you," responded Molly sincerely, placing her right fingertips below her neck. "That's very kind of you."

Molly turned to Anna.

"You must be so proud of her. All your daughters."

"I am."

"Rachel, what's your favorite school subject?" asked Molly, bending over slightly as she spoke.

"Spelling. It's easy."

"Easy for you, Rachel," said Molly, "but not for all young girls. Make sure, whether easy or difficult, you study diligently. What text books are you using?"

"McGuffey's Readers."

"Excellent. Those are the best," said Molly. "Rachel, I have to leave, but it has been a pleasure meeting you, and I hope we'll have a chance to chat in church."

Molly straightened up and looked at Anna.

"Thank you for taking the time to talk with me," said Molly. She studied Anna's eyes. "Perhaps we'll have time to talk after church."

"Yes, perhaps. It was nice to meet you."

Anna and Molly silently turned to walk in different directions, but after a few steps Molly stopped, turned and obliquely watched Anna and Rachel as they walked away. Molly stood for several moments, watching.

Having regal bearing, beauty, excellent business acumen and unique mental toughness, it was a challenge for Molly B'Dam' to work the Line in Murray when she could have more easily operated a Seattle parlor house. It was her conviction that employing the image of a parlor house madam on the Line in Murray, the last major gold strike south of Alaska, would enable her to monopolize the profession in a bull market, generating substantial wealth in significantly less time than would be required under more genteel circumstances. Molly was willing to pay what she initially considered a small price for the present worth of future benefits.

That afternoon Molly was alone in her cabin, again considering her options. She glanced at the trunk and traveling bags stacked in the corner, wondering if she might use them soon. She again thought of Anna Nordquist and what it would be like being married to a man like Amos Nordquist and to have three beautiful daughters. Molly was particularly attracted to Rachel who looked much like Molly did at the same age. Although she still mistrusted men, Molly enjoyed the vision of husband and children to the point where she wondered if, maybe, that could really happen.

Meanwhile, the pain of her waywardness remained unmedicated. The cure, she knew from her own reading of the Bible, and the sermons of church services she attended since leaving her husband, was in simple submission to God's will. Molly could feel the leading of the Holy Spirit, standing at the door of her heart, knocking, and knew she would ultimately open the door. With each day of unhappiness, she reconsidered leaving for a cultured community, using her maiden name, Margaret Hall, and taking up a respectable occupation, perhaps nursing or, more likely, teaching.

But not yet, she thought. Respectable occupations don't pay well and, while respectable, aren't always respected. To insure respectability and security in an unknown future, she believed she needed to take a lot of money with her when she left Murray. Just a little longer, she thought.

56

October 31, 1885, Saturday

November 1st, Sunday, was the day all Chinese were to be out of Tacoma. As October advanced, employers, even the Northern Pacific Railroad, were laying-off Chinese, replacing them with white workers. On October 30th, the Tacoma Mill and the salmon cannery laid-off remaining Chinese employees. Employers had fallen into lock step with the Sinophobes. By October 31st, seventy Chinese had been able to afford passenger train faire to Portland, and many others hopped freight trains heading south. Between fifty and one hundred, the *Ledger* estimated, had neither means nor destination, however, and were still in Tacoma. As would later become evident, the number was much larger.

On the eve of the November 1st deadline, another torchlight parade saw 700 men march up Pacific Avenue to the Alpha Opera House where the largest mass meeting to date, organized by the Knights of Labor, and attended by a Seattle delegation greeted by a cannon salute, would be held. For the occasion, Millie Bixler, wife of Committee of Fifteen member Henry Bixler, baked an enormous frosted cake decorated with the exclamation: "The Chinese Must Go!"

"Did you see that cake, Will?" one attendee asked another as they walked in.

"Hell, we don't need no meetin' now, George. Kinda like the Last Supper. We just eat the cake, and everything's fixed."

"Only if y' think y' c'n have yer cake and eat it too, airhead, cuz nothin's fixed…although it shoulda been fixed by now. I'm gettin' tired 'a meetin's an' more meetin's and nothin' done. Talk, talk, talk. Still plenty a' Chinee in town. Far as I c'n see, other than talk, that cake's the only thing actually been done," said the man, chagrined. "Know what I mean?"

Many others felt the same way, and the witching hour was fast approaching.

"November 1st, that's tomorrah," shouted carpenter Jacob Ralph to all in the Opera House. "Chinee were all supposed t' leave, but a bunch are still here; I sees 'em. So we need real action, and I recommend beginning with a November 3rd investigation to identify any Chinee remaining in Tacoma, and then devise the quick means to *make* 'em leave. Meanwhile, I propose a resolution that, after the Tacoma Chinee are gone, the Committee of Fifteen becomes a permanent governing body, coordinating expulsion up and down the whole coast, so none 'em comes back."

After the resolution passed, it was further resolved the meeting would be followed by another meeting where, after determining how many Chinese still remained in Tacoma, the Committee of Fifteen would report their Tacoma investigative findings, and what they were going to do.

Another meeting. And it was too open-ended for several men present.

"This is horseshit," whispered Committee of Nine member, anarchist John Budlong to business partner Al Mills, secretly a member of both committees, as they sat listening. "These dam' people will meet-themselves-to-death before they ever do anything!"

"Yeeup," agreed Mills, comfortably leaning back in his chair, folding his arms. "I kinda figured this nonsense might go on forever. These dam' people don't know how t' get things done. They're 'committee' people. Talkers. 'Present their findings,'" snorted Mills. "What's t' find?" he asked in a loud whisper. "A buncha Chinee are still here, livin' in the same dam' places they been livin."

"Guess the committee [of Nine] needs t' step up, take over," smiled Budlong as he looked at the crowd in front and gestured widely, "give direction, an' just get things done."

"So, after this meetin's over," Mills looked at Budlong, "let's get Bill Christie an' the boys together an' do what we planned."

Continuing to look at the speaker droning on, beaming, Budlong nodded.

The Committee of Nine met Sunday night, November 1st, and went over their plan – secret circles of nine – determining it would be put into action on Tuesday when the Committee of Fifteen was supposed to present their findings and figure out what to do next.

November 2, 1885 Monday

The Committee of Fifteen met that evening in Mayor Weisbach's office, with Chairman James Chilberg having second thoughts.

"Boys, I'm not so sure we're ever going to get all the Chinese t' leave," said Chilberg. "And a bigger legal issue might be awaitin." Chilberg held out his hands. "Look, they got no money, no place t' go, an' we don't wanna be buyin' 'em any train tickets. I figure what we got now, a handful of Chinamen in Tacoma, is as good as it'll get. They ain't takin' nobody's jobs any more; thems that remain are self-employed – merchants and laundrymen – an' they'll be gone when they can't make any money, cuz from now on nobody's gonna use 'em." Chilberg folded his hands. "Let's tell everyone what we planned to do is what we done; call it a day." Chilberg sat back. "Simple enough."

"I got somethin' simpler," said Al Mills in a low voice, staring darts at Chilberg. "Why don't we get ourselves a new chairman?"

Chilberg was voted off the Committee of Fifteen, and Mills recommended Chilberg's replacement be Mills' partner John Budlong. All agreed, expecting Budlong to be the last person in Tacoma who might get cold feet. Chilberg's removal and Budlong's selection signalled expulsion was inevitable, indirectly validating the Mills, Budlong, Christie and Committee of Nine decision to take action immediately.

The Committee of Nine met again after midnight at Lister Foundry molder Mike Gillis's house, then Committee of Nine members went out about the town and aroused from bed each member of their preestablished circles-of-nine. Members of each circle then went out into the community, waking everyone up and telling them what to do when the foundry whistle blew at 9:30 a.m. the next morning.

November 3, 1885 Tuesday 9:30 a.m.

For no scheduled reason, a prolonged blast from Lister Foundry steam whistle was heard all over Tacoma at 9:30 a.m., a militant signal to the Sinophobes that the time had come to escort the remaining Chinese out of town.

Fifteen hundred men and women with wagons and carts, some containing vegetables, fruit, coffee, tea, bread and butter, headed toward the Northern Pacific wharf, "C" Street from 11th Street to 13th Street, and Railroad Street from 7th Street to 9th Street, the Half Moon yards and Old Town settlements.

"Okay folks, here we are," said William Christie as he pointed to the small shanties ahead. By this time, practiced oratory on the subject was rote: "This area is infested with the Oriental incubus, the pest of the Pacific Coast, the thralldom of Chinese filth," acerbic phrases that had been used and reused like honey buckets.

The leaders walked toward wide-eyed Chinese in the street watching the approaching Sinophobe masses.

"Listen t' me! Listen t' me!" shouted the Sinophobe leader. He grabbed a wooden box, set in place, and stood on it. "Ya listenin'?!"

He waited until other Chinese, most of whom could not speak English, came out to the street. Some did not; some, terrified, stayed inside, locking their doors.

"Here's what we're gonna do! We'll help you load your stuff on these wagons!" The leader's arm swept in the direction of the carts lined up behind him. "We also brought food for ya! Kinda like a picnic! When the carts are loaded, we'll escort you to the railroad station south of town. Then you leave. The carts stay. Savvy?!" The Chinese looked back expressionlessly.

"We don't particularly care where you go. Seattle. Centralia. Portland. Maybe Victoria up in Canada, since that's where a lot of ya last come from. Just get goin' an' keep goin'. We don't wanna see none a' ya back here again."

The few Chinese men who understood what he said spoke among themselves as the others listened. The men eyed the mob. There was no alternative. They spoke to the others who looked at the mob with expressionless resentment. The group broke apart, and men, women and children began going into their shanties to get readily transportable belongings.

As the Chinese began to load their belongings into carts and wagons, Sinophobes assigned to the task began giving them food to eat as the Chinese loaded up. At that moment, however, many Chinese weren't hungry, and uneaten food was put in the carts for the trip to wherever the Chinese found themselves going. For the townspeople, whatever the Chinese did after they left was irrelevant; the food acted as a moral anesthetic, a get-out-of-town, going-away present, proof expulsion somehow wasn't personal.

"It was probably the best meal some had ever had in their lives," remarked one woman as she watched the Chinese families carry and pull their belongings in an exodus along the waterfront.

Some Chinese unwisely remained locked in their shanties, however.

"Some of these doors are locked," said one Sinophobe as he pulled on a latch.

"Well, just bust 'em down. Either someone's in there or they ain't. If they ain't, all well and good. If they are, we toss 'em out."

The Sinophobes went to work breaking down doors, physically throwing occupants out into the street, chasing them in the direction others were already heading out of town. The Sinophobes then helped themselves to remaining Chinese belongings, apparently of value after being liberated from "the thralldom of Chinese filth."

As this was happening, Pastor McFarland, returning to First Presbyterian Church, momentarily stopped on a corner and watched in stunned disbelief. He turned and ran to Albert Whyte's office nearby.

"My God, Captain, this is America!" cried McFarland as he entered. "We must do something!"

Standing next to his desk, Whyte looked at McFarland, solemnly folded his arms, but made no other response.

"Why do we stand and do nothing?" asked McFarland, wide-eyed, unable to come to grips with the moment.

Whyte looked back and still made no response.

"Well, I must *do* something!" McFarland said exasperatedly as he turned, feeling for his .45s, and walked briskly to the door.

"Whoa! Whoa! Wait a minute, Pastor!" said Whyte, racing after McFarland. McFarland stopped. Gently hooking his right hand around McFarland's left arm, Whyte led McFarland over to the window.

"Pastor, look down there."

Bending at the waist, McFarland looked down at the street.

"See that man?" said Whyte, pointing. "He's the mayor. Remember? And that man?" Whyte pointed a little to the left. "He's a judge. And that man?" Whyte pointed a little further to the left. "He's on the council. And that man?" Whyte pointed to the right. "He's the sheriff. And most of the rest of them have been deputized." Whyte turned to McFarland who continued to stare at the street scene below. "Pastor, you've already made yourself plenty of enemies. Every man out there would just love to see you start something. Over the last several months they've built and fortified the conviction that what they're doing is morally justified; that someone attempting to stop them would be acting immorally and, in your case, hypocritically. It doesn't matter what you do, you can't stop this thing. You can only make it worse."

Still bent at the waist, McFarland studied the crowd below. He stood upright, continuing to watch. After a moment his angry visage became somber. He took a deep breath, sighed, and whispered to himself, "Merciful God."

Two hundred and fifty Tacoma Chinese were taken to the Northern Pacific Lake View station eight miles south of Tacoma. A few were able to buy tickets to Portland. With the cooperation of another engineer, the rest were put aboard empty freight cars. Many left possessions at the station.

November 4, 1885 Wednesday

The Wednesday edition of the Portland *Oregonian* did not mince words:

> *The Chinese have been driven out of Tacoma by methods that would disgrace barbarians. The act is a crime against civilization and mankind, on the level with the expulsion of the Jews and the Moors from Spain, and the Huguenots from France. Such a thing would not be possible in any community governed by principles of justice and civilization. It is characteristic of a mushrooming railroad town.*

The expulsion was reported nationally, and when Pastor Nordquist read about it, he wondered why, seemingly, no one had opposed such a thing, although some had. He reasoned to himself that he would have been at the oppositional fore, unaware that he was going to be granted that chance.

November 5, 1885 Thursday

The next day, all personal belongings of value having been taken, the shanties were burned to the ground, and ladies of European descent were again willing to be employed as domestic servants.

57

Three months passed. In Seattle, there was a knock on Mr. Chong's door. Surprised to have visitors, Mr. Chong hesitated, waited.

There was a second knock.

No one had visited in several weeks. Mr. Chong walked to his front door and cautiously opened it.

Five men stood looking back at him.

"You Chong T.. T's...?" The tall man with a gray mustache, round spectacles, and a battered, black bowler looked down, flustered, and turned to his left. "Here, you read it."

He handed a piece of paper to the big man next to him who was adjusting his suspenders over his checkered flannel shirt. Taking the paper, the man reached in his vest pocket for his reading glasses.

"You Chong T'sing Wei?" asked the large second man with a florid complexion, looking up from the piece of paper.

Mr. Chong looked at the man and his four companions who looked back seriously but without malice.

"Yes."

Pronouncing a long, rather than short, "a", the big man haltingly read, "'This is a legal notice. Your residence has failed to pass the hea…health laws of the City of Seattle, and the laws of the Territory.'"

He looked up, done reading.

"Please get your coat and hat, and anything else that you may want to take with you, and come with us."

Mr. Chong looked at the men perplexed, and kept the obvious motive at bay as he glanced around his home. The construction and cleanliness were superior to many nearby residences.

"I do not understand."

"Well, now," the tall, bespectacled man said, "we think y' do. We hear y' speak English pretty good."

"No," clarified Mr. Chong, "I mean I do not understand why you want me to get my coat and hat…and whatever I want to take with me." Mr. Chong looked back and forth. "Take with me where?"

The big man took off his reading glasses and cleared his throat, looking obliquely at Mr. Chong. It seemed the man was preparing to make a speech.

"We're from the Order Committee," the man explained. "We intend to do this orderly. Don't be givin' us no trouble. An' don't take this personal." He cleared his throat again. "The steamer *Queen of the Pacific* is presently moored at the Main Street dock. It'll be sailin' t' San Fr'ncisca in two days. You're t' be on it when it does."

The "Order Committee," as each Seattle Sinophobe congress sub-group of five was designated, stood and watched dispassionately, waiting for Mr. Chong to go back inside and get his things.

"Excuse me but…," Mr. Chong was finding difficulty groping his way through the irrational fog, "…why? For what purpose?"

The five men glanced at one another. The tall man with the large, gray mustache spoke. "You may not 'a noticed, but yore Chinee. That's why."

To him that answered the question, while to Mr. Chong it resurrected many others. Mr. Chong was not going to be formally arrested – the Order Committee had neither reason nor right to make an arrest – but he was going to be exiled. To San Francisco.

Realizing he had no choice, Mr. Chong went inside the house, carefully checked a certain area of the living room, put on two heavy sweaters and an overcoat, got his hat and gloves, and emerged with nothing else other than his wallet and house key. He locked the house, and put the key in his pants pocket.

'Y' might as well hand me that," said one of the other Committeemen. 'Y won't be needin' it no more."

After handing the man the house key, Mr. Chong went with the men down the hill toward the waterfront, stopping near the base of the hill where the men knocked on other doors. As they got closer to the shoreline, Mr. Chong could see a Chinese exodus, tributaries merging into a wide stream flowing toward the Ocean Dock.

"Y'know, Josh," said one Order Committee member to another, "this makes a lotta sense. Put all the Chinese on board the *Queen of the Pacific* and send 'em to San Francisco. Let San Francisco figger out what t' do with 'em." He nodded in agreement with himself. "Dunno why we didn't think a' this a long time ago."

"We *did* think a' this long time ago, Al. Just took forever t' do it."

A simple plan. With a simple flaw.

Black-and-gray-bearded Captain Jack Alexander, encapsulated in a thick, boot-length, black seafarer's coat, stood solemnly at the head of the gangplank, his graying hair covered by a sea captain's cap. In the light drizzle, he raised his right hand to get the crowd's attention, and pointed out an oversight.

"I don't necessarily blame you for what you're doing," Captain Alexander said loudly, "but, you see, there's a small problem. I won't do this *pro bono*. And I don't know where you got the idea that I might. If you want to send these Chinamen to San Francisco, I'll be glad to accommodate you. For $7.00 a head."

"Now, now, Captain Alexander," argued an Order Committee leader; "under the circumstances mightn't you be a bit more lenient?"

Captain Alexander bristled as he looked back at the man. He had considered charging more.

"I am being lenient," he responded, containing his anger. "$7.00 a head. Don't question my generosity," he growled loudly, "or I'll withdraw the offer altogether."

After extensive questioning, it was determined that only nine of the Chinese, including Mr. Chong, had enough money to pay their fare.

"Well, now what?" muttered one of the Sinophobe leaders.

"We can't just leave 'em here," answered another.

"Well, then what do you propose we do?"

"Dunno," shrugged the second man. "Guess we'll have t' send 'em home."

"Hell, no, we won't send 'em home!" countered the first. "We got 'em this far, now let's git 'em outta here."

"An' how do y' propose we do that?"

"I dunno," he began as he looked at the others. "Wait! Let's pass the hat."

"'Pass the hat'?"

"Y' want 'em outta here or not?"

"Of course we want 'em out 'a here." The men and women all looked at one another and murmured in agreement.

"Well, then, here…put up or shut up. Take this hat and put your money where your mouths is. After they're gone, in a couple a' weeks you'll have earned your money back."

The initial offering was modest, but later, after many left and returned with more money, the total increased to $600.

"Captain Alexander! We got $600 in hard cash here. That should cover it. That's $600 more 'n y' woulda had. An' you're goin' t' San Francisca with cargo anyway."

"$600." Captain Alexander did a mental calculation. "That'll take care of 85 of 'em."

There were approximately 380 Chinese on the Ocean Dock. Captain Alexander, a competent commanding officer, able businessman and experienced card player, leaned against a stanchion, hands folded, and waited for whatever the Sinophobes would do next.

Mary Kenworthy, a high-strung, militant anti-capitalist whose speeches about coming class warfare could wake the dead, challenged the others to keep the faith by signing a personal note guaranteeing an additional $1,500 in order to place the remainder of the Chinese on board the *Queen of the Pacific*. $1,500. Only Mary Kenworthy understood the reasoning behind that amount.

"Would you men accommodate those dog salmon capitalists by keeping these Asiatics in Seattle?" asked Mary Kenworthy loudly. "I say talk's cheap, but our working class labor should not be! Put your honor and good faith where it will do the most good!" She continued to challenge the men, questioning their commitment and manhood, and firing socialist platitudes aloft like Antietam cannon shells until a dozen men, gradually withering under the bombardment, finally agreed to sign.

"Mary! Just give me the damned note!" said one man angrily as he grabbed the piece of paper from her upraised hand. After the signatures were made, Mary Kenworthy turned triumphantly and walked toward the gangway.

"Captain Alexander!" shrilled Mary Kenworthy, "I have a note for $1,500 signed by 12 of Seattle's most reputable citizens! A $1,500 promissory note! Good as gold itself! Would you insult these fine people – people who purchase the goods you ship – while failing to exercise common decency with respect to organized labor? Would you support the traitorous capitalists who have placed us all in this despicable position of having to defend our sovereign rights as American tradesmen?" She looked wide-eyed at Captain Alexnder. "No? Then, here! Show one and all that you are a friend of labor! Take this promissory note and demonstrate your solidarity with the workers of this community!"

Leaning on a stanchion, Captain Alexander studied the scene before him, removed his pipe for a moment and almost chuckled. Although $1,500 wasn't nearly enough, Captain Alexander figured this was probably as good as he could do, and the odds of collecting something from Mary Kenworthy and 12 others were better than collecting from one or two. And he wouldn't have to listen to Mary Kenworthy any longer.

Just as the Chinese were beginning to be ushered toward the ship, however, a representative of Judge Roger Greene's court raced up the gangplank to Captain Alexander and handed him another paper. As the first few Chinese started to file on board, Captain Alexander read what the paper said, and then waved his right arm in the direction of the boarding Chinese.

"Whoa! Hold it! Everyone back on the dock."

He mechanically waved his arm, pointing again and again in the direction of the pier. "You heard me; back on the dock! You savvy?" He pointed at the Chinese, and then at the dock. "Back on the dock!"

"What's goin' on, Captain? What's that say?"

"This is a *writ of habeas corpus*," explained Captain Alexander. "It orders me to appear in court with my, uh, passengers at 8:00 tomorrow morning."

"What's *that* mean?"

"It means," Captain Alexander raised his eyebrows, "that we will not be getting underway until after 8:00 tomorrow morning."

Captain Alexander beamed at the chaos before him.

"Here's your chance to raise another $2,000 in cash," he said. "That's what it'll take."

Captain Alexander, friend of labor, was dealt a new hand. Mr. Chong and the others, confused, were herded into an empty warehouse on the dock.

It was early afternoon by the time everyone within the 79-man anti-Sino-phobe Home Guard militia gathered at the firehouse, well after the 380 Seattle Chinese had been rounded up by Sinophobes and marched down to the *Queen of the Pacific*. Joining the Home Guard were army cadets from the Territorial University, later the University of Washington. After discussing what they should do, the Guardsmen left the firehouse, reassembling at 2nd and Washington near the Ocean Dock. Meanwhile, the deputized Seattle Rifles, also Sinophobe opposition, assembled at the courthouse.

From a distance, unaware of gathering opposition, three Sinophobes sat down leisurely on the hillside above the docks and watched, reasoning among themselves.

"Think this whole thing'll work out? Seems like an awful lot of trouble considering how simple this whole thing should be."

"Yeah. Seems like nothin' goes as planned."

"Hell, 'nothin' goes as planned' 'cuz nothin's planned."

"Well now, some things is planned, okay? But other things, well, some things y' just can't plan for. Y' know?" The other two Sinophobes looked back with resignation. "So what d' we do now?"

"Guess we just sit 'n wait. Can't do much else." He put a chaw in his mouth.

One of the others was thinking pretty hard about something without coming up with an answer. "Can I ask you boys somethin'?"

"What's that?"

"How come Tacoma and Seattle don't get along much?"

"Only thing I ever heard was they think they got more brothels," said the first man. "Those boys say they got more brothels 'n us – and they're proud of that!"

The second man looked at the first man as if he had mice hanging from his eyebrows. "Why would that matter; how do they *know* they got more brothels?" asked the second man incredulously. "Someone *countin*'?"

"Dunno," responded the first man.

"Can I ask you fellers somethin' else? What's a *writ of habeas corpus*?"

"Dunno. Some legal nonsense about not bein' able t' board the *Queen of the Pacific*."

"But that don't mean they can't be put on board somethin' else. Hell, put 'em all on a train. People hitch rides on trains alla time. Hitchin' ain't expensive."

"We could do that – put 'em all on a train!"

The man thought for a moment, grinned and leaned forward, suppressing a laugh.

"Y' know where we could send 'em?"

"Where?"

"Tacoma!"

The men looked back and forth at one another and a spontaneous howl went up. The concept was inspired. Brilliant. Tacoma. Send the Chinese to *Tacoma*!

"We'll get the whole lot of 'em on board a train and headin' to Tacoma for a lot less'n $600. Let's go get the others."

The idea spread with contagion and soon Sheriff John McGraw was told of the plan. He summoned the railroad superintendent to the Sheriff's office.

Seated at his desk, McGraw folded his hands on his desk, and looked levelly at the superintendent seated across from him. "Can you tell me what you call it when you take a person or group of persons somewhere against their will?" asked Sheriff McGraw.

"Eh, well, no, not off-hand."

"Kidnapping," said the sheriff, his eyebrows raised. "If you put any of those Chinese on board your train without their free consent, I will arrest you for kidnapping. Now, what do you intend to do?"

"Well, we're scheduled t'…send our rollin' stock south."

"South to where?"

"Tacoma."

"With or without the Chinese."

"Oh, *without*! Without," he repeated more softly, massaging his chin with his thumb and forefinger. "Unless some of 'em wanna go."

"Tacoma? Unlikely," said Sheriff McGraw.

McGraw took a short, deep breath and expelled it. "Good. Thank you for your cooperation," said Sheriff McGraw as stood up and began to put on his hat and coat. "I'm glad we have an understanding, and I am very sure there will be no future misunderstanding. Now, you're very clear on this?"

"Oh, yes," the superintendent said. "Very clear."

The two of them headed toward the sheriff's office front door. As Sheriff McGraw opened the door, he turned, looked intently at the superintendent, and said, "I need to get some people together now. We have a large number of Seattleites convinced their liberty is in jeopardy."

The sheriff followed the superintendent out the door and locked the door behind him.

Unaware of Sheriff McGraw's meeting with the railroad superintendent, around midnight the Sinophobe guards at the Ocean Dock began to wake sleeping Chinese as other Sinophobes gathered at the train station several blocks away to assist getting the Chinese on board the train leaving for Tacoma, then further south. Already prepared for such a move, at Sheriff McGraw's direction, the Seattle Rifles were at the train station. They blocked the entrance to the train station while the railroad superintendent got the train underway ahead of schedule before the Sinophobes and Chinese left the pier.

Meanwhile, Home Guardsmen and the University Cadets formed up in the dark at the foot of Main Street and moved out to block the two exits from the Ocean Dock. After the train left, the Seattle Rifles ran from the train station to the waterfront where they joined the Home Guardsmen and the University Cadets.

The dock blocked off, the Sinophobe guards were trapped on the dock.

"Boys, you're probably confused about what's going on here," said Home Guard Captain George Kinnear to the Sinophobe guards. "Well, you have two options: stay here or head on home. We won't keep you, but I want you all to know these Chinese won't be on any train tonight." The Sinophobes quickly left, anxious to tell the others what was happening.

They met a few other Sinophobes who, having been frustrated at the train station, were returning to the dock. Upon being told the Guardsmen, Cadets and Seattle Rifles had taken over the dock, the Sinophobes were incensed, but it was well after midnight, and they were too tired and too few to change things at that moment. Angry for having been tricked, the tired Sinophobes went home intent on dealing with the matter during daylight hours after a night's sleep the Guardsmen, Cadets and Rifles would not get.

Apprised of what was happening, Territorial Governor Watson Squire telegraphed Secretary of War William C. Endicott and General John Gibbon at Ft. Vancouver about the growing crisis. Squire said the situation was nearing a boiling point, and he needed help at once. Upon being given the message the following morning, Secretary of War Endicott passed the message on to President Grover Cleveland.

After sunrise the next morning, sullen Sinophobes began heading toward the docks, their numbers growing ominously while the sleepless Seattle Rifles, Home Guardsmen and University Cadets formed a shoulder-to-shoulder barricade the length of the block between Washington St. and Main St in front of the Ocean Dock.

More Sinophobes came from their homes and, as the mob grew, bravado and anger also grew. Like gamblers in Murray, many of the men on facing sides knew one another. Past antagonisms smoldered and rekindled as verbal exchanges grew more heated. Further fueling Sinophobe confidence was their belief that opposition rifles, in the interest of preventing bloodshed, were not loaded…although they suspected some rifles might be loaded because there was Judge Thomas Burke with his double-barreled shotgun and coat pockets obviously full of shells, standing solemnly next to Territorial University professor Edmond Meany, glaring at the voluble Sinophobes. Since Burke was not the type of man to carry a gun he did not intend to use, the Sinophobes figured the shotgun was loaded. Loaded or not, Burke was castigated by mob members who believed extricating the Chinese from Seattle would never have become this difficult – Tacoma had no problem – were it not for Burke.

"Hey, Judge!" yelled a younger Sinophobe, now almost hoarse from shouting at the Home Guardsmen. "Whatcha got there? A shotgun? What's the problem? Your daughter gettin' married?" Others nearby snorted derisively. "You bein' a judge and all, maybe this is what you mean by 'the law.'"

Judge Burke glared at the younger man and said nothing.

"The law's a shotgun, huh Judge? No more, no less? Forget about all those fancy books, right? Just get a shotgun. Well, you know what, Judge? I think I'll do that." The younger man looked around him. "Mebbe we'll all do that; then we'll see whose side the law's on!"

Another Sinophobe, a large man with a reddish brown mustache took the opportunity to badger Seattle's leading banker.

"Hey, Horton! Yeah, you! Remember me?" The man laughed as he held his palms out. "Oh, hell no! For people like you, guys like me don't exist." The man spit chewing tobacco contemptuously in Dexter Horton's direction. "But, still, I'd like to make a deposit, Horton! Deposit my foot up your pompous keister!" The man glowered at the Dexter Horton National Bank president as the men around him guffawed and looked to see Horton's reaction. Horton looked back apprehensively but did not move.

"You down here guardin' the Chinese, Horton? Hope you made sure some-one's guardin' the bank? At the moment, you bein' here ain't good for business, so you'd better get your fanny back over t' the bank, y'know? Oh yeah, Horton. Sure as shootin', that bank's gonna need guardin', and real soon. Stockholders won't understand why you were down here guardin' the dam' Chinese when you shoulda been guardin' the bank. Now is that bein' a responsible banker, Horton?" the man asked. "What d'ya think, Horton? The Chinese or your bank? What's more important?"

Dexter Horton still did not move.

"Ohhhh, now who have we here?" asked a bewhiskered man looking at Pastor Louis Banks querulously. "Now how about this?" The man histrionically placed his hands on his hips as he looked at Banks who stood with Methodist Pastor Clark Davis and Congregational Pastor H. L. Bates, all armed. "Gun-totin' preachers. God a'mighty." The man dropped his hands and at a short distance badgered the men, especially Banks. "Hey, gun-totin' preachers, you plan on shootin' someone? That it? Or are you three down here for some pheasant huntin'?" The man sneered. "Lotta pheasants…or should I say 'peasants,'" he added, spitting out the "p", "down here." The man glanced about him. "Take a look around. Which peasant ya gonna shoot?"

Reverend Banks looked back with a defensive but intrepid gaze.

"So tell me, yer holiness," asked the man, looking at Banks, "how would you answer the Lord if He were standin' here and He asks y' why you're carryin' a gun, getting' ready t' shoot someone?"

"I know where my duty lies," responded Banks. "I'd much rather answer that question than if God asked me, as He will no doubt ask many of my peers with respect to various events in history, why I did nothing."

Reverend Banks raised his cradled rifle, its barrel pointed at the man. The man looked at the rifle, studied Banks' eyes, shoved his hands in his pockets, and said nothing more, obliquely glaring at Banks.

The general jeering and denigration continued. The mob knew, however, law enforcement didn't end with the men standing before them. The memory of Maj. Gen. John Gibbon last fall and the specter of martial law complicated the matter and restrained men who might otherwise have acted more impulsively. The mob grew and epithets increased as the Guardsmen, the Seattle Rifles and the University Cadets stood their ground.

"Think those boys are eventually gonna go away peacefully?" muttered a Home Guardsman named Preston to his brother. "I don't. Not for a moment."

"Well, what choice do they have?" responded the brother. "We're the law. Sheriff McGraw says we take over…so, we take over. Pure 'n simple."

"'Pure 'n simple', my eye," the first brother responded with a glance at the second. "Yeah, we're the law…if you don't consider the city police. Some of them are in that mob."

"Got a feelin' somethin's gonna happen," muttered another Home Guards-man named Bell who had a farm north of town. "As long as we do nothing, no need for them t' do anything. But pretty soon, we gotta do somethin.'"

Mr. Chong huddled in the warehouse among the others. His thoughts at the moment were about something he had left at the house and which, if possible, he needed to retrieve. An old woman shivered in the cold beside him. He removed his thick overcoat, gave it to her, joined several others huddling together to share and conserve body heat, and hugged himself to stay warm.

It came time for the Guards to lead the Chinese from the docks to Territorial Supreme Court Judge Roger Sherman Greene's courtroom. As the Guardsmen formed up and began to bring the Chinese out of the warehouse and on to the open dock, the Sinophobes jeered, although they knew a *writ of habeas corpus* had been issued and what it meant.

As the Guards began to march the Chinese column away from the Ocean Dock to the courthouse, although the mob continued to jeer and yell, the Sinophobes made no attempt to block the Guardsmen and Chinese, expecting the Chinese would be brought back to the dock when court was dismissed and, in spite of what went on in the courtroom, the Chinese would have the good sense to board the *Queen of the Pacific*.

As many of the 380 Chinese as could fit were cramped into the 3rd Avenue courtroom north of Yesler Way, and directed to take seats on benches. Others stood, many outside. Those inside watched as Judge Greene, a descendant of Declaration of Independence signer Roger Sherman, entered and took his seat. From his bench in the courtroom, Judge Greene looked out over a sea of Chinese faces.

As Judge Greene's words were translated for the Chinese, their stoic expressions failed to conceal their skepticism; it was as if Judge Greene had just told them China would merge with Ireland. "…will be arrested and brought to trial." Like George Venable Smith. "…you will be protected." On a dock in a warehouse waiting for a ship.

With the exception of sixteen persons, including Chong Tsing Wei, the Chinese elected to leave Seattle.

The Seattle Home Guardsmen marched the Chinese from the courthouse back to the dock either to be escorted aboard the *Queen of the Pacific* or, for the courageous 16, to collect any belongings still at the dock and return to their homes.

58

During the past two days, Captain Alexander had known the *Queen* was legally allowed to carry only 196 passengers. He would have taken many more initially but, with increased exposure, it would now be unwise to push his luck.

"Okay, single file. One at a time," instructed Captain Alexander as he motioned for the Chinese to begin boarding, and he counted as they filed on board. The number of Chinese boarding was considerable, but so was the number gathered on the dock.

"Hold it! Stop!" ordered Captain Alexander as the number aboard reached 196. "That's all I am legally allowed to take! No more." Captain Alexander motioned for those Chinese on the gang plank to turn around and go back to the dock. Expressionless, they turned and did so as Home Guardsmen and Sinophobes watched.

"What are we supposed t' do with the rest of 'em?" asked a Home Guardsman.

"The *George W. Elder* will be here in six days," said Captain Alexander. "See what kind of deal the *Elder* captain will give you."

"Six days? What'll we do until then?" There were 168 Chinese still on the dock.

"How should I know?" asked Alexander. "It's your problem. Deal with it."

The Home Guardsmen herded the remaining Chinese back into the warehouse. No food was available. Non-existent sanitation facilities were behind the warehouse. The rain continued.

"We obviously can't leave 'em here for six days," said Sheriff McGraw.

"You're right," agreed Guardsman Captain George Kinnear who had recently donated land for a city park on Queen Anne Hill. "I suppose the only alternative is to bring them back to their homes until the *Elder* arrives, and then, I guess, bring them all back down here and see what happens."

"Think we'll have any problem with that gang over there?" asked another Guardsman, nodding toward Sinophobes standing on the nearby street, watching.

"Probably," said Judge Burke. "They're not the world's most reasonable bunch. Even if we explain, they'll want the Chinese left in the warehouse. Those boys don't care about these people," Burke glanced at the Chinese huddled about the warehouse, "but these Chinese need to be fed and afforded sanitation. They're not cattle. If we can't take care of them, we can't leave them here."

"Well, then," began Kinnear, grimly glancing at the on-looking Sinophobes, "let's get started."

The Guardsmen summoned the cold and hungry Chinese out of the warehouse and ordered them to form columns. With Kinnear and Sheriff McGraw leading the Home Guard in the front, the Seattle Rifles guarding the flanks, and Cadets guarding the rear, the column began walking up Main Street toward Chinatown.

Sinophobes throughout downtown Seattle saw a large crowd of Chinese leaving the docks.

"Now what the hell is goin' on?" asked one wide-eyed Sinophobe of another.

"I dunno. Looks like they're tryin' t' bring the Chinese back home. Pull a fast one. We better get a few boys down here, pronto."

As the word spread like flood waters, Sinophobes angrily left saloons, homes, businesses, box houses and brothels, and walked briskly in the direction of the Ocean Dock. Many Sinophobes still harbored the mistaken idea that the Home Guardsmen, Seattle Rifles and Territorial University Cadets carried unloaded rifles.

As the column of frightened Chinese families carrying belongings walked up Main Street, Guardsmen's stomachs felt like twisted wet towels, and apprehension grew commensurately with Sinophobe mob expansion. More and more Sinophobes arrived, many becoming belligerent, and the mob noise set Guardsmen on edge.

The voluble Sinophobe crowd packed along Main Street with subsequent arrivals backed up north to Yesler Way. At the front of the Home Guard were Capt. George Kinnear, Lieutenant J. A. Hatfield, Lieutenant Bill Latimer, Sergeant Ed Carr and Deputy "Big Dave" Webster, along with Sheriff McGraw. As they marched eastward, all guardsmen apprehensively felt their rifle triggers as Sinophobe belligerency became louder and closer. As the column approached the Commercial Street intersection adjacent to the New England Hotel, the Sinophobes closed in on the Guardsmen's forward left flank and into the intersection, blocking the way of the leading Guardsmen.

"Hold on, gentlemen!" hoarsely hollered a big, bearded logger, Charles Stewart, 30, as the Guardsmen came to a halt. "What are you going to do with these Chinamen?"

In the Home Guard front row, Big Dave Webster, a little bigger than Stewart, and convinced that any attempt to intimidate the Home Guard should to be countered immediately, grabbed Stewart by the arm and ordered, "You come with us!"

"No, sir!" retorted Stewart, yanking his arm away defiantly and glaring at Webster. "I have done nothing to go with you for!" As the Sinophobe crowd edged in; each Guardsman turned toward the nearest Sinophobe, triggers fingered tightly. "No, we don't intend to, not a man of us!" Stewart continued, loosening his arms and looking uneasily at the forces of law, some of who were aiming their rifles.

Them guns must be loaded, thought Stewart as he looked at the eyes of surrounding adversaries. Stewart softened his tone slightly while remaining adamant.

"But we want to move the Chinamen out of Seattle and do it decently and quietly if we can."

Sensing Stewart's emotional retreat, Webster again grabbed Stewart – "Come with me!" – and again attempted to jerk the big logger to one side, but Stewart had the strength of someone who worked in the woods, and he jerked back. The Sinophobe mob, some of whom were also armed, edged closer.

"You men, get back!" shouted Sheriff McGraw at the crowd as Webster grabbed Stewart with both hands. "Murphy!" McGraw yelled at the acting Seattle Chief of Police, James Murphy, who was among the Sinophobe leaders and there with some of his force. "This is intolerable! Call off your dogs! You should know better!"

"I do know better, McGraw!" shouted Murphy angrily. "You're the dam' fool! Get those &%$#@ Asiatics back down to the docks!"

Before McGraw could explain, Stewart again wrenched free, angrily grabbed Webster and with a roar threw Webster to one side. Losing his balance, Big Dave fell as the frightened Chinese cowered behind the Guardsman. Guardsman Sergeant Ed Carr jumped in and grabbed Stewart from behind with both arms, attempting to hold Stewart as Webster got back on his feet. Enraged, Stewart again wrenched loose and went after Carr as Webster grabbed his rifle and slammed the butt into the back of the big logger's head, knocking Stewart into Carr who fell backwards into the Sinophobe crowd. Carr quickly jumped to his feet.

Momentarily stunned, Stewart staggered, regained his senses and, along with Sinophobe Bernie Muraine, angrily tried to grab Webster's rifle, intent on reciprocal bashing. As Stewart and Muraine went for Webster's rifle, other Sinophobes simultaneously jumped into the melee, attempting to grab Guardsmen's rifles that most Sinophobes believed were unloaded.

The lid was off. Loud reports cracked from several Guardmen's rifles, and nearby armed Sinophobes fired back while Chinese men quickly knelt, sheltering their women and children who were crying, covering their heads and ears with their hands in panic.

Hit in the arm, body and head, Stewart dropped to the ground as another bullet hit Muraine in the chest, puncturing his right lung, and he careened into wounded, staggering James Murphy, acting Seattle Police Chief. Both fell, sprawling on the ground near Stewart. Most of the Sinophobe mob instinctively crouched or backed away.

While a bullet passed through Sheriff McGraw's coat within an inch of his body, there were no casualties among those enforcing the law.

On either side, the Seattle Rifles swept their guns back and forth at the Sinophobes who froze or quickly crouched but did not step forward.

Eyes intense, the University Cadets, as trained, each dropped to one knee and aimed, expecting to fire, wanting to fire. They all knew about the Civil War Battle of New Market where Confederate General John Breckinridge sent in VMI cadets – "Put the boys in, and may God forgive me for the order" – and the Battle of New Market was won. Fingers squeezing triggers, the University Cadets hoped it was their turn.

The shooting stopped, however, with the two sides glaring wide-eyed at each other as the Guardsmen, Rifles and Cadets all continued to aim.

Slowly the stunned Sinophobes, many with hands in the air, stood up, eyes wide, apprehensively staring at the forces of law like a herd of elk staring at a mountain lion staring at a herd of elk. The defenseless, petrified Chinese remained on the ground. As gun smoke drifted to the east, rifles remained aimed, the Guardsmen anticipating an order. Stand at the ready. Or maybe, thought the Cadets, someone in the mob would do something stupid. At the front of the column, Captain George Kinnear began to give direction.

"Whitworth. Hanford," Kinnear said to County Engineer Frank Whitworth and Assistant U.S. Attorney Cornelius H. "Con" Hanford, after whom the town of Hanford would later be named, "now that they know we mean business, get out in front and get those people to step aside."

"You men should know we can't keep the Chinese at the docks," Hanford said loudly and formally to the Sinophobes. "There are no sanitation facilities and we have nothing to feed them. We're taking them to their homes until the next ship comes in six days. So, step aside!"

The belligerent crowd looked back, but did not move. A rumor began to spread from the rear to the front of the Sinophobe mob that Judge Thomas Burke gave the order to fire. Reflecting the Sinophobe hatred for Burke, one took the rumor a step further by speculating Burke did the actual shooting with his shotgun.

"Gentlemen, listen to reason," said Whitworth loudly, making eye contact with many Sinophobes disinclined to listen to reason. "Move aside so we can finish doing the only sensible thing to do. Make room."

Except for two or three men trying to treat Charles Stewart, Bermie Muraine and the others, the recalcitrant Sinophobes stared at Whitworth and Hanford, deaf to any request. Stubborn anger trumped clear thinking. The illogical imperative of mob ignorance inflamed, a mindless chant began, modest at first, but crescendoing as more men regained courage.

"Burke! Burke! We want Burke!"

Others joined in, shouting, "Burke! Burke! We want Burke!!" as if frenetically repeating the chant would assure the righteousness of their position and the guilt of Judge Thomas Burke.

As the chant crescendoed, Company D of the National Washington Guards finally arrived, led by Captain John C. Haines. In civilian life Haines was an attorney who successfully defended several men accused of killing Chinese laborers in the Squak (Issaquah) Valley, east of Seattle, the previous fall. The Sinophobes stopped chanting and began to cheer as Haines rode up. Knowing Haines was one of them, as evidenced by not having participated with the

Guards, Rifles and Cadets, the mob was anxious to see what Haines would do.

Captain Haines reined his horse to the right and cut a dash as he rode to the head of the Home Guard, looking past Burke, McGraw and Kinnear as if they weren't there, pulled on the reins, turned toward the Sinophobe crowd and shouted, "I promise you…! I promise you that whoever has acted illegally, he will be arrested and prosecuted!"

In the subsequent hush, no one responded. They waited. Haines said nothing else and rode back to the head of his troops.

That's it?

The Sinophobes had no option, however, other than believe Captain Haines's statement that justice would be served – although most knew that "whoever has acted illegally" was them. The Sinophobes were emotionally disarmed, had no legal position, and were facing the Home Guard, the Seattle Rifles, and the University Cadets in addition to the absurdity of their own irrational behavior. Most lost their desire to continue the confrontation, concluding this was becoming nonsense, and began backing away. There was always later.

As the crowd grudgingly dispersed, the Home Guard, relieved, returned to escorting the Chinese to their homes. Hoping that someone would still become belligerent at the last moment, the University Cadets kept their weapons raised, but when the Sinophobes only looked or backed away, Cadet Captain Charles Kinnear, son of Home Guard Captain George Kinnear, gave orders to reform ranks, and the disappointed Cadets guarded the rear of the procession until the Chinese were in their homes.

Charlie Stewart, the big logger, would die later that day, becoming a Sinophobe martyr.

Captain John Hatfield of the Home Guard subsequently sought out Sheriff McGraw. After opening the Sheriff's office door, Hatfield stood for a moment in the doorway. His expression was crestfallen.

"Sheriff. I have something to tell you."

"Hello, Hatfield." Seated at his desk, Sheriff McGraw smiled and pushed some paperwork aside. "What do you want to tell me?"

"It was me, not Judge Burke," began Hatfield. "I was the one who shot Stewart. Sheriff, I… Sheriff, I feel sick all over." Hatfield's dry mouth was open and his face had the pallid complexion of a man condemned. "I want to turn myself in."

Sheriff McGraw, weighing the consequences of Hatfield's confession, looked at him searchingly. Like a large hall immediately after everyone has left, the contrasting silence was loud.

"John," began Sheriff McGraw, "no one really believes Judge Burke did it, and I'm not entirely sure you did it, even though you may believe you did. With the way things are, I'd have my hands full trying to keep you alive if I were to arrest you and put you in jail to stand trial. Frankly, sir, things are such a mess out there that I have all I can handle as it is."

Sheriff McGraw looked at Hatfield and chose his words carefully.

"Now, you can be arrested and wait to stand trial, and probably be lynched, with me and a few of my boys gettin' killed tryin' to keep you alive, or, preferably, you can just keep this all to yourself. I know the last option may seem like a miscarriage of justice but, right now, it's the only sensible thing to do. I was only a few feet away from you. We didn't fire first and after I find out who did, then we'll sort this out." Sheriff McGraw folded his hands. "John, go on home."

Without looking up, Hatfield stood for a moment, then turned and, emotionally overburdened, walked slowly to the door. His two hands would not leave his hat until he had to turn the doorknob to leave the Sheriff's office.

After nearly three days without food, and only rainwater to drink, Chong Tsing Wei returned to his home weak from hunger, and physically ill. He retrieved a hidden key from under a rock aside the house, unlocked the front door, and as the door swung open, Mr. Chong could feel the stares of unseen eyes peering from behind neighborhood curtains. For a moment he stood dejectedly in the front doorway of a home that was no longer his.

Stepping inside the house, Mr. Chong looked around. The man who took his regular key had not returned to help himself; everything was as Mr. Chong had left it. He approached an apparent built-in bookcase – more than just a bookcase and not stationary. It hid a secret closet that contained his family shrine and his money. In 1886, Mr. Chong did not have faith in banks; and many banks did not welcome Mr. Chong. He kept his savings in a strong box concealed in the secret closet. As Mr Chong rolled the bookcase away from the wall, he decided he could not stay in Seattle, but neither would he board the *George W. Elder* for San Francisco. He would take his money, leave the city, and somehow later return for the hidden shrine.

⸺ ◆ ⸺

The day after the shooting, President Grover Cleveland declared a state of martial law in Seattle. A curfew was imposed. Shortly, Brigadier General John Gibbon and his troops, eight companies of the 14th Division, would return. Law again reigned and Gibbon's men had little to attract their attention other than an occasional curfew violator.

Judge Thomas Burke, Reverend Louis Banks, Ed Carr, Con Hanford and Big Dave Webster were arrested by the pro-Sinophobe Seattle police, taken before the police justice, released on bail, but never brought to trial. Neither was John Hatfield. Conventional wisdom, unaware of Hatfield's confession to Sheriff McGraw, continued to hold Burke responsible for Stewart's death, a lie that would follow Burke to his grave.

Meanwhile, Hanford continued to advise Seattle Mayor Henry Yesler on legal matters. After discussion of the arrest of Judge Burke and the others, Yesler forced the resignation of acting Seattle Police Chief James Murphy along with several city policemen.

59

May 1886

In mid-April through late-May, 1886, deadly smallpox found its way to Murray. Murray had become civilized with conventional law enforcement and city government but, while the town fathers talked about action to combat smallpox, action was not forthcoming. City fathers indecisiveness did not set well with the Queen of Murray as she walked into the small courthouse to attend a civic meeting. She sat at the end of the second row of chairs and looked attentively at the city officials seated at the front of the small room. When the opportunity came for her to speak, Molly was on her feet.

"Gentlemen," Molly began, "with all due respect, as a great American once said, 'This is no time for ceremony.' It is commendable you consider community stratagems to combat smallpox, but obviously we must do more than 'consider.' We have to take action, and you, as the city fathers, need to be at the forefront of that action. I realize everyone wants to keep their distance where smallpox is involved, but obviously smallpox does not keep its distance and, therefore, attempting to avoid it by not taking action will only make matters worse. You need to stop talking about organizing the townspeople, and actually do it.

"You need to establish ordinances so that cleanliness is mandated. You need to order vaccine. We need to isolate those who have smallpox but, at the same time, petition Christians among us to voluntarily care for those who are ill. Importantly," Molly said adamantly, her eyes narrowing, "if the town's doctor has any competency, any sympathy for the sick and dying, he needs to stop drinking long enough to attend to them."

The city fathers looked about at the faces gathered before them. In a public meeting where the primary subject was smallpox, the town doctor was conspicuously absent.

"We have all given the matter considerable thought," said Molly. "I expect… we all expect…that tonight will be an evening of resolve, and that definite plans will be put into place. It is mandatory that we do so." As she finished, she looked directly into the eyes of each man. "My girls and I are willing to follow your lead. Certainly it is in our, in everyone's, best interests to get started immediately."

Without taking her eyes off the men before her, Molly sat down.

Throughout the rest of the meeting the city fathers talked about general action, talked about organization, talked about the responsibilities of the citizenry, and proffered lofty platitudes. When the meeting ended, no specific actions were yet determined.

Molly, feeling a sense of urgency, and disgusted with the elected politicians' lack of imagination and action, took matters into her own hands and organized the citizens of Murray in combating the epidemic.

Some townsfolk died but, largely because of Molly's effort and direction, the epidemic passed. While exhausting herself in the battle, Molly justifiably received credit for saving the lives of many. Citizens of the defended realm held their Queen in even greater esteem.

For Molly, however, an end to the performance was becoming exigent. Her leadership in the successful, smallpox epidemic battle chased off questions of selfworth but, as the battle distanced itself, with annoying familiarity the emptiness returned, now deeper, exacerbated by the contrast between conditional respectability in Murray and a deep-seated desire for a respectable life in a respectable community. The dilemma, a result of her profession, was a continual source of angst. And there was another problem that would soon become an obstacle to her goals.

"Pastor, have you been noticin' that things seem t' be slowin' down a mite around here?" asked Angus as the two walked to the parsonage.

"I have, Angus," answered Amos. "There was a time when people were continually coming into town in droves, and staying. Lately, while they're still coming, they're not staying."

"I'll tell you what it is," said Angus. "First, you haven't heard much about any new gold strikes around Murray, now, have you?"

"No."

"No one else is hearin' either because there've been none. All the news is over in the Silver Valley. Y' notice? An' the men that are comin' here are stayin' for a moment, but then movin' on through," said Angus. "And where are they're goin'?"

"To the new settlements in the Silver Valley," answered Amos.

"Correct. Now let me ask y': if this continues, what happens t' Murray?"

"I know what you mean, Angus." Amos folded his hands. "We're at slack tide; next the tide will start going out. With a combination of declining gold around here, and prospectors leaving Murray for the Silver Valley, the odds of another big strike around Murray are getting smaller. With little reason to stay, and reason to go elsewhere, Murray population starts declining."

"Remember how business increased immediately followin' Kellogg's silver strike, Pastor? There was no place else t' go. Murray bein' all there was, Murray was where business was done. Now there's another new store down in the Silver Valley, an' new buildings bein' built, an' business here'll start t' wane. You know where it will lead."

Molly B'dam' also saw the changing tide, and realized her time was running out. A sense of urgency suffused her and she knew that, to reach her financial goal, she needed to do something extraordinary in a hurry. In addition, she was tired and it seemed she never felt well. She privately began to wonder, leave? Yes. But leave for where? She needed to go where growth was not dependent on mineral wealth, and there were families, churches and polite society. From several men passing through, she heard favorable things about Seattle and Tacoma population growth and economic activity. She began thinking about Seattle and Tacoma.

Polite society.

60

Polite society in Murray was as prevalent as bone china.

Late one morning as Molly adjusted her makeup in Cabin 1, and Anna took bread out of the oven in the parsonage, an Italian gypsy rode down Main Street in an elaborately painted wagon, large and colorful, as was the driver, Giuseppe. On the front of the wagon was a large, golden harp next to which sat a trained monkey named Napoleon, dressed in a little Italian grenadier costume. What caught the townfolk's attention, however, was on the back of the wagon inside a barred cage: a dancing bear named Josephina.

Giuseppe went from western town to western town with Napoleon, the harp and Josephina. A crowd, including the Nordquist family, soon gathered. Inga, Esther and Rachel, now 13, 9, and 6, had never seen a one-man traveling show, much less a circus.

"Momma, what's he going to do with the bear?" asked Rachel.

"I don't know," said Anna. "Let people look at it, I guess."

Although it made sense at the moment, Anna's guess was inaccurate.

As Amos, Anna and the girls looked on, using his wagon as a performance stage, Giuseppe juggled, performed simple fetes of legerdemain, played the harp, and, a strong tenor, sang songs from Italian operas.

> *...La donna è mobil'*
> *Qual piuma al vento,*
> *muta d'accento*
> *e di pensier'!*
> *e di pensier'!*
> *e di pensier'!*

After theatric Giuseppe finished holding out both arms and the improvised high last note, Inga smiled as she glanced at her mother. "He's really good."

"He is," replied Anna.

Opera in Murray? As the gathered crowd loudly applauded, Napoleon the monkey raced about the crowd with a tin cup wherein appreciative spectators dropped coins or small nuggets.

The grand finale came when Giuseppe went to the cage and, as Rachel,

Esther, Inga and the rest of the crowd watched wide-eyed, led collared, muzzled Josephina down from the wagon, placing a grenadier hat, matching Napolean the monkey's, on her head.

Then Giuseppe began to play the large, golden harp. He played a waltz, and Josephina performed, standing and turning slowly in circles. Giuseppe's astute tempo made Josephina look like dancing was second nature to bears.

"Momma," said Rachel, "the bear can really dance!"

When finished, Josephina sat on her haunches like a huge family pet and happily padded her front paws together several times. Unused to entertainment, especially from a domesticated bear, the appreciative crowd looked at one another smiling and applauding loudly, and Napoleon the monkey raced about with his tin cup.

As the crowd wondered what would happen next, Giuseppe led Josephina to a large, nearby tree, pointed upward, and encouraged Josephina to climb the tree. The crowd watched as the large animal slowly climbed the trunk up through the branches to a height of around 20 feet. When Josephine stopped, Giuseppe, smiling, nodded at the crowd as he gestured with his hand in Josephina's direction, the crowd again applauded, and Napoleon capitalized on their appreciation.

"Atsa good, Josephina," called Giuseppe. "You come 'a down now."

While the audience watched, some town dogs gathered at the tree base and began barking and yelping at Josephina, attracting other dogs in the town, and soon there was a pack of dogs racing about, looking up at the treed bear, all barking and howling.

Giuseppe and a few men attempted to disperse the growing pack of dogs, throwing rocks and sticks at them, kicking at them, but the frenzy of each was fed by the frenzy of the others, the pack mentality was introduced, and they became dangerous. With the dogs below, Josephina, frightened, stayed high in the tree as Giuseppe pleaded and cajoled without success while men in the audience continued unsuccessfully trying to disperse the dogs.

At that moment, something terrible happened.

While the dogs continued to howl, and the confused bear looked down at Giuseppe, from the nearby trees on the other side of Prichard Creek a shot rang out, followed by two more in quick succession, and Josephina shuddered in pain as she was hit by rifle fire.

The crowd turned and looked in the direction of the sound as the culprit(s) disappeared into the woods. Stunned and confused, Josephina looked down pleadingly toward Giuseppe whose face blanched as he realized what was happening. His beloved Josephina hugged the tree for a moment longer before her eyes turned up, looked inward and went blank. Giuseppe watched in stunned disbelief as, like a great, stuffed toy, Josephina began to fall, hitting the ground with a loud, sickening thud as Rachel screamed while Esther and Inga both burst into tears, turning to their wide-eyed mother covering her mouth.

As the dogs barked and nipped at the dead body, Giuseppe raced over to Josephina and threw his arms around the neck, hugging her and attempting to somehow revive her, but she was dead. As if he had lost a daughter, Giuseppe was beside himself with grief, sobbing loudly and uncontrollably. Shortly someone began to pass a hat, hoping to somehow alleviate Giuseppe's suffering with extra cash. As the man stood before Giuseppe with the hat containing money, Giuseppe stood up and looked at the crowd.

"No. I don't want the mon," he cried. "I go all over. I go to Virginia City. I go to Nevada City. Nothing like this happen." He looked sadly at Josephina. "What kind of people do this?"

He wiped his eyes, turned, and with frightened Napoleon by his side, walked toward the brightly painted wagon. He stopped, turned around and with deep sorrow took one last look at the body of Josephina. He turned again and upon reaching the wagon, sadly closed the cage door, got up on the driver's seat, and slowly drove off.

Later that afternoon, Murray townspeople skinned and quartered Josephina, and had a community barbeque.

The Silver Valley, July 4, 1886

"Line 'em up and *shoot* 'em!" shouted the big, grimy miner.

Before him burned a bonfire ringed at a comfortable distance with coarse men of similar suasion in varying states of inebriation. Adding angry exclamation to his statement, he fired his rifle in the air twice, precipitating a bullet fusillade from other rifles that hot, 4th of July evening. Line 'em up and shoot 'em. It was a solution unfettered in its simplicity and finality, similar to other final solutions in history.

"There's a rumor going around that mining management wants to recruit Chinese," said Angus as he sat with Amos and Anna that Sunday afternoon.

"To do what?" asked Amos.

"Work the mines."

"Why would they do that?" asked Anna as she sat folding some dishtowels she had just finished embroidering. "It makes no sense. The owners would also have to hire an army of security guards to protect the Chinese miners." She seemed uncharacteristically annoyed. "Recruiting security guards would be difficult and expensive because anyone foolhardy enough to work as a security guard here would require extraordinarily high compensation before endangering their lives guarding a race of men for whom many have only contempt in the first place…and because of this, the guards could not be trusted. And, secondly, with these people the way they are, why would Chinese want to come here?

"Any owner that would seriously consider doing that would have to have half a brain," added Anna with an undertone of irritation. "Can you imagine how much trouble that would cause? If that's what the miners truly believe, it's not the owners who are half-brains."

Amos looked at his wife. Something deeper than the subject of discussion was bothering her, and although she said nothing specific, like seeing a star with peripheral vision, Amos discerned censure in her tone.

"Aye, well, brains smaller than normal size are found everywhere," said

Angus, folding his hands. "You remember a few years ago they found some skulls in France – Cro Magnon men – that they believed must have predated homo sapiens in part because the skulls had brain cavities smaller than modern humans. I wondered at the time just what they expected to find in France."

Amos laughed.

"Angus, what if those bones were found in Scotland?" asked Anna humorlessly. "What would you have thought then?"

"Some French wandered into Scotland."

"Well, Angus, these people around Murray," said Amos, smiling, "are primarily Italian, Irish, and Scotch. How would you explain the smaller brains here?"

"Scotch, you say?"

"Well, yes, of course. You know the men around here…where they came from."

"Well, then," said Angus, again stroking his beard, "Frenchmen definitely wandered into Scotland. How else do you explain it?"

"Angus, the French are…oh, why do I waste my time?" muttered Anna.

Amos again studied Anna as Angus wisely changed the subject, figuring it might be well if he left Anna alone for a while.

"As we speak, there be an assembly up on the hill," Angus said as he got up from his chair. "Givin' liquored speeches, no doubt, about the Chinese. 4th of July. Fireworks of a sort, y' know. I thought I might go up and watch."

"Do as you wish," said Amos, "but be careful and keep your distance. You know how those men get."

Anna shot a heated glance at Amos.

⎯⎯⎯⎯⎯ ●◦● ⎯⎯⎯⎯⎯

"Hell! It's simple," shouted the man who took a swig of whisky, spat the mouthful at the bonfire, and the whiskey exploded as the fire spat back. "Jes' line 'em up and shoot 'em! You want someone to pull the trigger? Well, then, here," he said, reaching out with his right hand benevolently, "this here hand is available. Got another one too."

He's pretty sure of it, Angus thought, watching from a distance.

When the men grew tired of the repetition or were too hoarse or drunk to shout any longer, they collectively resolved to keep Chinese labor out of the Coeur d'Alene mining region. No action was planned; any action was sanctioned.

Although no Chinese miners would come to the Coeur d'Alenes, there was already a Chinese laundry in town. Days after the bonfire, another rumor circulated that three Chinese were murdered. Weighing the Murray moral atmosphere, Anna believed the rumor true.

Murray immorality was eating away at Anna like lye on calico; there were few families and, other than her own, no children to teach in a church school. The spiritual climate in Murray had become so heavy that at times Anna found it hard to breath, and, like Molly B'Dam', she privately began entertaining thoughts about leaving.

61

Anna finished patching a pair of Amos's work pants, and placed them in a bedroom closet. She returned to the living room, sat down, folded her hands, and looked impatiently at Amos seated near the fireplace discussing weak church attendance with Angus.

"People in Murray don't come to church because most people in Murray aren't church people," uncharacteristically interrupted Anna.

The two men turned and looked at her.

"I didn't expect to find Philadelphia socialites when I came here, Amos, but at the same time, there was a great deal you didn't tell me about Murray before I left. Things you should have told me."

"Murray was in its infancy – there was much I couldn't know," answered Amos. "You were alone with the girls. I wanted to write strengthening, supportive letters in my absence."

"I appreciate that, Amos, and I completely understand. But I'm not nine-years-old. It would have made no difference, of course, as far as my coming here. Still, I would like to have been more prepared for what I would face when I arrived. Hearts need to be changed, but I don't see that happening. There's that rumor – probably not a rumor – three Chinese were murdered…probably just because they were Chinese. Murdered. How much sense does that make?"

Neither Amos nor Angus spoke.

"This town is a moral cesspool," continued Anna. "The first lady of Murray, revered by all, is a high-priced prostitute giving discounts. And she's the Queen of England in comparison to the other women. Disagreements among men – and women – are settled with fists or, worse, knives, clubs and firearms. Oh, and that incident with the poor bear. Good grief, Amos. The basest of men, men unwanted – or wanted – elsewhere, seem to flock here. I would like to have known this and to have been prepared when we came."

"I didn't want to concern you," said Amos. "Things are in transition here. It was worse before you arrived. I didn't think it wise to make you worry."

"I'm a woman, Amos. If I don't worry and plan accordingly, it means I'm dead."

"But, in general, you needn't worry," responded Amos. "As you know, Jesus said, 'Look at the birds of the air. They do not sow or reap or store away in barns, and yet your heavenly Father feeds them. Are you not much more valuable than they? Who among you by worrying can add a single hour to his life?' and He finished by saying, 'Therefore, do not worry about tomorrow…'"

"Jesus was a man…the second person of the Trinity, but still a man," interrupted Anna. "His mother wouldn't say that."

Seated nearby, Angus chuckled. "Perhaps, then, Catholics worry more than Protestants."

"Not Protestant mothers," responded Anna brusquely.

"Jesus, of course, was talking to women too," said Amos.

"Women worry, Amos," said Anna with deprecation. "Worry is what we do. We worry if we're not worried. Angus, I worry about what might happen around here if I weren't here to do the worrying. No one would consider possible future problems – Amos, you might worry a little, and you, Angus, wouldn't worry at all – and the lack of worry would result in some disaster that, if someone had worried a little about it in the first place, would never have happened. Life doesn't just wander blindly on without mishap. Bad things happen! 'Each day has enough trouble of its own.' But someone has to plan for tomorrow, to consider the 'what if's. You say I needn't worry, Amos. Okay, tell me what part of the worry-burden you're bearing, and I'll figure out what I don't need to worry about."

"All I'm saying, of course, is trust God, Anna," said Amos with mild exasperation.

"I do trust God," answered Anna. "And I believe in some sense God enables trust in me, and the extent of this trust dictates I worry. To assume things will invariably take care of themselves is foolish."

"But, of course, Anna," said Amos comfortingly, "trusting God is very beneficial. You can't control everything, and He can."

Amos stood up, walked over to Anna, took her hands, gently pulling her to her feet. When she stood, he pulled her to him, placed his arms around her and embraced her supportively.

"I don't expect to control everything, and I don't plan on worrying about everything," continued Anna, her head on Amos's shoulder, "but I do plan on worrying about what I can control." She tilted her head back and looked into his eyes. "I'm a mother, Amos. A mother, wife, sister, cook, nurse, administrator, teacher, and all the things I do, and to get things done and done without calamity, I worry. To dodge disaster, I worry. Worry thwarts injury, scarcity, illness…all the things a woman thinks about. I'm a woman, Amos. Telling a woman not to worry is like telling salmon not to spawn."

"Very well, then," said Amos calmly. He could sense that she wanted to step away and talk seriously. He let his arms slide down her sides, and she stepped back. "What are you specifically worried about?"

"I'm worried we're wasting our time here," said Anna. "In Minnesota we would build a church, go out into the surrounding community, grow the congregation to the point where the church and school became a focal point in the community, and go elsewhere and do it again. Here, we've no surrounding community because everyone is in transition…people are here to either find gold or make money off those who do, and the vast majority of people who come here have no intention of taking up permanent residency.

"In Minnesota there were closely-knit families, the salt of the earth, working against the odds, building a future, the kind of people who make this country a beacon for hopeful and hardworking men and women elsewhere. People who know who they are and what they believe in, and if the going gets rough, they don't complain. They stay, make the hard decisions, do the hard work, and if disaster strikes, they weather the storm and then rebuild." Amos thought of the Shenandoah Valley. "Here in Murray," added Anna, "it's just the opposite: we have men and women all hoping to just get rich quick and leave, without commitment, without loyalty, without conviction." She looked away. "It's almost a sickness."

She pushed her hair back along the sides of her head and looked at Amos with a determined expression.

"Although I know you have been trying hard to get people to worship," she continued, "church attendance has not changed since I arrived with the girls. The people coming to Murray are of an entirely different mindset than the people coming to Minnesota. You're a very talented man, Amos, and your talent is not being used wisely in this place. The seeds you sow are falling on hard ground."

Looking at the floor with his arms folded, Amos nodded.

"My second worry should not come as a surprise," continued Anna. "At the pace we're progressing, to reach any respectable congregation size could take years, and that would mean that our girls would reach maturity here in Murray, perhaps marry one of the many single men who populate this area. Of the young men you have met, have there been any that are well-educated, God-fearing, socially cultivated, and have a profession? The type of man we would want Inga to marry, Amos?"

"I don't know the vast majority of young men in town," said Amos.

"That eliminates the 'God-fearing' part," said Anna, looking impatiently at her husband.

"Yes, you're right," Amos shrugged. "No, as a practical matter I haven't met anyone that fits that description. I haven't worried too much about it because Inga is not yet of marrying age."

"But the time will pass quickly, Amos. It seems only a moment ago that Inga was born. It all goes too quickly, and I don't want to waste your time and talent, and my daughters' precious futures, in a place where there is mineral wealth but spiritual poverty."

Anna stepped back again while still looking at Amos.

"Honestly, Amos, lately my heart has been so heavy I don't know how to describe it. I want to do God's work, but, ideally, I want to do it where we can make a difference, and where our daughters' futures will be brightest. I worry about that. Let's face it, Amos, Murray may someday become a wonderfully cultured area, but, at best, that would take decades. Or, if the gold runs out, it may become a ghost town. That's happening elsewhere: when the gold runs out, the prospectors, miners, gamblers, merchants, and working women all leave. Look around," Anna gestured from window to window with her right hand. "Besides gold, what would keep people here?"

Amos gently took Anna's hand and led her to the couch where they sat down, still holding hands.

"Nels Hanseth gave me the option of Eagle City because of the extraordinary population growth, and it made sense then. Considering what we know now, poor church attendance is unsurprising. The community stability associated with church attendance is missing because, as you say, everyone is passing through. Proportionately few of the townspeople are God-fearing, and of those that are, even fewer want to become associated with a Lutheran church." Amos sighed. "Our biggest societal problem in Minnesota was trying to accommodate both Swedish and Norwegian immigrants. In Murray, of the thousands of people here, I may be the only one from Scandinavia. That, I'm afraid, has not helped."

"Aye, birds of a feather," said Angus.

"As you recall, Nels didn't send me to Eagle City – now Murray effectively – with the expectation I must stay here but, rather, sent me to this region, following the leading of the Holy Spirit, to deliver God's word where it was most needed. Certainly it is needed here in Murray, but, considering the obstacles we've encountered, it appears I'm being directed elsewhere. If I contact Nels, he'll want us to make the decision to do what is best. And that, as always, is the problem, Anna." Amos stepped forward and gently squeezed her hand. "What is best? Move to the Silver Valley? Leave for somewhere else? Stay? God may have something in store of which we're presently unaware. Understandably, we'll need to pray extensively about this."

Anna nodded neutrally.

Anna and Molly B'Dam were thinking the same thoughts. While mining and prospecting activity around Murray were still active, people were beginning to leave Murray for the Silver Valley. Molly continued to think about what she should do next. When should the Murray population exodus include the Queen of Murray? And if the queen leaves, what happens to the realm? Were I to move to the Silver Valley, she thought, the throne would be relocated, but the realm would remain the same. She thought about that expressionlessly. She had come to care about the town and the men who populated it. The ache in her heart, however, said she had to get far away from both Murray and the Silver Valley. On the other hand, another part of her, a forceful companion with folded arms, said anxiously, no. Not yet. She had unfinished business. The ache stubbornly countered that this business might finish her. Murray felt like a card game where she held an above-average hand and needed to quickly decide whether to call or raise. It would seem that she should call. Now? In a week? When was soon enough, but when was too late?

62

Fall, 1886

In the fall, the U.S. Congress appropriated $276,619.50 to compensate the Chinese for any loss sustained as the result of what began in Eureka and ended in Seattle. The money was paid to the Chinese government.

Summer, 1887

The heat inside the dark cabin was uncomfortable in spite of tree shade outside. On the edge of the sink next to the hot stove, a cracked lye soap bar filled the immediate air space with an acrid fragrance. The cabin inconveniences had been expected; sacrifices to be endured until Molly reached her financial goals. As Molly approached the hot water kettle blowing steam like an immense insect blowing smoke, she cautiously picked it up, making certain not to spill while turning carefully to her right, her soft silk slippers slip-sliding aside the porcelain sink. She poured the hot water on the rubber stopper, and mixed in cold water to get the temperature right. Splashing water on her face preparatory to putting on make-up, she patted her face. She rose to study her reflection in the mirror, and froze.

Her reflection. Her eyes. How hardened her face suddenly looked. She stared.

Without changing her gaze, she relaxed, reached for the towel next to the soap dish and carefully dried the areas around her eyes and mouth…and again stared at herself.

Then it came. The hair on her forearms rose. Fear swept over her as Old Evil kneaded her shoulders with frigid fingers, then squeezed her lustfully. Molly spun around, mouth open, and backed against the sink, her eyes flashing wildly, probing every corner of the room.

She stood rigidly, every muscle tense, looking. Nothing. She slowly turned back to the mirror, watching the reflection of the room behind her.

After a moment her eyes drifted back to her image. "I don't…," she began to whisper confidentially to the face-in-the-mirror, "I.." She steeled her heart. But this time her conscience penetrated the steely veneer like a .45 caliber bullet, crying, "Listen to me!"

As her inner cauldron boiled and the pain in her heart became more pronounced, she winced, dropping her head. The reflection in the water looked back at her darkly. She lifted her head, biting her lip, looked in the mirror, and looked away for a second before being drawn back to her watery image. She reached down, pulled up the basin plug chain and, as the face in the water contorted and disappeared, she turned to the side, dried her hands and wiped her forehead.

Turning back to the mirror, her eyes narrowed as she tried to toughen up. She perfunctorily fixed her hair, but stopped, motionless, seeing her face as if it wasn't her.

She began a quiet conversation as if discussing her predicament with a trusted confidante, and as she spoke, securely sequestered convictions, left momentarily unguarded, clambered to the surface of her heart like imprisoned men escaping through a momentarily unlocked cell door.

"This was not supposed to take so long," she said softly, a quaver in her voice. "Don't you remember, Margaret?" she asked slightly above a whisper, using her real name. "It was only temporary – an unpleasant sacrificial step enabling the next step and a better life."

Expressionlessly, she daubed her damp face with the towel. Dropping her arms, she stood motionlessly, not taking her eyes off the face in the mirror. She inhaled deeply through her nose, held her breath a moment, and forcefully exhaled through pursed lips as if attempting to purge her soul's lamp stand of accumulated soot.

Inside her, as the face in the mirror watched, she felt a fleeting moment's relief.

Molly quickly dried the wetness beneath her eyes, and placed the towel aside.

"This pretense… It's all pretense. You pretend to be well off." She put both hands on the edge of the basin and stood up straight, looking directly at the face. "And are you?"

The face looked back and said nothing.

You pretend to be many things, she thought to herself. The Queen. Her fingertips absently rose to her cheeks as she thought. Comical when we consider that all you are is a well dressed Colombina among Harlequins? Her hands fell. "It's easy when you're surrounded by men," she murmured out loud, "whose loneliness and need for a woman – and to believe in you – makes them ascribe favorable traits you lack." She absently folded a washcloth she was about to use.

"Let them believe," said the face in the mirror. Molly looked at her image as it looked back discerningly.

"But we know better," was Molly's soft response. The face stifled a smile as if to suggest it knew her secret. "There's the rub, to be respected for yourself."

"Yes, well," sighed the face impassively, "that's what we're after, Molly." The lack of conviction was obvious and her conscience pressed for her attention. 'Listen to me! Listen to…' The heartache would not retreat. Molly paused, her sigh turned to a shudder, and again her head fell.

She wiped her eyes again quickly and looked at herself.

"Something must be of value. What is there in Murray?" Her lips pursed as her imagination lifted up the Murray bed skirt and searched beneath the obvious.

"Men," blurted the blurred face in the mirror. "Lonely men."

Molly laughed softly, but the laughter was too quick and unnatural.

There are better men in better places than here, she thought.

"…and better competition," the face said. The poker face in the mirror looked at Molly as if studying the backs of her cards. "It's why you're here, Margaret," said the face, again using her real name, "weaker competition, many men…more money. It's what you do." The face stared icily.

Molly wiped her eyes and began brushing her hair again.

"No. I also play the Queen. And one should not be caught out of character," said Molly. The face feigned sweetness, and the brush strokes accelerated. "Character," Molly repeated, as if not having clearly said the word.

The brushing stopped. She stared at her image. Her teeth clenched and without taking taking her eyes off her image, in one quick motion she threw down the hairbrush that loudly bounced off a wooden floorboard and against her leg, resting next to her foot.

Catching herself, she knelt gracefully to pick up the hairbrush. As she grasped the hairbrush, she stopped, thinking about how she was debating with herself.

Standing up, she continued brushing the ends of her hair as if no conversation took place, and the face in the mirror watched expressionlessly. Then the hand with the hairbrush fell to her side.

For a moment the face in the mirror looked back in mute anticipation before the hairbrush slipped from her fingers and fell to the floor, and the most suppressed thought in her heart fought to the surface, blurting out that while she no longer needed men – she was so weary of men – she needed a man.

She was desired by many, but truly loved by none. Her capacity to love was great, but she was afraid to focus love on one man. Her emotional needs would not be met in Murray, and her spiritual needs would only be fulfilled if she did as Pastor Nordquist constantly encouraged.

She buried her head in her hands.

Who was the lonelier, she wondered, the men or her? Her simple goal in Murray was to make a big killing, leave Murray, and start over – living according to convictions she carried around like a suitcase full of summer clothes, waiting for the sun – but Murray was beginning to grow on her. She looked up and thought of her ex-husband, and then of the rough-but-adoring men of Murray. A captivating rose among thorns, she filled the otherwise distaff emptiness in a town barren of refined women – girlfriends, wives and mothers. And my actions are not all pretense. Although the contrast is stark, I dress well because I prefer to dress well, and would regardless of where I am. Her eyes grew larger. And I do care about the men in the town. There were many she had gotten to know apart from business, and about whom, for her, it was impossible not to care and worry; it was how she was. My spiritual and emotional needs cannot be met in Murray?

She knew they might be met anywhere if she unlocked the door to her heart. And I'm valued and wanted in Murray – would it necessarily be so somewhere else? Her uniquely beautiful, ice blue eyes expressionlessly stared at the mirror. If she did not leave soon, she sensed, she might not.

"Yes, of course," she said out loud. "I must leave. We agree. That is obvious."

But not without one last Herculean effort to do what she did best: remove men from their money. She had been thinking about this for some time. It would require one last major sacrifice of self-esteem, and she would be gone.

Gold mining around Murray involved not only individual miners with their burros and grubstakes, but also mining teams using pressurized hoses to wash down gold-bearing hillside gravel. This was called hydraulic placer mining or just placer digging. A couple of extensive placer clean-ups were scheduled for the following week in the Murray mining area, a fact not lost on Molly. Many participating placer miners and their employers, having experienced little success otherwise, might see gold dust and nuggets that normally eluded them, and for a moment the pre-placer fortunate few would be joined by others.

At such a moment in the Murray support system, timing was everything. To attract the additional gold in circulation, merchants used loss-leaders, bait-and-switch, three-for-the-price-of-two, cheap giveaways, or complimentary services with any substantial purchase. In the theater that was Murray, these moments captured the complete attention of a participating audience.

To capitalize on this pending, short-lived expansion of circulating gold, at the right moment Molly B'Dam planned to assume center stage on Gold Street, her script both imaginative and depraved.

When the curtain went up, she would take a public bath – not in water, but in gold dust and gold nuggets. Provided by theater patrons.

Were this poker, the gold accumulated in this single act could be the equivalent of hundreds, perhaps thousands of more conventional winning hands. Margaret "Maggie" Hall would have to play Molly B'Dam spectacularly, and the size of the pot would depend on the response of theater patrons. If patrons responded favorably, it would be her last hurrah, "not yet" would become "now," and the curtain would fall. If they did not respond as hoped, however, the gamble would fail, and she would need to remain in Murray, her self-esteem and public image having suffered. But it was a gamble she had to take.

The next day, notices were placed conspicuously throughout Murray in locations used earlier by Pastor Nordquist to announce his first church service. When Pastor Nordquist was told of Molly's intention, he at first refused to believe it. Many things were said about Molly B'Dam. Many were true. Anna Nordquist found the prospect incredible but, with a woman's intuition, did not dismiss it.

When queried about the notices, Molly silently responded with veiled looks of seductiveness. Sensuous under any circumstances, her mannerisms became subtly more exaggerated, and she seemed to take more interest in the miners and prospectors on the street, and card games in Dutch Jake's Saloon.

Two weeks later, after the placer clean-ups were well underway, Molly B'Dam instructed her girls to remind everyone that the performance was scheduled to begin at 1:00 p.m. the following day. Those told, as expected, quickly passed the word to others until all of Murray and the Silver Valley knew.

Out of curiosity, miners and prospectors came into town the following morning. Shortly after noon, Molly completed some finishing touches prior to taking stage for what she hoped would be her grand finale.

Curtain time approached. A purple velvet, blanket-covered, portable platform with a full-sized, oval tin-tub across two poles was carried to the center of Gold Street by four patrons of the arts accompanied by Molly's girls who smiled at the men gathering. The crowd began to expand rapidly with men jockeying for position. Molly's girls asked them to step back to a distance that would allow others to see.

Girls began coming out of other saloons to watch. Storekeepers and bartenders locked up their establishments and joined the crowd.

As Molly's girls stood beside the tub, smiling at onlookers, most of the men only stood and looked back.

"Ready for a show, boys?" asked one of the girls, her mouth slightly open. She studied the nearest miner, his weather-beaten face watching intently. "Think your heart can stand it, honey?" she asked.

"M' heart?" His eyes grew wide. "Hell, don't have no heart problem," rasped the miner, as if he needed to explain.

Realizing she was having fun, the miner smirked as he reached into his pocket for a chaw. His gold tooth and the missing incisor were distracting as he smiled broadly after digging into the chewing tobacco. "In fact, my heart ain' gonna mind this at all." He smiled another distracting smile. "An' neither is the rest of me!" he laughed, dancing for a moment. The men nearby also laughed, easing the atmosphere and attracting others at a distance.

The banter between the girls and the men continued, and the crowd continued to expand as latecomers joined, some men standing on boxes and barrels, until it seemed like all of Murray and the Silver Valley was there.

Molly was usually gorgeous, but with a little effort she could be breathtaking. In moments the men would be mesmerized.

The tin tub stage was set. As had been implied, the mere shadow of her well-proportioned anatomy, tightly enveloped in an attractive, white robe, was a potential cause of heart failure. In the shaded confine of Cabin No. 1, she knew she looked good. Part of her fought back, but while making minor hair adjustments in front of her dresser mirror, she countered that the end justified the means, and the end was in sight.

"You must do what you must do, Maggie," whispered the mirror. "This is what you came for, dear." She deftly slipped away from her conscience attempting to restrain her.

Tightening the cloth waistband around her robe, she pulled her shoulders back slightly, and then walked toward the door. The moment seemed like a dream. She held the latch in her hand, looking down at it as she again steeled her heart preparatory to going on stage.

Once in character, she opened the door and Molly B'Dam, the Queen of

Murray, regally stepped forward to a raucous welcome from the crowd of miners, prospectors, merchants, drifters and bargirls. Now the last act would begin. She was escorted to the tub by two more of her girls, ladies in waiting who glanced about, smiling, making eye contact with as many men as possible. Molly held her head erectly, and the crowd noise continued to grow. At a distance, more girls from various saloons ran to watch, jumping up and down or pushing against men in an unsuccessful attempt to get a better view as the swarm surrounded the queen bee.

Still tightly wrapped and acting as her own cheerleader, as Molly approached the tub, she began cajoling and cooing seductively. She openly dared the onlookers to begin placing gold in the tub. She affronted their manhood and flaunted her sensuality in order to accelerate the momentum of gold being placed in the tub, offerings that would need to be sufficient in size and quantity before she would disrobe and bathe.

Although most of the men were not consciously aware of it, Molly had become essential to the image of Murray, indispensable to Murray's identity, and indirectly, by extension, their own. Without being obsequious, the men revered her, desiring her attention, were it available, while uneasy at the prospect of her rejection. So the offerings came. Men began tithing gold nuggets and gold dust as if they were making offerings to a goddess, simultaneously displaying and strengthening their faith, in the absence of any other. With each offering, Molly nodded approvingly at the honored donor. They were all so familiar with the Queen of Murray that each felt he knew her. Surprisingly to many, she knew them as well; their names, who they were. Reservation dissipated. She sensuously looked about, a glittering island in a sea of drab, begrimed miners and prospectors, as expensive minerals continued to wash up on the beach. She bantered with the miners, and their excitement increased as her language became more indelicate. For a moment a lull occurred, and Molly looked about disapprovingly. When others stepped up to the tub, not wanting to disappoint their queen, the approving expression returned. Miners and prospectors who could not afford to do so, incautiously placed gold or gold dust into the tub until, finally, the offering was sufficient, and she prepared to do what they were gathered to see.

Molly was center stage, about to perform her most spectacular role.

"Gentlemen," she first cautioned, looking from man to man and sighing, "once this performance begins, it will only go on as long as your manly generosity continues."

Mouth open slightly, she looked about and slowly, ever so slowly, licked the bottom of her upper lip. Wide-eyed, slack-jawed, the anxious men stared at her while jockeying for position.

"Remember, gentlemen," she reminded them, "no gold, no show."

She stepped into the tub, acting as excited as the men around her, standing perfectly erect with hands on her hips, and looked about coyly. More men with gold stepped forward, enabling them to get in front. Apprehension increased, eyes grew wider, mouths fell open, and the noise died.

She smiled at the wide-eyed men, and her hands slowly slipped from her hips inward, grasping the waistband of her robe. The men – those not struggling to get a better view – watched mesmerized as she unloosened the waistband, and cautiously let it fall, her hands remaining in front of her. As men to the rear further jockeyed for position, her hands slowly rose upward along the seams of her still-closed robe. Pulling the robe slowly apart, exposing her anatomy bit-by-bit, her hands slowly slid down the seams until, at a level just above her waist, she simultaneously arched her back and threw open the robe with rehearsed flair, allowing it to slide off her back and fall behind her, her hands instantly coming to her hips.

The split second "whoosh" as men spontaneously gasped, was followed by a roar that careened about the surrounding ancient hillsides like a reverberating explosion, echoing and re-echoing like rolling thunder as the men erupted in an emotionally transparent celebration of dissolute ecstasy. Hands still on her hips, back arched slightly, Molly smiled broadly. As men clapped and cheered, statuesque Molly looked about, took a slow, deep breath and assumed a variety of poses, the howling miners acting possessed, as if other than themselves.

She positioned herself in the tub with movements as graceful as when she retrieved her hairbrush.

"Gentlemen, remember, again: no gold, no show."

Crude statements made by the laughing, excited miners were met with equally crude responses by Molly as, naked, she managed their investments and maintained the bull market by stroking their male egos, further inflaming already excited passions.

The excited miners, prospectors and merchants laughed, danced, hooted and swore; some fighting their way to the front, Molly's girls maintaining the inner perimeter. Other girls looked on in astonishment; amazed regal Molly would conceive this, but admiring how well it was working. Other men only stood with mouths open, unbelievably staring at the vision – normally found only in dreams – convinced no other woman on earth looked that good. No one – it wasn't possible.

They were men whose limited cultural, academic and social backgrounds dictated a livelihood in long hours of hard, backbreaking, dirty, monotonous work that would either slowly or instantly kill many. They were sacrificing thousands of dollars of their hard-earned reward on an altar occupied by gorgeous Molly B'Dam' milking the moment for all it was worth.

Eventually the offerings began to subside. As miner benevolence waned, and additional encouragement was of no avail, Molly decided the final act should draw to a close. It was a superb performance and, Molly thought, while they did not receive their money's worth, they got what they paid for. For a lifetime, all would remember this moment.

Molly stood up, beamed at the men as she stood, placed her hands on her hips, shoulders back, gave one last series of poses, then carefully dusted herself off, put on her robe, cinched up the waistband, and dusted off each foot as she stepped out of the tub. She instructed the four art patrons to carry the tub to her cabin, turned, smiled, bowed, stood upright and blew kisses to an excited audience giving her an ovation as the curtain descended.

Nearing the cabin door, no longer in character, Margaret Hall embraced herself while walking head down and looking at no one.

That evening, sensing his wife's concern, Amos Nordquist brought up Molly's fundraiser.

"The events of this afternoon," began Amos, "I'm not sure I underst…"

"Amos…," Anna began, looking up from her knitting. Her jaws clenched. She looked down at her knitting, and back up. "Amos… Why are we here?"

Amos looked at Anna, not knowing what to say.

"I can't begin to imagine what this most recent performance did to Molly's heart," said Anna, "but I know what it did to mine.

"We only have one life to live…on behalf of ourselves, on behalf of the Lord," said Anna. "As I've asked before, is this the best use of your talent, here in Murray? Is this where we want to continue to raise our daughters? Are there men in this community to whom we would want to see Inga and Esther married? Is this where we want Rachel to grow up? Will this place even be around in five years?"

"No, this is not where I want little Rachel to grow up," answered Pastor Nordquist. "Nor do I know of any young men whom I would want Inga or Esther to marry," he concluded. "Where I want or do not want to be is, of course, not what matters. What matters is where God wants me. And the universal ministry enigma is where to be, spreading God's word, when God's word is needed everywhere. I have prayed a great deal about this."

Anna listened to this statement, looking at Amos as he stood at the window watching the people outside on the street.

"So have I," said Anna. "I know that the Lord works miracles, and I must tell you, Amos, that, as I see it, a miracle would be required to justify our remaining in this mining camp."

Amos turned and looked at Anna. Mining camp? Amos unfolded his arms, and said, "Excuse me for a moment." He walked to the kitchen. Amos washed his hands, thinking. But Murray desperately needs the gospel.

So one more time, after drying his hands, he again stood alone and prayed another of many prayers for God's direction, as Anna watched from the living room.

Nothing more was said that week about Anna's concerns; Anna knew Amos needed to wait on the Lord, and only wished the Lord would hurry.

The next Sunday morning worship service was again held in the living room. Except for saddler Charlie O'Toole attending for the first time, those in attendance were not much different than usual, including Angus MacGregor and Molly Burdan who, in the offering plate, placed a small pouch of gold dust. Her demeanor and behavior during the worship service were almost as if nothing unusual happened during the previous week, as if Molly Burdan nee Margaret Hall were one person, and Molly B'Dam another. Pastor Nordquist noticed that in contrast to the indelicate language and flamboyant behavior he heard about, however, Molly was demure and quiet. Her beautiful eyes looked straight ahead, but not up, as she listened. In the past when Pastor Nordquist and Molly had conversations about her profession, Molly knew what Amos was going to say before he said it, and would deflect his questions; she already knew the correct decision, but would pick the time. To Pastor Nordquist, now was the time, and he decided to meet with her after church.

At the close of the service, Pastor Nordquist stood by his front door in order to shake hands with all who had attended. Molly filed out with the others, and as she approached Pastor Nordquist, her mouth opened to speak, but she could not. Her eyes fell as she asked herself, why did I come? She came, she knew, because she needed to come, but as Pastor Nordquist reached down and took her hand (she did not offer it), she looked up at him with forced pleasantry, nodded, politely pulled her hand back, and continued out the door.

Remembering Anna's words about damage to Molly's heart, Amos watched Molly walk away, and thought how, like a mine shaft, the hole she has dug is too deep to disappear just like that.

The last one to leave was Charlie O'Toole.

"Hi, Pastor," said Charlie as he approached the door.

"It's nice to see you this morning, Charlie. I can't recall you having attended before."

"No. First time. I've been thinkin'. I haven't been to church since I was a kid, and I remember thinkin' about religious stuff back then, and a lot of it didn't make sense."

"What denomination did you attend?"

"Catholic. But I suppose it could have been any church, for all the attention I paid."

"What can I tell you?"

"Well, I guess, what is the whole Christian thing about? We went to mass, but I don't know. Seems like I was too busy daydreaming and looking at stuff, pictures and statues. People. Watching the priest."

"And you felt compelled to come to church this morning?"

"Well, yeah. I started thinking a lot about it. For some reason, I really wanted to come – and I'm sorta happy I did. Just kind of surprising because I never really wanted to come before."

'The Lord is drawing you to Him, Charlie, not to church."

"Well, why do you say that? If, like you say, I'm drawn to Him, that means church."

"We worship God in church, but sometimes people get the cart before the horse. God is the focus of our worship, and the reason for our being in church. The measure of anything is the extent to which it glorifies God. You ask what is this whole Christian thing about? God dwells in holy light – that's the best I can describe it – and sin cannot be in his presence. We are sinners, and our sins preclude our spending eternity with God, except that Christ's sacrifice was a provision for forgiveness where the slate is wiped clean, our sin vanishes – 'as far as the east is from the west' – providing a new, meaningful life here on earth, and the eternal life with God that we would not otherwise have. Eternity, Charlie."

Charlie continued to ask Pastor Nordquist questions long after the rest of the congregation left, reminding Amos of the conversations he had with Blade, Fur Man, and so many others.

"Charlie, there's no point standing in the doorway. C'mon back in and sit down. Anna?!" Amos hollered toward the kitchen. "Charlie O'Toole is joining us for lunch."

"Wonderful!" said Anna as she peeked out of the kitchen, wiping her hands. In public she had observed Charlie, an attractive young man, and had always sensed he was different from the others. After church, Charlie and Amos talked for hours, Amos answering Charlie's questions with occasional assistance from Angus MacGregor.

Amos had not quite made up his mind whether or not to leave Murray, when something happened that evening, making the decision easier. As Amos sat reading the *Murray Sun*, and Anna began reading a new novel, *Kidnapped*, reticent Inga, tall and attractive like her mother, and looking older than her 14 years, came up to them, obviously troubled.

"Dad and mom," began Inga, "could I talk to you, please?"

Amos and Anna looked up at Inga with surprise.

"Of course," said Amos, growing serious as he put down the paper. "Always. Sit down. What seems to be the problem?" Inga seldom had problems.

Inga sat down and took a deep breath. "A man has been following me," said Inga. Amos's eyes narrowed as Inga, hands folded in her lap, looked down and began telling what was happening.

63

I don't know how long he's been doing this," Inga began, "but I first noticed it two weeks ago when I went to the store. He was waiting on the corner across the street, and I noticed him watching me as I walked out the door. It's not that I mind men looking at me – it's spontaneous and I just don't look back – but it was as if he were standing there waiting for me to leave so he could watch.

"Two days later, I saw him again, and I got the same sensation that he was only there to watch me walk out the door and down the street." Inga continued to look down. "It it felt strange. Three days ago after I left the house, I turned around, and he was about a half block behind me. I quickened my pace and when I got to the store, I looked back. He wasn't there.

"Today the same thing happened and he was there. It would be one thing if he walked up and introduced himself, but he doesn't, he follows me. Each time he seems to be getting closer and, well, this has begun to make me very uncomfortable."

"What does he look like?" asked Anna as Esther and Rachel also listened.

"He's tall, about as tall as Dad, but not as big. He's slim, has a huge, brown mustache that probably hasn't been trimmed in months and it covers his mouth. He wears a big, gray hat, and his eyes are round and small. He's probably, oh, older than 20 and younger than 30. Whenever I've seen him, he's just staring at me." Inga looked away.

"When did this happen today?" asked Amos.

"When I was walking over to the livery stable to check on our horses."

"And he followed you from where?" asked Anna.

"I'm not sure. He wasn't across the street…I think he quit doing that. When I reached the livery stable, however, I could feel something – you know – behind me, and I looked around, and there he was, maybe twenty feet away, walking toward me with that stare. He doesn't smile or nod or anything – there's no expression. The others all smile and try to be friendly, but this man just…stares." Inga shrugged her shoulders. "So I turned and went into the stable, walked immediately over to Mr. O'Toole, and began talking to him about the horses while I watched the entrance."

"Did he walk by the entrance…or walk in?"

"No," said Inga, "he did neither. After I talked to Mr. O'Toole, I curried the horses, then went to the entrance and looked out. I saw him again – on the other side of the street down the block, sitting in a chair on the boardwalk, watching the livery stable. I had to go home, so I did. As I walked by him, I could feel his eyes almost as if they were part of my dress. There were other people around, but I actually wanted to run. I didn't, but I walked faster. As I got to our front door, I looked back, and he was walking behind me."

"Inga," said Anna, "all men like to look – they'd be dead if they didn't – but this is a little more; this is odd behavior."

"It certainly feels odd," said Inga.

"Why does he just stare at you?" asked Rachel, now seven.

"Some people," began Anna, "get a strange, heightened sense of pleasure from furtively watching. They're called 'voyeurs' – if that's all he is. My concern is that, if he seems to be coming closer, he might be someone capable of doing more than just looking."

"Inga," said Amos, standing up, "let's go for a walk. It's still light out. There are plenty of men on the street. Why don't we see if we can spy him instead of vice versa?"

"Very well…," said Inga apprehensively – Inga knew what her father's temper could be like, "…if…are you sure?"

"Very," said Amos. "Even if we do not see him, he might see us, and I think he'll be able to deduce why an angry father and his attractive daughter are out walking about Murray in the evening."

Amos and Inga went out the front door, and Inga looked across the street where the man stood in the past, but he was not there. Inga took her father's arm.

As Amos and Inga walked down the street, Amos glanced about for a man his height with a big mustache, round narrow eyes, and a large gray hat. Some men who passed by nodded a greeting to Amos; two well-mannered men removed their hats and nodded toward Inga. Inga and Amos continued to walk a block and a half and were approaching the Daisy Saloon when a man of Amos's height with a big, gray hat, who obviously had been drinking heavily, walked unsteadily out the open door. The man had no mustache, however.

When the man looked at Inga, he froze as Inga looked back startled. The mustache was gone, perhaps to intentionally alter his appearance, but it was him. Amos glanced at Inga, and gathered from her expression that this was the man who had been following her. Amos's face clouded over and, as Inga stopped walking, he left her side. Amos walked quickly toward the man as Inga watched wide-eyed.

As Amos approached him, the man awkwardly bolted, almost falling down as he started to run. Amos started to sprint after him, but changed his mind, stopped and watched the man clambering awkwardly down the street. For a moment, Amos stood watching, then turned around and walked back to Inga. As he approached her in front of the Daisy Saloon, a short, ovate, older man with oversized pants, frayed suspenders, and a tattered hat, came out of the saloon and approached Amos. The man turned and looked down the street.

"You're Pastor Nordquist?" asked the man without looking up.

"I am. Did you see that man who just came out of the saloon? Do you know who he is?"

"Only name I've heard is 'Mulligan,'" said the short man. "Works in the mines. Otherwise, spends his time in the Daisy. Real infatuated with your daughter there," the man added, nodding toward Inga. "Not surprisin' considerin' she's so attractive and ain't a workin' girl. That Mulligan's odd though. Don't say much, but after a few drinks he'll say a little, and your daughter's usually what he talks about. Lotta 'what-if's.'" The man looked knowingly at Amos out of the corner of his eye, and then in the distance again. "Ain't unusual. Bein' how attractive your daughter is…I mean, let's be honest. She'd be attractive anywhere, but especially here where there ain't no more like her…well, what can I say? Your daughter gets talked about." The man looked up at Amos. "Know what I mean?"

As Amos looked down at him, the short man looked off in the distance again and shrugged. "The Cabots and the Lodges don't live in Murray."

Amos glanced at the entrance to the Daisy Saloon, saw the eyes looking out the door – not at him, at Inga – and, as the eyes watched, offered Inga his arm.

"Thank you," he said to the short man. "You've been extremely helpful."

Pastor Nordquist turned, and he and Inga began walking home.

With a sense of peace, that evening he told his wife, "We should leave this area altogether. I will need to contact Nels Hanseth for approval and direction."

Anna silently looked at him, and her stomach unwound like a released rubber band after being twisted to the point of snapping. *We're leaving.* Greatly relieved, for the moment she allowed herself to stop worrying. Later in the evening, however, she began wondering: *to where?*

64

In response to his letter to Nels Hanseth, Pastor Nordquist received a surprisingly urgent reply requesting Amos and his family leave for Seattle as soon as possible.

A new congregation was forming in Seattle and, while the Murray population was transient and tied to remaining mineral wealth, Seattle had timber, rail, agriculture, a deep water port, and exports. Families. People came to stay. The Seattle congregation was already building a sanctuary. They needed a pastor, in contrast to Murray where the pastor needed a congregation.

"We'll keep this community in our prayers; Molly in particular. I worry about her," Amos said quietly to Anna. "But then, I worry about them all." Then he smiled. "You get to worry about everything else."

"Thank you."

The following morning, Pastor Nordquist told Angus MacGregor of his plans to leave Murray. "Where do y' plan to go?" asked Angus, his face losing expression.

"Seattle, 300 miles west of here. It is growing much faster than either Murray or even the Silver Valley."

"Seattle. Aye, I've heard people speak well of it," said Angus. His expression remained unchanged as he massaged his beard while looking to one side. Then a light went on in his eyes.

"Now – and this be a fair and reasonable question t' ask – would it be pleasin' t' y' if I were t' join y' on your journey?"

Pastor Nordquist looked back at Angus, unprepared for the question. The thought of having Angus accompany them, however, appealed to Pastor Nordquist. Angus had enough money to pay his own way; his presence would contribute to the security of the trip and, with Angus along, no doubt the trip would go much faster. Amos looked at Anna who shrugged: why not?

"Certainly," Amos smiled. "Why not join us?"

Pastor Nordquist attempted to make himself comfortable in the grasp of a spontaneous, one-arm hug from bearish Angus MacGregor.

Charlie O'Toole, the saddler, had continued to meet and discuss the gospel with Amos. Charlie's spiritual growth was rapid. After Amos made his decision, he visited Charlie, asking him to watch over the small flock after Amos left, leading them in Bible studies, perhaps even worship.

Later that week, Pastor Nordquist received word that four additional men in the ministry, a Catholic priest and three Protestant ministers, were coming to Murray to establish congregations. Pastor Nordquist accepted this news with pleasure and relief. His departure would not mean the absence of God's word being taught. Amos encouraged Charlie O'Toole to assist parishioners in finding the right church for them. Charlie began to think that while he would continue to make saddles, train horses, and work in the livery stable, in addition he might try to pick up where Amos left off.

"Charlie, pray about that, and then follow God's leading," Amos said simply, expecting that Charlie would nod and follow his advice. But Charlie was beyond that point.

"I already have been praying, and I think right now is like when I had this new desire to attend church. Except now I have a desire to lead church."

"Charlie, I have no doubt you would make a wonderful pastor," smiled Anna. "I've sensed something for a while. Why don't you take it a step further and seriously consider full-time ministry?"

"You'll need to attend seminary," smiled Amos. "I'll give you Nels Hanseth's address in Minnesota, and you can write to him, as will I, and begin a new life following your new birth."

Charlie wanted to begin getting a feel for leading worship, and the next Sunday Amos let him participate in the service. Although attendance was no greater than normal, with a head pastor and a quasi-assistant pastor, the church service seemed more prominent than in the past. At the same time, due to declining gold strikes around Murray, together with Mr. Kellogg's silver strike to the southwest, more people were leaving Murray, joining those passing through, and Pastor Nordquist told Charlie to plan on serving in the Great Silver Valley when he was done with seminary because, by the time he returned, there might be no Murray. Charlie nodded. Murray was atrophying; Eagle City was already on its death bed.

Amos would suggest to the priest and ministers that they also consider the small-but-growing Silver Valley towns of Kellogg and Wallace.

While Pastor Nordquist sold his house without much difficulty, two years later the same house would be worth a small fraction of what Pastor Nordquist received.

As Pastor Nordquist and his family started preparing for the journey, one of Amos's infrequent parishioners, Frank Cesarelli, stopped by. Frank, a hotel and restaurant supply salesman from Seattle, just came from Spokane Falls.

"Goin' t' Seattle?" asked Frank.

"Yes. A new congregation needs a pastor," Amos smiled. "Seattle should be quite a change from Murray."

Frank looked down and smoothed his trim mustache with his index finger, then looked up at Pastor Nordquist. "You think Murray's bad," Frank remarked, "wait until you see the Lava Bed."

"What's the 'Lava Bed'?" asked Pastor Nordquist.

Frank chuckled with an insider inflection, glanced at Amos's wife and daughters, and decided not to go into detail. "You'll find out soon enough, pastor."

Seattle, late summer, 1887

In the brothel parlor, the Victorian chandelier, its brass and crystal coated with tobacco smoke film, hung high above the floor as if wanting to keep its distance from the men below. The overweight, middle-aged, painted woman, as much a fixture as the chandelier, attended to guests, her breathing labored.

As she walked about in the weakly illuminated room, her partially exposed bosom, a fleshy sign advertising sin, heaved heavily. About her, cigar and pipe smoke drifted through the pyramid light beams radiating downward from suspended parlor lamps. Older Seattle men, cherishing cheap drinks and ogling younger girls, glanced in the woman's direction if she sought their attention; otherwise she was of no interest. Her blotched, white skin glistened in the weak chandelier light as she moved slowly, ambulating through the smoke shroud, wheezing in her discomfort. Late evening's mascara showed hairline fractures not evident earlier in the day. Uncomfortably packed into her crimson-stained, red satin dress with yellowed lace, her overheated bulk was soft, contrasting with a heart grown hard as polar ice.

A wisp of a woman, still nearly a girl, emerged from the vapor, appearing as if by magic before the large woman. The small woman's long coat draped over her like a navy blanket; her hands hid in the dark, worn sleeves. Men nearby, seemingly sober, watched curiously.

"Are you the madam?" the girl asked.

To the men, it was an odd question. No one called the large woman "the madam." She was Lil'. None knew her last name.

"Call me Lil', sweetie," came the husky reply. "What can I do for you?" Lil' sounded pleasant when she talked business.

"My husband left me," said the girl. "I need a job." The girl said nothing more.

Without expression, Lil' studied the delicate features before her, the large brown eyes looking up with no outward sign of emotion. Lil' had long since dispensed with feelings of pity at this moment.

"What's your name, honey?" Lil' asked, unsuccessfully stifling a cough.

"Mary," was all the girl said, not certain she was expected to say more.

"What's your last name, Mary?" asked Lil'.

Her last name. Repressed emotion tripped her controlled composure.

"Sullivan." She had difficulty saying the name. Her eyes were downcast.

"Sullivan," repeated Lil', as if to be sure.

"It was my husband's name," Mary unnecessarily volunteered, looking up.

"It makes no difference to me, Mary," Lil' replied, certain the name, which once must have been a source of joy for this Mary, now cavorted with different emotions. "Sullivan's as good a name as any." Lil' roughly coughed again.

Mary looked back. Unable to overlook the soft, attractive, innocent face before her, Lil' asked a question she usually didn't ask.

"Are you sure you want to work in a brothel?"

Mary repeated the question in her mind, as if she was dreaming. "It's what I can do," Mary responded without emotion, turning her head, again looking down.

"Your timing is good," said Lil'. "One of my girls must have run off last night." Lil' added logically, "She ain't here now. Some rube probably promised her the moon."

Lil' laughed hoarsely, coughing, and shrugged her shoulders. Mary did not look up.

"I'll show you your room," Lil' said, beckoning Mary to follow her. "Here's how it works here…"

The manikin men, expressions drawn, silently watched the two women turn and leave the parlor.

Lil' and Mary walked to the stair landing, and up the stairs. At the top of the stairs was a hall corridor leading to a room, a place where Mary would live to work with no scheduled hours, a world wherein Mary would learn survival and grow hard, gradually emulating her mentor. Mary saw everything as in a dream while she walked, about to vitiate her life.

Lil stopped, opened a door and, as Lil waited to one side, Mary stepped in.

October 12, 1887

Pastor Nordquist had spent three difficult years in Murray. With an inexplicable twinge of melancholy in spite of his frustrated efforts – or perhaps, he thought paradoxically, because of those efforts – Amos realized he had become attached to the rough and tumble mining town. Now that he was leaving, it was as if the unpleasant memories never occurred. Why this one-sided twinge of fondness? Why is this? he wondered to himself as he walked along Main Street. He looked about as he crossed the street. It was not a rewarding experience, yet, as I look around, I also look back with fondness. He smiled and in his mind concluded that while the recipe for nostalgia requires a pinch of deception, his time in Murray was anything but dull. And perhaps I did more to accomplish the Lord's work, the Holy Spirit working through me, than I realize.

Pastor Nordquist made his rounds for the last time with some reluctance, cornering and thanking Dutch Jake for the use of his extra saloon chairs that would continue to provide seating for the small congregation during its waning existence. Dutch Jake's conscience tugged lightly at his heart, but quickly let go.

Amos encouraged Charlie O'Toole to place himself under one of the newly arrived, ordained ministers. Charlie agreed to do this, but assured Amos that as soon as he could afford to go to seminary, he would enter the ministry himself. He had been corresponding with Nels Hanseth.

Pastor Nordquist again made visits to the Catholic priest and Methodist minister who recently arrived, leaving the forwarding address of the new congregation where Amos would become pastor upon arriving in Seattle.

Meanwhile, Anna stood in front of the kitchen sink looking out the window, thinking, and made the decision to go down to Gold Street to say goodbye to the Queen of Murray who had not been in church for two weeks.

In the cold, overcast afternoon, arriving at the door of Cabin 1, Anna knocked politely and waited.

No answer. She knocked again.

Anna waited for another moment and then knocked again, harder. Except for the sweep of easy wind, it was quiet. From a gray cloud cover that enveloped the hillsides, a cold mist began to descend, turning to light drizzle. Anna adjusted her bonnet, raised her collar, put her hands in the pockets of her coat as she turned and began to walk back to Main Street, shoulders hunched in the falling rain.

"Mrs. Nordquist?"

Anna stopped. Turning around, she saw no one. But then, shadowed behind the front door that had opened a couple of inches, Anna recognized the attractive features of Molly B'Dam. Anna again adjusted the brim of her bonnet and walked back to Cabin 1 as mixed rain and snow fell, insuring that in moments, once again the streets of Murray would be thick with mud until freezing temperatures became more common.

"Hello, Molly. I am sorry to tell you this but..."

"Yes, I heard; you are leaving for Seattle," said Molly softly. She turned her head and covered her mouth to cough. "And I am sincerely sorry to see you go, but I understand." Her tone was quietly forward, unaffected and unguarded. She paused for a second. "In fact, after I get over this illness, whatever it is, I might be leaving for Seattle myself." She turned to the side and coughed again.

Anna noticed with some alarm how softly Molly spoke and how delicate she looked. She was under the weather, yes, but also seemed like someone else...or perhaps what Anna saw up to this moment was someone else. Molly's face was pale and her hair unkempt. Even for being sick, she looked withdrawn. Most unsettling, the regal air was absent.

"Do you need a doctor?" asked Anna.

"I'll be fine," whispered Molly, not looking at Anna, before clearing her throat. "The girls check in on me regularly." Murray medical service left something to be desired. Molly knew everyone. She did not want the doctor.

"Molly, if you are going to Seattle..."

"Please, don't tell anyone; I don't want the town to know just yet. At least not until I'm well. And I still have mixed feelings. But probably because I'm under the weather, not thinking clearly."

"When you are in Seattle, I expect to see you in our new congregation."

"Oh, yes, I'll be there."

Perhaps it was the softness in Molly's voice and demeanor that troubled Anna. Whatever it was that bothered Anna was not directly evident, but Anna sensed Molly's illness was more than simply being under the weather, and the sensation concerned Anna.

Mixed rain and snow continued to fall, becoming heavier. Out of courtesy,

Anna was compelled to keep the conversation brief so that Molly could shut her door.

Molly admired Anna. Anna was loving and uncondemning, while her behavior reflected high standards. An attractive, intelligent woman of character, were more women like Anna Nordquist, Molly thought, and more men like her husband, Amos, how different might life be. Indeed, how different the world would be. She sighed when first thinking this two years earlier.

It is remarkable, Anna thought as she stood in front of Molly, in spite of her self-sufficiency and independence, how much she needs a loving husband – an odd thought to some, Anna mused, who have not experienced or seen what Amos and I have.

"As, no doubt, you already know," Anna said, "other men of God have come to Murray. In my husband's absence, I encourage you to place yourself within the ministry of one. And spend time in the Word. Amos has instructed Charlie O'Toole to help anyone in our small congregation with whatever spiritual needs they may have. Charlie is making arrangements to attend seminary," Anna smiled. "In the meantime, he's there for you. In Amos's absence, use him. He has the address of our new congregation in Seattle where I hope to see you soon."

For a moment Anna studied Molly's features quietly as Anna received what appeared to be a presentiment that, actually, this would be the last time Anna would see Molly.

Pray, said Anna's inner voice. Anna heard it, and said to Molly, "Let me pray with you." Molly closed her eyes, the door slightly open.

"Heavenly father," prayed Anna as directed, "we pray you will give Molly the inner peace and salvation she needs, and may she receive the contentment and happiness she desires." Anna paused. "Amen."

It was a simple prayer, but covered everything. For a moment, Molly kept her eyes closed, then crossed herself.

"God bless you," Anna smiled.

She was about to walk away in the cold sleet when Molly said, "Anna, stop." It was the first time Molly had called Mrs. Nordquist, "Anna."

Anna turned toward Molly.

"Anna, for my own reasons, I've done what I've done, and have never completely submitted to God, even though Pastor Nordquist has so often encouraged me to do so. But I'm completely tired of what I've been doing; I'm done." Molly looked intently at Anna. "I want what you have."

Anna looked back at Molly and nodded knowingly. "Take my hands," Anna said after a moment, her voice soft, her rejoicing eyes never leaving Molly's. Molly reached out and took Anna's hands. "Now, you pray, Molly. Pray what is on your heart. I'll pray with you – 'where two or more…' – but this is between you and God. He has drawn you to Him. Jesus says that He stands at the door and knocks. At this moment He's at the door, knocking, and God has unlocked the door." Anna lightly squeezed Molly's hands. "Open it."

As mixed rain and sleet began to fall, Molly almost inaudibly prayed what was on her heart, giving herself to God. In spite of all the times she had put it off, it was surprisingly easy.

When she was done, still holding Molly's hands, Anna beamed at her and said, "For some, conversion is a matter of a few days or moments, but, for you, my guess is that conversion has been gradually approached during a lifetime, culminating a moment ago, and now you have salvation." Anna again smiled as Molly looked back, both women memorizing the moment, and then Anna let go of Molly's hands.

"Amos and I will be gone, but that is a small matter," Anna said. "God is with you. Meanwhile, standing here with this cold coming in is not good for you. Be assured, Amos and I will continue to pray for you."

"I shall miss you both," said Molly. "Please tell your husband this town will never be the same without him."

Anna nodded politely, sensing Molly's statement reflected a wishful reverie, perhaps the same reverie of many Murray working girls who had observed Amos at a distance.

"I must go now," said Anna as she stepped back. "Good bye, Molly. May God give you the love your heart needs."

Molly's expression became distant; she said nothing as Anna turned and walked away, the rain and sleet beginning to fall more heavily. As Anna walked in the downpour, she could feel Molly watching through the slightly open door. Several moments passed before Anna heard the door latch behind her.

The Sunset Stage route over the Nine-Mile Road to Wallace was still not complete and, as a consequence, in late November the Nordquists left Murray by pack train along the snow-covered Jackass Trail down to the South Fork of the Coeur d'Alene River and then to the Mission. From there, the *Amelia Wheaton* would take them down river to Lake Coeur d'Alene, and to the Third Street dock in Coeur d'Alene City at the north end of the lake.

The weather was cold but clear. The sunlit scenery through which the *Amelia Wheaton* passed was covered with snow, the reflection of which danced on the blue lake surface. Angus MacGregor enjoyed the view and his ongoing descriptions insured that the others were attentive to the landscape around them. At one point Angus became unusually animated because of the extent to which a certain area reminded him of similar scenery around Loch Lomond, northwest of Glasgow, Scotland. The constant offering of descriptions, reminiscences, anecdotes and insights shortened the trip considerably.

The Nordquist family took a stage from Coeur d'Alene City to Rathdrum where they caught the Northern Pacific train ultimately destined for Seattle.

Seattle, December 1, 1887

During the Eocene Period 34 to 56 million years ago when an epochal cycle of global warming was pushing the top of the thermometer, crocodiles wiled away under Alaskan palm trees, and early lemurs raced around Arctic Circle redwoods. Off the coast of Washington state, what there was of it, through seafloor volcanic activity, the Olympic Mountains were beginning to rise beneath the Pacific Ocean surface as if bread in a great aquatic oven. Subduction plates subsequently pushed the volcanoes out of the oven and up into the atmosphere where, over epochs, they were turned into jagged mountains by continental ice sheets, glaciers, and all manner of un-Eocene-like activity during subsequent cycles.

Meanwhile, to the east, convergence of the small Juan de Fuca tectonic plate with the larger North American plate raised geological havoc along the Cascadia subduction zone, creating the Cascade Volcanic Arc where volcanoes erupted, re-erupted, and erupted again. And again. For good measure, they continued to erupt periodically, even into the present at the end of the recent Ice Age, forming the Cascade Mountains.

Proximity of the Cascade and Olympic mountain ranges to the Pacific Ocean, coupled with the coriolis effect of the earth's rotation, resulted in prevailing westerly winds carrying substantial moisture over Puget Sound, with predictable atmospheric consequences.

***

It was raining in Seattle. The low hanging, marbled overcast didn't move. The three men huddled motionlessly in the dreary drizzle, hiding beneath their oilskin overcoats and broad brimmed southwesters as the ubiquitous rain continually soaked into fields, roads, docks, boardwalks, roofs, trees, siding, pilings, and clothing. Miniature streams converged into tiny cascades racing down Seattle hillsides to see which would reach Elliott Bay first, and in the constant rainfall, Elliott Bay seemed to become wetter.

When the three men began their vigil, looking down the railroad tracks, they attempted conversation but, after a half hour, all subjects of mutual interest were exhausted, and each man carried on imaginary conversations within himself, each alone in his thoughts, the only motion and sound being the falling rain. Growing impatient, one man, Einar, moaned irritably.

"Now, Einar, don't be too anxious," Gunnar Olsson responded, his Scandinavian accent as thick as his blonde mustache. "Dese t'ings are never on time."

"Vell, yah, but I have other t'ings to do, you know."

"It'll be worth the wait," countered the third man. "We just about have a real church building; in a little bit we'll have a real pastor." He returned his gaze down the track. "It's important to make a good first impression, start things off on the right foot." He pulled up his oilskin coat collar, adjusting it for comfort. "Keep your shirt on, Einar."

"In dis veather, vhat vould you expect me to do?" Einar's drowned appearance – exasperated eyes, soaked clothes, and drooping, dripping mustache – was comical as he looked down the tracks.

"Vhat's dat old saying about not having enough brains to come in out of the rain?"

"That old saying doesn't apply here," said the third man.

Gunnar Olsson laughed, as he often did. A fisherman, the waning fragrance of salmon, halibut, red snapper and cod followed him around like an invisible aura. People gradually associated the smell with his warm demeanor and quick smile. As a consequence, those who knew Gunnar unconsciously welcomed the smell. It made them feel good. When Gunnar laughed, as he did that moment, worry and care stepped away and stood at a respectable distance.

The men were soaking statues, hands dug deep in their pockets, staring down the wet stretch of railroad track as if the act of wishing could bring results. Gunnar began rocking back and forth on the heels of his thick boots, humming a Norwegian folk tune. He was not bari-tenor Mattia Battistini, but the sound was pleasant. The other men looked down the railroad tracks and listened to Gunnar's voice accompanied by the drizzle's sibilance.

Gunnar stopped singing as something grabbed his attention.

There. Smoke shooting above a distant tapering hillside. A train would appear any moment. Gunnar glanced over his shoulder at the wagon and horses to reassure everything was ready. The others did the same.

All other sensation was chased away by the approaching train with black smoke billowing over a trailing queue of passenger cars. The smoke, hissing steam, and thunderous noise made the iron horse seem more like a fire-breathing dragon as it approached the train station. The emotional intensity produced by the vision of locomotive, smoke and steam, and the cacophony accompanying them, magnified the impression of arriving royalty. The men stood anxiously, awaiting the new pastor and his family as the big, black locomotive pulled into the station.

65

Pastor Nordquist stepped down to the landing platform and scanned the small crowd, awkwardly looking for anyone who might be awkwardly looking for him.

The angst from thinking there might be no one quickly disappeared when a big fisherman with a thick, blond mustache and a quizzical look approached him. What if this big, blond fisherman and his two companions were waiting for Bill Smith, a railroad executive from Wallula? What if this man who sure-as-punch looks like he might be a pastor is actually Bill Smith, a railroad executive from Wallula?

"Yah, Pastor Nordquist?"

"Yah!" responded Amos with relief.

"How do you do?" Gunnar said excitedly. "I am Gunnar Olsson." The receiving committee chairman stuck out his large right hand and, smiling, shook Pastor Nordquist's hand repeatedly. "And these two yentlemen are Curt Larsen and Einar Skoglund."

Amos smiled as he pulled his hand out of Gunnar's calloused grip to shake hands with the others.

In the distance Pastor Nordquist noticed a frail but attractive young woman, not dressed warmly enough for this weather, strolling aimlessly along a boardwalk. She stopped as if having reached a predetermined point, furtively studied train passengers on the landing, turned and began walking slowly the other way.

"Let's load the Nordquist's baggage onto the vagon," said Gunnar.

"Thanks, Gunnar. I vasn't shoor vhy ve vere down here," mumbled Einar.

The wagon was large enough to carry the Nordquist family, their baggage, Angus MacGregor and the receiving party of three men. With the baggage loaded and covered with an oiled canvas tarp as protection against the rain, beaming, Gunnar lightly snapped the reins, and the wagon began to roll up the hillside away from the train station and the waterfront.

"Vell, ve are sure pleased to see you and yoor family," said Gunnar excitedly, clapping his large fisherman hands together for emphasis. One of the rear horses started. "Ve have everything all arranged. Ve even have a parsonage for you – a furnished parsonage," exclaimed Gunnar.

"'Furnished'?" repeated Anna Nordquist.

"Yah, furnished," echoed Gunnar Olsson with a big smile. "Chairs, beds, silvervare." Pleased, he smiled at Anna. "Vere ve prepared for your arrival? Yah!"

"Well, we certainly did not expect so much," said Amos, also pleased. "We expected that we would stay with parishioners until we found our own place. This is much more than we expected. We certainly appreciate your being so accommodating."

"Ve appreciate your coming," responded Gunnar Olsson amid similar responses by other receiving committee members.

This is certainly in stark contrast to Murray, thought Anna.

While a vague glimpse of trees could be seen through the distant mist, years earlier, loggers shaved the hillside. There were muddy streets in varying repair, and wooden buildings, either new or under construction, but no trees except at distances. As rain fell, the four horses pulled the wagon like a large plow through the eroded, muddy street, inducing greater erosion.

Gunnar Olsson explained that church members belonged to a large number of Scandinavian families who settled in Seattle within the past five years and who, believing they were well established, decided a Lutheran church nearby was mandatory for reasons both spiritual and social. They formed a committee that, in turn, contacted Nels Hanseth in Minneapolis and, prior to receiving notification that Pastor Nordquist and his family would soon be leaving Murray for Seattle, began construction of a hillside church on a donated site using volunteer labor. Lumber, in large supply, was obtained relatively inexpensively from Henry Yesler's mill, a short distance down the hill. The construction of the church was nearly done and, as the horses pulled the wagon up the hillside away from the waterfront, the parsonage was waiting.

The rain did nothing to dampen the enthusiasm of Anna Nordquist and her daughters who managed to contain their joy at the prospect of a new home with a new but established congregation in a new and thriving city.

Pastor Nordquist felt this same elation, but, for inexplicable reasons, his inner voice was less than joyful, his sense of peace disturbed. In the face of unexpected good fortune, once again he was feeling something was not right. Or maybe I am just used to Murray. A false alarm? The sensation had not been so in the past.

Angus MacGregor was uncharacteristically silent, keeping his collar turned up, almost touching the brim of his hat in order to protect him from the drizzle falling quietly all about them. As the wagon moved further up the hillside, Angus looked westward toward Elliott Bay and Duwamish Head, attempting to imagine what they would look like in good weather.

The wagon came to a slow, creaking stop next to the attractive parsonage. In contrast to the smaller homes with two-step porches at the base of the hill, the parsonage was much larger and more striking than they expected moments ago.

Amos jumped down and helped his wife climb down; Anna was very anxious to see the inside of the house – both out of curiosity and as a practical matter. Bedrooms needed to be assigned, luggage needed to be unloaded, and the contents placed or stored where most appropriate. Although the parsonage design and fenestration were not ostentatious, Amos Nordquist the carpenter was struck by the workmanship. Amos nodded approvingly.

Being careful not to track in mud, after laying a tarp on the foyer floor, Gunnar Olsson and the other committee members deposited boxes of belongings that would either find a home on the main floor, be brought down to the basement for storage, or carried upstairs.

"This is a very fine home," said Pastor Nordquist as he stood in the large living room looking about. "This is a nicer home than I would have expected were I expecting a home," he smiled. Helping Anna unload boxes, the three members of the receiving committee smiled in response, but said nothing.

Pastor Nordquist wandered through the living room into the dining room, his hands in his pockets. Through dining room leaded glass windows he looked down on mist-obscured Elliott Bay.

"Was this house also donated?"

Amos could not see how a young congregation, even if they were established Seattle residents, could afford to purchase this attractive Victorian home. The fixtures had an unpretentious elegance and, from his carpentry expertise, Pastor Nordquist recognized excellent finish work. On second thought, Amos believed that a wealthy church member was allowing the church to use the house as a parsonage, but certainly could not be expected to donate a 2½ story home with a full basement.

"Vell, yah. In a manner of speaking," responded Gunnar Olsson.

Gunnar and the other committee members did not bother to look up from the boxes they were helping to unpack, seemingly more focused on the effort at hand than the question Pastor Nordquist posed. Amos sensed, however, that the question instantly commandeered the thoughts of each, and concluded that there was more to this. Pastor Nordquist changed his tone of voice from pleasant to authoritative. He was now the church leader, the pastor, the teaching elder, and would at this moment assume that position.

"'In a manner of speaking'? Would you mind telling me more?" No one spoke.

"Gunnar?"

"Vell, the previous owner left," responded Gunnar as he opened another box. Gunnar paused again and, straightening up, looked at Amos. "He vill not be back," Gunnar added.

"What happened?" asked Pastor Nordquist. "Was he in trouble with the law?"

"Vell…yah." As Gunnar Olsson spoke, the two other committee members, without expression, stood up. "The former owner broke a law."

The other two men continued to look at Gunnar who said nothing more – although it was obvious that his mind was working.

"Well, what did he *do*?" Pastor Nordquist asked in exasperation.

Gunnar Olsson glanced at the other two men.

"He broke a law saying no property could be owned by anyone who vas

Chinese."

"He broke…he was Chinese?"

"Yah," said Gunnar.

"Where is he now?"

"No one knows," said Gunnar, shrugging his shoulders. "The city donated the house to the new congregation."

"No one questioned the morality of accepting such a donation?" asked Pastor Nordquist.

"Ve could not change vhat happened," said Einar, "and many in the congregation thought it vas a good thing. If ve could not change vhat happened, and the house vas going to someone, why not us? Ve vanted to have a pastor, and thought this house vould be best used as a parsonage."

Amos accepted this explanation, but felt his stomach tighten.

"When you said that 'many in the congregation thought it was a good thing," asked Pastor Nordquist, "did any think that taking the house away from someone simply because they were Chinese was a good thing?"

"Yah," Gunnar nodded, "some did."

Amos silently prayed that he would be able to locate the former owner and that, somehow, the injustice could be reversed; and he began to worry about "some" in his new congregation.

February 1, 1888

A letter arrived. Mail always caused some excitement because few letters came to the Nordquist residence. Until today, no mail came from Idaho, and it was some time since the Nordquists had left Murray. Amos felt a rush of excitement as he looked at the letter from Charlie O'Toole, and opened it anxiously, eager to know what was happening since he and his family left. Phil O'Roarke, Noah Kellogg, Dutch Jake? It was evident why part of him became attached to Murray. Murray was not a quiet town where ordinary people led simple lives. Murray was theater.

"Anna, we received a letter from Murray!" Amos called to his wife as he walked into the kitchen, the letter in his hand.

"Oh," she responded and turned toward Amos. While she did not want to live in Murray, the prospect of hearing about events in Murray piqued her interest.

As Amos stood silently reading the letter, his head fell slightly and his expression went blank. He continued to read, and Anna waited for some response, but he said nothing.

Done reading, he looked up, his facial expression gravely solemn, his mind somewhere else, the edges of his eyes lined with sorrow.

"Amos?" Anna attempted to get her husband's attention.

She walked over to him as his right hand, holding the letter, fell to his side. He took a deep breath, expelled it, and looked away. He looked down at his wife for a second, attempting to properly phrase the words, but could think of nothing other than the difficult fact.

"Molly is dead."

Anna's eyes grew wide and her mouth dropped open. "What?"

She looked at Amos, stunned. Anna could not believe what she just heard. "Dead? What…? How did she die?"

Anna looked toward the other side of the living room at nothing in particular, her mind's eye completely focused on the last time she and Molly spoke. Why didn't I see it? she thought. She would not have asked for help.

Anna gently took the letter from his hand and, serious to the point of frowning, read it herself as Amos, deep in thought, wandered slowly toward the living room front windows.

In the letter, there was news of how gold discoveries were few and insignificant, and how an exodus of prospectors was leaving Murray for the nearby Silver Valley in hopes of better fortune. The letter said Molly had contracted a lingering illness; no further explanation was given. Charlie O'Toole also said he went to the new Catholic priest in Murray requesting absolution for Molly, but this was refused. Before her death, he said, she requested she be called posthumously by her maiden name growing up, "Maggie" Hall. The funeral service was nondenominational, conducted by the Methodist minister, and his eulogy, enclosed, simple.

> *…She flashed like a diamond among us, until she herself was laid low by a lingering illness which brought her untimely end in a humble cabin which was home to her.*
>
> *And to the credit of Him in whom she placed her trust, her last days were made comfortable, if not happy; and her every want was readily met. To the lasting credit of our Christian ladies… whatever could be done by them was done without ostentation, in the pure and noble spirit.*
>
> *God rest your soul, Maggie Hall, through eternity.*
> *Amen.*

Charlie wrote, "I spent as much time with her as I could. When I visited, we would talk – not much because it became hard for her to talk. Sometimes I just held her hand, and she held mine, even though she was weak. Maybe it's just wishful thinking, but while I could never have had a relationship with her before she got sick, based on our time together in her last days, I can't help wonder whether we could have had something if she got well. But Molly knew her time had come. She was not only prepared to meet her Maker, but looked forward to it. She did not agonize over her wayward life, but accepted what it had been, believing when she stood before the throne of God, she would be blameless as the result of Christ's sacrifice on her behalf, and an eternity of love would be hers. She passed away peacefully."

Charlie also enclosed a copy of the obituary printed in the Murray *Sun* the day before the funeral, a brief summary of her life.

> *"Maggie Hall, for that was her maiden name, was known to all of us as Molly Burdan, her married name. She was born in*

Dublin, Ireland, on December 26, 1853, which made her only a few weeks past 34 years of age at the time of her death. She came to New York in 1873, at the age of 20, and made her own way in life from that time on.

"She arrived in Murray in January of 1884, almost exactly four years ago, coming in over the frozen, snow-bound trail from Thompson Falls. And it is safe to state that no one person has made such an imprint on our community as this warm hearted, forthright woman, whose sacrificing generosity was known even before she had arrived, when she stopped on the wintery trail to share her fur coat and her horse with a woman and child.

"She has drawn more public attention than any other woman in this part of the country, for her many generous deeds towards others. We will never forget Maggie Hall, nee Molly Burdan.

"It is not to her shame that she was the mistress of a million-aire in New York; rather to her credit for what she was while she lived among us.

"Simple graveside services will be held at the new burial grounds tomorrow (Thursday) afternoon at 3:30 o'clock, conducted by our three Protestant ministers. Those attending will gather at the end of South Second Street for the procession to the cemetery."

Charlie wrote that the county courthouse on Main Street closed, as did all businesses. Flags in Murray were flown at half-mast, and the edition of the Murray *Sun* had a reverse image with white print on a black front page. Charlie said the Methodist minister was actually the only speaker at the funeral although nearly all of Murray was there. Phil O'Rourke and Con Sullivan were two of the pallbearers.

Anna Nordquist folded the contents, replacing them in the envelope. She walked over to where her husband was standing, looking out the large window that framed the adolescent city and Elliott Bay below. She stood for a moment, letter at her side, looking up at him as dozens of self-condemning thoughts darted through his mind like fish among fronds, suggesting Murray was unfinished business, his motives for leaving were selfish, and he left when he was still needed.

Amos looked down at Anna, took her other hand, and led her slowly to the couch where they both sat down, continuing to hold hands. The thoughts were irrational, he knew. His first responsibility was to his family. But he wished he were at Molly's funeral and could have spoken. After all, he really knew her.

Pastor Nordquist lowered his eyes, lifted his palms and prayed, thanking God for Molly's salvation and asking for discernment when dealing with others. He was grateful for many things. He was grateful for the leading and intervention of the Holy Spirit, and in his mind he repeated John 15:5: "I am the vine, you are the branches; he who abides in Me and I in him, he bears much fruit; for apart from me you can do nothing." While he knew his own efforts would be pointless without the Holy Spirit, at the moment, however, thinking of others in Murray, he still questioned: was it enough?

He knew he could always do more, but also that he was a tool in the hands of God. Yet at moments like this, he felt his efforts should be greater, that he was not trying hard enough, and was inadequately attending to the harvest for which he was given five talents of responsibility.

He simultaneously gently bit both lips for a moment, and then silently sighed. Molly was with her Lord. Amos believed this, as did Charlie O'Toole. Realizing the implications of what he had been thinking a moment earlier, Amos became angry with himself. While it seemed imperative he do as much as possible, at the same time who was he? None of this was up to him.

The letter was on the reading table. He looked at Anna and studied her features. In spite of his shortcomings, God surely loved him: he had Anna. He felt a twinge of heartache as a related thought stepped to the front of his mind: when Molly died she had an admiring community of men, and Charlie O'Toole sat at her bedside as she slowly faded, but there was inadequate time; he could only be a caring man while she approached death. The seat reserved for the love of her life was empty.

Turning to his left and putting his arms around Anna's shoulders, as emotions of sadness and thankfulness rose like a creek during heavy rain, Amos's eyes began to mist, and he pulled Anna toward himself. The love a man needed to give, he gave, wrapping his powerful arms around her; and the love a woman needed to get, she absorbed as she spontaneously leaned into his gift of affection, pressing the side of her head along his neck and shoulder.

66

As Pastor Nordquist stood beside muddy Yesler Way, looking at the beehive of activity south of Yesler, someone patted him on the shoulder.

"Hiya, pastor."

Amos turned around and was startled to see the smiling, familiar face of affable Frank Cesarelli, the hotel and restaurant supply salesman he last saw in Murray. A little shorter than Amos, Frank was good-looking, always East Coast well-dressed for success, and at that moment he never looked better.

"Frank!" exclaimed Amos, sticking out his hand. "Great to see you!"

"Good to see you too, pastor," smiled Frank, smiling as he shook hands. "And I see you have found the Lava Bed."

"Lava bed? Ah, I haven't found it yet, Frank."

Amos remembered the comment, but was uncertain as to what it meant.

"Then you haven't been in Seattle long enough to learn your way around. All you see down there," said Frank, pointing toward the buildings to the south of them, "is called 'the Lava Bed.'"

"I didn't know that," answered Amos, looking at the activity along the streets. "From here it seems like most of the women in Seattle live there."

"Accurate assessment, pastor."

Frank folded his arms as they both looked southward.

"I supply a lot of those places with their restaurant and hotel needs – everything from bottle stoppers to bedspreads. I was just going down there to call on a couple of clients." Frank knew that once Pastor Nordquist understood the Lava Bed, Amos would consider it his duty to regularly visit Lava Bed establishments.

"Pastor, why don't you join me? Considering how well you fit in when you were in Murray, I don't think you'll be bothered too much by what you see in the Lava Bed – at least you won't see anything you haven't seen before."

"What is it I should not be bothered *by…*" asked Amos, curious, looking southward, "…'too much'?"

Frank smiled.

"Yesler Way, formerly called 'Skid Road,'" said Frank, motioning at the road in front of them, "is now commonly referred to as 'The Deadline,' a phrase I first learned in a Confederate prison."

Amos looked at Frank, remembering what Shorty had said when they were trying to find their way in the woods near Wilmington. "You were in a Confederate prison?"

"Camp Sumter [Andersonville]," Frank said.

"Camp Sumter?" said Amos. "I didn't know."

"It's not something I talk about – people listen politely, but whatever I say doesn't resonate; I can't communicate what it was like…and, really, most people don't care anyway."

"I care." Amos then looked at Frank and nodded encouragingly.

"I'll tell you a little. Camp Sumter," Frank said as he turned and directly faced Amos, "was an open stockade, no buildings except some tents, and at first it had 16.5 acres, part of which was swamp – that became more like an open cesspool – and was built to hold a maximum of 10,000 prisoners. But that capacity estimate was someone's pipedream, and well before I got there, prison population quickly reached 10,000, continuing to climb. So, of necessity, Camp Sumter was expanded to 26 acres. That was a little before the time I wound up in there, all 18 years of me." Frank folded his arms.

"There were, maybe 20,000-25,000 of us in there when I got captured," Frank said, looking seriously at Amos. "You wouldn't *believe* the stench! Dysentary!" Frank's expression contorted. "God! At its worst point there were around 33,000 prisoners, and I'm bettin' at least half of 'em had dysentary. Hell, it's always a problem – before I got captured, dysentery was sometimes as big a problem as the rebs – but back then we'd do something about it. If we camped anywhere for a spell, every two or three days the waste pit'd be burned using crude oil to kill flies, larvae and whatever else was hatchin' down there. Boys still got typhus, cholera, you name it. But at Camp Sumter, they didn't do anything. Stink?" Frank's eyes screwed tight and his nostrils flared as if he'd just inhaled chloride gas. "God almighty it stunk! Some guys said they got used to it. Not me."

"My golly."

"Around 20 feet inside the stockade wall was a little fence the sentries in pigeon roosts called 'the dead line.'" Frank looked off in the distance. "Prisoners were told to stay behind the 'dead line,' the crossing of which meant that the prisoner was dead: if they didn't stay behind the line, sentries would pick 'em off from the roosts. Just leave 'em lying there for a burial detail to pick up. Sometimes no detail would come – too busy with other dead bodies – and the bodies 'd start t' rot." Frank looked back at Amos.

"During the worst time, around 3,000 prisoners a month were dyin' in Camp Sumter, mostly from disease resulting from overcrowding…death was the overcrowding solution. Any inmate still strong enough to use a shovel was assigned to the burial detail." Frank shoved his hands in his pockets as he again looked off in the distance.

"I was fortunate, I guess, to be tossed in toward the end of the war; earlier guys were all in pretty rough shape.

"To make matters worse" continued Frank, "there was a group of prisoners, called themselves the 'Raiders,' who went around taking anything of value other prisoners had, mostly little bits of food. Food was more valuable than gold, there was so damned little of it. Lotta guys were so weak, they couldn't fight back, and some of 'em died from getting rousted by the Raiders."

Amos was listening unastonished, reminded of the tales of hurricane survivors adrift at sea.

"When we saw that, a bunch of us newer boys," continued Frank, looking at the ground, then up at Amos, "still strong enough t' do something, got together and formed our own little police force – called ourselves the Regulators because that place needed some regulatin' – rounded up the Raiders, cleared an area, and put 'em on trial."

Frank looked at Amos who looked back, thinking about the Committee in Murray.

"Trial?" nodded Frank. "Yeah, I know that sounds odd, but we wanted to maintain some semblance of civilization in there. So we voted on a judge, selected a jury – nine guys – had one guy be the prosecuting attorney. The Raiders were their own defense attorneys. We called witnesses, and tried the Raiders fair and square." Frank folded his arms again as he looked at Amos solemnly.

"Those bastards were all found guilty as hell – pretty hard to hide what you did when everyone saw you do it. We made a lot of 'em into a permanent burial detail, kinda like a chain gang. And we hung the worse ones." Frank looked away, thinking. "Bastards." Frank breathed sharply through his nose. "Hangin' was too good for 'em." Amos said nothing, listening.

"The Confederate superintendent, Hennery Wirz – he was from Sweden too," Frank glanced at Amos, "did nothin' to stop us. The Confederates didn't give him the authority, really, to administer justice himself, and he didn't want to go through the Confederate bureaucracy when we were already taking care of it, an' the outcome would be the same. Just like the Union, the Confederacy had its fair share of mindless bureaucrats, you know the type: opposed to doing anything about anything; can't stand innovation, new ideas."

Frank folded his arms again, looked at the building across the street, and said, "There are people, pastor, who sit on committees, and the whole time say: 'It can't be done.' Maybe they think they're actually accomplishing something by saying: 'It can't be done.' Over and over and over. Useless, mindless, wasted bastards. Should have a Camp Sumter for mindless bureaucrats. Hell, anything can be done."

"I agree," said Amos, folding his hands.

"So Wirz figured: why bother? We Regulators were doing a good job. Those boys were found guilty by a jury of their peers. What else could anyone ask for?

"Wirz couldn't use his right arm because of an earlier war wound. That's why he got assigned to prisoner-of-war duty. He evidently served the South to the best of his ability...but had the misfortune to get stuck at Camp Sumter." Frank looked at Amos and held his ands out questioningly. "I don't know what he could have done differently. He was assigned a rotten job, and he was stuck. If he wanted out – which I'm sure he did – no one else wanted in. In comparison to his needs, his funding and supplies were pathetic, made worse when Lincoln and

Grant discontinued prisoner exchanges, expanding prison population on both sides. The North, however, had the resources to take care of prisoners; the South didn't. So whose soldiers got the better end of that deal?" Frank folded his arms; Amos put his hands in his pockets.

"Wirz was a physician in civilian life," continued Frank. "Probably hated his military job, but was no angel with the inmates. Attempting to maintain a necessary level of discipline in what was a catastrophic hell hole, he even executed some inmates, but, well, probably not as many as the Raiders and us Regulators did.

"At the same time, I know from talking to one of the guards who hated it there," Frank held his hands out, "that Wirz was constantly requesting more supplies and food, but received only what the Confederacy had available to give, which was little more than nothing; and at one point, bypassing the Confederate government, Wirz sent five inmates to the North with a direct request to exchange prisoners – which would reduce the Camp Sumter population, probably save a few lives – and they were turned down."

Frank looked at the ground, thinking. He looked up at Amos.

"When the war ended, Union people walked in and saw, and the horrors of Camp Sumter, by then one big cesspool with everyone sick, dying or dead, necessitated someone be made to pay for what they found. Blaming the South who lost in part by being starved into submission wasn't going to satisfy the need for a sacrificial lamb. Prisoner exchanges would have helped tremendously, but no one could put any of the blame on Lincoln who'd just been assassinated. Or Grant, the Union Army hero. The most likely candidate was Wirz. He was put on trial.

"Who testified? No one I knew of. The government's key witness lied about who he was and what he'd seen. He was actually a big-talking, full-of-himself, goddamned Union deserter who'd seen nothin' – but I guess that small fact didn't come out until well after the trial, and everyone had moved on.

"So Wirz was sentenced to be hanged, but I learned they told Wirz that if he implicated Jeff Davis, Wirz's sentence would be commuted. He told them he had no interaction with Davis, and would not lie about it, even to spare his life.

"Three Confederates were tried and executed for war crimes after the war. Wirz? He was one of 'em. So, everyone's happy," said Frank, his voice sodden with cynicism.

Frank turned away, thinking about it.

"Camp Sumter. When the stockade walls were built, civility, decency, and truth stood well away; probably had their own Deadline." Frank nodded at Amos who, listening, felt emotions he had unknowingly repressed, and had not felt since 1865. His stomach was anxious, as if attempting to hide, escape, and his face was expressionless except for newly hardened eyes.

"Deadline. Tells you something about the Lava Bed," said Frank. "C'mon, pastor." Frank expelled a short breath. "Let's go for a little walk."

The two of them started across muddy Yesler Way, still used to skid logs to

Henry Yesler's Mill on the Seattle waterfront.

"Anything built south of the Deadline," continued Frank, "is considered part of the 'Lava Bed.'" Frank looked at Amos. "You've heard the phrase 'red light district'?"

"Of course."

"That phrase started in Dodge City, Kansas, where railroad workers, in order to discourage intruders, would hang brakemen's red lanterns outside the door."

"I thought it had its origins in France."

"Nope. Started here in the U S of A. The Lava Bed is the red light district of Seattle and, as is always the case, in addition to harboring individuals who are employed in gambling and sexually immoral pursuits, it also attracts a variety of seasoned criminals. Not such a good place to be late at night."

"So those buildings are all brothels?" said Pastor Nordquist, looking at all the buildings and thinking of Sodom and Gomorrah. "My golly."

"Yes but no, pastor. Let me tell you something. Not all 'brothels' are brothels. Prostitution's fee simple estate encompasses four categories in descending order: parlor houses, brothels, box houses, and, at the bottom, semi-isolated cabins known simply as 'the Line.'"

"Molly B'Dam'?" asked Frank. Pastor Nordquist glanced at Frank. "Those cabins where she and her girls live and work? Those are called 'the Line.' Molly works the Line in Murray. That's the bottom of the hierarchy. At the top are parlor houses."

Frank doesn't know about Molly, Amos thought. "What are parlor houses, exactly?" Amos asked, curious.

"There aren't any in Murray, pastor," said Frank good naturedly as they walked. "Parlor houses are lavishly-furnished, former private residences in larger cities. Patrons are often entertained with music, served wine and, upon waking in the morning, find their clothes were cleaned and pressed during the night. Girls who reside in parlor houses are attractive and relatively refined, accommodating parlor house clientele who typically consist of influential businessmen and politicians with demanding tastes."

Frank looked at Amos and winked; Amos looked back and said nothing.

"While a few girls marry those businessmen and politicians, for most girls relationships are just business."

"Does Seattle have any parlor houses?" asked Amos.

"Oh, yes," said Frank, wiping his mouth with the back of his hand. "Seattle has an elegant parlor house frequented by members of the city council."

Amos looked incredulously at Frank as Frank laughed for a second before his expression turned solemn.

"Politicians with clout are given reduced rates. Since those same politicians are often paid a stipend as the 'cost of doing business,' it's all a matter of accounting. They have their tentacles wrapped around everything. I have to deal with them too."

"'Deal with them'?"

"I pay unofficial fees to city officials so I can continue to sell hotel and restaurant supplies." Frank's eyes narrowed and the ridges of his upper and lower teeth exposed themselves as he looked obliquely at Amos. "City hall. No different in Seattle than anywhere else. Arrogant, greedy, exploitive, grafting, insensitive, inflexible, unimaginative, stupid, incompetent, manipulative, senseless, ungodly and corrupt – a ravenous spider in the center of an expansive, expensive web, sucking blood out of the citizenry." Frank stared straight ahead. "A racket," he summarized acidly.

Amos's expression was a combination of incredulity and curiosity, but Frank did not want to elaborate.

"Molly B'Dam," continued Frank, straightening his lapels and looking obliquely at Amos as they walked, "*should* be a parlor house madam. Actual parlor house madams are often…"

"Frank, I hate to tell you this," Amos interrupted, "but Molly passed away a few weeks ago."

Frank's eyes flashed wide, his jaw went slack. "What?"

"Yah, I felt terrible when I found out."

"How did she die?" asked Frank, stopping and looking seriously at Amos.

"Sickness. Never went away. I don't know specifically what."

Frank looked at Amos somberly. "That's a real tragedy. She was a good woman. You know, I was about to head back over there. New establishments in Kellogg and Wallace." The two men turned and walked in silence, reminiscing, before Amos turned to Frank.

"She's with the Lord, Frank."

"If anyone is, she is," Frank nodded.

For a moment the two men walked without talking until Amos broke the silence.

"Frank, you were saying?"

"What?"

"Parlor houses."

"Ah. Yeah." Looking straight ahead expressionlessly as they walked, Frank sighed as he released the thought of Molly Burdan and returned to the moment.

"Well, parlor house madams are active in the community. Public relations are ongoing, and civic affairs are frequently on their agenda, occasionally being held at the parlor house." Frank nodded at Amos for emphasis. "In growing communities with few women, the most outwardly genteel ladies – like Molly – are often found in parlor houses. Their expense certifies their upper class status. The madams of parlor houses are *grand dames* in a lot of towns out west."

"I imagine."

"Since most towns can't support more than one or two high-end parlor houses, brothels, the next tier, are more prevalent."

"This is quite an education," said Amos.

"What do you think a brothel is?" asked Frank.

"I'm not certain I want to guess," said Amos.

"Well, pastor, they're probably about what you would expect. That's one there," said Frank, pointing toward a three-story building a block away. "Outwardly, brothels appear to be either small hotels or small apartments over saloons," Frank explained as he glanced at Amos who continued to look at the t-story building, "or rooming houses with community social rooms."

Amos thought the building looked innocuous, but wasn't surprised. It's no different with people, he again thought.

"Brothel madams and their girls," continued Frank, "are less sophisticated, less attractive, and more negotiable than their parlor house sisters. They work longer hours with lower class patronage from whom they receive more grief for less money." Frank nodded, thinking.

"'Box houses.' You said box houses. What's a box house?" asked Amos.

"Box houses are big business, Amos. Box houses are variety theaters…and I do mean 'variety.' You see that building over there, the Bijou," Frank pointed to a theater building with elaborate fenestration, "and that one, the Theatre Comique…and that one over there, the Palace?" Frank pointed at each as they walked. "Those are box houses. And that one down there," Frank again pointed, "that's the Illahee. It was the first one in Seattle. In the beginning, the proprietor traded some blankets to the local *Tyee*, or chief, in order to borrow *tokatee klooch*, or pretty women. I guess that made the chief a…well, never mind," smiled Frank. Pastor Nordquist's left eyebrow rose briefly as he looked at Frank, but he said nothing, returning his attention to the box houses; they made the brothel look insignificant. "They look much more elaborate, important, than brothels," said Amos as they walked. "Why would they be beneath brothels in the hierarchy?"

"I'll explain," said Frank. "A typical box house has a concert hall with a glitzy burlesque/vaudeville stage at one end," said Frank, "and a noisy saloon area at the other. In between the saloon and the stage is a smoke-filled casino where sporting men drink cheap liquor, play cards and make the acquaintance of the nearest 'seamstress,' as most of the girls call themselves when in polite company."

Frank and Amos walked along the street to a larger theater building where some girls were outside bantering with men.

The reason they're called box houses is…" Frank paused. "I need to call on the People's Theater manager, pastor. Let's go inside. I'll only be a few minutes… just following up on a previous order to make sure he got everything he wanted. You don't get repeat orders if you don't service your clients. You can make yourself scarce, pastor; just stand near the door," said Frank as they walked inside. "I'll be back in a moment."

Frank hadn't finished his explanation. Pastor Nordquist stood and looked around. The dark, smoke-filled room smelled rank. Four men at a poker table sat motionlessly, staring straight ahead or obliquely, not speaking. One of the four men, a slender man with a heavy mustache, leather coat and a black John Bull hat, was staring darts across the table at a heavy, balding man wearing a gray vest and bow tie. The slender man had a relatively small amount of cash on the table while the heavy, balding man had accumulated extensive winnings.

With a look of defiance the slender man was going to bet all he had left.

Pastor Nordquist sensed the man was in trouble already and, by betting the house, could either get out of trouble or exacerbate his difficulty. From the mezzanine stairs a girl watched the game without expression. Pastor Nordquist sensed she knew the men and was weighing how to capitalize on the heavy man's luck.

Below her was a striped-shirted piano player perfunctorily banging "tonk" on the keys while thinking of something unrelated to what he was doing. He wore sleeve garters on both arms because his shirt sleeves would otherwise slide down too far.

On the other side of the room, off to the side of the stage, was an indiscreet dance floor where some men, after a few drinks and a game of cards, were discussing mutual interests with some of the girls. While holding one another, most weren't trying to dance.

A girl walked toward Amos with a pleasant expression, and he nodded formally. She kept walking; Amos didn't look like someone who needed to pay for it.

He looked up at the mezzanine floors. There were rows of cubicles on both upper and lower mezzanines. Frank returned and stood next to Amos for a moment.

"Was he satisfied with the order?" asked Amos.

"Yes. In fact, he needed some more things. That's usually the case. Another reason to stop by."

"Good thing," agreed Amos without conviction. "You were saying…"

"What?"

"Box houses."

"Oh, yeah. Well, what you're looking at is entertainment. Card games, stage shows, music, and female…companionship," said Frank, looking at Amos out of the corner of his eye. "It's all about entertainment."

Frank pointed toward the mezzanine.

"You see those cubicles up on the mezzanine? The mezzanine is where entertainment reaches its climax," he said and laughed. "Privacy is minimal. Business is business. Those cubicles are the 'boxes' and, therefore, this," said Frank with a sweeping gesture, "is the 'box house.'"

"I see."

"Amos, as you also can see, box house girls range from attractive to less-than-attractive. They don't get paid a lot, but if they work hard, they can still make decent money. How? Get 'em in and get 'em out." Frank looked up at the first mezzanine. "Those cubicles see a lot of activity." He looked at Amos. "The formula is simple: the more men, the more money."

With his convictions about the relationships between men, women, and happiness, to Amos the formula was repulsive.

"Do they like what they do," asked Amos, studying the woman on the stairwell, "or is it similar to Murray?"

"From what the owners tell me, the girls that stay a while stay for a long while, but in general, turnover is frequent. Women get work in places like these because most have few other options. Let's face it, Amos, it's not a happy profession," said Frank. "Although suicides are infrequent," added Frank without expression. Amos turned his head and looked at Frank. "Let's go back outside," said Frank.

The two of them walked outside and headed toward Frank's next sales call.

"And the law, such as it must be, doesn't mind any of this?" asked Amos, looking about as they walked down the street to the Theatre Comique. "I would have thought Seattle would be much different than Murray."

"More like 'much worse," answered Frank. "Thriving prostitution and gambling, while frowned upon by the better element, are typical. San Francisco. Portland. Tacoma. Seattle. When a buck can be made, prostitution and gambling are not only allowed but promoted and protected by public servants with no reservations about graft. The owners pay those guys pretty well. The Seattle Chief of Police not only gets paid a bundle but, I'm told, has muscled silent interests in several establishments."

"You're kidding."

"Nope," said Frank. "He sends his men around to collect for him. The Seattle Police Department has become his personal collection agency."

They reached the entrance to the Theatre Comique.

"Do you want to come in or wait outside?"

"I'll wait here for you," said Amos.

Frank turned and went inside as Amos stood aside the glitzy Theatre Comique entrance, looking at a comparatively drab, smaller, brothel across the street.

Wednesday, October 3, 1888

Ever since the incident with the Russians when he was eighteen, Amos Nordquist learned to control his anger and was normally patient and forgiving. It was not that he never became angry but, rather, on those rare occasions when a display of temper was justified, he would use it, not lose it. When he used it, the extent of Amos's anger, especially evident in his countenance, could be frightening. On the evening of October 3, 1888 in the heat of the moment, Amos's repressed anger blew the lid off.

67

October 3, 1888

Early in his ministry Amos came to the conclusion that while original sin was the beginning of sinful behavior, the remaining history of human behavior finds little original sinning – regardless of how depraved, debauched, shameless, or cruel, it has been done before. To Amos Nordquist, the straight and narrow way was neither lighted nor paved, and at this stage of his career, need not be, because he could walk it blindfolded while describing long-since repetitive behavior on either side.

As in Murray, Amos had no reservations about mingling with sinners in Seattle. He made several visits to Lava Bed establishments in an attempt to befriend and redirect wayward young women and their clientele. His efforts were largely unsuccessful. If his immediate success was greater, he would have been shown the door by more than one proprietor. As long as his presence did not hurt business, no one cared. As in Murray, he conscientiously attempted witnessing without becoming a bother. Since most men and women he approached were unwilling to converse at any length, opportunities were minimal for advancement to a bother.

There was one notable exception, however. A woman young in years but ancient in demeanor would readily speak at length with Amos. Her intellect vaguely reminded Amos of the Queen of Murray. She was much smaller, however; fragile and not as attractive. She had no regal air; in fact, no air at all. When not on duty in a brothel where she split her earnings with the establishment, on days off she occasionally worked the streets. If a client took her to his place, she would charge less, but keep whatever she made.

Shortly before sunset, Pastor Nordquist saw her leaning against a wall near the intersection of Commercial and Yesler. He found it remarkable that, although only leaning motionlessly against a wooden wall, staring straight ahead, she could amplify what she was and why she was there. How does that work? Pastor Nordquist wondered as he walked toward her. Although many others were walking by, as he came closer she sensed his presence and turned her head toward him.

"Mary Sullivan," Pastor Nordquist warmly greeted the young woman as he approached, "how are you getting along?"

How am I getting along? she asked herself as she looked at the street. I'm a whore; he's a pastor. Does he really want to know that? "How should I be getting along?" she responded in a neutral voice.

"You know the answer to that," Pastor Nordquist said. "It isn't like we have never spoken before. You should be getting along somewhere else in a different occupation, don't you think? As I have said, it would be very good for you if you were in a position where you could meet a good Christian man and settle down. You would be much happier. We both know that."

"You're correct," she answered. "However, I do what I can do." Her eyes shifted between Amos and the street. "This certainly isn't what I planned." She looked at men walking by. Pastor Nordquist was bad for business.

"What did you plan?"

Mary continued to lean against the wall, inwardly debating whether to tell the truth that seemed so distant, or make up a more plausible lie. Why not tell the truth? she thought. Who could possibly care? Her quiet laugh died quickly and she looked up at Pastor Nordquist. "To please my husband," she said, turning her head toward the street. "I planned…to please."

Her eyes again shifted toward Amos, and back to the street.

"I pleased him so much, he left me for another woman. As you know, I'm a divorcée," she added with cynical sweetness, bitterness in her focused eyes, as she stared toward the opposite side of the street.

As her eyes slowly softened, she again looked at Amos. While she did not want to miss a trick, a customer, there was part of her that enjoyed her brief conversations with Pastor Nordquist, a decent man interested only in her welfare. Among men, he was the exception.

"A lot of us girls have been married," she said. "We all tried to do the same thing. Obviously with the same results." Her voice was soft and thin. She looked up at Pastor Nordquist neutrally.

"I loved my husband," she added without apparent emotion. For a moment she looked at Pastor Nordquist intently.

Changing her mind, she returned her gaze toward the street.

"For as much good as it did either one of us, why did I do it at all?" she asked. She paused, looking downward, reasoning to herself. "We all do that," she continued. "Women just do that." She sighed subtly, the sound barely audible. "It's a mistake we all make. In the end, we love too much by loving at all."

"No one loves too much," Pastor Nordquist countered as the sun drifted downward toward the Olympic Mountain skyline behind him. "And the Bible says that there is no greater love than to lay down one's life for another. Jesus did this for you, Mary. His death resulted in your salvation."

"I've never met him. Does he spend time south of Yesler?"

She looked up at Pastor Nordquist whose expression was neutral.

"I'm sorry, sir," she responded. "When I hear you say things like that, I get this feeling, almost like someone pushes a button in me, and I think, 'nonsense.'"

Mary shrugged her shoulders. "I know you're a sincere man – maybe the only sincere man I know – certainly the only man who cares about me. Maybe it's not nonsense, but that's not what I feel." Mary's chest rose and fell.

"Sir, you want me to meet a good Christian man. But I don't need to go to church to meet your men of God. They cross the Deadline every night."

Mary waited for Pastor Nordquist's reaction. He stood listening.

"The girls and I get to see the other side of the double standard," said Mary, looking at men walking by. "They come down here with their hypocritical smirks – that syrupy expression that says, 'Oh, everything is so lovely', while their hearts rot with deceit. I hate that. Later, after they've had a few drinks, I also hate their drunken eyes rubbering from one girl to another. Like that Earl. He goes to your church."

Mary looked up at Pastor Nordquist.

"He was upstairs last night."

Mary saw Amos's features stiffen, and sensed dark clouds gathering. Amos knew Earl's wife, Virginia, was devoted, a good mother and worthy of much more – spiritually, emotionally and physically – than Earl provided. Earl's father, Amos knew, was a grifter and philanderer who drank heavily and, passing out one night, fell face-first into a swollen side gutter, his death from drowning when Earl was 12. Amos was afraid Earl was becoming his father. Pastor Nordquist carried many burdens for his congregation and Earl's wayward venery would be another.

"I get satisfaction knowing," continued Mary, "they are more jaded than I. Men. In varying degrees, all men have the same problem. Men need to have their lust continually satisfied, but are…never seem satisfied with the passion, the love available right before them."

"I know at moments that may seem true," responded Pastor Nordquist. "Many men are strong physically, but weak morally. When it comes to their responsibility to women, they fall short. It is unfair, however, to men in general and to you, to believe all men are this way. Many women in this town thank God daily for blessing them with loving, devoted husbands. Even if it were not so, it is still true that Jesus died for you, that he is alive and continually intercedes with the Father on your behalf. If, to this, you think 'nonsense', my prayer is that you will reconsider your salvation with an open mind."

Pastor Nordquist stepped directly in front of Mary, blocking her view of the street, and looked down at her.

"Are you happy?" he asked pointedly. "Do you have inner peace?" They both knew the answers. Again, the responsive pain in her eyes spoke to him. "If," said Pastor Nordquist, "you were to say 'yes,' then I would also say 'nonsense.' Sin never satisfies. These men will take what you sell, giving only money in return, and the life you now lead will slowly destroy you. What I sell requires no money," said Pastor Nordquist, "will bring you inner peace, and assures eternal salvation." Pastor Nordquist studied Mary's eyes. "What choice will you make, Mary?"

Mary said nothing in response, but continued to stand motionlessly, her hands clasped behind her. While she enjoyed engaging Pastor Nordquist whom she genuinely respected, in the back of her mind a voice whispered that continued conversation was bad for business. For a moment, she ignored the voice, thinking about her life to this point, wondering where it was going.

"Why did God make me?" she wondered softly out loud. She folded her arms around herself, suddenly cold. "Why was I born? I feel like a..."

"You can leave," said Pastor Nordquist. "You can go with me this...'

"Not today," she interrupted a little too loudly, her hands falling to her side. Catching herself, she looked up at Amos and repeated in her normal tone of voice. "Not today."

"Then when? If not today, when?" asked Pastor Nordquist firmly.

She momentarily put the back of her right hand over her forehead. As she looked down the street again, a well-dressed, middle-aged man walking in their direction caught her eye. Her hand fell as her expression became very pleasant, inviting. Pastor Nordquist saw the changed expression, looked at the middle-aged man for longer than was comfortable for either of them and, controlling his gathering anger, returned his attention to Mary.

"Could you leave now?" she quickly whispered, continuing to look pleasantly at the approaching man.

"Very well, then," concluded Pastor Nordquist. "As you wish." The man stopped on the edge of the busy sidewalk about 20 feet away, waiting. "I look forward to talking to you again soon."

Frustrated and angry, Amos glared at the man, but knew that to stay could destroy the inroads he made with Mary. It would be better to return tomorrow. "Thank you for your time," said Amos politely.

"You're welcome." She glanced up for a split second as the sun drifted closer to the Olympic Mountains skyline. "Thank you."

Pastor Nordquist nodded, adjusted his hat, and walked away, inwardly praying for Mary. Amos knew that if he was doing his job conscientiously, rejection would summarize a major part of his job description, and he knew this when God called him. God's call, he thought. The opposite of rejection.

As another part of his job, he would need to talk with Earl.

68

Certain Lava Bed clientele were, as Mary just indicated, also members of Pastor Nordquist's congregation. They appreciated Pastor Nordquist's devotion to duty, but did not want that devotion interfering with their sinning. Whether out of traditional habit or to enhance social standing, they attended church on Sunday morning, and attended to more worldly activities during the remainder of the week. When Pastor Nordquist met with these men privately in a forceful effort to change their ways, all promised they would. And several did.

Walking northward on the east side of 2nd Avenue, as Amos approached the intersection he saw Earl, the wayward parishioner of whom Mary spoke, beginning to cross the intersection ahead.

Earl did not see the already frustrated, angry pastor, the "big preacher," who, rather than also crossing the intersection, backed up against the side of a building and waited as Earl approached.

"Earl!" Pastor Nordquist shouted loudly.

"Wha? Oh, ah, hello, pastor." Earl stopped obligatorily for a moment, wanting to continue, to leave. "Uh, Pastor, I'd like to talk but I'm supposed t' be…"

"Earl," Pastor Nordquist interrupted, "I understand that last night you were someplace you should not have been."

His heart suddenly filled with guilt, Earl's face went blank, his eyes becoming expressionless. "I was home with Virginia last night, Pastor," responded Earl quietly, his mouth slightly open.

Pastor Nordquist took a step closer to Earl.

"That's not what I heard."

"Well, I don't know what you heard," said Earl, looking about for any familiar faces, hoping there were none. "And I don't know who said it. But it ain't true."

"What isn't true?" asked Pastor Nordquist.

"Well, Pastor, you know…" Earl searched for non-incriminating words, "… what you said."

"Earl, where were you last night?" asked Pastor Nordquist.

Earl took off his hat and scratched his head, his face taking on an orange hue as the sun began slowly dropping behind the Olympic Mountains. Trying to think of an answer, Earl's eyes bounced about like little fishing floats as his pursed mouth peaked out from behind his walrus mustache.

"Uh, Pastor, I don't know what you heard but, well, whatever it was, it weren't true." Earl glanced up at Pastor Nordquist for a split second before his eyes shifted away. Earl's eyes took on an ugly light as his heart began to fill with defensive sullenness. He put his hat back on, adding three inches to his shadow on the wall behind him.

"I'm going to ask you again," said Pastor Nordquist, "and this time I want the truth." His upper and lower teeth showing slightly, Amos formed the subsequent words slowly and deliberately: "Where – were – you – last – night?"

Earl fidgeted and put his hands on his hips, fists closed. He glanced up at Pastor Nordquist and off in the distance again.

"Well, all right," Earl muttered. "We both know where I was."

"You were down at the Lava Bed." said Pastor Nordquist loudly.

Upon hearing the words "…the Lava Bed" stated incriminatingly, two passersby, curious, stopped at a short distance to listen.

Earl's inherent self-righteousness was being severely challenged. Earl wanted to leave. His jaw clenched, Earl said nothing.

"You weren't home with Virginia," Pastor Nordquist added.

Earl sullenly glanced from the two onlookers to Pastor Nordquist and then to the street.

"Earl," asked Pastor Nordquist loudly, "what did you find in the Lava Bed that was better than your bed at home?!"

No response. Overhearing, and seeing two men already listening, two other passersby stopped to listen.

"Someone who loves you more?" asked Pastor Nordquist. "Someone who loves your children more? Someone who takes care of your home? Someone who gives of herself and wants love and security – not money – in return?!"

Earl remained defiantly silent. In part from curiosity as to what caused the others, already standing and listening, to gather, and in part to what Pastor Nordquist just loudly asked, more people – men and women – stopped to listen and watch.

"Well, now, I am also a man," added Pastor Nordquist, raising his eyebrows and folding his arms as he looked down at Earl. "If I was to go down to the Lava Bed, what should I look for?! What thing – that I don't have at home – should I expect to find?!"

Earl looked at Pastor Nordquist and decided to talk, if just to get this over with. Those in the small crowd leaned forward to better hear the response. Curious about why a small group had gathered, another pedestrian stopped, and then another.

"A chance t' cut loose," Earl retorted, looking up at Amos. "Don't you ever feel like doin' a little…wanderin'? You say you're also a man. Well, don't you ever get those feelings like…you just want to have…a good time? Ain't nothin' destructive intended by it. Just a night out…havin' a few…some fun with the boys, a little…gamblin' and…" Earl stopped himself. For a few seconds he didn't breathe before taking a deep breath and letting the air rapidly escape – making it obvious he'd been drinking.

"'And' what?" asked Pastor Nordquist.

Earl looked up at Pastor Amos annoyed. "What do you think, Pastor?" asked Earl evasively, unconsciously squeezing his fists.

"A woman," responded Pastor Nordquist.

"Yeah," said Earl, momentarily relaxing. "A woman. Jane, Jean, Joan, somethin'. Don't know if I'll ever see her again. Just wanted…somethin' new. Different. Keep things from gittin' stale at home, y' understand. Nothin' permanent. Just a quick change of scenery, y' might say. Variety. The spice of life. It's why sheiks have harems. So I did…what I did."

"If a man loves and cherishes his wife, he has a harem of one," said Amos angrily. "No woman gets 'stale.' You don't understand that. Worse, last night you put your family in jeopardy, Earl."

"How do I jeopardize my family by lettin' off a little steam? Seems to me I done just the opposite."

Amos found conversations like this incredible. How is it, he asked himself, some church-going people have so few spiritual convictions? To what church – if they went to church – did Earl's father take him during Earl's formative years, and what did they teach? It's obvious what they didn't teach.

"For at least one night, probably more," explained Amos, "you left your wife, Virginia, for a prostitute. And, in so doing, you corrupted the bond between Virginia and yourself, further diminished what love and respect you have for Virginia, and increased the temptation to do it again in a few nights! That temptation hangs around. It always does. And if continued, you will dig a hole out of which you cannot climb."

Amos intimidatingly stepped closer to Earl and continued looking down at him, struggling to maintain his composure in view of Earl's nonchalant attitude. The growing, surrounding crowd inched closer. Stonewalling, Earl folded his arms again and, as if nonplused, looked up the street. Pastor Nordquist was uncomfortably close, but Earl did not move.

"Figgered God 'd forgive me." Earl glanced at the listening, watching people, and back at Pastor Nordquist. "What d'ya think, Pastor? Think God 'll forgive me? Suspect He'll forgive me a lot sooner 'n you'll forgive me."

"Have you asked God to forgive you?" asked Pastor Nordquist.

"No," answered Earl, shifting his weight from one leg to the other. "Not yet."

"He knows your heart, of course," Pastor Nordquist stated in light of Earl's lack of sincerity. "Lying to God is pointless."

"Pastor," Earl turned his head to the other side and wiped his forehead with his shirtsleeve, "I'm about ready to end this here conversation." Earl stood up straight, hands at his side, and looked directly at Amos. "You let God take care of forgivin', okay? I'll worry about me 'n the Lord. I figure that someone who preaches forgiveness oughta practice it."

Amos's anger was like little bubbles first appearing in the bottom of a pot prior to boiling. And I figure," said Pastor Nordquist, "anyone who stands before God and says marriage vows should also practice them!"

As Earl continued to give no indication of caring. Amos's stomach began to churn. "I also think that men should not intentionally sin!" added Pastor Nordquist, even more angrily. Annoyed at Earl's self-righteous subterfuge, Amos's tone of voice became heated. "I don't think a man should be one thing one moment and another the next! And I don't think immoral behavior is ever any less than destructive! It may seem free and easy but, in the long run, immorality demands and always receives recompense! Just like the woman you were with last night!" Pastor Nordquist glared at Earl. "Your wife deserved that affection! Your family needed that money! And you, as a man, need the subsequent respect and self-respect!"

His hands again at his side, Earl stood uncomfortably leaning in the direction he wanted to go, but was frozen in place, knowing he would have to endure whatever followed.

"And I'll tell you something else, Earl! Unforgiven sin is never left unpunished! It's not a matter of 'if' but 'how' and 'when.' When do you want to be punished, Earl? And how?!" Shifting his weight, his back nearly against the wooden building wall, Earl folded his arms sullenly, looked up at Pastor Nordquist, then the listening crowd, then the boardwalk, and, lips tight, waited.

Pastor Nordquist wanted to throttle Earl whose attitude was the same ignorant attitude, and responses the same ignorant responses stated as if they were novel ideas, that Pastor Nordquist heard many times before.

"And as far as forgiveness goes," Amos continued angrily, "in my position I am constantly forgiving! Daily! Being a pastor is a very difficult profession!"

When Earl skeptically looked up the street, his expression questioning Amos's last statement, Amos's anger came to a boil.

"The world," said Pastor Nordquist, his voice louder, "doesn't like men like me – who remind men like you what sin is! People don't want to hear the truth about right and wrong! Earl, you who know so much, what do you know about me?!"

Earl's mouth was partially open and his eyes glassy as he ground away on his chewing tobacco while looking down the street with a desultory, bovine expression. Earl still didn't give a damn, and his dullard demeanor made Amos nearly apoplectic.

As the sun set behind the Olympic Mountains, black piranha teeth biting into a blood orange sky, Amos pulled hard on the emotional bridle keeping his temper in check as it wrenched and jerked, but the fetters suddenly snapped, and teeth bared wolf-like, with hands like vice clamps Amos grabbed Earl by the shirt, yanked him several inches off the ground and violently slammed him up against the building wall, pinning him in place.

"Do you think I take satisfaction from the disappointments I encounter?!" Amos shouted in Earl's face as Earl quailed. Without putting Earl down, teeth still bared, Amos pulled Earl face-to-face like Earl was a rag doll, and again slammed Earl against the wall, causing Earl to cry out in pain.

"Uuhhh!"

"You don't know what I see, what I hear!"

As more strangers stopped to see what was happening, those in front obscured the view, but the rear of the crowd could still hear. Amos's face, inches from Earl's, was seething. Filled with fear, mouth open, Earl's eyes were huge as he looked back, his boots four inches off the ground, a sinner in the hands of an angry pastor. To emphasize each subsequent, shouted statement, Amos again violently slammed Earl against the wall without letting go.

"You don't know the heartache this job carries with it!"

"Uuhhh!" groaned wide-eyed Earl as his body hit the wall.

"You don't know the patience that is required when I see the same sinful behavior bring the same painful consequences over and over again!"

"Uuhhh!"

"It's bad enough that men place themselves in harm's way by intentionally sinning. It is even worse when, in doing so, they harm their families!"

"Uuhhh!" Earl's hat flew off to one side as he gritted his teeth in pain.

"Earl!" shouted Pastor Nordquist, holding Earl off the ground directly in front of his face. "Do you think that Virginia has no idea what you are doing?! No idea where you have been at night?! Do you think she is that stupid?! Do you think that she does not perceive that you think she is that stupid?!"

"Uuhhh!"

As Pastor Nordquist angrily spoke, slamming Earl against the wall, more men and women joined the side and rear of the crowd. Others at a distance, attracted by the gathering crowd and the commotion, turned and walked rapidly toward the crowd to see what was going on.

"Earl!" shouted Pastor Nordquist, teeth clenched, ignoring the crowd. "There are consequences for doing what God does not *allow*!" As Earl bounced off the building behind him, and Amos's voice bounced off surrounding buildings, Earl again groaned in pain.

"Uuhhh!"

"Do you think the commandment against adultery was a mistake?!

'Uuhhh!"

"That the God who created both men and women doesn't understand what he created?!"

"Uuhhh!" Amos stopped, holding Earl off the ground six inches in front of Amos's face.

"Well?!!!"

At that moment, something emotionally shook Amos as the normally still, small voice inside Amos became almost audible.

"*Put – him – down.*"

As Amos's eyes and features instantly softened, Amos let go, and Earl dropped like a sack of grain, losing his balance, bouncing against the wooden building wall as he fell to the ground.

Earl staggered to his feet, wide-eyed, open-mouthed, cowering, unused to seeing the angry side of a usually mild-mannered pastor – isn't that how pastors are supposed to act? From what Pastor Nordquist said, the on-lookers knew the big man was a minister. Frozen, perspiring, Earl looked up, fearing what Pastor Nordquist was going to do next.

"You stay out of the Lava Bed, Earl!" Amos ordered. "And you stay home with your wife! And don't insult my intelligence with this 'keep things from gettin' stale' nonsense!"

Earl saw the wrath of Amos, something some in Göteborg, but no one in Murray – or Minnesota – had seen. As Amos stood over Earl, the surrounding men and women waited breathlessly for what would happen next. Was it possible "Earl" might get the hell beat out of him, even if the big guy was a pastor?

"I spend my waking moments," added Amos, "spreading the truth of God, and I get sick and tired of ungrateful people who are so stupid that they continue to intentionally sin, destroying themselves and those around them!" Amos took a deep breath. "I get sick of it!"

Pastor Nordquist glared silently in anger at Earl who was prepared to bolt and run, but whose feet felt like they were set in cement.

Amos let his hands fall at his side. Still cowering, Earl, who had gone through the motions of being a Christian without giving Christ much thought, looked up at Amos. The pedestrians looked hard, waiting.

Earl's mouth was dry and he suddenly felt like a perfidious little boy caught torturing a small animal. He had no excuse. He felt guilt, stupidity, disappointment.

"Pastor, I was lettin' off a little steam." Earl looked to the side as one of the surrounding men folded his arms. "It was wrong of me." Then came the Great Rationalization. "But I warn't the only one."

"And who else is doing this?"

Earl stepped to his left, looking off into the distance. The bystanders waited for Earl to sell-out his friends, if they were. Earl's mouth was again open slightly. His shoulders drooped, and his head fell.

"Pastor, for right now…c'n I just take care of my own…problem before I get others involved?"

"If you promise me you will take care of the problem – go home to Virginia, tell her you love her, that she is an amazing woman, that she means more than anything in the world to you, that you are the man in her life, and then, Earl, show her you are a man! Tell her honestly what you have been doing, tell her you've made a terrible mistake, and ask her forgiveness! If she forgives you, do everything within your ability to show her you love her. Daily. Hourly. Minute by minute. It won't be easy, Earl. If you aren't sure what to do, find me; I will give you direction."

Earl's eyes became wider and the perspiration on his forehead became more pronounced even in the growing darkness. The surrounding men and women listened.

"Pastor, I don't know," he responded in disbelief. "That's askin' a lot."

"'Askin' a lot,'" Amos said disgustedly. "Yes, asking forgiveness is never as easy as the act needing forgiveness."

Amos, his temper still simmering, put his hands in his pockets and glowered at Earl.

"Earl, do you have any idea of what you've been doing to Virginia?"

Pastor Nordquist stared at Earl for a moment, and lowered his head without taking his eyes off Earl. His voice softened. The men and women leaned forward.

"I have seen this time and time again," said Pastor Nordquist. "Even if she suspected nothing, your deceitful actions, your betrayal, will cause unhappiness. But invariably she suspects, and through you, the marriage, which could have been the most wonderful thing you have ever known, has instead been severely weakened, frayed. To restore that bond between you and Virginia, if you are a man, you will tell her what you have done, and sincerely ask her forgiveness."

"I don't know what she'll do," said Earl nervously.

"What have you already done?" asked Pastor Nordquist, his eyebrows knitted. "This will not go away of its own accord…that is not how things work. It is your responsibility. You cannot leave this unattended. You need to exercise the will to stop this now. Even if she did not already know, the damage will be wreaked in some other way. I do not know how this will specifically happen. I only know it will. It always does. Always. Changes in you – a million different things – come into play. What you have done will have consequences," Pastor Nordquist said adamantly. "To obviate those consequences, you must take responsibility for what you have done. And this is never easy; it's hard. Either you have the courage to do it or you do not."

"She'll get mad as hell."

"Cheated wives do that."

Pastor Nordquist paused, glancing at the surrounding men and women before addressing Earl again. The expressions on the faces of some men were blank, telling, while some women looked back with veiled gratitude.

"Go home," commanded Pastor Nordquist, "and do what I have told you to do. Then, on Sunday after church, I want to meet with both you and Virginia… and, if you have not had the courage to confess and ask forgiveness – from both God and Virginia – I will help you."

As if frozen in place, Earl at first stood motionlessly looking back at Pastor Nordquist. The crowd was also motionless.

Earl turned, took a few steps, but stopped. He turned back slightly and looked at Pastor Nordquist. Without expression, Pastor Nordquist nodded. Along with the bystanders, he watched Earl take a deep breath, turn and walk into the evening.

As the crowd slowly began to disperse, each with their own thoughts, several women furtively studied Pastor Nordquist. While leaving, one male acquaintance quietly asked another, "Who was that?"

"Name's Nordquist. Pastor up on the hill."

The first man glanced at Pastor Nordquist as the two men walked away and, after a prolonged pause while looking at the ground, his succinct, "Mmmh," spoke volumes.

69

December 24, 1888: Christmas Eve

In the kitchen, Anna and Esther bantered while planning a *pepparkakorhus*, a gingerbread house. The previous evening they made the dough from flour, butter, molasses, cinnamon, sugar, salt, pepper, and ginger, let it sit in the cooler overnight, and as Anna and Esther flattened the dough for the walls and roof, they discussed fenestration options once the residence was erected. The *pepparkakorhus* would again be the coffee table centerpiece with chimney, shingles, windows, doors, porches, steps…and residents.

"How many gingerbread men should we have on the porch and in the 'yard'?" asked Esther.

"Don't overdo it," said Anna as she deftly placed a few finishing touches with her rolling pin.

"Yes," replied Esther with an undercurrent of restiveness, "but maybe that doesn't apply to Christmas gingerbread houses."

Having read of the Tower Building under construction in New York, and which would eventually reach 11 stories, Esther wanted to create an extraordinary *pepparkakorhus*, but perfection bridled by simplicity would require more discipline she wanted to exercise.

Combined kitchen aromas of hot cider and Inga's *pepparnotter* cookies baking on the wood-heated stovetop visited a lively yuletide ambiance on the Nordquist living room. Adding to the aroma was the fragrant, eight-foot, Douglas fir that Angus cut from the forest edge by Lake Washington that morning, placing it in the corner of the living room at a short distance from the fireplace. In addition, fir boughs were festooned above the living room entrance and above the mantle.

Logs crackled in the fireplace, throwing a golden glow across the living room. As her *pepparnotter* cookies and *julekage* Christmas bread began baking in the kitchen, quiet Inga walked to the front door, stepped outside into the cold air of the dark front porch and hung a sheaf of grain on a corner porch post, a Swedish tradition enabling neighborhood birds to have Christmas Eve dinner as well. Escaping the cold, she ducked back inside, quickly closing the door, and walked to the rocker facing the fireplace.

Inga loved fireplaces. When it's bleak, cold, wet and cheerless outside, thought Inga as she sat down, a fireplace warms home, body and soul. She relaxed, staring at the fire, listening to the angry rain beating against window panes, until her attention was diverted by eight-year-old Rachel and Angus Mac-Gregor decorating the Christmas tree. Inga was entertained as Angus annoyed Rachel, and Rachel annoyed back.

"Now, it be fittin' we place an angel near the top of the tree," said Angus while hanging a small, decorative glass angel from a high branch, "for t'is on treetops that angels live."

"What? Like bats? Angels do *not* live on treetops, Mr. MacGregor. They spend most of their time in heaven, of course," said Rachel with a slight tone of exasperation as she fastened an ornament, a Christmas star cookie with a ribbon attached, to a low-hanging bough.

"And I'm supposin' now you'll be tellin' me," said Angus, pointing to the large, decorative gingerbread star Rachel wanted him to put at the top of the tree, "that stars don't live on treetops either."

"No, they don't live on treetops; they're in the sky, of course." Auburn-haired Rachel sighed as she shrugged her shoulders. "But we bake fake stars and put them on the tops of Christmas trees."

"And if stars don't live on treetops, why do we put them up there?"

"It's a high place like the sky. The Christmas star was in the sky over Bethlehem." Rachel looked at Angus in frustration. "It's symbolic, Mr. MacGregor."

"Aye, but how might a fake star be properly symbolic? Was the first Christmas star a fake star?"

"Noooo," responded Rachel petulantly. "Mr. MacGregor, read your Bible."

"T'is good advice," Angus chuckled.

Normally reserved Esther, momentarily standing and looking out from the kitchen entrance, absorbing the cornucopia of visual delights complemented by aromas and sounds that magnified the happiness of the moment, danced quietly on her toes, ebulliently swaying back and forth.

Pastor Nordquist entered from the study and placed a few finely wrapped and decorated boxes beneath the tree. While Scandinavian tradition dictated opening presents on Christmas eve, like most in America the Nordquists had a adopted a tradition of allowing Santa Claus adequate time to deliver the gifts. The boxes Amos placed by the tree were for show; the real presents would not materialize until Santa came that night.

Outside the house in the cold darkness, rain was drumming on the porch roof. The darkness and downpour deformed silhouettes of houses, the weakly-visible parsonage seemingly bent over like a half-starved horse enduring the cold and wet.

Glowing parsonage windows were beacons in the dark, however, as Chong Tsing Wei stood hunched over, shivering, holding the lapels of his coat close to his neck, staring from the opposite side of the street, enduring the downpour. Diminutive streams converged on his hat's broad brim, rushing toward a singular, miniature waterfall cascading in front of his stark stare. In the dark, Mr. Chong's heart welled with anxiety as, in contrast to the rain's snare drumming on slick shingles, he was a silent, transparent block of ice, frozen in place, unable to move.

It was only moments ago that he lived there alone. Yet he never felt alone. It was always home. As the drum roll continued, part of him wanted to march forward, but another part wanted to retreat. What can I hope to accomplish by coming here? But he could not leave. He unnecessarily reminded himself of his reason for coming and, a wooden soldier, began stiffly walking across the street through the downpour.

Before him rose the first step of the wide, front porch stairway that always provided an initial "welcome home" but which now showed no sign of recognition. Mr. Chong stopped in front of it. Shivering, Mr. Chong momentarily thought to himself. Who am I? I am of no value.

For the past few days, gnawing depression, like a rat shadowing a nighttime garbage wagon, followed Mr. Chong around. It stood with him now as he revisited the scene of government trespass whitewashed by official fiat. The drum roll downpour, oblique sheets of rain occasionally driven sideways by gusts of wind, formed an opaque wall between the front porch and Mr. Chong, a barrier discouraging him from reaching the bottom step. But he would need to mount the first step, and the second…and the third. Regardless of how he felt, he had to do it. Momentarily chained in place, he would need to break the bonds of growing discouragement and timidity increasingly constricting like a hangman's noose. And he would, he would break them. He had come further than this before.

Expressionless in the dark, he took the first step up. The emotional burden seemed to grow heavier. As if two people, he forced himself to take the next step up. And the next. And the next. And in a moment he was standing on the dark porch at the top of the steps, although he felt far from the door. Again, he forced his recalcitrant feet to do what was necessary.

Exhausted from walking long distances with no food, little sleep, and constant fear of Sinophobes, as Mr. Chong knocked, his heart pounded lightly at first, but then louder and louder, seemingly louder than his knocking on the door, and as his heartbeat grew louder, he became light-headed, almost vertiginous.

At that late hour on Christmas Eve, 1888, Pastor Nordquist was not only surprised to hear a knock at the front door, but also concerned. A pastor's responsibility to his congregation dictated 24-hour working days, and unexpected visits after 9 p.m. were usually caused by unexpected mishaps or suffering befalling a member of the congregation. On such occasions, regardless of the hour, Pastor Nordquist was expected to be present for provision of labor, direction, prayer, wisdom, comfort or any of the many virtues a pastor is expected to carry around like loose change. Walking briskly to the front door, Amos grabbed and put on the overcoat hanging from a rung by the door, saddled his hat to his head, reached down and turned the doorknob.

As the door swung open, a wide-eyed unfamiliar face with a panicked expression looked up at the pastor, bringing Amos to an abrupt halt, his hands slowly coming to rest like two miniature ships docking on the center flaps of his coat. Pastor Nordquist and Chong Tsing Wei stared at one another, Mr. Chong unable to speak out of shear anxiety, and Amos Nordquist dumbfounded for the moment.

"Well...yah. What can I do for you?" asked Pastor Nordquist politely.

Shivering, Mr. Chong struggled to speak, looked away, but again looked up at Pastor Nordquist. Mr. Chong began by summarizing volumes in two sentences.

"I am Chong Tsing Wei. I built this house."

Mr. Chong proceeded to tell Pastor Nordquist why Mr. Chong no longer lived there. As Mr. Chong spoke, Anna Nordquist came to the side of her husband, listening intently while the two youngest girls vied for position beside their parents, acting like they had never seen another human being before.

"Girls, it's bedtime. Please go to your room," said Mrs. Nordquist calmly but firmly. Esther and Rachel hesitated. "*Now*, please."

As the disappointed girls slowly walked to the stairs, they glanced back as Mr. Chong concluded his brief summary of what had happened almost three years earlier. Although not intending to be disobedient, they stopped at the foot of the stairwell to listen.

Mr. Chong paused, not certain of what to say next. He needed to get inside, but could not bring himself to ask. Again, part of him did not want to go inside. The rain, the cold and the dark stood shivering behind Mr. Chong, bringing Pastor Nordquist to Mr. Chong's aid.

"Won't you come in?" offered Pastor Nordquist as he opened the door wider and stepped to one side.

The part of Mr. Chong that wanted to leave was outmatched; the dark and the cold at his back were abruptly abandoned for the contrast of the warm Nordquist living room full of wonderful aromas and Christmas cheer.

This is my living room, said the First Thought as Mr. Chong stepped inside. It was an undisciplined thought, disinclined toward discretion. It is not, countered the Second Thought, more discerning.

"May I take your hat and coat?" offered Anna sympathetically as her two youngest daughters remained motionless, watching from the foot of the stairwell.

Again, Mr. Chong hesitated, but then handed Anna his hat and, as she held out her other hand, removed his coat, both dripping.

"Where will you be staying tonight?" Anna asked, furtively shooting a sharp look at her restive daughters as she hung Mr. Chong's coat on an entry closet door hook apart from the other hooks, keeping other coats dry.

"I...am not...," responded Mr. Chong hesitantly.

"He could stay *here!*" excitedly volunteered Rachel from the base of the stairs. "If he built this house, then it would be nice for him to stay *here*."

"And, besides, it's Christmas," added Esther before either Pastor Nordquist or his wife had a chance to respond to Rachel's suggestion. From the head of the stairs, Inga looked sympathetically at Mr. Chong, sporadically shivering, who had the appearance of having just drowned, slightly shrugging her shoulders as if to say, "We should."

Not wanting to impose, Mr. Chong interjected: "I can find..."

"Well, fine," interrupted Pastor Nordquist, who silently wondered who, under the circumstances, was the host and who was the guest. He smiled as he added, "We had hoped to eventually meet you and we would be happy – honored – we would be honored if you would spend Christmas with us in this house – which belongs more to you than to us."

Pastor Nordquist extended his hand, and Mr. Chong, after hesitating, looked at the hand and weakly shook it. Amos politely stepped back and turned slightly to his right.

"I am Pastor Amos Nordquist and this is my wife, Anna." Anna nodded pleasantly.

"And these," said Pastor Nordquist, gesturing toward his stairwell-bound daughters, "are my daughters Inga, Esther and Rachel."

Like their mother, Inga and Esther nodded pleasantly. Rachel chirped, "Pleased to meet you!"

"I...am pleased to meet you...too," Mr. Chong managed to respond awkwardly, bowing reflexively.

"Now, then, girls," said Anna solemnly as she went to the kitchen to get a towel for Mr. Chong, "you have had an opportunity to see a *real* human being... who came from beyond the front porch. And, as you can see, he has two arms and two eyes just like you. I'm sure the excitement of *seeing* another human being has worn you out; so, if you don't mind...please do what you were told a few moments ago."

Esther and Rachel started up the stairs. Pastor Nordquist observed that the trek up the stairs became progressively slower with each riser, probably due to declining oxygen levels.

At that moment Angus MacGregor, who made a second residence out of the basement, opened the basement door beneath the stairwell. He had been reading in poor light and, spectacles in his left hand, was rubbing his eyes with his right.

"And what might all the commotion be about?" asked Angus, turning to Amos and Anna.

Esther and Rachel stopped at the head of the stairs and looked over the railing that guarded the upstairs landing.

"Oh, Mr. MacGregor!" announced Rachel, startling Angus. "A wonderful thing has happened." Rachel was energetically rising up and down on her toes as she informed Angus of the latest events. "Mr. Chong, who built this house, has come to visit us and he will be staying for Christmas!" Inadvertently, Rachel correctly referred to her guest as "Mr. Chong," for his "last" name was Chong. "Isn't that wonderful, Mr. MacGregor?" asked Rachel rhetorically. "God wanted Mr. Chong to spend this Christmas with us. It's almost like Mr. Chong is Santa Claus..." Angus looked at Mr. Chong and smiled, "...because," continued Rachel,

"Mr. Chong built this house as a gift for us to live in. And now he's come on Christmas Eve to live in it too!" concluded Rachel. It made perfect sense to Rachel.

"Does that make the rest of us elves?" asked Esther snidely as she leaned back from the upstairs railing.

"'Does that make the rest of us elllvves?'" mimicked Rachel sarcastically as Angus looked up at Esther and Rachel, amused.

"Indeed it does, ladies. Indeed it does." laughed Angus. "Every Christmas!"

He turned to Chong Tsing Wei.

"Y' built this house, did y'? Well, it's a handsome residence we be livin' in, Mr. Chong. I'm very appreciative of your generosity, as are we all. And I expect," continued Angus, looking at Pastor Nordquist, "we'll be returnin' that generosity."

Pastor Nordquist looked at Angus, and glanced at his wife. Adequately returning Chong Tsing Wei's involuntary charity, if even possible, would take considerable time and effort. As a practical matter, if Mr. Chong wanted to stay the night, he could.

"Mr. Chong," asked Anna, "would you like something to eat?"

A few minutes ago, standing in the cold rain and darkness, Chong dreaded what he believed he must do, what the reaction of the resident might be, and now moments later he saw the humor in what was happening. An effort was being made to make him feel welcome in his own house.

It is not my home, he thought, not any more. These are good people, but they are only one family. Other families will not be so charitable. He did not believe his treatment in the community would be any different than it was almost three years ago. Perhaps things had changed, but any change would be modest. Mr. Chong had a good track record of not being where he was not wanted, and the Nordquist's unexpected warm welcome would, no doubt, be overshadowed by, at best, a cold shoulder from others. In the morning he would take what he came for, and he would leave.

"Go to bed, Esther and Rachel."

Mr. Chong, wiping his face and hands on the towel Anna gave him, looked around the room and marveled at the Christmas decorations Anna and her three daughters, working inspiredly, had created. He had seen nothing like this. To the right of the fireplace was a miniature nativity scene. Earlier that week, Pastor Nordquist built it, singing softly – "*Borta i en krubba, ingen spjälsäng som säng...*" – as he painstakingly reconstructed a traditional tiny manger. Mr. Chong looked at the crèche – apparently a cattle shed – with curiosity. The focal point of the cattle shed was a baby in a feeding trough. Who is this baby? he wondered. And why is it in a cattle shed, a feeding trough?

At the top of a decorated tree was an ornately decorated gingerbread star. This seemed to have some significance, he thought. From having spent several Christmas seasons in the American West, Mr. Chong knew that Christmas was a day for giving gifts, but never previously participated. Only now was he directly exposed to the Christmas family traditions that European Christians celebrated for centuries. Mr. Chong continued to survey the room, full of wonder at the lamps, candles, wreaths, ribbons, garlands and a few brightly wrapped presents beneath a decorated tree. As he would find out, there would be more presents in the morning,

"Off to bed with you now, girls," ordered Anna, as she walked out of the kitchen with a tray of Scandinavian Christmas cookies and breads, and coffee. "Now. Be good or Santa won't come."

"Oh, I don't believe that Santa Claus stuff," volunteered Rachel as she compulsively raced toward her bedroom ahead of Esther.

"You mustn't say that," countered Esther, now eleven, motivated by desires to both protect a time-honored tradition as well as prolong her little sister's childhood.

"Oh, all right," responded Rachel as she slowed near the bedroom door, allowing Esther to catch up. "But," said Rachel, watching her steps in the dark, "this is the *last* year I'm going to believe that Santa Claus stuff."

After watching the children disappear into their bedrooms, Mr. Chong returned his attention to the bright decorations in the otherwise dimly lit living room with a continued look of wonder. The nativity scene was placed in front of the bookcase that served as a front for the secret closet within which, unknown to the Nordquists, Mr. Chong's family shrine rested.

"Mr. Chong, after you've had something to eat, please let me show you to your room for the evening," said Anna, nodding in the direction of the main floor guest bedroom that Pastor Nordquist also used as a study.

Anna placed the tray on the coffee table and, smiling, motioned for Mr. Chong to be seated on the couch. He politely sat down and ate slowly at first. At first. But the combination of hunger and culinary delights hastened his pace until nothing was left.

"Mr. Chong, would you follow me?" Anna motioned for Mr. Chong to come with her

Mr. Chong followed Anna and, once inside the guest bedroom, looked about. The furnishings were much the same as when he left. While he lived there, this room was never used, and probably would never have been used if he stayed. The Nordquists were making use of the entire house, even the basement. This is good, Mr. Chong thought. This was meant to be. The house is a good house, and should receive great use. Here I am, back in this house after it is being put to great use. To Mr. Chong it seemed as if there was a controlling higher power that, perhaps for entertainment, moved men about like pieces on a game board to make their situation better, or worse, and who brought about this present situation. Sometimes things happen in ways for which there is no other explanation, he thought.

"Good night, Mr. Chong," said Anna pleasantly. "Thank you for coming tonight. You could not have picked a better evening of the year." Believing as he did, Mr. Chong was not surprised by this statement and, from the implication, was secretly pleased. "And tomorrow morning," continued Anna, "will be an enjoyable experience for you, but will come very early. So sleep soundly."

She closed the door. Mr. Chong stood motionlessly in the lamp-lit room seemingly for the first time. Is this a dream?

While the Nordquist's hospitality was totally unexpected, and Mr. Chong welcomed it, he believed he no longer belonged here. He would tell them about the shrine in the morning and, with the shrine, he would leave.

December 25, 1888

Chong Tsing Wei seldom had dreams. He was not certain why. He speculated that because he worked so hard, he was too tired to dream at night. At the moment, however, he seemed to be dreaming. People were running. At first he heard the sound of soft, rapid footsteps slapping the floor – no shoes. Moments later a second pair of softer, slower footsteps followed. The second pair of feet must be wearing thick stockings. And not running. Mr. Chong awoke as a third pair of feet approached, sounding like the second pair. The stairs. They were coming down the stairs.

He sat up in bed and realized what he heard was not part of a dream. He quickly got up, lit the lamp next to the bed, put on his clothes, straightened his hair while inspecting himself in the dresser mirror, and opened the door cautiously in order that no one be disturbed. He need not have worried.

Robed Esther was sliding comfortably into the rocking chair, watching Rachel, barefooted in her pajamas and nightgown, tear into her presents. As if considerately informing an audience of everything that was happening, Rachel chattered excitedly as she opened each gift.

"Now this is just what I've always wanted. Ever since I was three I've wanted one of these. They're not only fun to play with, but also useful. You can actually make pies – small pies – with one of these. Do you know what this is?" asked Rachel, holding up the object for the others to see. "Why, of course! It's a miniature rolling pin. But don't let the 'miniature' fool you," she added. "They can do everything a bigger rolling pin can do. Aaand," she paused for breath, "as you can imagine, they're much easier to hold. I shall be using this one for a few years until my hands are big enough to use an adult rolling pin. I believe that is how becoming an adult woman is decided. You have to have hands that are…"

"Your hands are already almost big enough," interrupted Esther. "You can prob…"

"That will be just enough out of you, young lady," Rachel interrupted back, repeating the admonition she had heard so many times herself.

In a nearby side chair, Inga sat passively, being entertained by Rachel's antics.

Quiet Inga's beauty was wholesome – so much so, it was distracting. Her reticence was usually accompanied by limited facial expression often mistaken for either taciturn wisdom or muted indifference. Her combination of quietness and lack of expression could give an impression which did not correspond with Inga's emotion of the moment. She could be deeply troubled about something, immure those feelings, and, unless someone knew Inga as well as a sister might, her emotion would not be evident.

Standing together along the second floor railing overlooking the living room, Pastor and Mrs. Nordquist chuckled appreciatively at Rachel's behavior;

this might be the last Christmas where these antics could be enjoyed. While the presents were neither extensive nor expensive, there were more than during previous years. With the girls another year older, and so much room within their present residence, Pastor Nordquist encouraged Santa to be a little more generous.

Amos and Anna walked down the stairs, and Amos lit a morning fire in the large living room fireplace.

"Come on over and join us, Mr. Chong," Anna called to Chong Tsing Wei, standing by the guest bedroom door, watching Rachel's excited antics with interest.

As Mr. Chong walked toward the others, Anna tried to reconstruct some order in Rachel's wake.

"Okay, Rachel, now it's Esther's turn," said Mrs. Nordquist.

"No, first I have a present for Mr. Chong," responded Rachel.

Anna, Amos, Inga and Esther looked surprised, curious to know what Rachel, never known to follow the adage "t'is more blessed to give than receive," was about to give.

From under the tree, Rachel picked up a small, awkwardly wrapped red package, and marched over to Mr. Chong. Written with a green Franklin crayon on the wrapping paper were the words: "For: Mr. Chong. From: Rachel Ruth Nordquist."

"Here you are, Mr. Chong," said Rachel as she held the package up with outstretched arms.

Mr. Chong took the package with both hands, studying it.

"That's okay. You can open it," encouraged Rachel anxiously. "Hurry up… please."

70

Self-consciously, Mr. Chong slowly tore the wrapping paper, provoking Rachel to rhythmically rise and fall on her toes in order to generate the extra energy needed to hasten his laggard pace. Pastor Nordquist and Anna leaned forward to see what was inside. It was a book, and Anna's head nodded as she realized which book.

Mr. Chong had heard of the Bible, but had never seen one until Rachel gave him hers. Most English-speaking railroad workers were either illiterate or semi-literate, although there were some exceptions and, in a few cases, major exceptions. Mr. Chong's own English literacy was fortified by engineering manuals and conversations with English-speaking railroad bosses.

"You promise me you'll read it?" asked Rachel, still rising up and down on her toes.

"This is a nice gift," Mr. Chong stated, appreciating something that held the potential for intellectual stimulation. "I like this gift."

"Then you'll read it?" responded Rachel, now also swinging her arms back and forth while rising up and down on her toes.

"Yes, I will read it."

"Good; read it right now," said Rachel, taking Mr. Chong's hand and leading him to the overstuffed chair near the fireplace and next to the crèche.

"Read 'Romans' first," suggested Rachel with uncharacteristic seriousness. "Then you'll know what the rest of the Bible is about and it will be easier to understand."

Pastor Nordquist's mouth fell open. This was the first indication Rachel listened to, much less absorbed, any of his sermons.

As Esther and then Inga opened their presents, Mr. Chong made himself at home. He turned through the pages, uncertain of what "Romans" was. He subsequently returned to the beginning of the Bible and began reading.

> *1. In the beginning, God created the heavens and the earth. 2. And the earth was formless and void, and darkness was over the surface of the deep; and the Spirit of God was moving over the surface of the waters. 3. Then God said, "Let there be light"; and there was light.*

"…formless and void…" Meaning there was no thing – nothing? "Waters"? If there is nothing, what is meant by "waters"? The universe – what? What was there? Mr. Chong was fascinated. This means more than it seems, he thought as he continued to read, becoming oblivious to what was happening around him.

Inga and Esther each received a new dress, compliments of mom the seamstress. And then Anna opened her package to find…a new dress. Store bought. She did not expect to receive anything. After the obligatory, "You shouldn't have," Anna went to the upstairs bedroom to try it on. Facing the mirror, she beamed; she looked good. As he stood in the background, arms folded, Amos smiled. They returned downstairs and the girls were also impressed.

Moments later, Mr. Chong walked over to Pastor Nordquist.

"Do you know this book?" asked Mr. Chong.

"Yah, I teach this book," said Pastor Nordquist.

"Ohhh." Mr. Chong looked at Pastor Nordquist for a moment. "You teach this book?"

"Yah, it is what I do," said Pastor Nordquist, turning to face Mr. Chong directly.

Mr. Chong looked down at the Bible. "Who write this book?"

"The books in the Bible had many authors, but all were inspired by the Holy Spirit, that is, the Spirit of God, the creator of all things, and the giver of life."

"I do not understand this – 'God created man in His own image…' What does this mean?" asked Mr. Chong.

"When you look in a mirror," said Pastor Nordquist, nodding toward a decorative living room mirror, "you see an image, an image of yourself, and it looks exactly like you." Mr. Chong nodded, realizing Pastor Nordquist was unfamiliar with Chinese superstition about mirrors. "But, of course," continued Pastor Nordquist, "reality is not what is in the mirror, and without reality, there would be nothing in the mirror…and no mirror. That's a crude analogy of how we conceptually relate to the Creator. To continue the analogy, like what appears in the mirror is not reality, what we consider reality is also an image, perhaps a mirage falling far short of the dimension – the true reality – in which we find God. And then, beyond the difficulty of dimension, what are the characteristics of this 'image?' The Bible says, in the 4th chapter of John," Pastor Nordquist pointed at the Bible, "that God is spirit. The 'image' of which the Bible speaks would then be spiritual. But beyond that, what is God? 'God.' What are we talking about?

"We have words to describe attributes of God such as 'omniscient' or 'omnipotent', but the truth is that we do not understand what these words mean. We *do* understand more limited attributes applicable to man like 'knowledgeable' and 'powerful', words from which divine, infinite attributes such as 'omniscient' and 'omnipotent' are extrapolated. As a consequence of dimensional, epistemic, conceptual and linguistic challenges, however, it is impossible to bridge the gap between our characteristics, the 'image', and those of God. We are left reasoning from what we know about us to what we can believe about God. From this limited perspective, we are left with faith which, according to the book you are holding, was evidently God's intention in the first place."

Amos studied Mr. Chong's expression to discern understanding. Mr. Chong looked back at Pastor Nordquist with an expression of confused perplexity.

"This simple image is how most Christians conceive God: an omniloving, omniscient, omnipotent, spiritual father. What are we if created in that image? Obviously, far less. We are often unloving children capable of betrayal – furtive, feeble and flawed in our physicality."

Mr. Chong had difficulty understanding what Pastor Nordquist was saying. Words like "omniscient' and "omnipotent" were completely unfamiliar. Amos said much that Mr. Chong understood, however. After musing a moment, Mr. Chong bowed slightly, turned, and walked back to the overstuffed chair, deep in thought, sat down and resumed reading.

Shortly, Angus MacGregor walked into the room, visibly upset. He celebrated Christmas Eve in his usual fashion, and slept through the Christmas morning opening of presents.

"And why, might I ask, was no one here considerate enough to wake me?" Angus asked, rubbing his head. "Do I not contribute to family matters? Do I not matter to family members?"

"It was Christmas morning, Mr. MacGregor," responded Rachel. "On Christmas morning you're supposed to wake yourself up."

"And why is that, may I ask?" responded Angus.

"It's just like Santa Claus. Maybe it's not true, but on Christmas morning it's what you're supposed to believe. You were supposed to believe that you could get yourself out of bed…'oh ye of little faith.'"

"Rachel, that's enough," interjected Anna. "You apologize to Mr. MacGregor."

"I'm sorry," said Rachel both convincingly and unconvincingly. She glanced at Esther who responded by looking smug.

"Rachel is still young enough to give Christmas morning a good dose of chaos," said Anna, sensitive to how Angus felt, "but we could have been more thoughtful."

"Yes, well, I suppose if I had gotten myself up," responded Angus, "I'd have nothin' t' complain about now, would I?"

Mr. Chong noticed none of this and continued undisturbed, lost in his reading. While Chong Tsing Wei could not know it, for the purpose of having biblical questions answered, between Pastor Nordquist and Angus MacGregor, Mr. Chong was in the right place. While refastening a fir bough, Pastor Nordquist looked at Mr. Chong and his serious facial expression, realizing what was happening beyond the activities of the moment. *God is drawing this man to Him.* The feeling inside Amos was warm. With respect to Mr. Chong, Amos would follow the leading of the Holy Spirit.

As the family prepared to leave for the Christmas morning service, no one disturbed Mr. Chong, allowing him to continue reading the Bible rather than attending a worship service governed by traditional and seemingly sempiternal stand-up/sit-down liturgy that did little to enliven the service or glorify God. Considering his newfound interest in the Bible, and his limited knowledge of

Christianity, it was well that he stayed home. In a limited sense, it was home. In the near future, although neither Mr. Chong nor the Nordquists foresaw it, the residence would become more so.

The Nordquists and Angus MacGregor returned two hours later to find Mr. Chong had not moved. He finished *Genesis* and was into *Exodus*. He had many questions to ask, a fact that delighted Angus MacGregor, for there was nothing Angus loved more than discussions about the Bible. The problem was that Angus wanted to give more answers than Mr. Chong asked questions. Angus's good intentions were restrained at times by Pastor Nordquist.

"Angus, he's just learning. This is all new to him. Leave free will and determinism for later," suggested Amos.

The remainder of the afternoon and evening, Pastor and Mrs. Nordquist, as well as Angus MacGregor, were available to answer Mr. Chong's questions. And as the hour grew late, Pastor Nordquist again asked Chong Tsing Wei to stay the night.

April 28, 1889

Months passed. Chong Tsing Wei became part of the Nordquist family. The concepts of redemption and grace were not difficult for Mr. Chong to grasp, and when he did, the simplicity of salvation was enlightening, and he was grateful God had led him on the long journey that now inexplicably found him in the family of a devoted Christian minister. This was not… He fought to remember the English word. "Coincidence." Mr. Chong thought that this word might be eliminated from the English lexicon.

Once Mr. Chong understood salvation by grace, conversion came simultaneously. He uncharacteristically smiled, thinking about how things are so often not as they seem. It seemed Pastor Nordquist had led him to Christ, but Amos told Mr. Chong, no, no one comes to Christ unless God first draws them. "You're here because He loves you. I might have been like a welcoming doorman, but God unlocked the door. He's the only One who can."

While Mr. Chong began to feel the love of God, and love from the Nordquists, he was, however, still apprehensive about others in the growing Seattle community, an apprehension again soon justified.

-------------------- ●▬ --------------------

Puget Sound, a great, natural moderator of temperature extremes, after having kept most winter snow at a distance, was preparing to do the same with summer heat. This spring morning found a refreshing breeze wafting up from the Duwamish River valley. Across the street, dozens of goldfinches, chirping excitedly, flitted from branch to branch in the yellow Scotch broom.

Resembling the goldfinches, some members chatted animatedly on the church steps. Shortly, a church usher appeared and, with an impatient wave of his hand, motioned them inside. "If you're coming to church, come to church," he muttered as he turned around and disappeared inside the sanctuary.

Filtering through simple, stained and opaque glass panes, sunlight cast a fine, multi-hued veil over pews and the modest chancel. The air inside remained cold and still, and the pleasant aroma of hymnals, curtains, old books, and wooden pews was preserved in the cold air. As parishioners entered, silence demanded silence. Once comfortable, each person looked toward pastor's family in front. But that morning something unusual had happened.

Seated parishioners stared.

Antipathy groped from family to family and, within the normally solemn sanctuary, the ecclesiastical elements associated with peace, love and under-standing – the alter, baptismal font, chalice, votives, and the symbolic cross affixed to the front of the chancel – could not alleviate or conceal the tension. Lack of spontaneous movement before and during the service was typical. While no one moved, however, thoughts darted about like spectators before a 15th century heresy hanging.

Seated beside Mrs. Nordquist, Chong Tsing Wei nervously fingered the pages of the Bible he carried to his first worship service. He did not want to attend, fearing his presence would cause problems for both himself and the Nordquists. Although parishioners never saw him, they knew he lived in the Nordquist home that, they also knew, was previously his home. That seemed justification enough, and as long as he remained out of sight, they did not think about him. On this beautiful Sunday morning, however, in response to Pastor Nordquist's oft repeated encouragement, Mr. Chong agreed to accompany the Nordquists to church.

Sitting directly behind the two front pews traditionally left vacant in Chris-tian churches, he was apprehensive, uncomfortable. He felt the stares from behind, and in defense rationalized he was, for the moment, secure, protected. He seemed accepted, even liked, by the Nordquists and Angus MacGregor. In light of his earlier experience, however, he was uncertain of the others in the congregation. It has been a short time, he thought.

He duplicated Mrs. Nordquist's actions as the church service progressed. She would share her hymnal with Mr. Chong as they stood singing, and she was obviously very familiar with the songs in this book. Mr. Chong was not; and could not sing well in any event. He listened to Mrs. Nordquist's attractive alto voice, cultivated and refined by years of singing hymns such as the one before him.

> *Blest be the tie that binds*
> *Our hearts in…*

After the second verse in Swedish, Mr. Chong found himself quietly humming the melody. The hymnal had an English translation beneath the Swedish words, and this translation contributed modestly to a growing but guarded optimism; the message complemented the reception he unexpectedly received from the Nordquist family.

The end of the service eventually drew near. Following the sermon and the singing of another hymn, Pastor Nordquist lifted his right arm, his two smallest fingers tucked beneath his thumb into his palm. Pointing above the congregation before him, he said the benediction.

"*Herren kan välsigna du och hålla dig,*" he intoned in Swedish, "and may the Lord make His face to shine upon you…"

After blessing the congregation, solemnly finishing with the sign of the cross, Pastor Nordquist turned and stepped down the two steps from the pulpit. He walked down the aisle toward the narthex as the congregation stood, some very slowly, and waited for him to pass by. Soon parishioners filed up the center aisle to shake hands with Pastor Nordquist as they left the sanctuary.

At first Mr. Chong, at the rear of the procession with the Nordquist family, only looked at the aisle floor. Apprehensive of what might be done or said, he would not make eye contact with other parishioners. Feeling a stabbing stare, however, he reflexively looked up to see the face of a large, older man six feet in front of him coldly looking over the heads of other parishioners. Mr. Chong's heart sank. The large, gray mustache. It was the man from the corner in Tacoma. As Mr. Chong's eyes met the man's, the man's virulent expression faintly contorted. The man turned his head and joined the slow procession up the center aisle as Mr. Chong watched him, wide eyed.

As Pastor Nordquist shook the hands of numerous parishioners, he noticed others, expressions severe, walk around the reception area and out the door without speaking. While Amos shook hands, he thought about the implication: he brought a Samaritan to temple.

Outside the door, a small group of church elders and deacons gathered and, during conversation, made periodic, furtive glances at Amos inside.

The following week, defying evident membership disapprobation, Pastor Nordquist would take Mr. Chong's church attendance a step further.

"Angus, the right thing to do is for the church to deed the house back to Mr. Chong," said Pastor Nordquist, seated on the living room couch. "It rightly belongs to him."

"I agree but, as you know," replied Angus, sitting in a nearby rocker, "it's against the law for him to own his own house."

Pastor Nordquist ran his hands along the sides of his head as he thought for a moment. "Perhaps I should talk with some of the other Seattle pastors and Judge Burke about organizing an effort to repeal that law. I would think a good constitutional lawyer…"

"If you think a quick solution is possible, think yet again," politely interjected Angus, folding his hands in his lap. "As far as that law is concerned, the ink is still wet on the page. At present, we'd have more success tryin' t' drain Elliott Bay. Even with Judge Burke leadin' the effort, t'would probably take years to succeed – probably have t' go all the way t' the Supreme Court. I can go see Judge Burke and ask if he'd be willing t' get things started. I'd like t' see Mr. Chong eventually get his house back. But don't hold your breath. For these people right now, repealin' that law'd be too much too soon."

Amos took a deep breath and slowly let it out. "I also have another idea."

"What's that?"

"Any pending maintenance costs," began Amos, "have to be approved by the elders. Relying on the elders to determine what work is necessary, and when and who to do it, has been a slow, inefficient way of handling ongoing maintenance. Sanctuary cleaning is done by volunteers – usually you, me and the family. In my opinion, the church needs a part-time janitor and maintenance man, and Mr. Chong is the best candidate. The construction quality and appearance of the parsonage provide ample evidence that Mr. Chong is capable of handling any repair, remodel or expansion project considered necessary by the elders."

"If the elders went along with it – which isn't likely – what would you expect to pay him?"

Amos looked at the floor. "As a practical matter, the church can provide little more than the room and board already being provided but, if formally hired, Mr. Chong will be recognized as part of the congregation, gradually parishioners will get to know him, and who knows where things eventually will lead? Perhaps someday he'll get his house back." Amos looked at Angus and shrugged. "I think I'll introduce the idea at the Wednesday elders meeting."

Angus kneaded his hat brim, looking at the floor in front of him. "Commendable idea, pastor, but don't hold your breath."

71

While the irony of Chong Tsing Wei being offered free room and board in his own house did not escape Pastor Nordquist, he knew that Angus was right: attempting to reverse the course of earlier events would be a fruitless task at best.

The prospect of Mr. Chong living comfortably in the parsonage provided some vindication for what occurred before the Nordquists arrived, and this was, in Pastor Nordquist's estimation, the best that could be done under the circumstances. Many in the community openly spoke of the Chinese with hostility. Amos believed his church was obligated to provide safe haven for Mr. Chong, however, and that Mr. Chong's potential position as the church maintenance man – assuming Mr. Chong was willing to take the job – would give parishioners the opportunity to know Mr. Chong personally, thereby dispelling erroneous perceptions many held. Amos expected this suggestion might be contested, but it was the right and practical thing to do.

On Wednesday, at noon, the church elders sat with folded arms and puzzled expressions as they listened to Pastor Nordquist present Mr. Chong's background including design and construction of what was now the parsonage.

Between last Sunday and this meeting, while little was said to Pastor Nordquist, condemning conversation among some parishioners was unbridled, and the elders heard the denunciation. Invective begat invective, and the elders knew, like rising flood waters, rising parishioner discontent would need to find an outlet at this elders' session.

The elders sat silently as Pastor Nordquist, speaking forcefully, closed his recommendation by reminding the elders of who they were, their obligation to lead by example, and Who they served, punctuating his concluding remarks with lyrics from one of the hymns sung during that previous Sunday.

> *Blest be the tie that binds*
> *Our hearts in Christian love;*
> *The fellowship of kindred minds*
> *Is like to that above.*

When asked to vote, of the six, three raised their hands in response to "all in favor" while three responded to "all opposed." Pastor Nordquist's vote was the tie-breaker.

Mr. Chong had the job if he wanted it, or so it seemed. Amos sensed weak conviction from one elder who voted in favor of hiring Mr. Chong, and repressed hostility from the three who voted against. Amos made a mental note to speak with each of those four elders privately before the following Wednesday evening elder's meeting in order to resolve whatever unvoiced concerns existed.

The elders moved more quickly, however. At noon the next day they met again…without Pastor Nordquist.

"It makes sense, I think, to go forward with this," said Elder Curt Larson. "This Chong's pretty good with tools, it looks like, and he's sure to be familiar with the parsonage. Room 'n board – in the house he built himself. Can't do too much better than that, don't you think?"

"Can't say as I agree, Curt," countered a second elder, Ole Bergdahl. Staring imperiously at Curt, Ole took an intensely long puff on his pipe and blew smoke in the air above the table. Ole was the head elder and his wife was in charge of the youth ministry. Much of what was done in the church was their idea. Hiring Mr. Chong was not their idea.

"Seems t' me we'd be stirrin' up a hornets' nest, by golly, if we brought him on board," said Ole. "People I talk to don't want no part of it. Don't open that door even a crack. We have to represent the congregation. If we don't, we got no congregation."

"I agree with Ole," added a third elder, Elmer "Bud" Olson, Ole's cousin. Ole had privately discussed the topic at length with Bud. "This whole thing is just one big problem waitin' t' get bigger, and we don't need no big problems, Curt. Y' see what I mean? As elders, we're supposed to solve problems, not make 'em. This bringin' in some Chinee, even if he's a good carpenter, would bring more trouble than all the Chinee carpenters in the world could fix."

"But, gentlemen," responded Curt, "on the other hand, as Christians, don't you think we should set an example?"

"Okay then, let's set an example," said Bud. "Let's say, 'No, we can't do this.' Are we representing the will of the congregation or not? Curt, there's people in this congregation who don't even like Danes and Norwegians. Danes and Norwegians is close…well, Norwegians anyway. Chinee ain't."

"Now wait a minute," Curt countered as he sat up. "We *are* supposed do what's best for the congregation, sure, but that may not necessarily be what some of them want."

"Isn't what they want? Is that what you said?" asked Ole with hauteur. "How do y' figure that? What do *you* want? You want a *Chinee* handyman? Do we need a *Chinee* handyman?"

"He's a little more'n a 'handyman,' Ole," countered Curt firmly. "He designed and built the parsonage. He's designed and built bridges. Room and board, livin' with the pastor. We're getting' a good deal, and that's all that should be considered."

"Well, by golly, more'n a few of us in the congregation think somethin' else should be considered too." Ole glared. Seeing his bullying tactic wasn't working, however, he leaned back, breathed in heavily through his nose, sharply exhaled and, as his expression transformed, leaned forward and folded his hands, looking both self-righteous and self-effacing, a man proud of his humility. "We'd be wise," said Ole in a treacly tone, pausing at the end of each phrase, "to consider…the will… of the congregation."

"I agree that we are supposed to represent someone's will," countered Curt, "but it isn't the congregation's and it isn't ours."

"The Lord's will," said Bud, glancing at Ole. "Well, I always wondered somethin'. How does someone know the Lord's will matter-a-factly beyond a doubt? How do you know that sayin', 'No,' ain't doin' the will of the Lord? How do you know what God knows or what He wants done?"

"Look Curt," impatiently interjected the fourth elder, leaning forward with his elbows resting on his worn overalls, rubbing his callused hands together, "this is a *bad* idear. Y' unnerstand; a bad idear. Don't need no big philosophical discussion t' know that. Now, jes' believe me when I tell ya, this is a bad idear."

Listening, the fifth elder periodically drew on his pipe in an already smoke-filled room.

"Here, gentlemen," responded Curt, "I think we can find the will of the Lord from the Good Book…"

"We all read the Bible, Curt. We're elders," said Ole, "if you haven't forgotten. We don't need no one tellin' us what it says."

"Curt, all we're 'a sayin'," added Bud, "is that we should do whatever is gonna keep things peaceful. Bible says that. 'Blessed are the peacemakers.' Let's not stir things up and get people all mad and up in arms. People are mighty sensitive about this. So let's keep the peace here."

"Gentlemen," countered the sixth elder, Einar Skoglund, speaking for the first time, "Christian history is full of examples where peace is disrupted because of principle."

Ole looked back as if to skeptically ask, "Like what?"

"If you need examples, well, there are plenty. Jesus was crucified." Einar let that sink in. "Peter was crucified upside down. All but one disciple was murdered. James, the brother of Jesus, was stoned to death. Paul was beheaded. If compromising were okay, they all would have lived. What you're saying, well, that isn't what the Lord meant."

"Now, like I said before," quickly interjected Elmer, "how do you know what the Lord meant?"

Einar Skoglund began to read.

> *Blessed are ye, when men shall revile you, and persecute you,*
> *and say all manner of evil against you falsely, for my sake. Re-*
> *joice, and be exceeding glad: for great is your reward in heaven: for*
> *so persecuted they the prophets which were…*

"Einar, what did I just say?!" Ole interrupted, shaking his head. "Einar. Put that down. We know what it says."

"Einar, you're no help," added Bud. "What kind of an attitude is that? We're tryin' t' get somethin' done here. That's annoyin'. Stop doin' it."

As if he hadn't heard a word, Einar read again.

> *"Therefore, all things whatsoever ye would that men should do to you, do ye even so…"*

"Einar! Enough!" Ole glared angrily at Einar who looked back as if Ole had lost his mind. If Ole won't even listen to what the Bible says, Einar thought, what…? "Now look, you're makin' me lose my composure," said Ole, his face flushed and his forehead damp. "Einar. Just…keep quiet."

My responsibility is not to keep quiet, Einar thought.

"What has Pastor Nordquist emphasized ever since he arrived?" countered Einar. "Submitting to the power and leading of the Holy Spirit." Einar looked directly at Ole. "But that's not what I'm feelin' now, Ole – I've got this feeling of oppression like what's happening here is just totally wrong, just the opposite of what it should be."

"I got the same feelin'," said Curt.

"Gentlemen, what are we doin'?" asked Einar, holding out his hands questioningly.

"Tryin' t' get something done, Einar!"

"We're doin' a little more'n that, Ole," said Einar heatedly, "we're *rejectin'* the leading of the Holy Spirit – we're doin' things *our* way."

"Einar's right," said Curt. "We're tasked with serving God according to biblical principle – like Einar just read – which means opening our hearts to the leading of the Holy Spirit. It's there for us. But, Ole, are we doin' that?"

"Well, now, hold your horses," said Bud. "First of all, not everyone agrees on what you wanna call 'biblical principle'. And frankly, Curt, a few of us think this 'leadin' of the Holy Spirit' stuff is a lot of hooey. God gave us minds; we're supposed t' use 'em."

"Not a bad idea," said Einar. "Use 'em to understand what the Bible says, maybe."

"Curt, Einar," responded Bud, folding his hands prayer-like, "I go t' church regular. I been baptized. I take communion. Sing in the choir. Here," Bud opened his hands and held his palms up, gesturing toward the others, "I'm servin' on the elder board. And," added Bud, again folding his hands, "as some of ya already know, I give a lotta money t' this church. A lotta money. I figure all that's more'n 'good' enough. How many other people do all that?" His expression studious, Bud cocked his head slightly. "'Born again.' 'Born again,'" he repeated. "What's that religious mumbo jumbo s'pose t' mean?"

"Now, that's another thing that annoys people about Amos Nordquist," said Ole while looking steely-eyed at Einar. "It's like he's sayin' that in spite of all we do, Einar, we're still goin' t' hell. That's bothered me ever since he got here. I'm curious who he thinks he is? Jesus Christ himself?"

After an hour-long, heated debate, their respective positions didn't change. While letting the others know they were grateful for Pastor Nordquist's convictions, Curt and Einar were still in favor of accepting Mr. Chong into the congregation and offering him the job of maintenance man.

The remaining four opposed employing Mr. Chong, ostensibly concerned about the potential effect this act would have on the congregation and the church's position within the young Seattle community, while Ole and Bud also criticized Pastor Nordquist's emphasis on conversion and the leading of the Holy Spirit.

The meeting ended with Curt and Einar convinced that what Pastor Nordquist wanted to do was right, and the others reasoning that something needed to be done.

Acrimony quickly sprouted from seeds of dissension planted in fertile places. Amos knew accommodation and compromise would encourage the dissenting alliance and undermine the authority of the Bible, but although angry, Pastor Nordquist concluded that meeting individually with the dissenting elders would accomplish nothing, because their personal biases mirrored congregational convictions. Instead, he would speak directly to the congregation, and he began preparing a sermon for Sunday with the hope the Holy Spirit would use that moment to change congregational hearts – for Mr. Chong's benefit and the congregational members themselves.

While preparing the sermon, Pastor Nordquist considered the Apostle Paul's single-minded conviction and unwillingness to compromise the truth. As the first elder said, for his unwillingness to compromise, Paul was beheaded. In conviction and action, Pastor Nordquist attempted to emulate Paul.

Amos was normally quick to listen, and measured when speaking. He worked hard and prided himself as a devoted husband and a loving father. After being converted, his personal relationship with God, hope in Christ, and dependence on the Holy Spirit resulted in a behavior that was consistently reserved.

A part of Amos still existed, however, that, having been seen once, was never forgotten. The Messina sailor whose jaw Amos broke when Amos was 16, saw it. Earl, husband of Virginia, saw it on the 2nd Ave. boardwalk. The Rebel soldier attempting to saber Amos died because of it. What normally slept quietly in the bosom of Amos Nordquist was something akin to dynamite before the fuse is lit. When aroused during a sermon, this anger gave Amos a presence remarkable in the extent to which it stirred the souls of believers while commanding the undivided attention of even the most callused skeptics. His congregation did not know this; had not seen it. They thought of Amos as an average, innocuous preacher.

Anna mused quietly to herself as she watched her husband making notes from his Bible. When she saw his countenance darken and felt his spirit become distant and quiet, she knew it was best to leave him alone, allowing God to work through her husband uninterrupted.

Amos pored through his Bible, looking at relevant, underlined passages, silently asking God for the proper message, when he came upon Matthew 25:42-45. He read and reread the passages.

> *For I was hungry and you gave Me nothing to eat; I was thirsty*
> *and you gave Me nothing to drink; I was a stranger, and ye took*
> *me not in: naked, and ye clothed me not: sick, and in prison, and*
> *ye visited me not. Then shall he answer them, saying, Verily I say*
> *unto you, Inasmuch as ye did it not to one of the least of these, ye*
> *did it not to me.*

There is much more to this than employing Mr. Chong, Amos thought, and read verse 41.

> *Then shall he say also unto them on the left hand, Depart from*
> *me, ye cursed, into everlasting fire, prepared for the devil and his*
> *angels.*

Pastor Nordquist leaned back in his chair, expressionless. What is at the heart of the problem, Amos thought, is what is always at the heart of the problem. The actions of the church elders are symptomatic of what's in their hearts…or, more to the point, not in their hearts, and this is what condemns them, not their actions.

> *"…And in thy name done many wonderful works? And then will*
> *I profess unto them, 'I never knew you; depart from me, ye that*
> *work iniquity."*

A change of heart is needed. Amos stared at his folded hands as his jaws tightened. But I can't do that; only God can do that…if He chooses. Dealing with unconverted elders cynical about spiritual rebirth, he thought, is like attempting to harmonize with someone tone deaf. Yet 'the old, old story' is so simple, mused Amos. These elders, believing in God and active in the church but without belief in their sanctification through Jesus' sacrifice that first Easter, are trying to earn their way into heaven, which is impossible.

Christians. Pastor Nordquist considered how little else frustrated him more than some who call themselves "Christians." Placing his hands behind his head, he thought of one dissenting elder who was also a Seattle real estate broker, and who made a point of letting clients know he was a Christian businessman. From a distance, Pastor Nordquist judged the man to be a self-serving opportunist, and found it amazing how many other Christians were drawn to this elder whose unconventional business practices, tinged with spiritual overtones, bordered on flimflam. When Pastor Nordquist spoke to the elder about this, the elder justified his "unusual style" as a form of witnessing. And what was it, Amos wondered, people witnessed?

How should these elders – wolves dressed as sheep – be handled? Pastor Nordquist wondered.

> *Behold I send you out as sheep in the midst of wolves; therefore, be*
> *shrewd as serpents, and innocent as doves.*

After a moment of recalling Yuri the Russian, and thinking of Pastor Olafson's discussions of "living water" and prayer many years earlier, Pastor

Nordquist folded his hands on the table. Pastor Nordquist believed that while God answers prayer, the Holy Spirit would tell him what to pray for. As direction stepped up, Amos closed his eyes, bowed his head, almost touching his folded hands, and prayed as led.

Meanwhile, news of the two Elders meetings spread with contagion, gossip begat gossip, and dissension piled up like a Cascade Mountain avalanche. Shortly everyone knew everything – all aware Pastor Nordquist would resign next Sunday and return to Minnesota.

The following Sunday morning as Pastor Nordquist made his usual sanctuary entrance from the pastor's study, the church was full…even the first two rows filled. The stand-up/sit-down liturgy was dramatically offset by several hymns, lustily sung in time-honored tradition. During the middle of the last verse of the last hymn before the sermon, Pastor Nordquist rose from his chair on the dais and climbed the two, high, cedar steps into the pulpit. He solemnly folded his hands and, as soon as the last note ended, immediately led the congregation in prayer.

"May it be that this house has been built upon a rock," he began forcefully in Swedish, the word for "rock" – *vagga* – reverberating about the sanctuary, "so that when the rain descends, the floods come, and the winds blow and beat upon this house, it will withstand those forces that would destroy it. As in all things, Your will be done," he concluded. "Amen."

The prayer was succinct. After saying "Amen," Pastor Nordquist, with his hands remaining folded on the edge of the pulpit, looked up and his eyes raked the sea of faces before him. The church became as silent as ice, the congregation looking back in anticipation.

72

Amos began quietly, logically, sounding almost as Judge Thomas Burke had begun three years earlier. But as Pastor Nordquist continued, his tone of voice, tinged with anger, demanded answers to questions. And as he raised more questions, his anger grew and his voice amplified.

"...and where does the Bible justify exclusion from Christendom based on *race*?! Someone tell me!" As his voice reverberated about the sanctuary, he paused, glaring at the men and women before him.

"And when Jesus said, 'A new commandment I give to you, that you love one another, as I have loved you...' what were the exceptions he gave?! Who did He say we need not love? The Chinese?! The Samaritans!?"

A few in the normally motionless, emotionless congregation uncharacteristically shook their heads in response. Consciences and biases vied with one another.

"And *where*," he asked as he defiantly glared at the congregation, his eyes ablaze, "does it say that there are times where it is correct to ignore, even reject, the leading of the Holy Spirit?" He leaned toward the front of the pulpit. "Well?!" he asked loudly enough to make some in the congregation flinch. "You seem to know!" he said as he slapped the podium with his right hand, the sound reverberating about the sanctuary like a rifle shot. "You've all read the Bible. Tell me!"

As mouths dropped and eyes grew larger, the congregation would have noticed their discomfort if not for the mesmerizing effect of his words and fearful countenance.

Taking the offensive, Pastor Nordquist used related Bible passages from the Old and New Testaments, from Exodus and Proverbs, and Matthew and Ephesians. Women cringed as his voice thundered like a storm above the north Cascades; and when it fell to almost the murmur of a late summer creek, even the parishioners in the front row leaned forward to catch each word.

The message hammered those members who opposed Mr. Chong's involvement in the church, but they still sat dispassionately, hearing what Pastor Nordquist said, steeling their hearts, binding their consciences. Looking down at the dullard expressions tinged with defiance, Pastor Nordquist became more annoyed.

"From the faces before me, I see a few of you have difficulty hearing! So let me help you!"

Pastor Nordquist, who never liked pulpits anyway because they were a physical barrier between him and the congregation, took his Bible, stepped down the two cedar steps, and walked to the front of the center aisle.

"Perhaps you'll hear me better now!" he said to obdurate dissidents seated at a distance and immediately nearby, as he began slowly walking up the aisle, making eye contact as he spoke. When approaching those who did not look at him, he stopped and raised his voice until in their discomfort they were forced to look up.

Looking at members seating on either side of the aisle, as he read, he continued walking slowly toward the rear where those with the weakest conviction sat every Sunday.

"In the Bible, Jesus says, 'By their fruit you shall know them'! And He says, 'I am the vine, ye are the branches: He that abideth in me, and I in him, the same bringeth forth much fruit: for without me ye can do nothing. If a man abideth not in me, he is cast forth as a branch, and is withered; and men gather them, and cast them into the fire, and they are burned' [John 15:5-6]."

He stopped and held out his hand, looking about at the staring eyes of his congregation. "Church, do you understand your total dependence on Jesus for salvation?!" he asked loudly. He studied faces as the words echoed about the sanctuary. "And do you understand that you will be judged based on what you did with talents you were given?!" The congregation sat motionless.

"Evidently not!

"The fruit of this congregation," said Pastor Nordquist as he began walking again, "is scarce, desiccated, evidence of not abiding in Christ, and unless something changes, many here will be cut from the vine that is Christ! This sermon is not about a maintenance man, it's about you! Your eternal salvation is at stake, and this salvation, as I have said time and time again, comes from abiding, believing, in Christ through regeneration by the Holy Spirit. How much sense do your convictions make – rejecting 'the least of these' and, therefore, the Savior – evidence the Holy Spirit is far from you?!" He stopped and looked about. "Do you think about *that*?"

As if ignorant of the reason for the first Easter, the congregation sat like Easter Island statues as Pastor Nordquist reached the end of the aisle, turned, facing the front, and began walking back down the aisle.

"I would like to tell you you're all saved. I would love to say that! Nothing would give me greater pleasure…as a friend and as your pastor. But the evidence – your actions – suggest otherwise! At this moment my heart is heavy because your hearts are hard, and while I cannot save you anymore than you can save yourself, still it is my job to direct you toward the One who can. But you refuse direction!

"God is not interested in formality, ritual and pretense. The Bible says,

'…let justice roll down like waters/And righteousness like an

*ever-flowing steam!…Yet you have turned justice into poison/And
the fruit of righteousness into wormwood.'*

"Church, I am talking about more than symptoms. I am talking about God's saving grace being rejected by hearts hard as hammers. You know – because I've said it often enough – while giving an appearance of piety, you cannot serve yourself and ignore God, spurning the Holy Spirit.

I have told you what will result!

*"Alas, you who are longing for the day of the Lord,
For what purpose will the day of the Lord be to you?
It will be darkness and not light.'*

*"'And then will I profess unto them, I never knew you: depart from
me, ye that work iniquity!'*

"Is that what you *want!*?" Standing in the aisle, eyes afire, Pastor Nordquist slowly turned 360 degrees, looking at parishioners. "I said: Is that what you *want*?!" The congregation sat fearfully rigid as the last word bounced off the sanctuary walls.

"Some of you," Pastor Nordquist swept his finger around the sanctuary, "do not believe in the Holy Spirit, much less open your heart to Him. Trust me; at a coming moment *you will believe.*

"I had a neighbor – some of you knew him – who recently passed away. He would not come to church, even delighting in the least defensible theistic conviction: proud he did *not* believe." Pastor Nordquist's face remained grim as he said: "He's a believer now."

Pastor Nordquist's expression was anguished as he reached the front of the aisle, and he turned to face the congregation. Studying the faces before him, some wide-eyed and attentive but others impassive and convictionless, he sensed that for many this was just another sermon, as apparently were all sermons. Amos felt like Moses upon descending Mt. Sinai and finding the Israelites in idol worship.

For a second he stared at the congregation, then loudly slammed his Bible shut!

While many remained obstinate, others were moved by Pastor Nordquist's uncompromising compassion and adamancy. Up until that morning, for many parishioners Pastor Nordquist was just the pastor – were he not the pastor, there would be another. The passion of Pastor Nordquist, however, convicted many of his remarkable spiritual leadership. Where followers gather – sheep in need of a shepherd – the leadership void is quickly filled. Self-serving, secular leaders like George Venable Smith searched for opportunities to lead but, inner directed and holding themselves to no greater standard, wandered blindly, misleading their flock in the process. Pastor Nordquist was an emissary of the Good Shepherd, equipped to lead the parishioners along the straight and narrow way. But many did not want to go there.

At the end of the service, Pastor Nordquist led the congregation in a closing hymn, said the benediction, and again walked up the aisle to the rear of the church where he turned and began shaking hands with parishioners as they left the service. Some parishioners, however, sat without moving.

He had not resigned.

Was he going to stay? Although attendance that morning was the largest ever, the center aisle line of parishioners was three fourths of what assembled two weeks earlier. While shaking hands with the faithful, gratefully hearing some ask about conversion, Pastor Nordquist noticed a large group of men outside encircling four partially obscured elders in discreet discussion. Out of earshot from Amos, the elders agreed that, since he didn't resign, they would ask for his resignation.

Monday, April 29, 1889

What is the obstacle here? wondered Pastor Nordquist when rereading Mathew 22 at his desk. It seems simple, he thought to himself. When a scribe asked which was the great commandment, Jesus did not hesitate in responding:

> *"'YOU SHALL LOVE THE LORD YOUR GOD WITH ALL*
> *YOUR HEART, AND WITH ALL YOUR SOUL, AND WITH*
> *ALL YOUR MIND.' This is the great and foremost commandment.*
> *And a second is like it, 'YOU SHALL LOVE YOUR NEIGHBOR*
> *AS YOURSELF.' On these two commandments depend the whole*
> *Law and the Prophets.*

Why is this directive so difficult to follow? Pastor Nordquist asked himself, reflecting more on human history than the Seattle congregation. While Christ's response is simple and direct, the commandment to love our neighbor seems all-too-easily subverted, he thought, not by selective determination of who is our neighbor, but who is not.

Pastor Nordquist faced an increased elevation in the intolerance cycle. Human nature and irrational intolerance, he thought, go together like contaminated drinking water and cholera. In contrast to his immediate problem, Amos thought of bigger examples where the intolerance cycle has continued for centuries. Oppression always comes down to two things, he thought.

Us.

Them.

If historic intolerance upheaval were charted, Amos mused, it might look like the Olympic Mountains just after sunset: up, down, up, down…peaks and valleys. No, he thought, topographical intolerance has always been continually constant. Hejaz, Abyssinia, Esdraelon, antiquities now renamed but still the same. Ignorance and insecurity, sullen soul mates, have long spread the intolerance virus, infecting them-nots. Those four elders no longer consider me one of them, Amos thought, but one of them.

***

"Well, dear, where do we move to now?" asked Anna Nordquist, showing no outward sign of emotion as her rolling pin flowed freely forward, obliquely right, obliquely left, the pie dough inching outward incrementally.

"At the moment we are not going anywhere." Amos sounded inattentive as he arranged parts of the clock he brought in to repair on the kitchen table.

Anna looked down at her nearly-finished artistry, moving the rolling pin more slowly and delicately to insure that the dough thickness was uniform. For a moment she said nothing, focusing on the knot in her stomach.

"Are you going to compromise?" asked Anna. "Are they going to compromise?" Anna put down the rolling pin, and turned toward Amos. Amos was a man of action often because of Anna's unwillingness to procrastinate when her intuition demanded an immediate response to a problem. Anna walked toward him. "Of course," she added, openly stating the obvious, "I agree with you, Amos." Her eyes were wide and sincere. "But what do erroneously principled people do when those principles are challenged? Act rationally? Behave sensibly? Are we so naïve that we would expect that now? As far as the others are concerned, at this point neither logic nor appeal to Christian charity will change anyone's heart. While their position is without moral justification, Amos, it isn't going to change."

"Should I immediately entertain thoughts of leaving?" asked Amos as he looked at Anna solemnly. "As Jesus said in the Beatitudes, 'Blessed are those who have been persecuted for the sake of righteousness, for theirs is the kingdom of heaven.' If I am an effective servant of the Lord, persecution in some form invariably follows."

Anna looked back at him for a moment as if to say, "Of course, but…" but said nothing. The knot in her stomach was not growing any smaller.

"What are you going to do now, Amos?"

A lesser man might have said nothing, or might have said, "Nothing." Amos did neither. He loved Anna for many reasons including how she made him, a good man, a better man. He knew she loved him and respected him, and he would do nothing to weaken her love and respect. Her intuition in important affairs was never to be ignored. She had come to depend on his willingness to stride to the fore in defense of things cherished when she sensed those things were being challenged. So now, again, he would.

"I will pray about this," he said. She nodded.

Outside of the Nordquist residence, in homes of church members, others were weighing the same ideals. While members who agreed with Pastor Nordquist's position were pusillanimous, their position was evidence Amos's sermon had an effect. Most opposed were obstreperous, however, giving the impression that many more were opposed than was the case. Many on either side believed there would be some form of compromise.

⸺•⸺

"You know, Ulma," began Ode, a church deacon, as he balanced his pipe stem in his teeth, "Pastor Nordquist is a good man and you can't fault his having the courage of his convictions." Ode then sat motionlessly, smoke levitating from his pipe bowl, as he looked intently at his wife and waited for a second thought. "But, now, what about his wife and kids?" Ode continued. "Do they mean anything to him? Of course they do." Ode puffed passively. "Of course they do," he reiterated. "So, if you ask me, he'll back down. He has that fine home to live in. Has a small salary now. It isn't much but, here, it isn't much more than the rest of us make. He'd be downright foolish to continue supporting this Chinaman."

"I couldn't agree more, Ode," said Ulma. "In fact, I was talking with Florence Joergensen and Delores Bakken this morning, and we all agreed – Delores, Florence and I all agreed – that, as a man of God, he should just be a pastor, take care of church matters, and don't try to do all this stirring-things-up. No call for it. Pastors aren't supposed to do that. Delores looked at me and asked, 'What the devil has gotten into that man?' We all laughed. 'What the devil has gotten into that man?' And he's a *pastor*. That was hilarious, Ode. Ode? Don't you think that was funny?"

Ode drew from his pipe.

"Ode?"

"Huh? What's that?"

"Wasn't that funny, Ode?"

"Oh. Yah, sure. That was funny."

"I certainly thought so," said Ulma. "So did Florence and Delores. Well, that is, Delores thought it was funny after she figured out why we were laughing. Anyway, we agreed Pastor Nordquist needs to be more like a pastor should be, and not be taking these stands on matters that don't concern him. And Delores told us she heard – you won't believe this – the reason they left Minnesota was because Pastor Nordquist had an affair!"

"An affair?" questioned Ode. "Are you sure?"

"Delores heard from Myrtle Swenson that he had an affair! And that's why he came all the way out here." Ode questioningly looked over his bifocals at his wife. "But Ode, it only stands to reason. Why else would he come all the way out here if not to get away from something in his past."

"Myrtle Swenson?" asked Ode. "How would Myrtle Swenson know?"

"I don't know – but I wouldn't put it past him," said Elma. "He is, after all, very good looking; and he practically hid that Chinaman for months – we all knew that man was living with him in the parsonage, *our* parsonage. I don't know who Pastor Nordquist thought he was fooling. Then he brought that man to church, thinking we wouldn't notice." Ulma folded her arms. "As if we're all fools. Well we're not fools, Ode. You seem to trust him, and I don't know why." Ulma walked over to Ode. "And I have no doubt that Myrtle is right. He had an affair and, true to form, told no one. But what do you expect, Ode?"

"Maybe so," Ode shrugged as he glanced at his paper lying on his lap.

"I know so. Everyone knows so."

"Even if that's not true," said Ode, "he's running out of aces. If he doesn't toe the line here, he won't be able to go anywhere else. Kind of a shame. Seems like a good man."

Ode picked up his newspaper and shook it, returning to the article he had been reading.

"Well, good man or not, I think he's painted himself into a corner," said

Ulma. "Pastor Nordquist is in no position to aggravate the church membership just to help some Chinaman."

———————————————●●———————————————

Pastor Nordquist would have continued in the face of adverse spiritual conditions, but he sensed the problem had gone beyond the point of no return. Initially, Chong Tsing Wei was interested in the job as maintenance man, but when it became evident there was strong opposition to this idea, Mr. Chong told Pastor Nordquist he did not want the job. Rather, he would return to his original plan of offering his services to James J. Hill who had begun construction of the Great Northern Railroad.

———————————————●●———————————————

The church was in turmoil. While the four elders demanded Amos's resignation, some in the congregation wanted him to stay under any circumstances. He told the elders he would "consider it" and had not submitted a resignation, waiting on direction from the Holy Spirit, not the elders.

The struggle over Mr. Chong was not the only problem. The lie about Pastor Nordquist having an affair in Minnesota gained traction. The Lava Bed lost none of its appeal to some male parishioners. In Murray, Pastor Nordquist had a tiny congregation, but was respected in the community. In Seattle, the congregation was greater, but the respect was less. Although Jesus stated one must be "born again" to enter heaven, and Pastor Nordquist was clear on this matter, he was flummoxed that some in church leadership were antagonized by the concept, considering it "unfair" – one used the term "unChristian" – criticizing Pastor Nordquist for preaching it. The attitudes and perceptions of some congregation members at times made Amos ask himself the same question Pastor Olafson asked decades earlier: Where does Jesus fit into any of this?

———————————————●●———————————————

The waterfront was awash with transient men in a hurry. The saltwater aroma was pungent, and Amos stopped to take a deep breath as if to re-energize. As Amos and Angus continued to walk down Marion Street toward the waterfront, Angus was the second to broach the obvious.

"Pastor, too many of this bunch worships God with their mouths, but their hearts are far from 'im." Angus shaded his eyes as he walked. "They go through the motions like stage actors. In my opinion, you'd be better off to dump the whole bloomin' bunch."

Angus solemnly glanced at his friend as the two crossed the intersection at Front and Marion where they would attempt to pass the time of day with men going in and out of the Dietz and Mayer liquor store, perhaps finding the opportunity to help someone less fortunate, an intent contrasting with the attitudes of some in his congregation whose interest was not in the less-fortunate but the more-fortunate. Coming to a halt in front of the store, Amos adjusted his hat and put his hands on his hips as he looked around him. Determined men from all walks-of-life passed by, generating a cacophonous, hollow clomping on the boardwalk. Angus, standing three feet away, studied Pastor Nordquist's face.

"The Lord led y' to Murray, He did," said Angus. "Then He led y' here. Now don't y' think that He may still be leadin' y'? D' y' not think that things would be a lot better if the Lord determined this was where y' were to stay, m' friend?"

"Well, no, not necessarily," responded Pastor Nordquist. "You know what Jesus said, how His yoke is easy and his burden is light." Amos sighed. "The Bible did not say there would be no yoke and no burden. A pastor's burden is heavier than most and this is to be expected. This calling is too important for the burden to be light. As I've said before, a pastor with no burden is not doing his job."

"Y' know, however," countered Angus, "that the Lord did not spend a great deal o' time rubbin' elbows with the Pharisees, now did He?"

"No," agreed Pastor Nordquist. "But neither did He avoid or ignore them."

Amos stared at the boardwalk and thought, Angus is right; many merely go through the motions – until, perhaps, that moment when the fear of the Lord makes it necessary to summon conviction. Amos raised his eyes, studying the silhouettes of the men hurriedly walking about him, oblivious to his presence. Where were they going; what could be so earthly important? He dropped his hands from his hips and turned toward an approaching man.

"Excuse, me. I'm Pastor Amos Nordquist."

The man walking toward Amos stopped.

"Well?" The man paused, puzzled. "Wha' d'ya want?"

"Where are you from?"

"Tennessee. Why?"

"I pastor the church up on the hill," said Amos, pointing in the direction of the church. "You're quite a ways from home and we would be happy to have you to join us this Sunday."

"Won't be here this Sunday. Goin' north. Dawson Creek."

"Aye, Dawson Creek," said Angus. "Gets a mite cold. Nothin' like Tennessee."

The man looked mutely at Angus, formally touched the tip of his hat brim and walked away. The look in his eyes said nothing was more important than what he was set on doing. Possibly getting rich. Ultimately what happened was far different. Like a cat with a small mouse, the frozen North played with the man for a while before tiring of the sport. Beneath a lean-to aside a frozen lake 65 miles east southeast of Dawson City, with the temperature 35 degrees below zero, weak and out of food, the *cheechako* spent his last semiconscious moments hallucinating about being home in Clarksville by the Cumberland River. Angus and Amos watched him walk away as another man approached.

"Excuse me, I'm Pastor Amos Nordquist," smiled Amos.

"Heh!" came the disgusted response. The man stopped in mid-stride long enough to vent. "An' I'm in no mood to talk to no slick-talkin' preacher! Already lost enough money to one o' you scoundrels in San Fr'ncisca. Said he needed it right then. Sounded as sincere as my mother. Said it was to help feed a family of six in desperate need, an' that he'd repay me the next Monday after church offerin' was taken. 'Bless thee, brother,' he says. 'See thee first thing Monday mornin',' he says.

"Never saw 'im again. Help the needy. Hell. Help the needy preacher!"

The man gave Pastor Nordquist a parting look of contempt. "G'day!"

Amos looked at Angus.

"A preacher, he says," responded Angus, chuckling. Angus looked up in the sky and down at the boardwalk beneath his feet. "As if we don't have enough obstacles as it is." Angus shook his head and muttered inaudibly as Pastor Nordquist began speaking to another man walking by.

"Excuse me, I'm…"

"Not interested," interjected the man as he brushed by Pastor Nordquist without making eye contact.

Amos turned and watched him disappear into the store.

On the opposite street corner was a man selling something he claimed cured everything from backache to poor eyesight. A few feet away was a beggar, eyes rolled up under his eyelids, a hat on the boardwalk in front of him, and around his neck a sign that said, "Blind. Please help." Next to the hat was a small sign that said, "God bless."

It's a believable act, thought Pastor Nordquist who had seen it done before. His eyes seem perfectly white. Some people will assume he has no pupils. Pastor Nordquist momentarily studied the scene. The "blind" man sat in a chair on the boardwalk next to the intersection, very visible aside foot traffic. People had to walk right next to him. Perfect location. As a passerby tossed a coin into the man's hat, Pastor Nordquist wondered who was blind and who was not.

"Pastor," Angus's voice broke Pastor Nordquist's reverie, "we're like a rock tryin' t' roll uphill. I tell y', we'll get nowhere with this bunch. Now, are y' sure this is your callin' – this corner in this place at this moment?" Angus MacGregor's voice was almost pleading. "Does this seem t' be the right place, here, now?" Angus looked at Pastor Nordquist without blinking.

Amos looked at Angus. While Angus had his shortcomings, his spiritual sensitivity was strong. And for all the time that Angus wasted, he was obviously an intelligent man. Pastor Nordquist sighed. Many intelligent men waste a lot of time. Am I wasting time in Seattle? Is this only a stop en route to a parish prepared for me? The feeling inside Pastor Nordquist seemed to quietly say, "Obviously."

Angus remained silent, watching Pastor Nordquist. As another man brushed by him, Pastor Nordquist lightly bit his lips while gazing at the boardwalk. He relaxed and for a second looked back at Angus, nodded, and without a word the two of them turned and silently walked back up the hill. As they walked, Amos considered the present situation, believing it was as bad as it was going to get, misjudging the extent to which things were deteriorating.

73

Friday, May 18, 1889

Bye Esther." The words were venomous.

Esther Nordquist continued walking rapidly, trying to act as if she neither saw nor heard anything. But what she felt made it seem as if the confrontation was still happening.

"*Byyye* Esther," came again from a greater distance, making Esther involuntarily cringe, as if being struck from behind.

It was Pastor Nordquist's perception that the loneliest and most vulnerable people in the world were girls between the ages of twelve and fifteen. In the various churches he pastored, he noticed that most young girls keenly felt loneliness, and often imagined rejection. The need and drive to be loved and accepted seemed strongest among these blossoming, young women. Ironically, they could also be uncommonly cruel to one another.

The three girls watched Esther continue to walk away, but for a moment did nothing. Then the voice said it again.

What is she *saying*? thought Esther defensively. Once Esther safely distanced herself from the three girls, tears welled in her eyes, but she fought them off – sticks and stones may… Why did they have to *say* those things? They don't even *know* me.

In spite of present circumstances, Pastor Nordquist also concluded that maturity, tolerance and recognition of common bonds could enable adults with widely differing convictions to create and maintain a pacific social fabric in spite of those differences. It was uncommon, but it happened. Under identical conditions, however, young adults almost never could.

Esther didn't know the lanky, older boy with the large, brown eyes who was standing on the corner watching the interaction between Esther and the three girls. As she approached him he turned and walked next to her, acting as if they were familiar with one another. At a distance, the three girls watched with interest. The boy was aware of this.

"Watcha gonna do? Yer not gonna stay, are ya?" asked the older boy, his thumbs hooked in his suspenders. His tone of voice made the question seem an ultimatum.

"I don't know what you're talking about," responded Esther, although she did.

"Well, ya can't stay," he said with finality as he walked closer to her. "Chinee lovers don't belong here. Ya might as well be Cath'lic, y' know *that*?"

Esther looked straight ahead, focusing on a distant hillside, trying to block the boy out of her consciousness. For a few moments neither said anything as they walked stride-for-stride, the boy's gaze swinging from Esther to the road and back.

"Well?" he asked, staring at her as they walked.

Esther made no response, but began to walk faster. This angered the boy who began walking even closer, herding Ester toward the ditch, until Esther stopped. Wide-eyed, she looked up at him, frightened and trapped. No thoughts or words came as she looked into his acrimonious eyes. Her composure snapped under the strain and her mouth fell open. She began backing away, turned and ran, terrified, toward home.

At a distance, the three girls watched.

When her front porch appeared a half block away, Esther slowed, exhausted, stopped and quickly glanced around, her chest heaving as her lungs begged for oxygen. If the boy had been chasing her, he was no longer. Tears burst forth like Seattle rain as, head down, and breathing heavily, she turned and walked the remaining half block, sobbing to herself. Before reaching the front porch, she cut to the side of the house where she intended to regain her composure and dry her tears before going inside. She didn't want to worry her mom or dad.

Quiet Inga, standing at the front window, watched Esther walk across the street and run to the side of the house; saw the tears. Moments later, as Esther stood alone, desperately trying to stifle her sobs, Inga came up and stood looking compassionately at Esther. Inga's eyes, as always, radiated kindness. The stark contrast between the three girls' bullying cruelty and the boy's acrimony on one hand, and Inga's compassion and love on the other, caused the release of remaining pent-up emotion and instead of regaining her composure, Esther again began sobbing uncontrollably as she reached out and held on to her older sister as if to keep from drowning. As the two embraced, Esther's fear and angst gradually gave in to Inga's lovingkindness.

After a while, Esther let go and stepped back, wiping her eyes. Inga continued to look down at her sister, but still said nothing. At that moment it seemed clear to Esther that Inga, who was always so quiet, didn't talk because Inga didn't have to talk.

"It's okay, Inga…I'll be fine." Inga didn't move as Esther tried to choke her sobs. "I'll…I'll tell you about it later."

Finally regaining her composure, Esther looked to one side and dried her eyes with her right sleeve as Inga took Esther's left hand, and the two slowly walked around the corner of the house to the large, front porch.

Later that day, Inga looked pensively out the window, studying several men on the opposite side of the street who, while engaged in conversation, made furtive glances in the direction of the Nordquist residence, appearing like vultures anticipating a carcass. Who were they? Inga learned from the bear incident in Murray that dogs, when alone in a domestic setting, were usually docile, often protective, but when becoming part of a pack and beginning to run, would revert to primal behavior and become dangerous to other animals and people. Inga wondered whether the pack mentality, masked in communal self-righteousness, was about to isolate a victim?

Rachel was washing the dishes while Esther, with glazed, emotionless eyes and clenched jaw, solemnly attended to her homework. The fact that she was deeply upset was apparent not only by her countenance but also her uncharacteristic reticence over the past few days. She seldom spoke, and usually only when spoken to.

While it seemed that Esther was closely studying her textbook, Mrs. Nordquist could not help but notice that, for the past five minutes, Esther's hands did not move. From the intense expression on Esther's face and an occasional arm or shoulder twitch, it was evident her imagination was racing pell-mell like a frightened rabbit.

"What are you thinking about?" asked Anna.

Rachel looked toward Esther in anticipation of what Esther would say.

"Oh, nothing really," responded Esther as she resumed reading. There was an awkward silence as Mrs. Nordquist waited.

"Nothing?"

Without raising her head, Esther looked up at her mother for a moment, and her eyes returned to her text.

"Why don't you tell her?" interjected Rachel impatiently. "If you don't, I will."

"Then go ahead," said Esther, looking sullenly at her open book.

"It's those kids!" exclaimed Rachel as she walked toward her mother. She put her hands on her hips. "When you're not around, they're mean. They won't talk to us. Except when they call us names. Lillian Swenson took my brush and wouldn't give it back, and when I told her to, Ingrid Bergquist made a face at me and said that if I didn't like it, I could leave Seattle." This would be the first but not the last time that Mrs. Nordquist was to hear this suggestion. The cruel taunts of children echoed adult conversations overheard at home. "Jonny Johnson says that we're different and that we shouldn't be here. And Ona Larsen says 'chinky, chinky Chinaman' when she sees me. That's so stupid! She just does it to impress her stupid friends."

"Rachel, regardless of what they say, as a general rule I do not want to hear you calling others 'stupid,'" said Anna as she placed silverware pieces on the table.

"Well, they are," responded Rachel.

"Rachel, I want you three, as Christians," countered Mrs. Nordquist, "to set good examples."

"They're Christians too!" Rachel responded, eyebrows raised, as she took her hands off her waist and held out her palms. "But they sure don't act like it."

"All the more reason why you should," said Mrs. Nordquist in a disciplined, neutral voice.

"But they're really mean to us, Mama," reiterated Rachel. "They say that Daddy is a bad pastor, that he had 'an affair' with a woman in Minnesota, and that we're not really Christians because we support heathens."

"An affair?" Anna's mouth fell open as she looked at Rachel, disbelieving what she heard.

"They say we don't understand things," continued Rachel, "and we think we're better than they are when we're really worse." Rachel paused. "I didn't use to think we were better, but I do now."

"Rachel," responded Mrs. Nordquist with a calm voice that belied her true feelings at that moment, "this is, of course, all nonsense. Do you know what an affair is?"

"Mmm, no," Rachel shrugged.

"Good. And presently there is no point in knowing…other than to know there are a number of lies being told about your father."

"Mama," said Esther in a monotone as she looked up at her mother acerbically, her voice tinged with bitterness, "they call Mr. Chong a heathen, but they really only say that because he's Chinese. Sometimes I think that if I weren't already a Christian, and I looked at how some Christians behave, I wouldn't be one."

Anna's lips again parted as she looked at Esther, trying to think of an appropriate response.

"Let me just say," Anna began, "that Mr. Chong is not a heathen. He was once not a Christian simply because he was never exposed to the Bible, to Jesus. Reading biblical history and teachings changed his life. Now he is a Christian; the Holy Spirit resides in his heart. You can see the change in him in spite of these difficulties we are having with others."

Her stomach suddenly feeling like she had drunk spoiled cider, Anna walked to the large living room table, sat down and began sketching a quilt design that had been formulating in her imagination for several days.

"Girls," concluded Anna firmly, arising momentarily from the depths of her thought, "at present I have nothing more to say on this matter." Anna seemed to be looking through whatever it was she was sketching. "I'll discuss it with your father this evening."

Later that evening, as Mr. Chong sat reading in the living room, he glanced up at Anna as she purposefully walked to the guest bedroom where Amos also had his desk. Mr. Chong watched as she stepped inside, turned and quietly closed the door. Mr. Chong looked at the closed door and wondered what was happening.

Amos, sat at his desk, hunched over a reference source, writing notes to himself. The sound of her entrance did not make its way into his consciousness.

"Dear," Anna said quietly, "I have something I need to discuss with you."

At the sound of Anna's voice, Amos turned around and noticed the door was closed. If Anna came into the study to talk after closing the door, the "something" she wanted to discuss would be important.

Amos got up and went to the chair next to the bedroom door, picked it up and brought it over to his desk, placing it next to his own chair. He turned it so that the two chairs faced one another, and nodded for Anna to sit down. As the two took their seats, Anna's expression reflected her inner alarm.

"Esther and Rachel," Anna began, "have been the target of name-calling and cruel behavior by other children." Anna folded her hands in her lap. "Our relationship with Mr. Chong is at the heart of the matter. There is evidently also a rumor that you had an affair with a woman in Minnesota."

Pastor Nordquist sat back, and his eyes narrowed as his head dropped slightly while he continued to look levelly at Anna.

"It seems serious because the other children parrot what their parents say," continued Anna, "and, consequently, this cruel behavior is implicitly countenanced, perhaps even encouraged, by the adults." Anna began to speak even more softly. "The name-calling and ostracizing are bad enough, but I am fearful that as the intensity of antisocial behavior increases, one of our girls may come to physical harm. I agree that we need to stand our ground as far as Mr. Chong is concerned, but while we do, we will need a plan of immediate defense and," Anna looked intently at Amos as her words became more deliberate, "a plan to move elsewhere."

For a moment Amos sat looking at Anna.

"But why should I be surprised?" he said, looking at Anna. He thought of the apostle Paul who faced similar problems with church leaders, and Martin Luther who would have been martyred like John Hus if Luther was not a popular instructor at Wittenberg. "How is it that church leaders can get so stiff-necked?" Amos angrily wondered aloud.

Anna looked at him for a moment before answering.

"It's not just the leaders. The reason," she replied, "is that those who call themselves Lutherans...or Methodists...or Episcopalians...or Catholics...are whatever they are."

"'Are whatever they are'?"

"Are merely Lutherans...so on and so forth. It comes down to what you go to church for," said Anna. "Church may be no more than a social club. It is different to consider yourself a Christian. Christians have a relationship with the Lord; others are sectarians with a sanctuary."

Amos's forehead furrowed. "Lutherans have traditions," responded Amos defensively, "but we are, of course, Christians. I don't need to tell you that."

"Are we – you and I – Lutherans first or Christians first?" asked Anna.

"Christians, of course."

"That is true for us," Anna said. "But for many, as you know, it's not that way." Anna looked at Amos for a moment before speaking. "Priorities...what comes first...obviously have much to do with our present problem."

Pastor Nordquist thought of his conversation with Blade, the formidable cavalry veteran, about motive – what's in a person's heart. Amos folded his hands and, feeling disquietude, looked back at Anna.

"Amos," said Anna, getting to the point, "there is a reason for this, as you know. It is painful to say this but," Anna chose her words carefully, "many of our parishioners are so far from being led by the Holy Spirit, and emulating the love of Christ, that labeling them Christians may be a mistake."

"Now, now," responded Amos, looking levelly at Anna. "Labeling makes matters worse."

"That's not what I mean," replied Anna. "I'm talking about believing that Christ is who the Bible said He is, and that He did what He came to do, and His admonition to love God and to love one another – and the behavior that follows from the Holy Spirit taking residence in one's heart. Besides, with neither faith nor commitment, it really doesn't matter what they call themselves…Lutherans, Catholics, Baptists, Methodists… If they don't have the Holy Spirit in their heart, all they have is their denomination and whatever that might mean to them. In this case, we have too few Christians and too many 'Lutherans.'"

As he thought about this, Amos began to chuckle. It occurred to him that the priest at the small Catholic church a few blocks away also had his fair share of "Lutherans." So did the Presbyterian teaching elder. Or maybe Amos had too many "Catholics." As he actually began to laugh, Amos stood up and took his bewildered wife's hands, bringing her to her feet. The unexpected laughter was, as always, cathartic. He could have stopped but, feeling buoyant, he allowed the therapeutic hilarity to continue. Amos momentarily felt better, emotionally, physically and spiritually. Still laughing, he put his arms around Anna, rocking her back and forth.

"What in heaven's name is so funny?" She looked at him like he had lost his senses. He squeezed her, kissed her forehead and held her close.

"Oh, I just thought of something funny," he answered, pressing his cheek against her forehead. "That's all. I'll tell you later. But you're right. We need more Christians."

Amos released Anna and sat down. Anna re-took her seat, looking at Amos.

Amos put his right elbow on the arm of his chair with his right thumb supporting his chin, his right middle finger partially covering lips still holding a waning smile. "Can you imagine," he wondered out loud, "what the world would be like if everyone who said they were a Christian, was?" His imagination racing, Amos's facial perplexity while thinking about the implications of what he just asked, caused him to stare at the guest room fireplace as if someone were sitting in it.

Anna glanced at the fireplace and back at Amos, responding spontaneously, "We certainly would have no problem bringing Mr. Chong into the congregation. In fact, not only would no one think twice about it, all the Chinese would be welcome."

"And we would not," added Amos, smiling again, "have to think twice about what we are going to do next – which is the next question you will ask me." Amos folded his arms.

"Well, what *are* we going to do?" Anna wanted to know.

"I'll tell you tomorrow," said Amos who also wanted to know. He was reasonably certain of which direction to take, but uncertain of where it would lead. He would think things over this evening, pray extensively, and with a clear head and a light heart in the morning, make the decision.

74

Based on the events and the names he heard from his girls, Pastor Nordquist concluded that the situation was as grim as it seemed. Early in the morning, the two elders who sided with Pastor Nordquist at the previous elders meeting came to the parsonage accompanied by Earl Jensen whom Amos excoriated on the downtown boardwalk months earlier, and whose heart was changed.

"Well, hello!" said Pastor Nordquist as he opened the front door. "Curt…" He shook Curt's hand. "Einar…Earl? How are you?" Earl nodded. None of the men smiled. Out of custom, each walked to the large, living room couch where they stood waiting for Pastor Nordquist to ask them to sit down.

"Gentlemen, won't you sit down?" In unison the three sat down, each holding their hats with both hands. Earl sat comfortably, his demeanor one of quietude and gratitude. "Anna," Pastor Nordquist began, "could you…"

"I'll be right back with some coffee," interjected Anna, smiling. She enjoyed having people over. She was an excellent cook, noteworthy particularly for her baking, and loved to serve guests who were always openly appreciative of what they received, in contrast to her children whose appreciation fell short of what it would be later in life. Serving guests was a treat for both the guests and Anna; having coffee would include a culinary treasure trove of homemade delights.

"Pastor," Curt began, "we know what your kids are goin' through. Our kids are having similar experiences. Seems that kids never have restraints about being mean to one another."

"Well, yah," Pastor Nordquist replied, musing. "In adolescence, the walls of human nature have not yet known wallpaper."

"I'm not sure how much paperin'-over adults have either," added Einar.

"Einar and I," began Curt, getting to the reason for coming, "are sorry about what's happenin'. It isn't easy for you. And, well, it hasn't been easy for us either. It's been like a dam has busted all at once." Curt paused, kneading the brim of the hat on his lap. "Frankly, Pastor," he said, "my kids have heard the words 'white Chinee' more'n they need to."

Anna came into the room with a coffee tray holding china cups and saucers, compliments of Mr. Chong, as well as a silver coffee pot and a variety of Scandinavian pastries and cookies.

"Oh, will you look at this," said Earl under his breath.

"The reason we're here," Einar began after everyone was settled, "is we believe we can no longer serve as elders. This is all nonsense, by golly. These people – who read the Bible and seem t' believe it – don't want to hear anything the Bible might have to say on this matter. Seriously, they *don't* want to hear it. Get real annoyed. And this church is becoming the talk of the town. Men in bars, everyone, got nothing good to say about us – you, me, Curt – one way or the other. Too many people think they know what's going on. Naturally, they side against us. All I know is we can't stay where we are."

"Pastor," Curt added, "this is a big problem. It's been a big problem for quite awhile, and it's gonna be a big problem for quite awhile longer. We can't have our families going through this. You understand?"

"Pastor," said Einar, "it's one thing when it's just us men, but when the wife and kids are being made to feel like…well…"

At that moment, Angus MacGregor walked into the room and took a seat near the window a short distance from the four men.

"Pastor," Curt continued, "we would all be better serving the Lord somewhere else. *You* would be, *I* would be, *Einar* would be, and so would Earl. In fact, it would be a real waste for you to continue where you are, swimming upstream again a horrendous current. You won't be getting the work of the Lord done because, under present circumstances, you won't be getting anything done."

Angus nodded in agreement.

"There's a new congregation starting over in Ballard," said Einar. "We were thinking we would go over and see if the love of God was with them. If it is, you're sure welcome to join us…maybe even lead us."

These were good Christian men, Pastor Nordquist thought to himself. He appreciated their offer and suggestion, but at the moment he wanted the leading of the Lord, not only Curt and Einar.

"I appreciate your concern," said Amos to Einar. "At the moment I'm not certain we are to stay in Seattle…or Ballard. My good friend," added Pastor Nordquist, nodding in the direction of Angus MacGregor, "thinks the Almighty may be leading me somewhere else."

"Where is He leading you?" asked Curt, looking first at Amos, and then at Angus.

"I believe somewhere other than Seattle," answered Angus, looking at Pastor Nordquist, "somewhere in western Washington. This pilgrimage may nearly be over."

Einar, a moment ago encapsulated in disconsolate gloom, suddenly sat up.

"Well, you know," said Einar, "I just thought of a good place, by golly!" Einar looked at the others, puzzled. "Now why didn't I think of it before? Before I tell you, let me find out some things."

"Thank you, Einar," said Pastor Nordquist, wondering what had entered Einar's mind. "Obviously I need to make a decision soon. Your help is appreciated."

Regardless of where he would go next, it was obvious to Pastor Nordquist that he should prepare a formal resignation. How would his resignation be received by many in the congregation? he wondered. To what level might the euphoria rise?

Thursday, May 30, 1889

A flurry of knocks on the door signaled an emergency. Amos and Anna both stared at the door for a moment, and looked at one another. Now what? A knock on the door was an insignificant occurrence during normal times. These were not normal times, and Amos did not know what to expect. With guarded concern, Amos went to the door and opened it.

"Well, by yiminy, I have some good news!" said Einar, clapping his hands together as he smiled and looked up at Amos. Amos looked at Einar, startled. Good news?

"Come in," said Amos, returning Einar's smile. "I could stand some good news."

"It seems there are more Swedes and Norwegians up north than salmon in Puget Sound, by golly." Einar waved his arms, "Well, that's mostly all there are up there, you know."

Einar turned and pointed north.

"So many Lutherans, but no Lutheran pastor," Einar clarified. "Well, no, that is not entirely true. There is a circuit rider who, I am told, is about to die of exhaustion." Einar tilted his head to his right, crossed his eyes and stuck his tongue out the side of his mouth, feigning his death – and the others could not help but laugh.

"Einar, I can tell from your happy delirium that you are pleased to bring me this information," Pastor Nordquist understated. He had not seen Einar this buoyant since meeting him.

"Aye, we both be pleased," said Angus who had come to Amos's side when hearing the news. Nodding sagaciously, Angus looked at Amos with an I-told-you-so expression. "Now this may be what we're expectin'; this may be where the Lord wants y' t' go, finally."

"If you go up north to the Skagit River valley," continued Einar, "you will be welcomed with open arms."

Amos wrote down "Scajit [the way it sounded] River valley," preparatory to studying it on a map.

"I'll need to contact church official Nels Hanseth in Minnesota about this," said Amos.

Amos showed Einar what he wrote. "Is this correct?'

"No, it is spelled with a "k" and a 'g' – S-k-a-g-i-t," corrected Einar. "Oh, and some more good news: my cousin and her family have a big farm and farm-house, and will be glad to put you up for a spell."

"That's very generous."

"Well, just between you and me, they might need some help around the farm."

"Ah, that makes more sense. If we head north, we'd be happy to help, of course."

"My cousin's husband can do the work of five men. He just can't be everywhere at once. And my cousin, Erika Odegaard, she is a strong believer. You'll be very welcome there."

"What's her husband's name?" asked Amos.

"Ode, but folks call him 'Big Swede'."

"Sounds like someone I would like to meet." Before making plans to head north, however, Pastor Nordquist needed to publicly resign from the pulpit.

75

Sunday, June 2, 1889

Marinating in pretentious piety near the front of the church, the four dissenting elders sat solemnly, arms folded like inquisition adjudicators. They would meet with Pastor Nordquist after the service ended and again request his resignation. If he did not comply, they would fire him.

For his sermon that morning, Pastor Nordquist used as his text the verses from Luke 10:25 – 37, the lawyer's "neighbor" question, and Christ's response of the Good Samaritan parable. Attendance that morning was half of what it was a month ago.

At the sermon conclusion Pastor Nordquist prayed with the congregation. In the prolonged silence following the prayer, standing in the pulpit like a captain on the bridge of a ship, he studied the faces gradually crowded toward the back of the church. The sanctuary floor seemed to float in the stillness.

He spoke solemnly with an overtone of finality.

"Just as our senses are quickened with use, worshipping God quickens our hearts. While God is unchanging, from worshipping Him we change by growing more aware of God's presence and of His majesty, bringing us closer to God, causing us to become more Christ-like, more loving of one another and God Himself. It is why you worship; for it is worshipping that cultivates the ability to *'LOVE THE LORD YOUR GOD WITH ALL YOUR HEART AND WITH ALL YOUR SOUL AND WITH ALL YOUR STRENGTH AND WITH ALL YOUR MIND,' and to 'LOVE YOUR NEIGHBOR AS YOURSELF'* and to serve the Lord. It is through worship from the heart that you attain a heart for the Lord. Sadly, however, worship for many in this congregation has been a formality."

Pastor Nordquist looked about the sanctuary.

"I have been with you for a very short time. In the beginning, my hope and expectations were great. I hoped that in this new and growing community, I would be used by the Holy Spirit in a manner by which many of you could be drawn to Jesus to be born again, to salvation." He placed his hands on the outer edges of the pulpit and leaned forward.

"I understand some of you believe the difficulty of the moment can be resolved through compromise. If, in order to remain pastor of this congregation, I would need to compromise biblical principles – such as Luke 6:31: 'And just as you want people to treat you, treat them in the same way' – I must disappoint you, for this I will not do."

The congregation looked back at him with manikin motionlessness.

"If I did not take my position, profession, and the word of God seriously," Pastor Nordquist continued, "the compromise which some of you expect would be no obstacle. I will not indulge in pretense, however.

"I have spoken to other church leaders in this new community. Several encouraged me to remain in this pulpit. I considered what they said. I have also carefully considered, however, what others, converted men, have advised." Pastor Nordquist placed his hands on the front of the pulpit. "With regret I am formally submitting my resignation as pastor of this congregation." The announcement met with continued silence. Pastor Nordquist sensed that the consciences of some parishioners were aching at that moment. Gunnar Olsson, the big fisherman who had met Pastor Nordquist and his family at the train depot, sat dejected, feeling somehow responsible. "And I assume," Pastor Nordquist concluded, "there would be no objection if the resignation were effective immediately."

Silence.

The four elders remained as motionless as spiders outside a kitchen window, watching Pastor Nordquist.

Pastor Nordquist looked down at his wife, daughters, and Angus MacGregor in the second pew. Mr. Chong was not with them. Pastor Nordquist looked about the sanctuary for the last time and raised his right hand for the benediction that he intoned with sincerity.

"May the Lord bless you and keep you. May the Lord make His face to…"

Pastor Nordquist greeted each person who filed up the aisle that warm summer morning. Gunnar Olsson reached out with a callused hand, and attempted to tell Pastor Nordquist how bad he felt, but Gunnar could not find the words as hard as he tried. Looking down, Gunnar shook Pastor Nordquist's hand again and again as if trying to recharge a dry pump. Letting go, Gunnar gave Pastor Nordquist a look of profound sorrow that said everything. Gunnar turned and walked toward his awaiting family whose expressions were equally glum.

Some parishioners acted as if no announcement was made; that hearing a pastor's resignation was just part of what they did in church on Sunday mornings.

Only one, a stout, elderly woman, Alma Erikson, asked the obvious question: "How will we find another pastor who ministers as you do? We shall be given a new pastor who emphasizes sacraments and liturgy, with little emphasis on God's saving grace. What will become of us when you leave?"

"I'm honored, but I am merely the messenger, Mrs. Erikson, and I'm certain God will answer your prayers for direction. You may need to find another congregation. It seems most here expect the Lord to continually stand at the door and knock."

As congregation families dispersed in the various directions, the Nordquists remained behind. After helping the ushers clean the pews and floors, and insuring that everything was in its proper place, Pastor Nordquist and the family exited the church and began walking the few blocks to the parsonage. It was a warm, sunny day, one of many such days in the growing town of Seattle. The weather and Angus MacGregor's frame of mind were in union.

"Is it *not* lovely weather?" laughed Angus. "Aye but it is. Indeed it is," said Angus as he looked about him. "T'is a great day to have a heavy burden lifted." Angus MacGregor marveled at the blue skies and Elliott Bay. "God has given this as a sign, He has."

"A sign of what, Angus?" asked Amos.

"A sign that the difficulties with these Pharisees are behind us."

"Well, forgive my lack of faith," responded Pastor Nordquist after a moment's thought, "but I'm not sure this weather is a sign of anything in particular, and I'm not certain we are out of the Pharisaic woods yet."

"Pastor Nordquist," said Angus, "if we be not out of the woods, we be close to the edge. Can y' not see the trees for the forest? And all the sunlight streamin' through the trees?" Angus laughed and lifted his arms toward the clear Seattle sky. "Ah, indeed. 'T'is a beautiful day."

In his happiness at that moment, Angus MacGregor stopped to drink in the scenery while the others proceeded ahead. The sky was simultaneously a dark azure blue while being incredibly bright. An unbelievable color, Angus thought. Head tilted slightly back, unaware of the fortuitous incident about to occur, Angus studied the cloudless sky dotted with seabirds flying above Elliott Bay. Angus looked at Duwamish Head tucked between the blue-green Elliott Bay foreground and the Olympic Mountain range beneath the bright blue sky.

Suddenly a white light flashed and all went black.

Immediately the colors returned, but were hazy as Angus found himself on his knees, pitching forward. He caught himself, got back up, and the fingertips of his right hand reflexively went to the back of his head. Momentarily stunned, Angus bent down, picked up his hat and looked around, confused.

It was there behind him, lying in the dirt. His reverie was shattered like glass by a rock about the size of Angus's fist hitting him in the back of the head, knocking his hat to the ground. Angus looked incredulously at the crimson fingertips of his right hand. His head hurt badly. Grimacing, he looked about anxiously for the assailant? There was no one, nothing. Only blues and greens, and no sound other than seabirds and goldfinches.

"Pastor Nordquist!" Amos shouted as he began running awkwardly while holding the back of his head. "Pastor Nordquist!" The others turned around. "Watch out! Someone just hit m' head with a stone!"

Pastor Nordquist jogged quickly to meet approaching Angus and took his arm, leading Angus toward the others, looking about but seeing no one. As they walked rapidly toward the women, Amos continued to glance about. Still nothing.

Pastor Nordquist and his wife looked at one another mutely. The girls looked down, their lips forming thin lines, upset and frightened at what was happening. Tears welled in Rachel's eyes. Anna turned and looked straight ahead, her posture erect and her expression determined, wanting to get her family away from there as quickly as possible. They began walking rapidly, Amos and Angus at the rear. Angus held the back of his aching head with his right hand, looking at the ground as the small group approached the house.

Once inside the house, the air was cool. No one spoke; no one noticed the change in temperature. The girls began attending to Angus who sat slumped forward on a kitchen chair while Amos took Anna by the arm and gently guided her to one corner of the living room. It was early Sunday afternoon, June 2, 1889. Pastor and Mrs. Nordquist spoke briefly, and then Pastor Nordquist gave a quiet command to the others in the living room.

"We'll start packing now."

Careful and deliberate packing of belongings began in earnest. At about 3:00 p.m., Angus, head bandaged, left for a short while and returned with some more boxes. As the books were removed from bookshelves, Chong Tsing Wei stood facing the bookshelves and finally began attending to the reason that led him back to this house: his family shrine. It was still secreted away on a single high shelf in a hidden closet behind the bookcase.

Over the past six months, Mr. Chong's spiritual beliefs evolved significantly; now Buddhism was a former family tradition. He was never a strong Buddhist and now not a Buddhist at all. At the same time, the shrine had been in his family for generations. While he no longer needed the shrine to satisfy his spiritual hunger, Mr. Chong had a cultivated reverence for tradition and posterity.

Mr. Chong walked to the emptied bookcase and, to the surprise of Angus and the Nordquists, pulled what appeared to be a built-in bookcase away from the wall, revealing the hidden closet door. As the others watched, Mr. Chong opened the door, entered the closet and emerged with the ornate family shrine centered with a small, seated jade statue of Buddha. He carefully took it over by the fireplace and set it on the coffee table. The Nordquists had never seen a shrine. Mr. Chong perfunctorily kneeled, expressionless, facing the shrine. He bowed.

Mr. Chong rose and stood up. Looking at the Nordquists for the first time, he was unprepared for the wide eyes. The others were as motionless as the Buddha statue. When Mr. Chong realized what the others thought they saw, he smiled and began to laugh.

"Ho, ho, ho." He momentarily stopped, continuing to smile, before resuming his staccato laughter. "Ho, ho, ho, ho."

The eyes of the nothers softened, but everything else remained frozen.

"Ah, no," began Mr. Chong smiling. "You see, I do not worship this shrine. I only pay respect to many generations who go before me. Why?" Chong shrugged. "I should." Then he looked apprehensively at the others. "I respect ancestors when I bow. It is harmful?"

Pastor Nordquist looked at the shrine inquisitively and answered, "No, respecting ancestors is a good thing, Mr. Chong. Posterity always wants to revere their ancestry. It's why we have cemeteries. But I'm…"

"'T' be truthful, pastor," interjected Angus, "if it be no more 'n a symbol of his forefathers… Mr. Chong, is this a symbol of your forefathers?"

"No, not a symbol," answered Mr. Chong. "Maybe a…reminder."

"You don't worship your ancestors," said Angus.

"No," said Mr. Chong. "They are dead. I am Christian now. I worship God." Mr. Chong held out his hands. "I do not worship ancestors or shrine; I show respect to ancestors."

Mr. Chong looked back and forth between Amos and Angus. "Bowing is Chinese tradition," said Mr. Chong. "To show respect is tradition. Those who show respect are strong. Those who do not show respect are not worthy of respect."

Pastor looked at Mr. Chong, and the shrine. "Well, then," concluded Pastor Nordquist, "there's no harm."

While relieved, Rachel and Esther continued to study the shrine somewhat apprehensively. Mr. Chong looked at them and, turning his head, looked at the shrine. Mr. Chong returned his gaze to the floor between himself and the Nordquists and shrugged his shoulders.

"It has been in my family many generations," said Mr. Chong.

He hoped they would understand. He said nothing more, walked to the secret closet door and closed it. Pushing the bookcase back against the wall, he returned to the task at hand, boxing books. Pastor Nordquist went to Mr. Chong's side, helping to sort the books before Mr. Chong placed them in the boxes.

As the others continued packing, Rachel began asking Mr. Chong dozens of questions about the shrine, chirping in her delightful way.

"Who's that?"

"Oh. That is a statue of Buddha."

"Who's he?"

Mr. Chong was pleased to answer and the others were interested. The experience was educational and made time fly. In addition, it provided a distraction from the lingering emotional pain following the events of that morning. When the Nordquists arrived in Seattle, many offered to help them get settled. Now, only a short while later, there were none, but it didn't seem to matter. Esther, in fact, seemed to be more concerned about the spiritual welfare of Seattle than her immediate efforts or future plans.

"Daddy, what's going to happen in Seattle when we leave?" asked Esther.

"People here will go on as usual," answered Pastor Nordquist, folding a shirt, "doing as they do. Probably nothing much will change," added Amos. "Why do you ask?"

"Oh," responded Esther, eyebrows raised, "I just wondered."

"No one just wonders," said Anna. "Why do you ask?"

"I thought if we weren't here, Seattle would be a worse place. Or God might punish Seattle," said Esther, shrugging her shoulders as she looked at her father. "Like He did Sodom and Gomorrah." Then she glanced at Angus who was obviously still in some pain. "He should at least punish whoever hit Mr. MacGregor with a rock."

"If God punishes Seattle," said Amos, smiling, "I don't think it will have much to do with us. I am not Abraham or one of the great prophets. Whatever I accomplish is actually accomplished by God working through me. In the greater scheme of God's plan, my role is relatively insignificant."

"What?" Rachel responded, turning toward her father and looking at him with disbelief. "Daddy, it's not insignificant! Just think! In 100 years this could all be viewed as really important. Like Mr. McGregor says, 'One thing leads to another.' Maybe this will be the 'one thing,' and people will read about you in history books some day."

"I think it is more likely they will read about you," responded Pastor Nordquist. "It is not, however, really important that they read about either of us. Many significant historical events and the people who participated in those events have either been forgotten or were never recognized for their importance in the first place – while on the other hand there are events and people whose importance has been exaggerated."

"Like who?" asked Rachel.

"Oh," paused Pastor Nordquist, smiling, "I can think of several generals and presidents. Historians can be creative…but not only historians. Do you remember that book you read, *Tales of a Wayside Inn* by Longfellow, and that poem about Paul Revere?" Pastor Nordquist knew it was Rachel's favorite.

"'Listen my children and you shall hear/,'" responded Rachel, "'Of the midnight ride of…'"

"Yes, that's the one," interrupted Amos who knew Rachel would repeat all 13 stanzas if allowed. "What did Paul Revere do?"

"He warned the villagers."

"All by himself?"

"No," responded Rachel. "Do you remember in the poem where he had a 'friend'? He said to his friend, 'If the British march/By land or sea from the town to-night,/Hang a lantern aloft in the…'"

"That's correct," interjected Amos. "He had a partner, William Dawes. Events are hazy but, in reality, both Paul Revere and William Dawes, not just Paul Revere, rode toward Lexington, quietly warning people along the way.

"Taking different routes, Dawes and Revere rode to Lexington to warn Samuel Adams and John Hancock that they were about to be captured, and both Adams and Hancock escaped. Then Paul Revere and William Dawes rode toward Concord to warn the colonialists that the British intended to capture a weapons storage building there. Along the way, Paul Revere and William Dawes were joined by Dr. Samuel Prescott who was riding home after visiting his fiancé. As the three men proceeded, a group of patrolling British regulars stopped Paul Revere, William Dawes and Samuel Prescott."

"They were captured?!" exclaimed Rachel incredulously.

"Two of the men were captured, but one of them escaped. Guess which one?"

"Paul Revere," said Rachel, folding her arms with satisfaction.

"No, both Paul Revere and William Dawes were captured and detained. Dr. Samuel Prescott got away and rode to Concord to alert the patriots."

"Dr. Samuel Prescott? Who's Dr. Samuel Prescott?"

"He's actually the one made the last leg of 'The Midnight Ride of Paul Revere;' he's the one who rode to Concord."

"Well, then," asked Rachel, arms still folded, "why didn't Longfellow write a poem about Dr. Samuel Prescott?"

Amos didn't get a chance to respond.

"Because it wouldn't rhyme with: 'Listen my children and you shall hear…,'" said Esther. "'Listen my children and you shall hear/Of the midnight ride of Dr. Samuel Prescott.' Dumb."

"Girls, it's just an example," smiled Pastor Nordquist. "Longfellow wrote a wonderful, inspiring, historic poem – I love reading it – and Paul Revere participated in a great event. Most people erroneously believe Paul Revere acted alone. Returning to what we were first discussing, my point is that it is not important what people believe happened, it is important what God knows happened. Ultimately, we must account to Him for what really occurred and what we really did."

"Well," said Rachel, referring to their befriending Mr. Chong and not compromising that friendship, "what we really did was the right thing." Her expression became serious. "So, you see, that's significant." She nodded her head again with finality as she looked judiciously at the light blue dress she held, made for her by her mother during the first month they were in Seattle. It doesn't fit any more, she frowned.

Neither did her family.

Monday, June 3, 1889

"You know how much I bring – I will not take much more," said Mr. Chong to Mrs. Nordquist. He looked at his knapsack stuffed with clothes, and chuckled. The shrine was small and in a box.

Angus MacGregor's needs were few and, consequently, when it came time to pack, he was done in 20 minutes. It took that long because there were a few items he needed to find, placed in locations that did not lend themselves to memory. The muffled, rhythmic thud – thud – thud of his big brown boots, aged by years of wear and repair, again preceded his appearance at the top of the basement stairs. After he stepped out the door, he placed his box of belongings on the floor beneath the flight of stairs to the second floor. His head throbbed slightly but was feeling a little better.

The time necessary for the Nordquists to pack could be reduced substantially with help from both Angus and Mr. Chong. Anna, however, wanted everything packed purposefully. "Mr. Chong, Angus," directed Anna Nordquist, "you two make yourselves comfortable while the girls and I do the packing. I want to make sure that everything is put away neatly…and I know where everything is. Not like last time. If I need you, I'll let you know."

Angus sat down next to Mr. Chong.

"Perhaps we should pack Mr. Chong's dishes and silverware," suggested Esther, standing beside her mother. "After all, they're really his."

"That's an interesting consideration," responded Mrs. Nordquist, placing a forefinger on her right cheek, her eyebrows lifted. She looked at the china for a moment. "When we moved in, they were here, property of the church," she murmured absently to herself, "but, of course, before then they belonged to Mr. Chong."

"Then let's do it," said Rachel. "Those people don't deserve this good stuff! We should take everything that is Mr. Chong's."

"I'm not sure we should," said Inga quietly. "They're not ours either." Inga looked at Mr. Chong. "First ask Mr. Chong."

"Oh, he'll say, 'It's just fine,'" said Rachel. "So let's just…"

"Rachel," said Mrs. Nordquist, "Inga is right. It is not our decision to make."

Anna turned to Mr. Chong. "Mr. Chong, what would you like to do?"

Mr. Chong stared at the china.

"This does not belong to me now," said Mr. Chong. "It was mine. But not now. Belong to someone, not Chong Tsing Wei. Maybe belong to police. If police say these are mine, and give them back to me, they are mine. But that is not to happen. These things are not important. They are…dirty." Mr. Chong paused. "Why do you want them?" Mr. Chong turned to the others.

"Well, they are very valuable," responded Anna somewhat awkwardly. "They are worth keeping."

"No," said Mr. Chong, nodding politely, "not valuable. Dirty. You know?"

Mr. Chong looked at the others to discern understanding. The others, with the exception of Pastor Nordquist, looked back puzzled.

"Not valuable," Mr. Chong repeated. "Maybe only valuable to leave them here."

⸺ ● ⸺

Nels Hanseth was distraught. From his vantage point in Minneapolis, he had seen occasional schisms, but the present problem in blossoming Seattle, together with the involvement of his long-time friend, Amos Nordquist, made this schism particularly frustrating.

When Pastor Nordquist also submitted his resignation to Nels Hanseth and requested permission to head north to the Skagit River valley, sixty miles north of Seattle, it was a dilemma. In fact, a permanent Lutheran pastor was desperately needed in Skagit County, but the loss in Seattle was a significant reversal for church officials attempting to organize the community at a great distance. A new pastor would be called and hopefully the damage could be gradually repaired. Damage control, however, was never truly productive – the subsequent spiritual plateau would not approach what could have been if the church had opened its doors to Mr. Chong – and bringing in a new pastor sometimes only exacerbated the discontent while temporarily forestalling the inevitable.

Meanwhile, knowing the warm reception a permanent pastor's arrival in Skagit County would bring, Einar arranged for the Nordquist family to stay with

Einar's relatives, the Odegaards – "Big Swede" and his wife Erika, Einar's cousin – who welcomed the opportunity to temporarily host a Lutheran pastor and his family. Many families already settled in the Skagit River Valley would host friends or relatives until the latter could get settled. In a land filling up with newcomers, such arrangements were not unusual.

The Seattle population went from 3,500 in 1880 to approximately 31,000 in 1889. Due to the vagaries of the national economy, together with the expense incurred when traveling to Seattle from the East Coast, most arriving in Seattle were short on cash. Pastor Nordquist was able to find a teamster who would take them north to the Skagit River Valley for the same price as would be charged for a similar trip to Tacoma, even though the distance to the Skagit River Valley was greater and the road more difficult.

Mr. Chong surprised the others with an announcement of his plans which differed from theirs.

"When we get to Snohomish," said Mr. Chong, "I will not continue. I will wait or go east. Maybe soon I will work for James J. Hill. I want that for a long time. His Seattle agent said he will build a railroad over the Cascades to Snohomish. I will see. I will visit you in the future."

Mr. Chong's belief that he could work for Hill was not born of wishful thinking. Mr. Chong talked to J. J. Hill's Seattle agent, the one man outside of the Nordquists and Amos MacGregor whom Mr. Chong believed he could trust: Judge Thomas Burke. Until other arrangements were made, however, Judge Burke could not guarantee Mr. Chong physical safety in Seattle and, consequently, Mr. Chong would travel with the Nordquists north to Snohomish. Once in Snohomish, he would decide what he should do next. Mr. Chong promised that once his fate with the "Empire Builder" was decided, he would attempt to relocate his friends in the Skagit River Valley.

Meanwhile, the desire to immediately leave Seattle grew stronger in the mind of Pastor Nordquist. Why? What else could happen? he wondered, unaware of the disaster that would occur the next day.

Part Three

Heartbreak and Hope

1889–1918

76

Thursday, June 6, 1889, 2:00 p.m.

As Pastor Nordquist roughly pulled and cinched ropes on the wagon loaded with family belongings that clear June morning, Angus MacGregor stood silently, almost reverently, looking at Elliott Bay, the distant shores, and the snow-covered Olympic Mountains beyond. The view was like several small paintings of singular but beautiful composition, all placed adjacent to one another to form one larger painting with extensive variety in beauty, so much so that it seemed almost impossible to visually take it all in.

"Come, now, everyone!" shouted Pastor Nordquist, interrupting Angus's reverie. Amos had an overwhelming urge to leave immediately. "Let's get going, please."

"What's the hurry?" asked Angus. Amos looked at Angus, unamused.

"'The hurry' is I want to leave. Perhaps I'm fed-up. Or I don't like how my family has been treated. Or I am anxious to get started again. I don't know. I just want to get going."

Anna, already formally seated on the wagon, listened passively although her stomach was still tense. It was exactly as she felt.

"Very well," said Angus merrily, rechecking the tautness of a support rope at the rear of the wagon, "if it's leavin' y' want, it's leavin' we do."

"Everyone! Up on the wagon!" directed Pastor Nordquist. "Let's go!" Angus and the girls quickly climbed on board.

Once all were settled, the teamster shouted, "Yah!" and lightly snapped the reins. As the wagon began to roll, the anxiety on Anna's face began to fade in favor of hope. Pastor Nordquist was annoyed at the laggard pace, and stared at the road ahead, wishing they were further along, but said nothing to the teamster.

The overhead sun shone brightly as Amos and Anna Nordquist, the girls, and Angus MacGregor headed north out of Seattle. No rain had fallen for weeks, almost as if the month were not June, but July or August in other years. The roadbed was dry, covered with a powder of dust, and, although moving slowly, the wagon still forced up a light veil of dust behind it. The morning air was warming and Angus was already wiping the light perspiration from his forehead.

As the teamster pushed his team northward on Broadway Hill, tragedy was about to strike a few blocks away. Victor Clairmont's Cabinet Shop was in the basement of the downtown Pontius Building. Cabinetmaker Charlie Stoll was immersed in the effort at hand, unmindful of the slumbering presence Charlie's young assistant, John Back, was about to awaken. Stoll's attention was disrupted. He would need some hot glue in a moment but, staving off heat as long as possible, had not wanted to melt glue balls in the gluepot earlier. "John, I need some glue," Stoll said with resignation. "Toss some glue balls in the glue pot and light the stove."

"Argh!" started Ed Kittermaster, another cabinetmaker. "With this infernal heat, t'would be nice if we had no need of heatin' glue."

Back picked up the nearby gluepot and placed it on the wood stove, dropped in enough glue balls to fill it, lit a fire in the stove, and walked back across the floor – littered with wood shavings and sawdust inadvertently saturated over months with turpentine, kerosene and flammable solvents – to his workbench a short distance away.

Amos MacGregor looked westward toward Elliott Bay, Duwamish Head and the Olympics from the back of the wagon. Angus sighed nostalgically. In spite of maltreatment recently experienced, Angus found leaving difficult. If there were problems with those living in Seattle, there was very little wrong with Seattle itself. The teamster lightly snapped the reigns again, urging his team forward at a faster but controlled pace. All were prepared for a trip of several days.

As the wagon approached the northern end of town, Stoll the cabinetmaker was being careful not to over-bore a hole preparatory to cabinet shelf placement. As he worked, focused completely on what he was doing, the pot of glue on the corner stove began to bubble.

"Back, get me that drill by that wood vice," requested Stoll, glancing over at the wood vice. His assistant went to get the drill as Stoll wiped his forehead with his bandana. Behind Stoll, the glue-pot boiled over.

"Hey, Back! The glue!" shouted George Kirchener as the gobs of glue ran down the side of the pot, touched the hot stove surface and burst into flame, also setting the glue pot on fire.

Back turned around, looked and, wide-eyed, ran to the sink, filled a pot of water, dashed over to the stove and threw the water on the burning glue. When the water hit the pot, rather than putting out the fire, it splattered a small amount of hot, burning glue from the pot on to the floor covered with turpentine-saturated sawdust and wood shavings. As the small, flaming glob touched the floor, a slumbering presence awoke with a start, and a small fire shot up, stopping for a moment as if to look around.

Seeing the flame, wide-eyed, Stoll dropped the drill just handed to him. "Back, get more water!" Stoll quickly turned and grabbed a coat off a wall hook, and raced to the still-watching fire, swinging the coat downward again and again, attempting to beat out the fire, but the fire barely cringed from the blows, instead angrily surging across the floor as Stoll jumped to the side, thunderstruck, his stomach feeling like it was also afire. His tools. His equipment. His work.

"Lads!" Kirchener shouted, "Get out! Get out! It's no use!" Back was already running up the stairs when Stoll grabbed some nearby tools.

As Back, Stoll, Kirchener, and Kittermaster rushed from the building, the flames covered the floor, then climbed the board walls, and began hungrily eating through the wood ceiling. Outside someone noticed the smoke coming from the open basement windows, and verbally sounded the alarm, passed quickly from block to block to the small fire station.

The basement became a furnace, and the first floor above began to burn. Seeing the smoke and feeling the heat, most first floor tenants, grabbing belongings and valuables, quickly vacated the building as others raced up stairs, warning upper floor tenants. Smoke and heat began pouring out the first floor windows just after the building was completely vacated, and town folk began to gather along the street. As upper floors caught on fire, a hose cart, pulled by men and boys, clambered into position, the hose attached to the nearest fire hydrant on Madison Street. Moments later a clanging fire bell sounded the approach of a horse-drawn fire engine racing around the corner, smoke pouring from its stack, and sparks flying from its steel-rimmed wheels. It pulled into place and the firemen jumped off, moving furiously, getting hoses hooked up and into position. By the time the firemen began to use their hoses, however, the Pontius Building was ablaze and so hot, the firemen could not get close to it.

Tenants in the adjacent two-story wood building included the Crystal Palace Saloon, the Opera House Saloon, and the Dietz and Mayer Liquor Store, all housing dozens of whiskey barrels in the basement. As the fire raged into the adjacent building, the nearest whiskey barrels exploded, turning the neighboring basement into an oven rivaling the Pontius Building. As more and more whiskey was consumed, the Fire looked to ravage everything nearby.

The fire spread with breakneck speed. By 2:40 p.m. on June 6, 1889, ten minutes after the glue boiled over in Victor Clairmont's Cabinet Shop, half of a Seattle city block was in flames.

Volunteer firemen began hosing down the sides of tinder-dry buildings facing the fire. It was a good idea and would have worked except flaming firebrands, wafting high into the air from already burning buildings, came to rest on other nearby roofs. When the dry roofs caught on fire, the walls below followed.

"We can't get water fast enough!" shouted James Murphy, consummate public servant acting as fire marshal while the regular fire marshal was out or town. "Get more hoses! We can't get ahead of this thing at the rate we're goin'!"

What followed was a firefighter's nightmare. There were two sources of water. The first was obvious: fire hydrants. As more hoses were connected, water pressure at each hydrant gradually fell until hoses doing their job at the start of the firefighting effort were becoming useless.

"Murph!" hollered a fireman. "We've hooked up all the hydrants within reach! Ain't enough! And the water pressure 's a'fallin'! What d' we do? Murph?"

"Ah, lemme find out!" Murphy hollered, running to talk with someone else.

"Can we hook up to the bay?!" Murphy yelled to a seasoned fireman who just moved to Seattle from Newark.

"Hook up to the bay?!"

"Yeah!" shouted Murphy. "Pump water from Elliott Bay!"

"Yeah, I s'pose so!"

"Then don't just stand there," ordered Murphy, "get goin'!"

The fireman ran off, returning a short while later.

"Murph!" yelled the Newark fireman, perspiring heavily in the heat from the hot sun and the fire as he ran up the street. "Murph, the tide's out! We can't reach it!"

"What?!" yelled Murphy in panicked disbelief. "The tide should be comin' in! The tide should be comin' *in*!" The tide was coming in, as it invariably did that time of day, but, with the hoses available, would not be reachable for at least an hour.

"Murph, I can't do nothin' about what the dam' tide is doin'! It's out! The hoses from Steam Engine No. 2 on the wharf behind the Colman Building only stretch to the south side of the building – which is away from the fire. The tide's out! An' the water pressure is goin' down! That's all I know! Murph! What d'ya want us t' do?!"

Another firebrand landed on the Opera House roof, and the roof burst into flames as Murphy watched. Smoke filled the air and there was fire all around. Murphy stood aghast, mouth open, watching the blazing Opera House roof as the Masonic Hall next door caught on fire almost simultaneously with the north side of the Colman Building, seconds before the roof of the Commercial Mill burst into flames. It seemed there was nothing he could do except... Except what?

"Say, where's the regular fire chief?" asked one volunteer fireman. "We got an enormous problem here!"

"He's in San Francisco!" hollered another. "Takin' a class on bein' a fireman!"

"'Takin' a...'? Then Murph's the only one who knows anything?!"

"Murph's in charge...dunno what he knows!"

James Murphy, the acting fire chief with a history of past employment in various public offices, and no fire fighting experience, was faced with a conflagration for which the regular fire chief would not have been prepared. As the fire grew bolder, Murphy began to wither from the heat as Robert Moran, the cerebral Seattle mayor who arrived in Seattle alone 14 years earlier with $0.10, earning enough as a laborer to bring his two brothers and start a successful marine repair and boat building company on Yesler's wharf, stood watching the men battle the fire like a general watches his troops, studying movement, efficiency, intensity and morale. As a boy, Moran was inspired when reading about Union Army Gen. Phillip Sheridan who, in the Battle of Cedar Creek south of Winchester, Virginia, rode up to panicked, retreating Union troops, turned them around in the teeth of Confederate pursuit, and inspired them to victory.

"Hey, Murph!" shouted Moran. "You need help?!"

No reply.

"Murphy! Y' hear me?!"

There was no immediate response as the acting fire chief stood motionlessly attempting to assess a situation for which he was unprepared.

"Hey, Murph!!" shouted Moran a third time, stepping forward a few paces, "You need a hand here?!" Seeing the acting fire chief faltering, Mayor Moran strode toward Murphy. Moran had as little preparation in fire fighting as James Murphy, but Moran's self-confidence was the result of successfully overcoming major obstacles on multiple occasions.

"Murph, take a break," said the mayor, his arm around Murphy. "I'll take it from here."

Moran turned toward a group of firemen frustrated by the lack of water pressure as they feebly fought the fire.

"Johnson! McGuire!" Moran yelled, his voice sounding like Snoqualmie River gravel. "We need to get ahead of the fire and get water pressure back up! Order your men to disconnect at the hydrants where the fire is already out of control! It's like trying to build half a dam! Reconnect a few hoses a couple of blocks up the hill, but don't overdo it or we're back where we started! Do you have any dynamite?!"

"Yessir!" shouted Johnson, wide-eyed. "There's bunch of it in storage over near 4th and Pine."

"Get it! Get all of it!"

"What 'r we gonna do, mayor?"

Giving commands of which a lesser man would not have thought, Moran ordered the remaining Colman block blown up. On-looking Seattleites looked on dismayed as Moran brought down his arm, and the buildings not already ablaze in the Colman block exploded with tremendous noise, pieces of wood flying in different directions, structures collapsing to the ground.

But the fire was unintimidated by Robert Moran. The fire contemptuously hissed and, ambulatory through its own radiating heat, incinerated and nimbly swept across the hot wreckage, wounding the egos of his adversaries while consuming ravenously.

Reacting with fury fueled by wood, vulnerable opposition, and weeks without rain, the fire raced in all directions. From the Commercial Mill it sprinted along the waterfront, destroying Yesler's Wharf including Moran's boat building business. From the Opera House, it climbed rapidly eastward up the hill, consuming residences where Chong Tsing Wei was once a topic of conversation. It encircled buildings and ran down alleys, insuring nothing escaped.

The wind that day would have been mild. The fire voraciously sucked in ground level currents that, with combustion, rose like July 4th rockets. The rising heat from the burning city became so strong along the perimeter of the fire that distant breezes were created and sucked in, joining inferno-induced air currents, driving smoke, sparks, burning firebrands and ashes high into the sky as if from a volcano. Rising heat then radiated outward. The discomfort and frustration of fighting the fire became more and more vexing.

At first the Nordquists heard the sound of distant fire bells, but continued on their northerly trek. By the time they had reached the small Portage Bridge that spanned the 16-foot-wide channel between Lake Washington and Lake Union, they stopped the wagon and watched the smoke billowing over the rim of Broadway Hill into the late afternoon sky. In a few moments, the Fire would begin devouring both the Gordon Hardware Company building, which stored 30 tons of cartridges, and the Seattle Hardware Store where another 20 tons of ammunition was kept. Firefighters kept their distance as the ammunition began exploding, continuing for over a half an hour. Amazingly, no one was hurt although, at a distance, Rachel thought it sounded like a gun battle, and wondered out loud whether a war was being fought in Seattle.

Attempting to form an effective fire gap, Mayor Moran organized the destruction of more buildings. Taunted, the fire responded with ferocious rapacity, again leaping gaps with the aid of winds and hot, combustible materials. The fire reached the stately parsonage and, in a moment, evidence that Mr. Chong was capable of handling small maintenance projects or anything else, was ablaze. Minutes later the Lutheran church, bone-dry like everything else, caught fire. The siding and roof were quickly gone, leaving a white, skeleton of flaming framing with only the fireplace not on fire. The firemen made no further attempt to fight the fire, but stood in resigned exhaustion next to harried, dismayed citizens, and helplessly watched the devastating flames.

The fire enjoyed itself north of the Deadline, seeming to have little or no interest in the Lava Bed south of Yesler Way. As the expansive inferno north of the Deadline crackled and roared, checked only by lack of additional buildings, the fire turned and stared at the brothels and box houses some of Pastor Nordquist's restive male parishioners frequented. One-by-one the buildings were lightly tapped by the outstretched finger of the fire until all of the Seattle business district and residential periphery, 120 acres, 30 city blocks, were burning. With the torching of the Lava Bed, the fire spread no further, as if it stopped, like everyone else, to watch itself.

Rachel fell asleep in her mother's arms at around 9:00 p.m. After Anna told Amos she was not feeling well, she went to sleep while still holding Rachel. The others continued to sit motionlessly, looking back at the fire-illuminated smoke rising in the darkening sky. The teamster said they would spend the night where they were.

Pastor Nordquist thought of his former congregation and the difficulties he experienced. The Swensons. The Jonsons. The Bergquists. He thought of Murray underworld members who knew they were sinners, but did not want to hear about it, contrasted with Seattle polite society. Pastor Nordquist sighed. No, polite society did not want to hear about it either. Pastor Nordquist, although tired, continued to watch the distant embers shoot skyward, white ash descending around him like snowfall.

There were, he thought, many good people in Seattle – proportionately more than Nineveh. To Jonah's chagrin, God temporarily spared Nineveh. But He later allowed Nineveh, its buildings and people, to be utterly destroyed by Babylonians, Medes and Scythians. The destruction was so thorough that for centuries the location of Nineveh was lost, some believing Nineveh never existed. Has God spared Seattle? Amos joked to himself. The city will rebuild. Meanwhile, Amos wondered, was the fire the result of an accidental mishap, or was there more to it?

Pastor Nordquist put his hands behind his head, leaned back against a box filled with clothing, and stared skyward. All our belongings are in this wagon. It might have been otherwise. Is that why Angus was hit in the head with a rock? Without really seeing them, Amos looked down at the tips of his boots silhouetted in the fire-illuminated smoke cloud, and thought the rock must have been providential – although like most providential things, it didn't seem so at the time.

Pastor Nordquist's eyes were heavy. They closed, and he fell asleep.

The Great Seattle Fire continued to burn, peacefully absorbed in itself until at about 3:00 a.m. when all that remained of Seattle were isolated islands of glowing white and orange coals within a sea of ashes covered by darkness. The Lava Bed resembled its name. The fire gradually grew more fragmented and smaller, and still smaller, until, as the air cooled and early morning twilight outlined the crest of eastern hillsides, there were only tufts of smoke, as if from a thousand extinguished candles, rising from pocks in the ashes. Then the fire, so healthy and horrific hours earlier, quietly passed away.

There was a wake. When the fire first began to spread, several Lava Bed saloons rolled nearly 100 barrels of whiskey into Elliott Bay, hoping to retrieve them later. They recovered two.

As the sun rose, Anna still wasn't feeling well. Breakfast was made over a campfire.

"This is just like camping out!" said Rachel.

"It is camping out," said Esther.

"'It *is* camping…'"

"Girls, don't dawdle," said Anna, "the teamster says we need to get moving immediately if we expect to get to Snohomish City before dark.

ROUTE NORTH TO EQUALITY COLONY

77

June 5, 1889

The wagon began to roll, and by 9:00 a.m. the Nordquists were passing aside huge stumps in what had been great virgin forests north of Green Lake en route to somewhere that might include, Anna silently hoped, a permanent parish.

As the second afternoon neared its end, the wagon wound through forests where tree trunks six to nine axe handles in circumference supported arboreal giants looming high overhead. Seated on the edge of the wagon, Angus McGregor, nearly losing his balance, grabbed his hat as he looked up at the huge cedars and firs under which the wagon was slowly moving

Capt. George Vancouver, writing in his log 100 years earlier, described the area as "…a faire land, a goode place…" that needed only "…villages, mansions, cottages and other buildings, to render it the most lovely country that could be imagined." Vancouver's imagination must have been exceptional, thought Amos when he read Vancouver's words. How the land could be made lovelier was difficult to envision.

Amos looked about. The azure sky was pristine. The great, white-capped mountains occasionally visible in various directions were from a Bierstadt painting. Pastor Nordquist imagined Captain Vancouver sailing into Puget Sound, his long glass held to his eye, studying the shorelines and hillsides. In the foreground, waves lapped up on sand-and-pebble covered beaches where gray and white gulls looked back at Vancouver with indifference, and in the middle, beneath the mountains, from one end of the landscape to the other were emerald-hued hillsides and foothills robed in Douglas fir.

"God's country," summarized Angus, intuiting Amos's thoughts.

Passing through centuries-old, mammoth forests, Amos had the same sensation of insignificance he sometimes had when at sea – particularly poignant while studying the star-covered sky that first clear night in the lifeboat. Angus, however, had a different take.

"Aye," Angus began. "This looks like a good place for a lumber mill, does it not? Henry Yesler never saw trees the like of these."

"Don't be too sure," said Pastor Nordquist. "Seattle was once a forest just like you see here."

"You're correct, sir," Angus replied, although he wasn't entirely convinced. Head tilted back, Angus looked up at the boughs obstructing sunlight high above.

"Brobdingnagian trees these are," he said. "If there be a land of giants, these be their trees."

A moment later his expression became neutral as he stared at the trunk of a tree so large that it made other large trees appear like second growth.

"Look at the size of that," said Angus. The Nordquists looked at the monarch surrounded by other large trees, but each maintaining a respectable distance as if courtiers about a throne. As the wagon rolled forward and the tree's visibility became unobstructed, it was as if, between them and the tree, there was a huge, invisible magnifying glass.

"Now, pastor, in Seattle you saw some large stumps from early loggin', but Seattle never had stumps to compare with that," stated Angus. The others stared at the goliath. "None that I saw."

"If someone cut that down, they could build a whole house on the stump," said Rachel. "How old is that tree?" Rachel jumped off the slow-moving wagon, and ran into the woods until she stood about 20 feet from the great tree.

"How old d' y' think?" responded Angus loudly as the wagon passed where Rachel was standing.

Rachel turned toward Angus and yelled back, "I'll bet it's over...oh...I'll guess it's over...[she thought of Nels Hanseth, and deduced that the tree must be even older] 70 years old!" she concluded, clapping her hands together with finality.

She looked at Angus to see if she was close.

"Rachel, come here! Get back on the wagon!" yelled Pastor Nordquist.

"Rachel," said Angus as she climbed back on the wagon, "I spoke with men at Yesler's Mill on many occasions and, from its size, I can tell you that tree was well along in years before Columbus arrived…possibly alive even before the Norman Conquest."

"Really," said Inga in amazement. She stared at the tree. The Norman Conquest. The Battle of Hastings. 1066. Over 800 years ago. It's amazing anything could live that long, she thought.

"It's older than that, Angus," said Amos. "Remember that huge single log section down by Lake Washington? The loggers couldn't move it because it was too large, and just left it there."

"That's right," nodded Angus. "I remember that. It was enormous."

"Someone counted the rings, "Amos smiled.

"That would take all day. How many were there?"

"Nearly thirteen hundred."

"Nearly thirteen hundred rings?" said Inga, wide-eyed. "That would mean the tree started to grow in the seventh century." It seemed impossible.

"Could be. You've heard of Mohamed and Moslems." Amos folded his arms as he studied the tree. "Maybe the tree sprouted about the time Mohamed first heard what he believed to be voices of the *jinn*, or familiar spirits," said Amos, "giving him revelations. That experience scared him at first. But later he was convinced the revelations were sent by al-Ilah or Allah, the Moslem god. Thus began Islam in the 7th century, followed by Moslem conquests of Arabia, Egypt and Palestine. And they kept going from there. As directed by 'Allah,' conquest by the sword was to continue until all the earth was under Islam, and then there would be peace, but not until then. Now, we think of that time as ancient history." He looked at Rachel. "So long ago. But that tree," Amos nodded toward the huge monarch, "may have been alive then. Looking at that tree makes ancient history seem not-so-ancient, doesn't it?"

"I hope they don't cut it down," said Rachel with a frown.

"They might not," said Angus. "As the Seattle loggers found out, it's one thing t' fall a tree that size; another to haul it out. But, well, y' saw what they did to Seattle."

"Seattle was bald!" exclaimed Rachel, wide-eyed, baring her upper and lower teeth.

"Just a matter of time," said Angus as he nodded at the tree.

Rachel looked apprehensively at the big tree, studying it carefully so that if it were cut down, she could remember it. It seemed to Rachel that someone should remember it.

* * *

Meanwhile, several miles to the west on the bluff overlooking the Snohomish River where it empties into Port Gardner Bay, another conversation was taking place, a conversation between two millionaires about a grand concept.

It would be a unique undertaking.

Amos knew most inchoate cities initially received some degree of direction in the sense that street grids and, perhaps, zoning were mapped. London. Paris. Göteborg. Beginning with New Haven, Connecticut in 1639, most future American cities expanded according to similar planning, and over an extended time period a city would gradually take shape. Seattle. New Orleans. Washington, D.C. The planned city on Port Gardner Bay would go well beyond mere conceptual direction, however, with extensive industrial, commercial and residential construction all simultaneously underway while an army of prospective residents camped along the city periphery, waiting to move in. Why? What could possibly generate that much hope?

The movement began when Wisconsin millionaire Henry Hewitt painted a verbal portrait of a great industrial and metropolitan community for New York multimillionaire Charles Colby to envision.

***

"You see down there," Hewitt pointed below them. "The Snohomish River mouth could be readily dredged."

Hewitt pointed to his right.

"Over there, you see that long strip of land just off the shoreline?"

Solemnly, Colby nodded. The two men became acquainted years ago in Wisconsin when Colby, only in his early 30's, was president of Wisconsin Central Railroad, and Hewitt, a year younger than Colby, purchased timberland from the railroad. Both were intelligent, industrious and assiduous. Having worked well together, they subsequently had other business dealings.

Colby came from New York in his private Northern Pacific railroad car. Balding, his full, dark beard lightly streaked with gray, Colby looked older than his 50 years. When listening as he was now, his reticence was measured and, while his face was expressionless, his fierce-looking eyes, like those of an eagle, occasionally made him appear angry when he was not.

"Dredge this whole area starting well above the river mouth," said Hewitt, pointing to the east, "then downstream to the mouth," his finger swept from east to north, "and then along the inside of that natural jetty," he pointed west then southwest, "and we have freshwater moorage for dozens of sailing ships and steamships."

Charles Colby looked where Hewitt pointed, and saw what Hewitt saw. It looked physically feasible. Hewitt was speaking to the potential for passenger transportation and manufactured goods distribution. But what goods? wondered Colby. For whom? Colby had been thinking about the possibility of a major West Coast port, but the timing seemed premature.

As Hewitt spoke, Colby studied Hewitt who seemed more animated than usual. Henry Hewitt, 49, was a slender man of average height, and had kind, tired eyes with crow's feet that turned up at the end, the consequence of a ready smile. His slight limp was the result of a timber cruising accident north of Green Bay years earlier. He combed his thinning hair forward and then to the side to compensate for previous hair that abandoned ship. While having neither mustache nor sideburns, his brown 6" long beard grew from a 2" wide font beneath his lower lip, looking like a dark, miniature waterfall with nowhere to go.

Foreseeing the Puget Sound region as a logging paradise with civilization to follow, Hewitt recently came to Tacoma from Wisconsin with $400,000 to invest in virgin timberland that could be purchased for $5.00 an acre. Often at the leading edge of a venture, he would occasionally be frustrated when others couldn't, or wouldn't, see what he could see. While usually courteous to all, as with most wealthy men he was judiciously selective when choosing business partners. With Hewitt's money, an average man wouldn't need partners – except that an average man would not have Hewitt's vision. In 1889, Hewitt's imagination was busy envisioning the Puget Sound corridor as it could appear 50, 100 years later.

"Over there," Hewitt continued, pointing west toward the bay, "we have deep water moorage. Port Gardner Bay. Very deep. Sounded it myself to be sure."

Charles Colby looked at the bay. Port Gardner. His father's and grandfather's first name was Gardner. Waterville College in Maine was renamed Colby College to honor his grandfather's benevolence. Descended from the early Puritans and raised in a Boston brahmin family, Colby was refined and reserved. A prominent New York businessman, Colby was wealthier than Hewitt, lived in the mansion at 8 E. 69th St., "one of the finest in the upper 5th Avenue section," and moved within a small circle of very wealthy New York investors. He was constantly approached with investment schemes, and was always wary, becoming comfortable with few men. Hewitt was one. Colby looked at the bay without expression, his hands retiring to the pockets of his expensive leather jacket.

"Combine the freshwater moorage," Hewitt pointed below to the north, "and the deep water harbor," he pointed again toward the bay, "and of what East Coast city would you be reminded, Charles?"

Charles Colby had no doubt of the correct answer.

Although Colby was interested in West Coast shipbuilding potential, had Hewitt attempted to point out opportunities for shipbuilding and lumber mills and other industry, Hewitt probably would not have caught Colby's imagination. When Hewitt instantly filled Colby's mind's eye with the familiar Port of New York, Colby felt something.

He began to mentally backtrack over what Hewitt was saying. Colby began to see what Hewitt saw and even more; for Hewitt, born in England, raised in Wisconsin, and presently living in Tacoma, was not a New York insider, whereas Colby was among those at the center of New York capitalism.

As Hewitt talked, Colby continued to look around him, not always paying attention to what Hewitt was saying. Colby could see the possibilities. Not only could he see the possibilities, but with the financial resources he and his East Coast acquaintances had, he could make the possibilities happen.

Nothing would happen, however, until Colby's comfort level was high. This defensive screen worked well for Colby whose business acumen did not allow him to feel good about any but the best of speculative ventures. At the moment, the feeling was becoming comfortable. As Hewitt continued to talk, Colby's eagle eyes studied the geography of the immediate area and surrounding countryside.

Colby looked at the deep, protected harbor, and back at the river mouth. As president of American Steel Barge Company, Colby had practical knowledge of harbors. As he listened to Hewitt extol the same timber resources that had once captivated Capt. George Vancouver, Colby looked again at the surrounding hillsides covered with trees now 100 years larger.

"Douglas fir. Best lumber in the world." Hewitt looked at Colby with a beatific visage.

"What would tie all this together like a Christmas ribbon," stated Hewitt, "is a railroad – a deepwater port with a railroad terminus provided by James J. Hill, if we build a city Mr. Hill is unable to resist." Hewitt looked at Colby knowingly. "Success requires population centers, markets and, with a railroad, we could ship directly to the Midwest and East Coast. Hill would make even more money."

Hewitt put his hands on his hips as he looked eastward.

"Can you see it, Charles? With a direct railroad line, we – you and I – could tie major East Coast cities to a West Coast city as big as..." he gestured toward the Port Gardner waterfront as he looked at Colby studying the waterfront, "well you can imagine, sir."

Hands still in his pockets, Colby's incisive eyes continued to study the bay and river characteristics, as well as the surrounding topography and geography. James J. Hill recently purchased several railroads and intended to gradually expand to the Pacific Northwest.

Perhaps this is it, Colby thought. The "West Coast New York." Everyone expects there will be one. But here. Not San Francisco. Not Seattle. The logistics of trading with China, India and Japan are favorable, just as New York trades with Europe. The shipping distance is less than from San Francisco, even Seattle. And we could develop harbor resources Seattle and San Francisco could not match.

Like a Northern Pacific locomotive, Charles Colby's imagination began to gather speed.

"Seattle, sir," continued Hewitt, "has grown by nearly 40,000 people during the past 10 years. Seattle, however, well… just happened, Charles. With foresight and planning, considering the natural geography, a proper city where we stand could grow by far more than 40,000 in far less than 10 years. And after that?"

Hewitt's right index finger swung from east to west.

"Look at that bay. The navy has been considering Seattle for a safe harbor," Hewitt stated, and then chuckled as if there was obviously a better alternative. He looked to the north and pointed. "Right there is where America should put men-o'-war!"

Colby listened carefully; he had connections.

"Envision navy ships below you, sir," Hewitt encouraged, holding out his arm as if making an informal personal introduction. "Look at the freshwater moorage potential below you and imagine steamships at anchor. Imagine mills and industry, and dozens of ships, sir," said Hewitt pointing to the shoreline southwest of them. Colby looked, keeping his hands in his pockets.

"A railroad would tie it all together; a railroad and the causal effect it would have, could make us," concluded Hewitt animatedly, "not only extraordinarily wealthy, but, in the annals of history, legendary."

Looking at Hewitt without expression, in his mind Colby debated whether Hewitt's statement was hyperbole, or whether Hewitt could be right. As a Northern Pacific Railroad Executive Board member, Colby also knew railroad politics. Hewitt knew that. Hewitt hoped Colby would be able to imagine as much as Hewitt. Colby would.

Although Hewitt was acquainted with many wealthy men, Charles Colby was Hewitt's steel bridge to prominent New York investment capitalists. Walter Oakes, Chairman of the Northern Pacific Railway, was a friend of Colby's. Colgate Hoyt, a New York multimillionaire with a variety of interests, was also on the Northern Pacific board. Charles W. Wetmore, a wealthy New York financier, was a Colby investment partner. Charles Colby attended the 5th Avenue Baptist Church in New York. So did Colgate Hoyt. So did John D. Rockefeller.

Colby knew, as a general rule, a Rockefeller decision to participate in any venture would give already-participating partners euphoria. It wasn't just that Rockefeller made a lot of money, over $10,000,000 a year between 1888 and 1889, more than, at times, he could proficiently reinvest; it was the bigger-than-life Rockefeller mystique. He was America's richest man. More importantly to Colby, Rockefeller never lost money in any of a multitude of ventures.

As Rockefeller's millions and successes accumulated in an era where an income of $5,000/year was respectable, his reputation for success reached folklore proportions. By 1889, Rockefeller's intuition in business matters was considered as certain as the sunrise. Rockefeller participation in a venture implied no risk. If Rockefeller was in the deal, the deal was destined to succeed. As Hewitt continued to talk, Colby's mind raced like a thoroughbred at Belmont.

"Charles, if we were able to..."

"Henry...," interrupted Colby. "Forgive me for interrupting, but, understandably, there are too many generalities. I need to see details. I want to see numbers and the rationale for each one. Where are the markets for what? And what might their eventual profit and loss statements look like? How would you phase development? How much capital will you need? For what? What should my associates and I expect in return? How much will you personally contribute? Timing? You need to get specific. I want to see a very detailed plan in writing. Detailed."

"And you should expect no less," responded Hewitt, folding his hands. "I wouldn't expect a dime from you and your associates until every 't' has been crossed and every 'i' dotted to your satisfaction."

Before approaching Colby, Hewitt spent long hours weighing alternative development scenarios and preparing development cost estimates, potential profit and loss statements, and hypothetical real estate operating statements for various envisioned asset categories. He was planning to update and supplement the i's already dotted and the t's already crossed. From his numbers, the possibilities excited Hewitt. It was a colossal undertaking with colossal growth potential and profitability.

What Hewitt saw was a chance of a lifetime; a chance of many lifetimes.

"You know timber," said Colby, looking at Hewitt. "Timber would be the start. Mills? Who are the buyers? Shipping? What sort of revenues should we anticipate? Operating expenses? What can we expect in profits, Henry?"

"Local timber," responded Hewitt matter-of-factly, "has already been very profitable for men like Henry Yesler. I see no reason it should be any less profitable for us. They were the first to capitalize on this resource in areas south of us. We shall be the first to do the same here," he said, turning to the side, facing the hills and forests, and extending his arm, as if showing Colby the direction to success.

"Look at that timber," said Hewitt, pointing to the hillsides. "Sections and sections of untouched forest. The biggest trees you'll ever see, sir. Douglas fir. That's almost all you see on those hillsides, Charles, each tree an individual repository of the best lumber on earth, lumber needed throughout America. With a railroad to our community, we, like Mr. Hill, should do very well for ourselves."

"It seems so, Henry," responded Colby. "Nevertheless, I want a plan that is well thought-out, where every contingency is anticipated." Colby's eagle eyes looked piercingly at Hewitt. "Every contingency you can imagine, Henry."

Then Colby made an objection that Hewitt hadn't anticipated.

"Something bothers me." Colby seemed to study the ground. "Based on location, natural resources and geography, the potential seems so great that…" Colby stopped in mid-sentence and shoved his hands back in his jacket pockets. "This may seem like an odd reservation, Henry, but perhaps our vision is too good to be true."

"Too good to be true?"

Colby turned and looked at Hewitt judiciously. "A venture of this magnitude by its very nature would be rife with risk…more than any man can foresee. Apart from needing a railroad – which, if you're correct in your assumptions, Jim Hill should be more than happy to provide – what are we missing? What else might undermine development feasibility? You need to think about that and discover whatever it is that I sense being overlooked. Sit down and make a long list of what-if's. Factor those into your business plan and financial forecasts. To the extent possible, Henry, overlook nothing. Weigh several alternative scenarios from each investment component being considered. The complexity and scope of the projections should equal the complexity and scope of the undertaking."

Colby's right hand left its jacket pocket security as Colby raised an edictive finger. "Show all this to me on paper. Make no omissions or avoidable errors. Then…" Colby paused, staring at Hewitt, "but only then," Colby's right hand returned to the pocket as Hewitt looked back into Colby's stern, piercing eyes, "there may be some possibilities."

Colby would move forward if Hewitt provided adequate justification for doing so. Hewitt, who knew the timber and lumber industry, was confident he could. Colby and Hewitt walked away, with Hewitt making mental notes about production forecasts, and Colby wondering if involvement might prove to be a monumental blunder.

78

W hat's New York like?" echoed Rachel as she looked in the direction of the letter. "What did Aunt Sarah say? Has she been to any theaters?"

"No," responded Anna, not paying complete attention to Rachel.

"Why not?" asked Rachel, studying her mother's expression. "What's the matter?"

"Aunt Sarah makes New York sound…well…," Anna paused. "She and Uncle Charles are not in a nice part of town."

"Really? What does she say?"

"I'll read some of her letter," said Anna. "You'll understand my concern." Anna began to read.

> …*poor, foreign immigrants, "huddled masses," stuffed in noisy, rat-infested tenements like spoiled sausage. I see malnourished little boys, some orphans, living like feral cats, fight pitched battles using fists, rocks, boards, broken bottles, whatever might be available, before going at night into the bowels of miserable hovels – where the beatings they receive are worse than in the street.*
>
> *Stealing, swearing, gambling, even drinking are common among young boys. Filth, disease, illiteracy and debauchery swarm like flies around children who know nothing else. It seems enough here to survive; living is for the more fortunate.*
>
> *English is both greatly abused and greatly respected. My husband's English, as you know, is exact. When we knock on doors, often those doors will not open. Those inside will defiantly growl, "Hoo-iz'it?" When Charles answers and does so commandingly, the doors always open, not out of hospitality, but out of heightened respect for authority that the inhabitants associate with cultivated English. It is a form of God's protection I had not expected, but gratefully accept. Entire hallways grow quiet at the sound of Charles' voice. Who might that be? they must wonder. They associate proper English with power. Indeed, they should.*

Nevertheless, children are unschooled. Parents don't watch their children, and it seems the only communication – if you could call it that – among families is nerve-grating noise. It is terrible. Sometimes even at 4:00 in the morning you can hear them – women screaming, men shouting, children crying. From the families we have visited, I have learned that many children never live to adulthood, and that disease, alcoholism or murder take more than a few of the men. It seems that law enforcement is largely absent in the slums, as they are called.

Contributing to this combustible mixture are former farming families leaving rural poverty and farm foreclosures for subsistence jobs. The poor souls seem totally out of place. If the social order were arranged according to floor level, rural immigrants would live in the cellar. Ostracized and abused by the others, they are, nevertheless, most receptive to the Word of God. Their children, unfortunately, too often adapt to the ways of the street.

Available jobs are long, monotonous, injurious, even debilitating, and pay practically nothing. Yet competition for these menial jobs, as you might surmise, is extensive. Men wait in line for hours on the chance of getting one job – loading boxes on to wagons – lasting a day at best.

To escape the misery, some men spend food and rent money on drink, giving rise to more misery. In the morning I see women hanging wet clothes on clotheslines running between tenement buildings, and some of these women are bruised, black and blue, obviously having been beaten.

To make ends meet, young girls, believing they have no other options, entertain older men – many of whom are married – from the other side of town. Yet, the young girls despise the older men, and the older men view the girls with veiled contempt.

Where is the Good Book in all of this? Where is love? The contrast between the rich and the poor, the upper class and the lower class, the faithful and the unfaithful, is diabolically stark and…

"Will Seattle become like that?" asked Rachel, wide-eyed.

"It's possible, but I don't think so," answered Anna, looking at the letter. "Most of the people your Aunt Sarah writes about are in New York because they've been forced to leave difficult circumstances in Europe and, while hoping for the best, lack education, vision or skills – not to mention finances – needed to manage their immediate future. The Seattle people have come here from other areas of the country in pursuit of more specific opportunities. Settlement in Seattle is more considered and purposeful. Most come here with a plan…like we did."

"But that plan didn't work out," said Rachel.

"No, but according to God's purpose," smiled Anna as she straightened Rachel's glimmering auburn hair, "it will. I'm looking forward to seeing what God has in…"

"Oh!" interrupted Rachel. Rachel looked up at her mother apologetically and explained, "Excuse me. Daddy's back!"

Rachel stood up and ran in the direction of her father who was walking rapidly toward her.

"What did you get?" sang Rachel excitedly, stopping, then rising up and down on her toes.

"Not everything I wanted," answered her father, smiling at his youngest daughter's excitement. "I thought I would get some basic farming tools," Pastor Nordquist explained. "But most things are unreasonably expensive. I asked, 'Why so much?' and I was told railroad shipping costs were high." He turned to his wife. "The store owner said that even though farm tools are almost free in Kansas now – with so many farms in foreclosure, new tools and equipment just sit in warehouses – the cost to send them here is another matter. Whatever the reason, I'm not going to pay that much money for a hoe." Pastor Nordquist chuckled. "Railroads are a great idea – but apparently when planning, no one gave adequate thought to shipping costs."

"Actually, me friend," countered Angus, "that's not entirely true. Maybe the farmers didn't think about them, but railroad stockholders – the trusts, the big corporations – did. For the stockholders, shipping costs are what railroads are all about."

"I understand," responded Amos, sighing inaudibly. "I was in a similar business once. My father, mother, brother and I understood, however, that shipping costs needed to be equitable if manufacturers, suppliers and travelers were to continue using our services."

The railroad system, Amos would learn, was inside out. The cost of shipping grain from Chicago to Liverpool was less than from Dakota farms to Chicago while, conversely, railroads operating in the Dakotas earned less than needed to pay taxes after other operating expenses were deducted. Meanwhile, between 1889 and 1893 over 11,000 Kansas farms went into foreclosure.

"Ay, there be reasons for high shipping costs, and I'll be tellin' y' one. T'is the gold standard," said Angus, introducing a controversial topic.

"The 'gold standard,'" echoed Rachel. "What's that?"

"Do we have time for this?" asked Mrs. Nordquist, implying they did not. Angus looked about at the darkening forests and wondered what might be the hurry.

"Y'd rather not hear about the gold standard, now," responded Angus, putting his hands in his pockets. "Economic theory is dull stuff, t'is," Angus smiled as he sat down on the community log, "and has no audience in good times, only bad. Right now people are standin' in line t' get tickets."

He looked at Rachel.

"The Apostle Paul said the love of money is 'a root of all sorts of evil'; I read where Kansas farmers believe the shortage of money is another."

"It's very unfortunate," responded Anna. "We're not in Kansas, however, and even if we were, there is very little we could do about the shortage of money."

"Why do you care what Kansas farmers think, anyway?" Rachel asked Angus.

"'Why do…'," Angus' hands grasped the sides of his face as he feigned shock, "it would be a *sad* day, a sad day, when folks don't care what Kansas farmers think. A sad day, indeed. Farmers in Kansas or elsewhere are the salt of the earth. When farmers can't make ends meet, the rest of us be in trouble as well. Y' ought to bear some concern for the farmer, child. They can't pay their bills."

"Why not?" asked Esther.

"Well, now," began Angus, lightly kneading his beard with his right thumb and two forefingers as he looked sideways at Anna, "I could explain that t' y', but I suspect now's not the time."

"Very well, then," said Anna as she stitched a torn pocket on Angus's other pair of overalls, "but please make it brief."

"T'is simple, child," Angus said to Esther. "While the population of the United States has doubled since the end of the Civil War, and foreign trade has expanded greatly, dollars in circulation have actually declined. The consequence is the purchasing power of the dollar today is three times what it was in 1865 at the end of the Civil War. In other words, an 1865 $3.00 item costs $1.00 today. Now, this is very advantageous if you be among those with cash, but a great burden for debtors."

"Why?"

"The debtors borrowed a certain amount of dollars, y' see, and must pay back that same dollar amount with interest. But the 'new' dollars can buy more than the 'old' dollars they borrowed – that's what 'deflation' means, child. Since the 'new' dollars are effectively more valuable, the debtors pay back much more purchasing power than they borrowed. And most farmers are debtors." Angus held up his index finger, emphasizing each subsequent phrase. "Price fixin', rebatin', long-and-short-haul discrimination, traffic associations and double-digit deflation have erected walls impossible for many farmers to surmount. Now, if the gold standard could be relaxed…"

"Daddy," asked Rachel, confused and concerned, "we can pay our bills, can't we?"

"Yes," answered Pastor Nordquist. "Even if I had no money when I left Sweden, we made subsistence income in Minnesota. I worked hard in Murray, built our house out-of-pocket, and sold it at a fair price. There were some expenses traveling from Murray to Seattle, but in Seattle the Lord blessed us with a free home and a modest income so, presently, we owe no one, and we have money saved." A pleased look came over Amos. "Quite a bit. And, of course, your Uncle Anders has been profitably busy in Göteborg."

"So we're fine?" asked Rachel.

"Yes, we are fine. Even if we weren't, this life is not as important as the life hereafter." Amos sat down with the others on the community log and folded his hands. "In either case, the Lord is in control. His will be done. Remember, man is not the measure of all things." Amos concluded with his oft-repeated first principle. "The measure of anything is the extent to which it glorifies God."

Rachel looked at her father warmly and nodded. When she first heard the Bible verse about how men are created in God's image, the image she immediately envisioned was her father. God must be like Daddy, she thought, or maybe Daddy like God. She thought about orphans who didn't grow up with a father, and how her dad said he obviously wouldn't be the same person without Grandpa Stig. Having a dad is so important, she thought. She couldn't imagine what life would be like without her dad. And it was good, she believed, to have a father who was a pastor. As she began to consider how lucky she was, it occurred to her that luck had nothing to do with it.

"Dad," said Esther, after a moment, "you've built houses, and you used to be in the export business. And the shipping business. Now, in your responsibilities each day, do you ever…do you ever stop being a pastor?"

"No," responded Pastor Nordquist. "It is my calling, my profession. I deliver God's word because of what I believe. I will never stop serving as a means by which God draws people to Jesus – what others perceive as me leading people to God – although sometimes a congregation can wear me out. Day by day, hour by hour, minute by minute, my pastoral responsibility never ceases."

He began to place a canvas tarp over some goods on the wagon.

"When you became a believer," asked Esther, "did you feel differently?"

"I felt valued. And…renewed hope. All this could only come from God."

"But, daddy," asked Rachel, "didn't you already have a lot of money that Grandpa Stig made, and so weren't you already important, no matter what?"

"Again, I wish you had been able to meet your grandfather," answered Amos, "and he, you. As far as feeling valuable, sometimes wealth can actually have the opposite effect. Some of the most unhappy, empty men I have met have also been among the most wealthy and intelligent. Worldly possessions, accomplishments, which they believed should bring satisfaction, deep inside did not. If someone does not know the Lord, they can feel empty, even bitter, without knowing why. That is how it is when value is tied to worldly things. The more discerning ask themselves, 'What's the point?' When I gave my heart to God, I began to…"

"Didn't He really already have it?" interjected Esther.

"Yes, it was His…but that was not evident to me until my spiritual eyesight improved. When it did, I saw things around me differently, more clearly. What seemed important before was not important afterwards, while formerly unimportant things took on a new significance. Many of the things I once did…well, even though I was at a younger age, I could not believe I could have been so stu…," Amos stopped short, "uh, shortsighted."

"Did anything really special happen?" asked Rachel.

"Besides what I just told you?" Pastor Nordquist looked down at Rachel who nodded. "Yah. Many special things. God began moving me in different directions. I have told you the stories. Eventually your mother and I were brought together." Pastor Nordquist beamed at Anna. "That was wonderful!" Amos raised his eyebrows as he looked pleasantly at Rachel. "Then other special things happened."

Pastor Nordquist stood up, reached down for Rachel, picked her up and hugged her like a rag doll. Still holding her, he kissed her forehead and then, his head tilted back slightly, looked at her warmly.

"The last special thing was you."

Amos put Rachel down and looked at the others. "It's getting late. Let's get some sleep, and tomorrow we finish our journey."

The following morning the Nordquists continued northward, unaware that the last special thing was not the last special thing.

As the wagon rolled along, all were lost in thought. Anna reminisced about life after being led to Minnesota: meeting a handsome Lutheran pastor with whom she started schools and a school system, falling in love with that pastor, getting married, having Inga, then Esther, and Rachel, all the while watching her husband being used by the Lord to lead many to Him. Then moving to boomtown Murray, meeting Molly B'Dam', overcoming difficulties encountered there, and eventually how much she wanted to leave. And then Seattle. Everything began wonderfully, but they harbored Mr. Chong, precipitating a church schism leading to Amos's resignation. Although they barely escaped the Great Seattle Fire, they escaped. What if Angus hadn't been hit by that rock? Anna considered that while many in the Seattle congregation were critical of her husband, others must have been silently impressed with the strength of his conviction, leadership and faith. In spite of the obstacles and disappointment, she had no doubt many were drawn to Christ, while others grew stronger in the faith because Amos would not compromise.

And now God was leading them north in Washington Territory to further attend the harvest. What next?

She stared ahead as if trying to see where they were going, sensing a page turning to end another large chapter of her life, with a new chapter beginning on their arrival. Another new beginning. She looked about at the ancient trees. Time. The wagon seemed like time, moving slowly but constantly forward. Is that what time does? What is time? she wondered. She could never get her mind around it, but it seemed to be something God created to hold things together. Or at least give that appearance. She turned and looked behind her, then returned her attention to the road ahead and again wondered where they were going. She wanted to know. Could it be any more eventful than the road behind?

Oh yes, came the soft presentiment, almost as if spoken out loud.

79

As the wagon rolled forward, Rachel was wondering.

"Why isn't there a train from Seattle to Snohomish City?" she asked.

"There is," answered her mother. "In fact, the line was very recently completed."

"Then why didn't we take the *train* to Snohomish City?" Rachel asked, surprised, looking at the wagon with disdain.

"Our ultimate destination isn't Snohomish City," answered Pastor Nordquist. "If we took the train, we would need to unload and reload in Snohomish City before continuing northward. We spent considerable time painstakingly packing. I'd rather spend a little more time traveling than load the wagon at the parsonage, unload the wagon at the Seattle train station, load those belongings on a train, then unload from the train in Snohomish City, and reload another wagon. This wagon is also less expensive."

"This sure is slow," said Esther. "These trees will all die of old age before we get there."

"That is unlikely, child," said Angus MacGregor. "Aye, t'is best y' not complain. Y' be lucky that trees cannot laugh, for laugh they would if they heard y'. Now, y'd not want t' be laughed at, would, y'?"

"No," said Esther, although the prospect of laughing trees was interesting. But she was getting tired.

"We'll get there soon, don't worry," concluded Angus, smiling.

"Daddy," asked Rachel, "do you think that someday people will be able to take trains everywhere?"

"Probably."

"Do you think we'll ever fly in the air?"

"It's possible," said Pastor Nordquist. "Birds fly. We'll figure it out eventually."

"Daddy," said Esther after a moment, "after we learn to fly, I think we'll be done; then there won't be anything else to learn."

Amos thought of the sky that first clear night while in the lifeboat on the North Atlantic, and the enormity of the universe. "Esther, we'll never 'be done,' at least not until the Lord comes; and then I doubt we will have scratched the surface."

June 7, 1889

"'McGuffey.'" Rachel's eyes narrowed. "Hmmmmm."

Rachel peered intently at the print, her eyelashes fluttering like humming-bird wings as Inga and Esther did school lessons on a sunlit, grassy knoll nearby.

Suddenly the fluttering stopped, followed by a loud, "Ahah!" as Rachel remained motionless, pretending to be completely absorbed by her discovery. "'McGuffey.' No doubt a codeword."

Her intense facial expression suggested she was on to something. Through a magnifying glass Rachel carefully studied the words on the book cover.

"So," she whispered under her breath, "what might 'McGuffey' really mean? Mmmmmiguffey. What does it say, _reeally_?" asked Rachel as she surreptitiously picked up the book, turned to her left and, while glancing about in the event of spies, secretly showed the _Eclectic Second Reader_ to her unamused mother as Anna repacked some towels.

Anna had been reading a new suspense novel, _A Study in Scarlet_, with an intriguing primary character, an extraordinarily intuitive British detective. Earlier Anna told her daughters some of what she was reading. At a distance, Esther and Inga, amused, watched their little sister pretend to be Sherlock Holmes.

"Or if McGuffey's name is on this book," said Rachel, looking at the book, "he might be famous, but we should ask ourselves, is he as famous as Abraham Lincoln?" Anna looked at Rachel out of the corner of her eye. "But if so, that presents a problem," cautioned Rachel, "for if he is as famous as Abraham Lincoln, McGuffey might also get shot."

"William Holmes McGuffey was a very wise man," responded Mrs. Nordquist matter-of-factly. "Someone once called him, 'The schoolmaster of the nation.' Do you know who called him that?"

"No. Who?"

"Abraham Lincoln. Professor McGuffey passed away 16 years ago. And not from getting shot."

Anna began re-reading the letter received before they left Seattle.

"Well, Abraham Lincoln got shot," said Rachel, "and if McGuffey was a wise man and did not get shot, then we can only conclude that Abraham Lincoln must not have been a wise man."

"Wha…? Rachel, I swear," responded Anna.

"Yes, and in front of a 9-year-old, little girl," said Rachel wide-eyed with mock disgust, her lower teeth bared as she frowned at her mother and said emphatically, "The shame!"

"Rachel," said Anna, "perhaps you could take this lesson more seriously if you understood the significance of what you're doing."

Anna turned and faced Rachel directly. "Your father and Angus will be back soon, and before they get back we…"

Rachel had a sour look as she listened to her mother.

"Oh, I see. You're distracted," said Anna, touching the fingers of her hands together as she looked at her daughter. "You're expecting that when they return, your father and Mr. MacGregor will bring you gifts?"

Rachel shrugged as she looked to one side.

"Gold, frankincense and myrrh, perhaps?"

"No, mahhm."

"Were you," Anna began a playful deposition, "planning to sew?"

"No."

"Knit?"

"No."

"Anything?"

"No," mumbled Rachel almost inaudibly.

"I was wondering," said Anna pleasantly, her chin nestled between her thumb and forefinger as she looked off into the distance, "are any of us given time to waste?"

"No."

"Rachel, while you may not think so at the moment, McGuffey's *Readers* are a blessing. The most widely-read – not just the most widely-owned – book in the United States is, of course, the Bible," said Anna. Rachel nodded. "At the moment, McGuffey's *Readers* are, however, comfortably in second place – over 75 thousand sets of William Holmes McGuffey's *Readers* have been sold thus far, and the number is still climbing rapidly."

"Over 75 thousand," said Rachel who could count to 75,000, but never tried, and was uncertain of the magnitude of 75,000. "That's a lot. How many people are in the whole country?"

"The United States population is also expanding rapidly, and it's difficult to say exactly how many people live here, but I've read the population is over 50 million."

"Fifty million?" questioned Rachel as her eyes grew large. "That's…oh, that's way too many, mom. We should send some back."

"No doubt the Sioux agree, but we are not sending anyone back. That aside, Rachel, do you know why so many sets of McGuffey's *Readers* have sold? Ask yourself, 'What makes them so popular?'"

Rachel made a half-hearted shrug as she looked at her mother. "Partly so everyone, including the Sioux, can learn to read?"

"Everyone needs to be literate in English," answered Anna, ignoring Rachel's impertinent response. "There is no alternative. The Sioux…or, for that matter, the Norwegians and the Swedes…may want to maintain their present identity, to keep their traditions, which is understandable. Contrary to what some think, however, learning to read and write English should not eradicate those traditions, although obviously much will change, as is inevitable. Knowing English will enable the Norwegian and Swedish immigrants, and the Sioux, to better function in a changing world."

"But Mom, isn't the changing world due to more people speaking English?"

"Yes, to a considerable extent."

"Doesn't that mean that learning English will change the Sioux?"

"It gives them more options, and when a people has additional options, things usually do change." Anna looked at Rachel. "Now, is that good or bad? It depends on what the options are. Like it or not, it is to their advantage to learn English."

"Where did they learn their language?" asked Rachel. "Where did the Sioux come from? Siouxland? Like the Engs."

"The Engs?"

"Came from England and spoke English."

"There are theories," answered Anna, rolling her eyes. "I honestly don't know."

"Why wouldn't the Sioux want to learn English?"

"Your father says there are Sioux who are greatly resentful of having their way of life disrupted, and want nothing to do with those doing the disruption.

"Like Swedes and the English?"

"Yes."

"But while the Sioux don't like the English, there are Norwegians who don't like Swedes either," countered Rachel.

"Yes, there are…although the differences are so minor as to be almost non-existent. Too many narcissistic people can make much ado about nothing, unfortunately."

"So, which would the Sioux most *not* want to be like, the Swedes or the Norwegians?"

"Rachel, too many people discern differences that are really less-than-important. We left Seattle because we befriended Mr. Chong, while others could not even tolerate his presence in church. Rachel, aren't there more important things to worry about? Wouldn't it be much more constructive to learn things from Mr. Chong who comes from a much different background, than to ostracize Mr. Chong in part because of that background? There are many bigger questions and problems that need our attention. That is, in fact, one reason why we use McGuffey's *Readers*."

"McGuffey's *Readers*," repeated Rachel, looking at her nearby *Second Reader* as if spying a small skunk. "Ooyeeuu," she said quietly with a sour look, wrinkling her nose.

"I use McGuffey's *Readers*," continued Anna without pause, "not only to teach you to read, spell and write properly, but also to present historic events and why those events are significant. And the *Readers* expand your understanding of important ideas and concepts. Learning these things…as Esther and Inga are doing right now," Anna glanced in the direction of Esther and Inga who instantly returned to their texts, "is actually quite exciting. Inga and Esther are not only learning poetry and prose written by the best English and American authors, they are being exposed to challenging philosophical concepts as well as reinforcement of moral virtues such as honesty, thrift, charity and courage. Such writings are the underpinnings of civilized society."

"Because that's what we already do," said Rachel.

"You mean, 'honesty, thrift, charity…'? Yes, but some people do not behave accordingly, not realizing importance of these character traits. So, don't you think it would be wise if these things were made evident to all?"

"Yes," Rachel shrugged.

"I agree," said Anna. "We should make an effort to help others further their abilities. Not to do so would be selfish. In fact, Dr. McGuffey stressed that selfishness, laziness, greed and procrastination are to be avoided. I enjoy teaching others because the lessons in McGuffey's *Readers* are both instructive and edifying, for me and for everyone affected. And through teaching, I make the world a better place."

While listening, Rachel folded her hands, and was absently biting down on her lips between her teeth, giving the impression she had no lips.

"So, Rachel, as an additional example, do you know what else McGuffey teaches?" asked Anna.

"Mm-mm [no]."

"The *Readers* teach that inevitable harm occurs when young people become involved in drinking and gambling, because these are addictive, substituting moral weakness for the strength of character that comes from trust in God. Dr. McGuffey, you see, held the church, the school and the home as the core of American idealism. And at the core's center is the Bible."

"So, then, do Dr. McGuffey's *Readers* make us like we are?" asked Rachel after unbiting herself. At a short distance, Inga and Esther were listening again.

"They contribute greatly," Anna answered as she stood next to Rachel. "Many children, however, never directly learn the concepts presented in McGuffey's *Readers*. Many never even learn to read and write, and are at a great disadvantage later in life."

Refolding the letter she held in her hand, Anna sat down beside her daughter.

"They will never realize their God-given potential. Still, with over 75,000 sets sold, McGuffey's *Readers* have a significant effect on the national mindset including those who unfortunately remain illiterate. What the *Readers* contribute to," said Anna, looking intently at Rachel, "is an American folk belief: love one another, help the less fortunate, deal honestly with others, place God above self-interest, work hard, and if at first you don't succeed, try, try again. You've heard me say that."

Rachel nodded.

"Massachusetts Bay Colony Governor John Winthrop preached to the first immigrants in 1630 that this land should be a 'shining city on a hill,' using a phrase Jesus used in the Beatitudes. America should be an instrument of God protecting those persecuted for righteousness' sake, and providing refuge for those who hunger and thirst for righteousness. McGuffey's *Readers* encourage righteousness in America, glorifying God in the process.

"So, now, Rachel, put down the magnifying glass," said Anna. "It was useful for comparing maple, alder and willow leaf membranes earlier, but now you need to finish your lesson."

"Mom," said Rachel just above a whisper, furtively glancing about, "do I have to study still? Now? Here? By the forest?" Rachel looked at the thick forest with an exaggerated expression reflecting fear bordering on terror.

"Oh, you had other plans?" said Mrs. Nordquist with mock inquisitiveness.

"No."

"Before we left Seattle, did you finish *Lesson LXXII* about LaFayette?" asked Mrs. Nordquist.

Rachel sighed before speaking. "No."

"Then here and now," concluded Anna, feigning excitement as she turned and faced Rachel, "seems wonderfully appropriate, don't you think?"

"Mahhhm," moaned Rachel as she stood up, unable to think of a better reason than, "This *Second Reader* is too hard." With fingertips of her outstretched right arm, Rachel held the *Reader* slightly above her as if it were a small, dead rodent.

"Rachel," sighed Mrs. Nordquist, countering Rachel's nonsense with fact, "you went through the *Primer* faster than either of your sisters. You complained that the *First Reader* was 'borrrrring.'"

"I'll bet Inga and Esther have found things that are borrrring," said Rachel.

"Really? Perhaps I should ask them." Anna turned toward Inga and Esther who were listening. "Girls, have you found anything not to your liking?"

Inga simply shook her head as she looked obliquely at her mother. Esther adopted an acerbic expression. "Not boring but…" Esther paused.

"'But' what?" asked Anna.

"That dialogue about someone's deceased mother in the *Third Reader*," said Esther, "I could have gone my whole, entire life without reading that."

Rachel crossed her eyes and bared her upper and lower teeth in pretended revulsion. "Someone's deceased motherrrr…," repeated Rachel, ghoulishly shuddering as if she'd just returned from the dead.

"That dialogue," countered Mrs. Nordquist, patiently placing her hands in her lap as thespian Rachel pretended to become ill, about to vomit, "was intended not only to give an example of what is meant by 'dialogue' but also to emphasize, as it says, that death is inevitable. Death will not ignore us, will not pass us by. Every living thing dies, have you noticed? Some so much sooner than expected. And so, while we will go from the land of dying to the realm of living, wisdom dictates we be prepared for death's coming. In a small way, the *Reader* story was contributing to that preparation. Remember what the father told his child?" asked Mrs. Nordquist, raising her eyebrows. "That the suffering of that moment would be temporary, and that mother and child will be reunited after death? At your age, death is not a matter of concern. But it will become so when you get older."

"Is it a matter of concern for you?" asked Rachel.

"Yes," answered Anna. "Not so much for myself – in fact, I'm looking forward to spending eternity with Jesus – but, rather, for my family."

"Don't you think we'll be with Jesus?" asked Rachel.

"That's not what I meant, Rachel – as if you didn't know," answered Anna. "I worry about something happening to one of my children. Or my husband. The one who dies has everything to gain; but for those left behind, it's a great loss. The child in Esther's *Third Reader* had a very difficult time with the mother's death, and the father gave sound counsel; although no doubt he too was still having a difficult time dealing with his wife's death. I would have a very difficult time dealing with your death, Rachel."

"Mom, I'm not going to die," responded Rachel matter-of-factly, looking seriously toward the forest, "so don't worry about that." Rachel looked up at her mother. "And neither are you."

"I don't plan on dying any time soon, girls," countered Anna, looking at Esther and Inga, and back at Rachel, "but I will die, probably before you. When I do, I know you will be grief-stricken – it can't be helped – but at the same time I want you to be happy for me. You know where I will be. I want you to rejoice in that."

"I'll rejoice," mumbled Rachel weakly. "I guess."

Rachel wasn't sure how she would react to her mother's death, and at the moment did not want to think about it. It occurred to her that if she didn't want to think about it, she knew how she would react. Inside her a voice told her to think about it because later she would need to remember, unaware that many years later this moment would come back to haunt her. But in her mind Rachel changed the subject, and looked down at the small, dead rodent.

"I won't rejoice in this *Second Reader*, though," said Rachel, her nose wrinkled again – as if the rodent had been deceased for some time.

"Rachel," responded Anna, standing up and walking to the wagon, "you probably have more intelligence in your little finger than most people have in their brains." Anna turned and looked directly at Rachel. "I do wish you would try to use that intelligence."

Anna looked slightly peeved as Rachel pseudo-seriously studied her little finger.

"And Esther," added Anna as she took some sewing from the wagon where she left it earlier, "academically you could move mountains if you were not, in a word, 'lazy.'"

"Mahhhm," whined Esther unbecomingly, "who wants to study what some old, dead French guy wrote?"

Anna's face went blank as she patiently put down her sewing and walked over to where Esther was sitting. Anna picked up the *Eclectic Fourth Reader* and looked at what Esther had been reading.

"Rousseau," stated Anna, identifying the "old, dead French guy."

"Rousseau was slightly more than 'some old, dead French guy,'" continued Anna as she sat down next to Esther. "Really, Esther, I have no idea where you come up with these phrases you use."

"I talk like all the kids."

"The ones we left in Seattle?" responded Anna. Anna let that sink in. "You'd better spend more time in the *Fourth Reader*," suggested Mrs. Nordquist. "In fact, read again what Rousseau has written."

"Mahhhhm," came the anemic response.

"Ehhhhster," mimicked Anna, "you're trying my patience. Where would we be without the wisdom of our forefathers – 'old, dead' people, as you call them? Read what Rousseau has written. Read it again. Even at your age, it should prove insightful. Read it as if you were preparing to go on stage. You're quite theatrical. Then," added Anna, "do the vocabulary preparatory to solidify a con*vincing* performance."

Anna picked up her sewing, returned to the community log, and sat down.

Esther secretly wanted to become a stage actress. Apparently, she realized, it wasn't as big a secret as she thought.

"Who was Rousseau?" asked Rachel.

"A confused man," answered Anna. "His mother died shortly after he was born, his father would not allow him to have playmates – he obviously spent a great deal of time alone – his father abandoned him when he was 10, and Rousseau, himself, sent each of his children to an orphanage shortly after they were born."

The girls looked back at their mother incredulously.

"Didn't he like babies?" asked Rachel, eyes wide, lips again invisible.

"Evidently not. His father set that example. To a great extent it is questionable what Rousseau liked and did not like. He did not like any institution that, as he put it, set man against himself, that is, restricted natural impulse, and he did not consider Christians to be proper citizens because our standards are based on the Bible, not secular laws only. Yes, I know what you're wondering: don't many secular laws have their basis in biblical instruction?"

"Yes, mom," interjected Rachel, acting inane, "how about that?"

"Well, as a matter of fact, Rachel, yes, if you go back to the late 17th and early 18th centuries, they do." For a moment Anna thought of John Locke and the Presbyterian teaching elders from whom Locke received inspiration, and the early 18th century Great Awakening with pastors like George Whitfield. Anna nodded to herself.

"Rousseau. When I studied him in college, I had a very difficult time following what he was attempting to say," Anna smiled faintly as she returned to her sewing, "and I suspect he may have been as confused as I was."

"If he's so confused, why should we pay any attention to what he said?" asked Esther.

"What he says about Jesus is interesting, particularly from the perspective of someone who maintained strong skepticism about Christianity and Christian institutions…or anything else. While he and another French intellectual, Voltaire, greatly disliked Christianity as practiced in France at the time, it is well to remember there was only one official church: the French Catholic Church, and…"

"You mean, not a lot of different churches?" asked Rachel. "Like here?"

"No, just one. And it was doing very little to spread the word of God."

"But it was a church, wasn't it?"

"Yes, but not like American churches. The French population was divided into what they called estates," explained Anna. "There were three estates: the nobles, the church leaders, and the people. When France would vote, each estate had one vote. Church leaders had considerable political power, and many church leaders were interested only in furthering their personal fortunes here on earth. It was said at the time that they 'administered more provinces than sacraments.' In that regard, the French church leaders were not much different than the French nobility; in fact, some were nobility."

"So they used the church just to get money?"

"Yes, essentially, and the church leaders and nobles always voted the same. The third estate, the people, consequently was marginalized. And many of those people, like Voltaire and Rousseau, became very cynical about the French Catholic Church which they equated with Christianity – although for many church leaders, Christ was of secondary concern, if that."

"Then the people should have come to America," said Rachel.

"Many did, but not without the French Revolution first taking place."

"What was that?"

"The third estate, the people, rose up and overthrew King Louis XVI and the nobility, as well as all the church leaders."

"Church leaders?" asked Rachel. Although her dad was nothing like 18th century French clerics, Rachel naturally thought of her dad as a church leader. "What did the people do?"

"The king, nobles and church leaders were simply rounded up and beheaded."

"Oh, no." Wide-eyed, Rachel put her hands over her cheeks.

"One French intellectual," added Anna, "Denis Diderot, said that he would not be happy until he saw 'the last king strangled with the guts of the last priest.'"

"Gaghhh," exclaimed Esther. "That makes me ill."

"Yes, it was a terrible time. A group of men led by a man named Robespierre, considering themselves enlightened, and who disingenuously called themselves the Committee of Public Safety, took over and, among other things, set up a campaign to de-Christianize France, replacing Christianity with 'reason.'"

"Reason?" asked Esther, her eyes knitted. "What do you mean, 'reason'?"

"People would be ruled by 'reason' which essentially meant being ruled without a monarchy, without a nobility class, and without Christian principles or any other established religious tenets."

"Ruled by who?"

"The Committee of Public Safety utilizing 'reason.' The Cathedral of Notre Dame was subsequently renamed the Temple of Reason, and streets named after nobility or Christian saints – there were many such streets – were given new names. But what resulted was the state effectively also becoming the church, worshipping its collective self."

"How?" asked Esther, puzzled. "How would they do that?"

"They didn't have church services like Christians, of course – that would be the opposite of what they intended to accomplish – or a deified ruler like some ancient civilizations. The spiritual void, however, had to be filled, and, with the state outlawing worship of the God of Abraham, Isaac and Jacob, and secularism itself a religion complete with saints and creeds, and the state being above all else, the void was filled by the state."

"Did that work?"

"The experiment did not end well."

"What happened?" asked Rachel.

"Instead of '*Liberté, égalité, fraternité*' – liberty, equality and fraternity – the ostensible enlightened goals of the revolution, new sources of oppression, led by the misnamed Committee of Public Safety, insured just the opposite, and the opposite happened. Like most revolutions, the Committee of Public Safety in their conceit religiously believed their cause was so critical, so important, so righteously imperative, that anyone not falling into lockstep was an enemy, enemy of the revolution, enemy of the state. Those accused of failing to follow the revolutionary vision – at first dozens, but then hundreds, and then thousands – were murdered by the state in what became known as the Reign of Terror."

"We would never get that bad, would we?"

"America? No. We're a nation focused on liberty and governed by law. The American Revolution ended six years before the French Revolution began. But in the American Revolution, churches weren't the target of the revolution; they were part of the revolt. Our founding fathers, well aware of original sin and man's fallen nature, instituted governmental checks and balances that make it very hard for any one person or any one group to take power and subjugate others. If one person or one group is given the power to effectively regulate conscience, they receive a moral *carte blanche* – freedom to do whatever they like – and there is no means with which to restrain them. The result is tyranny. Alternatively, one service that our free Christian churches do for our country is to identify and question abuse of power by the state, calling the state to rectitude. The Christian church, in effect, can act as the conscience of America."

"Mom, we don't have any nobility, do we?" asked Rachel.

"No."

"And we don't have a king."

"No, contrary to what some newspapers would have us think, we don't have a king. We're a democracy with a republican form of representation."

"And lots of churches."

"Oh, yes. We have freedom of religion, attendance is voluntary, not compulsory, and most pastors in the Sunday pulpit preach what the Bible says."

"Phew."

"'Phew,' is right," Anna smiled. "Although Rousseau helped set the stage for the bloody French Revolution, he died 11 years before it all happened. My point is that in spite of Rousseau's skepticism, he still concluded Jesus was a real person whose purpose and history were as the Bible stated." Anna looked directly at Esther. "It is interesting that someone with Rousseau's perspective believed the life and character of Christ were as stated in the Bible, rather than suggesting the biblical story of Christ was a compilation of fabrications, or an adaptation of earlier Egyptian fables. A study of Rousseau gives enough perspective to make you think about these things. So, please return to your lesson."

At her mother's suggestion, Esther again read *Lesson XVIII*, "The Scriptures and the Savior" by Rousseau, from the *Fourth Reader* as if preparing to give a soliloquy.

> *...Shall we say that the evangelical history is a mere fiction – it does not bear the stamp of fiction, but the contrary. The history of Socrates, which no one doubts, is not as well attested as that of Jesus Christ. Such an assertion, in fact, only shifts the difficulty, without removing it. It is more inconceivable that a number of persons should have agreed to fabricate this book, than that one only should have furnished the subject of it.*

Esther continued to read and, when finished, reviewed the *Reader* questions she already answered in her notebook preparatory to diction, spelling and definitions.

"Mom," began Esther a few moments later, "what does 'inimitable' mean?"

"What does your dictionary say it means?" responded Anna.

"I couldn't find it."

"You looked?"

"Mmm, yes. But it's not in here," answered Esther, her hand on her dictionary. "It's going to get dark soon."

Anna got up from her sewing, walked over to Esther, picked up the dictionary and found "inimitable."

"It's here. Look," said Anna, holding the *Dictionary* by Noah Webster in her left hand and pointing to the word with her right. "'Inimitable.'" Anna read the definition. "It's something that's 'too good to be equaled or duplicated.' You could have found it if you tried."

While the sun was close to setting, the sky was still bright. Esther finished her lesson and looked at her mother.

"Have you finished *Lesson XVIII*?" she asked Esther.

"Yes," answered Esther who added, "but it's getting too late to start on lesson XIX," anticipating an unwanted suggestion from her mother.

"Then tomorrow," stated Anna.

"Will Uncle Charles and Aunt Sarah be in New York for a long time," asked Esther.

"Yes, Uncle Charles' and Aunt Sarah's involvement with the American Home Missionary Movement will require them to stay in New York for a while."

"I like to listen to Uncle Charles talk," said Rachel. "He speaks perfectly. Per'-fect-ly," she repeated while holding her forearm vertically and affectedly letting her right wrist go limp.

"Yes, he does," said Anna. "An Oxford education will have that effect. Aunt Sarah thought your Uncle Charles quite a catch."

"Did you think Dad to be quite a catch?"

"Once I got to know your father," answered Anna after a moment, "I thought I had never met a more gracious and sensitive man. He was – and still is – extremely good looking. I guess I jumped to conclusions. I must admit I had reservations about your father at first."

"Why?"

"I mistakenly assumed," Anna said as she shrugged her shoulders, "anyone that attractive would be vain and self-absorbed. He is not. In fact, he is very caring and unselfish. When I got to know him, I was reminded of the line in *Julius Caesar*: 'His life was gentle, and the elements/ So mixed in him that Nature might stand up/ And say to all the world, "This was a man!"'"

Anna looked at her daughters, smiled and nodded as Amos's daughters looked back, barely masking expressions of pride while thinking in unison: that's what I want.

80

June 8, 1889
The Odegaard farm

At the opposite end of the dark, plowed field, Ode Odegaard, whose shadow covered almost as much ground as a shadow from one of his massive workhorses, pushed hard on the Butcher and Gibbs plow, supplementing workhorse effort in front.

He let go with his left hand, and wiped his hand on his flannel shirtsleeve 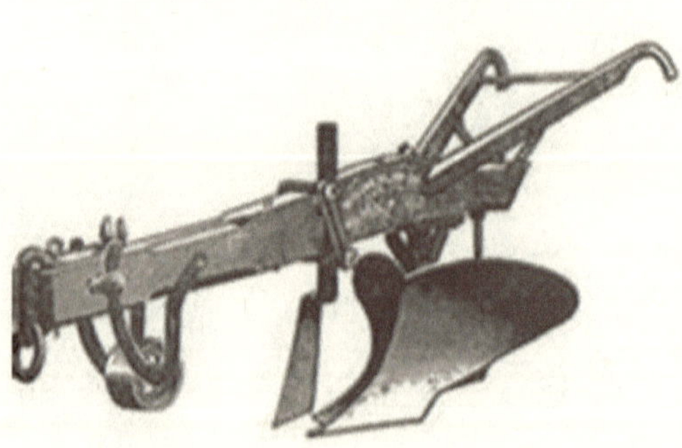 that, like his large bib overalls and big work boots, was permanently soiled from long hours in the fields, outbuildings and surrounding woodlands. With his left hand he again reached for the bandana that hung around his powerful neck like an embroidered ascot and wiped his forehead while continuing to push hard with his right.

He came to America unable to speak English, and at first could not respond when someone asked him his name. Although he learned to speak English and began introducing himself by his real name, Ode, most continued to call him "Big Swede."

While still a young boy, Big Swede saw widespread food shortages and unemployment in Sweden. He could remember the demoralized look of failure on his father's large weathered face when it was evident the family lost its race against hardship. It was at that moment, when all else was gone, that his father ran out of hope, and Swede watched his father's expression darken as if the Grim Reaper had entered the room, arms folded, waiting.

While Swede did not understand why the situation was so bleak, he understood his father's face…the contrast was stark, for his dad was always optimistic and confident. Swede would never forget going down into the cellar where, shaken, he cried alone, not wanting to further burden his father.

In America, Swede would be neither indolent nor a risk-taker. He planned carefully and worked extraordinarily hard, in part because he wanted his own family to never experience prolonged hardship and helpless impotence like his father, mother and he endured when he was little, and because of his conviction that his productivity was his identity. Swede worked from before sunrise to after sundown every day, seven days each week, each month, each year. His was the most productive farm in the Skagit River valley.

Swede's intellect was comparable to his physical size. While he did not believe in God, neither did he disbelieve, but, unlike most agnostics, rather than abandon the topic, interestingly, he continued to think a lot about "God," attempting to logically arrive at a conclusion one way or the other. Working and thinking simultaneously made his time doubly productive. Were indolence the only vice in the world, Swede would have no vices…except, perhaps, one. When he occasionally allowed himself to take his mind off farm work and epistemic challenges, he played checkers with Doc Torgeson.

Swede again loosened and removed the bandanna, wiped his forehead as he had done periodically since sunrise, pulled his blonde mustache up and outward at both ends, and watched the dust wafting up from the dirt road in the distance, a signal of someone approaching.

After tying the bandana, he grabbed the plow with both hands and simultaneously whistled shrilly, starting the horses while pushing the plow forward, beginning another furlong. Swede periodically glanced at the wagon rolling down the road, approaching the entrance to his long dirt driveway. These must be the Nordquists, Swede thought. Could use the help.

Swede continued to plow; there was still time to finish the field. As Swede completed the next furlong, the wagon turned into the driveway.

Mrs. Odegaard danced down the farmhouse porch steps to greet the Nordquists as the wagon slowed to a halt in front of the big farmhouse on the other side of the field. Erika Odegaard was taller than most women, her attractive face framed by blonde, shoulder-length hair when she did not have it tied in a bun, as she now did. The brightness of Erika Odegaard's smile at the approaching Nordquists was like the flash of sunlight off glass.

The two older Odegaard brothers, meanwhile, were high on the top of the big barn roof replacing shingles. It was precarious work, frightening to men with a greater instinct for survival. Mrs. Odeqaard knew her boys were the best ones for the job, but would berate her sons to be more careful. Yet, while cautious, they were unafraid. Like most young men their age, they would live forever, not yet aware of how quickly forever passes. Far below them, anxious for adult company, their mother approached the Nordquists excitedly.

"Velcome!" Mrs. Odegaard smiled, clapping her hands softly as she briskly walked toward the new pastor and his family.

Amos jumped down from the wagon, walked to Mrs. Odegaard and introduced himself, his family and Angus.

"We so much appreciate your willingness to put us up," began Anna Nordquist who remained seated, "– perhaps I should say 'put up with us' – while we…"

"Oh, vell, guudness," interrupted Mrs. Odegaard. "It iss no problem at all. Heavens, no."

"We are still indeed grateful for your hospitality," said Pastor Nordquist as he looked about for Mr. Odegaard. Anna Nordquist still made no effort to get down from the wagon.

"You must be exhausted," Mrs. Odeqaard said to Anna. Anna was physically in distress as she closed her eyes and lowered her head for a moment. "Come inside so you can clean up. Ve can unload after ve have visited."

Pastor Nordquist looked at the teamster who shrugged.

"Thank you so much," Anna Nordquist responded weakly, looking squeamish as she put her hand to her head. "I'm afraid that the trip, the heat and the rough road have made me nauseous."

Anna did not look well. After both Angus MacGregor and Pastor Nordquist gently helped Anna down from the wagon, Amos put his right hand around her waist, providing emotional and physical support as he guided her to the front steps leading up to the large front porch and into the big farmhouse where he asked the world's most well-meaning question having an obvious answer: "Are you okay?"

Big Swede turned the horses for another furlong as the others went inside. Socializing has its place and time, he thought. The furlongs lay side-by-side across the field, a design, a simple earth tapestry with near-perfect balance and symmetry. Once he began a new creation, he was always impatient to finish it, finding the imperfection of an unfinished design annoying. While Swede accepted imperfection in others, he was less than forgiving with himself.

Meanwhile, Anna Nordquist, white as a sheep, reached the center of the living room. Putting her hand partially over her mouth, she closed her eyes and, in a whisper, politely but desperately asked for directions to the nearest sink. Erika Odegaard quickly escorted Anna, who now had both hands over her mouth, to the bath chamber.

A moment later, hands on the sink rim, bending over the basin, Anna Nordquist became violently ill. Her physical state was made worse by the mortification she felt and the imposition she believed she was causing at the moment. Erika Odegaard wanted to help but felt helpless. After Anna vomited, her body gradually relaxed, almost as if nothing happened.

Believing she must appear like a little child to the Odegaards, Anna slowly straightened up as she pumped water into the sink to clear out the mess, and turned to apologize but, catching a glance of herself in the mirror, quickly pumped some water into her hand to wash off her mouth. She nervously reached for the towel Erika Odegaard offered. Agonizingly embarrassed beyond description, Anna turned and began apologizing as if her salvation depended on it.

"Oh, no, no. No," Mrs. Odegaard responded. "My guudness, you must come into the parlor and rest!"

Although Anna felt better, Pastor Nordquist and Angus helped Anna into the parlor adjacent to the living room where she sat down.

"Mrs. Odegaard, would you…"

"Oh, yust call me Erika."

"Would you mind if I were to lie here for a moment?"

"Oh, of course! Please do!"

Anna lay down, limp on the chesterfield, and through a window pane watched a cottonwood tree's sun-lit, silver leaves flash in the breeze.

"Mrs. Odegaard, Erika, I…," Pastor Nordquist began as he sat down aside Anna, "this is very unexpected. Perhaps, if you don't mind, could we have a wet washcloth? It would be soothing."

Without saying anything, Erika walked quickly to the linen closet, grateful she was there, wondering what might be happening if she were not. What if the Nordquists were still continuing their journey north?

Erika took out two washcloths, one of which she dampened with water from the bath chamber sink pump, quickly returned and handed both to Pastor Nordquist.

Meanwhile, Big Swede's symmetry was nearly finished. He glanced about, studying previous rows.

Angus, standing near the parlor door, looked at Anna without expression. She seemed recovered. Angus' eyes met Anna's and, when Anna's expression did not change, Angus' face softened. Anna turned her head and took her concerned husband's hand. She again looked out the window for a period that, from her husband's perspective, seemed inconsiderately prolonged.

Although Anna could not see it, the field was complete. Big Swede stood at the field's edge for several moments looking for noticeable imperfections. Nothing was ever perfect, but an acceptable job would come close. This job, Swede, concluded, came close. The modest mid-afternoon shadows subtly highlighted his artwork. Satisfied, he stood and looked at the symmetrical rows and coils of black earth for another minute before disconnecting the plow and leading the horses to the pasture behind the barn.

Removing the damp washcloth from her forehead, Anna turned her head and, for the first time since becoming sick, looked directly up at Amos, her eyes smiling.

"Do you still want a son?" she asked.

Sunday, June 9, 1889

Besides a Swedish homeland, Big Swede Odegaard and Pastor Amos Nordquist found many other things they had in common. Both men could usually do whatever they set their minds on doing. Pastor Nordquist's carpentry talents and ministry were witness of who he was. Big Swede's farm generated inspiration of a similar sort. The large, five-bedroom farmhouse interior was a home show of rough woodwork, and the river rock fireplace – large enough for a child to stand in – with its massive, elaborately carved mantel and raised slate hearth, was evidence of painstakingly meticulous effort. The crown molding around the living room ceiling proved that Big Swede could do more than turn dirt, shear sheep, dig wells or mesmerize any onlooker as he wielded spud, froe or adz like they were carving knives. Like the newly plowed field, the house was not perfect, but it was close, a testament to Swede's standards.

This was one of the few Sundays where Amos Nordquist led no church service. Relaxing in the Odegaard living room, he took advantage of the short vacation. And to the delight of the Nordquists that late afternoon, the expansive Odegaard country kitchen was becoming an arena where regal aromas vied for supremacy.

Ruth Odegaard, 16, coordinated dinner preparation with her 12-year-old twin sisters, Mary and Martha. With little effort, informal supper could become a formal dinner. Like her father, Ruth had a penchant for creativity and artistic perfection, but Ruth displayed this talent in the kitchen where she pursued flavor, aroma, balance, presentation and temperature perfection, allowing her mother the momentary freedom to weigh seating and table arrangements while socializing with Anna Nordquist in the dining room.

Ruth was a young version of Erika – a good thing, for Erika Odegaard was an extraordinary woman. Erika could sew beautifully, cook to perfection, milk cows, split rails, and work the plow if needed. She never complained; it never occurred to her that difficulties were unfair. They were temporary obstacles that, if not surmounted, would no longer be temporary. She was of the mind that the resource most wasted was time, and convinced she could always be more productive than she was, once told Swede in exasperation, "The additional time I need is exceeded only by the time I waste." Her home was beautiful. Between Erika, Swede, Ruth, Mary and Martha, this was unsurprising.

Erika's spiritual proclivity was evident from the names she chose for her children.

Each of the Odegaard brothers was unique. Even if the differences in their ages were ignored, to someone unacquainted with the family it would be surprising that Jacob, 18, Samuel, 15, and Luke, who had just turned 10, were related. Although Jacob and Samuel looked somewhat alike, their personalities gave little hint of identical parentage.

Jacob, over six feet tall and farm work strong, began drawing barnyard animals at an early age. He spent his meager spare moments drawing horses and, as time progressed, his horses looked exactly like horses looked, and eventually how they would look if they were perfect. After Jacob began carefully studying photographs of Rembrandt and da Vinci paintings, although unaware of the terms, Jacob experimented with *chiaroscuro, tenebrism* and *sfumato*. Stately horses found themselves spirited in Elysian Fields as Jacob became so adept with light and color that his artistry seemed to transcend reality.

As a child, Jacob thought he might become a doctor/veterinarian like Doc Torgeson who doubled both as family doctor according to his formal training, but also as veterinarian according to avocation and community need. Jacob still thought about it, but believed the occupation, at least the medical training, would not be his. Ironically, the time required tending farm animals gradually distanced Jacob from any formal education. Spiritually, Jacob walked in his mother's footsteps, as did all the children. Erika encouraged it, and Swede, the agnostic, did not discourage it.

While Jacob inherited his father's creativity, attention to detail, and intellect, not to mention, on a slightly smaller scale, his father's physique, he inherited his mother's facial features. Jacob was broad-shouldered, dark-skinned and blonde, with a smile that was distracting. His mother said it was a shame that they could not bottle Jacob's smile and sell it, laughingly suggesting that from these sales, first, they would become rich, and, secondly, the world would become a much happier place.

On the other hand, Samuel, the happy-go-lucky 15-year-old, was not concerned with details. He had two passions: hunting and fishing. From observing Samuel the fisherman over the years, Erika had phrased a natural law, "Samuel's Law," which was: "Those with a propensity to catch fish, will; and those without, get skunked."

Samuel always caught fish. Only God knew why Samuel was able to do this. If Samuel did not catch the only fish, he would catch the most fish and, usually among the fish caught, the largest. It wasn't luck. Luck has nothing to do with it, concluded Erika. No one is that lucky. In fact, if luck were the deciding factor, Samuel would have been the least likely candidate to catch fish, for in most other matters Samuel was inauspicious and, lost in thought, often oblivious to things around him, or inattentive to the matter at hand. At the moment he had a black eye, the result of absentmindedly forgetting to cinch the saddle before mounting his horse. When he put his foot in the stirrup to mount, he pulled the saddle off the horse, the saddle horn hitting him in the eye as the saddle fell on top of him. This added insult to a previous minor injury incurred two days earlier when, after getting instructions from his mother, he turned around, missed the first step, and fell down the porch steps. Many were the times where Erika, wide-eyed, held her head or cheeks while looking at Samuel, hoping he was all right.

When did this fishing *kismet* arise? Erika wondered. Could it be traced back through the family tree to prehistoric origin – subsequently cultivated by centuries of survival and passed down genetically to this day? If so, why didn't the rest of the family always catch fish? And what is it that is passed down? Or did God, simply feeling sorry for Samuel and his daily foibles, benevolently gift to Samuel a unique talent of no apparent origin. Occasionally Erika thought she should have named Samuel "Peter" or "Andrew" or "James" or "John," the net fishermen in Matthew 4, rather than Samuel which means "heard of God," because often Samuel didn't hear anything.

Luke, the ten-year-old, was both the youngest and, as the phrase goes, the runt of the litter. The thick, round-rim spectacles he wore did nothing for his self-image. While Jacob and Samuel were always bigger, stronger and more athletic than others of similar ages, Luke was of average height, overweight, unathletic and, in fact, struggled to complete his daily chores, much less do them well. His weak eyesight sometimes caused him to miss things that, to the others, appeared carelessly overlooked when, in fact, he could not see well enough to notice. His glasses helped but they were not strong enough to completely correct his weak vision. His parents did not know this because self-conscious Luke could not bring himself to tell them. Luke also thought he might like to become a doctor like Doc Torgeson. No one knew that either.

Luke tried hard, but his physical shortcomings were his burden to bear. On the other hand, Luke was unusually intelligent. Luke overcompensated by using his intellect, honed and sharpened through constant reading – his nose sometimes two inches from the page – and he often asked questions about how things worked around the farm. Occasionally he would think of a more-efficient way to accomplish something. For example, after studiously watching his father and brothers use an inefficient (to Luke) process of getting hay into the barn hayloft, Luke drew a sketch of what looked like a collapsible conveyor belt on which hay was pitched from the hay wagon and continually sent to the top where it was dropped, to be pitched to the rear of the hayloft. Turning from his work, Swede looked at Luke's sketch.

"Vhat did you draw?" he asked.

"It's a good way, I think," explained Luke self-consciously, "to get hay up to the hayloft and into any area of the hayloft. Just attach this to one side of the hay wagon and, if you pitch hay on this while someone turns this crank, over here," Luke pointed at the drawing, "the hay will continually go up, up, up," he motioned slowly upward with his finger to the hayloft. "You could get more hay up there faster, father."

He bit his lip nervously as, through his spectacles, he strained to see his father's facial expression.

"Maybe," Luke added as a defensive measure.

Swede looked at the drawing, and at the hayloft rigging presently used, and back at the drawing.

"You tought of dis yoorself?" asked Big Swede.

"Yes, father," responded Luke respectfully, almost standing at attention. The spectacles magnified Luke's eyes as Swede looked down at his youngest son. Big Swede beamed, rubbed the top of Luke's head, said no more, and Luke's anxiety instantly dissipated. Big Swede folded the drawing, put it in his pocket, and began walking toward the haystack by the barn but, before returning to the hay storage effort, he stopped and turned to Luke.

"I don't know vhy ve didn't think of dis sooner…ve'll see vhat ve can do vith dis," said Swede. "You do yoor chores now."

As Luke watched his father walk away, Luke's resolve rose like the morning sun. After he was finished with the conveyor drawings, he would think about a way to combat the farm's ubiquitous mice.

In the dimly lit barn, tiny spectral shadows raced along barn walls, tool racks, feeding troughs, feed bins and milking stalls, and scrabbled in all recesses of the hayloft. Not mere mice but demonic mice, thought Luke. Their mice numbers were, after all, legion. In Luke's imagination, having overwhelmed the cat, the mice thought they, not the Odegaards, ran the farm. Luke stared at the barn where mice seemed as prevalent as straw. His expression turned dark.

Luke silently walked toward the flowerbeds and their weeds, again thinking about his conveyor, and began to question its potential efficacy. After a few moments, he began to feel uncomfortable and believed his father might only be humoring him.

The idea is probably silly, he thought.

He hoped his father was not mad, although Big Swede seldom found himself becoming angry with others because, to begin with, he was slow to anger and, secondly, when Swede's anger boiled to the surface, those who witnessed never forgot. Consequently, the family behaved according to the Temperate Swede Law: never let dad's temperature reach the boiling point. Once, Luke saw his father, frustrated while fixing some farm equipment, stand up, teeth clenched, and throw something at the side of the barn. Luke watched his father angrily hitch up the wagon and drive off. Trips into town to obtain, or worse, order new parts, could waste hours. After Swede left, Luke went over and looked at the barn where the object was thrown. The object was a large wrench, the handle stuck in the side of the barn like a knife.

Although physically dissimilar, Luke was as imaginative as Jacob, and Luke's imagination served him both creatively and socially because Luke spent a great deal of time alone with himself. When no one else was near, he would pretend to be two people and would carry on quiet conversations. This would seem odd to some, but for Luke it was the best social outlet he had, and, besides, he was stimulating enough to enjoy his own company. He and Luke discussed matters large and small.

Luke's thoughts returned to catching mice. There were so many, they hid so well and, fearful he might accidentally step on one, sometimes they scared the daylights out of him as he walked cautiously through the barn, adjusting his spectacles. Luke knew the family cat was completely overwhelmed, and Luke's fragile ego had enough problems without having to deal with stealthy mice. There was nothing he disliked more than a mouse underfoot. As he weighed the problem, a novel idea percolated up Luke's brainstem.

He went cautiously to the mouse megatropolis, the barn, and got an old bucket. With the bucket, he left the barn and walked the short distance to the workshop where he drilled two side-holes opposite one another midway between the bucket handle fasteners near the top of the staves.

Luke used a hammer and nail to punch opposing holes of desired size in a tin can.

Finished with the hole punching, he pounded a small nail through the inside bottom of the can so that about a half inch stuck out the bottom.

Luke pushed a narrow, round stick into one bucket hole, through the side holes in the can, and pushed the protruding end of the stick through the opposite side hole of the bucket, leaving the tin can suspended above the bucket bottom.

Bucket in hand, Luke got a canned prune from the kitchen – he inadvertently had learned mice liked prunes – took the prune and the bucket with the suspended can to the irrigation well.

He filled the bucket with about 4" of water. He took the bucket into the barn and pushed a prune piece into the small nail protruding from the bottom of the can – suspended about 6" above the water.

He reasoned that mice, after smelling the prune and crawling along the stick

to the tin can, while attempting to reach the prune would lose their grip on the slick sides of the can, fall in the water and drown. All night long. I hope, Luke thought as, through his thick spectacles, he looked about for enemy reconnaissance mice. He saw none, certain evidence their spies were watching.

Luke carefully set the bucket next to the lower hay bin, and placed a two-foot piece of wood – a mouse-ramp – from the floor to the top of the bucket.

Luke stood up, looking at his mousetrap, and took a deep breath that he expelled slowly. "Will it work?" he wondered out loud as he turned and walked toward the barn door exit.

Luke had Luke. Mary and Martha, 12-year-old twins, had each other, and worked well as a team oddly because of a desire for individuality. As little girls, their relationship was difficult because, while inseparable, each wanted to be different. What one would do, therefore, the other would not. Mary fed the chickens and gathered the eggs, while Martha fed the pigs, and ignored the chickens. While chickens are found on every populated continent, in Martha's world there were no chickens. And in the kitchen, exceeding Darwinian expectations, Mary and Martha evolved into a formidable two-headed creature scurrying about, each head periodically peering at the other to assure an even pace.

Meanwhile, Luke stood on the back porch steps in the early evening twilight attempting to focus on the barn through his thick, round spectacles. Will my mousetrap work? Earlier at dinner, Anna read aloud the letter from her sister about New York slums and, as Luke stood looking at the barn, he imagined the huge barn as a vermin tenement building a hundred stories high. Mice York, he thought.

His lips taut, Luke took one more look at the barn, turned and went inside the house.

The next morning, before doing early morning, pre-breakfast chores, Luke ran to the barn.

As Luke looked down at the bucket contents, he could not believe the degree of his success. "Yeeeuck," he muttered as he looked at all the soggy, drowned mice. "We'll need a bigger bucket."

The evidence in the bucket indicated that one mouse simply followed another. Luke read about evolution and discerned that mice, like men, were like lemmings, perhaps all with a common ancestor in Ethiopia named Lucy, and because of common characteristics, the bucket mousetrap worked.

Later that morning, Swede looked at the bucket contents.

"You are going to put the cat out of business," said Swede.

He rubbed the top of Luke's head while looking down at Luke warmly, and nodded. As Swede picked up the bucket and turned to leave the barn, Luke beamed and, from behind his spectacles, his pupils dilated and redilated furiously, working to watch his father walk out into the bright, sunlit farmscape beyond the barn door opening.

———•———

While the Nordquists became comfortable at the Odegaard farm, on a cruise to Alaska, Henry Hewitt and Charles Colby continued discussing the proposed new city. In his free moments, Henry Hewitt expanded and refined his financial vision. The preliminary numbers continued to be encouraging.

Upon returning to Seattle, Hewitt and Colby went east in Colby's private railroad car. On the way to New York, Hewitt continued to work on his projections.

Like many wealthy men, Colby had a large number of acquaintances, but few friends. Hewitt and Colby had enough history to have developed a friendship, and when in New York, Hewitt stayed with Colby in Colby's mansion at 8 E. 69th Street.

One evening during dinner, Charles Colby's promising young son, Everett, 15, still overcoming learning and speaking disabilities, was nevertheless doing an excellent job of convincing his taciturn father that the dessert was superb, so much so that it would be a travesty if Everett were unable to have more of it. Everett was successful. Amused but impressed, Hewitt suggested they name the new city "Everett." Charles Colby looked at Hewitt, rolled his eyes, and nodded. Obviously, Colby already liked the name.

Before returning to the future location of Everett the city, Hewitt stated the obvious.

"I think, Charles, it's time to draw up the articles of incorporation for both our venture and the new city. It is only proper that we, as you suggested when we were back in Everett…," Hewitt winked and Colby nodded, recalling the dessert incident, "put things in writing."

"True enough," responded Colby, resting comfortably in his overstuffed chair. He puffed on his pipe. He still wasn't entirely sold on the venture but, nevertheless, repeated, "True enough."

With a serious countenance Colby lightly blew smoke in the direction of the study fireplace.

"We've been over the numbers so many times," continued Hewitt, "I'm to the point where I don't need the ledgers in front of me when having our discussions. I've analyzed the timber and lumber potential until I'm blue in the face. The rest? I've raised as many questions as I can think of, and have considered those questions in my projections. I've attempted to anticipate every contingency, and my forecasts range from conservative to very conservative. Still, it all points to success." Hewitt looked levelly at Colby. "Are you in favor of moving ahead with the venture?"

Colby stared at the fireplace. Hewitt was right.

"What corporation name do you propose?" asked Colby.

"Everett Land Company," said Hewitt.

"'Everett Land Company,'" nodded Colby. "Incorporation will establish direction, responsibility and an initial basis for value. Besides, I can't approach others without having formally incorporated. And providing a business plan." Colby spoke positively although, while wanting to feel good about the venture, inexplicably something still bothered him.

"Who were you thinking of involving," asked Hewitt.

"Well, actually," said Colby, "here's what I want to do first…before we incorporate." Colby needed a sedative for whatever was still bothering him. "I want to broach the subject with Colgate Hoyt. As you know, we have been in other ventures – quite successfully – and, if he agrees this is feasible, there would be no further reservation on my part."

Henry Hewitt nodded.

———●———

Colgate Hoyt, for reasons based as much on his respect for Charles Colby as the merit of the venture itself, subsequently agreed. Together, Colby, Hoyt and Hewitt formed the Everett Land Company.

———●———

Returning to the Everett area to buy more land, Hewitt found one landowner to be particularly difficult. Wyatt J. Rucker and his family purchased the Edmond Smith farm a year earlier and, together with two neighboring property owners, jointly platted a 50-acre parcel they envisioned as the eventual City of Port Gardner. Hewitt was able to purchase the portions of the plat owned by the two neighbors, but the Ruckers saw what Hewitt saw; the Ruckers did not want to sell. Hewitt was undaunted and offered the Ruckers a substantial amount for their portion. The Ruckers negotiated a quick but healthy profit, selling most of the land, but not all. The Ruckers kept certain strategically located blocks in the plat. In addition, the Ruckers determined that, besides money, the consideration for that portion sold to Hewitt would also include a contractual agreement requiring Hewitt to develop heavy industry along the waterfront, favorably affecting the future value of retained Rucker sites. Hewitt agreed to develop a lumber mill, a shipyard and a railroad, enterprises, with Colby's help, Hewitt expected to deliver anyway. The Ruckers became partners with Hewitt, Colby and Hoyt in the development of Everett.

July 17th, 1889

In the warm quiet of the night, alone again, the Ranger stood looking in the direction of his next assignment. Moonlight gilded the farm buildings in silver as he quietly dusted off his hat, reached down and fixed his cuffs, stood up, wiped his thick spectacles, and moved his buckets into the space beneath the chicken house. There's not enough room in this town for both me and the Mice York Gang. While law and order were being restored in the farm buildings, in the big farmhouse a more significant change was about to occur. Dinners were enjoyable, but the Nordquist and Odegaard families thus far maintained a spiritual separateness. Something wonderful was about to happen that would change that.

81

Saturday, July 20th, 1889

No rain had fallen for weeks.

Mid-July saw temperatures drop unseasonably. Thick, brooding storm clouds sullenly met and merged, and thunder claps sounded from distant Cascade foothills. Above the Skagit River valley the late afternoon sky became dark, and the air motionless as if waiting to see what would happen next. Barely visible at first, intermittent raindrops began to fall, tapping lightly on the porch roof. Inga watched through the window as young cornstalks stood erectly, leaves held out at their sides, as if preparing to bathe in the rain. Swede came up beside Rachel and also looked out the window. As they watched, with a loud rush the rain suddenly came down in buckets, drenching farm buildings, and forming instant puddles around the house and in the fields. Swede folded his arms as he watched dozens of runnels cascading off the barn roof. He nodded. Thanks to his sons' fearlessness, the roof was waterproof; the rain a Godsend.

Quietly humming as he straightened his blonde mustache with ham-sized hands, Swede turned and walked over to the huge, river rock fireplace, the focal point of the room, and lit the kindling that had been sitting inside for months. The heat was unneeded, but the cool wind, dark sky, and sudden downpour beckoned a small fire's ambiance even if it was July. The infant fire played peacefully, quietly flicking small wisps of bright light upward.

Swede added more kindling from the inglenook until small coals formed. He placed some of the smaller pieces of firewood in a miniature teepee about the coals and burning kindling. The new wood quickly caught fire, and the crackling sound complemented the early evening candles and flowers on the large, cedar dining room table. Country kitchen aromas wafted about the big room as the girls brought food to the table.

To Inga, standing alone after placing a large baked ham on the table for Swede to carve, the glowing coals looked like a small city of dancing lights surrounded by pulsating orange and platinum stars. Unlike the great Seattle fire, the fireplace fire seemed innocent, almost lovable. Inga walked to the fireplace, stopped and stared, musing. You're not so tough, she thought.

Inga's face glowed in the firelight. In winter, or even summer, Inga loved fireplaces and all they did. The flames were mesmerizing and, as she stared, Inga wondered how many people stood and stared at fireplace fires like she was doing. Caesar Augustus. Gustavus Adolphus. Adoph Menzel. Most of humanity. The human family constant: the heated hearth. She stared at the dancing flames. Why do I stare? she wondered. What makes it hard to pull your eyes away? Fireplaces are magic. Many remarkable ideas must have come from people standing before a fireplace. Or sitting. Thinking. In her mind, Inga asked God to bless whoever invented the fireplace, and then considered that perhaps she was asking God to bless Himself. She thought of fireplaces she had seen in photographs of great European castles; those in the Prussian Berg Hohenzollern castle were amazing. Inga often thought about royalty and what it would be like to belong to the House of Hohenzollern or the House of Windsor.

Returning to the kitchen, Inga helped with meal preparation while ruminating about historic figure Sophia Charlotte, radiant wife of Frederick III, founder and first King of Prussia. Living in an era when marriage contracts and chess pieces had much in common, and when all powerful men had, and were expected to have, mistresses, while Frederick III felt obligated to have a mistress, his heart wasn't in it. He cherished his extraordinary wife, Sophia Charlotte – beautiful, charming, intelligent, effervescent, musical, multilingual and ambitious – while still being kind to his mistress. Unlike Louis XIV and so many others, he loved his wife and wanted none other. Sophia, however, was interested in culture, prestige and power – upon meeting her, even normally indomitable 6' 7" Russian tsar Peter the Great was slightly awed – not the love she could have, and she largely ignored the wonderful, important man who truly loved her.

Humming, preparing gravy in a big pan on the stove, in Inga's imagination Inga consorted with Sophia Charlotte, attempting to understand Sophia – to Inga an enigma – while imagining, if Inga were to trade places, being loved by someone like Frederick III, and thanking God for such a husband.

Bolting into the dining room while balancing two plates of towel-wrapped hot loaves, trying not to trip, wide-eyed Rachel made a beeline for the closest place on the large dining room table. As she placed the hot bread on the table, she sighed with relief. Rachel looked at the ham brought in by Inga, and decided the bread would look good on either side of the baked ham. Stepping back and looking at the table as the Odegaard girls brought in more dishes, Rachel concluded that regardless of what else might occur during the Nordquist's stay, they wouldn't starve.

Rachel watched as Ruth, Mary and Martha placed dishes of hot candied yams, warm applesauce, and hot creamed corn on the large table. Plum pudding would eventually follow.

"This is so great. Look at how good this looks," volunteered Rachel, gesturing at the table. "This should be in a painting."

As Rachel spoke, Esther again approached the table, her hands cradling braided potholders flattened against a large, covered bowl filled with mashed potatoes topped with melting butter. At best noncommittal whenever Rachel spoke, Esther smiled agreeably as she carefully positioned a modest portion of the late fall potato harvest.

Before staying with the Odegaards, Rachel never saw so much food except at church dinners. She rose up and down on her toes as she thought. Church food is pretty good (Rachel then thought of *lutefisk*); most of it. Scandinavian grandmas certainly know how to cook. I guess that's why we never saw any Scandinavian restaurants in Seattle. No need for them.

Rachel walked over to the fire, lost in her reverie. But we ate from rickety, old tables, Rachel remembered, and sat on big, old benches. Yes, but when you're four, everything is big and old. After Rachel sighed, her lips tightened. But that was – she bent her elbow, and raised her right forearm, letting her wrist go limp as she affectedly extended her small finger – acceptable. She fluttered her eyelashes for an instant. She was getting good at it. Rachel looked at the Odegaard table and about the room. This, however, is like having Thanksgiving at a king's palace.

"Everyvun. Time to sit up." Erika Odegaard's pleasant alto voice interrupted the reverie. "Samuel, first vahsh yoor haaands, please."

The room was aglow. Six candles regally rose from the table centerpiece, and complemented the radiant fireplace. On either side were shorter candles yet to be lit. Inga savored the mingled aromas of baked ham, hot bread, warmed honey and fresh cedar kindling. Oh, heaven, thought Inga. Heaven. That aroma. The polished cedar crown molding which Mr. Odegaard meticulously carved by hand three winters ago subtly reflected the fireplace offering. Inga took a deep breath as if to absorb the atmosphere, and then slowly exhaled.

The euphoria, however, was stimulated by more than ambiance, more than aroma and warmth and light. At that moment a loving presence, as if a silent sylph, shepherded emotions, encouraging a greater wonder, a sacred conclusion that would become a basis for future miracles. In the kitchen, quiet Inga uncharacteristically smiled for no apparent reason. With two pitchers of milk she returned to the living room, still in a regal mindset, and after placing the pitchers at either end of the table, stood staring at the candles, thinking about what it would be like to have met Peter the Great or Sweden's Charles XII, nemeses with great mutual respect.

Swede and Angus MacGregor re-entered the room, politely interrupting the thoughts playing in Inga's head. Inga turned, faced Swede, and stepped forward, anticipating direction. Swede adjusted his suspenders with what Inga had decided were the largest hands in the world, and stood next to the table beaming down at the treasures upon it. He looked at Inga.

"Vell, young lady, you look lovely this evening."

Swede returned his attention to the setting in front of him, studying the centerpiece, tablecloth, candles and seating arrangements to insure proper balance. Unused to such familiarity, Inga blushed.

"Thank you."

"It iss too bad my sons are not so good looking," Swede added, still studying the table setting.

Not so good looking? Inga repeated in her mind, thinking of Jacob before responding. Your sons…she started to think but choked the silent counter. The thought was not diverted, however.

Sensing her thought, Swede again pleasantly looked down at her for a moment, but said nothing.

Inga responded with a polite smile, turned and joined his gaze toward the growing table cornucopia.

The seed was planted, and for the moment she continued to think of Jacob. Following the moment their eyes first met, Inga could not bring herself to look at Jacob. But in the beginning her memory served her well. He was not as big as his father, but he was still well over six feet tall. With broad shoulders and large hands, like his father. Inga looked at Jacob in her mind's eye. And a strong jaw. And honey blonde hair. And those eyes…Inga stopped herself.

Inga looked up at Mr. Odegaard who, huge forearms arms folded, returned her gaze with a fatherly look that told her he genuinely liked her…who and what she was. He knew her, she sensed. For a moment she was unnerved, but quickly regained her composure. She was, after all, proud of who she was. Mr. Odegaard seems so intelligent, masterful, she thought. In some respects, he seems almost superhuman. He may even think so, she silently considered. No, she countered herself; he wouldn't think that.

Swede took the large fork and carving knife that seemed to shrink in his hands, and began to slice the ham.

"I vill tell you somet'ing," Swede said as he carved the ham. "All the t'ings in this room are not so beautiful as you and yoor smile." He looked at her directly, his eyebrows raised. "You are strikingly beautiful," he said sincerely.

Inga's heart nearly stopped.

Swede beamed pleasantly for a moment and returned his attention to the ham. Angus, seated near the fireplace, nodded in agreement and smiled because, while the compliment was true, shy Inga was embarrassed. No one ever told her she was beautiful…not, well, "beautiful." How he said it. Her sisters never said anything because Inga's beauty was so obvious; why tell her what she already knew? Her father favorably complimented her "appearance" many times, and her mother remarked that she was very attractive, but no one had ever said she was, well...

Beautiful.

The word went straight to her heart. At that moment, the readiness to hear dictated the telling. Inga self-consciously turned back toward the fireplace, her mind racing, unaware that since the Nordquists arrived, Jacob had difficulty bringing himself to look directly at her as well.

"Inga, we need you to finish the gravy," Anna called from the kitchen.

Inga excused herself and hurried to the kitchen, passing Mrs. Odegaard who was walking anxiously into the dining room, intent on directing traffic.

Standing with his hands on the back of his extra large chair, Swede nodded at his wife. As her bright smile flashed knowingly in reply, competing with candles and the fireplace, she nodded back. She and Swede had discussed this moment earlier.

Erika Odegaard was convinced that she had the best husband alive. When, as a young woman, she was in a position to choose from among many young men, she quickly distanced herself from the others after she met Swede. She was attracted not so much by his good looks – she knew others who were equally good looking – but, rather, his intelligence, innate sensitivity, self-confidence, character and depth.

He conscientiously insured that she always felt loved and desired. That was what she needed. All the rest, the stuff, was frosting.

Swede nodded towards Amos who was standing near the table. "Amos, vould you and your family join us?" Swede asked with a wink. As if Amos and his family had a contingency plan.

"We would be honored," Pastor Nordquist smiled. "Girls…Anna…please come to the table now."

And it began.

"Erika, vould you light the rest of the candles, please," Swede said pleasantly in his low voice.

As Erika lit the remaining candles, the others walked toward the table.

The Odegaard daughters, as was their custom, begin to sit next to each other, but tonight their mother had other ideas.

"No," Mrs. Odegaard ordered. "Mary, Martha, vait yust a minute. Ve vill sit in different places now."

Mrs. Odegaard walked to her chair next to her husband who still stood at the head of the table.

"In polite society," explained Mrs. Odegaard, "it iss proper for men and women, boys and girls, to alternate seating around the table. I vill sit here. Jacob, vould you sit here next to me?" she asked in a tone of voice that implied there was no alternative. Swede, seemingly without expression, looked at his oldest son to indicate that Jacob had better move quickly, which Jacob did.

Erika stepped to the left behind the next chair, but passed to the next, leaving a place empty for the moment. She looked at Samuel with a pleasant continence and asked him to take the next seat. She nodded toward Esther who sat to the left of Samuel. And so it went.

Jacob eased into his chair as Inga cautiously passed through the kitchen door, her eyes firmly watching the porcelain gravy boat cradled in her hands. As she approached the table, her attention did not waver. Upon reaching the table, through the seating opening provided by the remaining empty chair space, she carefully centered the gravy boat in its proper moorage. Standing upright, she first took notice of the empty chair, left for her – there was only one remaining place to sit – and who was sitting next to it.

Inga flushed, then froze. She could not move…except for her heartbeat that nearly stopped, but instantly restarted, loud as Gettysburg artillery. As the battle became more pitched, the Boston Handel and Hayden Society embellished the cacophony with the Grande Finale of the *1812 Overture*. And she stood there. Hours turned into days, weeks. Centuries passed before a faint sign of life eked out.

"Where do you want me to sit?" she finally managed to gurgle, the empty chair obvious before her.

The humiliation was complete. After dinner (she resolved) while the others exchanged pleasantries, she would hang herself in the barn. Anna Nordquist smiled pleasantly at Inga who, not understanding, wanted only for the rapture to occur immediately. Jacob seemed not to notice, although he did. Inga pulled out the chair and sat down.

Swede reached out his big hands, to his wife on one side, and Rachel, on the other. At first his wife and Rachel were uncertain of his intentions. When it was evident that communal prayer would be said out loud, instead of individually and silently, Mrs. Odegaard, elated, took the hand of her husband and that of Jacob, then the others followed in kind, holding hands prior to praying. Erika Odegaard glanced thankfully at Swede. While his objective intellect allowed him to go no further than agnosticism, for the sake of his wife and guests he would make this easy compromise.

At Swede's request, as He listened, Amos Nordquist thanked Him for the food, the moment at hand, and all His blessings, concluding with, "Your will be done. Amen."

During the prayer, Inga, her left hand immersed in Samuel's firm grip and her right hand in the strong but sensitive possession of Jacob, was indeed thankful. It was the first time Inga held hands with anyone outside her immediate family since she was little. As she held Jacob's large hand, she fought against the growing ecstasy threatening to overwhelm her self-control. Social expediency, Lutheran asceticism, and supreme self-discipline won out. Her cover was not blown. With the fragrances of cedar, warm honey, baked ham, hot bread, tea and a variety of spices wafting about the table, in the glow of the candlelight and the fireplace, nothing was more radiant than Inga.

Inga stared over the centerpiece at the huge mouth of the river rock fireplace within which the harmless fire played, shadows and light dancing about. To her, everything in the room lightly glowed. So beautiful, so warm. She softly touched her hand where Jacob Odegaard just held it, before helping herself to food being passed around the table. There is, she thought, so much love here.

In the emotion of the moment, she turned and looked at Jacob. In her quiet way, she smiled politely.

Jacob stopped chewing, motionless, returning her gaze. Jacob remained still, mesmerized, taking the opportunity to politely drink in Inga's beauty, then continued chewing, masking the excitement he felt.

Again, it wasn't as if he had not noticed Inga. Or even Esther. He had. So had Samuel. But now in his growing excitement, Jacob's world-view began mutating rapidly. And what was before was no more. In its place was something similar but different, that again instantly changed. Inga's radiance played havoc with Jacob's senses and sensibility; momentarily he couldn't think. Like his father, he was usually the master of a situation. While Inga said nothing to him, the force of her momentary, pleasant smile left him emotionally disarmed. He would have felt more assured if he knew the unconditional disarmament was mutual.

Inga's attention was distracted to her left where Samuel indelicately pursued the food on his plate, insuring none of it could escape, until he glanced at his father whose expression was one of darkness similar to the storm outside.

Samuel immediately sat upright and began eating with more propriety than would be necessary at Stockholm Palace, obviously knowing how.

It was not only Samuel's table manners that beckoned Inga's eye but, beyond Samuel, her mother's gaze. Anna, seated next to her husband at the other end of the table, was watching. Inga turned her attention to the honey-baked ham on her plate, back to her father engaging her mother in conversation, and to Big Swede who seemed the size of two men.

Meanwhile Jacob, seated upright, relaxed with both wrists on the edge of the table, one hand with a fork, while again looking at Inga. In the next moment their eyes met and while Jacob enjoyed the view, Inga finally pulled her eyes away, glancing at her mother who, while continuing to listen to her husband, fielded Inga's glance like a shortstop, visually focusing on both Inga and Jacob.

As Inga looked momentarily down at her plate, part of Inga felt wonderful, but, unused to this kind of attention, even so subtle, another part felt self-conscious.

Jacob put down his fork, brought his hands up, folded them, rested his chin on them, and, like a pitcher looking at the runner at first, glanced momentarily at Anna Nordquist before returning his attention to Inga. He certainly is good looking, thought Anna. Pastor Nordquist stopped speaking and, following Anna's lead, also looked at Jacob. The outer placidness of the situation contrasted with emotions sprinting as if chasing a deep fly ball near the warning track.

Inga looked at the edge of her plate feeling for-all-the-world like all the world was watching. But, really, she silently queried herself, who is watching? Mom. Dad. Jacob. Inga sighed inwardly, made her decision, lifted her head and, like a hitter looking for a high fastball, ignored all else and gave an awaiting Jacob her complete attention.

As Jacob began asking her questions about herself, she started to enjoy this new position – how quickly things changed in a few minutes, she thought. She reveled in the feeling as she looked at Jacob and thought, really, could this evening be any better?

As dinner progressed, Samuel wanted to know everything about the Seattle fire and began asking questions. None of the Odegaard family was satisfied with partial answers. Farm life was long, demanding and repetitive. Exciting news, particularly from eyewitnesses, was stimulating, and the subject had not been introduced until now. Table conversation went back and forth like the ball in a double-play run-down. Where did the fire start? How did it start? How much smoke was there? Did everything burn? Was anyone hurt? How many were saved by the firemen? What did the fire engine look like? How many firemen were there?

As the questions flew, so did the responses, with Inga, like the rest of her family, although admitting she knew little, becoming uncharacteristically talkative and, occasionally, animated, although not as animated as Angus MacGregor who, like everyone else at the table, at times forgot to eat, an inactivity which would have seemed impossible moments earlier. The unexpected spontaneity of conversation generated an easy camaraderie, seeds of fondness effortlessly sprouting into friendships among adults, young adults and children.

Effervescent Rachel bantered with Luke, a good listener, encouraging Rachel to banter more. Luke and Rachel became anxious, wanting to end dinner so that they could go outside before it got too dark. Luke had several things he wanted to show Rachel.

"Have you noticed it iss raining?" countered Mrs. Odegaard, annoyed at the interruption. "You can play in the cellar."

"May we be excused?" asked Mary and Martha simultaneously.

"Yah," answered Erika Odegaard as she listened attentively to Anna Nordquist.

Luke, Rachel, Mary and Martha all got down from their chairs. Rachel and Luke walked toward the back door while Mary and Martha collected dishes and silverware (Mary), cups and glasses (Martha) from the table, and went to the kitchen.

Anna wanted to compare recipes. And the Odegaard *krumkake* iron, a family heirloom Erika brought to America, sounded identical to Anna's.

The harmony between Jacob, Samuel and Inga gradually went from a trio to a duet as Samuel found it easier to converse with Esther, seated on Samuel's left. Inga was now composed and uninhibited, finding it easy to talk to Jacob – toward whom earlier she could not turn her eyes, and whom only a moment ago, she reminded herself, she had trouble addressing. Addressing? You only "address" perfect strangers, she thought.

Beyond the happiness of the moment, more than becoming closely acquainted, Inga felt oddly like she and Jacob had always known one another. How is that?

Jacob, a shock of dark blonde hair flowing at an oblique angle across his bronzed forehead, and resting precariously on his dark left eyebrow, looked down intently at Inga, giving her an up-close view of those waterfall blue eyes she secretly admired from a distance. They were more beautiful than she imagined. This was all so new. Inga was spellbound.

"You know," Jacob offered, putting his right elbow on the table, "I like talking to you. You're very intelligent…" He paused and leaned close to her ear, in a low voice quietly adding, "...and so beautiful."

Inga's lips parted slightly as she looked back at him, his eyes continuing to smile down at her while he rested his chin on the back of his wrist, his large hand hanging loosely but cautiously like it was afraid of falling. Inga was not afraid of falling and, in fact, she was. Unable to think of a response in spite of all that intelligence, her feminine instincts took over and she said nothing, equally returning his pleasant gaze, almost defying him to do something about it. Momentum undisturbed by verbal trespassers, the ball left the park.

Watching, Anna Nordquist initially thought of her first personal moments with Amos. How often when remaining silent, she thought, so much is said.

What was said? At that moment, it was decided.

"And for His pleasure, they are created…," Anna sang softly as her eyes glanced upward and about, as if half-expecting to see the Holy Spirit leaving, before considering the unlikelihood of that ever happening.

82

Swede bent over and put his hands on his knees and maintained that position for longer than he wanted. Although the morning wasn't over, he was already exhausted, almost ready to return to bed.

The day before, he hauled lumber and river rock into the woods to begin building a bridge over the creek, and then worked on the bridge until the summer sunset. His wife saved him dinner. He left the woods and went to his workshop where, preparatory to the next day, he worked until after midnight on bridge braces and forms. Finally in bed and asleep, Swede awoke to the sound of panicked chickens making a terrible ruckus in the chicken house. Grabbing his rifle and a lantern, he ran out the back door and to the chicken house. Throwing open the chicken house door, he saw coyotes, mouths full of feathers, killing his chickens in the far roosting area. Quickly setting the lantern on the feed barrel cover, the roosting area illuminated, Swede took quick aim and angrily fired multiple times.

Swede stuffed the dead chickens and coyotes into separate large gunny sacks, grabbed the lantern, and went outside to inspect the chicken wire fence that surrounded the chicken house. Swede found the hole the coyotes dug under one of the logs that weighed down the base of the wire fence.

In the dark, he walked rapidly to the tool shed, grabbed his shovel, a maul and wood stakes, and returning to the shallow hole, in the lantern light, drove the stakes partially into the base of the hole, the protruding ends of the stakes forming a vertical barrier. He then packed the hole with large rocks and dirt.

Swede re-placed the chicken wire over the refilled hole and stakes, and the log over the extended base of the chicken wire.

Grabbing his rifle, shovel and the two large gunny sacks, he walked back to the tool shed, placed the shovel and dead coyotes and chickens in a corner, stepped outside, and closed the door behind him. Tired in spite of the adrenalin in his system, he would attend to the dead animals after daylight. He walked to the house, washed, went to bed and was asleep as soon as his head hit the pillow.

Two hours later he forced himself out of bed before daybreak to skin the coyotes, and bury the coyote carcasses and dead hens.

Finished, he pushed himself to the barn to help his sons, already in the barn, with the milking. He was late and one cow uncomfortably looked at him as if to say, "Where have you been?" In a nearby stall, a heifer, eyes distressed, was about to go into labor.

Normally Swede didn't allow his pigs to get much bigger than 200 to 250 lbs. before being butchered, but one pig – an unusual pet pig his daughters named Grover after President Grover Cleveland – was being allowed to live to a ripe old age. As a piglet, Grover was already intelligent and affable. And now Grover was huge, an enormous family pet, identifying more with humans than other pigs.

A couple years earlier when let out of his pen, Grover decided to go inside the house with the rest of the humans, but shortly Grover was shown the door by Swede's daughters, Mary and Martha.

"Get out of here, Grover! You can't come in here!" they told him.

Grover looked back questioningly. They can't be serious, he thought. Everyone else is here. Grover grunted several times attempting to make his case.

"Grover thinks he can talk."

"He *can* talk; we just can't understand him."

"Grover, if you're so smart, you should learn to knock," said Mary as she affectionately put her arms around Grover's neck. She knew Grover liked that. "We all love you, but you have to stay outside." Mary and Martha then gently pushed and pulled Grover who was obediently leaving, but at his own pace.

Grover was smaller then. The girls knew if Grover came inside now, and didn't want to leave, the only person who might get him out was their father, but more likely the effort would also require their brothers and maybe Angus McGregor and Pastor Nordquist too. With ropes and pulleys. No one could guess how much Grover weighed…other than: a lot.

The milking was done. Shortly, Angus and Amos came into the barn to get directions for the day. Swede gave Amos a short list that Amos began to read.

"Angus, here's your list," said Swede as he wearily wiped his forehead with his bandana. I needed more sleep, he thought.

Angus began mentally prioritizing the listed items. Among the list items was, "Inspect pigs' feet, and pens." Angus nodded, knowing that contrary to conventional wisdom, pigs didn't like their pens soiled.

Late in the morning, the heifer went into labor, and Swede, feeling last night's lack of sleep, grudgingly dropped other things he was doing.

By early afternoon, Amos was finished and joined Swede in the barn.

At mid-afternoon, Angus, finished with his chores, came into the barn to assist if needed, but labor was nearing its end. Although it was a difficult labor, both heifer and calf were in good health.

Swede, on the other hand, was ready to drop. He seldom took naps but, feeling as tired as he did, made a decision to do something very unusual for him: take a nap for about an hour.

As Amos stood next to the heifer and calf while Swede remained on one knee, Grover sauntered into the barn and came up behind Angus. Swede looked at Grover and looked up at Angus.

"Vhy did you let Grover out?"

Angus blinked, turned around and saw Grover. Angus had no idea how Grover got there, and looked back at Swede.

"I didn't let him out," said Angus with a surprised expression. "How he got out is a mystery to me."

For a moment, Swede, still on one knee, only looked up at Angus.

"It's not a mystery to me," said Swede. "If you did not intentionally let him out, there iss only vun vay he could have gotten out." Swede's forehead furrowed. "And if Grover is out, where are the other pigs?" Angus' expression went neutral.

Swede stood up and walked rapidly to the barn entrance, brushing by Angus.

Once outside, Swede disappeared for a moment. When he returned, his angry visage was unchanged.

"All the pigs are out – in the corn field. Eating."

The young corn stalks were a little over knee-high and the pigs were enjoying the moment.

Herding sheep, cattle – most farm animals – is not difficult. The person herding flanks the herd on the left if the herd is to go right; right to go left.

But Amos, as well as Angus and Swede, knew pigs are too smart for that.

Getting pigs back into their pen can take all day, and Swede, so tired he earlier considered taking a nap, at that moment had neither time nor patience.

"Angus, go in the house and get the women. Amos, my sons are vorking by the river. Get them. Ve'll need everyvun to get the pigs back inside the pen area."

Swede walked toward Grover near the entrance, reasoning that attempting to herd Grover would be pointless. He appealed to Grover's good nature and intelligence. "Grover, c'mon," Swede cajoled. "C'mon Grover. Follow me." Swede gently patted his thigh, encouraging Grover to follow, and Grover began to follow. Swede sighed with relief. The rest won't be this easy.

As Angus walked out the barn entrance, Swede and Grover were behind him. While Swede sounded pleasant when talking to Grover, inside Swede was fuming.

"C'mon, Grover. Follow me. That's good. You're a smart pig. I'm glad somevun here has a brain," said Swede to Grover, loud enough for both Amos and Angus to hear. Amos and Angus looked at one another.

"Angus," called Swede to Angus ahead of him, "try to remember to close the gate vhen you either enter or leave the pen area. Can you do that?"

Angus, still walking, turned his head, embarrassed and annoyed at Swede's jibe.

"Of course, I can do that," explained Angus. "In fact, I'm sure I did it."

"Then vhy is Grover behind me," asked Swede heatedly, "and other pigs in the cornfield? Obviously, Angus, you didn't do it. And the suggestion that you did only insults my intelligence…and raises some qvestion about your dependability."

"Well…I, I apologize," stammered Angus, not knowing what else to say as they walked. "I can't believe I…"

"Don't apologize," said Swede, exhausted, as he glanced toward the cornfield. "Apologize later vhen an apology might be sincere."

Angus, embarrassed, again didn't know what to say. He remembered closing the gate to the pen area. How did those pigs get out? Realizing Swede was too tired to think clearly and in no mood to listen, Angus said nothing.

"Swede," began Pastor Nordquist, "I'm certain Angus's apology is sincere. It's unnecessary to denigr..."

"Two days from now vhen we've managed to finally get all those pigs back vhere they belong," interrupted Swede impatiently, "ve'll discuss it. Meanwhile, I don't need to hear excuses. Vhat obviously happened is vhat obviously happened," added Swede querulously, glaring down at Amos as they walked. "Angus forgot to close the gate. It's yust that simple. Angus needs to remember things and spend less time daydreaming. It isn't like ve don't have better things to do, you know."

"I'm sure that Angus didn't intend..."

"Amos," interrupted Swede impatiently, "get the boys."

Neither Amos nor Angus said anything. Amos and Angus turned and rapidly walked away. Swede continued around the barn toward the pigs' pen area, disappearing from the sight.

"Angus," said Amos, "he's really tired. He was up late working on things for the bridge, and in the middle of the night had to deal with the coyotes killing the chickens…he got up a couple of hours later to start milking, and then the heifer went into labor, putting him way behind his schedule with..."

"Aye, but I'll tell you, I didn't let those pigs out," said Angus, looking at Amos as they walked. "How they got out is something of a mystery I'd like to know myself…both because I'm curious and also," Angus turned his head forward, "to reclaim some small bit of honor."

"I understand," said Amos as he put his hands in his pockets. "Swede is obviously not himself. He doesn't mean what he's saying."

"Aye, well," sighed Angus, "we've all done that." Angus looked blankly at the ground as he swallowed his pride. "It will be interesting when we find out..."

"*Fan* [damn]!" came the loud shout from the other side of the barn. For a moment there was silence. Almost blurry-eyed from sleeplessness, Swede stared at the collapsed fence. He looked down at Grover. A collapsed fence. The pigs were out, and forcing its way out from inside Swede's befogged brain was that he had just behaved disgracefully toward Angus and Amos. "*Fan! Fan! Fan!*" Swede uncharacteristically erupted, enraged.

Amos and Angus, hearing Swede, turned and ran toward the barn en route to the pigs' pen just as Swede came running around the barn, wide-eyed, angrily going the other direction. Angus and Amos stopped, turned and watched as Swede ran by them, reached the house, bounded up the back porch steps and disappeared inside.

As Amos and Angus started to trot in the direction of the house, Swede ran out again carrying his rifle, reloaded after shooting the coyotes.

"Swede! What are you going to do?" yelled Amos. "Swede, be calm!"

"I should have done this years ago," growled Swede to no one in particular as he raced toward Angus and Amos. Angus, wide-eyed, panicked and turned to run, fearful Swede had snapped, but Swede raced past Angus without stopping to explain, and Amos and Angus turned and watched incredulously as Swede ran around the barn. Angus looked anxiously at Amos.

"What in the world is going on?" Angus asked. "What's he doing?"

Swede was mad – mad at everything, but especially himself. He would deal with the immediate cause of his dilemma and then he'd deal with everything else. Swede was looking down at his rifle, making sure it was loaded, as he trotted into the pigs' pen area.

Grover saw.

Grover stared at the rifle; and Grover, having watched in the past, knew what would happen next. Grover looked to his left. None of the other pigs were nearby. It was his turn. Before Swede could aim, Grover began to lie down.

Angus and Amos flinched at the sound of the report. Anxiously, they ran around the barn and over to the pen area where Swede was standing, the rifle hanging slack at his side, looking at Grover who lay dead, his mouth partially open and an eye still looking at Swede, staring. Swede continued to stare back. Stepping to Swede's side, Amos and Angus apprehensively looked up at Swede, saying nothing, their expressions begging for explanation. Mouth partially open, looking unbelievingly at dead Grover, Swede slumped as he silently asked: what am I doing?

Swede lifted his eyes, placed the rifle over his shoulder, and again dropped his head as Amos and Angus looked at him. Swede silently motioned with his head toward the collapsed fence to their right.

"You say you are sorry," Swede said to Angus after a moment. "Vell...," Swede took a deep breath, expelled it, and looked down again, "you had no reason to be sorry. I vas the vun who vas wrong." Swede looked over toward the collapsed fence. "Grover vas so heavy – and smart – vhen he vanted out – he must have been curious about vhat vas going on in the barn – he leaned against that fence section until it fell over." Swede turned his head to the far right. "You see the gate?"

Amos and Angus looked. The gate was closed. As Angus said it was.

"Grover pushed over the fence, valked through the opening, and the other pigs followed." Swede looked down at Angus.

"Angus, you say you don't know how the gate got open. I don't know how my mouth got open; how the t'ings I said came out of it." Swede looked back at Grover's body, as if this was a dream. But it wasn't. "And I shot Grover." Amos and Angus looked at Swede without expression.

"I feel now...like I am not myself," added Swede. "You know? I don't know vhat iss happening to me. Dis iss not the sort of t'ing I do." Swede looked back and forth from Angus to Amos. "I feel vorthless. Useless." It was a strange feeling. Swede had never felt useless during his entire adult life. His mouth open, he again looked at Grover. "I am sorry," he said with a quaver in his voice. "Please, forgive me."

"You are tired, exhausted," replied Angus, "truly not yourself. Forgiveness is really unnecessary."

"That is not how I feel," said Swede, staring at Grover's lifeless body.

"You are forgiven…of course," said Pastor Nordquist. "But there is a deeper cause for your feeling of worthlessness, deeper than your actions of the last few minutes. To rid yourself of that feeling, worthlessness, you'll need more than our forgiveness."

Swede looked at Amos and knew what Amos meant. Deep inside, however, part of Swede ordered he not consider that. On the other hand, Swede felt like hell. Swede the perfectionist just did several extraordinarily imperfect things. He erroneously blamed someone for something they did not do; he unnecessarily insulted that man, Angus, as well as Amos; he lost his composure, behaving like a child; and he took out his anger by killing Mary and Martha's lovable pet pig. All in less than a minute.

Now how will I tell Erika? And Mary and Martha?

83

Y ou shot Grover?" replied Erika in Swedish as she joined the men to herd the pigs back into the pen area. "Why?" she asked. "Grover wasn't just one of the pigs. And why now? Why not, well, years ago…or in the late fall when we normally butcher pigs?" She shrugged. "I don't understand."

Swede explained.

"Mary and Martha will not be happy," said Erika grimly. "What are you going to do with Grover now? He'll never fit in the pig scalder."

"I'm…I'm not sure I want to treat Grover…like a regular pig…"

———— ◆ ————

"Oh, nooooo." Mary looked up at her father and put her hands to her cheeks.

"Grover vas getting so big that he vas becoming disruptive," explained Swede. "Vhen a pig can push over a fence, his days are numbered. It vas time," Swede added.

The verisimilitude was effective. He killed Grover, however, because he was mad, extraordinarily mad at himself for losing his composure, and wrongly insulting Angus and Amos, two men undeserving of censure. And he basely took his anger out on Grover, exacerbating an already-bad situation.

Mary looked at the floor and bit her lips as she fought to keep from crying. Grover was a pig, but a wonderful pig, she thought. Like a person. You could talk to Grover, and Grover would listen. He understood. Even knew. And he'd even try to talk back.

Martha looked at her father sadly, questioningly, her head cocked slightly, trying to pry some additional explanation – it seemed there must be more.

Dog-tired, Swede's spirits flagged further as he remained silent.

The two girls glanced sorrowfully at one another.

Butchering animals was part of farm life. Looking down, Mary and Martha sadly turned and walked away, tears welling up, thinking about Grover.

Continuing to feel like hell, Swede asked Amos what he thought about having funeral for an animal.

"It won't be the first time," said Amos, wiping his forehead. "I doubt it will be the last."

While Swede said nothing, the voice of his conscience was loud. Later as he chased pigs – some of which he was able to corner, catch and carry to the pen area – he thought about what just happened when talking to Mary and Martha. By wallowing in prevarication, he was guilty of the insincerity of which he accused Angus earlier. When Mary and Martha walked away, Swede's anger and disappointment remained and, while Angus, Amos, Erika, Mary and Martha were all forgiving, Swede was having difficulty obtaining forgiveness from Swede. By early evening, all the pigs were back in the pen area. The men were able to hoist Grover onto a hay wagon for burial in the back pasture the next day. Jacob and Samuel repaired the fence, but Swede felt like nothing was fixed.

Sunday, July 21, 1889, 9:00 a.m.

Early the next morning, in the workshop Swede made a grave marker for Grover before turning his attention to the barn. He was physically rested, but the previous day's behavior continued to weigh down his conscience.

Pastor Nordquist now sat quietly on the couch reading passages from the Book of Acts. Finished, Amos prayed for his new congregation and its future. Its first worship service would begin in half an hour, conducted in the Odegaard living room.

While Swede shoveled the milking and feeding areas, his expansive living room served as a sanctuary for a church service. Swede, at Erika's request, provided his home for worship, but he did not attend. He was at an impasse, his excellent reasoning still failing him. Had he not excellent reasoning, upon failing to convince himself of God's existence, he could have drawn the easy conclusion and given the matter no more thought. He had the intellectual integrity, however, to examine both sides of the question, and either way he logically came up empty-handed. He felt weary from fruitless mental exercises and silently wished for a resolution. His family and friends were inside his house worshipping something, someone, he could not prehend. What did they know that he did not?

Despondent because of Grover, and feeling empty, Swede shoveled more manure into the wheelbarrow. The putrid, uric stench made him nauseous, and the barn flies were indomitable, attacking from all sides in a manner that seemed coordinated, as if they were trained in aerial combat. Their behavior seemed more sentient than flies should be, and made him question what was going on?

He groaned slightly to relieve the pressure as he threw down the shovel. Then with hands that seemed powerful enough to turn coal into diamonds, he grabbed the wheelbarrow handles and pushed the wheelbarrow full of bovine excrement out of the barn toward the big compost wagon. The stench and attacking flies followed annoyingly as if telling him to put the manure back where he found it.

Running up the ramp built from the ground to the top of the compost wagon, Swede used inertia to flip the wheelbarrow contents forward onto the pile below.

One cow, two pregnant pigs in a holding pen, and two horses stood nearby watching this feat of dexterity.

"Do you t'ink dis iss great fun? Heh?" Swede said to the cow.

Swede began to back down the ramp as the cow continued to chew its cud, looking at Swede with blank, brown eyes. It looked away. The expressionless cow seemed indifferent, almost aloof, as if to say, "Manure collecting. Impressive."

"You know of a better vay to do dis? Perhaps you do it yourself. Hmm?" Swede stopped in the middle of the ramp and looked at the cow's eyes for some recognition, some indication the cow understood. The cow continued to chew.

Swede noticed the pigs watching him talk to the cow. Staring, they seemed incredulous, as if to say: "That's a stupid cow! Why in the world are you asking that brainless moron for advice? You must be as stupid as she is. We intelligent *porcinus* and these noble *equus* [the pigs glanced toward the horses] are beyond perplexed."

At this moment, the horses, Swede imagined, did look perplexed. Swede began to back down the ramp again. He stopped at the bottom of the ramp as he looked at the animals. The cow continued to chew, but the pigs and horses just looked away. Or did they? With horses one never…

"I am losing my mind," Swede muttered.

He turned around and started toward the milking area to shovel more manure, gripping the wheelbarrow staves so tightly they might break. Shoveling manure. The great agrarian equalizer.

"*Uhrrahhh!*" he growled loudly, frightening the pigs who quickly turned to face him as if to say, "Hey. Whoa, boss. Calm down."

As he stopped in front of a manure accumulation aside the milking stalls, he thought, I am master of much, but not this. This? But if not master of manure shoveling, of what *am* I master? He laughed painfully. "Why am I even…? Why am I talking to myself?"

His shovel – a child's toy in his big hands – moved like a metronome as, perspiring uncomfortably, he performed his mindless chore. Moments later, guiding the huge, home-made wheelbarrow out of the barn into the bright daylight toward the compost wagon, he drank in the beauty of the hillside forests, their twittering philistine residents flitting about, deaf to opposing viewpoints about the latest meager events and their weighty implications. Upon looking higher above him, his expression was one of ingenuous wonder.

"Could any artist duplicate that shade of blue," he said out loud, unknowingly echoing the sentiments of Angus MacGregor weeks earlier, "simultaneously dark and yet so bright?" He continued to study the sky. "No, no, not yet; maybe never. Another of man's unables," he mumbled. His neck began to ache from looking upward. The mountain gleamed white. Such majesty. His eyes began to feel pain from staring at the radiant whiteness and, after a moment, he looked down, raced forward and up the ramp, flipping another manure load.

Aggravatingly, the God question popped into his head although he didn't want to think about it. "I am tired of this. Is God? The answer is… How can anyone know?" Swede wondered out loud. "These people in my dining room? How do they know? My vife is there. She believes vithout reservation. My sons are there; they know little, but they too believe." Swede shrugged his shoulders.

"Yust do." And I am talking to myself.

As Swede pushed the wheelbarrow along a well-worn path to the barn, his confidence flagged further when it seemed the wheelbarrow was directing him, not vice versa. War with the flies continued. The pit of his stomach ached.

"Vhat am I doing?"

The question had nothing to do with cow manure, wheelbarrow or compost wagon but, rather, the overriding reason for his existence at all. What purpose did any of this serve? He stopped, continuing to hold the wheelbarrow handles. Looking about, he considered what he had accomplished. The home. The fields. The livestock. Here, he thought, are my reasons for being. Unexpectedly, however, these things that consumed so much of his waking moments seemed pointless.

"Vhat am I doing?"

Like the work behind him, the work that needed to be done seemed unimportant now, its prominence waning, reacting in fear to the angry commands of Swede's impatient soul. He unconsciously released the wheelbarrow handles. The thud of the rear supports hitting the ground startled some chickens close by, and made nearby workhorses turn their thick necks and look as if to ask, "What's wrong?"

What's wrong? I feel useless, he silently responded to the question. I'm a common, lying hypocrite. And my life pointless. That's what's wrong.

For Swede it was a terrible feeling. He grabbed the wheelbarrow handles again and rapidly plodded forward as if running from something, racing into the barn where following flies were joined by reinforcements. He filled the wheelbarrow, grabbed the handles, and ran out of the barn. Running up the ramp, at the edge of the compost wagon Swede flipped the wheelbarrow contents into the heap that lie beneath, waiting to be buried to be of value. Powerless. Decaying. He did not want to be by himself and, after returning the wheelbarrow to the barn, mouth partly open, he wearily wiped his forehead with his bandana before walking at a deliberate pace toward the temporary tabernacle.

On the porch, he removed his boots, opened the door, and on wool-socked feet, slipped into the foyer, silently closing the door behind him. The others were in prayer. His eyes tired and his mouth still slightly open, his huge frame filled the living room entrance. While he made no sound, his sons sensed his presence and simultaneously raised their eyes as Swede stood listening to his wife pray.

After hearing a few sentences, he realized she was praying for him. His confidence dropped further as his despondence grew even greater. His insides felt like a vortex above the Norwegian Trench, his mouth open and contorted in anguish. The perspiration on his face only partially camouflaged uncommon tears caused by his emotional turmoil, and yet he felt a sense of gratefulness that, like so much else now, he did not understand. What is happening? he asked himself.

His sons dropped their eyes, pretending not to notice.

He turned and faced the front entry, his back to the others, standing still, his head bowed as if praying, as his wife finished.

The silence was loud.

"Dad?" Jacob finally broke the silence. "Do you want to join us?"

"Vell...yah," Swede responded, wiping his face with his bandana before turning around. As he turned around, he smiled weakly. "Talking all morning vith cows and pigs iss not so good." He weakly laughed with the others. "How much longer is the service?"

"We were just about to sing the closing hymn," responded Pastor Nordquist. 'Beautiful Savior'. Do you know it?"

"It has been a few years," said Big Swede, walking toward the table. He had sung it many times as a boy growing up.

"My, Inga has a beautiful voice," remarked Erika Odegaard as her husband joined them, sitting in the big cedar chair he made for his own comfort, and which wouldn't be soiled by his work clothes. Indeed, Inga, a lyric soprano, did have a beautiful voice, extraordinarily beautiful. Inga silently nodded thanks, slightly embarrassed.

"Then let's all sing 'Beautiful Savior," said Anna. "Swede, will you join us?"

"Vell, I vill try to remember the vords," Swede said to the group, "but it has been a while. And after this iss over I need to spend some time vith Pastor Nordquist."

'Pastor Nordquist,' thought Amos. Not 'Amos.' I wonder what Swede wants.

Led by Erika, the others began singing "Beautiful Savior" *a cappella* but Swede only listened, primarily to Inga seated nearby to his left. Near the end of the first verse, he nodded appreciatively and joined the others, momentarily disrupting the flow by singing in Swedish, the way he learned the hymn as a boy, reducing the tempo. The adults joined him in Swedish while the children and young adults attempted to join in, self-testing their knowledge of the language. Samuel and Jacob simultaneously sang and listened to their dad who sounded not just good but formidable.

At the beginning of the second verse, Swede created a bass line and began singing the first verse again, but in Swedish, how he learned it as a boy. The others stopped. Then Erika dropped to the alto line while Anna and Inga continued the soprano melody and, although not a natural tenor, Pastor Nordquist joined in, improvising a tenor part. After listening, Samuel and Jacob also attempted singing bass, following their dad.

And when it sounded like his sons had the bass line covered, Swede incredibly dropped an octave.

Everyone stared at him, and for a moment Samuel and Jacob stopped singing, listening to their father who with an admonitory finger motioned circularly – continue. They awkwardly continued with the normal bass line. The others had never heard the word "oktavist," unaware there are few in the world, but, having crossed the Baltic to Russia while in his teens, Swede knew, and liked singing that low; it felt good, and at the moment he wanted to feel good.

The blend was surprisingly pleasurable; the younger children, listening, were enthralled. In timbre, Swede softly sang deeply and resonantly, laying a foundation the others built upon.

When they finished, the children looked at the adults excitedly.

"That was good," said Samuel adamantly. "That sounded good."

"Maybe we should all try harmonizing in English," Ester added wishfully, and the younger children agreed.

"We can all learn the Swedish version," deflected Jacob, thinking his father may not want to learn it in English.

"I can learn it in English," beamed Swede. "I speak English now."

Luke happily looked hard at the others through his thick glasses. This is so good, he thought. This feels so good. Luke weighed the reason: it's more than the singing; it's because Dad's here. His mother held Sunday morning Bible studies in the home while Swede worked outside. Luke never felt something was missing until that moment. Dad's here.

"Let's close with a prayer," Pastor Nordquist concluded, redirecting the communal thought. Swede wanted to talk with Amos, and the Holy Spirit wanted Amos to talk with Swede. Swede, having regained some sense of worth, however, felt a need to get back to work and finish what he had started earlier. The two would talk that evening.

84

The barn iss looking like a herd of goats spent the vinter there," said Swede, using a well-worn phrase he also occasionally applied to his sons' bedrooms or any other indoor area in a state of disarray. "Tomorrow vill be a good time to reorganize the barn, replace the straw on the main floor, put all the bee-keeping supplies in the small cellar, tools along the east wall, clean the mow [hayloft], and so on."

"What about Grover?" asked Jacob.

"Ve vill take care of Grover now," said Swede.

The men hitched up the hay wagon with Grover on it, as well as picks and shovels, and drove out into the far pasture to a place with wild flowers where they dug a deep grave for Grover.

While the other men wrangled Grover out of the wagon and into the grave, Samuel ran back to the farmhouse, went inside and got the women who joined the men in the field. Martha brought the grave marker.

Pastor Nordquist gave a sermonette used at previous funerals for other pets and when finished, the men pitched dirt over Grover's body. Martha pounded the grave marker into the ground, the last three strikes coming slowly, deliberately, like a death knell. The others understood. Crestfallen, Swede looked at the grave marker; while Grover was dead and buried, Swede's conscience remained alive and well.

After an early Sunday dinner, Amos and Angus prayed for God's leading during Amos' discussion with Swede that evening, then headed to the barn to make a separate itemization preparatory to Monday morning barn cleaning.

"Y'know, Swede works hard to be productive," said Angus, "but also because he is so restless, like a wave on a rough sea. There's no 'quiet' in the man. I could be wrong, but it seems t' me he's workin' feverishly tryin' to make his own inner peace."

Amos nodded pleasantly and shrugged. "Hopefully, he'll know inner peace this evening."

"Aye. He's a bit nervous about that."

"Angus, in my experience," said Amos, "coming to God is never as difficult as expected by the one being drawn."

"Difficult as openin' a Christmas present."

"Usually easier." Amos smiled. "One takes a spritual step of faith, seemingly difficult until the actual moment. And usually, Angus," Amos looked at Angus as they walked, "when someone has reached that point, God has drawn them close enough to where the gap is narrow and the step naturally follows."

"Aye," said Angus, looking back at Amos, "usually – but not always. It's God's timing, not ours."

"I agree but, at that point, the time has come."

"Expect so," Angus nodded.

"What never works well," added Amos, "is an attempt to reach either God or atheism the way Swede has been trying to do it: climbing hand-over-hand up a gradually increasing incline of failing logic under dimly lit apologetics before ultimately reaching a high agnostic bluff overlooking an apparent haze of faith." Amos held his hands out. "And then the searcher asks, 'Now what?' Often just giving up and saying, 'I can't know.'"

"But 'I can't know,'" said Angus, "doesn't answer the question – or any question."

"That's true," said Amos. "While agnosticism is intellectually honest, no epistemic void is filled, no answer received. And while the intellectual path ends, the spiritual path continues for those given the lamp of faith; enabling them to see it before them. Even then the next step forward can be difficult – sometimes discouraged by inner opposition."

"D'y expect that with Swede?" asked Angus.

"I'd be surprised if it were otherwise."

Sunday, July 21, 1889, 8:58 p.m. That evening.

After lighting kerosene lamps on either side of the back door, Big Swede walked over to his oversized rocking chair and sat down, slumping forward on the front edge in the faint, evening porch light, thinking about things he had read – some as murky as the lower Skagit River. Convivial frogs chorused in the distance. One of them stopped; and they all stopped. Moments passed. One started; and the others followed.

Swede's expansive front porch had enough floor area for two rooms. After removing his hat, Swede sat kneading the hat brim with his huge hands while watching a small ant making its way across the boards at his feet. First left, then right; stop; reconsider; forward again. No definite direction, but no time to waste. Swede sighed, continuing to finger his hat brim while waiting for Pastor Nordquist to join him in the cooler evening air.

Pastor Nordquist stepped through the door, his boots lightly clomping on the porch floorboards. He took his place next to Swede, sitting in the rocker where Mrs. Odegaard would often sit with her husband on evenings such as this, planning the next day, discussing the children, weighing the future. The porch heard conversations vaguely similar to that about to occur, but never a resolution.

Amos rested his elbow on the left rocker arm, looking intently at Swede as if to say, "Let's get started." He was comfortable, having hoped for this witnessing opportunity since first getting to know Swede. Amos had not expected the opportunity would come at the behest of Swede himself.

"I was surprised to have you join us," began Pastor Nordquist in Swedish. "Your wife has told me of your struggles with Christianity. What can I tell you?"

"It is not (cough, cough) – excuse me – just Christianity," Swede responded in Swedish, clearing his throat, but then coughing again. "It is belief in God. I cannot prove to my own satisfaction that God exists in the first place, and I (cough) cannot prove to my own satisfaction that (cough, cough)," Swede covered his mouth, "God does not (cough, cough, cough)."

Swede slowly leaned back in his chair, angry at himself for coughing. People cough unnecessarily when they're in over their heads, he thought, such as at concerts where the orchestra music is spellbinding, glorious, while, in contrast, course individuals seem strategically seated in the concert hall for the sole purpose of coughing, exhibiting the shallowness of their souls and ruining the moment for those absorbed in the performance. Why am I coughing? There is nothing wrong with me. As talking became difficult, Swede stiffened, glancing at Pastor Nordquist.

"The proofs for God's existence are not convincing?" Pastor Nordquist asked rhetorically, knowing the path Swede followed.

"Well, they may be convincing to some, but not to me." Swede loosened his bandana, although it was not too tight. "Too many questions are raised that cannot be answered. I beat my head against a wall (cough)." Swede put his hand over his mouth, and held his breath for a moment before expelling it. "And trying to convincingly prove God's non-existence is worse."

"I was unaware that there were proofs for God's non-existence," responded Pastor Nordquist. "Atheists normally don't get that far."

"They are not so much logical as cynical," began Swede. "They ask questions, but give no answers. It's puzzling that bright people negatively assume so much that is unsubstantiated. Pushing into the recesses of theological thought is stimulating at first but then," Swede wiped his right eyelid with the knuckle of his right index finger, "those recesses do not get any more illuminating; things get darker. People give up and assume as correct whatever they feel. I'm sensitive to the difference between fact, on one hand, and ignorance for the sake of convenience on the other, however." Swede shifted left and right, attempting to become more comfortable.

"Visibility becomes more difficult the deeper we search intellectually," said Pastor Nordquist. "People who have scoffed at me and my faith don't realize they cannot prove beyond a shadow of a doubt they are sitting there, much less prove beyond a doubt that God either does or does not exist."

Swede looked at Amos, puzzled.

"I take for granted I am sitting here," responded Swede. "Why would anyone think otherwise?"

"There is little point in doing otherwise," Amos agreed, looking toward the darkly silhouetted cornfield. "But we are talking about proof. Proof that God exists. Proof that anything exists." Amos watched the fields in the darkness as he spoke. "I have also studied these things and I have found, as you suggest, it is good we take much for granted because, actually, we have no choice."

"Go on," Swede said, hands folded.

Glancing sideways at Swede, Amos dropped his index finger, allowing his thumb and fingers to gently support his chin.

"We are more limited in our awareness than people realize," explained Pastor Nordquist. "Since before the time of Socrates, people have unsuccessfully attempted to come up with all the conditions for knowing, that is, the conditions under which we are confident that what is believed is also known, that is, true. There is good reason for lack of success over the centuries."

"What is that?"

"What we call 'knowledge,'" answered Pastor Nordquist, "is *not* knowledge. Let me explain. When I was in seminary studying these questions in one of my classes and using logic, we concluded that God did exist. It was interesting. I remember one student – he was much brighter than I was – pointing out, however, that by making some minor, valid changes in the form of the argument, but without changing the assumed premises, we could come up with the exact opposite conclusion: God did *not* exist." Amos smiled. "Logic."

Swede, frowning, said nothing, continuing to listen.

"What does that tell you about God?" asked Amos. He shrugged his shoulders. "Not much. But it says a great deal about our limitations."

"Limitations. Limits of knowledge?"

"Yes."

Swede's frown momentarily vanished, but then slowly repositioned itself.

"If there is knowledge," continued Pastor Nordquist, "that is, belief where there is no margin of error, then it is absolute knowledge and, by definition, would be a characteristic of Almighty God. Absolute knowledge is consequently unavailable to human beings; "knowledge" is a conceptual extrapolation of the highly justified belief we continually experience, such as the 'fact' we are sitting here."

"You say that knowledge is a characteristic of God, not men," interjected Swede. "It seems you might be assuming what you are expected to prove."

"No," responded Amos, "we can impute characteristics to the concept of God, but whether or not He exists is another matter. At the moment, I am talking about the limitations of human understanding."

Swede returned to kneading the brim of his hat, peering at the lower porch railing where, in the bright moonlight, antennae probing sensitively, the ant anxiously worked its way toward the next step.

"So, I think you are saying," said Swede, "if we have highly justified belief about something, we say it is true. We say we have 'knowledge' of whatever it is that is the object of our highly justified belief."

"Or some say knowledge," added Pastor Nordquist, "is justified *true* belief – but, if nothing can be proven beyond a shadow of a doubt, the insertion of the word "true" is another step of faith."

Swede, slumping slightly in his chair, reflected for a moment.

"What I think you are saying," said Swede, "is that all 'knowledge,' as we normally use the word, is actually faith of a sort."

"Yes. All perceptions involve varying degrees of justified faith." Amos looked levelly at Swede. "As we agreed earlier, however, it is impractical to continually doubt everything."

"1 + 1= 2. Why would that require faith?" asked Swede. "It is true by definition."

"1 + 1 = 2," repeated Pastor Nordquist. "I am not talking about, essentially, X = X, I am talking about the question of whether there is an X at all," said Amos. "Do you believe that 1 + 1 = 2?"

"Of course."

"Good for you," smiled Pastor Nordquist. "Does that give you any additional insight into reality?"

"No, I don't suppose so," said Swede after a moment, retying his bandana.

"If you want to discuss things that are true by definition, start with knowledge."

"I don't understand."

"We do not experience absolute knowledge," continued Amos. "By definition, only 'God' does, and that is the problem, but it is an insightful problem. It is merely another way of expressing that, as the Bible says, we are created in his image. Our awareness is built on a foundation of faith. Varying degrees of faith. God has the capacity for absolute knowledge. 'Absolute.' Ask yourself, what does that mean? Incomprehensible. Think of His capacity for love. Absolute love. Also incomprehensible. But it is there."

"We don't know this," responded Swede.

"And in this present state never will," answered Pastor Nordquist. "Your pursuit of knowledge in this matter will always be frustrated."

"You kn...," Swede stopped, now sensitive to the word "know." After pausing, he inaudibly muttered, pausing again. "You know, Amos...," began Swede, raising his voice as he sat up, looking sideways at Pastor Nordquist. He did not finish the sentence, however, but sat back again in his chair, still looking at Amos.

"What is the point in all this?" asked Swede.

"The point is that faith in God may not be an intellectual compromise. We literally have faith in – not knowledge of – all that is 'out there'…beyond our own consciousness, and even consciousness itself. All perception involves varying degrees of faith. Secondly, as you know, we do not seem to be able to generate adequate arguments to justify either of the alternative faiths about the existence or the non-existence of God to the satisfaction of the majority of persons who have objectively attempted to prove one or the other over the ages."

"If you cannot prove one or the other, how then is it not 'an intellectual compromise' to accept one or the other?" asked Swede.

"On one hand, as Angus and I agreed earlier today, while agnosticism is intellectually honest, it does not answer the question of "God." On the other hand, the Holy Spirit performs acts, miracles – some evident, some not evident at all – the source for which there is no other explanation. Those who experience these things have little doubt of the Source, however. And there is the Bible. Your wife says you have studied the Bible," responded Pastor Nordquist. "What does the Bible say about those who say there is no God?"

"They are fools." Swede slouched in his chair.

"Psalms 14:1: 'The fool has said in his heart, "There is no God."' Why might they be fools?" asked Pastor Nordquist.

"For one thing, they cannot prove there is no God. In that regard, they deceive themselves." Swede sat up. "But then, why would the same term, 'fools,' not apply to those who say there *is* a God? Believers cannot adequately justify their faith either."

"No," responded Amos matter-of-factly. "No, we agree that we are at a dead-end with respect to logical proof," answered Pastor Nordquist. "But why stop there?"

"What?" Swede sat upright again and turned toward Amos. "Because there is no place left to go. I kn... I know!"

Swede remained motionless, thinking, but just before Amos was about to speak, Swede heavily slumped again, turned his head toward the fields, silver crested in the moonlight, looking over them as if searching the dark eastern skyline, and said *sotto voce*, "Well, maybe I don't know. I'm not sure what I know. What does it mean to know?" Swede was aware of the answer; they had just discussed it. He stared at Pastor Nordquist for a moment. "I sit here with no place to go."

Pastor Nordquist looked back at Swede understandingly. Swede worked very hard, conscientiously accumulating the fruits of his labor and, unintentionally, the distant admiration although not necessarily friendship of many in the community. But it seemed his worldly success was increasing, even magnifying his inner emptiness, and while part of him longed for relief from this emptiness, another part was more frightened of the relief.

Realizing the strides that Swede was making in his understanding, and the spiritual significance of this conversation, Amos quietly complimented, "Good for you. But you are wrong about 'no place to go.' Jesus said that 'no one can come to me unless the Father who sent me draws him [John 6:44].' You are being drawn by the Father. We would not be having this conversation if you were not.

"Now you take the next step of faith. Spiritual faith. Faith is amazing," Pastor Nordquist added. "So much more powerful than most suspect. When Jesus walked on the Sea of Galilee, Simon Peter stepped out of the boat and, for a moment, also walked by faith, but then that faith was taken from him... and he began to sink. Bartimaeus, blind from birth, sat beside the road into Jericho and, as the Savior passed by, cried out to Jesus, 'Son of David, have mercy on me!' Jesus, who knew what Bartimaeus wanted, nevertheless, for the sake of the crowd around them, asked him what he wanted, and when Bartimaeus responded by saying, 'Rabboni, I want to regain my sight,' Jesus responded simply, 'Go your way; your faith has made you well.'" Amos reiterated: "Spiritual faith is amazing – but does not follow from logical arguments. Rather, it is a gift from God the Father through His Holy Spirit, a gift that is the consequence of the Christ's sacrifice on your behalf that first Easter. The complete trinity is at work in conversion."

"You are using examples from the Bible," said Swede in a skeptical monotone. "What other examples can you give?"

"Why not the Bible?" asked Amos. "Did those things happen or did they not happen?"

"I don't know."

"What do you believe? Which is more probable?"

"They happened."

"Good. I respect your intellectual integrity."

"But you just said probability isn't certainty."

"It's as close as we'll come."

"If 'close' was all that was necessary, I would believe…but how do you get close to 'God'?"

"Of your own volition, you don't. He gets close to you – by drawing you to Him. Swede, a month ago it seemed you were in complete control of your life and God was not in it, your excellent reasoning still sufficing. What has changed?"

"For one thing, you showed up."

"Yes, that is 'one thing,' but there were many other things working together to bring you to this moment. Coincidences?" Amos looked evenly at Swede. "No. God loves you, and the things that have happened are God herding you, perhaps like we herd pigs. It takes some doing," Amos nodded. "If you want a recent example outside of the Bible, consider what has gone on during the past week…outside of you, but also inside of you."

Swede studied the porch floor and subtly nodded.

"Belief in God? You can take that 'step of faith' but," Amos smiled, "ironically you need faith to do it." Swede looked at Amos seemingly without expression. In Swede's eyes, however, Amos saw something few ever saw in Swede: fear.

"Do you understand me?" Amos politely asked. Amos continued to look at Swede who looked back in silence. "Many will make no attempt to step over the line," added Pastor Nordquist, "because they do not have the faith which enables them to do so. The faith needed comes from God; you cannot bring it upon yourself."

"Well, now, how do you know that?" asked Swede.

"To begin with, I have witnessed conversion, including my own, many times. But even if I had not, the Bible says this. There is no other book comparable to the Bible; if rejected, no substitute. Throughout the Bible are verses speaking of the elect, those whom God has drawn to Him. The Bible also states that belief in God is itself a gift from God, and that belief in God is not possible apart from this benevolence. Jesus tells the disciples, 'You did not choose me, but I chose you.' Why do some men believe and others do not? The Bible says God chooses to harden the hearts of some and open the hearts of others. Why? To achieve His purposes, and, beyond that, I do not know the answer to this question. I wish I knew more."

Pastor Nordquist studied Swede for a moment, and asked, "How hard is your heart?"

Swede, otherwise motionless, absently massaged his chin between his thumb and forefinger, forehead furrowed, watching the ant anxiously searching along the top step. Swede's head was beginning to ache slightly, and again he unloosened his bandana, snapping it as he pulled it again from his neck. He wiped his forehead while watching the black-silhouetted army of short, thin corn-men standing shoulder to shoulder, seemingly listening in the moonlit field.

"But how do I…how do I know faith is there?" Swede, who was never at peace, put his hand over his heart. "If I receive it, do I feel a certain way one moment and another way the next?"

"No, not necessarily," answered Pastor Nordquist. "The act of my conversion ostensibly occurred the evening of my father's funeral, but it had been a long time in coming, and may have even occurred much earlier. When I was very young, I wanted to know more about Jesus, and I often felt the need to pray. Perhaps the conversion experience the evening of my father's funeral was a formality. Perhaps it's often that way when someone comes to Jesus. But for others the formality is an emotional moment."

Swede said nothing. At the name of "Jesus," however, his stomach tightened, hardening inside as if it was lined with soft clay that was beginning to dry. Part of him wanted to simply get up and go inside, but a more intrepid part of him would not allow this.

"Here is where you are," Pastor Nordquist summarized. "While you probably know as much about Christianity as any born-again Christian, the truth of God, Christ and eternal salvation are not evident to you because the Holy Spirit has not taken residence in your heart. Your excellent research and reasoning have led you as far as you can go. But God is taking you further, and you are now standing in front of a line separating you from accepting what you can neither prove nor disprove by rational methods. You can either do nothing, stay where you are – which I don't think you want to do – or you can step over the line and find out what is on the other side."

"What choice is that?" Swede asked. "I starve where I am." Part of him, however, preferred to starve.

"If you make this step of faith, it is the step that is the proof. You cannot take that step without having first received enough faith to take it. It won't happen. You can go through the motions – left or right so to speak – as many do, but that is not taking the step forward. And after the step is taken – perhaps not immediately, but at some time in the future – things will occur in your life that can only be explained by the presence of the Holy Spirit."

"Why?"

"That is how God works."

Swede was skeptical. "You are talking in circles."

"No. Faith is a seed planted by God. It starts with God. Where there is no seed, nothing grows. Faith, the seed, is a gift granted according to God's will, His love. His love for you. How did God most strongly demonstrate his love?"

"Golgatha," answered Swede, his head tilted to one side. "I know the story. But sometimes I question if it is true because, from what I have seen, dying for another is not typical Christian behavior."

Pastor Nordquist nodded his head.

"Let me ask you something," responded Pastor Nordquist. "What do offensive actions committed by people calling themselves Christians, or those whom others call 'Christians,' have to do with Jesus?"

"I'm not sure what you're getting at," said Swede.

"We don't worship men, we worship God. If we worshipped other Christians or things associated with Christians or Christianity, or believed in self-redemption, the Christian faith would have long ago become just another cult. The physical act of going to church, isolated from truly believing in Christ, does not make you a Christian any more than going to the milking shed makes you a cow. Don't focus on the weaknesses of men; focus on the strengths of God and the love of Jesus Christ. As your wife does." Amos looked at Swede intently. "You know the central theme of the Bible: sin separates you from God, and you are incapable of self-redemption so, by the grace of God, the sinless Christ died in your place. You can either accept Christ or reject Christ. Accept Christ," said Pastor Nordquist, "and you are a new man. Your feelings of emptiness, worthlessness, go away. Reject Christ and, at best, you stay where you are until death."

"Where I am."

"Jesus performed many miracles witnessed by thousands," said Pastor Nordquist. "And yet He allowed himself to be crucified. Other religious leaders – diversions – before and since, accumulated wealth, women and earthly power. But what did Jesus and his disciples accumulate? None got rich; no earthly kingdom; no women. None gained earthly prominence and power leading a new religion. That was never the intent. These men practiced what they preached, received no material gain, and were killed for their belief. And the miracles – and the intervention of the Holy Spirit – continue today." Pastor Nordquist paused, looking at Swede watching the ant near to his boot. "A man after the truth, seeking peace, cannot ignore these things," concluded Pastor Nordquist as he leaned toward Swede.

"Swede, ask yourself the most important question anyone can ask."

"What question is that?"

"Who is Jesus Christ?"

Swede looked at Amos. Amos added, "Who is He? Honestly ask yourself that. Is He who the Bible says He is?"

"Obviously," responded Swede as he tied his bandanna, "you think so."

"If you make a thorough, objective attempt to answer that question," responded Amos, "you come to the conclusion that He is who the Bible says He is, and He did what the Bible said He came to do. The evidence does not support another conclusion. Answer that question and you go way beyond where you now are hesitant to go." Swede continued to look at Amos. "What would motivate an innocent man," asked Amos, "to voluntarily suffer an excruciating death on behalf others? Fame?" His eyebrows rose. "You get fame from being crucified?

Hardly. Only one motivation would cause someone to voluntarily do this: love. Extraordinary love. Through excruciating sacrifice.

"Swede, few people actually know what 'excruciating' specifically means. Long before the birth of Christ, the Romans created the Latin word '*excruciatus*' because no other word adequately communicated crucifixion suffering. The word '*excruciatus*' has as its root the Latin word 'cru' or cross, and means literally torture 'out of the cross.' The effects were complex: after enduring long, terrible agony, victims usually died from a combination of slow asphyxiation and heart failure. Roman citizens could not be crucified because crucifixion was considered too horrible, 'excruciating,' for any Roman citizen sentenced to death. Even in an era where cruel and deadly punishment was often part of major sporting events, crucifixion was considered beyond the pale. Yet Jesus Christ, who fed the 10,000, calmed the Sea of Galilee, and performed many other miracles, voluntarily went through that experience as a sacrifice atoning for our sins, your sins. Were I in your shoes, I would be looking hard at Jesus the Christ, at Christianity."

Swede looked at Amos with gravity.

"Your wife said that God would deal with you when it was time," said Pastor Nordquist. "Well," Amos looked levelly at Swede, "it is time."

Swede's stomach tightened further, and he reflexively reached for his bandana, but then stopped. He let his hand drop as he sat motionlessly, staring toward the silhouetted corn men.

"It is time now," repeated Pastor Nordquist.

"I'm not sure it is," mumbled Swede. It was as if he had not said this. Something inside was pulling at him, pulling hard.

"It is," countered Pastor Nordquist. "What reason have you for waiting?" Pastor Nordquist studied Swede; even beneath the weak lantern light, Swede looked pale. "You feel nervous?"

"Well, not so much 'nervous,'" Swede responded with self-control. "I feel...I..." Swede coughed. "I guess I feel..." He coughed again.

"A man who has spent as many years as you have living only by reason," said Pastor Nordquist, "yet continually dissatisfied with the efforts of his own intellect, can still expect discomfort when asked to step completely outside that restricted comfort zone. But if you are to find rest, peace with God, that is where you must go. We have reasoned to that point where you need to make that step of faith."

Swede again unloosened his bandana and wiped his forehead while staring blankly at the silhouetted corn men. His head dropped slightly. "I don't know. This is not just... I can't explain it. For a while now I have had this overriding sense of weakness, imperfection, guilt I had not..."

"Sinfulness."

"...I had not felt before, and while part of me wants to move forward, on the other hand it is like something inside me is...more than anything, does not want to let go."

"Something inside you," repeated Pastor Nordquist, nodding as he spoke. "Well, something inside you has become very comfortable assuming this moment – as with many who walk the path you've been on – would never come...but God has been drawing you to Him, and now here you are. Your wife has been praying for you. Jesus said that prayer is inordinately powerful. The Bible says, 'Pray without ceasing.' Why? Because prayer is an act of faith, and faith is a gift from God. Prayer is powerful because the source of this power is God Himself. This 'something inside' has, until now, ignored your wife and her prayers. God, effectively the source of those prayers, *never* has. And God continues to draw you to Him...even at this moment."

Swede looked back, his forehead glistening.

"Swede, I want you to repeat after me words which will help you find peace. These words will *not* bring about your conversion but, as you speak, the Holy Spirit, softening your heart, will. My sense is that you don't have far to go to enjoy peace, peace with God. And isn't that what you want?"

Peace. How bad can it be? Swede sighed. Why not? It was a question he would not have asked one month ago. He looked at the porch floor, sat back looking at the cornfield, turned his head and looked at Pastor Nordquist.

"Yes."

"Repeat after me." Pastor Nordquist bowed his head and Swede did the same. "Lord God, I believe that You have created all things..." began Pastor Nordquist. Swede quietly repeated the words.

"...and that You have an incomprehensible ability to love..." Again, Swede repeated what Amos said.

"...and that You love *me*,'" Swede also concluded.

"I, therefore, accept Your will," Pastor Nordquist said, "and I also accept Your son, Jesus Christ, as my savior." Swede repeated this.

"I ask Your Holy Spirit to fill my heart and to guide my life," said Pastor Nordquist. There was no immediate response.

"What is the matter?"

"I... Swede coughed, and then coughed again several times. "I..." There was a quaver in his voice. Pastor Nordquist's eyes narrowed.

"Say it," said Pastor Nordquist, sensing the war going on inside Swede. "You must not falter." Pastor Nordquist said the words again, "I ask Your Holy Spirit to fill my heart and guide my life."

"I ask..." Swede looked at Amos. The struggle inside Swede was evident from the tension etched in the lines on his glistening face. What, wondered Swede, is happening?

"Swede, keep going," encouraged Amos softly. Amos repeated, "I ask Your Holy Spirit to fill my heart and guide my life."

"I ask Your Holy Spirit to fill my heart...and to guide my life," said Swede in a moment, as if having snapped a remaining fetter.

"Amen," smiled Pastor Nordquist.

"Amen."

"Thank you, Lord," said Amos. "Thank you. Now, Swede, how do you feel?"

"Well," laughed Swede nervously in his bass voice, "I don't know why that was so hard. I am okay But, at the same time, I still feel...annoyed, aggravated. Offended? Why? This seems odd, I think. I did what I did. If I didn't want to, I would not have."

"No, actually you did as God wanted, not what you wanted. And now with all you've done before – perhaps in spite of all you've done – I believe the most important thing in your life is being accomplished."

"I am confused," said Swede, continuing to speak in Swedish. "I said what I was asked to say. I took the step of faith. Why, then, is this gift-of-which-you-speak seem not forthcoming? Like I have taken the step of faith, but my foot has not landed."

"Faith is not an act of magic. Presto!" Pastor Nordquist filliped. "If you were chosen, you were chosen before the beginning of time. The moment of conversion is known only to God."

"How do you know…," began Swede. "Never mind."

"Again, faith in God, in Christ's redemption, comes from God. It is spiritually discerned. And if, when, and how we receive it is up to Him, not us," said Pastor Nordquist. "Now we wait upon the Lord. Your wife who has loved you for so long, and who has been praying faithfully during all that time, needs to experience the joy of this moment. I will go get her."

Pastor Nordquist stood up and went inside to tell Erika.

As Pastor Nordquist spoke, Swede, although listening, was distracted by the dissipation of his anxiety, so grave moments before. Swede cleared his throat as he thought to himself: is this working? He felt no apprehension, angst – "annoyed, aggravated. Offended" – in fact, he felt a new sensation. Optimism? Hope? Hope about what? That wasn't evident. But at that moment it seemed like he had spent his life running half blind through heavy fog, suddenly bursting into sunlight. In fact, everything somehow actually seemed oddly brighter. Is this Christian faith? Swede wondered.

Swede stood up, folded his large arms, and studied the empty porch steps for a moment. Turning and walking toward the back door, he felt a further uplifting sensation beyond optimism; a mixture of rectitude and ebullience together with optimism. Gratefulness. For a moment, he stood focusing on the feeling. Opening the door, he paused, hand on the doorknob, and looked in at the clean kitchen floor. As he heard Erika's joyful cry, he stepped inside, turned and closed the door.

85

August 24, 1889

A month later, leaning against the drain board, for the moment Swede was doing something uncharacteristic for Swede: nothing.

Listening to the others, a glass of water his defense against the hot stove and oven air congregating in the kitchen, he quietly beamed as it occurred to him that when he stepped into the kitchen that night a month earlier, he also stepped into his own family. And in contrast to the moments when shoveling manure, he now felt at peace, a fresh, novel feeling.

"I would like to start a Bible study on Wednesday nights," Swede said to Pastor Nordquist, standing nearby with Rachel, discussing the importance of table manners.

"We should start with Romans," interjected Rachel.

"That's not a bad idea," said Amos, nodding. "This Wednesday after dinner we'll start with the first chapter of Romans."

Pastor Nordquist was delighted by Swede's thirst for Bible study because this was an indication the Holy Spirit had taken full residency in Swede's heart. Thank you, Lord, Amos said to himself.

Wanting to escape the kitchen heat, Rachel asked Anna if they could go for a walk in the moonlight. Mother and daughter left the house and walked toward the nighttime cornfield, fringes of dark cornstalks daubed white by lunar light. The full moon outlined the Cascade Mountains and the path to the river.

"A lot of people are coming here," said Rachel as she held her mother's right hand and carefully watched the ground in front of her as moonlit shapes along the path passed within her peripheral vision. For Rachel, surrounding shadowed crops and trees seemed to come alive at night, and she imagined they were watching as Anna and Rachel walked. "Why are so many people coming here?"

The Odegaard family's bounty contrasted with what was happening nationally. Another depression. The national economy was failing again, if it ever recovered, and like prospectors moving to a new spot on a creek, many were reaffixing their hope in the Pacific Northwest.

"They're coming here motivated by among the strongest of emotions," answered Anna.

"Loathing and hatred," said Rachel as her lips grew exaggeratedly taut and her eyes filled with mock terror. By now it came naturally.

"No, Rachel. They come in search of future security, perhaps even prosperity, persuaded by hope. Hope," Anna repeated as she looked down at Rachel for a moment. "And this is good. People coming here are going to be very productive."

"How do you know?"

"Great expectations," said Anna. "When prolonged, difficult circumstances have been experienced, people will look hard for new opportunities. If they believe an opportunity for success is within their grasp, their productivity is often greatest. You remember the words of Emma Lazarus at the base of the Statue of Liberty. We learned those a few months ago."

"Yes," said Rachel who refreshed her memory for a moment before responding. "*The New Colossus*," said Rachel. "Everyone knows that." Rachel quoted the poem from memory.

> *Not like the brazen giant of Greek fame,*
> *With conquering limbs astride from land to land;*
> *Here at our sea-washed, sunset gates shall stand*
> *A mighty woman with a torch, whose flame*
> *Is the imprisoned lightning, and her name*
> *Mother of Exiles. From her beacon-hand*
> *Glows world-wide welcome; her mild eyes command*
> *The air-bridged harbor that twin cities frame.*
> *"Keep, ancient lands, your storied pomp!" cries she*
> *With silent lips. "Give me your tired, your poor,*
> *Your huddled masses yearning to breathe free,*
> *The wretched refuse of your teeming shore.*
> *Send these, the homeless, tempest-tost to me,*
> *I lift my lamp beside the golden door!"*

"Very good," said Anna, impressed. "And what was the 'brazen giant of Greek fame'?"

"The Colossus of Rhodes."

"And you remember Emma Lazarus' words," said Anna, "while humane in intent, were also pragmatic. In spite of national economic conditions, I expect that productivity resulting from expansion of a population intent on hard work will favor the Skagit River valley. Labor should be rewarded." Thinking of "labor," eyes smiling, Anna felt her expanding midsection as they walked. She became pregnant shortly before the Great Seattle Fire.

"Mom?" Rachel began, looking at her mother, "what are you going to name the babies? What will you call them if they're girls?"

"I'm not sure yet."

"What are some of the choices?" asked Rachel.

"We've named our children after my grandmother, Inga, or in the case of you and Esther, someone in the Bible. Perhaps we will again. As you can see from the names Mr. and Mrs. Odegaard gave their children, biblical names are not uncommon."

"Like 'Rachel' who was a very admirable person," said Rachel with slight affectation.

"Yes," smiled Anna. "She had many very favorable qualities."

Rachel was struck by her mother's vocabulary and how clearly her mother enunciated words.

"How come dad can't speak like you?" asked Rachel. "He's been here long enough."

"Your father," began Anna, "came over from Sweden when he was in his mid-20s and, consequently, still has a Swedish accent. I was born in Pennsylvania, and our family moved to Ohio, so I don't have an accent. As you know, your father and I met in Minnesota."

"I liked Minnesota. Will we ever go back?" asked Rachel.

"Perhaps to visit," answered Anna. "But, no, God willing, we will remain here the rest of our lives." Anna glanced about at silver outlined trees, crops and buildings. In the darkness, the evening air was quiet except for the occasional sound of a night bird. "It's a very beautiful place, don't you agree?"

Rachel didn't respond, inattentive to her mother's words after "no."

"What if they're boys?" asked Rachel. "You could name them Samuel and Jacob like the Odegaard brothers. Wouldn't that be interesting? Two sets of brothers in the same family with the same name."

"We will see about the names," responded Anna. "Boys would be nice for your father because he..."

"...because he already has three daughters," interjected Rachel.

"Yes." Anna paused.

"As for 'the same family,'" countered Anna, "I realize that it feels like we – the Odegaards and the Nordquists – are one family but, actually, Rachel, we are two families and we do not want to impose on the Odegaards any longer than is necessary. It is natural for a family to maintain their separate identity."

"But aren't we supposed to treat others with love like they are part of our family?" asked Rachel. "Aren't we all supposed to be part of the family of God? And Mr. Odeqaard said he was grateful that we were here to help with the harvest. Couldn't we become a family?" Rachel stepped over a mountain beaver hole. "I'd like that."

Anna thought for a moment. "Rachel, let's pretend that we were all the same family. We'll call this family the Odegaard-Nordquists and we'll pretend that we're all..."

"Or the Nordquist-Odegaards."

"Ah." Anna paused. "There, you see, we are by nature self-centered and inclined toward..."

"Why do you think we're 'self-centered'?" asked Rachel who already knew.

"We're self-centered because we identify all that is around us in terms of its relationship to us," answered Anna.

"Not God?" asked Rachel. Anna thought for a moment.

"As you know," began Anna, "many people such as your father and I try to place God and His principles ahead of their own self-interest...although we do not always succeed. Most people make no attempt. Our actions are substantially self-centered. It is our nature, human nature. It is, however, natural for us, through love, to extend our self-interest to our immediate families. Beyond that, while we want to be on the best of terms with all other people, the ties that bind become weaker. If we were to pretend that there was a family called the Nordquist-Odegaards – if you prefer – it would still be pretending."

Rachel thought about how her father would sometimes refer to someone as a brother or sister in the Lord, implying an extended spiritual family. "Couldn't we change that?" she asked.

"We could pretend to change it, but pretending is not the same as really changing it. God has structured families to insure that there is a stable social fabric...like a quilt of many pieces of cloth sewn together. Within the quilt the greatest strength is in each individual piece of cloth itself. Those individual pieces of cloth are the families. We have many earthly moral obligations, but the greatest is to take care of our immediate family."

"When would we take care of our families and not take care of someone else?" asked Rachel. "I mean: is there always a time where we don't take care of someone else because we have to take care of our family?"

"We take offerings in church to cover church expenses," began Anna. "But suppose a family barely had enough to eat. Should they use the money to buy food or should they put the money in the collection plate?"

"But didn't Jesus say that the widow who had given a 'mite,' had given most?" asked Rachel. "What if God liked what they did and gave them back a whole lot more?"

"And what if He chose not to?" countered Anna. "How much did he give the widow? Giving offerings is not a form of gambling. And God doesn't need our tithes and offerings; but we have need to give them. In the same vein, God wants fathers and mothers, husbands and wives, to take care of their families. Under normal circumstances, no one better understands the needs of a family than the family itself. If a family feels compelled to give money to the church, but then must return to the church for financial assistance, all that has been accomplished is unnecessary bookkeeping…unless the pastor or another elder sees something amiss, and is able to help them by giving them direction in handling their financial affairs."

"Amiss?"

"'Amiss' meaning that something wrong is happening. Perhaps the father drinks or gambles or even spends money on..." Anna stopped speaking and Rachel looked at her mother. "Perhaps the adult family members are not getting along – even shunning or rejecting one another or worse. Then it is wise for someone in the church, such as elders or the pastor, to step in and provide redirection."

Mother and daughter were approaching the river. At the edge of the riverbank they stood motionlessly mesmerized by the moon's image on the water's smooth surface except for the gentle sound of lightly lapping waves along the dimly lit bank. Nearby silhouetted trees rose up and bent forward as if they too were watching the moon's image.

At a short distance upriver, standing in the shadowed shallows along the steep river bank, a great blue heron watched the newcomers. Rachel picked up a small pebble and tossed it down into the river before them, briefly disrupting the tranquility on the surface. The disruption was nearly invisible and barely audible; the heron did not move.

"Mom?" Rachel took a breath and cleared her throat. "Will I ever be a good Lutheran?"

"What?"

"I mean, in church the good Lutherans never move. After they stand up, they're like herons, and after they sit down they're part of the pew. Wood, mom." Rachel sighed. "It's hard for me to sit perfectly still like that. Sometimes I want to stand up when it isn't time to stand up. And lots of times when daddy gives a sermon, I want to ask questions and nobody else ever does. It's like everybody already knows everything that daddy says and just sits silently agreeing."

Anna gently bit her lips together, glancing sideways at her daughter.

Rachel continued. "I like it when we sing 'I Love To Tell The Story,' even if it's in Swedish or Norwegian, because I know all the verses by heart, but when I look around, I see everyone using the hymnal, so I use it too because good Lutherans do it that way. Mom? If all those people seem to know what Dad is going to say, why can't they also learn the songs? *You* even use the hymnal. But you know the songs by heart, don't you?"

"Yes," Anna sighed. "I do. But I hold the hymnal as a formality."

"Why?" asked Rachel.

"To encourage others, who may be new and unfamiliar with the music or order of service, to use hymnals," answered Anna.

"You mean they might not?"

"Possibly," said Anna. "The pastor's wife has many responsibilities including showing correct liturgical behavior during worship service."

"But when we have worship services at the Odegaard house," responded Rachel, "we don't have correct behavior, we just...," Rachel turned toward the river and half shrugged her shoulders, "...do what seems natural."

"Do you like the way we worship God at the Odegaards?"

"Well, yes," responded Rachel, throwing another rock.

"I'll mention it to your father."

"He will not be pleased," said Rachel fearfully, gritting her teeth in feigned panic.

"Oh, nonsense. He *will* be pleased. Because you're right." Anna placed her hand gently on Rachel's shoulder. "Formal liturgy can sometimes become a barrier to worshipping God. And we can't let that happen. Your father will want to hear what we have talked about."

Rachel threw another pebble in the river, and studied the surface reaction while the heron studied Anna and Rachel.

"What does 'waterless places' mean?" asked Rachel. "In the Bible it says when demonic spirits leave a person, they go through 'waterless places,' but then might return and bring other demons with them. What or where are 'waterless places'?"

"Most Bible experts consider 'waterless places' to mean lifeless places because nothing lives without water, but as is often the case with the Bible, a waterless place might be beyond that, perhaps referring to a spiritual realm. Wherever it is, demons don't like being there, preferring to dwell in living creatures, especially man."

Standing at the top of the river embankment, staring down at the moon's reflection on the river surface, Rachel thought about her family, and her past and present circumstances, wondering what would happen next. She bent down, picked up and tossed another pebble into the river.

"The Holy Spirit sure seems important in all this."

Anna smiled at Rachel's understatement. "Oh, yes. Jesus said the only unforgivable sin is blaspheming the Holy Spirit, an act evidencing rejection of the Holy Spirit. And no Holy Spirit, no salvation."

"Then people should always want the Holy Spirit in them."

"Yes, but remember, we ask only if the Holy Spirit directs us."

"That seems backwards."

"Yes, if we were devising the system, we would be responsible. But we're not. God has not placed that responsibility in our hands. I can only imagine how muddled things would become if He did."

In the moonlight, the heron took flight, the tips of its six-foot wings at first beating in rapid syncopation against the river surface as the heron fought to gain momentum and altitude. In a moment the silhouetted heron lifted off a short distance below Anna and Rachel, fanning and rippling the moonlit river surface, gradually rising higher, flying downstream in the direction of a dark cedar tree along the riverbank. As the heron rose and landed on a high bough obscured in the darkness, Anna turned to walk back, looking down at Rachel as they walked. "Do you want to know a secret?"

"A secret? Yes!"

"I almost married someone else before I met your father."

"You did?" Rachel stopped walking and looked up at her mother wide-eyed. "Why?"

"Why? I'll tell you. My father – your Grandpa Lars – worked for Republic Iron and Steel as a senior manager. His boss, Mr. Chamberlain, was responsible for merging several smaller mills into Republic. The Chamberlains were very well off and had a son, Edward, my age. Edward and I were sort of romantically involved when I was in high school, and we corresponded when I went to college. My parents wanted me to marry Edward. While I was in college, I became involved with another young man, Charles, whose parents were also well off. My parents preferred Edward but liked Charles as well."

"So you were going to marry either Edward or Charles," said Rachel.

"No, Rachel, I wasn't sure I wanted to marry either one. They were, by conventional standards, great catches. Both, in fact, proposed marriage to me. Both couldn't understand what the problem was. Those were awkward moments because I wasn't sure, and was steeling my heart."

"Why?"

"Do you know that Bible verse about 'God and mammon'?"

"Yes…but what is 'mammon'?"

"The word 'mammon' is a transliteration of the Hebrew word for 'money.' The Bible verse essentially refers to love of wealth, material things. That would best describe the priorities of both Edward and Charles. I, however, wanted a man who valued spiritual wealth over earthly wealth."

"Not mammon."

"My parents pressured me. Edward pressured me. Charles pressured me. Mr. Chamberlain pressured my father – which was very unfair. I wanted to please everyone, but I could not make a decision. The whole thing became very wearying. I was beginning to feel like an apostate."

"What's an apostate?"

"A defector – someone who abandons or disavows something still highly valued by others." Anna looked down at Rachel. "A woman's heart should not be treated like that. I felt very uncomfortable, and at one point did not even want to be at home."

"What did you do?"

"I must admit at first I pressured my*self* – I tried to convince myself that I wanted to marry Edward – a marriage to Edward would have greatly pleased my father, and I wanted to please my father. As things progressed, however, I knew – as I really had all along – that neither Edward nor Charles was the right man for me. Meanwhile, my parents wanted me to make up my mind, and the pressure was becoming intolerable. I prayed a great deal, Rachel. I was very confused. I felt I had to do something; I had to step out in faith somehow. One night I prayed that God would send me someplace, a place where the right man was."

"One with money?"

"I didn't ask for that."

"Dad has money."

"For quite some time I didn't know that. When I met your father, I found him very attractive and congenial. And he was a godly man. As time progressed, we grew closer and closer, and it wasn't long before I knew your father was the one. Intelligent, sensitive, responsible, loving…always enjoyable to be around. We fit. He was everything I wanted, and he would have been everything I wanted even if he was broke because, frankly, Rachel, I had my fill of people whose priority was mammon. Never satisfied. Always wanting more."

"You must be happy Dad had money though."

"Have we lived in palaces, Rachel?" asked Anna, looking down at Rachel.

"No," said Rachel.

"I'm happy I have a man who is secure enough to where living in luxury need not cross his mind. I'm happy to have a man who loves me and our children with all his heart, and loves the Lord. The rest?" Anna shrugged her shoulders indifferently. "Rachel, when you become old enough to where you are interested in boys – and that time will come soon enough – remember what I just told you."

"I will." Rachel thought the subject, finding the right man for a husband, very interesting.

Anna took Rachel's hand and they continued back to the house. Anna's thoughts returned to the harvest effort. Her own involvement was being limited by her pregnancy. It was early in her pregnancy and, while one baby might not have been a cause for much concern, she was carrying twins and expected that, although she had no problems with prior deliveries, she should not exert herself.

The events of the next few weeks were torrid. The harvest was completed with one extensive canning and storing marathon. Angus, who was a natural salesman, made trips to Seattle to sell produce, and always came back with little or nothing remaining in the wagon. People bought from Angus when they could have bought from anyone or maybe no one. Angus also sold three of Jacob's paintings of horses in phantastic landscapes, making more money from the paintings than the produce. Swede began taking Jacob's paintings more seriously. In addition to money, Angus returned from Seattle with good news.

"Guess who I met on Occidental Street?" asked Angus.

"Angus," said Anna, "how could we possibly know who you met?"

"Our good friend, Earl the elder," said Angus. "And d' you know what he told me?"

Anna just looked at Angus. Amos chuckled.

"Remember Earl? Well, Pastor, after you left, Earl gathered together remnants of the old congregation and has been serving as their interim pastor. Curt says Earl doesn't mince words, and that Earl's sermons are inspirational – messages full of salvation, praising God, calls to repentance, and being converted by the Holy Spirit. When it comes to having been lost but then found, Curt uses himself as an example. He'd like it if maybe you could return occasionally as guest pastor."

"You know," said Amos, smiling, "some of the best pastors in Christendom, those with the greatest conviction, previously spent time in sinful living, and were then not just reformed but converted, and especially driven because they knew both sides of the fence."

For a moment Amos thought of the boardwalk incident with Earl, and shook his head, still sorry he had overreacted. But under the circumstances, he thought, should I be sorry? It wasn't seemly behavior, but God obviously used my temper to good advantage that day.

"Well, God bless Earl," Amos smiled. "I'm truly delighted. I couldn't be happier for him. And Virginia. The next time you're in Seattle, Angus, if you can find Curt or Earl, please tell them, with adequate advance notice, I'll be available." The prospect of preaching to the old congregation remnant excited Amos. Besides Earl, there were some good people in that bunch. Gunnar Olson. Curt Jensen. Einar Skoglund.

When the harvest came to an end, Amos, Swede and Angus began discussing construction of a parsonage on acreage Pastor Nordquist purchased during the summer.

"It iss good you should build your own home, of course," said Swede, "but a church should come first, you know."

"Our staying with you must cause some imposi…"

"You can stay longer," responded Swede. "It iss not a problem. It iss more important ve build a new church. Soon my living room vill not hold everyvun."

"Yes, Swede, but it would not take long to build a house. Then…"

"The harvest has been plentiful," interjected Swede, "your daughters are hard vorkers, your carpentry skills come in handy, and both Erika and I enjoy the adult companionship. You and your family should stay with us a little longer until ve get a new sanctuary built. Then you vill be under no pressure to build a parsonage in a hurry. Build the church first. Take your time. Do a good job. This is my suggestion."

"Well, okay. Arnie Arneson has some hillside land – impractical for crops but near the river – that he said he will donate," said Amos.

"That is good," nodded Swede. "I know Arnie's site. But there are no roads from the mill to that site. Lumber vill need to be towed on scows from the lumber mill to the mouth of the river and then upriver using oxen along the riverbank. The oxen vill also be used to pull the lumber on large carts from the river to the building site. In that sense, the location is good. The closer the building site is to the river, the better. But ve'll also need to clear a road from the north for future parishioners."

Pastor Nordquist designed a simple building. Adjacent to the northern and western sides of the church he incorporated an L-shaped cemetery. This would prove fortuitous.

<hr />

Knowing it takes money to make money, and usually a lot more money to make a lot more money, in addition to their own money, Colgate Hoyt and Charles Colby raised a substantial amount from select investors, but knew that, if they were to realize the grand metropolis of Everett as envisioned, they would need even more money to do bigger development faster.

"It makes you wonder, Colgate," began Colby, seated comfortably, wearing his smoking jacket, his feet resting on an ottoman as he relaxed in his E. 69th St. mansion. "An opportunity like this comes once in a lifetime – if at all. The possibilities are so enormous I sometimes feel like I'm dealing with a fantasy." Colby drew slowly on his pipe, oblivious to its presence. "It just seems like so much. Have you gone over the most recent numbers?" Colby asked Hoyt. Hoyt nodded. "Annual profits…" Colby shook his head. "Unbelievable," said Colby. "Seems too good to be true." Colby lightly blew smoke as he thought.

"It's odd," said Colby.

Hoyt, pipe firmly in his mouth, looked at Colby, wondering what was "odd."

"When we," Colby continued, "Hewitt and I, were standing on that bluff overlooking the river mouth, and he was explaining what he envisioned, the thought occurred to me." Hoyt waited. "Just came to me out of the blue. Standing there, looking at the forested hillsides, it was as if something inside me had to give a hint of what was to come." Colby removed his pipe. "I completely dismissed it at the time." Hoyt also removed his pipe, looking at Colby.

"I'm afraid I'm not following you," responded Hoyt. "What was it you dismissed?"

"I thought to myself," said Colby, looking at the floor, "this will involve Rockefeller."

Colby looked up at Hoyt.

"Why would I think that?" Colby asked, perplexed. "At that moment I had no clear idea of what we would be doing. Why would I even think about involving John at that moment when I wasn't entirely certain that I was going to be involved." Colby bit the stem as he took a slow draw, seemingly studying the radiator below the window. "Very odd."

"Rockefeller?" said Hoyt almost reverently. "You're thinking of talking to John?"

"The possibilities seem enormous," Colby reiterated. "We may not have enough capital to do it all ourselves. If that is the case, we'll need John's help."

"If you want to talk to John," said Hoyt, pipe aside his mouth, eyebrows knitted, "perhaps we should broach the subject with him after church."

"I have reservations about discussing business matters after church," responded Colby. "It's neither the time nor place."

"If you want to talk to Rockefeller," responded Hoyt, "you had better do so when the opportunity presents itself. You know there may be a long wait before the next opportunity comes along. Rockefeller is not an easily accessible man. Even for us."

Colby nodded.

<hr>

"John," began Colby after motioning Rockefeller aside outside the church steps, "good to see you." Hoyt joined them.

"Nice to see you too, Charles," Rockefeller nodded. "How's Everett? Ready to attend Brown like his old man?"

"Does he have a choice?" laughed Colby.

"No, I suppose not," said Rockefeller who turned to Hoyt. "Hello, Colgate," Rockefeller shook Hoyt's hand. "How's Reverend Wayland?" Rockefeller asked, referring to Hoyt's brother, Dr. Wayland Hoyt, pastor of Tabernacle Baptist Church in Brooklyn.

"He's been very busy, John," smiled Hoyt. "Spends a lot of time helping people understand the Lord's will. That can be time-consuming…especially when the Lord's will isn't their will."

"I'm sure that's a full-time job and then some," said Rockefeller. "I know how he feels." Rockefeller took a deep breath and slumped slightly.

"And Rev. Henry?" asked Rockefeller, referring to Colby's brother, Henry F. Colby, pastor of First Baptist Church in Dayton, Ohio.

"Like Wayland," said Colby, "it's amazing how busy Henry is. Being a pastor is a full-time job in itself, but Henry's involved in several charities, two colleges, community organizations, writing a book, raising a family... And Mary's pregnant again. I'm not sure how Henry does it all – must work a 25-hour day." Colby's smile disappeared as he studied Rockefeller. "How are you feeling, John?"

"Oh, fair to middlin," sighed Rockefeller. "My health could be better."

"You certainly have a lot to look after," understated Hoyt who already knew Rockefeller's doctor warned Rockefeller to slow down. "Everything okay?"

"Frankly, Colgate, I'm tired," Rockefeller stated quietly. "Worn out. Managing my businesses, my investments, all of these things, takes more time than there is. I could go without sleeping for weeks at a time. I hire an army of accountants and consultants, and they still can't keep track of everything. I don't know where all my money is going and, well, that is completely unacceptable. Wasteful. Immoral. Not knowing is irresponsible." Rockefeller looked at the ground. "Irresponsibility and inefficiency are for the *less* fortunate," muttered Rockefeller, almost to himself.

"Sorry, to hear of these problems, John," said Colby. "I'm sure you have challenges the average man cannot fathom."

"I'm so darned busy trying to manage my investments," said Rockefeller stoically, looking up at Colby, "I hardly have time to consider the relative merits of new investments. And, as you know, it's important I do." Colby and Hoyt listened. "As they say," continued Rockefeller, "'money doesn't grow on trees.' People look at me and think I have no financial worries because of my wealth. I do worry. The Good Lord has given me a tremendous responsibility. Standard Oil alone could consume my waking moments. The fundamental key to my success is maximizing the efficiency with which money is spent. I never deviate from that simple principle. But now," Rockefeller sighed, "it seems I don't have time to efficiently manage present investments, much less astutely invest in new ones. I'm worn-out from having to weigh poor investment schemes. And weary of trusting people who can't be trusted." Rockefeller took a deep breath, and looked down again. "The situation needs to get under control."

"John," began Colby, "we – you, Colgate and I – have found ourselves on the same investment path several times, of course, but we have never come to you with any substantial, independent investment proposal because, well," Colby looked down and then up, "we know how you're inundated by others. We have been business acquaintances, enjoying a distant friendship, and felt that our relationship should remain much as it has been. Colgate and I, however..."

"Gentlemen," interjected Rockefeller, "I greatly appreciate that. In fact, I'm glad you, and not someone else, pulled me aside. It seems that no matter where I go, almost no one sees me for anything other than a source of money. A walking dollar sign." Rockefeller glanced at the ground and laughed. "I have been approached," he looked up at the others, weakly smiling, "with investment schemes that would coddle an egg. Ridiculous, far-fetched delusions with no foundation in reality..." – Rockefeller looked back at the ground, agitated, as Colby and Hoyt stood motionlessly – "...wasting time I do not have." Rockefeller looked up at Hoyt and Colby. "Am I a fool?" Rockefeller asked quietly. "Did I generate a financial empire by being stupid?" Rockefeller laughed faintly and shook his head.

"Hardly, John," responded Colby.

"And these newspapers with their yellow journalism, 'robber baron' nonsense," complained Rockefeller, looking at Colby. "Do you read that slander?

Good gracious, Charles, I am blessed with the ability to make shrewd business decisions. Wise decisions. As I should. Is this such a bad thing? What other kind am I obligated to make? I have exhausted myself daily to the point where my mind does not want to think about these things I must get under control. I have amassed a fortune, yes, but through tremendous effort. I have robbed no one. These newspaper people sell lies at the expense of my personal reputation. *They* make money castigating *me* for making money." Rockefeller shook his head. "Ludicrous."

He paused and again looked at the ground.

"And so many others approach me wanting a contribution or just a hand-out. A few contribution requests are very worthy – I support those and wish more would approach me – but so many..." Rockefeller sighed, "...there are many more that are undeserving and a waste of time and money." Rockefeller put his hands in his pockets. "It's all so wearying," he concluded quietly. Although it was only late Sunday morning, Rockefeller already looked tired.

"John," began Colby, "Colgate and I believe we can help you with part of your problem. As I stated earlier, neither one of us has ever approached you with a substantial, independent, business proposition because we sensed what you just said about, as you put it, being seen only as a 'walking dollar sign.' And, frankly, with our own resources, it was never necessary to involve you. We, in a much more modest sense, of course, are also considered walking dollar signs by some."

"It's called 'inflation,' John," said Hoyt drolly, and the three men laughed.

"We have a business proposition we would like to discuss with you," said Colby.

At the age of 51, and with an 1889 income of $10 million, Rockefeller was in poor health, needed rest, and was on the verge of a nervous breakdown. When Colby and Hoyt, fellow communicants, suggested his involvement in what seemed to be a profitable venture, one in which Rockefeller was led to believe others would be investing more than he, a commitment seemed reasonable. He was searching for business relationships with honorable men. Hoyt and Colby were honorable men. So Rockefeller agreed. 26 Broadway would become involved.

When he agreed, he brought more than money to the venture – much more. He also contributed the Rockefeller mystique. With Rockefeller's blessing, the venture was providential, as good as gold, and for many common men, the proposed metropolis of Everett would become the next source of hope.

It was a source of hope for uncommon men as well. Dozens of investors approached the Everett Land Company like adolescents lining up at an amusement park carousel, wanting to get on the ride. With Rockefeller aboard, no one else could get on; there was no need for others. All seats were taken with the exception of one. Henry Hewitt had begun a campaign to entice railroad magnate James J. Hill into the circle of friends. Rockefeller's money assured Colby and Hoyt that the Everett Land Company could control Everett development. It enabled Hewitt to buy more land and begin marching toward his vision of a West Coast New York.

To reach that dream, however, he needed Hill's railroad.

For Everett to become what Hewitt envisioned, Everett needed to become a railroad terminus, and the Great Northern needed a West Coast terminus. What better location for a terminus than Everett? Hewitt believed. Alternatively, he might have encouraged Colby, Hoyt, Oakes, *et al*, to run a Northern Pacific line directly from Seattle, but did not want Everett to play second fiddle to Seattle and Tacoma. In addition, the Northern Pacific, although the others never mentioned it, was beginning to have trouble of its own. Running a Northern Pacific line from Seattle to a yet non-existent city was not going to happen.

The germane question that concerned Hewitt was: after manufacturing facilities were built, what then? Ships using new harbor facilities and manufacturing plants could service the West Coast. The greatest demand, however, was east of the Mississippi where the great population centers lie. Rockefeller involvement notwithstanding, distribution to the East Coast, Hewitt knew, was the key to success. Without Hill's railroad, all of Hewitt's other aces would become walls in a house of cards.

86

September 30, 1889 Monday morning

Dad, can we please go fishing in the [Puget] Sound? It was the third time Rachel had asked since Saturday.

"It's raining," said Amos, stating the obvious. Rain had been falling intermittently for two weeks. "The Sound is choppy. The lakes, creeks and the river also have fish."

"But not like the Sound. Those fish are big."

"Some are. Arnie Jensen caught an 80 lb. king last week."

"Eighty pounds?" exclaimed Rachel, eyes wide, feigning terror. "That's bigger than *me*."

"Have you finished your schoolwork?" asked Amos, warming to the idea.

"Yes, I'm even ahead on my assignments. Ask mom."

"That doesn't surprise me, Rachel. Your mother says you could be in the *Third Reader* now if you wanted to be."

Rachel shrugged.

"Very well," said Amos. "Grab the fishing poles. We'll go out in Mr. Odegaard's rowboat."

"The one tied to the log on the beach?" asked Rachel.

"Yes."

"And on the side is painted 'Big Swede'?" Rachel smirked, thinking "Big Swede" to be a funny name for a rowboat.

"Correct," said Amos. "Which is why it stays tied to the log on the beach."

"Do you think someone would steal it?"

"People around here are better behaved than that, but you never know; someone who does not live here might decide they need it more than Mr. Odegaard."

"Would they know who Mr. Odegaard is?"

"Not if they try to steal his boat."

Rachel beside him, Amos Nordquist adjusted his collar in the falling mist as small birds flitted and chattered under the cover of hillside boughs while eagles, terns, loons, herons, cormorants and ospreys spied for unwary fish in the shallow bay. It had always been so.

Fall, 1820

On the west side of the valley the river moved slowly with a single-minded purpose of filling the tidelands which, once again in the early fall, served as a temporary hostel for thousands of salmon journeying to the river mouth from all over the Pacific. Each salmon patiently waited for its appointed time to enter and continue upstream. Year after year, decade after decade, century after century, it had always been so.

Two Bears watched mesmerized as his hollowed cedar log canoe drifted slowly with the tide over the sea of sockeye. The sockeye was *siem* or "rich man, highly esteemed among all salmon." The salmon and Two Bears were kindred souls according to the tradition of Two Bears' people. But, at the same time, they were different. Salmon grew up in the same place as Two Bears, then left and seasons later returned. Two Bears and his people lived in the same location all of their lives. This was so for all tribes in the land of Two Bears.

The woodlands provided game, while the sea, rivers and lakes provided fish. The soil in the river valley was fertile. Unlike Native American tribes in other areas of North America, a nomadic way of life was foreign to the people of Two Bears. They did not need to follow animals on whom they were dependent for food; the animals came to them. Two Bears took his lifestyle for granted, and could not completely appreciate the incredible beauty of the mountains, islands, and lakes where he lived, for they were all he had known.

As the canoe drifted in the direction of the river mouth, the patient sockeye became thicker, so many it seemed to Two Bears he could step out into the water and walk on them.

"*Leyi*! [Watch them!]" yelped Two Bears, breaking the early morning silence.

The people of Two Bears believed that salmon were a race of supernatural beings who lived much like humans in longhouses under the sea. The most beautiful longhouses were inhabited by supernatural beings who at the time designated for the annual salmon run, would dress up as sockeye salmon and sacrifice themselves to fishermen in order to provide for the people of Two Bears. Lesser supernatural beings who lived under the sea would dress up as other forms of salmon. Among salmon, sockeye were held in high esteem, revered by the people of Two Bears.

Once the salmon were caught and had died, the supernatural beings returned to the sea. It was believed that if all of the bones of each salmon were returned to the sea after the salmon was eaten, the supernatural being would return to its human-like form. If some bones were missing, however, the supernatural being may lack toes or even an entire leg, become angry with the people of Two Bears, and refuse to dress up as a salmon at the appointed time during successive seasons.

The first sockeye salmon caught was always honored as a visiting *tyee* or chief. The people of Two Bears honored other animals and fish in their respective fashion, but the most formal ceremony was reserved for the sockeye salmon. To offend the *tyee* could result in great harm to the people of Two Bears.

As he watched the fish beneath the surface of the water, Two Bears glanced at the scars on his arms, the result of being cut by sharp bones when Two Bears was first becoming a man. His father did this on several occasions. It was a tradition among the people of Two Bears that young boys entering manhood endure severe hardship and discipline. The father of Two Bears forced Two Bears to submit to extensive and painful discipline including being beaten, being starved, and bathing two or three times each day in the icy waters of the great inlet during the winter months. Some young men were broken in spirit by the rigor of such discipline and abuse. Two Bears' resolve, however, increased...as was the will of his father. During this period of time and for several years after, Two Bears avoided his father, but now, as he floated in the direction of the river mouth, he understood his father's motive.

Among the people of Two Bears, it was believed that all animate objects – the raven, the wolf, the bear, even smoke, rain, and the wind – were inhabited by spirits who were once humans whose behavior had offended the Great Spirit, *Xelas*, the powerful transforming spirit who causes things to change.

The people of Two Bears had many taboos which they observed in order that *Xelas* not become angry with them. Other spirits were *Xhaltap*, the spirit of the "flying human being," *Stkayeolyt* or "spirit of the wolf," and *Sqalesan*, the "spirit having no pity." For other members of the spirit world, as with *Xelas*, the people of Two Bears had rituals and taboos religiously observed in order that no spirits be offended.

Two Bears stared at the sockeye salmon, attempting to objectively discern from their movements or behavior whether it was true that they were spirits, somehow similar to human beings, dressed as fish. He saw nothing which might verify the accuracy of this belief and silently wondered how much of what was believed by his people was true and when did these beliefs began?

Through all seasons, nearly all tribal behavior was governed by hundreds of taboos and superstitions. The customs which the people of Two Bears observed were constructed on a very elaborate foundation of fear of the unknown spirit world. The greatest taboo was to question these customs. Two Bears would keep his thoughts to himself.

The mouth of the river continually filled the vast tidelands. The head of the river began to the east flowing initially from the slopes of the mountain. Glancing up at the mountain beyond the folds of numerous foothills clothed with virgin Douglas fir, Two Bears watched steam slowly vent from its peak. The pure whiteness of the mountain, together with the tinge of orange among the trees in late autumn, was duplicated on the surface of the still water. Aside from the occasional lapping sound of water off his cedar paddle, no other sound reached the ears of Two Bears.

September 30, 1889 late Monday morning

Regardless of weather, Rachel liked the excitement of catching fish. There were all kinds of fish in the bays and channels, and while waiting for a fish to bite, she liked to watch the birds, especially ospreys. To her they were the most beautiful of birds.

The old Indian named Two Bears told her that in his language, the local

Lushootseed tongue, the name for the osprey meant "hawk from the sea," or seahawk. To Rachel, however, ospreys were more attractive than hawks and, as her father rowed, Rachel watched an osprey high above the water, searching for smaller fish below.

For a moment it almost stopped in mid-air, tilted, leaned sideways, and then dove like a lightning bolt, pulling up and skimming along the surface, plucking a small fish from the water's surface before the fish knew what was happening. Rachel sat fascinated as the osprey flew off with the fish in its talons. That's certainly more fun than how we do it, she thought.

Old Two Bears, who lived in a derelict longhouse near the mouth of the river where the elk herd grazed, said ospreys had always nested around the area lakes and bays. On walks with her sisters through the forests, Rachel had no problem finding their nests, for they were quite large and could be seen from just about any trail near a lake. Ospreys didn't seem to care if settlers were around and, like Two Bears, did things the way they always had.

Rachel befriended Two Bears who had neither friends nor family. He did not know how old he was ("many snows") but his teeth were bad and his eyes failing. Rachel would bring him soft bread and fruit whenever she walked to the river mouth. Reciprocating her generosity, he gave her what, Rachel could not know, was his most valuable possession, actually much more valuable than either one would know. It was an amulet or totem, a carved bone that Two Bears said would keep her from harm, and would help guide her.

Rachel turned it over in her hand. It looked worn, old. It was a carving of an elephant, the tiny grooves, almost no longer visible, down the sides suggesting a hairy elephant.

"Much old," said Two Bears. "Many fathers."

"It's a mammoth," said Anna when Rachel showed it to her. Anna then showed it to Amos. "Look at this, Amos. What do you think this is?"

Amos studied it for a moment.

"You're right," said Amos. "My golly."

"Two bears said it had been in his family a long time – 'many fathers.'"

"Mammoths. It's possible," Amos said, recalling the *Einar II* conversation many years ago with Second Mate Gustaf Johansen when they wondered what unknown sea creatures might still lurk beneath the surface of the Skagerrak. "We'll need to hold on to this, Rachel, until we can find someone who might be able to authenticate its significance." Rachel put the talisman on a bedroom shelf with her doll collection.

"Dad, I've a bite!"

"Go ahead and reel it in."

Excitedly, Rachel slowly reeled in the fish she caught using a sandworm as bait. The fish didn't fight much, but still generated pull, and Amos guessed it was a bottom fish. As she maneuvered it near the boat, Amos's guess was confirmed: a flounder. Once on board, the flounder flipped and flopped on the wet bottom of the rowboat as Amos attempted to grab it and hold it long enough to remove the hook.

"This isn't very large," said Amos, removing the hook and letting go of the fish's gill. Rachel sat back, avoiding the bizarre-looking fish with one eye almost on top of its head, and one eye close by, as it flopped some more. After a few moments, it lay still, its mouth opening and closing like a singer repeatedly mouthing the sounds "ohh… ahh…ohh… ahh…"

"Do you want to keep it?" asked Amos.

"No, I want to catch a real fish."

"This is a real fish."

"I mean one that's narrow, not flat. A salmon."

"Very well," said Amos as he reached down, hooked his finger through the gill, and flipped the flounder back into the Sound where it swam slowly downward, quickly vanishing in the dark water.

"We'll need to use something other than sandworms to catch a salmon."

'What do big salmon eat?" asked Rachel.

"What do most big fish eat?"

"Little fish."

"We'll need to make a lure that will attract a big salmon."

"Good."

"First we'll need to catch a small fish."

As Rachel wished she were an osprey, Pastor Nordquist baited another hook with a sandworm and, after rowing closer to shore, began casting it near some rocks, looking warily at nearby sea lions watching with interest. Within minutes he hooked a small perch and quickly reeled it into the boat.

Using a small shiny piece of metal with a heavy line, lead sinker, large hook, and the back half of the perch, Amos fashioned a rigging and lure. He rowed out into deeper water and began trolling. While nine-year-old Rachel held the pole, Amos wrapped a short line around the pole and tied the other end to a cleat, just in case.

"Maybe we'll catch a whale," said Rachel as she watched.

"In Puget Sound it is more likely a whale would catch us."

"*Are* there whales in Puget Sound?"

"Occasionally."

What kind?"

"Oh, minke whales; small gray whales once in a while. But usually what we see are killer whales." For a moment, Rachel looked seaward with concern but, seeing nothing, looked back at her father.

"What else?"

"Just the pain-in-the-neck seals and sea lions," said Amos, looking toward the shoreline.

"Because when you've hooked a salmon and it can't get away," said Rachel, knowing this had happened before, "a sea lion will come and try to steal it before you get it to the boat."

"Yes, sea lions are clever."

"Mr. MacGregor calls them 'rats of the ocean.' Is that why you brought the rifle?"

"One reason."

"What if we catch a salmon as big as the one Mr. Jensen caught?"

"If that happens, I – not you – will need to reel in the fish."

"Is the line strong enough?"

"Oh, yes. This line should be strong enough to catch even a huge halibut."

"Do you think we'll do that?"

"No. If we catch a 35 lb. salmon, I'll be pleased."

Minutes later as the falling mist turned to drizzle, Rachel's pole bent twice.

"Dad, I've got something." Her eyes grew large as the pole bent more. "Oh, I think I've caught a fish," said Rachel as she began reeling in the fish.

Instead of fighting the hook, however, the fish swam toward the boat, Rachel reeling as fast as she could.

"Dad, what's it doing?"

"I'm not sure. This is a new one," said Amos as the fish swam deeply to one side of the boat and continued in the opposite direction. In a moment, the line became taut.

"Dad, I can't reel it in anymore. It's too hard." Rachel was gritting her teeth as she gripped the reel with both hands, trying not to let go.

"I'll take the pole, Rachel."

Amos reached and grabbed the pole, gripping the reel tightly.

As Amos attempted to reel in the fish, from the force on the line the fish began to slowly turn the boat.

Whatever is at the end of the line is big, thought Amos. Amos struggled as he reeled. Afraid he might tire out before the fish did, Amos decided to stop reeling. The fish turned out away from the shoreline toward the middle of the Sound, swimming violently back and forth, finally making the usual effort to break free.

After a few minutes, Amos felt the fish tiring and began to reel in again.

"Rachel, don't lean over the edge, looking. Maintain a central balance. The fish will reach the surface soon enough."

Rachel sat up, but continued to study the quivering line knifing back and forth along the choppy surface. In a few moments I'll be able to see it, she thought – for Rachel the most exciting part of fishing. Maybe it's a monster! Then something in her peripheral vision caught her attention.

"Dad, a sea lion is swimming toward us."

"Rachel, you know how to use the gun. Don't wait. Take careful aim and shoot."

Although Rachel had been taught to load and shoot, she normally didn't like to shoot because of the noise. At that moment, however, she gave noise no thought, picked up the rifle, put it to her shoulder, slowly drew a bead on the sea lion and squeezed the trigger. As the rifle barked, the sea lion dove.

"I think I hit it," said Rachel as, mouth partially open, she stared in the direction of the sea lion ripples. "I'm not sure."

"The bullets are under the seat. Reload," said Amos, returning his eyes to the line.

As Amos gritted his teeth while slowly pulling and reeling the fish toward the surface, at a short distance he saw a large, silver flash beneath the dark waves, and Amos knew Rachel had hooked a big, king salmon.

Slowly Amos pulled the big fish to the surface perhaps 15 minutes after being hooked, and Amos thought, my golly, they always look smaller before being boated, but this thing still looks enormous under the water.

"Rachel, sit behind me on the other side of the boat."

Amos got the salmon next to the boat and gaffed it.

"Here, Rachel, hold the pole."

With a gaff and one hand, Amos attempted to pull the big fish, still thrashing and splashing saltwater on Amos and Rachel, up on the gunwale, but the fish thrashed enough to go back in the water.

"Rachel, hand me the club," Amos grimaced.

Holding the gaff with his left hand and reaching backwards with his right, Amos grabbed the club kept available for this purpose, and pulling up on the gaff, bashed the salmon's head several times, knocking it unconscious.

Amos repositioned himself and began pulling the big fish aboard. It was almost over the gunwale as a second sea lion, racing up from underneath, sank its teeth into the tail. As Amos fought to keep his balance, Rachel quickly put down the pole. For a split second Amos struggled in a tug-of-war battle with the sea lion, a battle the big sea lion was about to win except...

The rifle cracked, and Amos fell backward pulling the big fish over the gunwale, nearly falling overboard on the opposite side of the boat. For a moment he lay there looking up at Rachel kneeling with one knee on the rear seat, the rifle still against her shoulder, looking down at the dark water.

"Good work, Rachel," said Amos, regaining his position on the middle seat as other sea lions swam at a short distance, watching the boat. "That was fast thinking."

"Goodness, how big is that?" asked Rachel excitedly as she reached for the bullet box under the seat.

"I can't tell, but I will say it's the biggest salmon I've seen."

"Bigger than Mr. Jensen's?"

"Oh, yes." Amos studied the fish. "Most certainly."

As they rowed back to shore in the rain, Amos and Rachel watched a pod of killer whales approach at a distance, attracted by the scent of the wounded sea lions. Amos rowed faster, and reached the beach without difficulty.

After backing the wagon into the light waves along the shore, pulling the salmon from the boat onto the wagon, and repositioning the boat on the upper beach, Amos and Rachel returned to the farm where Rachel would learn she had hooked a 96 lb. king.

As the Odegaard sisters began cleaning the salmon preparatory to smoking fillets, Amos left to help excavate the church site on donated land sloping down to the river. A level building site was being dug out of the hillside, with men excavating from the uphill side and depositing the dirt on the downhill side, not anticipating the tragedy that would occur on November 9th.

November 9, 1889 Saturday

The daylight worked to penetrate a low, afternoon cloud cover dark enough to look like an inverted coal bin as the rain continued unrelentingly. For the past two weeks, whether showers, drizzle, mist, downpour or buckets, like Union troops at Sailor's Creek, rain just kept coming.

As Amos surveyed the steep, tree-covered hillside, he considered the pre-cariousness of digging out the side of a hill in weather like this. He recalled deer-hunting the previous summer, and walking through an isolated topograph-ical depression, a bowl-like area sequestering large 60-70-year-old alder. The bowl area was approximately five acres in size, above which fir and cedar looked down from the hillside rim. The soil was soft and wet with multiple springs running down from above. Amos surmised that 70 to 75 years earlier, probably in weather like today, the hillside collapsed in an enormous mudslide, uprooting former evergreen trees, the present alders being the result of re-seeding in the subsequent wet ground.

After working in the rain for a couple of hours, Pastor Nordquist loosened his coat collar and shivered for an instant. His breathing labored, Pastor Nord-quist pitched another shovel load of mud from the dark, northern embankment base into his wooden wheelbarrow, jammed the shovel firmly into the mucky ground, and grabbed the wheelbarrow handles. The axle and Amos groaned in unison as Amos lifted and swung the wheelbarrow in the mud, leaving a deep impression of an irreverent smile that immediately filled with rainwater.

Drenched, teeth clenched, Amos staggered forward, his forearms aching as he fought to keep the load balanced, his tired obedient legs two mechani-cal pistons. After dumping the load, he backed up to one side, and stopped to rest. Looking about, he again wondered about the soil stability in all this rain. He reasoned that upper hillside tree and brush cover held things together. And it's not like it never rains, he thought. As the river below crested, flooding the opposite flats to the south, he pushed through the mud and downpour back to the base of the upper hillside excavation.

As the late afternoon grew darker, rain still falling relentlessly, Ollie Dahlquist pushed his wheelbarrow with extreme difficulty for a few steps and, before he got to the boardwalk, stopped to rest, allowing Pastor Nordquist to pass in front of him.

"You know," Ollie said to Amos, "I teenk I poosh vun more lowed and den call it a day."

"Yah," responded Pastor Nordquist, breathing heavily as he half-pushed and half-plowed his way toward the edge of the embankment. "There is no point in continuing."

Ollie stood and watched the others in the waning daylight, the rain running off his hat. After a couple of minutes, Ollie felt rested enough to proceed. Knowing this would be his last load, he pushed forward vigorously, wanting little more than to finish this final effort.

As Ollie approached the south embankment, the ground beneath him hissed, and a surge of primordial fear shot through Ollie.

"Vhat vas dat?!" Ollie shouted, letting go of the wheelbarrow. In a heartbeat, with a moan the embankment gave way, breaking like a giant ocean wave, sucking Ollie and the wheelbarrow into disintegrating chaos.

With superhuman strength born of terror, Ollie blindly clawed and kicked, but his panic only quickened the mud that gave way more rapidly, slowly swallowing Ollie.

Ollie's unexpected cry was barely audible over the noise of the downpour but, feeling an odd sensation, Amos turned, saw what was happening, and began running toward the receding edge of the southern embankment before realizing what he was doing.

"No, no!" Amos yelled as he brought himself to a quick halt, seeing that he could become part of the problem, not the solution.

"Jacob!" Amos turned and loudly shouted to Jacob Odegaard who was 30 feet behind him. The rainfall on the building site and surrounding forest sounded like a loud, unending gasp and, above the noise, Amos again shouted, "Jacob!" The rain continued to beat on everything relentlessly when Jacob looked up as Pastor Nordquist ran toward him.

"Jacob!"

The incoming rain generated miniature explosions in mud puddles all around as Jacob's wide-eyed expression begged Pastor Nordquist for more. What? What is it? The words were loud in Jacob's mind.

"Get the rope! In the oxcart! Get the rope!"

Jacob saw the embankment, at once understood and, eyes wide, raced awkwardly in the mud back to the oxcart. In the waning daylight he slid and fell halfway over the rear oxcart edge, groping for the rope in the dark interior. Feeling the coil, he grabbed it, pushed himself backward and half-ran, half-slid toward approaching Pastor Nordquist who reached out and grabbed the loose end of the rope.

"The embankment collapsed, taking Ollie with it!" Amos yelled at Jacob. "Hold the other end of this rope real tight! I'm going over the embankment after him!"

Fighting to keep his balance in the mud and rivulets forming on the ground, Amos began slogging in the south embankment direction while tying the rope end tightly around his waist.

Swede, Angus, Omar Roehl and Will Bergstrom saw something was wrong and turned toward Amos and Jacob.

"Dad!" yelled Jacob while holding the other end of the rope, "The embankment collapsed with Mr. Dahlquist!" Swede watched Pastor Nordquist, the rope tied around Amos' waist, and intuited what Amos was about to do. Swede immediately ran over and grabbed the rope ahead of Jacob.

"Angus! Vill! Omar!" yelled Swede, motioning to the other three men and moving forward, "Grab the rope and stand behind me! Jacob, Samuel, get behind Omar!"

Meanwhile, racing to the disintegrating embankment edge, Amos did what he had to do: he jumped in the direction of Ollie and, using his momentum, slid and rolled down the mud surface, getting covered with mud but not allowing it to grip him.

"Dad!" yelled Jacob, "I'm going to the edge to make sure Pastor Nordquist is down far enough! Don't pull until I signal!"

Amos's momentum carried him to within three feet of Ollie who continued to flail with his free arm, his head partially submerged as the muck slowly sucked him under. Amos grabbed Ollie's mud-soaked jacket collar, then his arm.

Jacob signaled the others in the downpour, and with the northern embankment watching, the men began a tug-of-war with the sinking southern embankment.

"Ollie! Move your knees!" Amos began to feel the painful strain of the rope around his waist and prayed the knot would hold. The tension and angle of the rope at first kept Pastor Nordquist from sinking. "Ollie! Pump your knees!" shouted Pastor Nordquist. "Move them in or out, up or down! Bend your elbow, Ollie! Break the suction!"

As Pastor Nordquist yelled in the waning daylight and driving rain, he felt the mud slowly envelop his legs and lower torso as he battled against mud and panic. Ollie was becoming exhausted, but struggled with the energy he had, keeping his head from going under.

"Ollie!" yelled Amos. "Get your hands around my neck!"

Ollie's eyes were covered with mud as he groped for Pastor Nordquist's neck. Pastor Nordquist struggled to move his upper body close enough for Ollie to reach his neck while pulling on Ollie's left arm. Ollie, with strength cultivated by hours of pitching hay, carrying buckets, and lifting calves, kids, children, and farm equipment, clasped his strong hands around the back of Amos's neck. Drenched in panic, he would not let go.

Amos was in a rack, the pain from the rope around his ribs increasing as the six men at the other end of the rope pulled harder in the growing early darkness.

To Jacob Odegaard, having all six men pull on the rope seemed a waste of manpower, particularly when one, his dad, could do the job alone. Jacob let go of the rope and again ran to his father.

"Dad, I'm going to follow the rope to the edge, slide down part way, holding the rope, and also work to pull Mr. Dahlquist free!"

Swede knew 6' 5" 235 lb. Jacob was powerful – pound-for-pound almost as strong as Swede himself – and that Jacob the artist was a master of detail. If anyone could find a way, it would be Jacob.

"Yah!" responded Swede. "Go ahead! But do not go all the vay down to them; stay above them – use a hand, foot, to reach out to them if that iss possible!" he yelled over the downpour. "And you *vill not* let go of the rope for any reason! None!"

"Yes, dad!" yelled Jacob as he turned to run.

Jacob ran to the ox cart and found a large wood clamp, a mallet, a smaller strand of rope, and two stakes, and pulled the ladder from the ox cart. The smaller items wedged under his arms, dragging the ladder and looking over his shoulder, he walked backward through the dark mud awash with puddles to the edge of the embankment.

"Harder, Ollie!" Amos encouraged, his teeth clenched.

As the two men struggled against the mud, Amos could sense the mud's grip on Ollie weaken, but also sensed Ollie's fading ability to fight on.

"Ollie! Don't quit!"

Jacob was cautiously almost at the edge, looking down in the fading light at the two men below him, in his mind measuring the distance. Below Jacob, Ollie was giving everything he had remaining, but his energy was nearly spent. With every push, his next push became weaker, and the same was true for Pastor Nordquist whose ribs were in pain from the rope.

The rope holding Amos remained taut as Jacob slid the ladder laterally next to the embankment edge. Standing up, Jacob ran back about eight feet from the embankment edge, and drove the two stakes deep in the rain-soaked ground about four feet apart. He tied one end of the strand to one stake. Running forward, he quickly stopped, slipped the rope strand under the top ladder rung, turned, and raced back to the other stake where he tied the other end of the strand. The ladder partly secured, Jacob swung the ladder over the embankment edge, allowing it to drop down several feet, lying over the main rope. Jacob grabbed the large wood clamp, lid down the main rope a short way, and then stepped on the suspended ladder while still holding on to the main rope. He cautiously released his grip on the main rope; the ladder held. Jacob secured the main rope and wood ladder together with the wood clamp. The ladder was now fastened to the rope strand fastened to stakes behind the embankment edge, and clamped to the main rope.

It was becoming darker, the rain unrelenting, and Amos's muscles were nearly exhausted. His body was chilled to the bone and sinking in mud. His own intensity began to wane, not knowing Jacob was a few feet above him. Lifting his face skyward, Amos let the rain clean the mud out of his eyes when he saw Jacob begin descending Jacob's ladder.

Bending low, Jacob slid one leg over the bottom rung while holding on to the next rung with his left hand. He bent low, reached down and wrapped his proportionately large right hand around Pastor Nordquist's partially submerged right arm that, in turn, was tightly wrapped around Ollie. Applying pressure around Pastor Nordquist's arm, Jacob began pulling gradually at first, allowing Pastor Nordquist to become acclimated to what was happening. The constant pressure of the rope was becoming more painful for Amos, and would become even more so as Swede grew impatient.

"Kick!!" ordered Pastor Nordquist. "Kick, Ollie," he shouted. This would be all Ollie could give.

As if his right arm was part of a large machine, Jacob increased the upward pull, more concerned he might dislocate Pastor Nordquist's arm than fail in his effort to free the two men.

As the Swede and the men pulled on the rope, Jacob's hand gripped Amos' arm like a vice, and Amos gritted his teeth.

Swede was getting more anxious and pulled harder. Then harder. Then still harder to where the tension level for Amos was extreme, worsened by Jacob increasing his effort when pulling Amos' arm upwards.

Suddenly there came a prolonged "Sswwoooosssssssshh" and, as if in a dream, Amos found himself going up the side of the embankment nearly as fast as he had gone down, Ollie still clinging tightly. As Jacob, then Amos and Ollie, were pulled up and over the top of the embankment, the others lost their balance, falling down and becoming further covered with mud.

Jacob stood up; his left leg would be bruised but otherwise he was okay. Lying in the downpour, Ollie could not move; exhausted. The will to survive created and used more energy than would have been available under normal circumstances, and his anatomy was back in normal circumstances.

Amos attempted to get up, but sat back down, catching his breath and hoping the pain in his ribs would subside. He rolled over on his side, his head resting on his left arm in the downpour as Ollie, nearby, managed to slowly get to his feet. Seeing Amos falter, Swede ran to Amos and stooped down.

"Swede," muttered Amos through clenched teeth, "Ah… My ribs..." Jacob joined them.

"Pastor, ve all need to get home but especially you," said Swede, kneeling at Amos's side with Jacob. Swede paused for a moment, looking at Amos and thinking.

"This may hurt," Swede said as he slid both arms under Pastor Nordquist, picked him up and carried him to the ox cart. As the downpour again rinsed mud off his face, Amos gritted his teeth, unaware this would not be the last time Swede would need to pick him up and carry him.

━━━●━━━

The welt around Pastor Nordquist's right arm remained for two weeks. A cold was cured by rest, a strong disposition, a loving wife, a conscientious doctor, and chicken soup, but after his cold ended, Pastor Nordquist's cracked ribs and neck pain kept him inside, and the excavation continued without him.

"Y' know, Pastor," said Angus the following evening as Pastor Nordquist lay covered with blankets on the couch, "I feel responsible for you lyin' here. The potential for disaster, I could see it, I could. But, no, I just continued mindlessly pushin' m' wheelbarrow without stoppin' t' investigate, without mentionin' my concern t' anyone. But there it was: I could see plainly what might happen."

"We all could, Angus," said Pastor Nordquist, looking up at Angus. "Individually, we all expected embankment erosion might become a problem and yet we each threw caution to the wind."

Later that evening Pastor Nordquist lay in bed, and looked upward, silently wondering. You want us to build a church. Why this? Inside him a still, small voice responded, in effect: you knew the danger, you ignored it, you'll recover soon, and Ollie Dahlquist is alive. It could have been otherwise.

The foundation for the new church was started in late November on the solid portion of the excavated site, and by mid-December 1889, construction was about 60% done. Meanwhile, the growing congregation filled Swede's living room, women and children seated, and men lining the walls.

A letter from the Methodist minister in Murray, Idaho arrived, and Amos sat reading about how the small Methodist congregation would build a new church in nearby Wallace, nine miles south-southwest of Murray. Over the past three years, many had left Murray, and most Murray housing and commercial buildings, although nearly new, were now vacant. Names with which Amos was familiar were gone. The Methodist pastor said that on November 14th the decomposed bodies of three Chinese were found under some logs near the Wallace Northern Pacific Railroad Depot, and Pastor Nordquist remembered the rumor that three Chinese had been murdered.

On the construction site the following day, Angus expressed his impatience.

"We be movin' at the speed of molasses runnin' uphill," complained Angus as he worked on the church interior. "Before we reach Christmas, t'is time to wrap things up," he said, unintentionally punning.

"Well, yah" responded Pastor Nordquist, smiling in spite of his aching, wrapped ribs. "But," Amos sighed, "I don't think construction will be finished before Christmas, Angus."

Angus looked down and in frustration pounded his hammer against a wall stud.

"Y' know what t'was," said Angus. "It took far too long to get the site level. This hillside was free…," Angus looked upward, "thank you Lord, but we still paid a price."

Angus removed his hat with his left hand and cautiously smoothed back his hair with his right wrist, his hammer still in his right hand.

"You know where the gremlins live?" asked Angus rhetorically as if Amos should know.

"Where the gremlins live?"

"The gremlins live in the ground." Angus nodded several times. "Never been involved in building anything significant where the dirt wasn't somehow a problem."

"Yah. That is true," responded Pastor Nordquist, thinking back to several construction projects in Minnesota. As in Minnesota, his breath fogged in front of his face as he spoke. "Getting lumber up the river took time too."

Undaunted, the men continued, but while the end was approaching, so was Christmas. We'll need to work harder, was the common thought. A Christmas Eve candlelight service would be worth all this effort.

87

December 24, 1889

Born to raise the sons of earth,
Born to give them second birth.
Hark! The herald angels sing,
"Glory to the newborn King."

For Pastor Nordquist, it was the best the carol ever sounded.

Shunting seating practicality aside, throughout the Christmas Eve candlelight service all stood because there were no pews or chairs, and the floor and wall surfaces were still unfinished. No one seemed to mind, however, and many of the women and children were openly excited about the church being close to completion. The men, listening to the spontaneous comments, quietly absorbed the excitement of their families, becoming more determined to get the job completed.

December 29, 1889, Sunday

In the fields and meadows, low hanging chimney smoke combined with cold, damp grass to create the sweet, smoky smell of extinguished birthday candles. On the hillside above the meadows, the new steeple bell rang, calling the surrounding community to worship. Finally, thought Pastor Nordquist as he listened to the bell chime. With all the men pitching in, the church was finished Thursday, the day after Christmas.

On Friday, about a mile away and slightly above the floodplain, using Swede's workhorses, the men began clearing the future Nordquist homesite and periphery of Douglas fir. The big logs would be floated down the river to the mill, cut into lumber, and the lumber cured beside the mill in a large curing barn. A few months later, lumber would be planed as necessary, and the lumber barged back up the river. Once the logs were sent downriver, Angus, Amos, Swede, Jacob, Samuel and several volunteers would begin digging out the parsonage basement area – perhaps, Anna hoped, the last for the Nordquists.

In the meantime, another development was underway.

January 1, 1890

On New Year's Day, Anna looked down at her large abdominal area and wondered: Has any other woman been this big? She knew being pregnant with twins was more pregnant than most women got, but many women had similarly gone before her. This, however, did not alleviate the sensation she was becoming as large as the home she and her husband were planning.

"So, first, tell me, Rachel: boys or girls?"

"They're going to be boys," said Rachel as if she wanted no one else to know. "And their names will be," Rachel's self-confidence was having second thoughts, "Joshua and Jacob," names Amos and Anna had already considered.

"Joshua and Jacob," responded Anna, returning her attention to the remaining pans in the dishwater. "Those sound like good names to me too." Anna smiled as she looked out the kitchen window at the fields, meadows and woodlands, and considered that once the parsonage was completed, they might stay here.

January 2, 1890

Anna Nordquist went into labor and gave birth to fraternal twin boys whom she and Amos named Joshua and Jacob.

March 15, 1890

All was well until Anna noticed Jacob seemed to be developing more slowly than Joshua.

"Amos," began Anna, "I'm concerned about Jacob. Look at how small his eyes are. They don't seem to be developing like Joshua's. Do you think something might be wrong?"

"I hope not," answered Pastor Nordquist, looking closely at Jacob, "but I am not the one to say." He massaged his chin as he studied Jacob, who seemed to look back without really seeing. "We should visit Doc Torgeson."

Doc could diagnose a problem as well as any doctor in Seattle. Old Doc, a tall man with broad shoulders, a large head and thinning white hair, whether examining a patient or playing checkers with Swede, had a way of raising his eyebrows without opening his eyes any wider. Doc's reading glasses, sitting comfortably on the end of his nose, and the stethoscope continually hanging around his neck, made him look like the quintessential country doctor. Doc was like a grandfather to children, or favorite uncle to younger adults. His interest in each family went beyond medicine, especially after he began living alone following his wife's untimely death from bronchial pneumonia years earlier in North Dakota. They had no children, and he never remarried. His patients became his extended family.

In addition, no one in the valley knew horses better than Doc who had raised horses for years and doubled as a veterinarian. Whether he was treating people or animals, Doc always seemed to know what the problem was and, within the restrictions of medical knowledge in that era, always knew what could be done.

"Hmm," was all he said when first examining Jacob's eyes. As Joshua and Jacob lay still in their mother's arms, Doc probed and studied. Jacob simply looked back in wonder. Doc had an idea.

Sitting back on a stool, Doc took one more studied look at Jacob and then rose. Doc slowly took a seat on the couch next to Anna holding both boys.

"Yoor son, Yaycob, has an unusual condition that I cannot change."

"What is it?" asked Anna anxiously.

"Yaycob is Mongoloid." Doc Torgeson paused, watching Anna's reaction. "I don't know vhat causes this. He vill not be a difficult baby, but he vill require closer attention for longer period than vill Yoshua."

Doc cleaned his glasses on his handkerchief and looked at the little flower arrangement on the coffee table before him. "He vill require special attention. There is nothing I can do to change this."

Anna looked down at Little Jacob. "This one will need more love," was all she said.

As the Lutheran pastor's twin baby boys grew larger, gawking increased and, whereas other mothers were relaxed when holding Joshua, with Jacob some felt awkward. When meeting the eyes of someone with residual poker-faced solemnity, Anna knew they had been furtively studying Jacob.

As always, what a few adults said in private, their children would parrot publicly. Regardless of who said it, to Rachel it was stupid. If Jacob is different, Rachel thought, what of it? *I'm* different. *Everyone* is different. And that was certainly true – as evidenced by the odd convictions of a few Darwinian members in the community who privately considered little Jacob not only different, but a weakling to be culled from the herd.

⎯⎯⎯⎯⎯ ● ⎯⎯⎯⎯⎯

As the development effort progressed, Everett Land Company executives were making a strong first move that J. J. Hill would appreciate: to get the railroad, they were building a need for the railroad. In New York, Charles Colby and Colgate Hoyt got commitments for a paper mill and a nail factory. Colby convinced New York shipbuilder Charles Wetmore to build whaleback steamers in Everett. And Colby and Hoyt raised money to build a railroad line from Everett to Snohomish, connecting Everett with Seattle where city fathers looked north in awe at all that was happening. Momentum was strong. Hewitt named most Everett streets after Everett Land Company executives and stockholders and, anticipating the development of a West Coast New York, added Broadway and Wall Street.

Then came unexpected good news. Three prospectors approached Hewitt with evidence of a galena concentration in the Cascades, and Hewitt sent two mining engineers up into the hills with the prospectors. Upon returning, the engineers said the find showed promise. Hewitt contacted Colby in New York, and Colby and Hoyt, to be certain, sent another team of mining experts to the location. The experts returned with a report of silver, gold, lead and iron, although they cautioned that these findings were limited to surface samples, and the samples had a low mineral content. Adequate mineral extraction would require a railroad and a large concentrator, but if those costs were not prohibitive, a profitable mining operation could be possible.

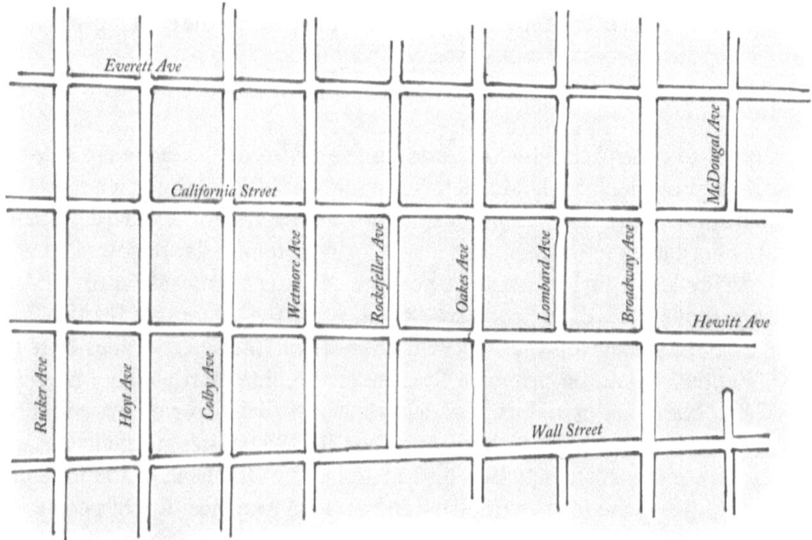

The three prospectors already named the location Monte Cristo after the island where fabulous treasure was found in the 24th chapter of Alexandre Dumas's popular novel *Le Comte de Monte Cristo*. Upon hearing the reports, Colby, Hoyt and the other investors were delighted; things were going from very good to excellent. Monte Cristo. They had all read the novel.

For reasons not entirely clear, mining expert Alton L. Dickerman made hyperbolic statements suggesting the new find would rival the Comstock Lode, and "should send down enough silver to pave the streets [of Everett]." Dickerman's statements were printed in the Everett *Times*. Hewitt mailed copies to Colby and Hoyt. The investors' vision began to include not only New York but also Pittsburgh. Using Rockefeller money, a railroad line between Everett and Monte Cristo was begun. The "possibilities" were brightening like an early morning sky.

Henry Hewitt knew he could not develop a stable manufacturing center worthy of James J. Hill's Great Northern Railroad, however, without bringing in the railroad late in the development effort. When "the need" was completed, the railroad had better be there.

The daily line between Seattle and Everett via Snohomish was useful, but favored Seattle, not Everett. Hewitt's window-of-opportunity to make Everett an independent terminus would be open briefly. The extent of the gamble was far greater than anyone, including Hewitt, realized, and it was a gamble of which Rockefeller in New York, busy with Standard Oil and a multitude of other investments, was unaware.

Soon streets, hotels, banks, office and retail buildings, homes, docks, the Puget Sound Pulp and Paper Company mill, Charles Wetmore's shipbuilding facility, the Everett Timber Company mill, another shipyard, a smelter, and the

Puget Sound Wire Nail and Steel Company manufacturing plant were all under construction simultaneously. With all that was happening, the earlier generalization, "The potential is enormous," seemed prophetic.

1892

Unable to control things alone, and on the advice of his doctors to delegate as much as possible, John D. Rockefeller made the decision to form a four-person board to oversee his investments, with the exception of Standard Oil, and, initially, charitable giving. Since January 21, 1889, Rockefeller had worked with Reverend Frederick Taylor Gates, previously a minister at Central Baptist Church in Minneapolis, and then Executive Secretary of the American Baptist Education Society, to develop the Baptist University of Chicago. Decades later the word "Baptist" would be dropped. Rockefeller became increasingly impressed with Gates' combination of business savvy and spiritual discernment, and hired Gates as a financial and philanthropic advisor. By 1892, Gates gradually became Rockefeller's most trusted advisor, and was placed at the head of the four-person board, giving the former minister an extraordinary position of power and responsibility. Rockefeller had not closely monitored developments in Everett. Gates would.

1893

Initial assessments of Monte Cristo mineral wealth proved to be overstated. Little ore was sent to the smelter, and minimal local iron was available for the nail factory. Construction of the *City of Everett,* a whaleback steamer design popularized by marine architect Alexander McDougall, began, but there were no further orders. Although the steamers had been profitably used on the Great Lakes, demand for vessels waned. In fact, orders for everything everywhere were falling.

Like water in an unplugged kitchen sink, the economy was circling the drain, and the source of the problem was not isolated in Everett. It wasn't the absence of a railroad terminus. Newspapers continually brought menacing news that the national economy was sliding rapidly into another depression, likely worse than any preceding depression.

The Panic of 1893 began.

Although Hewitt did not know it, the Northern Pacific Railroad was on the verge of bankruptcy, and there was no practical incentive for J. J. Hill to bring the Great Northern to Everett until economic conditions improved. Hoyt and Colby met with Hewitt and other investors in Everett.

"Needless to say," said Colgate Hoyt, "we're all greatly concerned."

"And I share your concern, Colgate," responded Hewitt, hands in his pockets, leaning against his secretarial desk. All of the men were having difficulties with investments everywhere. Trader's Bank, a Tacoma bank that Hewitt helped start, as well as the Everett bank that bore his name, were having difficulty keeping their doors open. "But gentlemen, we've read these sorts of headlines in the past when business activity dropped dramatically and eventually recovered. Headlines sell newspapers. We want them to sell newspapers…printed on Everett paper made from Everett pulp. With regard to what they print, however, how much of this is to be believed? We're in the middle of everything now. To shut it all down because of speculative newspaper headlines makes little sense."

"Henry, you know it's not just newspapers," countered Charles Colby, standing nearby and looking incisively at Hewitt. "Money is becoming tight. Demand for all goods and services is dropping rapidly. Things went well, we got caught up in the optimism, and now, unfortunately, we are in the throes of a major market correction. It has little to do with you, Henry, but people are being cautious. You know yourself how much demand has dropped for timber products. I'm not an alarmist, Henry," Colby folded his arms, "but I know a few people who are actually scared. We need to proceed with extreme caution, perhaps placing certain…"

"I could not agree more, Charles," interjected Hewitt, also folding his arms. "But, again, we're in the middle of everything. Do we just tell everyone to stop and go home? This *is* home. Homes are under construction everywhere, just as new manufacturing facilities are. At worst, we need to complete what we have started." Hewitt put his hands back in his pockets and looked at the others.

"I'm also concerned about John," added Colby with a look of apprehension. "His advisor, Fred Gates, has personally evaluated everything in which Rockefeller has money invested. We've used more of his money than we originally planned to use, and in due time he'll want to see a return on – and of – his investment. Using his money as we have, without showing a timely return, will make us seem incompetent at best or, at worst, we could look like crooks. I don't' want to…"

"Rockefeller will understand," countered Hewitt reassuringly. "'You have to spend money to make money.' Rockefeller knows that." Colby looked at Hewitt as if Hewitt had just crawled out from under a rock. "You know that from the Northern Pacific, gentlemen," Hewitt stated cheerily. The others looked back glumly and said nothing. "Rockefeller," insisted Hewitt more quietly, "will make money in this venture just like he has in every other venture. He's not in this by accident. He'll make money here too. You know the expression, 'In God and Rockefeller we trust.'"

"You'd be better served trusting God, Henry," said Colby quietly, his gray beard seeming whiter than the last time the two met. "Whereas God has infinite patience and forgiveness, in business matters Rockefeller has little of either. And Rockefeller won't save you."

"Charles, I suspect that if construction is completed," Hewitt responded, "and the economy has improved – which it will invariably do – we'll be very relieved, of course, but especially relieved we did not take the action we seem to be considering at this moment."

Hewitt wanted to convince the others that, if he moved fast, the wolf could be driven from the door. Regardless of what the national economy did, he believed a railroad with Everett as its terminus would preserve demand for Everett-manufactured products.

"Everett has such great potential," said Hewitt, annoyed he had to explain what to him was obvious. "With a railroad, while a depression might postpone realization of that potential, it will not kill that potential. I, we, need to force Hill's hand," said Hewitt. "I can't see why he procrastinates. We've built a railroad over 50 miles to the Cascades. All he has to do is go through the mountains and hook-up with it. Good Lord," added Hewitt, "it's effectively the only subsidy he will have received." The others forced a brief, half-hearted laugh.

"I simply want a commitment," concluded Hewitt. "What we've done – and are doing – is considerable. The potential is obvious to us. It must be obvious to Hill. This procrastination nonsense must end."

Hewitt, arms again folded and a slightly disgusted look replacing his normally pleasant expression, looked at the others who said nothing. Hewitt had driven this enormous development and had, as far as the others could see, done so competently. They realized Everett had become more to Hewitt than a potentially great city. Besides his fortune, Hewitt's heart and soul were in this. It meant more to him than to any of them, they knew, and they were not inclined to disrupt his efforts without sufficient justification. Presently, justification was still insufficient. What was the alternative?

"Here's what I would like to do," said Hewitt. "I want to throw a lavish banquet – one not seen since the days of Solomon – for James J. Hill. In the Bayview Hotel." The Bayview Hotel was just finished at the north end of Everett. Hewitt held his hands up defensively. "Granted," Hewitt said, "Hill as yet deserves no such festivity. If we put him up in front of our investors and good citizens, however, dressed in their best finery, following an extraordinary dinner, champagne toasts to the future of Everett – an *entre* prepared in champagne – I believe that in the gallantry of the moment it will be nearly impossible for him to do anything other than accommodate his gracious hosts. I wouldn't be able to pass it up. I can't see where he would pass up the opportunity to become the most popular man on the face of the earth by committing to become among the richest."

Hewitt consequently organized a lavish banquet in honor of The Empire Builder, James J. Hill, hoping that, in an instant of enormous popularity, Hill could not possibly disappoint his supporters, but, rather, would publicly commit to Everett. Then Everett, as Hewitt envisioned it, would become the West Coast New York.

— • —

Hill attended, spoke pleasantly but ambiguously, said little, committed to less, and left.

— • —

"I honestly don't know what to say," said Hewitt with difficulty to Colby and other Everett Land Company executives the next day. "He avoided the issue. I'm having a hard time understanding this. Does anyone understand why he would not commit?"

Colby stood quietly looking at Hewitt. But his mind was on Rockefeller.

"It's the economy, of course," said one of the executives morosely. "Nobody's doing anything, and the lack of market activity will probably get worse. Hill is waiting until things improve substantially. And that may take awhile."

"Henry, I don't know what other options there are," said another. "I wish I did. The banquet was first rate – we could not have done better in Boston – but it's quite understandable why Hill did not say, 'Yes.'"

The only sound was construction activity outside. Hewitt looked at the others. Busy with the business of Everett, the obstacles were not as apparent to Hewitt as they were to Hill – who wanted to go to Everett, but only when it was expedient to do so.

"However," countered Hewitt, "he did not say, 'No.'"

Colby remained expressionless, but his head tilted back slightly as the intensity of his gaze increased.

With worsening economic conditions, after procrastinating in hopes of being able to somehow accommodate Hewitt, Hill told Hewitt that until the national economic climate improved, the Great Northern Railroad would not be coming. This is as close to a commitment from Hill as Hewitt would get.

As market demand continually declined, previously avoidable difficulties became exacerbated. At first the problems were barely noticeable because Rockefeller money was being used to wallpaper over those problems. In business, Rockefeller was usually uncompromising. As he said, his success was due to the efficiency with which his money was spent or invested. Frederick T. Gates shared that simple conviction. In the long run, Rockefeller's money would not be used for wallpaper.

***

Colby, Hoyt, Oakes and others had their attention momentarily diverted away from Everett. Everything was gradually going from bad to worse. Later in 1893, the Northern Pacific Railroad went bankrupt. While economic conditions deteriorated, Rockefeller's health improved as his four-man board led by Reverend Gates attended to investment matters. As Rockefeller began to become more involved at the office, Gates kept him apprised of growing problems in Everett, advising expeditious extrication.

***

"Charles, I'm doing everything within my power to turn this whole thing around," explained Hewitt again. "I've invested all of my own money. The extent to which we needed to depend on Rockefeller is unfortunate and not as planned. We had no choice, however." Hewitt stood up and walked over to the window. "I didn't expect there would be a deep depression."

"In the beginning," responded Colby, who remained seated, "I asked you to present a plan which would consider every eventuality. We're in a depression. Your plan should have considered that possibility. It's not like there have been none during the past 20 years. I realize in hindsight," continued Colby, "we were all too optimistic for our own good. Wishful thinking. Such is human nature." Over the past several months the lines on Colby's face had increased; his beard was now white. "I remarked in the beginning that it seemed too good to be true. I should have paid closer attention to my intuition. In any event, a bit more caution on your part and mine might have kept us out of the mess in which we presently find ourselves." Colby's disconsolate gaze became almost angry, causing Hewitt to wait for Colby to finish what he was about to say.

"We have a bigger problem now," Colby stated with unease. "I have worried about this for some time. You have received an urgent telegram."

"As you know," said Hewitt, turning fully toward Colby, "lately I have received more urgent telegrams than I have time to read."

"You had better read this one," said Colby, looking down at the piece of paper in his hand. "Fred Gates has made his recommendation. The telegram is from Rockefeller." Colby looked up at Hewitt as Hewitt's heart began to sink. "He wants to meet with you at 26 Broadway in one week."

That meant leaving at once.

<hr>

The meeting involving Rockefeller, Gates and Hewitt was serious but not acrimonious, and Gates did most of the talking. Rockefeller relieved Hewitt of his responsibilities with the Everett Land Company, summarily assumed all of Hewitt's Everett debts and assets, and sent Hewitt on his way with $14,000, an amount which might keep Hewitt personally afloat for a little while. Rockefeller appreciated Hewitt's effort. Which wasn't good enough.

Demoralized, Hewitt left the meeting hoping his dream would not fade in the growing darkness of the depression. Before Hewitt returned to Everett, Rockefeller replaced him with Colby. Colby knew he could do no more than Hewitt. His eagle eyes stared as he tried to summon uncommon wisdom, an extraordinary plan, anything that might stem the tide. He conferred regularly with Hewitt who, because of their friendship and Hewitt's emotional involvement with Everett, helped to the extent he could. Colby talked with as many others as might offer insight. It was hopeless, however. They could think of nothing beyond the ordinary, and Colby continually expended one futile effort after another, each effort discarded and piled on a pyre of failure.

While Rockefeller began controlling ownership, the depression controlled everything else. As Hewitt's dream of a West Coast New York continued to fade, Rockefeller, who had yet to see Everett, eventually dismissed Colby. For good measure, Rockefeller removed Colgate Hoyt from the Everett Land Company's board of directors.

Colby, who lost millions between the Northern Pacific, the Everett Land Company, and a multitude of other ventures, became severely depressed. His depression resulted not just from the great financial losses, but also from feeling responsible for Hoyt's loss of money and face, and a certainty that, although Rockefeller did not say so, Rockefeller might have felt betrayed by Colby. Communications from Fred Gates had been terse. Including foreclosing on the large mortgage encumbering the Everett holdings, and buying the mortgage encumbering the Monte Cristo mines, Reverend Gates gradually took control of everything within which Rockefeller inadvertently invested. Except for the Rucker properties, Rockefeller would own Everett.

The emotional and physical trauma that burdened Charles Colby became more and more evident. His formerly piercing eyes became weak, even fearful, and he began to stoop as he walked, using a cane. He had been in high-pressure situations many times in the past, but they were situations he could control. Adding insult to injury, Gates became openly critical of Hewitt and Colby, considering them less-than-competent. The accumulating burden became too great for Colby and, at the age of 56, while walking in the garden beside his home, feeling the weight of failure upon failure, Colby clutched his chest, staggered, and collapsed to the ground where he died of a heart attack.

Rockefeller, who did not feel betrayed, but who made a business decision to remove Colby and Hoyt, was saddened. He personally liked and respected Colby and his family. Rockefeller's decision was based on the obvious difficulty Colby found himself in. When it became evident that Colby and Hoyt could not change things, Rockefeller simply took the next step.

Rockefeller sent Reverend Gates back to Everett with instructions to reevaluate the Everett assets and market conditions, and do whatever necessary to insure a profitable return – a seemingly impossible request. Gates shared Rockefeller's conviction that wealth was a trust from God, and unique measures were required. Whereas Colby and his Everett Land Company associates were unable to think of anything beyond the ordinary, Gates conceived a plan to move Rockefeller money laterally with a potential for profit.

Gates reinvestigated and monitored all operations, and over the course of several years gradually liquidated Rockefeller business and real estate holdings at losses. He unloaded the Monte Cristo mines, and sold the Everett-Monte Cristo Railroad, built to transport ore and labor, and eventually to be part of J.J. Hill's Great Northern Railroad, at a $2,000,000 loss.

Following Rockefeller's primary rule with respect to the efficiency with which money is spent, however, Gates did not accept the losses and head back east. While Rockefeller did business with Andrew Carnegie, J. P. Morgan and John Jacob Astor IV, Rockefeller considered Reverend Frederick T. Gates to have the best business mind in America, and believed Gates would find a way to realize Rockefeller's seemingly impossible request. A man of both faith and excellent business acumen, Reverend Gates would do the impossible.

88

April 12th, 1895

Five years passed since Joshua and Jacob were born. Pastor Nordquist sat in his front porch rocking chair thinking about how large the porch seemed, but how small it was in comparison to the front porch in Göteborg. Here he spent time watching his young sons play on the lawn before him. Life has been uneventful, Amos thought, unsurprising because normally things go normally. But there are also times, he mused, when normalcy almost seems forbidden, where on-going mishaps, even disasters, occur so frequently that normalcy is abnormal. Things went from bad to worse with the Seattle congregation, one problem after another; and then it only took an instant for the great Seattle fire to start. The unstable embankment gave way before either he or Ollie realized what was happening, and there were an abnormal number of problems when building the church.

Thinking about these events, Amos considered how mishaps always occur in matter of seconds, and then actions of the moment can mean the difference between safety and injury, achievement and disaster, and sometimes life and death. While thinking about this, the discomfort in the pit of Amos's stomach slowly grew and, while watching his sons, Amos looked upward and half-jokingly asked, "Oh, no. Now what?"

At home, as a mongoloid child, Jacob was almost always happy, wanting to please his mother and father to the greatest extent he could. By the time he was five years old, Jacob had two close friends: his brother, Joshua, and an infinitely patient collie named Shadow. When Shadow was a puppy, so that Shadow could have a twin too, the boys gave Shadow a cloth rag-doll puppy that Jacob received for Christmas. As Shadow grew larger, the cloth puppy was relegated to the floor next to her corner sleeping box, largely ignored.

When Shadow grew older and had her first litter late one afternoon, all were stillborn. Pastor Nordquist explained to the boys that God loves all creatures, even puppies, and would take care of them. It was left to Pastor Nordquist, however, to take care of the little bodies. With all present, the puppies were given a brief funeral service and buried next to the Nordquist barn. The next morning the boys found Shadow in her box next to the kitchen door, with one paw over the cloth puppy lying next to her.

Shadow would avoid the sometimes-playful Jacob indoors, but outdoors would, true to her name, shadow Jacob constantly. Joshua and Jacob were rarely out of their mother's sight for very long, but Shadow, in addition to a genetic predisposition to herd, felt an unceasing obligation to watch over Joshua and Jacob, insuring they stayed out of harm's way. When either boy wandered off, as Jacob occasionally did, Shadow's series of soft staccato barks would bring Anna Nordquist out of the house to investigate. Without realizing it, Anna began to depend on Shadow when other responsibilities took Anna away from the vicinity of the kitchen window for any extended period.

Joshua grew more active than Jacob, and occasionally engaged in activities where Jacob would only watch. During these times, Shadow would sit at Jacob's side, also watching; watching Jacob or anything else that needed watching.

Jacob became attached to Shadow. The two of them were occasionally joined by the family cat, Liddy. Now and then, Anna would take a moment to be entertained, watching Jacob and his mini-family – Shadow and Liddy – outside the kitchen window. Shadow, tongue tip protruding slightly from the front of her mouth, would walk alongside Jacob, while Liddy would tentatively negotiate the damp ground in order to be properly stroked in the manner Jacob's mom taught him.

Last night Shadow had a run-in with a porcupine. Sharp, hooked quills penetrated Shadow's chest and left front leg causing Shadow a great deal of suffering. Accompanied by a very concerned Joshua, that morning Pastor Nordquist loaded Shadow on the buggy and took Shadow to Doc Torgeson. In the absence of Joshua and Shadow, Jacob had only Liddy to keep him company when he played outside.

Liddy had an angular white tipped tail that seemed to inspect where Liddy had been, angling back and forth, looking first left then right like a tiny, furry sea serpent. When resting, Liddy had an alarmingly loud purr. Although the Luke Odegaard mouse exterminator was also employed at the Nordquist farm, Pastor Nordquist once told the boys that the absence of mice around their small farm was the result of Liddy's purr. The mice thought Liddy was a lion and they all ran away. Jacob loved to make Liddy purr. Whenever an adult studied Liddy, the thought was always the same: life is hard.

As the morning progressed, Anna peered out the window periodically, but always found everything in order. Jacob sat quietly absorbed in the effort of making Liddy purr. Jacob, without thinking, looked around for Shadow, and momentarily became anxious about Shadow's absence. But purring Liddy commanded Jacob's attention and, for the joy of the moment, Jacob forgot his worry.

Eventually Liddy, as with all cats, decided a moment of independence was needed, and began to walk away. The tool shed needed inspecting.

Jacob followed, alternately taking a few steps and bending down to pet Liddy who continued to walk according to an agenda known only to her.

It was a short distance to the tool shed/workshop and, although Pastor

Nordquist told Joshua and Jacob never to go in there, with the door slightly ajar, in a few moments Liddy and Jacob were inside.

To the left of the tool shed door, along the wall that ran to the workbench, hung racks of ropes, pulleys and leather strips used for various fastening, pulling and heavy lifting requirements around the farm. In front of a small block-and-tackle rigging sat an empty nail keg. Liddy jumped up on the keg lid, weighted in place by an ax head, paused, and jumped up to the waist-high workbench that Amos used for repairs, blade sharpening, and saw filing. Jacob watched from below.

Liddy stopped and sat on the workbench, looking down at Jacob. Liddy meowed. Then meowed again.

Jacob looked anxiously at Liddy and, not understanding, thought Liddy needed him. Jacob stepped forward and attempted to climb up on the empty nail keg, but, as he tried to get up on the lid, his weight caused the barrel to tip over, the lid scraping Jacob's forehead as it flew off, with the ax head barely missing Jacob's face. He fell awkwardly on his back.

Lying on the dirt and sawdust floor, hurt and confused, looking up at Liddy, Jacob began to cry. Jacob seldom cried, but now the scrape on his forehead, the scare from the nail keg overturn, and the concern for Liddy all worked in unison to engender fear.

Liddy meowed again, reclaiming Jacob's attention.

Climbing to his feet, Jacob again attempted to help Liddy, first pulling himself up on the overturned nail keg which was prevented from rolling in his direction by the ax head wedged between a barrel stave and the dirt floor.

"What…?" Anna said, placing her hand near her heart as she stood in the root cellar connected to the kitchen. It was as if something was shaking Anna from inside, trying to get her attention. Anna continued standing silently for a moment listening for a sound, but heard nothing. The feeling grew louder and, as the sense of apprehension grew greater, she turned and ran up the root cellar stairs into the kitchen. Icing her inexplicable anxiety, she looked out the window and saw no one.

Where was Jacob?

As she ran out into the yard, the buckboard with Pastor Nordquist, Joshua and a mended Shadow, turned into the driveway, a distance of about 150 feet from the road. Anna stopped and yelled in their direction.

"Amos! I can't find Jacob!"

She hadn't looked yet, but the sensation yelled this before she could think. The others couldn't hear her, but she was outside with her apron on and had a panicked look on her face. Pastor Nordquist immediately pushed the horse to a gallop over the short distance to his wife.

"Jacob! I can't find Jacob!"

"Where did you last see him?"

His chest and left leg bandaged, Shadow awkwardly jumped from the wagon and, upon making impact with the ground, yelped and fell, but immediately regained her feet and hobbled as fast as she could to the tool shed, Joshua running after her, quickly followed by Pastor Nordquist and Anna.

As Anna ran up the root cellar stairs, Jacob was tottering on the side of the overturned nail keg, turning awkwardly toward Liddy. As he turned, the unstable keg jerked in the opposite direction of the ax head, sending Jacob into the spidery maze of ropes hanging from the wall. Instinctively, Jacob grabbed the first thing he felt as he fell, the free rope on the small block and tackle, but as he fell sideways into the ropes, his neck became caught, as if in a sprung trap. The small block and tackle formed a noose that simultaneously closed and lifted upward as Jacob grabbed and pulled. Unaware of what he was doing while acting out of self-preservation, he reflexively clung to the rope.

As Jacob began to struggle in the noose, Anna was looking out the kitchen window at the empty side yard. When Pastor Nordquist pulled into the driveway, Jacob was beginning to lose consciousness. At the moment Shadow yelped, Jacob had lost consciousness. When the family reached and released his small body in the tool shed, they thought he was dead.

But the moment of imbalance passed. Pastor Nordquist realized that if little Jacob was unconscious a few moments longer, they could not have revived him. By the grace of God, the time of unconsciousness was limited just long enough to allow revival. Disaster was avoided, and the next day Pastor Nordquist went about the farm and made everything Jacob-safe. For months afterward, Anna would call both Joshua and Jacob to her in order to hug and hold them, unwilling to let them out of her sight for any more than a moment. But it only takes a moment.

89

September 1896

In September 1896, while the Odegaards and the Nordquists were preparing for the harvest, Everett Colby, after whom the City of Everett was named, was elected captain of the Brown football team. A star player because of his speed, athleticism and leadership, Colby overshadowed his friend and roommate, equipment manager John D. Rockefeller, Jr. Meanwhile, at a short distance south of Maine's Colby College, named after Everett Colby's great grandfather, two men, Norman Lermond and Ed Pelton, were in discussion about the economy, a discussion that would lead to life-changing events for Pastor Nordquist and, especially, his blossoming 16-year-old daughter, Rachel.

—— • ——

"Ed?"

The small living room was quiet except for the occasional sound of newspaper pages being turned. The voice waited and then broke a lengthy silence.

"Ed?"

"What's that, Norman?" responded Ed Pelton. Pelton, tall with sandy hair and mustache, looked up from a living room easy chair. Smoke wafted from his pipe, momentarily abandoned. Pelton was gifted with an amiable expression that made people feel good and, as Pelton put his pipe in his mouth, he reflexively beamed at Norman Lermond, his eyes somehow lightly coruscating, sparkling. Like most people, Lermond liked Pelton. But there were people Lermond didn't like.

"You read today's paper?" asked Norman Wallace Lermond as he swung his swivel chair to the right and looked over the top of the paper at his friend and business associate.

"No," replied Ed again puffing placidly on his pipe. "You read all the papers. You read enough for me and ten other people. I can worry enough from reading one paper, much less a dozen."

Norman Lermond let the paper slowly fall to his lap.

"You have to read a lot of papers to get a clear focus on the truth," said Lermond. "One paper alone won't give you the whole truth."

"You read one paper, you get lies; you read a bunch of papers, you get a pack of lies. I don't see how reading a pack of lies gets you any closer to the truth, Norman. At best, you'll get an extraordinary distortion of the truth." Pelton looked down at his hunting knife that he was about to sharpen. "Not that I care."

"Ed," retorted Lermond, "I can't understand how you can just sit and not care. All this…graft, bribery, outright larceny! What do those people use for ethics?"

"Very little, Norman."

"Damn' right 'very little,'" said Lermond, looking at the paper. "It's been one problem after another." He looked up at Pelton. "The first depression was between 1873 and 1878. Then there was a six-year hiatus until the next depression between 1884 and 1887. Remember? Then came another six-year lay-off until the panic in '93. And now poverty and disappointment are again epidemic among farmers, laborers, shopkeepers…guys like you, Ed. Guys who work long and hard just to keep a roof overhead."

"I know that, Norman," said Pelton, annoyed but not showing it. "I know that."

"In stark contrast," Lermond whacked the newspaper with the back of his hand, "there's the East Coast plutocracy whose wealth-flaunting is so practiced that if similarly continued, it might become an Olympic event, and I wouldn't be surprised if the vice president is selling secrets to the Chinese, or the president has a mistress in the White House!"

Ed Pelton looked perplexed. Lermond seemed to be blathering impossible twaddle. "What?" asked Pelton.

"Where's this all gonna end, Ed?" asked Lermond, who then repeated adamantly, "Where's it gonna end?"

"Norman, how am I going to answer that?" asked Pelton as he held his hands out questioningly. "What the hell are you talking about?"

"Well, start with William Marcy Tweed and the gang of Tammany politicians with their collective hand in the New York City treasury, an act made possible by a bunch of corrupt judges. Then go to the Crédit Mobilier scandal with government bribery leading all the way to the Vice President. The White House, Ed! Then the Star Route gang that included federal officials and congressmen defraudin' the government. One depression after another. One scandal after another. The country's bein' run by a bunch 'a crooks! It's becoming hard to keep track, Ed – the bleeding colors all run together!"

"I know that, Norman. I'm not Rip Van Winkle."

"Well then, Ed, seriously, where's it gonna end?" asked Lermond again as he sat at his desk, looking at Pelton. "Graft. Everywhere. And everyone wants a solution, but no one has a solution. Oh, well, no, I take that back. Shari Kerry down the road," Lermond leaned forward and whispered, "says the Lord will *not* put up with this much longer."

"Yup." Ed Pelton beamed. "Scary Shari. 'The end is near.'"

"Maybe she's right," Lermond muttered with no conviction. "If there was ever a time for the end to be near, it would be now."

"Wasn't there a bunch of people," wondered Ed out loud, "who were standing on some hill a while back expecting the Second Comin'?"

"Yeah, I remember reading about that."

"Sold all their belongings. Went and stood on the hill. Don't see how as anyone could know, but there they stood. Some religious leader said that was where the Lord was gonna land."

"Did He show up?" asked Lermond without a trace of sarcasm.

"Who?"

"The Lord."

"No. I don't believe that happened," understated Pelton, balancing his pipe in the side of his mouth while studying the edge of his hunting knife.

"Musta been the wrong hill," said Lermond.

"Right, Norman," said Pelton unamused. "But it's amazing what some people will believe."

"No kiddin'."

"I learned in Sunday school that no one knows when that's going to happen," said Pelton, his eyes smiling. "Can't believe how gullible some people are."

"Seems like sometimes religion and gullibility go hand-in-hand. 'Ignorance is bliss," replied Lermond. "Just go off and believe stuff that makes no sense at all."

"But what puzzles me is when a whole bunch of people do it. Some of 'em pretty smart."

"Well, Ed, that's what I'm talking about," responded Lermond. "We're in a big financial mess in this country, people who are supposed t' be smart keep doin' the same things that don't work, and everybody keeps hoping things will get better when they're getting worse. Ed," continued Lermond, again hitting the paper with the back of his right hand, "there are serious problems here. Serious, serious problems. We – you and I – need to get involved."

Pelton sighed.

"I have serious problems of my own," responded Pelton. "I have more'n enough right now, Norman. Thanks anyway. I don't know what you want me to do about that stuff in the paper."

"Do more than sit there. Don't you think we have to do somethin'?"

"Do somethin'? You keep wantin' to do something, Norman. Change things. Save the world. Hell, I'd sure like to change things. But we're stuck. I have to deal with my own problems. So, whatever it is you might have in mind, thanks, but no thanks."

"But it goes all the way to the White House!" countered Lermond in a shrill tone of voice. "The *White House*! Every damned politician everywhere is taking their cut. Fraud. Graft. Rich businessmen paying off politicians left and right. All those crooks getting richer. The average working man is lost in the shuffle, totally forgotten. *Totally* forgotten."

"I know that, Norman. I don't need anyone else telling me." Annoyed, Pelton blew a stream of pipe smoke as if intentionally filling the air before him, and added: "Good Lord, Norman."

"You know," responded Lermond, peering over the rim of his glasses at his friend, "sometimes, Ed, you disappoint me."

"What? Now what're you talking about?"

"Here you are. You're broke. In a financial bind – just like all of us – but all you can think of is yourself, and you don't – I repeat, *don't* – want to do anything that might get you, and a whole lot of other people, including your wife, out of this miserable state of affairs."

"Horse manure, Norman."

"Ed," continued Lermond, "if somebody doesn't do something soon…well, it'll get *worse*. May seem like it can't get any worse, but it can. Maybe to the point where no one except the millionaires and the banks and the thieving, lying politicians own anything."

"Norman, what am I supposed to do?" asked Pelton in exasperation.

"It's not like you to hide, Ed."

"Wha'…I'm not *hidin'*!" Pelton looked irately at Lermond. "Where do you come *up* with that *hidin'* nonsense?"

"Well, then, what are you gonna *do*?"

"Hell, I don't *know* what I'm gonna do. If I *knew* what t' do, I'd *do* it!"

"Now, there," responded Lermond, sitting upright, wide-eyed. "There. You see. That's the same answer 99% of Americans would give. No one knows what to do, but if someone showed them, they would. Right?"

"'If someone showed them,'" echoed Pelton sarcastically. "Sure, Norman. Someone'll just run out, stand on the damn' North Pole, and yell, 'Hey! Look up here! Listen to meeeee! I know what to dooooo!' The trouble is even if someone knew, he couldn't get the word out. And then if he did, well, who can you believe anymore? Half of what you read is just bull. Norman, I don't know why you bother readin' all those papers. Those boys don't know any more 'n you or me."

"They don't know more 'n *you*, maybe," said Lermond as he pressed tobacco into the bowl of his pipe.

"What's that supposed to mean?" asked Pelton.

"I know what to do," said Lermond just before he lit his pipe.

Pelton looked at Lermond as if two teams of enemy lice were shooting at each other from Lermond's thick eyebrows.

"What?" responded Pelton, not believing what he just heard.

"You heard me. I know what t' do!" repeated Lermond. "The damned *New York Times* and the *Chicago Tribune* don't know what to do, but *I* do!"

"Hell, the papers…," said Pelton, "but, now, here you're sayin' you know. No one else knows, but Norman 'the Genius of Chickawaukie Pond' Lermond knows." Then Pelton looked at Lermond curiously. "Are you talking about that book you wrote? *How to Build Here and Now a Cooperative Commonwealth*? I think I'm the only one who ever read it. I can't say it inspired me…"

"It should have inspired you. It should have inspired a lot of people. People don't necessarily understand what they read though," stated Lermond, staring darts at Pelton.

"Norman, you're about four letters short of a jackass."

"Thanks," retorted Lermond. "And, Ed, you're a real good friend."

"Who told you that?"

"Absolutely no one," said Lermond as he made himself more comfortable. "Look, Ed, trust me. What I wrote is just the beginning. The rest is all right there in these two books." Awash in determination, Lermond impatiently nodded toward the bookshelf above his desk. "Right there," he said as he pointed toward the shelf.

Lermond pushed his chair away from the desk and reached for the books.

"What two books?" asked Pelton philistinely as he watched Lermond. "Ah, let me guess. *Alice's Adventures in Wonderland*…and *Strange Case of Dr. Jekyl and Mr. Hyde*." Pelton laughed.

"Listen, Ed," replied Lermond as he reached up to the bookshelf over the desk, "I don't mean some fiction bouncin' around; I mean something that no one's ever tried."

He reached back up and pulled down the second book.

"Now, don't you think that if something worked, people would continue to follow that course of action?"

"Yes," answered Pelton skeptically. "But if it hasn't been tried, Norman, how do you know it will work?"

"It will work because people will make it work. If people follow the principles as presented in these two books, it will work."

"What about that book you wrote…and published…*How to Build Here and Now*…? I believe that's been tried."

"No it hasn't been tried; close, but not quite. The principles have always been utopian – which is commendable – but implementation has always been flawed in the past. Not like what these two books present." Lermond looked at Pelton with grave seriousness. "And what I plan now."

Norman Lermond walked over to Ed Pelton, and stood with the two books balanced deferentially on each palm like the books were ancient Greek medallions.

"Just like findin' something no one believed existed," explained Lermond, an amateur conchologist. "It's like findin' two 'extinct' mollusks, male and female, both alive, side-by-side."

Ed Pelton looked at Lermond, at the books, and back at Lermond.

"Well?" asked Pelton.

"'Well', what?"

"What do the mollusks tell you? If you put those books up to your ears, can you hear the ocean?"

"Let me tell you what these say," said Lermond, giving Pelton a sour look. Lermond returned to the bookshelf, replaced the books, and turned to Pelton. "What Edward Bellamy has written…"

"Edward Bellamy? I read that. *Looking Backward*? And his second book, *Equality*. Is that what you're talkin' about?"

"Yes, that's what I'm talkin' about. And it'll work. Someone has to do it, however."

"And what you're sayin' is that 'someone' is us?"

"Bellamy hits the nail square on the head, Ed. And I think a lot of other people think the same thing. So, if you'll excuse me, I'll just put on my hat and coat and head for the North Pole."

Lermond sat down and stopped talking long enough to relight his pipe.

"Well?" repeated Pelton.

"'Well' what?" asked Lermond as he blew out the match.

"Start headin'."

"Okay, I might just do that," said Lermond confidently as he sat back. "You see, after reading *Looking Backward* and *Equality*, I have become inspired, Ed. And I believe I have the solution to this deep international recession. So I am going to start organizing what will be the beginning of the end of world wide economic misfortune. Forever!"

"I have no doubt you can go on talking forever."

"It isn't just talk, Ed. You obviously have no idea what these books say."

"Norman, like I just said, I read *Looking Backward*."

"Then you didn't understand it."

"It had merits."

"So, do you believe that type of society will work?"

"I don't know," said Ed, removing his pipe. "Maybe; maybe not."

"You need to read these two books more carefully, good man."

"All right, Moses V. Debs," said Pelton, "how are you going to lead us out of the capitalistic wilderness?"

"Bellamy wrote these books about the future," said Lermond, miffed at Pelton's skepticism. "How things could be. Right now it's 1896. This book is about what the future will be after the year 2000!"

"Yeah but, hell, you don't know what's going to happen tomorrow morning, Norman."

Lermond looked at Pelton with disgust.

"No, but I have some ideas about what'll happen after that. The concept found in these books offers viable change. Change we can believe in! The fundamental tenet of these books, Ed, is that people have to envision cooperative civilization as an army."

"An army," echoed Pelton.

"Like the U.S. army," explained Lermond. "And everyone has to realize that the whole army is greater than the soldiers in the army. In other words, people have to know they're morally compelled to contribute but, on the other hand, can only receive what they need."

"I've never quite understood how that could work," said Pelton.

"Okay," responded Lermond, "let me put it this way. Pretend you're in the army. You're out on the battlefield. I'm running in front of you and – blam! – I get shot. I go down. Wounded real bad. The enemy's shooting at both you and me. What're you going to do?"

"I'd try to rescue you," answered Pelton, "first aid, something. Stop the bleeding, apply a tourniquet. Carry you to the rear."

"But you could get shot doing that," said Lermond. "If you try to carry me out of harm's way, you could get shot. Both of us would be up a creek. So, what are you gonna do?"

"Norman, I could get shot doin' anything then. Hell, the enemy is tryin' t' kill me. I have t' do what's right, and what's right is to try'n save you. Granted, you aren't *worth* savin' but, as far as what I should do, that's the honorable thing. So that's what I'd do. I'd hope you'd do the same for me."

"You wouldn't leave me to die?" asked Lermond.

"Hell, no, I wouldn't leave you to die!" retorted Ed Pelton. "Men in my family were at Vicksburg, Gettysburg... We're no cowards!"

"You'd do the right thing?" Norman Lermond asked. "The honorable thing?"

"What the hell is this all about, Norman?" asked Pelton. His normally affable, easygoing countenance was gone as he leaned back in his chair and stared at Lermond.

"Here's my point," answered Lermond. "If we get people to use the same principles in peacetime as in war – where we have no qualms about helping one another under difficult conditions, even to the point of risking our lives – we wouldn't have all this economic misery we have now."

"Act like we're at war?"

"That's the solution," said Lermond. "People have to feel like heroes when they sacrifice for the greater good, and feel like cowards when they act out of pure selfishness. You get it?"

"Um. Yeah," answered Pelton, "I get it. But I don't get how you would get others to get it."

"We start an army," answered Lermond. "A civilian army."

"'A civilian army,'" echoed Pelton, his face contorted.

"Yes. With the same rules of conduct as a real army. The army, like I said, is more important than the individual soldiers. And, like an army, the heroes are the ones who will sacrifice for their comrades in arms, and the cowards are the ones who only give a damn about themselves."

"Sacrifice," repeated Pelton. "Again, I read that book. Sounds like you mean sacrificin' everything. What about ownin' stuff? You know, people havin', say, cows?"

"In our army, nobody owns anything, but everybody, together, owns everything. It's the army. The goal is for everybody to work toward taking care of the army, that is, the country. Everybody working together to take care of the army means everybody is taken care of. Nobody stands alone. Nobody stays destitute, hungry."

"So, everybody owns everything," said Pelton, "and everybody takes care of everybody else. That it?"

"It's a reasonable summation," said Lermond.

"I can't see it. Everybody'll take care of everybody else until one opportunist decides everybody else should just take care of him."

"Not if we stick to the principles of a civilian army."

"I still can't see it."

"Then you're blind. And since you can't see, I'll tell you how things look now. It's a mess out there because nobody takes care of anybody. Everybody – like you – is too busy trying to take care of just himself. Get an army of people together, working together, taking care of the army, and everyone involved is productive, equal and happy. Equality. True equality and happiness." Lermond looked levelly at Pelton. "Are you tired of being broke, Ed?"

"Yup."

"Have you been in the army?"

"Yup."

"Have you ever wanted to go back in the army?"

"I've thought about it," said Ed. "Especially when things are really bad. I figure at least my wife and I'd eat...if it came to that."

"Well, right now, Ed, a lot of men think the same thing," said Lermond in an almost mystical tone-of-voice that made Pelton uneasy. "What this is called," Lermond began to explain, "is 'socialism'..."

"I know that, Norman."

"...where everybody owns everything, but nobody owns anything in particular. I tell you, this is something we have to do. People have to know."

"Most everyone knows."

"No they don't. Ed, if people really knew what this was, every American would get down on their knees and pray to God that some day they will have the opportunity to live in a socialist society because, I'm telling you, Ed, this world would be a far better place."

"How." Pelton cynically raised his right hand.

"Listen, Ed. I have some novel ideas," said Lermond animatedly. "I got those ideas from these books. Our goal is to get our own territory claimed for socialism." Lermond looked at Pelton solemnly. "Ed, we have to socialize an entire state."

"Wha'? 'An entire state'?" echoed Pelton, looking at Lermond like he had coots building a nest in his hair. "You mean one of the United States states?"

"Yeeup," responded Lermond. "We have to do that if we're to show the rest of the world how it works. Set an example. First one state, then, when everyone else sees how well we do, the entire United States will follow along." Lermond looked intently at Pelton. "You believe that, Ed?"

"Which state, Norman?"

"I don't know."

"Try Missouri," said Pelton skeptically. "If you can show them, no doubt everyone else will jump on board."

"Are you on board?" asked Lermond.

"We'll see."

Lermond formed the Brotherhood of Cooperative Commonwealth (BCC), the object of which was...

"...to educate the people in the principles of socialism; to unite all socialists into one fraternal organization; to establish cooperative colonies and industries, and so far as is possible, concentrate those colonies and industries in one state until said state is 'socialized.'"

———————————◆———————————

Lermond was so anxious to get started, he could hardly sleep.

"I've got the BCC pointed and ready to fire, Ed."

"So you're out to sell socialism?" responded Ed irreverently.

"Yes." Lermond felt giddy thinking he was finally there.

"An' who do you think is gonna buy it?"

"Lotsa people. It's not just what it is, but how it's packaged, Ed. The idea of socializing an entire state has never been tried. Unspoiled by large, existing capitalist enterprises, and attended by a host of like-minded men and women, we can build a brotherhood of unselfish camaraderie within the confines of a single state…our own socialist country." Norman gave Ed a look of sincerity. "I can sell that."

"What states are candidates for being socialized, Norman?"

"So that the movement isn't contaminated," replied Lermond, "it is necessary to colonize a state with a very modest population. We establish my system and we bring in the right people."

"Missouri?"

"No, not Missouri, Ed," said Lermond with some aggravation. "Too many people already. I'm thinking of the South. Tennessee, maybe."

Lermond obtained population and land area statistics for Tennessee, and concluded Tennessee was far too populated.

Arkansas? A lot of people already beat Lermond to the punch in Arkansas.

Although substantially rural, the South was too settled. Lermond hoped to stay east of the Mississippi River, enabling most prospective colonists shorter travel, but was forced to conclude the odds would be better if he looked west.

Oregon?

Again, already too many people.

While the effort was underway to determine which state should be colonized, Lermond milked the discontent of Populists, Christian Socialists and a growing number of new political organizations clamoring for social and economic reform. Contributions were slow at first. After a while, however, through propaganda tracts, promotional newsletters and word-of-mouth, momentum increased, and Norman Lermond began raising substantial sums of money from an exponentially growing number of supporters nationwide. Change they could believe in.

Ed Pelton was astounded.

"Norman," said Ed, resharpening his hunting knife, "I can't believe this. People are really sending you money. Not just a few bucks here and there, but real money. I suppose there's no hurry, Norman," said Ed as he stretched, "what with people sending money. The longer you take, the more money's available for whatever you need to do. Hell, you could take forever and then call the whole thing off."

"I would not do that, Ed. But it's good I have time. I don't want to make a mistake. The future of mankind depends on this – a chance like this will never come again." Lermond looked solemnly at Pelton. "People are sendin' money for a reason, Ed. The audacity of hope. Say what sounds good, avoid the complexity of the issue, generally promise in a manner that implies you understand people's needs, and they'll *want* to believe you. But in this case they have good reason to believe. Socialism, Ed." Lermond nodded sagely as if to suggest that America was finally waking up. Ed looked back, one eyebrow raised, and drew on his pipe.

June 1897

On the outskirts of Everett, two of the most powerful men in America, James J. Hill and John D. Rockefeller, joined by Reverend Frederick T. Gates, met in Rockefeller's private railway car.

It would have been a monumental occasion except no one knew they were there.

Hill, who was sold on Everett, but unwilling to commit to Everett until the national economy improved, agreed to buy remaining Rockefeller-owned Everett properties except the smelter. Hill wondered what anyone would do with the smelter since there was nothing to smelt.

As Gates and Hill talked, Rockefeller looked out the train window toward the hillside city of Everett with its struggling population. Everett. Named after his son's athletic, charismatic, college roommate who, out of curiosity, had already clandestinely been to Everett with Rockefeller's son, John Jr.

Rockefeller thought of Everett's father, Charles Colby, and sighed sadly. But philanthropy is philanthropy and business is business, and sometimes so is philanthropy. Compromising business principles only results in more trouble, he thought, as the Everett undertaking demonstrated. Hewitt, Colby and Hoyt left too much to chance. Inadvertenly so did I, Rockefeller thought. While Hill and Gates went over the assets, Rockefeller studied the young city's skyline. If not for the Panic of 1893, Rockefeller thought, Henry Hewitt would have realized his dream, and in future decades Everett would have been unrecognizable. The West Coast New York. Running along the top of the hill was Colby Avenue. It intersected with Wall Street and paralleled Broadway. And another arterial, he knew, was named Rockefeller Avenue. For a moment his studious expression relaxed. Everett. It was a grand scheme. In his heart, Rockefeller wished the young city well and, when through with the Empire Builder, he left.

———————— •———————

Meanwhile, Norman Lermond figured out which state to socialize.

90

O kay, Ed," said Lermond, "I've studied this long enough. I know which state it will be."

"Are you sure you don't just want to take the money and run?"

"Ed, you're about as idealistic as a fox in a henhouse." Lermond held his hands out. "Now, listen to me. I feel good about this. There is no doubt in my mind."

"So," responded Pelton, "where are you going next, Norman?"

"Not me, Ed. You."

"Me?"

"You're out of work, Ed. Nothing to do. Your wife wants something better. You know land better than I do. People naturally like you – I don't happen to enjoy that luxury." Lermond drew on his pipe. "I'll cover all your expenses while you're looking for a colony site, and I'll pay you to do it."

"Where would I be going?"

"Out west."

Pelton looked thoughtfully at Lermond for a moment and said, "Give me a day to think about it."

Pelton knew that Lermond received substantial donations. Organizational momentum was already going strong, and Lermond was receiving enough seed money to start and sustain his dream: start one colony, get it up and running, and start another…and then another. Pelton saw he could be in on the ground floor. Neither Pelton nor his wife wanted to move, but figured that if Lermond held up his end of the bargain, in the long run the move would be worth the effort.

"Okay," responded Pelton the next day. "I was about to die of boredom anyway. Where are you sending me?"

"To Washington," said Lermond with a self-satisfied expression.

"Washington?" Pelton looked puzzled for a moment. "D.C.?"

"No, Washington state!"

"Where *is* that?"

"Right here, Ed," said Lermond, showing Pelton a map.

"Few people. Lots of variety. Farmland, timberland, mountains, rivers, valleys, fish, wildlife. Plenty of water." Lermond looked at Pelton and with urgency added, "It's all there, Ed, and we need to get movin' immediately. My plan is to stay here in Maine fortifyin' the BCC while you go find the first colony site in Washington. Then I'll follow you out there."

Lermond dispatched Ed Pelton to locate and establish a colony site while Lermond remained in Warren, Maine, attending to the heady matters of the ballooning BCC.

Anna watched Rachel straining to pull on a pair of work pants that fit perfectly a couple of months ago. Rachel was preparing to help milk the cows and carry the pails of milk in from the barn. When in their early teens, Inga and Esther looked older than they were but quit maturing at around 15. As beautiful Rachel matured, Rachel's sisters' hand-me-down dresses quickly quit fitting her, being too loose around the waist, and too tight everywhere else. At 15, Rachel looked like she should quit maturing…but she did not. Nor did she stop at 16. Tall, long-legged, broad-shouldered, full-chested, strong and athletic with bronze-colored hair that shimmered in the light, she was expanding curves where curves were wanted but, thought Anna, my golly. It was as if God decided to make Rachel His pet art project, subtly refining a little here, adding a shade more there, spending considerably more time with Rachel than with His many other female projects.

Anna studied Rachel's face and shook her head; Rachel's facial symmetry would put a Greek statue to shame. From whom did she inherit all this? Anna wondered. Anna was very attractive at the same age, but Rachel had gone beyond being very attractive. Amos and his brother Anders were both good looking, thought Anna. I guess Rachel got it all. Anna was simultaneously proud but apprehensive.

Ed Pelton arrived in Seattle in August 1897 and wasted no time looking around. Based on conversations with local residents, he concluded the optimum location for a big logging and farming operation would be well north of Seattle up in Snohomish County or Skagit County. He rode north, and liked what he saw around Edison and Blanchard in northwest Skagit County. Reducing the possibility for the local rumor mill to warm up, Pelton made his first purchase, 280 acres for $10 an acre, in his own name, waited until any talk ran its course, and quietly transferred title to the BCC.

Using money from Lermond, Ed Pelton made several more purchases and by 1898 the BCC had 600 contiguous acres, some of which could be farmed, but most of which could be logged, then farmed.

While land was being accumulated, Lermond recruited prospective residents for his socialist Nirvana.

Summer 1898

While not as desperate as two years earlier, the times were still bad and for Lermond that was good. Lermond provided ads and articles in the socialist weekly *Coming Nation*, a national publication that mirrored his convictions and served his purposes. More money, more letters of interest flowed in from a nation filled with unhappy people in search of hope.

Norman Lermond moved the BCC national headquarters from Warren, Maine, across county to Edison, Washington. In conformity with the motivating ideology, Lermond named the new colony "Equality."

Industrial Freedom, the newsletter Lermond began, had over 2,000 subscribers, and sensationalized the merits of socialism and the plan to convert the entire Washington state to socialism. Lermond sold hope during difficult times, and the sales pitch was effective. From across the country, discontented idealists with the required $160 membership fee committed to Equality, flowing into the colony in a small but steady stream.

Fall 1898

Three years passed since the near-death of little Jacob. Mongoloid children, Doc had told Anna, can have short lifespans, and eventually Anna would have to deal with something similar to what almost happened.

Joshua and Jacob were eight. Inga and Esther now had the last name Odegaard, and 18-year-old Rachel was an aunt five times over.

"Mom, I'm not entirely certain of the meaning of the word 'colony'?" said Rachel, staring at a polished apple as she stood next to the kitchen sink while lost in thought, as she often was. "What does it mean exactly?"

"A colony," said Anna, sifting flour, "is formed when a small group of people from a larger city, or even country, move to an isolated, unpopulated area and begin what may eventually become a more prominent township; for example, the first 13 states – initially called colonies."

"I know, mom."

"And if you knew," Anna said as she put down the flour sifter, "why did you ask?"

"I just wondered."

"No one 'just wonder's," countered Anna. "Why did you ask?"

"There's a colony being started up north on the east hillside," said Rachel.

"A 'colony'?" responded Anna, trying to adjust her perception of what Rachel meant. "What do you mean a 'colony'?"

"I asked you first, mom," said Rachel. "I asked you what a colony was, you told me, and now you're asking *me* what a colony is." Rachel turned and raised her left hand, the back against her forehead. "I find this conversation very confusing."

"Young lady," responded Anna, "a 'colony' – as I understand the term – on that hillside is difficult to grasp. Why don't you tell me a little more about it?"

"A man named Mr. Pelton," began Rachel, "moved there along with a number of other people to start a colony. That's what they call it. A 'colony.' I met some of them this morning. They say they are going to rely only on themselves and no one else." Anna looked at Rachel without expression as Rachel turned back toward the drain board. "They're rather snobbish about the whole thing," continued Rachel, "as if the rest of the world were a bunch of idiots. They said they were going to start the colony here, and then gradually colonize the whole state. The whole, entire state."

Rachel continued to study the apple in the light of the kitchen window as Anna looked at her daughter, puzzled. Colonize the whole state? Anna wondered. It's already a state…what do they mean by "colonize."

"Do you think they can do that?" Rachel asked. "First they'd colonize Edison, then Snohomish, then Hamilton, then…"

"I'm still not certain what they mean when they use the term 'colonize.' I'm missing something. Why 'colonize' Hamilton when it's already there?"

"I guess they're going to set an example to show everyone else how to live together. And Snohomish, Hamilton and everywhere else will want to do exactly what the first colonists do."

"It sounds pretty far-fetched to me," responded Anna, clearing off the drain board.

"They sure talk like they can do it," said Rachel.

"Talk is one thing; doing is another," countered Anna. "We can talk about peeling apples, but that alone does not get them peeled. How old were these people with whom you spoke?"

"Some were kids; some young adults."

Rachel picked up another apple in her left hand, while still holding an apple in her right, and attempted to simultaneously toss each in the air and catch them with the opposite hand. The left apple landed in the right hand, but the right apple bounced from the left hand to the kitchen counter to the floor. Quickly bending over to pick it up, Rachel bounced her head on the edge of the drain board.

"Yeeouch!" exclaimed Rachel, dropping the apple in her right hand and momentarily grabbing her forehead with her left hand before groping for both apples with her right.

"Rachel, for goodness sakes watch yourself!" said Anna spontaneously.

"Watch myself? How can I watch myself?" retorted Rachel painfully. "I am myself!"

"Rachel," responded Anna calmly, "whoever you are, please be careful." Anna walked to Rachel and removed Rachel's hand from her forehead. "Here, let me see what you've done." Anna studied Rachel's forehead as Rachel looked back. "It's not too bad, Rachel. Minor cut. You'll probably have a not-so-minor bruise though."

Anna daubed the small cut with a clean washcloth dampened with hot water from the kettle.

"Tell me more about these colonists."

"'Colonist.' You know, that's a funny word," said Rachel.

"Why? What's funny about it?"

"It seems like a colonist should be someone who lives in a colon."

Anna resisted the impulse to compare what Rachel just said with what actually exists in a colon.

"Tell me about these colonists on the hillside, Rachel."

"I talked to them – ouch – for a half hour. One young man was rather strange in a pleasant, entertaining sort of way," continued Rachel, "and, eh hem, very good looking."

"I'm sure he was impressed with you," said Anna, lightly drying Rachel's forehead with another clean cloth. For good measure Anna put a cloth bandage over the cut, and began wrapping a cloth strip around Rachel's forehead to keep the bandage in place.

"Mom, now I'm sure to impress everyone," Rachel said after a moment, "seeing how I look like I just returned from the Civil War. Gettysburg. Mom."

"You'll only need this for a few minutes," said Anna, ignoring Rachel's complaining. "How many young men were there?"

"Three," answered Rachel in a normal tone of voice, polishing another apple. "They were all brothers. It doesn't hurt anymore. The good-looking, strange one is 19, and the others are around 17 and 14, I think."

"Just keep it on a moment longer. And I guess you were quite smitten by the 14-year-old."

"Yes!!" responded Rachel with exaggerated emotion. Rachel's eyes grew large. "He was *extremely* handsome," said Rachel. "I was so in love I could hardly speak. And he would have been so proud of me had he known I single-handedly took Little Round Top. Perhaps we shall elope this evening after dinner." Rachel looked at her nonplused mother with a wide-eyed, panicked expression. "But, oh! There..." The apple fell and bounced on the drain board as Rachel's left-hand shot up to join her right hand covering her cheeks. "I wasn't supposed to tell [the back of her left hand again rose to her bandaged forehead as her eyes closed] and look what I have done. How shall I ever explain my indiscretion to…to… oh, I am so overwhelmed, now I can't remember his name," she moaned as if grief stricken.

"I'm sure," said Anna, underwhelmed by the melodrama.

Hands returning to their normal positions, Rachel bit into the apple, and gave her mother a vinegary look.

"These are good for pies but…echh, this is sour!"

"Rachel, peel, don't eat. What *is* his name?" asked Anna.

"The 19-year-old?" answered Rachel, chewing. "Jared. Jared Young."

"What does he look like?"

Rachel looked out the window and imagined Jared in her mind's eye.

"He's about Dad's height and he has wavy brown hair, a mustache, but no beard, and very attractive facial features. Brown eyes; really nice brown eyes. His eyes continually sparkle. I'm not sure how that happens. He smiles a lot, and when he looks at you," Rachel looked at her mother, "you immediately feel happy."

"Does he seem intelligent?"

"I don't know for sure," said Rachel, thinking. "It's hard to tell because he has a weird sense-of-humor – it's difficult to know when he's serious." Rachel shrugged her shoulders. "An awful lot of what he says is off-the-wall, and you have to think, 'What did he just mean?' I guess with his odd sense-of-humor he must be intelligent. Dumb guys usually have little or no sense of humor, much less one that's…creative."

"Any girls?" asked Anna.

"Two," said Rachel, still chewing, but now absently re-polishing the uneaten 7/8's of the partly eaten apple. "They were little, maybe 9 or 10 or 11." Rachel peered at the highly polished, partially eaten apple as if it were a crystal ball. Her eyes grew large. "They saaaid," said Rachel in an eerie tone-of-voice, still gazing at the apple, "that the colony leaders didn't like girls as much as boys because girls couldn't do the hard work that needed to be done."

Rachel looked at her mother smugly. "They obviously don't know *us*."

Anna looked back at Rachel, at the partially-eaten apple in Rachel's hand, and at Rachel again.

"Peel those," said Anna. "What else did they say?"

"Mom, I washed the dishes, the kitchen floor, brought in the laundry and folded it," Rachel responded defensively, iterating what she had actually done before the embellishment: "I painted the living room, built a new back porch, and plowed the south pasture. All in less than two hours. Don't worry; I'll make short work of these apples. You will stand amazed."

Anna looked at Rachel out of the corner of her eye.

"They have their own money," continued Rachel. "I mean it's different, not gold, gold or silver certificates or United States Notes. Not real. I guess even if everything is owned in common, they still need money." Rachel shrugged her shoulders. "I don't know what it looks like – they didn't show me – but they said it was different. Mom, you know, I'd worry about that. Whoever is responsible for printing the money could easily make plenty for just him, and not tell the others."

"I'm sure that money-printing is not entrusted to one individual acting alone," said Anna.

After putting the perfectly polished, partly eaten apple down, Rachel hummed, picking up and inspecting another apple.

Anna stared at Rachel as if a tiny frog had just crawled out Rachel's nose. I'm losing my mind, thought Anna. Does this Martian hear *any*thing? Anna, shaking her head, began measuring three cups of flour, a tablespoon of sugar, and a teaspoon of salt. Anna's patience was waning.

"Rachel, please go outside and get the cold butter from the creek."

Rachel went outside to the creek to get the butter that her mother kept as cold as possible before using it in pie dough.

"There aren't many children," offered Rachel, upon returning. Rachel put down the butter and picked up the wooden spoon sitting in the bowl used to make cake frosting earlier. "Or women." She paused, her mouth forming an irreverent smirk. Rachel glanced at her already agitated mother and made a bad decision. Rachel feigned a gleam in her eye and said, "Mostly mennnnn" as she aggressively began sensuously licking frosting from the large wooden spoon, "mmmmm…."

"Rachel!!!"

Rachel's little act brought more than the intended consequence as Anna, her patience at an end, grabbed the spoon from Rachel's hand, flipped it into the sink, and reached for Rachel with both hands as Rachel, eyes exaggeratedly widened in mock terror, began back-peddling with her hands outstretched in protection against her aggravated, angry, disgusted, caring mother.

Regaining her self-control, Anna stopped, put her hands on her hips, and for a moment glowered at her daughter. Rachel looked back inquisitively as if this were part of Act III, Scene 2, as if wanting to know what would happen next.

"Young lady," Anna said in a monotone that did not belie the fact she was steaming inside, "your father and I both appreciate your very different sense of humor, but don't push it. You know that wasn't funny. What you just did…for cryin' out loud, I'm your mother. What in the world was going through your head, Rachel?"

"Momma, I wasn't… I was just…"

"'Just'?" interrupted Anna angrily, eyes wide, her intelligence insulted.

"But, Momma," said Rachel, "the Bible doesn't say: 'Thou shalt not jest and make mirth.'"

"We both know that 'mirth' was not what upset me – nor what you intended to use to upset me. I would never get upset about laughter as long as the basis was truly funny."

"Mother, you're too proper."

Anna paused, struggling to maintain her properness.

"'Proper?'" Anna looked intently at Rachel. "That's a bad thing?"

"Mom, I only…"

'Proper' simply demands that 'mirth', as you call it, must actually be funny. Not disgusting, stupid or vulgar."

"I know but…"

"Let me explain it," said Anna, looking at Rachel. "You're a very bright young lady, Rachel, but you need to exercise discretion. It is often unwise to act-out whatever just comes into your head. While I like to laugh – I *love* to laugh, in fact – sometimes what the world passes for humor simply isn't funny." Anna held her hands out before her. "Adult humor for example. Besides being a stretch as far as wit is concerned, what's 'adult' about adult humor? Stupid stuff," added Anna as she stepped back. "Within the bounds of 'proper,' humor is never stupid or offensive, and is truly funny."

"Mom, all I did…that wasn't 'adult humor.'"

"It wasn't adult behavior either. Rachel, maintain your standards."

"Mom, I'm not compromising anyth…"

"You're also not listening. Things that are truly funny are wonderful. Think. Only weaklings find humor in things jaded or crass. Weaklings. You're not a weakling. Don't behave like one."

"Mom, I'm sorry," said Rachel unconvincingly.

"You don't see what I see because you've not seen what I've seen." Anna looked apprehensively at Rachel, hoping that the 18-year-old's path in life would continue along the straight and narrow way.

"Rachel," said Anna, "I worry about you, and you know I do. You're extraordinarily attractive…and you know that too. I was your age not that long ago, and I was also quite attractive, but not like you are. Temptation is always around. The world searches for, entraps and ruins young women like you. It always begins innocently enough. Appearances at your age are deceiving. Until you're more discerning, it is my responsibility to protect you from the groping hands of a heartless world. I reacted as I did because I love you," emphasized Anna. "And you know that too."

Rachel said nothing.

"Again, you are a beautiful young woman," Anna said softly. "Outside and inside. I want you to stay that way."

Anna sighed, inwardly praying that the words inspired by her feelings of apprehension were not falling on deaf ears. Looking at Rachel, Anna knew Rachel could have any man she wanted, but that what she wanted should not be just any man.

91

Anna knew physical sensuality was a double-edged sword, and at that moment Anna wished Rachel had a more ordinary appearance, for it was eerie how much Rachel had grown to resemble Molly B'Dam.

"After you're through inspecting the apples," Anna said, referring to Rachel's crystal ball behavior earlier, "please peel them."

Returning to the task of making pie dough, Anna began dicing the cold butter.

"Now, what else did they say about the 'colony'?"

"Everyone owns everything," answered Rachel, as she picked up a knife for peeling, "...whatever that means."

"Who is responsible for decisions?" asked Anna.

"Everyone," answered Rachel. "I suppose. They make decisions as a community. And they work together for the mutual benefit of all."

"That sounds like a wonderful place," said Anna without conviction.

"They said the colony," added Rachel, "is organized according to two books called *Looking Backward* and *Equality*. In fact, that's what they call their colony: 'Equality.' They said everyone is equal."

"And what did you say about them preferring men instead of women because of the physical labor that needed to be done?" asked Anna as she added the water to the diced butter and reached for the eggbeater.

"I don't know," answered Rachel. "I'm not sure they know either."

"I'm not familiar with the book *Equality*," said Anna as she added the flour/sugar/salt/cinnamon and began beating the mixture with a thick, wooden spoon, "but I read *Looking Backward* shortly before we made the trip from Minnesota to Murray. It was quite popular back East. It was about a Bostonian placed in a trance in order to help him go to sleep at night. He was placed in such an extreme state of rest that he didn't wake up until the year 2000."

"2000?" echoed Rachel. "That's over a hundred years from now."

"Waking up in the 21st century, he goes through a difficult period getting used to how much Boston has changed in over 100 years."

"How much?"

"All the buildings are very tall, the government controls everything, and no one suffers for want of any material need. The country is run by an enlightened committee, and there is no currency in circulation. Everyone uses something called a credit card, and the committee gives them a certain amount of credit each year with which to purchase items at huge government-owned stores that, in theory, have anything you might want to buy."

"Anything? How fantastic," responded Rachel. "How much credit do they get? I mean, how does the committee determine how much each person is to receive?"

"By law, each person must work," answered Anna as she added about a half cup of cold water, "but each person receives the same amount of credit regardless of what their occupation is."

"So a pastor gets paid as much as a steel magnate," said Rachel.

"Yes," said Anna as she continued beating the mixture.

"Do they take collections in church?" asked Rachel.

"No," said Anna, grimacing from the effort of mixing the dense pie dough. "Hypothetically, there would be no need for offerings. Church operating expenses would be paid by the state."

Anna said nothing for a moment, concentrating on the task at hand. After the dough became more manageable, she continued the discussion.

"The pastor would receive a state credit card for support of his family," said Anna, "and the church buildings would all be owned by the state. The need for new church buildings would subsequently be determined by the state."

Rachel, listening, stood looking at her mother, uneasy about state control of churches. "There is no 'state,' mom, just the people who run it."

"True enough; and that would be a concern. Meanwhile, Rachel, apples."

"Yes, mom."

Rachel quickly began peeling an apple.

"Would the new buildings be for any denomination," asked Rachel, "or would there be a denominational preference?"

"The committee would determine that. I suppose." Anna thought for a moment. "I don't know. I suppose it would depend on which denomination was growing fastest in which locations. Or maybe just committee preference."

"Then, in order to start a new church, it would first be necessary to be part of an existing, growing denomination," added Rachel, "and approval would have to come from the committee. Just starting a new church, like you and daddy do, would not be possible."

"I suppose."

"There are an awful lot of 'I suppose's in all this," said Rachel. "Why would, say, a doctor want to work for the same wage as a chimney sweep? And what would be the incentive to work hard?"

"There would be an established and well-publicized job hierarchy," answered Anna, "but credit would not be awarded based on this hierarchy."

"Would that work?" asked Rachel skeptically.

Anna began kneading the dough in the bowl, feeling for correct texture.

"According to the book, *Looking Backward*, there would be a new morality."

"'New morality'?" responded Rachel. "Meaning what?"

"Awarding equal credit for all jobs met with no disfavor," replied Anna, "because the system of morality changed. In the 21st century, the book says, people would be willing to work hard out of a sense of patriotism…just as if they were in the army during wartime. Each person would be expected to treat strangers like members of their own outfit, and to work toward the support of others in the interest of the common good. It would be a source of shame to be found not working to one's potential.

"For example," continued Anna, "if one could *peel apples*, and one failed to do so, then failure to peel the apples would be a source of embarrassment. Much different than today, don't you think?"

"Uhm, yes mom," said Rachel as she began peeling another apple.

"In Bellamy's new world," said Anna, "not working to one's potential would be considered treasonous." Anna looked at Rachel who looked back incredulously. "Seriously," responded Anna. "Treasonous."

"So people could be shot for not working."

"I suppose."

"That might not be a bad idea," said Rachel semi-seriously after a moment. Anna looked at Rachel out of the corner of her eye, and then at the awaiting apples.

"In any event," Anna continued, "people would supposedly get more credit than they were expected to need, as determined by the central committee, and would never abuse the amount of credit available to them."

Anna rapidly brushed her hands together to remove small pieces of pie dough, but it seemed to Rachel that her mother's action was criticizing the last point.

"How much credit would they receive?" asked Rachel as she began peeling.

"I don't know."

"How does the committee know how much credit is more than needed?"

"I don't know. How do they do it at Equality?" asked Anna. "Perhaps you could find out?"

Rachel stopped peeling for a moment.

"If I lived under this system," volunteered Rachel, "I would choose to be a stage actress."

Rachel looked at her reflection in the kitchen window.

"Why not?" Rachel continued. "I would get as much credit for being an actress as I would for being a physician or pastor's wife. But I could become famous."

Rachel absentmindedly twirled a tress of her long hair as she studied her image in the window. She subtly pulled her shoulders back slightly.

"I could be a good actress."

"At the same time," Anna responded, ignoring Rachel's last proclamation, "I'm not sure that anyone who is *not* in the workforce receives credit. A pastor's wife would not receive a credit card, only her husband, the pastor."

"Hmm." Rachel thought some more. "What about people who are too old to work?"

"In the 21st century," answered Anna, with the base of her palms flattening the first half of the pie dough on the floured drain board, "according to the book, everyone reaches mandatory retirement at the ripe old age of 45. They keep using their credit card, however."

"After they retire, what do they do?" asked Rachel.

"Have fun. Whatever they like, I suppose."

"'I suppose,'" repeated Rachel.

"I suppose."

"Since, at age 45," Rachel began to ask, "they have probably reached the point where they're really good at whatever it is the committee has decided they should no longer do, shouldn't they continue to do it?"

"Apparently not."

"Why not?" asked Rachel, almost smiling.

"I'm not sure," answered Anna. "I su… I *suppose* there are people waiting to have that job."

"Who – for how long – has been sitting around waiting for a job?" asked Rachel.

"Persons who have tested as having a high aptitude, and have subsequently been trained for that profession. Some might be actresses."

"How does the committee determine how many people should be trained for what kind of jobs?" asked Rachel.

"Supposedly," answered Anna, "according to the relationship between the number of workers needed in any job category and the number of people already trained for that job. The government determines how many jobs are needed and who is trained for each job."

"How do they know how many jobs are needed? And who is really good and who isn't so good? General McClellan was supposed to be good, but he wasn't."

"That's a good question," responded Anna, expertly rolling out the pie dough, "the answer to which, I am afraid, was not made clear in the book. In fact, the author, obviously with the best of intentions, indulged in a great deal of wishful-thinking. He failed to give the concept enough critical consideration."

"The boys from Equality think he did," said Rachel. "They say people are coming from all over the world to be part of it. The boys are certain it will be successful and all others will want to join and, consequently, the whole state of Washington will adopt the same system. 'Socialism,' they called it. They said they were going to socialize the whole state."

"I wish them luck," responded Anna. "Let's first see if they can get Equality on firm footings."

"They said people send money from all over," said Rachel. "They're going to build a large number of buildings, plant hundreds of fruit trees, raise tons of corn and, within their own confines, be totally self-sufficient. And independent."

"Are they going to consume all that corn themselves?" asked Anna.

"No, I suppose they'll sell quite a bit of it," answered Rachel.

"Then they won't be totally independent," countered Anna. "No one ever is. And if the world is to become one, big, happy army, why would they be?"

"They seem to be doing very well presently," answered Rachel.

"With people sending money from all over," responded Anna, "I'm not surprised. Are they planning on contributions eventually waning? If people stopped sending money, could things continue?"

Anna measured the flattened pie dough while Rachel looked out the window and thought.

"The two biggest problems I have with this scheme, Rachel," said Anna as she rolled the pie dough up on the floured rolling pin, and unrolled it into the pie pan, "are, first, it doesn't realistically consider the self-centeredness of human nature and, second, innovation and new ideas are discouraged, innovation effectively outlawed. And no committee, no matter how wise or well-intended, is capable of accurately foreseeing the infinite minutiae of future needs and changes. Even at the colony level they would need to make hundreds, perhaps thousands, of well-informed decisions daily. But then, at the colony everyone makes the decisions, not just a committee."

"That's what they said."

"Chaos."

Rachel shrugged her shoulders.

"I suspect this experiment will come to an unhappy ending, Rachel." Rachel stood looking out the window. "I'm ready for the apples, Rachel." Rachel began to peel in earnest as Anna flattened the top crust dough with a rolling pin on the drain board.

After a few moments, looking sideways, Anna stared at Rachel who, in turn, was staring out the window.

"I have almost finished preparing the pie dough. See." Anna gestured toward the encrusted pie pan and flattened top crust on the floured drain board. "So, *could you* peel the rest of the apples?" Anna asked adamantly. "Then cut them up into small pieces."

"Here," replied Rachel, "I peeled four and am halfway done with a fifth."

"If you were me," asked Anna, "would you be impressed?"

Rachel made no reply.

"I hope someday, Rachel, you have a Rachel of your own and, when you do, I hope you are able to adequately exercise the patience and self-control you need to deal with you."

"Another Rachel?"

"Yes."

"Is that possible?" Rachel smiled.

Anna wiped some flour off the edge of the drain board.

"Actually, no."

● ● ●

"Socialism is the answer," said Jared Young, Rachel's handsome-but-eccentric new friend from the expanding nearby socialist colony.

"The answer to what?" asked Rachel coquettishly.

"'How many angels can dance on the head of a pin.'"

"What?"

"Angels are social…as in socialism. And for them, dancing is second nature. But pinheads, of course, come in a variety of sizes. So the number is not intuitive."

"I agree. In fact, your Lordship, I've known several pinheads."

"Impressive," responded Jared with mock seriousness.

"So, how many?"

"It depends on whether a waltz or foxtrot or flamenco." Jared's boots began convincingly pounding the ground as he loudly clapped his hands while simulating an angel doing the flamenco on the head of a pin.

"Ehhhmhmm," responded Rachel when he stopped. "'Impressive.'"

The ruts from wagon wheels in the country road were soft, but not muddy. Rain had not fallen for a few days. For his next fete of dexterity, Jared Young began entertaining beautiful Rachel Nordquist by walking in two wagon wheel ruts that were gradually diverging.

"Jared," Rachel began inquisitively as they walked, "I must admit I do not entirely understand how this is organized. The – what do you call it? – BCC wants to socialize the entire state of Washington, but the leader does not lead the colony. Why, Your Lordship, pardon me for asking, is not the leader leading?"

"I, Jared Charles Young, First Duke of Earl, herewith do thee pardon, m' lady.

"Sir Edward Pelton and the knights shall lead the colony," clarified Jared in a formal British accent although he was not British. "King Lermond is in charge of the BCC which, in turn, m' lady, will be responsible for establishing several similar colonies, ultimately leading the State of Washington to – ta da da DAH da DAHHHH – socialism." Jared concentrated on his balance.

"How 'm I doin'?" asked Jared, switching to his regular voice as his feet gradually became more distant from one another.

"Quite excellent," Rachel responded, pretending to be impressed. "Oh, I'm so proud of you," she added, clasping her hands together and fluttering her eyelashes. "And what does BCC stand for?" Rachel asked.

Jared switched to a Scottish brogue. "'Booll crrrap and cow paees', yoor majesty."

"Bull crap and cow pies." Rachel folded her arms as she looked at him sideways.

"Aye. T'insure equality and an adequate food supply – uh – ooh – we be formin' a fertile society using booll crrrap and cow paees and, well," Jason briefly waved his arms to keep his balance, "'t'is easy t' see why people join! Soon the entire state of Washington will be colonized as a consequence of the *prrroper* use of booll crrrap and cow paees as was foretold by…"

"What does BCC stand for, you cretin?" countered Rachel, her fists clenched, eyes wide.

"Ah, yes! Our motto!" answered Jason, his arms parallel to the ground as he maintained his balance. "'Crrretins of the World Unite!'"

"Ehhrrrhh," growled Rachel, sounding like a mad dog just awakened. "What! Does! It! *Stand* for?!" Rachel reached up, violently grabbed Jason around the throat and throttled him while, through clenched teeth, yelling, "*What*?! *What*?! *What*?!"

"Actually," gurgled Jason as he pulled maniacal Rachel's hands away from his throat, "Brotherhood of Cooperative Commonwealth. Ahh!" he yelped as he lost his balance and stepped to his left. "Now look what you made me do!" he said. "I (gasp) lost my balance. Had I made it another two feet, the world (gasp) would have been saved but now it's…"

"You're so weird! What does the BCC do?!"

"*I'm* weird?" sneered Jared. "Look at you? You're the one wearing a *dress*. Hah. Do you see me looking like that?"

"What! Does! The! B! B! C! *Do*!?" shouted Rachel loudly, baring her teeth and again going for Jared's throat.

Catching her wrists, Jared looked down at her, holding her wrists.

"The BCC creates socialist colonies," he whispered quickly, "first Equality," his voice gradually grew louder, "then the state of Washington, then the earth!" His eyes widened as he shouted, "Then Mars and Saturn and *Joo'piter* and the worrrldahahahahahaaaaaaah!!!"

"Let-go-of-my-wrists-or-I-will-kill-you," sneered Rachel through clenched teeth.

"How? I have hold of your wrists."

"My wrists contain a deadly venom that can be injected into your hands if I wish," said Rachel. "My great grandfather was a cobra."

"My great grandfather was in the Elks Club."

"My great grandfather *ate* your great grandfather."

"Ahah! As I suspected. Descended from mongeese. That explains every-thing. And you thought you could fool me with this descended-from-cobras nonsense." Jason released her wrists and, as the two continued their walk, added, "Although you had me going, there."

"You believe the BCC's efforts to socialize the state of Washington are in the best interests of everyone."

"Yup."

"But, then, you believe most of what the BCC tells you."

"Yup." Jared looked at Rachel, pointing upward with his right index finger. "The moon is made of green cheese, you know."

"Don't you ever think about it first?" asked Rachel. "I do," said Rachel. "I always wonder: 'Is this true? Or are there alternatives that need to be consid-ered?'"

"Me too," added Jared. "I said, 'C'mon, people, the moon isn't even *green*. So the moon must be made of *white* cheese.' But they…"

"Usually [!] I think of a few alternatives; then think about those, and usually I conclude with what seems most reasonable. Mom read *Looking Backward*," said Rachel as she looked at Jared, narrowed her eyes and flicked her tongue out several times. Eyes widening, Jared jumped back, putting up his hands in mock fear. "She said it did not adequately consider human nature, and that socialism will, ironically, always result in social inequalities that Bellamy suggests will be eradicated by his socialist system."

"How would she *know*?" asked Jared as they walked along the country road. "He just wrote the book. It's never been done before."

"Dad said it is not a new idea," said Rachel. "We sat around discussing it," Rachel again coquettishly batted her eyelashes at the flustered Jared, anticipating his physical and emotional responses, "shortly after I met…," she paused, giving a melodramatic sigh and pursing her lips, "…you."

Jared's heart and mind raced as Rachel momentarily looked off in the distance, smiling, and deliberately walked close to Jared, pushing hard against his upper arm, and Jared reflexively put his arm around her. Mission accomplished. Flushed with excitement, Jared looked down at Rachel while Rachel looked back.

She stopped, turned, reached over and took his hands, pulling him toward her as she held them. Looking down, Jared became momentarily speechless. Rachel looked deeply into his eyes, glancing from one to the other, and in a pseudo-treacly voice said, "By subordinating selfish desires to the general welfare, and caring for one another, while there will never be a perfect society, you could weave a social fabric which is nearly perfect in terms of meeting communal and individual material and emotional needs."

Jared continued to look down at Rachel, mouth half open, eyes wide.

"Yew shoor c'n talk guud."

Jared responded with what came naturally. For him. Jared would drive most people nuts, but not Rachel. She enjoyed His Royal Weirdness.

They started walking again. Still euphoric, Jared excitedly exaggerated his side-to-side gait and slapped the side of his pant leg with his imaginary straw hat. "Ah jes' never heard no one talk so guuud. Ah jes' never have. Ah… well, Ah jes' ain't never have. Nope, never, not once ever…"

"Yes [!]," interrupted Rachel, gritting her teeth, "well, may I again remind you," Rachel paused for effect and stopped walking, "I am absolutely brilliant."

With that she tossed her locks, blinking several times as she looked at him.

"Then you believe what we are doing could be successful?" asked Jared after a moment, smiling. Rachel loved his smile.

"Mmmm, I can't say that," answered Rachel. "My mother is convinced that because 'all have sinned and fallen short of the glory of God,' people will never be able to get along well enough to successfully effect such an idealistic movement. You're shooting for the moon."

"We're low on cheese."

"You know," added Rachel, "the biggest concern I have at the moment…"

"Don't be concerned," interrupted Jared. "Once we get to the moon, there will be more than enough cheese for every…"

"…*is* [!] that dad and mom are seldom wrong about things."

"Well, good for them," said Jared, folding his arms. "Bellamy should have consulted your folks first. What a dummy. Anyway, we already have a pastor and he already thinks it will work."

"Really?" responded Rachel. "You have a pastor?"

"Yes," said Jared. "He speaks just as you do. Well, perhaps not as well as you do." Jared's eyes got wider. "In fact, my father got the phrase 'Edict of Eden' from Reverend Candee."

"'Reverend Candee'? That's really his name? Where's he from?"

"That's really his name. Sent from God. With the Edict of Eden."

"What did he say was the Edict of Eden?"

"That, I guess, we *are* our 'brother's keeper.'"

"Ummm," Rachel responded. "Although *Genesis* doesn't say it specifically, it is implied in *Genesis*. And the Bible does say as much elsewhere. For example, the story of the Good Samaritan. So Reverend Candee could be right. On the other hand, the message is one of individual responsibility. Nothing is said about setting up a colony where everything is owned in common. Where does the Bible say that?"

"Second Jonah," gabbled Jared, "where Jonah goes fishing, catches a fish so big it swallows him, hook, line, sinker, and boat, and while he's floating around on the fish's stomach with nothing to do except think about what he'll do if he ever gets out, it occurs to him to start a socialist fishing fleet from the proceeds of First and Second Jonah that he will sell to the Lord to be part of the Bi..."

"*Then* [!]," interrupted Rachel loudly, startling Jared, "m' Lord, I shall review Second Jonah tonight!"

"Do that," said Jared, stepping in front of Rachel and again raising his right index finger, "and you shall be enlightened. Enlightened! You shall see signs and wonders. Socialism. Right there in the Good Book – that's why they call it the Good Book." Jared put his left palm out as if it had an open book resting in it. "Weirdliness is next to godliness." The Orthodox Eccentric pointed to the imaginary book. "Right here in Second Jonah."

"Then it is well I continue to walk with you," responded Rachel primly, taking Jared's arm.

"You've been receiving a lot of money," Rachel said. "How much land does the colony have? You must have quite an accumulation by now."

"It's a secret."

"How much of a secret?"

"About this much," said Jared with mock gravity, showing Rachel a ½ inch distance between his thumb and index finger.

"How much land?" asked Rachel through gritted teeth.

"Oh, dad says we have 600 acres." Jared smiled down at Rachel.

"And what are those buildings being constructed on the hillside?" asked Rachel. "Chicken houses? They can be seen from the bay."

"'Chicken houses'?" Jared stopped and looked at Rachel, as if in pain. "They're *apartment* houses for new members to live in." Jared turned and continued walking, seemingly annoyed. "Errrr," he growled. "My dad helped design them." Jared glanced at Rachel. "And what thou sayeth doth exceedingly grieveth me."

"Oh, forgive me, your Highness," Rachel said, her hands clasped together in front of her. "I, a lowly commoner, spoke out of turn. And what will they look like inside?" Rachel dropped her hands and looked at Jared. "I'm sure the chickens will be pleased."

"They – the people," answered Jared with exaggerated masculinity, "will have rooms, that is, bedrooms, one per family, with a central hallway. Each room will have about 170 square feet. They're temporary quarters until we begin building ha-ha-houses."

"'Ha-ha-houses,'" repeated Rachel. "Perhaps my father would be willing to ha-ha-help you. He is a very good carpenter. When do you intend to start doing that?"

"We've already started. The first members of the colony will receive the first houses," added Jared. "First come, first live."

"That would include you and your family."

"I'm not sure," said Jared. "My dad helps run the BCC and he thinks we should live separately from the colony because the BCC and Equality should remain distinct organizations. Equality is just the first of many colonies which the BCC will start."

"What do you live in now?"

"The Lewis house. It was donated to the colony by the Lewis family. It's a little south of the apartment buildings."

"You mean every BCC person lives in the Lewis house?" asked Rachel. "How many people live there now?"

"'T'is packed, m'lady. The last time I counted, there were 10. I'll be glad to get out of there. No privacy."

"It couldn't be," suggested Rachel as diplomatically as possible, "any worse than those apartment buildings *cum* chicken houses."

"You know Latin?"

"What might there be of which I know not, your Majesty?"

"Do you know how to get a colony up and running?"

"Does anyone?"

"Yes, there is a certain party who knows," stated idealistic Jared, becoming uncharacteristically serious. "You don't like our apartments, and I agree they're modest. We all have to endure some form of sacrifice to get momentum started and the movement established. That's what this is all about, Rachel: subordinating petty personal desires to the greater welfare of the community. If things are crowded at first, we simply put up with it because it will only be temporary. Eventually everyone will enjoy the lifestyle of which Bellamy foretold in *Looking Backward*, and then even skeptics like your parents will see the benefits of socialism."

While Rachel was not convinced that socialism would solve the world's economic problems, still she wondered: did Jared understand something she did not? Part of her found the high-minded idealism of Jared appealing. And he was far from dull. From a spiritual perspective, he wasn't what she had in mind, but he was good looking, charming, quite entertaining, and had a vision.

And what if this Equality experiment actually works? she asked herself.

As if in answer to this question, several odd events shortly took place.

92

April 1898

By April nearly 200 Equality memberships had been sold at $160 each. The BBC leaders structured the equality labor force in conformity with the *Looking Backward* and *Equality* paradigm. Carpentry, blacksmithing, shepherding…the list was extensive, and fishing was considered a necessary occupation, not recreation, a boon for the fortunate few official fishermen.

"Ed, excuse me." It was Horace the pea man, among those whose job was planting, cultivating and harvesting the pea crop. "Can I ask a question?"

"Certainly," answered Ed Pelton as he took a break from splitting firewood. Ed was a woodman; Ed's job was anything having to do with wood – from logging to lumber to firewood.

"I never see any of the BCC people around here," said Horace. "There's a lot of small changes, adjustments, that should be done an' I've a bunch of suggestions. Do you talk much with Lermond?"

"I try. He's always busy."

"Do you think you can get someone to come up here so's I can show 'em some problems, tell 'em my solutions, and they can tell us what's happenin' at their end? They're drivin' the buggy. I'd kinda want t' tell 'em some things."

"I'll certainly try, Horace. Honestly, I don't know any more than you at the moment."

"I thought you and Lermond were close."

"I'm not sure any more." Ed's face was expressionless.

"Well, anyway, thanks, Ed. Oh, Ed. Ah, one more thing." Horace walked up to Ed. "You know that Graef couple that's part of our team cultivatin' the peas?"

"Yes. Gerald and Jenny."

"They only show up about every other day. Gerald said Jenny ain't feelin' good, and at first that was understandable. But it seems Jenny ain't never feelin' good, so my wife, Alice, and I have t' do a lot more work than it seems we should. This has been goin' on for a spell. Could you say somethin' to those Graefs about pitchin' in every day? It's starting to make me mad, y' know. People shouldn't come here if they're not prepared t' pitch in and do their job. I can tell you about a few others who are the same way. Ain't good. There's some hard feelin's happenin' here."

"I'll talk to the Graefs," said Pelton who didn't think it was his place to talk to anyone, and resented being placed in this position. In the absence of a more formal arrangement, he was the colony's natural leader, and people came to him with problems. As disagreements increased, so did Ed Pelton's responsibilities, emotional burden and resentment.

"Buford, you'd better fix that harness," said Pelton as he walked by Buford Jones. Moving with the alacrity of a hot air balloon, Buford was leading one of the workhorses toward the fields. "Buford, I mentioned that two days ago," Ed added questioningly. "Remember?"

"I don't fix harnesses, Ed," said Buford. "I plow. I'm a plowman. That's my job. Full time. Plowin'. They's a lot of plowin' t' be done. I do my job regular. More'n I can say for some. I don't know who fixes harnesses."

Ed stopped and looked at Buford.

"What are you going to do if the harness snaps, Buford?"

Buford kept walking, leading the horse. "Nothin'," he said over his shoulder. "Wait until it's fixed by whoever is supposed t' fix harnesses."

"Buford, hold it right there!"

Buford stopped and turned around half way.

"Do you know how to fix the damned harness?"

"S'pose I could," answered Buford. "But I'm a plowman. Not a repairman. I plow. I do it all day long. Do my share."

"Buford, fix the harness," said Ed forcefully.

"Why me? It's not my job. I plow. That's my job. Send the harness repairman t' fix this."

"We have no harness repairman, Buford."

"How about the blacksmith?"

"Buford, the blacksmith is already complaining about being overworked. People bring all kinds of repairs to the blacksmith. His patience is wearing thin. Buford, just fix the harness."

"I'm a plowman," responded Buford defensively. "I don't think I should do more'n I'm supposed to."

"Neither does the blacksmith. Buford, if you don't fix that harness, it will get worse, and soon it will be beyond repair, and you will have no harness and, therefore, nothing to do."

"That's fine," said Buford woodenly. "Could use a break. D'ya know how many hours I work each day?"

"Buford, fix the harness," concluded Ed Pelton angrily as he walked off.

Ed Pelton had better things to do than argue with recalcitrant members about their responsibilities. Fixing the harness was intuitive. Why do people get it in their head they should be limited to just so much? He can fix the harness. Just do it. What would Buford do if there were nothing to eat? Plow?

I wish I could talk to Lermond about this sort of thing, Pelton thought as he walked. A saddler would be nice, but there's no saddler here. And maybe the blacksmith could do it but…Buford should just take care of it. We should have someone who formally adjudicates these things. Lermond should be involved, but I can't even talk to him because he's so busy – planning the next colony. Pelton's face darkened as he thought. Lermond's getting the cart before the horse…harness or no harness.

Pelton blew a deep, frustrated sigh. The colony is organized up to a point, but there is so much else that needs to be considered. Too many in this "army" of people – supposedly subordinating themselves to the whole army – think only of themselves. But so does most of the regular army, thought Pelton. He sighed. Every army has plenty of those guys. What army was Edward Bellamy in?

Ed Pelton wanted to keep the Equality and the BCC united, but found it difficult to communicate with Norman Lermond who was always too busy, occupied with things Lermond considered more important. After riding to the Lewis house several times in an attempt to speak with Lermond, and finding Lermond unreceptive to discussing the day-to-day problems of Equality, Pelton felt used. He subsequently gave up trying to see Lermond, enabling Pelton's irritation to build.

The BCC executives had big ideas, but felt no compulsion to discuss these ideas with the Equality members. To Ed Pelton, it would be wise to discuss future plans with present colony members, like Horace the pea man, in order to properly plan future colonies. First of all, every precaution should be made to insure people get along with one another. At that moment within the colony, as it became evident a few members were just along for the ride while others believed they were being made to work longer and harder than they should, formerly pacific relationships were deteriorating. Others, like Buford, would do one thing but, beyond that, refuse to lift a finger. The effect and perception of injustice damaged relationships and discouraged badly needed communication. The colony was like a dank cabin: spores of suspicion spreading a mildew of mistrust. When people finally talked, conversation was chafing and cold.

The lack of communication and extent of suspicion became painfully evident when Norman Lermond finally addressed the colonists on Good Friday, 1898. By that time, many colonists, including Ed Pelton, were upset about a lot of things.

April 10, 1898, Good Friday

At the request of Norman Lermond, the BCC executives and interested Equality members were invited to meet at the new Equality communal hall. Jared asked Rachel to join him, and they sat in the back row. The agenda had little to do with Equality itself. Norman Wallace Lermond, National Secretary, Brotherhood of Cooperative Commonwealth (BCC), got up to speak about his vision of additional colonies in Washington State.

"Friends," began Lermond, "timing is crucial. The Equality colony is but one of a mighty host of colonies which will ultimately grow together, blanketing the State of Washington with socialism and, to preclude capitalistic influences from without," Lermond solemnly raised both index fingers for emphasis, "it is crucial

– crucial! – that we proceed forward quickly to establish as many colonies as possible. I, therefore, am announcing our intention to formally establish what has already been informally established: a second colony in Edison within which present and future directors and officers of the Brotherhood of Cooperative Commonwealth will work diligently toward state socialization. That is the purpose of this colony."

Rather than bringing the BCC and Equality into lock step, this proposal would distance the BCC from Equality, clearly separating the identities of the two. A murmur felt its way through the crowd. The BCC isn't a colony, thought Pelton; it's a bunch of executives living in a house.

Near the front, a short, wrinkled prune of a man stood up. From behind the little man's suspenders his thumbs peaked out like baby opossums, gradually sliding up and down his suspenders as he got up the nerve to speak.

"You mean…you people are going to form your own separate colony?" he asked in a high-pitched, raspy voice.

"That is correct," answered Lermond. "We will continue our goals as stated in the preamble to our constitution adopted by national referendum on September 19th, 18 and 96 [1896]."

Lermond pulled a document out from under his notes.

"Let me read it to you. As you know, our goals are '(1) to educate the people in the principles of Socialism; (2) to unite all Socialists into one fraternal organization; (3) to establish cooperative colonies and industries in one State until said State is socialized.' That is what our constitution says and that is where our responsibilities lie."

"We all know that," said the little man, "but, as far as what we're doin' right now, wouldn't it be a lot smarter to make sure everything was runnin' smooth at Equality before y' start growing colonies all over hell and gone?"

Annoyed, Lermond pursed his lips while raising his head.

"I beg your pardon," responded Lermond solemnly. "Do I need to remind you we are in mixed company? If you cannot participate in a civil manner, I must ask you to keep your remarks to yourself."

"Well, now, jest a minute," responded the little man, "I ain't a gonna be saving my breath for no one. I been breakin' my neck every day and I ain't gonna jes' sit here an' be all genteel and quiet," he said as he looked around. "No sir. I'm jes' sayin' you should be treatin' us like equals. An' if you figure on leavin', well, don't be plannin' on takin' all that money with ya. That money," said the little man, "should stay right here to help finish what's been started."

"Establishing a second colony is evidence no one in the BCC," answered Lermond, further annoyed, "is intending to leave, and funds are available as needed."

Lermond shook the papers to smooth them out, and looked contemptuously at the little man. At that moment, the need to defend what he had created was to Lermond an insult. Had this little man, Lermond wondered, the vision and skill to create such an undertaking, an undertaking greatly benefitting all participants, eventually the nation, and ultimately many nations? He – they –

should be enormously grateful and unquestionably loyal.

"However," Lermond continued, "the greater need is as stated in the constitution, and it is the responsibility of the BCC to uphold that constitution. Those generous supporters who send contributions, do so expecting the constitution be upheld and, were it not, would be less-than-generous. So you see, sir, we are only doing what our position has required since the beginning of Equality. We will…"

"Excuse me!" came a voice from a man standing up three rows back. "Since I was there [at the beginning], I'd like to say something."

It was Ed Pelton. Unable to listen to Lermond any longer.

Pelton helped many a newcomer get established in the growing community; most were now friends with Pelton. While Lermond remained aloof in nearby Edison, Pelton put his heart and soul into Equality, and he and his wife were becoming increasingly angry with how things were going. The crowd, rigidly solemn, strained to hear the colony's natural leader.

"I agree with what you're tryin' to do, Norman," said Ed, "but I can't see the sense in how you're tryin' to do it. I can't see where callin' the BCC a 'colony' makes it a colony. Meanwhile, Equality hasn't reached the point where it can sail under its own power." Pelton looked down, thinking, and in a single, quick, downward motion, wiped his forehead with his outstretched thumb and forefinger, continuing over nose, mouth and chin, as if pulling off a mask. "You know," Norman," continued Pelton, while putting his hands in his pockets, "I sometimes wonder what you people do down there. What do you do? You're thinkin' about colonizin' the whole state, and we're workin' our tails off tryin' t' live half way decently. Obviously, when you're thinking about those things you just mentioned, you're not thinkin' about us. Of course, I appreciate your vision, but if Equality doesn't make it, Norman, none of those other colonies'll make it either. You have to make this one work first."

"They will survive," responded Lermond in a tight voice, staring at Pelton. "They will not only survive, but prosper."

Ed Pelton looked at Lermond; Lermond was not in touch with reality.

"They will survive and prosper," echoed Pelton, pulling his hands out of his pockets and folding his arms. "Well, I feel better already." Pelton's eyes became steely. "No. No, Norman, I don't feel better at all."

Pelton's stomach felt as knotted as fouled fishing line, and he was having difficulty forcing himself to say what needed to be said – what he wanted to say to Lermond privately, but was never given the opportunity.

"This new idea of yours," said Pelton, "shows you aren't too concerned about things that are needed now, things apparently you don't know about. Norman, we're obviously not all livin' in the same world. You live in some sort of fantasy world, not here in Equality. You have big ideas for the future, but don't have any idea about the here-and-now, and my fear is that all this effort is gonna be wasted because of your lack of action…here…at home.

"You live close," Pelton continued, "yet you never come up here, and have no idea of the sacrifices we make every day, the problems arisin' and the changes that need to be made." Lermond stared back at the last man he expected to say these things. "Norman, you won't take the time to come up here and get involved with your own brainchild. You prefer to stay down there, eh, apparently spendin' a lot of time tellin' yourself, well, I don't know – must be how important you are…certainly more important than the rest of us."

Pelton, who had brooded over the problem for some time, began to seethe and his pent-up anger overwhelmed his self-control.

"Norman, you are not behavin' like the leader of a socialist movement," Pelton pointed at Lermond, no longer attempting to hide his disillusionment. "Do you know what you act like? You act like a capitalist peddlin' socialism. You're makin' money sellin' Equality. You talk about donations and donors. Well, if you don't attend to the business at hand, this whole thing is gonna fall flat on its face. What'll you tell your donors then? And these members who've invested $160 and themselves?!"

"Financial stability is and always has been a concern, Ed," said Lermond. "This is not about money; it is about the growth of…"

"Norman I hear one thing and see another." Pelton glared at Lermond. "Right now, Norman, I'm not buyin' what you're sellin.'" Pelton's arms unfolded and dropped to his sides. "Because you're no different than the capitalists, Norman. What do capitalists do? They make money from the inability of the workingman to fend for himself. He needs to pay his bills, support his family; so when the capitalist offers a job that barely pays enough to feed the workingman's family, he has to take it. You've brought us all here, put us to work, collected the money and left us to fend for ourselves. Does that sound familiar? From where I stand, it seems you've become a publicity-seeking, long-winded opportunist with a heart almost black enough to shame some of the East Coast monied aristocracy that walk on the backs of the workingman like a Northern Pacific locomotive rides on the …"

"That's it!" interrupted Miss Helen Mason, BCC Treasurer, rising from her seat purse-lipped. "I have heard all I can stand!" Looking around her, she said angrily, "Not one word of what you have heard is true! In fact, this man," she pointed at Lermond, "is a saint! All he has ever been concerned with is the welfare of the downtrodden, the sick, the poor and the weak. This slanderous onslaught is despicable. Good Friday – yes! They also crucified Christ on Good Friday!"

"No one is bein' crucified here!" Pelton shouted back. "Unless it's us!" Like a pressure cooker, emotions in the room began boiling from the heat of suppressed acrimony. "Norman, when we were back in Maine, this seemed like a good idea, an idea whose time had come; maybe a chance of a lifetime. But unless you get directly involved and work out all the kinks in Equality, the idea could fail and, if it does, the whole plan fails, and the blame will rest squarely on your shoulders! If you don't like what I say, then make a total commitment to this colony. These people paid $160 that many couldn't afford, and they've invested themselves. Separating Equality from the BCC might be a good thing at some point in the future, but not now. We're still a long way from self-sufficiency. If you can't get down off your high horse and make a commitment to Equality now, you might as well take our money and head back to Maine!" Pelton glanced about him and then looked firmly at Lermond. "So that the rest of us can start making plans, make up your mind and do it soon."

As Pelton turned to sit down, Miss Mason gave Pelton a look that would freeze fire. The colony crowd was behind Pelton, and it would take more than Miss Mason's frigid presence to cool the passion of insecure men and women sensing betrayal.

After angry discussion, the Equality members voted to reject the idea of an Edison colony. The next day the Edison BCC continued business as if nothing happened. But something had happened, something akin to a ship glancing off an iceberg.

The colony social climate gradually grew more acrimonious and, as the relationship between the BCC people and colonists deteriorated, whenever anything was wrong, colonist fingers pointed toward the BCC people down the road. Becoming defensive, the BCC people began to consider the complaints as a lot of whining and hyperbole. Equality began to resemble a dragon with two heads, each bickering at the other, and neither listening.

His former passion doused by a stream of cold reality, Jared began to doubt the viability of this social experiment of which he was formerly so certain.

The relationship between the colonists and BCC people grew worse, and four months later Jared's fears were realized when Equality members, believing they would never have access to "all that money" anyway, drew up a constitutional amendment, passed by a vote of 298 to 176, severing Equality's relationship with the BCC.

August 1898

"These people have no vision, no commitment. I don't know what they'll do next," Lermond said to Arlen Young, BCC accountant and Jared Young's father, as Young sat looking up from his desk. Lermond leaned against the door jam, his hands in his pockets, and added, "Did they expect we would consider every detail, provide for every contingency? Didn't they know that would be impossible, that they would need to fill in gaps themselves? Equality would work wonderfully if we had innovative people." Lermond looked at Young. "Perhaps this is the crowd we would attract every time."

For a moment Lermond looked away, thinking about what happened, and his face angrily contorted.

"It's all very odd," said Young. "I can imagine problems arising, but the vilification of the BCC was so extreme and irrational, it gives me pause. I feel like when I look in the mirror I should see red skin and two horns."

Lermond attempted a chuckle, but no sound came out.

"I obviously assumed too much," said Lermond, looking at the floor. "I assumed people would behave resourcefully and responsibly." Lermond's expression again became angry and he snorted cynically. "It seems more like we populated the colony with school children."

Lermond put his hands back in his pockets.

"I must tell you I was devastated when Ed Pelton stood up and castigated me as being no different than an East Coast capitalist…selling socialism. How does one respond to a characterization like that? How did it get to that point? Arlen, he's an intelligent man. This certainly has turned out differently than planned… and I don't know how to fix it."

Lermond looked at the floor and Young studied him.

"What do you intend to do, Norman?"

"What can I do? We – you and I and the others here – have been shown the door. You, Arlen, should return to your accounting practice in Ohio." Lermond looked at Young solemnly. "I'm going to return to Maine. I still believe in what I attempted to do, but it is evident I need to take an entirely different approach. These people were uprooted, apparently expected more than what they were given, and behaved badly. The key may be to start on a much larger scale where people are already settled, and through education and legislation attempt to establish socialism."

"Do you think that will work?" asked Young. "You know there will be those who oppose socialism. It might take years, decades, to convince enough people to where socialism becomes part of the commonweal."

"I believe in socialism," answered Lermond. "It's a commendable ideal. If people only understood what socialism was, they would fall down on their knees and pray…well… I believe establishing socialism is my destiny."

"I wonder what will happen to the colony now," said Young. "I wonder if they'll make a go of it. I could offer my services…if they don't mind someone with horns and a bifurcated tongue."

"From my perspective, then you'd fit right in," said Lermond, "but I wouldn't get your hopes up. That's an odd bunch up there. I think I would have much better success if I focused on people in Maine. They're stellar. Hard working and independent, but they are usually receptive to new ideas." Young looked askance at Lermond. "Well, maybe not, but I think I know how it might work."

"What's your idea?"

"Rather than bringing people into a situation of instability, and attempting to socialize a state from the ground up, I should begin in a place where things are already stable, and I'll do it from the top down. I believe that would work better," said Lermond as he thought, "and that's what I'll do. Indeed, Maine would be a good place to start."

Lermond puffed on his pipe as he thought.

"If things are already stable," asked Young, "why would anyone want to make a switch to socialism?"

Lermond looked at Young for a moment, unwilling to allow any doubt to seep into his utopian dream. "Because of the inspired vision of Bellamy," said Lermond with asperity. "Given a chance, it will work."

Young looked back at Lermond. "Good luck," said Young without a trace of sarcasm.

Norman Wallace Lermond, National Secretary, Brotherhood of Cooperative Commonwealth, optimistic about the future, made preparations to return to

Maine where, "with all that money," he would begin again.

———————— • ————————

Between the two of them, Jared and Rachel normally provided as much entertainment as two people would need. Today's walk was the exception.

Rachel stopped and, having never been in that immediate spot before, looked about to discover what might be of interest. She did not talk – for, except at the start, there was little of that. As Rachel studied the surroundings, Jared, hands deep in his pockets, studied the ground.

"Jared, you have not spoken two words. Why this deep, mysterious silence?" Rachel asked, concerned about their relationship.

Hands still buried, Jared looked off in the distance.

"Have I said or done anything to annoy you?" Rachel asked.

"It's not you."

"He spoke!" exclaimed wide-eyed Rachel. She clasped her hands together. "The Prince of Equality spoke to a simple peasant." Open-mouthed, she looked about wildly. "Oh, I shall cherish this moment forever!"

Jared remained motionless, looking down the path they walked. He said nothing.

"Then what *is* it?" she asked, exasperated.

"Several people from the colony said some very unpleasant things to my father and Mr. Lermond at the meeting last night. This has been bothering me."

"Oh, you had another one of those wunnderful meetings," said Rachel, again clasping her hands together, "where everybody in the colony gets together, and anyone says whatever it is they feel like saying."

Jared said nothing.

"And no one whines and complains…with no alternative solution. Oh, but how could I even *think* of such a thing?" asked Rachel, turning to Jared. "Of course, no one whined and complained. It was," she added pleasantly, "merely a constructive meeting. Where *never* is heard a discouraging word." Jared made no response.

"Forgive me for asking, Your Highness," said Rachel with exasperation, "but could you tell me, her Lowness, what was said?"

"The people at the Equality colony," answered Jared quietly, "were upset about us, the BCC families, living in town in what the colonists think are pleasant surroundings, while the colonists live in the apartment building until the first houses are built."

"Vile commoners!" exclaimed Rachel, her right finger stabbing the air above her head. "Wrong-headed imbeciles! How totally insensitive of them!"

"No one said it would be easy," said Jared, unaffected by Rachel's levity. "But these people don't *care*. They're not willing to make initial sacrifices for the benefit of the community." For the first time in quite a while, Jared looked directly at Rachel. "All they care about is themselves."

Rachel struck her closed right fist below her left shoulder, and proclaimed, "A self-serving pack of unrueful, restive rats!"

"Unrueful? Wha..?"

"How could these vile vermin become involved in such a noble cause as yours? Incidentally," Rachel looked up at Jared with her very best Cheshire feline smile, "what sacrifices *are* you making?"

Jared only looked at her.

"You live packed but relatively comfortably," said Rachel, as the two of them turned around to begin walking back, "and you get aaahhhl that money from your supporters." Her mouth slightly open, she studied Jared. "How much did you receive last month?" she asked. "Over $16,000?"

Jared looked at the trees, and pretended to ignore her, an ostensible indifference that only encouraged Rachel to spoon-feed another dose of cold truth.

"You send out those *Industrial Freedom* newspapers," said Rachel, "emphasizing either how bright the future will be if true believers send money, or how dark the future will be if enemies gain an upper hand – an eventuality which can be thwarted only if true believers send money." Rachel gritted her teeth attempting not to smile. "You know, that's a very clever way of getting funds. We Christians should do that."

Jared momentarily glowered at Rachel. "It's not funny." He looked sourly down the road.

"I agree," responded Rachel.

"Mom was right," added Rachel, sighing. "You people in the BCC haven't completely thought this one out. What are you going to do about these people who recognize the present inequalities – pardon the pun – and suggest that things should be otherwise?"

Rachel let go of Jared's arm.

"I don't know," answered Jared, shoving his hands in his pockets again. "I should mention the colony and the BCC are going to go their separate ways."

"Really?"

"But I'm going to stay on here with the colony. I think my folks will move back to Ohio. Mr. Lermond told my dad..." Jared stopped in mid-sentence, glanced furtively at Rachel, and remained silent.

"Told your dad what?"

"Nothin'."

"Hold it, Sir Talkalot," said Rachel, grabbing Jared's right arm with both her hands, bringing their walk to a halt. "Don't tell me, 'Nothin'.' What did he say?"

"Mr. Lermond told my dad they had attracted the wrong people and that we need to..."

"Whoa!" interrupted Rachel, wide-eyed, stopping and letting go of Jared's arm. "Haven't I heard this 'wrong people' line before? People are people. Maybe there's something wrong with your organization or ideals that need fixing?"

Rachel took Jared's arm as they again began to walk.

"You fix it, Jared. You find what's wrong and *you* fix it."

"What? I'm 19."

"Almost 20," said Rachel, dropping his arm as they stopped again. "There were kings in Egypt younger than you when they took the throne."

"They had sage advisors," countered Jared, "people wise in the ways of the world or anywhere else."

"So," replied Rachel, looking at Jared and batting her eyelashes, "do you."

Jared released another short, agonized sigh. Injustice was complicated. Fix it. Easy to say. Jared knew that if what was formerly perceived as an injustice became integrated with the status quo, many would no longer see it as an injustice – especially people whose self-interest is served by the former injustice – and, consequently, eliminating the injustice would be considered as an injustice while the well-intended fixer is perceived as a nuisance.

"I'll do what I can."

Rachel again took Jared's arm and urged him to continue their stroll.

"So. What did Mr. Lermond say?" asked Rachel.

"Okay, I'll tell you what he said," sighed Jared. "He said we have – if you don't mind – 'attracted the wrong people,' unimaginative people who put their own self-interest ahead of the principles of socialism. Bellamy said when that happens, socialism won't work. A few days ago Mr. Lermond said if the attitude of the people in the colony didn't change, he would remove himself from the BCC. Equality's already gone because they voted to leave the BCC."

"Oh, wunnnderful," Rachel answered with sweetly refined sarcasm, delicately flicking her up-lifted right wrist to emphasize the last word. Rachel looked up at Jared with wide, theatric eyes and, jumping in front of him, clutched his jacket. "Wonderful Mr. Lermond," choked Rachel emotionally, "who would *never* put self-interest ahead of the principles of socialism, is thinking of abandoning something that doesn't fit his enlightened vision of how things should be. Such sacrifice! Why," Rachel gasped, throwing her hands over her chest, and looked star-stricken into the distance, "what a *saint* of a man!"

"Rachel, you don't understand," countered Jared. "Things don't appear to be going the way people think they should go, so people pontificate, questioning how things are done, without offering any alternatives, and everyone talks in glittering generalities and no one says anything specific, and then everybody blames everybody else for things that are, frankly, totally imagined."

"Sounds like Congress."

"Congress? Listen, it's hard as heck to defend yourself against charges that are totally without merit but, nonetheless, believed. Takes forever. Biggest waste of time. Have you ever had to sit and listen to a lot of nonsense – stupid, unfounded nonsense about your father – being spouted off in front of people who actually believe it?"

"Yeeup." Rachel twirled her glistening, bronze hair in her right fingers, holding Jared's hand in her left. "I have."

"You have?"

"I'm afraid so."

"Where?"

"Seattle. We had to leave the church down there."

"You did?"

"We befriended a man, let him live with us, that other people in the church didn't like."

"Why didn't they like him?"

"He was Chinese."

Jared studied Rachel, attempting to discern whether or not she was serious. "Oh."

"So, when Mr. Lermond leaves," asked Rachel, "what will you do?"

"I don't think he'll leave here," said Jared adamantly. "First, he's the founder of this organization. Second, he came all the way from Maine. Third, he's a committed socialist. He'll probably start another colony somewhere around here. Or maybe wait to see what happens with this one. He won't leave. I'd almost stake my life on that."

"Stake your life?"

"Almost."

"Considering your heritage, I'd avoid stakes," said Rachel.

"Heritage?"

"Vampires avoid stakes."

"I don't think he'll leave," said Jared in a haunting voice, giving Rachel a look of exaggerated lasciviousness as he leaned over and bit her neck.

93

I never thought in a million years Norman 'd do it," Ed Pelton said. "Up and leave."

"The first people in here were fine," said the bald man sitting next to Ed. "They worked hard, cooperated, didn't ask for much, and were patient. We were doin' good."

"But after that it seemed that new people expected more." Ed looked sideways at the bald man. "One reason could've been the paper."

"*Industrial Freedom?*"

"We made this place sound like more'n it was," said Ed. "A worker's paradise. A lot of clichés, slogans. Catchy slogans leave something to be desired where facts are concerned."

"Ya mean like totally distort the truth?"

"Yeah, like that. Many people came, took one look around, and left."

"Not to mention the ones who came, stayed awhile, and then left," said the bald man.

"Got tired of carrying the load for both themselves and a number of malingerers I can think of."

"Yup," agreed the bald man, inspecting a loose patch. "That's the truth."

"Ain't this somethin'? We start a colony to get away from economic and labor problems, and what do we get? Economic and labor problems."

Pelton put on his hat, folded his hands, and rested his chin on them as he looked off toward the bay. "You know, I could sure go for a cigar right about now."

The bald man just looked at Pelton. Neither man had seen a cigar in months.

———————————————•———————————————

"You'd think they could understand that by helping one another they help themselves, but, no, they can't see that," said Jared, head in his hands.

"But don't some enjoy helping others?" asked Rachel.

"Most think of themselves first," said Jared, "and they can't get beyond that."

"So, mom's right again. Sometimes even the most selfish man will be willing to help someone else. But only a saintly few are willing to do it all the time. What are you going to do now?"

"Figure out what I'm going to do next."

"While you're trying to figure things out here, I've decided to figure out things in Seattle college classes."

Jared looked at Rachel.

"What?"

Sales of Rockefeller Everett assets closed at losses, but Reverend Fred Gates took advantage of a buyer's market and, with the accumulated receipts from sales of Everett real estate holdings, moved Rockefeller's money from speculative municipal development into a real estate/commodity combination: thousands of acres of timberland in western Washington and British Columbia, adding substantially to timberland already owned. Gradually, almost the entire investment portfolio was timberland. The remaining exception was the smelter. In the absence of ore deposits, Reverend Gates was having difficulty finding a buyer for the smelter at any price.

Fall, 1898

Neither Inga nor Esther chose to go to college, but Rachel decided to emulate her mother.

There were no colleges nearby, but higher education was gaining a foothold in nascent Seattle. In 1894, the Territorial University moved north from its small Capitol Hill spot to a remote, 600-acre location with extensive marshy Lake Washington frontage teaming with biology specimens.

"I don't know what classes to take, mom, because I don't know enough to know what to take."

"That's not uncommon, Rachel," said Anna. "Besides required curriculum, take classes you believe will be interesting, and gradually attempt to determine what subject area you like best."

"Any recommendations?"

"Only generally. History, English, science, and math."

"Whoa. I already know enough to not take one of those."

"Take math anyway, Rachel," said Anna. "College isn't just for taking what you enjoy, but also for strengthening areas in which you may be weak."

"Trust me. I'll stay weak in math no matter how many classes I take."

"A lot of that will depend on your professors, Rachel. A good introductory math instructor will not only teach you math, but will inculcate an interest in mathematics. You might be surprised. Take an introductory math class and see what happens. And, as far as recommendations go, I'd also suggest considering political science or economics."

"Economics sounds interesting," said Rachel as she looked down at the curriculum, not seeing the suppressed pained expression on Anna's face.

Preparatory to attending the Territorial University, Rachel talked a lot with her parents about economics, attempting to have a small foundation before arriving at school.

Rachel's classes were in the first Territorial University building, Denny Hall, which served a variety of purposes academically and socially. By fall 1898 the student body had grown to over 200 students – to Rachel a small town. Rachel moved to the new campus and, deciding to forego math at first, began attending classes in biology, English literature, and an introductory economics course.

———————⬤———————

"Socialism," said the economics professor, standing in the front of the room as he reached for his pipe, "is the answer."

I've heard this before, was Rachel's first thought.

As the professor paused to study his pipe bowl, the students looked back neutrally. The bearded, balding professor looked pleasantly at his students as he absentmindedly placed the pipe stem in his mouth for a moment before removing it to add tobacco. "A capital idea, socialism," he added, winking mischievously at the students in front including Rachel. As most students chuckled obligatorily, he leaned against his desk, lightly tapping his pipe bowl in the middle of the large ashtray adjacent the tobacco canister as he looked at Rachel. The professor was older, but not to the point where Rachel was not a distraction. His gray eyes searched other eyes in the room. "Commendable concept, socialism. Yet history shows there have been problems. Quickly, would someone be willing to explain *why* there have been problems?"

Rachel raised her hand.

"Yes," nodded the professor.

"I can give you some examples including one that is occurring presently," began Rachel. The professor packed his pipe bowl tightly as he listened to Rachel's complete response. Taking a long match from the match case beside the classroom fireplace, the professor patiently held one end toward the fire for a moment until spontaneous combustion did its work. Wafting the match over the pipe bowl, he drew slowly on the pipe stem, continuing to listen patiently. A young man seated nearby lit his own pipe. The other students listened intently. Rachel's story about socialism was interesting.

"Ah, yes," the professor responded as he walked around the desk and sat down, settling comfortably in his chair. "But those blunders were…well… just that: blunders." Rachel listened without expression as the professor drew on his pipe, looking astutely at the others who sat politely mute, looking back attentively. "Without a doubt, to properly succeed, socialism must be properly practiced. If socialistic ideals are compromised – *compromised*," the professor repeated as if he had invented the word, "so too is any chance of success. In point of fact, history has shown that compromise leads invariably to disaster. *Disaster*," he repeated with cultured emphasis.

"Oh, certainly a point or two," the professor pointed the pipe stem in the direction of the students, "can be said for free enterprise," he sighed, "but look at the fog we're in now. Appalling." The professor looked away, putting the pipe in his mouth for only a second before adding, "*Appalling.*"

He returned his gaze toward the class and nodded several times until most students unwittingly nodded back, ostensibly in agreement. Rachel remained motionless.

"Of what is our most recent national economic depression evidence?" the professor asked. "Is it not evidence that something is fundamentally wrong with our present system; that something more enlightened must be available? Is this," the professor gestured with his pipe toward the window and the world outside, "as good as it gets?"

The professor turned, facing the others more directly.

"Does not the present economic state of affairs imply that there *must* be something better? Are we sheep who just follow the herd, pathetically bleating, or are we, the intelligent men and women of this campus, perhaps capable of finding a higher and better alternative, something less base – indeed, of much greater consequence – than mere capitalism."

He looked at Rachel as he drew on his pipe.

"Are we so ignorant that we would indefinitely employ an economic system that doesn't work? Or is it time for us to step to the fore and lead the flock to something better?"

Again the professor nodded several times and, again, almost all of the students reciprocated. Rachel just looked at him. Questions. Questions. No answers.

"Practiced properly, true socialism could result in a veritable paradise," the professor posited. "*Veritable.*" He looked about the room. "Is there anyone who might disagree?"

"I have no doubt that many present things should be done differently," said Rachel, "but I'm not sure, as you suggest, socialism is the answer. What has made America great has not been heavy-handed, short-sighted, inefficient, central planning but, rather, just the opposite…"

As the professor listened to Rachel's monologue, the professor's pipe bowl glow weakly pulsated with each slow puff. Rachel finished by reiterating the inequities that arise in a socialist system.

"Oh?" was the professor's incredulous response at one point. His voice sounded deeply dubious. "What were the results then?" came the question.

As the professor listened, the pipe in his mouth momentarily became inactive.

"You don't say?" he responded softly with veiled irritation. The professor again attempted to become more comfortable as the pipe suddenly gave modest simulation of the smokestacks a mile southwest.

"Well, compromise – there, 'compromise,' again I say – no doubt was rampant. Slipshod organization. We all agree," he looked about the room, "it is important that the ideals be religiously followed; no compromise be allowed." The professor pointed his pipe stem at the others and said solemnly, "Considering the importance of conformity, principle compromise in economics would be tantamount to, say, heresy in religion." Rachel showed almost no expression although the others could sense her dismay. "American socialists," continued the professor, "have agreed that the time has come for socialism to be properly undertaken and subsequently given its due. If properly undertaken, well…then see if the others scoff. While socialists are, indeed, mindful that earlier attempts at socialism were less-than-successful, what of it? The popular adage of our era admonishes, 'If at first you don't succeed, try, try again.' Acceptance of failure is no longer American. Do we all agree?"

Rachel said nothing.

"Socialism will work if properly executed. The time has come to 'try again.'"

Rachel disagreed and attempted to clarify her position. "I don't see what has changed. If socialism has discouraged productivity and innovation in the past, why would it not do the same…"

"Yes, yes, young lady. I heard you the first time," replied the professor immediately. "My hearing is still good. I must remind you to keep an open mind to alternative ideas, however. So you believe socialism has been less than stellar anywhere it has been tried?" Pipe smoke was no longer visible from the pipe itself. The bowl would need to be relit. "Has it," he asked poignantly, "been tried here?"

The professor's gray eyebrows rose as the students sat silently, not understanding.

"Has it been tried in the United States?" he clarified with subtle defiance. Then they understood. The United States. Manifest destiny. "…huddled masses yearning to breathe free…" Succeeding where others had failed…although reasons for success or failure did not occur to the students at that moment.

It seemed only that any responsive contradiction from an unbeliever would somehow be un-American and, therefore, incorrect, at least politically. Students looked down or glanced at one another; none looked directly at the professor. Rachel glared at him. As the professor waited, no response came.

"Well, then, there you have it," he said as he stood up, reaching for another match from the case beside the fireplace.

"I trust the matter is clear to all of you," he added as he re-lit his pipe.

"And I needn't remind you that this subject will be covered extensively on the mid-term."

⎯⎯⎯ • ⎯⎯⎯

Beautiful, effervescent Rachel made friends quickly, including Deacon Reese and Clarence Larson, members of the University's 14-man football team. She cheered for them during their two games. They lost the first and won the second.

At the end of fall quarter, Rachel returned home for Christmas vacation, and renewed her friendship with Jared Young, now as familiar as a nearby lake. While she had made friends with others, she had missed Jared. And he had missed her. After spending time at home, Rachel decided to put off returning to the Territorial University.

January 1899

Pastor Nordquist perused an older letter from Anders in Göteborg.

The merger with White Star Line was complete and, while the Nordquists greatly benefited financially, there was no more Nordquist Shipping Co. While ships of sail still roamed the seven seas, the ships that once flew Captain Stig Nordquist's flag were gone. Anders' responsibilities revolved around transporting Scandinavian emigrants and cargo to America on huge steam-powered ocean liners. Anders wrote of a new passenger liner under construction, the *Olympic II*, which, while not as fast as some others, would be more beautiful and combine greater comfort and luxury – providing second-class quarters that were finer than first-class quarters on competing steamships – with greater economy of operation and, consequently, greater profitability.

A more recent letter from Anders indicated that White Star Line also expected to build four more beautiful Olympic-class steamships, all weighing over 20,000 tons. The first, to be named the Celtic, was to be launched in 1901. Anders added that White Star Line was talking with representatives of other shipping companies for the purpose of reaching an operating agreement where, while operating independently, they would also operate interdependently, effectively controlling passenger rates. Anders told Amos to keep that to himself.

In 1899, the depression was nearing its end. After years of litigation, the Everett Land Company's few remaining assets, mostly a large bond portfolio of modest value, were auctioned off on the county courthouse steps, steps built by Everett Land Company. The purchaser was Wyatt J. Rucker, the remaining power in Everett, acting on behalf of James J. Hill. With the economy getting back on its feet, Hill would bring his railroad to Everett. A valuable employee in the construction effort would be Chong Tsing Wei.

When the Great Northern Railroad was completed, Mr. Chong, like all others involved, was proud of the results, because James J. Hill built both a railroad and a need for a railroad, and kept his fares low, enabling customers to price their goods competitively and, subsequently, profitably, increasing productivity and the need to use Mr. Hill's railroad again. Unlike the Union Pacific and Northern Pacific developers, James J. Hill began construction of the Great Northern Railroad without government subsidies. Mr. Chong watched the Northern Pacific and Union Pacific railroads go bankrupt while Hill's Great Northern Railroad made money because Hill established small profit centers for others along the route, importing beef cattle and placing them, occasionally for free, where they would be most suitably raised by resolute ranchers. He chose railroad corridors that were heavily forested, and joint ventured subsequent logging operations with his friend and St. Paul next door neighbor, Frederick

Weyerhaeuser. Mr. Hill captured a large market share by creating and girding sustainable en route submarkets. Along the Great Northern corridor, most participants made money, but especially James J. Hill.

Working to a similar end, in 1899 Reverend Frederick T. Gates began selling the extensive Rockefeller timberland holdings.

February 1901

Following Norman Lermond's departure, feeling obligated, Ed Pelton stayed in Equality for two more years, but as time progressed, Pelton's wife became more discontented. Ed was becoming burned out, and finally Pelton also left the colony, moving to Seattle.

While in Seattle, however, Ed Pelton missed the feeling of being needed, being part of a team. Equality missed Pelton. In early 1901, when again asked if he would reconsider returning, he and his wife agreed to return to the immediate area, where he would help with colony affairs, but not continually, and would live at a distance.

During a February 1901 logging exercise as two exhausted fallers, being close to done, continued to swing their axes in syncopated rhythm, the 500-year-old Douglas fir began to creak and slowly tilt in the direction of the fall line planned three days earlier. Aside a creek rushing down the hillside, Ed Pelton was on his hands and knees getting a drink, his attention diverted. Ed didn't hear the yell "Timmberrrrrr" as the huge tree began to lean in slow motion as if hoping Ed Pelton would get out of the way. Others at a short distance downhill looked in horror and gasped while one man nearby ran toward Pelton shouting, "Ed! Ed!" The moment was heart stopping. The big tree's momentum accelerated until thousands of pounds came crashing down to the ground with such velocity that Ed Pelton had no time to look up, and for Ed Pelton, time stopped. Men ran to Pelton's body, pinned beneath the tree, but he was gone. They looked at one another in stunned disbelief. One moment Ed was with them, nothing different, all was well. A moment later...

Mild depression hung over the colony like a pall, and the death of Ed Pelton reopened a void begging to be filled. There was no one in the colony with the stature to do so, however, and things got worse when Harry Ault, *Industrial Freedom* editor, disgruntled with the decline of ideality, leadership and circulation, left the next year. By mid-1902, the colony population was less than 100.

August 15, 1902

The communal effort was dying, and former principles of socialism were being neglected. Meanwhile, outside of Equality, capitalism was faring better.

A letter from Anders indicated White Star Line was absorbed into International Mercantile Marine Co., a huge corporate trust whose reins were held by New York financier J. P. Morgan. Seven years earlier in 1895 when the U. S. Treasury found itself nearly out of gold, Anders wrote, Morgan created a private syndicate that supplied the U.S. Treasury with $65 million in gold, and floated a bond issue that restored the treasury surplus of $100 million. Anders, thought

Amos, is involved with some very powerful men.

Meanwhile, in Equality where day-to-day living involved less-powerful men, their far-less-important problems seemed equally enormous.

"Now what, Your Highness?" asked Rachel as she and Jared sat on a blanket eating a picnic dinner above the river near the bay.

"What do you mean: 'Now what'?"

"Are you going to go or are you going to stay?"

"I won't leave," said Jared, clinging to the last vestige of hope. "The colony deserves to continue and succeed, if only to honor the memory of Ed Pelton. I've put so much of me into this colony, I don't want to quit. We still have some good people. It can still work."

Jared glared at Rachel as she looked back at him with a Cheshire Cat smile.

"It's lucky for you that I love hopeless romantics," responded Rachel.

"Well, that's where you're wrong, m'lady. I am *not* romantic."

"Ah, but I disagree, m' Lord," countered Rachel. "You are but most romantic. Incurably so, and it is this trait I find so attractive."

"I could live without Equality," said Jared, "and all the nonsense that's gone on here, so I guess I'm not a complete romantic – and I may not have much, but I have you. So I'm not 'hopeless' either." As he said that, emotion began welling up inside him and, although it wasn't supposed to happen yet, the moment felt right, and Jared decided to ask something he had been giving considerable thought.

"Rachel, we've never discussed this..." He stood up and reached down with his right hand, taking her left hand and urging her to her feet.

"Discussed what?" responded Rachel as she got up.

"I wanted to be a lot further ahead by now," explained Jared as he took both her hands in his. "I expected the difficulties with the colony would be worked out and, by now, the system in Bellamy's *Looking Backward* would be operational, and I would have participated in building a utopia. That was my plan."

Rachel stared at Jared.

"I wanted the best," said Jared, "for both of us. I wanted to get it done first. But now I can't say it will happen. Maybe I *am* a hopeless romantic… He turned his head to the side, then back toward Rachel's beautiful eyes.

"Ever since the first day we met…gosh you were so beautiful…I know I clown around, but I had to do that to grab your attention." Jared drank in Rachel's beauty.

"Rachel, I have always been in love with you." Rachel's lips parted as looked back at Jared. "I have always loved you, and I know I will always love you. Through the difficult times you have been an incredible source of inspiration for me, a gift from God."

God? He had never before referred to God, thought Rachel.

Sensing Rachel's thoughts, Jared, added, "The greatest testimony you have is not what you say about God, but who you are. For example, when I look at you, I know there must be angels.

"I'm not an angel."

"Yes, you are." As he said this, he gently drew Rachel to him and said, "I can prove it scientifically."

He put his arms around her and, constricting forcefully, kissed her long and passionately. Rachel closed her eyes, immersed in his affection until they both needed to come up for air.

"There," said Jared, holding gorgeous Rachel tightly. "You kiss like an angel. Proof."

"Whatever you say," said Rachel, wondering how many angels Jared had kissed.

Jared put his arm around Rachel's waist, turned and walked a few steps closer to the river bank, then stopped, looking at the waning sunset.

"Rachel, do you see all the beautiful things around us that are the handiwork of God? Do you see them all?"

"Yes, I do," said Rachel, looking at the sunset reflection on the bay beyond the darkening foreground and silhouetted trees, again marveling at Jared's reference to God.

"Of all of these things," said Jared, "you, Rachel, are the most beautiful."

In the twilight, Jared paused, wanting to savor the moment, wishing he could stop time. In only a few short seconds the highlight of my life will have come and gone, he thought. But postponing the moment would not bring the moment, so he quietly asked the question.

"Rachel," Rachel's face was aglow in the twilight, and Jared committed the vision to memory, "will you marry me?"

Normally never at a loss for words and, theater or no theater, frequently on stage, Rachel looked up at Jared and was mute. In her heart she was saying, "Yes, yes, yes!" But no sound came out of her mouth.

"Rachel?"

Her eyes beginning to glisten, and the words finally tumbled out.

"Yes, yes, oh yes!"

As with Jared's proposal, what she said wasn't what she had planned when often thinking about when this moment might come, but was what she felt when it came. Jared again kissed her long and deeply, savoring the moment, insuring that while this moment could not be repeated, it would never be forgotten. As their lips parted and they looked at one another, they felt like a single being, each an extension of the other. Jared relaxed his arms, feeling her love and his love intertwining like strands of a rope.

"I love you, Rachel."

"I love you too."

Jared slowly let go of Rachel, put his right hand around her waist as he stepped to her side, and they walked back to the picnic blanket.

After folding the blanket and putting remaining items in the picnic basket, Jared and Rachel turned to walk home in the twilight.

"Jared, I want to bring dad up to Equality and show him around," said Rachel as they left the wooded path and began walking along the country road. "He's done a lot of things, and always successfully. He might have some ideas about how things could be improved."

"Sure…if he wants to come."

"He will," said Rachel pleasantly as, without looking up at Jared, she took his arm with both hands, "especially now."

———————•———————

The next day Pastor Nordquist's daughter and future son-in-law took Amos up to the colony for the first time. Out of curiosity, Amos was anxious to see what was there for, between Rachel and Jared, he heard a great deal, but until now had never seen anything.

After a half hour, Pastor Nordquist stopped and looked about the disorderly site, visually summarizing what he had seen. He smiled, and Jared's heart sank while Rachel only wondered what her father found to smile about.

"Jared," said Pastor Nordquist, "you have, what, 620 acres and no indebtedness? You have oats, corn, cattle, pigs and chickens. Orchards. There's a dairy, a shingle mill, a flour mill, a saw mill…" Amos turned toward Jared and comfortably folded his arms. "Jared, you have all these things and all underutilized. Forget about socialism. Put together a business plan and follow it."

Jared looked at Pastor Nordquist and then Rachel.

"Use your God-given talents wisely," added Pastor Nordquist, "not leaving anything to chance; plan carefully." Pastor Nordquist looked about. "Swede hasn't anything like this. You could do extremely well here, Jared. This is like Nordquist Shipping 30 years ago. And I will be happy to provide business counsel whenever needed."

"Do pastors do that?"

"Oh, yes. Having insight into human nature and value is important for business success. And efficient economics is much simpler than economists make it. The extent to which pastors provide sage business advice would surprise many."

1903

Reverend Frederick T. Gates finally sold the smelter. Gates knew there was a buyer for everything; it was just a matter of discovering the motive for purchasing. The smelter was sold for pennies on the dollar to an international trust controlled by Guggenheim Steel, and eventually dismantled to insure it would never become a competitor.

Reverend Gates took the money received and added it to all the timberland sales receipts. At that moment, the only evidence of Rockefeller in Everett was the avenue that bore his name, parallel with Hoyt Ave. and Colby Ave., and intersecting with Hewitt Ave. All who invested in Everett suffered extensive losses.

Except one.

Reverend Gates' finger went down the ledger as he made one last overview of all the expenses and income received from the Everett venture. Satisfied nothing had been overlooked, Gates deducted total Everett expenses from total receipts. Like the light of dawn, a look of pleasure gradually spread across Gates' face. He leaned forward and made the last accounting entry, deducting the sum of Rockefeller's total investment. He sat back in his chair, looking at the bottom line.

"John will be pleased," Gates understated to an associate assisting Gates with the Everett venture accounting. The associate got up from his desk and walked over to Gates.

"How pleased?"

Gates showed the associate the bottom line, the amount remaining after all business expenses and investment monies were deducted. The associate nodded twice, smiled, and shook his head. In a venture that transformed as continually as the aurora borealis, thanks to Reverend Gates, Rockefeller made $2,000,000 before taxes.

After Rockefeller was extricated from the entire Everett venture, he philosophically summarized the episode as: "Unfortunate." Those hearing this statement considered that, while others lost fortunes, in the literal sense of the word, for Rockefeller the conclusion was untrue. His fortune increased. And his reputation was untarnished. He still had lost no money in any venture.

⬤

At Equality, a free enterprise atmosphere gradually developed where people who knew what they were doing, did it; people who did not, let them; and no one seemed too worried about doing too much. Jared believed he was too young to assume leadership, but he and several others informally became a leadership body directing various aspects of the colony operation, an executive team. During the four years after Ed Pelton's death, the raised fist of socialism clutching a copy of Bellamy's *Looking Backward* was joined by Adam Smith's "invisible hand" holding a ledger, and in the face of potentially crippling adversity, the colony managed its affairs favorably.

As economic conditions on the outside improved, however, more people left, until by 1904 there were only 38 colonists remaining.

The colony was treading water, neither prospering nor failing. The progressive image hung around – and the occasional newcomer was attracted more by this image than the reality of Equality day-to-day living. There was no strong leader and, while things worked adequately, the progressive image lent itself to either the rise of an authoritarian leader or, in the absence of a dominant autocrat, a leadership void waiting to be filled. In early 1904, underutilized Colony assets were nevertheless extensive, the void left by Norman Lermond and Ed Pelton was still open, and, consequently, Equality was ripe for takeover.

94

Jared focused on becoming the best at one thing and, consequently, through repetition and focus, Jared's proficiency as a trainer of prehistoric animals was now second to none.

No one was better, especially at night when the two monsters would rage at their keeper or anything else, a reminder that no matter how well-fed the beasts were, or how carefully their environment was controlled, turning one's back for a moment could spell disaster.

Armed with the necessary instruments, Jared advanced cautiously. Ten seconds were available to get the job done. Only ten seconds.

Seven…six…five…

With four seconds to go, feeling the hot breath of the beast, Jared pulled the second safety pin from his mouth, slipped it through the two remaining diaper corners, and with lightning speed slipped on the rubber pants.

Eight seconds total.

"Zip, zap, zop, done!"

The monster roared, wanting to get down from the changing table.

"Hyahhh! Get back!" barked Jared, jumping backward and momentarily wielding an imaginary whip while making credible whip-cracking noises.

"It's a long drop to the floor, buddy," Jared said. "You monsters fly too?" Jared looked about fearfully.

Jared lifted Caleb and lowered him to the floor where he clambered away on all fours while making ear-splitting turtle noises. Jared reached for Thomas, insatiably salivating, digging his powerful claws into Jared's pant leg while awaiting the same ritual within the same time restriction.

Life had returned to abnormal in the Young residence.

Finished with Thomas, the skilled handler quickly redirected the two beasts back to the reinforced concrete holding pen where Jared quickly bundled them in preparation for the buckboard ride to grandma's house. Hurry. Under the circumstances, to be late would be inexcusable.

The twins became excited as the buckboard pulled up in front of grandma's house. Normally everyone else would be happy too, but not today. Something was wrong; everyone was somber.

While Grandma Anna waited outside not far from the buckboard, memories politely patted her heart as they rose in her consciousness. Jacob died of heart failure a year ago. The memory of Jacob, however, remained Anna's companion, clinging to her much as Jacob himself, in her imagination wrapping his arms around her neck, and exchanging as much love as possible. The memory never let go. And when she would sit knitting, and the memory of Jacob would hug a little tighter than normal, Shadow would raise her head and look at Anna. It seemed Shadow sensed Anna's heartache. It was odd. The others never noticed. And now, with Shadow's death, no one would.

Anna Nordquist wiped a tear from her eye with the tip of her finger as she watched the proceedings in the chill, fall air. It was so, oh, silly on one hand, but on the other, Shadow had become almost like one of the children. This is not the first funeral for an animal that the girls have attended. There were Shadow's stillborn puppies. And Grover. Before that, there was the bag of drowned kittens Inga and Esther accidentally snagged while fishing in Minnesota, a discovery causing no small amount of unhappiness. They brought the small creatures home, and Amos gave them a funeral.

And now the girls are all grown with children of their own, thought Anna. And loving, God-fearing husbands. Life is both so full and rich, short and fleeting. While her eyes were seemingly inexpressive, her lips, aided by her teeth, lightly pressed inward against one another.

Considering Shadow was a family pet for years, it was a formal affair. Jacob and Samuel Odegaard lowered the small casket – a gift from Swede who stood quietly watching – into the ground, the physical resting place for the body of Shadow.

Inga, Esther and Rachel, like Anna, felt foolish as tears slowly formed in the corners of their eyes, but Shadow was part of the family and this was his final moment with them.

Joshua Nordquist also could not subdue his emotions as he thought of his best friend. Do dogs have souls? wondered Joshua. It seemed Shadow must.

After giving a 3-minute eulogy, reminisces of Shadow's life with the family, Amos comforted his angelic wife and his 14-year-old son, and openly thanked God for the tender hearts in his family, again reminding them that if God cares for sparrows, cats and dogs, He certainly cares for us. As the last shovel of dirt was tossed, Amos once again mused that funerals are not for the deceased. He blessed those that mourned, and ended with a brief prayer.

Jared carried Caleb and Thomas as he and Rachel walked slowly to the buckboard. Rachel was quiet as she pulled herself up into the seat and, around her shoulders, strapped a special front harness for carrying the twins. Her hands would support the harness base. Jared first handed her each boy and, after climbing up himself, strapped the twins comfortably in the harness. Rachel put her arms around Caleb and Thomas, and gently hugged them.

"I love you two," she said, and alternatively and rapidly kissed each one until they began to yuckle.

"A bunch of new people arrived at the colony yesterday," said Jared as the horse trotted forward.

"Really." Rachel didn't look up. "How many?"

"Oh, I guess about a dozen." Jared turned the horse down an intersecting dirt road.

Rachel looked at Jared. "Did they stay?"

"Stay?" responded Jared. "They not only stayed, they have more ideas to revitalize the colony than anyone already there." Jared leaned forward, allowing the reigns to slack slightly. "I don't know; maybe they're a godsend. They sure have everyone excited. Maybe the colony will be like a cormorant about to rise from the ashes," said Jared.

"Phoenix," corrected Rachel.

"No. No cormorants there. Too hot."

"Aghhh," Rachel gagged. "Why didn't you tell me this last night?"

"Didn't learn until this morning. Cormorants migrate to Seattle where the weather is…"

"Jared!" Rachel looked at Jared, teeth bared. How much unhappier the world would be without Jared, she thought. Then she smiled, laughed softly and looked down again, shaking her head.

"Well," began Jared, taking a deep breath, "what with your dog dyin', I didn't think you'd care to hear anything about the colony. Especially considering that every time something got me optimistic in the past, it always turned out to be a wild goose chase." Jared looked at Rachel. "Did I get that right? 'Wild goose'?"

"You did," said Rachel with a melodramatic sigh. "I'm so proud of you."

"Oh, thank you. Thankyouthankyouthankyou."

The horse trotted at an even gait, knowing the way home.

"So," Jared continued, "I thought I'd hold off saying anything. But this time, we might have something. These people aren't like anyone else who has arrived."

"Where are they from?"

"New York."

"Did they bring anything with them besides big ideas?"

"You mean money?" asked Jared. "Stuff?"

"Anything of value."

"Nothing much," answered Jared.

"What do they intend to do?" asked Rachel. "What's their plan?"

"No plan. Just the opposite. They emphasize freedom." Jared looked intently at Rachel. "Freedom," Jared repeated.

Rachel looked sideways at Jared, her lips parting, but made no response.

"They're from the Freeland Central Association – that's what they called it – and they say they know all sorts of people they can bring to rejuvenate the colony," said Jared. "They say the most important thing is there has to be in an environment where people can be free."

"Free," Rachel echoed, still looking obliquely at Jared as the horse trotted along.

"Yeah," said Jared, "they say freedom is the solution to everyone's problems."

"Free. Free from what?" Rachel said in a low tone of voice, turning and looking at Jared discerningly.

"Well," Jared shrugged his shoulders without moving the reigns, "anything, I guess. Do what you wanna do."

"Martin Luther would have something to say about that," smiled Rachel. "The will is in bondage."

"To what?"

"Sin," said Rachel.

"How does being free to do whatever you like, as long as it doesn't hurt anyone else, lead to sin?"

"The natural man is inclined to sin," said Rachel. "Read history – or just the papers. It's like an apple falling from a tree. It only falls in one direction. The natural man has neither desire nor ability to go the other direction. Going the other direction requires help from a Greater Power. So 'free' means free from God, conscience, and that opens the door to all kinds of misery."

"But we can set standards that…"

"You said, 'free'. Remember?"

Jared flicked the reins.

"But, yes, whenever you reject existing standards," said Rachel, "viable and venerable, it doesn't mean you have *no* standards, Jason, it means the way, as you just suggested, is open for alternatives – alternatives usually touted as new and, ta dummm, 'revolutionary,' but which are probably as old as these hills. My fear, Jared, is these alternatives would already be existing standards if they worked, but they aren't and probably don't and, consequently, what will result are the usual results: acrimony, strife and Lord knows what."

"And you know all this by virtue of…?"

Rachel's lips tightened for a moment as she looked at Jared.

"Free. Freedom. It's an ancient scam. The Godless void usually attracts a heavy-handed leader who wants followers unencumbered by standards and, therefore, free to do whatever he wants." Rachel looked at Jared intently. "Do we have a dominant leader with gaggle of followers?"

"Uh, the man who does all the talking," answered Jared, "is named Alexander Horr. He's very n…"

"Jared?" Rachel looked at Jared skeptically. "That's his real name?"

"'Fraid so," Jared shrugged. "He's kinda nervous," continued Jared, reins in his hands. "Never stands still. And he continually uses his hands when he talks, like our lives depend on hearing what he has to say."

Jared pulled on the reins as the buckboard approached the modest house in which he and Rachel resided near the colony.

Jared climbed down from the buckboard, took the twins from Rachel who removed the twin-harness, and Jared stood rigidly as Rachel placed her hand on his shoulder while climbing down. As Rachel and Jared walked toward the house, Jared adjusted his hold on the twins whose weight increased proportionately with the decline in distance to the front door.

"Horr is about as tall as you, Rachel, and his hair is a dark, rusty color. He's from Hungary and has a strong accent. He says that Bellamy was too idealistic, impractical, and that a book called *Freiland* written by someone named Hertzka, is more pragmatic. He says we're doing things all wrong and we need reorganize according to what people do in *Freiland*.

Rachel walked up the three porch steps and opened the front door for Jared and the twins. After closing the door, Rachel took off her coat and hung it on a hook next to the door. "What else does Mr. Horr have to say?" Rachel asked.

"He said he had been following our experiences in Equality ever since it was founded," said Jared as he handed over Thomas whose cocoon Rachel removed.

"Probably waiting to see if it worked, and, if not, to take over," said Rachel.

Jared glanced at her.

"No, he had already concluded it wouldn't work. He said he knew things would not work out, why, and how things should be done differently."

"Did he tell you what should be done differently?" asked Rachel, putting Thomas on the floor.

"Oh, yes," answered Jared. "No one else could get a word in. He seems very sure of himself. One general rule was that…"

"Rule?"

"…was that in order to advance economic freedom, interest must be abolished."

"He can abolish interest, but not self-interest," said Rachel. "As has already been demonstrated in Equality, no one abolishes self-interest…which will make it difficult to abolish interest."

Jared placed Caleb next to Thomas on the floor, and the two boys set about entertaining one another.

"Maybe if you need money," added Jared, "you must convince the source of capital to invest in whatever you need money for. Sell stock. Pay dividends. In any event, Freiland, in the book, is an imaginary place in Africa where everything is own…"

"…is so advanced."

"…where everything is owned in common by all citizens, but each individual gets paid according to seniority and how many hours they work."

"What a novel idea," said Rachel, intentionally punning, and obviously unimpressed.

"After expenses and salaries," continued Jared, "any money remaining is divided among the populace like dividends. In Freiland the primary rule, if you will, is that everyone is allowed to do whatever they want, as long as – like you said earlier – it does no harm to others."

Rachel laughed as she looked up at Jared. "I can do anything except what would harm someone else."

"Yes," answered Jared. "That's simple enough."

"Suppose, for fun, I wanted to go to bed with, oh, the barber in Stanwood," said gorgeous Rachel, subtly flaunting her chest and looking at Jared coquettishly. "That's simple enough. No harm there. And I just luhhhv big, black mustaches."

"No harm? Of course, there's harm."

"How?"

"I'd be devastated," said Jared, putting his hands on his hips. "It would ruin our marriage!"

"I wouldn't tell you."

"Wha'...it's still wrong."

"Not if you don't know. If you don't know, you won't be hurt...and, therefore, it's not wrong."

"What if I find out?"

"Then it's wrong," said Rachel.

"That's dumb."

"Beyond dumb," said Rachel. "And what might the barber have been doing if I hadn't, eh hem, intervened?" Looking up at Jared with partially closed eyes, she slooowly licked her upper lip. "In his barber chair, he might have had a doctor who was working on a cure for, say, consumption, and in the course of conversation the barber may have given the doctor advice that would have led the doctor to make a decision that would, in turn, lead to saving the lives of millions! The world would be a better place!

"But, no! Rachel Ruth Nordquist Young," Rachel turned her head and pretended to spit on the floor, "felt like seducing the barber – perfectly harmless because you were never going to know – with millions of lives lost!" Rachel turned toward Jared, wide-eyed. "And it's all my fault! Don't you see?" Rachel raised her forearm to her forehead. "I should be put in jail!"

"That's..."

"I'm so *rotten!*" shouted Rachel, striking her left shoulder with her right hand.

"You're not rotten!"

"I *am!*" yelled Rachel. "I'm such a *wretch!*"

The twins looked up at their mom and laughed.

"What's the point in all this?!" shouted Jared, waving his arms. "I don't... Rachel, judgment lapses happen all the time."

"Jared, that's – the – point!" stated Rachel, standing directly in front of Jared with her index finger on his chest. "In a system where there are no restraints and no direction, more wrong decisions, bad decisions, oversights will happen. I made a judgment error. Surpraeez! In a 'no rules, feel good' system, judgment errors are encouraged. It's like putting a blind pig in a fenceless pen." Rachel jabbed her finger into Jared's chest. "The result of my action was *harm*, [stab] moose breath! I didn't intend for harm to result but it *did*, [stab] ant brain! And now I feel terrible! Terrible! In doing a feel-good thing, I ruined people's lives," said Rachel, throwing her arms in the air in mock despair. "*C'est la vie.*"

"La vee."

"My point," growled Rachel, "is the Freiland golden rule, this 'if it harm none, do as you will' idea is an invitation to disaster. It's just like socialism. It sounds good; it doesn't work. After a while there will have to be absolute Thou Shalts and Shalt Nots, correct behavior actually becomes restrained and rigid...

but it won't make any difference."

"What do you mean, 'After a while there will be…'?"

"If the system is unfettered as it apparently is in Freiland, after people do whatever they want for a while, they naturally start making their own personal standards, rules, based on outcomes of previous actions. Those self-serving standards will vary, of course, with personal experience. And with subjective standards," continued Rachel, affectionately taking Jared's arm, "and no absolutes, people will begin to infringe on one another's rules of behavior." Rachel's eyebrows rose. "Then," she pointed upward with her free hand, "everyone begins to see themselves as either repressed or a victim of the self-centered indiscretion of others."

"But I'm discrete," stated Jared as he turned toward the door. "For example, I have to discretely put the buckboard out back and put Star…"

"Then like-minded individuals eventually aggregate," interrupted Rachel, "and confrontations between individuals evolve to confrontations between groups. Stronger persons attempt to dominate. And the wheels fall off the wagon."

"Not if I put it out back. And, okay, but doesn't the Bible say the same about doing unto…"

"'Do unto others as you would have them do unto you' is different than 'if it harm none, do as you will," said Rachel, continuing to hold Jared's arm, forcing him to hear her out. "The former requires that you put the welfare of others first – an extension of Christ's admonition to love one another – while the latter puts you first in line every time. It doesn't sound that way; I'm sure it's never presented that way – probably just the opposite – but it works that way. No question, it's still about you. In the framework of self-oriented judgments and lack of formal moral restraint, others become either vehicles for, or annoying obstacles to, self-serving, hedonistic behavior inevitably leading to trouble."

"Well, I never cared for Hedons anyway."

"Hedons?"

"Running around serving themselves. Champagne mostly. Hedons. Worse than Cretins. After I return from discretely corralling Star," said Jared with contrasting mock pedantry, "we shall continue this enlightening discussion."

They walked the short distance toward the door.

"I hate to be a big, verbal, wet blanket," concluded Rachel, opening the door, "but, Jared, in my opinion, here we go again. And, if you don't mind, I don't want to go through another experiment."

On the other side of the room the turtles crawled frantically toward the root cellar door, excitedly anticipating the inevitable.

"Hey, you two!" yelled Jared. "Get away from there! No. No. No. The cellar door is off-limits, so just head on over to the other end of the kitchen." Jared pointed toward the kitchen.

Caleb and Thomas stopped dead in their knee and hand tracks at the sound of "No. No. No." And, looking backward in a mirror image, grinned semi-toothlessly at their father and then at one another, obviously both thinking about the object of "No. No. No."

How fascinating, Rachel intuited. Infants who haven't mastered a language must think with an intrinsic language that apparently works perfectly well while it lasts. Infantese. I wonder what it sounds like? If it sounds at all. And what if we could somehow bridle that language and continue it into adolescence and adulthood?

We'll go to the kitchen, the turtles thought in Infantese, looking toward the kitchen area. Beats going to the bedroom because, although it is that time of day, we're not tired.

Jared opened the door and looked outside.

"Don't think there are any Hedons around," he said to himself fearfully. "But maybe I should get my rifle."

"Get Star into the corral." Rachel watched Jared grin, step outside and close the door.

Rachel enjoined the turtles, "Stay away from the cellar door. In fact, I have an idea. C'mon you two, it's time for a nap."

But we're not tired!

Rachel picked up the twins and turned toward the bedroom as the boys looked up at their young mother and thought: children's naps are not for children. Children's naps are for adults needing rest. You're very old. You don't remember being forced to take a nap. You don't remember that you didn't really sleep. Like us, you were a good child, so you pretended to sleep. Day after day, week after week, month after month, pretending. Remember? No, of course not.

Rachel approached the bedroom door. The twins looked at one another as their fears were about to be realized. Abusive oppression! This gross injustice can only be countered with...

The reverberating cries would have arrested the attention of even the most disinterested student of the Jurassic Period.

September 16, 1904

"Uhhrrh."

It was a schnauzer-like growl, weakly audible in the littered little room.

Nauseating kerosene fumes blended with the odors of sweat-saturated work clothes, and uric cow manure tracked-in on the black, oiled wood floor. From one dark corner, the smell of sour, spilled milk contended with other noxious odors. Underfed cats, wonting for comfort on a ripped and worn couch, skirmished with biting fleas. The pan at the table corner had rancid leftover beans sustaining fungi and flies, and smelling similar to the moldy cat feces in the corner by the door. The air seemed tinted green as if the sickly room were about to vomit.

In the dimness it was impossible to estimate how many flies had died – died on the floor, died on the soiled shelf above the washbowl or the dirty plates next to it. A few dead flies even littered the small table and the end of the broken bench where Alexander Horr sat grinding his teeth, ignoring the atrophy about him. Dead flies. Upside down. Beelzebub bound. Considering the means by which flies thrive when alive, Rachel once wondered, why do they die? In Alexander Horr's cubicle apartment, dead flies fit.

"Uhhrrh," Horr growled again as he rolled a cigarette. The cigarette completed, he struck a Lucifer, lighting the cigarette, and took a puff, dropping the smoking match on the floor. Holding the cigarette in his left hand, he grabbed his pen with his right.

Leaning over his writing, Alexander Horr's lank, rust-colored hair hung over his right eye, obstructing his vision and his concentration. With the back of his right hand, being careful not to jab himself with his pen, he agitatedly brushed away the obstruction, taking no time to put it permanently in place. It interfered with his writing, but didn't everything?

"Tam nuisintz," he breathed.

His Hungarian accent told others only that, like them, he was new here.

Attempting to recover his train of thought, he flicked his head upward, looking straight ahead. Where? Where was he? The dark convolutions of his brain were warrens where countercultural thoughts lived and multiplied like mountain rabbits. In the cerebral dimness, grinding his teeth, Horr attempted to entrap his elusive initial thought.

"Uhrrh!" He sucked in some smoke and, eyes wide, blew it out while placing the cigarette on a used canning lid.

His narrow shoulders began to twitch as his head moved slightly to the left and the right and back. His right hand again dutifully brushed back his hair while the nervous fingers of his unburdened left hand drummed on the table, foreigners in a land of otherwise dull appendages. Tired of drumming, the fingers jumped up and began sifting through the sedimentary layers of Horr's scalp, probing for artifacts, as strands of dark corn silk hair again fell over his right eye.

"Uhhrrrr-tam!" he spat, aggravated, taking his pen hand from the paper.

"Tam nuisintz!" he yelled, startling flies still alive. In Horr's mind, the words seemed to echo about the room ("Tam nuisintz! Tam nuisintz! Tam nuisintz!…"). He looked about wildly (as if sensing someone else in the room) and, seeing nothing, returned to his writing.

Books by Spencer and Marx lay on a nearby shelf. On Horr's small table was a worn copy of fellow Hungarian Theodor Hertzka's *Freilandein soziales Zukenftsbild* [*Freeland: An Image of Future Society*], Horr's obsession.

After arriving in Equality, Horr and his soiled sycophants excitedly sniffed about like mice in a larder. Jared watched Horr scurry about the colony, burrowing in Equality politics, digging in everyone's dirt, his secretive, insensitive behavior, his narcissistic blindness to alternative convictions, causing several colonists to become openly critical of Horr, but with a mole's aversion to light, it didn't matter, for he saw only what he wanted to see. After a few weeks, Jared considered Horr irrational, garrulous, and abrasive, and began avoiding him.

Bent over the table, Horr squinted through narrow, jack-o'-lantern eyes at the brown writing paper lying submissively before him. His left hand rose, reached for the cigarette, and he sucked in some more smoke which drifted down into his lungs to be violently discharged, shooting through his teeth as if exploding in his mouth, while he pushed the pen like a plow across the brown paper, preparing another inspired lecture to recalcitrant membership. By sheer force of will, like a small-but-indefatiguable army of ants in a decaying log, Horr and his followers would transform the environment to their liking.

Horr's horde coerced one insignificant triumph after another until the sum of the insignificant triumphs was significant, enough to place Horr at the front of the colony. He became the *de facto* colony leader, Ed Pelton's successor. While many did not like it, all gradually became acclimated to it.

Horr began his reign by changing the colony name. *Equality* became *Freeland*, and over a period of a few weeks Alexander Horr successfully coerced, cajoled and manipulated enough to be elected colony Secretary, the leader *de jure*.

He had control and like hundreds of similar leaders before him, was tolerant of any point of view except those not his own.

By the summer of 1905, as more pliable members became used to Horr's agenda, enough votes were available to amend the BCC constitution. Horr's revised constitution wording made future changes to the constitution, as well replacing officers like Alexander Horr, very difficult. Horr had his fiefdom which he labeled "libertarian," a political, economic and social system wherein people were free to do whatever he liked.

Remaining dissenters among established colony members wondered why, of all people, Alexander Horr arrived in Equality? The colony had been doing well. Horr's arrival seemed almost as if there was some providential vendetta at work. It was illogical to think such thoughts but, at the same time, thus far events in the Equality experiment defied logic and, although concerned about the future, Jared was completely unprepared for what would happen next.

95

After Church, Pastor Nordquist came up to the colony with Jared to see how Jared's experiment was coming along.

"That's a fine barn," said Amos, looking at the huge colony barn that housed dairy cattle, horses and 100 tons of hay. "Swede would be impressed."

"It was a communal effort," said Jared.

"Barn raisings usually are," smiled Amos.

"Yes, but we knew that if our goal – self-sufficiency and that none would suffer want – was to be realized, we would need an enormous barn. That barn symbolizes our socialist ideals. If the colony was a wheel, it would revolve around that barn."

"Yes, it looks to be the heart of the colony."

Jared stood silently, arms folded, looking up at the huge barn with pride.

"It is, however, only a barn," said Pastor Nordquist. "You might redirect communal focus toward something a little more meaningful, permanent."

"Like what?" asked Jared, looking at Pastor Nordquist who looked back.

"Jesus Christ."

"That would first require everyone believing in God Almighty."

"My prayer is these people all either have or receive that belief."

Jared shrugged. Why is the god of socialism anything but God?

"You have an impressive enterprise here, Jared," said Amos. "Self-sufficiency is admirable, but you would more effectively capitalize on your labor and resources by creating a wide trading radius and utilizing the primary strengths of the colony – doing a few things extremely well – rather than trying to do everything."

"But the colonists still don't trust the outside community. This whole undertaking was started because what is out there is not dependable."

"As far as depending is concerned, first, depend on the Holy Spirit. That's the foundation. Everything else can be built upon it." Pastor Nordquist smiled at Jared's expression of puzzlement. "Secondly, with respect to production, it isn't necessary to entirely depend on the outside community but…"

"Excuze me!"

Jared and Amos turned around to face the man standing behind them.

"Vhadar you talking about?" asked the person who looked up at Amos. "Vhadar you doing here?"

"We were talking about efficiently utilizing our resources," said Jared.

"You, Jared, should be verking," said Alexander Horr with asperity. The jack o'lantern eyes in his narrow, hatchet face seemed to bulge as if being pushed against from the inside. Horr turned to Amos. "And you should not be here not minding your business."

Amos' expression also became perplexed while Jared's visage darkened.

"It's a free country," said Jared, "and this is a free colony. Free. Isn't that what you keep telling us?"

"Id izn't free for men who talk nonzenze," said Horr, waving his hands. "This colony vill only verk if ve do what Hertzka says, not vhat dis man says. 'God.' 'Holy Spirit.' 'Capitalize.' I hear. You should not listen. He is not da solution; he cause da problem!"

"I'm not trying to interfere in your affairs," said Amos. "I was making helpful suggestions."

"Ve don't vant suggestions. You should go!"

"He's my guest," said Jared.

"You should bring other guests," said Horr, arms folded. "Not dis man. He iz not somevun ve vant here!"

"I beg your pardon," said Jared, "I don't know who you think…"

"Jared, Jared." Amos turned and looked at Horr. "I just came to visit."

"Don't visit," said Horr who made the mistake of pushing against Amos' shoulder for emphasis. It was like a mountain beaver pushing against a mountain lion – Amos did not move – except to grab Jared's arm just before Jared got to Horr. Amos firmly-but-gently pulled Jared back to one side, and looked down at Alexander Horr.

"Conducting an unemotional, objective discussion with someone who takes a stand based on nothing but negatives is difficult," said Amos to Horr as Amos flashed back to Sunny and Sol. "You go nowhere because you've nowhere to go. What you don't believe doesn't impress me. I might be more impressed if you tell me what you do believe."

Horr looked back defiantly.

"I didn't become a Christian pastor based on negatives. The power of the Holy Spirit is not evident to you and, since it isn't evident, you think, no, there is no such thing. It is, however, extraordinarily evident to many others, Alexander. Like the ground we stand on."

Amos studied Horr. "Alexander, have you been to Alaska?"

"Alaska?" Horr's stern expression took on a tinge of perplexity. "No!" he said gruffly.

"Since you've never seen Alaska, then it must not exist. Is that correct?"

"Nonzenze," said Horr in a monotone.

"Don't you ever worry about your soul, Alexander?" Amos asked sincerely.

"Zoul? You can walk on Alaska. You can zee it. 'Zoul' is nonzenze. You die, you die. Nut'ing lives when you die! This," Horr angrily kicked the dirt, "is vhere ve go vhen ve die. But, now, you go!"

"Then how are we having this conversation, Alexander? Does your inability to sense anything apart from the here-and-now determine it doesn't exist? Intelligence? No such thing? Presentiment? Prescience? Genius?" Amos folded his arms. "Pure fantasy?" Amos stared at Horr. "Shakespeare, Milton, Bach, Handel, Rembrandt? All just incredibly lucky? Holy? Sacred? Divine?" Amos held out his hands questioningly. "Just imaginative illusions? And what about honesty, thrift, charity and courage? All senseless, meaningless?" Amos pressed his fingers together. "Love?" Amos's eyes grew wide as he looked down at Horr. "Life itself?"Amos's head tilted to one side. "Somehow consequences of coincidences?"

Horr looked back, flummoxed, angry and not understanding.

"Alexander," said Amos as he turned intimidatingly toward the smaller man, his eyes boring into Horr's, "you need to tell me: who was Jesus Christ?!"

"He vaz…he *vaz*…!" screeched Horr defiantly in his discomfort, "…*he vas nut'ing*! You *leave*! *Now*!" Horr shrieked, waving his arms.

"Very well," said Amos, "but you need to think about these things, Alexander, because they exist as surely as the dirt you just kicked. Meanwhile, Christlessness and emptiness walk hand-in-hand. I'll inquire about you from time-to-time, and I will pray for you during the interim."

"Don't inquire! Don't…," Horr shuddered, "*pray*…yust *go!*"

"No, Alexander, I'll inquire, and I'll pray," said Amos. "That's what I'll do." This guy's so anxious for me to leave, he's nearly hysterical, thought Amos as he turned to Jared, and the two began walking away. I'm glad he's not carrying a gun.

Amos glanced back at Horr who was nervously fumbling with cigarette papers. Amos stopped and turned around. "Alexander? Do you believe the matter will end if I leave?" asked Amos.

Tensely rolling his cigarette, Horr glanced up for a moment, wide-eyed. "I said, you go! *You* go, it goes!"

Amos smiled and in his mind repeated, Nonzenze. He turned around and walked away with Jared, thinking: for better or worse, I just sowed another seed. While the ground is as hard as concrete, sometimes there are cracks wide enough for a seed to take root.

As Amos and Jared walked away, Horr awkwardly lit a poorly rolled cigarette, his hands shaking.

"That miserable rat," muttered Jared as the two men walked away, "He really gets under my skin!"

"He obviously doesn't care for me," said Amos.

"On the other hand, a lot of people don't care for him."

"But it appears that many are disposed to follow him."

"Some people – maybe more than 'some' – are followers…and in Equality there doesn't seem to be much middle ground."

"Sounds like a teakettle beginning to simmer."

"We'll get it worked out tonight."

That evening as the remaining colony members waited for the community meeting to get underway, Charles F. Hart sat whittling, glowering, wondering how he might rid the colony of what he considered a parasitic plague from beyond society's fringe. Hart despised Horr.

Wielding his pocket knife aggressively, Hart whittled small chunks out of a stick as he talked to Jared, seated next to Hart in the front row.

"I'm telling you, Jared," grimaced Hart, "I can't take much more of that slimy dogfish. Somethin's gotta give or this whole colony will be stolen by that dam' *ló tolvaj.*"

"*Ló tolvaj?*"

"'*Ló*' means 'horse' in Magyar, Hungarian. '*Tolvaj*' means 'thief.'"

"Where did you learn Hungarian?"

"Hungaria." Charlie muttered as he mutilated the stick until it broke. "Next to Barbaria." Charlie folded his knife, put it in his pocket, and then folded his arms. "No, I learned it in south Chicago. In south Chicago, one Hungarian mad at another would call the other a *ló tolvaj.*" Charlie looked straight ahead as the glower returned, and he muttered, "Hungaria. Send that bastard back there."

The atmosphere was tense, as it usually was when Alexander Horr and the public met in the same room. Hart sat and stewed. It was too early for speeches, many had not yet arrived, but Hart, anxious, thought someone should set the tone for this meeting. Things are going from bad to worse, he thought, and I should say so.

"Okay, Charlie," he said to himself, putting his hands on his knees, "why not? Let's go."

Standing up and whirling 180 degrees in order to face his neighbors, Charlie shouted,

"Who got us this far?!!"

Instantly, the room grew quiet. Faces went expressionless as everyone stared at Charlie.

"*We* did!" shouted Hart. "For years we did it all. Put up with those hard times. Lermond left us and went back to Maine. Ed Pelton got killed loggin'." Hart thought of the difficult past that, in light of present problems, seemed better than it was. The contrast increased his anger. "And now this slithering *snake*, this slimy, little Horr, wants it all for him*self!*"

As the others watched, Hart took the stick remnant, stuck it between his teeth, and broke it in two.

"That's what someone needs t' do t' that slimey bastard!!" shouted Hart in his gravelly voice to a wide-eyed audience. "I been around too many of his kind. That dogfish, Horr, has only one interest in mind: his own! Tonight, we have to do something to change things! We have to get rid of that vermin! Am I the only one who thinks so or does anyone else agree?!"

A murmur swept through the room and several men nodded. Satisfied, Hart looked at the people, some just taking seats to the rear, unaware they had missed the Cross of Gold sequel, and Hart turned and took his front row seat, his anger momentarily subsiding.

Even Charlie Hart, however, was unaware of the extent of Horr's convictions. Horr was unlike most people, even in Equality/Freeland. Horr kept pictures of famous dissidents in his room including loner Leon Czolgosz, the anarchist who, believing economic conditions necessitated extreme violence, assassinated President William McKinley three years earlier. Colgosz's last words before being electrocuted were: "I killed the President because he was the enemy of the good people – the good working people. I am not sorry for my crime."

Horr was also a narcissistic misfit, with misfit associates, intent on leading colonists along a path many wanted no part of.

Minutes later, Horr walked briskly back and forth from acquaintance to acquaintance, stopping to speak with the vague sententiousness of a Delphic oracle, talking only long enough to insure that the acquaintance – who at first thought they understood what was being said – began questioning that understanding. Horr smiled and abruptly turned as he marched to the next confusion custodian candidate. When the time comes that I speak, Horr thought, they should know what I said I would say.

Horr was suspicious of Pastor Nordquist who espoused an ideology that favored God, not any man, countervailing Horr's agenda. Horr chose to believe Christianity, which he called "religion," was a tool of the elite used to subjugate the common man. To the extent that Horr gave the Bible any consideration, he found it annoying. Horr wanted to do what he wanted to do, including things the Bible forbade or discouraged. Christianity-underpinned society got in his way.

In response to Pastor Nordquist again accompanying Jared about the colony, phobic Horr told his inner circle Amos was plotting to take over the colony.

"Mark my verds. Dis iz vhadee iz doing. He seez vhat iz here and he vahntzit for himself."

Horr said Amos promised Amos' followers an earthly paradise…including "spiritual wifery," something some religious sect leaders advocated, where any woman in the colony, married or single, acting as a proxy for Pastor Nordquist's wife, Anna, must sleep with Amos if he wished, a big enough lie to be believed.

Amos might have been upset, but he considered Horr to be like a shell casing on the floor of a buckboard: Horr rattled a lot but was harmless. Others did not consider Horr quite so innocuous, however.

The meeting began when Horr stood at the podium and, naturally trilling his r's, spoke adamantly with theatric aplomb and vexed emotion. He beat his chest with his right hand as he shouted upward at the ceiling. He cut lofty images out of English borrowed from translations of Hertzka, stringing slogans together like dead crappie. Eyes wide, his hair blurring his vision, he pushed his head over the podium, countering imagined criticism from potential critics in the front row. He called for an end to failure, and a beginning to success, which could come from his leadership, ideology, and a socio-economic system modeled after Hertzka's *Freiland*.

"To be sooksesful ve mus' reorganize into many small parteezzz. An' each small vun mus' try to beat all d' other vuns. Den ve all get better and ve all get more. But you cannot do it by yourself; you must follow me. I vill show you. If you do not follow, you vill be like you vere."

"What's wrong with *that*?!" shouted Charlie Hart as he stood, becoming angry just trying to understand what Horr was saying.

"You, Hart," said Horr, "are not so shmart as to know vhat vas wrong. You…"

"Whoa! Wait a minute, dogfish," Hart shouted, "one more word out of…!"

"*You* vait, stoopid, beeg horse!!" shouted Horr. "Vhat did you know about…"

"*I'll tell you what I know*!" roared Hart. Hart, livid, eyes wide, was continually pulling himself away from the edge since the beginning of the evening. "I know," shouted Hart, taking a step forward, "how hard we all worked and all the hard times we went through before you got here and started turning everything upside down! I know I could depend on certain things before you got here and now I don't know what the hell's gonna happen!"

Hart took another step forward, shaking his finger at Horr.

"What's this lease that's supposed to be giving you sole control of 160 acres and the colony buildings?" shouted Hart. "What gives you the right t' do that?!"

In the emotion of the moment, other concerned, angry men spontaneously stood up. Wide-eyed Hart struck his left hand with his right fist, his teeth clenched and bared as more men stood up.

The lid was off.

During prior weeks, Horr representatives pushed for power, and honorable colony men had their honor questioned and their integrity challenged. Every uncomfortable incident, regardless of how insignificant, increased the antagonism between neighbors – some of whom opposed Horr and some of whom took the side of the Horr faction – until the colony on the hill came to resemble a social Krakatoa.

The pro-Horr faction began trading angry words with anti-Horr neighbors. For personal as well as ideological reasons, other neighbors joined in. Submerged hostilities surfaced with neighbor confronting neighbor. Antagonisms, simmering on low heat when the meeting began, began boiling over.

"I can't control d' prodookshun vithout having control of the means of prodookshun!" Horr screamed at Hart over the din.

"Who said you have the right to control anyth…?!"

At that moment, someone turned out the lights.

When the lights went out, natural impulses exploded. Acid oaths, epithets, curses, lefts and rights filled the darkened room as hate-filled, angry men and women, like beings possessed, bitterly struggled with unidentified antagonists whom, in the absence of either light or enlightenment, were sometimes protagonists. Libertarian Freeland became unfettered Bedlam and the moment's violent chaos was extraordinary.

The lights came on again, stopping hostilities as if a bell rang to end Round 1. Bruised, bleeding, cursing men, even women, realizing the senselessness of their actions, began to work at recovering their wounded dignity, with one notable exception.

When the lights went out, Hart raced in the direction of the podium, knocking down people in his way. In the podium's vicinity, Hart groped about but couldn't find Horr…until the lights came back on. Looking about wildly, Hart saw Horr partially sticking out from his hiding place, and raced toward the speaker's three-sided lectern.

Feeling Hart coming, Horr bolted for the front row, Hart right behind him, attempting to duck through several people standing in front, when Hart's big right hand caught Horr's shoulder, pulling him back. Screeching like an orangutan, Horr wrenched free but fell. With rattlesnake speed, Hart's left hand shot down and clamped Horr's upper left arm like a bear trap, attempting to pull Horr up from the floor, but Horr not only resisted, struggling with all his might, but did so while clinging to the lower leg of a large woman who in turn was shrieking and violently shaking and kicking her leg as if having been attacked by an animal. As the woman shrieked and kicked, five men quickly jumped in and began to pry Hart loose from Horr. While the rest of the room watched, Charlie Hart finally gave in and, with the men still holding him, stood glaring at Horr. Released from Hart's grip, Horr let go of the woman and scrambled to his feet, standing open-mouthed and wide-eyed about five feet away, staring apprehensively at Hart. Paying no attention to the woman, Horr did not see her angrily pick up her large purse and, teeth bared, using two hands, with all of her might shellelagh Horr, knocking him down. Again, however, he staggered to his feet while never taking his eyes off of Hart.

While Horr held the right side of his head where he was just hit, Hart made no further attempt to resist, and the five men holding him gradually released their grip.

"This doesn't end here," said Hart, pressing his right fist into his left palm in a rotational motion. "You gotta sleep sometime, dogfish."

With the apparent cessation of hostilities, the warring factions stood glaring at one another, and then slowly returned to the business at hand.

People sat down and the meeting recommenced, beginning an emotional struggle that gradually grew to a single-minded intensity as each side angrily leaned heavily into the other. One side made a concerted effort to oust the hated Horr, but became bogged down under enemy sniper fire in the form of technicalities and confusing, illogical counterarguments, and indeed Horr was as slippery as his enemies claimed. After an hour and a half, the anti-Horr forces, exhausted, fell back.

Horr aroused the worst and the best in those he alienated. Disgusted with the mud in which they found themselves wallowing when forced to confront Horr, many simply discontinued the face off, and began plans for leaving. Among those present, however, were hostile men with a willingness to take their hostility to another level, manifesting an atrocious act that would precipitate the end of the colony.

February 6, 1906

The day proceeded normally. Fallen leaves preserved by low and freezing temperatures were still visible on the ground beneath the black outlines of spidery deciduous tree branches in the cold air. As shadows of day merged with the advancing gloom of late afternoon, 20 colony cows, after standing indifferently for hours, were herded into the big barn to be fed with a portion of the 100 tons of stored hay.

The big barn, a monument to the dreams and self-sufficiency of the original colonists, was constructed of beams, boards and shingles cut from 1898 virgin Douglas fir growing on colony woodlands; the barn walls and roof erected by idealists consumed with hope for a better life.

Throughout the county, as the cold darkness advanced slowly, more logs were placed in fireplaces, fortifying farmhouses in self-defense. Darkness soon covered the colony hillside, blending vague black forms into surreal shapes and silhouettes.

Inside the barn, walking toward the lower hayloft after opening one of the huge barn doors, grandfatherly "Daddy" Giles, looking like Santa Claus in bib overalls, pitched hay into the feeding troughs. The barn was his responsibility, and this late afternoon he tended to the horses and cows. He hummed softly as he pitched hay and, occasionally, in his fine British accent, carried on one-sided conversations with the animals.

The animals, especially the workhorses, always listened even if the monologue produced nothing not heard before. Daddy never considered the topics of discussion monotonous. He felt good just talking to someone who didn't argue. Other than the animals, no one in the colony listened any more.

Earlier, others came in to help with the milking and, feeding and milking done, in the lantern-light, Daddy Giles now sat alone on a milking stool, stroking his white beard, contentedly watching the animals still feeding. After a while his backside began to hurt, causing him to slowly straighten up until he was standing. One of the cows turned to look, but the others, finishing dinner, paid no attention. In the cold weather, Daddy Giles's hip always bothered him. Figuring the evening's socializing was over, Daddy picked up his lantern with his left hand and limped toward the big barn door.

Reaching the doors, one open, Daddy placed the pitchfork against the wall and, after stepping outside, shuffled to his right and grabbed the short rope shank attached to the open door. As he pulled the open door toward the barn, the hinges eerily groaned in alarm.

Daddy Giles stared at the hinges, holding his lantern high enough to see as much as he could. He pulled the heavy latch bar over, uniting the two big doors for the night. He couldn't understand why the hinges made that sound. I haven't heard that before, he thought. Just sounded strange. Something that should be checked in the morning, he concluded as, facing the barn, he continued to study the hinges in the lantern light.

It was growing colder as Daddy, holding a lantern high in front of him, turned and walked up the dark path back to the colony apartment building, feeling the fingers of the damp night. His breath preceded him as he thought of how the cold made the barn smell better. Daddy Giles thought again about the eerie sound of the hinges and, chuckling, chided himself for his fears.

He shivered.

Very cold tonight, he rationalized silently, and then chuckled at irrationally feeling as if men were hiding somewhere nearby.

"Bogey men? Daddy, you are much too old for this sort of thing," he said out loud.

He glanced around slowly and seemingly without concern, exercising supreme self-discipline.

The hidden men, barely breathing, waited until he was out of sight, and waited a moment longer to insure an improbable return would not happen.

"I gotta tell y' agin," quietly whispered the first man, reviving a subject already thoroughly discussed, "that stunt at the meetin' was a good'n." Discussion of the previous success bolstered their courage. "Lights out. An' ya' just thought that up?" the whisper said bravely, barely audible.

"Yeah," came the whispered reply.

"Couldn't 'a worked better if we planned it," countered the first whisper.

"I don't think Giles is comin' back," whispered the second man.

"Let's get goin.'"

The workhorses listened to the approaching sounds – quiet, not like humans. At first there was no entrance. The horses inside followed the sounds around the barn. Then the latch bar was raised and the big door opened slightly.

The men stepped in. One raised his lantern, looking about the barn. He started toward the hay bin, but stopped. The horses were watching him. The man – his singular thought commanding his total attention – and the horses exchanged stares.

Lowering his lantern, he woodenly pushed himself forward, and pulled some straw from the bin. The horses looked at the straw as if to say, "What are you going to do with that?"

Looking back at the horses, the man felt like he needed to explain, to allay any fears by minimizing the gravity of what he was about to do (Oh, nothing much. Gotta be done. Just get back to eating). He said nothing, staring uncomfortably at the horses, holding the lantern in one hand and the straw in the other. Gotta be done. The horses turned their heads away while still watching the man.

Turning his back to the horses, the man held the lantern at chest level. Lantern shadows created a ghoulish countenance as he gripped the handful of straw tightly, and carefully stuck the end of the straw into the kerosene lantern. The straw hissed as the end caught on fire, and the man quickly turned around, facing the barn animals, all staring at the man and his fire. The man defiantly looked back and, without turning his head, reached sideways toward the lower hay bin to his right. He looked down and carefully set fire to the hay, as if his conscientious attention to detail would ameliorate the heinousness of his act.

The damp air caused the flames to sputter and crackle at first but, as the heat infused the dry, lower strands of straw and hay, the fire exploded. For a moment, the men watched, mesmerized.

Regaining their wits, the first man dropped the lantern, and they ran for the door, ignoring the frightened animals. Sprinting outside, they slipped and skidded on the wet ground to an abrupt halt. One turned, stepped forward and pushed the big door shut, slamming the latch bar down in one panicked motion as the other man watched in horrified excitement. The big door latched, the men sprinted away, diving under the cover of darkness.

As the flames enveloped the barn, gorging gluttonously on wood, stores, and 100 tons of hay, turning the barn into an enormous pyre, the screams of terrified animals were horrific. From a distance, the concealed men watched the cinders shoot into the sky as the inferno raged uncontested. When the heat grew more intense, the large root house next to the barn began to smolder, growing hotter until it burst into flame. Inside the root house was the remaining winter food supply for the colony. By the time an alarm was sounded and colonists came running, all was lost except three horses somehow not in the barn.

Arriving colonists stood paralyzed as they watched in agonized disbelief. The heat from the huge fire kept them at a distance in the cold dampness.

The big barn, the heart of the colony, together with the root house, would be gone shortly. Much of what the colony owned, and most of what they had produced from months of toil, were gone, taken from them in one demented moment. Within the already venomous atmosphere that enveloped Equality/ Freeland, as the devastated colonists stood watching the roaring fire, each silently vowed: someone will pay for this.

Horr supporters blamed Horr opponents, and Horr opponents despised them even more. Since none were entirely certain of who did it, none were above suspicion. The already acrimonious atmosphere was exacerbated as greater anger, hatred and now fear enveloped the colony like a toxic mist, poisoning hearts and bringing colony affairs to an *impasse* because members could no longer stand to live with one another.

Arguments became physical, and each confrontation increased the division and enmity between the two embattled camps. Men began arming themselves, and a "reign of terror" resulted. Many, out of fear, did the reasonable thing: they picked up and left – a few at first, but, as the caldron continued to boil, the exodus became greater. Alexander Horr gave no thought to leaving.

Jared, having lost all faith in what was once Equality and now Freeland, determined that under these circumstances the colony should be formally dissolved, remaining colony assets sold, and sales proceeds equitably redistributed. Without much difficulty, he and other colonists easily convinced less-emotional members that continuing the *status quo* could be suicidal.

At the last community meeting, Alexander Horr, attempting to capitalize on the misfortune, again proposed to privately lease 160 acres with most colony improvements. The reaction was predictable, and if he pushed as was his wont, he might have been killed. As violence was about to erupt, Horr backed off.

The deteriorating situation deprived Horr and his followers of further triumphs. The colonists were simply unwilling to continue either the experiment or any attempt at conciliation. All wanted out. But with at least as much as they brought in. All wrangled over what was left, and consequent litigation prolonged the sordid affair longer than anyone wanted.

June 17, 1907

Judge George S. Joiner approved the sale of the remaining 400 acres owned by the colony and, officially, the experiment fashioned after Edward Bellamy's novel, *Equality*, and modified to accommodate Hertzka's novel, *Freiland*, was over.

Daddy Giles continued to mourn the loss of his animals, his "family." He was the last to see them alive. Having grown close to his animals, he used his share of the sales proceeds to stay on the colony site, living near where his animals died. Following his death a short while later, his burial, presided over by Pastor Nordquist, was the last act of former colonists, and the end of the last chapter of Equality.

October 9, 1907

Pastor Nordquist sat in the living room reading a letter from Anders. Since 1899, the *Oceanic II* was joined by the *Celtic, Cedric, Baltic* and *Adriatic*, all over 20,000 tons, while rival Cunard had launched the 31,550 ton *Lusitania* and the 31,938 ton *Mauretania*, both of which took their maiden voyages the previous month. Anders wondered if there might be more passenger liners than demand required. Anders wrote that White Star Line was committed to building more ships, however. Amos studied the enclosed postcard of the 709 ft., 24,542-ton *Adriatic* with smoke flowing easily skyward from its two huge stacks. That is enormous, Amos thought.

———————●———————

Anna and Amos suggested Jared and Rachel visit often, occasionally even stay for the night or a weekend. Joshua, 17, was the only Nordquist child still at home. Anna and Amos believed the brief respites would allow Jared and Rachel a chance to catch their emotional breath, and give Jared an opportunity to add another bedroom to the Young house because the twins were getting bigger, Jared and Rachel expected to have more children, and the day would come soon enough when another bedroom was needed.

For Anna, there was another motive: when Jared and Rachel visited, so did the grandchildren, Caleb and Thomas. Anna was "Grandma," assurance that a third generation is never without love.

The first time they stayed overnight, Rachel lay in bed and thought about when she lived in this house. As Rachel lay still, eyes open, thinking about this, she realized spending time in her parent's home made her feel happy and hopeful. There was a permeating essence of love, belonging and security, she thought, and when growing up she took this for granted because she knew nothing else. Rachel's own home did not have that same feeling and, sensing the contrast between Equality/Freeland mutating instability, on one hand, and the tranquil love and stability in her parents' traditional, God-fearing home, on the other, Rachel decided a change must be made. Perhaps it was already underway, she considered, with the end of Equality. What her parents had, she wanted – the presence of biblically-based family structure and the continued sensation that the Holy Spirit was present; Rachel wanted that again.

"Jared, we need to make some changes," said Rachel, sitting in front of a bath chamber mirror. Jared leaned against the chamber wall relishing how beautiful Rachel's hair was, and the natural scent of sweetness her skin had.

"What? You want to add a third story? We don't even have a second story yet. Do you know how much hot air would be required to fill balloons needed to lift a third story?"

"What?"

"What 'What'? If I build a third story on the ground and must lift it up to third story level because there is no second story, how else do you expect me to do that other than with hot air balloons?"

"Jared, you're so full of hot air it would be simple, but, as you know, that isn't what I'm talking about."

"It isn't? Well, once again, you could have fooled me," said Jared with feigned indignation, folding his arms. "I don't know who to believe anymore."

"Well, for starters, let's start with God, not some half-baked experiment," said Rachel, her expression tensing. "Not socialism. These things all feel like attic cobwebs." Rachel's shoulders flinched and she cringed and shuddered. "Get off of me." After a moment her expression relaxed. "And what *is* socialism, by the way? I don't think 'socialism' has ever existed, really. I know I initially encouraged whatever-it-was we did, but if we never become involved in another experiment, I'll be grateful."

"Well, okay, Equality was…well, you know…,"

"No I don't," countered Rachel. "It was like chewing spoiled cod." Rachel made a face and stuck out her tongue.

"Yup," replied Jared, "I was just going to say the same thing. Rachel, I can't change what happened, but we both can learn from it. I know how much you miss Equality, but I'd like to move on."

"To where?" Rachel asked Jared's mirror image. Jared stepped behind Rachel and began massaging her shoulders while allowing Rachel room to continue grooming. Her hand with the hairbrush, however, continued to rest on the edge of the sink.

"Okay, in the future, m'lady, we'll pattern our life after your folks," said Jared to the face in the mirror. "Are they happy? I believe that is what you asked. The answer – don't argue – is, ta dummm: they are. So we'll do it the way your folks do it." Jared added seriously, "Everyone being happy is all I really ever wanted." He folded his arms and looked at the floor, uncharacteristically out of words.

But what he said was enough. The promise of a familiar, stable life flooded Rachel's heart with relief, and the clinging Equality burden – acrimony and hopelessness – fell away. No more social experiments; a normal life. Putting down her hairbrush, gorgeous Rachel Young stood, turned and aggressively hugged her husband hard enough to make him ecstatically moan.

"I love you too," he said as she drove his libido beyond the hypothetical third floor. Jared began thinking concupiscent thoughts about proving his love, but the romance of the moment was broken when visiting Erika Odegaard's melodic voice rang from the kitchen.

"Raaachel! Could you come here, pleeease?!"

With the gravity of the sun, Erika's force of will pulled Jared and Rachel into the kitchen where they witnessed… What is this? thought Rachel. A meeting of the Ku Klux Klan children's auxiliary?

With the incredible ahah!-the-adults-are-absent timing God gives those between the ages of two and four, Caleb and Thomas, pulled out the flour drawer. The flour drawer. The ultimate "No. No. No."

Rachel knew wheat flour was ground for millennia. Flour was found in Egyptian tombs and in ancient Middle Eastern caves. Flour is mentioned several times in the Old Testament. The New Testament. Why the significance of flour? What is flour for?

You play in it, of course. You take hands full and pour them over your head or, if you have a twin brother, his head because, as it is written, two heads are better than one. Barnum and Bailey were joined by Caleb and Thomas, at the moment vaguely resembling two demon-possessed clowns needing only a burning cross to complete the ruse.

"Vell, my goodness," Erika Odegaard sighed, "if you t'ink you haf problems now, you yust vait. Next they vill be falling out of trees."

Ah, the thought, Jared envisioned to himself: two demon-possessed, Klan clowns falling out of trees. His face contorted as he stared at the two floured faces ghoulishly grinning back.

Rachel began laughing. "This…must… have been…how…you started out," Rachel laughed uncontollably at Jared, tears in her eyes.

"Not exactly," said Jared with mock contrasting seriousness. "I didn't have a twin brother."

The levity of the moment went on for several minutes. The mess on the floor and the boys would be cleaned up. The time was coming, however, when Rachel's hysteria would assume a different form, emanating from an event that was no laughing matter.

96

As fall was transitioning to winter, the season allowed time for planning farm and farmhouse expansion. Jared finished the third bedroom, but Rachel also wanted a bigger kitchen, and Jared needed more land. Neighboring farmer Arnie Jorgensen owned several hundred acres of river bottom, and was willing to sell a small amount to Jared.

The Nordquists with the twins and Angus MacGregor arrived at the Jorgensen residence, and the Jorgensen's youngest son, Billie, greeted the guests at the door, with his mother, Helen, close behind.

"Hello everyone, please come in," smiled Helen as Billie held the door open. "Let me take your coats. Billie, would you go play with the twins, please?" Billie dutifully walked over to toddlers Caleb and Thomas and took them to the large, bright red toy chest in his bedroom while Anna, Rachel and Helen chatted in the kitchen.

"Pastor, come on in the living room," said Arnie, extending his hand.

"Angus, Jared, good to see you."

When everyone gathered in the living room, Jared agreed to pay the going rate for 50 acres. By the standards of the day, the amount of land wasn't significant, and neither was the price. Pastor Nordquist offered to help with payment, but Jared and Rachel respectfully declined his offer.

As the adults discussed the land purchase, Billy Jorgensen found Caleb and Thomas entertaining because the twins naturally imitated the behavior of other children and adults, and imitated everything Billie Jorgensen did, laughing excitedly after doing it.

Caleb's and Thomas's antics began two summers ago when, at an early age, they were taken to a nearby lake. It was then that they became known as "the turtles" because of their short frenzied crawl through the water along the edge of the beach. They loved "swimming."

⬤

Five days had passed since the Jorgensen visit. While Jared was doing some uphill excavation by their house, Rachel took the twins on a morning buckboard ride to visit grandma and grandpa. Around noon, Pastor Nordquist and Anna left to visit parishioners, leaving Rachel alone with the boys.

"It's time for a nap, you two," ordered Rachel shortly after 1:00 p.m. Both boys immediately began to whimper.

"Noooo," responded Rachel. "You need a rest now. C'mon."

Rachel took the hands of her recalcitrant charges and began the walk to the spare downstairs bedroom where cribs were. They needed a nap and she looked forward to planning the expansion and partial enclosure of the kitchen while they slept. Rachel was trying to plan exactly what she needed. Getting Caleb and Thomas down for a nap would eliminate interruptions.

"Goodness, you two are warm!" Rachel said as she lifted the boys into their cribs. "You obviously have been playing hard. Also, I suspect you're not feeling too good." Rachel felt their foreheads. "This nap will be good for you." Surprisingly, there was little further protest.

Rachel stood silently, absorbing the moment. They seem fine. Maybe a little under the weather.

Rachel insured that each boy wore socks and was completely covered by blankets. Then she walked softly to the bedroom door, stepped into the hallway, and quietly closed the door part-way in a time-honored effort to keep outside noise from entering while allowing inside noise to exit. By the time Rachel returned to her parents' kitchen to resume her planning, the twins were asleep.

Two and one half hours passed quickly while, seated at her mother's kitchen table, facing the window, Rachel immersed herself in ideas, sketching alternative layouts, straining her imagination. Every detail commanded her attention which she gladly gave. To help matters, Caleb and Thomas slept soundly.

Her concentration was interrupted by a knock at the front door in the entry hallway

Upon opening the door Rachel's mouth fell open and her eyes grew large as she looked up at the calming, quiet face of Doc Torgeson who carried two acquaintances in either arm.

"Vell, Rachel, boys vill be boys," said Doc, attempting to introduce levity into a potentially grave situation. "They vere out by the road. It's a vonder they didn't freeze to death," Doc Torgeson added with concern. "My guess is that they yoost got to the end of the drivevay. Didn't seem to know vhere to go next; yoost standing next to the road. Probably been outside a little too long, though," he tactfully understated as he handed first one and then the other snow-blue, shivering little boy to Rachel who couldn't believe what had happened.

They awakened and simultaneously came upon the idea to go swimming. Why? They were hot. Swimming is what people do when it gets hot.

"You get them into bed," said Doc. "I'll be right back."

Doc went out to his buggy and got his medical carrying case as Rachel mutely hugged her two sons in an attempt to warm them up. In contrast to how warm they were when she put them down for their naps, both were chilled to the bone.

How did I not notice they were up? How long have they been outside? How long does it take two three-year-olds to navigate over 150 feet of wet driveway? Two minutes? Three minutes? Four…? How long had they stood at the end of the driveway? Rachel tried to stay her concern, but in her heart her maternal fears barged to the fore.

Both boys were limp. Caleb whimpered weakly as she returned them to their cribs.

"Ve haf to be careful, Rachel," warned Dr. Torgeson as he returned to Rachel's side. "I yoost came from the Yorgensen's. Young Billie has the measles."

"Measles?" responded Rachel, her mouth not closing.

It was a time when crop failure and natural disasters, but especially sickness and disease, claimed lives of all ages everywhere. While preventive medicine was just learning to tie its shoes, nutritional deficiency and poor sanitation still roamed far and wide, leading many to an early grave. Historically, wealth and influence had never guaranteed longevity. In earlier centuries, Queen Anne of England gave birth 16 times and none of her children lived beyond the age of 10. Peter the Great of Russia and his wife Catherine had 12 children, but only two reached adulthood. Louis XIV and Maria Theresa lost five of their six children either shortly after childbirth or early in childhood, and, much later in life, Louis XIV saw three heirs to his throne – his son, his oldest grandson, and his oldest great grandson – all die from measles within a 14-month period. Stockholm lost one third of its population during an early 18th century plague; 10 years later Marseilles lost half. While medicine was improving – emetics and blood-letting were finally out of favor – during the late 19th and early 20th centuries, health-care had not advanced to the point where the suggestion of measles did not strike fear in a mother's heart.

"Yah," said Doc solemnly. "Pretty obvious now. During the first veek it isn't so obvious. For about the first veek after a child catches the measles, he doesn't know he has them. Dangerous time. Can spread the disease all over hill and dale before it's diagnosed."

"Dr. Torgeson," said Rachel apprehensively, "Billie was playing with Thomas and Caleb last week."

"How long did they play together?" asked Doc, looking at her over his reading spectacles.

"About an hour," responded Rachel, her fingers turning white and beet red as she folded her hands tightly together.

"Then they have the measles too," said Doc as he and Rachel returned to the living room and sat down. "Have you had the measles?"

"Yes."

"Your husband?"

"Yes."

"That is good," said Doc, trying to sound slightly relieved. He apprehensively glanced toward the boys' bedroom.

"Keep those two in bed," said Doc, "keep them warm and give them a lot of diluted warm milk. They're tough little guys, and in a couple of veeks they should be fine. But in the meantime – probably vithin the next four days – they're going to get a rash, and their temperature is going to get very high. In about a veek, maybe sooner, they'll start getting those little blotches behind the ears, on the neck, upper forehead, vorking downward. Those boys vill cough, and need their noses viped, and they vill cry a little. That fever vill stay right up there. This vill be no fun for them or you.

"As long as no other form of illness takes advantage of their veakness, this could be over in three veeks."

Doc looked out the window.

"Being outside in the cold is about the worst thing they could have done though."

Doc stood up and walked toward his worn medical carrying case sitting on a corner chair.

"I have to go now. The Arnestads have three sick kids…and the Van Huizens…" Doc glanced at Rachel as he reached the chair.

"Got to go," he reaffirmed. "I'll be by tomorrow."

He began putting on his heavy overcoat.

"I have some carpentry vork that needs to be done," said Doc. "I'll talk to Jared about payment arrangements vhen I come by tomorrow." Looking toward the boys' bedroom, he said, "I don't t'ink you vill need to vorry about them escaping again."

Picking-up his carrying case, he walked somberly down the hallway to the front door. Doc Torgeson opened the door and touched the brim of his hat as he said, "Good bye, Rachel."

He headed out the door to visit his next patient, thinking about the challenges he had seen so many young mothers face during his 40 years of practice. He had seen so much.

Rachel walked into the guest bedroom, bent over Caleb who was sound asleep, and listened to his breathing. Any sound was inaudible. Thomas was no different.

How long were they outside? Rachel continued to wonder as she sat down again at the table. It just seems incomprehensible that they could get up, walk to the front door, reach up, open it and leave, without my hearing. She put her right elbow on the table, resting her chin on her right palm, and looked at the drawings, plans which absorbed her total attention. Are the spatial relationships between the root cellar door, stove, back door, cooler, sink, cabinets, counters, and kitchen window that all-consuming? Her conscience assaulted her. A house. She turned her head sideways, thinking. God will provide, she reminded herself.

The Bible verse about "the birds of the air…" came to her and, sitting up, she got up, walked into her parents' living room to the coffee table where the family Bible always was. She reached down for the Bible to find the verse and read it. Measles, she thought, turning the pages. I just hope it's nothing else. Hopefully all will go as Doc Torgeson said. Finding the familiar verse, she read to herself.

> *Look at the birds of the air, that they do not sow, neither do they reap, nor gather into barns, and yet your heavenly Father feeds them. Are you not worth much more than they?*

The verses seemed to say to Rachel, "Don't worry about the house. Don't worry about anything. Everything will be fine." The verses did not say that, but "everything will be fine" was what Rachel wanted them to say.

Everything is never fine.

Satisfied, Rachel closed the Bible, returned to the kitchen, sat down, pulled the beckoning sketches toward her and revisited the kitchen plan.

When Rachel didn't come home at the end of the afternoon, Jared rode to his in-law's home. Rachel told Jared about the events of the day, and Jared closely inspected the twins who continued to sleep.

"They're sound asleep," said Jared. "When will Doc stop by tomorrow?"

"I don't know," said Rachel, standing next to her husband. "He didn't say."

"What did he say?" asked Jared, worried, as he felt each boy's forehead. "Their temperatures must each be 130 degrees."

"He said," began Rachel, "that since you and I… you've had the measles, right?

"Yes."

"Since we've both had measles, we wouldn't get sick. He said that the boys would be very sick for a couple of weeks, but then they should start getting well."

"Anything else?" asked Jared, looking down at Caleb.

"Yes, there was…," said Rachel, looking up at Jared, "but don't worry, honey. God will take care of this."

"'This' what?"

"Don't worry."

Jared and Rachel stayed the night. The next day, Doc Torgeson stopped by at around 8:30 a.m. shortly after Anna and Amos had gone into town. Angus was out back, cleaning the barn.

"Vell, Billie Yorgenson's temperature vas 103 degrees," said Doc raising his eyebrows as he would often do, his eyes remaining unchanged. "That vasn't too surprising. Let's see vhat temperatures the boys have."

Doc put a thermometer in Caleb's mouth and, using his stethoscope, listened to Caleb's heart.

"His heartbeat is veaker than I vould like," said Doc solemnly. Jared and Rachel inched closer.

Doc sat motionlessly beside the bed looking at Caleb. The thermometer in Caleb's mouth was still. Caleb's eyes seemed like they were almost open but could open no further.

Doc took out the thermometer and looked at it, remained motionless, studying Caleb for a moment, and finally spoke.

"105."

Rachel's lips parted and her eyes grew wide.

Doc put the back of his right hand on Caleb's forehead, lost in thought. "This is a sick young man," he said to himself.

"Sicker than Billy Jorgenson," affirmed Jared.

"Yes," Doc said almost inaudibly. The room was deathly quiet. Caleb was awake, but lay motionlessly, too weak to do anything. "Let's see how Thomas is faring."

Doc took out another thermometer, studied it, shook it several times and very gently slid it into Thomas's mouth. Doc began using his stethoscope as Thomas remained motionless. After a short while of silence, Doc again informed Rachel and Jared that the heartbeat was weaker than expected. As Rachel sat exercising maximum self-discipline, Doc delicately removed the thermometer.

"Also 105."

As if shouldering a heavy weight, Doc slowly stood, his large frame dwarfing the two children. Again, their eyes seemed to be almost open, attempting to look at him. Or were they looking at anything?

Doc slowly walked the short distance from the bed to his medical carrying case sitting on a nearby chair.

"Yesterday, vhen did you put the boys down for their nap?" asked Doc.

"It was around 1:00," answered Rachel after a moment.

"Were they…in hindsight, could they have been sick then? Did they feel like they might each have had a temperature?"

"Yes," said Rachel.

"Ve don't know vhen they got up…but I drove by and found them around 3:30" said Doc. "Rachel, could you bring the lamp over here for a moment?"

"Yes," Rachel answered. Rachel quickly brought the lamp to Doc.

"Hold it right above Caleb." Doc opened Caleb's mouth with the handle of a teaspoon, probing and carefully studying.

"Now Thomas."

Again Doc probed, looking inside the mouth of Thomas.

"You vould be a good nurse," said Doc.

Rachel said nothing at first. The suggestion reintroduced a series of thoughts in Rachel's mind, and she put her free hand over her tearing eyes as her head dropped. "Doc, I can't believe I…"

"Now, you must not blame yourself," Doc softly interrupted. "You cannot be like God, vith eyes and ears everyvhere to see and hear all t'ings."

Doc Torgeson knew and understood her belief although he did not believe in God as Rachel did. When he was younger, he never wondered about "God," but now occasionally he would. Regardless, his beliefs were secondary at the moment. It was important that Rachel not be allowed to assign herself responsibility. Who else was to blame? No one. But what purpose would it serve to blame anyone at this moment? thought Doc. She is sick with fear. It could have been prevented. Many things have happened that could have been prevented. My purpose is to prevent or alleviate misery, and already too much misery is in this room.

Doc looked in his worn, medical carrying case, sat down and reread some literature. Turning his head away from the others, he sighed softly and thought for a while. Doc stood up, quietly took a deep breath, and walked back to Jared and Rachel.

"Measles come and go," Doc began. "Vhen sick with measles, yoor body becomes very veak and yoor chances of fighting off other forms of illness are reduced. Vhen yoor sons vere sick vith the measles, and then vent outside, they contracted pneumonia. The combination of the two iss very serious."

"How serious?" asked Jared in a low monotone.

Doc looked at Jared and then down at Rachel grimly. The answer he would give, for him, was hard, but it was a succinct, direct answer and, at the moment, Doc did not feel much like talking.

"My vife died of pneumonia," answered Doc, unwavering. "Yoor sons haf measles and pneumonia. That is how serious. If their temperatures do not go down... They need to eat and, especially, drink as much as possible."

"They don't eat or drink anything," responded Rachel. "I can't get them to."

"Give them some of this," Doc said, taking out a bottle of medicine. "Use the dropper."

'I... They don't...,' stammered Rachel.

She knew.

It was October 16, 1907, still a time when many life spans did not extend beyond childhood. As Doc raised the eyelids of each boy, Rachel looked at her sons. To her, they seemed already lifeless. She struggled to maintain her composure.

And could not.

As her teeth clenched, her face contorted in pain, and the tears flowing were accompanied by masquerading sobs that inside her were screams. Doc stopped his inspection of the twins, and watched Rachel gravely.

In an effort to divert her attention, Rachel picked up a doily from the side table, attempting to reset it properly, when it fell from her fingers. She put the back of her hand over her eyes, her head again bowed but quivering. Without moving her hand, as Jared and Doc apprehensively watched, she shuffled across the floor to a chair, and sat down. As Jared walked toward her, she sat head bowed, tears running into her clenched teeth, her hand over her eyes.

My babies. My babies.

Just before Jared reached her, the sobs stopped as her head raised, teeth gritted, her face contorted with pain. Tossing her head back, from the depths of her soul came a prolonged wail, a loud, anguished cry, notifying all mothers of dead children that the grim reaper was at another door.

Jared, mouth open, pulled up a second chair and, sitting down, wrapped his arms around her, wanting to hug away her pain, wanting to change what he could not change. In spite of Jared's effort, her anguished sobs became uncontrollable as Rachel wept for her children.

"Vhy in God's name," Doc muttered absently as he looked at sobbing Rachel being held tightly by an anguished husband who was choking back his own tears, "if there iss, vould He allow such a t'ing?" The boys, he also knew, were no longer hers.

Doc stood next to Rachel and Jared, and asked Jared to stand up. When Jared stood up, the two men slowly helped Rachel stand, led her to the living room, and helped her into a resting position on the couch, lying on her side, her head on her arm. Jared placed a pillow under her head. Trancelike, staring vacantly toward the doorway, except for her intermittent sobs it was as if she were lifeless herself. As Doc stood watching her, and Jared bent over and again held Rachel, she was unaware of either man's presence.

Doc returned to the bedroom and again took the pulses of both children. Their heartbeats were weaker. His own pulse increased in response. Doc wiped their foreheads and his own with a wet cloth. How I wish I knew more. How I hate feeling helpless, being only able to forestall the inevitable. What good is that? he silently asked himself. He began to feel sick emotionally. How much good is someone whose ability only enables people to become less miserable? The thought was overly severe, summarizing all he could do at the moment. He had other calls to make, but could not leave. He could not leave the twins. He could not leave Rachel or Jared. Doc gently adjusted the blankets over the bodies of Caleb and Thomas.

Returning to the living room, Doc removed his carrying case from the chair, and sat down near motionless Rachel. Doc stretched his legs out, placing his right foot over his left ankle, folded his hands in his lap and, while staring at his shoes, began thinking of his wife.

Standing aside and slightly behind Rachel, Jared massaged her shoulders – she would love it under normal circumstances – while looking toward the twins' bedroom door. Rachel gave no indication of noticing. She stared straight ahead with swollen, pain-filled eyes, an occasional sob breaking the silence as Jared continued to massage, hoping.

97

October 17, 1907

In Pastor Nordquist's spare bedroom during the night, holding a lamp overhead, Doc Torgeson occasionally checked on the children using his free hand to feel their foreheads, and stethoscope when listening to their heartbeats. Doc's quiet face was calming for the others, and occasionally Jared, Amos or Anna joined him when he inspected the twins. Otherwise, the adults prayed or dozed fitfully, never completely asleep.

Dawn cracked the eastern horizon, and backlit black Cascade Mountain ridges. Soon gray daylight filtered into the spare downstairs bedroom, giving Caleb and Thomas a ghostly appearance as they lay still.

Emotionally drained and physically tired, as the early dawn segued into daylight, and the world outside the window became more apparent, the world inside grew dimmer. The Nordquists sat motionlessly in the living room. Tired and disillusioned, his expression as gray as the overcast sky outside, Jared was still attempting to comfort Rachel, his arm gently around her as she sat upright. Unresponsive, she sat with her hands flat on her lap, her bloodshot eyes narrow with fatigue, expressionlessly staring straight ahead like the Sphinx.

Grandma Anna sat at one end of the couch, awake, her eyes closed in prayer. All except Doc Torgeson and Rachel had prayed intermittently throughout the night. Filled with despair, Pastor Nordquist prayed fervently that it be God's will to spare his grandsons but, in his prayers, dutifully accepted God's will, whatever it might be. They prayed for the twins and one another, including Doc.

As the hours passed, Doc not only watched the twins, but also Rachel who continued to stare vacantly.

Shortly before 8:00 a.m., Thomas' soul waited a few moments for Caleb, and the two again left the house, and the dimensional world.

At 8:04 a.m., Doc slowly got up from his chair and walked into the bedroom. He leaned over the cribs, briefly checking the boys, his back to the living room. It seemed to Amos that Doc was taking longer than usual.

After Doc straightened up, he did not turn around and return to the living room as he had before, but stood silently looking downward.

Beginning with Pastor Nordquist, one-by-one, all except Rachel got up and went to the bedroom. Wearing weariness like an oversized winter coat, at 8:05 a.m. Doc confirmed the inevitable.

"It iss over," he whispered.

Fatigue born from the weight of sleeplessness and powerlessness caused Doc to slump and, as he did, he slid the small blankets the remaining distance over the faces of the still, small bodies, expecting that the others, grieving, would leave the bedroom, perhaps to comfort one another. None did.

Then he felt the soft presence of Rachel standing next to him, oblivious to his company, as she looked at the covered forms. Her bloodshot eyes were enigmatic, unemotive and unblinking. Her mouth was relaxed and expressionless. She showed no signs of anguish, no emotion at all. As the others watched apprehensively, she reached down and slid the covers back from the boys' faces and stood looking at them as if studying items on a pantry shelf. Just as quietly, Rachel turned and walked away, away from the lifeless bodies of her only children.

⎯⎯⎯⎯⎯◗●◖⎯⎯⎯⎯⎯

Doc knew what Rachel was experiencing. It wasn't in any medical texts, but he knew about it because it happened to him. To combat excruciating emotional pain that, like a terrible burn, hurts to the point of disability, Rachel might have responded with anger and prolonged grief. Were she able to do this, her pain, suffering and grieving would have been horrible, but would have gradually subsided and, while she would be scarred, and things would be much different, her life would go on. When a heart is so badly burned that anger and grief provide no relief from intolerable pain, however, the other solution is: to not feel at all. No happiness. No unhappiness. The Sphinx.

Doc worried as he studied Rachel at a short distance, knowing that when feeling is turned off, it is nearly impossible to turn back on. For Rachel to again experience normal emotional behavior, offsetting emotional conditions would have to accumulate to a similar magnitude. This would require considerable time, and during the interim period there was the chance that others who did not understand what happened might behave unseemingly toward her lack of emotion, further reinforcing her state of feelinglessness. It would have been better, thought Doc, if Rachel had cursed God, if that's what it took, and gone on with her life. Instead of devoting herself to her kitchen, formerly effervescent Rachel walked down a long, dark passageway into a black dungeon where her heart was tightly bound and gagged, and her sensitivity to the day's events drained from her as if letting blood. How long will she remain there? Doc wondered. Sometimes, depending on life's circumstances, feelings never return or, if they do, years pass until that moment.

Rachel never spoke about it. During the funeral she stood motionlessly, blankly looking straight ahead as those around her, not comprehending what had occurred inside of her, admired her strength.

All except Doc.

Jared was finding out. He couldn't reach her, and it became apparent his wife was completely different from the woman he married. Her soul had gone dark.

January 16, 1910

Almost two and a half years passed; the constant love of husband and parents, together with a lack of any pain inflicted by others, caused Rachel's bindings to loosen. Restraining bonds began to unravel, and when hope and love became stronger than bondage, Rachel's heart broke free. Weakly walking back up the dungeon passageway, she stared apprehensively at the light shining through the door at the top. Could she bear the pain? How different she had become. But she wanted to live again. This meant accepting what was under the blankets.

The twins had been dead for over two years but, for Rachel, it could have been two minutes. Opening the dungeon door, she walked out of her parents' bath chamber, where she had been crying, seemingly forever, and into the living room where her husband and her parents were sitting that normal Sunday afternoon. Her eyes ran with tears, and her mouth contorted as, in an effort to maintain some self-control, her teeth clenched, damming her sobs, her emotion a dramatic contrast to the inexpressiveness to which the others had become accustomed.

Surprised, almost stunned upon first seeing her, Pastor Nordquist's lips parted as his eyes narrowed.

"Rachel?"

"Is something wrong?" asked Mrs. Nordquist. Rachel looked at her mother through blurring tears as Amos, Anna, Jared and Angus stood up.

Is something wrong?

As she sobbed against her will, Rachel thought of failing to notice her boys going out in the cold that day, of Doc's succinct prognosis, of the emotional war waged that night, followed by her emotional incarceration the next morning; of repressed memories of her only children; the changes in herself; and her motherless void of over two years.

"No," she whispered, neither able nor wanting to explain. Rachel's tears began to burn.

"I'm not so sure that is true," Amos quietly understated.

Rachel walked to the sofa across from the others and sat down slowly as if uncertain of where she was, still fighting to regain her composure. For a moment she sat still and swallowed. Still intermittently sobbing, the flow of tears was momentarily stemmed, and she looked up at the others who looked back in angst. Jared began to step toward Rachel, but Rachel put up her hand, motioning him to stop as her head dropped and her lips again began to quiver. He stopped for a moment, but as Rachel's body began to quiver, Jared, Amos and Anna all stepped toward her with mounting concern. Rachel quickly rose to her feet, slightly bent over, fists clenched, and stopped them from coming any further when she erupted.

"Why?!"

Knitting fell out of Anna's startled hands, the ball of yarn rolling out on the floor. Rachel's face flushed. Pushing her tear-dampened hair away from her eyes, she angrily walked to her father. As a child wondering what God must be like, she had thought of her father, and now, standing in front of Pastor Nordquist, her eyes wide, her fists clenched, she demanded to know whatever he knew. What was in the logical gap?

"Tell me! Why did God allow this to happen?!"

Before Pastor Nordquist had a chance to respond, what little remained of Rachel's disintegrating composure failed and she fell violently upon her father, the Lutheran pastor, sobbing uncontrollably and hitting him over and over with her fists, simultaneously gasping for breath and, with each attempted blow, angrily shouting: "Why?!..."

Rachel's father deflected her blows, feeling tears within, the result of his empathy with his daughter's anguish and disillusionment, as well as the return of sorrow and pain for grandpa.

She regained her composure and pulled back her damp hair, now also angry at herself. As she looked up at her father through a blur of tears, the repressed memories, the inner wounds, the regret, the anguish all seemed to wash over her as she inexplicably thought of everything at once.

"Look what this has done." Rachel stepped back, turned and looked at her mother. Jared wanted to hold her, but she was so distraught, no one dared move. "Look what this has done!" Dislodging clenched teeth, tears distorting her vision, she shouted what she had never accepted. Until now. "My children are dead!!"

Her face still contorted, fists clenched, tears blurring her vision, she was still defiantly bent forward as she choked back the sobs. The others stood facing her in tormented silence, wanting to explain what they could not, to help, to do something, but there was nothing they could do. Standing in front of her, her father wanted to hold her, but could not, for fear her emotions would again overrule her better judgment.

"They're dead," she whimpered in stark contrast to her voice a moment ago.

As the sobbing came back, Rachel collapsed, reflexively grabbing and holding on to Pastor Nordquist as she continued to uncontrollably weep, and his powerful arms quickly embraced her as Jared walked over, putting his arms around her shoulders, pressing the side of his head against hers.

Still sobbing out of control, Rachel weakly removed the arms of her husband and her father. She did not want comfort now; she wanted resolution. Pulling herself away, she turned, took three unstable steps in the opposite direction, and stood still, bent slightly forward, her tear-soaked hair partially covering her face. She pushed her hair back again and turned to face the others who stood looking at her in anguished helplessness.

Anna Nordquist, her graying hair in a bun, and her apron tied tightly, also had tears running down her cheeks. Her grandsons were dead. Her daughter experienced emotional incarceration that Anna could not understand. Anna blinked away tears and looked at her daughter with profound sadness as Rachel's swollen eyes ran with suffering.

"Is this God's plan?" asked Rachel. The room was still quiet. "Is this…something that furthers the Kingdom of God here on earth? Glorifies God?" she choked.

"Well, is it?!!"

Part of her was angry, livid, at God, at her father the pastor, for the seeming pointlessness of what happened, while another part believed there must have been a reason and someone should say what it was. There was no logic for this moment, however.

Anna Nordquist walked slowly to her daughter until, standing behind her, Anna delicately put her hands on Rachel's shoulders, carefully introducing a mother's presence and love to a daughter who needed both, but who was so distraught as to reject what was needed.

"Nothing that happens is outside of the will of God," answered Anna. "All that we have, our children, our grandchildren, our belongings, are a trust from God." She leaned forward and put her cheek aside Rachel's head. "Little Jacob was a trust from God." Several years earlier when little Jacob died of heart failure, they knew it might come – Doc Torgeson had told them – but it was still great cause for grief, and a mother's heart never completely mends. With that statement, the souls of both women momentarily became the soul of one.

Rachel turned around and the two women embraced one another, each sharing solace for a common grief. "You cannot control everything that happens," added Anna in a whisper, tears running down her cheeks. "The Creator of Life has chosen to do what He has done for reasons we neither know nor understand."

Slowly releasing Rachel, Anna put her hand aside Rachel's head, sequentially caressing Rachel, pushing back her wet hair and wiping away her tears as Rachel, eyes closed and mouth slightly open, sporadically shuddered involuntarily while she allowed her mother's healing love to wipe away inside tears as well.

"God loves you," said Anna. "And he loves Thomas and Caleb, and Jacob, who are now in much better circumstances than are we." Anna looked at Rachel as if there were no one else in the room, no one else in the world, seemingly looking through Rachel's eyes into her soul. "And it may be that all else is or will be in better circumstances as a result of their deaths. Trust that God, in His infinite wisdom, will attend to the best interests of us all preparatory to a place of which we know very little and wherein before Him we will all eventually stand." Anna weakly wiped her eyes, glancing toward the bedroom where the boys had died. "Some sooner than later."

Rachel held her mother tightly, and Anna gently embraced Rachel, both women softly swaying in unison, comforting one another as women have from the beginning.

98

October 16, 1910

Nine months passed and late fall embraced the landscape. Outside the church, winter began nosing about, absently clucking its tongue while peering in the side windows.

Inside the church, quiet Inga more than compensated for her natural reticence, gracing each Sunday with her beautiful, lyric soprano voice that moved parishioners and offset the Lutheran liturgy which occasionally became a spiritual substitute for taps.

Her personal version of *Beautiful Savior* was the favorite of the parish. There were "three" verses. Inga would sing the first verse in Swedish…

> *Härlig är jorden/Härlig är Guds himmel/Skön är själens/Pilgrims gang…*

…and again in Norwegian…

> *Deilig er jorden/Prektig er Guds himel/Skjøn er sjellenes/Pilgrims gang…*

…and then Inga would sing the English version.

> *Fair are the meadows/Fairer still the woodlands/Robed in blooming flowers of spring…*

The sentences were obviously different, but so too were the statements. Each verse – familiarity with which depended on nationality – after centuries of use and sometime modification, arrived in modest variations. The lilting melody, different from the traditional, just came to Inga one day while she did housework. It fit, showcasing her talent, enchanting her listeners. Elderly members of the congregation asked for it often and, with church choral music being a primary source of community entertainment, Inga's reputation spread.

One Sunday morning, nobility unexpectedly attended the service. Theater-owner Pericles Pantages, now calling himself Alexander, after Alexander the Great, came north to hear Inga sing. After the service, he introduced himself and offered her the opportunity to sing in one of his three Seattle theaters. He intimated that the compensation would be handsome, and the opportunity would be extraordinarily satisfying for an artist of her talent – not to mention the chance for stardom. She was, he stated, much more talented and attractive than Fanny Brice, the new star of the Ziegfeld Follies in New York, and could become a legend with his help. Between his promotional efficacy and her talent, he said, it was an opportunity of a lifetime for them both.

Alexander Pantages, however, went home disappointed.

———————— • ————————

"Inga, are you completely insane?" asked Rachel, eyes wide.

"No," Inga said quietly, looking up at her sister, annoyed. "Not completely."

"Inga, it's the stage! And you're so good!"

"Thank you."

"'Thank you'? You'd be famous!"

"Rachel, that's not important to me."

"'Not impor...' You *are* crazy! If I had an opportunity like this…"

"There are more important things," Inga stated with finality.

"But Inga, you have this God-given talent. Think of what your husband is doing with his artistic talents. Jacob makes as much from his paintings as he does from farming – he'd make *more* if he didn't spend so much time with the farm. You're supposed to use those talents."

"I know. I read the Bible too."

"Then, why won't you do it? Okay, okay, I know. Then why isn't it important to you?"

"I have considered it," said Inga calmly. "I have read at length about Fanny Brice and Marie Lloyd, and what they do to maintain their popularity in those places with those patrons, and I have concluded that the stage is not where I want to be. It's not for me." Inga looked at Rachel knowingly. "And it's not for you either, Rachel. You shouldn't judge a profession by the chance for fame…or how much it might pay. You should ask: how will this help me become the person I should be?" To Inga, singing for the Lord in a small rural church was more honorable than instant fame performing secular, occasionally bawdy, songs in front of nameless faces at any of the Pantages theaters. "You must give to get, Rachel," explained Inga. "What, in turn, might I have to give – or give-up – over the long run? What compromises would need to be made, what forfeits, what needless pains? You know? Would the worldly gains offset the spiritual losses?" Inga shook her head. "That never happens."

Rachel just shrugged but, secretly believing audiences would much rather watch Rachel Nordquist Young than Lillian Gish, knew if she were in Inga's place, she would ignore the pitfalls. To Inga, however, the value was less than the price.

———————— • ————————

Pastor Nordquist was in his workshop attending to the weekly duty of filing saws. It was a mindless but necessary chore, and gave him time to think; he was thinking of Rachel. She seemed so much better, he thought. They had talked about what she experienced nearly three years ago, and in his mind's eye he watched her seated alone on the couch; how she would occasionally look pensively to one side, and it was evident the events of that morning three years ago were being recalled ("As I stood looking down at the faces – that's all they were at that moment, faces – I said to myself: That's not Thomas. That's not Caleb.").

Previously crippled with heartbreak and guilt, and now scarred, yet she had moved on, looking to the future. For this, Pastor Nordquist was grateful, and thankful that, while time marches forward, it doesn't retreat. Pastor Nordquist grimaced as he unclamped a crosscut saw in the dual vices. Through faith, peace exchanged places with the overwhelming duress that homesteaded in Rachel's heart. Pastor Nordquist again nodded as he very lightly ran his fingernail along the filed saw teeth edges to insure the teeth were as sharp as they could be.

God takes relationships between parents and children, men and women, far more seriously than do his creatures, thought Amos. He wondered about his son, Joshua, and who Joshua would eventually meet and marry. Although 20, Joshua had no girlfriends, there were no prospects on the horizon, and it seemed Joshua often preferred to be alone. Meanwhile, as Pastor Nordquist stood filing and ruminating, Joshua was being uncharacteristically indolent this cold, late afternoon as he sat on the riverbank watching the grand, fall parade before him. The river was teaming with spawning salmon, some extraordinarily large, and watching the fish swim upstream was mesmerizing.

Joshua looked at the rippling surface, and knew many salmon would become food before reaching their spawning ground. Bears just waded into the river, but often fall rains caused the river to rise, flooding surrounding farmland, leaving stranded salmon as a feast for scavengers.

The old Indian, Two Bears, told Joshua the salmon and Two Bears were kindred souls according to the tradition of Two Bears' people. The people of Two Bears believed salmon were a race of supernatural beings and, once caught, while the body died, the supernatural beings returned to the sea.

Joshua stared at the water, daydreaming, at the moment unmindful of the salmon. He came to the river to be alone, although loneliness was never far from him. He began these treks shortly after his twin brother Jacob's death and, Jacob spiritually beside him, Joshua silently talked with Jacob much as Joshua did when Jacob was alive. Jacob was mongoloid, but when they were little, it had not mattered. Now, as when they were young boys, Jacob said little. Precise word selection and phrasing were unnecessary because ideas flowed between the two, precluding what might be tediously worded conversation between normal siblings. Even though their path split and diverged as they grew older, the initial bond remained. Now, as in the past, when no one else would be there, Jacob would.

The low clouds began slowly exhaling, softly showering mist over Skagit lowlands. A half-mile down the river road, Angela Engberg's horse, a gift from her father, Lars, the blacksmith, had gone lame. Angela, who would be late for dinner, walked slowly in the falling mist, leading her horse back to a barn two miles distant. Her dark brown eyes were uniquely large, as if she were suddenly surprised or jubilant. When surprised or jubilant, they would become even larger, brightening her face and the emotions of those around her. Her hair was thick, black and slightly longer than shoulder-length, and her jaw set in a way reflecting confidence and determination.

"How could this happen now?" she asked herself, and silently thought of answers. The falling mist gently glossed her elegant facial features. She was cutting things close enough without this. Forty minutes passed. Soon it would start getting dark and her mother and father would begin to worry.

Joshua's reverie along the riverbank suddenly spooked. Good grief! Enough! Go! It wasn't as if before his very eyes the salmon were transforming into supernatural beings, and the weather wasn't getting any drier. He turned and at first walked rapidly over the wet grass, but then began to run. His balance was excellent, allowing him to keep his hands dug deep in his pockets, head down, as he danced rapidly forward, breaking into a sprint along the path through the thick woods and, moments later, being propelled out the other end to the road in front of startled Angela Engberg.

"Oh," Joshua stopped. "Hello."

"Hello." Angela nervously studied the large, rain-drenched figure before her.

"I'm Joshua Nordquist," he said in a tone unintentionally implying that many people knew him. Angela tilted her head slightly to one side. The corners of her mouth turned up, presenting a very bright contrast to the dismal surroundings. Joshua smiled in response, the best thing he could have done, even if he was aware of what he was doing.

"I'm Angela Engberg. How do you do?"

"Fine," Joshua said, thinking the name sounded familiar. "Your father's the blacksmith?"

"Yes." She maintained the tilt and the charming expression, continuing to study Joshua carefully. "And your father's the Lutheran pastor south of town," she responded.

"Yes," said Joshua. "How did you know that?"

"I heard your father speak at a Chautauqua meeting in Mt. Vernon…you look much like your father," answered Angela. "Also Doctor Torgeson has mentioned your father many times. Doc and papa spend a great deal of time together. Doc raises horses. As you can see, I have a problem with this one. It seems so odd. I just got her and here she is, lame."

Joshua perfunctorily took the reins from Angela, pulling the horse in the direction of home. Angela walked beside him.

"Dad will talk to anyone, anywhere," said Joshua. "You wouldn't believe some of the places he's been and some of the experiences he's had," Joshua added with weakly veiled pride.

"I enjoyed his homily," said Angela, looking at the road before them. "He seemed like a knowledgeable man." She returned to her study of Joshua. "He seemed especially sensitive to the relationships between men and women. What he said was very insightful."

"It's one of his favorite subjects: how the Bible says men should treat women, and vice versa," said Joshua. Angela's heartbeat increased slightly.

"How would you summarize what he said?" asked Angela.

"Dad believes God wants us to be happy," answered Joshua, "and has given us ways of maintaining happiness even when everything suggests we should not be happy." Joshua paused, uncertain of how much he should say.

"And…"

"Well, about relationships, just to summarize, Dad always reminds the congregation of what Jesus and Paul said. Pray without ceasing, love God above all things, and love one another. Paul also said that husbands must love, cherish, their wives. With respect to happiness, Dad says the relationships between men and women are crucial – another "cru" word – and if a husband loves and cherishes his wife, his wife will respond in kind. It obviously works for mom. 'Husbands, love your wives, just as Christ also loved the church and gave himself up for her.' Dad calls it the 12th commandment, although it's more a corollary of the 11th."

"The 11th?"

"Yes, you know: 'A new commandment I give you that you love one another. As I have loved you, so must you love one another.' The 11th commandment."

"Very true," nodded Angela.

"So, those are the keys for remaining happy in the worst of circumstances… although, Dad says, adhering to the 12th commandment usually prevents the worst of circumstances." Joshua smiled.

Angela listened. What a coincidence, she thought. I was impressed with Pastor Nordquist. What are the odds of meeting his son two years later? Or, perhaps, what were the odds of listening to Joshua's father two years before? Angela looked up at Joshua. He obviously has been listening to his father. Joshua looked down at Angela pleasantly. The horse plodded along. The instant familiarity and affability she felt were intriguing to Angela. Angela stifled the urge to take Joshua's arm.

"Have you ever thought of going into the ministry?" asked Angela.

"Yes," responded Joshua, "but I'm not sure that's my calling. Maybe. But I don't know. There's so much out there I don't know about."

Joshua looked through the falling mist at the road ahead, mist-drenched trees hunched over on either side. Neither Angela nor Joshua was conscious of the weather.

Angela's mother, Johanna Engberg, a large woman, pulled back the edge of the Engberg living room curtain. After worrying about Angela, Johanna was greatly relieved to see her daughter coming up the driveway. Johanna studied the scene for a moment. Oh, dear. Angela's horse is lame, she thought. And who is this handsome Sir Galahad who has come to her rescue? Oh, my goodness.

"Lars," called Johanna to her husband who was reading next to the kitchen stove.

No answer.

"Lars! Angela's home. Her horse seems to be lame and there's…"

"Her horse is *what*?"

"Her horse is…"

"I just bought that horse! Good night! If it's not one thing, it's another." Lars, a short, powerful, dark-complexioned man with handsome features, put his book in his lap. "I'll have to pay Al Olson a visit and see what he thinks he's doing selling me a horse that's about to go lame."

"Now Lars," countered Johanna, "you know Al wouldn't have sold you the horse if he thought that it was going to go lame. What good would that have done? I'm sure that whatever you want to do will be fine with Al. And I also wanted to tell you that…"

"If he doesn't want to do business fair and square, well, he won't do business. He can sell horses in Bellingham or Hamilton, but not around here."

"Yes, dear. Lars, I was also about to tell you that Angela has a…"

"Looked fine when I bought it. Should've had Doc take a look. If I had done that, I wouldn't be in this pickle!"

"Lars, you're not in a pickle," Johanna responded as she opened the door for Angela and her companion who were just coming from the barn. Lars Engberg seemed like a curmudgeon, but this was mostly an act.

"And, Lars, I want you to come in here…"

"Johanna speak up! You know my hearing isn't what it used to be."

"I said, could you," cupping her hands and lifting them to shoulder level, she sang, "come *innnnn heeeere*?"

"What in heaven's name for," mumbled Lars as he put down his book and walked toward the living room.

"I believe Angela has someone for you to meet."

"What? You know I can't…Who's this?"

"I'm not sure," answered Mrs. Engberg sweetly. "Angela, would you introduce this young man?"

"I was riding down the river road and Starlight went lame," answered Angela. "It started to rain. I was walking along the road and Joshua…this is Joshua Nordquist…"

"How do you do?" responded Joshua. Lars Engberg's right hand was buried in Joshua's.

"Just fine. Lars Engberg. How are you, Joshua?"

"Very well, thank you. My grandfather's name was Lars."

"There's a few of us around."

Turning to Johanna Engberg, Joshua bowed his head slightly. Johanna was taller than her husband, as was Angela.

"As I was saying," continued Angela, "after Starlight went lame, I was walking down the road just as Joshua came running out of the river trail…," she turned to Joshua, "I guess you were in a hurry to get home because it was raining."

"I…yes, I was in a hurry."

"But," Angela turned to her parents, "when he saw my horse was lame, he offered to accompany me back to the house."

"Well, that was very considerate of you, Joshua," said Mrs. Engberg.

"It seemed like the right thing to do," said Joshua, shrugging. Was that what I did?

"Indeed, it was," agreed Lars Engberg. "Indeed. How bad is the horse?"

Angela looked at Joshua, implying that he, not she, answer the question.

"From the way she walks," guessed Joshua, "the problem might be the hind tendon above the left hock but," he added, "I'd suggest that you have Doc Torgeson take a look at her."

"An excellent suggestion," agreed Lars Engberg. "Doc and I are old friends. Say, you're…" Lars' voice trailed off quickly when he realized who Joshua was. Doc had talked about the deaths of Jacob, and Thomas and Caleb, with Lars.

"You're Pastor Nordquist's boy," said Lars. Lars became solemn. "I, we, should go to church more often…"

"Yes, we should," agreed his wife, interrupting. Lars looked at her for a moment, clearing his throat.

"…'more often' but horses," continued Mr. Engberg, "can keep a blacksmith going seven days a week."

"We're happy to have you whenever you can come," said Joshua.

"Thank you. I'll try to make it more often," Lars replied sincerely. Johanna looked at her husband hopefully.

"Well, I should be going," said Joshua. "My parents may be wondering where I am as well."

"Yes," said Mr. Engberg. "Well, thanks for escorting Angela home." Out of the corner of his eye, Lars Engberg caught a glimpse of how Angela looked at Joshua. "Say 'hello' to your father for me and tell him he'll be seeing more of us in the future."

"I'll do that," said Joshua.

"Ah, say," added Mr. Engberg, "ah, since we know you now, and since you were kind enough to escort Angela home, do you think you could come by next Sunday for dinner?"

Angela's large eyes grew even larger as her heart leaped, and it took a considerable amount of self-discipline to hide her eternal gratitude to her father who was acting like himself, but not in character. "I get kind of tired being the only male in this house and Johanna, here, she's a great cook."

Lars glanced at beautiful Angela, his only child. Looking at Joshua, he asked earnestly, "Can you make it?"

"I can't think of anything else I would rather do more," Joshua replied with sincerity.

"Wonderful!" responded Johanna Engberg. "I'll do my best to not disappoint you."

"Don't let her fool ya, son," said Lars. "I don't know where she developed this sudden streak of modesty, but if anyone can cook, it's Johanna. You come prepared to eat."

"That has never been a problem, sir," said Joshua. "Perhaps I will see you in church on Sunday and we can come directly here after church?"

"Sounds just fine," said Mr. Engberg, taking the door handle and shooting a wry glance at his beaming wife and his daughter. Lars made points with everyone.

"'Night now."

The seeds of the relationship were planted and, although there would be some rocks in the soil, like spring's daffodils, the relationship would sprout and blossom in full, regardless.

March 28, 1911

Winter was gone. The snow geese were thick in a nearby field, each having a quick bite before heading further north. Barely aboveground, little green heads sneaked a peek to see if winter was still pacing about. No, no sign of him. So the infant daffodils rose higher, following the lead of the crocuses who had been out for quite some time and were, in fact, tiring of the tedium. It was early spring, 1911, and the fields and woodlands of the Skagit River valley were preparing to do what they did best: burst into bloom.

After several months, beautiful Angela Engberg knew what she wanted and, in her heart, Angela made her commitment. But Joshua was not one to hurry things. Commitment could occur in due course. He was young – he just turned 21 – and there was a lot of world to see before settling down. Perhaps they were rushing things. But for Angela, if Joshua wanted to see the world, that was all fine and good, but he would see it with her.

Joshua's emotional foot-dragging began to try Angela's patience until one evening as Angela and Joshua walked along a large pond, quieting the amphibian residents therein, she came to the conclusion that his intentions needed to be questioned.

"Are you serious about us, Joshua?" asked Angela.

"What?" responded Joshua as he looked down at her. "Yes, I'm serious."

"I am committed to you," countered Angela as she stopped and turned toward him, her large eyes boring into his, "but it does not seem that you are committed to me."

"Uh," responded Joshua uncomfortably, "am I committed to someone else?"

"Apparently."

"Oh." Joshua looked at her incredulously. "And who might that be?"

"You," responded Angela. "I don't have your heart; you do." Joshua continued to look at Angela, still trying to come to grips with the conversation topic. "I think," continued Angela, "that either you take some responsibility for the health of our relationship or stop seeing me so I can go on with my life."

"What? I don't want to stop seeing you. What do you mean, 'go on with…'"

"Either you make a sincere commitment or we go our separate ways," said Angela firmly. "I don't like this shilly-shallying one bit."

Joshua was speechless. "'Shilly-sha…'"

"It's very simple," interjected Angela, sensing Joshua was having some difficulty. "We've been seeing one another daily for five months. The first month was wonderful; but in the second month you seemed to hit an emotional brick wall…and things haven't changed since then. To get off dead center, I am asking you to make a decision between *you* and *us*."

Angela looked solemnly at Joshua, and his lips parted slightly.

"I love you," said Angela sincerely, "but I have been feeling unloved and I don't like it. And I won't continue this way. Either love me or leave me. We can be inseparable or we can be acquaintances. As much as I will not like it, if you choose to leave, you will still have done me a great favor for I believe there are men who will be much more appreciative of me than you appear to be."

"I am appreciative," countered Joshua in a raised voice, putting his hands on his hips. "I don't want to stop seeing you."

"I am committed to you," said Angela as if not having heard. "Either you make a commitment to me or leave me so that I can go on with my life."

Joshua tried to marshal his thoughts through a counterintuitive fogbank. "You can't be serious about th..."

"I am serious!" Angela interrupted loudly, her patience at an end. "Very serious!" She glared at him for a second, but turned her head and looked at the sunset reflection on the still pond. Before he could think of something else to say, she looked back up at him and stated, "If you're going to be the man in my life, act like it. Otherwise..."

"I *am* the man in your life, Angela, and I'll tell you this," Joshua retorted angrily, the ends of his eyebrows rising, "I'm not going anywhere! And if I hear anymore of this lack-of-commitment nonsense, then the less-masculine of us is going to get paddled!"

Under such circumstances Angela would gladly be paddled. These words – not the words themselves but the emotion behind them – were what she needed to hear. Joshua not only talked conviction, he sounded conviction.

"Very well then," Angela beamed, her beautiful eyes studying his dark face, "I look forward to my first spanking."

Looming above her, Joshua suppressed a smile. As she stood motionlessly in front of him, he stepped forward and, taking her in his arms, bent her over backwards, constricting and kissing her with such passion that she became almost limp.

He stood upright, intently savoring both her beauty and reaction. She was dumbstruck and elated. You want commitment, Joshua thought, you got commitment. With his left hand, he gently turned her to her right while with his right hand he gave her well-proportioned tush a firm "whack!"

"Owh!" Her dark eyes flashed. That hurt.

She regained her composure quickly as the sting subsided, almost as if nothing happened. But that was hardly the case.

Joshua took her left hand, slipped it over his right forearm, placed his left hand over hers, and led her homeward. As the two of them began to disappear in the distance, the eavesdropping spring pond audience responded, modestly at first, gradually crescendoing to a raucous chorus sounding for all the world like applause.

April 25, 1911

Three weeks later, in the warm, early evening, Joshua and Angela rode up the trail high into the steep woodland hills which overlook the bay and just about everything else worth seeing. The orange sky over the horizon contrasted the black-silhouetted islands below. A crescent moon hung in the southwest, and Skagit Bay shimmered navy blue and gold in the warm sunset air. At Joshua's suggestion the two dismounted.

"Isn't this beautiful?" asked Angela. "I can't imagine a more beautiful place. Why have you never taken me here before?"

"I thought I'd wait for a special occasion."

"What special occasion would that be?" Angela responded without thinking. Then she looked up at Joshua, studying his face, hers expressionless.

"Three weeks ago you questioned my commitment to you and suggested I may not be as serious about our relationship as you are." He paused, looking at Angela. "You suggested it might be better that we separate, go our own ways." Angela's heart almost stopped. "But how could I leave the world's most beautiful woman?" Joshua smiled. "Perhaps she could leave me but, when thinking about these things during the past three weeks, I couldn't imagine leaving her."

Angela's eyes glistened as Joshua continued to speak. As the first few evening stars entered the sky high above shimmering Skagit Bay, Joshua asked Angela to marry him.

"Yes!"

He again kissed her tenderly but forcefully…he had become quite good at it, as she had remarked more than once.

The kiss of a lifetime awaited.

99

The bride is the focal point of a wedding," Anna smiled, "the groom an afterthought given a substantial supporting role as evidence the bride has decided correctly."

Amos beamed and said nothing. Joshua Nordquist, listening, had attended several weddings, but couldn't remember much about them, and never envisioned his own.

Angela had no problem with either memory or imagination. Anna Nordquist, wedding planner, provided the options, Johanna Engberg made suggestions, and Angela Engberg made the choices. This was Angela's ceremony to direct and, with a passion rarely equaled on Broadway, direct it she would. One, after all, only gets married once.

June 18, 1912

Pastor Nordquist was reading a letter from Anders about the latest White Star Line ship, a sister ship to the *Olympic*. The *Olympic* had been launched last year and subsequently had a collision with a British warship.

> *Even in poor visibility, you would think the HMS Hawke would use a little more sense. There she was, the Olympic: 882 feet long weighing roughly 50,000 tons; you would think they would notice her. Everyone else did.*

And now the *Olympic*'s even more luxurious sister ship, the *Titanic*, Anders wrote, was about to take its maiden voyage.

The letter had been composed over a period of a week, Anders was slow to send it, and the mail was slow to arrive.

By the time Amos received the letter, the *Titanic* was already at the bottom of the North Atlantic along with 89 of the 123 Swedes who booked passage. Amos frowned, thinking of the tragedy and what it must have been like for those with the character and courage, in the absence of adequate lifeboat availability, to voluntarily remain on board as the great ship sank, the string quartet on deck playing "Nearer My God to Thee."

In the kitchen, Anna Nordquist squeezed the mop water into the bucket. It was continual warfare, Anna versus the dirt. As Anna mopped the floor, there was a knock at the front door. Resting the mop handle against the kitchen counter, she wiped her hands on her apron, and walked to the door. Opening the door, she stepped back, momentarily startled, and stared open-mouthed as if seeing Jacob Marley's ghost.

"Mr. Chong!" she exclaimed.

The flow of words was momentarily blocked as Anna stared at the affable apparition whom she had not seen in… Has it been…22 years? she asked herself, bringing her hands to her cheeks.

"Good gracious, where have you *been*?" she finally asked excitedly. Others in the house, pieces of iron attracted by the magnetic exclamation, "Mr. Chong!" came quickly to the front door.

From the front porch, Mr. Chong looked up at Anna, smiling happily, triggering a torrent of memories that flooded Anna's orderly mind with cerebral flotsam.

"I wanted to come back and see you," Mr. Chong sang. "You are not hard to find. Everybody knows you."

Mr. Chong laughed obligatorily, and looked excitedly from face to face, not recognizing Joshua and Angela. Theirs were not the only unfamiliar faces present. Amos stepped next to Anna.

"And who is this, Mr. Chong?" Amos asked respectfully, looking down at the small, young woman standing next to Mr. Chong with bowed head and large, downcast eyes, dressed in a traditional light-colored Chinese *shen-i*.

"Ohhh," began Mr. Chong. "This is my wife. I went to China and, to satisfy her parents, I gave them money, and we went through the Chinese marriage ritual. But I want to have a Christian wedding. We want to be married here. Can you do that?"

"Mr. Chong, could you introduce us?" asked Anna tactfully.

"Oh. This is Yi [Yee]," said Mr. Chong as he turned to look at Yi.

Yi did not move at the sound of her name. The others looked back at Mr. Chong who returned their gaze, volunteering nothing else. Pastor Nordquist broke the silence.

"You want me to marry the two of you?" he asked.

"Yes. Is it possible you can?"

Amos looked at Mr. Chong's fiancé who remained motionlessly looking downward, not understanding English. Amos returned his attention to Mr. Chong, studying the apprehensive expression before him. Amos chuckled and smiled.

"I'd be honored," said Pastor Nordquist.

Amos looked at Anna who nodded approvingly.

"How long have you known one another?" asked Amos.

"Ohhh, one week," Mr. Chong responded respectfully. Pastor Nordquist looked back perplexed. "But Yi came back with me to Seattle, so we know each other better."

Yi stood like a fragile porcelain figurine.

"Is such a short period a Chinese tradition?" Anna asked.

"Oh, no, not short," answered Mr. Chong. "Her parents already knew my parents. We were engaged when she was two."

Mr. Chong looked back and forth at the confused looks of the others. "They know I was going to be away for a long time. I paid them a lot of money. My parents also presented a very good dowry. So now we will get married here. You should be the one who will marry us because you teach me about God," Mr. Chong concluded with finality. He searched Amos's face as if to ask what else was necessary to know?

"Please, come in," Amos said. "We should not be standing in the doorway letting in flies."

The others stepped aside allowing Mr. Chong and Yi to enter. The diminutive Yi followed like a small shadow as they quietly entered the house. It was the first Western house she had entered, and part of her fought to see the unusual things flashing in and out of her peripheral vision. In China she was frequently reminded of her insignificance, and the strange surroundings and comfortable lifestyle unintentionally exacerbated this feeling.

"Won't you all sit down," said Anna. Mr. Chong sat down on the wall sofa, and Yi, after a moment, sat down next to him, not looking up.

Sensing Yi's emotional isolation, Anna excused herself and went to the kitchen as the others took seats in the living room. Anna returned with a tray of small plates of freshly made *fatemann*. She put a plate in front of everyone, making a special effort to stoop low enough to make eye contact with Yi when putting a plate before her. Anna smiled warmly as she did this. Yi would not look up, but understood the significance of what was happening, and while showing no outward emotion, was both self-conscious and appreciative of this unexpected attention.

As Anna walked away, without lifting her head Yi glanced out of the corner of her eye at this attractive woman who had informally welcomed Yi into Western society. Yi had been treated with some importance when Mr. Chong became her fiancé, but this was mostly due to tradition and the exchange of wealth. This moment in this room was the first time Yi was unconditionally treated as important, and the experience heightened her interest in all that was happening around her.

"When would you like to be married?" Amos asked Mr. Chong.

"Ohhh. Soon." Mr. Chong's eyebrows rose. "Now, maybe."

Mr. Chong's answer caught Amos off-guard.

"Wouldn't you rather wait a short while and have a church ceremony?" Amos responded politely.

"Ohhh. Yes. That would be good," answered Mr. Chong, nodding. "We could be married on Sunday?"

"Well, maybe in a few Sundays," said Amos. "Weddings take some preparation. How about three Sundays from now, if you like?"

"I do," said Mr. Chong. "And you?"

"Oh, it's fine with me." Amos looked at Mr. Chong with a fatherly countenance. "I know your reverence of tradition. I know you will be a devoted husband, and I sense that Yi will do all she can to be a good wife." Pastor Nordquist looked pleasantly at Yi, wishing she could somehow engage in the conversation.

"I'm in reasonably good practice," added Pastor Nordquist, smiling. "It's not like we never have weddings around here." Amos glanced at Joshua and Angela, seated nearby.

"I'd be happy to take care of arrangements," volunteered Anna before she was asked. "Sunday afternoon, July 7th, at 2:00 p.m. would be fine. That will give me time to get things ready." Anna said nothing more, but glanced at Angela who sat quietly holding Joshua's hand.

"Oh," Angela started awkwardly. "I'll help you." Although over a year passed since the wedding of Angela and Joshua, Angela remembered everything like it happened yesterday, and it had gone wonderfully. "We did well together the last time around, Anna," smiled Angela.

"It was fun," responded Anna.

Mr. Chong punctuated Anna's concluding sentence by nodding several times. Yi remained motionless, concentrating on a small braid in the rug under the coffee table. She glanced at but did not touch her *fatemann*.

"Then it is decided," concluded Amos. "July 7th at 2:00 p. m. we will witness the wedding of Mr. Chong and Yi."

The others looked at the couple, each secretly wishing Yi, the prospective bride, could share in the joy of the moment. Weddings *are* fun, Anna thought.

———◦———

As the American melting pot continued to fill, former Europeans mistreated one another along former national lines. On several occasions, Pastor Nordquist saw human nature stoke sparks into fires, many small and short lived, but some large and enduring when fuel was continually replenished. In Pastor Nordquist's opinion, the acrimony was all nonsense. Pointless. Given a little time and patience everyone could get along. It's so much easier than the alternative. Since the congregation formed, however, there were new people, including former railroad workers, moving into the small community. The vernacular "Chinee" was revived. The fact that Mr. Chong was the first person in Seattle whom Pastor Nordquist led to the Lord seemed an adequate explanation among parishioners for the wedding to be held here; it was the right and loving thing to do. Christian charity seemed to prevail. A church wedding provided legitimacy, however, which was more than some unchurched newcomers could accept, including Jake O'Bannion.

June 23, 1912, 5:30 p.m.

The mustachioed bartender didn't look up from the glass he was drying. Although the room was empty, the rancid smell of cheap cigars and a thousand spilled drinks suffused the saloon that afternoon. A soiled pail, used to mop up vomit and blood from the floor the night before, stood by the door. In the corner, next to a high stool was an old, beat-up guitar leaning against the wall. Two men entered, walked to the bar, and stood in front of Joe the bartender.

"What'll it be, boys?" asked Joe.

The smaller man almost secretively asked the larger man, "Th' usual?"

Joe made a quick study of both. The short man had shot-glass eyes as if seeing everything for the first time. Bits of his matted hair stuck out from under a worn hat someone else probably threw away. His mustache hung down like a frayed, horse blanket on a clothesline, covering much of his lower face, and it appeared he tried to trim his beard recently, perhaps with a jackknife. He continually wiped his nose on his coat sleeve.

The big man, head and shoulders taller than the smaller man, had sinister eyes with an ugly light flickering on an dark ocular background. Although nothing was funny, his mouth maintained a frozen smirk. Being too close to loud dynamite explosions, and having been hit on the side of his head, once with an axe handle and on several occasions with billy clubs, made his ears continually ring, impairing his hearing and causing some brain damage. Emotionally scarred, viewing an adversarial world, the big man's eyes glittered with mistrust.

Both men were covered with grime, not from the day's toil, but because neither man changed clothes in a long while. Their odor, of which neither was any longer aware, preceded their approach to the bar. Theirs was a feral, desultory existence.

"Yeah, lez jiz 'ave a couple a beeyers!" amplified the bigger man, loud enough to startle the usually unflappable bartender. The bartender looked back at a satyr-like face with the texture of scraped cowhide. Like his partner, the big man's beard and mustache were matted. The seasoned bartender, although unaware of the big man's encounters with truncheons, sensed the big man's ongoing alcohol consumption was enough to cause cerebral corrosion, and figured the bigger man's brain cavity was festooned with cobwebs. The bartender poured two beers.

Putting one boot on the bar rail, in the afternoon sunlight filtering through the film-covered windows, the bigger man looked down at his small companion.

"Ya know," the big man continued a constant conversational topic, "thas why I don't go to no dam' church."

He cleared his sinuses, then coarsely coughed, subsequently searching for a spittoon. Seeing one nearby, he spat loudly, missing his mark by less than an inch. He turned to his companion.

"One dam' week." People talk. "He only knows her one dam' week, an' d' dam' preacher says 's'all right t' git married."

As the bartender pushed the two beers in front of the men, out of the corner of his eye he could not help but study the bigger man. This guy's dirt is a lot deeper than his skin, thought the bartender.

Jimmy Dunleavey looked up at his bigger companion. "Wull, I dunno. One week might be long enough. I r'member when..."

"Shaddup!" The big man's impatience snapped like a defective guitar string and he swore angrily at the small man. "Shaddup! I don' need none a yer goddam 'I r'member's. I'm tellin' ya dat one week ain' long enough! See!"

"Yeah, sure, Jake."

"Gawdeny money?" asked Jake O'Bannion loudly.

"Yeah," said Jimmy.

"Den pay da bartender!" Jake leaned on one elbow and laughed sadistically, his maniacal, menacing laughter making Jimmy Dunleavy quail.

"Yeah, okay, Jake," Dunleavy replied weakly.

The bartender stood in front of the two men, arms stretched forward with both hands on the bar as if to insure it didn't come any closer.

"H're," Jimmy mumbled.

The bartender took the change, rang up the sale in the large, brass cash register and, without a word, went to the other end of the bar.

"Hey, dis is good." Jake held his breath, took another gulp, and discharged a loud, satisfied belch. "Ain' dis good? Huh, Jimmy?"

"Yeah, sure, Jake."

"Dam' right." Jake wiped his black mustache and upper beard partially dry with his right sleeve, his eyes maintaining their frozen smile.

"So wha' d' we got here?" asked Jake. "Who built the dam' rai'road? Huh? *We* built the dam' rai'road. Built it with the sweat a' our brow."

Jake took another healthy swig as if drinking to his past success.

"An' dis preacher thinks some dam' Chinee did it," growled Jake. "Ignoran' bas'erd. Hell, dey didn' do nothin', did dey?"

Jake's pocked nose bulged over his mustache that was again dripping beer that soaked into his ratted beard. His eyes continued to laugh.

"Huh? Well, hell, did dey?" Jake grew annoyed. "What 'm I *doin'* here? Talkin' t' *m'self? We* built th' dam' *rai'road, right?*"

"Yeah, sure, Jake."

"'Yeah, sure,' *dam'* right. An' I did more'n my share." Jake ruminated for a moment. "Hell, I saved your gawddam hide. Saved your dam' life, by gawd."

Jake took another big swig.

"Hell, accidents happen alla time. Didn't wanna lose ol' Jimmy. No sir, by gawd. Close call dere. Dam' good thing I was dere, huh?"

"Yeah. It was," Jimmy answered quietly.

"You' dam' righ' it was." Jake again wiped the lower half of his face with the back of his sleeve and again belched as the bartender did his best to ignore the two men. "That was good. Hey, wan' another? Hey, bartender, two more!"

Jimmy reached for his wallet.

"Dam' preacher," mumbled Jake. "Turnin' on his own kind. Turning wha's ours over t' d' infeedels. Dam' turncoat! Y' r'member wha' I did t' dat dam' turncoat 'n Por'land. Tha's one turncoat 'at'll ne'er turn on 'is fren's ag'in."

Jake stared straight ahead as he thought about that night outside a Portland bar shortly after the train terminal was finished. In a drunken argument, another ex-laborer, his inebriated courage overtaking his common sense, called Jake "'n Irish pig! Worse'n'a dam' Chinee." Jake's face grew dark, dimming the flickering in his eyes. Jimmy winced and tried to think of something else.

"Y' don' turn on yer fren's," growled Jake. "Dam' trait'r deserved t' die! Serve' 'im righ'!"

Jake mumbled for a moment. He stopped. His glass was empty again. He looked at Jimmy.

"Gawdeny more money?"

"I'm yer fren."

"Yeah. An' y' better not turn trait'r either."

"Ain' gonna do that, Jake."

"Sure's hell better nah." Jake stared at Jimmy for a moment, and at his empty beer glass. "Gawdeny more money?"

"Not much."

"How much?"

"Jake, we don't want to go through th…"

"How *much*?!" Jake shouted. His eyes wild, Jake turned towards the smaller man.

"I don't know," answered Jimmy who stepped back, looking fearfully at Jake. "A couple of bucks."

"A couple o' bucks?!" yelped Jake. "Hell! We're rich!"

"Jake, that's gotta last for at least another…"

"Bartender! 'Nother roun'!" Jake looked at Jimmy with humorless, frightening black eyes. The flicker came back.

Jimmy quietly put money on the bar, and stared at his full glass.

As was his habit since arriving in Murray years earlier, Pastor Nordquist included local bars among his rounds. Pastor Nordquist did as he always did: befriended someone who needed befriending, kept the conversations short, planted the seed, invited the person to church that Sunday, and left. This day would be different. This day, as if it was any other day, would find Pastor Nordquist entering the Night Owl Saloon down by the river with the intention of encouraging some lonely soul in need of companionship, but at this hour on this day there would be only two patrons present, and one would be Jake O'Bannion.

"Joe, how's it going?" Pastor Nordquist asked the bartender as Amos walked toward the bar, sensing an unnerving, crawling sensation. He shrugged his shoulders a couple times, attempting to slough off the uncomfortable feeling.

Most ministers dressed like ministers. Amos usually didn't, except on Sunday morning. Dressed in dirty work boots, work pants, suspenders and a heavy shirt, Amos looked toward O'Bannion and Dunleavy, and the crawling sensation grew.

"Hi, Amos," responded Joe, the bartender, glancing nervously at Jake O'Bannion. "Say, uh, Amos, can I talk to you privately for a moment?"

"Shayyy. Aymish. Aymish. Wha' kinda name izzat?" asked Jake O'Bannion loudly.

"Amos, could you come here for a moment?" said Joe quickly.

"Well, I was named after someone in the Old Testament," responded Amos. "Are either of you gentlemen familiar with the Bible?"

When Amos said the word "Bible," the sensation clearly identified itself. The Old Evil.

"Amos, for gosh sakes…"

"Th' Bible?" replied Jake, looking at a blurred Amos Nordquist. "Yeah, I heared abou' th' Bible. Why?"

"Have either of you gentlemen ever read any of the Bible?" asked Amos as pleasantly as possible, hoping to herd the conversation in the right direction.

Voices rushed to speak with Jake O'Bannion, and there was a pause before the answer came.

"Wha' th' hell's it *to* ya?!" said Jake, turning toward Amos. "Somethin' wrong with not *readin'*?!"

Jake straightened up like a charged fire hose.

"Hell, I built d' gawddam' rai'road! Beats th' hell outa any gawddam readin', fr'en'!"

Jake swore crassly as he took his boot off the rail and walked unsteadily over to Amos who stood slack-jawed, stunned by the verbal onslaught. Amos looked at Jake's wicked, laughing eyes. The maniacal light reminded him of Mombasa hyenas, and Jake's eyes unnaturally bulged as if something inside was pushing out, trying to get a better look. Amos realized this man was big trouble, and knew he needed to do some fast talking.

"I was just asking if you had read the Bible," Amos said calmly. "It's the book of…"

"I knows what y' wuz askin', an' I knows why!" said Jake loudly. "It's cuz yer a high-falootin', smart-ass bas'erd. An' I don' like smart-ass bas'erds. Especially smart-ass bas'erds who think dey know so gawddam' much more den d' res' uv us. An' think dat anyone who built a gawddam' rai'road is an 'ignorant jackash'. You callin' me a – *up* – a jackash? Mister, you'd be'er naw be." Jake stepped closer to Amos and stood grinding his teeth menacingly under his matted black mustache and beard. Jake's eyes continued to flicker, glinting with hatred. "Where y' from, smart ass? Y' cain't speak English worth a dam'. You got no call givin' me trouble 'bou' readin' when you cain' even talk."

Jimmy watched apprehensively. He'd seen it all before. Last week Jake got mad at his horse, tied it up, and beat it to death, then stole the one now tied to the hitching rail outside. Jake's temper went off like short-fused dynamite. Amos's took longer.

The bartender's mouth was half open, and his eyes intense. He didn't want trouble and especially did not want to see a minister come to harm in his saloon. Jake did not know that Amos was a minister, and the bartender was not about to tell Jake.

"I am sorry I upset you," began Pastor Nordquist, backing away. "It's just that I am a pastor and so it is natural for me to talk about spiritual matters. If you will excuse me, I'll be going."

Pastor Nordquist turned and began walking toward the door.

Jake stood unsteadily. As Pastor Nordquist walked toward the door, he touched the brim of his hat respectfully while looking at the bartender, and increased his pace, anxious to be out of there.

"What did y' say y' wuz?!" Jake hollered.

There were few pastors around. Pastor Nordquist continued toward the door.

"Hey!" Jake shouted. "I'm talking t' y', gahhhddammit; y' look a' me!"

His boots clomping loudly, Jake awkwardly started after Amos, who was nearing the door.

"Wha' did y' say y' wuz? A dam' preacher? Turnaroun' 'n' look a' me when I'm talkin'. Yer not dat dam' preacher what's gonna marry dem two…"

"Jake, Jake, let 'im be!" shouted Jimmy. "Don't be causin' trouble wi' no man o' God, Jake. C'mon!"

Jake stopped; his eyes quickly expanding like a bomb going off, his mouth open slightly as the flicker in his eyes went out. He turned slowly and stared at Jimmy.

"Shuddup, Jimmy," Jake snarled. "You make me sick! Shouldn't'a saved yer gawddam' hide. Now yer turnin' on me jes' like this here Chinee-lovin' preacher. Y' know wha' I do t' turncoats, Jimmy, y' miserable sack a gawddam…!"

"Jake, c'mon, I'm jes' sayin' tha…"

"Shaddap!" Jake bellowed, convicted of another pending betrayal. "Shaddap! Shaddap, y' lyin' li'l bas'erd!" he roared.

Teeth clenched like pliers, Jake staggered in Jimmy's direction, intent on executing judgment according to O'Bannion's First Law which was to beat turncoats to death.

"Aw." Jimmy despondently looked down, but quickly returned his attention to the approaching big man. Jimmy pleaded as he started to move away, his round eyes wide with terror. "Aw, c'mon, Jake," said Jimmy, his voice quavering with fear.

The saloon interior was growing dimmer as the sunlight coming through the windows headed further west. Jimmy began backing toward the stove, never taking his eyes off Jake.

"Jake, yer drunk as a skunk," said Jimmy, sounding as calm as he felt, "and y' know how yez git when y' drink. C'mon Jake," Jimmy pleaded again. Jimmy had twice seen Jake in drunken brawls kill other laborers whom Jake thought had turned against him. The hate in Jake never knew when to let up.

Jimmy stumbled over a chair as he evaded Jake the Betrayed, his scarred heart a repository for decades of bitterness that ate at Jake's soul like acid on iron.

Seeing Jake unleashed, Joe the bartender panicked, ran to the storeroom behind the bar and grabbed his loaded rifle, accidentally firing a round into the ceiling. The accidental discharge further unnerved an already nervous Joe, but Jake didn't seem to hear the report as he crashed through tables and chairs, falling like a mountain boulder in his single minded effort to get to Jimmy.

Jake became even angrier as he awkwardly got to his feet and raged forward.

Behind the bar, Joe stood frozen, his rifle pointed in the direction of the careening big man. In a moment, Joe would fire a bullet into Jake, possibly killing him. It would, no doubt, be judged a justifiable homicide, self-defense of some sort, but Joe was having difficulty coming to grips with the moment. Part of him did not want to pull the trigger.

Standing near the door, Amos sensed Joe's limited options and his unwillingness to pursue them. Jake was about to grab Jimmy, and Amos could see from

Jimmy's eyes that Jimmy was scared to death. Who in the world is this Jake? wondered Amos as he walked quickly toward the two men.

"Jake, c'mon," Jimmy whimpered. "C'mon Jake. We – you, me – been through a lot together. I ain't no traitor."

"Boo'shit, y' lyin' basserd," said Jake, grimacing as he grabbed Jimmy by the front of Jimmy's coat. "You wuz never my fren'. Naw once. Y' thought y' could fool me? Zaddit? You lyin' piece a gawddam…"

"Jake! Jake! Ehhuhh," cried Jimmy, kicking and flailing in an attempt to get loose as Jake, scattering tables and chairs like bowling pins, dragged Jimmy toward the open dance floor where Jake would take his best shots. Afraid of dying, Jimmy struggled with all the strength in him, his terror and adrenalin making it hard for Jake to maintain his grip.

"Ehhhhh," Jimmy cried, as he struggled. "Ahhuhhh…ain't no…ehh… traitor," Jimmy gasped.

"Shaddup!" Jake roared. "Shaddup, Jimmy. This'll settle it!" Jake said as they reached the dance floor.

Jake spun Jimmy around, holding Jimmy by the front of his collar, raising his right fist as Amos, his long dormant anger now wide awake, sprinted the remaining few feet and grabbed Jake by the back of his shirt. Amos angrily yanked a surprised Jake backwards – enabling Jimmy to wrench free – wrapping his arms around Jake's arms and mid-section, constricting so hard that Jake cried out. Amos picked up Jake and carried him to the bar, insuring that Jake saw Joe pointing his rifle at Jake's head.

Amos was a big man, but a man of the cloth, while Jake, equal to Amos in size but not strength, had the compassion and forgiveness of a wounded wolverine. With emotional and spiritual maturity, it was no longer the nature of Amos to come to blows, while in the unchurched world of Jake O'Bannion this was how things were settled. Over the years, Jake became proficient at settling things. To Jake, Amos was not a peacemaker, but another backstabber with whom Jake would deal as he did with every betrayer.

As Amos roughly put Jake down, Jake was struggling and swearing demonically. When Amos let go, as Amos stepped back, Jake turned around and swung at unwary Amos, catching Amos flush on the left eye. A bright light flashed, and Amos could not recall falling, but found himself on the floor a moment later looking up at the ugly, perpetual flicker in Jake O'Bannion's eyes. As Amos started to get up, Jake, struggling to maintain his balance, attempted to kick Amos in the head, but Amos dodged Jake's foot, and Jake lost his balance, swearing as he fell.

As Jake got to his feet, he attempted another haymaker, but Pastor Nordquist's left hand caught Jake's right wrist in midair and twisted it. Amos' right hand joined the left, applying enough pressure to make Jake again cry out, his knees buckling, bringing Jake to his knees.

Crouching in the corner, Jimmy stared in amazement. He had never seen Jake manhandled…much less imagined a pastor who could do that. Joe the bartender, who also had no idea Pastor Nordquist had that kind of strength, continued to stare down the barrel of his rifle, momentarily forgetting it was there.

Gritting his teeth, Amos angrily wrenched Jake's wrist, almost breaking it, sending the message Jake needed to start behaving himself.

"I'm going to let you up," said Amos, controlling explosive anger not felt for years, "and when you stand up, you will either stand still or I will, beginning with your right hand, break your fingers one at a time. Do you understand that?" Amos gave Jake's wrist a second wrench.

"Ehhhyeahyeah!" grimaced Jake. "Unnerstan'!"

From the corner, Jimmy breathed a sigh of relief, and stood up. Joe slowly put down his rifle. Amos let go.

Jake stood up, rubbing his wrist, his eyes brimming with hatred. Amos responded by giving Jake a withering look, and turned to see where Jimmy was.

"Amos, look out!" shouted Joe the bartender as Jake grabbed and swung a wooden chair with both hands. Amos quickly looked around as the weapon of war hurled downward, and a chair leg caught Amos' nose, breaking both. Amos again dropped to one knee, stunned. Joe was aghast.

Amos's nose began to bleed profusely. This seemed a nightmare, not reality, to the dazed Lutheran pastor, and Amos was slow to get up and defend himself.

At that moment, a large dark silhouette filled the saloon entrance, outlined in the fading sunlight.

His slurred cursing spewing like lava, Jake raced forward and bashed his big right boot into the side of Amos's head, knocking Amos over on his side, unconscious on the floor.

"Jake! Jake!" shouted Jimmy. "He's a pastor!"

Jimmy's shouting infuriated Jake even further. He could kill a pastor; he would kill this one.

Joe the bartender, his eyes wide and mouth half open, suddenly remembered what he was holding. He had to do it. Looking down his gun sights like a Civil War statue, Joe took aim at the laughing, staggering target. Jake stepped back to unleash another kick to Amos' head as Joe squeezed the trigger slightly. One second more. Steady. Steady. Joe softly squeezed the trigger.

Jake never saw what hit him.

It flashed from east to west, exploding on contact, lifting Jake upward and sending him spinning end-over-end like a barroom chair until the wall stopped him.

Joe lowered his rifle, unfired, and again stood frozen behind the bar, while Jimmy stood wide-eyed in the corner behind the pot-bellied stove.

Standing over Jake O'Bannion was the last man in the world Jake would ever want to face: Swede Odegaard.

100

Big Swede stood over Jake O'Bannion, half hoping O'Bannion could somehow get up, while Erika Odegaard ran to Amos who lay bleeding on the barroom floor.

Joe quickly filled a water pitcher, grabbed several towels, and ran around the bar to Erika. Reintroducing civilization, Erika, fighting back tears, began cleaning Amos's bloodied face.

Eventually Amos regained consciousness. It might have been otherwise, thought Swede as he angrily glanced at Jake. That guy would have killed Amos. Jimmy stood nearby looking back and forth at Jake and Amos, silently confirming Swede's thought.

"You poor, dear man," Erika Odegaard said to Amos, his teeth clenched tightly in response to the pain. "Your wife vill be worried to death!"

Pastor Nordquist was having trouble recalling what had happened, but knew with certainty that his head hurt something awful, and his nose felt like a horse had kicked it.

Jimmy sat down on a chair, slumped over, head down, his hands behind his neck, bobbing slightly while staring wide-eyed at the floor, waiting for the inevitable visit from the local sheriff. When with Jake, Jimmy had always felt secure because Jake was protection. Jake was always obstreperous, but this was the first time Jimmy was the target of Jake's urge-to-kill, and Jimmy determined it would be the last.

"Ve vere passing by," explained Swede, "vhen ve saw your horse and heard some commotion. It vas fortunate ve vere going by. Ve usually don't go dis vay."

Swede kneeled beside Pastor Nordquist.

"Where does it hurt the most?" Swede asked.

"Head," said Amos with difficulty.

"Can you stand up?" asked Swede.

"Yah, sure." Amos started to get up. "Agh!" Pain suddenly shot through his head, and feeling vertiginous, he dropped back to a sitting position. "Eh, I don't know. This might take some…" He gasped.

"Lie back. Lie still," comforted Swede. "I vill carry you to the vagon."

His left hand gently cradling Amos's head at angle, Swede carefully picked up Amos, carried him to the wagon, set Amos, grimacing, on the seat with his head against Erika's shoulder, and started to return to the tavern. "Vhere are you going?" Erika asked.

"He iss also coming with us," responded Swede in a monotone, motioning with his head toward the saloon.

Stepping inside and looking at Jimmy, Swede asked in a low, flat voice, "Von't you also join us?"

Swede walked over to where Jake was lying unconscious, grabbed Jake's right arm with his left hand, placed his right arm beneath Jake's upper legs, lifted and tossed Jake over his shoulder like a large sack of grain while motioning with his head for Jimmy to follow.

As Joe the bartender mopped the blood-stained floor and reset the chairs, the first evening patrons coming to the door stopped and watched Big Swede carry Jake O'Bannion while Jimmy followed. They turned and watched slack-jawed as Swede tossed Jake O'Bannion into the back of the wagon like an extra saddle. Oh, m'gawd, they thought in unison. Oh, m'gawd. Someone got in a fight with Swede?

Once seated in the wagon, Swede explained to Amos, "You're both going to see Doc Torgeson. Then vun of you vill go to yail."

As the wagon rolled away, the patrons turned and went inside. Joe the bartender, emotionally exhausted, glumly returned their inquisitive expressions, anticipating the question he did not want to hear.

"What happened, Joe?"

What happened was bad enough, but Pastor Nordquist, who was to perform a wedding in a few days, soon discovered Jake O'Bannion's right boot had caused severe damage not immediately evident.

June 24, 1912, 2:34 a.m.

"He won't be eating for a while," Doc understated.

Doc was disgusted by Jake's absence of hygiene. Even though no surgical procedure was undertaken, resetting Jake O'Bannion's dislocated jaw would involve more attention to cleanliness than should be necessary for resetting a jaw.

"Jake, do you see this?" asked Doc as he showed Jake a bottle that appeared full of whiskey. "Does this look familiar?"

Jake, whose face was black and blue, nodded.

"I vant you to thoroughly gargle this – get it everyvhere in the inside of yoor mouth for as long as possible – and then I vant you to svallow. It's a homemade elixir vun of my upriver patients sometimes uses for payment; it tastes like bad bourbon. I vould guess it's at least 100 proof. I don't drink it, mind you, but others have and you should. So after you've gargled, svallow. Do this several times."

Jake complied…Doc twice reminded Jake to gargle longer.

"I vant to kill everything in his mouth," Doc explained to the sheriff, "because in a moment I'll need to stick my left hand in there."

When Jake was about halfway through the bottle and feeling no pain, Doc made certain he would. As the sheriff cocked and placed his revolver against the side of Jake's temple to insure Jake did nothing stupid, Doc reached into Jake's mouth with his left hand, and pressed against the outside of Jake's jaw with his right. Using both hands, Doc indelicately rammed – reset – Jake's jaw as Jake cried out, sounding like an angry crow.

The job completed, the sheriff uncocked and reholstered his pistol while Doc went to the sink and poured some "bourbon" over his hand to kill anything from Jake's mouth still alive. Finished with the bourbon, Doc thoroughly washed his hands.

Earlier, Doc cut off Jake's beard, and shaved aound and beneath Jake's chin. As the sheriff leaned comfortably against the doctor's office doorjamb looking at O'Bannion, the sheriff chuckled as Doc, to restrict jaw movement, put a cloth sling under Jake's lower jaw, pulled the cloth up on either side of Jake's face, and tied the cloth tightly at the top of Jake's head. It reminded the sheriff of those drawings of a stork delivering a baby, with the baby in a cloth sling hanging from the stork's beak – only the baby was Jake's jaw. Yeah, he may not chew for a while, thought the sheriff. Serves him right.

After Doc Torgeson secured Jake's jaw, Jake accompanied the sheriff to jail. Jake spent a lot of time in jails, but this time alone. Jimmy left town with what little money they had, hoping to never see Jake again.

Amos was left in the care of angelic Anna, the Good Lord and natural healing processes that always take longer than wished. Lying in bed, propped up by pillows, Amos reread letters from Anders who never slowed down. A lifetime of fast living, however, was catching up with him. His health was going from average to fair, and Amos worried about where it might go from there. Amos frowned and ruminated.

It had been too long since he was in Göteborg, and he thought about all that had happened since he left. He should visit soon; neither he nor Anders was getting any younger. With a severe concussion and a broken nose, Amos' immediate health wasn't good either, and while he might begin planning a trip, he would not be going anywhere soon.

That night, eyes tightly closed, his teeth weakly clenched, Amos lay half awake. Where his head was kicked, a great bruise of variable colors ranging from brown-tinged yellow to purplish magenta gradually recruited darker hued companions as the bruise sluggishly expanded over his right temple. It marked the origin of hyperactive pain drumming in the night. Sleeping was impossible.

In the morning before church, the temple pain had companions. While Amos said he could walk, he found it difficult. Feeling had abandoned the left side of his body and he wished the same were true for the right side of his head. In addition to immobility and variability of feeling, Amos sensed another problem take residence.

Words did not spontaneously come forth.

Amos could not speak normally.

Ideas would beckon, but the expressive words, always eager in the past, sat back restively. Sometimes only a few would respond. Amos spoke haltingly, sometimes pausing for several seconds, or sometimes unable to speak at all. So many words, particularly nouns, close friends in the past, were absent. Whether on a brief respite until the pain went away, or restive forever, Amos could only wait to know. In the meantime, speaking was a source of frustration.

That morning, Joshua and Jared, who knew the worship service well, took turns in front of the congregation.

This is pretty good, thought one parishioner as she marveled at how Joshua's understanding of biblical history and principle was reinforced by Jared's showmanship. The service moved along quickly until it came time for the Most Reverend Angus McGregor to give the sermon. Mounting the pulpit, believing he had spent a lifetime preparing for this moment, Angus looked severely solemn.

Angus had little sense of timing, however, and less sense of time. Adding to temporal stress was the topic: free will and determinism. It was Angus's favorite, but not a topic adequately covered during a normal Sunday morning attention span. Eventually one older woman, snoring loudly, could not be awakened with any gentleness, and Angus, although half finished, decided to wrap it up – taking another ten minutes.

Finally finished, the sermon was a lesson for Angus, but few others.

That afternoon, Amos decided to postpone the much-discussed wedding between Mr. Chong and Yi because Amos could not yet speak well enough, and considering the events that brought Mr. Chong and Yi to this place, Anna did not want them married by a second-stringer.

"But why not let me do it?" asked Jared. "I've already done it once myself."

"During the wedding," Joshua asked, "what would you say?"

"Do you, Jared Young, take this woman to be yo…'"

"Exactly. That's exactly what you *would* do. You should see a psychiatrist."

"There's nothing wrong with my eyes."

"Boys," said Anna hoarsely, "let's wait until my husband, the pastor, feels better," arms folded as she cleared her throat. "We'll wait."

The next day a letter arrived from Anders who, widowed and semi-retired, was writing quite often. The letter described the reaction of many in ostensibly neutral Sweden to the Battle of Jutland involving 151 British ships against 99 German ships. It was the largest naval battle in history, and occurred at the mouth of the Skagerrak. While the British exited the battle with continued numerical superiority and rule of the seas, Anders wrote that the British Royal Navy "was outmaneuvered and outfought by the Germans, losing 14 ships with many others seriously damaged, while sinking only 11 German ships. The formidable navy of Sir Francis Drake and Admiral Lord Nelson," wrote Anders, "was not present at the Battle of Jutland, but, rather, a British navy infused with timidity, stupidity and, in my opinion, callousness to the great British naval tradition."

The letter became quite heated, and the judgments therein seemed a bit severe to Amos who had read about the battle in the Seattle and Everett newspapers. As always, accounts varied.

Amos reflected how those present (much less those not) still often fail to get the story straight. And besides, Amos smiled as he read, Anders isn't even British. A resident of "Little London," evidently Anders had spent considerable time in, and grown attached to, big London.

Putting the Battle of Jutland letter on the table, Amos began thinking about the Skagerrak. He clearly remembered leaving the last time, and remembered the superstitious apprehension of some because of his presence on board. Sunny and Sol. Probably still somewhere foisting their *schadenfreude* on other unsuspecting victims. Amos chuckled. He turned his imagination toward Göteborg. Looking at Göteborg in his mind's eye, he knew what he saw was Göteborg 48 years ago, and said aloud, "I wonder what…Göteborg looks like now."

A week passed. The bruise grew to maturity, covering the right side of Pastor Nordquist's head with intermingling purple and black blotches which made his skin look like a partially composted cabbage leaf. Sensation on the left side of his body gradually returned; and now his nose and head did not feel nearly as badly as they looked.

But where are the words? How will I be able to…? Amos wondered, intentionally failing to complete the thought.

Pastor Nordquist weighed how candidate occupations beckon from many directions including heritage, market demand, opportunity and natural talent, but regardless of origin, occupational proficiency depends on obtaining and maintaining skills that create value. Deprived of key skills, productivity suffers, and so does the producer. A century later, medicine would discover that Alzheimer's patients, when memory is emptied of all else, still recognize the thing they did best. Amos Nordquist, the Christian minister, was doing what he did best. Yet now, within his occupation, his most outwardly important skill was compromised.

The effort of winning souls for God is never without disappointment and pain, Amos stoically thought as his head ached. Suffering seems essential and, to further God's puposes, Satan is allowed his temporary victories.

The still, small voice inside him disrupted his reverie. Prayer. Pray. Amos felt the compulsion to pray. "If God already knows what you're going to pray," Rachel once asked him, "why pray?" Amos responded, "If all that is to be done in the universe was caused by what God already knew, why would we be here? What would be the point? But, to answer your question, I don't know the answer other than somehow our prayer helps facilitate what the Holy Spirit already intends to do."

Amos again shrugged his shoulders. The internal mechanism of the eternal system was a mystery far beyond his understanding. Prayer is the sustaining act of faith, he thought, and nodded, thinking of the biblical admonition, "Pray without ceasing." Good idea.

Amos got down on his knees, as the Holy Spirit led him to do, and prayed as he was led to pray. Amos prayed for a solution to his problem, knowing the ways of God are unfathomable.

A letter mailed a week earlier from Nels Hanseth at church headquarters in Minneapolis arrived the next day.

June 15, 1912

Dear Amos,
Greetings in the name of Jesus.

We trust all is well with you and your family. It has been such a long time since we have seen one another. I write you as an aging, old friend and as a fellow servant of God. This letter expresses our great need and anticipation, but also our fondness and excitement.

As you know there have been many other churches of our denomination formed throughout western Washington. These new congregations, as well as those to follow, need local coordination. The distance between Minnesota and Washington State, together with the amount of correspondence we have been receiving, make it difficult for us to adequately serve new congregations in your area. With so much enthusiasm, it is important that needs be met.

Since you are senior among pastors in western Washington, and are a capable administrator, we are asking you to become president of the newly formed Pacific District presently covering the entire Puget Sound region. You will shepherd new congregations as well as all established churches in your area. Their joys will be your joys, but their sorrows will be your sorrows. You will be required to help initiate or coordinate worship service format, worship materials purchases, programs, installations of pastors, holiday celebrations, parsonage and parish construction.

Your responsibility before the Lord will be greater than it presently is. You will direct salvation efforts throughout the region rather than only in the Skagit River valley. In addition to the increased burden of responsibility, you should relocate in Everett in order to reduce the distance to the majority of congregations you will oversee, enhancing your/their accessibility.

I know this will not be an easy decision to make. Such is the burden of all men of God. Please consider this new position prayerfully. As always, let God's leading be your beacon and guide.

I look forward to your response, both as a fellow servant of God and as one who finds it difficult to watch the years pass so quickly without seeing old friends. You are, and have always been, in our prayers, Amos – in Murray, in Seattle, and in your present parish.

Please give my best wishes to your wonderful wife, Anna.

I remain
Your servant in Christ,
Nels Hanseth

Amos stared at the letter for several minutes. As he sat on the couch, he reread it again as if for the first time.

"What does it say, Amos?" asked Anna as she entered the room, intrigued by his perplexed expression. Amos looked up at her.

"Do you want to move to Everett?"

"What?"

101

I have been offered the position of President of the…Pacific District in charge of all Pacific Northwest Lutheran…congregations."

"That's wonderful. I'm sure that the position is important," responded Anna, "but, well, Amos, you know how much…" Anna bit her lip and said nothing more, returning to the folding she had brought inside from the clothesline. Earlier the sky had been blue, but the blue was gone, the sky looking like charcoal brushed cotton tufts. It would start raining soon.

"You don't seem too…enthused," said Amos.

"I am at peace here," said Anna, looking at Amos sincerely. "We have close friends. The grandchildren are all here. I, well, I love it here. It was so easy to leave Murray, and Seattle. I wanted to leave. But, here…"

"We wouldn't be too far away," countered Amos. "Everett is just a little bit down the road."

"How are you feeling, dear?" asked Anna, glancing at Amos as she snapped a folded sheet in mid-air to smooth out a crease.

"I still have difficulty…speaking."

"It seems there has been no change."

"I'm afraid," said Amos, "to think about it. But I do not see myself…improving in this regard. Anna, speaking for me is constantly a…struggle. It is like the words are there in my head but won't…come out."

Anna sat down on the edge of the couch near the ironing board and looked at Amos.

"That man did a great deal of harm," said Anna.

"Well, yes," responded Amos. "But maybe no." Amos sighed. "We have two choices before us. My…affliction makes the decision easier. It is not our…choice alone, however. We always followed the…leading of God in the past and this should be no different. We must pray about this. Again." He looked fondly at Anna, but was greeted with no change in expression.

Anna knew a decision to sow unselfish charity on moral high ground would be bountiful. And so, while absently gazing at the folded laundry stacked on the ironing board, she thought the requisite thoughts. Neither Amos nor I are getting any younger. This farm, although small, requires much of our time. It isn't like the children and 11 grandchildren and pets are always around anyway.

"You should accept the position; we should move," said Anna unemotionally, surprising Amos. Anna said nothing for a moment as stood up, walked to the laundry basket, and began folding a tablecloth. "When you consider that, at the moment, there are more Lutherans north of Seattle than in Seattle and Tacoma combined, having headquarters in Everett makes sense."

Amos nodded.

"Before we seriously plan a move, however," said Anna out loud, "we have a wedding to perform."

"Yah, well," said Amos, "we better start…preparing. Mr. Chong deserves a fine…ceremony."

"Not to mention Mr. Chong's fiancé," added Anna.

"Yah," Amos laughed. "Anyone who would come all that way to get married to someone she was…engaged to since the age of two should have a fine…wedding."

Anna picked up her sewing basket. "I do hope she'll understand much of it."

Amos looked fondly at Anna, his wife and best friend these many years. "Weddings and women are…kindred souls, dear," said Pastor Nordquist. "The groom may feel out of place, but never the bride, even when she doesn't understand the…language. How are you coming with her…bridal gown?"

"Oh, quite nicely." Anna walked over to her sewing table and studied her handiwork. "She is *so* petite."

Anna turned the fabric over, feeling the texture of the white satin and lace bodice. Anna smiled, imagining what Yi would look like.

"Who should give away the bride?" asked Anna.

"I have someone in mind," responded Pastor Nordquist, "who has attended several weddings over the last few years."

"Angus?"

"Uh, no," said Pastor Nordquist with a smile. "Angus has another role to play…one that he might consider more appropriate. But you're close."

Sunday, August 4, 1912

On the day of the wedding, the honor of giving away the bride belonged to Big Swede. Pastor Nordquist was concerned that Swede's massive presence would overwhelm diminutive Yi. Such was not the case. Yi was radiant. Her hair was done by the church ladies in the best Gibson girl style of the day and, after doing her hair, they applied mascara, rouge and lipstick, tittering in unison when viewing the splendid finished product. Yi, the daughter of a Chinese merchant, was transformed into something Mr. Chong had never seen, and would not see according to tradition, until she took Swede's arm and, protected from all other suitors, began walking down the aisle.

After glancing down the aisle at the pastor, groom and best man, Big Swede looked at Yi, nodded and held out his arm. She looked back, her countenance beatific, understanding his heart. She was not his daughter, yet at that moment he relished feeling as if she was. She placed her small, right hand on his left forearm, and Swede responded by placing his right hand over hers. As the church organist pumped out the *allegro vivace* notes of *The Wedding March*, Yi and Swede began walking down the aisle while all in attendance stood. As she walked, Yi's eyes, once continually downcast, focused straight ahead toward her fiancé, the pastor and the best man.

Mr. Chong, standing beside the best man, Angus McGregor, was overwhelmed by Yi's transformation and struggled to control feelings of excitement. Meanwhile, Yi knew what and who she was, and nothing in her past or the present could interfere with this moment. Swede beside her, her heart filled, Yi stopped in front of the chancel.

"Who gives this…?"

⸻ • ⸻

The following week Angela Nordquist went into labor and delivered a little boy, Lars, named after Kathleen's father, and Joshua's maternal grandfather and paternal great grandfather. Joshua was a dairy farmer now, working in partnership with his brothers-in-law, Jared Young and Samuel Odegaard, and Arnie Jorgensen. Jacob Odegaard helped part-time while also concentrating on his paintings. Luke Odegaard, interning under Doc Torgeson, hoped to eventually specialize in ophthalmology.

During that week, as Amos and Anna began planning the move to Everett, Amos received a letter from Minnesota notifying him that his friend and colleague, Nels Hanseth, had passed away.

Pastor Nordquist was deeply saddened by the news although Nels had led a full, productive life. In his late 80's, it was amazing Nels continued the work of the Lord for so long. The letter in his hand at his waist, Amos stood looking at the floor, thinking. Nels Hanseth was a committed man of God whose greatest witness was his love for others, and an inspiration. I will certainly miss his counsel; I will miss him.

Within a month, Amos sold his farm to Arnie Jorgenson, and began the Everett chapter of his life's journey. Amos believed the Civil War was the last and only occasion where he would witness men in the heat of battle. The Everett chapter would prove that belief premature.

102

August 6th, 1913, 3:00 p.m.

Amos and Anna had lived in Everett nearly a year. On this hot August afternoon as pets napped beneath exhausted shade trees, inside the Nordquist home, thick walls, high ceilings, and 2½ stories insulated the Nordquist living room from outside temperatures. Next to the corner table, Anna and Amos sat on the couch reading while eating the last of the applesauce cake prepared for his 72nd birthday party, celebrated with family the day before.

The Nordquists' new home, on the west side of Colby Ave. several blocks south of the Hewitt Avenue intersection, was equidistant to both waterfront and the Riverside district. It was a location allowing respectability in Everett social circles which, depending on where one lived and what one did, could open warmly or close impenetrably. Amos was a Lutheran Church administrator; royalty to some, commoner to others.

While growing up in Göteborg, Amos was continually around foreign ships. In contact with sailors from foreign ports, Amos had learned several languages. In Everett, ships from a variety of foreign lands also sailed into port. That evening after the air cooled, Amos walked down to the docks where he studied an older schooner brig aside a three-masted barque, much as he would have as a boy. Works of art, he thought.

He thought about how he once wanted to be a sea captain like his father, reminding himself that it was at sea where he concluded the Lord's work was most important. After looking for a while at the different ships in port, he turned and began to walk home, thinking about missing the pulpit, former parishioners, shepherding the flock.

After all these years, and knowing as much as I do… But now I have no church and…*no*… That is not true. He looked around him at people, buildings, and the ships below. "The whole world is a church," he said out loud…with opportunities for ministry every moment, everywhere, came the thought.

While the sun hung over the western horizon, dockhands cast off the lines of an old freighter, a three-masted, full-rigged ship. "The *Northstar*," Amos read out-loud. Amos thought of the *Polstjärnan*, and smiled. "No doubt the *Northstar* would have some…tales to tell if she could talk."

But now I am talking to myself, he thought, shaking his head.

He turned and walked up Hewitt Avenue. Approaching the Colby Avenue intersection along the crest of the hill, Amos again turned around to look at the ships in the harbor now many blocks away. He watched the ship drift free of the harbor tug, and thought of how people drift, never anticipating the moment when this life segues with all eternity.

November 2, 1916

Pastor Nordquist continued to think about these things. In November 1916, the urge to pastor remained strong in Amos, but the largest obstacle, his speaking difficulty, also remained.

"Anna, once again I am missing having a…congregation." Amos smiled at Anna as she rearranged the kitchen cabinet shelves.

"You're a good pastor, Amos," she responded, standing on a stepladder while moving jars of canned beans into compact rows.

"I was."

"Nonsense. You've always been good. You still are," she said softly.

Anna looked lovingly down at him from her perch, placed her hand over her mouth, but unsuccessfully stifled a cough. Amos looked back affectionately; her full head of white hair was not there yesterday, was it? And still, she looks good.

"I have found a…substitute," Amos offered.

"A substitute?"

"Yah," responded Pastor Nordquist. "Let me tell you what I did this morning."

The previous evening, Amos watched a Dutch ship enter Port Gardner Bay and, convinced that worship and prayer would be a welcome blessing to believers among the crew, decided to ask permission to conduct a worship service on board. With limited English-speaking ability, where can they worship ashore? he thought. There is no Dutch synod ashore. Ah, but normally sailors do not take time to worship ashore. My coming aboard would be the solution.

After the in-port watch was set and initial business completed in preparation for the next day, Amos was allowed to come aboard. He smiled, passing greetings in Dutch, as the majority of the crew passed him while going ashore.

"May I see the captain," he asked a seaman on watch at the head of the gangplank.

The bronzed, leathery face of Captain Christiaan van der Zee contrasted with his trimmed, white beard and mustache. He looks like a weathered Robert E. Lee, Pastor Nordquist thought.

"Captain," began Pastor Nordquist in Dutch, "I am Pastor Amos Nordquist. I live here in Everett. I speak…Dutch." Pastor Nordquist smiled warmly. "With your permission, I would like to come aboard Sunday morning and conduct a worship service if that is…agreeable to you."

Captain van der Zee considered the request for a moment, nodded and granted permission.

"Worship on the Sabbath would benefit the crew," said Captain van der Zee. "There are some who would come out of conviction and, hopefully, a few who might come out of curiosity. I can guarantee the attendance of only one person, however," concluded Captain Van der Zee, "me."

Dutch Reformed Captain Christiaan van der Zee said he would notify the crew. After determining the exact time Pastor Nordquist would come aboard on Sunday morning, Captain van der Zee shook Amos' hand, nodded and returned to his quarters.

Ebullient, Amos walked down the gangplank to the pier. The moment reminded him of how he felt before his initial Murray church service many years earlier. Pastor Nordquist silently thanked God for another opportunity to face the challenge.

━━━━━●━━━━━

"Do you still speak Dutch well, Amos?" asked Anna.

"Yah," answered Amos with slight smile. "After speaking with the Dutch… captain for awhile, it started coming back. Tomorrow," Amos smiled, "I will give a sermon while…converting English words with a Swedish accent into Dutch," Amos joked. "With my…slowness of speech in English, I will have more time to convert words to Dutch."

"You mean you might be twice as slow."

"Well, maybe. Maybe not." Amos knew Anna was kidding, but the subject concerned him. "God has given me this opportunity. He will give me the words to say," said Amos, unaware that when that moment came, he would be at a loss for words.

103

Big events usually start as small events. During brief infancy, the Great Seattle Fire burned on a wood stove. Noah Kellogg was only looking for his mule. And when Annie Miller, diminutive under her fashionable hat, mounted her portable stand on Seattle's Occidental Avenue to deliver a speech opposing U.S. involvement in WWI, at first no one paid much attention. When later told about the events, Amos only shook his head, unaware that those events would soon lead to his involvement.

"I can only wonder in dismay," said Annie Miller as loud as she could, constantly clearing her throat, "why we would consider sending our young men to fight a war – in which many of them will die – that does not directly threaten our land." Her hands clasped together as if she were singing a solo. "Is it patriotic to kill our fellow man simply to appease the British crown? No," she answered. "Patriotism has no role in this grand disagreement between…who knows who?'"

Three inebriated sailors from Whidbey Island Naval Station northwest of Everett were walking by, but then stood and listened for a few moments. Annoyed at what they were hearing, they took exception to Mrs. Miller's comments.

"Nonsense," said one loudly. "We should be over there. You like krauts? Take your soap box and go over there with the krauts!"

This attracted some attention. By behaving disrespectfully, the three seamen annoyed those (some of German ancestry) nearby. People expected more from uniformed servicemen. Although most of the small crowd had no idea what she said, their sympathy at the moment was with Mrs. Miller. In a pique, Mrs. Miller quickly finished her oration and stepped down from her portable stand.

One of the sailors immediately stepped up on Mrs. Miller's stand to defend his country.

Mrs. Miller angrily waited but, as the sailor droned on, her patience left, and she asked the sailor to weigh anchor so she could pick up her stand and leave. The sailor responded by further questioning both Mrs. Miller's character and patriotism. None of this would have mattered except that, for emphasis, in the heat of battle he unnecessarily shook his fist at the much smaller woman.

A large, well-dressed passer-by, a Spanish-American War army veteran already in a foul mood from earlier, unrelated events, saw what he perceived was a drunken sailor threatening a woman.

"See here!" shouted the man. "You would strike a woman?!"

"Hey shove off!"

The angry passer-by shoved the sailor off Annie Miller's speaker's stand, prompting shipmates to come to the sailor's defense. Amos was told that several men in the crowd, rallying behind the chivalrous passer-by, took umbrage with the sailors. For the navy, all was not lost, however, as into this maw of anti-American sentiment – theirs was not to reason why – two soldiers charged in defense of their comrades-in-arms.

There were more annoyed civilians than military personnel, and more verbal salvos than anything else. Minutes later, upon arrival of the police to restore order, the armed forces representatives had sustained modest combat casualties.

While they would lose the battle, they would not lose the war. Through the ideologically informative efforts of the press, Annie Miller would transform into the socialist IWW, the Industrial Workers of the World, a national labor organization begun by radical Big Bill Haywood, and who were more militant than any of the servicemen. An uncivil war was about to start.

Members of the IWW were nicknamed "Wobblies," and raised either the ire or sympathy of most. From Amos' conversations with several men, he realized that unemotionally discussing the Wobblies was nearly impossible. What kept the Wobblies standing? Their slogans, long and short. Wobblies had slogans for anything they deemed of importance, and if there was no slogan for a matter, it was by definition a matter of unimportance even if important. Slogans dictated mindset, behavior and correct communication: what to say, how to shout... how to wear signs. From reading their tracts, Amos learned Wobblies were of the conviction that "the working class and the employing class have nothing in common," and that workers needed to "take possession of the means of production," and, instead of the American Federation of Labor motto, "A fair day's wage for a fair day's work," the workers' motto should be, "Abolition of the wage system," *viz.*, capitalism. From what Amos read, Wobblies were militant socialists who believed in the inevitability of class warfare. To win this war, the Wobbly goal was to organize all workers into one big union where the worker would dictate the days and hours of labor, as well as the amount of compensation in a system that was somehow not a wage system. Lack of employer cooperation could result in a general strike, the ultimate Wobbly weapon of Marxist "expropriation in the war with business owners."

Amos read this and asked himself, "How would a general strike actually work as a means of expropriation?" He asked others. No one knew. Many Everett men wanted no part of an organization where unskilled laborers were considered no different than skilled technicians.

But it was a slogan. And from their slogans every Wobbly knew who they were and what was expected of them. How important did the Wobblies consider their slogans? Amos often observed that Almighty God was not the focal point of all religiosity. As with many militant social movements, what Wobblies believed was their religion. And Wobblies were zealots.

The Wobbly parish was any street corner although, in the spirit of the era, modest parades were a form of demonstration. Accommodating the humanist mystique, parades allowed the Wobbly to feel good by being seen doing what, according to Wobbly ideology, was right – whether it was or not. The good feeling was intensified by a perception of defiant self-sacrifice in response to persecution since, as all Wobblies knew, their convictions were less than universal.

A year earlier, Wobblies paraded down Seattle streets in the middle of the day with their red flag flying next to Old Glory. Up to that day, while the publisher of a large Seattle newspaper considered Wobblies as anarchists and no better than the rats around the Seattle wharves, he felt little compulsion to do much about them except to negatively report an occasional IWW event. Watching the parade from his office, that changed.

"Mattison," said the publisher, looking out the window. "Come here and look at this," he motioned. "Look at this."

Matthew Mattison, political reporter, walked over to the publisher and stood looking down toward the street below.

"I don't know what it is," continued the publisher, "but watching those damned arrogant people, and seeing the stars and stripes – as if held *captive* – being flown next to that red anarchist ensign, gives me heartburn."

The publisher turned and glared at Mattison who stood solemnly watching the parade below, his hands in his pockets.

"This is a travesty," the publisher muttered under his breath as he turned again to look out the window.

"This is intolerable," he added after a moment of watching. "Seriously, those stupid people cause more confusion, more damage, than…God only knows who. If that American flag could talk, you'd damned well better believe it would be screaming: 'Get me out of this!'"

The two men stared as the Wobblies marched into the intersection, bystanders watching sullenly.

"Well," said the publisher, pausing for a moment as he studied the scene below, "let's do that."

The publisher looked intently at Mattison who looked back, his serious expression changing to an almost pleasant demeanor as he sensed what was coming next.

"The people of this fair town," continued the publisher, "need to know who those anarchists really are, Mr. Mattison, and I want you to take the bull by the horns, pull out the stops, and completely expose those crackpots."

Through the window, the publisher glanced once more up the street as the small parade moved into the next block.

"Enough is enough," the publisher muttered. Over the next year, as opportunities presented themselves, the paper lampooned the IWW. The Annie Miller story would generate the greatest reaction.

While to err is human, to significantly distort the truth – as Jack Comerford, interim editor of the *Tacoma Ledger,* demonstrated decades earlier – requires media bias. Little would have resulted from the Annie Miller melee were it not for the fact that political reporter Matthew Mattison never met a story he couldn't like. If it appeared plain and unkempt, dressed in glad rags, he could spin a tuxedo of stereotypes. Mattison pioneered the dangerously false axiom that good journalists do not report the news, they make the news.

> *…at the very moment a gang* [no gang] *of red-flag worshippers and anarchists* [wrong people] *were brutally* [no brutality] *beating two bluejackets and three soldiers* [wrong numbers] *who had dared protest against the insults heaped* [no insults, no heap] *on the American flag* [no flag] *at a soap-box meeting* [no meeting] *on Washington Street* [wrong street] *last night…*

Woven into the Mattison fabric was the thread that Mrs. Miller and the others involved were Wobblies, an assertion that carried credibility since the IWW was opposed to U.S. involvement in WWI.

In the same article, Amos read that the Secretary of the Navy, Josephus Daniels, who spoke in Seattle that same evening, berated Seattle Mayor George Cotterill by making "…a merciless denunciation of the cowardly un-American [Cotterill] who…fosters anarchy in the streets by permitting the display of the red [IWW] flag…" Daniels said nothing of the sort, and Cotterill, by not repressing the IWW, was following constitutional mandate.

Amos did not question the credibility of Mattison's report because Wobblies beat up opposition in other cities, and such events were widely reported. But servicemen? The American flag? This is new, and this seemed treasonous. To solidify his credibility, Mattison provided quotes from a National Guard representative, veterans of the Spanish American War, as well as "anonymous sources" whom, according to the article, promised that the next evening, if Seattle's better element was further incited, retaliation would be swift and sure. All based on fiction. Besides Amos, 7,000 subscribers read the story.

As Mr. Mattison's anonymous sources duly warned, retaliation was swift and sure. The next evening the mob gathered around sunset.

"C'mon, boys! Let's get started," cried the man at the head of the mob, club held high, his back to the Seattle IWW headquarters front door. "The Wobs wanna beat up American soldiers and sailors?!" The others inched forward. "We'll show 'em what comes of *that*!!" he turned and headed toward the front door. The others followed in a rage. The mob, more than a few of whom were members of the U.S. Navy, demolished Wobbly headquarters in less than a half hour.

The publisher was delighted and, in his opinion, justice was served. With flare that impressed even the least biased media members, Mattison subsequently wrote:

> *The smashing of chairs and tables, the rending of yielding timbers, the creaking and groaning of sundered walls, and above the*

rest the crash of glass of the windows on the east side all blended together in one grand Wagnerian cacophony. And all the while the crowd outside just howled and cheered. It was almost more joy than they could stand.

It was more than Mayor Cotterill could stand and, fearful of the potential for anarchy fostered by newspaper anti-anarchists, the next day the mayor undertook strong counter measures.

"Harrison," Mayor Cotterill asked an assistant firmly, "could you find [Police] Chief Bannick and ask him to see me at once?"

Mayor Cotterill stood looking through his office window at people on the street below. This is a thankless job, he thought. These people cause trouble. Trouble, trouble, trouble. And then they blame the trouble on me.

He returned to his desk and re-read the newspaper article. Moments later Chief Bannick came through the door.

"Chief, hello," began Cotterill. "Have you read what the paper says about the Wobbly headquarters demolition?"

"Yessir," replied Chief Bannick. "Very creative, those newspaper people."

"Well, their creativity could make your job very difficult, Chief."

"I don't like the Wobs any more 'n the newspaper does," responded Chief Bannick. "Hell, you don't like 'em either.

"No," agreed Cotterill, "I don't. They're an odd bunch with a knack for bringing out the worst in others. They make our job a lot more difficult than it would be otherwise. But we have a responsibility. Chief, I normally don't tell you how to do your job, and I really don't want to start now. But the paper has these people all steamed up, and things could get out of hand in a hurry. So I'm giving you some orders. Once you proceed to execute these orders, if people ask you, 'what right do you have' to do these things, just say, 'Mayor's orders' or 'to keep from implementing martial law.'"

Chief Bannick stood silently, anxiously waiting for Cotterill to say what he wanted done.

"First," began Cotterill, "I want you to close all the liquor stores."

"Close the liquor stores?" responded Chief Bannick incredulously. "Have they ever been closed?"

"I want those liquor stores closed!" repeated Cotterill. "I don't need a bunch of drunks beating up Wobblies, or people they *think* are Wobblies, or anyone else for that matter. Get a few of your boys out on the streets and close the liquor stores. It isn't like your boys don't know where the damned liquor stores are, so just get them closed."

"Yessir," responded Bannick. Closing liquor stores is a new one, but shouldn't be too hard, he thought to himself.

"And I also don't want any street meetings or public speaking," said Cotterill. In an emotionally charged era of budding labor reform, many street speeches ended in violence. As a practical matter, some towns would not allow unrestricted speaking in public. Everett didn't. "No one gets to harangue anyone else, y' understand. No Wobblies, no pacifists, no socialists. No one! While your boys are out shutting down the liquor stores, they can bust up street meetings. Hell, all those people do is run off at the mouth. Whine. Whine. Whine. So, no runnin' off at the mouth. Tell your boys to let people know it's time to simmer down for a while." Cotterill studied Bannick. "You okay with that?"

"Yessir," said Chief Bannick who wondered for a moment about the First Amendment, but, under the circumstances, what the Mayor requested seemed necessary.

"You're probably wondering about the First Amendment," said Mayor Cotterill. "Well, I'm all for the First Amendment. But it's against the law to incite violence. That's what we're tryin' to stop." Chief Bannick nodded.

"One more thing," added Mayor Cotterill, who got up from his seat and walked toward Bannick. Cotterill stopped about three feet in front of Bannick and, for a moment, looked at him levelly. "To insure law and order," said Mayor Cotterill firmly, "and to insure some cooling off, I want you to take as many of your boys as you need, and I want you to surround our largest newspaper's building, and I don't want one damned paper to get out of there until Monday morning. Monday morning," he repeated. "I think things will have cooled off by then."

Chief Bannick looked at Mayor Cotterill for a moment. "Lord," said Bannick, "you'd think we were at war."

"We are not at war," responded Cotterill, "and we aren't about to be at war. At least, not if I can do anything to stop it." Cotterill turned, walked over to the window and looked down at the street. He hooked his thumbs around his suspenders and said, "I don't know who might start it, but after what happened yesterday, sure as shootin' someone will." Mayor Cotterill turned and looked at Chief Bannick. "You've got your orders. Any questions?"

"No, sir."

Without another word spoken, Chief Bannick left Mayor Cotterill's office with the single-minded purpose of carrying out his orders.

⸻ ◆ ⸻

The publisher was livid. He called his attorney.

"Who does he think he *is*?" the publisher shouted into the phone while pounding his free hand on the desk. "This is *my* newspaper, and this is *my* town, and these are *my* readers, and he has no right whatsoever to interfere with the distribution of my paper in *my town!*" The publisher's teeth clenched. "You get that @$%&!! arrested and thrown in his own *jail*, and I don't care who you get to do it!"

The publisher's attorney contacted Judge Humphries, the only judge he could find that Saturday morning. Humphries wrote out bench warrants for Cotterill and Bannick, ordering them to appear in court.

By noon, the blockade was lifted. Later that day, Amos had the opportunity to read the objective editorial follow-up to the riot story that – in an initially uncharacteristic spirit of good will – began by calling Cotterill "...a loathsome louse..." but went on to say less complimentary things about the mayor.

Doing anything it could to advance socialism and instigate the inevitable class warfare, the IWW seemed irrationally intent on vilification of its public image. The publisher made hay with all the news the IWW gave him, the newspaper continuing to fire a daily barrage at the IWW, insuring declining popularity. Unpopularity, however, seldom deterred a Wobbly.

Amos and Anna had lived in Everett for four years and made many new friends. Most men worked with their hands, and Amos would learn a great deal about the difficulties of working conditions. In 1916, the unskilled laborer worked in jobs ranging from tedious to dangerous, especially in the logging camps where men working long hours for subsistence wages were occasionally maimed or killed in largely preventable accidents. Mill workers also worked long, exhausting hours in order to barely support their families. The IWW expected their ideals and methods would command sympathy in Everett where Pastor Nordquist followed Wobbly activities in the *Herald* or the *Tribune*, but support was limited. The Industrial Workers of the World, who wanted to unite all labor unions, were not having much success doing so because their radical politics, overbearing manner, and strident speeches alienated regular union members. The big Everett Shingle Weavers union, for example, never recognized the IWW.

In lumber mills, Amos learned, the phrase "shingle weaver" generally covered shingle packers, sawyers and saw filers, but was directly applicable to packers. Shingles in the hands of an experienced packer were like cards in the hands of a croupier. An experienced shingle packer, when stacking cedar shingles into overlapping bundles, would work so fast it appeared he was weaving shingles together. The Shingle Weavers Union was the strongest and largest representative body on the Trades Council in Everett. For years, their secretary-treasurer was Donald McRae until he was elected Snohomish County Sheriff in 1912 when Amos and Anna moved to Everett.

For a year after Mrs. Miller's speech, the Seattle newspaper wasted few opportunities to lambaste the IWW. The Wobblies did not care but, motivated by an expectation of inevitable class warfare, were intent on fueling the fire. In this vein, the IWW decided to lend moral support to the striking shingle weavers in Everett. While the shingle weavers did not ask for IWW support, to the Wobblies a request was irrelevant; the opportunity arose. Following an August 29th evening shingle weaver attack on replacement workers who were leaving an Everett theater, the IWW decided to make a show of speech on behalf of the shingle weavers. The Shingle Weavers Union leadership advocated non-violence, and condemned the attack by some striking members. Sheriff Donald McRae was convinced the attack was unsanctioned.

But who unofficially planned it? The number of attackers justified the assumption someone did. If not union leadership, McRae wanted to know, who was behind this?

104

The IWW reputation being what it was, Sheriff McRae suspected IWW involvement although there was no evidence they took part in the attack on replacement workers.

The Everett waterfront mills should have been within the city limits and, to Amos, it seemed they were. Henry Hewitt, however, drew up the Everett city limits so that the waterfront mills, including lumber and shingle mills, were technically in the county, outside of city jurisdiction and city taxation. The city/county border went along the street providing access to the waterfront mills and, because the docks and mills were in the county, the Snohomish County Sheriff's Department was responsible for the waterfront area, the war-zone where pickets and replacement workers would clash. The Snohomish County Sheriff's Department, which could see more trouble in a day than the Everett Police Department saw in a month, effectively became the primary Everett law enforcement agency.

In early 1916, Sheriff McRae, former Shingle Weavers Union Secretary-Treasurer, was well-liked among union men because of his amiability, concern for others, and continued loyalty. For example, he donated $25, a decent sum at the time for an average man, to the strike fund in May 1916. McRae was convinced that Everett people were good people, and that workers and management could work out their differences if left alone to do so. By August, arrests, inmate statements and a Pinkerton investigation convinced Sheriff McRae that outside agitation was behind local violence which, in McRae's opinion, would not be happening if things were left to local union leaders, friends of McRae. McRae decided to combat the unwelcome demonstrations and interference creating obstacles to peaceful Everett negotiations, interference that included Wobblies – in McRae's opinion, primarily Wobblies.

November 4, 1916

Anna went to the front door after hearing a knock, opened the door and looked down to find a familiar face.

"Hello, Mrs. Nordquist," said the man nervously, holding his hat in both hands.

"Oh, hello Freddie. My, I haven't seen you for a while."

"I just got back in town," said Freddie, standing back from the door, his worn hat in his hands and his brindle on the porch floor beside him. Freddie looked like he normally did whenever Anna saw him this time of year: tired, grimy, and depressed, with a foul smell that came from walking great distances, sleeping in box cars and hobo jungles, and having one change of clothes but no bath.

"Nice to see ya, Mrs. Nordquist. Eh, I've been down around Bakersfield and south of Los Angeles helpin' with the harvests. Came back up here t' see if there wasn't any wood cuttin' jobs." Freddie, who spent much of his life hopping trains to wherever work was available according to season, kneaded his ragged hat brim and looked down. "Eh, I was wonderin' if, uh," he looked up, "I might, uh…"

"Certainly, Freddie," said Anna politely. "Come in. I'll fix you a sandwich, and a little extra to take back with you for the Mulligan stew down at the jungle." She assumed there was a pot of Mulligan stew – communal stew continually resupplied from anything available – at the Riverside district hobo jungle, a camp area by the Snohomish River where transients lived when in Everett. She looked at Freddie to see if her assumption was correct.

"Thanks, ma'am. It's nice t' know y' can count on some people," said Freddie, his expression pleasant and respectful as he continued to hold his ragged hat in his hands. Freddie followed Anna inside and, responding to Anna's directive gesture, sat down on a wooden kitchen chair not far from the sink.

"Well, Freddie, how is your wife? Have you been able to see her at all recently?"

"I did see her toward the end of summer. She gets the money I send and don't spend a nickel more'n she needs to." Freddie took a deep breath and expelled it as he looked wistfully at the kitchen floor cabinets, thinking of his wife. "Wish I could spend more time at home, but I gotta go where there's work."

"I see you have a full brindle with you," said Anna.

"Uh, yes ma'am. I, uh, I don't want to wear out my welcome like everything else, but, uh, I was wonderin' if I might boil down [wash, including boiling] some of my clothes," said Freddie with a hopeful look. "I ain't done it for a while and I'd be much obliged."

"Let's see what you have," said Anna.

"Just these," said Freddie as he showed her the clothes in his brindle. What Freddie had was modest – his glad rags, hobo argot for a set of clothes in better condition than the other set, the ones he had on.

"We'll take care of these first," said Anna, implying that tomorrow he could also wash what he presently wore after the glad rags were dry. "Put those in the sink, run some cold water over them, and first try to get as much dirt out as possible." Anna went to the wood-heated oven/range as Freddie got up and put his glad rags in the sink. She refilled the kettle and added a second kettle and a big pot of water on the stove before beginning to fix Freddie two hearty beef sandwiches and a large glass of milk. Freddie washed his clothes with an effort equal to how dirty they were.

"I really appreciate it, ma'am," said Freddie as he scrubbed away. "You know I'll do whatever you need done."

"Yes, I do. Actually, my husband is not as young as he once was, and we have a load of firewood that needs to be split. Also the cellar needs cleaning, and the front porch needs to be scrubbed. Could you help us with any of those?"

"Oh, yes ma'am," said Freddie happily. "Absolutely." The more he did, the more he'd get; hopefully even enough extra cash to send to his wife.

"Since we won't get to the clothes you have on until tomorrow, you should try to get as much work done today as you can. There's no point in washing clothes and immediately soiling them again if it can be avoided. And Pastor Nordquist might have some other odds and ends that need attention."

Anna sliced some homemade bread, got butter and meat out of the ice box, and made two large sandwiches for Freddie.

"How long have you been in town, Freddie?"

"I got here Tuesday night. Didn't want t' bother you but…" Freddie looked down at the clothes in the sink before him, "a man's gotta eat. Mulligan stew's okay, but, well, things are kinda sparse down at the jungle." Freddie had a hangdog look. "November ain't such a good time for food."

Anna nodded as she thought about Thanksgiving for most Everett families.

"How many men are down at the jungle?"

"Oh, maybe 15 or so right now. Lookin' for odd jobs. They keep the place clean like they're s'pose t' and, near as I can tell, there ain't no brindle stiff [hobo that steals from other hoboes] around. You hardly ever find that anyway. A man that's hungry is too weak, eh, emotionally weak, uh…"

"Impotent, powerless?" clarified Anna.

"Yeah. You have t' have a certain amount a' bein' all high 'n mighty t' be a real thief, out deliberately takin' what ain't yours t' take. Bein' a real thief and bein' down-and-out don't mix well. We get blamed for a lot a' what we don't do." He twisted a wet shirt, squeezing water from it. "I don't do it. Oh, I suppose if I was starvin' and there was an apple I could pinch, I'd do it, but that ain't like goin' out lookin' for somethin' t' steal, you know?"

"Was there anyone at the jungle who you know?"

"There are a few locals, a few guys that come up from California like me, and a couple a' Wobblies. I was told that Ed McNeil – you remember when I brought him by last year?"

"Yes, I do."

"Anyway, Ed got killed in Modesto tryin' t' hop a train. Got flung under the wheels." Anna winced. "Joe Clark was a guy I got chummy with when I was here a couple of years ago. I was told Joe caught the westbound [died] over in Spokane. Froze t' death sleepin' under a trestle. That happens…especially with the single boys. Dunno. Can't help but think they must know what's gonna happen if they go to sleep not dressed warm enough in that kinda cold."

"Have you been writing?" asked Anna.

"Yeah, I wrote a story about a guy like myself – pickin' fruit, cuttin' wood, cleanin', diggin' – and his friend. The two of 'em would hop trains and go around the country lookin' for work together. Interestin' stuff. And I made 'em both a little nuts, especially the friend. The guy can't be completely trusted 'cuz he's looney. But I guess you gotta be a little nuts to be a 'bo."

"Sounds interesting."

"I used real life experiences – toned 'em down a bit so they'd be more believable."

Anna beamed as Freddie continued to scrub.

"I'd like to read your story later."

"It's in my brindle. That'd be fine. I'd like you t' read it. You'd be the first."

"Maybe not the last," said Anna.

"Maybe not."

After Freddie completed the initial scrubbing, Anna pushed Freddie's clothes around in hot water with the handle of a mop, thinking about how there were between 500,000 and 700,000 hoboes like Freddie, as common as commas, trying to survive. She could understand why so many people were searching for alternatives to the present economic situation and system. After a moment she discontinued, put down the mop handle, drained the sink and sat down opposite Freddie.

"So Wobblies are in the jungle," said Anna. "What do the Wobblies have to say?"

"The usual, ma'am." Freddie thought for a moment. "You've heard it all before, I think," said Freddie. "I'd like to find a way to fix things, but I've read enough history to know what the Wobs are shootin' for is all wishful thinkin'… hope, sorta. Interestin' t' talk to sometimes. They get all jacked up while most 'bo's just sit. Sharin' t'bacco and contributin' t' the stew is about as close to socialism as I get, but I can understand how those boys think." Freddie nodded. "Don't agree, but I understand, y' know."

Anna nodded as Freddie continued.

"They talk about Sheriff McRae…talk about him like he's the devil incarnate. The locals argue that McRae's a fine man. The Wobs don't buy none a' that. That's the problem with the Wobs: their minds're totally made up and it don't matter whether they're right or wrong. No alternative point of view with them – t'ain't allowed. Ain't like they're a'goin' by what's true and what ain't, it's more like what's correct t' believe and what ain't. Kinda like religious. That attitude gets real annoyin'." Freddie looked to one side. "I don't like being around the Wobs much. Times're depressin' enough."

"I understand," said Anna as she stood up, walked to the stove, lifted the pot lid, and saw the large pot of water on the stove was beginning to bubble. "Freddie, could you put your glad rags in the pot?" The clothes would remain in the pot for about 10-15 minutes until any remaining lice were dead and most ground-in dirt loosened.

After making certain the sink stopper was tightly inserted, using a mop handle, Freddie took the clothes out of the pot and transferred them to the sink. Anna began pouring hot water from both kettles over Freddie's clothes until they were submerged. Freddie began to stir his clothes with soap in the hot water. After a while the water gradually cooled to a lukewarm temperature; gritting his teeth, Freddie wrung out his clothes, then rinsed them in cold water, wrung them out again, rinsed them again, wrung them out and hung them on the clothes rack near the oven.

He nodded respectfully to Anna and went out the back door to the wood shed where he began splitting firewood with an old, double-blade axe Amos bought from a Mt. Index lumberjack.

Finished, before it became too dark outside, Anna gave Freddie meat, vegetables, flour and salt for the Mulligan stew, and Freddie headed back to the jungle.

The next day, Freddie returned and told Anna how appreciative the "bo's" were for the meat, vegetables and all. "The boys were real happy. You shoulda seen 'em. The Mulligan stew was far better than usual. Most of the bo's hadn't eaten anything decent for a spell.

"They all want to know where you live," added Freddie, "but those boys don't always appreciate sky pilots [pastors], y' know, and even though one or two 'bo's ain't so bad, a whole bunch can become a nuisance. Besides, I don't want them thinking of you as an easy mark." Freddie looked at Anna protectively. "Too many for that. Although if there's any angel food [church dinner leftovers] somewhere, the boys'd be happy t' get in line. As long as they still don't know where you live, I don't see no problem there."

"I'll be happy to let you know of any Lutheran church events, Freddie," said Anna. "You and the others probably already know which other churches provide food and when." Anna glanced out the window. "Certainly, I'll keep it in mind. And I'm certain Amos will again want to go down to the jungle and give brief sermon for anyone who might want to listen, as well as individually pray for the men."

"I don't know about the others, but I sure appreciate that he does that. No one else thinks like that. Seems like he's about the only person who cares about us."

Freddie went outside to scrub the porch. Later he began cleaning the cellar. Finished, he went back upstairs. Anna didn't bother going down in the cellar to inspect the job; Freddie had proven himself dependable in the past.

"You've finished with the firewood, the cellar and the porch," Anna summarized at the end of the second afternoon. "You've taken a bath, and both sets of clothes have been washed. Before I pay you something, would you talk with Pastor Nordquist and see if he has anything else for you to do?"

Freddie went outside to the back yard where Pastor Nordquist was working in the flowerbeds preparatory to next spring.

"Freddie, grab that cultivator and dig along the edge of the foundation down to the end of the flower bed, then back up along the outside edge."

Freddie began as instructed.

"What did you do when you first got into town, Freddie?" asked Pastor Nordquist.

"Got in last Tuesday and started goin' from house-t'-house hopin' t' make a dollar or two choppin' firewood. Also been down in the jungle or over at the mills – the waterfront in general – hopin' they might need someone t' clean up. I've been talkin' with a lot of people." Freddie's eyebrows rose. "Interestin' things goin' on here in Everett." Freddie continued to dig. "You know Sheriff McRae?"

"I know who he is, of course. I've met him."

"He seems t' be the center of a big controversy a'brewin' around here."

"Freddie, dig a little…harder. I need the weeds loosened at the roots." Freddie dug harder.

"And y' know, pastor," said Freddie, pushing himself, "from what I have been told, I can't say I'd wanna be in Sheriff McRae's place for anything."

"Yah," answered Pastor Nordquist, on his hands and knees, mulching flowerbed soil with a trowel. "Enforcing the law is a thankless…profession."

"No," responded Freddie, "I mean some folks don't like him at all, but then, of course, there's a bunch who do. Just depends on the whole Wobbly thing."

"Who doesn't like him?" asked Pastor Nordquist. "As I say, I've met him. He seems straight forward, a man of…character."

"Well, it's hard t' figure out," responded Freddie. "I've been told that Sheriff McRae and the unions are tight. But the Wobblies started coming around and, well, Sheriff McRae don't like no outsiders coming into Everett startin' trouble."

"I can't blame him," said Amos. "Who would want that?"

"You wouldn't think anyone would, Pastor. I was told that Sheriff McRae'll stand by locals, regardless of which side they're on, but he don't want anybody coming into Everett and unnecessarily meddling in Everett affairs, stirrin' things up." Freddie looked at Amos and, still digging, shrugged.

"So why don't some people like him?"

"It depends on who you're talkin' to. Some people think the Wobs are a good thing," answered Freddie. "Some people, especially Wobs, think the mill bosses couldn't give a darn about the working man, and that the Wobs are 'help on the way,' not 'trouble a brewin.' And, well, some people do more 'n complain, you know. Some people go further." Freddie looked down at his cultivator chewing up the flowerbed along the foundation, and said nothing else.

"Like what?" asked Pastor Nordquist, who knew there were problems, but not the extent of those problems. Freddie talked to people who evidently did.

"Well," began Freddie, standing upright and studying the flowerbed edge, "this is what I was told: I heard his wife can't take no more threatening phone calls. Guess it's really upsettin' her."

"Phone calls? Who? Who are the callers?" asked Pastor Nordquist, standing up.

"I dunno," said Freddie, looking at Pastor Nordquist. "They, of course, don't tell her who they are. I was told they just call at night, 'specially when McRae ain't home, and make threats."

"What kind of threats?"

"Someone poisoned Sheriff McRae's dogs a few nights ago," said Freddie, turning toward Amos. "Both dead." Pastor Nordquist looked back incredulously. "Those kind of threats…and worse, I guess." Freddie's expression was a contortion of puzzlement and disgust. "I go to a lot of places, and I see a lot of people, and you know what?" Freddie looked at Pastor Nordquist seriously. "Some people are nuts." Freddie started to dig again. "No matter which side you're on," said Freddie, "people should be civil, you know? 'Bo's are more civil 'n that. People should look at one another's position. I guess that's the way it used to be. What's his name, the union leader?"

"Ernest Marsh?" responded Amos as he knelt down along the next section of flowerbed.

"Yeah, that's him. I was told by one of the locals that Ernest Marsh always tried to see the side of the mill owners. I'm told that things are changin' and the cooperative spirit Everett used to have seems to have hopped the last train. Seems Mr. Marsh is having trouble feeling any sympathy for…what's the main mill owner's name?"

"Well, there's David Clough."

"Yes, that's the name. Mr. Marsh can't feel any sympathy for Mr. Clough and the rest of the owners, and vice versa, and I think Sheriff McRae is askin' himself, 'What's different now? Where's the change?'"

"What do you think?" Pastor Nordquist asked Freddie.

Freddie stood upright again, looking down at the flowerbed. "I hear and can see both sides." Freddie stepped to his left and began digging again. "And Sheriff McRae, he can see both sides. And I think he wants everyone to do the same like always, but now something's different. Bit by bit, somethin's hardening hearts on both sides. 'What is it?' he asks himself. 'Why the growing standoff? No sense to any of it.' To Sheriff McRae there's only one answer."

Freddie took an unearthed earthworm and carefully buried it where he'd already dug.

"I know Sheriff McRae believes it's the Wobs. Lotta boys pay no mind to the Wobs, but then there's a bunch that do. The Wobs just stick their nose in and stir things up. That's what they do."

Freddie sensed Pastor Nordquist's thoughts.

"Mediate?" Freddie held his left hand out questioningly. "Not with the Wobs. No reasonin' with those boys down at the jungle. Not with their slogans and screwball ideas about class warfare. So, Sheriff McRae figures Everett people can work things out, but the fly-in-the-soup is the Wobs."

Freddie stood back, holding the cultivator with his right hand, and studied the flowerbed beneath the Nordquist's window boxes.

"Maybe so, maybe not," continued Freddie. "I guess Sheriff McRae's committed, though. He's doin' what he thinks is right. Might as well be carrying around a sign that says, 'No Wobs.' That's the stand he's a' taking, but a few people don't like it. Then, again, there's a bunch that think Sheriff McRae's the best lawman in the state. That's what I hear. Courage. Conviction. Character. Dependability. Greatest thing since swell fork saddles."

Freddie continued to dig in earnest as Pastor Nordquist studied Freddie with a pleasant expression. Freddie knows more about what is going on in Everett than most Everett residents, thought Amos. Like others, however, Freddie does not know a solution.

"Wish I knew what to do," Freddie concluded. "Wish I knew more. Heck, if I knew more, I could probably be the sheriff. Heck – 'sheriff' – I'd be mayor." Freddie laughed for a moment and thought about Sheriff McRae. "Guess you just gotta go with what ya think is right, an' hope it is."

"There is an excellent book," said Pastor Nordquist, "that is very useful when attempting to discern what is right."

"What book is that?" asked Freddie without thinking. "Oh. That book. Yeah." Freddie pinched his bushy mustache nervously. "Um. Hope Sheriff McRae reads it."

"Everyone should read it carefully," responded Pastor Nordquist, now leaning on his shovel. "People would get along."

Freddie looked at Pastor Nordquist and thought for a moment.

"Didn't your wife tell me that a while back you had some problems with a congregation in Seattle?" asked Freddie.

"Yes. I did."

"Weren't those people reading the Bible? And people still didn't get along?"

"I can't tell you how many read the Bible and took it to heart," said Pastor Nordquist. "When it comes to Christians, as Lincoln said, 'Calling a horse's tail a leg doesn't make it one.' Unfortunately, the Bible was not seriously consulted. If it was, Freddie, as much as I enjoy your company, we wouldn't be having this conversation."

Freddie thought some more, shrugged his shoulders and massaged his mustache with his right thumb and forefinger.

"Seems sometimes people just can't get along no matter what," said Freddie.

"Our fallen nature."

"Well, from what I hear, the growing friction between the Sheriff's Department and the IWW is creating enough heat to cause some real smolderin'," said Freddie. "Where there's smoke, there isn't always fire, but, well, with a little time and effort, sometimes smolderin' can do more than just ignite, it can explode, and people wind up in the bone orchard [cemetery]." Freddie looked at Pastor Nordquist knowingly. "Hope that doesn't happen. Guess it depends on whether or not the Wobs stay out of Everett."

<hr>

About a month earlier, however, on behalf of the Shingle Weavers who had requested no assistance, the Wobblies planned a free speech offensive in Everett.

"Miserable damn' mill owners," muttered the first Wobbly, sitting on his haunches near a Seattle jungle campfire.

He spat chewing tobacco on one of the rocks surrounding the small fire pit, and the spittle sizzled with a rank aroma.

"Dunno how those Everett 'brothers' put up with it." He turned to the others – some sitting, some standing. "We should show 'em what we did in Spokane, don't y' think?"

"Yeah, Spokane!" yelped a second Wobbly with a laugh. "You was there, Bill. Lord! I can't believe how well that worked. Better'n anyone coulda *ever* dreamed!

People just kept on comin'. Formed a line a' Wobs. Step up on a soapbox, say a few words, and then, zip, the next cop would send you off to jail…"

"Cops were as organized as we were."

"…and the next speaker would step up."

"Had a regular machine there."

"Filled the jail, and they put the rest of us in a school nearby – kinda cold, no heat – and when the school was full, they put us in army barracks…"

"Until there was so many of us they couldn't afford t' keep us anymore. Had t' let us all out." He laughed. "Free room an' board for a while. What 'd that cost 'em?" he asked as he began straining used coffee grounds from the boiled coffee.

A third Wobbly, seated to the left on a short log, while lighting his pipe said, "For the food, cops, everything, someone told me it ran up to $25,000."

"You're kidding! $25,000? That much? Nah."

"Yup."

"I could start a whole world for $25,000."

"Yup."

"Hell, the City of Spokane shoulda just put us all to work!"

"Yup.

"Well, hell. Wanna do it again?" asked the second Wobbly.

"Yyyup," said the third Wobbly with greater emphasis, as he drew on his pipe.

"How many people we got here?" asked the first Wobbly, looking around at the small group.

"Oh, counting those that ain't here at the moment," answered the second Wobbly, "well, maybe 20 or so."

"Hell, that ain't anywhere near enough," muttered the first Wobbly. "They arrested 1,200 in Spokane."

"'Course it ain't near enough," said the second Wobbly. "We gotta recruit a few boys."

"There's a lot of boys coming in from east of the mountains," volunteered a fourth Wobbly. "Fruit picking and shipping season's done. Long been done. No snow in Seattle yet so no snow shoveling jobs. Lotta boys with nothing to do."

"Let's give 'em somethin' t' do," said the first Wobbly. "How long do y' think it'll take?"

"Gonna need a little time," said the fourth. "Some of these new boys ain't quite as inspired as the rest of us."

One month later, 41 Wobblies – rookies and veterans – boarded a passenger ferry for Everett where, again, public speaking was restricted. The Everett Commercial Club Pinkerton detective called Sheriff McRae.

"May I speak to Sheriff McRae, please," said the Pinkerton detective into the Bell telephone.

"Hi, Al. How are you?" responded Sheriff McRae as he held the receiver to his ear.

"I'm fine," answered the detective. "But not everything else is fine. Everett's gonna get some visitors."

"Who?" asked Sheriff McRae.

"Wobblies. About 40 or so," said the detective. "Mostly unemployed transients. Bums. Stiffs in need of something to do. Something righteous." As Sheriff McRae listened, his stomach began to tighten. "They plan on a small version of what they did in Spokane. You know, how they filled the jails? So many of them got arrested and jailed, Spokane couldn't afford to keep them locked up. Wiped out the city treasury."

"Can I ask a question?" asked McRae in a quiet monotone.

"Sure."

"If you were a Wobbly," began McRae, "and you went to Spokane, and were part of that, what would you say you accomplished?"

"Can't say as I know," said the detective.

"What about the working man?" asked McRae. "The Wobs make a big deal out of helping the working man. What about the little guy? The guy who can barely afford to pay union dues. In Spokane, how was he helped?"

"Well, as I said," responded the detective, "can't say as I know. They closed down a few bogus employment agencies that were taking fees from stiffs, and doin' nothing in return. Beyond that, I don't know. What do you think? As far as labor is concerned, what do you think they accomplished?"

"As far as the working man is concerned," said Sheriff McRae, "considering the number of people involved, I can't see where the Wobs accomplished anything. Got a lot of time on their hands. I wish that weren't so. They'd…hell, we'd *all* be a lot better off. Seems to me this is just one big party for most of those boys. They get a great deal of satisfaction just raising hell under the guise of some high-minded nonsense that none of them really gives much thought."

"I can't see where they give it *any* thought," said the Pinkerton detective. "You think about this stuff and it makes no sense."

"'Class warfare,'" Sheriff McRae responded, giving an example. "It's all moonshine. But, you know what? I think most of them must know that."

"So, what's the motivation?"

"Something to do; maybe somehow feel better about themselves," said McRae. "But some are just nuts. The ideal solution is for them to all find jobs, but, well, things are as they are. How do we get things fixed? From where I see it, under present circumstances the Everett mill owners and the Everett union leaders can interact better, get things done quicker, and get men back to work a lot sooner without Wobs buttin' in."

"What do you plan to do?" asked the detective.

"I don't expect we'll be seeing anyone making any speeches," said Sheriff McRae, "and we won't jail anyone. This won't be Spokane."

———————————◆———————————

Meeting the boat as it tied up to the pier, Sheriff McRae and deputies rounded up the 41 speakers, bound them and shoved them into deputies' automobiles.

"Hope your jail is comfortable," said one Wobbly. "I plan on staying awhile."

"Ain't going t' jail. Gotta private club, though. And tonight you get to be initiated!"

"Initiated?" echoed the Wobbly. "What's that?"

"You'll find out soon enough," said the deputy.

It was dark and raining as the caravan rolled to the rural Beverly Park neighborhood south of town. Other deputies were already waiting. Some had 3' hose sections, some had rubber tubing filled with sand or rocks. Others had clubs. Headlights from Packards, Dodges, Studebakers, Fords, and Chevrolets lit a path on either side of which two lines of deputies began to form.

In moments, the Wobblies were made to run a gauntlet of club-wielding deputies ladling out early 20th century justice. All 41 Wobblies were subsequently beaten, some severely, and made to walk the 25-mile Interurban tracks back to Seattle.

----------●----------

"I hope they got the message," said one deputy in conversation with Sheriff McRae the next morning as they stood around the sheriff's desk.

"I don't think we could have made it clearer," added a second deputy. "I know we were pretty hard on 'em but, damn, everyone knows they…I don't know…it seems they expect to get hurt. They're just nuts. How do you handle lunatics? I just hope they don't come back."

"I hope they don't either," agreed the sheriff. "But they're trouble." Sheriff McRae turned and walked behind his desk where he stood for a moment. "That's what they're all about. 'Class warfare'? Hell, most of them don't know how that could happen. I'm not sure anyone does. But to them I suspect it really doesn't matter.

"If the Wobs come back," added McRae as he sat down, "which for those people is not out of the question, and they violate our laws – which they would expect to do – there will be hell to pay."

In spite of this experience, the Wobblies refused to accept the message. Beaten but not defeated, they straggled back to Seattle and considered how to retaliate, their lumps and bruises inspiration to others of like mind. Calls went out to IWW locals all over the state. Courage begat courage. There were subsequently many more than 41 willing to help in the retaliation. Within one week, the IWW had raised a small army for a return confrontation that IWW leaders said would decide "the entire history of the organization."

105

November 5, 1916

The next week on the morning of November 5th, the Seattle IWW chartered two large boats, and filled them with 280 solid Wobblies.

The men and women, many chattering and exchanging pleasantries, boarded the two boats and, once on deck, some broke into song, proving their mettle by lustily singing militant labor anthems.

> *Then raise the scarlet standard high!*
> *Beneath its folds we'll live and die.*
> *Though cowards flinch and traitors sneer*
> *We'll keep the red flag flying here.*

As the boats left a Seattle pier, the Wobblies were enveloped in celebration. While many gave little thought to what they would encounter in Everett, others were prepared for trouble. The trouble would have been far less if the Pinkerton agent and, consequently, Sheriff McRae did not know the Wobblies were coming.

The size and intent of the IWW retaliation was Sheriff McRae's initial fear when he learned of the call to other locals. Subsequently, the Everett Commercial Club, a private downtown men's club comprised of local businessmen, became a command center to which, throughout the week, citizens came voluntarily to be sworn in as deputies. For years Commercial Club membership also included union men. As the rift between mill-owners and shingle-weavers grew larger, however, union members began to give up Commercial Club membership. In this case, however, the place of enlistment did not matter; both union and non-union citizens volunteered.

The incentive to be deputized increased when the Everett *Tribune* got wind of the IWW retaliation plan, and portrayed the approaching Wobblies as intent upon the destruction of Everett. Most volunteer deputies believed they were protecting their homes and livelihood. The Seattle *Industrial Worker*, on the other hand, said Everett deputies were intent upon the destruction of the IWW, a portrayal actually gaining traction in Everett. Pastor Nordquist heard about the deputizing but, as a minister, gave no thought to offering his services

After leaving church where he was usually part of the congregation, Pastor Nordquist returned home for lunch, but because of his anticipation of leading another worship service (not to mention in Dutch), had no appetite. He was anxious to get down to the docks. Later in the day, Jared and Rachel, and Joshua and Angela, were coming down – with the grandchildren.

"Oh, wait a minute dear," Anna hollered in a rasping voice from the kitchen as she saw Amos putting on his coat to leave. "I need some things down at the store." Seeing his impatience, she quickly resorted to reason. "Dear, it's within walking distance, and I need some of these items…butter, eggs, milk, pork and ground beef – and any fruit – for dinner this afternoon. I'd go myself except I have so much to do before everyone arrives.

"The weather is better," she added, "but still wet and cold; I want dinner to be worth the long ride. And, of course, after ministering, you'll deserve a good dinner."

"We wouldn't do this when we lived up north," reminisced Amos. "We raised all these things ourselves."

"Yes," agreed Anna, "but now we go to the store. It's convenient; right up the street. When we lived up north, nothing was within walking distance. And the store carries more than groceries. Since I still have this infernal headache, I also put aspirin – and cough medicine again – on the list."

"Very well," sighed Amos patiently, "let me have the list."

Amos took the list and left quickly. The early afternoon overcast was turning darker.

Upon returning from the store, Amos set the groceries on the kitchen counter and, once again, began heading for the door followed by Anna.

"As you know from Rachel's letter, Jared and Joshua have a surprise announcement for us," said Anna, "but especially you."

Amos stopped for a moment and looked at her, wondering.

"I don't know what it is," Anna added, shrugging her shoulders.

"If it's that Rachel and Angela are both pregnant," responded Amos, smiling, "that won't be too much of a surprise…although I will be happy to hear it."

As he approached the door, Amos kissed awaiting Anna who never missed an opportunity to lovingly respond in kind. He held his hug longer than usual, his eyes closed, reaffirming their mutual love. After a moment, he let go and beamed down at her with the same loving look she had seen since he first kissed her. She is a beautiful woman, Amos thought to himself. Inside and out.

Anna sensed the thought and looked at him in kind. Amos stepped back and, after straightening his hat, opened the door and went out into the cold afternoon, unaware of the tragedy about to unfold.

Westerly winds softly hissed in the falling mist. Pulling up his collar, Amos cautiously walked down the wet cobblestone lane toward the distant docks. He expected to be on board the Dutch ship by now, and was anxious, hoping impatient crewmen had not gone ashore.

Hands in his pockets, Amos walked head down along the glistening cobblestone roadway, careful not to slip.

The dull sound of wet boots clomping, almost in unison, on the slick street gradually grew greater like a growing chorus of distant drums. Amos looked up and glanced about him. Several men merged and walked beside him single mindedly looking at the docks in the distance. As Amos continued, tributary streets and alleys jettisoned other men onto the main arterial. Still others joined ahead, while more fell in behind. It was Sunday, and the weather was cold.

The mills, even in good times, never employed this many men during a Sunday afternoon shift, thought Amos.

These men were not walking as men normally do, as he was walking. They were purposeful, erect, and intense as if marching. They were armed. Amos looked about him. In the cold November grayness, an armed force was gathering at the foot of the hill along the waterfront.

The combined forces of the sea breeze and piling tar overpowered the mill odors close to the docks, invigorating the armed men gathering in the cold, their senses on full alert, adrenalin pumping, focused like soldiers awaiting battle.

At the pier, Amos walked away from the gathering and toward the Dutch ship where he would lead worship services. As he walked up the gangplank to the quarterdeck, two boats carrying 280 passengers steamed around the bend into Possession Sound, heading toward Everett's Port Gardner docks.

The sight of the black smoke billowing from the stacks of the two distant boats silenced superficial conversation among the men crowded in the cold November air, and they turned and stared. On the pier, it seemed quiet forever as the boats gradually drew closer. Deputies fingered their weapons. A white-haired man wearing a ragged, wool, Civil War tunic, haversack, and cavalry cap, double-checked his .54-caliber Spencer repeater. He looked older than Amos who was 75.

Amos asked to see Captain van der Zee who, from the pilothouse port hatchway, watched the merging men meld an amoebaeic unity below. Seeing Amos approach, the captain walked quickly to the bridge ladder and down the ladder to the quarterdeck, the noise from his blurred feet sounding like a snare drum. Stopping next to Amos, Captain van der Zee shook Pastor Nordquist's hand, but said nothing, turned to his left and watched the large congregation of armed men on the pier.

The men's stares were affixed on the approaching boats. Amos was about to introduce conversation when a shout was heard as Sheriff McRae, standing on a stack of lumber, addressed the men before him.

"Listen to me!" shouted Sheriff McRae. "I don't want this thing getting out of hand!" The others listened. "We'll arrest their leaders! And the rest we'll send sailing for home!" He studied the men. He knew many of them, some better than others, and they all knew him. "Once we've arrested their leaders, if the others don't want to leave, we'll give them reason to!" A few in the crowd spontaneously cheered, but most looked back in baleful silence as the sheriff glanced from face to face.

"They have women aboard!"

Women?

"They know we mean business!" Sheriff McRae shouted. "I just want 'em *out* of here! Again, first thing we do is to make an example out of their leaders!" Sheriff McRae studied the rear of the crowd.

On the embankment to the east, a small audience was forming. People wanted to watch.

"Now, any questions?!" asked McRae. "Anyone here who doesn't understand what we're gonna do?!"

There was no response. No response from the deputies. The nearby but isolated lumber company guards, whose principle responsibility was to help break the shingle weaver's strike, just watched.

"Boys, spread out!" McRae shouted to the deputies. "You're all bunched up here! Spread out!" The sheriff whipped his arms out, palms down, like an umpire calling a runner safe. He knew the Wobbly mentality. He knew there could be trouble, and he wanted to insure the Wobblies would have no doubt there were more men – armed men – on the pier than on those boats.

The Everett deputies spread out along the pier and nearby warehouse. The rain stopped. On the two boats, Wobbly faces, some stone cold and some radiating irrational excitement, all reflected determination. They were getting close enough to study the tenseness on the faces of armed Everett deputies. Many Wobblies were also armed. The deputies expected the Wobblies would bring guns, but didn't know to what extent. Most Wobblies were also unaware of how much firepower they brought with them. This was supposed to be an invasion of free speech.

"That's quite bunch of lawmen on the dock," said the first Wobbly, leaning on a forward railing as the boat came closer and closer to its destination. The sun momentarily broke through the clouds, lighting the stage for the audience gathering on the embankment.

"I dunno," said the second Wobbly. "Looks like there's a lot more of them than us. Can you see 'em? My eyes ain't so good. Any of 'em got guns?"

"All of 'em," said the third Wobbly matter-of-factly, attempting to light his pipe in the sea breeze. Around the three men, other Wobblies were loudly singing songs of the militant left.

"They all got guns?" said the first Wobbly.

"Yyyup," repeated the third Wobbly quietly. He gave up attempting to relight his pipe for a moment, and just stared contemptuously at the enemy.

"Think we ought to turn back?" asked the second Wobbly. "I mean, I don't wanna go through that initiation line like last time. Damn, that hurt. Dark. Couldn't see nothin' but some headlights in front of the line. I thought I was gonna die. I really did. I thought I was gonna die. And I asked myself, 'Is this worth dying for?'" He looked at the dock. "Those boys all got guns?"

"We're getting mighty close," the first Wobbly nervously interjected. "I recollect someone once saying something about 'the whites of their eyes.' Well, that's about now."

"We're in for it," said the second Wobbly. "Can't turn back now. Besides, no one here would give that order."

"Why not?"

"No one's in charge," was the answer. "We just…"

"There's 280 of us," interjected the first Wobbly. "How many of them do you suppose is standing there? Think it's more than 280?"

"Yyyup," said the third Wobbly matter-of-factly, staring at the dock. "They got an army too. Mebbe 400."

"*How* many?" asked the second Wobbly incredulously.

"You heard me," said the third Wobbly, studying the men on the dock.

"This could get out of hand in a hurry," said the second Wobbly. "This was just supposed t' be an invasion of free speech…like Spokane. Remember?" He looked wide-eyed at the dock and then at the third Wobbly. "Weren't no army t' greet us in Spokane. I don't like this. Look at 'em. People could get shot."

The third Wobbly stared at the pier. He glanced at the second Wobbly and muttered, "Everybody's gotta die sometime."

The second Wobbly looked back in disbelief.

The three IWW men grew silent as the boat slowly approached the pier populated by solemn, armed locals, all deputized and led by the man who despised outside intruders, painfully running 41 Wobblies out of Everett a month ago. Other Wobblies on board, seemingly oblivious to what awaited, continued to sing as if rehearsing for a county fair. The noise aboard was a stark contrast to the silence on the pier where men listened and said nothing.

"We're in for it," the second Wobbly said, wrapping his arms around himself.

"Not this time," muttered the third Wobbly, putting his pipe in his right coat pocket. His right hand felt the left side of his vest under his heavy coat. "We're not going through any initiation line this time."

The first boat, the *Verona*, approached the pier. The crowd of local spectators, some of whom supported the Wobblies, grew on the hillside behind the pier.

Sheriff McRae walked forward to the dock edge, and gave a signal for approximately 100 additional deputies, waiting in the adjacent warehouse, to come out and take their station behind him. His hope was that this would psychologically unnerve the Wobblies, making them more receptive to his demands.

It had no such effect. The Wobblies, already boisterous, booed and jeered as if the pier were a vaudeville stage.

"Those people are nuts," one deputy muttered. Many deputies were more ready to shoot than a moment before.

As Sheriff McRae began to address the approaching boat, he was met with a barrage of denunciation and epithets

"Boys!" shouted McRae, undeterred. "Who's in charge here?"

"We're all in charge!" shouted one Wobbly above the noise.

The boat was nearly to the pier. McRae was running out of time. Pulling a pistol, he pointed it toward the boat's gangplank as the *Verona* slowed to a crawl.

"I'm the Snohomish County Sheriff!" shouted McRae. "Some of you already know that! I'm here to enforce the law! You can't land here!!"

"The hell we can't!!"

The countdown started. Ten, nine…

As Amos watched the unfolding drama, he thought of how bravery and foolhardiness can be mirror images. Without a word, the third Wobbly jumped from the main deck to the pier in order to secure the first line as the boat came alongside. Deputies on the pier raised their rifles as the first line was made fast, but just as the third Wobbly finished, two larger deputies moved quickly and roughly grabbed the third Wobbly. He started to fight back, but this only further angered the two men and they dragged him, cursing, struggling and kicking, through the crowd to the rear where they and others took turns beating him. The third Wobbly's defiant behavior set the crowd of deputies further on edge, and the embankment crowd watched slack-jawed.

As the second boat at a short distance began to approach the pier, the Wobbly passengers in the first boat started to put down the gangplank, and were about to secure another line to the pier while others started toward the rails, intent on going ashore. One carried the red IWW flag. Held it high.

The countdown continued…six, five…

At the rear of the deputies, the beaten third Wobbly was still railing – "Someone shut that @&%$! up!" – at his captors, while in front more defiant Wobblies advanced toward the gangway as Sheriff McRae shouted, "Hey! Get back!" McRae drew his second pistol. Jeff Beard, Charlie Curtis and other surrounding deputies not carrying rifles, did the same.

As Freddie the hobo intuited might happen, emotional heat on each side was about to cause spontaneous combustion.

…three, two, one…

A single shot rang out like a starter's gun at the beginning of a race, and simultaneously from the dock and the boats, opposing fusillades exploded. Stunned, Amos Nordquist and Captain Christian van der Zee gripped the railing as the two sides flew into a rage before them. Wobblies hit the deck while deputies dove, crouched and scattered as gunfire was met with gunfire, loud and continual, and so much gun smoke filled the air that it obscured men on both sides.

Wide-eyed, the second boat skipper approaching the pier reversed engines, slowed to a stop, and began backing down rapidly as men on board fired at deputies who fired back. The din of battle was heard throughout the town and surrounding countryside, and while most of the embankment audience ran for cover, a few remained, mesmerized.

Deputies crouched behind barrels, logs, lumber and ox carts fired in the direction of the boats, while Wobblies bobbed up and down returning fire. When unarmed Wobblies rushed to the opposite side of the boat away from the gunfire, the boat began to list and, as the crowd crushed against Wobbly passengers next to the boat's rail, passengers were pushed over the side and into the icy water. Flailing, several who couldn't swim sank beneath the surface.

Taking his life in his hands, the *Verona* captain, Chance Wiman, jumped out from behind the ship's safe where he was hiding and raced into the *Verona* wheelhouse. The air was full of gun smoke when he ordered the engineman to back down at full speed as volley after volley of reciprocal gunfire continued to burst from decks and dock. The *Verona* engine responded, and when the *Verona* pulled rapidly away from the pier, the *Verona* line attached to a pier cleat stretched taut, parted and snapped, with the *Verona* pulling the line through the water as if having caught and lost something huge while fishing.

Dark clouds again covered the sun, and the pier grew darker. Gun smoke blanketing the decks gave the appearance the *Verona* was on fire, and armed men on both sides continually reloaded and fired, reloaded and fired. The old Civil War veteran with the Spencer repeater, back in a place he never left, gritted his teeth as he fired repeatedly but carefully. One shot, one kill. Although vision was obscured, the deputies could see the deck of the *Verona*, and the Wobblies could see a multitude of rifle flashes at specific dockside locations. As remaining rear hillside onlookers took cover, both sides continued to fire relentlessly at one another until the *Verona* was out of firing range.

After the last shot was fired, one-by-one the deputies stood and watched as the *Verona*, following the lead of the second boat, turned in the middle of Port Gardner Bay.

"Run, y' bas'erds," growled the old man with the Spencer repeater, his feet spread apart, his rifle hanging from his right hand as he watched the two boats turn and head south toward Seattle.

Gun smoke gradually drifted away and, through the waning haze, deputies nearest the water stood motionlessly attempting to ascertain the extent of Wobbly casualties as other deputies tended to the casualties on the dock.

Who fired first? According to the deputies, the Wobblies who wanted class warfare. According to the Wobblies, the deputies who wanted the Wobblies out of Everett. According to the *New York Post*, the lumber guards. According to the lumber guards…no one asked the lumber guards. No one knew who fired first. Lying on the pier were bloodied men, including Sheriff Donald McRae. Captain Christiaan van der Zee returned to his quarterdeck, but went no further as Amos stepped quickly but cautiously down the wet gangplank, grabbing the railings to keep from slipping as rain began to fall again.

For Amos it was almost as if he was back in Appomattox attending the wounded. No medical supplies were available on the Everett pier, however. No one expected what happened.

While 19 wounded deputies and Sheriff McRae would live, Jeff Beard and Charlie Curtis, in the forward line when the firing started, would die. That night in Seattle the Wobblies would carry ashore five dead and 31 wounded. The IWW at last experienced class warfare, pitting the workingman against other working-men.

Amos, who expected to be tending his new flock, rejuvenating tired souls with the peace that passes all understanding, instead was treating bleeding men.

Captain van der Zee stood leaning on his ship's railing, continuing to watch the aftermath until, as the late afternoon sky grew gradually darker, the deputies had all gone home. For a few moments he remained, motionlessly bent over the quarterdeck railing. Rain ran off the front of his cap. He took a deep breath and let it out as he stood erectly, his arms falling motionless at his sides. His placered thoughts were refined to one, short Dutch word as he turned and disappeared below deck. The English translation was: "Madness."

Amos's tortured heart beat hard as he walked up Hewitt Avenue in the early darkness. He felt physically and emotionally spent. The few blocks seemed like miles. Midway up the hill, Amos began struggling, slowly dragging himself along like a dying grasshopper. The effort made him think of pushing forward through the blizzard between Thompson Falls and Murray, but there was no Molly b'Dam, no Good Samaritan around.

Rising winds whipped the cold downpour in the dark, rinsing blood from Amos's sleeves, chest and pant legs. As he walked, occasionally stumbling, his lungs felt like they were failing. He was chilled and spent – so weakened he could barely think. Putting one foot in front of the other was becoming almost more than he could do. Meanwhile, Anna, who had heard the gunfire in the direction of the waterfront, was worrying about him.

"What is keeping him away? His worship service ended long ago." Anna looked at Joshua. "And he knew you were coming. He should have been home."

Alone, Amos stopped. Over the sound of the rain pounding the cobblestones, distant sobs joined the wailing of a young girl. A door slam severed both. Had he ever been this tired? He involuntarily sank to his knees, looking heavenward, the cold rain lacerating his face. The sky was only darker. Exhausted, thinking of the carnage he had just witnessed, his head fell, and he spontaneously whispered simple, selfless words of faith. "Forgive us, Lord." His head involuntarily fell further. Pastor Nordquist coughed twice and put his hands on the wet ground. Too weak to maintain that position, Amos's hands slid forward and he found himself lying on his front, unable to move. He tried to call for help, but could manage only a weak moan. The only sound was indifferent downpour, falling as if none of this mattered.

A short time passed before Amos vaguely heard approaching footsteps, and one set of hands on Amos's left joined another set on his right, attempting to get him to his feet.

"Dad, are you all right?"

He was not all right. Barely conscious, he could not respond. He could not get up.

"Pastor Nordquist, we've got to get you home. Here, try to stand while we help you up."

The two sets of hands were joined by strong arms and backs as Joshua and Jared each bent down, ducked under each of Amos's arms, and wrapped each arm around their necks, lifting Amos to his feet. Something was wrong. If they did not do this, he would not be standing. His head did not hurt as it did following the confrontation with Jake O'Bannion, but the lack of feeling elsewhere was similar.

"Dad, we expected you home a long time ago. What happened?"

"Y'know, Josh," said Jared, "he can't walk or talk. We're practically dragging him. We'll just have to carry him home, okay?"

"Yeah." Josh looked around. "There's a ladder over by that porch. Let's borrow it; put him on it. You take the front and I'll take the back."

The two young men rapidly carried Amos to his home where his wife, daughter, and daughter-in-law made him as comfortable as possible. Unable to respond, his breathing labored, he lay there as they asked him questions he could not answer.

Is it my time? He weakly wondered.

He could hear, but could not respond. Anna looked at her husband, her eyes constricted, her mouth slightly open.

"Dad," said Joshua as he sat next to the bed, the women standing behind them, "Dad, can you hear me?"

Amos could not move his head or any part of his body other than his facial features. Eyes closed, he weakly tightened his lips in what would have been the beginning of a smile if he could smile, and moved his eyebrows enough to where Joshua knew the answer was, "Yes."

Joshua and Jared looked at each other. Joshua thought that if anything could raise his father's spirits, rejuvenate him, what Joshua and Jared wanted to tell Pastor Nordquist when they arrived would.

"Dad? Last week Jared and I have decided to phase out of the dairy business, and into the ministry," said Joshua.

"Samuel decided to do the same thing," said Jared, looking hard at his father-in-law. "It seemed like it was time."

Amos's expression hardly changed, but the corners of his eyes began to tear; tears ran lightly down the sides of his cheeks as the others looked at him in silence until Rachel put her right hand over her mouth and, turning away, began to quietly weep. Worried earlier that his father might have lost consciousness, Joshua studied his father carefully. Amos's eyelids squeezed lightly, tears running, and it was evident to Joshua and Jared that Amos was attempting to communicate, that he was lucid. Joshua was slightly relieved his father could hear and understand but, as Rachel wiped her eyes, head bowed, all felt the oppressive sense of Death standing among them. As Anna left the room, Jared stepped forward and sat down next to his father-in-law.

"Pastor Nordquist, can you hear me?"

Amos squinted almost imperceptibly in reply.

"We're here with you, next to your bed, sir. Joshua and me…," Jared stopped and looked at Joshua, "through the two of us, and Samuel, the message will continue."

Joshua, Jared and Samuel were going to follow in Amos's footsteps, leaving successful enterprise in order to enter the ministry, just as he did. In the warm room, resting, some feeling was returning to Amos's body and face. Amos's facial expression remained unchanged but, to Jared, Joshua and the others, something was wrong, an annoying, apprehensive gut-wrenching feeling that would not leave. Amos still said nothing.

"Dad, are you Okay?" asked Joshua.

Jared and Rachel inched forward.

For the first time, Amos attempted to mouth words.

Joshua bent over his father in order to hear what Pastor Nordquist was trying to say.

"Where's…your…mother?" came the whisper, barely audible.

"Rachel," said Joshua, "could you go get mom?"

As the others remained in the room with Pastor Nordquist, Rachel got up from a bedside chair and went to the kitchen.

Her mother wasn't there.

She turned and walked to the living room, and the others suddenly jumped, startled by Rachel's panicked screams.

106

November 9, 1916

The old wind wheezed softly beneath dark wool clouds as if sleeping, and fir trees gently nodded at bypassing mourners warmly dressed in November's chill. The end brought friends and loved ones together, and all were family. Little Emma Larsen, bundled warmly, held her mother's gloved hand and watched somberly, trying to understand the deep mystery. Being big means you shouldn't cry, doesn't it?

Seeing grown-ups cry was very unsettling for three-year-old Emma. As Emma watched women comfort one another, she became very serious. The pastor's daughters were crying. Emma thought a grown pastor's daughter never cried.

At a short distance, four-year-old Lars Nordquist, the pastor's grandson, hugged his grandfather, seated in a chair. As Pastor Nordquist reached out and responded in kind, Emma was impressed that a little boy could give an adult emotional support, and looked at her mother. Emma wished she could make them all happy, but intuited that whatever made Mrs. Nordquist die was beyond anything she could do or say.

Anna continued to lead a normal life and attributed aches and pains to aging. Cancer research would not begin for many decades. Anna initially developed lung cancer, the cancer cells metastasized, spreading first to her throat, and then to her brain where she developed brain tumors. The "headache," about which she did not complain, killed her.

Why do people have to die? Emma wondered. Why did God do it like that? Emma asked herself silently. Why didn't God just have people grow up and then stay like…? Emma paused. Stay like what? When would be best to stop…when should we not change anymore? Emma thought hard for an answer, but found none. While she understood differences between little kids, big kids, adults and old people, drawing a line seemed impossible. I don't even know how to count to 20 yet, she demurred, rubbing her eye with her mittened left hand while still holding her mother's hand with her right.

Not far from little Emma, Rachel stood quietly wiping tears from her face, trying to be stoic. Rachel remembered the moment 27 years earlier alongside the wagon road next to the forest, waiting for her father to return from Snohomish Hardware. Esther complained about a story in McGuffey's *Third Reader*, a story about a mother dying. Rachel remembered Anna wanted her girls to "rejoice" in Anna's death when that time came, knowing that Anna would be in heaven with Jesus. Rachel remembered how she didn't want to think about her mother's death then, but knew if she didn't want to think about it, how she would react when that time came. And now it had come.

Attempting to accommodate her mother's wishes, Rachel tried to rejoice, to think about where her beautiful mother's spirit was. But the weight of what was in the casket was breaking Rachel's heart – as her mother said would happen – and the tears would not go away. Head down, she blinked her tears to the cold ground, and wished she could better remember the *Third Reader* lesson.

Little Emma noticed the white-haired, old man who spoke funny was not crying. No, just the opposite. Emma watched him with great curiosity. He seems happy, Emma thought after a moment. Why is he happy? Emma wondered. She looked about. No one else was happy. The old man stood silently with his hands in his pockets, looking at the casket, and nodding affably almost as if he were carrying on a conversation with Mrs. Nordquist.

Emma again looked about her at the adults. The nice old doctor with the quiet face, leaning heavily on his cane, also watched the old man who talked funny. The doctor is studying the old man, Emma thought. The old man knows something the doctor wants to know. The old man looked at the doctor and warmly nodded. Yes, Emma thought, that is it.

At first, it sounded like the hushed sound of birds rushing from bushes along the north hillside, but it continued uninterrupted, growing louder. Emma looked about, and up at her mother who showed no sign of hearing anything. Emma again looked at Doctor Torgeson. The old doctor doesn't hear it either, Emma thought. That noise. She quickly looked behind her. Nothing. Except the noise was becoming more audible.

"Momma, what's that sound?"

A snare drum roll. Joined by another. And another. And another… Where? wondered Emma, looking about. The sound seemed to be everywhere at once. The old man who talked funny also looked about, his eyes becoming wide and his mouth partially open, listening. Emma looked up at her mother again, and her father. They don't hear it. How come they don't hear it? she again wondered.

"Momma, do you hear that?"

"Shhh, Emma."

As men began to lower the casket into its grave, little Emma watched Inga, Esther and Rachel dissolve in tears. Rachel, especially, seemed to suffer to the point of torment.

The old man who talked funny suddenly took the arm of the seated, distraught pastor. Not understanding, the pastor only searched the face of the old man. But Emma heard it too. In disbelief, she glanced about at the others who stared at the excited old man as if he had temporarily taken leave of his senses. But it was louder than ever.

The old man stiffened, as if coming to attention, and looking up, cried out, "The pipes!"

He looked at Pastor Nordquist, and then looked upward and listened.

"D' y' hear 'em, pastor?!" he asked loudly, quivering. "Aye, she's with th' Lord now, she is!" said the old man, still looking upward. His heart overwhelmed with emotion, the old man's face streamed with tears. As the others watched, the old man, his white hair gently massaged by the reawakened wind, cried joyfully.

Christmas 1916

For weeks after the death of Anna, although physically improving, Amos languished emotionally, trying to ignore the pain in his heart and body, and the emptiness in his soul. He felt old, and looked down at the skin on his arms, wrinkled as if his body was deflating. Do I have much time left? Although he needed a cane to walk, he recovered from the night of the Everett Massacre, but, his emotions and thoughts confused, wondered why? Might it not have been better if we left together?

At that moment, in his sorrow it was what he wanted, but with the passing of time, he determined his life should go on, as it would anyway. While he was seemingly alone now, with a gradually expanding family he was never alone for long and, with the Holy Spirit, not alone at all.

Once again he sat reading a letter from his brother, Anders. The brothers corresponded more frequently because both had more time, and each sensed their extended time apart was overwhelming reason for reuniting.

Pastor Nordquist was 75, and Anders 73.

How did this happen? Amos chuckled to himself. The letter discussed the sister ship of the *Titanic*, the *Britannic*, requisitioned for wartime use as a hospital ship shortly after being launched (and subsequently never having carried a paying passenger), and how it recently went the way of the *Titanic*. The huge, converted luxury liner had struck a German mine in the Aegean Sea's Kea Channel not far from Athens, and another huge asset of the White Star Line lay on the ocean floor.

Anders angrily questioned whether the *HMHS Britannic* was sunk by a mine, asking whether a German mine could cause the damage done to the huge *Britannic*, the hull of which, after the *Titanic* disaster, was substantially reinforced against sinking. No, Amos read, the likely cause, Anders believed, was German torpedoes. After all, Anders argued, the Germans torpedoed the *Lusitania* and, more recently, the hospital ships *Drina*, *Dover Castle*, *Rewa*, and *Glenart Castle*. Describing the incident, Anders used the Swedish word "*förakt-liga*" (despicable).

As Amos read, he sighed and recalled his Civil War experience with the young, widowed mother on the porch ("…they shot him raht whay'ah you stand now"), and her two, deeply scarred children, and he thought again of Matthew 24:6: "And you will be hearing of wars and rumors of wars; see that you are not frightened for those things must take place…" War and "despicable," Amos considered. Rifled muskets and Minié balls.

Amos again looked down at the letter, took a slow, deep breath, and expelled it before beginning to read again.

Anders wrote that a starboard bunker serving *Titanic* Boiler Room No. 6 had a large coal fire, not uncommon, burning before the *Titanic* left Southampton, and speculated that between the increased heat on the inside and the below-freezing saltwater on the outside, bulkhead structural integrity may have been stressed to where, were there no fire, the damage to the *Titanic* might not have been as immediate and great when it struck the iceberg.

Anders wrote about his children and grandchildren, none of whom Amos had seen in person. Anders wanted Amos to come to Göteborg to visit. Anders wanted all the relatives – nephews, nieces and their children – to meet him, meet the infamous Uncle Amos who "was with Grant at Appomattox" and, of course, Anders very much wanted to see Amos again.

But how much time was there? Perhaps, as always, not enough, for Amos resumed his responsibilities to the Lutheran Church…the Puget Sound Lutheran population and church congregations continued to grow, and new congregations were continually being formed. It might take some time before Amos could free himself to travel back to Göteborg. But at the same time, his physical disabilities dictated Amos consider retirement soon. Waiting became a gamble; at his age, procrastination meant taking a chance the trip would never happen. No, he thought, I must go now.

Further encouraging Amos' return to Göteborg, Anders suggested that, using Anders' White Star Line connections, perhaps the whole Göteborg family could accompany Amos on a return trip – the war should be over soon, Anders said – then traveling across America and seeing some many things they read about. The Statue of Liberty. The Shenandoah Valley. Congressman William H. Clagett's Grand Canyon. The Cascades and the Olympic Mountains. To facilitate Amos' eastbound trip across the Atlantic, Anders said he would get Amos the equivalent of a first-class berth on the second *Titanic* sister ship, the *Olympic* – presently being used as a troop transport ship by the British navy, bringing both Canadian and American troops to England. Anders wrote that the *Olympic* was nearly identical to the *Titanic* except for fine art and other extraordinary accessories that gave the *Titanic* its luxury status. Anders seemed quite serious, and Amos thought about a trip, wishing Anna were alive. The war? Damn the war. I should have done this much sooner.

Amos spent Christmas with his children and grandchildren, and wished that, alternatively, Anders were there to see everyone.

Amos wrote Anders, telling Anders that Amos wanted to come, but needed to extricate himself from his present responsibilities, and that would take a little while. In a year or so, hopefully less, he could sail for Göteborg.

April 28, 1918

Amos went through the gradual exercise of replacing himself with someone else, and was ostensibly retired – where people no longer do what they must but, rather, what they wanted to do all along. Amos had done what he really wanted all along, however, and his life's story proved it.

Other members of the family were up ahead near the boarding platform, waiting for their father, their grandfather. Amos smiled as he looked ahead at family members whose pleasant facial expressions belied anxiousness, resigned to his trip, wanting him to have an enjoyable voyage, but not leave.

"Dad," said Esther as she walked with him toward the Seattle Great Northern boarding area, "I'm worried about this." She stopped walking. "I know you want to go, and I understand why you're going, but, Dad….we're at war." Esther looked up at her father leaning on his cane. "When you get to New York, and sail into the Atlantic…the German U-boats…well, you read the papers. The *Olympic* is the sister ship of the *Britannic* and *Titanic*. The *Olympic* might as well have a bull's-eye painted on each side. Dad, I wish you wouldn't go. It's too dangerous. Wait until the war is over."

"Under the circumstances, I go, not tempting God, but trusting God. What I am about to do is not foolhardy. And if nothing happens, and I live, well, I live. But if something happens, and I live, perhaps I live even more. And should I die," Pastor Nordquist shrugged, "I've lived a full life. And as far as dying goes, who doesn't?"

"Dad," said Esther. "Dad," she began again, "Dad, all I'm saying…"

"I understand. I love you too." Amos tousled her hair as if she were 10. "After I leave, please don't get hit by a train." With his right arm Pastor Nordquist gave his daughter a hug as they continued walking again, and smiled down at her.

Looking at the others ahead, Esther said nothing and gently bit her lip.

"What do you think happens in death?" asked Pastor Nordquist, his forehead furrowed. "What do you think it is like?"

"We go to heaven," responded Esther.

"Like I am going to Sweden?" asked Pastor Nordquist. "Is it that simple?"

"I don't know, Dad." Esther looked at her dad for an explanation. "What do you think?"

"I think the reason proximity to death magnifies life is because 'Death' is so much bigger than life. Think of Seattle. Isn't Seattle large?" Esther nodded. "Now think of the universe." He again looked directly at Esther. "Death is bigger than life. While bodies die, for the soul the moment of death is transitional blink, but that transition leads to an indescribable transformation…where the faith God gave us on earth leads to His presence in heaven – and where we are rewarded for what we did with the talents we were given."

Esther shrugged her shoulders. "I guess… I don't know."

"I don't either," said her father, "but we have been given clues. And I have a feeling life is all about faith. All of it. I look forward to the return to Göteborg in part because of the memories – memories having to do with faith – this trip will resurrect."

Pastor Nordquist hugged his children and grandchildren. If this trip was enjoyable, edifying, some of them might go with him on a second trip, but U-boats or no U-boats, he felt this trip needed to be taken alone; he wanted to return to Göteborg in the same manner he had left.

Amos bid the others a final farewell at Seattle's impressive King Street Station with its 242-foot tower, the tallest structure in Seattle, a replica of the bell tower at St. Mark's Basilica in Venice, Italy. As the conductor sounded the time-honored announcement, using his cane for support and leverage, Pastor Nordquist stepped up on the stairs to the boarding platform, turned and waved brightly to the others. He would travel cross-country to New York, catch the *RMS Olympic* sailing for Southampton, and from Southampton catch a smaller vessel east through the Strait of Dover and north to the North Sea, then into the Skagerrak.

May 5, 1918

Upon arriving in New York, Pastor Nordquist checked-in to the remarkable Algonquin Hotel where, before going to his room, he asked the concierge to make dinner reservations at a restaurant he had read about on the train. Early that evening he walked to Delmonico's where he dined alone, but was entertained by the spectacle about him. Seated with other guests at a table nearby was actor John Barrymore who appeared to be holding court as much as having dinner.

After returning to his hotel room briefly, Amos walked around the corner to the Hippodrome Theatre to take in the Ziegfeld Follies – which turned out to be a little risqué for his taste – and returned to his room, passing Algonquin manager Frank Case who inquired about his stay.

"Excellent," responded Pastor Nordquist. "What else can I say? The Algonquin is wonderful, and 1918 downtown New York is almost a dream world."

The next morning, a bellboy took Pastor Nordquist's luggage to the hotel entrance where the bell captain hailed the next cab, and Pastor Nordquist was on his way to the harbor. Upon arriving, the cab driver opened the door for Amos, and took his luggage out of the trunk. After paying the driver, Amos awkwardly carried his luggage (gaining insight into the root word in "luggage") as he walked slowly toward the head of the pier, studying the *Olympic* from a distance.

The ship was enormous, the biggest thing he had ever seen, a floating colossus. While at the hotel, Pastor Nordquist read the *Olympic* was slightly longer than 882 feet from stem to stern, and weighed over 52,000 tons, but those numbers only became relevant when first seeing the enormous ocean liner. It was longer than the height of the Woolworth Building, at 770 feet the tallest building in New York.

"My golly," said Pastor Nordquist under his breath. He whistled softly, staring with wonder at the enormous ship as if it were a mirage. How does something that big float? *Titanic* passengers who believed the *Titanic* was unsinkable must have had a great deal of faith. The *Olympic*'s giant expansion engines, Amos had read, required a vertical space equivalent of four decks, and were the largest of their type ever built. We've come a long way from the *Einar II*, he thought.

The big ship's hull looked queer, having been painted with an odd sort of design that was considered camouflage, supposedly making the *Olympic* less visible to U-boats. A boondoggle, Pastor Nordquist thought. The odd-looking paint job made the *Olympic* more visible. Who approves these things? he wondered.

Since being converted to a troop transport ship, besides the paint, there were other additions to the *Olympic* including installation of a big 12-pounder gun on the forecastle, a 4.7" gun aft, and several 6" guns about the main deck. Amos looked at the relative positioning of the new armament high above him, and tried to imagine specific circumstances under which they would be effective.

A few hours later, after all lines were brought aboard, the big ship was underway with the help of several harbor tugs. For a moment, the ship's master, Captain Bertram Fox Hayes, appeared outside the bridge looking down, visually measuring the distance between the ship's bow and the pier. Amos was told Captain Hayes was a competent commanding officer and a gracious gentleman, well-respected by those above and below him…although Amos read that some in the British Admiralty criticized Hayes for stopping to pick up lifeboat survivors of a French ship, the *Provincia*, sunk by a German U-boat three years earlier. Admiralty critics claimed that by stopping in U-boat infested waters, Hayes greatly jeopardized the welfare of the *Olympic* and her 6,000 passengers…and he had. Pastor Nordquist chuckled. "Too dangerous." Captain Hayes did, Amos thought, exactly what another great master, Jesus Christ, would have done, and had no doubt that at that fortuitous moment, while U-boats weren't present, the Holy Spirit was.

As Amos watched him from a distance, Hayes appeared like a natural leader, tall, almost statuesque, with a determined jaw, and intelligent but sad eyes. He looked familiar. It struck Amos that Captain Hayes resembled his father, Captain Stig Nordquist. Amos would be told that Hayes knew most of the *Titanic* officers well, and was acquainted with officers on other White Star Line ships such as the *Arabic*, the *Delphic*, and the *Afric*, all sunk by German U-boats, and, of course, *Olympic's* other sister ship, the *Britannic*. Of the three, huge sister ships, only the *Olympic* was still afloat, and there were those who believed its day was coming soon.

Amos looked at the Olympic; it was a huge target, inviting and difficult to miss. Pastor Nordquist wondered about the thoughts that must go through the mind of Captain Bertram Fox Hayes. Amos almost felt like reassuring Captain Hayes, "Everything will be fine." But, again, Amos thought, everything is never fine.

Once at sea, the voyage seemed relatively uneventful. The weather was favorable, but Amos couldn't help wonder, when you're 882 feet long and weigh over 52,000 tons, if the weather gets bad, so what? He caught himself, realizing that what he was thinking was painfully naïve…he had been on land too long. Even at 882 feet, an angry North Atlantic can still make a seemingly huge ship seem like a small log.

But that would not happen during this voyage. Four days passed, and soon they would be rendezvousing with four American destroyers who would escort them through the English Channel to Southampton. Everything was fine.

107

May 12, 1918

It was Mother's Day as the RMS *Olympic* approached the entrance to the English Channel off the coast of France en route to the Isle of Wight and Southampton. Early in the morning before sunrise, anxious to arrive in Göteborg and unable sleep, Pastor Nordquist went up on deck. He again stood leaning on a railing near the head of the forecastle, looking down at blips of phosphorus blinking in and out of existence in the froth fanning obliquely off the ship's bow, and feeling buoyant, knowing Southampton was only a few more hours away. Soon the *Olympic* would be joined by American destroyers.

In the dark, Pastor Nordquist attempted to see the waves loudly radiating diagonally away from the ship's waterline far below, and for several moments did not look up. The night ocean's surface was not visible in the darkness except for the phosphorous in the froth. The moment was so peaceful. How he wished…

As he thought of Anna, his imagination took over. Soon Anna will meet all the Nordquists, and beautiful Anna will see Göteborg. Amos had not been there in 54 years himself. Thinking about Anna, for a moment he looked up again.

The *Olympic* was running at darkened ship in order to avoid detection by German U-boats at night, and the only light anywhere was a thin line along the eastern horizon. Eventually sunrise would occur.

His left hand on his cane, his gray hair disheveled by the wind, he quickly lifted his head as a frisson of dread shot through his system. His eyes became narrow as he felt compelled to study at the distant horizon east off the starboard bow.

Now…what is that?

Fifteen minutes ago it would have been invisible, but in the faint, predawn glow above the horizon, Amos could see the silhouette of something on the surface, and as the Olympic gradually drew nearer the silhouette, from photographs in newspaper articles read before leaving New York, Amos recognized it: a predatory German U-boat lying in wait for Allied shipping.

"Merciful God."

Panicked fear surged through Amos as he let go of the railing, turned and, bouncing his cane as he walked, in the darkness moved as fast as his legs would allow over the deck toward one of the *Olympic* lookout stations.

"U-boat! 2:00 o'clock!" shouted Pastor Nordquist as he pointed in the U-boat's direction with his cane. Leaning against a stanchion, the startled lookout spun around. Amos cupped his left hand next to his mouth, and again shouted, "U-boat! 2:00 o'clock!"

The lookout turned toward the starboard bow, studied the horizon, saw, pushed away from the railing and over to the speaking tube to the bridge, where he yelled into the horn, "U-Boat at 2:00 o'clock!" several times just as the crow's-nest lookout relayed the same message. In moments, the ship's on-watch boatswain piped "general quarters," and the order was passed throughout the ship. Crewmembers began waking Canadian and American soldiers, directing them topside and toward lifeboats, anticipating the worst.

Captain Bertram Fox Hayes, also a member of the Royal Navy reserve, quickly arrived on the bridge and took command, ordering Royal Navy gunner's mates assigned to the *Olympic* to man those guns positioned in areas where they might be effective, and fire at the U-boat. Captain Hayes was certain the U-boat saw the huge *Olympic* in the growing predawn glow and was about to launch torpedoes.

While some on board believed the U-boat might not have seen the *Olympic* in the dark, this was wishful thinking.

After being awakened in his small rack, the U-boat 103 commanding officer, Captain Claus Rücker, peered through the periscope and, feeling like a veteran elk hunter upon spotting world-record bull, gave the order to ready torpedoes, as Captain Hayes ordered *Olympic* gunner's mates to open fire on the enemy. During the time between the U-boat sighting and the present moment, the Olympic made enough headway to where the U-boat was within range of *Olympic* guns. At nearly nine stories above the waterline, however, the stationary forward gunners had difficulty attaining accuracy due to the downward angle and, in any event, would be unable to do anything about torpedoes. Amos, watching, thought of the Spanish Armada. Captain Hayes quickly weighed his options.

"Captain Hayes," volunteered the anxious mate, "I recommend turning hard to port, reversing course in the dark, reducing our exposure and visibility, and we can outrun them, captain."

At the moment, it seemed the only option. But was that proper judgment?

No, thought Hayes. A 52,000-ton ship is not a gazelle. I could turn to port and, during the time required to arrive at an appropriate heading and distance, provide German torpedoes with 882 feet of broadside from which to choose… and subsequently join the *Titanic* and *Britannic* on the ocean's floor as many expect.

"All ahead full, right 10 degrees rudder!" ordered Captain Hayes.

"All ahead full, Captain" echoed the engineman on the bridge.

"Right 10 degrees rudder, Captain" repeated the helmsman.

The first mate and other officers were flummoxed. Right 10 degrees rudder?

"Rudder 10 degrees right, Captain," said the helmsman.

Meanwhile, on the boat deck American soldiers arriving from berthing spaces below were lining up near lifeboats, experiencing emotions ranging from grave apprehension to near-panic, attempting to see any U-boat torpedoes streaking near the surface in the dim light as the horizon slowly became brighter.

"What's he doing?!" wondered one out loud, voicing communal thought about the changing ship's course.

Following Capt. Hayes's order, the ship's stern began to swing to the left, redirecting the bow toward the right as the enormous *Titanic* sister-ship plowed through the water.

"Rudder amidships," ordered Capt. Hayes after a moment. "Mr. Anderson, have the Marconi room radio our position to the Americans, and tell the Americans that support would be greatly appreciated as we engage the enemy."

"Yes, captain."

What?

At that moment, Pastor Nordquist glanced up at the bridge, but turned and again watched the submarine silhouette apprehensively. How many torpedoes can a U-boat launch…and how fast? Pastor Nordquist had no idea but, remembering Anders' letter about the *Britannic,* Amos continued to fearfully watch the submarine, looking for any sign of torpedoes in the black water as the ship's deck hands began to ready the lifeboats.

As Amos and the American and Canadian soldiers watched, seconds raced by, and the huge ship still made no attempt to evade the submarine. Quite the opposite. Almost of a single mind, all passengers on deck suddenly realized what the commanding officer was doing.

Attacking.

Hayes was using the largest weapon at his disposal. *Lusitania, Britannic* be damned, thought Capt. Hayes. That will not happen to the *Olympic.*

Meanwhile, wide-eyed U-boat commander Captain Claus Rücker also realized the incredibly bold and improbable action Captain Bertram Fox Hayes was taking, and the U-boat captain ordered full speed ahead in an attempt to get inside *Olympic's* turning radius, avoiding the oncoming behemoth. In the light swells, the U-boat began to move forward to the right of the big ship's heading in a frantic attempt to get out of the way.

"Rudder hard right!" ordered Captain Hayes as the big ship approached full speed.

"Rudder hard right, Captain."

The big ship's stern responded by swinging to the left, directing the bow to the right, closing the big ship's turning circle. Rücker could not believe what he was seeing and at the last moment gave a hasty order – "*Mein Gott! Bereiten sie das schiff zu verlassen* [prepare to abandon ship]!"

"Rudder amidships!" commanded Captain Hayes.

"Rudder amidships, aye."

The mammouth *Olympic* plowed through the waves directly toward the hapless U-boat, and at full speed the enormous, 52,000 ton *Olympic* slammed into *Unterseeboot 103* with an explosive report and shudder felt throughout the big ship. The impact magnitude startled Hayes and those on the bridge. Until that moment, Captain Hayes had underestimated how well U-boats were constructed.

As the wounded U-boat passed by the *Olympic's* starboard side, the U-boat took on water so rapidly that it stood on its end – German sailors falling out of the superstructure hatch like the U-boat was an enormous, hollow pen – before beginning to slide slowly at first and then more rapidly into the deep, eventually coming to rest on the bottom like the eight Allied ships it sank during previous weeks, having fully expected the number would be nine.

His jaw set, Captain Hayes turned to the helmsman.

"Left 15 degrees rudder."

"Left 15 degrees, aye, captain," barked the normally taciturn helmsman, age 18, who watched the rudder angle indicator, smiling. His grandchildren would hear about this.

And so would Pastor Amos Nordquist's…although much sooner.

The big ship began to slowly turn to port and again in the direction of Southampton. With satisfaction, Captain Bertram Fox Hayes watched the U-boat sink astern, and for a moment said nothing. He turned to the radio officer.

"Mr. Anderson, radio the American destroyers. Tell them to pick up the German survivors – as per our [British] standards." Captain Hayes was well aware that after sinking English ships, some German U-boats surfaced and had target practice on survivors floating helplessly in the ocean.

The *USS Davis* (DD-65), the first American destroyer on the scene, picked up 31 U-boat survivors. Ten German sailors went down with the submarine.

Sinking U-boat 103 was a measure far short of anything that would make up for the White Star Line ships sunk by so many U-boats, but Captain Hayes also took pleasure in the fact that the *Olympic*, her crew and passengers were miraculously still safe on the surface.

Once again, Pastor Nordquist would subsequently learn, some in England complained that Captain Hayes jeopardized his ship, crew and passengers by such a "reckless" action, ramming a U-boat. Amos wondered whether there was anything about which some in England would *not* complain.

Amos considered the charge to be without merit – it was not an option of which many men would have thought, but it was the only option – and Amos read in subsequent newspaper reports that the majority of Parliament, as well as the Monarchy, agreed. Captain Hayes was awarded the Distinguished Service Order (DSO) for valor while in command during combat. Months later, Amos also read that the DSO was awarded to Thomas Edward Lawrence, "Lawrence of Arabia," questionably sensationalized by American journalist Lowell Thomas for action in the 1918 raid at Dara'a during the Arab Revolt. There would be, however, hard evidence of Captain Hayes' actions, Amos thought. 52,000 tons of it.

Captain Hayes was also knighted, later given the title Commodore, and henceforth called Sir Bertram Fox Hayes…when not on the bridge of the *Olympic* which, in turn, became popularly known in England as "Old Reliable."

Much later, while in the shipyard to determine the cause of a leak, shipyard divers found an 18-inch diameter dent in the *Olympic's* hull beneath the water-line. She had been hit by a torpedo that did not detonate. Thank you, Lord, Amos thought gratefully, as he read about it.

After watching the U-boat sink in the light of the morning sunrise, Pastor Nordquist, the soldiers and many of the crew went back to bed. To the extent they could, they would get as much sleep as possible before reaching Southampton in a few hours. The disruption in sleep would be partially offset by arriving later than expected.

May 17, 1918

The Skagerrak

Upon arriving at Southampton, Pastor Nordquist took a train to London.

London looked good; he had not been there in over 50 years, but concluded with satisfaction that London was still London and, God willing, always would be.

Amos caught a small steamer, the *Thule*, a member of the Swedish Lloyd Line, for the short remaining distance to Göteborg. Since the Thule was *Swedish*, and Sweden was neutral, U-boats should not be a problem, Amos thought (although, ironically, the *Thule* would be sold in 1925 to Italian ownership, renamed *Franca Fassio*, and torpedoed by a British submarine during WWII). In 1918, off the north coast of Denmark the *Thule* began to retrace the 1864 path of the *Nordland* and the *Kringflackande* of the former Nordquist Shipping Co.

Pastor Nordquist again leaned on the railing while sailing easterly through the Skagerrak, the high-seas highway under which lived all manner of treachery, mostly imagined, but even then only weakly comparable to what, with no imagination, could be found on land. From the forecastle, Pastor Nordquist watched the steamship's bow plow through the brine, and looked about at eddies amid the waves. The surface was similar to what he saw when leaving and, thinking about Skagerrak folk beliefs, he chuckled to himself. Some misguided souls, he thought, taking already odd convictions a step further, actually root for the sea monsters. Pastor Nordquist shook his head. What goes on in the minds of those who delight in the destruction of man's works? he wondered. While in London, he had encountered a self-absorbed man, quite British, who expressed disappointment that the *Olympic* sank the U-boat…that Captain Hayes succeeded, and the *Olympic* did not find itself in a watery grave like the *Titanic* and *Britannic*. Had such people any idea of the implications? What is inside such men, Pastor Nordquist absently wondered, men whose perceptions in life favor death with no concept of it? His eyes narrowed. What, indeed.

Approaching where he was born, Amos sensed the final upstream swim begin. How much longer did he have? he wondered. He would make the most of this visit; it could be the last.

The *Thule* entered the Göteborg outer harbor, for safety's sake travelling at slow headway, giving Pastor Nordquist time to look around at all the things.

Much of what he saw was new. Coming closer to the pier where they were to land, Amos judged it was in proximity to the pier location where he last stood when leaving, but was substantially larger, accommodating the transition from small ships of sail to large steamships.

As the *Thule* began to come alongside the pier, Pastor Nordquist searched the small crowd on the pier for a familiar face.

Oh, good grief. Amos studied him: the old guy who looked so much like Anders.

Good night. Who is that old guy who looks so much like Amos? came the reciprocal thought on the pier.

At a distance, both brothers chuckled simultaneously in what was for both an emotional, bittersweet moment.

As he reached the bottom of the gangway, Amos walked toward Anders who, dressed for the occasion, was wearing a Savile Row suit, Prince Albert black frock coat, and black top hat. Flanked by two other men on the pier, Anders stood smiling, joyfully studying the so-much-older vision of Amos approaching him.

His cane moving rapidly, Amos's pace quickened…he was away an irresponsibly long time, and a few more lost seconds were too many. Anders stepped forward and the brothers embraced one another in a fit of exuberance, pressing out misgivings of this being a dream.

At that moment, a thought flashed through Anders' mind, recalling the conversation many years ago in the parlor. Amos told Anders of his intention to go into the ministry, and during the conversation essentially forgave Anders for taking Karin Olafsdotter while Amos was at sea. It was as if it happened this morning: meeting Amos on that former pier at this location, Anders was in a great state of anxiety, having seemingly betrayed his brother. A few hours later, all was far better than what might have been had Anders done what it seemed he should have done, because Amos was who he was. Anders was grateful then, and was grateful now, these many years later as, again, he happily embraced his older brother.

"I suppose," began Anders as he stepped back, straightening his top hat, "you'll be coming up with some cock-and-bull story about being in a leaking lifeboat in a horrendous hurricane …and how you spent 54 years considering what you would do if you ever returned to Göteborg alive. Were I you, I'd advise not attempting to sell that nonsense because," Anders smartly tugged on his topcoat lapels to insure they lay flat, "54 years, dear brother, is entirely too…"

"It has been too long. I apologize," said Amos. "I very much agree. I should have returned to visit much sooner and then more often." Facing Anders, Amos affectionately grasped Anders by the shoulders with both hands, fully looked at Anders as if to certify that this moment was truly happening, and smiled. It is good to be here, he thought. Letting go of Anders, he looked around him. "Where, might I ask, is everyone else?"

"Going about their business," said Anders formally. "No point in them coming down here to see you. It obviously wouldn't enable you to get here any sooner."

"Again, I apologize," Amos laughed. He looked about at the hillsides and wharves. Everything was different. Well, no. There on the hillside was the house that Captain Stig Nordquist built. Amos smiled. "I look forward to seeing the old home again, Anders. Is the frigate bird still next to the fireplace?"

"Did you miss the frigate bird?" asked Anders in a condescending tone of voice. "I'm sorry to hear that. I am, however, pleased to hear you missed someone. I mean, Amos, it's not…"

"What are you babbling about?! I missed everyone! I missed people I haven't even met! I intend to make up for lost time. I really wish there…no offense, Anders, but I hoped to see a few more people here on the pier when I arrived. I guess they must…"

"There *were* other people," Anders replied, looking up at Amos. "Didn't you notice? There was, in particular, that very attractive honey-blonde with the great looking…"

"Ah, yes, well," interrupted Amos, "by golly, some things sure *don't* change, do they? I was referring to my immediate family…as if you didn't know."

"You'll get to meet everyone sooner or later," said Anders. "They'll be dropping by as time allows.

"Amos," Anders faced Amos sincerely, "frankly, no one remembers you. You've been gone so long, you're this fictional character they've heard or read about, but beyond that, well, I'm afraid you've been mostly forgotten. They give you no thought whatsoever. So, let's you and I just head up to the house."

Anders turned to the two well-dressed men standing nearby, and instructed them to wait for Amos's luggage and bring it up in the limousine. "We'll walk up," Anders said formally to the men, and returned his attention to Amos.

"Yes, the frigate bird is still there…along with the chandelier and some other stuff. And we'll have a glass of sherry…what'o."

"You're still doing business in London and Liverpool?"

"And occasionally drinking ale in Southampton. I suppose I could have met you there. But here seemed more appropriate. I'm supposed to be retired." Anders again smiled and tipped his hat as they walked past an attractive young woman on the sidewalk.

"Somehow retirement doesn't fit you," said Amos, "but I can recall the day when, before *you* did anything, attractive young women would tip their hats and smile at you."

"Actually, that's not true, Amos. They never tipped their hats."

"Yes, that would have been inappropriate. Forgive me."

"Forgiven. Oh, once again."

The two brothers walked up the street, now paved lanes lined with sidewalks and trees, that Stig Nordquist walked as he weighed retirement and the prospect of staying at home and enjoying his family.

"But, obviously, most things *have* changed, haven't they?" observed Amos, looking about.

"Not necessarily. I've always had a thing for honey-blondes. I'm not sure what did it for Copernicus, but beautiful women – and, I have concluded in my old age, God did not make any women who are *not* beautiful – have always made the world go around."

"Well, I'm happy for you." Amos shook his head and chuckled. Somehow, Anders made it this far.

They reached the huge front porch with the many steps, and Amos stopped for a moment at the base, remembering.

He joined Anders as they walked up the steps to the landing and to the large, front door.

"After you," volunteered Anders.

Amos opened the door and stepped inside.

"*Grattis* [congratulations]!!!" they all shouted giddily on cue, just as they rehearsed it, the adults raising wine glasses in Amos' direction, smiling excitedly, some dissolving in laughter from the look on his face.

The place was packed with a great many relatives and a few old friends – all smiling, laughing and chattering joyfully. Amos, making no attempt to mask his emotions, hugged everyone, everyone in the room, young and old. Then, wiping his eyes, he gratefully took the glass of Spanish sherry Anders held out to him as Anders put down the bottle.

The last bottle.

Aged far beyond perfection, but still drinkable, especially under the circumstances.

"Ladies! Children! Try to find a seat," ordered Anders. As the women sat down on chairs, davenport, love seats and ottoman while the men stood and the children took seats on the floor, Anders held out his glass of sherry and, in Swedish, intoned a toast.

"To Amos Nordquist, a fine gentleman, a wonderful brother, and a man of God." Turning to Amos, Anders raised his glass, smiling while fighting back tears. "Amos, welcome home."

"*Välkommen hem!*" the others echoed, the adults holding up their raised glasses.

Anders turned to the others and said, "Thank you, all, for coming!

"And now, here is your chance to get to know this fine man, my brother, come back from America. He has children and grandchildren of his own. He has experienced many things. He has pastored many congregations, and has been used by God to lead many to Jesus. In fact, you may," Anders added, glancing about at the children present, "call him 'Pastor Amos,' as those in America do."

Gesturing to the others with both arms, Anders encouraged them. "Why don't you ask him some questions?"

"Great Uncle Pastor Amos," began one of Anders' anxious grandchildren, unconsciously raising his hand as if needing permission to speak, "were you really the only one who survived Little Big Horn?"

Epilogue

conversation with Anders early in Amos's life was playing in Amos's mind.

"My conclusion is that, if the measure of anything is the extent to which it glorifies God, the Creator of the stars and the seas and the insignificant men who sail them, I should, therefore, place myself in the best position to glorify God, to become more like the servant with five talents than those with two or one."

"Isn't that rather dangerous?"

"Why would it be dangerous?"

"Because God expects much from those to whom much is given," answered Anders. "The Bible says that. And remember the foolish servant buried his one talent in the ground, and was consequently cast into outer darkness. What if God determines that you have effectively buried all five talents in the ground? What then? On judgment day, instead of saying, 'Well done, wise and faithful servant' – whatever it is He says – He says, 'You should have stuck with the one talent, buddy. But no, you had to have five. Well, outer darkness is too good for you.'

"You're screwed, Amos."

Amos was given five talents, and he painstakingly cultivated and profitably invested them all. He did much for the harvest; he did much to replace preying on one another with praying for one another, the Holy Spirit using him to bring many to love God and each other. Anders need not have worried.

By most standards it was a good life. Again, the nostalgia recipe requires a pinch of deception, but that's pretty much how it happened, how I remember it. The opportunities made available, the things enabled, the challenges, the chances…chances of a lifetime.

Some might ask where I am now, writing this. Someone might ask: when a lifetime ends, is it instantly no more, like a snowflake hitting a lake, or does a life continue, transform, and become part of a larger essence, like a snowflake hitting a lake? As I told Anders, the measure of anything is the extent to which it glorifies God and, to that end, in my lifetime I wanted full measure, five talents, as it were, in order that if God were to glorify Himself through me, He would be greatly glorified.

In spite of my extensive flaws and sinful nature, by the love and grace of God, I am where I hoped to be, and that, to say the least, is both a happy ending and beginning. Five talents? I was consequently given many opportunities, chances to step out in faith, the Holy Spirit working through me. I was expected to do much.

And I did.

The End

Acknowledgments

Thank you to historians Chris Calkins (Appomattox Campaign), David Dilgard (Everett), Marie Hayden (Tacoma), Charles LeWarne (Seattle and Equality Colony), and Ernie Price (Appomattox Courthouse). Thanks also to Angelo Albertini who grew up in the Great Silver Valley.

www.ingramcontent.com/pod-product-compliance
Lightning Source LLC
Chambersburg PA
CBHW022013120726
47902CB00012B/6